MORE PRAISE FOR JUDITH KRANTZ AND . . .

Mistral's Daughter

"High-gloss romance. . . I loved every minute of it."

—*Chicago Tribune*

"Entertaining celebration of power, money, lust, and lineage."

—*Detroit Free Press*

Princess Daisy

"This page-turner is a champion."

—*People*

"*Princess Daisy* soars to the heights of escapist entertainment."

—*Philadelphia Inquirer*

I'll Take Manhattan

"This one outperforms Scruples. . . . It is crème de la Krantz."

—*New Woman*

"Delicious."

—*New York Daily News*

THREE COMPLETE NOVELS

JUDITH KRANTZ

THREE COMPLETE NOVELS

JUDITH KRANTZ

Mistral's Daughter

Princess Daisy

I'll Take Manhattan

WINGS BOOKS
New York • Avenel, New Jersey

This omnibus was originally published in separate volumes under the titles:

This edition contains the complete and unabridged texts of the original editions. They have been completely reset for this volume.

This 1994 edition is published by Wings Books, distributed by Outlet Book Company, Inc., a Random House Company, 40 Engelhard Avenue, Avenel, New Jersey 07001, by arrangement with Crown Publishers, Inc.

Random House
New York • Toronto • London • Sydney • Auckland

Printed and bound in the United States of America

Library of Congress Cataloging-in-Publication Data

Krantz, Judith.
[Novels. Selections]
Judith Krantz : three complete novels.
p. cm.
Contents: I'll take Manhattan — Mistral's daughter — Princess Daisy.
ISBN 0-517-10180-7
1. Man-woman relationships—Fiction. 2. Upper classes—Fiction. 3. Women—Fiction. I. Title. II. Title: Three complete novels.
PS3561.R264A6 1994 93-42236
813'.54—dc20 CIP

8 7 6 5 4 3 2 1

Contents

Mistral's Daughter
1

Princess Daisy
363

I'll Take Manhattan
697

Mistral's Daughter

For Ginette Spanier
Who opened the doors of Paris for me.
With much love and the memory of many years of friendship.

For Steve
Who has all my love.
This book could never have been written without him.

I feel deep gratitude to these friends for their answers to my questions.

Jean Garcin, *Le Président, Conseil Général de Vaucluse*
Jacques and Marie-France Mille of *Le Prieuré*,
Villeneuve-les-Avignon
Bill Weinberg of the Wilhelmina Agency
Karen Hilton and Faith Kates of the Wilhelmina Agency
Joe Downing
Aaron Shikler
Micheline Swift
Betty Dorso
Grace Mirabella of *Vogue*
Ann Heilperin of Van Cleef and Arpels

1

Fauve dashed through the lobby, her Stop-sign red slicker flapping around her, and managed to squeeze her way through the elevator doors a split second before they closed. Panting, she tried to furl her big striped umbrella so that it wouldn't drip on the other people who were jammed in with her, but, in the crowd, her arms were pinned to her sides.

Earlier in the morning Fauve would have had the elevator pretty much to herself, but there hadn't been a single empty taxi in Manhattan on this rainy September morning in 1975. She'd had to wait endlessly for a bus on Madison Avenue and run the rest of the way across Fifty-seventh Street. Soaking and uncomfortable, she cautiously swiveled her neck around to survey the mob that hemmed her in. Would any of them get off before the tenth floor? No hope of that, she realized. The creaky, ancient elevator that rose so slowly in the Carnegie Hall office building was charged with a palpable cloud of tension and terror. Except for the operator, the small space was packed with young women who were gripped in silent, fierce and frightened concentration. Each one of them had grown up knowing that she was, beyond any question, the most beautiful girl in her high school, in her hometown, in her state.

This elevator trip was the last step toward a goal they had been dreaming of feverishly for years. Before them lay an audition at the Lunel Agency, the most famous of all the modeling agencies in the world, the agency with the most prestige and the most power. Fauve felt the almost unbearable weight of the quivering anxiety and nervous anticipation that palpitated around her, and, closing her eyes, she prayed for the ride to be over.

"Casey asked if I'd seen you," the elevator operator said to Fauve, so loudly that everyone heard him. "She's waiting for you upstairs."

"Thanks, Harry." Fauve hunched deeper into her coat collar, trying to disappear as she felt twenty pairs of eyes immediately turn toward her in a wave of hostile awareness. On each side her profile was being evaluated in naked competitiveness, her neighbors sweeping their glances from her forehead to her chin and finding no flaw. Behind her they were estimating her height and noting, with a misery that vibrated clearly, that she was as tall or taller than any of them. Even in the rear of the elevator there was no girl whose view was so completely blocked that she couldn't see the conflagration of Fauve's tumult of hair, of a red so extravagant that it could only be natural.

There was absolute silence as Fauve was inspected.

"You're a model, aren't you?" the girl on Fauve's right asked her, accusation and desperate envy clear in her tone.

"No, I just work there." Fauve could feel the relief in the elevator as if it were a solid substance. She straightened up, invisible now and blessedly unimportant. As soon as the elevator doors opened on the tenth floor she sprinted out into the corridor and ran through the entrance to the Lunel Agency without a backward glance.

She knew precisely what the girls behind her would do. Each one of them would take her place on the line that had begun to form a half-hour ago for the open auditions that were held three mornings a week at the agency that had been founded more than forty years earlier by Maggy Lunel, Fauve Lunel's grandmother. Out of the many thousands who auditioned each year, only thirty were accepted.

As Fauve walked rapidly to her office she thought that perhaps one of those girls in the elevator might have the slightest breath of a faint percentage of a chance to succeed. Perhaps one of them had that quality everyone in the agency called "lightning." How could they know, she wondered, as she pushed open the door to her office on which the sign said, "Director, Women's Division," that it had never been enough just to be beautiful?

Casey d'Augustino, Fauve's assistant, looked up in surprise from the chair on which she was perched, leafing through an advance copy of *Vogue.* Tiny and curly haired, Casey, at twenty-five, was older than Fauve by several years.

"You look as if you're wanted by the Mounties," she chortled, amused by Fauve's expression.

"I've just escaped the furies . . . got caught in the elevator with a large batch of young hopefuls."

"Serves you right for being late."

"How often does that happen?" Fauve asked with mild belligerence, shucking off her raincoat and sinking, with a sigh of relief, into her chair. She pulled off her wet boots and put her feet, in their kelly green tights, on her desk. She always dressed to defy bad weather and today she wore an orange turtleneck sweater and purple tweed trousers.

"Rarely," Casey admitted, "but no need to apologize, you're still right on time for the emergency of the week."

"Emergency?" Fauve looked out through the glass door of her office, her red eyebrows raised in inquiry. Everywhere she looked she saw the normal activity of the agency, dozens of bookers talking into their batteries of phones. As long as the telephones functioned, there could be no real emergency at Lunel.

"Trouble with Jane," Casey said, looking unnervingly serious.

"*Again!*" Fauve, who had started to doodle on the pad on her desk, slammed down her pencil with as much force as if it were the gavel of a hanging judge. "After that warning I gave her last week. Trouble *again?*"

"She was booked for *Bazaar* yesterday—Arthur Brown was shooting. Bunny, his stylist, called first thing this morning, absolutely livid . . ."

"Did you know that livid means black and blue?" Fauve interrupted hastily, not anxious to have her already harried day utterly ruined by hearing the latest about Jane, Lunel's top model, a girl who worked only under her plain first name, needing none of the catchy, inventive appellations of others, for she was the best blue-eyed blonde in the world, possessing a cataclysmic beauty about which there could be no ifs, ands or buts. It was all there with Jane, locked into the bone, irrefutable. She was the only model Fauve had ever known who was completely satisfied with how she looked, insufferable Jane, who knew she was perfect.

"Livid as in furious," Casey went on. "Jane showed up two hours late yesterday which Bunny had anticipated, since she's always late. So that wasn't the problem. Her hair was filthy. That wasn't the problem either because the stylist washed it. She proceeded to mortally insult the makeup man but he forgave her because he's heavily into being insulted. Then she felt too shaky to work because she hadn't had lunch so they fed her, sending out for three different kinds of yogurt before she was happy. After that she had to make a half-hour phone call to her personal astrological adviser. All par for the course, so far. The thing Bunny was livid about was that after fawning over Jane all day *Bazaar* still didn't get the picture. She wouldn't let them cut her hair."

Fauve leapt to her feet, her lovely, vivid face a study in disbelief, her great gray eyes wide with outrage. "Jane *knew* it was a beauty editorial. She knew they had to cut her hair two inches—that was the whole point. Damnation! The difference in hair next season is a *mere* two inches—I had it all out with her last month when she accepted the booking."

"Ah, but our Jane changed her mind, you see. Her astrologer told her not to make any changes until the sun moves into Neptune."

"That's it! Jane's got to go. I'm going to terminate her contract today."

"Oh, Fauve . . ." Casey moaned, thinking of the next three solid months' worth of bookings on Jane's schedule.

"Nope. Jane's made us look bad once too often. How can I expect the other girls to behave and work hard if I let her get away with this?"

"If you terminate her she'll be working for Ford or Wilhelmina tomorrow. People will put up with anything to get her—there's only one Jane," Casey warned solemnly.

"Wrong, Casey. There'll always be another Jane, sooner or later," Fauve said quietly. "But there's only one Lunel."

"Point well made. Point taken. Still, aren't you going to talk it over with Maggy first?" Casey asked.

"Maggy!" Fauve said, astonished. "She's not supposed to be in today—it's Friday." When her grandmother was away on her habitual long weekends, Fauve was in full charge of the business.

"She told me it was raining too hard to go up to the country until tomorrow. The Boss is in her office," Casey informed her.

"Of course I'll tell her about Jane," Fauve said thoughtfully. "Any more emergencies?"

"Only one you can't do anything about. Pete's working on it now," Casey said, referring to the telephone repair man who spent half of every week unscrambling their hundred outside lines and dozens of intercoms. "One of the bookers' phones is screwed up—she's getting some shrink's calls and he's getting ours. She's telling everyone to have a good cry, then take a cold shower, two aspirins . . . and pray."

"Couldn't hurt," said Fauve as she pushed open the office door and headed in the direction of the big corner office where Maggy Lunel had long reigned over the world of fashion modeling.

Certain great beauties age gracefully; others hang on relentlessly to a particular period in their past and try to maintain themselves there, withering, nevertheless, just a little every year; and still others lose their beauty quite suddenly, so that it can only be fleetingly reconstructed in the imagination of those who meet them. Maggy Lunel had aged *agelessly*. From twenty feet away she was still that seventeen-year-old who had once been the loveliest artists' model in all Montparnasse. At a distance of ten feet she was clearly the most sophisticated woman in New York, a woman who held her slim body with an élan that generations of women had tried to copy. From a closer view it was impossible to realize that she was in her sixties, for her charm was too potent to leave room for such mean-spirited calculations.

"Magali! What a shame about the country . . . was Darcy very disappointed?" Fauve rushed forward to kiss her grandmother, calling her by her true first name as no one else had the right to.

"He was a bit grumpy but then he called Herb Mayes and they made a date for lunch at '21' which cheered him up immediately," Maggy answered, hugging her. "Last night the radio said the power lines were out so I refused to budge . . . I tend to lose my famously sweet disposition when I have to creep around by candlelight and grill a hot dog in the fireplace."

"And I thought you'd be more romantic—another illusion gone. Anyway, I'm awfully glad you're here. I've decided to cut Jane loose . . ." Fauve looked at Maggy with a mixture of inquiry and determination.

"I rather wondered when it would happen. Loulou and I've had a bet on it for the last three months."

Fauve's mouth opened in surprise. Loulou, the head booker and Maggy's particular crony, had never indicated anything but resignation over Jane's unpredictable behavior.

"Who won?" she gasped.

"Loulou, of course. In five years of trying I have yet to win a bet from Loulou. Still . . . someday . . ." Maggy grinned and shrugged. Fauve, she thought, was looking particularly enchanting on this gloomy morning, in her wild combination of clothes, and her green feet. Any of *Les Fauves*, the school of painters after whom she'd been named, would have been overcome by her. Indeed, in Maggy's opinion, any man at all would be overcome by her, although it wouldn't quite do to tell Fauve that. Not that she was vain, but it might sound like some ordinary grandmother's normal prejudice. For decades Maggy had possessed the most expertly trained eye in the world for spotting beauty and she was deeply thankful that Fauve hadn't decided to be a model. She could have been the best of them all—in her own way outclassing Jane—but Maggy had never wanted that particular career for her.

"What time is it?" Fauve asked suddenly. "I left my watch at home—that's what comes from dressing in a hurry, and I don't want to miss Angel's new cottage cheese commercial."

"It's almost ten-thirty."

"Good. We're just in time. Shall I switch on your set?" Fauve gestured toward the television set that Maggy kept to monitor the various commercials in which her girls appeared. "Or are you busy? I can watch on my own set if you are."

"No, stay here, darling. I'd like to see it and I don't have all that much to do today. I hear that Angel's interviewing business managers . . . she's doing as well as you thought she would."

Fauve turned on the set and sat down in the chair in front of Maggy's desk. The two women both turned their eyes to the screen and watched as Angel managed to convince even them, for thirty astonishing seconds, that skim milk cottage cheese could be an object of gourmet devotion.

When the commercial was over they shook hands in congratulations, laughing together, each on the same rollicking thrilling note of freedom from all convention, a laugh that made everyone who heard it stop to listen and wish fervently to hear it again.

"You were right to move Angel to the Big Board," Maggy said. "That spot should run forever."

"I can just see her trying to decide whether to buy an apartment house or a herd of cattle with the residuals. She'll probably settle for a Jaguar."

As Fauve reached up to turn off the set, the words "News Center Flash" popped onto the screen and she kept it on to see what had happened. An anchorwoman appeared, speaking rapidly.

> "Julien Mistral, considered to be France's greatest living painter, died today of pneumonia at his home in the South of France. The artist was seventy-five years old. His daughter, Madame Nadine Dalmas, was with him at the time of his death. Details at noon."

Neither Fauve nor Maggy moved. Shock held them in their chairs as another commercial ran its course. Suddenly Maggy jumped up and turned the set off but Fauve still sat immobilized, the light of her eyes extinguished. Maggy went to her, leaned down, put her arms around her shoulders and pulled the motionless red head to her breast.

"My God, my God, to hear it like that," she murmured, rocking Fauve in her arms.

"I don't feel anything. Absolutely nothing. I should feel something, shouldn't I?" Fauve said, almost too softly for Maggy to hear.

"It's the suddenness . . . I don't feel anything either, but I will." For a moment they were both silent, clinging together, listening to the wail of a siren in traffic on Fifty-seventh Street without hearing it. Julien Mistral was dead and time had come to a stop for the two women, both of whom had loved him.

On Maggy's desk there was one framed photograph. As if they were joining her in their shock, each of them found herself looking toward that picture of Teddy, the greatest fashion model of all time; the girl who had been Maggy's daughter, Julien Mistral's mistress and Fauve's mother.

Finally Maggy stood up and released Fauve as her French practicality swept over her arrested emotions and told her what had to happen next.

"Fauve, the funeral . . . you'll have to go. Come on—I'll go back to the apartment with you. I'll help you pack. Casey can get your plane ticket."

Fauve moved for the first time since the television announcement. She walked over to one of the windows and looked out at the rain. She spoke without turning her head to Maggy.

"No."

"What do you mean 'no'? I don't understand."

"No, Magali, I can't go."

"Fauve, you're in shock. Your father is dead. I know you haven't spoken to him in more than six years but of course you must go to his funeral."

"No, Magali, no, I won't. I'm not going. I *can't*."

2

Paris was *en fête*, in love with itself. It was a Monday in May 1925 and everywhere neighbors agreed with each other that never, in their memories, had the chestnut trees carried so many creamy pyramids of flowers. But they only stopped to notice the parade of blue days and star-filled nights when they weren't busy gossiping, for never, even in the history of this capital city of all capital cities, had the ferment of the worlds of art and fashion and society yielded such a pungent, intoxicating wine.

In her workroom on that morning in May, Chanel was busy creating the very first little black suit; on that morning Colette was putting the finishing touches to the scandalous manuscript of *La Fin de Chéri*. Young Hemingway and the half-blind James Joyce had been out on that dawn, drinking together, while Mistinguette had opened the night before at the Casino de Paris, proving once again, as surely as a great bullfighter claims the applause of the crowd, that the art of descending a staircase belonged to her. The Cartier brothers had bought the most extraordinary necklace in the world, three perfect strands of pink pearls that had taken two centuries to gather—and many people wondered to whom they would sell it.

Maggy Lunel cared nothing about pearl necklaces as she stood on a street corner in Montparnasse, called the Carrefour Vavin. She was devouring her second breakfast, a handful of hot fried potatoes she had just bought for four centimes from a street vendor. She had been in Paris less than twenty-four hours and, at seventeen, she found that running away from home in Tours to seek her destiny was an infernally hungry business.

Passersby on the rue de la Grande Chaumière turned to cast a second and often third glance at her, planted there as if she owned the pavement, tall, long-limbed, unselfconscious and apparently totally unaware of the contradiction between her face and her clothing. She wore the boyish, athletic silhouette of the day following the latest mode in a trim skirt of pleated navy serge that covered her knees and a white crêpe overblouse, which was belted below her waist.

But, in a day when no lady, rich or poor, was seen on the street without a hat, she was bareheaded and her face had not been tweaked and painted into the cupid-bowed, heavily powdered, highly rouged version of a Kewpie doll that was so in favor that women everywhere had managed to make themselves all look alike. She had the strong, bold beauty of a day in the future, of an era that wouldn't dawn for another quarter-century. Her cheekbones were twin scimitars under the white stretch of her skin and she carried her head on her long neck as proudly as a war flag.

In a time when all women had cut their hair, hers was a long, straight fall of shiny stuff, the dark orange of apricot jam, and her thick, unfashionably unplucked eyebrows were only a few shades deeper over eyes that were set almost too far apart. They were frank and spangled and wide open, the whites fresh and bright, the irises the yellow-green of a glass of Pernod before it has been diluted by water. Maggy's lips were so full and well marked that they were the focus of her face, a signal as emphatic as a signpost.

As Maggy Lunel regretfully chewed the last of the potatoes she looked like a large golden cat who had walked into a breeze. Nothing about her self-confident stance would have revealed her age to an observer, but her skin was as tender and new as a baby's palms and where it lay over her well-formed, straight nose, it was dappled with faint freckles.

Maggy dusted her hands off with her handkerchief and looked about the Carrefour Vavin. She was standing a step away from the boulevard Raspail. Across that wide thoroughfare was the beginning of the rue Delambre. From her spot on the sidewalk every other street seemed to be going downhill. She had the feeling of being on top of a gentle hill in the center of a great open place, as if this crossroad were the main avenue of a great city, complete in itself. In every direction she had large views of the fresh, blowing sky of spring, pierced by the tops of the chestnut trees. But there was nothing peaceful in the prospect. The very air was charged with sparks of energy, and even the pigeons looked busy. It seemed to Maggy that the passersby were almost running to get to their mysterious destinations.

Oh, she thought, how madly she wanted to crunch Paris between her teeth, to chew and chew until she possessed this city, this unopened treasure chest crammed with objects of desire. She shifted from one foot to another with impatience to *begin*, tapping her neat, "Louis" heeled pump with the instep strap buttoned on one side, swinging her head to try to look into the windows of each passing taxi, so overwhelmed with curiosity and eagerness that she didn't notice that she herself had become the object of the attention of a growing group of people who had clustered around her. They were an oddly assorted band: young women in cheap, brightly colored clothes, old women in aprons and slippers; grandfathers smoking and small children tugging at their mothers' hands; boys and girls who should, surely, have been in school, all waiting with an air of resigned patience that made Maggy look like a nervous filly straining at a starting gate.

Gradually they formed a rough circle around her and their conversation trailed off as they looked at the stranger and nudged each other.

"Are you waiting for someone?" asked a buxom woman of thirty-five.

Maggy looked up in surprise, glanced around the circle and smiled.

"I certainly hope so, Madame. I'm in the right place, aren't I?"

"That depends."

"The models' fair? Isn't it here that I wait to get work as an artist's model?"

"It's the spot," said a twelve-year-old boy, peering at her with ardent interest. "Me, I'm of the *métier*. I wasn't even born when I was painted for the first time," he boasted. "But my ma, she was in her last month."

"Shut up, imbecile," said his mother, shoving him behind her.

"You're no model," she said to Maggy, accusingly.

The *foire aux modeles* was an institution that had started in Montmartre some seventy-five years earlier, when professional artists' models gathered to be hired around the fountain of the Place Pigalle. As the artists had moved to Montparnasse the models had followed them, still standing on the street waiting for work every Monday morning.

Entire families had lived by this trade for generations and Maggy's appearance among them was greeted with the deep resentment any group of professionals shows toward an obvious amateur.

"If someone will pay to paint me," Maggy retorted, "won't that make me a model?"

"So you think that's all there is to it, do you? It's a stinking hard job of work, my fine young lady."

"Good," Maggy said decisively, jamming her hands into the pockets of her skirt and standing straight and sure in her tight new shoes.

The models who had gathered closely around to hear this exchange, blocking the pavement, suddenly drew back as they all turned to watch a pretty girl wearing a close-fitting, jade green cloche over her shingled dark hair, who was swinging along the street with an admiring man on each arm. As she caught sight of Maggy she looked her up and down with a sharp eye. She raised her eyebrows in surprise and then shrugged her shoulders in dismissal. Loudly enough for all of them to hear she commented, "So that's the kind of savage coming from the provinces these days, is it? That beanpole's never seen a pair of scissors obviously. I wonder if she's even heard of soap and water . . . there's a strong air of the farmyard somewhere." She laughed in contempt, pretending not to hear the wave of sniggers her comments had caused and disappeared down the street.

"Who is that . . . individual?" Maggy asked indignantly.

"That's Kiki of Montparnasse, and you didn't even recognize her? Now *there's* a model—the queen of us all." The woman was glad to underscore Maggy's ignorance. "Everybody knows Kiki, and Kiki knows everybody. You *are* wet behind the ears and no mistake."

As Maggy was about to reply she felt a hand fall on her arm and turn her around abruptly. "What have we here?" Two men were looking at her. The one who had spoken was shorter than she, dressed in a dandy's piped jacket and perfectly pressed trousers, a stickpin in his tie and a straw hat tipped to one side of his head. He had small, clever eyes and a grin that showed tiny, yellow teeth.

The second man was as monumental as the massive tree trunk against which he leaned. His eyes, as blue as open water, were disconcerting in the steadiness and the fixity of their gaze. He was six feet four inches tall, and there was a wild, yet noble air about him that was doubly startling in. this crowded city scene because it was untamed by urban custom or consideration. He might have been a mountain climber surveying the world below from the height of a conquered peak. He had a splendid head set arrogantly on a thick, strong neck, a broad open brow, a dominant, high-bridged, confident nose and a wide mouth. His hair was dark red, curly and unkempt. As he looked appraisingly at Maggy he had the air of a gallant, battle-bound cavalier riding out of the past, in spite of his working-man's brown corduroy trousers and open-necked blue shirt.

"Mistral," the smaller man said to him, "what do you think?" He put his hand under Maggy's chin and slowly turned her head from one side to another. "Very interesting, eh? The eyes—a most curious color. And decidedly there's something unusual—even odd—about this mouth, just a touch cannibalistic, wouldn't you say? Van Dongen couldn't make much of it." He fingered Maggy's hair as if it were fabric in a shop, rubbing it between his thumb and index finger. "Hmmm—at least it's clean and she hasn't cut it."

Maggy stood rigid in shock. No man had touched her like this in her lifetime. In automatic self-defense she focused on a neutral object, three bunches of leeks the taller man was carrying under his arm as if they were a book. As the shorter man's fingers lifted her hair away from her ears so that he could inspect her profile, she stepped forward, reached out and snatched a big white leek by its hairy, grayish roots. She held it up to her mouth and bit the vegetable cleanly in half, its long green leaves falling to the pavement. The man in the piped vest, Vadim Legrand, known to all as "Vava," let his hand fall as he watched her chewing. She took another bite.

"You could say 'please,' " said Julien Mistral.

"When you look at the animals in the zoo, you must also feed them," Maggy answered, her jaw moving vigorously. Mistral didn't smile.

"Mistral," Vava said with an air of decision, "I'm going to take her into the academy and see what she looks like. Come on." He motioned to Maggy to follow him into the painting academy of La Grande Chaumière, a few steps away.

"Why? You've been looking at me. What more do you want?" Maggy demanded.

"He wants to see your tits," the boy told her with an air of importance.

"In there? Now?" she asked, bewildered.

The boy's mother laughed with malice. "Get your ass moving, my girl. Go strip down in any empty classroom just like the rest of us. Do you think you're hiding something special that they've never seen before? Oh, these debutantes! She thinks it's made of mother-of-pearl."

"Are you coming or aren't you? Make up your mind," Vava insisted. "I don't really need a model today."

"Yes," Maggy heard herself saying. "Of course."

She turned and followed him rapidly, trying to get out of sight of the crowd of models before they could notice the wave of heat she felt rising on her face, the blush that tormented her life.

"Wait up, Vava." Mistral passed her in one stride and stopped the smaller artist. "I'll take this girl."

"I saw her first."

"What the hell difference does that make? Do you have me confused with someone who gives a shit, Vava?"

Vava gave his yellow grin. "That makes a dozen times you've done this to me."

"When I want something, not merely to annoy you."

"Ah, bravo! That's as close to an apology that anyone has ever had from you, Mistral. Take her. Take her! I have to work on the portrait of Madame Blanche anyway. Nobody buys your stuff so you have the time to indulge your curiosity; just tell me, can you afford to pay a model?"

"Who the hell can? But I can't afford to spend my time doing flattering portraits of rich women either," Mistral said with indifference, not caring if Vava was insulted or not.

"Come along," Mistral said to Maggy, giving Vava's hand a quick shake of farewell. He took out his pocketknife, sliced the roots off another leek, handed it to her, and began to walk down the boulevard du Montparnasse without turning to see if she was following. Maggy took the leek and tucked it like a handkerchief into the pocket of the young boy who had talked to her, and rushed after him, whistling a phrase from the melody of the Java—an insistent catchy dance tune that she had heard the night before, floating up to her window from the open door of the *bal musette* next to her cheap hotel.

Julien Mistral was in a filthy mood as he took the shortcuts to his studio on the boulevard Arago. For years now he'd been pounding at his painting as if he were a convict in chains, given a mighty rock and a small hammer and ordered to reduce the rock to dust. He was engaged in the struggle that had become his only goal from the day he had walked out of a class in the École des Beaux-Arts of the Sorbonne and decided to paint his own way, to paint from his feelings and not from his brain. In the four years since that day, Mistral had found that it was almost impossible to turn off his head, to escape from the narrow prison of French education, to go freely beyond the classicism that has always dominated the core of French painting. He was consumed with the attempt to get the paint on the canvas *without* the rule of his trained French brain.

The tall man hurried under the ancient trees of the park of the Cochin hospital, ignoring the girl who had to run to keep up with him. He forgot her existence as he thought wrathfully of the exhibition he had visited with Vava earlier that morning.

Even that bugger Matisse, even *he* is stuck in chess playing, not painting. He uses the contrast of two colors to create a third color—one that just isn't *there*, damn his eyes—why doesn't he call himself a mathematician and be done with it? Or an interior decorator? And as for that damned acrobat Picasso and his friend Braque, gray, boring, imitative, *dreary* Braque, the two of them are no better—chasing Cézanne's bullshit about reducing all nature into a cone, a square and a circle, beating it right down into the ground until they drain out all the life, all the air—to the lowest circle of hell with all of them!

He was so angry that he walked right past number 65 and only realized that he had passed his destination after half a block. He turned abruptly, with a curse, and, with Maggy close on his heels, flung through the open doors that led to a covered passage.

The artists' *cité* of the boulevard Arago, built in 1878, was like a village in Normandy. A cobbled street led to rows of two-story, half-timbered houses with high gabled roofs and walls of glass. Long gravel walks bordered an overgrown garden filled with apple trees, hollyhocks and geraniums. Each of the small studios also had its own small private garden, enclosed by boxwood hedges and low gates.

Maggy followed Mistral as he climbed three steep steps and opened his front door. He went to his shambles of a kitchen and looked angrily about for a place to put the leeks while she stood just inside the doorway, intimidated by his silence and the way he seemed to project himself through the air as if it were an enemy. She was flushed from the long, fast walk, her chin tilted high to cover her sudden and inhabitual shyness.

Finally, Mistral threw the leeks on the floor and turned into the big studio, jerking his head at Maggy to follow him. She looked around in amazement. Everywhere there were canvases and everywhere there was color, such color as she had never seen before, such color as she had not known existed within any walls of any room, color on which she felt she could swim as on a great river. There were rainbows and clouds and stars and giant flowers; there were children and circuses and pinwheels; there were soldiers and naked women and flags and horses jumping and a fallen jockey and always there was the river of color torn from the sun itself.

"That's the bedroom," Mistral told her, pointing the way. "Go get ready. The robe's in there." Maggy found herself in a small room containing little more than a bed. On a hook behind the door hung the dusty red silk kimono Mistral kept for models.

Maggy took off her skirt and blouse, folded them neatly and put them on the bed. She stopped, dry-mouthed. "Painters paint *skin*," she told herself in a panic, turning to her high school art lessons for reassurance. "Rubens painted mountains of white skin with red patches. Rembrandt painted yellow-green skin. Boucher painted pink and white skin. Skin is the single most painted substance in the history of painting." With shaking fingers she unrolled her lovely new silk stockings. "Painters are like doctors—a body is only a body—an object, not a person," she told herself in a rising inner wail.

Many times in her life Maggy had propelled herself into a situation through which only her inborn self-confidence could carry her. She had realized, when she first determined to run away to Paris and become an artists' model, that of course she would have to pose naked. With her usual bravado she had decided that she could do it, and gone on with her plans.

Now, on a sunny morning in May, she found herself shivering and trembling and sweating all at once. She had reckoned without taking into account her life's experience. No man had ever seen her naked, not even a doctor, since she'd never been sick in her life.

She tried to whistle a phrase from the tune of last night's Java as, with frantic resolution, she let the straps of her chemise slip off her shoulders, but her mouth was too parched by fear to whistle as she shrugged out of the garment she had only possessed for a few days, her first grown-up underwear. Underneath the white batiste chemise, oh, the shame of it, she had on only a new pair of wide-legged, white knickers, as flimsy as the new style dictated. Nothing, no power on earth, could make her take them off she realized.

"What the hell is taking so long?" Mistral called roughly from the studio.

"Coming," she answered faintly. The impatience of his voice made her throw on the kimono over the knickers and wrap it tightly around her waist. The floor was so cold under her bare feet that she put her shoes back on. Flustered, she fumbled with the little buttons, gave up and walked out of the bedroom with the straps of her shoes flapping and making a little noise at each step she took. She stopped ten feet away from Mistral, who stood ready before an easel, and waited for instructions. All the light of the room was sucked toward the clash of her orange hair and the red Japanese silk.

"Go stand by the window, one hand on the back of that chair."

She obeyed and stood very still.

"For Christ's sake, the kimono," Mistral snapped.

Maggy bit the inside of her lip and felt her hands trembling as she undid the sash and let the robe fall to the floor.

Maggy had broad shoulders and the long vertical curve of her neck, as it met the sweeping horizontal of her collarbones, was strong and passionate. Her breasts were tenderly alive, so young that they were almost like cones, high and well separated, with tiny nipples that stood out in firm points. The line of her rib cage from armpit to waist had a fine tension and a perfect clarity. Her skin was so polished, so white, that it drew the lapping, splashing light into it and then reflected it back so that she glowed as if she were illuminated from within.

Instinctively Mistral reacted against her beauty. He was accustomed to the easily proffered nakedness of the professional model who wore her skin as casually as an old dress. Nakedness to him had value only because painting the nude body was an intensely serious business. Maggy, who stood as resolute as Joan of Arc at the stake, seemed instantly, furiously erotic. As he realized that she had aroused him, he became angry in self-defense.

"What the hell do you think this is—the Folies Bergère? Since when does a model pose in her knickers and shoes? Eh?" He glared at Maggy. She kicked off her shoes and began to undo the buttons that held her knickers together at the waist. A tear of humiliation and rage slipped out of each eye.

"Now what? A striptease? Is this a whorehouse? Is that what you think I hired you for?" Mistral shouted. "Enough, don't bother!"

"It's all right," Maggy muttered, her head bowed. A button resisted her fingers and she struggled with it.

"Out!" ordered Mistral. "I said enough. I can't paint a model who is embarrassed. You're absurd, ridiculous! You should never have come. You've wasted my time, damn it. Out!" He gestured to her as angrily as he might have chased away a cat who had walked over a freshly painted canvas, sending her rushing back into the bedroom with the kimono bundled around her like a blanket.

"Fool, fool, *fool!*" Maggy lashed at herself as she scurried, fully dressed, out of Mistral's studio. She had not dared to look at him again before she left, but if she had she would have seen him staring at the chair by the window, the image of her naked body imprinted on his unwilling mind.

3

Shaking and furious with herself, Maggy fled in the direction of the Luxembourg Gardens and almost fell onto the first empty chair she could find, indifferent to the scampering world of children at play. In the space of the last half-hour the dream that had ruled her for four years had turned into such a stinging misery of failure that she wrapped her arms protectively around herself and bowed her head in shame.

A young mother sat down next to Maggy and busied herself with tending her baby. Her feelings of importance and pride communicated themselves to Maggy even through her own emotions. She raised her head and gazed about her at a dappled world in which the old sunned themselves as the young ran about intent on their games. Her heart began to lift when a small boy tottered over to her and laid a big rubber ball in her lap. She unlocked her arms and rolled it along the path for him. He brought it back, as hopefully as a dog with a stick, and soon she found herself the center of a group of children who were attracted by the novelty of a grown-up who would condescend to play with them, so unlike their own mothers whose words were a litany of French childhood: "Don't touch; shake hands nicely; don't get dirty; don't run too fast; take that out of your mouth."

Maggy played for an hour, escaping into a world of simple games that carried the flavor of her early schooldays when she had been a hoyden, a tomboy with a fan of wild hair that flew in the wind like the wings of a big bird, the only girl in school who could throw a stone better than any of the boys, catch any ball, climb any wall.

Soon after the last child had been dragged home for the midday meal, Maggy, too, left the park. Hunger drove her back to the Carrefour Vavin but every restaurant she passed was full. It was just after noon and on the terraces of Le Dôme and La Rotonde there wasn't an empty chair to be found. Waiters whisked about adding extra chairs and tables so that the terraces sprawled out almost to the edge of the pavement, but there was no place for the uninitiated to sit, since no one was fool enough to leave a front-row seat at the most exciting theater in the world.

Maggy stopped at a street vendor and bought one red carnation and pinned it to her blouse. Her spirits rose abruptly and she turned, head high, into the Select, hoping that the smaller café might have room for her inside. She zigzagged sharply left at the door to avoid the crowd of men standing in front of the long bar and discovered a tiny empty table in the far corner of the room, next to the big, lace-curtained window, sheltered and inconspicuous.

Thriftily, she ordered only a cheese sandwich and a lemonade, staring at the crowd of rowdy, roaring, bizarrely dressed, carefree people packed in together behind the little wooden bar tables as if they intended to spend the day. The sound of raucous, high-pitched conversation, swelling like a river in spring, mounted around her. As the room grew smokier she caught snatches of French spoken in a dozen different accents, for this was the era in which foreign artists dominated Montparnasse; the days of Picasso, Chagall, Soutine, Zadkine, and Kisling; the years of de Chirico and Brancusi and Mondrian, of Diego Rivera and Foujita. French artists, like Léger and Matisse, were in the minority as Americans, Germans, Scandinavians and Russians flocked to the *quartier.*

Happy in her anonymity, feeling invisible because she knew no one, Maggy didn't notice the interested glances that were directed at her. Here at last was the exotic spectacle she had expected to find. This was the life Constantine Moreau, her high school art teacher, had talked about. A failed artist, he had filled his pupils' minds with high-flown tales of the cultural life of Montparnasse, stuffing their heads with half-accurate stories of parties to which he had never been invited and feuds in which he had never been involved. What he lacked in teaching ability he had made up for in the passion he felt for the life of the artist, in the aching exile he conveyed as he made real the violently pigmented, tempestuous drama of a Paris to which he had so vainly yearned to belong. It was Moreau who had given Maggy's imagination the home it had been seeking, Moreau who made a bohemian life in Montparnasse her ever-present fantasy, he who had assured her that Renoir himself would have wanted to paint her even if she were taller than most of the other women in the world. She gazed, almost open-mouthed in wonder, at the display of deliberate eccentricity inside the Select. This is what heaven must be like, she thought. If only she were part of it.

"Well, my little one, so you're the new girl, no? Let me offer you a drink."

Maggy turned, startled. She hadn't even noticed a woman who sat at the next table, inspecting her closely from the outrageous orange of her hair to the remarkable and almost equally outrageous boldness of her features.

"Well, are you or aren't you?" the woman asked.

"Oh, I'm new, that's for sure," Maggy said, startled, looking around at the stranger. She must be over forty, Maggy thought, and yet still so rosily pretty, even though she was more than just plump, like one of the luscious girls Fragonard painted, who had grown middle-aged and fat.

"I am Paula Deslandes," the woman announced, with an air of importance. "And you?"

"Maggy Lunel."

"Maggy Lunel," she repeated slowly, as if she were tasting the name. Her shortsighted eyes, the warm brown of an expensive cigar, peered intently at Maggy. "Not bad. It has a certain charm, a certain dash, a brio—perhaps it will do. In any case it has the essential two syllables and since there isn't another Maggy working in the *quartier*, that I know of, and I know everything there is to know, I approve, in principle, for the moment anyway."

"What luck for me. And if I hadn't met with your approval?"

"*Tiens, tiens!* She sits up and barks." Paula's smile, which had the power to banish all despondence, broadened. "You're cheeky for a provincial."

"A provincial!" Maggy exploded. "That's the second time in one day. Oh, it's too much!" Although she had never known a Parisian other than Moreau, she understood that the provincial is a matter of constant superior amusement to anyone who has the sovereign luck to be born in Paris.

"But it jumps right out, my poor little pigeon," Paula said without apology. "Never mind. Ninety-nine percent of the people in the *quartier* are provincial. But I—I am the exception." She was intensely proud of herself, this child of the streets of Montparnasse, a "flower of the pavement" as she liked to say with a romantic sigh, the daughter of a framemaker who had been brought up within a few hundred feet of the Carrefour Vavin. All Paula Deslandes knew or ever wanted to know of nature was contained within the walls of the Luxembourg Gardens, all she knew of mankind, and she was steeped in the subject like a cherry at the bottom of a bottle of old brandy, she had learned during the thousands of hours she had spent posing in the studios of painters or seated in a café. Paula represented, in her round, abundant and buxom form, the embodiment of the passion for gossip, endless gossip, that was embedded so deeply in the artistic life of Montparnasse.

Meeting Maggy put Paula into the highest category of the only three moods she permitted herself. She rated her emotional temperature every morning and never admitted to a mood that was not good, better or superb. Superb had long been reserved for an addition to her list of lovers—there were and would always be men who appreciated a woman who embodied that classic trio of pleasures: fair, fat and forty. Recently she had found that uncovering a fresh item of news before anyone else in the *quartier* had wind of it was able to make her feel a mood that deserved the designation of superb, and Maggy promised a great feast of novelty.

Every Monday, when her restaurant, La Pomme d'Or, was closed, Paula treated herself to a tour of her village of Montparnasse, knitting together the many threads of gossip to which she had been privy during the busy week. Each night she presided over the dinners of artists and art collectors from all over the world who had made her restaurant so profitable. Paula Deslandes was a natural, untutored historian, who could easily put stray bits and pieces of information together so that they formed a coherent social fabric.

"Well then, Maggy Lunel—so it didn't go well this morning with Mistral, eh?"

"Oh!" Maggy cried. "How could you possibly know anything about that? You've never even seen me before!"

"The word travels fast in this little corner of Paris," Paula answered smugly.

"But . . . who told you?"

"Vava. He dropped in on Mistral right after that big bastard threw you out, poor thing, and being Vava, naturally he couldn't wait to spread the story. He's an old woman, I always say."

"Oh, no!" Maggy hammered on her new skirt with both fists, punishing her bold pink knees. She felt drenched in a blush, once more intolerably shamed, shown up again as a childish little prude from the country.

"It's not important," Paula said urgently. "You mustn't take it seriously—everyone has to start somewhere."

But Maggy had stopped paying attention. Two women and three men had just taken complacent possession of a table in the center of the room. One of the women was Kiki de Montparnasse, who stared openly at her, elbowed her friends and pointed toward Maggy and Paula. Her male companions fixed Maggy with their eyes and raised their hats to her with satiric politeness while the women giggled.

"That one again! Just what I needed," Maggy muttered angrily.

"What has Kiki to do with you?" Paula asked.

"She insulted me this morning when she passed me in the street."

"Ah. Did she indeed?" Paula murmured.

"I don't find it amusing," Maggy said, not liking Paula's thoughtful tone.

"Nor do I, I assure you. I find it fascinating . . . that bitch is too condescending to bother to insult just anyone . . . so she's noticed you already . . . well, I have to grant her an eye."

"So you know her, too?"

"Yes. I know her. Let's get out of here. There is a bad odor suddenly in this café. I'm inviting you to a real lunch. Come on—last night I won three hundred francs at poker, took them off Zborowski and God knows that dealer can afford it. Stop looking at that slut and her riffraff. Pretend they don't exist. We're going to Dominique's for a *chachlik.* Sound good?"

"*Chachlik?* What is it? Something to eat I hope—I'm starving—I'm always starving." Maggy stood up quickly, desperate to leave, unfolding to her full five feet nine inches. Paula's eyes squinted as she looked up.

"My God, how much will it take to fill you up? Never mind, come along, it's crowded there but they'll find a place for us." Paula herded Maggy out of the Select as briskly as a terrier, never glancing at the table of Kiki's friends who watched them maliciously until they reached the door.

Around the corner, halfway down the rue Bréa, the two women turned in at an inconspicuous door that seemed to lead to a *charcuterie.* But beyond the display cases, filled with selections of cold Russian hors d'oeuvres, was a small, low-ceilinged, red-walled room with marble counters and high stools.

Once they were perched before a counter and Paula had ordered for both of them, she returned to her questioning of Maggy. "Tell me all about yourself. Mind you. I'll know if you leave something out."

Maggy hesitated, not knowing how to begin. No one in her seventeen years had ever asked her this question. In Tours, where she had lived all of her life, everyone knew everything there was to know about her. Should she gloss over the facts? Something about Paula's eyes disposed her to tell the truth. They were infinitely knowing, yet infinitely kind and Maggy needed someone to talk to even more than she needed food. She took a deep breath for courage and plunged in to get the worst of it said as quickly as possible.

"The most important thing about me has always been that my father died a week before he was supposed to marry my mother—he had smallpox. If he'd lived, I'd have been just another premature child—as it was—I'm illegitimate."

"Evidently—but these things happen, even in the best of families."

"But not in respectable Jewish families. They just *never* happen. I'm the only bastard in the whole Jewish community of Tours and I've always had my nose rubbed in it."

"Your mother then, why didn't she just leave Tours and go to live somewhere else, pretend that she was a widow like so many other women?"

"She died when I was born. Aunt Esther always blamed her for dying and escaping the scandal of her conduct."

"Charming! Such sympathy! Did this agreeable aunt bring you up?"

"No, I lived with my grandmother until she died four months ago." Maggy thought wistfully of the gentle old woman who had raised her so tenderly in her small house, who had been made happy by Maggy's smiles, whose uncritical love had made Maggy brave, who had always resisted Aunt Esther's irrational conviction that somehow Maggy had to pay for the shame of her birth.

"It was my grandmother Cecile, my mother's mother, who named me Magali. She always called me that, even though everyone else calls me Maggy, because it was one of her family's favorite names. The Lunels moved to Tours from Provence after the Revolution and in Provençal Magali means '*Marguerite*' . . ."

"So you're from the South, when it gets down to it?"

"Yes, on my father's side too. His name was David Astruc. Astruc means 'born under a lucky star' in Provençal . . . but not for him! My grandmother used to tell me stories about my family to cheer me up when the other kids called me a bastard. She said that even though my parents had made a mistake they came from the oldest Jewish families in France—from many hundreds of years before the Crusades—and that I should always remember it with pride."

Maggy gestured with her long arms in an ardent arabesque, fired by memories of the tales her grandmother had woven of a life in cities with musical names: Nîmes, Cavaillon, Avignon.

"But what happened after she died?" Paula asked, touched by Maggy's almost childish sense of vanished grandeur.

"Ah, that's why I'm here, that's why I had to leave Tours forever and why I'll never go back. My aunt couldn't wait to get rid of me. The funeral was hardly over before the hunt for a husband began. Not in Tours of course—there I'd always be the Lunel bastard—but in other cities. Finally she found a family in Lille whose son was so ugly that they couldn't find a girl who would even go out with him, much less marry him . . . and they arranged it!"

Furiously, Maggy pushed her hair away from her elegantly positioned ears. "An arranged marriage. In this day and age . . . yes, they still do it. As soon as I heard I started to make my plans."

As she paused to eat the marinated lamb she remembered the day on which her rebellion had changed from an insubstantial dream into a necessary act. The proposed marriage took the idea of running away to Paris out of the realm of fantasy. She had saved five hundred francs over the years out of her grandmother's little gifts and she spent three hundred of them in the department stores on the rue Bordeaux for a cheap suitcase and a few ready-made garments. Her only extravagance had been the silk stockings, three pairs of them, but how could she confront Paris in black cotton?

"So," Paula interrupted her thoughts, "you are, in short, a beautiful, orphaned Jewish virgin."

Maggy laughed at this interpretation, on a rising, blithe note, showing the glint of her perfect teeth, her yellow-green eyes sparkling like the target of a treasure hunt in the dimness of the restaurant.

"Nobody ever put it precisely like that before and I've been called a lot of things. My grandmother used to send me to the rabbi of our town, Rabbi Taradash, to be properly scolded because she knew that she could never do it convincingly. And I'd go to him in disgrace at least once a month—it gave him a change, he said, from preparing bar mitzvah boys—and he'd get so involved in the logic of my explanations that finally he'd just make me promise not to do it again and I never did. I'd do something worse. But 'beautiful'—no, nobody but my poor grandmother ever called me that. Or 'virgin' either."

"Are you a virgin then?"

"Of course I am!" Maggy looked startled. She'd been in trouble all of her life for running wild with a bunch of boys but they had been companions only, partners in troublemaking.

"So much the better," Paula said, "at least for the moment. You have everything still ahead of you and that's the best way to begin in Paris."

Paula had seen generations of Montparnasse girls come and go. She had seen them drive off in Bugattis with millionaires and never return and she had seen them die in a week of a raging form of syphilis; she had seen them marry artists and turn into proud housewives, and more often, she had seen them marry artists and turn into harpies. She didn't believe she'd ever seen a girl with the promise of Maggy Lunel. This girl, she thought consideringly, was someone inevitable.

"Well, that's it, that's all there is to me. Except that I've made the worst possible start." Not even a full stomach, not even the novelty of a listener as interested as Paula, had made Maggy forget her experience with the painter she knew was called Mistral.

"Listen to me, my little one. You must put Mistral and his abominable manners out of your mind. Vava tells me he's a genius but if that's true, I ask, why doesn't he sell? How much of a genius can he be if he can't afford to eat at my restaurant?" Clearly this was Paula's yardstick of worldly achievement.

"That woman, Kiki de Montparnasse, does she eat at your place?" Maggy asked curiously.

"She wouldn't dare to put her foot in the door, that dough-faced bundle of bones and pretensions. And her name is Alice Prin. 'Kiki de Montparnasse' indeed!" Paula's face grew as grim as its round contours would allow. "To call herself that when she wasn't even born in Paris—it's too disgusting."

"But they told me she was queen of the models . . ."

"They told you a lie. They know nothing. Once, and not so long ago either, I was queen of the models but Alice Prin has never rivaled what I was, she hasn't come close." Paula's lips closed in an unforgiving line. She could hardly explain to the innocence of Maggy that the one who called herself Kiki had stolen not just one but many of Paula's lovers, and then, not content with those victories, she had boasted to all Montparnasse of them.

"I wonder why she insulted me? I've never done anything to her."

"Because she is so proud of herself that she has to make fun of every other woman she sees. But her little group of sycophants mean nothing. Listen to me, Maggy, you look like no one else in the world. You were *born* to be painted."

"Born?" Maggy stopped. Paula's words, stated with such authority, were so unexpected that they robbed her of speech.

"Yes, born, as a hummingbird is born to seek nectar, as a bee is born to sting, as a chicken is born to be roasted. But this business of offering yourself in the street in the *foire aux modeles*, that's out of the question for you, understand? I'll introduce you to the painters who can afford to pay more than fifteen francs for a three-hour pose—they're all my pals. Did Mistral pay you anything, by the way? No, of course he wouldn't—that doesn't astonish me. But from now on you work only for the maximum. Of course you have to learn a thing or two first, but nothing I can't teach you. It's all a matter of making up your mind to take off your knickers—how difficult can that be, after all? You see, it is a painter's business to learn how each woman is made. Whatever we may think, they need us far more than we need them."

"They do?" Maggy's voice was astonished.

"But yes. Just imagine it, Maggy. For fifteen hundred years, ever since the Dark Ages ended, artists have been running after this ordinary thing, the body of a naked woman. Nothing calls more upon an artist's strength, nothing shows up his weakness as quickly. Show me a man who cannot paint a naked woman and I'll show you a man who cannot truly paint."

"Constantine Moreau never told us that. He only said . . . that, well, that Renoir would have wanted to paint me."

"Perhaps Moreau merely wanted to keep his job. What, I wonder, would you schoolgirls have repeated at home? Well, what do you say? I propose to *launch* you! Not just out of the goodness of my heart, mind you. I want you to beat that bitch, that insufferable, intolerable Alice Prin who has the arrogance to think that because my youth is gone, because I've put on perhaps a kilo or two, that she has taken my place. Mine! She can't see into the future, but I can, and one day her youth will go too—as will yours, my seventeen-year-old pigeon—even yours. Well, Maggy?"

Before the girl could answer Paula held up a warning hand. "Are you sure you're up to it? I don't want to waste my time if you're not. It's boring work, you'll always feel too cold or too hot, and most of all it's far more difficult than anyone realizes to hold a pose. You'll want to cry with pain but you must never let your client know it. When the half-hour is up, then, and only then, may you move. And ten minutes later, back to work. So. Shall we make Alice Prin regret the day she insulted you? Shall we attack?"

"Oh, yes . . . yes, *please!*" Maggy sent her glass of tea crashing to the floor with her instantaneous gesture of impatient acceptance. Suddenly the old dream lay within her grasp again all the more precious for the fiasco of the morning, suddenly she felt that she had only to reach out to hold Paris between her arms. What did it matter, after all, if Renoir was dead?

4

"Listen to me, Maggy Lunel," Paula said severely. "Does an egg wear a skirt?"

"Not the eggs I know," Maggy answered, rolling her eyes disrespectfully. In less than a week's acquaintance she had learned to love Paula—and those she loved, she teased.

"Don't make the mistake of not taking me seriously, my girl! You must imagine, with all the power you possess, that your body is a *basket of eggs*, eggs of different colors and sizes, your breasts the eggs of an ostrich, your pubic hair the spotted egg of a gull, your nipples the eggs of an undernourished sparrow. A naked egg is the most natural thing in the world. It is so basic, so complete that not even Brillat-Savarin ever suggested that an eggshell should be decorated."

"What about Russian Easter eggs?" Maggy protested, but sooner than she would have believed possible, she learned how to feel genuinely unconcerned as she exposed her body to the eyes of the painters who first gave her work as Paula's *protégée*, only to quickly find themselves in hot competition with each other for her time. If she felt a blush about to betray her, Maggy learned to shield her face with her hair for the few seconds it took to recover the egg image, but within weeks she moved easily from pose to pose, her body just an object.

Pascin painted her with roses in her lap, an icon of sensual authority; Chagall painted her as a bride flying in wonder through a purple sky; Picasso painted her over and over again in his monumental, neoclassic style and she became the preferred odalisque of Matisse. "You, *popotte*," she said to him, "are my favorite client. Not for your beautiful eyes, but for your oriental carpet. Here, at least, I can sit down—it's like a week's vacation."

The day after she met Paula, Maggy moved out of her hotel into one room with a fireplace and a sink and a bidet, high up in the building next to La Pomme d'Or, Paula's restaurant. It cost her eighty-five francs a month, furnished only with a big, gilt-trimmed bed. Maggy bought herself fresh new bedding. Paula gave her an overstuffed chair, she picked up a battered table and an old armoire in a junk shop and once they were installed she had no more space for anything but a mirror above the sink. When Maggy looked out of her window at the mansards and chimney pots of the gray-white roofs of Montparnasse, outlined against the ever-changing skies of Paris, she wished for no other view on earth.

The building in which she lived boasted that rarest of creatures, a good-natured, happy concierge. Madame Poulard sat in her dark *loge* working all day at her Singer sewing machine, toes up, heels down, toes up, heels down, *petite couturière* to the immediate neighborhood. Childless, she adopted all the girls for whom she sewed, pouring over *Le Journal des Modes* with Maggy as they looked for designs to copy, since the two ready-made skirts and two blouses Maggy had brought from Tours were totally inadequate for her new life.

By October of 1925 Maggy had established herself as Kiki's only rival and equal and even if Kiki was still "*de*" Montparnasse, Paula gloated over the fact that Maggy needed no such qualification after her own name.

It was just as Maggy, unique Maggy, the one and only Maggy, who always sported a fresh red carnation in her buttonhole, that she jumped in and out of taxis, too busy to walk from one job to another; it was as Maggy that she danced all night at Le Jockey and La Jungle to the music of a tango or a shimmy; as Maggy that she moved to the insinuating melody of the beguine at La Bal Nègre where she felt as foreign to that world of dancers who had been born in Martinique and Guadeloupe, as did Cocteau and Scott Fitzgerald, who danced there as well.

Maggy was invited to the twenty-round boxing matches at the Cirque d'Hiver, which she attended with several masculine admirers to protect her from the rough crowd, and she went often to the steeplechases at Auteuil, cheering when her horse cleared all the jumps and lavishing all her winnings afterward on champagne for her pals. She never went to the races without a tip on a horse and she rarely lost because the tips were excellent, given in return for a smile and a sudden hug from her strong, slim arms.

When Maggy arrived at La Rotonde or La Coupole, there was always a chair for her as she joined first one table and then another of her *copains*. Now Montparnasse felt like her own village too and that fall she celebrated her eighteenth birthday with a party in her room. Maggy decorated the bidet by filling it with bunches of red carnations, piled the one table high with bottles of wine and invited a hundred people. Everyone came, bringing friends, and they sat drinking and singing on the staircase until the police finally arrived.

Occasionally she would spend an evening alone at home, on her quilt, watching the sky from her window and trying to arrange in her mind all the new things she had seen, all the new people she had met. Rabbi Taradash would have disapproved deeply, Maggy smiled to herself, if he knew how she earned her living, in fact he wouldn't have believed it possible, but she suspected that he would still call her, as he used to, "my little *mazik*," a Hebrew word used to describe a beloved child who is also a swift, clever prankster.

She wasn't homesick although she still grieved for her grandmother, particularly on Friday evenings when, on the eve of the Sabbath, peace and cheer had filled their small house with the illumination of the two candles on the dining room table and the blessing of the light and the wine. None of the Lunels had been particularly observant or pious Jews yet this weekly ceremony had been comforting to Maggy and every year she had looked forward eagerly to kindling an additional candle on her grandmother's fine Chanukah menorah day by day, until all the candles blazed sweetly in memory of those flames that had once burned in the Temple in Jerusalem for eight days with only one day's supply of oil. Now all that belonged to a life she had put behind her. Certainly, she thought, she didn't miss the family seder on the eve of Passover that had always taken place at Aunt Esther's house. Maggy's gathered relatives had somehow never failed to make her remember her shameful status; each year she would once again feel that her mere existence was a stain on their family's good name . . . no, she thought defiantly, no, I couldn't have endured that existence a minute longer and now I can forget it forever.

Maggy needed these occasional quiet hours of reflection as a balance to the many nights of dancing when she escaped from the immobility of her hours of posing into the wholehearted dash toward pleasure, ever more pleasure, never *enough* pleasure, that made Montparnasse the center of all that was mad and joyous and abandoned in Paris.

As Paula never failed to point out to her, there was a dark side to Montparnasse life, a world in which drink and drugs were a constant. But even without her warnings, Maggy would have gamboled immune through the never-ending party of Montparnasse nights. She would have been untainted by that sky that burned so red, illuminated as it was by the dozens of nightclubs and bars that attracted all of Paris to its lights. She still was shielded by essential and untouchable innocence, the legacy of seventeen years in her grandmother's house.

Often Maggy danced barefoot, not just for comfort, but because she was taller than many of her partners. She still refused to cut her hair. Before she went out at night, in one of the simple sleeveless chemise dresses with low necklines that Madame Poulard made from the ends of bolts of material Maggy found on sale at Le Bon Marché, she parted her hair in the middle and coiled it over her ears, or she wrapped a sequined scarf around her head, knotting it on one side and letting it fall over a shoulder. But do what she would to simulate the hairstyle of the time, after half an hour on a dance floor, Maggy would find that the scarf had slipped off, or that the tight coils of hair had somehow come undone and the masses of her hair were swinging from side to side as if she were galloping about in open fields.

It was not just a whim that prevented her from adopting a more modish hairstyle; the painters she posed for preferred it long, and even paid a few francs extra because of it. An artist's joy in a woman is based on her flesh in all its manifestations, from her toenails to the crown of her head, and, to a man, they detested the style that decreed that a woman's hair should be cropped and flat. However, like most of the other women in the Western world, Maggy had adopted the line of dress imposed by fashion, the waist barely marked at the hips, the breasts flattened. That whimsical painter, Marie Laurençin, protested that a woman was not a stick, but Chanel and Patou and Molyneux had decreed that she must try to look as much like one as possible, and within her limited means, Maggy tried to follow fashion.

"You needn't give yourself airs and graces," she cheerfully assured Picasso, as she cocked an eye at the way he had distorted her body in his paintings. "It's not only your own idea, *chouchou*, for we women too can reinvent anatomy. Did you notice my new dress, eh? And don't forget it, they belong strictly to us, those breasts and thighs and all the other bits and pieces you play fast and loose with. *No touching*!"

For her work she had bought herself an apple-green silk robe and during her minutes of rest she would often wrap it around her body and walk around the artist's studio, stalking the unfinished canvas like a heron.

"So that's the way I look to you, is it? Well, I may not have a full-length mirror in my place but I have only to look down to see that both my nipples are the same color. D'y' see that you made the right one look like a raspberry and the other like a strawberry out of season? And my eyes—do they really have so many different shapes? I've heard that the Eskimos have twenty-five different words for snow—are you of the Eskimo school then? Still, you might have a lick of talent. Who knows? I'm no expert certainly."

On her clients, "*mes popottes*," Maggy lavished her sarcasm, her generosity and her incurable impudence. On Paula she bestowed a solid love that was untouched by capriciousness and suited the older woman very well. She regarded all of Maggy's triumphs as if they were her own and from time to time, as the two women ate an early dinner together in the kitchen of La Pomme d'Or, Paula noted that the girl had still not found a man. Not with that monstrous appetite of hers, the appetite of someone who had never known a lovesick day. Time enough, she thought to herself approvingly.

While Maggy conquered Montparnasse, Julien Mistral found himself facing a financial crisis. For years he had carefully eked out the modest patrimony he had inherited at the death of his mother, almost three years earlier, but now, he realized with a shock, it was almost gone. Yet no strict economies were possible to an artist who used paint and canvas as lavishly as he did.

He had always bought in such quantities that he had persuaded Lucien Lefebvre, the owner of Lefebvre-Foinet, the art supply store on the rue Bréa, to give him a small discount. There were cheaper paints to be sure, but only Lefebvre ground his by hand and mixed them with poppy-seed oil instead of the usual linseed oil so that they smelled like honey, and possessed, Mistral was convinced, a richness of tone that other paints didn't have. But even with the discount he had run up an uncomfortably large bill. Yet to limit himself? Impossible!

Restraint, economy, husbanding of resources, living within his means; all of these virtues Mistral practiced in his daily life, drinking only a little cheap red wine in cafés, and paying almost nothing for rent or food. Women, he thought, as he got ready to leave home on the evening of the Surrealist costume ball, to which he'd been invited by a rich young American woman, Kate Browning, were no expense. As plentiful in his life as the burrs on a dog, not one of them had yet cost him a centime.

Mistral stretched and almost hit his head on the ceiling of his bedroom. He decided not to bother shaving or brushing his tangled red curls, since his only concession to the need for a costume was an old-fashioned, wide-brimmed, black hat he had picked up in some secondhand clothes store. He was not disposed to take any more trouble for the Surrealists whose definition of beauty—"the chance encounter of a sewing machine and an umbrella on a dissection table"—was, to him, an abomination.

All "isms" were equally loathsome to him, and in that group he included political parties of every type, all religious groups and anyone who believed in some clearly formulated system of morals. Art had nothing to do with words like morality or immorality; it was above morality, above definitions of beauty. Why, he often wondered, did people bugger themselves up by getting involved in ideas instead of paint?

Still, he was willing to take the time to go to the ball. Kate Browning might buy another painting soon, he thought, and God knows he could use the money. She was not unattractive in her severely groomed, almost ascetically pretty, blond, and obviously American way. In the last months he'd sold her two small canvases, which made her even more attractive to him than perhaps she deserved—he liked a less austere type.

In any case, he would not, could not skimp on his materials. Mistral hurried out, rolling the Lefebvre-Foinet bill into a ball and flipping it into the garden next door. There was no artist so serious or so busy that he didn't go to costume balls, not even Julien Mistral.

Were there more costume balls in 1926 than there had been in 1925? Or would there be more in 1927? No one could be sure during those fine festive years for no one could keep track. Every week there was another ball sponsored by a different group. In this second week of April 1926, the Russian artists had already given their *Bal Banal* and the homosexual international had held their *Bal des Lopes* at Magic City. When the Surrealists organized a *Bal Sans Raison d'Etre* to celebrate nothing at all and everything at once, everyone agreed it was not to be missed.

Just a year before, the Surrealists had created a great scandal at a banquet given at the Closerie des Lilas that ended in an attempted lynching only broken up by the police. Freethinkers of the most doctrinaire kind, they made a violent stand against the government, the military, the church, and for full measure, against business as well, glorying in their nickname "The Terror of the Boulevard Montparnasse." When two of their number, Miró and Max Ernst, created the decor for Diaghilev's *Ballet Russe*, dozens of Surrealists broke up the performance by blowing trumpets, making speeches and attacking the spectators.

With their exciting reputation who, with any pretense to position in the world of art or letters or fashion, could possibly stay home that night?

"Surrealist or not," Paula had announced a week earlier, "I'm going in what suits me best, just as I always do."

"Not the Pompadour? Not again!" asked Maggy. "You're impossible—I'm tired of your costumes and you should be too."

"There is only one reason to go to a costume ball," Paula said serenely. "You go to show off whatever part of your body the accident of living in this banal era has prevented you from revealing in your everyday clothes. I'm not trying to be clever—I leave that for those with nothing special to reveal, who don't have my magnificent white shoulders, my delicious pair of breasts, my still small waist. But—just for a change—I'm going as Du Barry, to make a little change from the Pompadour, no?"

"So little that it's unimportant. Again your wide pink taffeta skirts, the tight blue satin bodice, a lace fichu, more lace at your wrists, your powdered wig and your beauty patch—you disgrace me!"

"Ah, I'm always underestimated," Paula sighed. "Instead of the lace fichu I will wear a stuffed python attached at my right shoulder, passing under my bare breasts and fastened securely along my left shoulder until the tongue of the beast licks my ear."

"Bare breasts?"

"But naturally—I thought I'd explained."

"*Félicitations!* I'm proud of you."

"It's a small effort. Only the python to be borrowed, and I'm set. What about you?"

"I'm going as a bowl of fruit."

"What a horror! Lemons in your hair and a dress like an apple? Maggy, that's unworthy of you."

"Wait and see." Maggy stirred her coffee and lowered her lids over her eyes. The thick, straight sweep of her lashes, darkened with mascara, looked like two long, spiky caterpillars on her cheeks.

"Who are you going with—Alain?"

"Alain and three of his friends—four men to be precise."

"As always, safety in numbers, isn't that so?"

Maggy puffed out her lips and blew at an imaginary hair as she did when she was embarrassed, a childish habit she had often been teased for in the past. Paula, as usual, was right.

Montparnasse was like an overstocked sexual zoo. Every possible kind and variety and assortment of sexual partnership was to be found there in examples by the dozens. From the domestic household of the heterosexual couple, to the most unrestrained cases of fetishism, no aspect of Eros was foreign or antipathetical to the *quartier*. Everything was possible and permitted.

In this atmosphere of unbounded, and therefore frightening, permissiveness, Maggy had found herself, from the beginning, more comfortable as a spectator than a participant. She scolded herself as the months slipped past, berating herself for virginity of which nobody but Paula suspected her, but in spite of all the arguments she found in favor of having a lover, the fact was that she remained a virgin although her eighteenth birthday was months past.

Maggy concealed her state of stubborn, unfashionable chastity from everyone. Only Paula was not misled by her free and easy airs, the saucy impertinence with which she treated her men, her laughing rejoinders to their importuning, her casual nakedness. Since everyone assumed that she must have a lover, the fact that Maggy rejected every man's attention whenever it became serious, simply gave her the reputation of being some fortunate man's faithful and secretive mistress.

It took Alain and his friends all afternoon and evening to create Maggy's *trompe l'oeil* costume. Her right breast was painted as a bunch of pale green grapes, her left as a small melon of Cavaillon, the kind that is served whole, with sweet wine in its cavity. Her arms and shoulders became bunches of bananas, some ripe, some still showing a hint of green, and a pineapple grew down under her breasts and over her navel, its sharp leaves losing themselves in her pubic hair. Each hip was a slice of pumpkin and her thighs were stalks of rhubarb. From her knees to her feet she was entwined in painted grapevines and her armpits held apples.

Her face was left unpainted except for two honey bees on her forehead, her hair was held back by a garland of flowers. She had refused to bow to the protests of the artists who insisted that the green chiffon scarf she intended to wear as an improvised G-string was incompatible with the spirit of the occasion.

The artists had constructed an oval, wooden fruit bowl, six feet long, covered with silver paint, on which they planned to carry Maggy at shoulder height. Each of the four men wore painted sandwich boards, over black tights and sweaters. André represented a Brie, Pierre an entire Camembert, Henri a slice of Roquefort and Alain half of a Chevre . . . each huge block of cheese painted so realistically that they looked edible. The four artists were part of a school of Realist painters and their ensemble of cheese and fruit was meant as a protest against the Surrealists and their distortions.

"Wait," Maggy protested as they made a trial attempt to hoist the fruit bowl, "I need something to do with my hands. Can't I carry a flower or something?"

"No, you'll ruin it. Just rest your head on one elbow and lie absolutely still and don't, for the love of God, sweat. Damn it, Maggy, why wouldn't you let us use oils instead of water colors?"

"Because I don't intend to spend tomorrow bathing in turpentine," Maggy answered. "As it is, Alain, the silver paint feels a bit sticky. I'm not sure it dried properly. Didn't some king paint slaves with gold paint once? I believe they died of it."

"Rumor, rumor. Anyway it's only going to come off on your ass, if at all. Now let's go—the ball started an hour ago. Maggy, get off there and walk with us. When we get to Bullier we'll put this miracle together."

"Just let me put on my coat and shoes."

"Why bother—it's warm out," André protested.

"But it's three streets away."

"Don't you dare smudge anything," Pierre said anxiously.

"On second thought, I'm taking a taxi—in a coat. I'll meet you there."

"Oh, the little bourgeoise," André mocked.

Maggy advanced on the little artist menacingly. "Do you want to die, mosquito? Strangled by two bananas? Take that back."

"You wouldn't get mad if it weren't true," he cried, dancing out of her reach.

"Hey, there's no time for lovemaking," Alain shouted. "If we get there too late everybody'll be too far gone to notice us—onward! Everybody to the barricades!"

Five hundred people were jammed together at the Bullier by the time Maggy arrived. In the crowd were Darius Milhaud, Satie and Massine. The Comtesse de Noailles was there and so were Paul Poiret and Schiaparelli, joined by Picasso wearing his picador's costume. Gromaire had put on the habit of a Spanish Jesuit to which he had added balloonlike woman's underpants trimmed with rose red ribbons and Brancusi had gotten himself up as an Oriental prince with beads to his knees and a Persian carpet around his shoulders. Pascin, followed as always by his tame troop of gypsies, jazz musicians and pretty girls, wore his usual black.

Astonished "Bravos" sounded at the first sight of Maggy at the tip of the great staircase. She made her entrance borne aloft and perfectly balanced during the perilous descent. One by one the musicians caught sight of Maggy through the smoke, and with a toot and a blare and a blast of every instrument in the orchestra they heralded her slow passage around the huge ballroom, lying motionless on the silver platter. Everywhere she passed sections of the crowd stopped dancing to press around the group of Realists, applauding and screaming their approval. Maggy had been so skillfully painted that only little by little did everyone realize that, except for a wisp of chiffon, she was utterly naked, a realization that only added to the roar of approbation.

"What on earth is *that*?" Kate Browning asked Mistral, from her vantage point at one of the raised tables that circled the dance floor.

"A Realist manifesto," he shrugged. He had recognized Maggy as soon as she appeared. No one else in Montparnasse had ever flaunted hair of such a flamboyant shade of orange, a color he'd never forgotten. But he could scarcely reconcile the awkward, embarrassed girl who didn't know the first thing about posing with this shamelessly revealed creature, lounging naked before a thousand eyes, and laughing. *Laughing!*

He had heard about her from dozens of people as she became well known, he had often glimpsed her hurrying about the streets from a distance, but they had never exchanged a word in the eleven months that had passed since her first day as a model. If he had been honest he might have admitted to himself that he had avoided her, he might even have recognized that he was ashamed of the manner in which he had chased her away—but such thoughts were foreign to Mistral's attitude toward life. Second thoughts about a silly girl? No, life was too short, there was too much work to do.

"Julien! Do you know how to dance?" Kate Browning asked in the quietly imperious manner that she was unaware she possessed, although she was only twenty-three.

"Dance? Of course I dance. But not well. I warn you."

"Well, don't you *want* to dance?"

"In this mob?"

"Come on, I'm in the mood," she said, not to be frustrated.

"What's that they're playing now?" he asked.

" 'Mountain Greenery.' It's nice and bouncy and you can't just sit here."

Reluctantly he got to his feet, inches taller than anyone in the room, and followed the trim American onto the infernal dance floor on which the bodies were so pressed together that his lack of dancing skills wasn't important. For a few minutes they moved inexpertly almost at the edge of the crowd as the music changed to a pulsing ragtime beat. Suddenly Mistral and Kate were squeezed from both sides by scores of dancers crowding to get a better look at Maggy, whose four bearers were approaching.

Maggy, on her perch, was wrapped in a mounting delirium induced by the warm bath of cheering admiration whirling around her. There was an immense liberation in being naked yet covered by paint as if she were visible and invisible at the same moment. She felt as if she were hovering over the ballroom floating free. From every side hands reached out to try to touch her but she was aware of no menace as the artists raised the silver oval higher and higher to keep her out of reach.

Suddenly, from the crowd, a voice shouted, "Down with the Realists!"

"Down with the Surrealists!" screamed a dozen other voices.

The crowd, which only a second before had been good-natured in spite of the suffocating pressure of the dance floor, joined battle vigorously—this is what they had been waiting for all evening. Kate Browning, aware of danger, adroitly slipped out of Mistral's arms and threaded her way to the edge of the crowd, leaving Mistral to follow her.

Jostling, shoving, elbowing each other, howling slogans, the dancers closed in on Maggy's four artists, almost knocking Alain and André off their feet. Pierre and Henri, the Camembert and Roquefort, still struggled manfully. However, without the careful balance the four artists had achieved, the big wooden platform tilted alarmingly and, with a start, Maggy realized that she was in danger of falling and being trampled underfoot. She looked around, suddenly alert, keeping her wits about her. Everywhere there was a mass of bodies, men punching each other, women ducking and screeching. The place had erupted into a riot.

Crouching, Maggy gathered herself together, coiled herself up into a tight ball and launched herself off the platter with a strong leap sideways, aimed right at the only point in the room that seemed stable—Mistral's black hat.

He caught her with an "Ouf!" of surprise but he stood rocklike, too strong to lose his feet in the mob. Maggy lay in his arms like a child on a swing, no fear, no alarm in her eyes, still under the spell of the moment in spite of her instinctive spring to safety.

She curled her arms around Mistral's neck and let her head fall on his shoulder. Automatically he tightened his arms and held her to him as she compressed herself into a compact oval, bending her knees sharply so that her legs and feet protected the backs of her thighs and her bare, silver-splotched bottom.

Finally, Mistral moved. There was a door to the street not more than a hundred feet away and he pushed strongly toward it through the swarm, clutching Maggy as if she were someone he had rescued from the sea.

As he reached the street, Maggy spoke.

"Where are we going?"

"Not far."

"I hope it's an unpretentious place."

"Oh, it is."

Mistral crossed the street, turned a corner and walked into a large building with an ornate, sham-Moroccan façade. Inside there was a counter behind which a woman stood waiting for customers.

"Good evening, Monsieur. For one or two?" She showed no surprise at the sight of a man carrying a multicolored, naked woman.

"One, please. Do we have to wait?"

"No, you're in luck tonight. I have something ready—just follow me, Monsieur, 'Dame."

The woman led the way down a hallway lined with doors at regular intervals. She opened one of the doors, ushered him in and shut the door behind them.

In the middle of the bare room stood a huge tub filled to the brim with hot water. On a chair by the tub lay a towel, a cake of soap and a washcloth. Still holding Maggy, with a rapid movement Mistral bent down and tested the temperature with one finger. Satisfied, without letting her feet touch the floor, he plunged her into the water, getting his arms wet above the elbows.

"*Assassin!*" Maggy sputtered.

"It's not that I don't admire your costume but it was coming off all over my shirt," he said, vigorously lathering the washcloth.

"Give me that."

"Certainly not. It's man's work." He took off his damp jacket, rolled up his wet sleeves and knelt on the floor by the tub. Maggy tried to stand up in the water but she couldn't get the right leverage in the deep tub. She floundered, heaving herself halfway out only to slip back again. Mistral ignored her struggles and briskly applied the washcloth to whatever part of her body presented itself. Within seconds the water turned a murky gray.

Maggy started to laugh helplessly. She let herself lie back in the water and watch uncomplainingly while he scrubbed her shoulders and her legs. Only when he approached her breasts did she pounce, with an overhand blow from her two hands, her fingers firmly interlaced, right to the back of his neck. His hat fell into the water and he let go of the washcloth just long enough for her to grab it. She slung a hatful of soapy water directly into his eyes and, while he swore vilely, half blinded, into the towel, drying them as best he could, she finished scrubbing off the last of the watercolor from her body, laughing harder than ever at the sight of him kneeling on the floor, dripping onto his shirt, his eyes red and smarting.

At last Maggy dropped the washcloth on the wooden floor and sat in the opaque water that rose to her shoulders, her arms folded on the rim of the tub, her chin on her hands. Her damp hair clung to her shoulders, her eyes wet with tears of mirth, but her lips were curved in an old tomboy grin, and she'd clapped Mistral's sopping hat on the back of her head.

"Nice work," she congratulated him. "But what have you planned for the rest of the evening?"

Mistral sat back on his heels. What indeed?

"I'm getting cold and I'm getting hungry," Maggy menaced. "And when I'm cold and hungry I get mean. D'y' want to risk it?" There was challenge in her voice, in her eyes, in the cock of her head—even her red eyebrows were challenging. She might be naked and submerged but the very way she'd appropriated his hat defied him.

"Don't go away," Mistral said, jumped to his feet and walked out of the room, taking his jacket and the damp towel, closing the door behind him.

"Oh, that son of a bitch!" Maggy cried out loud. She looked disgustedly at the rim of the tub where a gray ring was forming. She tried to let in some more water but the faucet was locked. She shrugged and stood up in the tub, sloshing water over herself with the palms of her hands. She was reassured to see that she hadn't turned gray. She stepped carefully onto the floor and shook herself mightily, shuddering like a great dog, wringing water out of her hair. Fortunately the night was warm and the room was even warmer, filled, as it was, with the steam of the bath.

Suddenly, the door opened and Mistral walked back into the room. Maggy straightened up, shielding her lower belly with the big hat, one arm over her breasts.

"You forgot to knock."

"Sorry." He passed her two fresh towels. "Dry yourself off—go on—I won't look. And here's my jacket—put it on when you're finished. I have a taxi waiting."

"I hope we're going somewhere nice for dinner."

"Eventually."

"You *do* know how to treat a girl." Maggy struggled into his jacket. The sleeves dangled below her knees, hiding her hands. Clumsily, she wrapped her arms around herself to hold the jacket together. She was entirely covered up except for her bare legs and feet. "Well, I'm all set, and rather grand too, but you don't look like much. Your shirt's all wet," she grumbled.

"I think we both look . . . clean," Mistral said, leading the way to the front door of the public baths. "As long as you're clean, the rest isn't important."

Padding in her bare feet, Maggy followed him to the street door of the public bathhouse. They darted across the pavement into the taxi that waited outside.

"Sixty-five boulevard Arago," Mistral told the startled driver.

Still barefoot, but wearing the red kimono, which she had put on with a smile of surprise at finding it just where it had been a year before, surprised that it could still hang from the same hook like a remote memory, Maggy entered the studio, dimly lit at night when the work lights were off, and looked for a place to sit down.

The studio was as crowded as the bedroom was bare. Mistral had the habit of visiting the *brocantes* of the neighborhood, the dealers in objects that could not be called antiques, yet were certainly not new, and picking up odd bits and pieces that caught his questing eye; a huge casserole of Quimper pottery with a hole in it; a ship's figurehead, half eaten by worms; the last remaining piece of a once splendid set of painted tin soldiers; a Victorian chair of purple satin trimmed with moth-eaten braid.

However, although his discoveries filled a room they fell short of furnishing it. Maggy picked her way toward the Victorian chair, which at least seemed to have a recognizable function, and sat in it with a sigh of pleasure. She was brimming with a mixture of curiosity and adventure. She had never expected to find herself here again and the evening seemed filled with tentative wonder.

"Soup?" she called into the tiny kitchen in which she heard Mistral moving about.

"What do you think this is, a restaurant? If I want soup I go out for it. You'll get bread and cheese and sausage and wine and be glad for them."

"You're not much of a host."

"I don't entertain often," Mistral said, looking with irritation at the sausage he was slicing. It had an air of antiquity to it. On a tray, he hastily arranged a few mismated dishes, a bottle of wine and two glasses, one of them chipped, and carried it out to the studio. He stopped in mid-stride at the sight of Maggy in the purple chair, her orange hair spread out on the red Japanese silk. It was as if a fire had been lit in the corner of his studio.

"You can't sit there."

"Why not?"

"That chair is about to fall apart."

"What do you suggest then—the floor?"

"I have a little table outside in the garden—I thought we'd eat out there."

"But do you also have little chairs out there in the garden?" she asked with a flick of laughter in her voice.

"Yes, believe it or not."

"Ah, well in that case, who could resist such magnificence?" Maggy followed Mistral outside where overgrown lilacs, their white blooms just in full bloom, hung glimmering faintly over a table of white painted wood. Two bentwood chairs stood in the unmown grass, with heart-shaped backs and striped cotton cushions on their wooden seats. Mistral lit a tall candle in a short, twisted copper candlestick while Maggy bent over the plate and inspected the sausage.

"Go on, take a slice," he urged her.

"It lacks . . . how shall I put it . . . a certain youth."

"Better not eat it," he said, hastily putting the plate on the grass. "I think the cheese is probably safe. Are you really hungry? I can go and get something—there's a *charcuterie* that stays open late . . ."

"No, no, I'm teasing you. But did you have dinner?"

"Oh."

"What is it?"

"I just remembered where I had dinner."

"And?"

"It was with a woman . . . a rich American art collector of sorts who invited me to that Surrealist madhouse."

"In that case she has serious reason for complaint." Maggy raised her wineglass, gravely leaning forward and gesturing to Mistral to raise his glass to hers. "To the lady, let's drink to the lady who began the evening with Monsieur Mistral. Who knows with whom she will end it? I wish her good fortune."

"Good fortune," said Mistral, touching her glass with his. And as he drank all memory of Kate Browning disappeared. Nothing existed outside of this still, dim corner of a fragrant little garden, this space that seemed to have been dreamed into an existence far from the real world, a space in which the music of Maggy's voice, impudent, low and as free as running water, insulated him from his former life; a space in which his familiar plot of garden seemed to be newly created, as fresh-minted, secret and hidden as if it were the floor of a rain forest.

He felt his will, his reliable, intractable will, slipping away from him like a heavy garment he had worn for too long. He felt ten years younger, he found himself aware of the warm touch of the April air and the lush whisper of the tall grass and the sweet scent of the lilacs and the harsh taste of the wine. Maggy was a lovely shock. He hadn't been prepared for her. He hadn't expected her. What was she doing here? He drank again and the question dissolved, not in wine, because he hadn't had much wine, but in the sight of her.

Without any light but that of the single candle, she decorated the night. Her skin reflected the moon when she moved. The flame of the candle kindled an answering spark in the green of her eyes, a spark so alive that it made the April moon, tucked among the trees, look insignificant and far away. The sound of her voice seemed to be arousing him to feelings of confused mutiny . . . against what he could not have said.

Almost reluctantly, as if obeying an order, he yielded to an unfamiliar yet irresistible command. He flung himself on the grass and took Maggy's bare feet in his hands, rubbing gently.

"Poor feet—they're cold," he murmured.

She didn't answer. The touch of his hands, big, flexible, powerful, the heat and the slight roughness of his skin, made her shudder with an emotion she didn't understand. She flung back her head and it seemed to her that the haze of stars was humming.

Now his lips were on the soles of her feet, tentative, questioning, barely brushing the skin. She caught her breath, afraid to move, spellbound by the sensations that shot from her feet to the very roots of her hair, piercingly urgent sensations that were like a foreign language, heard for the first time and, mysteriously, understood. She bit her lips as his tongue touched the arch of her foot, outlining, exploring, bolder each second. She moaned out loud as she felt his teeth graze her heel, and she tried feebly to pull her feet out of his grasp, but he only tightened his hold. She felt her knees falling apart under the Japanese silk as his tongue ran up the calf of one leg then up the other, finding that soft, private curve behind her knees.

"Stop it," she gasped. "Please."

Mistral stood up, a huge figure in the dark, and gathered her in his arms. He looked at her with a frown of concentration.

"Stop? Are you sure?" He kissed her lips fleetingly and drew back so that he could see her face. "Ah, not so sure, not completely sure," he sighed and kissed her mouth, its succulence both carnal and innocent, slowly kissed those lips that stood out from her pale face like an opulent flower.

Maggy's confusion and sudden alarm disappeared under his kisses. She laughed, not just with pleasure, but with a new note in her voice, the outlaw that had always lived within her rising to the surface. Her lips became an outlaw's lips, her hands an outlaw's hands as she caressed his powerful neck, and reached up for his curly head to pull it down to her again. She wriggled out of his arms, finding her feet, and boldly pressed all her long length against his body. They stood together for a long, long moment, growing together like two tall trees, swaying slightly as their lips parted, then almost immobile as they strained together, seeking a knowledge beyond knowledge. With a grunt of need, Mistral parted the heavy silk kimono, mad to touch the body he knew only through his eyes, mad to feel her skin, to hold her breasts in his hands, to learn the tight buds of her nipples with his fingertips. She spoke in a trance. "Not here—inside." Stumbling, unbuttoning his shirt as he walked, he followed her to his bedroom, to that wide bed under the window through which moonlight fell on the sheets. In seconds he stood naked, erect, magnificent.

"Let me look," she commanded in such a tone of urgent curiosity that he stood still while she approached, all her coltishness gone as she delicately ran her fingers over his shoulders and his chest and down to his waist, lingering over the unfamiliar shapes and textures, the sinewy muscles of his arms, the astonishingly hard points of nipples that hid in the springy hair in his chest. Only when she had satisfied herself, when his body was no longer completely strange to her, did she untie the sash of the kimono and let it fall to the floor. She lay down on the bed, waiting for him.

At last, Maggy thought, at last. She didn't submit to his hands, she encouraged them. Arching and stretching like a cat she played with him, holding her breasts in her hands and offering them to his mouth, letting him raven on them until, with a swift, lithe movement she withdrew and flung herself at his chest, her lips seeking his nipples. Imitating him, she sucked on them until he almost screamed and held her off, unable to endure the excitement. "Ah, so two can't play at that game?" she murmured and soon she had her answer, as with unsteady hands, he parted her legs and bent over her, kneeling on the bed, his hot open mouth questing between her thighs, his tongue flickering. A vast silence seemed to envelop them. Maggy found herself immobile, rigid, almost without breath, as she waited, all playfulness gone.

Still kneeling, sitting on his heels, holding her waist in both hands, Mistral launched himself into her body. She was so moist that he was able to advance several inches before he reached the barrier. He persisted, not understanding, and got no farther.

"What . . . ?" he murmured, heat consuming him as he looked down at the darkness of the triangle where they were joined. He tried again, without success. Now, the spell of inaction broken, Maggy gathered herself up with all her courage and pressed forward, willing herself to open to him. Every muscle in her long, strong legs was tensed, her toes were pointed, her hands clutched the mattress and her back arched as she raised her pelvis upward, his jutting, hot spur of flesh the only focus in the universe. There was a flash of pain but she ignored it, launching herself anew, met halfway by his mighty thrust. Suddenly he was inside of her, suddenly the spear, point and shaft and hilt, now a heavy fullness of mortal flesh, was encompassed by her body and they lay still, panting like two gladiators evenly matched who pause to salute each other before renewing the struggle.

"I didn't know," he whispered, his astonishment so great that it had only commonplace words.

"I didn't tell you. Would it have made a difference?"

"No, *no*." Now they lay on their sides, looking into each other's eyes. One of Mistral's arms supported her shoulders and, with his free hand, he gently probed the damp tangle of her pubic hair, finding the tender flesh he sought, and caressed it stealthily, steadily, without stopping, even when she begged, until she cried out in bewildered joy. Only then did he take his own serious pleasure, but still carefully, with an unaccustomed caution, that added to the swelling, rising fever that shocked him with its power when at last he burst into her as potent as a great bull.

5

The first time Julien Mistral painted Maggy, the first time he went after the shadow between her breasts, the first time he dipped his brush, unthinkingly, into vermilion and painted that shadow, he heard a cosmic "Ah ha!" rock his brain. Stunned, almost knocked off his feet, he *saw*, he saw as he had never seen before, he saw with his entrails as he ravished the canvas, his brush flying almost out of control, his fingers numb with discovery, the temperature of his body rising so that he had to tear off his shirt, his impatience to follow his vision so great that finally he dropped his brushes and squeezed paint onto the canvas directly from the tubes.

He was painting at last as he had always known he could paint, without inhibition, without calculation, with freedom so vast that it was as if the walls and the ceiling of the studio had been knocked away and he was standing under the blue, open sky.

Fascinated, Maggy watched him, as she lay motionless on a heap of green pillows, not daring to move until, long after an hour had passed, he finally stopped his attack on the canvas and dropped at her side, radiant, bathed in sweat.

In a gesture he had never dreamed of before he wiped his paint-smeared hands on her pubic hair, branding her with smears of green and Titian red as if she were another kind of canvas. He tore open his pants, without taking them off, and plunged into her violently, grinding her down on the pillows with his big, hot, wet body until he found a huge release that he met with a sound that was a roar of triumph.

Weeks passed while Mistral painted Maggy. He knew that something about the way light interacted with her flesh had been the inspiration for his breakthrough. It was not only a technical matter, a phenomenon that could be explained by the translucent whiteness of her skin or the way her hair broke into shafts of fire or the fact that his imagination was prepared, why he did not know and did not ask, to seize on her particular physical qualities and use them to make the leap forward. It was also his spiritual conviction that light poured out from the inside of her body, *emanating from it*, so that when he painted her the very canvas became a source of light. Maggy knew that something surpassingly important had happened to him but when she asked him about it the few words he found were not enough. Since the experience was not an intellectual one, it escaped words, and Mistral felt a superstitious awe that prevented him from wanting to talk about it.

After that first night in April it was the one perfect spring of Maggy's life. It was the spring by which all other springs would be judged and found wanting, and while Maggy lived it she also watched herself living it. She knew, in the part of her brain that felt no emotion, that only recorded and filed memory, that this was her age of gold. She knew, with the knowledge born in all women, that nothing as glorious ever lasted forever, and yet, as day followed day, she never looked ahead, never considered the future, never asked herself what would happen tomorrow. Each day was enough, round and full and as complete as an apple of the sun.

For Mistral, too, it was a time of surpassing joy, but before he was a man he was a painter, and his happiness sprang more from the work he was doing than from Maggy herself.

It never occurred to Julien Mistral, following the night of the Surrealist ball, that Maggy had a life that could prevent her from posing solely for him seven days a week. He took all her time as his right, expecting her to hold her pose for abnormally long periods since he was tireless and never stopped until she was in such muscle pain that she had to beg for a rest. He assumed, with a selfishness so total that it was regal, that she was entirely content to leave her own life behind, to abandon her room and share his studio, to forsake her circle of friends, to go without normal diversions, to give up any vestige of personal freedom. When he dropped his brushes it was only natural that she be there waiting to relieve the nervous tension of creation by opening her body to his hungry, violent love-making.

Maggy questioned none of his careless convictions. She offered herself to him on every level with simple generosity, as if she were a field filled with tall, blowing flowers, that grew only to be gathered at his pleasure.

Hour after hour, she gladly endured the concentration of his gaze, knowing that he wasn't thinking of her or even seeing her as Maggy. Her love asked nothing for itself but the satisfaction of watching him work. He was a man consumed, a man filled with so high a passion for creation that she thought of it as holy. The two months during which Mistral painted the seven pictures of Maggy, the series that later came to be called simply *La Rouquinne*, "The Redhead," were months that soon would become isolated from all that Maggy or Mistral knew of ordinary life. They would become as legendary, to each of them, as if they had once been joined together in some heroic adventure never before attempted by man. The series became a milestone in the history of art, but neither of them was ever to discuss it.

By the end of May of 1926, Mistral felt sure enough of his new powers to attack other subjects. When he had finished the seventh portrait of Maggy he abandoned his concentration on the nude as suddenly as he had begun. Now he turned to still life. His neglected garden, heavy with June flowers; each corner of his junk-filled studio, bright with tatters as a flea market; a vase of purple and white asters; a melon split in half—all these objects presented themselves to his freshly inspired vision as if he had never seen them before. They *lived*, as surely as Maggy lived. Light fell on them and they breathed it in. The world was new.

Mistral never painted except from life, and, as his mind danced he changed forever the way people would focus their eyes. With the rhythm of a bandit, with the bravura of a pirate, he let loose that sense of play he had not been in touch with since childhood. He plundered the secret clearings of his spirit, opening them to sun and air and wind, using his brushes as if they were a trumpet on which he could blow his way to the gates of heaven.

Maggy's disappearance with Mistral from the life of the *quartier* had provoked a storm of gossip and, when Mistral released her from posing for him, her reappearance was a cause for more questions.

"Of course," Paula said, "you did it all in the name of love?"

"Paula!" Maggy said, shocked. "You don't expect me to ask him for money!"

"No, unfortunately, I don't suppose I can. God, what fools women are."

"But you just don't understand," Maggy said mildly. She was too happy to get angry.

"On the contrary. I understand perfectly and I disapprove totally. It's *la folie furieuse*—only to be expected—but don't think I'm going to congratulate you. I thought you'd learned to be a professional."

"As for that—you old cynic—Julien has given me my favorite picture—the largest and the best of them all and the one I love more than any other—the first one he ever painted of me, on the green cushions."

"Wonderful! Months of work and you own a painting by an artist for whose work there is no demand! Oh, Maggy, I never thought you'd end up a painter's maid of all work. That's for other girls, not for you," Paula scolded, too upset to hide her feelings. "And now that he's finished painting you for the moment, now that you have time to go back to work where you get paid, I suppose you give him the money you make posing for others?"

"That's just not fair," Maggy protested. "Julien is working like a demon and he hasn't a sou—naturally I'm pitching in and paying for things—it's only natural, but just until he begins to sell, Paula."

"Tell me this, what does Julien Mistral do for you besides paint you and permit you to share his bed?"

"*Oh!*" Maggy could hardly believe that Paula could have misunderstood so utterly the nature of the ties that bound her to Mistral.

" 'Oh,' says the goose," Paula echoed her severely. "And who cooks the meals and who cleans the studio and who takes the dirty laundry to be washed—or perhaps, heaven forbid, washes it herself—and who makes sure there's enough wine and goes out for the morning croissant and brews the coffee and makes that much-used bed? Does Monsieur Mistral do all this in return for the money you bring home?"

"Paula, how ridiculous you can be. Of course he doesn't have time to do those things. Why, I hardly have time myself—I just buy something at the *charcuterie* and we have a picnic—"

"Not another word!" Paula said. It was worse than she suspected. The women she had known, and there were many of them, who lived with painters, had, with almost no exceptions, finished badly. Painters, even bad painters, had the egos of giant babies. Monstrous infants, each was the center of his own universe and other people existed in orbit around him only to gratify his needs.

Sometimes, when Paula was in a charitable mood, she conceded that the struggle to be recognized as a painter in a world in which, in her private opinion, the greatest work had already been done, was so great that *only* a man with an enormous ego could possibly take himself seriously enough to persist. Perhaps *without* those egos they would have to give up and become bank clerks. Perhaps their ego was all that stood between them and utter panic. But she didn't give a damn what kept them painting when, to her wisely unexpressed way of thinking, one trip to the Louvre would compel them all to cut their wrists in despair. She didn't have a sou's worth of sympathy to spare for them when a woman's fate was concerned. Sometimes, for one had to be fair, sometimes a painter married his model and sometimes a painter and his wife even stayed married, like good old Monet, who painted gardens and lily pads because his wife threatened to leave him if he brought a model into the house, but that was long ago.

Paula had no illusions about Mistral. She didn't trust such careless, indisputable beauty in a man. It was disquieting and indecent. Beauty, she told herself, should be reserved for women who had need of it in dealing with the world. Why, even she, Paula Deslandes, who didn't like Mistral, had found herself staring at him in the street when he passed like a highwayman, wondering what it would be like to lie warm and sticky after love, in the fierce protection of that huge, well-muscled body; even she had caught herself thinking that if she were still young she would tame him, that arrogant swaggerer who had, to her sure knowledge, fallen into short seasons of passion with a dozen girls around Montparnasse. No, this man was not a potential husband for anyone. And as a lover—oh, why couldn't Maggy have found a less selfish man?

La vie bohème, thought Paula with a sinking heart, has never been more than a poet's pea-green fantasy and here was her Maggy, her own dear Maggy, still innocent, thinking that she was living it.

"Never mind," Paula said, pulling herself out of her reverie. "I lost fifty francs at liar's dice last night and I'm suspicious of human nature, particularly my own. Pay no attention."

"I hadn't," Maggy answered truthfully.

Had Paula known more about Julien Mistral she might have understood him better but she would have been no less concerned about Maggy's love for him.

The painter had been born and raised in Versailles, an only child. If both of his parents had been at home while he was growing up, he might have been drawn into a normal family atmosphere but his childhood had been oddly barren, empty of laughter.

His father, an engineer, a builder of bridges in the service of the French government, was away much, if not quite all, of every year, working in the Colonies, and his mother seemed quite content with this arrangement. She would probably have accepted any way of life that left her alone to pursue the needlework that was her only real interest. She embroidered magnificent ecclesiastical garments with a passion that had nothing to do with religion although she might well have been happier as a nun. Without a piece of embroidery in her hands she quickly grew restless, plaintive and eventually angry.

Madame Mistral had attended to her son's needs while he was a baby but as soon as Julien could be sent to the Ecole Maternelle she left him to fend largely for himself with a clear conscience. The boy was healthy and well formed, there was a servant to keep him fed and clean and to take him to school.

From a point in the past that went as far back as he could remember, Julien had always known that most of what he could learn at school was not worth the trouble. He lived for other information, the lessons he taught himself. Like all children he was a natural artist, with a basic set of symbols at his command to represent people, houses, trees, the sun.

By the time he was six, before most children become enamored of realism in their drawings, Julien had started to use his eyes to put the elements he drew into a coherent whole, a composition. Soon he lived for the sheets of paper he carried about in his schoolbag, the precious pencils he kept so sharp, the colored crayons on which he spent all his pocket money. As drawing became the focus of his being he grew less verbal, less aware of the passage of time as he bent himself to the ultimate questions: *the shape of things*, the relation of one shape to another and the relation of all the shapes to the whole. Grammar, spelling, mathematics and even reading itself had nothing to do with the crucial problems of pattern and structure with which his mind was concerned.

When his teachers protested to his mother she agreed that Julien's inattention was deplorable. But even the formidable French educational system can't force a child to do well when he doesn't care about the opinion of others, when punishment is merely a minor annoyance and when his mother forgets his crimes as soon as she escapes from the principal's office.

Uncaring, soon given up as a dolt by his teachers, he held down the place at the bottom of every class until he was old enough to leave school. Years earlier his schoolmates had given up trying to communicate with the absent boy whose remoteness was so complete that it had long ago ceased to be a challenge for them. If he had been shy, he might have been victimized, but his undisguised lack of interest in his schoolmates protected him from them quite as well as his unusual height and strength.

At seventeen when his schoolmates were volunteering to fight the Kaiser, Mistral entered a private art school in Paris where, he worked brilliantly within the academic tradition until he passed the exam for the École des Beaux-Arts. After a few years at the Sorbonne he began to find himself at odds with any traditional approach to art. First only to himself, then openly, he said that art cannot be taught. "Technique, yes; color, yes; anatomy, yes . . . as for the rest, no." He abandoned the Beaux-Arts when he was barely twenty-one and his father, from Algeria, unprotestingly sent him enough to live on until he died a year later. When Mistral was twenty-three his mother, too, died, and except for a legacy to her best friend, she had left the little she possessed to her son and only child.

Now Julien Mistral was almost twenty-six and still unknown in the art world except for the reputation he had earned among some of his contemporaries. To him all gallery owners and dealers came under the category of the enemy. When Mistral heard that Marcel Duchamp had called art dealers "lice on the backs of the artists" he roared that Duchamp hadn't gone far enough.

"What about Cheron, who paid Zadkine ten francs for sixty drawings? He's the same shit who threw Foujita seven francs fifty centimes for a watercolor! *Merely* a louse? He should be hung, taken down while still breathing and disemboweled. Twenty francs to Modigliani for a portrait—it's unspeakable."

Yet his inheritance was almost gone and Kate Browning, the prim, rich American who had invited him to the Surrealist ball, hadn't returned to buy another painting. Should he perhaps, Mistral wondered, have written her an apology for his disappearance? He considered the thought briefly and then dismissed it to return to his easel.

Katherine Maxwell Browning of New York City had a small talent. A very, very small talent, and what was infinitely worse, she *almost* knew it. Her intelligence was keen, her eye for the beautiful acute; she had been born with the painful capacity to appreciate the best, to aspire toward it, but without the ability to produce it. She referred to herself as a sculptress, her family of rich stockbrokers thought of her with admiration and puzzlement as a true artist since none of them had any intimate knowledge of art nor cared to have. Even her professors at college had been encouraging. She had always been able to trap and stamp upon the truth about her own talent before it rose to her consciousness.

Kate Browning had come to Paris in early 1925 to study with Brancusi, but he would have none of her. However, the professor in charge of the *atelier* at the Beaux-Arts, where Kate next presented herself, was lenient enough to allow her to join, even after she had shown him the required photos of her best college work. He expected that once she had bought the obligatory round of drinks for the other students, she would attend a few classes and then quietly drop out as so many Americans did in those days.

His attitude was dictated not by any un-French, untraditional desire to be nice to foreigners but by a very French appreciation of her immaculate prettiness—a look as quietly emphatic as the power of will which had driven this essentially ungifted woman to position herself in the heart of the artistic life of the world.

She was twenty-two, and she had the rare kind of perfect oval skull that permitted her to part her short ash-blond hair in the middle with impunity. Her high forehead loomed over eyebrows plucked into a thin line and the prominent bones of the clearly marked sockets around her gray eyes gave her face a distinction that might otherwise have escaped it because of the relentless regularity of her features. Kate's nose was slim, her lips were thin, her chin was sharp, yet it was these very hard edges that, in the ensemble of her wonderfully shaped skull, made her a striking woman.

In the early spring of 1926, Kate Browning, who spoke French with a tutored fluency that made up in vocabulary what she lacked in gesture, was taken to visit Mistral in his studio by one of her fellow students at the Beaux-Arts.

With the first savage pounce that his canvases made on her trained yet unrigid eye she was consumed by a rage to possess this man's work. She *knew*. She looked at his work, she let herself plunge into the great river of color and she knew for once and for all. There was never any doubt in her mind, then or ever, that Julien Mistral was the greatest painter of his day, nor that others would eventually agree with her.

Yet Kate was clever enough and disciplined enough to resist the voracious impulse she felt to buy as much of Mistral's work as possible. At their first meeting she had quietly listened to him fulminating against private collectors.

"I've known some who buy everything a poor wretch of an artist will give them, they take everything, at bargain prices, and wait until the market catches up with their tastes. Then, hup! Huge profits! They're even worse than dealers—at least with a dealer you know it when you're being robbed."

Julien Mistral would have shouted with outrage if anyone had suggested that even as he spoke Kate was seeing herself as his future patroness, the custodian of his talent, the protector of his career. Yet, from that day on, she found herself waking in the middle of the night thinking of him, planning how she could make him as famous as she knew he deserved to be.

Her acquisitive nature was covered only lightly by a smooth fabric of civilized rules. She was cunning, deeply cunning, and as tenacious as she was cunning. There were primitive forces alive under the spareness of the personality she presented to the world and she directed the flow of this power to biding her time. Carefully she chose one of Mistral's works and then, a month later, bought another. She held herself in check for she had understood from the beginning that in spite of his financial need—of which the perceptive antenna of the rich had immediately informed her—Mistral was intensely suspicious of anyone who seemed to want to own a piece of him. And what was his work but himself, flung raw onto canvas?

She had contrived to invite Mistral to the Surrealist ball in the most casual manner and when he decamped with Maggy she merely murmured "Patience" to herself, refusing to take his act as an insult.

Was Kate Browning's decision born of the fact that her devotion to Mistral's work enabled her to put aside her own utterly minor abilities without having to make any excuse, even to herself? Was it born of this perfect opportunity to lay down with honor her own, fruitless struggle to create? Or was it the prize of Mistral himself that she sought, rather than his work? Was not this rough, lawless, remote man the most essential part of her interest? This redheaded man whose tall body moved with such an outdoorsman's grace, whose face was so unforgettable in its beauty, its strength?

She never asked herself these questions in the middle of the night, nor would the answers have mattered. Everything had come together for her in one instant of awareness and in her spare, predatory and absolutely determined way, Kate Browning dedicated herself for life.

As Maggy stood in the kitchen of Mistral's studio, humming to herself and peeling potatoes on a Saturday afternoon in early July, she heard a knock on the front door. She glanced into the studio where Julien was working. When the knock was repeated he didn't hear it. Maggy opened the door with a feeling of mild curiosity. Outside stood a young, finely boned, obviously self-possessed woman who looked much too elegant for the neighborhood. She was dressed in an immaculate, white, crêpe-de-chine dress intricately fagoted and scalloped with a deep white cloche of the finest straw covering her head. The man with her, Maggy thought, had the look of a farmer dressed for a visit to the big city, as if he'd just had a good scrub and struggled into his only proper suit.

"Is Monsieur Mistral at home?" the woman asked.

"Yes, but he's working." Maggy wouldn't dare disturb him at the whim of a casual caller.

"But I am expected, Mademoiselle," Kate said with a polite smile.

"He didn't tell me . . ." Maggy broke off as Kate brushed quickly by her. Openmouthed, she watched the pair advance into the studio. Mistral put down his brushes with ill grace, but he walked forward and shook Kate's hand, frowning as he loomed over her.

"So! You did forget, Julien. Never mind—I told Adrien that I didn't think you'd be expecting us. Adrien, this is Julien Mistral—Julien, this is the friend I told you about in my note, Adrien Avigdor." As the two men shook hands Kate laughed a social laugh, a drawing-room laugh, a laugh that could cover any situation with its characteristic note of total confidence and perfect assurance that anything the owner of that laugh did or said was correct.

Maggy hastily took off her apron and dried her hands on it. She was barefoot, as usual, and wearing a sleeveless, flowered, cotton smock she wore only in the kitchen. She pulled back her shoulders and marched into the studio with her limber, long tread. Thank God I'm tall, she thought as she shook hands with Kate Browning and Avigdor, both of whom were shorter than she. Why, she wondered, hadn't Julien warned her that he expected visitors? That was what must have been in the little blue telegraph message he'd received earlier that day and tossed away with a grunt of annoyance.

"A glass of red?" she heard Mistral offer. "Sit down somewhere," he said gesturing vaguely. "Maggy, bring the wine."

As she searched the kitchen for four intact glasses Maggy felt a wave of heat rise from her throat to her forehead. *Damn* him for not telling her. That woman looked as if she had just stepped off a yacht—so that was the American he'd ditched the night of the ball. He'd never said she was young and good-looking. And that marvelous dress! Oh, what a dress! Why were they slumming? Avigdor couldn't be her boyfriend—he looked too simple to even know her—yet his name was familiar somehow. She found an almost full bottle of red wine, settled on four glasses, unmatched, two chipped and two unchipped glasses—to hell with being a scullery maid—and brought them into the studio.

As Mistral poured the wine, Kate kept up a flow of chatter, her voice with its level American drawl charmingly at odds with the formal correctness of her French. Adrien Avigdor looked around the studio, Maggy noticed, with the inattentive eye of a man who was thinking about his vegetables and wondering if it would rain before evening. He seemed to scarcely listen to Kate yet, as soon as she left a pause in her observations, he spoke directly to Mistral.

"I've seen the two paintings Kate bought from you. They pleased me very much."

"That's what she wrote me," Mistral replied in brusque dismissal, as if the compliment were false.

And damn him again, Maggy thought. If this farmer is even possibly a customer Julien could at least be courteous. What does he expect us to use for money when I go to market? The shopkeepers won't let me put food on account the way he does his paints. It's my francs we spend.

"Would you mind if I looked around?" Avigdor asked, his open and guileless light blue eyes beaming with frank good nature in his round face. He had an air of trusting pleasantness, a kind of decency and kindness that Maggy responded to in spite of her annoyance at this surprise visit.

"Look, Avigdor, *dealers* like you don't just 'look around,' " Mistral said, suddenly vicious. "You don't go visiting artists to kill time on a Saturday afternoon, not unless it's to put something in your pocket, don't think I'm a fool. Why, it's dealers like you who . . ."

"Monsieur Mistral, you're making a mistake," Avigdor interrupted mildly. "Don't lump all dealers together, that's really not at all fair of you, you know. What about Zborowski—why, he finally got Modigliani's price up to four hundred and fifty francs for a portrait, eh? And who else would have been able to get that American, Barnes, interested in Soutine? And consider a few of the other decent middlemen of art. What about Basler, and Couquiot and Francis Carco, the poet—you can't tell me that they're all dishonest, now can you?"

"All right, there are some, one or two maybe, exceptions—but as far as I'm concerned, dealers, as a group, are common thieves, whoremasters and first-class shits!"

Kate's calm, tinkling laugh greeted his words. "Well said, Julien! But as I wrote you, Adrien is another of the exceptions. I wouldn't have presumed to bring him otherwise. So may he have his look around? And for that matter, may I? I haven't seen your work in months."

"Go ahead, go ahead, since you're here," Mistral grumbled, ungraciously. "But don't expect me to stay around and watch you. I have a horror of people saying the kinds of things they think they have to say when they look at pictures. I'll be out in the garden until you've finished. Come along, Maggy. And bring the bottle."

Alone in the studio, Avigdor started to walk around the room, looking intently at the pictures on the wall.

"No, Adrien," Kate said impatiently, "let's see the new work . . . you can look at the rest later." She started to pull at a large canvas that was standing on the floor, tilted toward the wall, its front hidden. "Help me with this."

Quickly, expertly, Avigdor turned all the paintings Mistral had propped carelessly against the wall, so that they faced into the room. He didn't stop to look at them as he placed them side by side. He worked with the rapidity of a cat burglar, fearing that Mistral would change his mind and come back into the studio at any minute. Finally all the canvases were in place and he and Kate stood surrounded by them, each silently looking, Avigdor panting from exertion, Kate trembling from excitement, and an emotion she couldn't identify, an emotion that made her feel angry, furiously angry.

As his eyes went from one of Mistral's paintings of Maggy to another, Adrien Avigdor thought that it was like pressing himself naked on living flesh, like feasting, gorging, literally eating youth. He wanted to roll on the canvases, he realized with amazement, he who trusted only his calm judgment, he ached to throw himself down and roll all over them and kick up his heels with spurting excitement. The pictures of the girl—ah, he could mount her! They excited him far more than Maggy did in living flesh.

Finally, he tore himself away from the seven large canvases and turned toward the still lifes. Looking at them, he felt as if he were outdoors, lying in long, sweet grass, pagan, blissful, innocent of everything but the flood of his senses. As eager as a young dog after a bone, he rushed from one canvas to another, unable to contemplate each one for more than a few seconds because another beckoned out of the corner of his eye.

As Kate watched him, crystals of triumph hardened within her. Certain as she had been of Mistral's genius, she had waited tensely for Avigdor's reaction. He was, in the opinion of many people, the shrewdest of the avant-garde art dealers of the day. In only one year his new gallery on the rue de Seine had been the scene of a series of successful exhibitions of work by a group of new artists who had not been widely exhibited before and he had created a fast-moving market for his discoveries.

She turned her back on the nudes. There was something about them, she thought, that utterly disgusted her, something sickening. But the other work! She was astounded by it. Mistral's earlier work that still hung on the walls, and her own two paintings as well, all faded in comparison with the new energy, the explosion of vitality that charged his still lifes. Here a single huge zinnia, with its double circle of stiff pink petals, hovered against the sky, drawing into itself the essence of every flower that ever grew. Next to the zinnia, a big canvas showed a corner of the studio, in which every object radiated a life force so powerful that the canvas grew in mystery the longer she looked at it until, finally, it blotted out its surroundings and she felt dizzy, mystified, overwhelmed. Everywhere in the studio she felt as if there were holes that had been punched into wonderment.

"So?" Kate said at last to Avigdor in English, which he spoke well. To her it would always be the language of business and business was what she had brought him here for.

"I am indebted to you, my dear," he said vaguely, as if in a dream turning back to the pictures of Maggy on the green cushions.

"Adrien, pay attention." Kate walked up to him and snapped her fingers under his nose. "I know the way you feel but I didn't bring you here just to gape."

"My God, Kate, my knees are weak, my eyeballs are popping. I feel as if I've been struck by lightning—give me a chance to recover, I can almost smell thunder," Avigdor said with his countryman's open smile.

"So," Kate pounced, "you agree with me?"

"Without reservation."

"Then what about the one-man show? You said you were totally committed for the next year, that you had absolutely no way to fit in another artist—what do you say now?"

"I have suddenly discovered a new month in 1926—we will baptize it October."

"The opening show of the season?" Kate's thin eyebrows flew upward.

"But naturally," he said with the simplicity of a prosperous peasant discussing the price of beets.

"Naturally," Kate echoed, breathless with the magnitude of her victory. She had been buying from Avigdor since he opened and her respect for his astuteness had grown as she watched him moving from strength to strength in the risky waters of the art market. Now, as she saw him make a decision with the same swiftness and commitment with which she operated, she understood the man better than she ever had.

How right had been the calculation she had made to bring him here without even giving Julien a chance to say he didn't want to see him. Avigdor, like many dealers, bought outright the paintings he planned to exhibit. The difference between the price that he paid for them, and the price that he sold them for, represented not only the risk he took but his potential for profit.

He would, she knew, pay Mistral the least he could get away with, in all due fairness, but that suited her perfectly. Mistral's financial independence was the last thing she wanted. A painter who can control his dealer needs no patroness, Kate thought, and when the time came, as it soon would, for his prices to go up, she intended to be the agent of that particular piece of good news.

They stood in a sudden silence, conspiratorial yet with an edge of caution, each waiting for the other to speak. Finally Avigdor said, "I'd better go and talk to him."

"Oh, no, Adrien."

"But, my dear Kate, one thing must be understood. This Mistral of yours may be allergic to talk of money, as you told me, but unless I have signed him to an exclusive contract we have nothing to discuss."

"Adrien, trust me. Today isn't the right time to mention the contract to him. Today isn't the right time to tell him *anything* except that three months from now you're going to give him a one-man show. I haven't been wrong so far, have I?"

"Kate, I can't tell this man that I'm going to go ahead and do everything I can to establish him unless I have an absolute assurance that he's not going to leave me and go off to another gallery someday," Avigdor said, with a firmness of a breeder discussing the stud fee of a prize bull.

"You have *my* assurance."

"Do you expect me to go all-out on nothing but your promise? What makes you so sure that you speak for him?"

"You just take my word for it," Kate insisted, quietly.

Adrien considered her for a moment. He was not certain that he liked Kate Browning but he admired her. She had a sureness of taste that was remarkable for someone not in the business, and she had distinction. Could Mistral, that haughty, impatient, rude giant be under her influence? There had been nothing in the way he greeted her to indicate it, and yet . . . and yet . . . it was impossible to doubt Kate, as she spoke with such fine, clear determination. It was a risk worth taking. In fact he did not see how he could avoid it. The same instinct that had led Avigdor to decide to open his season with the paintings of a man whose recent work he had never seen until little more than an hour ago, told him that he could not get to Mistral except through Kate. He made a gesture of acceptance and turned toward the door to the garden.

"Shall I tell him, Kate, or will you?"

"Adrien! *You*, of course. It's your decision, your gallery." Kate's precise mouth curved in delicate mirth.

Oh, *yes*, Avigdor thought, she *was* clever. A tiny shiver touched his spine. No wonder she had never appealed to him physically. He didn't like women who were as clever as he. Or more clever.

6

Adrien Avigdor was only twenty-eight when he first met Julien Mistral, but he might, with truth, have said that he had spent his life preparing for the day when he would be able to change a painter's future in a single moment of decision.

He had been brought up in the antique business. "We," his father used to say, gesturing grandly toward his flourishing shop on the quai Voltaire, "were selling them antiques before they built Notre Dame." "We" were the Jewish Avigdors, "they" everyone else in France. Adrien, who loved his grandiose father, as much as he laughed at him, wondered why he had stopped short of saying the Avigdors had been selling the Pharaoh antiques while *they* built the Pyramids.

As a child, Adrien traveled about the countryside with his father on buying trips. So quickly that he seemed to be drinking rather than learning, young Adrien had grasped the profound difference between the way antique dealers think and the way antique *buyers* think. When he was only eight, he could judge merchandise by imagining himself looking through the window of his father's shop and *having to have* a certain pair of goblets. Better yet, by the time he was ten, he could just as easily distinguish the teapot or inlaid box that would never call out to be bought, that would be admired, even picked up and discussed for a quarter of an hour, but was destined somehow to never change hands. Presented with two dozen Limoges teacups, his hand, as if of its own volition, would pick up and turn over the only cup with a tiny crack on its base.

When his father died, rather than work in the family business with his two older brothers, Adrien opened his own shop, in the rue Jacob, only a few steps from the church of St. Germain-des-Prés. He was convinced that people bought more freely from a shop that was built in the shadow of a church, preferably a cathedral. By the time he was twenty-five, his fortune was made and, unheard of for an Avigdor, the traffic in antiques had ceased to fascinate him. He realized he had reached a dangerous point in his life when he sold a chocolate service that might not have—perhaps—belonged to the Empress Josephine, but should and could have. He got five times what he paid for it, and had trouble keeping awake during the transaction.

"We," he said to himself, looking as if one of his pigs had died, "have been selling them the debris of centuries for too long." Within a matter of hours he had determined to make a change of *métier*. He would move from the world of antiques, in which everything that could be sold already existed, to the world of art in which profits beckoned on works as yet uncreated. His well-trained assistants could continue to run his business, with an occasional visit from him.

All threat of boredom vanished as Avigdor contemplated the challenge of making a place for himself in a trade that already included such giants as Paul Rosenberg, the Bernheim brothers, Réné Gimpel, Wildenstein and, richest of them all, Vollard, whose fortune was based on the two hundred and fifty Cézannes he had once managed to buy from the artist for an average of fifty francs apiece. It wouldn't be easy, starting from scratch, in a profession dominated by establishment dealers who handled the work of the most important modern painters, such as Matisse and Picasso, and who at the same time were able to attract the custom of the biggest customers, many of them American millionaires, by the ease with which they could conjure out from their storerooms a Velásquez, a Goya drawing, or a work by one of the great Impressionists.

In spite of the dignified solemnity of these great dealers, with their gray-velvet-covered walls, Avigdor knew that their tightly knit world was a snakepit of snarling envy and open, spiteful rivalry which mounted as news grew of the success of the New York branches of French dealers. What tearing of hair there had been at the news that the Bernheims had gotten twenty thousand dollars for a Matisse, that Wildenstein had sold a large Cézanne for sixty thousand dollars, both prices previously unheard of in France.

Clearly, Adrien Avigdor calculated, if there's that kind of money to be made in men who were absolutely unknown only twenty-five years ago, there's going to be a similar market for the work of men who don't yet interest the major dealers. Only a few princely collectors can afford to purchase old masters to ensure their own immortality. Nor are there many collectors who will risk thousands on artists with reputations that have been freshly made. Yet there must exist many would-be collectors who will risk lesser sums than those needed to own a Matisse.

Yes, he told himself, as he walked along the rue de Seine on which busier Left Bank galleries were already located, buyers come in three sizes: the Andrew Mellon size who only want artists who have stood the test of time, the Picasso size, in the medium range, and the Avigdor size, who want to get in on the coming thing, on the ground floor.

As he scanned the people sauntering along, he realized that the world had been organized so that men like him could prosper. After all, nobody needed to own works of art to survive. And yet, human nature is so constituted that once survival is ensured, once a level of comfort is established, proprietorship of nonessential objects becomes an immediate desire. The savage who adds a second necklace to the first, and John D. Rockefeller buying the Unicorn tapestries, weren't that different from each other, were they now? And the peasant's wife who waits for a good harvest and promptly buys a painted jug to adorn the top of a chest—how different is she from Henry Clay Frick, that cold-eyed Maecenas, who spent a million dollars for the eleven Fragonard panels that Madame Du Barry, thinking them too suggestive, had refused to accept from Louis XV? Yes, falling somewhere between the peasant's wife and the Rockefellers, there are a lot of potential customers out here, Adrien Avigdor told himself happily.

For two years he dedicated himself to learning his new trade. Outwardly he seemed as leisurely as that fixture of the eighteenth century, the gentleman amateur. He visited and revisited every one of the best galleries where he was welcomed as a wealthy, cultivated colleague from the world of antiques. He smiled his honorably intentioned, if countrified, smile and spoke of thinking about taking up collecting paintings . . . about which, alas, he had to confess himself a complete neophyte.

At Gimpel's he said shyly that he wasn't thinking of anything as rare as a Greuze drawing or even a tiny Marie Laurencin—too rich for his blood—but perhaps something by a younger man? At Rosenberg's he reflected sadly on Picasso. He admired Picasso but he didn't think he could afford him—not at a hundred thousand francs a picture. If only he could afford three hundred thousand francs for the Monet, the one of the red boat—but of course the day to buy Monet was long past, was it not? Perhaps a younger man? At Zborowski's he admitted that he was sorely tempted by the Soutines. Was it true that they couldn't give them away a year ago and now they were fifteen thousand francs each? Fascinating! That's what he heard. What an unpredictable affair the art market was, to be sure.

Avigdor sought out the advice of a number of carefully chosen art critics, those who worked for specialized publications with readers who bought art regularly. Flatteringly, he asked for their guidance in forming his projected collection. Some, as was common practice, undertook to advise him for a fee, others he was able to lead to exceptionally fine bargains in antiques. What man does not enjoy living with a bit of fine old silver, an Empire chair, a few Meissen plates? They became his friends and well-wishers.

Eventually he plunged into the sordid warrens of the artists' studios in Montparnasse, working his way through La Ruche and the *cité* of Denfert Rochereau and number 3 rue Joseph-Bara, neither rejecting nor accepting, but looking, always looking.

By 1925 Avigdor, now twenty-seven, was ready to open the gallery he had rented and handsomely renovated on the rue de Seine. He picked seven artists who interested him, a stable of men who still had a long way to go, and in choosing them he was lucky, he was brilliant, his eyes functioned sublimely—and again, he was lucky. In a year he was considered an avant-garde dealer of exceptional discernment. Soon the entire art world buzzed with news of his every move. His good friends among the critics applauded, for had they not taught him everything he knew? Was he not a good fellow? Those critics who were not his friends attacked him viciously and that brought even more sales, for in Paris if new art does not cause a scandal it is hardly worth bothering to look at it.

With well-concealed relief Mistral agreed to the one-man show. Somehow, once that had been settled, it seemed relatively unimportant, as Kate explained it to him, to sign the contract of exclusivity. It stood to reason that you couldn't have one without the other, she said in a matter-of-fact way that shortened the discussion, particularly as she had advised him that he had not set high enough prices on his work.

"Let me bargain with Avigdor for you," she said. "Everyone knows that nobody asks enough for his own work—you need somebody who isn't emotionally involved. And I like doing it—that's the sort of thing we're good at in my family—really, Julien, you'd be doing me a favor." Mistral, who hated even to think about money and didn't relish the idea of a haggle with Avigdor, put his financial affairs in her hands with gratitude. Now he was able to supervise the mounting of his exhibition with growing attention.

For years he'd been careless with his finished canvases, impatiently leaving them unstretched and unvarnished, propped against his walls or stuck up on a nail anywhere he could find a space, but now, his pride in the work he had done in the last few months was so great that no detail was too unimportant to demand his full attention. In the three months before the date of the exhibition, he was almost too busy to paint. Maggy continued to support him by modeling as he allowed himself to be interrupted at any time by Kate, who came by frequently and carried him off in her blue Talbot convertible to inspect the proofs for the catalog, to choose a type style for the cards of invitation to the opening, or to meet Avigdor for a drink.

Kate established an excellent working rapport with the framemakers who had to be handled carefully, for their craftsmen's testiness was notorious. Mistral found himself more and more dependent on her services as a go-between between himself and these artisans who took no badgering from impatient painters, but who seemed to enjoy cooperating with the charming American girl who spoke to them with such proper deference.

Maggy watched and waited, with an unadmitted premonition of fearful grief daily growing in her heart. She had no weapons except her body and her love, but Mistral's attention was focused on the exhibition and he turned to her less and less often. When he did make love to her there were shadows between them, the shadows of her unadmitted jealousy, the shadows of his scarcely surfaced feelings about the exhibition.

He lived in an unsorted jumble of exultation and worry in which anxiety mixed with hope, excitement was tinged with panic. Underlying it all was a growing, swelling, terrifyingly strong intimation of victory. This man who had sneered at his fellow artists for so long, who had gone his own uncivil way, who had railed contemptuously at the commerciality of the art world, now found himself craving desperately with all the power of his barbaric, famished character to take his rightful place in that world, to be recognized at last.

As the date of the opening of the exhibition, the *vernissage*, grew closer, Mistral grew more and more agitated.

Somehow Kate, with her utter conviction of his genius, was able to find just the right words he needed to hear to feel a momentary reassurance, a solace for which he asked her more and more frequently although he affected to almost ignore her when she spoke.

Even if Maggy had known what to say he wouldn't have paid attention to her. She was too young, too ignorant for her opinion to carry any weight with Mistral. Naturally Maggy thought his work was wonderful. Why shouldn't she? What did she know of the painting that she didn't pick up as a pigeon picks up crumbs in the street? How could the judgment of an eighteen-year-old model give him the support he found in conversation with a cultivated woman of the world, a rich man's daughter who, at twenty-three, had quickly come to know everyone who counted in the artistic circles of Paris? Kate's delicate fingers seemed formed to take the pulse of that world and judge its condition.

That past June, Paul Rosenberg had exhibited Picasso's work of the last twenty years. On October 5th of 1926, when Avigdor first exhibited Mistral, it was clear that the second major artistic event of the year had taken place. The crowds who are invited to a *vernissage* are as without pity as they are without false pride. If they find work uninteresting they quickly turn their backs to the walls and chat with each other, take a quick glass of wine if it's available, and leave for something more interesting without even a word of apology to the dealer.

But when the work speaks to them, when they smell new talent, they are capable of shoving each other aside to get a better look with as little courtesy as if they were snatching the last taxi on a rainy night. And when they decide to buy, a wave of desire begins to mount in the gallery, rocketing from one spectator to another, as infectious as hysteria, as if these finely dressed collectors were badly behaved children at a birthday party, openly covetous, grabbing for the last slice of a delicious, but inadequately large, yet essential cake.

Avigdor, besieged, put a small red "sold" sticker on the last of the fifty canvases less than two hours after the collectors and the merely curious had begun to trickle into the gallery, many of them alerted by the critics who knew that Avigdor would provide them with the occasion for a rousing debate. He needed all his patience and good nature to deal with the complaints of former customers who were angered at the unavailability of the pictures they insisted on having.

"Come back tomorrow," he repeated, with a confiding appeal in his kind eyes, "and I'll see if there's something I can spare you—but I can't promise miracles—it will be small. Forgive me, my friend. No, I assure you, I didn't reserve any for myself—you know I never do that. Tomorrow—yes, I'll try to find something." He would, he thought, get rid of all of Mistral's earlier work at this rate.

Mistral brooded, a silent island in the middle of the long crowded room. He understood his success intellectually, but instead of the glory he expected to feel, there was blankness, emptiness, confusion. And there was something worse—there was fear. Success, disdained for so long, then sought at last with such an unleashed need, success was too great a change for him to accept. The territory was too unfamiliar, the position too exposed, the prize too rich.

Each time another stranger came up to him to congratulate him the words seemed to mean less and less. The people surging excitedly around him, chattering at him and at each other, didn't connect in his mind with the pictures on the walls. He couldn't forge a link between his work, the work he did alone, the work that poured from his belly, with any of the compliments that were being paid him. He muttered his thanks, keeping his eyes focused above the heads of the people who talked to him, absently pushing his dark red curls away from his forehead that was damp from the heat of the room.

Only with Kate who slipped effortlessly through the throng and returned to his side from time to time, was he able to look down and grin faintly. They exchanged a few words, unimportant comments on the size of the crowd and the success of the frames, but the less they said the more intimate was their communication. Mistral drew strength from Kate, who felt none of the unwelcome emotion that was poisoning the moment for him. For her the victory was at second hand, removed enough to be under control, yet close enough to fill her with the sweetness of being the instrument of it all.

Maggy stood in a corner, holding herself particularly tall and proud. A ferocious malaise had gripped her as she watched the crowd cluster excitedly around at the seven canvases that displayed her in all her nakedness. It was one thing to pose for an artist, but quite another to be displayed for laymen to see, she thought. If she had known how she was going to feel, she wouldn't have come to the *vernissage* at all. She mustered all the experience of the past year to calmly accept the congratulations that accompanied the perfunctory shakes of her hand, the rapacious, avidly inquisitive, scrutinizing glances.

It was almost, she thought, as if she were an animal, a horse who had just won a race or a dog that had been named "best in show." "Magnificent, Mademoiselle," or "splendid, quite splendid," they said to her, and passed quickly on, as if she were not a human being to whom one could talk reasonably. Soon, she speculated, some man would doubtless try to pop a lump of sugar in her mouth—that one would lose a finger.

If only Julien would come and stand by her, if only he would even catch her eye, but he was as immobile in his position in the center of the room as if he'd been planted there. Why did he ignore her so, today of all days? she asked herself, and a cramp of misery settled behind her eyes.

Even Paula, who had first stayed close to her side, had drifted off to inspect the crowd of collectors, artists and critics, the very people who came to her restaurant every night. It was as if this was a party in Paula's honor, for if it had not been for her, none of it would be happening. If Paula Deslandes had not launched Maggy Lunel, Mistral might well still be unknown, she meditated, not at all sure she was pleased with her largesse. She was looking about with that indefinable air of the insider, the person in the know at a public event, when a man she'd never seen before spoke to her.

"It's an extraordinary event, Madame, don't you agree?"

"I do indeed," said Paula with a subtle inclination of her head that Madame the Marquise du Pompadour would not have found unworthy. She could tell immediately from that one sentence that the man was the particular kind of American who speaks acceptable French but still has enough trouble with the language not to have the insupportable pretension to imagine himself fluent.

"Is Madame a collector?"

"In a minor way," Paula answered, looking at the man with interest. "And Monsieur?" As always, she responded first to his masculinity, his good looks. Then she noticed that he was exceptionally well turned out, yet he wore his expensive clothes with American forthrightness, a kind of brusque immaculateness that proclaimed his origins.

"In a minor way also—can one live in Paris and not collect something?"

"Some do . . . but I have no use for them," Paula said with a disdainful sniff of her pert nose.

"May I present myself? Perry Kilkullen."

"Paula Deslandes."

As they shook hands she took stock of her new acquaintance. He was probably close to forty, and his aura of prosperity contrasted pleasingly with his thick blond hair that was just beginning to go gray at the temples and his gray eyes that held a youthful enthusiasm. He was, Paula thought, the sort of splendid American that the English are regretfully forced to concede is a gentleman in spite of his birthplace.

"Have you bought anything in the show?" Paula asked.

"Unfortunately, no. The only pictures I really wanted were all sold."

"Which ones would you have chosen?" Paula asked with her most adorable pout.

"Any one of the nudes—I think they're the finest things here."

"Monsieur has a taste for the sublime," Paula teased.

"I noticed you talking to the young lady," Perry Kilkullen said, indicating Maggy across the room. "She's the model, isn't she?"

"Surely you don't imagine there are two like her in the world?"

"I suppose she's the artist's wife?"

"God forbid!"

"His friend then?" he asked delicately, giving the word "friend" the particular tiny nuance of pronunciation, a mere fragment of a tone that to the French indicates a sexual partner.

"Certainly not," Paula said protectively. "Maggy is a professional artists' model—the best one in Paris as anyone will tell you. She works for many painters."

"Maggy?"

"Maggy Lunel—my *protégée*," Paula said preeningly.

"She's so very beautiful. A girl apart," Perry Kilkullen said in such a voice that Paula glanced at him sharply. He was staring openly at Maggy with a look of such poleaxed yearning that Paula would have laughed if her self-esteem hadn't required a split second to regain its equilibrium. Ah, but what did she take herself for? Her forty-three years, luscious as they were, would seem nothing when compared to

Maggy's resplendent eighteen, Paula thought, shaking herself mentally.

"How does she come to be your *protégée*?" the stranger continued, not trying to hide his curiosity.

"Ah, that's a long story," Paula said evasively. She had to grant eighteen its full glory, she reflected, but she didn't have to humble herself before it. This handsome Kilkullen would have to try much harder to find out anything he wished to know.

Maggy, still trapped in the corner, looked at Mistral who stood some twenty feet away. Oh, this was intolerable. She couldn't endure another minute without some contact with him. Perhaps he would put his arm around her, or at least take her hand in his. She needed some loving word, some gesture. Why was she so childish? Even a single smile would help her to get through these moments. Maggy began to struggle through the mob in Mistral's direction. She found her passage blocked by Avigdor, who had been collared by a stout man with dyed black hair.

"Adrien, who owns that nude lying on the green cushions? I want to find the lucky son of a bitch and get it from him. It's only a question of how much he wants—I'll pay anything—be a good chap and tell me."

"It's not for sale," Maggy said gently.

"Mademoiselle Lunel is right," Avigdor agreed. "It belongs to Miss Browning."

"The hell it does!" the stout man said. "Where is she—I'd like to talk to her."

"Monsieur Avigdor is mistaken," Maggy spoke up firmly. "I've owned that particular painting from the very day it was painted. Julien gave it to me and it has no price because I'll never sell it."

"What do *you* say, Avigdor?" the man insisted, unimpressed.

"There seems to be some confusion . . . ah, perhaps Miss Browning can . . . I don't . . ." Avigdor looked as if the heavens had opened and hail had ruined his hay.

"Look, just follow me," Maggy told the stout man. Avigdor obviously didn't know what he was doing or saying. With difficulty she cleared the way toward Mistral, and clutched his arm.

"Julien, that dealer of yours has just told this gentleman that my picture doesn't belong to me—explain to him, would you, please?"

Mistral turned his head and glared at both of them from under his frowning brows. His mouth, always set in a stern line, was tight with annoyance.

"What's this nonsense, Maggy? You sound as crazy as everyone else in this lousy menagerie."

"Julien, listen. It's about *my* picture, the first one you painted of me on the green cushions. Avigdor told this man that Mademoiselle Browning owns it."

"That's perfectly true." Kate spoke calmly. She had appeared at Mistral's side just as Maggy reached him.

Mistral shook his head angrily. "What the hell is going on!"

"It's quite simple, Julien," Kate proclaimed in her unimpassioned voice. "I reserved all the nudes for myself before the exhibition opened. Obviously they are far too important to be sold separately. I wanted to make sure they'd be preserved as a series—it was the only way to insure it. Otherwise, they'd be dispersed in the hands of seven different people by now."

Maggy let go of Mistral's arm. "You *couldn't* have bought it for yourself, Mademoiselle Browning. It was *never* for sale. It's mine. Ask Julien! Julien, *tell* her! You remember, you must remember—"

Mistral closed his eyes as if to blot out her words and Maggy saw, in a flash, that moment when he had fallen on her with that pounce of absolute possession, his great hands, still sticky with paint, rubbing with rough victory on her pubic hair.

"He'll paint you another," Kate said without raising her voice. "Won't you, Julien? Be reasonable, Mademoiselle, calm yourself. You simply can't expect him to keep any hasty promise he may have made about that first canvas—it's too significant to the body of his work. I'm sure we all agree."

"Julien! Why don't you say something? You know you gave me that picture." Maggy's voice rose furiously, suddenly out of control.

Mistral looked from one woman to the other. Maggy's face had flushed with anguish and disbelief, she was immobilized, ineffective in the tightly packed crowd and her prominent mouth was thrust forward in a grimace of emotion. Kate stood quietly, fastidious and graceful, the pure oval of her head poised on her neck in a way that indicated, as no word could have, that the rightness of her position was beyond dispute.

"Stop carrying on like a child, Maggy!" Mistral commanded roughly. "Kate's absolutely right, the seven pictures belong together. I'll make it up to you, damn it! It's not going to kill you to give up one picture, for Christ's sake!"

For the space of a long moment Maggy looked straight at his face. She had grown absolutely still and severe composure fell like a mask over her vivid outrage as she listened to his words. The clatter of voices dimmed around her as she absorbed the stance of Kate and the meaning of what Mistral had said. She knew more about them in that instant than they knew about themselves—perhaps more than they would ever know.

Maggy had always recognized that Kate was an antagonist—now she saw that the American had the eyes of a wolverine. She had not bought the paintings because she loved them but because she hated them, because she wanted to make them disappear. Mistral, whom she had willed herself to trust, because to do otherwise would have been against all her loving nature, had turned on her in a spurious irritation that amounted to a shameful lie.

Here, in what should have been his moment of triumph, it seemed to her that he reeked of the furtive and the diminished—a wild animal trapped, tamed and caged. In Kate, Maggy smelled a ruthlessness the size of which she could only begin to understand. She stood powerless, friendless, in an arena in which there could be no victory, from which there was no escape except an honorable retreat. She felt as if some essential plug in her body had been pulled. If she stayed facing them any longer she would begin to howl in outrageous, indecent pain . . . and to no purpose.

Slowly, quietly now, she spoke to Kate.

"Since you want my portrait so badly, Mademoiselle, that you are ready to steal it, I give it to you. There is no price. Keep it where you can always see it but remember—it will never really belong to you." She turned to Mistral. "You can't 'make up' anything to me, Julien. You gave me a gift, you've changed your mind, now you've taken it back . . . it's so simple that even I, child though I am, can understand such an action."

"Shit! Maggy, stop exaggerating . . ."

"Farewell, Julien." She nodded formally at Avigdor and Kate, turned and walked out of the gallery, as stiffly as if her legs had turned to ice, but with her head high on the long stem of her neck. As Maggy moved, in cold dignity, people found themselves moving aside to let her pass and looking after her. Surely, more than one of them thought, she isn't, after all, the same girl who modeled for those nude paintings. That model had been a laughing, erotic creature, and so young, so succulent. But this was a woman, austerely beautiful, untouchable, regal, above all, adult.

7

When Perry Mackay Kilkullen finally tore himself away from Mistral's *vernissage* he knew that he should find a taxi since he was running behind schedule. It is equally far to travel, either as the crow flies, or on foot, from Avigdor's gallery to the Hotel Ritz, where Kilkullen lived, or in the other direction, to the Carrefour Vavin. The heart of the art world and the center of the grandeur of the Right Bank are both a comfortable walk from the rue de Seine. They are an even shorter taxi ride but Perry Kilkullen found himself unable to make the physical leap out of the Paris evening into the enclosed interior of one of the square, dark red Renault taxis. The early October dusk had a dreaminess, a warmth still lulled by summer's scents, fruity with promise, that it would be criminal to miss.

As he walked back to the Ritz to change for a business dinner he stopped for a minute on the Pont du Carrousel and looked toward the great ship of the Île de la Cité, that noble island in the Seine that bore aloft the crouching silhouette of the façade of Notre Dame. He turned his back on that immemorial reminder of his faith and looked west, into the lemon distance, along the winding river bordered by tall, narrow, gray buildings on the left and the alluring shadows of the blue Tuileries garden on the right, a sight that usually made him concentrate with all his senses in order to engrave once more on his memory the view he considered civilized man's crowning achievement.

Tonight he saw nothing except a girl, a tall girl like a young queen with red hair, with a mouth that looked as if it had been formed for him alone, and a body he felt he would die if he never touched. He was all longing and torment, and even in his flood of emotion he remembered Shelley's phrase, "the desire of the moth for the star," and laughed for happiness at feeling an emotion he had never known before, an emotion he had thought poets described with deliberate malice in order to make nonpoets envious.

Perry Kilkullen, at forty-two, was an example of the flower of American Irish Catholic aristocracy. Related to the Mackay family of the vast Comstock Lode riches, he had been married young to one of the vast and distinguished McDonnell clan, a graceful and intensely pious young lady who could prove that her particular branch of the big, important family was directly descended from the Lord of the Isles himself, and spoke of the thirteenth-century McDonnells as if they were first cousins.

As the years went by, Mary Jane Kilkullen's love of genealogy had to substitute for a love of progeny as she and Perry found themselves almost alone among their contemporaries in having no children. Like their many friends, they sailed at Southampton in the summer and skied at the Lake Placid Club and went to Pinehurst for golf in the spring, but the absence of those sons and daughters who would have united them as staunch Catholic parents did not make them turn to each other for solace, as so often happens in childless marriages.

At first their barrenness was a frustrating, inexplicable absence and then, as it was prolonged into an acid acceptance, they turned away from their personal relationship, which had been founded on a mere fleeting, youthful attraction, and plunged, separately, into matters that guaranteed them some fulfillment.

Mary Jane Kilkullen became indispensable to the Guild of the Infant Saviour, the Catholic Big Sisters, the Catholic Center for the Blind, and the Foundling Hospital. Perry Kilkullen immersed himself in his firm of international bankers, and by 1926 he spent more of the year in Paris than he did in their large apartment at 1008 Park Avenue.

Paris had become his true love, his consolation for the aridity of his personal life and Paris had kept him young, as she does all who truly love her. As love of London will give a man mellowness, as love of Rome will impart to a man a patina of history, love of Paris will guarantee an available heart.

Perry Kilkullen kept a three-room suite facing an inner garden of the Ritz and although his Parisian life was filled with cables and conferences and business lunches and formal dinners with other members of the international banking community, he often dismissed his chauffeur and set out on foot, at random, to walk the endlessly alluring streets of his city.

Now women, many women, glanced at him as he hurried, already late, toward the Place Vendôme. While Paula had scrutinized his voice and clothes and his manner, the women who noticed him, although deprived of such clues, all knew he was not French as they were caught by the sight of his tall outline, by an impression of casualness and litheness and vitality. There was something about his step, quick, martial, confident, that looked as if he were walking to the beat of drums.

Perry Kilkullen saw none of them as he approached the Ritz and dashed up the steps, already crowded by men in tailcoats and women in brocade evening capes, their many bracelets clinking and clashing together. He rushed through the buzzing, perfumed, gray and gold lobby, forgot to nod to the stately concierge, neglected his usual greeting to the white-gloved lift boy, brushed wordlessly past his valet, ignored the handful of letters waiting for him and flung himself into his dinner clothes with only two words beating in his head. Maggy Lunel. Maggy Lunel!

It took only a half-hour of inquiry the next morning to find out that Madame Paula Deslandes was the owner of La Pomme d'Or. She had said that Maggy Lunel was her *protégée*, Perry Kilkullen thought. Just what would that mean?

He had his secretary book a table for him for that night, and he dined alone, not noticing the excellence of the rare *gigot* or the ripeness of the Brie, waiting for the moment when Madame Deslandes would condescend to stop by his table. She had greeted him pleasantly as he arrived but as she made her way from one table to another in her crowded restaurant, each party seemed to demand an endless amount of her attention. She watched him sit impatiently, scarcely eating, out of the corner of her eye as she chatted with her regulars at greater length than usual. Let him wait, she thought, not without a small but undeniable residue of offended pride. As he drank his second cup of coffee Paula approached his table and nodded. Perry sprang to his feet.

"Will you take a brandy with me, Madame?"

"Willingly." Paula sat down opposite him, put her plump elbows on the table and thoughtfully rested her saucy chin on her folded hands. How, she wondered, was he going to get around to the matter that brought him here without being obvious?

"Madame, I must meet her."

Paula raised one eyebrow in admiration. The attack direct. Not bad for an American.

"Can you help me, Madame?"

She raised her other eyebrow, her cosily distributed features arranged midway between receptivity and hesitation.

"Madame, I'm in love."

She snapped her fingers dismissively. "Like that? It's not possible."

"Madame, I am a serious man, I'm not whimsical, you understand, not given to flights of fancy. Things like this have never happened to me . . . but now it has. I'm a banker . . ."

"A banker? *Tiens*—more and more impossible."

"I assure you—please don't laugh—look, I'm a partner with the Kilkullen International Trust—here's my card—all I ask is an opportunity to meet her."

Paula looked at the card as long and as seriously as if she were trying to read the future in it. Maggy had spent the night in Paula's apartment and they had talked long past midnight. Maggy was through with Mistral. It didn't matter if he had made love to Kate or not, she had said, and Paula had recognized unmistakable truth in her voice. It was a matter of Maggy's own pride. She had been treated as if she were of no worth. She had been rejected slowly for weeks and she had refused to acknowledge what was happening. Now that she knew that Mistral held her in less esteem than the American woman, now that she finally understood, she would never again seek the slightest gesture from him. Nothing. Ever. It was one thing to be made a fool of by love—that could happen to anybody—and there was no dishonor in it, but it was totally different to make a fool of oneself.

Paula had listened, careful not to encourage her at first, since she knew that a wise woman takes no sides in lovers' quarrels. If Maggy went back to Mistral after all these brave words, Paula's agreement would ultimately be held against her.

But as the hours passed she saw that Maggy had truly gone too far to turn back, that events had tutored her slowly, unconsciously, over the past weeks, in an unwilling comprehension of Mistral's character; that she had no reservoir of illusion to drain, no stored-up years of shared emotions to comfort her with false hope.

Paula didn't doubt that Maggy still loved Mistral. A passion, a first passion, like the one she had lived with him, marks a woman for life. No woman truly recovers from such a love. But the loss of the painting had, as no other event could ever have done, shown her his true nature. It was a conclusive proof that Julien Mistral had never had the commitment to her that Maggy had made to him. She could never love him blindly again. The generosity that she had bestowed so purely on Mistral depended on her belief—no matter if it had been hasty or foolish or even utterly false—that he had loved her as she loved him. With that belief destroyed there was nothing left for her to hold on to.

Maggy was beyond anger now. Mistral had, in all fairness, never said that he felt as she did. She had taken it for granted with a credulity that now seemed to belong to a childish innocent she hardly knew. She was dry-eyed, firm and decisive. It was the only way she could deal with the situation. To wail would have been to injure herself even further, and that would have been unendurable. She had sent a boy to pick up the belongings she had left at Mistral's studio, and, even now, she was resettling herself in her own little place.

"Madame . . ." Perry Kilkullen thought that if she looked at his card any longer it would turn yellow at the edges and wither with age.

Paula looked up. He was a good man. She could hardly be mistaken about something so basic. He was rich—that jumped out from every thread on his vest. He was sincere. Whether he could really be in love with Maggy without having spoken one word to her was a matter for debate, but he certainly thought he was. Lust—of course—but love was another matter. He was probably married but that was not an issue. The rawness of Maggy's wounds shouldn't be allowed to go without some salve, and the sooner the better. God knows this Kilkullen was marvelous to look at. What better tonic to help Maggy begin her recovery from a stupid misadventure with Julien Mistral than a good, rich, handsome American? Even if he was a little crazy? Every Frenchwoman should have at least one American—at least once.

"Tomorrow night, Monsieur Kilkullen, you may invite us to dine with you," she said gravely, feeling a bit like Juliet's nurse.

"Ah . . ." he sighed with huge relief. He had been prepared to go to Avigdor next if Madame Deslandes refused him but he felt less ridiculous talking to a woman.

"At Marius and Janette," Paula continued, "since oysters are in season." And, she thought, since Maggy doesn't have the clothes for Maxim's. Madame Poulard's creations could only carry her so far—certainly not into Maxim's.

"How can I thank you?" he implored.

"By not noticing when I order a second dozen Belons—by begging me to have a third dozen—but not permitting me dessert. I'm not a difficult woman. I prefer the simple pleasures."

"I *wish* I had a brother," he said, with admiration.

"Oh, so do I!"

During that first awkward dinner, as Paula devoted herself to her oysters—for one may bring people together but after that they must fend for themselves—Perry Kilkullen saw clearly that underneath Maggy's tense exterior there was a deep and terrible grief, a heavy burden of sadness she could hardly attempt to hide. This encouraged him more than if she had been gay because it meant that she must be suffering, and whatever it was, he meant to cure it. The operetta of sound that filled the bright, busy restaurant just off the place d'Alma was a background for the luxurious low charm of her sad voice in which there was a mourning note of which she was unaware. He was prepared for enchantment but, as the dinner went on, he was appalled by the recklessness of his emotions, appalled and unafraid.

In the weeks that followed he courted her as gentlemen had courted ladies when he had been unmarried, in the early years of the 1900s. For all the youthfulness of his forty-two years, Perry Kilkullen's manners were marked by Edwardian grace, by the restraint of a period in which there was ample time for all things.

Maggy's apartment was filled with baskets of flowers that arrived every day from Lachaume, but he did not permit himself to offer her anything else. He walked up the rue de la Paix every morning as he left the Ritz and looked wistfully at the entrance to Cartier. He would have liked to rush in and buy her—anything, everything!—but he knew it was utterly inappropriate. As often as she would agree, he took her out to dinner. In an era in which evening clothes were the rule at the grand restaurants, he bowed to her desire to go to simpler places where she was comfortable in her little chemises and her black cape. Gently, as if she were a rare, wild bird, he led her to talk to him of her childhood, of her grandmother, of Rabbi

Taradash and the gang of young rascals she had been a member of less than two years before. In turn he told her of his legendary relative, "Honest Ned Kilkullen," who took on the power of Tammany Hall and won—for a while—and he explained to her the difference between the Irish and all other immigrants to the United States.

"They love a good fight, Maggy, and they love a good song. They're scrappy and devilishly proud and they'll do anything to win freedom and justice as they see it. They always think they're in the right, of course, even when they're wrong, but that's just Irish fire."

"I think I'd like the Irish," she said, amused at his fervor.

Suddenly Perry saw a vision of his wife in whom the Irish fire had been quenched years ago, if indeed, the Eastern seaboard stiffness that had been drilled into her by her governess had left any fire burning. Mary Jane Kilkullen had turned into a dry, duty-bound committee woman whose name evoked dim images of a big antique-filled apartment in which the valuable silver was always highly polished and the fine linen sheets freshly ironed; of a golf ball neatly hit; a cocktail perfectly mixed, but no memories came to him of the feeling of her hair under his hand, of her scent or her lips. As quickly as her image had drifted into his mind it faded. Reality was the roundness of Maggy's shoulder, the unquenchable spangled flash of her eyes, set so far apart on her face that they had that touch of peculiarity without which mere beauty is empty.

Two weeks of this gracious courtship passed and Perry Kilkullen, who had been able to be so direct with Paula, began to damn himself more as day followed day and he realized that he was paralyzed by the power of his feeling for Maggy. He felt that he'd been turned back into a timid adolescent who hesitates to even reach out a hand to the girl he loves for fear of rebuff. How, he asked himself, as he neglected his correspondence and forgot to return phone calls, how had he allowed a situation to develop between them in which he was behaving like some sort of benign, doting *uncle?*

Another week went by before Maggy, who couldn't avoid realizing how much he seemed to cherish her, started observing him for signs of what Paula, as inquisitive as an old concierge, called his "intentions." She had never known a man could be so gallant or so shy. One night, as they finished a massively gastronomic dinner at Le Grand Véfour, Maggy discovered that she suddenly felt like dancing. It was more than a feeling, she explained gravely to Perry, it was a physical necessity.

"Where?" he asked, delighted at an interruption in what seemed to be an endless series of meals.

"Le Jockey," she answered. Maggy hadn't returned to any of the Montparnasse nightclubs or bistros or cafés since the *vernissage.* On the Right Bank, she had been as unlikely to bump into Mistral or any of their scandal-loving friends as if she'd taken an ocean voyage, but tonight when she chose Le Jockey it was a sign that she didn't care whom she might encounter, for it was the artists' favorite nightclub, so casual that they often went there in their painting clothes.

Perry and Maggy soon found themselves jammed into the narrow, dark room that was perhaps the noisiest place in Paris. Owned by two men, one a painter, the other a former steamship steward, the walls and ceiling of the first and most famous Montparnasse nightclub were decorated like a Western saloon, covered with posters pasted up in every direction, punctuated here and there by blackboards on which saucy limericks were written in American slang. Lee Copeland, an ex-cowboy, played the piano, accompanied by two Hawaiian guitarists, and if they grew tired, a phonograph beat out the latest jazz and blues records from the United States.

A tribal and primitive excitement throbbed in the tiny Jockey for the four years of its brief, legendary existence, and every night limousines, like Perry's, swung to a stop before the black walls of the club, on which Indians and cowboys had been painted in bright colors, and couples who had fled formal balls quickly disappeared inside to drink endless glasses of whiskey and dance in a delirium all night long. A record was blaring out the "Black Bottom" from George White's *Scandals* as Maggy and Perry sat down. On the tiny dance floor couples were flailing around madly.

"Hell—I don't know how to do that one!" Perry said in exasperation.

"I don't either—I haven't been here in months." Maggy sipped her whiskey. "You could break an arm out there."

Then Lee Copeland slid into the first phrase of "Someone to Watch Over Me" and Perry grinned in relief. "I can manage that—shall we?"

Maggy rose, and in a reflex, kicked off her shoes. It was the first time he had held her in his arms and the eloquence of the body was never more immediate as in that moment when they touched. Physical compatibility is a question of skin first and foremost. If the contact of one skin on another isn't *immediately* pleasing nothing else can possibly matter, but if it is, all other things may follow.

One of the great simplifications of life took place when ballroom dancing was invented. It was no accident that for years farsighted matrons refused to let their daughters waltz. Once a man is permitted to put his arms around a woman and move to music with her, an infinitude of additional arrangements can be contemplated that no gavotte or minuet had ever led to.

Of all dances known to Western man in the twenties, the fox-trot, or the "Slow" as it is called in France, was the most dangerous, more fatal by far than the sexual explicitness of the athletic tango or the exuberant shimmy. A "Slow" is simply an embrace to a simple step, and the size of the dance floor at Le Jockey made even that simple step almost impossible to take.

As the Hawaiian guitars wailed out the Gershwin masterpiece, Maggy became magically accessible to Perry as the constraints he had been imprisoned by for the last three weeks simply vanished into the melody.

"I'm a little lamb that's lost in the wood . . .
Oh, how I would try to be good."

The lyric of the imperishably banal words would be, for Perry, the source of an unreasonable happiness as long as he lived. They held each other until the music ended and as the piano glided into the next song, they stood still, clasped together, and looked into each other's eyes. Without moving a muscle Maggy gave Perry the feeling that she was in motion, leaning against a spring wind.

"I could ask him to play that song again," Perry said longingly.

"Or you could take me home," Maggy whispered with a curving, poignant note in her voice. Without letting go of each other's hand, pausing just long enough to drop money at the table and for Maggy to retrieve her shoes, they walked out of Le Jockey and into the waiting limousine that took them the few streets to Maggy's tall, narrow building next to La Pomme d'Or.

Maggy still hummed the melody as wordlessly, hand in hand, they climbed the dilapidated badly lit staircase, toward her fifth-floor room. As they reached the third floor they had to pick their way carefully between baskets of flowers, still fresh, that had been carefully deposited on each tread of the stairs. The corridor to Maggy's rooms was lined with more baskets and when she opened the door Perry gasped—the huge, gilt-trimmed bed in her bedroom was born aloft, entirely adrift on a sea of flowers.

"I guess I overdid it," he muttered.

"A girl can never have too many flowers."

"There's no place to sit," he said, bemused.

"And there's no room for me to make you a cup of coffee."

"And you can't get to the fireplace to toast a marshmallow."

"And I can't open the door of the armoire to hang up your coat."

"I'm not wearing a coat."

"Ah, but that simplifies things. We have no choice, do we?"

"No. We have to lie down on the bed or stand here all night."

"My feet hurt," she said plaintively.

"Then the alternative—the alternative . . ."

In the pause before he kissed the lips she raised, in that humming second in which everything seemed possible, in which every happiness was offered, he thought he was approaching a destination toward which all unknowing he had been traveling all of his life. And when he bent his mouth to hers and felt her breath mingle with his, he knew he had arrived.

They stood, kissing in a field of flowers, for a long time, until their hearts beat so turbulently that they were both shaking.

"The alternative?" she murmured and at last they lay down together on top of the quilt and slowly, with trembling fingers and many kisses Perry got undressed as Maggy watched him by the dim, pale gold of the streetlamp that filtered up to her window. Naked, he stood startlingly young; without the fine suit, the vest, the starched linen, he was a man with rumpled thick blond hair and the long, flat muscles of a skier.

He slipped the thin straps of her chemise off her shoulders and pushed her dress down to her waist. With one arm he held her up so that she was half reclining on the bed, as he stroked her from her neck to her waist, his warm hand taking possession of her body inch by inch, gentling her down until she relaxed completely, her head thrown back on the pillow. Now he slid her dress off, threw it down over a basket of violets and soon she was as naked as he was, her body calm yet filled with riotous promise as she waited, deliberately and deliciously passive, for whatever he would do next. He looked long at the perfect and untroubled youth of her body. Then he molded himself closely to her as they lay facing each other, side by side, almost equal in height, lips to lips, nipples to nipples, heart to heart.

"Maggy, I love you so. Will you let me love you?"

"If you don't . . . if you don't," she threatened with a quiver of a shivering laugh. "Oh, yes, love me . . . darling Perry . . . love me . . . don't ask any more questions."

At first there was a dissonance in their rhythms. Maggy, accustomed only to Mistral's urgency and roughness, was several paces ahead of Perry, who brought a grave, slow rapture to his caresses, taking one step at a time and lingering over it, but, as she felt herself swelling with readiness, budding hotly and wantingly, and then swelling even more demandingly, Maggy realized that she had no need to hurry toward quick satisfaction. She matched herself to him, abandoned her haste for languorous waiting, almost holding her breath, proffering herself to his fingertips and his mouth with blissful curiosity. Each moment was enough in itself, one blending into another like notes of music. He smelled like honey, she thought, driftingly, as he finally took her, sure of himself, strongly. As they strained together, suddenly she felt as if a fluttering flight of bright butterflies had just been released from her body, borne in soft surprise between her thighs, launched into the quivering air.

Twice during that perfect night they woke from sleep and turned toward each other, deepening and confirming their need.

When Maggy finally woke it was bright daylight outside and Perry was sleeping as if nothing could possibly arouse him. She slid out of bed, put on her silver-kid evening shoes, and, stark naked under her black cape, she dashed down the stairs to the bakery at the corner where she bought six still-warm croissants. He was sleeping when she returned and picked her way carefully through the flower baskets toward her single gas ring to make coffee and heat milk. Maggy filled two enormous cups half-full of the strong brew, put them on a tray with a pitcher of the steaming milk, a bowl of sugar, and the croissants and cleared a place for the tray on the floor next to the bed.

Perry lay flat on his stomach and, at some point in the night, he had dragged the quilt so far up that everything was hidden but the top of his head and one outflung hand. Should she pull his hair or . . . Maggy bent her head and licked the knuckles of his little finger. He groaned and lapsed back into sleep. She slipped her tongue between the top of his little finger and his ring finger and slid it back and forth between his fingers. He moved his hand away but she imprisoned it and sucked the tip of his index finger. The quilted mass rose from the bed as if a bell had been rung in his ear.

"What the hell? . . . where? Maggy, you devil!" He lunged for her and threw her on the bed. "Why are you wearing your coat? Take it off! Kiss me! Kiss me!"

He captured her, and pushed her back on the pillow so that her hair spread like red banners against a white cloud. It seemed to him, as he felt her lips open against his, that he had awakened as a child again, with every hour full of possibility, every moment stretching before him, free and shining and ready to be filled with his dreams, with no day yet used up, none tarnished or forgotten.

"The coffee!" she managed to gasp finally. "It'll get cold."

"Why didn't you say *coffee?*" he demanded, releasing her. "I smell it but I don't see it."

Maggy squirmed to the edge of the bed and managed to raise the tray carefully so that nothing spilled.

"My God! Where did it come from?" he asked, as she poured the hot milk into the big cups. "Last night you said there wasn't room to make a cup of coffee . . . this morning there's a feast!"

"In the morning certain things become . . . more important, so I reconsidered. Have a croissant."

"It's so *good.* It's the best thing I've ever eaten in my life. How did you get them?"

"I went down to the bakery before you woke up," she said hungrily, taking another.

When everything on the tray had been consumed Perry lay back on the bed and stretched. He looked around him and really observed his surroundings for the first time. The only beauty of the room was in the flower baskets and now his clothes, cast aside so hastily, covered a number of them. The walls were covered with a faded and splotched wallpaper, the gilt of the bed was scratched and tarnished. Maggy's tenth-hand armoire sagged in the middle and the ceiling was low and confining in spite of the sun that poured in from the two open windows.

"Could I use your bathroom?" he asked.

"Down the hall, second door on the left."

"You don't have your own?"

"One to a floor, sir. I have a sink and a bidet—cold water only—but whenever I want a bath I have to go to Paula's. And when I want to go to the bathroom I go down the hall."

"You don't happen to remember what happened to my trousers?" he asked, casting his eyes around the room.

"They must be here somewhere."

"If they're not, I'll have to piss in the bidet," he threatened, surprising himself. He'd never spoken to Mary Jane so freely in twenty years of marriage.

"There they are on those pink roses—no, stay, I'll get them." Maggy prowled catlike among the flowers, at ease in her miraculous nakedness, with a total lack of modesty that made Perry waver an instant between awe and shock. Never in all of his married life had his convent-bred wife walked around like that.

By the time he had returned from the bathroom Maggy had hastily brushed her teeth, washed her face and made a collection of his clothes on the bed, where she was perched, covered now in her peignoir of lilac silk.

"Maggy." He sat on the bed with the air of someone about to make an announcement.

"Was the bathroom all you had hoped?"

"And more. Listen, my darling love, you can't stay here."

"But why not—I have the best view in Paris."

"Because we can't live on coffee and croissants. Because I can't stand to think that you don't have a bathroom. Because there are so many things I want to give you. Because I can't sleep here every night and get to work in the morning without going back to the Ritz to bathe and shave and change and I don't have time for that. Because there isn't enough room for your flowers."

"Sleep here every night?" she asked, seizing on the one phrase he'd used that had really caught her attention.

"Don't you want me?"

"Oh, yes, I want you!"

"Every night?" His gray eyes insisted on affirmation.

"I'm not sure about *every* night." She caught him around the waist and lay in his lap, looking up at the thatch of blond hair that covered his chest. "But certainly tonight, and tomorrow, and the day after . . ."

"Then, you see, my beautiful girl, you have to move. There isn't room here for my clothes."

"Or your valet."

"Especially my valet. Would you like to live at the Ritz? No, forget that—in five minutes the whole hotel staff would be talking about it and I don't see why anybody should know our business. Maggy—will you let me find an apartment for you? Will you let me make the arrangements so that we have a decent place?"

"But you're so proper," she protested. "Here you have a chance for an adventure in the real Paris, the part of Paris only the artists and the French really know—the place all those other visiting Americans are trying so hard to make their own—but immediately you want to change it into something else; a nice place to live, to sleep, with servants no doubt, and the best meat from the best butcher and all the bills paid on time . . . this 'decent place,' would it be for me or for us?"

"What's the difference?"

"I won't move into *any* man's apartment or house or suite—I'd rather keep my little room here. It suits me. But if it's a place of my own, a place to which I alone have the key, my own, private place, like this one, I might begin, *just begin*, mind you, to consider it . . ."

"I promise! Your own, absolutely. Only one key. I'll call for an appointment. Is Mademoiselle free this evening? Would Mademoiselle care to receive Monsieur Kilkullen? Is Mademoiselle in the mood to entertain a gentleman caller? Does Mademoiselle want to be kissed on the back of her neck or does Mademoiselle have more unorthodox desires? Does Mademoiselle want to be touched between . . ."

"Stop!" Maggy wriggled away. "Mademoiselle has no desires left this morning."

"But do *you* promise, Maggy? Will you move? You still haven't said yes." He looked at her anxiously. She was so unpredictable, he thought, so *unownable*, that he feared she might prefer a way of life that offered her complete freedom. There was not a domestic hair on her head. But he couldn't bear to think of her living here in this impossible room in which he'd spent the most beautiful night of his life. Daylight did not become it.

"Perry, what you want, put quite plainly and without chichi," Maggy said, with sudden seriousness, "is to *keep* me. My own key or no key, I'll be a kept woman if I agree, won't I?"

"That's such a sordid word!" he said, horrified. "Why put it like that?"

"But am I correct? Isn't that exactly what other people would say? What else would I be but a kept woman, *une femme entretenue?*" she kept on, relentlessly.

"Oh, Maggy, you're impossible," he said wretchedly.

"And I suppose you'd want me to dress in couture clothes—you wouldn't think my own things are good enough—and you'd want to buy me jewels and furs . . ."

"*Yes!* Goddamn it, I would! What's so terrible about that? Damn!"

Maggy jumped on the bed and a wide smile began to appear on her lips as she whirled around and around with her lilac peignoir swirling about her bare legs. "Diamond bracelets all the way to my elbows? Chinchilla to the floor? Trips to Deauville? My own car?"

Perry looked up at the mischief in her face. "Bracelets on both arms, to your shoulder if that's possible . . . ten fur coats . . . a coach and four . . . six tall footmen . . . one of each number in the new Chanel collection . . . and that's only the beginning!"

"Oh . . . oh!" She whirled faster and faster until she collapsed on top of him. "I've *always* wanted to be a kept woman! It was the dream of my depraved youth—oh, the thrill of it . . . *kept* . . . just like in *la Belle Époque.*" She shivered deliciously. "What would Aunt Esther say if she only knew?"

"Let's not tell her," Perry said hastily.

"I wouldn't dream of it. Listen, darling—how soon do you intend to start keeping me? To tell you the truth, I want to leave Montparnasse and never come back. I'm finished with my life here. It's over, this chapter, and done with . . . everything except Paula."

"Today, this morning. I'll get a suite for you at the Lotti—it's just a few steps from the Ritz and we'll start looking for a place."

"Oh, *yes!* I knew being kept would be heaven—but kept by a rich, tall, handsome, generous, crazy American!" Maggy covered his face with a torrent of kisses. "*Ça, alors, Ça c'est la vie, mon chéri—la bonne vie!*"

"The good life," Perry echoed, "yes, my beloved, I promise."

8

"He isn't working," Kate said as she sat with Avigdor in a café. "He hasn't even been able to pick up a brush since the *vernissage*." The dealer stiffened. An artist who doesn't paint regularly, as if he were going to an office, may prove as bad an investment as a vein of gold that dwindles into rock.

"It's that damned girl. She never came back, did she?"

"It wasn't that at all," Kate snapped. "Naturally he was furious after she kicked up such a stupid fuss—that revolting little scene she made was disgraceful—but he's hardly the type to pine away over a woman. He doesn't need her as a model anymore and I gather they'd only been together a few months—not enough to make a man like him stop work. She's essentially unimportant."

"As you say." Avigdor, in agreeing, reserved his thoughts. Could an unimportant girl have been the inspiration for such impassioned work? But something forbidding about the smoothness of Kate's high forehead, an icy note in her voice, told him not to speculate further, at least not out loud.

"I have a theory that it's some sort of letdown—postpartum blues. The *vernissage* was such a high point that afterward there had to be a reaction. I've been feeling a bit . . . flat . . . myself so I can imagine how it must have affected him."

"Has he even tried to paint?" Avigdor asked.

"Yes. That's the thing that worries me most. It's been two weeks now and he stands in front of his easel and just looks at it, hour after hour, day after day, while the paint dries on his palette. Every time I drop in I see him there with nothing on the canvas. Then, at night, he gets reeling drunk on red wine—he never did that before. And he won't talk about it. Adrien, he looks . . . *frightened*—that's the only word I can think of to describe his eyes. It's almost as if he's in some sort of private panic . . . I just don't understand it."

"He's got to get away for a while, see something besides his studio walls. He isn't the first artist to be unable to lift a brush after a big success."

"I've been suggesting that he should take a trip somewhere."

"And?"

"He says he's not in the mood. He says he's not the kind of man who takes vacations. He says he hasn't done a decent minute's work in months and he has to keep at it until it begins to come again."

"Shall I talk to him?"

"I wish you would, Adrien. He thinks you did a good job on the exhibition."

"Thanks," Adrien said dryly. He'd *made* the man into the sensation of the season. But if dealers expected normal gratitude from artists they'd go to bed every night severely disappointed. Any dealer who was in business for gratitude should abandon his gallery and become a breeder of dogs, nice big slobbery ones.

Two days later, early one morning in mid-October, Mistral left for Provence. The night before while they were having a farewell drink, as if it were an afterthought, Kate had offered to drive him down.

"I only know Paris and a little of Normandy. I'd like to see Aix and Avignon myself but I don't like traveling alone . . . and you wouldn't have to take the train . . ."

Mistral was affronted. "You take too much for granted, Kate. Do you think I want you driving me all over the place?"

"*You* drive . . . I don't care," Kate said, exasperated.

"I don't know how—how typically American to think that I would, as if I had a car."

"I'll teach you in half an hour as soon as we get into the country. There's nothing to it."

As soon as they had passed Fontainebleau, Kate turned off the main road and, after the briefest of demonstrations and instructions, turned the Talbot two-seater sports car over to Mistral. She knew that he possessed instantaneous reflexes, that his reactions were as fast as if he were in danger, and that his concentration on anything visual was prodigious. She was curious to see what he would make of this challenge. Without giving him a word of guidance she watched his big, exceptionally elongated hands with their finely articulated fingers deal deftly with the wheel and the shift.

He mastered the machine in ten minutes and they turned back to the main road and sped toward Saulieu, going southwest along an almost deserted route at ninety kilometers an hour.

Kate sat silently, relaxed and warm in her beautifully cut brown-and-rust tweeds, wearing soft leather gloves and a felt cloche. They drove through the countryside of the flat *département* of the Yonne, between endless rows of plane trees bordering fields from which the last wheat had almost all been gathered. It was the kind of fall day that contains no touch of melancholy, the kind of day on which some tantalizing promise lies almost visible in the depth of the sky and the snap of the air, particularly when the traveler's destination is south.

In Avallon they had a quick lunch and continued on their wordless, swift flight until the destination she had planned for that night lay behind them. Mistral seemed to have fallen into a trance of motion in which thought or memory played no part.

From time to time Kate looked at his profile and noted that his mouth, normally held in a commanding, peremptory line, had relaxed. She couldn't see his expression because his eyes were so deeply hooded, but nothing about the set of his imperious head invited conversation.

"How far are we going?" Kate finally asked as the afternoon drew on and she began to feel the chill of evening in the open car, in spite of her heavy suit and sweater.

"Until we get to Lyon, where the Saône joins the Rhône. Long ago it was a sacred place. For me it's the true beginning of Provence, although any Provençal would say it's too far north. No stopping until Lyon."

"That's almost two hundred kilometers," Kate protested.

"Yes, but it's all downhill," Mistral assured her. "South is always downhill."

In Lyon they found a small hotel, ate excellently for little money and went to their rooms windburned and exhausted. The next day they followed the majestic

Rhône, that quickly moving and unpredictable river that has been venerated for millennia, driving through villages whose names followed each other like a great wine list, a prodigious pathway of vineyards, one more precious than the next, from Lyon to Valence to Orange and finally to Avignon. There they crossed the river to Villeneuve-les-Avignon, where they stopped at last almost at midnight, at a *pension* Mistral had visited once before, during a vacation trip while he was still at the Beaux-Arts.

Madame Blé had bought her *pension* from a gentleman farmer. The original building had been a cardinal's palace and then a priory from 1333 until the Revolution, when it had returned to secular use. Yet it still basked in an atmosphere of utter peace. It was built in a U-shape around a courtyard where the mossy marble columns of the former cloister stood sentinel in the dark garden. This ancient priory had nothing of the monastic about it, nothing ecclesiastical. Its warm tranquillity was that of a refuge from the world, but not from the fruits or the joys of the earth. The center of the courtyard was punctuated by a flight of steps that descended into a wine cellar as old as Cardinal Arnaud de Via's palace, and this was the true heart of the building.

"I've got to find some sort of guidebook to this area," Kate said the next morning after a late breakfast.

"Why?"

"We've been traveling so fast I feel utterly disoriented. I don't know what's to the east or to the west of this place but I do know it's terribly historic and I don't like feeling ignorant."

"Historic?" Mistral lifted his heavy eyebrows in feigned surprise.

"Oh, for heaven's sakes, Julien—full of ruins, churches, museums, all sorts of things we should see. Stop looking so amazed. What's wrong with my wanting to know? We've driven damn near the whole way from Paris to the Mediterranean in two days and I want to know why you picked this one particular place to stop in, out of all the rest of France."

"And will a book tell you that?"

"Well . . . why not? We can't just wander around without knowing."

"We can't?"

"Obviously it's possible, but that way we're sure to miss things," she said tartly.

"You could have ten guidebooks and ten years in which to follow them and you'd still miss something marvelous right under your very American nose. Why don't you relax and look around. That's what I came to do—just look around."

Kate abandoned the discussion. Although her fundamental sense of order was put out of joint by the idea of drifting about without some authority to refer to, she didn't want to argue with him about anything.

All the rest of the day and the following one they wandered around Villeneuve-les-Avignon on foot, exploring the city that had grown up during the fourteenth century when the pope moved from Rome to Avignon. Church dignitaries had settled in Villeneuve and created a bustling city with a great monastery and a magnificent fort, a city that had now retreated into a few sleepy, fragrant squares and several narrow, arcaded streets where the last stones of episcopal palaces could still be distinguished.

On the third day, they headed east past Avignon itself and took the road that led to the market town of Apt and bisected the Apt basin, a rich fruitful valley that lay cupped between two mountain ranges some six miles apart. Far away to the north lay the Monts de Vaucluse and, to the south, almost bordering the road, was the Montagne du Lubéron. It was this side of the Lubéron, *Le Versant Nord*, that had captivated Mistral on his previous visit. He had never forgotten those fantastically eroded limestone cliffs, on which sparse vegetation clung as fiercely as did the huddled villages that perched a thousand feet above the main route, apparently unreachable until Mistral found the thread of narrow dirt road that led to each one of them: Maubec, Oppède-le-Vieux, Félice, Ménerbes, Lacoste and Bonnieux.

In prehistory man had lived where these fortified hill villages now stood, each one of them nearly invisible from the road along which enemies had so often come marching in the past. For hundreds of years they had endured bloody battles against tyranny from the north, these tiny, sleepy villages with streets as steep as stepladders, whose houses tumbled close together, soft gray and softer ocher, mantled with vines, splashed with the fluttering, mythological silver of olive groves and the deep coral of the flowers of the vine called "Fairy's Fingers." From these villages, at night, rose a mist, peopled, it was said, by the ghosts of the former inhabitants, Protestant dissenters who were mercilessly slaughtered by their countrymen in the Wars of Religion. These now peaceful villages were the homes of shopkeepers and craftsmen whose trade came from the many small, prosperous farms of the Apt basin.

Mistral was wildly excited. He had no sooner climbed up to the white marble ruins of the château-fortress in Oppède-le-Vieux, where he would see, from that steep vantage point, some particularly enticing farm that lay down below and he'd hurry down the precipitous path he and Kate had just climbed, dragging her protestingly behind him, to throw himself back into the car and drive back to the rolling, richly cultivated valley searching for the farmhouse he had spied from above.

Each big farmhouse, or *mas*, as it was called in Provence, was a collection of stone buildings, built roughly in a square around a central courtyard, with so many connected outbuildings and small towers, so many different heights of roof and such a diverse, asymmetrical collection of shuttered windows and arched doorways that it resembled a small hamlet set in the middle of a wealth of fields and vines that grew till they touched the walls of the buildings on every side.

Mistral would ignore the signs that warned that the road to a *mas* was private property and drive right up to it, get out of the car and circle around lost in admiration, ignoring the warning barking of the farm dogs, until a peasant woman would come out to investigate. Then, while Kate watched from the car, he'd engage her in conversation. Invariably she'd invite them both in for a glass of wine. He was passionately intent on penetrating into the interiors of these rural strongholds, no two of which were alike, with their three-foot-thick walls and fireplaces so large that he could stand in them.

The Provençal peasant women, taciturn and wary of anyone unknown, would never normally have asked two strangers into their homes, but Mistral's robust appreciation and interest charmed them as much as did the sight of him, so much a fine cavalier in spite of his rough workingman's clothes. The farm women's suspicions were replaced by friendliness and curiosity for they could sense in this tall man of the north, with his red hair and ocean-blue eyes, an emotional rapport, an immediate sensitivity to their way of life that made him seem not quite a stranger even though they clannishly called their own neighbors from the next village "foreigners."

"There isn't a more beautiful place in the world," he told Kate after they had spent three days driving about the mountains and plains of the north Lubéron, returning the forty kilometers to Villeneuve each night before dinner. "At least in my opinion."

"Have you seen enough of the world that you can be a fair judge?" Kate couldn't prevent herself from wondering.

"I don't need to. Some things are self-evident. What more could you ask of nature, Kate, and what more of man, than these villages, this sky, these trees and stones and earth? I was right to come back here. In Paris I'd forgotten the horizon—I'd forgotten green. Nothing, Kate, *nothing* on earth is as green as the leaves of a vineyard with the late afternoon sun on them."

Kate had never seen him so expansive with visible pleasure. He looked as if every pore of his being was flooded with the particularly pure and vivid light of the Provençal countryside, that land, the poet Frédéric Mistral had called "The Empire of the Sun."

She felt different herself. These days outside in air that smelled of heather, rosemary and thyme had made her shed the thick layer of sophistication within which she normally moved. The hard edges of her features, which she had always before covered with pale ivory powder, were all softened by a sunburn that rounded and warmed her face. Her thin lips, no longer touched carefully with bright red lipstick, looked fuller and softer against the flush of her cheeks and her high forehead was covered by the fine ash-blond hair that had been so blown about by the wind of the open car that she had abandoned any attempt to maintain her neat center part, forgot to wear her hat and just let it fly about as it wanted to. The perfection of the shape of her face was enhanced by this new abandon. Now, as she slid into a country mood, she seemed less formidable and as young as her twenty-three years.

"You were right about the guidebook," she admitted as they finished dinner in the garden of the *pension* of Madame Blé.

"But, Kate, think of what you've missed! There's the Popes' Palace in Avignon—we haven't even been inside and it's just across the river—and the Roman Arena in Arles and the fountains of Aix—oh, don't forget the Maison Carrée in Nîmes—here you are in the middle of a hundred famous antiquities that tourists have been visiting for centuries and all you've seen is a few sleepy villages and a dozen farms."

"Why do you keep teasing me, Julien? I said you were right; do you want a formal apology?"

"An apology? From you, the haughty New York lady, the rich and elegant American who darts about organizing people so neatly that they hardly know she's doing it?" He gave her a condescending grin.

"Now that's just not fair. I resent that." Kate spoke calmly but she felt anger grip her. Why did he turn on her the minute she made a concession? What made him so contrary?

"Fair? Of course it's fair—you just don't want to see yourself as you are. You're different here, I'll grant that, but in Paris when you're in your element, I've never known a woman who managed to have things more her own way. You're remarkable, Kate. What's wrong with being rich and perfectly dressed and looking down your nose and making life turn out the way you want it to? There are a lot of women who would like a chance to change places with you."

"God*damn* you, Julien! Who the hell are you to tell me what sort of person you think I am? Nothing, no one, matters to you, does it? Besides your work, is there anything you truly care about? If so, I haven't seen it. You're a *monster*." Kate could hardly believe the words she heard pour out of her lips. Her composure, her sense of proportion, the neat stitches of her normal speech had all disappeared in a storm of fury.

Mistral smiled like a small boy provoking a kitten.

"And you, dear Kate, will of course, permit anyone to walk all over you because you're too good-hearted to stop them. Flexible, soft-minded Kate, undemanding Kate Browning who only asks from life the small fruit that falls from the tree to her feet."

Too angry to reply, she fell silent, biting the inside of her lips, fighting back a bellyful of rage.

Lazily he spoke. "Two such thoroughly decent people, two such splendid characters as we, might make an interesting combination. What do you say, Kate? Shall we experiment?"

Kate jumped up from the table and walked into the dark garden, outside of the pool of light. Mistral followed her, and with his powerful hands, turned her toward him. She stiffened her body in resistance and averted her head, her jaw tense. With one hand he held her in place and with the other he forced her head around to face him but she didn't raise her eyes, whether still in resentment or not, he couldn't be sure, nor did he care. She had begun to appeal to him these last few days and surely she hadn't invited herself along on this trip just for the sake of the scenery. Women didn't work like that, in his experience. Not even rich Americans in expensive tweeds.

"Kate, let's go to my room. I want to see you naked, spread out on my bed."

"Julien!"

"Now don't tell me you're shocked. Was I too direct for Miss Browning? Do you want pretty words, Kate? I want to fuck you. If that doesn't suit you, you have only to say so. I won't ask again. So . . . yes or no?"

"How typical, how romantic," she muttered.

"I said 'yes' or 'no.' "

In the little light there was he saw her whole face take on such a complex, shivering expression of unwilling but irrepressible yearning that it made him put his arm around her, without another word. All the way up the curving flight of stairs they said nothing to each other, their only contact was the light pressure of his arm across her back and his hand at her waist. Through his fingers he could feel her rigidity, her refusal to lean against him, her insistence on walking as self-containedly as if he weren't touching her, yet Kate didn't hesitate or resist him in any way. It was almost as if she were mounting the steps to his bed without thinking about what she was doing, yet her silence was charged with something so tight, so secret, so much stronger than ordinary sexual tension, that Mistral found himself puzzled by it.

He released her to lock the door of his room. When he turned back to her he found that she had retreated to the window and seemed to be looking in complete fascination at something in the garden. He crossed the room and stood behind her and brushed the back of her neck with one finger. She didn't jump or turn around but her hands grasped the window frame with determination.

"Kate, how can we begin to experiment if you won't even turn around?" he whispered to her teasingly. She didn't move, or indicate that she had heard him. Mistral bent and brushed the back of her neck with his lips. Kate gripped the window frame convulsively. He smiled faintly, and with the tip of his tongue he touched the nape of her neck at the exact spot where her bobbed hair came to a neat point and then he drew his tongue slowly down the back of her neck along the delicate ridge of her spinal column to a place between her shoulder blades. There he fastened his mouth against her skin and breathed gently, patiently, without a single additional motion, until her hands dropped to her sides and she turned around and faced him, white and shaking.

"You've never kissed me, Julien. Never even kissed me."

"A mistake, Kate . . . one of the few I'll admit to," he said as he reached down and lifted her chin toward him. Her lips were cool and held together so tensely, so ungivingly, that he drew back in surprise. "Kate, you don't have to go ahead with this—I don't force myself on unwilling women."

"No, no, Julien, I *want* to," she insisted although her words were contradicted by the timidity of her voice. She flung herself toward him, throwing her arms around his neck and pressing her lips on his in quick, short kisses that were almost like pecks.

For a moment Mistral, amused, let this awkward assault continue, but soon he held her off at arm's length.

"Not so fast and furious, Kate."

"Christ! Don't you ever stop making fun of me?"

For an answer he picked her up and carried her over to the bed. Still holding her in his arms he lay down next to her. "I'll admit to another mistake . . . I forgot how impatient you are . . . I'm going to teach you patience, Kate, you need to learn it badly—so badly." As she lay there stiffly he ran his hands lightly down the length of her body. She flinched but didn't protest. "I have no intention of undressing you, Kate, not for a long time," Julien murmured as he bent over her lips. "Lie still," he commanded and he kissed her closed mouth, concentrating all his curiosity, all his need—for it had been weeks since he'd made love to any woman—on her finely shaped lips, until they grew warm and swollen and finally parted willingly to allow his tongue to enter her mouth. He held himself back, touching only lightly along the inside of her lips, languorously sweeping from one corner of her mouth to the other, resisting her when she began to try to trap his tongue and draw it further into her mouth, then letting her have it for one brief second before he withdrew it completely and covered her whole mouth with his, his mouth that always looked so stern until it turned hot and tender in love. As he played with her, his tongue flicking in and out of her lips, pressing forward for only a tiny fraction of a moment, he could feel all the muscles of her body beginning to relax until she lay passively, no longer clenched in anxious anticipation, her entire being centered on his mouth and what it was doing to her. Soon that stage of abandon passed away and he could sense the gradual tightening of her arm and leg and pelvic muscles as she began to want more than mere kisses, but still he confined himself to her lips, laughing inwardly at the lesson he was forcing her to endure. She groaned and ground her teeth as he tantalized her. You'll beg for it, he promised himself, you'll have to beg for it, you cool American bitch, even as he felt himself growing almost unbearably excited.

"Julien . . ." Kate gasped. "Undress me."

"No, Kate."

"Julien . . . *please.*"

"If you want me . . . undress me," he demanded, flinging himself back on the quilt and kicking off his shoes and lying quite still. Kate looked at the splendid man who offered himself to her in such a maddening way and in a sudden, resolute fury of determination, with trembling fingers, ignoring her self-consciousness, she threw herself at the buttons of his shirt, almost ripping them open. He helped her to ease his arms out of his sleeves and she scarcely paused to run her hands greedily down over his chest before she attacked his belt buckle. But then she reached the buttons of his fly and she became conscious of the great hard outline of his penis straining under the cloth. She was seized by a sudden inability to continue and her hands fell to her sides. "You . . . Julien . . . *you* do it," she implored.

"Lost your nerve, Kate?" he taunted her, watching her carefully even though every impulse in his body was urging him to throw her on the bed and take her just as she was, her hair wet at the roots with the sweat of lust, her lips bruised, her fists clenched.

"No! Damn you!" she responded violently and took a deep breath before setting herself the task of opening his fly, revealing him rearing and naked, for he wore nothing under his corduroy trousers. Mistral was breathing as rapidly as she while Kate forced herself to unbutton each button. When she had reached the last one he ripped off his trousers in one swift movement and threw her back on the bed. "Good, Kate, good . . . you were patient . . ." he grunted as, with experienced fingers, he began to take off her clothes, finding, as he had expected, that her breasts and hips were small, her waist slender and her blond pubic hair as fine as that of a young girl's.

Soon they were both entirely naked and Kate lay on the bed in such a posture of modesty restrained by sheer willpower that Mistral had difficulty in not laughing at her. "Lovely Kate," he murmured as he grasped her slim body and hugged it, covering as much of her flesh with his own as he could. He held her, quietly warming her with his nakedness until he felt her begin to relax against him. Had she been another female he would already have entered her, but Kate, this unsensual, inexperienced woman presented him with a challenge he had no wish to resist. She wanted *him*—oh, yes, but she wanted to get it over with as quickly as possible, without losing herself, and that was something he had no intention of permitting.

Eventually, when her body felt as warm as his own, he began to trace her backbone with his fingertips while he continued to hold her locked tightly against him. He caressed her almost boyishly trim buttocks with a rapid movement and when she immediately grew tense, he muttered, "Patience, patience, Kate," and withdrew his fingers to the small of her back. Each time his hand returned to her buttocks he lingered there for a second longer until finally he felt her pressing them against his hands, offering themselves. "Patience . . . patience," he repeated, taking an altogether new pleasure in this leisurely arousal, he who had never bothered to gauge so carefully the state of readiness of any woman, he who had never explored the delicious, self-inflicted pain of holding himself back when release was there for the taking. With one arm he held Kate immobile as he finally probed between her buttocks, finding her astonishingly ready, although, as his fingers parted her, she jerked away in a halfhearted protest. Now he grew merciless as his long fingers advanced further between her slim thighs and found the precise spot he was seeking. His middle finger became as agile, as delicate as the tip of a tongue as he returned again and again to the attack, now pressing softly and moving slowly, now darting quickly and purposefully, all his lust centered on that one fingertip and the flesh it was awakening with such cleverness.

"Julien . . . my God . . . stop!" Kate cried out, but he answered only "Patience," and soon he felt her gathering herself together in an unmistakable clenching and hardening of her pelvic muscles. More rapidly, ever more rapidly his finger flickered until finally, he felt her shuddering and leaping, out of control, her shriek of release smothered against his neck. His fingers didn't leave her until the last spasm had left her body. She lay back, drained but wide-eyed. "You see what patience will earn, Kate?" Mistral whispered to her but she didn't nod or smile but looked at him gravely.

"That's never happened to me before," she whispered.

"Then our experiment is half a success—now, it's my turn, Kate," Julien answered and gave himself up to his own fierce mastery of her willing, open, pliant body.

Later, Kate, like someone coming out of a trance, began to cover his hands with fluttering kisses of gratitude. It was a long while before she realized that Mistral was sleeping deeply.

9

Kate Browning was in torment. Every night for the next week, after Mistral fell away from her and went to sleep she lay awake, her sleekly fashioned body echoing with a passion she had never known existed, for she had always been too cautious before. The thoughts of the pleasures Mistral had taught her so quickly pierced through her entrails like honeyed arrows that she would never want to pluck from her body. She put her fingers between her legs, to that tender kernel of flesh that was so unfamiliar to her touch. It was still alive, still ready to quiver again. All day long she had felt it distended, burning, aching for his hands and his lips. At meals she watched those hands tear bread and cut meat and found, to her mortified surprise, that she was rubbing her thighs together under the table. She moaned aloud at the sight of his mouth, so firm now, soon to be so hot and soft on her skin. Her nipples were sore yet she rubbed them stealthily across Mistral's arm.

The foundation of her life shifted and she felt heavy with inevitability. Her mind could not rest, probing Mistral's inner inaccessibility. How could she dare to swim, to just float along, in this mindless rapture when the man himself did not *belong* to her? The only moments when Kate felt certain that Julien's full attention was on her was during the actual act of love. But even in those moments he had never once wholly *given* himself to her, never once betrayed a need of her, never once said that he loved her. Was he holding back, as she was, she wondered, or was she simply a female body in a bed?

"*Je t'aime bien*, Kate," he said—that careless phrase with that careful nuance, that "*bien*" that turned the word "love" into "like." She was desperate to hear him say the simple, *necessary* words, "*Je t'aime*," but until he did she would not say those words to him. Yet every day she realized that she was falling deeper and deeper in love. Mistral had become the only prize the whole wide world had to offer her. There was an insatiable, ruthless completeness about her feelings that included everything she knew about him; all the difficulties he presented; all the faults clearly observed in him; the women he had had before she met him. They didn't matter. Nothing mattered except an avid, addictive obsession that would accept nothing less than possession.

Kate was a woman of enormous strength, proud, devious and subtle, yet her nerves were pulled so tightly by the strain of concealing her emotions that she wept, lying there next to the superb body of the man who slept without thought of her. But after she wept she stayed awake and scrutinized the situation with the cold, farsighted intelligence that no fire could extinguish.

Frustration was alien to Kate's deepest nature. She did not and never had believed that there was anything she couldn't have if she really wanted it.

During the second week in Provence, Mistral decided to drive west to Nîmes, that mellow city that had been declining with delicious serenity since the reign of Hadrian. There he and Kate went walking in the park, climbing up the many steep stone steps that finally led to the base of the Tour Magne, the ruin of a Roman watchtower that looked out over a vast panorama. They lay on the grass, agreeably tired, observing the few citizens of Nîmes who had sought out this high, cool place, from which, almost two thousand years ago, Roman soldiers had been able to see for a hundred kilometers. After a long silence, Mistral spoke.

"I couldn't, I wouldn't begin, or even dream of beginning to paint this view. It's too complete, too vast, it answers every question I might ask of it, it has no need of man."

"You haven't found anything . . . anything you feel like painting, in Provence?" Kate asked carefully. This was the first time he had mentioned painting since they had left Paris. She had obeyed his unspoken rule of silence on the subject.

"No," he said. No, he thought, no, I haven't *wanted* to paint—that's what terrifies me the most. *Not to want, not to need to paint*—I've never known such emptiness! That young couple on the bench over there, their hands are almost touching—they're not seeing the view, they've probably grown up on it, probably their mothers brought them here for years and years to play—and today they've realized that the other is *another*, a mystery, that strangest of things, another human being. Once . . . once I could have painted their hands not quite touching, painted those hands a dozen times, ten dozen times and never come to the end of what they make me feel, those four hands that don't quite touch, that don't yet dare to touch, that *will* touch—and perhaps—who knows?—change the world. But I don't *want* to paint those hands . . . I don't *have* to paint them. And if I'm not a painter, *why am I alive?*

"I suppose," ventured Kate, "that this country has been painted too often? Everything's so—picturesque . . . that it doesn't interest you?"

"Something like that, yes," Mistral answered briefly. The last time I was here, he thought, I wouldn't walk around a corner without my sketchbook, I was wild with excitement, nothing looked as if anyone had ever laid eyes on it before—much less painted it—all Provence was calling me until I thought I'd go as mad as Van Gogh. "Picturesque" my ass. You can't understand, Kate, and I can't explain. "Picturesque" will do as well as any other explanation but the fact is that I've lost it, *lost it*, and even Provence hasn't brought it back.

"Come on, Kate," he said abruptly, getting up. "This grass is still wet."

More and more often during the next week Mistral turned the car in the direction of Félice, the village that lay on the north flank of the Lubéron, east of Ménerbes and west of Lacoste. Félice held an attraction with which he became more and more obsessed as the urge to paint refused to return: the game of boules.

In the single café of the town every man who could walk and belonged to the village gathered each evening and each noon to have a *pastis* or two. Now, in autumn, their ranks were swelled by many farmers, who were making the most of this short, leisurely time of the year after the crops were in and before the hunting season opened. After a few rounds the men all wandered off to the flat, shady ground behind the café and played endless games of boules, that bowling game which is the equivalent, throughout the South of France, of soccer, bicycle racing and billiards put together, a game so complicated that its rules cover three pages of tiny print.

One of the farmers, a young man named Josephe Bernard, had looked Mistral up and down the second time he and Kate had gone to the café.

"Do you play boules?" he asked finally.

"I'm just a tourist," Mistral said to excuse himself.

"No matter. Would you like to try?"

In spite of the rules, boules is basically so simple that Mistral was able to acquit himself honorably with a minimum of instruction. His coordination and eye were so well developed that although he had never held one of the steel balls before, within an hour he was making a respectable showing and on that first day he managed to knock away the boule of another man from its position close to the target, delighting his sponsor who invited him to be part of the game any time he was in the neighborhood.

Mistral had returned often, charmed by the high drama of the game, which involved endless arguments, filled with wit, insults, laughter and shrewdness, as well as the never-failing pleasure of throwing a ball, that one skill all men love to use.

Kate watched from the sidelines, amazed at Mistral's ability to lose himself in a game that she found infinitely boring. But while he played she was able to look at him without his realizing it. How easily he fell into the manners of the boules players, she thought. He threw his arm into the air as widely as they did, argued as earnestly, laughed as loudly, played without noticing the passage of time, and every day his command of his boule grew greater.

"You're sure you're not from this country?" Josephe Bernard asked his new friend. "Provence must be in your blood . . . and in your name. Mistral—that's 'master wind' in Provençal. I have some cousins named Mistral from over near Mérindol, on the south side of the mountain . . . perhaps we're related?"

"Maybe I am but I can't prove it. I don't know where my great-grandparents came from. I wish I did, but my family's all dead and while they were alive I never listened—never bothered to ask."

"Most strangers, if they try to throw a boule, they make fools of themselves. It only looks easy. If you practiced for a few more weeks you could be on my team. There's a tournament the last Saturday in November."

Mistral threw his arm around the young farmer's shoulders and ordered a round of drinks for everyone in the café. He knew how much such an offer meant from a man to whom each boules tournament was a matter that would be discussed with an intensity of interest for years to come.

"I wish I could, Josephe, but I have to work for a living." But how, Mistral wondered, am I going to go back to work? Boules had let him forget for a few hours, boules had let him stop trying to find someone whom he could blame for the fire that had gone out: Avigdor because he was a dealer and all he wanted was product to sell; Kate because she had caused the exhibition to happen and before the exhibition he had been painting as simply as he breathed; Maggy because she was a fool and a child and the only woman who had ever left him; the exhibition itself because it opened his eyes to the cupidity of collectors who buy in a minute what it takes a man months of labor to create, collectors who don't respect, don't understand, but just open their purses and purchase a piece of him—he realized that none of them was to blame but still he circled them in his mind, trying to find the culprit.

"We have to work too," Josephe replied, "but there's always time for boules—if not, why bother to work?"

Besides the café and the game, Félice held another lure. Below the village in the valley not too far from the main road, Mistral had discovered a deserted *mas*. One day, spurred only by idle interest, he had followed a deeply rutted path that wound up and around a low knoll covered by an orchard of precious live oaks, the only trees at whose roots truffles grow. The shade of the orchard opened into an avenue of excited, pointed, green-black cypress beyond which stood a high wall surrounding a *mas*.

Mistral parked the Talbot on the strip of meadow that lay between the cypress and the walls of the house, a sunny, dry stretch of tiny yellow thistles and wild grasses. Tall, broad, double doors barred them from seeing inside. There was a silence, laced, as always, by the sound of the cicadas, a dry but pleasant crackle that was so much a part of the countryside that it was a part of the silence itself. None of the familiar sounds of a farm rose from behind the walls that surrounded the buildings; no dogs yapped, there were no kitchen noises nor the calling of children. Honeysuckle, growing thickly and curling over the walls, released an intense sweetness that was almost as tangible as if it were visible; a swarm of red and orange butterflies hung above the meadow like a Chinese kite and a sleepy, swarming hum indicated that here was a paradise of bees.

Together Mistral and Kate walked around trying to peer inside, but the walls were surrounded at their base by wicked brambles and the tendrils of honeysuckle grew up into the air just above Mistral's head.

At one point the wall turned into the bottom of a big round tower with two unshuttered windows open high above them, but whoever had abandoned the *mas* had made sure that there would be no intruders for there was no gap anywhere. As they made the circuit they could see five tilted roofs of various heights, and the tops of some window frames. The walled *mas* was the hub of a wheel of wedge-shaped fields, each separated from the other by tall windbreaks of cypress or cane. One section of the wheel was an olive grove, the next an unworked expanse of red earth; then came a vineyard heavy with unpicked grapes; and next to this lay an apricot orchard, laden with rotting fruits; then another vineyard and more sections of unplanted fields, the earth clumped as if a plow had never passed over it.

"It's incredible!" Mistral exploded. "Here, in a land whose every millimeter of good soil is used—I can't believe the shame of it! Look at those grapes, look at the olives! And the apricots! They grew and ripened and no one picked them. It's a disgrace!"

"It must be for sale," Kate ventured.

"There's no sign posted. All I saw was the name on the mailbox. *La Tourrello*—a Provençal word—must mean tower—little tower, or something like that," he said angrily. "It's probably part of an estate and the heirs are fighting about it—that's what often happens. If they don't agree to work the land in shares they have to sell it at auction."

"Why don't we find out? They must know in Félice," Kate suggested. "If it's for sale, we could at least ask to visit it."

"No, I don't think so. I don't want to go in." Mistral sounded troubled.

"You? You've been inside every *mas* from Maubec to Bonnieux. Why not this one?"

"I can't explain it. It's just a feeling." He was protecting himself. An intuition told him that he would never forget the look of this securely locked, valuable, walled domain. Even though he had seen only the outline of the shallow slant of the tilted roofs inside, their simple geometry had such a rightness that they had touched his heart. The *mas* on the knoll was perfectly at one with nature and he preferred to see no more of it than the outside since it was empty and therefore available.

Mistral had never owned a house and the house-lust that most of the human race feels had never touched him before. He had been content to look at the farms of Provence with the simple understanding that they were the only possible structure that could be perfectly mated with this wondrous countryside. It was an esthetic joy, not tainted by the itch to own; but one step inside the doors of this *mas* would change him forever.

"All right," Kate said, respecting his wish. Both she and Mistral were profoundly alike in the limitation they placed on the things they did not want to know.

In the week that followed, they returned four times to the deserted *mas* and she never repeated her suggestion although she was irritated almost beyond bearing at his fascination with the place. He's courting that old farmhouse, she thought jealously, wooing it as if it were a woman, prowling around the walls like a lovesick adolescent. Between the café and the boules and mooning around this farm he manages to put in a full day without accomplishing one damn thing. When will he paint again?

In the café in Félice, several days later, Josephe Bernard questioned Mistral.

"You say you're a painter, eh, Julien? We've seen them come and go for years—there's always a painter hanging around in these parts. But I never saw one who did anything but paint the countryside. I say that a real painter should be able to make a picture of another human being that looked *exactly* like him. What do you say to that?"

"Not every painter does portraits, Josephe, and not every portrait looks like its subject, or the way he thinks he looks, which is never the same thing at all."

"I was afraid you'd come out with high-class crap like that," Josephe replied, disappointment evident in his open face. "So you couldn't paint me the way I look in the mirror, is that it?"

"Maybe yes, maybe no, but I can do something that will make you smile, my friend." Mistral took a pencil from the bar and drew rapidly on the back of a slip of paper used for the game of Lotto. "What do you think of this?" He shoved the paper over to Bernard. In a few spare lines, in less than a minute, using a knack he had had since he was a teenager, a knack he never thought twice about, he had distilled the essence of Josephe Bernard into a caricature.

"Damn if it's not me!—big nose and all!" Bernard bellowed with laughter. "Now do Henri—he's got another ugly mug!" He grabbed an old farmer and thrust him in front of Mistral and slid another piece of paper at him. Soon Mistral was surrounded by men, all clamoring for their caricatures, vying with each other like schoolboys for the next turn. He ripped them off with an ease that astonished the crowd.

Now that was something, they told each other, an image that looked so much like you that it could be no one else in the world, and done so quickly that it seemed like magic. Each one of them pored over his caricature—how had the painter managed it? Those of them who lived near the café hurried home to bring their wives and children back with them, all waiting in line for one of the amazing slips of paper. Better than a game of *belotte*, this was. Soon Mistral had to take another pencil and then another, as the points wore down, but nothing stopped the slashing strokes of his cunning hand. Finally there was no one left in Félice who hadn't been caricatured, who hadn't carefully carried away a slip of Lotto paper, to look at over dinner and compare with many a friendly insult.

It was late, almost seven o'clock, when Mistral and Kate finally left Félice to go back to Villeneuve. His heart was so swollen with thanksgiving that he didn't want to talk. Caricatures, a simple party trick he had forgotten he could do, *caricatures*, by all the saints in heaven, had given him back the demon of creation. His fingers itched for the feel of a brush, his nose craved the smell of oil paint and turpentine, his gut was alive again with images he *had* to throw on canvas—and all because he'd taken a pencil without thinking and spilled out foolishness to entertain those simple folk he liked so much. They had responded with such wholehearted appreciation, the caricatures had gone directly from his hand into their hands. Theirs was the only reward he could accept with ease, without feeling disconnected from his work.

For the first time Mistral enjoyed that feeling of triumph he had not been able to absorb into himself on the night of the *vernissage*. Every muscle, every nerve and sinew of his body was newborn, as full of power as it had ever been. Mistral could scarcely contain his excitement. How could he wait till morning?

After dinner that night Mistral set out by himself for a walk. He felt a wild energy that was too great to be contained under a roof and his jubilation was all the companion he wanted as he roamed along the banks of the Rhône, accepting with pleasure the feeling of the chill of the air against his skin, rejoicing in the free rustle of the trees, the tumble of water. As he walked he understood, with so clear a conviction that he marveled that it had not come to him sooner, that he must never leave Provence.

Never again, he thought, never again the loneliness of cities. Never again the anthill of Montparnasse, where too many people spoke too many languages in too many cafés, and talked too much rot about government and religion and schools of painting. Never again the cold Parisian winter with the dismal rain killing the light. Never again a day without a view of the horizon.

Even as he enumerated for himself the reasons for not going back, he knew that he didn't need them, they were only the outward expression of an inward feeling that held him in the tightest grip. *He must not leave Provence because here he could work.* It was as if he had had a revelation, as if he had seen a vision, it was stronger than any superstition and clearer than any logic.

At dawn he awakened Kate.

"The vacation's over, Kate. I'm going back to work."

Kate blinked with relief. "Give me half an hour—I'll dress and pack as quickly as I can."

"No, don't rush, no need. Stay on awhile if you like."

"But you just said you're going back to work. What are you talking about?"

"I'm staying here, Kate."

"What?"

"Right here. Madame Blé is open all year around, which solves one problem and there are plenty of empty houses in Villeneuve to rent as a studio. As soon as the store's open, I'll telephone old Lefebvre and have him ship down all the supplies

I need on the next train and send the bill to Avigdor—nothing could be easier. I've got it all planned."

"I suppose you're doing all this to be on that damn boules team," Kate said viciously.

"That wouldn't be a bad reason, but no, I have a better one." Mistral paced restlessly around the room, not seeing Kate's face, white with shock. "It's this place, Kate, this place." He didn't know how to explain his conviction to her, and, he realized, he didn't need to. "It's the light here, don't you understand?"

"I see perfectly," she said evenly. Nothing could be gained by further discussion. One thing Kate was never wrong about was the strength of another's position and Mistral's was of unquarried marble. "I'll stay on a day or so then."

"You don't have to rush back—stay as long as you like, unless you'd be bored when I start working all day. I'd enjoy having you here Kate, very much."

"We'll see." Did he think she'd hang around like a house cat? she thought furiously. Kate realized that his announcement snapped her out of a coma. Love, concealed with so much difficulty, had made her inattentive. She'd been dreaming the days away, dangerously sidetracked by her body. "Since you're staying, I don't think I'll go sight-seeing today, Julien. I'll be in that car long enough on the way back. I've got a few things to put together—and I have to go into Avignon to buy some heavy sweaters for the trip, or a decent coat if they have such a thing. I'll get the taxi to take me into town."

"No, you can have the car. I'm going to walk around and see what's for rent." He didn't try to conceal his eagerness.

Kate was out all day, not returning for lunch. When she finally appeared late in the afternoon Mistral was impatient. It was a good forty-minute drive to Félice and he was anxious to announce his decision to his friends in the café.

A thousand meters along the small road that led to Félice Kate put her hand over Mistral's. "Turn left," she said.

"Why? We'll be late for the game. I can visit *La Tourrello* any time now."

"There's something I want to show you. It won't take long. Please."

He turned the car onto the path and parked, as usual, on the strip of meadow.

"A last look?" he asked. "I didn't know you cared that much about it."

Kate slipped out of her seat, walked to the big wooden double doors set in the wall and took a key out of her pocket. She put it into the lock and turned it with difficulty. As Mistral watched, astonished, she pushed one of the heavy doors open wide. She beckoned at him. "Come on!"

"What are you doing? Where'd you get that key?" he called, not moving from the driver's seat. He had no intention of going in.

Kate walked back to the car and held out the key to Mistral. "Take it. It's mine. Or rather it's yours. To be precise, it's my dowry."

He snorted with astonishment. She certainly had the capacity to surprise. And how grand was her scale! She did nothing by half and somehow, he realized as he looked at her grave and hopeful eyes, she was never preposterous, even now. Dignified, serious, intent, she made her extraordinary proposition a possibility just by her assumption that it could happen.

"Will you marry me, Julien?" Kate asked.

He was silent. He knew she had more to say and he found her profoundly interesting.

"I love you and you need a wife. You need a home, I saw the notary in Félice today and bought this farm. The former owner died leaving only a granddaughter who was anxious to sell. Next week a young farmer and his wife will move into the wing on the left and start hiring men to get the land back in shape, the groves, the orchards, the vineyards." She paused but still he said nothing so she continued, spreading out a delicious life before him as clearly, as distinctly as if she had flung a bright cloth on the grass and placed generous platters of fine food and bottles of wine upon it and invited him to a feast. "I'm looking for an architect to design your studio. I've already hired a master mason in Avignon. He's meeting me here tomorrow. A plumber and an electrician will come with him—there's a great deal of work to be done before the house is—"

"Could *you* live here—in the country—at *La Tourrello*?" he interrupted at last.

"It seems that I can't imagine living happily anywhere you are not. God help me. I find myself curiously unable to go back to Paris and leave you here for the winter and drive down to visit in February pretending that I want to see the almond trees in flower."

"But I've never thought of marriage," Mistral said.

"Think of it then," Kate said with a flash of humor. "It's time to get started on our lives. It's time to do the real work. You've begun well, so that part's over, but now the harder part comes . . . to keep going forward, to enlarge, to reinforce, to gain new territory and make it absolutely your own . . . years and years of work that will take all your strength. Didn't Flaubert tell artists to be regular and ordinary in their lives so they could be violent and original in their work?"

"I've never read Flaubert," Mistral said. The important thing, the only thing, he thought, is that I want to paint again and I must not leave this place.

"Julien, imagine having your studio built here, looking up toward Félice."

She didn't gesture. The immoderate bounty that lay before his eyes all spoke for her. Her love needed no other adornment to make itself evident. He looked about and saw a future of order and peace and plenty, saw that it was possible.

"Think," she added in a voice that danced with nerves, as he remained silent, "think of the boules tournaments, the many boules tournaments, year after year."

"You're trying to bribe me, Kate."

"Of course." She stood her ground resolutely, the key still in her outstretched hand, the wind blowing her hair, the grave gray eyes warmed by the emotion she no longer hid. In her expression, her blind faith in him mingled with vulnerability.

"I'm trying to think of a single reason . . . to say no," Mistral said slowly.

"And . . . ?"

He jumped out of the car and took the key from her. He grasped it tightly, feeling the heavy, smooth iron press into his palm. Recognition flooded him. This piece of land, this woman . . . they were his future. They laughed together, complicit laughter and not for the first time. It had been so from the first day they had met.

"But how strange life is!" he exclaimed in wonder.

" 'Pray love me little, so you love me long,' " she murmured in English.

"What does that mean, my clever bossy American girl?" he asked as he pulled her into his arms.

"A poet long ago . . . someday I'll tell you . . . someday you'll understand."

10

"No, decidedly no! Impossible, totally impossible. It's out of the question," Paula proclaimed to Maggy, looking more scandalized than Maggy would have thought possible for a woman who, self-admittedly, had seen everything.

"But why?" Maggy wailed.

"Two catastrophic reasons. Your lingerie and your shoes. They simply will not do! Oh, Maggy, just look at this. It's enough to make me cry." Paula waved distractedly at the scant pile of undergarments she had taken out of Maggy's armoire and spread over the bed, and held up three petticoats as accusingly as if they were dustcloths.

"This one is patched, this one is frayed at the hem, this one is missing half its ribbon as far as I can tell. You don't have a single complete set of lingerie in suitable condition," she continued, warming to her grievances, "and where, may I ask, are your corselettes and *soutien-gorges*? All I see here are ill-assorted garters, mended stockings, knickers that you must have brought with you when you left home and these disgraceful petticoats. I will admit that they're clean but beyond that!" She threw up her hands.

Maggy blew hair out of her eyes. "Oh, why are you acting like a duchess? You don't seriously think I bothered with all that, do you? I don't need them in my work surely. Or to go dancing. On the contrary! And as for my petticoats, they're perfectly good with just a stitch here and there . . . Madame Poulard can fix them up in no time."

Paula sat down on the bed with finality.

"Maggy, you must be mad. How do you expect to be treated with respect, when you go to Patou or Molyneux, if they see you in these rags? What would Mademoiselle Chanel say to such a beggar woman? I don't care how much money you have to spend, no coutourier, no *vendeuse* and no fitter is ever going to take you seriously unless you have proper lingerie, proper shoes and a proper hat as well."

"Well, so much for my glorious career as a kept woman. Over before it began. I don't have the right clothes to wear in order to go and buy the right clothes, so how can I possibly move into a suite at the Lotti? Maybe I could tell Monsieur Patou that I've been in a shipwreck and lost everything? Or convince Mademoiselle Chanel that I was stolen by the gypsies who kept all my clothes and returned me unharmed? How *do* people ever manage to buy made-to-order clothes if they have never bought them before? It's worse than a Chinese puzzle."

Maggy flopped down on the floor of her room, crossed her bare legs and leaned rebelliously forward, her chin on her hands.

"It all seemed so simple this morning and now you've made it so complicated that I don't even want to think about it. A year ago you were instructing me in how to hop out of my knickers, now you want to put me in corsets! I'll just tell Perry we have to stay here and to hell with his valet and his business. If he doesn't like me the way I am, it's just too bad. Corsets be damned."

"Now, now," said Paula, hastily, "it's not that insoluble. Calm yourself, little one. It merely demands thought and planning, like all important events in life. For the lingerie we start from the beginning. Everything must be new. There is a shop, just off the rue St. Honoré—it's run by three Russian emigrées, all titled ladies, of great discretion and understanding and—what is more important—promptitude. They specialize in cases like yours . . ."

"What! Now I'm a 'case,' am I?" Maggy said indignantly.

"In this particular matter, yes." Paula went on imperturbably.

"If they get the order this afternoon, and I explain to them the nature of the emergency, you should have exquisite lingerie made within a week. And as for the shoes, there is a splendid little Italian *bottier* I know who is not far from them. Rue St. Florentin, up two flights, a very reliable address. For him there is no need to worry about the lingerie so we can go there today."

"I could just pop off to Raoul . . ."

"Raoul? That dreadful little place in the arcade with the shoes for eighty francs that have ruined your feet?" Paula was mortified.

"That's what I've been wearing all along and you never objected before."

"Forget what you endured before—don't you want Perry to be proud of you?"

"He is already." Maggy brooded, pulling her tender orange plumage around her face, all but hiding it. Her romantic fantasy of the life of a kept woman was rapidly falling apart in the face of Paula's practicality. It sounded like work, and work of the most boring kind; endless fittings; days wasted running around from one special workroom to another; *corsets*, all so that she could impress a saleswoman who would probably see through her anyway. She hated that saleswoman already, she thought in dejection.

Suddenly the memory of Kate Browning as she had looked the first time she came to Mistral's studio came into her mind, Kate Browning so sure of herself in cool, white silk, every stitch of which had to have been made by hand, Kate Browning with her spotless white gloves who always looked so stylish, so self-confident and self-possessed that it was impossible to doubt that she had tiptoed daintily out of her mother's womb in a pair of tiny perfect shoes and a marvelous hat from Rose Descat.

Galvanized, Maggy jumped up with a suddenness that startled Paula: "What about gloves?" she demanded, taking Paula by the shoulders and shaking her. "Foolish female, have you been in that kitchen of yours for so long that you don't know that without gloves no lady is dressed for the street? While you drivel on about corsets you have forgotten gloves. How can I start my new life without at least six *dozen* pairs of gloves since I intend to never wear a pair more than once, *once*, do you hear?"

She released Paula and danced around her room, picking up a stocking here and another there, inspecting them for darns and finally taking two that were intact. All the others she swept into a wastebasket. "Twelve dozen pairs of silk stockings, before lunch! Then on to the Russian aristocrats—I *crave* lingerie: all silk chiffon and stupendous appliqués of lace; peach-colored crêpe de chine; garter belts, teddies, *soutiengorges* to flatten my tits, flared tap pants in pale green and lavender and mocha, red chiffon nightgowns . . . what else? Chinese pajamas! But no corsets!" Maggy halted her capering progress around her tiny room in front of the mirror she had hung above the sink. She studied herself intently, shaking her hair around her head. She pulled it all back behind her ears, then she lifted it in both hands and piled it on top of her head. Slowly she shook her head from side to side in disapproval.

"I need a haircut."

"Of course you do. You can't wear hats properly with all that hair and without the right hats . . ."

"Don't tell me—I know. Without the right hats no self-respecting *vendeuse* will even let me in the salon. Now just tell me one thing, Paula. Do I have to go and get my hair cut off *before* I go for a haircut by Antoine, or will Antoine deign to cut my hair in its present lamentably unfashionable condition?"

Paula's eyes widened. Antoine was the most famous hairdresser in the world. Twenty years before he had invented bobbed hair when the great actress, Eve Lavallière, let him sacrifice her hair to his scissors, an experiment that so unnerved him that he didn't try it again for another six years. Now he ruled supreme in his salon on the rue Didier that he had inaugurated by a ball for fourteen hundred guests with each woman dressed in white. Every female creature in France dreamed of presenting her head before the master.

"Antoine," Paula breathed, respectfully.

"But of course," Maggy said. "He will know, just by looking at me, that I am worthy of his scissors, poor though I have been and temporarily between one pair of knickers and another."

"How will you get an appointment?"

"I'll just go and see him. Will he be able to resist the chance to cut off this hair?"

"I don't see how he could," Paula said truthfully. Antoine was so impulsive that he had recently bid five thousand francs at a charity auction for a single glove that had been donated by his client, the poetess Vicomtesse Marie-Laure de Noailles.

"Then on your feet, my *coco*. You don't think I'm going without you?"

"I wouldn't let you—what if you changed your mind halfway through?"

"My thought exactly." With a caressing hand Maggy touched her hair. It had to go, that much was clear, but she was not nearly as brave about the prospect as she sounded. In fact her heart was fluttering in a way that made her want to give little yelps of anguish, but she flung on her best daytime clothes and bundled Paula into a taxi before she had a chance to change her mind.

It was never more difficult for a woman to be beautiful than during the 1920s. Fashion flattered no one, femininity in all its manifestations was truncated, hidden, distorted. Hats hid the forehead and the eyes; eyebrows were unnaturally tweezed, bodies forced ruthlessly into unflattering boyish forms; cosmetics used badly. Only three colors of lipsticks existed and hairstyles were so ugly that only the most authentic beauty could overcome them.

In this period a haircut could make or break a woman. Women who only ten years before had been considered lovely in their Edwardian draperies and the floating clouds of their elaborately dressed hair, were denuded and exposed to the cruel light of day without any grace or charm left to them—all in the name of fashion. Women who would once have been reigning beauties were revealed as scarecrows, with scalped heads perched like knobs on top of unfashionably plump shoulders. A poorly shaped skull could ruin a young woman's future.

Maggy sat in the chair before Antoine's mirror while the hairdresser hovered behind her, surrounded by a small crown of apprentices and assistants. Paula sat grimly off to one side.

"My God . . . your hairline," he said in excitement in his Polish-accented French.

"What's wrong with it?" Maggy asked, ready to explode. Any excuse would do if she could only leave with dignity. Leave *now* before he started. She looked around in a dizzy panic. The walls of the salon were made of great sheets of plate glass, the staircases themselves were constructed of glass, the chairs and tables of the salon and the decorations and lights were all made of glass to please this tall, pale Pole who lived in a crystal abode above the salon and slept in a glass coffin which, he claimed, protected him from dangerous electric radiation in the night air.

"How *could* you have kept it hidden for so long?" he asked reproachfully. "Elegance starts with the hairline, Madame, and yours is—a *poem.* This," he said, tracing a long thin finger high across her forehead, "is the essential shape without which no other elegance matters, without which no true elegance can begin. It must be *exposed.*"

"Whatever you say," Maggy muttered, closing her eyes as she saw him pick up his scissors. They made a horrible, softly shrieking sound as they flashed through her wings of hair, each lock of which was carefully caught before it fell to the floor by an assistant whose job it was to preserve long hair and make it into switches and chignons and braids that the shorn client could pin on in the evening. Maggy opened one eye and saw her head hunched into her shoulders as she cringed in the chair.

She sat up bravely for it was entirely too late now to act the coward, and forced a smile onto her lips. Was that her neck, that endlessly long, white *thing*? Were those her ears, those poor little pink projections? Now Antoine wet her head and took up a razor that glittered relentlessly as he gradually shaped her hair into a shining cap, as short as that of an English public schoolboy, the extreme Eton cut which only the most beautiful women could wear. It was combed straight back, parted precisely on one side, and in front of each exposed ear the cap came to a sleek point on her cheek. At her nape her hair was shingled so that the fine shape of her whole skull was clearly seen. Maggy's large yellow-green eyes, set so far apart, looked twice as big as they ever had and her sharp, fiercely curved cheekbones now had competition in the totally revealed, long, pliant column of her neck.

She threw off the cloth that covered her and stood up, gazing into the mirror, turning this way and that so that she could see herself from each side and from the back. There was a hushed silence from the crowd of onlookers. Even Antoine himself said nothing as Maggy anxiously looked at the new personage who faced her in the mirrors.

She felt faint. Her head seemed quite separate from her shoulders, as if it had been detached and allowed to fly upward like a balloon. The woman in the mirror was bold; the woman in the mirror was older than Maggy and absolutely in command of herself; the woman in the mirror was supremely chic even though she was wearing Maggy's suit and Maggy's deplorable shoes. Her head, that sleek, superbly cropped head, so bright that it looked painted on, a magnificent red punctuation mark, dominated the room.

Maggy stood expressionless. Paula held her breath. Slowly Maggy moved closer and closer to the mirror, her eyes never leaving it. The images she saw grew huge and she looked at it questioningly until her eyes merged and her nose touched the mirror. She remained there a second, misting the mirror with her breath and then, with a decisive motion, she kissed the mirror with her big, delicious mouth.

"Ah!" all the watchers breathed in relief.

"Madame is content," Antoine stated with an air of proprietorship.

"Madame is enchanted!" Maggy seized the astonished Pole, squeezed him hard and pressed a kiss on his ear. "Madame is to be addressed as Monsieur from now on." She took the carnation that was pinned to her jacket and put it behind Antoine's ear. "From one Monsieur to another, I love you," she told him.

Perry Kilkullen did not know the first thing about keeping a woman. It all sounded so easy, the phrase fell so naturally off the tongue; men, after all, had been keeping women for thousands of years, Perry reassured himself. The ancient Greeks and Romans had kept women or young boys, depending on their tastes. Perhaps both? Who knew? The history of any country was filled with legendary kept women and the ranks of the aristocracy were eventually filled with their children. How did the various Louises do it—XIV, XV and XVI? How on earth did they make the *arrangements?*

Feeling more American than he had for years in Paris, slightly abashed but infinitely determined, he went to a real-estate agent. A place to live had to be the first step for a Kilkullen, as for a Louis. Or did they just slip the lady into a set of spare rooms at the palace?

"In what quarter does Monsieur desire to live? How many reception rooms does Monsieur require? How many bedrooms? And how many will there be in staff? Does Monsieur wish a house or a flat?"

"Look, I simply won't know until I see it. Just show me the very best of what you've got."

He inspected a dozen houses and apartments in the fashionable parts of the Right Bank and rejected them all for one reason or another. He didn't include Maggy on these expeditions because he wanted it to be a surprise. Finally, on the avenue Vélasquez he walked into a vast, second-floor flat that opened directly onto the noble, green, lopsided rectangle of the Parc Monceau. As if he were a person with perfect pitch hearing the right chord, Perry felt at home in the empty rooms.

He took her there that evening at twilight and led her through the apartment. She was struck dumb as he proudly displayed chamber after chamber.

"Oh, my God!" Maggy burst out at last.

"Don't you like it?" Perry asked anxiously.

"Have you counted the rooms?" she asked on a wild note.

"No, not exactly. It seemed okay to me."

"There are *eleven* rooms, and at least two dozen closets. Heaven knows how many baths and that's not counting the kitchen and the pantries and laundry room or the servants' rooms you said are up in the attic," she quavered.

"Is that too big?" he couldn't help sounding dejected.

"Anything more than two rooms is too big as far as I'm concerned. And one of them should have a bathtub in it."

"But . . . but, you said you dreamed of being kept in style."

"Oh, Perry," she cried, huddling close to him, "I'm so *scared*! I know what I said but that was a fantasy and this is reality. I just want to go back to the Left Bank and find a tiny room in a tiny hotel and get into bed and pull up the covers over my head and not come out! Ever!"

Perry pulled her close to him and stroked her as firmly and as gently as if she were a large, terrified animal. He realized, as he held her, that he had grown up among rich New York women who had always expected that one day they would rule large establishments; women who had been in training all of their lives to move effortlessly, with quiet authority, through rooms far larger and more numerous than these on the Parc Monceau. But what did Maggy, his wonderful girl, his first, his only love, know of such things? It only made her more precious to him that she was reduced to terror by an eleven-room apartment, this girl who had had the courage to run away from home at seventeen, who took risks by nature, who was still at heart almost a tomboy.

"Look," he whispered to her, as if he were talking to a child, "if you want to, we'll keep living in hotels, don't worry. But why not give this place a chance? It isn't as if you have to move in tomorrow, darling. It'll take time to furnish and then, when it's finished, if you have even the slightest doubt, if you still feel it's too big, I'll simply get rid of it. What do you say to that?" As he spoke he knew how desperately he wanted to make a real home for Maggy, not in a hotel, but here, in this lovely space, where they could be together permanently, just the two of them.

Maggy's voice was muffled because her head was pressed to his vest.

"How many months will it take?" she asked suspiciously.

"Oh, a long time," Perry assured her, "a very long time." He wondered how people actually did furnish apartments. His wife and his mother-in-law and his mother had all been in a feminine tizzy for a while before his wedding, so long ago, and he supposed that it was apartment stuff that they were rushing around about but he hadn't paid any attention. Apartments, to men of his generation, *came* furnished, new of course, but somehow to a chap's taste. All that just got taken care of—was that not one of the things women spent their time on?

During the next six months it seemed to Maggy that she learned an amazing number of new things every day. First there was English. She had determined to learn English because it wasn't fair, it seemed to her, for Perry always to be at the disadvantage when they talked together, and anyway, no matter where they went, whether it was to the Bal Tabarin to watch the cancan, or to dine at Maxim's or to Frederick's for pressed duck, all around her she heard English spoken and it was infuriating not to understand the jokes.

The buying power of the American dollar was so high that Paris was filled with expatriates living well on fifteen dollars a week. They intrigued Maggy with their carelessness, their rambunctious gaiety, their way of irreverently throwing themselves on Paris, as if it were the world's biggest playpen. Who but Americans would play tennis inside Josephine Baker's nightclub with paper rackets and balls? Who but Americans could sit in with the musicians at Bricktop's and make such wild jazz as she'd never heard before? Not speaking English in 1926 in Paris was to miss the best party given in history.

Every morning, right after breakfast, Maggy took an English lesson from the earnest Bostonian wife of an American writer who couldn't seem to finish his novel. One of the first expressions Maggy learned was "writer's block" and, for the rest of her life, whenever she heard those words they would bring back the expensively draped, pale blue satin sitting room of her suite at the Lotti.

Perry had engaged Jean Michel Frank, the most talked about of the decorator-designers of the day—the leader of the practitioners of *Les Arts Décoratifs*—to work on the apartment, and while he went about his business, Maggy went about hers.

"Do you have any idea, Paula," she asked querulously, "how hard a kept woman has to work? It's a job and a half. Why, you can't leave the house in the morning if you're not in a suit from O'Rosen or Chanel, you don't dare show yourself in the afternoon unless you're in Patou, you can't just drink a cocktail, you have to dress for it, in something from Molyneux with tiny shoulder straps and a handkerchief-pointed hemline . . ."

"I hope you're not complaining," Paula said severely. "Every *métier* has its price."

"Being kept seems to amount to spending one percent of your time naked in bed and changing your clothes the other ninety-nine percent," Maggy said thoughtfully. "Aren't there any *métiers* that allow you to wear the same thing from morning till night? And the hats, Paula—a different one for each outfit and three fittings on each hat, all that fuss over the tilt of a brim or the width of a ribbon—who would have guessed it?"

"I could have warned you," Paula said knowingly, "but I was afraid you'd back out of the whole thing while you still had time."

"It's too late now," Maggy said, restored to her high spirits.

"Interview a butler?" she said incredulously.

"The apartment will be furnished next month," Perry replied reasonably. "We have to have a staff, and a staff means a butler—he can help you with the rest of the interviews."

"How would I know what to ask him?" Maggy huffed in indignation. "What do I know of the care and feeding of cigars, of the intimate love life of cases of wine, the protocol of announcing dinner or of the right way to polish silver? Or of the wrong way either, for that matter? If you want a butler, you must find him yourself and that goes for all the other 'staff' as well. I'm not sure yet that I'll ever move in."

"You haven't even been to see what's going on—aren't you curious?"

"No," Maggy lied. She found herself wondering at odd moments of every day just what Monsieur Frank was up to, but she didn't want to be drawn into the process because as soon as she expressed a taste or a preference it would be as good as agreeing to live in that enormous, deeply alarming, oppressively grand apartment Perry had bought. Hotel life, even in the high style of the Lotti, had something enchantingly harum-scarum about it. The elevators were crammed with amorous couples who couldn't possibly be married, the lobby echoed with music and laughter, the maids were always ready to chat for a moment and as for the dignified concierges, they pored over the racing form with her every day.

"Well then, I'll do it," Perry said with resignation.

"I know—let Paula. It's the sort of thing she does best. She can read character, that one—you can't fool her. At least I never could. And don't forget the last *shiddach* she made."

"*Shiddach*?"

"An introduction—as in you and me—well, only used loosely. Actually it's an arranged marriage, like the one my Aunt Esther wanted me to make. It comes from a Hebrew word '*shidukh*,' " Maggy said learnedly.

"And that bit of lore came, I assume, from Rabbi Taradash?" Perry was charmed by Maggy's rare use of Jewish expressions. They seemed as piquant and chipper to him as the red carnation in her buttonhole.

"Don't remind me of my poor sweet rabbi. A kept woman living in sin with a Catholic? Oh, I can't even think what he'd say."

"Would he explode?"

"Explode with anger, split with aggravation, burst with suffering—you can take your pick. But he would not understand, any more than your priest if you had one, would. However, I refuse to feel guilty! The Talmud says 'When a man faces his Maker, he will have to account for those pleasures of life he failed to experience.' That's one part of the Talmud I know and the one part I agree with entirely. It's probably contradicted in another part—I'm basically ignorant about religion and where we're concerned, I don't see that it has any relevance."

"Is that the only reason you don't feel guilty about me?" he asked, with sudden gravity.

"Oh, my darling, no. I don't feel guilty because I love you so much." There was no way to truly tell him, she thought, how she felt about him.

It was a love without mystifications, free of surprises or harshness, a love that could never wound her. Perry's arms were a bulwark against ever being hurt again. With him she was utterly safe, and now she knew the value of safety.

There were moments, she admitted to herself, when she was flooded by memories of Julien Mistral, when she would feel again just how the stern line of his mouth became so surprisingly tender under her lips. But then she would turn away resolutely from the unwelcome memory and count her blessings. What if she had lived with Mistral for years? What if she had been saturated with him, her heart stained through and through by the paint-obsessed man who cared for no one. How astonishingly lucky she'd been. Her brief months with Mistral had left her badly bruised, but she believed that she possessed a core that he had never touched. She bent her head to the back of Perry's hand and rubbed her cheek over it so gently that she could feel the tiny blond hairs tickle her skin. "About that butler . . ." she murmured.

"I'll attend to it."

"I knew you would."

"Close your eyes tight and promise not to peek. I'll lead you into the salon—I want you to see that first," Perry said to Maggy. It was April of 1927 and they stood outside the front door of the Parc Monceau flat.

"But that's so silly. Still, after all, why not? This whole thing is ridiculous." Maggy squeezed her eyes shut and took Perry's arm. It seemed to her that they walked a long time before he said, in a voice tight with emotion, "You can look now."

She opened her eyes on one of the first of the truly modern rooms of the twentieth century. She felt as if a fresh breeze had blown her into a new world, a gold and beige and ivory and white world in which the utmost luxury was expressed in the purest of forms. Nothing looked like anything she had ever seen before. The gloomy walls, that she had remembered as paneled in dark wood, had been stripped from floor to ceiling and covered with hundreds of squares of parchment, each one slightly different from all of the others. Uninterrupted by a single picture, they formed, in their assembly, a deliberate and masterful work of art that glowed, pale gold, in the light of the boldly shaped white plaster lamps.

The room, which had seemed impossibly big when she first saw it, now embraced her in its unexpected festivity. As she walked around on the white rugs she realized that she was moving in a new *sort* of space, a space in which she had never imagined people living, a space suffused with freshness and openness, that immediately made all other interiors seem crowded and fussy and old-fashioned. Maggy trailed her fingers along the backs of the simple armchairs, covered in the plainest, heaviest ivory silk imaginable, she caressed the tops of the low, gold lacquered tables and then dizzily, she dropped down to one of the large sofas. She lay full length on the soft, natural beige leather and, eyes half-closed, contemplated the essential shapes of everything in the room.

"What do you think? Isn't it terrific?" Perry asked anxiously, his words rushing. "The lamps are designed by Giacometti, there are forty coats of gold lacquer on the tables, the rugs are hand knotted in Grasse . . ."

"Don't bother me with details, my darling," Maggy said. "Just come lie with me here, it's like floating."

They moved in three days later. Jean Michel Frank, delighted with his American client, since a rich, open-pocketed single man—particularly if he is in love—is always the most desirable client any artist can have, had bent his great talent to making the Parc Monceau apartment a total expression of his revolutionary vision, a vision that would still be fresh and meaningful a half-century later.

On the first night in the new apartment Maggy found herself unable to sleep. Quietly, she got out of bed and wrapped herself in her maribou negligee. As she wandered around the apartment she had the nagging feeling that something was missing, something was not quite right. Yet Monsieur Frank had neglected no detail.

Never, Maggy thought as she passed by the linen and silver closets, had she dreamed that anyone could own so many objects. It would be weeks before she felt familiar with their contents. Nothing that could make life supremely comfortable was missing and everywhere immense cleanness reigned, a cleanness that made the satin-draped luxury of her suite at the Lotti seem shabby and even grimy by contrast.

Maggy drifted into the salon and stood by the French doors that looked out into the park. From the vantage point of the second floor she could see much of that most frolicsome of Parisian parks, the classic colonnade and the oval pond and the pyramid that the Duke of Orléans had caused to be brought there in 1778. Empty now, the park, surrounded by elaborate wrought-iron railings tipped with gilded arrows, was like a stage set, she thought, ready for some masque or entertainment of an archaic kind. It looked as if it were waiting for a procession of goddesses in Grecian robes or a band of fantastical fairies from a poet's imagination. But she knew that nothing would go on in the locked park until the children, those well-behaved children of this elegant quarter, arrived in the morning with their nurses. Restlessly she walked from room to room but in spite of her growing sense of something lacking that *should* be there, she could find no human need unaccounted for. Finally Maggy went back to bed and drifted into a troubled sleep filled with fragments of dreams.

The following day, toward twilight, Maggy let herself into the apartment, using her new key for the first time. Rosy with the coolness of the April evening, she didn't even bother to take off her coat as she crossed the entrance hall and almost ran through the long corridor to the dining room. Under her arm was a large, lumpy package wrapped in newspaper.

She had spent the afternoon poking through certain shops on the rue des Rosiers and the package contained the object she had gone searching for, the one thing, she had realized as she had awakened late that morning, that was missing from the apartment. Maggy stood in front of the vellum-covered sideboard. On it stood two heavy silver and lapis lazuli candelabras that had been designed by the famous silversmith, Jean Puiforcat, especially for the room. They matched the great covered silver and lapis bowl that stood on the dining table. Maggy took each of the candelabras from the sideboard and placed them on the table, on either side of the bowl. Then, very carefully she unwrapped the newspaper and uncovered a large, rather battered brass candlestick with seven branches.

"There! That's more like it," she said out loud as she put the menorah in the place of honor in her home.

11

Perry Mackay Kilkullen did not give one good goddamn. Not a damn for the shocked letters from his mother and his sisters and brothers. Not a damn for what the church had already said, would continue to say, was presently saying. Not a damn for the unspoken disapproval of his partners and the thrilled gossip of their wives. Not a damn for the rising tide of whispers at the Turf and Field, the Piping Rock or the New York Yacht Club. Not a damn for the opinion of anyone he had ever known or liked or even loved before he met Maggy. He was utterly indifferent to these shadowy figures, who had once seemed important, and to what they thought about a matter that was so fundamentally his own. He was forty-two, he had lived more than half of the years any man could expect on earth, and only now did he understand what it meant to be alive. *Maggy*. Without her he would have been an approximation of a man, and never known it.

He still performed his banking functions with precision; no one could accuse him of neglecting the firm, but otherwise he cut himself off from his past life deliberately and effectively. He no longer accepted invitations to dinner from his circle of friends within the Parisian banking community; when his Yale classmates visited Paris with their wives he avoided them. Carefully he arranged his business matters so that he didn't have to spend time in New York, where his wife, clad in her dignity and her religious convictions, waited with seeming serenity for him to outgrow a stage in life through which, as her mother assured her, many other fine men had passed. Mary Jane McDonnell Kilkullen was too proud to give her friends any indication of how she felt about the open scandal of Perry's keeping a French mistress. She continued on her rounds of good works, a slim, jeweled, gracious woman who refused, by her brisk yet bland bearing, to let anyone feel sorry for her. Nothing would ever make her descend to the vulgarity of acting like an outraged and deceived wife.

In the fall of 1927 Maggy turned twenty. She looked more worldly than her age, as she always had, with the urbane eyelids and bold mouth that made her, in any crowd of women, the most fascinating to watch, even if she was unlike the ideal beauty of the time. She was not, had never been, a "young thing," prettily engaging, nor did she fit into the fashionably childish and brittle flapper mode. In the past few months during which she had been able to indulge her taste, she had achieved a timeless, enigmatic, never-to-be-dated elegance.

To celebrate her birthday Perry took her to Marius and Janette, where they had dined together for the first time, and then they went on to their favorite Montmartre nightclub, Chez Josephine, where the absurdity of the nanny goat and the pig, Josephine Baker's bizarre pets, who ran about being spoiled by royalty from a dozen European countries, never failed to amuse Maggy.

Tonight however she felt oddly thoughtful. Twenty was very different from nineteen. It was a woman's age, not a girl's age. Her girlhood was over, Maggy reflected, and didn't know whether to be cast down or delighted. She sighed and twisted the double rope of pearls that Perry had given her for her birthday.

"Is something wrong, my baby?" he asked.

"I'll never be young—*really* young—again. And don't you dare tell me I'm being silly."

"Was being 'really young' so very wonderful?"

She shook her head at his misunderstanding her meaning.

"It meant that everything lay ahead of me. It meant that I didn't have to think about the future because it was so far off. Somehow the choices I made didn't really *count.* Nothing was final because everything was going to change anyway. But now, now I feel so . . . so," she gestured ineffectively and shook her head because the words disappeared even as she tried to find them.

"As if you have to make decisions?" he asked tenderly.

"Something almost like that. As if I'm *in* my future—as if my life should be going somewhere." She smiled wistfully and shrugged her shoulders with an uncharacteristically helpless air.

"You are going somewhere. You're going to marry me."

Maggy's hands flew up incredulously. "Don't say that! You know it's impossible! How can you say that, even as a joke? I've never thought of it!"

"I know you haven't but I have. It's all I've been thinking about, almost from the day I met you—the theoretically unthinkable plan of getting a divorce and marrying you and living with you for the rest of my life. Nothing else is natural or right or true. We belong together."

"You're a Catholic and you're married!" Maggy objected in wild consternation. She had acquiesced in all his arrangements for her even as she understood that nothing more was ever going to be possible. Every barrier stood between them; he was as little likely to marry her as if he had been the Prince of Wales, and she had loved him enough to accept the situation.

"My wife and I have been as good as separated for years—you know that. We don't have children to keep us together . . ."

"Oh, why did you have to bring this up?" Maggy cried. "You know you can't get a divorce."

"That's what they said to Henry the Eighth." Perry grinned at her. True, Catholics should not get divorced. But that was not to say that they *did* not divorce on rare occasions, through the use of infinite willpower and patience and a great deal of money and influence. Of course such Catholics were not what his family or anyone he knew would consider *good* Catholics. He himself would not consider a divorced Catholic a good Catholic.

But to marry Maggy, Perry Kilkullen was willing to become a bad Catholic. He had discovered that his faith was not nearly as strong as his love. Once the wheels of his imagination had begun to turn, once he had seen his life as barren, his marriage as merely the arid continuation of something that was long dead, no more than a social and theological convenience, he had become impatient with the laws of the church. Could rules that demanded that he be false to his deepest needs be right? Did he have to surrender all the good years that were left of his life as a man to a web of "musts" and "must nots" that had been decreed by Rome? Every time he made love to Maggy it was, by all the dogma he had learned, an occasion of sin. Yet when he lay within her he felt consecrated. Her breasts, her belly, her thighs—all were a benediction. Nothing as beautiful could be unblessed.

"Oh, how can you smile like that? Don't you know what you're saying?" Maggy cried, deeply shocked. "You've gone crazy."

"Wouldn't you want to marry me if it were possible?" Finally, Perry was struck by her reaction. He had expected wonderment, confusion, but not this refusal to be happy about his plans.

"I don't want to be the cause of all sorts of trouble for you," Maggy said stubbornly.

"I was *parched* before I met you!" Perry said violently. "I was dying of thirst and you saved me. I could have gone on for years and ended up withered, dry, bleached, as empty of sap as a piece of driftwood."

"But won't it cause trouble? Bad trouble?" Maggy insisted.

"Big, bad, terrible trouble." He grinned in relief. That was all that had upset her. "Almost the worst trouble you can imagine. But worth every minute of it, if you'll be there to marry me, if you'll say you'll love me always no matter how long it takes."

"You know I will," she said slowly. His utter need dissolved her fears.

"Even though you're not really young anymore? Are you sure you're not too long in the tooth to make such a decision? After all, it may well take a few years and you don't want to risk being an old maid."

"I may be reaching maturity," Maggy said, "but I'm not yet too old to take a chance."

"Then it's settled?" he said eagerly.

"Between us, yes, *yes*, my darling. As for the rest . . ."

"I'll leave for New York on the next crossing . . ." Perry promised.

"But now—while I'm still young enough, let's dance."

Less than ten days after Maggy's twentieth birthday Perry Kilkullen and his wife confronted each other in the library of their Park Avenue apartment. For two hours Mary Jane had not once raised her voice in anger or let an unguarded word escape her lips. She had listened quietly and without interruption to everything he had to say, her trim legs crossed neatly at the ankle, her pretty face almost expressionless, her hands lying quietly in her lap. She didn't even fiddle with any of her many rings. She wasn't making it tough for him, Perry thought, as he poured out all his arguments, all his reasons, all his pain at what he had to do to them. She seemed to be listening, really listening, to what he was telling her. Perhaps she, too, was anxious to make a true life for herself. Perhaps, in all the time he'd been gone, she had found someone who could love her as every woman should be loved. Finally he stopped, hoarse from talking. There was nothing now that she didn't know, nothing he hadn't confessed, and tried to explain.

A silence fell and lasted for so long that he almost began to speak again, to repeat himself, when she said, gently and so softly that he could barely hear her. "A divorce? I couldn't do that to you, Perry."

"But you'd be doing *nothing*. I'm totally to blame."

"I couldn't possibly abandon you, Perry. How could you expect me to be so cruel?" she said with a look of compassion.

"Mary Jane, stop twisting things. You wouldn't be abandoning me, I've abandoned you."

"You haven't done anything that can't be put right, Perry," she said, as kindly as if she were reassuring a frightened child. "You—oh, I suppose people would say that you've 'strayed'—people love to say things like that, I find—but as I see it, you've just made a mistake. It's serious but far from irreparable. Fortunately the church understands, the church will take you back when this is over."

"I thought you were *listening*, damn it!"

"I was. I heard every word. But Perry, poor Perry, you seem to forget that you have an immortal soul."

"Mary Jane, I'm a grown-up man. I'm forty-two—let me worry about my own soul."

"You're asking the impossible, Perry. Is it for *me* to decide that you are to be denied the life to come? If I *were* to agree, if you were able to get a divorce, if you married this girl during my lifetime, you'd be excommunicated. And it would be through my fault as much as your own."

"I'm willing to take that chance, Mary Jane."

"But I'm not willing to condemn you. And you know that you have no right to ask me to do so."

He looked at her narrowly. Was there the merest hint that she was playing a game with him, hiding behind piety? But on Mary Jane's face he saw only conviction and resolution and tranquillity, a fatal calmness that told him that there was no hope. She existed in a parallel world from his and there was no bridge of words that could be spun between them. Her belief negated the existence of his passion. Maggy and his love for her were not real to Mary Jane. They were merely an abstraction, a "state of sin" from which he could be redeemed by confession and penance and a return to her. He knew he had lost even as he continued to reason, to argue, to plead.

At last Perry left, defeated. Mary Jane looked at her watch and frowned. She had missed a meeting of the Guild of the Infant Saviour at which she had been supposed to preside. Still, nothing could be more important than making Perry understand that there was no circumstance under which she would weaken and doom him to an eternity without salvation.

As she picked up the phone to call and excuse her absence, she told herself that she could almost weep for him, for his pitiful delusion that he could hope to spend a single day of happiness outside of the church. Poor deluded, corrupted, dishonored Perry, so far gone that he was actually capable of imagining that Mary Jane McDonnell would ever allow herself to become the first woman in the long history of her clan to be divorced. That, she mused, as the phone rang, showed, more than anything else, how far into error he had fallen.

Perry lingered in New York for a few weeks, attempting to persuade members of his family who had influence with his wife to plead his cause for him. He failed utterly. The ranks of the Kilkullens and the Mackays were closed as far as the question of divorce was concerned. When he attempted to speak of Maggy only one of his sisters was even willing to listen, and she had always been the biggest gossip of the lot who just couldn't restrain her curiosity. He turned away from her, easily able to imagine what she would repeat in a horrified, delighted whisper, to one and then to another of his relatives. "A twenty-year-old artists' model, my dear—you know what *that* means."

How could he possibly convey Maggy's pure essence to them? How could he ever hope to make them understand? A few of his male relatives showed themselves not unsympathetic to his problem so long as he limited it to being nuts about some girl who wasn't his wife. It had happened to them too. To most of them, for that matter. But it had never led to divorce, not even to any thought of divorce. Why, several of them asked, wasn't he willing to just let things go as they had before? Many a Catholic had a girl on the side, why the hell was he rocking the boat?

Almost eight weeks passed before Perry was able to extricate himself from the business demands made on him by his partners now that he was in New York. He was buying time, he wrote Maggy. It would be at least another year before he had to return to the United States—perhaps longer.

He arranged for his Paris lawyer, *Maître* Jacques Hulot, to take charge of the household, so that she need never give it a thought. Hulot paid the servants, checked and settled all the household accounts and took care of Maggy's personal bills as well. One of the lawyer's clerks delivered a supply of cash to Maggy every week since no Frenchwoman was allowed to have a bank account in her own name. He didn't know what she might want to spend cash on, Perry wrote, but he wanted her purse always to be so full that any folly, any caprice could be satisfied. The only matter he neglected to recount in his daily letters to his love was the result of his meeting with his wife, and Maggy, in her own letters, didn't press for details.

Her mood was high-hearted, she assured him, she saw Paula frequently, she'd ordered a sable coat as he'd insisted before he left, she'd gone back to her English lessons and was becoming genuinely fluent; yes, she missed him terribly but since there was no one she truly wanted to be with but him, it wasn't quite the same feeling as being *lonely*, it wasn't as if he weren't coming back as soon as he could.

As he reread Maggy's letters in his rooms at the Yale Club, Perry Kilkullen thanked God that he was rich. So very, very rich that he need never worry about the approval of the rest of the world. His family could close its doors to them socially, but they couldn't prevent him from creating his own world with Maggy, a sweet, wide, adventurous world in which every desire could be fulfilled with the exception of a legal marriage. It would be a permanent arrangement of the kind that the French had a knack for understanding; Maggy would never feel that he was less than a true husband to her, divorce or no divorce. Of course she'd be bitterly disappointed when he finally had to tell her, but she was French, so she'd accept reality.

And as for the life to come and his immortal soul, about which Mary Jane was so damnably concerned, when he thought of Maggy, Perry Kilkullen knew that he was indestructible. His immortal soul could shift for itself.

Maggy came to meet him at Cherbourg. While Perry waited for his baggage to be cleared he saw her on the other side of the barrier, her face tense, almost drawn, with excitement. This was the moment he had conjured up, over and over during the long days of the stormy ocean crossing. Now, all at once, just seconds away, was the end of the painful weeks of separation, but even as he longed impatiently to take her in his arms he found himself wishing that she had not driven out to Cherbourg but had let him take the boat train into Paris. That train trip, those four dull hours of gentle progression, would surely have inspired him to find the precise words in which to present the future to Maggy in its best light. Mary Jane's refusal still hadn't formed itself into just the right, optimistic yet final, sequence of explanation, try as he would to find it.

Suddenly Maggy slipped under the barrier and ran toward him, throwing herself into his arms, covering his face with kisses. To the protesting customs inspector

Maggy said something in such rapid slang that Perry couldn't understand it, but it left the man chuckling, blushing and unexpectedly benign.

"Oh, my darling, I have such news! It can't wait, really it can't! I was up at four in the morning to make sure to be here on time . . . oh, Perry!" She stopped abruptly and fell suddenly silent.

He scarcely made sense out of her words as he felt himself enter the circle of enchantment that her charm had created for him from the moment he had first seen her. Automatically he fell back into their teasing mode, as if they were continuing a conversation that had just been interrupted, even while he pressed her head closely between his hands, tenderly caressing her cheeks. "If it can't wait why don't you tell me?"

"I'm too shy," she said, her face rising out of the high collar of her fluffy, silky dark fur like a bunch of white violets.

"Since when have you been shy?" he asked. He had forgotten exactly how young her skin felt under his fingertips, he thought abstractedly.

"I've always been terribly shy. I just don't act it. People don't understand that about me because I don't have a shy look, I'm too tall," Maggy said rapidly, nervously.

"Is that what you got up so early in the morning to tell me? It's a fascinating subject, your height, but to lose half a night's sleep over it . . ."

"Guess," she demanded, drawing back a little, and putting a finger over his lips.

"You fired the cook?"

"Be serious," she pleaded.

"Darling, I haven't seen you in almost two months and your letters haven't hinted at the smallest mystery. Wait—I have it! You found a pearl in your oyster at Prunier's yesterday and you're having it made into a tiepin for me?"

"That's close, very close," she murmured.

"You've discovered a brilliant new little milliner no woman in Paris knows about yet, you've been offered a part in a film with Valentino, and you're leaving me to go to Hollywood, you've found a little château in the country that we can buy for weekends, you've learned to ice skate, you won a tango contest . . . must I go on or can I just kiss you again?"

Maggy took a deep breath and switched from French to English. "I am going to have a baby. No, *we* are going to have a baby."

"*That's impossible!*"

"I already have sickness in the morning," she said with timid pride.

"Maggy, you *can't* be pregnant . . . I've never been able to father a child . . ."

"When you change your woman, you change that possibility." Her mouth smiled but her eyes were tremendously anxious.

"I just can't believe it," he said numbly.

"Then you aren't happy? Oh, I've been so afraid you wouldn't be happy about it, oh, Perry, I'm so sorry . . ."

"*No!* My God, no! Don't be sorry, don't ever say that . . . it's the most incredible, the most—oh, darling, Maggy, you can't possibly know how much I've always wanted a child. I gave up hope so long ago . . . this is the most glorious news . . . sweet Jesus, I can't even begin to tell you . . ." Tears of joy sprang into his eyes, and fell down his cheeks and when she saw them, a touch of color came into her white face.

For weeks, Maggy had been caught between terror and exultance, between wild excitement and a million fears. Yet was she not to be his wife? It hadn't been until

Perry had left for the United States that she began to wonder if she might be pregnant. Somehow she didn't dare to write about it. What if she were? What if she weren't? She had waited until a few weeks ago to see a doctor, as if not knowing for sure would make the whole situation disappear. Yet now Maggy was almost three months into her pregnancy as far as she and the doctor had been able to determine.

"Just thank heaven that it didn't happen sooner," Paula had said to her when she heard the news. "If Mistral, God forbid, had given you a baby, my girl, I'd advise you to get rid of it and don't think I don't know a dozen fancy doctors who'd do the job. But Perry is a man you can trust, an honest man, a good man, if I've ever met one. Granted, this matter of a divorce is inconvenient, but everything will be arranged, sooner or later, I don't doubt—Americans get divorced right and left, day and night, as far as I can make out. And then think, Maggy, a fine husband and a baby too, ah . . . a baby's the only good thing I've ever missed in my life, the only regret I have. But you my little one, you are going to have everything—and in such style! I have to admit it, I envy you."

Maggy had held on tightly to Paula's words, willing them to be true. Now she lay her head on Perry's shoulder. "Hug me, hug me, you don't know how much I've needed you." It wasn't until the chauffeur was driving the big Voisin steadily toward Paris that she brought herself to ask with studied lightness, "What happened, then, with your wife?"

"It's going to be absolutely all right, darling," he responded instantly. "It's just a question of time, that's our only problem."

"The Vatican can't be persuaded to rush, I suppose? Just a little tiny nudge?"

"Are you asking if I'll be divorced by the time the baby is born?"

"I guess . . . I *was* hoping for it," she admitted.

He hesitated before he spoke. "I'm afraid that will be impossible. But, Maggy, there's nothing, absolutely nothing to worry about—I swear, I *promise.* By the time our baby is grown up enough to know the difference it'll be ancient history—we'll be just another old married couple. The important thing is to take care of yourself so that nothing goes wrong."

"Wrong?"

"*I want this baby so much, Maggy.*"

In May of 1928 Théodora Lunel was born. The name means "Gift of God" in Greek and both Maggy and Perry thought it perfect. She was a wise baby from her first day on earth, a baby who rarely cried, nursed efficiently, slept in the most satisfactorily thorough way and woke without a moment's crankiness. And she was extraordinarily beautiful. People who think all babies are beautiful have only to walk through a hospital nursery to discover that while all babies may be endearing in their smallness and helplessness, almost none are beautiful. Teddy, whose features were already arranged in a classic pattern of excellence, whose light red hair curled entrancingly, whose limbs were straight and perfect in every way, was the wonder of the nursery.

Perry Kilkullen felt marvelously justified. That undeniable, atavistic need for a continuation of his own existence that he had repressed for so long, burst forth with more power than any emotion he had ever known, until he had met Maggy. The deep human magic of a baby, his baby, absorbed him so completely that Maggy, confined to bed for the two weeks that were deemed necessary for a new mother, felt almost jealous, and then felt ashamed of herself as she recognized the source of her irritation.

The moments she most enjoyed were in the middle of the night when she was left alone to nurse for twenty minutes at a time. "Little bastard," she told the child in a low, loving whisper, "little adorable bastard, how can you look so contemplative? Such dignity, such a look of meditation on your face, even as you empty my breast, anyone would think you were born an heiress to a throne. Aah, but you take yourself seriously, don't you? Not even a thought for your poor old mother. Bastard that you are, and daughter of a bastard—little double bastard—you should pay me more attention. Just look at all the trouble that has gone into putting you in the world. I demand some respect. But what do you care about it? I didn't have a mother to nurse me, yet I survived. You are a luckier baby in every way, but . . . nevertheless—a bastard."

When Maggy and Perry were together they never talked of the fact that the baby bore Maggy's name. All that, as Perry repeatedly assured her, would be changed as soon as they got married. However, it preyed on Maggie's mind to a degree that surprised her. She had not thought often of her own illegitimacy once she had put Tours and all those who knew her history behind her forever, but giving birth had brought it back as if she were still in the cruel schoolyard, fighting anyone who taunted her with such ferocity that even the strongest of them had learned to leave her alone. It seemed to her that if she called Teddy a bastard, no one else would do so . . . she was drawing out the poison before it had a chance to circulate in the baby's veins.

The only person to whom she revealed her fears and anxieties was Paula. Shortly after they had brought the baby home, Paula, who had often visited at the hospital, came to call for tea and scolded her roundly.

"For a Frenchwoman you are a proper fool, my girl, worrying about something that you know will be regularized. *Regularized*, I tell you! We have a national genius for regularization, we French. Why, just look around you—what could be more solidly luxurious, more perfectly organized, more *comme il faut* in every way than this magnificent establishment of yours? I personally cannot find the slightest fault with it, from the little Théodora's English Nanny Butterfield to those superb pearls you wear so casually around your neck. Look about you, Maggy. You are surrounded by everything a woman could possibly want to make her feel secure, by every evidence that Perry intends you to become his wife. You should be ashamed to even *think* the word 'bastard' about that glorious baby. All these legal details will be put right in a twinkling when the time comes. It's your unfortunate childhood that makes you so nervous, that's all." She helped herself to another miniature chocolate éclair. "Why, you even possess a pastry chef who has no equal, right in your own kitchen, you ungrateful girl."

"How materialistic you are, Paula," Maggy protested, laughing.

"Of course I am. And what is wrong with that? Now, where are you hiding that delicious scrap of an *enfant?* I want to take just one tiny bite out of her. You owe me that much."

Teddy had been born in a vintage year, a year in which the Kellogg-Briand Anti-War Pact was signed in Paris by fifteen nations, the pact that outlawed war forever. The sensation of the salon of 1928 was a full-length nude of Josephine Baker. The French public flocked to the movies to see Mary Pickford, Charlie Chaplin and Gloria Swanson, the house of Hermès made the first useful handbag that any woman had ever carried and Coco Chanel had become the mistress of the Duke of Westminster, the richest man in England. Jean Patou, who had had the idea of importing pretty young American girls on whom to show his clothes, was enjoying a great success with the development of a strong bias cut, and a new neutral called "greige" became the color for the most stylish women.

It was such a gentle, fruitful year that Maggy forgot her apprehensions and relaxed into the absorbed and playful life of a pampered young mother. The great world seemed to have nothing to do with her. Perry would read out loud to her from the newspapers as she lay watching Teddy perform the incredible act of sitting up and she would reply with an abstracted noise to the fact that two American men had gone around the world in the record time of twenty-three days, fifteen hours, twenty-one minutes and three seconds by steamer and airplane. She seemed to have abdicated an interest in the immediacy of his divorce, Perry decided, listening to her sing as she fed the baby on Nanny's day off. Maggy could wait placidly for it to come about, certain that wheels were turning mysteriously but surely in the Vatican, but he was not self-deluded enough to share the optimism for which he had been responsible.

Divorce was the first thing he thought about when he woke each morning and every day he resolved to take some action, but then, as each day wore on, he remembered the adamantine rejection with which Mary Jane had responded to the proposal and he allowed himself to be seduced into immobility because he was living the happiest life any man could hope for.

Teddy's first birthday passed and still he did nothing, in a trance of peace. During the summer of 1929 Perry and Maggy took the baby, her nurse and Maggy's personal maid to spend six weeks in a great beachfront hotel in Concarneau, where the cool air of Brittany was known to be so good for growing children. Teddy had become mobile, not a toddler but a swift-running little creature who remained miraculously upright until she reached the object of her lovely flight.

As Perry rolled a ball to her one day at the beach he noticed a group of four people sitting on a blanket not far away, under a big umbrella. He glanced at them and, in the instant that he did so, they glanced away. As Teddy ran up to him with the ball and collapsed in his lap with a laughing cry of "Papa, Papa!" his heart drained of blood. On the blanket sat two of his business associates and their wives. He looked at them again and saw that they had rearranged themselves adroitly so that none of them was facing in his direction. In spite of their tactful backs Perry knew that all they could be thinking about was the sight of him and his child, that all they would talk about as soon as they left the beach was Perry Kilkullen and his bastard daughter.

He picked Teddy up and walked off the beach, holding her in such a tightly protective grasp that she squirmed. Bitterly, savagely he damned himself for a coward. Oh, he had bought happiness all right, bought it for almost two years at the cost of lying to Maggy every minute of every day although she didn't know it. Yes, she had been willing to live with him before there had been any question of marriage. But reminding himself of that didn't help him to feel less ignoble. Maggy had exercised her right to choose. But what rights did Teddy have? What future was there for her? What kind of father was he to his child, his only child, the child of his heart?

Perry went to consult the lawyer, *Maître* Jacques Hulot, before he returned to do battle with Mary Jane in New York. If there was the slightest chance of some legal wrinkle that he could take advantage of by becoming a French citizen, he was ready to change nationalities. Hulot ponderously announced that he was unable to help him, he could not use French law for his convenience. As Perry rose to go, the lawyer leaned forward over his immense desk. "One moment, Monsieur Kilkullen," he said, raising his hand commandingly.

For two years he had supervised the payments of enormous sums of money that this rich and headstrong American spent so easily to maintain what must be a juicy and accomplished mistress. He had resented being used to expedite the man's private life, so that no one of his American world would know how he lived and with whom. How dare Kilkullen, who could afford to dissipate such vast amounts without thinking twice, presume to discuss French citizenship? Why did he not avail himself of his own Reno, Nevada?

"We are both men of the world, are we not?" Hulot said with satisfaction. "This need not, after all, be considered a tragedy. It must seem to you now that everything is conspiring against you to deny you your wish to marry Mademoiselle Lunel. Yet, in ten years, in even five perhaps, will you not be grateful that the church and the state, which possess more wisdom than you realize, have prevented you from escaping into this impetuous liaison? When the day comes that you find a new, different . . . *friend* . . . will you not be glad for the restrictions . . . ?" He stopped, as Perry came around the desk and grabbed him by the lapels until he was pulled out of his chair.

"Never, *never* speak of Mademoiselle Lunel again!" He released the lawyer. Until he could engage another one, he still needed this man's services, damn him. Hulot had all the financial reins of the household in his hands. Perry Kilkullen rushed out of the legal chambers and stalked, enraged, through the streets of Paris. Perfumed gusts of insinuating air drifted alluringly around every corner. When, Perry asked himself in angry despair, did the cynical French, the mean-minded, hard-hearted French, *keep* all the promises that they made implicit by the fatal fairness of their skies and the wanton intoxication of their city? When a man and woman who should not fall in love, did fall in love, as everything French invited them to do, then God help them.

As soon as it was possible after his conversation with Hulot, Perry left once more for New York, determined to wrest a consent for a divorce from Mary Jane. It was the middle of October before she would agree to see him. He found her thinner than ever and looking far older than the passage of two years should warrant. She was a graying, middle-aged woman, only dimly pretty now, he thought with surprise, while she gazed at him with her pale blue eyes and noted, with a searing flash of bitterness, that he looked positively young. She could see in him too much of the man she had married. Time had treated him lightly. Unfair, oh, *unfair.*

"Mary Jane, I have a daughter."

"Surely you don't think that's news to me, Perry? I don't believe I have a friend in the world who hasn't managed to let slip that information. Do you expect me to congratulate you?"

"Doesn't her existence change the picture, for Christ's sake? It's no longer just a matter of your religious convictions or my excommunication, it's a matter of my only child's future. If I'm willing to risk hellfire and eternal damnation and any and all punishments the church promises me, why won't you let go?"

"I feel no responsibility for her future. She was conceived in sin and born in sin and she is nothing to me. But God's law is clear and I, at least, intend to obey it."

"Mary Jane, I can't believe you mean that. You're not a hard woman . . ."

"How would you know? How would you know what kind of woman I've become? How many years has it been since you turned away from me? Go away, Perry. You and your bastard disgust me!"

She left Perry alone in the library looking out at the unfriendly gray stones of Park Avenue, touching in his pocket the photographs of Teddy he had brought with him to soften the heart of this woman who, he now realized, would only have been further inflamed by them. He was glad Mary Jane had finally gotten angry. Now that she had vented some of her real feelings, now that she had given up her pose of the saint who was thinking only of his salvation, they could surely find a way to work it out. He would be back, in a week, in two weeks, every week for a year if that was what it took. The essential thing was not to give up. Eventually she must give in. He went back to the Yale Club and tried to exorcise his frustration on the squash court. It was that or howl out loud.

Two weeks later, on October 29, 1929, the stock market collapsed. "Coolidge prosperity" vanished as almost seventeen million shares of stock were sold at steadily declining prices. For the next frantic weeks Perry had all he could do to help cope with the panic of the investors whose money he and his partners handled. He saw no chance of leaving New York at any time in the near future, so he wrote Maggy to leave Paris and come to the United States with Teddy.

"Thank heaven I learned English," Maggy said to Paula as she supervised the packing of one of her six steamer trunks.

"Has this American financial trouble affected Perry's fortune?" Paula asked in concern. In just a few weeks the number of free-spending American customers at her restaurant had dwindled to almost nothing.

"I don't know, but I shouldn't think so, he's so clever, after all. I've never discussed money with him. It's been like a magic carpet—often I have even forgotten to ask a price when I buy something."

"No!" Paula was horrified. It was one thing to be kept in the manner of a duchess but not to ask a price was un-French.

"But yes." Maggy giggled. "Like one of those American tourists. I'm so glad to see I've finally shocked you. I knew there was something that could."

Paula sniffed dismissively. She didn't really believe Maggy . . . it was too exaggerated to be true, she thought, looking at Maggy, who was holding a drift, a river of gauzy, quicksilver luxuriance, the silks and velvets and metallic brightness of her dresses rustling and shimmering as they dripped softly from her arms.

Maggy dropped the clothes on the bed and darted over to Paula and gave her a hug. "Why don't you come with me? I invite you—you've never been anywhere outside of Paris, darling sewer rat."

"Thank you but no. I'm too old to displace myself. Why should I travel to see skyscrapers when I've successfully resisted the temptation to view Mont St. Michel? Paris will always be sufficient for me. But when will you be back?"

"I can't really be sure—as soon as all this quiets down."

"I hope it's soon," Paula grumbled. "It's bad for business, this stock market nonsense."

Nine days later Maggy disembarked in New York. She walked down the gangplank holding Teddy's hand firmly, trying to control her own excitement and leaping anticipation. Behind her followed Nanny Butterfield, the pleasant English-woman who was still Teddy's nurse. The passage had been quiet and uneventful, the ship crowded with subdued, worried passengers, many of them expatriates coming back to see what had happened to the investments that enabled them to live in Europe. Perry had arranged to meet them at the pier and take them directly to the furnished apartment he'd rented.

Maggy stood under an enormous letter *L* in the long, dark customs shed, looking about her with wide, smiling eyes. She had dressed so carefully for this reunion. The tiny veil of her green satin cloche just reached to the tip of her nose. Her slim, sable-collared, green wool coat had a short attached cape, trimmed in another wide band of dark sable—nothing, she thought, could be more romantic, yet she couldn't help but shiver in the New York wind, a chill, whirling dirty wind that smelled so unfamiliar. Her smile faded after a while as an officious inspector insisted that she open every last trunk and suitcase. Teddy was whimpering, and Nanny Butterfield was anxious to feed her lunch. Where was Perry? Why wasn't he here to take charge? All around her people were directing porters to put their luggage on trolleys. The gloomy shed was almost empty before Maggy was cleared to leave. Three porters loaded her belongings and one of them asked her, "Where to, lady? Is there a car waiting for you or do you need a taxi? All this stuff won't fit in less than two cabs."

"I must telephone," Maggy said distractedly, looking everywhere for Perry's tall figure.

"Right over there."

She was in the phone booth before she realized that she had no American money in her handbag. How could Perry be so late? So inconsiderate? It was inexcusable Maggy went back to the porter. "Could you please lend me the necessary coin fo the telephone? And please, could you also show me how it works?"

"Sure, lady. Your first visit, right? Come on, follow me." He put the nickel in the slot for her and gave the operator the number she told him, that of Perry's office in Wall Street. Then he shut the door of the phone booth and waited outside, wondering with what she expected to tip him.

"May I speak to Mr. Perry Kilkullen, please?"

"Oh. Oh, I'll let you speak to his secretary. Who may I say is calling?"

"Miss Lunel."

"Just a moment."

When a second woman's voice answered, Maggy said impatiently, "Please, this is Miss Lunel. Can you tell me where Mr. Kilkullen is? He was supposed to meet me hours ago."

"Is this one of Mr. Kilkullen's clients?" the woman asked, uncertainty and caution in her voice.

"Certainly not," Maggy said in mounting anger.

"Are you a friend of his, Miss Lunel?"

"Yes, of course," Maggie snapped. "Now may I speak to him? This is absurd!"

"You don't know," the voice said blankly. It was not a question, yet not a statement.

"Know . . . know what?"

"I'm sorry to be the one . . . it's most . . . everyone here is so upset . . . Mr. Kilkullen had a heart attack playing squash four days ago. I'm afraid . . . he didn't survive."

"Mr. Perry Kilkullen?" Maggy said mechanically. It must be one of his relatives, one of the other Kilkullens. The mouth of the telephone gaped at her, like a crucial organ that has been chopped in half. Blood would gush from it.

"Yes. I'm so sorry. The funeral took place yesterday, it was in all the newspapers. Is there nobody else here you'd like to speak to? Is there anything I can do to help you?"

"No, no, no."

12

If it had not been for Nanny Butterfield, Maggy asked herself when she was again able to think coherently, how could she have lived through the next minutes, the next hours, the next days? The sensible English-woman had taken over completely, coping with all the practical necessities while Maggy was made mute and blank with shock, and all but paralyzed by a disbelieving grief, a rending anguish that snapped through her flesh and bone like the metal jaws of a trap set for an unwary animal.

Nanny Butterfield hunted up the ship's purser and changed Maggy's sum of francs into dollars, she asked him for the name of a hotel and settled them in two adjoining rooms at the Dorset and she put Maggy to bed with the aid of the hotel doctor. For the next few days she treated the shattered woman as if she were the age of Teddy, coaxing her to eat a few mouthfuls and sitting with her until she fell into a drugged sleep.

When Maggy woke in the morning it was to raw pain, so brutal that she couldn't bear to remain under the covers because of the thoughts that attacked her there. Trembling with cold, no matter how warm her robe, she stood in front of the bathroom mirror, afraid to meet her image, tears draining from her eyes into the washbasin for long moments before she could bring herself to make the necessary movements to brush her teeth and wash her face. Every detail of grooming was like a pinnacle of ice over which she had to haul the burden of her bruised, aching body.

Getting dressed was impossible. Maggy spent the week in a nightgown and robe, pacing her overheated room gazing at the walls obsessively, as if their bland cream surfaces could blot out the unbearable. For hours on end, with the curtains tightly drawn and the lamps lit all day long, Maggy walked, shivering, shoulders hunched, toiling back and forth, as if she might die of the torment if she dared to stop her ceaseless movement. She was afraid to go to bed until she dropped on it from exhaustion.

Only when she was worn out did Nanny bring in Teddy to cuddle for a minute in her arms. Maggy held the child in weary blankness until Teddy, lively and easily bored, climbed out of her arms and ran off to play. Her baby was the only warm thing in the world, Maggy thought, her brain working slowly. Her hands were freezing even when she put them in her armpits to warm them. Her feet were icy, although they were snug in her fur-lined slippers. She was like someone who had been skating, fearless and agile, on a sunlit silver lake, until, in the space of an instant, she had fallen through the ice into the lethal chill of Arctic water. Drowned . . . drowned. But Teddy was warm. She could not drown, she must not drown because Teddy was still warm.

"Are we to return to Paris, Madame?" Nanny Butterfield asked, seeing that Maggy was ready to face the future.

"How much money do I have left?"

"About three hundred dollars, Madame."

"I must cable *Maître* Hulot for more—that won't be enough for the tickets," Maggy said dully.

His answering cable arrived the next day.

DEEPEST REGRETS FOR YOUR LOSS. MR. PERRY KILKULLEN LEFT NO INSTRUCTIONS TO DISBURSE MONIES BEYOND THAT OF PAYING HOUSEHOLD AND PERSONAL BILLS ON A MONTHLY BASIS. THESE HAVE BEEN ALL SETTLED. NO FURTHER SUMS CAN BE ADVANCED. HAVE TURNED ALL ESTATE MATTERS OVER TO HIS NEW YORK ATTORNEY MR. LOUIS FAIRCHILD OF 45 BROADWAY, ADVISE YOU CONTACT HIM FOR ANY FURTHER ASSISTANCE.

MAÎTRE JACQUES HULOT

"Look at this," Maggy said, handing the cable to Nanny Butterfield, too stunned for indignation.

"He's washing his hands of us," the Englishwoman said bluntly.

"I'd better go and see Mr. Fairchild," she said listlessly.

"Quite so, and soon . . ." She looked at Maggy, dead pale, standing helplessly, her eyes raw and rimmed with red, her face swollen from the endless, futile tears. "Why don't you write to him and make an appointment? And, Madame, today you really should get dressed and take a nice walk with Teddy and me. It's very pleasant in the park and it will make a change for you. Lovely, brisk weather they have here."

"Oh, no, Nanny, I couldn't."

"Indeed you *must*," she said with a mild authority that no child and few adults had ever questioned.

Three days later Maggy faced Louis Fairchild in his office. She had spent hours every day in the park with Teddy and that morning she had had her hair done in Richard Block's salon where they were able to set it almost as well as Antoine had in another life. Maggy had put on her bravest red lipstick for this interview.

"Thank you for making the time to see me," she said to the worried-looking, gray-haired man.

"Not at all. I must say I was astonished when I received your letter . . ."

"You *do* know who I am?" she asked anxiously.

"Of course, but poor Perry never told me you were coming to New York. May I say how terribly, terribly sorry I am. He was a very good friend, a dear friend. I still can't believe it . . . such a young man and with no history of . . ."

"Mr. Fairchild," Maggy begged, "please stop. I can't talk about it. I've come to you for advice. Would you read this cable and tell me what I am to do?"

He looked at it carefully for long, considering minutes and then shook his head. "I *told* Perry to make a will! I told him once if I told him a dozen times, but he just never got around to it. Like most men of his age he thought he had all the time in the world."

"I don't understand . . . just tell me please what is my *position?*"

"Position? I'm very much afraid that you have . . . none."

"But he was getting divorced! We were going to be married!" she cried.

"He died a married man, Miss Lunel. Legally you don't have any claims. Unfortunately there's nothing on paper."

"But Teddy, our daughter! What about her? Doesn't she have any rights?" Maggy's voice was incredulous.

"I'm sorry—but no." Louis Fairchild thought that if Mary Jane Kilkullen wasn't so bitter he might have been able to persuade her into giving the child something, however little. But it was because of the bastard, she insisted, that her husband had died in a state of mortal sin, that Frenchwoman and her bastard.

"*But he promised . . .*" Maggy broke off. The only emotion she had felt since she had arrived in New York was loss, endless loss. Now rage closed her throat. She saw herself as she must look, sitting there keening "he promised," like millions of other women since the beginning of time. Foolish women, childlike women, victimized women, stupid, *inexcusably, criminally stupid* women who believed in their men, those careless men who took what they wanted, those loving men who failed to make the most basic provisions for the women they should have protected. Men who lied and lied and lied. Julien Mistral and Perry Kilkullen. She pulled herself up tall in her chair and looked at the unhappy lawyer.

"Please, Mr. Fairchild, what precisely do I own in the world?"

"Your personal property, such as jewelry and furs and any other specific gifts Mr. Kilkullen may have made to you, a car perhaps?"

"Our apartment in Paris?"

"It will be disposed of, with all its contents, before the estate is settled."

"Disposed of," Maggy said, fury making her voice calm and businesslike. "I hope somebody remembered to pay the servants."

"*Maître* Hulot is in correspondence with me about that."

"They, I trust, will get some compensation for being thrown out of work without warning? That's only proper, is it not? And, fortunately for them, they have lost only their jobs. *Tiens*, I should have taken lessons in something useful."

"What are you going to do?" Louis Fairchild said. He really didn't want to know, he didn't want to sit and contemplate the future of this dazzling, but utterly dispossessed woman. However, mere decency demanded that he try to be helpful.

"Ah, that is something I shall have to consider carefully." Maggy gathered her silver fox furs about her and began to put on her long, gray gloves.

"If there's any advice I can give you . . ."

"Perhaps you could give me the name of an honest jeweler. I think that it would be sensible to get rid of some of those small pieces I never seem to find time to wear," Maggy said as casually as she could. The hotel bill was due again at the end of the week.

Fairchild scribbled a name on his card. "This is the fellow I always go to for my wife's birthday. Tell him you're a friend of mine. Look . . ." he hesitated, embarrassed to propose a loan to the most desirable woman he'd ever seen in his life, "if you need some cash, I'd be glad to be of service . . ."

"Thank you, that's very kind, but it won't be necessary," Maggy said with a reflex of pride. There were some things she just could not do. Not yet at least.

Louis Fairchild saw her to the elevator and then returned to his desk miserably. What an unholy mess. He supposed she'd go back to Paris and find a husband. Girls like that could always find husbands. And if he were to be honest with himself, he didn't really blame Kilkullen. If he'd had a chance at a girl like that himself, he'd have grabbed it too. Only he'd have had the common sense to make a will. At least he hoped he would. A girl like that could make you forget a lot of things you were supposed to do.

That night Maggy opened her jewel case for the first time since she'd been in the United States. The pretty, flashing pieces looked like childhood toys, long forgotten. Thoughtfully she put the real jewels into one pile. In another heap, much larger than the first, she laid the costume jewelry she much preferred for its cleverness; the lapel pins and necklaces she had collected from Chanel, who dictated, "Wear anything you like so long as it looks like junk."

Nevertheless, there should be enough here to keep them in comfort for a long, long time, she mused. Perry had loved to take her into a jeweler's for no reason at all, when they were out walking in the neighborhood of Place Vendôme, and demand that she pick out something to celebrate the sheer joy of the moment. "To celebrate Teddy's fourth tooth," he'd declare, or "Because you have the pinkest nipples in Paris."

Resolutely she took all the real jewels, with the exception of her pearls—a woman had to have her pearls—and her favorite bracelet, out of their velvet cases and tucked them into her handbag. She couldn't afford to be sentimental and, besides, she was finished, utterly finished, with sentiment, finished with an emotion that led, sooner or later, to mortal weakness.

Maggy found it impossible to forgive herself. She had been a "*poire,*" that classic French laughingstock, the foolish true believer, the butt of practical jokes, the person who almost asks people to take advantage of her. Since her interview with Louis Fairchild, Maggy felt as if she had grown centuries wiser and harder. She would never believe in a man again, Maggy knew in her soul, and as the knowledge flowed into her she felt warmed, strengthened and oddly alert. It was not a happy thing to find out, at twenty-two, that no man—whether he loved you truly or not—could ever be trusted. It was not a happy thing to finally realize that you could depend on no one but yourself. But it was a clean realization without the possibility of question marks or exceptions. The dirty, freezing, winter water in which she had been struggling receded, leaving her on dry land, barren and unwelcoming land perhaps, but so much less frightening now that she understood that she had only her own two feet to support her. She had been in that situation before and survived . . . it was familiar territory.

Maggy drew herself up to her full height and looked at herself sternly in the mirror. You have nowhere to go but straight ahead, she told herself, and firmly put her mind to planning the perfect costume in which to sell her jewelry. First the black, plainly cut, Vionnet dress. Then her black Schiaparelli coat, a complete transformation from last season, with its wide, padded epaulet shoulders and double-breasted, wooden-soldier silhouette. It looked as martial as she wanted to feel, severe, dashing and above all, absolutely new. With it she'd wear a strict black Caroline Reboux felt hat, its angular line strikingly defined. Did she look widowed? Surely that was the effect all that black gave—but not a pathetic widow who could be led into a mistake of judgment.

The next day, clad in her arrogant armor, Maggy walked calmly into Tiffany's in search of the salesman whose name Louis Fairchild had given her. He brightened as she introduced herself.

"I find myself with some jewels that no longer suit me," Maggy said casually. "Mr. Louis Fairchild told me that you might be able to help me dispose of them."

The salesman's face fell. "You mean buy them back from you?"

"They weren't bought here—they were made in Paris."

"But, Madame, we never buy back even our own jewelry, it's a policy of the company."

"Do other American jewelers have the same policy?" Maggy asked casually, allowing herself to sound mildly surprised.

"So far as I know. Particularly these days, Madame. There are so many ladies who are discovering that they have more jewelry than they need."

"Indeed. Ah well—how—inconvenient." She hesitated, sighed and then gave him a lightning, sideways look, overtly conspiratorial and mischievous.

He coughed discreetly. "Look, you'd have more luck in a smaller store. Those little jewelers are more flexible. They're in business for themselves so they're always on the lookout for a good buy."

"Do you recommend any of them?" Maggy asked with a wicked appealing note in her voice that made him yearn to kill dragons for her.

"Recommend? No, I wish I could go that far. But there's a fellow around the corner, on Madison, down a couple of blocks, who's got a nice little place—Harry C. Klein. But it is only a suggestion, not a recommendation, you understand."

"Of course, and I'm grateful to you. You've been most kind."

"Say, listen, it was a pleasure. You're the first person I've talked to all day. But this Wall Street panic can't last. So when you're in the market again come back and see me. Tiffany's will still be here." He looked after Maggy with wistful lust. He'd give almost anything to see her wearing that new ruby and diamond necklace with the matching earrings. And nothing else, no, not even a pair of high-heeled shoes.

Harry C. Klein had had a bad morning. An old customer had come in to have a sapphire ring he'd sold her a number of years ago put into a new setting. She had insisted on "sitting with" her stone while the work went on so that it couldn't be switched for one of less value. Paranoid! Everybody was going bananas. He'd almost told her to go away and find a jeweler she could trust but, business being what it was, he'd agreed. The men in the workroom would be furious. And now this young woman had just tipped out a bunch of pieces on his counter. Did she think he was Santa Claus? Nobody in his right mind was interested in adding to his inventory. He looked at the clips and earrings and bracelets with a quickly appraising eye.

"I can see you're definitely no gold digger," he sighed to Maggy. "Too bad. *Melée*—that's what you've got."

"*Melée*—but in French that means a fight, a struggle in a crowd," she said puzzled.

"For jewelers it just means a lot of little stones." Morosely he flipped over a pair of large clips thickly paved in tiny diamonds. "See, no big stones."

"But big stones are dull!" Maggy exclaimed. "I only wanted to wear amusing pieces, the witty ones—big stones are for old princesses at the Opera or for the Dolly Sisters—they are too serious for me."

"Big stones are for *resale*," he said, wagging a lecturing finger in her face.

"I never thought of jewelry as an investment," Maggy said in a low voice. She pushed out of her mind the gay lunches in the Ritz garden followed by the light-hearted search for a glittering folly in a jeweler's window. So even there she had been a *poire*—Perry would have given her anything she fancied; acres of those thick diamond bracelets she had scorned as "service stripes."

"Lady, lady, don't you know that jewelry is only an investment if you plan to hold onto it for fifty years? And even then it's a crapshoot. Sure you can always sew it into the lining of your skirt and flee the country. But where would you go? I'm talking *resale*, lady, not investment. I'm talking about getting something *close* to what you paid for it. Resale means big stones and even then only if they're good quality, good clarity. Better a two-carat ruby with the right strawberry gleam than a five-carat ruby that's a bit off."

"But look at these designs, this workmanship!" Maggy exclaimed angrily. Could all her treasures be worthless? This man must be trying to rob her.

"Means nothing. Only the weight of the stones and the value of the metal settings count when you go to sell *melée*. Look, I have a safe full of loose stones upstairs, little ones like these, maybe not as fine, but fine enough. I bought them at wholesale. I couldn't offer you anything except considerably less than wholesale, because with your fancy, funny piece there's a lot of labor involved just to break them up to get the stones out. Anyway, I can't buy them because my business is strictly a question of supply and demand and ever since the Crash, demand has disappeared." He looked at her pearls and nodded in regret. "Those cost a fortune, didn't they? Burmese, I'll bet? And then the Japanese learned how to cultivate them and now . . ." He sighed mournfully at the sight of the gleaming, once coveted objects that even Maggy had known were impossible to sell.

"So," Maggy sighed, echoing his mood, touching her lovely, devalued fantasies, "*Bubkes* . . . nothing."

"*Bubkes*?" he said, startled. "You're a Jewish girl?"

"But of course. Does that turn my *melée* into one big valuable ruby?"

"No such luck. But what's a beautiful Jewish girl like you doing without her basic diamond solitaire?" Harry C. Klein demanded severely. "How come you didn't get, at least, your major sapphire, your important ruby? Smart you weren't."

"Smart I wasn't," Maggy agreed emphatically, grinning in spite of herself at his outrage. She unfastened the row of big brass curtain-ring clips that Schiaparelli had used in place of coat buttons and slipped out of her narrow sleeves. Mr. Klein's shop was overheated and it had occurred to her that in her black dress she looked even more definitely widowed than with her coat on. Perhaps this nice man had a soft spot for Jewish widows? It was worth trying to sell her *melée*, even for next to nothing.

"Wait a minute—what's this?" He grasped her arm and took a look at the bracelet she had decided to keep.

"More *melée*, I suppose, plus some emeralds."

"Those emeralds look interesting. Take it off, I'll take a better look—with your luck there's something wrong with them." He examined the bracelets with his jeweler's loupe, scrutinizing each emerald in turn. Finally, with a grunt of satisfaction he gave it back to Maggy. "Good, very good. For these emeralds I don't mind making an exception. So what if I don't sell them for a long time?"

"You mean you want to buy the bracelet?"

"Definitely, and I'll give you the fairest possible price. Have it appraised first if that'll make you happier, be my guest."

"But Mr. Klein," Maggy said sharply, "I don't want to sell just the bracelet, I want to sell everything. The person who buys the bracelet has to take the other pieces too."

Totally dumb she wasn't, Harry C. Klein thought with a mixture of pleasure and gloom. The chances of a small jeweler like himself ever being able to buy four perfectly matched emeralds of two carats each was remote. An important jeweler might have to wait a long while before laying his hands on such a set. You could make two pairs of magnificent earrings from them or even a necklace—no, *two* necklaces with two emeralds in each, surrounded by diamonds. If stones like that ever lost their value, nothing they've dug up since the days of King Solomon's Mines would be worth anything. Even if he had to sit on the emeralds for years, he couldn't pass them up.

Maggy put the bracelet back on and reached for her coat.

"Where are you going?"

"To find somebody who'll buy the lot."

"All right, all right. Don't start to shop around, it'll only confuse you. We'll make a deal . . . don't be in such a hurry."

She looked at him suspiciously and then relaxed. He hadn't had to tell her that the emeralds were good . . . but first she'd get that appraisal.

By the time Maggy concluded the sale of her jewelry to Harry C. Klein they had become good friends. He knew her sad history: the French husband, handsome David Lunel, who had invested so unwisely in the United States and, while investigating the extent of his losses in New York, had died in an automobile crash, leaving her stranded with their baby daughter. He knew of Rabbi Taradash and of her grandmother and even of her grandmother's secret recipe for *pot-au-feu*, but he knew nothing of the fevers of Montparnasse nights or of a painter named Mistral or of a comic carefree girl who had let her green silk kimono slip off her naked body unconcernedly in front of the eyes of anyone who would pay to paint her. When the time came for the delivery of the twelve thousand dollars that Maggy's jewels finally fetched, of which the lion's share was paid for the emeralds, Harry C. Klein took a proprietary interest in her future.

"I suppose you're going to take the little girl and go back home? Maybe start a little business? You can do a lot with that much cash these days."

"I haven't really decided."

Maggy walked up Madison Avenue slowly, deep in thought, her check safely tucked inside her brassiere. She had a nest egg, enough to provide for herself and Teddy for four or five years in moderate comfort if she found a small flat in an unfashionable part of Paris. But when her money ran out, what would she do? What sort of small business could she establish, untrained as she was? And what if the business failed and she lost all her money? Could she get a job as a *vendeuse* perhaps, in one of those shops in which she used to lavish Perry's money without asking the prices?

She looked around her and sniffed the air. It was a few weeks before Christmas: the bright blue day flapped around her like a flag. New York was stunningly alive with a crackle of promise, an irresistible rush of vitality that made Paris seem old-fashioned, tradition-laden, unbeckoning. Why not make a clean break? Why not stay here where she was Mrs. Lunel, a widow, rather than go back to a country where too many people knew too much about her? Excitedly she turned and almost ran the short blocks back to the jewelry store.

"It's too late to change your mind. We agreed, fair market value," Mr. Klein said, looking up as she burst in, cheeks flaming.

"I've got to get a job! Here in New York! I'm not going back to France, I've just decided . . ."

"Doing what?"

"I don't know. Do you have any ideas for me?"

"A girl who's never worked a day in her life—are you kidding?"

"Well, I have done a little modeling."

"What kind of model?"

"For . . . fashion designers."

"So." He looked her over carefully. He didn't know anything about fashion models but he knew a stunner when he saw one. "I have a friend who's in the fashion business, we play poker twice a month, Italian fellow. He's done very well—a boy from the old neighborhood but today you'd never know it. Alberto Bianchi—we used to play stickball, today he's pretty fancy. I'll give him a call, see if there's anything doing." He retreated to his back office to telephone and returned beaming. "Maybe they can use a girl—just maybe. One of their regular models took off with the husband of their best client. The fellow decided to give himself a Christmas present for a change. Go quick—these days jobs don't stay empty long. Here's the address and here's," he said, giving Maggy a quick kiss on her cheek, "a kiss for good luck."

Maggy was as nervous as a goldfish as she approached the entrance to Bianchi's. The glass doors on East Fifty-fifth Street were smoked, and there were no show windows flanking them, merely the discreet bricks of a modernized townhouse.

She entered through the doors and, for the first moment since she'd been in New York, she felt immediately at home. Shocked, she stood still and breathed deeply. All around her the pulse of the establishment beat with a rhythm so familiar that she recognized it in her blood, the rhythm of a *maison de couture*. The sounds were the ones she knew: the voices behind fitting-room doors, those of the saleswomen deferential and unruffled, those of the customers high-pitched, indecisive and spoiled. The smells were the same; the mingled perfumes of a hundred rich women lingered in the air mixed with the smoke from their cigarettes, underlaid by the pungent aromas of new fabric and fur.

Her heart lurched as she drank in the atmosphere, that special distillation, that intensity that goes to a woman's head like a bolt of electricity, compounded of the million fantasies that had been brought to this place; fantasies of how a woman might look if she found that right, that perfect dress; of how that perfect dress would transform her; fantasies that placed a greater belief on the power of clothes than clothes could ever fulfill.

It was the Lourdes of vanity, Maggy thought. Here they came, not to be cured but to be made into their dreams of themselves; younger, more beautiful, thinner, more desirable. The concentrated force of these fantasies seemed strong enough to blow the walls of the dressmaker's apart, yet a controlled calm reigned over the gray-velvet, mirrored reception room.

Patricia Falkland, a beautifully tailored, dark-haired middle-aged woman, sat behind a polished desk on which stood only a single bud vase containing one white rose. She had worked for Alberto Bianchi for years, supervising all the salespeople and fulfilling the absolutely necessary role of mediator between saleswomen and clients. She never acted as a saleswoman herself but she was responsible for giving advice to vacillating customers, and for dealing with all the personnel of the house. Sizing up new customers was her specialty.

Miss Falkland could spot, in a dowdy, middle-aged woman, the wife of a major meat packer from Chicago who would spend thousands of dollars, as easily as she could pick out the young society woman, dressed in the latest fashion, wearing every evidence of luxury, who would never settle her bills. She knew each one of the wealthy women of New York who preferred to come to Bianchi for his brilliantly edited copies of Chanel and Vionnet and Lanvin, rather than going to Paris for their clothes. Throughout the 1920s, although fashion was dictated absolutely by Paris, there were many American women who refused to devote several months of each crowded year to traveling back and forth to France and subjecting themselves to the exhausting round of collections and fittings.

As Maggy entered, Patricia Falkland pursed her lips in an inaudible imperceptible whistle, that whistle of unqualified approval that few women ever elicited from her. Maggy embodied an ideal that the richest women couldn't buy. As Patricia Falkland's eyes traveled their customary swift path upward, taking in all the details of Maggy's ensemble, from the exquisite, perfectly polished shoes to the cunningly wrought hat, she knew that she was looking at someone who was dressed in the original of the clothes that Alberto Bianchi would be reproducing for his customers, someone who was dressed in the *real thing,* that uncapturable essence of Paris that could never be duplicated, no matter how closely they copied fabric for fabric, seam for seam, button for button. *How the hell do those bastards do it?* She always asked herself that question when she saw Parisian dressmaking at its best, and it was still the only question for which she had no answer.

For a second, neither of the women spoke. Maggy stood, looking around the reception room, with that inimitable air of a prospective customer that the atmosphere of the room had brought out in her, that stance; appraising, judgmental, yet absolutely sure of her welcome, which she had grown into during the last two luxurious years. It was a stance that could never be achieved by deliberate practice, never assumed by anyone who wasn't accustomed to spending a great deal of money. It came from an inner, unconscious attitude toward clothes. It said, as if she had spoken aloud, "There isn't anything you have to sell me that I cannot buy if I choose. But will I? It is for you to tempt me. And even then I may be so sated that I will refuse to be lured. Spread your best out in front of me. If I want it I will have it. Or perhaps not—that is for me to decide."

The instant of silence passed as Patricia Falkland rose deferentially and advanced toward Maggy. "May I help you, Madame?" she asked in the voice she reserved for the best customers.

"I hope so," Maggy replied.

"If you'd like to sit down, I'll call a saleslady immediately." Miss Falkland smiled as if to apologize because a saleslady had not materialized out of the floor at Maggy's arrival.

"No, please do not trouble. I would like to speak to someone about the modeling job."

"A job?" she repeated as her smile vanished.

"I understand that you need a model. I would like to apply for the position."

"That's quite impossible," Miss Falkland said sharply, a clear note of anger in her voice. How dare this woman waltz in the salon giving herself the airs and graces of a customer when she wanted a job? It was quite outrageous. It was unforgivable. Absolutely unheard of. Her heart hardened toward Maggy who had caused her to make a mistake in the judgment of which she was so proud. It was infuriating to have been caught putting on her most welcoming manner for a mere job hunter.

"I was informed by my friend Mr. Harry Klein that the House of Bianchi needs a dress model. Mr. Klein talked to Mr. Bianchi himself, no more than a quarter of an hour ago, so I came immediately."

"Mr. Bianchi is looking for a professional model, a working girl, not a dilettante. We pay thirty-five dollars a week, which wouldn't buy one of your shoes, and our girls work like brutes for that money, or they don't last a week. We'd never even consider someone without experience."

"Please, give me a trial," Maggy insisted. This female, she thought, is not going to get rid of me. I'm no longer a sniveling child who is too modest to take off her knickers. "Mr. Bianchi told Mr. Klein he needed . . ."

Patricia Falkland heard and noted the determination and stubbornness in Maggy's tone. For years she had deplored the masculine aberration that led her employer to continue to keep up an association with his poker-playing friends from his past, but she knew perfectly well how sentimental he was about it. She bowed to the fact that she couldn't brush Maggy off without trouble from Bianchi.

"Follow me," she said brusquely. "But it's a waste of your time." She led the way up one flight of stairs into a room, empty at the moment, where the new French originals hung on long racks next to the tables the models used for their makeup. She picked out a white satin evening dress, intricately cut on the bias, so low in front and in back that it was difficult to tell which was which. With a gathered peplum flounce that projected between the hip and the knee, it was, quite possibly, the most unwearable gown that Madame Jeanne Lanvin had ever created. She handed it to Maggy without a word and went back to her desk.

Damn that creature, Patricia Falkland fumed. She knew enough to wave Klein's name around like a sword, but she didn't have the sense to realize that she was totally unsuited to showing clothes. The last thing a model must do is to seem like competition to the customer. No matter how good-looking she is, she must not stir up any response of *envy* in the customer, she must never appear to be on the customer's social or economic level. The customer must be encouraged to feel superior. It was something bone deep, understood by everyone who sold clothes.

She was still immersed in angry thought when Maggy appeared at the top of the stairs, wrapped in an ermine cape she had appropriated from another rack in the model room. Her bare head revealed hair like a carefully tended bonfire, still parted at the side as Antoine had first styled it, but longer now and waved tightly over her ears. A living statue, she advanced at a subtle, gliding pace that was neither slow nor rapid, a pace calculated to allow the spectator to absorb the details of what she was wearing with ease, yet her eyes, looking serenely into the middle distance, did not permit any personal contact. Vanished, as if it could never have existed, was the unconscious, privileged challenge with which Maggy had entered the reception room and in its place was a demeanor that indicated clearly that she was there only and uniquely for the pleasure and service of others.

Look, look not at me, she seemed to be saying, but at what I'm wearing, because if it tempts you then it can be yours. I am only the medium who indicates to you how you can realize your dreams. I am neutral, the clothes are everything, and are they not beautiful? I am proud to wear them, for a few minutes. But they do not belong to me. Think how marvelous *you* could look in this.

Maggy reached the last step and walked across the reception room. Miss Falkland, regarding her with an unfriendly, impassive eye, noted that she had found a pair of white satin evening shoes from some model's cache. But anyone, even a born frump, could wrap herself in ermine and create something of an effect. There hadn't been a model who worked for Bianchi who hadn't fought to show that wrap and they'd all looked well in it. The test, the trial had been sidetracked and she was unimpressed.

Maggy turned in front of the desk and walked back to the foot of the staircase. There, slowly, with a gesture to which she gave all that she had ever learned of allure, a gesture that told all that could ever be learned about handling fur, she threw back the cape, unfolding it as easily as if it had been made of organdy, and let it trail from one hand as she revealed herself in the white satin dress that had, by the act of her having put it on, become ultimately desirable.

One of two fake diamond clips Maggy had picked up at Chanel marked the lowest point of the décolletage in the front, and as she turned again, another was clasped at the V of the dress in the back in a manner that no one in New York had yet seen. She circled the room, the ermine whispering on the carpet, and now a small, dreamlike smile warmed her face, enough, just precisely enough, exactly enough of a smile to gather the spectator into the sensuous pleasure of wearing such a dress, a smile that guaranteed temptation. She didn't look at Patricia Falkland for approval or disapproval as she walked, but if she had, she would have seen the woman's lips set grimly.

"Who's this?" a man's voice demanded. Miss Falkland jumped but Maggy stood still imperturbably, and waited, offering herself absolutely yet not losing her distance.

"Someone applying for a model job, Mr. Bianchi," she said. "I don't think she's suitable."

"Maybe you should have your eyes checked, Patsy. What's your name, Miss?" Maggy's neutral, bland look disappeared as she unfurled her unauthorized charm.

"Magali Lunel, but I am called simply Maggy in the business."

"You're the girl Harry called about—I didn't expect . . . when can you start?"

"Whenever you like. Tomorrow if that suits you."

"How about now? Patsy, Mrs. Townsend just called. She's changed her mind about leaving for Palm Beach after all, so she's desperate for new clothes for the Christmas parties in Tuxedo Park, and we're shorthanded."

"Now is even better than tomorrow," Maggy said. She liked the look of Mr. Bianchi, who had once been a boy in Harry Klein's old neighborhood. He had a perfectly tended look, splendid linen, a glossiness of hair and sleekness that was more continental than American. He was plump, as bright-eyed as a boy, and obviously a master at his trade. She understood a man like this one. He would be a demon if she disappointed him but kind, even generous, if she could give him the perfection he expected.

Several hours later, after she had modeled dozens of dresses and suits and coats for Mrs. Townsend, Maggy left the House of Alberto Bianchi with a job that paid thirty-five dollars a week. Her heart jumped as she thought gleefully that she had, after all, been trained for something useful. Years of taking her clothes off as quickly as possible for her artists, followed by years of watching fashion shows—and the ability to imitate the best models in Paris—had added up to a salable commodity. She would be making enough money to pay Nanny Butterfield and still have fifteen dollars left over.

Maggy arrived at the corner of Fifth Avenue and Fifty-seventh Street and paused to look around her, to absorb the almost tangible pledge made by the long, brightly lit thoroughfare in the winter twilight. Another Maggy, the seventeen-year-old girl who had stood in the center of springtime Montparnasse, and waited impatiently for her life to begin, seemed to join her, to stand by her side and say, "Courage." How little you knew then, Maggy whispered to herself. How little I know now. How much, how very much I am going to learn. She wondered where she could find a florist's shop. She needed to buy a red carnation for her buttonhole.

13

What was the reason for the hold Lavinia Longbridge had over the younger members of New York society? Even bridge-playing dowagers at the Southampton Beach Club bestirred themselves to ask each other. Mrs. Condé Nast posed the question to Mrs. William de Rahm, and Cecil Beaton, on his frequent visits to New York, had become enough aware of her power to inquire of Mrs. Herbert Weston if she understood the reason for it.

One cynic had said that in all of nature there were only fourteen different patterns into which objects from crystals to pineapples could stack themselves, but that at the top of each stack one would be sure to find Lally Longbridge. Yet this was too simple an answer, although it had first been observed when, as Lavinia Pendennis, she became the most fêted debutante of her year, her spectacular entrance into society so far outpaced the next contender as to make all the other girls seem to fall into one undifferentiated group.

When she married Cornwallis Longbridge she might have been expected to fall into the traditional role of rich young wife, but this she refused to do, maintaining in an era of couples, a separate identity, so that Cornie Longbridge became another, although the most favored, of her subjects.

Lally was as beautiful as she was miniature, with black eyes and black hair that sprang away from her white delicate face like a wreath above the whitest arms and shoulders and back in New York, and the reddest lips, the only touch of color she allowed herself; but there were many beautiful girls in society: Mary Taylor, Isabel Henry, Helen Kellogg, Justine Allen and Alice Doubleday all had their champions for the queen of beauty.

No, it was not just popularity and beauty that accounted for her enormous influence—it was the generous manner in which she had pledged her life to having a good time. For the only way Lally could have a good time was when she bestowed it on others.

In Lally Longbridge the reckless gaiety of that great party of the twenties had danced right on into the first frightening year of the thirties. Cornie Longbridge's fortune was secure and her life was devoted seriously to entertaining unseriously; her home was like a reassuring campfire that could be counted on to warm everyone who came near. Lally was considered the best bartender in the city and certainly she knew all the best bootleggers. She invented the buffet supper; meals at her house always had the charm of picnics; and her roving taste for people was the spice that made her parties go like rockets. Lally asked jazz musicians to her parties and newspaper reporters and professional boxers and tap dancers from Broadway shows and songwriters from Tin Pan Alley and, jealous hostesses whispered, even gangsters, which only made the parties more thrilling. She welded them all into one bright unit by her laughter and friendliness.

Often after a party had taken off, Lally would step back into the shadow of an alcove and watch for minutes at a time the new and unexpected groupings she had caused to happen, feeling like the most successful of stage directors. Her entertainments were as frequent as they were spontaneous, never planned more than a day or two in advance, with the knowledge that her household was organized around hospitality, her servants chosen for their capacity to cope with large groups as carefully as if she were an ambassador's wife.

Lally Longbridge had had dresses made at Bianchi's since her debut. She was one of those exceedingly rare short women who possess the gift of dressing in a way that made her look tall. The heart of it lay in the fact that Lally never perceived herself as tiny—everybody else she felt was simply too big. Until Maggy came to work at Bianchi's she had never found a model who understood this and who would willingly show her dresses that, in theory, only tall women could wear.

In the last year and a half she had become increasingly interested in Maggy. Mrs. Lunel was far from being the usual house model, obviously, but what *was* the mystery of this widowed Frenchwoman who couldn't be drawn into speaking of herself? Everybody she took an interest in was *supposed* to tell Lally all about herself—it really was most curious, almost vexing.

One day in the spring of 1931, she astonished Maggy by inviting her to a party the following evening.

"Say you'll come, Maggy, do! After dinner we're having a scavenger hunt and there'll be a fabulous prize for the winning team—it'll be great fun."

Maggy hesitated. The house models never mingled with the customers. A social gulf, which everyone acknowledged, separated them.

"Now don't be stuffy! I know what you're thinking and it's too silly for words. Lots of women work these days—it's getting rather smart. That doesn't mean that you're prohibited from having a good time."

"I'd love to," Maggy said decisively. She owed herself some kind of romp. For the past year and a half she'd led a life of discipline and hard work, at the beck and call of Bianchi and his customers for as long as ten hours a day, rarely off her feet for more than a few minutes at a time.

But it was healing work that kept her from thinking about the past, exhausting work that let her sleep soundly, waking only occasionally to dreams of Perry Kilkullen, which made her weep, waking too often to dream of Julien Mistral, which made her rage. How could she still dream about a man she hated? She'd ask herself that uncomfortable question furiously, trying to deny the profound, rolling orgasm that had awakened her. She was, on those mornings, particularly glad to run off to a job that left no time for uncomfortable introspection.

Maggy was now the leading model at Alberto Bianchi's and the other nine models all looked up to her. Even Patricia Falkland had been forced to admit, if only to herself, that no one could show and sell a dress like Maggy. In the scattered moments that the models had to congregate in their dressing room the other girls asked Maggy's advice and there was nothing about which she didn't express firm, immediate approval or disapproval, from the line of a new hairstyle to the shade of a pair of stockings. Somehow Maggy found herself calming the girls when they had jitters or complaints or quarreled among themselves. She listened to their accounts of their many romances and administered stiff but compassionate doses of tough-minded advice in which her own hard-learned wisdom was mixed with bits of Paula's well-remembered admonitions. She even found herself scolding the girls who put on a pound or two, and advising them about the placement of their rouge and eyeshadow.

Charity fashion shows had become a rage in New York and the House of Bianchi was constantly asked to participate in them. Soon Maggy found herself in demand by the organizers of these shows who were all amateurs. She was able to run herd on the models, most of them dithering, nervous, awkward society women who had never walked on a runway before.

Because of this extra work Maggy's salary was raised to fifty dollars a week. She had had to dip into her precious nest egg to furnish the small apartment just off Central Park West, on Sixty-third Street, that she'd taken for her little family.

Nevertheless, Maggy's salary was just enough to support Teddy and Nanny Butterfield. Her own expenses were minimal; her Paris clothes were still in style, chosen as they had been from advanced designs that embodied ideas that were still fresh to the American eye . . . not that it mattered really, Maggy thought, since she had no occasion to get really dressed up.

The other manikins at Bianchi's had, in her first days there, invited her to go out to speakeasies and nightclubs with them—there were always many young men who wanted to meet her. But she had refused time after time, and eventually they stopped asking. She never mentioned her choice of solitude in her letters to Paula, who would, she knew, have disapproved deeply. As soon as work was over Maggy hurried home every night to have an early dinner with Teddy and soak her feet.

Now, reacting to the flattering surprise of Lally Long-bridge's invitation, she felt that she'd gone as long as she could endure without an evening's break, just one night of sheer *fun*. The Jazz Age was finished, killed by the Depression, but an unsubdued audaciousness in Maggy told her how badly she still thirsted for the sound of a saxophone, the thrum of a guitar. The melody of "Sweet Georgia Brown," forgotten for six years, came back to her lips. As she dressed for the party she realized that on a May evening, even New York, that lonely, tense city of metal and concrete, could turn electric and rosy with expectation.

When the impulsive business of inviting guests was over, Lally Longbridge gave an hour's concentration to the composition of the teams for her scavenger hunt. There was no point in putting the same kind of people together, people who already knew each other—a scavenger hunt was only as much fun as the team members made it.

Maggy Lunel, she thought, was so smart that she should be on the team with Gay Barnes, who spun nothing but nonsense in her bubbly blond head. Gay had been the most famous of the showgirls in Earl Carroll's *Vanities* before she married Henry Oliver Barnes, who must be thirty-five years older than she. Lally, who was always interested in how others packaged their personalities, realized that Gay had managed to win over stuffy New York society by two simple means: she was amazingly decorative and she had a killingly funny way of seeming to never know when a man made a risqué remark—remarks she had most definitely provoked.

Which two men with those two women? She bit her thumb pensively. Why not Jerry Holt? The entertainment column he wrote for the *World* was read by everybody in town and he was as witty as his reputation was dubious. And . . . yes . . . it would serve him right for being so hard to pin down; the other man would be Darcy, Jason Darcy, whom everyone called by his last name.

How amusingly outraged that rather too self-satisfied twenty-nine-year-old *wunderkind* of the publishing business would be to find himself teamed up with an ex-showgirl, a dress house model and a, probably, pansy columnist. It was the kind of team that would give Lally a special kind of good time. At every party she gave she arranged for at least one such ill-assorted group, a secret game she played, for her own delectation.

Hours later, after dinner, the ten teams gathered in Lally's fashionably sterile chrome and glass drawing room, filled with white tulips. There was groaning and protesting over the lists she had handed them.

One debutante of this season, only beautiful ones count
One of Miss Ethel Barrymore's shoes
One dog, must be pure white
One program from *Smiles* signed by both Adele and Fred Astaire
One tablecloth from the Colony Restaurant
One English butler—no fakes
One brand-new copy of *A Farewell to Arms*
One single yellow glove
One New York City policeman's hat
One waiter's jacket from Jack and Charlie's

"This is simply fiendish," Gay Barnes wailed. "We'll never win, never."

"How long do we have?" Maggy asked.

"Two hours," Jerry Holt explained. "The team wins that brings in the most by the deadline."

"I've had an inspiration!" Gay Barnes announced. "It doesn't say anywhere that we can't split up, does it? What's the point in all four of us going after the same things? I think Jerry and I should take the first five and you two take the others. How about it?"

"All I know is that somewhere I must have a yellow glove, I'm a much-gloved woman," Maggy said, wondering, why on earth, if she were going to plot to be alone with a man, the blond girl had picked out a *pédé*.

"Whatever you all decide," Darcy agreed. "But let's get going—we've wasted five minutes already."

Downstairs, on Park Avenue, Darcy handed Maggy into a long limousine. "Twenty-one East Fifty-second Street," he said to the chauffeur sitting in an open box.

"I suspected Lally was going to spring another scavenger hunt so I told the car to wait," he told Maggy.

The enormous dark blue Packard, which would have seemed appropriate for J. P. Morgan himself, was only one of the ways in which Jason Darcy set himself apart from other young men of his age. The only son of a wealthy Hartford insurance company owner, he'd been considered one of the most brilliant men of his class at Harvard, graduating at eighteen. In the following years he had borrowed family money to launch three new magazines, each of which had become immediately successful in that booming era.

The money soon repaid, Darcy used his large income to live as well as a pasha entitled to display three horsetails. He had affairs with an astonishing percentage of all the prettiest women in New York, whom he bothered only to divide into two basic categories, treating the society ladies like chorus girls, and the chorus girls like society ladies, an arrangement that somehow ensured everyone's pleasure. No one woman had managed to catch him and the ever-growing band of his disappointed, temporary flames all drifted toward the face-saving conclusion that he was married to his work.

Jason Darcy was a genuinely influential man who risked becoming self-important. Unfortunately for his character, he'd never wanted anything he couldn't manage to obtain; not the admiration of his peers or his own self-esteem. For the moment Maggy was the bauble he had decided to acquire. Twice, during dinner, he had caught her eye although they had been seated at different tables. Gay Barnes, nitwit that she was, had shown a most convenient sense of timing in splitting up the team, although if there hadn't been the excuse of the scavenger hunt he would simply have taken more direct measures.

Maggy was jolted by the memory of Perry's dove-gray Voisin as she leaned back into the deep, soft cushion of the Packard. She'd forgotten how such a car made her feel, cosseted, a rare object made of precious materials, fitted into a velvet nest. Nothing, no perfume she knew, smelled as sensuous as the interior of a limousine.

She glanced at Darcy with mild interest. He had a long, thin face of infinite distinction, a scientist's face or a philosopher's face, she thought, in spite of his youth. It was a face that was sharp with cool curiosity, yet he looked as if he could never be surprised. He moved with economy and grace; he had a straight, gray gaze in which she suspected some humor must lurk, and a straight hard mouth that looked as if it could be capable of great scorn. His dark hair fit closely to his head, and he was easily a few inches taller than she was. A man like a blade, she thought, and dismissed him from her mind. The limousine was so much more potent an excitement than any mere man could be.

She was disappointed when the ride ended too quickly and they entered the permanent carnival of Jack and Charlie's, the most clublike and most expensive speakeasy in New York, a wood-paneled cave of jovial shouts and hearty defiance of the Volstead Act, which opened at lunch and didn't close until dawn. It was the daily hangout for a merry mix of Ivy League undergraduates, sports writers and stockbrokers and it roared with the complex, excited noise that can only be made by a lot of happy people drinking, eating, laughing and flirting in an overcrowded room.

They were quickly shown to a table and Darcy ordered champagne, conferring a moment with the waiter. Maggy, still longing to return to the limousine, sat restlessly, until the waiter poured the wine.

"Isn't that a waste?" she asked. "We can't drink the whole bottle—just look at this list—the English butler, the policeman's hat . . . what time is it?" Her competitive spirit had begun to rise. This was hardly an appropriate moment in which to sit around lazily and sip bootleg booze, no matter how authentically French it was.

Darcy gave her a complacent, rather too lofty look. "I've just arranged to rent our waiter's jacket. I'll phone home and tell my butler to meet us on Lally's sidewalk with my copy of Hemingway—Clarkson used to work for the Duke of Sutherland—and we can pick up that yellow glove you said you had on the way back."

"Is that your idea of sportsmanship?" Maggy frowned. This man was draining all the fun out of it, with his smugness and his showing off.

"I call it basic wisdom. We didn't take a blood oath to win—just to play. Anyway, aren't you bored stiff by scavenger hunts?"

"Most certainly not! I've never been on one before. What gives you the right to turn this evening into drinks for two?" she snapped. How she hated them, men who thought they could dominate women.

He didn't answer but drank his wine and looked intently into the world of her angry, challenging green eyes. He could feel himself respond to her quality, one which seemed to him to be untamed in the deepest sense but yet well under control. He didn't know anything about her, but she could never be anonymous.

"Where did Lally discover you?" he asked. "And why have we never met before?"

"I work at Alberto Bianchi's," she said curtly.

"What do you do there?" So she was another one of those women who never worked a day in their lives before, who had accepted a "funny little job" to show how undaunted they were by the Depression.

"I model dresses . . . other women buy them."

"I rather tend to doubt that."

"It's quite true."

"You mean you're a *genuine* victim of the Crash, you work for a *living?*"

"For fifty dollars a week. I do very well, as it happens."

"Tell me everything," he invited, confident that she'd like nothing more. What woman didn't?

"Everything? You're *damned* rude, do you know that? Why should I tell you anything at all? I don't even think I caught your name, whatever it may be. You've ruined my scavenger hunt and now you're being utterly presumptuous. What's more, you didn't even ask me if I like champagne before you ordered it."

"You're absolutely right," he said, taken aback. "I apologize profoundly. Would you like something else to drink?"

"This is quite enough, thank you," Maggy said. She looked around her, paying him no further attention.

"Mrs. Lunel, I'm Jason Darcy and I'm twenty-nine years old and I was born in Hartford, Connecticut, of a respectable family. I've never been to jail, I don't cheat at poker, I love animals, my mother speaks highly of me, and I usually have better manners than I've led you to believe."

"Is that quite 'everything'?" Maggy asked, permitting him a small smile.

I'm a publisher, *Mode, Women's Journal* and *City and Country Life.*"

"*Tiens, tiens*, three magazines for just one man," she said. "Just what precisely does a publisher do? Besides being obnoxiously inquisitive with unknown ladies?"

"Precisely? I'm the boss."

"What an unilluminating explanation. Who do you boss and why do you boss? Be more exact, if you please."

He looked at her, catching her scarcely hidden mockery.

"Couldn't you be a little more impressed?"

"Should I be? I have no idea just what a publisher does."

"I invented the magazines, I decided how they should look, I targeted in on my public, I established the standards, the formats. The editors report to me, and so do the business departments and everybody who physically produces the magazines."

"Is that a publishing empire?" Maggy asked. "Like the publishing empire of Mr. Hearst, for example?"

"Mine's more like a kingdom than an empire," Darcy admitted.

"How modest of you, Mr. Darcy."

"You don't feel any particular delight at drinking champagne with a fairly important publisher?"

"I'm far too old and too wise for astonished delight, Mr. Darcy."

"Darcy."

"Darcy. What little I've seen of the world has left me blasé, jaded, spoiled and, worst of all, hungry."

"So soon after dinner?"

"Dinner is a meal that invariably leaves me hungry."

"How about some chicken hash? It's a specialty here."

"Leftovers, how childishly barbarian." Maggy hadn't felt so impulsive, so to-hell-with-it-all, so intoxicatingly, splendidly silly since she had arrived in the United States. Ah, but it was droll to make an utter fool of a man again, she thought. Men had been invented to become fools—that was *all* they were good for, that and no more. Paula had said so and Paula had been right.

Jason Darcy couldn't stop looking at Maggy. She shot off more flames than a black opal, with those golden-greeny eyes and her orange hair, shining smooth over the lovely shape of her skull, breaking into deep waves just under her chin—she had the flushed brilliance of a child running loose in the first snow of winter. Who the hell *was* Maggy Lunel? Not a chorus girl or a society woman. And yet he was sure he knew all of the most beautiful women of the city.

"I've got it! You're a new Powers girl."

"And what might that be?" Maggy asked curiously. Recently she'd heard the phrase flung about more and more but she'd never had the time or interest to ask about this odd Americanism.

"A photographic model, with the John Robert Powers agency—come on, stop looking as if you didn't know."

"Truly, I'm not involved in that world. I merely model copies of Paris originals and help to run society fashion shows. The House of Bianchi has never used a Powers girl."

"Well, it's just a question of time before you do because Powers is getting bigger all the time. He's been in business for a couple of years, ever since the ad agencies and magazines all started using photographs instead of drawings."

"And what do these Powers girls make when they work?"

"As I remember they started at five dollars an hour in the first days but now the top girls are getting fifteen."

"Fifteen an hour! That's a fortune!" Maggy was awed.

"Damn right, especially if a girl works a lot and they're all getting busier and busier in spite of the Depression. Today either a business has to advertise or it goes under, and nothing sells a product like a pretty girl."

"And Mr. John Robert Powers, what does he earn?"

"Ten percent of whatever his models make."

"And how many models does he have working for him?" she persisted.

"I'm not sure—I'd imagine about a hundred, including the men and the kids. If you're really only a fifty-dollar-a-week dress model, you should be working for him."

"Thank you," Maggy said absently.

Jason Darcy was still far from convinced that Maggy Lunel was what she said she was, not because anything she'd told him was impossible but because there was something about her that was so unique in his own experience that it made him suspicious.

Maggy Lunel was not behaving normally. There was nothing in her manner, in her eyes or her words that indicated that she was trying to attract him, and this, to Darcy, was incredible. He knew, as well—or better—than anyone else that he was one of the most eligible men in the United States. He had everything: first of all, at only twenty-nine, he had accumulated enough influence to make him eligible if he'd been a gnome. In addition he was unattached and rich, which would have made him eligible if he'd been a werewolf. But he was neither gnome nor werewolf, he was a man who admitted, each time he looked in the mirror, that he was handsome, an accident of genetics to be sure but not to be despised.

Why then, *how* then, could this woman sit here drinking his champagne while she interrogated him about the Powers Agency as if he were a conduit of information and nothing more?

Perhaps she was in love? That was the only reasonable explanation. And yet she had come to the party alone. A fury to know more about Maggy stirred in him, as she seemed to engrave a pattern on the air with a gesture of her eloquent hands. "And where is this famous chicken hash?" she suddenly asked him. "And why is my glass empty? Shall we go dancing?" She was matter-of-fact, not provocative, he noted with fresh wonderment, but her vividness was a triumph.

"What about Lally's scavenger hunt?"

"But it's a ridiculous and boring American custom—isn't that what you think?"

"Where would you like to go? The St. Regis Roof, the Embassy, the Cotton Club?"

"Le Jockey," Maggy murmured.

"The Jockey?" he said puzzled.

"Did I say that? Never mind it's been closed for years. Let's go on up to Harlem."

Adrien Avigdor was sure of his ground. Since Julien Mistral had gone to live in Félice five years ago, since that improbable marriage to Kate Browning, the man had had three sell-out, one-man shows in Paris, each one a greater triumph than the one of the year before.

Now, in the spring of 1931, it was time for him to show in New York. His production of paintings was small, or, to be precise, he painted a great deal and showed very little. Mistral exercised to the full the legal position possessed by every French artist to obtain, by writing a simple phrase on the back of a painting—*ne pas à vendre*—the right to withhold from sale any canvas or even to prohibit the exhibition of the canvas, although he was under contract to Avigdor for all he agreed to actually sell.

Each year, four months before the planned exhibition, Avigdor drove down to Provence and spent a draining, difficult week living at *La Tourrello* and arguing with Mistral about his new work. Once in 1928, Mistral had not been satisfied with a single painting and there had been no show in the autumn of that year, Avigdor remembered gloomily. Mistral destroyed the work he didn't like in an annual bonfire, capering around and feeding canvas after canvas into the flames like a devil out of Hieronymus Bosch, a man who heartlessly, gleefully, invited Avigdor to watch as hundreds of thousands of francs of marvelous painting turned into oily smoke.

"That's in case I should fall down dead, Adrien, and you got your hands on stuff I never meant anybody to see—who would make sure that you wouldn't sell them, eh?" He was as suspicious as the peasants he lived among and trusted no one except Kate. And he trusted her only so far. Obviously not far enough to believe that she would obey the prohibitions he scrawled in large letters on the backs of hundreds of paintings.

It was agony for Avigdor to watch Mistral's mountainous bonfires but there was a miserable measure of satisfaction to be derived from the fact that while he never had any extra Mistrals left to sell when an exhibition was over, no other dealer in Paris ever had so much as a single one. As far as Avigdor knew, no collector who had ever bought a Mistral had resold it. Mistral himself always retained his favorites.

The man's prices had mounted far beyond anything Adrien had planned because of the scarcity of his available work. But, after all, Avigdor mused, there were only thirty-six Vermeers in existence, so perhaps Mistral knew what he was doing?

In any case, artists should not be allowed to marry rich women, it gave them too much freedom. No matter, Mistral had finally agreed to a New York show of new work and of selections from his output since 1926. Various American collectors were lending canvases so the show would be a large one. Many art critics from American newspapers and magazines were already in busy contact with Avigdor. *Vanity Fair* had commissioned a long article on him and Man Ray had gone to Félice to photograph Mistral in his studio. Mark Nathen, whose gallery was one of the best in New York, was planning a *vernissage* that would attract all of artistic and social New York. The show would be one of the major events of the spring of 1931 since everybody in the small, inbred world of art was extraordinarily curious to see the work of this man, who lived like a hermit stuck away in the Lubéron, indifferent to his gathering fame, his growing legend.

"Before dinner I thought we might drop into the opening of the new show at Nathen's," Darcy proposed to Maggy on the telephone.

"What show?" she asked idly. She had no time to keep up with the wide-ranging cultural life of the city.

"Mistral—the French painter—you must have heard of him."

She held the telephone in one hand, and with the other she steadied herself against the mantelpiece, feeling the cruel beat of her heart knock against her breasts. The shock of Mistral's name, spoken so unexpectedly, had made her mind a blank of ice. Her stomach contracted in fear. Why fear? she wondered. Automatically she said, "Yes, I know who he is, but I don't feel up to going out tonight."

"Maggy, what's the matter?"

"I'm just so tired I can't move, too tired to dress . . . I think I'm catching cold."

"I'm very, very disappointed," he said gravely.

"I am too."

In the three weeks since he had met Maggy, Darcy had asked her out far more frequently than she had been willing to go. Each time he saw her he grew increasingly baffled by her deep reserve, her gentle but obstinate refusal to speak of herself. She seemed to have told him all she was ever going to tell him on the night of the scavenger hunt. She always insisted on meeting him at a speakeasy or a restaurant. She never offered him any hospitality, and when he left her at the elevator of her apartment house—for she didn't ask him to come up—Maggy shook hands briskly, not even coming close enough for him to risk a brief kiss.

In his limousine, she sat far away from him, her hands folded tightly in her lap, she danced with a tension in her body that imposed a delicate but insistent formality that turned a song like "The Night Was Made for Love" into a satire. Was she frigid, was she frightened, was she suffering from some damn French neurosis he hadn't heard of? Did it have something to do with her being a widow?

Darcy thought about her in obsessive curiosity, for her widowhood and the existence of Teddy were two of the few details of her life that she had let escape.

He examined the little he knew about her with as much fascination as if it were a piece of a map that would lead to buried treasure, but she remained tart, aloof, serenely and mysteriously unknowable. What was worse, damn it to hell, was that she was as untouchable as a princess in a tower. Every now and then, as he talked to her, he had the almost unendurable suspicion that something he had said was making her go through a polite agony of suppressed laughter, but he'd never actually caught her at it. What colossal nerve she had!

"Look, I'll call you tomorrow, but take care of yourself, don't get sick. Will you go to bed early?" he asked anxiously.

"Yes," she agreed tonelessly, "I will, I promise."

As Jason Darcy wandered disconsolately into the Nathen Gallery he found he was reassuring himself that, at the very minimum, Maggy Lunel must *like* him. Darcy, sought after, hard-to-get, powerful, proud Darcy, started to review his virtues to balance the fact that he had never even been allowed to come close to her lips. Then quickly, like a man touching his tie to make sure that it's properly centered, he told himself how preposterous he was, piling one worldly asset on top of another, listing his magazines, his well-staffed household, his Harvard summa cum laude, his youth, his health, his desk piled high with invitations and solicitations from every part of the worlds that were touched by his publications, as if to prove that he had enough value to be allowed into the hidden garden of Maggy Lunel's private, guarded world.

He surveyed the crowd in the Nathen Gallery, surprised at the broad cross section of New York he saw there. He knew a great many of the people and, as he listened to the moneyed hum of conversation he thought that it sounded more like the Metropolitan Opera at intermission than an artistic event. He supposed that the unusual number of society women he recognized and greeted were there because the show had been organized as a benefit for the Children's Hospital; it was rare to find the Whitneys, the Ochses, the Kilkullens, the Gimbels, the Jays, the Rutherfords and the Vanderbilts all mixed up with the most famous faces of Greenwich Village and Southampton.

Then as Darcy began to look at the pictures, his mild interest at the composition of the crowd vanished in an instant. He had the sudden sensation of being picked up by a pair of great strong hands and set down under a new horizon. Each painting was like a step along a pathway into another world, an alternate world, a better world. Reasoning, deliberation, logic, time, and space itself all dissolved into an unqualified radiance, a splendor of paint that had the texture of a living, breathing substance.

And yet, Darcy asked himself, stunned, what has the man chosen to paint after all? A café table and chairs under an orange awning, a stand of poplars quivering in the heat, a market basket filled with bread, radishes and a bunch of dahlias, a woman bending down in a garden in the morning—the simplest of subject matter, nothing that had not been painted by a thousand painters before Mistral.

Yet the emotion of the artist as he looked at his subjects had so merged with the images he put on canvas that a transparency was created, through which a bridge was flung from the world in which Mistral *felt* to the world in which the spectator *lived*, so that for an essential moment, Darcy existed with Mistral's eyes, Darcy entered into Mistral's vision.

Wondering, amazed, buoyant with the blooming of his senses, feeling as if he had left New York and walked into open, sunlit, cloud-dappled country, Darcy went through the big gallery not noticing, as he entered the far room, that it was unusually crowded and filled with buzzing conversation.

Maggy! He shivered violently, the hair rose on his neck as he confronted the big canvases of Maggy on every wall, naked and so utterly abandoned as she offered the glory of her flesh, exposed, shameless, happier than he had ever dreamed she could be, available to every eye, Maggy, more erotic, more violently and generously sensual than any woman he had ever seen in paint or in the flesh.

Lust, palpable as smoke, a pungent, hungry, raw lust quivered on the canvases of Maggy with her legs sprawled wide apart lying on an unmade bed, one arm dangling to the floor; Maggy with wet hair washing between her legs with a soapy cloth; Maggy thrown down on a pile of green cushions, laughing, her nipples tender and inflamed, her pubic hair caught in a shaft of light so that each red filament was alive and separate.

As Darcy stood immobile, frozen, unable to look away from the pictures, he caught words rising from the talk in the room. There was a delighted, high-pitched, scarcely repressed excitement in the babble that greets any out-and-out scandal.

"Bianchi's model, my dear, that French girl . . . mistress . . . Perry Kilkullen, of course . . . what *skin* . . . I saw them together in Maxim's . . . did you say Bianchi?. . . . widow, my foot . . . incredible breasts . . . didn't they have a child? . . . met her at Lally's, yes, I'm sure . . . a child surely . . . how the hospital committee let this pass I'll never . . . the Kilkullens will . . . shocking . . . don't be so provincial . . . shocking . . . painted when, you say? . . . Bianchi's model . . . poor Mary Jane . . . Perry's *what?*"

Why the hell didn't he paint them in sperm? Darcy thought to himself, why not just fuck the canvas? He shook with uncontrolled laughter. Life had never attacked him so unexpectedly. That lily maid, that contained and elusive princess—oh, how beautifully she had outfoxed him! What a formidable woman she was! His admiration for Maggy swelled within him like a great chuckle as he watched the faces of all the men in the room, their eyes greedily roving the canvases—he'd bet that half of them were trying to control stiffening cocks—he knew he was. Oh, Maggy, darling Maggy, so you "had heard of Mistral" had you—and how many times did he stop painting to fuck you? How, in fact, was he able to pay any attention to his paint and brushes? The man must have had the concentration of a diamond cutter to get any work done at all under the circumstances—oh, Maggy, no woman has ever surprised me like this—I feel a virgin fifteen again. *Bravo!*

By noon of the next day Maggy was without a job. She didn't blame Bianchi; her usefulness to him was clearly over. He'd received a dozen outraged phone calls before he'd asked to see her and if none of them had actually used the term "scarlet woman" it was only because they knew it was old-fashioned. Obviously Maggy couldn't possibly organize another society fashion show and as for normal modeling for the house, her notoriety would get in the way of the dresses. People would come to see the cause of the scandal but they wouldn't dream of ordering the garments she wore. Just by putting a dress on, she would invalidate it.

As he said goodbye to Maggy, with a check for two weeks' salary, Alberto Bianchi felt two emotions; sorrow at losing this valuable model and a burning impatience to run up to the Nathen Gallery to see for himself what Maggy looked like stark naked—God knows, he'd wasted enough time wondering.

Darcy tried to reach Maggy at Bianchi's as soon as he left the Nathen Gallery, without success. She'd gone to bed, Nanny Butterfield had told him. He phoned her at home repeatedly but Maggy refused to take any calls, not even from Lally, who also had called several times. She asked Nanny Butterfield to answer the phone and say that she was out of town and wouldn't be back for a while.

When he couldn't reach Maggy by phone Darcy went to her apartment but the doorman had firm orders to allow no one upstairs but deliveries. He sent flowers twice a day with notes begging her to call him at the office or at home, but she did neither. He stood impatiently on the street outside of her apartment house for hours, but she never emerged. He did everything but disguise himself as a delivery boy. He could hardly believe his own behavior, yet he couldn't stay put.

Four days after the opening of Mistral's exhibition Darcy telephoned once more in the late afternoon, hoping that by now she might be ready to come out of her isolation. Maggy was in her bathroom when the phone rang, Nanny Butterfield was making Teddy's supper, and Teddy herself dared to answer the phone, something she was forbidden to do.

She was three, a prime age for little girls, one of their peak years. Teddy had already grown accustomed to the exclamations of strangers in the park who saw her beauty for the first time, she had already learned that there were certain laws that she could break without being reprimanded just because of how she looked. However, these laws still applied at home; Nanny and Maggy tried to be strict with her because they were joined in a conviction that it would be fatally easy to spoil her. A ringing phone was already an object of greedy veneration for Teddy. She picked it up with guilty delight and said a muffled hello.

"Who is this?" Darcy asked, thinking he had the wrong number.

"Teddy Lunel. Who are you?"

"A friend of your mother's. Hello, Teddy."

"Hello, hello, hello." She giggled and arched her neck. "I have new red shoes."

"Teddy, is your mother there?"

"Yes, but don't you want to talk to me? What's your name?"

"Darcy."

"Hello, Darcy, hello, Darcy. How old are you?"

"Hello, Teddy—I'm—oh, never mind—is your mother there?"

"In the bathroom . . . no, here she is . . . Mommy, telephone for you."

Hastily Teddy held out the phone to Maggy, who looked around wildly for Nanny Butterfield, almost replaced the receiver, but finally snapped her fingers in anger and answered curtly, "Yes?"

"Maggy, thank goodness, I thought you'd never come out of hiding."

"I'm not hiding!" she said furiously.

"Hibernating then. Your daughter sounds charming, much nicer than you. How about dinner tonight?"

"Absolutely not. I'm not going out."

"But you're the toast of New York."

"Darcy, you were never malicious before."

"I'm telling you the truth. The gallery is mobbed with people who've heard how luscious you are. You're considered the beauty of the decade."

"A *succès de scandale*—do you think I want that?"

"This is New York, Maggy, any success is a success, nobody really cares what it's based on as long as they talk about you," he said, trying hard to make her feel better in the only way he knew how.

"If that were so, I'd still have a job," Maggy answered, bruised by his practicality. Didn't he understand how embarrassed, how humiliated she was?

"That's different, Bianchi has to mollify his clients, but they aren't everybody in town . . . oh, they think they are, but they really don't count except in their own world."

"Nevertheless, Darcy, I earned a living in that world, such as it was."

"Maggy, remember what I thought about your being a Powers girl . . . why don't you go see him?"

"No!" Maggy exclaimed sharply. "I'll *never* model again, not for any reason. I've been a painters' model and a fashion model—I was seventeen when I started and now I'm twenty-three and out of work—and I've never made more than fifty dollars a week—no, thank you, that's not for me, it hasn't done much for me, has it? On the other hand . . . well . . . I suppose it's silly of me . . ." She stopped, unwilling to continue.

"Tell me, Maggy, come on."

"It's a foolish idea. No, no—perhaps not absolutely, totally foolish . . . do you remember telling me that Powers had a hundred models working for him and that he took ten percent of what they made?"

"Sure I do. What about it?"

"I'm used to telling models what to do and how to do it. At Bianchi's, all the girls came to me for advice—it's something I seem to know in my nerve endings. I haven't any idea what photographers require of a girl but it can't be so different from what painters expect, so, well . . . I thought I might . . . try . . . to open an agency myself!" she finished on a burst of bravado.

"*Compete* with John Robert Powers?" he asked doubtfully.

"And why not? Just what does some man do that I could not do? And perhaps better? He's only another kind of dealer and I've known dozens—believe me, there's no magic to them." She rushed on, spurred on by his reaction of doubt. "As it happens, Darcy, I have a little capital to risk."

"Maggy, you're bloody marvelous! Do you want some business from *Mode* and *Women's Journal* and *City and Country Life?*"

"Of course I do! Oh, Darcy, it *could* happen, it could really happen, couldn't it?"

"*It's already happened!*" How he'd missed that laugh of hers! It made the world dance. "Maggy, come out with me tonight and celebrate—champagne to baptize the new agency?"

"On one condition—you must allow me to pay."

"Why, for God's sake?"

"The Lunel Agency wishes to offer champagne to its first customer."

Oh, shit, he thought, *shit!* He realized too late, far, far too late, that he *adored* this impossible woman whom he'd as good as started in her own business. "You're right, Maggy," Darcy said glumly, "you don't have much to learn after all."

14

Maggy's Girls, as everyone called the Lunel Agency models, at first were only a choice handful, but soon their ranks grew to many dozens; exquisite girls, butterfly girls who were so much more glamorous, so clearly more sophisticated than their only rivals, Powers's often corn-fed "Long-Stemmed American Beauties."

Maggy's Girls pranced through the thirties as if there were no Great Depression. Wearing corsages of big lavender orchids pinned to their wide-skirted strapless ball gowns, they banished reality as they danced at the Stork Club and at El Morocco, escorted by at least two men on each arm. They embodied escape for millions of Americans who crowded the movie theaters to see films about rich people in whose lives all telephones were white. Like *Vogue*'s earnest report that the silly new hats have "killed discussion of the Stock Exchange and the rise of Mr. Hitler," Maggy's Girls filled the public's avid need to have fun, even if it was only vicariously. A *New York Daily News* poll asked women if they would rather be a movie star, a debutante or one of the Lunel models and 42 percent decided they would prefer to work for Maggy.

While Maggy prospered in New York, Julien Mistral painted in a fever of energy in Félice. He had entered into his "Middle Period" which was to last for the next twenty years. No longer, as he had in the twenties, did he paint at random the scenes or objects that caught his eye. Now he devoted himself, for two or three years at a time, to one subject, and out of this concentration, out of the thousands of studies and work sketches he made and eventually destroyed, would emerge a series of paintings, as few as a dozen, as many as thirty-five.

Défense d'Afficher, his series of paintings of walls covered with layer upon layer of peeling posters, was the first of these historic series. Next came *Vendredi Matin*, images of the bounty of the weekly outdoor market that took place in Apt. *Stella Artois*, the series that was named after Mistral's favorite brand of beer, illuminated as it had never been before, the intense inner life of the men of the village as they passed their evenings in the café of Félice, drinking, gambling, talking. *Jours de Fête*, the most important of the Middle Period series, was inspired by the celebrations that took place in each village of the Lubéron on the day of its patron saint, a day of mountains of cotton candy and dizzy children riding wooden horses, of processions and fireworks, of wild overexcitement and budding country passions.

Mistral spent every day in his studio from breakfast till dinner. Cold meat, bread and a bottle of wine were brought to him on a tray, and he devoured everything standing up in front of a canvas, unaware of what he was tasting. Kate took the opportunity given her by her husband's abdication of interest in anything but his work, to take more and more control of his business life. She handled all the contracts with Avigdor, she carried on the correspondence with the galleries in many foreign countries who wanted to show Mistral's work, and it was she who made the decisions about the management of the farm.

Once a year, at the time of the harvest, Mistral abandoned his studio and worked in his fields with his men, but otherwise he lived in a world entirely his own. He had no time for newspapers. The changing political tides in Europe were no more his concern than the train of cock feathers on the latest Paris evening gown. As for the boules tournament in Félice, yes, that still meant something to him, but the burning of the Reichstag was an event utterly without interest. If he found that he was down to his tenth tube of raw umber he raged, but the catastrophe of the Dust Bowl, when Mistral heard about it from the farmers in the café, didn't touch him enough to cause him to mutter a word of commiseration. He had as little interest in the Italian aggression in Ethiopia as he did in "Amos n' Andy."

Julien Mistral was at the height of his powers, at peace with himself at last, and his natural selfishness was only reinforced by the knowledge that never had he painted as well. How could anything that was happening in the world have the slightest importance, when he woke up each morning with an absolute need to stand in front of his easel burning strong inside every cell of his body? No human fate, no current of history had the power to affect him so long as he knew that nothing could stop him from spending the day in his studio.

Kate Mistral, on the other hand, never lost touch with life beyond Félice. She went to Paris several times a year to keep in touch with the art world and buy clothes, for live in the country as she might, she continued to be well dressed at all times. She worked closely with Avigdor on Mistral's shows, as she had on his first one, and she represented her husband at the *vernissages* he always refused to attend. Occasionally she left him alone for a month at a time and returned to New York to visit her family. He scarcely noticed these absences.

In the aftermath of the Crash, Kate was no longer rich. In hindsight, she had been lucky to use so much of her own capital on buying the domain of *La Tourrello.* Although she had fulfilled the pledge she had made to win Mistral and given him the title to the land as her dowry, it had been an excellent investment. Her husband had absolutely no idea of how rich they were growing. The many fertile hectares that surrounded the *mas* were crowded and orderly and sweet with fruits and vegetables destined for the wholesalers of Apt. They had fine pigs, flocks of chickens and ducks, a few horses, the latest in farm machinery and many hands to cultivate the crops. Whenever new, adjoining land came on the market, Kate snapped it up. The farm itself could support them in comfort, she thought with satisfaction, even as she counted and recounted the ever-growing sums from the sale of paintings that she deposited in the bank in Avignon.

Although the bank account was, of course, in Mistral's name, Kate's financial expertise compensated in many ways for the lack of close communion that she was dimly aware of at the heart of her life with Mistral. He rarely spoke to her of his work, he never asked to paint her because of what he explained was a "matte" finish to her skin that prevented the light from entering into it, and he almost never invited her to visit the studio. However, Kate had become a famous hostess. The *mas* was superbly comfortable and everyone she or Mistral had ever known in Paris was eventually invited to spend long weekends. She was house-proud and gloried in showing off *La Tourrello.*

During those periods of the year when the boules players were gathered outside behind the café, Mistral almost always joined them after he finished painting, coming home for dinner only when the last game was over. In the winter, when it was too cold for boules, he worked all day and went to bed early, like an exhausted farmer. Yet she possessed his body, that ever-hungry massively passionate body and the rough direct greed with which he frequently turned to her and satisfied himself was always enough to bring her to a climax, for Kate existed in a state of ready arousal caused by living within the field of sensuality that enveloped her whenever she thought of her husband. All he had to do was murmur "Patience, Kate, patience," and she was ready for him.

She was as addicted to Julien Mistral as she had ever been, Kate realized, as she sat downstairs alone by the great fireplace after he had gone to bed. She regretted nothing she had given up of the worldly life she had led before she met him. What little there was of Julien Mistral that did not belong to his work was, she felt certain, entirely hers. She smiled into the embers, safe within the thick walls of *La Tourrello* as the leaves of autumn flew outside and a low, red moon rose above the frosty, bare fields, the stripped vines.

Kate made as little as she could of the Spanish Civil War in 1936—"Spaniards against Spaniards," she said, guarding her peace of mind, for she, unlike Julien, read the newspapers. On September 29, 1938, the Munich agreement was signed and millions of French, English, and Germans as well, told themselves, in relief, that there would be no war.

In the summer of 1939, Kate, who hadn't seen her family in two years, went to New York for a visit. The city of her birth was particularly gay because of the World's Fair with its theme of the "World of Tomorrow."

Hitler had occupied Czechoslovakia two months earlier but every day twenty-eight thousand people, to whom this distant event had no particular significance, waited on line to visit the "Futurama" where they were treated to General Motors's wonderfully convincing version of the year 1960. It was to be an era in which diesel automobiles costing two hundred dollars each and shaped like raindrops, would race on accident-free highways; there would be a cure for cancer; Federal laws would protect every forest, lake and valley; everybody would have two-month vacations each year and women would possess perfect skin at the age of seventy-five.

"Kate, you absolutely must come back home," said Maxwell Woodson Browning, Kate's favorite uncle, who had been a career diplomat before his retirement. "It's dangerous to stay in Europe."

"Uncle Max, why are you so pessimistic? What about the Munich Pact? Surely Hitler has what he wants? And he couldn't be so foolish as to try anything against France—we have the Maginot Line, and Hitler's soldiers are nothing but a poor, ill-equipped rabble—everyone knows that. The Germans haven't got arms, even their uniforms aren't made out of real wool."

"Propaganda! Don't believe what you hear."

"How silly! Why would French newspapers and radio be full of propaganda? Aren't they free to print whatever they believe?"

"Kate, the situation is dreadfully serious. I'm in contact with a number of men who believe as I do that it is only a question of time before Hitler will try to invade the rest of Europe. You could easily be trapped over there during a war."

"But, Uncle Max, nobody wants a war, *nobody* wants to fight again, aren't you being an alarmist?"

"Kate, you've turned into a fool!" At such words from a man whom she had always admired and respected, Kate Mistral began to pay attention to what he was trying to tell her. By the end of the evening she was so convinced that she immediately wrote Julien to come to the United States.

When Mistral received this first letter he put it aside without rereading it. Such aberration was not worth the postage she had put on the letter. He was busy developing a concept for a new series of paintings of olive groves. At such a time he became ferociously protective of his mental processes. Nothing must intrude on that slow, steady fermentation. Her second and third letters, increasingly shrill, finally forced him to reply and he wrote angrily and briefly that no one in the village believed that there would be a war. Hitler didn't have the stomach to face the French Army. Weren't Kate's relatives aware that the English had fixed things up with surprisingly good sense for once in their history?

Now Kate took matters into her own hands and started to search north of Danbury for the kind of farm on which Mistral could be happy. She was sure that as events grew more ominous, he would see that she was right, as she had been throughout their life together. Knowing Julien she understood that it was crucial to find a comfortable studio before she could expect him to move. But then he would follow her, as he always had, reluctant to the last. She would return to Félice to drag him back with her as soon as a studio was organized.

On the first of September 1939, Germany invaded Poland, and, two days later, England and France, bound by treaty to defend the Poles, reluctantly declared war on Germany.

There was still time for Julien Mistral to get out of France if he had really wanted to, and thousands of Frenchmen did, but now he had begun painting in earnest the series that would be called *Les Oliviers*. The light had turned that limpid, deep golden color that meant that the summer was over, the wind, that rough, icy exhilarating mistral that he loved, had blown all the glare away from the groves of olive trees and he was plunged in ruthless, blind concentration. Mistral could no more pick up and move away from Félice than if he had been a woman in the last stages of childbirth.

All winter long in his studio, Mistral painted the olives of the summer, those strange mythic trees, hermaphrodites, with their ancient, masculine trunks, twisted, brutal, almost ugly, above which sprang feminine branches and leaves, silver and slender as they joined in a constant dialogue with the sun.

When Mistral visited Félice he found the mood in the café calm. After the defeat of Poland there had been no further aggression on either side and everyone agreed that there must certainly be a way short of actually fighting to get out of this *drôle de guerre* that the Germans themselves called the *Sitzkrieg*. But while Mistral was thinking of nothing but his olive trees, the Germans, refreshed and rested, overran Europe. On the seventeenth of June 1940, Pétain, the old marshal of the French Army, now premier of France, asked for an armistice or a truce, or a surrender, or a cease-fire, depending on each man's political convictions. The trap was closed.

Why now, Mistral raged violently, cursing his evil luck. *Why now*, when I have so much to do! *Why now*, when I haven't a second to spare, *why now*, when I'm painting as never before, *why now*, this stinking, foul *interruption?* What if I can't get any more supplies from Paris? There still isn't a decent paint store in Avignon. And what the hell am I supposed to do about new canvases?

He rampaged about his studio, stacking up empty canvases and grimly taking count of how few remained. There had been no shipments from Paris for months. He, like all painters, hoarded paint, but who could tell when he'd start to need more? And if that wasn't bad enough, if that wasn't enough damnable, ill-begotten trouble for him to worry about, there was the matter of the *mas*. Ever since Kate had gone on her trip to New York the farm had deteriorated steadily.

Jean Pollison, the young farmer Kate had engaged before their marriage to work the land, had always hired many additional men to help him during the time of heavy work, in the spring and in the fall, but since last spring there had been no men to hire; either they had been drafted and were now in German prison camps, or they were needed on their own farms to replace other men who had left for the army. Pollison had done his best by himself, assisted by the farm machinery Kate had bought which the other farmers of the region so envied, but now he had come to Mistral—actually *broke into his work*, Mistral thought incredulously—and told him that he feared a shortage of petrol to run the cultivators. The new government in Vichy was beginning to ration everything.

"*Merde*, Pollison! Is that my affair?" he roared.

"I'm sorry, Monsieur Mistral, but I thought I must tell you, since Madame is not here."

"Pollison, do whatever you can, but *never* bother me in my studio again, you understand?"

"But Monsieur Mistral . . ."

"Pollison," he shouted, "enough! Figure it out yourself, that's what you're here for."

As Jean Pollison hastily retreated from the studio he thought to himself that no matter how Monsieur Mistral played at being a part of the life of the village, no matter that he was the boules champion of the region, no matter how many rounds of drinks he bought for everyone at the café, he was still a stranger from Paris, and nothing would ever change that.

Five days after the cease-fire of June 17, Marte Pollison knocked timidly at the door of Mistral's studio late one afternoon. Normally she just left his lunch tray outside the studio, but today her errand was so important that it overcame her terror of angering him.

"What is it?" he barked.

"Monsieur Mistral, I must speak to you."

"Come in, damn it! What the hell is it?"

"People have arrived in a car filled with baggage asking to spend the night. It's Monsieur and Madame Behrman with their three children. I told them to wait outside until I spoke to you. They're driving to the border, trying to get into Spain. He said it's no longer safe for Jews to stay in France."

Mistral punched one big fist into the palm of his other hand in rage. Charles Behrman, and his wife, Toupette, were old friends. He had known Behrman, a sculptor, since the days of Montparnasse. They had rented the studio next to his on the boulevard Arago and often fed Mistral when he was broke. But now they had three small children, and when Kate had invited them down for a weekend several years before, Mistral found the children annoyingly boisterous. Mistral thought quickly. It was intolerable, Behrman's thinking that he could just drop in with his whole irritating family, expecting food and lodging. And who knew how long they might stay once they were comfortable? If he chose to chase off to Spain because he was a Jew, that was his own problem. The war, after all, was over, the cease-fire established all over France.

"Did you tell him I was here?" he asked Marte Pollison.

"Not exactly, just that I would have to ask you before I let them in."

"Go back and tell them you can't find me, that I've gone out and you don't know when I'll be back. Tell them that you have no authority to allow them to spend the night without my permission. *Get rid of them one way or another.* You didn't let them inside the gate?"

"No, it was closed."

"Good. Make sure that they drive off, keep a good eye on them until they've gone beyond the oak forest."

"Yes, Monsieur Mistral."

The day after the Behrmans had been turned away from *La Tourrello*, Mistral went up to the café in Félice and bought a round of *pastis* for his friends. He listened with unusual care to the words of the men at the bar. Genuine ill feeling and bitterness had begun to divide them for the first time since he had met them. Men who had enjoyed good-natured, long-running, political arguments for years now had formed into two angry camps, those who thought Pétain's cease-fire had saved France and those who thought he was a traitor.

There was only one subject on which everyone seemed to agree, the infuriating invasion of the countryside by the blasted northerners, people who had escaped from the Occupied Zone into the South before the line of demarkation had closed, and those others, amazing in their numbers, who were still managing to filter through the line illegally. The strangers were everywhere, ill prepared, often in panic, desperate for unobtainable food and petrol, swamping the local authorities with their presence, a pest and a plague on villages and farms. Resentment was high against these hordes who couldn't stay peacefully where they belonged.

Mistral returned home thoughtfully. He knew too many people in Paris. He knew many too many Jews. Because of Kate and her constant hospitality, her years of exhibiting their contentment at the *mas*, too many friends had learned the road to *La Tourrello*. They knew how many extra bedrooms it had, how rich its fields were, how self-sufficient the property had become. There were bound to be many more unexpected visitors like the Behrmans and there was no way to know when they would arrive, or in what condition of need.

He called Marte and Jean Pollison together in the kitchen.

"Pollison," he said to the man, "I want you to build a high fence where the road to the *mas* branches off from the road to Félice. I don't want anyone coming here and disturbing me at my work—the whole country is crawling with people who will try to take advantage, and I must *not* be bothered by them."

"Yes, Monsieur Mistral."

"And, Madame Pollison, I don't want any more interruptions of my work. If anyone should ignore the gate and come through the woods, don't come to let me know. Tell them that I haven't been here for a while and that you can't receive them. Don't open the gate for anyone, under any circumstances, use only the little postman's window. For no one. Do you understand?"

"Yes, Monsieur."

In the two years that followed, a number of old friends and acquaintances who had known Mistral for years were to make their dangerous, laborious, terrified way to *La Tourrello*, sometimes aided by Frenchmen and Frenchwomen who risked their lives to help them. All of them hoped for just a single night's shelter from those who hunted them so efficiently and mercilessly. Many of these despairing and hounded refugees disregarded the stout fence and managed to make their way to the *mas*, but the great wooden doors were always kept tightly locked and Marte Pollison responded grimly and negatively to the frantic ringing of the doorbell that sounded in the kitchen.

Most of those who came were Jews and only a few of them survived the war.

In June of 1942, as he followed his mother's small funeral procession, Adrien Avigdor realized that now he was free to leave Paris . . . if free was a word that could be used at all at such a time. He made sure that the yellow Star of David bordered in black, as big as the palm of his hand, with the word *Juif* inscribed on it in black letters, was clearly visible on his jacket. Women were being picked up all over Paris for carrying their handbags in a way that obscured the star; a man had been arrested only yesterday for wearing a star that wasn't sewn on tightly; last week an old lady who lived near him had been caught and taken away when she ventured outside to pick up her mail in her bathrobe, forgetting that it bore no star at all. Three stars for each Jew, the order of the twenty-ninth of May 1942 had decreed, and he had been made to give up tickets from his textile ration card for each of them.

He had not foreseen this, no one had foreseen this, when Avigdor had made his decision to stay in Paris. His mother was too crippled by arthritis to move, and together, during those hot weeks in June, two years earlier, they had watched the exodus from behind the closed shutters of Avigdor's apartment on the boulevard St.-Germain.

By night and by day they had watched the mute, terrified herd struggling southward. Most of Paris, entire villages to the north and the east, hundreds of miles of countryside, were abandoned to the oncoming enemy. The population had taken to the roads in whatever vehicles they possessed, only to leave them when they ran out of petrol and to continue on foot, carrying miserable children, umbrellas and Sunday hats, pushing baby carriages filled with pathetic, useless household treasures; farmers lugged chickens in cages and prodded cows bellowing with thirst.

"Go Adrien, go!" Madame Avigdor had begged him. "I'm an old woman. You mustn't stay to be with me . . . Madame Blanchet across the hall has offered to fetch me whatever I want. Leave now, Adrien, while you can!"

"*Maman*, don't be foolish. Just look at those people—bedraggled, hypnotized, a rabble—I assure you that I have no intention of joining them. How can I abandon my artists, how can I leave my gallery?"

He didn't tell her that he had no confidence in her neighbor's promises, that he could not possibly leave her alone to face the arrival of the Germans. And it was true enough that he was busily engaged in saving the hundreds of paintings that had been entrusted to him by many who had decided to flee. They represented the finest works of the artists for whom he was a dealer and it was up to him to make sure that they were securely secreted. Who knew what the Germans would do when they came? Hitler hated new art. Even old Picasso was a "degenerate" in Nazi eyes. Someone had to stay.

Now, two years later, he could only smile grimly at his bravado, yet he would make that same decision today. He had been able to make his mother's last years bearable and he was glad she had not lived long after the decree that made the wearing of the Star of David mandatory for every French Jew over the age of six.

She had lived long enough, however, to have had to be helped stand on her crippled legs to line up to register as a Jew at the Préfecture of Police; long enough to have seen the word *Juif* written in large letters on her identity card, long enough to have learned that all non-French Jews had been rounded up and sent away.

Thank God she had not lived to know, as he did, that now all French Jews, even those who had lived in France for many centuries, were forbidden to practice any profession, to work in any business, prohibited from using the telephone, from buying a stamp, from going to restaurants, cafés, libraries and films. Even from sitting in public squares. Nevertheless, we retain one right, Avigdor told himself in grim humor, we can buy food during one hour each day, from three to four o'clock—when most shops are closed.

The trains still ran from time to time and civilians traveled, but not without the *ausweis*, or German permit. As Avigdor thought over the possibilities open to him he realized that all over France millions of people were traveling to weddings, funerals and christenings, were visiting sick relatives or moving to another part of the country for their health or their business. Life, under the Germans, for most Frenchmen, continued under the meanest and most miserable of terms from the point of view of nourishment and heat and rationing and restrictions of every kind, but nevertheless they were allowed to *try* to survive.

Soutine, he knew, had sought refuge in Touraine, Max Jacob in St.-Benôit-sur-Loire, Braque was in l'Isle sur la Sorgue, his friend, the great art dealer Kahnweiller, lived in Limousin under the name of Kersaint, Picasso was still working busily in Paris and so were the collaborators, Vlaminck and Cocteau.

Avigdor's gallery had been confiscated and turned over, by order of the Germans, to a non-Jewish dealer who now did a lively trade with the enemy, selling the daubs of tenth-rate artists. During the last months Avigdor had sought information on the best way to escape from Paris, although that great source of all valuable gossip, Paula Deslandes, had died several months ago of a heart attack and La Pomme d'Or was closed for good.

From the earliest days of the Resistance Paula had been busy helping people who were in danger. "I've been in training for this all my life," she'd told Avigdor gaily. "I knew there were many reasons never to leave Paris and now I've found the best one of all—I stay put and find ways to get others out."

Most Parisians had soon returned to their city after the first fright; pretty women wore new hats, and those with money could eat openly in black-market restaurants without feeling guilty since 10 percent of their check went to the national charity. In the cafés the intellectuals still talked; people still fell in love and went to church; and women gave birth. Nevertheless, there was no one whose life had not been profoundly changed.

Each Frenchman and Frenchwoman reacted differently to the presence of the Germans, and Avigdor, whose understanding of other humans had once been directed toward selling them antiques and paintings, now used his sharp instincts to decide to whom it was safe to go for a false identity card and an *ausweis. Everything* was obtainable, every degree of false card, including the "real" false card that came from the police, right down to the most lamentable and obvious forgeries.

As he had cared for his ailing mother, Adrien Avigdor took note of the comings and goings of the neighborhood. Like almost every other Frenchman, Avigdor had been able to keep from starving by recourse to the *Marché Parallèle*, an institution which might have been called the black market except that almost everyone who could afford to make use of it, did so. The rations permitted by the Germans were simply not enough to maintain life and, in any case, were rarely available.

Oh, he had his sources, he had his friends, he had been reserving them for a long while for this eventuality. Thank God he had the money to pay to escape the prison of Paris.

More than two weeks later, armed with an identity card that did not bear the word *Juif*, the indispensable ration cards for food and textiles, and a valid *ausweis*, Adrien Avigdor, wearing the blue garb of a farmworker, and clutching a precious bicycle, was jammed into a train carriage traveling south. He had been en route for days, most of the time spent waiting for a train in various squalid, overflowing stations, packed with people whose unscheduled trains had not yet appeared and who waited patiently, exhausted, sitting on their bundles and packages all night. Once nine o'clock came, the curfew imprisoned them in the stations until the next morning.

Several times, Germans working their way through the trains had inspected his papers methodically, checking his face against his photograph. Open, amiable, frank, not too clever, his ordinary farmer's face had never aroused the slightest suspicion, his new cards, adroitly "aged," which had cost him as much as a country estate, were impeccable. Avigdor was on his way to make contact with the large Resistance operation in the mountains near Aix-en-Provence but he had resolved first to stop and see Mistral.

Who knew if he would ever see the painter again? He had to satisfy himself that the man was safe. What if he had been sent to Germany for forced labor as so many had been? There had been no communication between them since the fall of France. What if Kate, who had always retained her American citizenship, had been rounded up and deported? Avigdor had kept in touch as much as possible with what had happened to most of his artists under the Occupation—somehow news filtered through—but he had been deeply troubled by the lack of the slightest scrap of information about Mistral.

It was a long and wearying bicycle ride from the station in Avignon to Félice, but Adrien Avigdor relished it. Being in the open country after years of confined city life was pure joy. He realized that he would be lucky to reach *La Tourrello* by curfew as he toiled up the road from the hamlet of Beaumettes. Everywhere he saw fields left untilled, vines neglected. In every corner of France, the Vichy regime, who had done the Germans' work for them in the Unoccupied Zone since the armistice, had taken away many able-bodied men to work in German factories, replacing German soldiers. However, the production of food was always a necessity and Avigdor saw many people still in the fields, women and children as well as men of his age, old men and boys.

Exhausted, he pushed his bike up the hill leading to the *mas*, through the forest of live oaks, crossed the meadow and pounded on the tall gates he knew so well. After a long wait Madame Pollison opened the small window of wood and looked out forbiddingly.

Avigdor smiled at the familiar face he had come to know so well during his visits of the past years. "So you think you've seen a ghost, do you? It's wonderful to lay eyes on you, Madame Pollison, absolutely wonderful! I hope you still have a bottle of wine left in the cellar for me? Well, come on, open up—where is Monsieur Mistral?"

"You can't come in, Monsieur Avigdor," the woman said.

"Is there something wrong?" he asked, instantly alarmed by her expression.

"No one is to come in, Monsieur."

"What are you talking about? I've cycled all the way from Avignon. Are you afraid of something, Madame Pollison?"

"Nothing, Monsieur, but I have my orders. We can receive no one."

"But I must see Monsieur Mistral!"

"He is away."

"But, Madame Pollison, you *know* me! How many times have I stayed here, for God's sake? I'm a friend—more than a friend. Come on, let me in—what's the matter with you?"

"That was before. Monsieur Mistral is not here and I can't admit you."

"*Where is he?* Was he taken away for labor? Where is Madame?"

"I told you, Monsieur is out. Madame stayed in her own country. *Au revoir*, Monsieur Avigdor." The housekeeper drew back from the door and closed the window of wood in his face.

Avigdor stood there incredulously. The *mas* was shut as tight as any walled village of the Middle Ages. That beastly woman! He'd never liked her but it was incredible that she had not welcomed him. She knew perfectly well how close he was to the family. Where could Mistral have gone? What would Mistral do to her when he found out that she had sent him away? He started to pound on the door again but looked up at the sky first. It was still light, but darkness and the curfew were coming soon. There was just enough time to get back to Beaumettes with its one country inn.

Furiously, cursing, Avigdor quickly headed the bicycle down the hill but before plunging into the oak forest, he stopped, turned and gave one last unbelieving look backward toward the *mas*.

There, in the high window of the *pigeonnier* was a massive, unmistakable head. Julien Mistral stood watching him depart. With his keen sight, Avigdor could even see the fierce, determined, set expression on the painter's face. He stopped as abruptly as if he'd been shot and gave a great shout of relief. Their eyes met for a long minute over the distance. Mistral withdrew from the window. Avigdor, his heart pounding, rushed back to the gate and waited for him to come and open the gate. It was all that moronic housekeeper's fault. She had acted on her own without ever asking Mistral.

Minutes passed in the twilight hush, long minutes during which the silence of the *mas* grew more solid, long minutes before Adrien Avigdor finally understood and remounted his bicycle. He had not wept when the Germans marched down the Champs Elysées, he had not wept when he sewed on his yellow star, he had not wept when his mother had died, but he wept now.

Five months after Avigdor started to work with the Resistance, the Allies landed in North Africa and the Germans took over all of France. The Unoccupied Zone no longer existed, a large German garrison with its inevitable branch of the Gestapo was established in Avignon, and troops were stationed five kilometers from Félice, at Nôtre Dame-des-Lumières.

For almost two years Julien Mistral had worked in the fields. Even he had been forced to accept the fact that unless he worked officially at food production, as did everyone in Provence, he risked forced labor. In any case if he expected to eat he had to till the soil. The shopkeepers of Félice had almost no food to sell at any price. The farmer was now the one who ate, if not his fill, at least better than people in the big towns who were dying of hunger every day while the crops, the butter, the milk and the meat of France went to the Germans.

Mistral gave his toil of the day for the promise of painting at night, the shutters of the studio tightly closed, so as not to show the mild illumination he managed to create with the candles that had been stockpiled before the war by Kate, who believed as firmly as any French *châtelaine* in a bulging larder, far-sighted Kate who had piled up bars of soap as if they were gold ingots; who, much to Mistral's scorn, had filled armoires with blankets and dozens of heavy, hand-woven linen sheets that had never been used.

Now these sheets, treated with a kind of sizing made by boiling rabbit bones into a glue, served him as canvases. They were priceless, his most precious possessions. Bitterly he regretted the bonfires of former years. What would he not have given to have those paintings back so that he could paint over them? With growing despair he saw his stock of paints dwindle, although he rationed himself as severely as possible. Still, while he was working, sometimes he would forget, and lost in the trance of creation he would use paint as he always had. Then, as the candles guttered, Mistral was overwhelmed with the blackest misery as he confronted the half-empty tubes that had been almost full mere hours before.

A few weeks after the Germans came to Avignon a black Citroën stopped before the gates to Mistral's *mas*. A German officer in his green uniform got out, followed by two soldiers with cocked machine guns. Rigid and pale, Marte Pollison made haste to open the gates so that they could drive in.

"Is this the home of Julien Mistral?" the officer asked in passable French.

"Yes, sir."

"Go and get him."

No Frenchman answered the summons of a German officer without fear, even Mistral, who had no hidden radio tuned to the BBC wavelength, who had taken no part in any Resistance effort, who was perfectly *en règle* with the Vichy authorities.

The captain introduced himself with a flourish. "Kapitän Schmitt." He extended his hand and Mistral shook it. The German waved his arm at the soldiers and they lowered their guns.

"It is a great honor to meet you, Monsieur Mistral," Schmitt said. "For years I have admired your work. In fact I am a bit of a painter myself—only an amateur, of course, but nevertheless I have a great love of all art."

"Thank you," Mistral replied. The man sounded like one of the dozens of daubers he had taken pains to avoid in the past. His uniform seemed totally at odds with his friendly words.

"I was stationed in Paris until recently and I had the pleasure of visiting Picasso in his studio. I had hoped that if it wasn't inconvenient you might allow me to see your own studio—I have read so much about it."

"Certainly," Mistral answered. He led the way to the studio wing of the *mas.* Schmitt looked carefully at the canvases Mistral had piled against the walls. His exclamations of pleasure were perceptive and intelligent and showed a thorough knowledge of the body of Mistral's work. Before the war, he explained, growing more talkative, he had visited Paris every year in the autumn to see the new exhibitions and tour the museums. At his home outside Frankfurt he had his own little studio, and even now, in Avignon, whenever he had the time, he worked at his portable easel. "I can't resist painting, it's my weakness. I painted in Paris every weekend for two years, you understand how it is."

"Perfectly."

The captain gave his soldiers an order and one of them ran out to the black car and returned a minute later with a bottle of cognac.

"I thought . . ." the officer said with a trace of shyness, presenting the bottle to Mistral, "please allow me—I would be honored."

Mistral stared hard at this polite, enthusiastic, cultivated man who was the only person to have seen his new paintings in two and a half years. Paintings that were his body, his heartbeats, his breath, his every vital function. The soldiers had disappeared.

"Sit down," Mistral said, "I'll get some glasses. Let's have a drink."

Kapitän Schmitt became a regular visitor, dropping by every two or three weeks. On his first visit he offered to bring Mistral tubes of paint and Mistral accepted them eagerly.

Later in the year, when the Todt Organization, which was fast becoming the largest employer in France, swept through the Lubéron, drafting thousands of farmers to build submarine bases, blockhouses and airfields, Schmitt took Mistral's dossier and marked it in such a way that he was exempt from the work which would have finally forced him to leave his studio.

If his neighbors concerned themselves with his friendship—for that was what it had become—with a German officer, Mistral never knew about it, for he no longer went to the café in Félice. The atmosphere there was closed, suspicious and dismal, there was nothing left to drink, and only a few old men and young boys ever ventured out to play boules.

One day as he came back late from his cabbages, Mistral found Madame Pollison shrieking with anger.

"They came and took everything! *Everything.* The last chicken, the turnips, the jam, the ration books—they searched the house, the young bandits, they even searched me! Oh, Monsieur Mistral, if only you'd been here—"

"Who came?" Mistral demanded roughly.

"I don't know, I've never seen them before, not anyone from around here—young savages, gangsters, criminals—they went toward Lacoste through the woods . . ."

"Did they go into the studio?"

"They went everywhere, there wasn't a door they didn't open . . ."

Mistral ran to the studio and examined it quickly. He came out screaming, "*Where are my sheets?*"

"They took those too, and the ones in the house as well, and all the blankets . . ."

"*All the sheets?*"

"What could I do, Monsieur Mistral? I ask you?" she cried, indignation mingled with fury. "I tell you they were gangsters."

When Kapitän Schmitt came, the next day, on one of his regular visits, bringing as usual a painting he had completed for Mistral to look at and criticize, he found the painter haggard.

"What's wrong? Has anything happened?"

"I've been robbed," Mistral answered grimly.

"Was it Germans? If so, I'll look into it, rest assured."

"No, I don't know who they were—young bandits, my housekeeper says. A bunch of thugs."

"The *Maquis?*"

"All I know is that they were strangers, she'd never seen them before."

"What did they take?" Schmitt asked, concerned over the mask of despair that was Mistral's face.

"Many things, of no importance, damn them to bloody, eternal hell, but why did they take my *sheets?* How can I work? I haven't a single canvas left. I could kill them! Bastards! Scum!"

"Where did they go?"

"I don't know—Madame Pollison said toward Lacoste, on the forest road. By now they could be anywhere."

"I'll see what I can do to get you some canvases—it isn't easy, there is almost none anywhere, but I'll try."

Two days later Schmitt returned with his car filled with the wide linen bedsheets.

"No canvas—but I got you your sheets back," he said beaming.

"How . . . ?"

"We found the thieves in the woods, near where you said they'd gone—a regular nest of them . . . they were loaded with stuff—they'd been out" requisitioning' all over, or so it looked. *Maquis.*"

"*They weren't Maquis!*"

"Oh, yes, Julien, they were. Twenty of them. Don't worry, the little swine won't bother anyone ever again."

15

Shortness, Teddy Lunel thought with wistful, hopeless longing as she looked about her in the classroom, shortness is the answer. It must be.

There had been so many times in the past seven years at the Elm School, a small, private school just off Central Park West, when she had finally decided that her lack of popularity must be due to one or another of the things about her that made her different.

She didn't, like all the other girls, have a father or a family. Her mother, unlike any of theirs, worked all day. She had skipped third grade and was a year younger than her classmates. Eventually Teddy had worked it out that it had to be her height that caused her to be relegated to the ranks of the outsiders, the few girls who were lumped together like untouchables by the formidable band of the acceptable girls, who decided, with as much gravity as if they were electing a pope, which of them was the most popular, which the next most popular, right on down to that fatal line that excluded Teddy forever.

She had never been invited to a birthday party unless some mother democratically insisted on inviting the entire class; during the lunch hour no group ever saved a seat for her in the cafeteria; when clumps of girls formed to giggle at secrets during recess, Teddy had never been beckoned to join their priceless intimacy.

This exclusion seemed to have reached back to the first day of first grade, there was no appeal that could be made to change it, no person from whom she could seek an explanation—it simply existed, with mysterious finality.

There was no one wise in the ways of little girls who could have told Teddy that her extraordinary beauty was, at her age, a calamity that set her apart; nobody to point out that her peers weren't able to deal with a beauty so uncompromising, so inescapable, that it made her seem to belong to a different species from their own. When adults complimented her, and few of them could resist, she completely discounted whatever they said for they didn't know that no matter how she looked no one liked her.

Just as Teddy couldn't see herself in the mirror and know that she was already a classic beauty, neither could she draw back from the situation and understand the ways of school. How could a thirteen-year-old girl be philosophical about the need that exists in children, as it does in all other social groups, to form up into layers of clubbiness and that in order for any of the layers to seem ultimately desirable, there must always be one group that does not belong to any of them?

This same phenomenon operates in leper colonies, among whores, in jails and on the sidewalks of Calcutta. None of this knowledge would have comforted Teddy Lunel, who, at thirteen, had reached her full growth of five feet ten and a half inches, standing three inches above Mr. Simon, her eighth-grade teacher.

Maggy had no understanding of Teddy's position as one of the pariahs of the class. Teddy had never been able to admit it to her mother, who loved her with such a proud love, a love that made an implicit demand that Teddy be happy, be exceptional, be all that Maggy had ever dreamed of in a child. Teddy was terrorized by the possibility of jeopardizing her position as the joy of her mother's life if she diluted that love with the reality of her sad, lonely chagrin and bewilderment. She hid her wounds from Maggy as if she had indeed done something so awful that she deserved them. Very early in her life she learned to deceive, quickly she discovered that she could create a fantasy of an untroubled day that Maggy would believe and find reassuring.

Maggy often thought that Teddy lacked normal vanity. But perhaps it was just as well, considering how young her daughter was, she concluded, feeling wise and careful, for to Maggy, whose business was based on women's beauty, it seemed that Teddy had been designed by witchcraft. She was a creature of the most romantic contrasts, her hair, a dark red, its curling strands held a bewilderment of colors from almost brown to almost gold, her skin was so pale that when she flushed she seemed to flash into a moment of passionate fever, her delicate mouth was so mobile, so firmly outlined, such a riotous natural pink that it looked as if she were wearing lipstick. Under wonderfully astonished eyebrows, she had her father's eyes, blue and green and gray by turn, but they were set as far apart as Maggy's own. Her nose was splendid, a real nose, Maggy thought proudly, a fine, shapely firm nose that gave Teddy a faintly haughty air. It was, admittedly, perhaps too important a nose for a face without makeup, a child's face, to carry, but time would take care of that. Maggy never really saw Teddy as another child among children, because her practiced eye, alert to detect beauty, saw the woman she would become, not the too tall, too proud, too different-looking girl she was.

Although Maggy had no idea that Teddy would have joyfully traded her beauty to be little and cute, she had always been concerned about the fact that Teddy had not one relative in the world, no family but herself.

In the earliest days of the Lunel Agency, when Maggy was still working from home, she had watched with gratitude as her first models treated Teddy as if she were their baby sister. Soon, when Maggy moved to a suite of offices in the Carnegie Hall building, adding more phone lines and more assistants and more office space every year, she had asked Nanny Butterfield, and later Mademoiselle Gallirand, who replaced her, to bring Teddy to the office after school to play for a few hours several times a week.

Later, when Teddy had homework, there was a special desk set up for her in a quiet corner and the Lunel girls, who now numbered a hundred and twenty, would pop into Teddy's "office" to give her a quick hug, show her a new picture of themselves, complain about their aching feet or ask for an apple from the pile that Maggy kept heaped in a basket on Teddy's desk. They were a wonderful band of honorary relatives, Maggy thought defiantly, as she shopped at Saks and De Pinna on Saturday, when the office was closed, for yet more pastel cashmere sweaters, yet another expensive imported tweed or flannel skirt for Teddy to wear to school.

The Elm School was only a short walk away from the big high apartment Maggy rented in the handsome San Remo, at Seventy-fourth and Central Park West, overlooking the park. The towers of Fifth Avenue rose facing them across the entire width of the park and it was precisely this separation that had made Maggy decide upon the apartment, although she could easily have afforded to live in the most elegant part of the East Sixties or Seventies and sent her daughter to one of the better known, more fashionable schools. But on the East Side, Teddy would have been in constant danger of bumping into a Kilkullen or a McDonnell or a Murray, or a Buckley: the East Side was the *quartier* of the Establishment Catholics, and after Maggy had lost her job at Bianchi's, after the scandal of the Mistral exhibition, she had tried to keep her child at a distance. It is ridiculously easy in any city to just drop out of the small circle of fashionable neighborhoods and schools. Particularly, Maggy thought, when you have never been a part of it.

Teddy roamed the Sam Remo as if it were her fief. There wasn't one of the black elevator operators whose life history she didn't know; she was a favorite with the doormen who were always ready to lend her a piece of chalk for sidewalk hopscotch, at which, with her long legs, she was a natural champion. When she wasn't in school she was a volatile, talkative girl, always in motion, on roller skates, on her bike, or belly-flopping down the hills of the park on her sled in winter. Like the Pied Piper, she often led a romping file of children much younger than she, and when they were tired of playing, Teddy told them complicated stories about tropical jungles and raft trips down the Amazon.

There were other days, usually in the spring when a soft rain fell and the first forsythia splashed its yellow promise over the gray park, on which Teddy would take solitary refuge in Anne Hathaway's Garden, at the foot of an old stone tower. There, her imagination flaming, her hopes dancing, her heart high, she would dream her vague, glorious silvery dreams of love, and wonder when, oh, when, would it happen to her?

When Teddy, at thirteen, graduated from eighth grade, she led the class into the auditorium, a decision reached in a half-hour of wrangling among the teachers about whether her height would be less noticeable if she were first in line or last, since putting her in the middle was obviously unthinkable.

As she walked across the stage in her white dress to get her diploma there was an outburst of applause from the audience. Maggy had invited Darcy, the Longworths, Gay and Oliver Barnes, and a dozen of her favorite models to come and see her daughter finish elementary school. The twelve top cover girls of 1941, decked out in their best hats, whooped and hollered and whistled as they watched Teddy, her eyes downcast so that she wouldn't trip, walk with a grace that some of them would never be able to learn. "My God, Doe," said one of them who had just had her twenty-fourth birthday, "wouldn't it be wonderful to be young again?" "I still am, darling," Doe replied but a sudden finger of doubt touched her heart. She, too, was twenty-four.

In high school Teddy resolutely forged an alliance with a few of the unpopular girls. Sally was a bookworm who wore thick glasses and sweated too much; Harriet stuttered and wore orthopedic shoes, and Mary-Anne was the teacher's pet, always sitting in the front row of every class, ready to wave her hand triumphantly when others failed to know the answers, but the three of them became her best friends.

Teddy stopped going to the park or to the Lunel Agency after school in favor of doing her homework with her new allies. The four of them would gather at one another's houses and finish their assignments as quickly as possible so that they could get down to the real business of these afternoons, the discussion, in unfailingly fascinating detail, of their romantic dreams. They had no actual boy in mind, just a vague notion of someone male, somewhere in the distant future. The most burning question they dealt with was that of the wedding night. How could you wear a nightgown like those their mothers possessed? After all, it was possible to *see through* those nightgowns—they had all sneaked into their mothers' drawers and held the pretty, fancy things up and made sure of this incomprehensible, frighteningly strange fact. How could you get from the bathroom to the bed wearing a gown that was almost transparent? How could you, assuming that you wore a bathrobe over the nightgown, *ever* take the bathrobe off? Would you actually get *into* the bed? Or would you just lie on top of it? *And then what*? At that point they all stopped talking in a flurry of giggles and went into the kitchen for brownies and Cokes.

One day Teddy had tried to tell them what happened next. "The father takes his penis and puts it in the mother's vagina and seeds come out that swim . . ." She was interrupted by a chorus of disgusted shrieks and squeals. Her friends didn't want to hear such revolting details and they could not believe that Teddy's mother—even if she did work—had ever really sat down with her and told her these horrible things. At barely fourteen they hadn't really recovered from the shock of their first periods and what Maggy called "the facts of life" were far too unromantic and entirely too clinical for them to bear.

What then, Teddy wondered, would they think if they knew the whole truth about *her*? If they couldn't even listen to how a baby was made, what would they say if they knew she was a bastard? Oh, Mom had used a different term, of course, but it didn't change the truth.

She couldn't remember how old she had been when Maggy, finding it easier to express herself in the French they spoke together than in the English they spoke with everyone else, had told her that she was "*une enfante naturelle*"—but it was so long ago that she had had to *grow up* to the knowledge, gradually working out what exactly it meant long after she had first heard the words. How had Maggy let her know that her background was something she must not investigate? How had she been taught to know how to say, in a way that stopped all further questions, that her father was dead? She couldn't explain it even to herself, but it was long ago and she accepted it absolutely.

Like some Melanesian native confronted with a dish of sacred food that is consecrated to the use of priests, Teddy stepped instantly, self-protectively away from the forbidden subject. It was an interdiction so strong, so total, that she dared not ask Maggy more about it. This taboo set squarely in the living center of her life kept Teddy apart from her friends. None of them had any real secrets. Indeed the prime objective of their friendship was to share secrets, to confide, to reassure each other, to be companions and comrades in the difficult business of puberty.

Maggy had offered Teddy few details about her father. When she thought Teddy was old enough to understand, she told her that he had been an Irish Catholic who, before he died of a heart attack, had been prevented from marrying her by the laws of his church. Her manner as she said these few, halting words was strained, tense and so forbiddingly sad that it would have warded off any demands to know more, even if Teddy had dared to make them.

Teddy worshipped her mother but she was a little afraid of her. Many people were.

The habit of command, of being in total charge of a growing, prosperous business had added a formidable dimension to Maggy's character that was lacking in almost every other woman of the 1940s. It was a dimension that if it made it hard to think of her as maternal, made it easy to think of her as "The Boss" as all her girls called her, except when she was angry. Then they whispered to each other that "Marie Antoinette" was at large. On those days any girl who had gained more than a single pound invented excuses to avoid coming into the agency, every model who had stayed out too late at the Stork Club or El Morocco the night before took special care with her makeup and no one, absolutely no one, was a minute late for any booking.

At thirty-four Maggy had the authentically proud, bravura air of the acknowledged great beauty. When she was seventeen she had looked years older than her age; now she looked younger than her peers. Time had only accentuated the daring line of the bones under her taut, still luminous skin. She had grown into her self-confidence of movement, the spangles of her Pernod-colored eyes were brightened by wit and experience.

At the office Maggy dressed in black and gray suits and, in the summer, white suits, tailored to an almost inhuman perfection of line by Hattie Carnegie. The Burmese pearls she had received for her twentieth birthday were always around her neck, a fresh red carnation always pinned to her lapel. Titania of Saks Fifth Avenue designed the enchanting hats which she wore even when she was seated at her desk, as did most of the top fashion editors of the day. Maggy was friendly with all of them; she often had lunch with one or another at the Pavillon where Henri Soulé reserved one of his best tables for her every day. If by chance she were not planning to go there, she would have her secretary telephone to free the table.

And at night, there was always Jason Darcy, her best friend, her lover of many years, her co-conspirator, the man whom she would never marry. It was something Maggy hadn't even been able to make her dearest woman friend, Lally Longworth, understand. She had tried, God knows, when Lally took her to task years ago. "Are you totally mad, Maggy Lunel?" she had demanded. "Darcy's dying to marry you. What on earth is stopping you from saying yes?"

"Oh, Lally, Lally, I must never depend on a man. If we got married I know just what would happen. Slowly, inevitably, I'd have to spend less and less time at work until one day I'd just give up the business and be Darcy's hostess and travel with him and worry about our houses and our servants and our dinner parties—maybe even our children. I'd be *in his power*, Lally, and I don't want that ever to happen. I can *not* depend on any man to support me." Maggy put down her drink and almost shook Lally to make her understand.

"What if we found out that we couldn't be happy together and we got a divorce? Then, just tell me, where would I be? You can't build a business like mine and then drop it and expect it to be waiting for you when you get back . . . it isn't possible. It's much better to go on as we have—Darcy knows that he has me, there's no other man I care about. If that's not enough for him I'm sorry, but that's the only way it can be."

"And I was going to give you the wedding," Lally said in a tone of exaggerated disappointment, but she was privately appalled by Maggy's grim view of marriage. Lord have mercy, if every woman thought so clear-mindedly about divorce before she got married the human race would die out in a generation.

Maggy knew that Teddy must speculate on her relationship with Darcy, but if she couldn't explain it successfully to a woman as sophisticated as Lally Longworth, she wasn't going to try to make it comprehensible to a teenager. Oh, there was so much that she couldn't quite explain to Teddy, she thought with a familiar, guilty fear. She had never told Teddy that she, Maggy, was illegitimate herself. Instead she had invented a story of being orphaned early. Teddy, who was lost in *Wuthering Heights*, whose bible became *Gone With the Wind* and who saw *The Philadelphia Story* a dozen times, was too befuddled by high romance to question her mother closely.

And then there was the problem of Teddy's lack of a defined religion. Maggy's own Jewish identity had never depended on religious observance, although she had lived in a closely knit Jewish community during her early years, and Rabbi Taradash had been her example of the dignity and wisdom of Judaism. From the time she ran away from home she felt no personal need to carry on specific traditions that, to her, were somehow unnecessary. She felt that she *was* a Jew—but she had no obligation to be an observant one. The menorah she had left behind in Paris had never been sent for and she hadn't had the heart to replace it.

Years too late for it to have been worthwhile, she sent Teddy to Sunday school at the Spanish and Portuguese Synagogue on Central Park West. Teddy spent one bewildered morning discovering that everyone else seemed to belong there, to know and care about what they were learning. She decided that nothing could make her return to a place that made even the pecking order at the Elm School seem comfortable in comparison. As soon as she was old enough to take a bus by herself she ventured into St. Patrick's Cathedral, sat down in an inconspicuous pew and looked about in frightened curiosity.

This immensity of stone, this softly buzzing cave of blue and red and golden lights, these ranks of candles, the many sober, self-contained people going about their business so confidently—what had they to do with her? No more than the Synagogue school, she decided. She was no more Catholic than Jewish—no more and no less. To Maggy she announced that she thought she was a pantheist, or perhaps a pagan, whichever it was that felt more strongly about apple trees in bloom, the Brontë sisters, weeping willows, Siamese cats, the hot dogs at Jones Beach, and the Staten Island ferry.

"Patsy Berg touched a boy's *thing!*" Sally said with an air of fascinated incredulity.

"I don't believe you!" Mary-Anne said, stunned.

"If she did, he must have *forced* her," Harriet said with the look of someone with superior knowledge.

Teddy said nothing. She would give almost anything just to *see* a boy's thing. Touching it was even too much to dream about. She roamed the corridors of the Metropolitan Museum looking in vain for a statue that would possess a penis that was more than a marble curlicue, as insignificant as if it were a decoration on a birthday cake. Mostly they were broken off like the noses on the Greek statues. She *knew* that there had to be more to the whole mystery than the museum revealed.

But she was almost sixteen and only one boy had ever asked her out on a date, Harriet's second cousin, Melvin Allenberg. Melvin was short, almost elfin, and he wore thick glasses, but he was a senior at Collegiate, and when he smiled she told herself there was something about his grin that reminded her, for a split second, of

Van Johnson, except that he wasn't blond or tall or handsome. But on the other hand, he didn't have pimples. The next time that little Melvin Allenberg asked Teddy to go to the movies with him she accepted.

From the moment Melvin had first seen Teddy, his rampaging imagination had grasped her in a hold in which reverence mingled with longing. Her height only seemed one more uniquely wonderful thing about her. His fantasy was to live on an island peopled only by tall, beautiful women, who would, at his command, do anything he asked.

Before her date Teddy shaved the fine golden hair on her legs, the first of her friends to do so. The others watched in gloomy depression. "The hairs will grow back in like the stubble of a man's beard—real tough and scratchy," Mary-Anne warned. "Now you'll have to do it every week," Sally said with malice, "for the rest of your whole life." "I can't believe you're going through this for my icky, second cousin, Melvin, even if he is eighteen—you're crazy, Teddy Lunel," said Harriet, the most disapproving of the lot. "Do you know what his mother told my mother about him? He's *weird*, that's what. He's supposed to have this terrific I.Q. but he says he doesn't want to go to college, he's not interested in any sports, he doesn't care about anything except his stupid camera and that darkroom he's fixed up in his closet—Aunt Ethel can't keep a decent maid because Melvin is always bothering them to pose for him—the maid, for goodness sake—that's *bizarre*, Teddy. My aunt found hundreds of dirty magazines in his room once. You'd better watch out with him. He may only come up to your shoulder but who knows what goes on in his mind?"

Teddy smiled at Harriet and started on her left leg. They're all envious, she thought. None of them has ever had a date.

She sat through *See Here, Private Hargrove* without daring to meet Melvin's eyes, but she was conscious from time to time he would stare at her profile with something considering and earnest in the attitude of his round, curly head.

As they had waffles after the movie Melvin said solemnly, "You *are* the most beautiful girl in the world, Teddy Lunel."

"*I am?*" she gasped.

"Without any doubt." His glasses glittered at her. "I'm an acknowledged connoisseur of feminine loveliness, ask anyone at Collegiate."

"I don't believe you!"

"It doesn't matter what you believe. That has nothing to do with it."

Teddy blushed, her ears buzzed and she was afraid that tears were about to come into her eyes. None of the compliments she had received in her life from grown-ups had ever meant anything, but this! It was impossible not to know that Melvin meant what he said. He spoke as if he were making a documented academic pronouncement, there was an evaluating quality in his voice and she saw that behind his glasses he had bright, clever and very big, very clear blue eyes. His whole funny little face was set in an expression of total conviction. He looked like some kind of fluffy bird concentrating on an exceptionally fat worm.

"I've decided to call you Red," he continued. "Every beautiful woman needs a nickname that keeps her from being too intimidating and Teddy makes me think of Theodore Roosevelt. When a guy looks at you, Red, he sees something he never really believed existed except maybe on the movie screen, so he gets terrified that he won't have anything interesting enough to say to you. That's going to be one of your problems, getting people to treat you normally . . . to make ordinary human contact . . . in fact it's going to be damn near impossible. All the most beautiful women suffer from the same thing. It takes a special kind of man to understand them."

"You're nuts, Melvin Allenberg." Teddy was overcome with the intimate, flattering things he was saying to her so calmly, with such authority.

"Think about it, Red, just think about it," he said quietly. "One day, when we're both rich and famous, you'll tell me I was right."

Teddy couldn't answer. His words, that casual "one day" had acted on her as if they had been a beam of light that shot all the way into the future, illuminating undreamed-of vistas, as though Teddy Lunel was someone else who moved lightly in a world where the impossible became possible. Teddy looked down and slowly drew lines in her maple syrup with her fork. With the first absolutely calculated provocativeness of her life she asked, "What's a dirty magazine, Melvin?"

"Oh, so Harriet told you. I can't even make a collection of art photos without my family thinking I'm a dirty old man. Red, do I look like a dirty old man to you?"

"Harriet never said you were a dirty old man," Teddy said hastily, to defend her friend. "She never talked about you at all until you asked me to the movies."

"Well, she certainly never mentioned you either so that's fair. Anyway I never see her—our mothers have a mutual avoidance pact."

"Did Harriet never tell you about my family . . . my father?"

"No—should she have?"

"Well . . . he was a member of the Abraham Lincoln Brigade . . . he died fighting the Fascists in Spain . . . he was a great hero."

Melvin blinked with emotion. "God, you must be proud of him!"

"I am. My mother . . . she hasn't really gotten over it. She buries herself in her work . . . carrying on. She's French, you know. Her family was noble—there was a marquis who lost his head in the French Revolution . . . then all their land and money was confiscated . . . but not their pride. Mom's the last of her line . . . or rather I am . . ." Teddy said in a dreamy voice.

Melvin swallowed three times in awe. No wonder Red was not like any girl he'd ever met before. "Do you go out much?" he ventured, after a silence that seemed a fitting tribute to the unfortunate marquis.

"Mom's terribly strict. She only lets me have two dates a week on Friday and Saturday. She makes me go to bed early on Sunday because of school."

Reminded of the time, Melvin looked at his watch. "Come on, Red. She said home by eleven-thirty. I don't want to get you in any trouble."

At the door to Teddy's apartment Melvin Allenberg looked up at Teddy, who had been strangely quiet during the walk home.

"Have you seen *Jane Eyre* yet?" he asked. He might be short and funny-looking but he believed in always asking for what he wanted, no matter what the odds.

"No," said Teddy, who had seen it three times.

"Would you like to go next Saturday? If you're not busy already?"

"Umm . . . could we make it Friday? Saturday's taken I'm afraid."

"It's a date," he beamed. Once again his simple approach, unknown to most boys of eighteen, had let him achieve his goal.

"Thank you for a lovely evening," said Teddy, who had been grudgingly coached in this ritualistic phrase by her three friends.

Melvin grinned his not-quite-Van Johnson grin, reassured by this conventionality. "I hope you had as good a time as I did. Listen, I can tell that you're not the kind of girl who lets a guy kiss her good night before the third date, but don't you think it would be good for your soul to make one exception?"

Teddy didn't hesitate. She took off his glasses, and wrapped her long arms around him tightly, crushing his face into her collarbone with passionate gratitude. He struggled free. "Not like that, Red! Come on, bend down, and hold still." He planted a chaste kiss on her lips. "There! Now don't let anybody else get away with that. Promise?"

"I promise," Teddy whispered. Male lips felt different from female lips, they were prickly at their edges. Who would have guessed it? With her first conscious smile as a flirt she swayed forward and kissed him fleetingly before she gave him his glasses back. "Just don't tell anybody," she murmured. "It'd ruin my reputation."

16

"You told him *what?*" Bunny Abbott, Teddy's roommate at Wellesley was astonished. Just as she thought she had gotten used to the glorious excesses that had made Teddy an instant legend among the four hundred freshmen who had entered college with her in the fall of 1945, another caprice surfaced.

"I simply lied by an inch and a half and said I was six feet tall," Teddy repeated calmly, as she came back from the phone booth in the corridor. "When they hear that they suddenly lose interest unless they're six two or three—it eliminates the shrimps."

"Why do you still bother with blind dates?" Bunny asked. "You can't even fit them into your datebook anymore."

"Oh, they just amuse me . . . it's like opening a Christmas present." Teddy sounded casual because she knew she could never possibly explain the feelings of embarrassingly violent love she felt for everything about her new life, for every detail of college, from blind dates to each and every girl in her dormitory. From the very first day she had arrived at Wellesley she had been reborn into an intoxication so unexpected that at night she lay awake to try to pin down and fully explore the dimensions of the unbounded joy that possessed her.

Teddy's life had become a high drama of popularity; every afternoon the dormitory phone rang at least a dozen times for her and the girl on "Bells" who answered it would come to the head of the corridor and shout "Lunel" in ironic resignation, yet without any growing trace of resentment. At Wellesley, Teddy had found at last the miraculous arena where it was acceptable to be different.

Her class had its share of brilliant girls who studied half the night; other girls were dedicated to winning a place on the crew that rowed against Radcliffe; there were those girls who clearly arrived at college already running for president of the class, girls who cared for little except art or music or philosophy, and still others who played fierce bridge all afternoon while simultaneously knitting argyle socks. If Teddy Lunel was almost exclusively interested in boys, who cared, as long as she didn't flunk out? She was smart enough to have been admitted to Wellesley so she was automatically one of them, her identity was, before all else, a member of the class of 1949.

The Wellesley campus was the noble proscenium for the epidemic of dating that had unfolded ever since the distribution of the little red Freshman Handbook, which contained photographs of each member of the class above their names and hometowns. The book was printed to help the freshman get to know each other but before it had been out for twenty-four hours, copies found their way to every man's campus in New England, now swollen by the ranks of newly returning veterans of World War II as well as the usual freshmen.

At the second week of freshman year, Teddy had been invited to every major Ivy League football weekend until Christmas vacation; she had her choice of nine dates for the Dartmouth Winter Carnival and, if her studies had permitted it, she could have gone out to dinner with a different man from nearby Harvard every night of the week.

When she went home for Christmas vacation that year, Maggy realized that her tall child had become a young woman who beckoned and tempted even when she stood still. The refrigerator held a heap of orchid corsages, love letters arrived in the mail every morning, Teddy went out every night and slept till noon. Still, better to be a prom queen, Maggy decided, and from what she observed, an utterly heartless and merciless flirt, than to be a girl who could be taken advantage of by a man because she imagined that he loved her.

Teddy waltzed through the first years of college, amorous, fanciful, vainglorious, as memorable as a first kiss and as impossible to recapture. She whirled from romance to romance as changeably as the tides, developing an authentic affectation of personality as she felt her power grow. She began to acquire a kind of learned self-confidence that was translated into a bewitching air of happiness as if nothing on earth had ever caused her to feel ruffled, or flustered or perturbed. She started to enter every room with a buoyant certainty of welcome, she accepted any change as if it had been planned for her enjoyment, there seemed to be no disappointment in her world, no potential for diminished expectations.

I don't believe this is happening to me, she whispered to herself, over and over, but she never said it out loud, for under all her triumphs always lurked the fear that she might suddenly find herself again the outsider just as suddenly as she had attained her fantasies of popularity.

Reality was never enough for Teddy. Somehow reality didn't manage to penetrate her unconscious in a way that allowed it to become a rock of experience on which she could base her emotions. She had been just a child, only six, when she learned the habit of changing reality into something brighter in recounting her days at school to Maggy. Now reality was as highly colored as she could ever have imagined, and it still didn't satisfy her. Outer success did not, could never, translate fully into an inner self-image that allowed her peace. Little by little the fantasy that dwelled within Teddy, that had inspired her to invent a father who died in Spain and a noble French background for Melvin Allenberg, was allowed to grow, to blossom.

At a Harvard-Yale game Teddy told her date, "My father went to Harvard, you know. Before he died he used to take me to all the Harvard games that were played near New York. He was mountain climbing in Tibet when he was killed—but he managed to save all the others." At Princeton, in a group that was discussing summer plans she grew nostalgic. "While I was growing up I spent every summer at my family's château in the Dordogne—the Lunels have lived in the Dordogne for as long as anyone can remember—the château has a hundred rooms, half of them in ruins—I haven't been back since my grandfather died." At the Dartmouth Winter Carnival she confided in her date. "Would you mind if I didn't go to the ski jumping? You see my father was killed right before my mother's eyes—he was ski jumping in the Alps, training for the Olympics . . . she's never been the same." When the talk turned to Christmas vacation Teddy remembered her own. "We used to go to my great-great-grandmother's in Quebec. She always had the tallest tree I've ever seen—a living pine, at least thirty feet tall—and I'd dance around it with all my little cousins—there must have been two dozen of them—no, I don't see them anymore—my mother quarreled with my father's family after he died. They blamed her for letting him join the Free French when France was invaded. He was killed when his plane was shot down—he was on a special secret mission for General de Gaulle . . . no one's ever known what it was about, to this day."

Her tales were never questioned; a girl so extraordinary to look at must surely have tragedy and romance in her life, and she talked this way only to men she didn't intend to see in New York where they might meet Maggy when they came to call for her.

Maggy made it a point to inspect Teddy's dates as often as she could. She was reassured by the ever-changing parade of polo coated youths who looked so fresh-faced, so respectful and essentially innocent. They were only children, she thought, and harmless.

"There's no question that there's safety in numbers," she told Lally Longworth. "I'm happier that Teddy's going out with dozens of boys than just one or two. And she treats them all so badly . . . I don't understand her anymore . . . if I ever did. I know it's too late now that she's gone away to school but I feel uneasy, as if I've lost touch with her . . . as if there's a beat missing . . . I keep thinking that there must have been something that I should have done to be closer to Teddy, to know her better. She mystifies me, Lally, and yet I gave her everything I could . . . I love her so, she has a comfortable home, she's always been beautifully looked after, I bought her the best clothes . . . oh, I just don't know . . ."

"Half the mothers I know say the same thing about their girls," Lally said comfortably, speaking from within the untroubled fortress of her little-regretted childlessness which entitled her to tell her friends how to bring up their offspring. "Once they go to college they become strangers. Are you sure there isn't anybody serious in Teddy's life? She'll be twenty soon. What were you doing at that age, I wonder?"

"Having fittings all day—and living like a woman," Maggy said thoughtfully. "We grew up so much faster in France. Or maybe it was just the twenties—I don't know, but her boyfriends all seem barely hatched to me. They're still groping their way out of the shell. Teddy assures me that these boys don't even expect—much less try—to make love to her . . . do you suppose that's really true?"

"Of course it is! What *are* you talking about, Maggy Lunel? Nice boys *never* expect to make love to nice girls."

It all depends on your definition of nice, Maggy thought, remembering how the blue frenzy of the Hawaiian guitars used to sound in her blood, remembering the wildness of the red sky of Montparnasse, remembering the melody of a Java that had the power to make a girl of seventeen be embarrassed by her virginity, remembering a spring night on which five hundred people had howled their delight at the sight of her naked body.

But Lally Longworth was right, at least for the second half of the 1940s, that profoundly conservative period. An overwhelming majority of the class of 1949 at Wellesley remained virgins until their marriages, and in that era of the tease, Teddy Lunel was responsible for more aching groins than any other girl in greater Boston. She had been influenced more than she realized by Maggy's deep suspicion of men.

A few of her favorite dates were allowed to kiss her for hours, rubbing themselves frantically against her in the back seats of convertibles or on the sofas of darkened rooms in eating clubs or fraternities, striving to gain their orgasms through the thickness of the clothes that separated their two bodies, for Teddy would never permit any of them to unzip his fly, to insinuate his hand under her skirt. She triumphed over their desire by refusing it any release except whatever they could gain without her seeming to notice. None of them was calm enough to guess that Teddy always had an orgasm too, easily, without a sound or a movement that could be detected, produced magically just by the pressure of a rigid penis straining inside a pair of trousers, a secret orgasm that could happen even on a dance floor. She never granted any of them the closeness to her that knowledge of this would have produced and, for her cruelty to them, she received the tribute of their proposals of marriage.

Teddy was not indifferent to the men who loved her, but somewhere deep within her there was a profound lack of concern with their pain. She was so in love with the idea of her popularity that she never fell in love with any one individual man. This inaccessible, heedless, faraway sensuality was like a few drops of water to men longing to drink their fill; it drove them mad, far more than if she had refused them the kisses she spent so lavishly. To have felt the points of her breasts through her dress, to have held her tumbled fragrance so closely, to have made her lips swell with too many kisses, but to be stopped there as if by an iron will . . . "I just hope, Teddy Lunel," one of them had said in a rage, "that someday somebody makes you suffer the way you make me."

She looked suitably regretful but she knew it could never happen.

If premarital Ivy League sex was rare in the late 1940s, drinking was the rule. At the very first football game Teddy ever attended in the Harvard stadium, she had been initiated with a paper cup of the powerful rum punch that was smuggled up into the stands in one of the red fire buckets that usually stood along the corridors of Eliot House. The buckets were intended to be filled with sand to throw on flaming wastepaper baskets but they were most often used as cocktail shakers or punch bowls.

After the game everybody went from party to party, sampling the various lethal, fruity concoctions, based on the cheapest available gin, which were served in each suite of rooms. Drunkenness was a normal way to end a Saturday night throughout the Ivy League, but Wellesley was a resolutely dry campus. Once there had been rumors of a single beer party in Munger given by a group known as the Lousy Eleven, but nobody believed them because the risk was too great: immediate expulsion for anybody drinking on college property.

Teddy loved to drink. Really loved it. There were few better feelings than the shift in perception that only liquor could produce, that sudden sense that the world was finally comprehensible and that it lay within her hands. Teddy studied, because it was essential, and dated and drank her way through three years at college, each more memorable than the last.

On a Sunday afternoon in the early fall of her senior year five members of a Harvard singing group, the Dunster Funsters, drove out to Wellesley to visit Teddy. They went frolicking about the famously beautiful campus, and after they decided not to walk all the way around the lake, Teddy showed them the Arboretum, an almost hidden, little-explored collection of rare trees behind the science building. Part of the Arboretum is a thicket of pine trees, wonderfully scented, its floor covered with inches of fallen needles, slippery and soft underfoot. Instinctively they lowered their voices and slowed their pace. They seemed to have arrived at a place that was no longer Wellesley, that wasn't connected to the Gothic towers and the high sense of purpose that always hung over that marvelously lovely campus no matter how lazy the day.

"Drink, Théodora?" asked one of the boys, pulling a flask out of his pocket and sitting down under a tree.

"Harry! Are you mad?"

"Nothing like a schnapps in the fresh air—come on, there's nobody here but us and you know we're harmless, alas."

"*Don't you dare!*" she shouted, but the boys were already passing the flask around. The first time they offered it to Teddy she refused, but soon, under the soothing influence of the aroma of the pine needles and the out-of-season softness of the early October air, she dared to accept one small sip. And then another, and then a third. Harry was absolutely right about drinking outdoors, it heightened senses that didn't get properly exercised unless you were a part of nature. And oh, how blissful, how truly blissful it is to be a part of nature, she thought as she had a generous swallow of Scotch from a second flask.

"Gin smells bad, bourbon is too strong, rye is utterly horrid, but whoever invented Scotch was a good man and true," she announced. She felt that she'd made an important discovery.

"Robert Graves survived the trenches in World War One by drinking a whole bottle of Scotch every day," Harry's roommate, Luther, told her. "I can get by on less than a half of that."

"And you can't even write," Harry said.

"But I can sing, can't I, Harry?"

"Luther, you can sing, we all can damn well sing, we all *should* damn well sing!"

And sing they did, softly at first, harmonizing sweetly on old ballads, their voices so low that the birds could still be heard. Teddy lay back and listened in a haze of pleasure. How fine it was! One by one they sang all the Funster specialties. Really, she mused, it would only be fair of Harvard to give me a diploma when these boys graduate—I'm as much a part of their classes as they are. When they started singing football songs none of them noticed that their voices now rang loudly through the little pine forest. "With the Crimson in Triumph Flashing . . ." Teddy found herself joining in but her voice was drowned out by the boys' voices, so she rose from the pine needles and did a little wild and antic dance. The five Funsters applauded wildly.

"More, Teddy, more!"

"Sing the Yale song—then I'll dance more."

"Never."

"Traitor—you're a traitor to the Crimson, Théodora."

"Sing the Notre Dame song," Teddy insisted, capering wickedly.

"What the hell—we don't play the Irish—give the little lady Notre Dame—take it off, Teddy, take it off!" Their voices rose in the Notre Dame fight song and Teddy cavorted like a shooting star, a captivating demon in Bermuda shorts, hair-raisingly graceful and quite, quite drunk.

It was during her bacchic encore, performed to a roaring Navy finale, "Beat the Army, Beat the Army Grey!" that Teddy's philosophy professor and his wife, out for an afternoon's stroll, attracted by the noise, wandered into the pine grove.

Two days later Teddy left Wellesley for good. Her case had been investigated and settled with due formality but there had never been any real question of the outcome. The sin was too grave.

At Back Bay Station, Teddy waved a last goodbye to all the grieving and guilty

Funsters who had come to the station to see her off. But, as the train gathered speed in the outskirts of Boston, she dropped her aching, hot head to her hands and thought, silly bitch, *silly bitch*, STUPID BITCH! My fault, totally and absolutely my fault, I knew better! Did I think I could get away with anything? Did I think I was invulnerable? Fool, fool, bloody, bloody *fool!* I've lost it all, all lost, all gone, kicked out of paradise for good and for ever . . . I'll never be happy again. She would have groaned out loud but she was in the club car and it was filled with passengers. She had never known such paralyzing hopelessness. All the fears that had ever plagued her, all the premonitions that life was too good to be true, that nothing so wonderful could endure, gathered together in one lump that bulged rawly in her chest and rose up into her throat.

Teddy sat quite still for three hours, lanced by misery, drowning in self-reproach as the train traveled along the route that she had taken so triumphantly to Brown and Yale and Princeton. All the way to Hartford she stared unseeingly out of the grimy window. Finally she roused herself enough to order a sandwich and coffee. As she ate she looked around the club car for the first time since she had entered it.

At first her gaze was indifferent, unthinking, her mind didn't process what her eyes took in, but after a few minutes she focused, narrowed her concentration. The club car was filled with businessmen and wherever she looked there was approval. More than approval, there was intense interest, there was frank invitation, there was fascination. Teddy felt the first faint relief from pain that she had known since that moment in the pine grove when Professor Tompkins stopped dead and said, incredulously, "Miss Lunel!" Some instinct made Teddy get up and walk the length of the club car to the little toilet. She pushed open the door impatiently and confronted her eyes in the cracked mirror over the washstand. No matter how she felt inside, she looked no different than she had only two days ago. She braced herself against the walls, swaying with the train, as each mile brought her nearer to New York and the confrontation with Maggy that she dreaded with a fear so great that she couldn't even begin to face it.

You have to do *something*, she told herself grimly, looking in the mirror. You can't just show up and say that three years have gone down the drain. You have to have some project for the future, some idea of how you plan to lead your life. Three years toward a degree in history is useless on the job market—but I can't come home without a scheme. I've got nothing left but my face, it's as simple as that. But am I right?

In her mind Teddy checked over every comment she had ever heard Maggy make as she pored over models' photographs at home in the evening. It had been seven years since Teddy had spent much time at her mother's agency, seven years of being absorbed in herself, seven years in which an entire generation of models had retired, their places taken by new faces, seven years during which she had only given rare glances to fashion magazines except for the yearly back-to-school issues. Yet she had never forgotten the indispensable requisites for a model's face. How often had she heard Maggy repeat them as she discarded photograph after photograph?

Peering desperately into the grimy mirror, she went down the list, her heart beating faster and faster. Definite cheekbones; eyes set far apart; a nose with a distinct shape to it; but not too big or too small; hair that anything could be done with; clear skin; perfect teeth; a long, long neck; a small chin, clearly cut; wide jawbones; a high forehead; a well-shaped hairline; an *uncrowded* face . . . yes, oh, *yes*, she had them all. She knew she was more than tall enough, she had always been skinny enough . . . but was she photogenic?

Teddy knew that only the camera could decide this. The crucial question of whether the sum of all the parts, no matter how good, will add up to a face that *matters* in only two dimensions, without the third dimension of depth, and minus the help of color, can never be settled by the eye alone. Maggy never let herself get too optimistic about a new model's potential until she had seen the test shots because so many girls didn't photograph as well as they looked in person, just as some of the best models were oddly unexciting in the flesh.

No, I just can't be sure, Teddy thought, as she went back to her seat, but at least it's something to try for, something Mother might approve of . . . oh, you bloody, silly bitch, who are you kidding? If she wanted me to become a model, why would she have never mentioned it? Why would she have sent me to Wellesley? But better a straw than nothing.

After her disappointment, after her anger, Maggy asked herself a sudden question. Why was her daughter so punished, in such disgrace for drinking on campus when, at Teddy's age, she had been living in sin with a married man and bearing an illegitimate child? A little historical perspective, please, she said to herself grimly. It won't kill her not to graduate. From this, as Rabbi Taradash used to say, little children don't die. And it would be good discipline for Teddy to try her hand at modeling.

The Lunel girls were a regiment of foot soldiers, hardworking, motivated and unspoiled. No one, looking at the fashion pictures and advertisements they posed for would have guessed at the vast amounts of grit and energy and willingness to endure discomfort that the frivolous images represented.

With a few flighty exceptions, every successful model went to bed early to get eight hours' sleep to prepare herself for the difficult day ahead. Without nonsense, businesslike, and as cheerfully as possible, she got up early so as to be ready on the dot of her first appointment; punctuality was vitally important to editors and clients and photographers who expected to see every model arrive, made-up and ready to work, on the stroke of the hour. Dependability was the sister virtue to punctuality; a model wouldn't cancel a booking for anything less than hospitalization, and even if she shook with fatigue between shots, she never let herself show it when the camera was on her. Tiredness was something she accepted as part of the money she earned, now as much as forty dollars an hour for top models.

Forty dollars an hour. The sum still astonished Maggy even as she fought to push it still higher. In Montparnasse, when she'd arrived there, the average artist's model worked for the equivalent of sixty cents for three hours of posing. Of course, once Paula had taken her in hand, she'd made double that, forty cents an hour for standing naked in an unheated studio in the middle of a Paris winter. She'd managed to live on it, even to pay her rent, buy her clothes, wear a fresh carnation every day—even to support Julien Mistral for one unforgettable perfect spring. Maggy paused and tried hard to imagine herself back in the skin of that girl. What had she thought about, how had she felt? Flashes of memory were vivid, the rest was lost.

She shrugged. There must still be artists' models, poor souls, but those of her girls who posed for lingerie photographs made double the money of those who worked only in fashion although they paid dearly for it in a loss of status. Her top girls even refused to pose in nightgowns and peignoirs. At least no budding Julien Mistral of a photographer could ever order Teddy to drop *her* knickers. In that there was some comfort.

Maggy pondered the question of the photographer to whom Teddy should be sent for her test shots. Normally she no longer concerned herself with this sort of decision. She had twenty-two employees and among them there were six who could have settled the matter with one phone call. Maggy knew, of course, that she was being overprotective, but these pictures were crucial. If they were disappointing, Teddy's future as a model would vanish. If they were good they would be used for Teddy's first "composite," a glossy 8 × 10 collage of photographs that would be her calling card, passport and temporary identity papers until she had painstakingly, over months, built up a portfolio of a variety of pictures, her "book" that she would carry everywhere so that it could be shown to magazine editors, advertising agencies and photographers.

Suddenly Maggy, who was in the habit of hardening her heart toward the ambitions, hopes and dreams of a thousand girls a year, Maggy, who never took the model's point of view until she had the pictures to look at that would speak louder than any human voice, found herself as eager to get the pictures right as if she were trying to break into the business herself. She imagined herself flipping through Teddy's test shots, imagined herself weighing and considering Teddy's merits as against those of—oh, say, that great model, Sunny Harnett, whose chin and nose were far too prominent for beauty, whose mouth was entirely too wide, but who had a smile that swept you right into the page with her, a smile of such pure gaiety that it was transferable to the reader; Sunny Harnett, who projected a blond blast of Southampton chic, who looked as if she were out-of-doors and dashing after a tennis ball even when she was sitting down. Did Teddy have any of that energy? Maggy, for all her expertise, found that all she could really do to help Teddy in a practical way was to work on her rudimentary makeup which was fine for college but not remotely right for photography.

Coffin, Toni Frisell, Horst, Rawlings, Bill Helburn, Milton Greene, Jimmy Abbe, Roger Prigent—she could ask a favor like this of any of these top photographers, but even as Maggy ran their names over in her head she knew that she was not going to be able to resist asking one of the three photographers she considered the most gifted in the world: Avedon, Falk and Penn. But it was collection time in Paris and this particular season Avedon, whose star had risen so rapidly in the past few years, was there for *Bazaar*, and Penn was in Paris for *Vogue*. So Falk it would be because Maggy couldn't endure this suspense, even if Teddy could.

It was like being in a tumbrel on the way to the guillotine, Teddy thought, or standing on the edge of the high diving board looking down into the ring of fire in the water below. She stood, frozen with self-consciousness outside a converted coachhouse that housed Falk's studio between Lexington and Third Avenue. It was after five on a Friday evening and the street was crowded with people rushing away from their jobs, the weekend beckoning.

It was football weather, Teddy realized, as she shivered in the breeze, and she should be hundreds of miles away, dressing for a date—oh, Dunster, Leverett, Winthrop and Eliot! She mumbled an incantation of the names of the fabled Harvard residence houses on the Charles River—that's where she should be! Instead she was primped and polished, brushed and painted and dressed in new clothes, up from her shoes and out from her skin, as perfect as her mother had been able to make her. She had never looked better, and she knew it, but the knowledge didn't help.

Her eyelashes were covered in unfamiliar mascara, her skin in powder, base and rouge, artfully applied, and her hair had just been done at Elizabeth Arden. Maggy had turned Teddy out in the flawless, adult elegance of Dior's "New Look," choosing a tightly fitted, double-breasted, gray flannel suit with black velvet lapels. The jacket was nipped in savagely at the waist, the hips exaggeratedly rounded by a buckrum lining above a slim skirt that stopped a few inches above her ankles. Teddy wore high-heeled black antelope pumps, a small black velvet hat with a veil that reached below her nose, and pale gray kid gloves. Under her expensive new blouse, in spite of the antiperspirant that she had frantically applied three times since the morning, she was beginning to sweat from nerves. She jabbed at the doorbell. Maybe action would keep her dry.

Falk had agreed to take the test shots of the new girl from Lunel so long as she came after he was finished shooting for the week. If Dora Mazlin, Maggy's chief booker, hadn't called to beg this personal favor from Falk's secretary he would never have been bothered to make the time, but his secretary owed Dora that favor for help in past emergencies. Every photographer, even those in Falk's position, sometimes needed a top model in five minutes and Dora was *the* pipeline.

The door was opened, to Teddy's ring, by a small cheerful woman.

"You're the new girl from Lunel, right? Come on in."

Teddy looked around the reception room. There was a general air of casual comfort but nothing about the room was exceptional except the photographs on the walls. "May I look?" she asked the secretary, because she was too nervous to sit still.

"Sure, go ahead."

Teddy walked from one photo to another, growing more tense with each second. She had always paid a fraction more attention to fashion photographs than other girls her age, but these pictures were like certain dreams that reveal a world that is similar to the real world, but mystically heightened, more significant, filled with a magic power. She recognized many of the faces; most of the models were from Lunel, but surely none of the girls she was familiar with had ever been quite so interesting. The camera's eye had caught a millisecond of a revelation of personality. Behind the patterns of beautiful features Teddy could sense the intimate *self* of each model. These were not merely fashion photographs, they were fully realized portraits of women thinking their most personal thoughts.

"Listen," the secretary said suddenly. "If I hang around any longer I'm going to be late for my date. The phone isn't going to ring again today so I'm leaving. Will you tell him I'll see him Monday morning bright and early?" She grabbed her coat, and rushed out the door with a brisk wave, slamming it behind her.

Teddy sat down on the edge of a chair in the empty reception room. Beyond an open door she could see a slice of studio, brilliantly lit. For twenty, quite nearly unendurable minutes, nothing at all happened. The coachhouse was quiet with that special late-Friday-afternoon hush that says so clearly that work is over for the week. Could there be a mistake? Could she be alone here? Teddy wondered at last.

Finally, hesitating at every step, Teddy got up stiffly and ventured slowly into the studio, stopping a few feet on the other side of the door. She tried to peel off the tight gloves that seemed to be stuck to her hands. There was no place to sit, nothing in the room but an intense, waiting blaze of lights, a camera on a tripod and a sheet of virgin white paper that stretched right across one wall and was spread out on the floor. Sweat, yes, definitely more sweat, she thought in horror, trickled down her sides under her new waist cincher. She realized that she wasn't breathing and drew in two deep breaths.

"Is anybody at home?" she quavered in a small voice. There was no answer. Suddenly the door to the darkroom was flung open and a man popped out, holding a sheet of paper in his hand and looking at it. He gave her a glance. "I'll be right with you," he said, frowning at the paper. Then he looked up again and dropped the wet photograph. He peered at her from the other side of the sea of white paper.

"Red?"

Teddy jumped and squinted but she couldn't see him clearly.

"*Red!*"

The expression on Teddy's face changed and grew as complicated as the moment before a spring storm. She stepped firmly on the unspotted paper and took a big stride forward, shielding her eyes.

"Only one person has ever called me Red and that's a son of a bitch rat-fink who took me to seven movies, taught me how to French kiss and then dropped me without a word of explanation."

"Red . . . I can explain."

"*Ah ha!*" Galvanized, her nervous anxiety forgotten, Teddy took five swift steps forward and grabbed his shirt. "I cried my eyes out for you, you louse! I thought I was a total failure for months, I pretended to my mother that I was fed up with you, I told your cousin that you'd tried to get fresh . . . why didn't you ever call, Melvin Allenberg?"

"Were you really sorry?" he asked.

"Oh, what a shit you turned out to be! Now you want to *revel* in how awful I felt. That stinks! Anyway, what are you doing here?"

"Working late."

"So, you talked your way into a photographer's studio after all . . . the black sheep of the Allenbergs . . . I'll bet your mother's still upset?"

"She's made an adjustment."

"Where's Falk? I've been here a half-hour," Teddy said imperiously.

"I'm Falk."

"Bullshit."

"Do you see anybody else here?"

"Prove it."

Melvin Allenberg began to laugh. "Oh, God, Red, you don't change." Teddy hadn't loosened her grip on his shirt and now she tried to shake him, but try as she would he was impossible to budge. Solid as a small bear, he roared with laughter at her efforts, making her so angry that tears came into her eyes. He reached up and forced her arms down at her sides and pinned them there.

"Come on upstairs . . . I live over the store. I'll show you all the evidence that you want."

He released Teddy and quickly walked out of the studio into the reception room. She followed, beginning to believe him because of the way he moved. There was, in the casual sureness of his tread, that unmistakable modulation that reveals proprietorship, and when she climbed the stairs behind him and saw the large room that seemed to have been made out of the entire second floor of the coachhouse, she knew instantly that he was in his own home. The room fit Melvin Allenberg. It was messy and warm and crowded everywhere with enormous blow-ups of photographs of beautiful women, some of them on the walls, some on the floor, others piled in corners. Dozens of books lay open, a desk was piled three feet high with magazines and the big low couches and armchairs were all covered in dark green tufted leather.

"Drink?" he asked, going over to a tray covered with bottles and glasses that stood on top of an old seachest.

"Scotch on the rocks, but it won't improve your case, Melvin Allenberg."

"Melvin Falk Allenberg."

Teddy narrowed her eyes without comment, in a way that let him know that he was on strict probation. He poured two drinks and sat down on a chair by the couch, leaning forward, his elbows on his knees and his hands folded under his chin. He looked at Teddy quietly for a while. "Take off your hat," he said finally.

"What?" She was outraged.

"Take off your hat . . . I don't like that veil, I can't really see you."

"I don't even know if I'm staying," she said with what she hoped was a completely colorless smile, a smile such as she had never given in her life, nor would ever be able to give in the future. She was restored to the fine bravado that three years of unopposed tampering with malleable masculine hearts had given her. "I don't even know yet if I'm going to let you take my test shots. It all depends on the reason why you never called me again. I don't give a damn that you're rich and famous, you bastard, just the way you said you'd be."

"I said that *we'd* be," he answered.

"You remember that? After five years?"

"I remember everything. When we met you were entering into your destructive phase. Even though I was just nineteen I could see it coming, as sure as sunrise, and I didn't want to be your first victim . . . it was rough enough being your first triumph. So I bailed out when I knew that one more date, one more of those wild kissing sessions standing up outside of your front door, would finish me off, probably for life." He fell silent, and then he added, "Needless to say I was wrong." It was already far too late for self-preservation.

"Hmmm." Teddy had heard this sort of declaration before, in every variety of version, but there was an enduring patience and a kind of accepting calm about his statement that was more convincing than the most passionate phrases. He continued to scrutinize her as she took off her hat with care and pushed her fingers artfully through her hair, redistributing the carefully set waves until the lamplight dodged through its bewilderment of reds.

Teddy sipped her Scotch, which would always taste like danger, and returned his steady gaze. Melvin Allenberg had grown up well. He still looked like a bird, with his beaky nose and his big glasses, but his big bright eyes dominated his face with an intelligence that was infused with the kind of energy that is the essence of charm itself. His was a completed face: years would only confirm its shape, the firm chin, the broad brow, the curly halo of dark hair. She'd never forgotten his mouth, the first she'd ever kissed. Cleverness and whimsy were stamped as clearly on his well-formed lips as if he'd been a warlock.

"I suppose . . ." she began, with something quivering on the corners of her own mouth that showed that she was inclined to forgive him. Then she stopped, stung by a sudden memory. "And I'd been planning to ask you to the junior prom the very next time I saw you. Oh! When I never heard from you again I was too proud to call."

"What about all those other guys you were dating?"

"I decided not to ask any of them . . . so I didn't go. I missed it," she replied sadly.

Abruptly he got up, crossed the space between them, sat down on the couch, took her firmly in his arms and kissed her mouth.

"Oh, my sweet Red, my poor baby, I'm so sorry . . . I should have called but what could I have said? There was no way then to explain . . . I was too dumb to know the right words." Tenderly he wiped her lipstick off with his handkerchief and kissed her again. In his arms she felt him as solid as a tree, his lips were familiar. Her lips had received thousands of kisses in the last years but sensory memory retrieved his particular touch and taste and warmth; yet he was so changed, different in a way she suddenly understood with a leap of gladness. He was a man and he kissed like a man, not a boy. Teddy kicked off her shoes and lay back on the couch, her eyes open, looking at the pink Tiepolo twilight on the ceiling. She sighed deliciously and let him lift her hair off her neck and kiss her behind the ears. They'd never kissed sitting down before, she thought, and childishly, willfully, she eluded him and rubbed noses vigorously.

"Friends?" he asked anxiously.

"I forgive you. Only for old times' sake," Teddy growled crooningly. He ran his hands over her smart jacket, a garment so stiffly interlined and boned that it could stand up by itself. "All those buttons," he complained, as he started to undo them carefully, "between me and my girl."

The attempted unbuttoning of any single button was like an instant alarm signal to Teddy but she permitted it because the blouse under her jacket protected her with yet another double row of tiny taffeta buttons. Soon she lay on the couch in her elaborate blouse and new skirt, floating and lifting and melting under the storm of his kisses. She gasped for breath. This suddenness, this lack of prelude, of courtship, this brevity; the realization that she was alone in the house with him, not in a fraternity surrounded by a dozen kissing couples, was abruptly dangerous until she looked at Melvin's face and relaxed again. He'd taken his glasses off, and he looked so dear and reassuring that she plunged back into the flood of his caresses, enjoying the heady sense of power she always felt as whatever man who was kissing her grew more and more excited, as the beat of his passion grew quicker and the rhythm of his heart quickened. But now Melvin did something that had never happened to her before in three years of dedicated necking. He lifted her right off the couch, without any preliminary warning, and he carried her with ease, across the big room and through a door she hadn't noticed before, into what was his small bedroom.

"Melvin!" she protested, kicking wildly. "Stop that! What do you think you're doing? I never lie down on boys' beds!"

"There's always a first time, and I'm not a boy," he said, his voice muffled with love but determined. Teddy struggled to heave herself up off the quilt but he was so strong that it was like fighting against an undertow, and all the while he kept kissing wherever he could: her fingertips, her chin, her hairline, her eyes, a skillful arsonist setting a hundred tiny fires. Many minutes later, when she was blazing from head to toe, he started on the buttons of her blouse. She protested feebly. Her trusted iron wall, beyond which no male could penetrate, seemed to have crumbled and Teddy found herself without boundaries.

This just isn't happening, she thought, as he took off her blouse and opened the waistband of her skirt and slid it down over her feet. When his warm hands deftly unhooked her waist cincher and freed her breasts, when his warm mouth bent to her nipples, those inviolate virgin nipples that had never been touched in their nakedness, she thought, again, no, it isn't happening, but soon, as he drew them up into tiny points of brilliant sensation with his mouth, she thought, maybe it is happening after all. When she found Melvin Allenberg naked, pressing every sturdy inch of his body along her own nakedness, when she felt his penis, leaping like a fish, against her lower belly, she knew that it must at last and absolutely be happening, and that, although unbelievingly, she was ready. Lying down they fit together as if they were exactly the same height. Melvin was supremely slow, quivering with control, exquisitely patient but relentless. He took her inch by inch, took Teddy Lunel with a thoroughness that banished all her habits of withholding, took her with a completeness that left her without any secrets. And, at last, relieved of her baggage of rigid chastity, she lay next to him and was glad and grateful.

17

One hundred and fifty Molyneux spring dresses, each with its own pair of gloves painted to match. Odd, the details that popped into her mind whenever she was nervous, Marietta Norton thought, as the Lockheed Constellation broke through the clouds and the sun blazed in—that must have been back in 1933.

The senior fashion associate of *Mode* took a breath of relief as the plane steadied. She never admitted it to anyone but she was terrified of flying and it had been a rough takeoff from Idlewild on this windy September morning in 1952. She thought longingly of the days when editing a fashion magazine was still a fairly civilized procedure, those years during which everyone took the *Normandie* over to France for the collections: first class it had been, five days of pâté, caviar, champagne and a chance to refresh the spirit. But now she was expected to flop and lurch back and forth through the horrid skies as if it were nothing special.

This trip for instance: to France for next year's resort clothes that would be shown on twelve pages of the January issue—it could have been done perfectly well out in the Hamptons, in her opinion—after all, the clothes were all American designs—but no, Darcy had insisted on a full-scale production. "Marietta," he had said in that grand seigneur manner of his which never failed to annoy her, "we've consistently stayed ahead of *Vogue* and *Bazaar* because we're not afraid to go allout. *Vogue* is shooting resort in Portugal, I hear, and you're going to France for *Mode*—let's not discuss it further." Marietta Norton shrugged. It was an old argument between them and she never won.

However, she knew that she was the most experienced fashion editor in the business and Darcy appreciated her in the only way she wanted to be acknowledged, by paying her generously in a field in which salaries were normally low. God knows, after thirty years in fashion she was working only for the money that had enabled her to send her four daughters to the best schools, not for the joy of it. The glamour was long gone as far as she was concerned, gone as totally as Lanvin's evening jacket with mufflike shoulders of silver fox and lunch for two for ten dollars at the Colony and Cobina Wright's circus party and floor-length dresses for the races in the afternoon and Mrs. Harrison Williams costumed in Winterhalter crinolines as the Duchess of Wellington for the Chicago Opera Ball.

There had simply been too many Paris collections, too many Christmas bathrobe pages shot in July, too many jolting taxi trips down to Seventh Avenue, too many fattening lunches with manufacturers who advertised in *Mode*, too many days on which she had had to find the words to announce that fashion had turned yet another new leaf and now women had to throw out the old and ring in the new, when Marietta Norton herself didn't give a hoot in hell what she wore and, what was worse, looked it, and knew she looked it.

Like many of the best fashion editors Marietta Norton was unabashedly dowdy. She had spent most of her life inspecting all the clothes of the Western world and deciding which were the best of them; she had an instinct for choice that, had it belonged to a young and slim and very rich woman, would have guaranteed that woman a place on the Best Dressed List, but Marietta Norton never had the time, interest or energy to waste on picking out things for herself. Worse, she reflected, she was short and plump, the kind of woman the English always said "looked like a cook" although even the English didn't seem to have many cooks anymore.

Still, she counted on this trip to produce resort pages that would make *Vogue's* Portugal stuff look downright dull, if none of the bugs that plagued location trips came raging out of the woodwork.

Bill Hatfield, the rangy, flip photographer, was, for her money, one of the most tasteful boys in the business. Berry Banning, her assistant, seemed unusually efficient so far, although the jury was still out on Berry until they came back without incident to New York. Often girls from her moneyed Locust Valley, Bar Harbor, Spence-Chapin background didn't have what it took to succeed in the magazine world.

The only detail that hadn't been nailed down to Marietta's complete satisfaction was the model's haircut. She cast a baleful glance at the back of Teddy's head. The incomparable Miss Lunel, damn her glorious eyes, had adamantly refused to let her hair be cut in the new petaled chrysanthemum shape. It was the coiffure of the decade, Marietta was convinced of it, but when did Teddy Lunel ever do anything she didn't want to do?

She had never had to compromise from the very first day she started working, four years ago. Like Norman Norell and Mainbocher, the two star designers who had so much power that they allowed their clothes to be photographed only on the condition that four entire pages were devoted to each of them exclusively, Teddy Lunel was the only model alive who was never photographed with another model. Still, it was probably better that way, Marietta thought, forgiving Teddy her stubbornness about her hair, since even the greatest of the other models looked—well, perhaps "diminished" was the best way to put it, next to Teddy.

This was the sixth time Marietta had used Teddy for Europe. Only last spring they'd gone to Paris together for the Fall Collections and if anybody had ever been as supremely, heartbreakingly beautiful as Teddy in Balenciaga's hat of black tulle and roses, with the tulle spun out in the back like sugar candy, she'd like very much to know about it because it would be a bloody miracle. And just where, she wondered, was the stewardess with her martini? New York to Paris, an eighteen-hour flight, with refueling stops at Gander, in Iceland, God alone knew where, and again at Shannon, was at least an eight-martini trip . . . if only no one had told her that the most dangerous moments were landing and takeoff she might have been able to get by with only two or three.

Bill Hatfield didn't need a drink although he'd ordered one anyway. He'd been a Navy pilot in the war and he could get on any commercial plane and fall asleep before takeoff and wake in time for landing—just so long as he was carrying his three good-luck charms, the ones that kept the plane up. He was glad that Marietta, a smart old broad if ever there was, had booked him for this trip. Things were getting sticky back at the studio. Ann had finally moved out and if she did as she had promised, was arranging for her lawyer to meet with his lawyer about the divorce. All well and good. But Monique planned to move in and so did Elsa. Had he really suggested it to both of them? They certainly seemed to think so. The only thing wrong with being a fashion photographer was the models. Great girls they were, he'd never met one he didn't like—that was the trouble. He'd be out of danger for this trip at any rate—he'd already had his waltz with Teddy Lunel.

Out of the corner of his eye he watched her as she bent over a book. It had been the most marvelous six months of his life, way back when she'd stopped being Falk's steady girl, three years ago, but with Teddy, when it was over, it was fucking finished, stone cold dead, no embers, no remember whens. She didn't look back, that one. He wondered how many affairs she'd had since him. The mystique of sexual promiscuity was like a velvet cape that she drew about herself with a smile that could send a man straight to hell. Still, he'd lived through it . . . barely.

He thought of the other models who might have been making this trip with the *Mode* bunch. There was Jean Patchett, whose eyebrows were drawn by a master calligrapher, whose little round black beauty mark just above her right eye was the most famous beauty mark in the history of photography. Patchett's look was sophistication pushed to its outer limits—wrong for the kind of pictures he planned to take. Dovima, with her passionate face, her black hair and blue eyes, would have been a good choice for ball gowns, but he couldn't quite see her for resort clothes. Lisa Fonsegrieves, with her lunar loveliness, her porcelain princess face, that witty tilted nose and curly blond hair—yes, she would have been wonderful . . . but still a shade less perfect than Teddy. The only other possibility had been Suzy Parker. You just thought that no girl had ever been born more beautiful than Suzy . . . until you looked at Teddy.

Strange how beauty divided itself into levels. There were the hundred and fifty models in New York who were the pick of the loveliest girls in all of America and there were the halfdozen of those hundred and fifty who had broken away from the pack and stood alone, each a superb champion with her own special beauty, and *then* there was Teddy Lunel. He had never heard a better description of her than one he remembered reading in college, "O thou art fairer than the evening air, Clad in the beauty of a thousand stars," a line of Marlowe's that had somehow stayed with him, professional beauty watcher that he had always been, even before he became a photographer. You could add up all the parts but you still couldn't express the mysterious harmony of her beauty without resorting to poetry.

Bill Hatfield looked forward to working with her although there would be none of the undercurrent of sexual potential between them that there would certainly have been if he were working with a model he hadn't slept with yet.

Teddy had the knack of never looking the same that made his work an adventure in mutual creativity rather than a technical process. With each new change of clothes, Teddy drew on the life of another woman, a woman who would one day buy that particular dress and in it meet a man who would become the great love of her life, a woman who would remember until she died just what she had been wearing at that particular moment. How the hell she did it he had never understood. A sense of *authentic existence*, nothing less, was what Teddy produced for the camera. Still, that was, after all, what she got seventy bucks an hour for, more than any model in the world. And worth every nickel.

Where, he wondered, was the stewardess with his martini? The nice thing about flying commercial was that you could drink without worrying about your coordination. Landing on an aircraft carrier with alcohol in your bloodstream had never been recommended . . . although it *had* been done, and by him, now that he thought about it.

Berry Banning was too excited to notice the bumpy air as they took off. This was her most important assignment since she'd joined *Mode* three years ago. She'd never been on a European location trip before and her responsibilities were terrifying. Marietta had decided on the clothes, of course, and they'd all been fitted on Teddy before they left, but Berry had been in complete charge of every detail from that time on.

She had done all the complicated, cross-indexed packing of twelve large suitcases so that each outfit traveled with the wide range of choices of shoes, handbags, jewelry, scarves, hats, nylon stockings and sunglasses that Marietta Norton demanded on a fashion sitting.

Like Diana Vreeland of *Bazaar* and Babs Rawlings of *Vogue*, Marietta Norton approached each photograph as if it were an art form. Even when she was planning to photograph only a single hat she would make sure that the model was wearing perfume that complemented the mood of the hat, had on perfectly fitting shoes, untouched white gloves and fresh stockings. She could tie a scarf to convey a hundred variations of style, with a flick of her wrist transforming any model from an Apache to a Gainsborough. She played games with accessories like a theatrical set decorator, but God help her assistant if Marietta didn't have enough choice. Should even a single suitcase be lost . . . one such slip, no matter if it was the porter's fault, and Berry would never be trusted again. Marietta Norton, whom she worshipped, could unquestionably improvise something because there had never been a Marietta Norton location trip that hadn't been successful, but her own career would die before it had been properly born and there was nothing in life that she wanted but a future in the world of fashion.

From the time that she had been a little girl Berry Banning had saved every copy of *Vogue* and *Mode* and *Bazaar* and, recently, *Charm* and *Glamour* and *Mademoiselle* as well, and studied their pages as if they were her one and only prayer book and she were a cloistered nun.

It had never occurred to her that how a woman dressed could be a legitimate expression of the woman's *own* personality that depended on her point of view toward life. Fashion to Berry was a *law* and the happiest of beings were those, like herself, who were rich enough to live under this law, who could dedicate themselves to carrying out every subtle shading of its marvelously inconstant dictates. She never stopped trying to be worthy of high fashion. She spent hours peering unhappily at herself in a full-length mirror, unsuccessfully practicing the frozen and eternally quizzical expressions of remote self-love that appeared on the pages of the magazines, as if the models were asking "Will I do?" and then giving themselves the secret answer "Of course." Every dress she owned was exactly as *Mode* said it should be; a triumph of architecture, constructed as carefully as a bridge, insistently feminine, creating a tiny-waisted, low-cut, full-skirted line that looked natural unless you were trapped inside it.

But alas, Berry Banning had rich-girl hair, brown-brown and without direction, the kind of hair that only looked good drawn back and bundled under a tiara. Worse, she had rich-girl limbs, formed by the genes of generations of athletic Bannings, and she was too sturdy for the almost Victorian paper-doll elegance of the New Look. And worst of all, she had stubbornly rich-girl features, good but plain, pleasant enough but too straightforward to lend themselves to change through the use of cosmetics.

She always looked the *same*, Berry thought, with familiar despair, no matter what she did. She kept her eyes away from Teddy, who sat only one row in front of her.

It was going to be bad enough having to look at her for ten whole working days. She had often worked with Teddy before, although only for a day at a time in various New York studios, and she was familiar with the hideous sick headache that she always developed after such a day when she came home and confronted her own face in the mirror.

It wasn't, she told herself scrupulously, that she envied Teddy exactly, nor that she was jealous of her—as a matter of fact she genuinely liked her—but simply that it just didn't seem *fair* that two girls of the same age could both have the same things on their faces, like eyes and noses and lips, and yet with such utterly different results. It was as if Teddy belonged to an absolutely different form of life. What must it be like for her to wake up in the morning and catch sight of herself in the mirror—*that face*—and know it was hers? Oh, where was the stewardess with her martini?

Sam Newman, Bill Hatfield's assistant, was watching Berry Banning without seeming to. Christ, but he *loved* her kind of woman! Nice full breasts, great legs, long and tan from the summer, the kind of laugh that rang with self-assurance that was bred in the bone, a laugh as rich as she was. There was, in his large experience, no fuck so satisfactory as a rich girl—they just seemed to enjoy it more, probably because it didn't really count when they were making it with the assistant instead of with the photographer himself, so they just let themselves go and had fun. He'd had rich girls from the staff of every fashion book in the business, and from the fashion departments of all the women's magazines too and he'd take them over models any day, and he'd had models aplenty, although, of course, never the likes of Teddy Lunel.

Rich girls were much less neurotic than models, for one thing; less worried about getting to sleep on time; they enjoyed their food more; held their liquor better; often insisted on paying the check because they knew perfectly well how little he made, and they all felt guilty because none of them had to live on their salaries. Oh, but he liked their immaculate underwear, and their good shoes and their clean, unfussed hair and their strong passionate bodies, developed by years of swimming lessons and skiing lessons and riding lessons. One day he'd have his own studio and he'd marry a nice, plain, *grateful* rich girl and have a bunch of rich kids. Meanwhile, where the hell was the stewardess with his martini?

Teddy put down her book, sat back and closed her eyes. She let her mind fill with the loud noise of the aircraft, those familiar racketing vibrations that still gave her a great splurging sense of freedom although she'd made this flight to Europe more than a dozen times since she started modeling. On one level she felt as if she were still working in New York, her mind filled with drifting thoughts of the details that constituted the sum of her life.

There were the taxis, as many as ten or twelve in a day. Half the cabdrivers in Manhattan knew her for a big tipper and could recognize her silhouette as she dashed out of a building to the curb, always in a tearing hurry, weighed down by her huge Lederer bag, and they stopped in an instant when she gave her traffic-piercing whistle.

Inside the taxi, her magnifying mirror clutched firmly between her knees, she applied different makeup or put on a pair of false eyelashes on the way from one job to another. If she had an extra minute she tried to organize the handbag out of which she lived. Certainly it could do everything but give milk, full as it was with her bulging cosmetic case, her hairpieces, her three kinds of bras, her collection of slips to wear under any kind of dress, her own assortment of scarves, gloves and jewelry for those advertising sittings where there was no accessory editor, her three pairs of shoes of different style and heel height for the occasions when nobody had thought to get shoes in her size.

Of course for a job like this location trip she had only to travel with a lipstick and her own clothes because Marietta and Berry had provided everything else, but the ordinary working day always held at least one emergency. As the sun touched her face through the window of the plane Teddy remembered a trip to Nassau with Micheline Swift, the superb Swiss model, and John Rawlings the photographer. He had bet the two of them that if they could list the contents of their bags without looking he would give them each a hundred dollars in cash and, as a handicap, he allowed them each to forget thirty items. They'd both lost by a mile.

She sighed and tried to forget the routine of her life but the sun through her eyelids only made her think of the lights of a studio. Whenever she looked in a mirror it was to make a routine inspection of the texture of a serviceable fabric. Her face was no more than a machine she owned, a machine that had only a certain, limited life span.

Had she danced too late at the St. Regis Roof last night? If so, tonight it must be bed at nine, no matter what she had planned. Nobody would keep paying seventy dollars an hour for Teddy Lunel if there was even the faintest hint of fatigue under her eyes.

Did anyone who envied a professional beauty ever think about the cost of maintaining the façade; the hours of upkeep, the ringing of the alarm at six-thirty every morning, the cold hamburgers that had to be eaten on the run for their power to keep her standing on her weary legs as long as ten hours a day? It was the exhaustion that finally got to you, the exhaustion that made you wait without too much fear for that first wrinkle. If a model's father had died, if she was going through a divorce, or if she had just discovered she was pregnant when she shouldn't be, she still had to be fully *there* for the camera. Only the camera mattered. Did anyone fully understand, besides another model, that there could be no narcissism in a business that demanded total concentration on what the photographer wanted from you, allied to a total lack of self-consciousness, so that you forgot yourself for hours as you gave it to him, moving constantly as you poured out pure energy? It was almost like dance when it went well but good God in heaven, *it was so endlessly boring.*

Still, it bought freedom. Her weekly paycheck had been almost three thousand dollars for several years now, she had moved from her little apartment where she had first been safe from Maggy's scrutiny, to an elegant set of rooms on East Sixty-third Street and, if she kept in training, there was no reason why she shouldn't work at this rate for another three or four years, or maybe more, depending on how well the face held up.

But was that what she wanted? When had she signed on for this? Teddy had celebrated her twenty-fourth birthday last spring and as far as she knew there wasn't a girl with whom she'd been at college who wasn't married by now and didn't have at least one child. She didn't want *that*, Teddy thought, or rather, not exactly that, not a bunch of kids in the suburbs. But she didn't want to end up like her mother either, still consumed by her business, beginning to feel just a trifle threatened by some of the new agencies that had opened in the late 1940s like the Fords and Frances Gill and Plaza 5.

As the sound of the motors changed and settled down Teddy wished that she were making this long trip alone. Lately there seemed never to be a time to just sit and look up at the sky and dream. Day tumbled after day, completely filled, crowded with obligations and appointments. Each evening after she came home from her last booking she'd phone the agency and find out what she would be doing during every hour tomorrow.

Then, if she wasn't so tired that she needed to go to bed early, she'd hurry to bathe and dress and go out to the Stork Club or "21" or L'Aiglon or Voisin for dinner with any of the twenty men she could summon at the last minute. There hadn't been anybody she wanted to make love to, for, oh, two months or more, she thought with dismay. Why were men all so alike?

This summer she had spent weekend after weekend in Connecticut or out on Long Island where all the house parties seemed, in the end, to be the same. Teddy didn't miss spending those hot summer weekends in the city, although they could have their special charm—ah, but only if you were in love and the city seemed to have been emptied just for you. Or rather, only if you *thought* you were in love, Teddy reflected sadly. She had almost believed she was in love a few times in her life but it had never come true, not even with Melvin, her darling Melvin whom she still loved but with whom she had never been in love no matter how hard she had tried to be.

It had lasted for an entire year and there was no friend more dear, no lover more tender, but Melvin had never fit her dream, although he had come achingly close, so close that when he realized that his kind of love and her kind of love were never going to lock together he had been so desperately unhappy that they had had to part.

Every time she had been seriously involved with a man, Teddy thought, there had come a moment when she realized that she was like a stranger in a foreign country who tries to pay in an unacceptable currency. The coins of her emotions, on which she planned to live, turned out to be worthless. She could search her pockets, empty her wallet, as if she were in a nightmare, but she could never seem to find the right amount of . . . oh, of whatever it took to be in love really and truly. Her deepest fear, so buried that she failed to articulate it, was that something in her, some incurable emptiness, had already doomed her to inspire love but never to feel it.

Teddy's most excessive fantasies had all been fulfilled many times over. She'd had everything the world of high fashion could offer, more adulation and attention in eight average working hours than any bride on her wedding day. But more and more often she felt the surfacing of a long neglected but unappeased child in her, a timid little girl who wanted to be taken care of, who craved some vaguely seen but all-powerful man on whom she could depend. Teddy snorted at her own absurdity. She made more money than almost any man she knew . . . but recently a lot of her days had felt like one long, dreary, late Sunday afternoon.

She stood up abruptly, smoothing down the white capeskin jacket cut exactly like a man's button-down shirt that she wore over gray flannel slacks. She surveyed the next rows of the first-class cabin of the Constellation and shook her head severely at her traveling companions. "I guess all you people just don't give a damn," she said, "but I'd like to know what the hell has happened to my martini?

I'm going to find that stewardess. Does anybody want anything while I'm on my feet?"

Julien Mistral stood poised on the edge of the diving board. His powerful, tanned body was bisected only by the thin strap of narrow elastic bikini that men in Europe had been wearing for the past four years. He was fifty-two and his heroic proportions were those of a man of thirty. He had painter's muscles, the firm solid legs of a man who spends his life standing before a canvas or walking around a studio, and the well-developed arms and back of any man who wields a tool, whether it be a paintbrush or a shovel.

The look of a gentleman trained to knightly swaggering, that he had worn so haughtily in his youth, had not changed with years of ever-growing fame, greater mastery. But the arrogance with which he had held his head, that air of a conqueror, was no longer perceived as arrogance but as the outward sign of validated genius. His neck had grown somewhat thicker, there were deep lines around his eyes and others that led from his high-bridged nose to his mouth, yet the prodigious blaze of blue that had been imprisoned in his eyes had not changed in its fixity or intensity. His thick dark red hair was cut short, at the temples it was almost sandy, and his mouth was still hard, dominating, uncompromising. Mistral had the face of a chieftain.

He paused before diving into the pool that had been built two years before and looked about him, his hands on his hips. He frowned and seemed to forget the invitation of the water on this hot September day in 1952, as he listened to the sounds around him. The buzzing silence, that paradise of bees that had once surrounded *La Tourrello*, had vanished long before, almost from the first day that Kate had bought the farm and organized a battalion of builders and plumbers and electricians.

Now, new noises invaded the air of Provence; a half-mile away automobiles passed frequently on the road to Apt where once they had been rare; a tractor ground and rattled in a distant field where so recently men had worked with their hands; from time to time the plane from Paris to Nice passed directly overhead; in the kitchen of the *mas* the voices of three servants were raised in a sudden quarrel as they prepared for the dinner party that Kate had planned for that evening. The door of Kate's new Citroën could be heard on the other side of the house as she slammed it briskly and drove off with a squealing abruptness that indicated her habitual pre-party discovery that some detail had been neglected that made necessary a last minute trip to set it right. While Mistral stood there, his senses concentrated on all the sounds that were eroding the peace of his countryside, he didn't hear the light footsteps that approached cautiously along the length of the diving board.

"Papa!" shrieked a child's voice right behind him.

"*Merde!*" Startled, Mistral jumped, slipped, lost his balance and fell into the pool.

Three months following Kate Mistral's return to France after the war she discovered she was pregnant again. She had had several miscarriages during their marriage but Mistral hadn't been particularly disappointed. He had never wanted a child the way other men did. Children, he would have said if he'd given it any thought, were disruptive, time-consuming, probably disappointing and certainly the source of unforgivable interruptions.

He had deeply begrudged the need to worry about Kate's new pregnancy at the ridiculously late age of forty-three. He wanted her full attention to be turned to putting the *mas* back in working order. He never intended to have to deal with practical matters again, and when Kate had arrived in the spring of 1945, her two suitcases crammed with Ivory soap, Kleenex, toilet paper, instant coffee, needles, thread, flashlights, and white sugar, luxuries unimaginable in France for five years, he drew a breath of relief. He wanted only to disappear into his studio at first light and forget the nagging problems of daily existence. A child would complicate his life—but certainly she would miscarry again. Ordinary men needed sons to prove to themselves that they had existed and left something behind on the face of the earth. Julien Mistral knew that he was immortal and that a son could add nothing to his place in the history of art.

However, when Kate gave birth, in February of 1946, to a skinny, solemn and somehow sour-faced baby girl, she was so proud of herself that even Mistral felt a certain sense of participation in her happiness. Kate named the baby Nadine and reassured Mistral by promptly putting her on a bottle and getting her own strength back in a few weeks.

In the next years Kate's organizational abilities were taxed to the fullest. Jean Pollison returned from Germany with teeth missing, skeletal from malnutrition, but he recovered rapidly and *La Tourrello* was the first farm in the Lubéron to bloom again, thanks to Mistral's money that Kate spent so liberally as soon as there was anything available for sale after the war. A Swiss nurse was imported to take care of Nadine while Kate dealt with the renewed explosion of interest in Mistral.

As early as 1946 France swarmed again with American dealers greedy to see what had been painted during the war, and Mistral's studio contained more canvases that he considered worthy to be sold than it had ever held before: all the paintings he had done in the five years since *Les Oliviers* had been completed.

"Have you heard from Avigdor yet?" Kate asked Mistral soon after her return.

"No, I've decided to change dealers," Mistral answered. "The man has always been more interested in discovering new talent than in getting the best prices for the artists to whom he owes his success—why did he never open an American branch, I ask you? That alone has cost me a great deal. My contract with him lapsed during the war—take advantage of it."

As Mistral had known she would, Kate obeyed him without further question. He had calculated from the beginning of their marriage that as long as he allowed her to feel powerful in certain areas she would be satisfied. Any dealer would have to reckon with Kate before he even got near Mistral. He wasn't giving up any authority he wanted to retain in letting Kate choose a new gallery, since it was the sort of necessary business that he loathed, on a level with coping with the neighboring farmers who were beginning to think of forming a cooperative to which they would all sell their grapes. An artist choosing a dealer, he told Kate, was like an elephant picking out a favorite louse. The dealer Kate finally settled on, Étienne Delage of New York, Paris and London, soon discovered that Julien Mistral was an exception to the rule that most painters only grow rich in the grave.

When the São Paulo Museum of Modern Art had its major Mistral exhibition in 1948 he didn't bother to make the trip although Kate was there for weeks in advance, overseeing the installation of the canvases. A year later she went to New York for the opening of the big Mistral retrospective at The Museum of Modern Art, but again Mistral preferred to stay at home. In 1950 and 1951 he had finally been persuaded to be present at the important exhibition at the Stedelijk Museum of Amsterdam, the Kunsthaus in Zurich, the Palazzo Reale in Milan, and the two-month-long celebration of the twenty-fifth anniversary of his first show which was celebrated by an exhibition that took over the entire Maison de la Pensée Française, in Paris.

Once that was over Mistral declared that he would never go to another museum show, no matter how significant. He detested the kind of elbow-rubbing and ceremonial duties of these occasions, he loathed the crowds of strangers who felt that because they loved his work they had the right to talk to him about their reactions to particular paintings. "Let Picasso, that mountebank, that marketplace of every kind of art—not excluding pots and pans—encourage the lionizers—I have better things to do than act like the ringmaster at a circus."

He kept to his resolve but each exhibition—and each major art auction—saw a dramatic rise in his prices. Étienne Delage discovered, as Adrien Avigdor had before him, that the very scarcity of Mistral's paintings made them unusually valuable. After his wartime paintings were sold, he took to retaining most of his new work that survived his annual bonfire, but in 1951 alone he earned the equivalent of a quarter of a million dollars in American money without having to part with more than a half-dozen canvases.

In the late 1940s and early 1950s more and more journalists found their way to Félice and for the many dozens who were denied entry to *La Tourrello* there were invariably several so important that Kate eventually persuaded Mistral to grant a few grudging interviews. On the other hand, she protected him from art historians who were writing books on him, tourists who wanted to have their photographs taken with him, college girls who wanted his autograph, scholars who were doing monographs on his work, collectors who thought that he might be charmed into selling them a picture when Delage had nothing to offer. Yet nothing was so disruptive, so distracting to him as Kate's growing interest in playing the hostess.

Perhaps it was the swimming pool, put in by a special company from Cannes, Mistral thought, that had set her off but during the last two years she had become the social queen of the region. Aristocrats from England had bought a château near Uzès, a great American expert on Cézanne had settled in Ménerbes, the Gimpels, art dealers for generations, had bought another château not far from Félice, and now all of them and others like them were entertaining each other and being entertained by Kate.

Mistral had lost any interest in her body soon after Nadine's birth. Otherwise he would have stopped her—what did he care to meet strangers, no matter how famous, what possible interest could he have in listening to their absurd, excited chatter about the new, so-called Abstract Expressionists, a scum-filled sewer of hopeless drooling idiots, every last one of them, who, lacking talent, vomited up their last meals and called it art, as if an apple could be abstract, or a full moon or a mountain or a naked woman . . . why waste time talking about them any more than telling malicious stories about that *pauvre con* of a Picasso and his ludicrous involvement with the Communists who used him to paint propaganda portraits of Stalin, but never understood what his work was trying to do . . . not that he had ever succeeded.

No, the only thing he agreed with Picasso about was Dubuffet. Picasso loathed him as much as Mistral did. And the only thing he agreed with Dubuffet about was Monet—they both liked him. Degas had had the right idea, Mistral thought. When he knew he was dying he'd said to his artist friend, Forain, that there was to be no funeral oration, but, "If there has to be one, you, Forain, get up and say," He greatly loved drawing. So do I.' And then go home." There was a man!

But Degas had not had an American wife to whom he made love less and less. There was just enough guilt in that, he admitted to himself, to make him feel that Kate had to be allowed the pleasure she got in dining with Charlie Chaplin and the Duchess of Windsor.

Yes, ambition came to a woman as the life of the body was denied to her, he mused. He had his women, of course, in Avignon now, for the sake of decency, one young and willing girl after another, no more important than a pair of shoelaces, yet indispensable as shoelaces are when you don't have them.

But Kate seemed content with her ever-expanding guest list and with Nadine, who was growing into more of a chatterbox every day. He had tried, once or twice, to let Nadine sit quietly in a corner of his studio because she had begged to be allowed to see him work, but the child had never learned to maintain a decent quiet. "Why are you using all that red, Papa? Is that big yellow thing a sun, Papa? Can you paint a bird, Papa? Paint me a dog!" And even, God help him, "Why are you standing so still, Papa . . . is it because you are thinking?" No! It was too much to be endured. He forbade her the studio although her tiny chin trembled and she pouted in the way the servants thought was adorable and pulled ever so wistfully on her pale blond hair.

Nadine, at six, already had all sorts of little tricks to get what she wanted. Frequently Mistral caught her out in lies, especially against the servants. When he insisted that she should be punished Kate grew angry. "She's just imaginative, oversensitive, at her age she can't be expected to know the difference—don't be so moralistic, Julien." Mistral thought otherwise. Like all adults he knew how easy it was to lie and he was deeply suspicious of a child who had learned so young to do it so well. But Marte Pollison, who had no children of her own, conspired with Kate to spoil Nadine in spite of the discipline that the nurse tried vainly to impose. When Mistral talked to Kate about it she just laughed and said that it was typically French to expect children to be like little adults. Didn't he realize that her daughter was not an ordinary child? She was special and she had a wonderfully inquisitive little mind.

As he swam underwater after he fell into the pool Mistral thought grimly that inquisitive mind or not, he would teach her not to creep up behind him on the diving board, but when he surfaced Nadine had prudently vanished. Sly. She had been born sly and manipulative he told himself and dismissed her from his mind.

As Julien Mistral floated in his pool he thought about his work. It had been six months now that he had been groping toward the beginnings of a series of paintings inspired by shapes of grapevines in winter. His studio floor was covered with sketches and studies but only he knew that when he woke up each morning he no longer felt the gut-filling urge to leap out of bed and paint until the light faded. Only he knew that he lay under the quilt of the bed with the taste of fear in his mouth, with a churning in his stomach, with a weak and contemptible desire to fall asleep again so that he wouldn't have to face the fact that his fire burned lower and lower. Nevertheless, Mistral sketched all day, every day, wandering through his vineyards and those of his neighbors, each stroke of his charcoal based on a fear of death. He worked to keep death away, every motion of his fingers a useless protest against even thinking about death.

Ever since his fiftieth birthday he had been obsessed by this thought. Which came first? he wondered. The idea of death or the loss of that urge to paint that was the same as death itself? Mistral had always cared nothing for the lives or opinions of other artists but he found himself wondering if any of them had ever lived through the arid stretch of sand and rock in which he found himself wandering. It was not that he could not paint . . . technically he had such mastery that he could continue to paint for as long as he lived, but something had disappeared from his work, and he could not deny it to himself even if the public could be fooled—who could not fool those credulous cretins?

He searched and searched for the reason. The nerves of his eyes were as alert as ever; he *saw* with the vision that had always possessed him . . . but he was not *driven* to record what he saw, except by that fear that he would die if he stopped. Where was the failure, he wondered, where was the lack of connection, no, no . . . not lack of connection but lack of *appetite.* Yes, that was it, that was what it was.

Julien Mistral shuddered even though the water he floated in was warm, for he knew that there were many things in life that could be learned and many that could be achieved with hard work but that *appetite* must spring from within a man, and well forth without his conscious effort. Just as no wise doctor has ever been able to explain why, at the end of nine months, the womb begins to work to expel the child, no one knows what causes the divine hunger of the artist, no one can tell you what temptation must be put before him to drive him to appease his appetite day after day. Should that appetite falter . . . should that appetite dry up . . . if he had believed in God, Julien Mistral would have prayed.

18

"It's the oddest thing," said Marietta Norton to Bill Hatfield, "but I believe I'm actually feeling a bit apprehensive. I haven't felt apprehensive since I heard about Pearl Harbor."

"Apprehensive, hell, I'm terrified . . . The last three guys who tried to get Mistral's picture came home empty-handed—all they had on film was the back of his head. But they didn't have our secret weapon—La Belle Théodora."

The fashion editor and the photographer leaned back against the cushions of the suitcase-filled old Renault taxi they were taking to *La Tourrello* from Le Prieuré—the hotel that had once been the pension of Madame Blé—in Villeneuve-les-Avignon, where they had spent the previous night. Behind them in another taxi were Berry, Sam and Teddy. They had been in France for almost ten days and after this afternoon's work they would be ready to return to Paris, and a day later fly back to New York with their objectives accomplished. Marietta Norton's intention had been to photograph her resort fashions in the studios of the three greatest living French artists—Picasso, Matisse and Mistral—and through Darcy's connections in the art world she had been granted permission by all of them.

In one day, in Vallauris, Bill Hatfield had shot fifteen rolls of film of Picasso and Teddy. There, on the Chemin du Fournas, Picasso rented two large studios in a building and split them in half, one part devoted to sculpture and the other to painting and engraving.

In the sculpture studio Berry had hooked Teddy into a strapless, black silk organdy dress printed with enormous white bows. Balancing lightly on her thin, high-heeled, black sandals, she stood amidst the mountain of spare metal parts that Picasso collected for his sculpture: bicycle chains and handlebars, wheels and pulleys of every size, any piece of odd iron that he could find discarded on a junk heap, some of which would be transformed into his animal heads and female forms and the great *She-Goat*, while Picasso, an aging Pan in a boiler room, flirted delightedly as she tried to avoid snagging her thin stockings on nails and barbed wire. Teddy quickly changed into a cornflower printed silk and the entire entourage moved into his painting studio where Picasso, peeking out from behind a pot-bellied stove, proudly pointed out the thick spiderwebs he encouraged to swing everywhere in the forty-foot room. Bill Hatfield went mad with excitement, trying to capture the expressions on Picasso's face as he talked to Teddy. Whenever he dared, he shot picture after picture of the messy, crowded studio itself, filled with the pots of paint and tools and old cans and equipment of all sorts from which the wizardry was distilled.

From Vallauris they had driven to Nice to find Matisse, bedridden in his bright hotel room at the Regina, living in a magnificent muddle of plants, singing birds, cooing doves and the brilliant fantasia of the bright paper cutouts he made now that he could no longer paint.

Matisse had welcomed them with the sweetness for which he was famous, enchanted with Teddy in her harem-bright dress, a shocking pink shantung splashed with an orange print, with her lovely bare arms making an arabesque that, he told her, none of his odalisques could equal. Teddy's clothes had been changed often enough to fill eight pages of *Mode* with the new spring prints. Now, at Mistral's domain, Marietta Norton planned to wind up with shots of the packable clothes that would travel everywhere next winter, four more pages of pictures in all.

In the second taxi Teddy sat in the front seat next to the driver. She was happy to leave the back seat to Berry and Sam, who seemed to be achieving an interesting relationship based on the limp and dazed condition in which Berry had staggered back last night into the room she shared with Teddy. Happy Berry, thought Teddy, I envy you. This is a country for lovers.

As the taxi passed l'Isle sur la Sorgue, with its ancient waterwheels still turning in the canals that surrounded the city, Teddy consulted the map. At least another half-hour to Félice, she thought, and her stomach clutched into a ball of nerves. Did all the others know that her mother had posed for Mistral? she wondered once again. The seven paintings that formed the *Rouquinne* series had never been publicly exhibited since the show in New York in 1931, but anybody with any knowledge of the history of modern art must have seen them in countless reproductions. Yet how many people in 1952 would ever connect them to Maggy?

Teddy had been in college in a darkened auditorium in the art building when a color slide of one of the series had been flashed on the screen in Art 101. She had never really looked at the picture before with close attention, but then, as the lecturer talked on about Mistral, she had scrutinized the model's face and realized, with a hot black flash of sureness, that the abandoned redheaded girl who displayed herself with such ripe sensuality had the same features as her remote, businesslike, stiffly coiffed, perfectly dressed mother.

On her next vacation Teddy had screwed up her nerve and ventured to ask Maggy about the painting but she had been granted only a few careless words. "I modeled briefly for artists when I was very young—it was so long ago that I've forgotten the details. Naturally we all posed naked—I thought you knew that," Maggy had said in a way that clearly indicated that she had no intention of discussing her life in Paris in any further detail. Teddy had been too intimidated to try to find out any more. Somehow her mother's existence before she came to the United States was almost as much of a taboo as the mystery of her own birth, the never-to-be-asked questions about her father.

Did Maggy have any understanding of the baffled, tongue-tied bruised frustration that Teddy had felt for so long? Or, to be fair, Teddy told herself, was she not a coward herself? Why had she been unable to confront Maggy with her questions, to insist on getting answers, no matter how much it might have shamed her mother? Oh, the old dilemma, the two sides to the argument that she had held with herself all those years while she was growing up.

In the past four years, living on her own, financially free of Maggy, she had almost forgotten the tormented, twisted bewilderments of her childhood. They had come to seem less and less important as her life grew more crowded and self-centered. It was only because she would be in the presence of Mistral so soon, that now they were filling her mind again. Yet, had this entire trip not been a kind of search?

Maggy had struggled to prevent her from taking the *Mode* booking as soon as she had learned what it was to involve, but Teddy had insisted. She waited to see if Maggy would finally come right out and say *why* she didn't want Teddy to go to Provence, but Maggy had given a dozen reasons that had nothing to do with

Mistral and in revenge, Teddy had resisted all her arguments.

What could Maggy be afraid of? Teddy wondered, her heart beating faster as the taxi turned off the road to Apt. What secret could she have that would still shock anyone after all these years? Could she possibly be so naive as to imagine that because she had once posed naked for a painter who must be an old man by now, that it would horrify her worldly daughter?

"Berry," she said softly, "we're almost there. Better put on some lipstick before Marietta gets a look at *you*."

"I'm sorry to keep you waiting," Kate Mistral explained to Marietta Norton, "but Julien is still working and I don't dare to tell him you're here."

"I hope the light doesn't go," Bill Hatfield said anxiously.

"Don't worry. I made him promise to stop at five tonight and I reminded him again at breakfast—he rarely agrees to do this sort of thing, you know, but when I can get him to say yes he's usually very good about it."

"We're awfully indebted to you," Marietta said, praying that one more expression of gratitude might hasten the emergence of Julien Mistral. Picasso had given them a whole day but Mistral had only agreed to the hours of the late afternoon.

"Not a bit—I've been a *Mode* reader all my life—I get it here by mail," Kate said, smiling, charming, very much the wife of the great painter. She had led them all through the *mas*, with its profusion of high, white-plastered, dark-beamed rooms, fashionably spare and shining with hexagonal terracotta tile floors. Baskets of dried lavender stood here and there amid the fine country antiques. At the rear of the house, two large wings, built of old stones, and connected by a high stone wall that protected them from the winds, faced each other across a central swimming pool surrounded by grass. One of the wings was Mistral's studio, its doors closed, and the other was the new pool pavilion where a room had been set aside in which Teddy could change. For almost an hour they all waited, drinking tall glasses of cassis-flavored lemonade in the shade of a vine-heaped trellis.

Kate Mistral took no interest in any of them but Marietta Norton. She had an unerring capacity to pick out the most important person in any group and as far as she was concerned the only one of this band worth talking to was the fashion editor. Not only could she catch up on news of some of her carefully tended friendships with people who shaped opinion in New York, but she could lay the foundations for a connection to Marietta that would someday, somehow be valuable.

Kate had watched with disgust as the attention of the art world turned toward the new painters, particularly those of the New York School, and although she had no fears that Mistral was not secure in the fame that had grown since 1926, she was too clear-eyed not to notice how Picasso, as firmly enthroned as Mistral, was no longer considered to have any relevance to what the new painters were doing, how he was attacked on every side by the younger generation of art critics.

It was not enough for Kate that the major museums of the world competed to give Mistral shows, that art historians took the most serious interest in him, that he sold every painting he allowed to be shown. She wanted continuing publicity, particularly in the most fashionable publications, that would prevent any public slackening of interest in Mistral.

She knew that Mistral had never given a damn whether his art was fashionable—she would never have dared to use the word in front of him when speaking of anything but a dress—but she, Madame Julien Mistral, did not intend ever to find herself the wife of a painter in whom the fashionable world had lost interest. The Impressionists had ignored the great Delacroix and the public had followed their lead. The new Abstractionists must never presume to discount Mistral. These pages in *Mode* would be helpful—all top-flight publicity was helpful, although "publicity" was a word she would have feared to use even more than "fashionable" in talking to Mistral.

While Kate chatted effusively on a wicker sofa with Marietta, the rest of the *Mode* group sat at a little distance. Only Teddy stood up the entire time in her sleeveless, white jersey Anne Fogarty dress. The top of the dress was tightly molded and finely pleated, crisscrossing over her breasts into a deeply wrapped *décolleté*, and spreading into a vast ballerina skirt that stopped less than ten inches from the floor.

To emphasize the illusion that Teddy belonged to some unseen *corps-de-ballet*, Marietta had added a belt like a tight gold ring, gold ballet slippers from Capezio and a gold band that held her mass of red hair back off her brow. Teddy looked as insubstantial as an iridescent soap bubble in the dress that, in theory, was uncrushable. However, Berry hadn't dared risk letting her sit down in it for there were eight stiffly starched crinolines underneath holding out the light fabric. Teddy leaned over carefully and sipped a mouthful of liquid from a glass that Berry held for her. All she needed was to spill the pink lemonade over the dress, she thought. Ridiculously her hands were shaking. Why the hell didn't he come out?

"Stage wait," Berry muttered sympathetically. It was odd to see Teddy visibly nervous. She'd treated Picasso and Matisse as if they'd been old beaux from dancing school days.

"How are my eyebrows?" Teddy asked. The style of 1952 demanded heavy, arched and strongly emphasized eyebrows placed halfway between anyone's normal brows and the forehead. No model, not even Teddy, could depart from this cosmetic convention, but unlike other models, Teddy had refused to shave or pluck her own light red eyebrows. She had covered them with makeup and penciled false brows above them, a delicate, painstaking process that took at least a half-hour to do perfectly.

"Still on," Berry reassured her.

"I have this awful feeling that they're slipping."

"Don't worry, I'd tell you if they were."

The tall doors of the studio opened and Julien Mistral walked slowly toward them along the side of the swimming pool wiping his hands on a paint-stained rag that he stuffed in the pocket of his corduroy pants. Kate introduced him to Marietta Norton and then she asked the fashion editor to introduce her colleagues. Marietta, flustered by Mistral's martial bearing, by his unmistakable look of a man who would prefer to be elsewhere, presented them as quickly as possible, using only their first names. When Mistral took Teddy's hand he looked at her a shade more closely than he looked at the others.

"Come into the studio," he said in French. "Let's get this over with."

They understood him. Berry had finishing school French; Marietta, Paris Collection French; Teddy, her mother's French and Bill Hatfield, photographer's French.

Inside the great space of the studio they all fell silent. Here reigned a kind of sublime disorder that made the mess of Picasso's studio seem almost banal.

Only Bill, cursing to himself at the need to choose between looking at the paintings and taking his pictures before the sun dimmed, was able to move. The others simply stood as speechlessly shy as schoolchildren, not daring to venture a word because anything they said would sound inadequate as they gazed from one big canvas to another. Each canvas was a meditation on a world in which the commonplace became a marvel, each a meditation on a human vision that could articulate the commonplace so that it was perceived for the first time.

Finally Bill picked his spot. "Come on, Teddy," he said, grabbing her arm. "Go stand over there next to him and make like you're having fun." Mistral was waiting impatiently in front of his easel, on which stood an empty canvas.

Gathering all her professionalism about her, Teddy walked over to him, the skirts of her Swan Queen dress swaying as she moved so lightly in her ballet slippers. He was so tall that she had to stretch her neck the full length of its supple ivory arch to look up at him. She had never felt so small next to any man, Teddy realized, as she tilted her finely cut chin, her head pulled backward by the heavy mass of her hair. Her changeable eyes were an unnameable color that held in it the bewitchment of a thousand twilights. Her smile was an adventure.

Mistral took her chin in his hand and turned it to one side and then to the other, expressionlessly. His blue eyes, blazing twin conflagrations, scanned her face. He pulled the rag on which he'd wiped his hands out of his pocket. It smelled of turpentine, Teddy had just time enough to think, before she realized that he was holding her head firmly in one big hand and wiping off her eyebrows with the other. In unison, Marietta squawked, Berry shrieked, Bill cursed and Sam hooted.

"That's better. You use too much paint," Mistral said so softly that only Teddy heard him. "Just like your mother." He smiled for the first time. "But you are a thousand times more beautiful."

After the furor had quieted down, everyone from *Mode* went back to the room in which Teddy had changed and Marietta Norton inspected the damage. She told them all to wait while she went off to straighten things out. She found Kate with the cook.

"Madame Mistral, we have a problem," she said grimly.

"Oh, no—is there anything I can do?"

"Monsieur Mistral has, unfortunately, removed my model's eyebrows."

"What!"

"They were penciled on and he wiped them off. He also seems to have messed up the makeup base on her forehead. It's going to take her at least an hour to match the top of her face to the bottom—by that time the light will be too low for color pictures."

"But why on earth . . . ?" Kate was furious with him. How could he be such a boor—and after all her careful arrangements?

"I haven't the slightest idea—an artistic decision no doubt—but the fact is that it puts us in a devil of a spot—we have four pages left to fill, and nothing to fill them with."

"I can't tell you how sorry—I can't imagine what he thought he was up to. Look, I wouldn't dream of disappointing you, not after you came all this way—I'll go and talk to him. If he could give you some time tomorrow morning, would that work out or do you have to be somewhere else?"

"We're not going anywhere," Marietta said grimly.

"Let me give you a gin and tonic and get this sorted out."

"Don't bother with the tonic," Marietta said with a sigh of relief. She understood Kate Mistral's kind of woman. They were both equally professional. She'd get her four pages and that was the only thing that mattered.

The next day, after breakfast, as they drove back to *La Tourrello* Teddy was more confused than she had ever been in her life. That moment, that brief moment when Julien Mistral had held her chin in his hand, was embedded in her mind as if she'd been shot between the eyes and the bullet had lodged there. He hadn't said another word to her—bedlam had taken over—but she thought about nothing else since it had happened. It was as if her life were a film and when Julien Mistral had touched her the director had yelled "Cut." Until she saw him again the screen must remain blank, waiting.

As soon as Teddy saw Mistral frowning impatiently at the invasion of their troop into his studio, she knew that he had been waiting for her as eagerly as she had been waiting for him. There could be no doubt about such passionate certainty. She walked over to the easel, holding her breath. He put out his hand and she took it and their hands clasped each other tightly without moving for a long second until they both remembered that they were supposed to be giving the conventional handshake greeting of France.

"Bonjour, Mademoiselle Lunel. Did you sleep well?"

"Bonjour, Monsieur Mistral. I didn't sleep."

"Nor did I."

"Teddy," Bill Hatfield said, "turn a bit—we can't see the dress."

I must touch his face, thought Teddy, as she moved a few inches to her right. I must put my hands on either side of his head and feel the place at his temples where his hair starts to grow and the skin looks so smooth.

Chin down a little," Bill called, "as if you're looking at the canvas."

I want to kiss his eyes. I want to feel his eyelids with my lips, Teddy thought, as she stared blankly at the canvas.

"Teddy, could we have a little more animation?" Bill asked.

I want to put my lips on his chest where his shirt is unbuttoned at the neck. I want to unbutton his shirt and lay my head on his chest and then button the shirt up again so that I'm inside it. I want to breathe with his breathing, I want my heart to beat with his heart.

"Teddy, back to me, please—I'm getting a rear view of the dress again."

I want to make his mouth grow sweet. I want to feel him laugh under my mouth, I want to beg him for kisses, I want him to beg me for kisses.

"Damn it, Teddy." Bill was more surprised than impatient, Teddy never needed this kind of direction.

"He is not happy, your photographer," Mistral said quietly.

"His happiness does not concern me."

"But he won't stop until he has the photographs he wants."

"No, you're right."

"And the sooner he stops the sooner we can talk."

"What are we going to talk about?"

"Teddy! You know I can't get anything with your lips moving, for Christ's sake!"

"What are we going to talk about?" she repeated.

"The rest of our lives."

"I'm leaving for New York tomorrow."

"You will stay here with me."

"Can that be true?"

"You know it is true."

"Look, guys, Monsieur Mistral I mean, this isn't working. What if you both went over to the table in the middle of the room and you show Teddy your palette?" Bill said with exaggerated calm.

"Where can we talk?" she asked.

"At the Hiely Restaurant in Avignon, at eight-thirty tonight. Understood?"

"Understood." Teddy gave Bill a smile that he spent the rest of his life wishing he'd captured on film and began to go through her poses as automatically as a well-trained animal, her head tipped so that she could look at Julien Mistral without meeting his eyes, because if she met his eyes she would not be able to stand up.

All these years, she thought, all these long years of dreaming and dreaming and falling and falling through the dream to this place, this minute. No one has ever been real before. No one else will ever be real again.

As soon as Teddy put herself seriously to work Bill Hatfield was able to get his photographs quickly. Kate Mistral, who returned from Félice just as they finished, asked them all to stay for lunch but Marietta had to refuse because she was afraid of missing the afternoon train for Paris, and all their luggage still had to be collected back at Le Prieuré.

"Are you all packed?" Berry asked over her shoulder. Teddy was lying on the bed in the comfortable room they had shared, with its walls covered in pale yellow fabric printed in a tiny Provençal flower design.

"I'm staying."

"Please, Teddy, you know that I have no sense of humor about anything to do with *arrangements*."

"I'm not going back with you."

"Did you see my list? I've got all the suitcases, but oh, God, I can't find the *list*. Why are you just lying there?"

"You weren't listening—I'm staying on in Provence . . . for a while. I've never seen any place I like as much as this."

"But you can't just do that!"

"Why not?" Teddy's voice was calm yet it was filled with a kind of feverish necessity, and there was a bright flare of pink under her cheekbones. Berry looked at her anxiously.

"Are you sick? Don't you feel well enough to make the trip?"

"Of course not. It's a whim . . . don't you ever have whims, Berry?"

"Certainly not. I won't be able to have them for a dozen years. Well, okay—so stay . . . I've found that list—God must have listened. Your return ticket's right here—I'll put it on the bureau. You could have mentioned it earlier, that's all."

"I didn't know earlier," Teddy said in a voice from a dream. "I'll send the agency a cable so they'll have the news before you get home."

"What about your mother? She's not going to like this, is she?"

"Oh, she'll understand," Teddy said slowly. "I have the feeling that she'll understand better than anyone."

In a French city of medium size the best restaurant in town is often characterized by a straightforward lack of decor that announces clearly that here everything is focused on great food.

The restaurant Hiely in Avignon was located in one large but unassuming rectangular room, plainly paneled in wood, its comfortably large tables spread with plain yellow cloths, its plain parquet floor highly polished. On a center table stood a whole smoked ham surrounded by bowls of fresh fruit, and platters of cooked lobsters and bottles of wine reclining in individual baskets. However, there was no other display, the windows were undraped, there were no flowers on the tables and the unupholstered wooden chairs stood around the table in a dignified and reasonable manner that indicated that this place was devoted to gastronomy with a philosophy of total concentration.

As Julien Mistral and Teddy Lunel sat facing each other at a quiet table in a window alcove Teddy wondered why nobody had ever warned her that love at first sight would strike her dumb. Veteran of thousands of first dinners she had never found herself so at a loss for speech. They had already said so much to each other, in front of other people and protected from its consequences by the fact that they were in public, even though unheard, that now that they were finally alone together she was tongue-tied, reduced to a few banal words about the food.

Julien Mistral, who had never hesitated to make his opinions known, a man to whom shyness was the most unfamiliar of states, found himself almost as silent as Teddy. A lamentable performance, he told himself. He was choking with things that had to be said but he too scarcely managed to push his food around on his plate. Where to start? Not at the beginning because this had started a long time ago; yesterday seemed another era of his life. He couldn't begin in the middle because this strangely solemn, awkward dinner *was* the middle. They didn't know each other after all, yet he could see no future for them that was not a continuation. The necessary presence of this woman must never be withdrawn from him.

To Teddy the rather ordinary lamplight in the room seemed to tremble as much as her hands as she tried to make a show of eating. She found herself singularly unwilling to use any of her easily summoned arsenal of allure. She wanted only to touch Mistral, to hold him. She had no impulse to flirt because they had gone beyond flirtation the instant that they had admitted to each other that neither of them had slept the night before.

Mistral's face, that famous face, so much more beautiful than she had ever imagined, was grave. He didn't try to joke, he seemed to be thinking, and the inconsequential comments she might have used to bridge this moment stuck to her lips before they were spoken. The questions that she wanted to ask him were either too unimportant or too important. There was no middle ground. Teddy had to know everything about Julien Mistral from the day he had been born—his life was dense, complicated, foreign—yet something informed her that only the thinnest of veils separated them from knowing each other better than either of them had ever known anyone.

When the meal was almost over Teddy looked up from her wineglass and confronted Mistral's gaze, dropping even the pretense of speech. One single tear, of some emotion she didn't dare to name, ran slowly down her cheek. He touched it with his finger, let it be absorbed by his skin, and around them there fell a web of confused, hesitant joy that was so fine and fierce that he was freed to talk to her at last.

"Last week," he said, "I was sure I'd never feel young again. I looked up at the sky that I used to love and the sunlight was glaring through a thin layer of clouds and the light had a flat skin of utter hopelessness. I told myself that it was the human condition and that all that was wrong with me was that I'd had the ego to think that the human condition could never apply to me."

"And now?" Teddy asked gravely.

"I feel as if I had never been young before, never known what it was, as if all the years of my youth were spent in a kind of emptiness. I thought it was being alive because I couldn't envision anything better. I wasn't unhappy—I worked and I lived like any other man and I didn't ask myself questions because I was painting and I've always believed that was the only thing I wanted. I can't tell you that I missed you then because I didn't know you existed. It's only now that I understand how incomplete I was."

"But during half of your life I didn't exist." She smiled gently as she spoke.

"Does that seem even remotely possible to you? I know it's true, but I can't make myself *feel* it."

"We should have been born on the same day," Teddy cried passionately. "We should have grown up together! You could always have been with me—oh, I've been waiting for you *forever.* Those hours in which I felt unhappy and only half a person—oh, so many hours—it was because you weren't there. I was afraid this could never happen to me," she said, liberated by a great wind of gladness. "I never expected to be a girl like this."

"And I," Julien Mistral said incredulously, "I never expected to be *a man like this* . . . it is so . . . *thorough* . . . it makes me understand other men, men who give up everything for a woman, men I used to be so scornful of—it makes me feel . . . *human*, just like everyone else."

"Is that a blow?" Teddy said, her laugh a promise.

"It would have been until yesterday. Now it is such an extraordinary . . . *relief* . . ." Even as he spoke he listened to himself and marveled. He had never talked to any woman like this, never dreamed it was possible, never known that these words could come to his lips, never imagined himself swept up by an emotion that clearly announced itself as the most important feeling he had ever experienced, a rapture.

"I can't survive you." His declaration was a mixture of wonder and certainty.

"You don't have to."

"You will not leave me." It was an elated command, not a question.

"How could I?" Teddy asked. Her entire face was illuminated by such an unconditional declaration of love that it was as if she had taken her heart and was holding it in her eyes for him to see.

"You could not."

Together they laughed like pagan gods. In the space of five phrases they had agreed to banish the outside world, they had swept away all the problems they would face, resolved, even as they saw the consequences, for neither of them was so simple as to imagine that they would be allowed to escape, that nothing could stop them. Chaos had been accepted, madness—that *folie à deux* that overcomes lovers—was to be their daily bread.

"Come with me now," Mistral said.

"Where?"

For an instant Mistral looked blank. He thought of the Hotel Europe, once the magnificent residence of a nobleman of the sixteenth century, built around a courtyard with splashing fountains. It had been turned into a hotel a century before. At this time of the year they would have empty rooms. Tomorrow he would make arrangements, permanent ones, but for tonight the Europe would harbor them as it had so often welcomed lovers in this profoundly sensuous city where the papal court had known many joyous sinners.

"Just come," he said to Teddy. "I'll take care of you, don't you know that?"

She flushed with a new kind of happiness. None of the men in her life had seemed to know that she wanted to be told what to do, yes, even to be ordered to do it. Melvin almost understood . . . a thought of him drifted into her memory and then was extinguished utterly.

She stood up and walked across the restaurant with him, not noticing that dozens of Frenchmen had paid her the ultimate honor of ceasing to eat or drink so that they could look at her undistracted.

Irrevocable. The word beat in her mind as Julien Mistral entered her for the first time. *Irrevocable.* Once inside the door of the hotel room they had fallen on the bed together without a second's hesitation, their madness of desire too severe to leave time for any conventional, ritualistic approach to each other. Almost fully dressed they made love with a clumsiness, an urgency that was final and necessary. It had to be done quickly, their pact to be sealed by this act.

Only when it was over did he undress her and take off his own clothes and make her lie quietly on the pillows while he touched her softly with his long hands, felt her as slowly and delicately and deliberately as if he were blind and could know her only from his fingertips.

Now Teddy delighted in being docile, taking a rare pleasure in not moaning or moving, as if he had ordered her to be still and wait. Now that she belonged to him they had all the time in the world. She let him move his hands back and forth with infinite care, never quite reaching that tender flesh that lay between her legs, until she burned too hotly to endure it any longer. She rose up and covered his body with her own, discovering him as urgent as a boy.

Irrevocable. He moved powerfully within her as he filled her in a way in which she had never been filled before. She clasped him deep within her, every one of her senses expanding until she knew that she had floated free beyond her own boundaries, that she had dissolved and he had dissolved and that together they had formed one being. Forever, she thought. *Forever.*

19

Even in the middle of winter a particular gaiety always rules in Avignon. As Teddy hurried down the rue Joseph Vernet to the hairdresser she was bundled up warmly against the brisk, dry cold that covered the South of France. But a festive sun shone out of a clear sky on to all the ancient stones of the town, stones of silver, stones like brown sugar, stones the gold of champagne, stones of rose and soft faded purple. Rue Joseph Vernet, curving and narrow, was as chic as a small street of Paris, bordered by townhouses whose ground floors were converted into *salons de coiffures*, flower shops, antique stores, and elegant little clothing boutiques. Teddy had a Friday morning appointment to get her hair done, the only fixed appointment in any of her weeks, for Teddy Lunel and Julien Mistral had made a life together that existed outside of ordinary time.

From the first night they spent together they had not once been parted. He had never returned to *La Tourrello*, he had abandoned it as if his house, his studio, his wife and his child were but a single worn-out sock, and they had lived together in a condition of astonished happiness that, in the last four months, had isolated them from the realities of everyday existence. They were so untouched by ordinary considerations that together they were like one sailing ship, lifted by a keen and steady wind, endlessly headed toward a rosy island.

After their first days at the Hotel Europe they had discovered a big apartment for rent inside the medieval walls of this queenly city with its opulent Tuscan light, its hundred bell towers, its history of pageantry and jubilation stretching from the days when seven popes had held lavish court, taking under their protection—for a price—those who did not feel safe outside the borders of the town: Jews, smugglers, escaped prisoners and, Teddy imagined, many other lovers like themselves. Avignon, lively, prosperous, laughing within its golden ramparts, contained everything to make life delightful, she thought, as she lay back and felt the expert hands of the shampoo assistant brush out her hair.

The apartment they occupied formed the entire second floor of an eighteenth-century mansion that had formerly belonged to a rich merchant in the fashionable Préfecture quarter. Its tall windows opened onto the flower beds and lawns, dotted with strutting peacocks of the Calvet Museum. Mistral had turned the largest room into a studio and next to it, in the bedroom, they had installed an enormous canopied bed with royal blue velvet hangings embroidered on the inside with scenes from a stag hunt. On chilly nights the hangings could be closed to shelter the bed on all sides.

There was no central heating in the apartment and each of the rooms had a huge fireplace, where, from early November on, fires of spicy eucalyptus and pine burned all day and all night. The studio was kept warmer than any of the other rooms of the house by a baroque Viennese stove, made of white porcelain, like a mound of whipped cream, taller than Mistral himself, that he had bought from an antique dealer to keep Teddy warm as she posed for him, as she did almost every day in the afternoons.

Never before in his life, he told Teddy, had he stayed up as late as he did now, sitting with her captive in his arms in front of their bedroom fire, talking and laughing far into the night, cracking walnuts, roasting chestnuts and sipping from the contents of the tall, slender-necked bottles of the colorless brandies distilled from fruits, which she bought for their irresistible names: *prunelle de buissons, mûre sauvage, églantine* and *myrtille des bois*. Nor had he ever slept so late. Now, when he woke, he lay and watched Teddy sleep until she opened her eyes. Then, often, they made love in luxurious forgetfulness of time and even space. Afterward Teddy would discover that she had so lost herself that she didn't know where she was for an instant, as she looked up into the embroidered forest with its running huntsmen, leaping hounds and tiny-petaled wild flowers.

"Does Madame want another soaping?" the assistant asked. Teddy nodded in assent and relaxed even more deeply as she contemplated the details of her new life. They lived like sovereigns, secure in their whirlwind of love, content to kiss and look at each other and know that they were right.

Every day before lunch they went for an *apéritif* to the Café du Palais, where they never wearied of the spectacle of the Place de l'Horloge, a vast, open square bordered by rows of venerable plane trees with their motley, piebald bark, filled with swooping flocks of pigeons and animated by the citizens of Avignon who promenaded there every midday, crowding the many cafés. At twilight they often walked to the top of the Rocher des Doms, where they found a park planted in roses that flowered till Christmas. Sometimes, when there was a film starring Gérard Phillipe or Jean Gabin or Michele Morgan, they went to one of the local movie houses, and in the intermission, when the ice cream sellers sold their wares up and down the aisles, Teddy would eat two Eskimos and Mistral would eat four.

It seemed to Teddy that although she sometimes noticed people glancing at them on the street or in a restaurant, no one in Avignon concerned himself with them. Mistral was a figure they had been accustomed to seeing for many years, coming and going, and if he now appeared with a young woman, it would be indiscreet and impolite to stare.

They had made no friends except for the doctor and his wife who occupied the *rez-de-chaussée* just below them. Two friends were all they needed, for Julien Mistral knew painful primitive feelings. He wanted to stand guard over Teddy and never let her out of his sight. He hid his suffering every time she left the apartment on an errand, he woke in the night to listen to her breathing; when men looked at her he would have gnashed his teeth at them if he could have. She was all woman to him, his bride, his child, sometimes as tender as a mother or as playful as the sister he'd never had, always his treasure, unknowable by anyone but him.

Under her turban of soapsuds Teddy made a wry face as she remembered the letter she had received today from Maggy. It had been conciliatory, very different from the first cruel and angry letters Maggy had sent after Teddy had written about her new life with Julien. Now, Maggy wrote, her only concern was Teddy's future. She was terrified that in some way history might repeat itself, as if Julien's intention to get a divorce would be no more successful than Teddy's father's had been.

How could she compare the cases? Teddy wondered. Kate Mistral was a Protestant, not a Catholic, and she had married Julien in a civil ceremony, not a religious one. Teddy tried to reconcile the Kate Mistral her mother described, a woman Maggy said she had feared from the moment she met her, a woman she described as having a willpower greater than Mistral's own, with the woman she herself had met; colorless, rather fragile, middle-aged and all but fawning over Marietta Norton.

No, Teddy assured herself as her head was gently massaged, her mother was wrong, she was seeing ghosts. Times had changed. Surely no woman today would continue to hang on to a man she had utterly lost?

It took the hairdresser a long time to towel-dry and brush out the long hair that Teddy no longer bothered to have set. Nor did she wear any makeup now, except for mascara. She looked younger than she had since she had started modeling, and her face was rosy from all the time she spent with Julien in the open air. All the eating and drinking, all the lazy parade of her days in which the only work she did was to pose for three or four hours, basking in the heat of the Viennese stove, had made her gain weight. The Korrigan skirts she had bought once she had decided to stay in Provence were growing tight, the slacks she had worn over in the plane from New York were difficult to zip.

I could never work for *Mode* today, Teddy thought, as she strolled to the Café du Palais to meet Mistral. Marietta Norton would faint if she saw me now. She stopped in a market to buy a jar of Mont Ventoux lavender honey, a long loaf of warm bread, a chalk-white cylinder of goat cheese and a half-kilo of pale yellow farm butter. The only meal she made was breakfast, the others they took in restaurants or bought from the *charcuterie* and ate as a picnic in their dining room where the only furniture was two wide, deep *bergère* armchairs covered in faded yellow brocade and an old, elaborately inlaid card table on which stood four unmatched, heavy silver candlesticks. After Kate's immaculate, well-appointed house Mistral delighted in this approximation of bohemia.

Teddy looked at her watch and began to walk quickly toward the Place de l'Horloge. As she swung the shopping net that held her few purchases she saw Mistral hurrying down the street to meet her, the top of his curly red head, tilted as cavalierly as ever, clearly visible from a distance above the crowd. Scattering the pigeons on the street by the force of her eagerness, Teddy began to run.

Kate Mistral stood thoughtfully in the big, windowless, fireproof room off Mistral's studio where sliding metal racks had been installed for storage of his paintings. There, in row after row, protected from the daylight and from dust, stretched, dated and varnished, but not signed or framed, stood the best of over a quarter-century of his work. Mistral had never sold the pictures he thought were the most successful of each year's work. Some years he had kept a half-dozen canvases, some years only one or two, some years as many as twenty. Kate knew each canvas by heart, knew on which rack it was held, knew almost to the penny how much each would bring if Étienne Delage were ever allowed to offer it for sale. She turned on all the lights and walked through the aisles that had been created to give easy access to the paintings and slid out a rack from the very back of the storage room. On it stood the painting of Maggy, naked on the pile of green cushions, the most famous of the *Rouquinne* series. Kate had not looked at that painting since 1931 when it had come back from exhibition in New York but she had never forgotten that it was there, along with the six others, like a growing lethal radioactive substance inside a metal container, unseen but alive.

Oh, yes, she thought, it's easy to understand. What man wouldn't, after all, what man could resist? Young flesh, they all want it at his age, and if they could all afford it they would line up at the market to buy it by the pound. Julien is no different—if anything he's more susceptible than others, I've always known that nothing matters to him more than the way things look, than what his eyes can see, surfaces, nothing but surfaces. But what a fool he is, what a vast, childlike, typically middle-aged fool. You don't *marry* this, you don't throw away your life for *flesh!*

How long did it take him to realize that about the mother? Only months. How I loathed her, that sulky Jewish girl with nothing but a pouting mouth and a ripe body, that girl who had never understood what a genius like Julien needed from a woman. Kate's mouth turned sour in disgust as she thought of Maggy. That greedy loose-living girl must have had many lovers after Julien, for obviously this American was a bastard, why else did she bear her mother's name?

Could it be the mother that Julien saw in the daughter? Did the man think he could travel back in time and become young again just by pressing himself into firm young flesh once more? Her hands were clenched with the effort not to rend the canvas, not to attack it with one of the sharp tools that lay about in the studio only a few feet away.

Abruptly, she pushed the rack back into place. In the seven years since the war, the seven *Rouquinne* canvases had tripled in price as the finest examples of Mistral's early work. It was the best investment she'd ever made, she thought grimly, and she'd sell them tomorrow if she wasn't certain that they'd triple or even quadruple in value again in the next ten years. She had nothing to gain by parting with them now at any price. But if she did sell, if she finally decided she couldn't endure their presence on her property any longer, even hidden in the storage room, she wished she could do it through Adrien Avigdor. If she had to do business with Jews—and in the art world it was impossible not to—better to deal with the smartest of them.

Kate remembered her trip to Paris after the war and her last interview with Avigdor. It had been necessary to see him because he still had a number of Mistral's paintings that he had sequestered before the Occupation. She had been afraid that he would insist that they were still his to sell although his contract with Mistral had expired, but the man had been more than willing to hand them over to Delage.

She hadn't understood until he had told her why he would never do business with Mistral again. Turned away from *La Tourrello*, had he been? Well, what of it? Any Frenchman sheltering Jews did it at the risk of his life, didn't Avigdor appreciate that? And what did she care that he had discovered that the same thing had happened to other Jews who had come to Julien for help? She didn't give a damn if there had been a dozen or a hundred or only one Jew.

What right had they had to jeopardize Julien, she demanded of Avigdor as he sat sternly behind his desk in his sumptuous Right Bank Gallery, wearing the ribbon of the Legion of Honor in his buttonhole, won, he didn't fail to tell her, for his activities in the Resistance. She had asked him angrily if he thought that a genius like her husband had to live by the rules Avigdor had made for himself? Did he know so little of artists, after all these years, as to think that they concerned themselves with politics unless it suited their need for subject matter? Avigdor was a fool, too, she told herself, and she would forget him. He had served his purpose.

Kate wandered down the aisle at random, stopping to pull out a large canvas of an apple tree in flower, the hidden voice of the painting speaking of an atmosphere so dense with spring that she could have heard the sap rising in the branches if she had looked at it with any attention. But Kate saw it without seeing it, as she remembered a conversation she had had with a notary she had gone to see in Nice only a week ago. One of her few friends in Félice was the notary's wife and since she suspected that her friend might hear things from her husband, she had made the long trip out of Haute Provence to the large city where she could be certain to find a notary who had no idea of who she was.

The visit itself had not taken long, and answers to her questions were simple. The institution of civil marriage in France he assured her was respected as in few countries of the world. Since 1866 divorce had been possible only *pour faute.* He had leaned back in his chair expectantly, knowing that he had not yet earned his fee. "*Pour faute?*" she had asked, skillfully hiding her anxiety.

"After the presentation of facts that constitute serious and repeated violations, my dear Madame, of the duties and obligations of marriage which make continued conjugal life intolerable." He obviously enjoyed the sonorous rhythm of his words as he rolled them out.

"I don't quite understand," she had said. "Does that mean that if my husband has given me grounds for divorce, if he is at fault, I can divorce him?"

"Indeed, yes, Madame. It is only a question of time, and of the proof."

"But if I don't want to divorce him, in spite of the fault?"

"Then no divorce is possible," he answered.

"None? No matter if he should want a divorce?"

"Never, Madame, it is completely impossible." She had thanked the notary, paid him, and taken the long, winding road back to Félice, climbing slowly through the bare meadows of winter. She need not worry, she need not act, she need not respond. She was protected by the weight of almost a hundred years of French law.

Did that despicable imbecile, her husband, know? Had he learned the truth from another notary yet? She had no intention of telling him. Let him find out for himself, let him learn the facts and slowly grow to understand—for he would not believe them at first, he would rage and shout and declare that nothing could stop him from getting what he wanted—let him realize that he was utterly impotent, totally powerless for the first time in his life. She could almost feel sorry for him if she chose. But that she did not. He must have forgotten how patient she was, he must really not remember that she never gave up.

I didn't let you go when I was young, Kate thought, when I could have had any man I wanted, when I could have had any life I cared to lead, when I could have shaped my future in any direction, I chose you, Julien. Is it likely, when I've spent my life *making* your career, that I'll let you go now? Oh, no, you contemptible man, why did you even bother to write and ask? How can you dare to imagine that I'll ever give you to that sly, thieving girl who came and took you away? Do you truly understand me so little? You belong to me. I own you just as I own these paintings. I paid for them, I still have the receipted bill, they are my property. And like it or not, so are you.

Mistral put down his brushes suddenly and stood very still. Teddy still looked dreamily at the ceiling moldings of the studio, her half-focused eyes resting on the garlands of flowers, the bows and cupids that she had grown so familiar with during the hours of posing. Surely it wasn't time for the break yet? It seemed to her as if she had just lain down on the model stand—but perhaps she'd dozed off as she sometimes did after a particularly heavy lunch. He walked over and stood looking down at her in abstraction.

"What is it, my darling?" she asked. "Don't tell me that I was snoring."

He sat on his heels and put out his hand and traced a line on her naked body from between her breasts down over her belly.

"No, not snoring . . . you never snore, but you're putting on weight."

"I know. It's all this good living. I'm going to be a Rubens one day. But I can't seem to really care . . . do you?"

"No . . . no . . . of course not." He sounded just a bit unsure. Perhaps he really did want her to be as skinny as she had been when she was modeling. Perhaps her nice new voluptuousness that she found so pleasant was making her less paintable in some way. The French were always so worried about *la ligne*—Frenchwomen anyway. Mistral took each of her breasts in his big hands and stroked them thoughtfully. Then he put his hands at her waistline, his thumbs touching, his long fingers spanning her waist. He looked as if he were listening to something.

"Hey, what's going on?" Teddy laughed. "Your hands are cold."

"You're pregnant," he said in a voice of incredulous joy.

"Oh, no, I'm not!" She sat up, her eyes wide in alarm.

"Oh, yes, you are. That's not fat, not the way it's distributed—believe me, I know the difference." He plunged his face into her stomach and kissed her skin in wild excitement. "My God, my God, you can't imagine how happy I am."

"You! You!" Teddy sputtered. "Oh, Julien, you're frightening me—how the hell can you know?"

"Isn't it possible? Think, Teddy."

"No! . . . yes . . . I suppose . . . oh, no! It *is* possible. Oh, shit, no, it can't be!"

"I'm right," he said triumphantly. "I knew it."

"*What am I going to do!*" Teddy grabbed a shawl and covered herself frantically.

"Do—why should you do anything?"

"Julien! You aren't even divorced, for God's sake . . ."

"Teddy, *I will be.* I promised you that on my life, on my love for you, on my work, on anything you hold sacred. I will be! Especially now that you're pregnant. When Kate learns about the baby she'll see that there is no use in clinging to me any longer. I know how she thinks, I know her well enough to tell you just what's going through her mind. But she doesn't yet understand about us. She still *will not* realize that you are the only woman—the only *person*—I have ever loved in my whole life."

He stood up and looked down at Teddy huddled in her shawl. "I'm still so amazed by it myself, I bless every day when I find you in bed with me! And when we form a *family*, when I recognize the child at the city hall and tell the world about it, when the news becomes public, Kate's pride won't permit her to be passive. Or even much sooner, as soon as she learns the baby's on the way, quietly, sensibly, she'll take action . . . for the sake of Nadine, for the sake of her own name, to stop people from talking. Yes, that's what *will* happen, I'm convinced of it."

"Do you know what you remind me of?" Teddy demanded ferociously. "Those stories I used to read in *National Geographic* about certain tribes where the men don't even consider a woman to be wife material until she gets pregnant and proves that she's not barren." Teddy's voice rose violently. "Julien, you're talking about *me*, Teddy Lunel, having an illegitimate baby! 'Recognizing a child'—at the city hall no less—that's barbaric! I'm a New Yorker, not some peasant girl. I make seventy dollars an hour! *I make three thousand dollars a week!* . . . Oh, Julien, you don't understand . . ." She faltered, stopped and burst into a passion of tears, clutching him like a child, feeling his arms enfold her and clasp her and mold her firmly, possessively to his body.

As she wept she realized that she wasn't Teddy Lunel who made seventy dollars an hour anymore—that Teddy Lunel who crossed Fifty-seventh Street and all but stopped traffic—she had turned into somebody else, a woman who loved a man, a woman who was pregnant with that man's baby, a woman who had become part of that man's history.

Her mind skittered about as she thought of how easy it would be to have an abortion. There were a dozen models in New York she could telephone for a certain well-known address in Sweden. It would be two hours by air from the Marseilles airport, a weekend in a spotless Stockholm clinic and back by next Tuesday or Wednesday. But even as she thought about it she knew that she wouldn't do it. Julien would understand if she did, his happiness with her didn't need a child to make it complete.

No, it was something else, an emotion she had felt only once before, a sense of inevitability that welled up within her. Already she felt changed, truly a woman now, no longer a girl. It was the same feeling she had had on that first night in the Hotel Europe . . . it was irrevocable, as irrevocable as her love for Mistral and therefore it must be as right.

Month by month Teddy traveled across the winter and spring of 1953, her destination growing closer and closer. The baby was due sometime in June, her obstetrician told her, and she lived, from the moment she had accepted the child, within a circle of enchanted harmony. She knew that Mistral was working hard on getting his divorce but she refused to worry herself with the details of the negotiations that she assumed were going on in an atmosphere of unpleasantness. Nothing disagreeable could touch her now. To ensure that Maggy didn't suddenly fly over and make a fuss she simply didn't write her about the baby in the monthly letters she mailed to New York. Time enough for that information when she could also announce her wedding day.

Now Julien insisted that they hire servants to live in several of the apartment's empty rooms and Teddy chose a young married couple, not because they were particularly well qualified for houseman and cook but because they were so visibly in love. Teddy was obedient, giving in to all Mistral's protectiveness, even letting him come to the doctor with her every month although she had never been in more robust health. She was one hell of a healthy animal, she congratulated her image, admiring herself as she never had when she sat before the mirrors in the dressing rooms of the world's best photographers. Her only complaint was that she couldn't keep from falling asleep over her *eau-de-vie* at night and Julien had to carry her tenderly to bed, lifting her, easily and tenderly, in spite of her bulk.

In the mornings they went for long walks and in the afternoons Teddy still posed. Mistral had never been captured by any subject as totally as he was by her budding body. His work had never been unreachable or enigmatic, drunk as he was on the mute rhapsody of form and color, but now, as he painted Teddy growing slowly big with child he began to interpret, to search, to think in paint, to penetrate the surface more deeply than he ever had. Maternity had not been a subject that had interested him before. When Kate had been pregnant he had been vaguely repelled by the way her womb seemed to stick out without reference to the rest of her spare frame, as if it were a growth rather than an organic part of her body. It had drained her face of energy and color and though she had endured it without complaint the child within her had been a stranger to him.

But Teddy flowered so rapturously: her breasts, once fashionably small, burgeoned in unabashed lushness; the blue veins showed clearly through the translucent whiteness of her skin; her nipples spread and grew pinker and softer; her arms and legs were less angular, more delicately rounded. Her body was a miracle of beauty, and in its swelling volume he felt the power of nature as he had never felt it in any landscape. No storm, no sky or star-filled night, no ripe orchards or grapeheavy vineyards had ever moved him so. It was an inexhaustible subject, a painter could paint nothing else but the mysterious volume of that glorious curve of her belly that was never the same from one day to another. Often he finished a painting in a single week and soon the studio was filled with the sight of canvases propped against the wall, more canvases in any one time than he had painted since he had first painted Maggy.

In the middle of June, Teddy went into labor. Mistral drove her to the nearby maternity hospital and, as was the age-old tradition in Provence, he was permitted to stay with Teddy while she gave birth. Teddy clung tightly to his hand but her labor was only six hours long and she bore it easily and bravely. When the baby emerged, the doctor had to give it several sharp smacks before it began to cry and when it finally did, it howled with outrage. A nurse wrapped it quickly in one of the pink blankets that were kept especially for the newborn and presented it to Mistral.

"A girl, Monsieur," she said as proudly as if she had had the baby herself. Mistral, stunned, overcome, stared at the amazing bundle. A purple face from which energetic yells of anger continued to emerge, bright orange hair, all wrapped in vivid pink wool. He studied his daughter intently and then he roared with delight.

"A *fauve*, by God. My darling, you've had a little wild beast. That's what we'll call her, eh? Fauve? Do you like that name?"

Teddy nodded her assent but the nurse protested. "Monsieur Mistral, that's not a saint's name . . . aren't you going to follow the custom?"

"A saint's name? The devil I will! Fauve's a painter's daughter!"

20

"Maman," wailed Nadine, "Arlette said I had a new little sister. I told her she was a liar. I'll never play with her again, she's wicked and I hate her."

"Why did she say that? Come, Nadine, remember."

"She said that her mother heard about it from her sister who works in a hospital in Avignon."

"When did she tell you this?"

"Today in Félice when I went with Monsieur Pollison to pick up a package at the post office. Arlette told everybody."

"She lied, Nadine. You don't have a new sister, you'll never have a new sister. But your father has a bastard child. You tell Arlette that the next time she says something."

Nadine's eyes grew wide and she pulled her curls with both hands. She knew what the word meant, any seven-year-old of the neighborhood knew what it meant, for illegitimate birth was far from unknown in Félice and the children of the village were brought up listening to adult talk from the time they were old enough to be held on a lap at mealtime.

"I don't understand, *Maman*."

"Remember how long your father's been away? While he's been gone he's been with a bad woman and now that woman has had a child. That child is a bastard."

"When will Papa come back?"

"You know perfectly well that I'm not sure, but if you're patient, he'll come home sooner or later."

"Will he bring the bad woman with him?"

"Now you're just being silly, Nadine."

"Will he bring the bastard?" Nadine asked jealously, daring to use the word because her mother had. The household had cosseted her so much since Mistral had disappeared that she had almost stopped thinking about her father. He had always seen through her fabrications—she found him terrifying. While he was away no one corrected her table manners or told her to stop chattering at the table. But many of her friends in school had baby brothers and sisters and she knew that once a baby was born the older children were expected to make way for the youngest in their parents' affections.

"Of course not! Nadine, don't say stupid things!" Kate jumped up and left her daughter beginning to whimper without attempting to comfort her. She rushed to her room, locked the door, sat in her favorite chair and stared sightlessly in front of her. She had expected this news daily but she had never imagined that she'd learn it from her own child. How many other rumors had Nadine heard that she'd never spoken of?

Obviously the grapevine that fed news to the inhabitants of Félice, most of whom were related in one way or another to people in every hamlet and city for fifty miles around, functioned more effectively than her own lawyer in Avignon. She had heard from Mistral about the Lunel woman's pregnancy six months ago. She had even gone through the formality of meeting with his lawyer and laying out her position for once and for all. Her husband was the victim of an aberration, an illusion, a temporary madness that a million men of his age experienced, she told the man. Her own position was immovable.

But Mistral had never accepted this. He had continued to send her urgent, deluded, insane letters, attempting to convince her that she had nothing to lose by giving him a divorce since he would never again be a husband to her.

Nothing to lose? Her contempt for him was so absolute that she could have laughed. She, Madame Julien Mistral, who had received the deepest respect throughout the world of international art, whose power was legendary because she controlled Mistral; she to whom museum curators came begging; she who could make the name of any gallery by lending pictures for a Mistral exhibition; she who alone could refuse or grant permission to reproduce one of Mistral's paintings; she who had to be won over before any scholar or reporter could get near Mistral; she who was in complete charge of his complicated business affairs—*she* had nothing to lose?

What if she had never brought Avigdor to see his work? With Mistral's hatred of dealers he might never have had his first show. How many other painters had been buried long before their work was appreciated? Far too many to count. It was she who had given him that first indispensable chance and it was her money that paid for *La Tourrello* and later her clever watchfulness that had made it possible for him to work for the last quarter of a century in a total freedom from worry that no other artist could even dream of. Oh, no, she didn't intend to abdicate, to throw away all that, to let some little whore of a model move into her position. *He owed her his life.*

Kate made an inarticulate, grinding sound of rage and began to walk from one window to another. How could a man think that one drop of his sperm deposited in the body of that Lunel bitch could influence her to give up all she'd worked for? How little he had ever really known her. There was nothing that could make her more determined to hold on to her rights than the birth of that bastard child. Julien's letters had offered her everything; *La Tourrello*, which she had once given him as her dowry; all the paintings, the money in their bank accounts; as if it were only a question of finding the right price to pay her to give up her identity. She was Madame Julien Mistral. Nothing could ever be allowed to change that.

Kate smoothed her hair and unlocked the door. She had handled Nadine badly. It would only make things worse if the child repeated her words. The scandal had undoubtedly already given the people of the village the finest entertainment that they'd had for years. They lived to discuss their neighbors and none with more malicious interest than the ones who didn't really belong to the village.

Kate found Nadine, sitting dismally in a corner of the kitchen while Marte Pollison directed the cook and her helper in preparation for the big meal that the men who worked in the fields would expect to find waiting for them at the end of the day.

She led the child back to her room and took her on her knees.

"Nadine, darling, what I just said to you was wrong. Don't pay any attention. Mother was just being foolish . . . sometimes mothers are foolish, you know, just like other people. I don't want you to say a single word to Arlette if she asks you anything about your father or me—everything will be all right soon, Papa will be back with us, but it isn't a good idea to talk to people about it. They get it all mixed up and it isn't any of their business. It doesn't concern them. I don't want you to go into Félice for a while . . ."

"But, *Maman*, school isn't over till July."

"I know, baby, but I'll speak to your teacher and she'll understand. You're doing so well at your lessons that it won't matter. We'll just have a good time by ourselves, we'll go on little trips in Mommy's big car and you'll eat in restaurants with me and see new things and every day I'll buy a special surprise for you, something extra pretty. Won't that be fun?"

Nadine looked unconvinced. If only I could take her away to Paris or New York, Kate thought. If only I could get away from this damn valley where everybody knows everything. But I can't leave, not for more than a few hours at a time. If Julien heard that we'd gone away—and he would know the same day—he'd think I'd given up. No, I must act as if nothing has happened, as if I've heard nothing, as if there is nothing to hear. I must not react, I must go on as always. He must not provoke me into the slightest action. One day it will be over, an ancient, confused, unimportant story. But now no one, *no one* may be allowed to pity me.

"What are you thinking, *Maman?*" Nadine asked.

"I'm deciding what to wear tonight. There's a big party at the Gimpels—what do you think, darling, shall I wear my white suit, or that dress you like so much, the blue?"

Teddy and Mistral sat drinking *pastis* before dinner on the terrace of the Sennequier in St. Tropez. A year earlier *Vogue* had discovered the "happy life, the undemanding ease, the lotus calm" of this little fishing village, but it was still unspoiled. As soon as Fauve was two weeks old they had packed her up, with her nurse, driven down to the coast and taken a suite of rooms at the Hotel l'Aioli for the summer.

"I'm restless, Julien," Teddy said moodily.

"I know, my darling, I can feel it jumping out at me. Did I play boules too long this afternoon? I'm sorry—it's just that these old men here are fantastically good. I wonder why it never occurred to me to come here before? It's been a perfect vacation."

"And why not?" Teddy said in a sudden burst of irritation. "Even if Fauve doesn't hold still for long, she and I are the best models you could ask for. The artist's mistress and his illegitimate daughter—a classic subject, isn't it? You must have enough paintings of us now for at least three of your series."

"Teddy!"

"I know, I know, it's not your fault, I'm not accusing you of anything, for God's sake, but how long is this supposed to drag on? I loathe this situation, Julien!"

"Darling, be reasonable. Fauve's only two months old. You don't seriously imagine that Kate can hold out for years and years, do you? One day soon she'll understand how dog-in-the-manger she looks, how hopeless it is—we only have to endure."

"You make it sound like Napoleon's retreat from Moscow. What do I see ahead of me, Julien? Listen to me! Last year I was in a state of hormonally induced passivity—I was hibernating, holed up in the apartment like that, eating and sleeping and dreaming whole months away like some sort of mama bear. That's nature's little trick, but now I'm right back to normal again and I just can't stand not having any idea of what to expect."

"You've had another letter from your mother." He groaned.

"Damn right. And I'm beginning to wonder if she might have been on the button after all. What if history *is* repeating itself? She never managed to get herself married and most people would agree that she's one hell of a lot smarter than I am."

Mistral took both of her hands in his and pressed his lips into her palms. "Don't say things like that, my love, it's only making it worse than . . ."

"Teddy! Teddy Lunel! I absolutely do *not* believe it!" a girl's voice squealed. Startled, Teddy pulled her hands away and looked up. There on the sidewalk in front of the café stood two men and two women. Peggy Arnold, who had recognized her, had been a star model with the Lunel Agency for the past two years. Teddy jumped up and enfolded her in a big hug. She was amazed at how happy she was to see a familiar face. Suddenly Peggy Arnold seemed like her best friend.

"So this is where you've been hiding out! Everyone's been wondering for so long that they've almost given you up for lost. Your mother said you'd fallen in love with France, but good Lord! Teddy, this is Ginny Maxwell—she's with Lunel too—and Bill Clark and Chase Talbot—we're all here for the weekend."

Mistral rose and approached them. "This is Julien Mistral," Teddy said, possession plain in her voice. The sun-dappled shade of the Sennequier suddenly seemed to turn into the stage of a theater as she watched Julien shake hands with the four tanned, white-clad, startled Americans who had grown suddenly shy, stiff—definitely in awe of him. It reminded her of that day, so many months before, when she had first met Mistral and, looking at him now, she was moved again by his heroic head, his splendid height and the contained force of his eyes. She was proud and glad that someone from her old life had seen them together at last, and, by God, she wanted to show him off.

"Oh, Peggy, I have a billion questions to ask you!" Teddy cried. "Listen, can the four of you have dinner with Julien and me tonight?"

"We can't, honey, we've promised to go to a party, but listen, Chase has his sailboat or yacht or whatever you call it when it's seventy feet long, anchored right here in the harbor—why don't you both come on out and sail with us tomorrow and have lunch on board?"

"We'd absolutely adore it, wouldn't we, Julien?"

"We would enjoy nothing more," Mistral said to Peggy Arnold. He welcomed any distraction at this moment. He was convinced that Kate would give in eventually but he had begun to realize that it would take longer than he'd expected and he didn't dare to share his suspicions with Teddy. It was growing harder to reassure her with every passing day.

The next day Teddy and Mistral boarded *The Baron*, Chase Talbot's chartered yacht, at ten in the morning. A crew of four, including a cook, had been hired to sail the yacht on a leisurely cruise from one port to another, along the French and Italian coastlines.

As *The Baron* moved smoothly out of the St. Tropez harbor into the Mediterranean, all six passengers lounged on cushions in the sun, close to the bow of the ship. Teddy allowed her hand to fall casually on Mistral's arm as she chatted with Ginny and Peggy, dropping back with relish into news of the world she had abandoned without a backward glance.

She had been lonely for women friends of her own kind, she realized, as they talked. She and Julien had lived in such a purposeful solitude that it felt good, just for a little while, to get back into an atmosphere where the difference between Ben Zuckerman and Norman Norell was, if not critical, at least acknowledged, a world full of assumptions and references that had once been so important to her, that was still important to them.

As they talked eagerly, catching up on the news of New York, with one finger she caressed the firm muscles on Julien's forearm. Just that light touch made her understand that nothing her old life had ever offered was more than a shallow facsimile of existence. She abandoned the conversation and half closed her eyes. Reality was Julien Mistral, the man who had made her life whole, the man who had turned her from a girl who feared she could never love, to a woman who knew that she could love forever. Reality was Fauve, the daughter she was bound to by a feeling that was so different in texture and power from anything she had ever thought of as love. When she took her baby, naked except for a diaper, in her arms and tucked Fauve into her neck and felt that silky, plump, soft and incredibly strong little body relax in complete trust against her, Teddy knew an emotion for which she had no words.

Reality was Julien and Fauve. Reality was the end of this vacation and the trip back to Avignon. Reality was settling in for the fall and winter in that champagne-colored city, hunting through antique shops for more furniture for the big apartment, taking Fauve for promenades in the park, getting in a huge supply of firewood, going to market—oh, reality was so full of lovely things to do and eat and drink and smell and touch! And if reality should include another child, Teddy grinned to herself, Kate would have to admit defeat. Why hadn't she thought of that sooner? It was a brilliant idea!

"Let's throw over the lunch hook," Bill suggested.

"What's that?" Teddy asked, roused from her reverie.

"It's a light anchor, a Danforth. We use it whenever we just want to stop for an hour or so and swim or eat. The other one—the Plough—is simply too much trouble to bother with unless we're staying for the night—it's a big heavy bastard and I keep it lashed under the bow as much as I can. I'm your average lazy sailor."

"Oh." Yachtsmen always told you more than you needed to know, Teddy remembered from her summers in the Hamptons.

"Do we want to swim or drink or both?" Chase Talbot inquired of the group.

"How's the water?" asked Ginny.

"Great. If you want your swim, now's the best time."

The yacht lay several miles off the coast, in quiet water. The sun was hot on the deck and everyone voted to swim first and drink later. For half an hour the six of them took turns diving from the pulpit, a U-shaped chrome structure above the bow from which two lifelines were rigged. The deck of *The Baron* was far enough above the Mediterranean so that the pulpit, which rose three and a half additional feet above the bow, made a good diving platform.

Teddy hadn't had a chance to dive into deep water for two years but after a few attempts all her muscle memory returned as she clambered up, using the lifelines, and curled her toes expertly around the top railing of the pulpit until it was time to let go of the jib stay and plunge into the ocean.

"Gin and tonic for all hands," Peggy called to her as Teddy took her place at the bow. She looked behind her. All four of her American friends had collapsed, laughing, on the cushions on deck, gathered around a tray of glasses brought by one of the crew. She looked out to the ocean. Some twenty-five feet away Julien waved to her from the water.

"Just one more quick one," she called. She'd swim out to Julien and put her arms on his shoulders and float there with him and kiss him and kiss him, and whisper her marvelous new idea to him.

A big fishing boat, unnoticed in all their noisy rollicking, had passed behind the stern of *The Baron* moments before. Just as Teddy let go of the jib stay, gracefully poised to dive, the heavy wake of the fishing boat smacked into the yacht. The whole boat rolled sharply. Teddy lost her balance, teetered in the air for a split second and somersaulted awkwardly. There were two sharp steel flukes, nine inches long, that protruded from the big Plough anchor lashed directly under the bow. As Teddy fell, her head smashed sideways into one of the wickedly pointed flukes. Mistral launched himself underwater as soon as he saw that she'd been hit. He found her almost immediately, caught her easily under one arm and brought her to the surface with a powerful stroke of his free arm. Chase and Bill helped him bring Teddy up to the deck. She had not drowned. There had not been time for that. Teddy had been dead before she entered the water.

Three days later, in the American Cemetery in Nice, Teddy was buried. Maggy and Julien Mistral had been the only mourners. Mistral had forbidden the four Americans from the yacht to come and they had been too much in dread of his monstrous anguish to insist.

Maggy had not yet, and would not now bring herself to look directly at Mistral. She felt such a surpassing hatred of him that it was almost impossible to utter even a few necessary words. She knew she had to stay calm enough to convince him that he must give her granddaughter to her. He had already killed her daughter.

"I want to take Fauve with me," she said at last.

"Of course," he muttered.

"Did you understand what I mean?" He couldn't have realized. He must not have listened.

"Naturally, you must take her. There is no one else. I have no home for her, I will never go back to Avignon, I never want to see *La Tourrello* again—I'm going away, I don't know where, I don't know for how long . . ."

"If I take her now, if you agree, you won't be able to change your mind," she said fiercely.

Mistral got up with a groping movement, hesitant, almost sightless, his monumental body shambling, his hands shaking and fumbling. His cheeks were covered in gray stubble, for he had not shaved or slept or eaten in the three days since the accident. His eyes weren't red for he had not been able to weep but the blue fire that they had always held was utterly gone. He was an old man with dead eyes.

"Go back to your home, Maggy. I can't talk anymore. Leave." He made his unsure way out of the hotel lobby and, a minute later, Maggy heard him drive off in his car.

She sat immobile for a moment, not daring to move lest she hear the car return. Then, galvanized, she went to the front desk and made a reservation on the next plane to Paris, ordered a taxi, and went to her room to pack.

"Madame?" It was the nurse, tiptoeing into the room.

"Pack one suitcase with the baby's things. Do you have a formula for her?"

"She drinks ordinary milk, Madame, for the last two weeks. But don't forget to warm the bottle."

"Thank you, Mademoiselle. I do remember that much."

A day later, trailed by a junior concierge from the Ritz who had been delegated to accompany her to the departure gate, Maggy crossed Orly Airport in Paris on her way to board the plane for New York. Fauve was in her arms. As she passed a newsstand she stopped suddenly, clutching Fauve to her so tightly that the baby started to cry. A pile of copies of the new issue of *Paris Match* had just been deposited on the counter. The cover photo, in black and white, had been taken on board *The Baron*. There looking into each other's eyes, stood Teddy and Julien Mistral. They were laughing in the most careless happiness, utterly absorbed in each other. A lock of Teddy's wet hair lay on his muscular shoulder and he held her possessively close to his bare chest with both his arms.

How many minutes, at that moment, Maggy asked herself did Teddy have left to live? She felt as if a crucial membrane inside of her chest had been ripped away.

"What is it, Madame?" the junior concierge asked in alarm as he saw her face.

"Please get me a copy of *Match*," Maggy said tightly. She would have to face the story. She couldn't pretend it didn't exist, not when everybody in the world would read one version of it or another.

Maggy sat in the first-class waiting room, cradling Fauve in one arm, and fumbled with the magazine, her hands shaking so badly that the slick pages were almost impossible to turn. The cover headline had announced "La Mort de la Compagne de Mistral"—at least they had called Teddy his companion, not his mistress, Maggy thought numbly.

Apparently there was no other major story in the world that week, or at least none that so appealed to the shrewd editors of the great French magazine, for they had devoted twelve pages of pictures and text to it.

Beyond surprise, or so she thought, but not beyond despair, Maggy turned the pages. There were three electrifying photographs that Bill Hatfield had taken of Teddy and Mistral in the studio, not the pictures *Mode* had published, but pictures of them talking to each other, ignoring the camera, already entranced, already lost. There were pages of photographs taken at *La Tourrello* of Mistral, Kate and Nadine, the artist and his devoted family, only two years earlier. Among the great pictures of Teddy that had been taken while she was modeling was a dignified portrait of Maggy, surrounded by her most famous models, which had been taken for *Life* three years earlier, and yes, there, just as she had assumed it would be, was a reproduction of that most notorious of the *Rouquinne* series, Maggy herself, on those damn cushions spread in full color across two pages. She didn't have to read the caption to know what it would say. *Match* rarely missed a trick.

She scanned the main body of the text, holding her breath in fearful apprehension. Until now there had been no news leaks anywhere about Fauve's existence. Maggy herself had only learned of Fauve's birth three weeks after it had happened . . . Teddy had waited until they had all arrived in St. Tropez to write to her. She had been too shocked, too outraged to bring herself to answer that letter. Now there was no need to, she realized in a grief so profound that it gave her the strength of utter loss that allowed her to search the *Match* story.

There, in the second paragraph, was the account of the investigation of the register of births at the town hall in Avignon. Fauve Lunel, *enfante adulterine*, was the civil status of her granddaughter. The baby was a child of adultery who, under French law, must remain forever unacknowledged, so different from the status of an *enfante naturelle*, a merely illegitimate child whose parents were free to marry each other if they wished, whose father could give her his name even without marrying her mother.

Teddy had long ago acquired American citizenship, at the time that Maggy herself had become a citizen, but Maggy knew that if the reporters had managed to search the right register in Paris they would have found still another fact: the record of the birth of Théodora Lunel: *enfante adulterine*. But the celebrated *Match* thoroughness had not operated at its full efficiency. This much at least they hadn't discovered.

Maggy let the magazine close without finishing the story. After all, what difference did it make? Why should anything so minor matter, now that Teddy no longer existed on this earth? Teddy was gone, her lovely, dreamy, heedless, sweet girl and nothing she had ever feared might happen to her had been even a shadow of the reality.

The baby in Maggy's arms woke up. Her eyes, a delicate, clear, smoke gray, were endless in their depth. She looked straight at Maggy with shocking clarity for such a young being. She blinked twice under her carrot fluff and when nothing happened she made a small but distinctly hungry noise. As Maggy searched her shoulder bag for the bottle that must be warmed, she remembered a saying that every French child repeats after two unplanned events of hazard of any kind: two bottles of spilled ink, two tumbles in the schoolyard, two splinters in the same finger. "*Jamais deux sans trois*." Never two without a third. Magali Lunel. Théodora Lunel. And now—Fauve Lunel.

The baby howled so loudly that every passenger in the lounge turned to look at Maggy. She glared back at them. Had they nothing better to do? Did they expect her to give her granddaughter cold milk? "Listen to me, you little bastard," she whispered to Fauve, "shut up, it's coming, it's coming." The infant stopped screaming immediately. "So, you'd rather listen than eat? That, at least, is a sign of intelligence. Perhaps you'll be the lucky third." As she signaled the lounge attendant to heat the bottle, she held the baby close and, as softly as she could, sang her a lullaby with half the words missing. Where had it come from, this song? It was in French and she had no idea how she knew it. She didn't remember ever singing it to Teddy. It must come from her own grandmother, Maggy thought. Her gentle grandmother, Cecile Lunel.

21

"How," Maggy asked Darcy, "do you expect a child who still hasn't learned how to walk, to play with a panda that is twice as big as she is?"

"It was irresistible—I was passing F.A.O. Schwarz and it was there in the window . . ."

"That trap—why, they probably sell a half-dozen every Saturday."

"No, this is the prototype, there isn't a bigger one in the whole store," he said proudly. "I checked it out."

"Well, I put it in her playpen and I haven't heard a sound from her room since, so obviously she liked it. That makes almost a half-hour of peace today. Let's enjoy it while it lasts."

A year had passed since Maggy had returned from France with Fauve. She and Darcy were sitting in the great drawing room of her resplendent new apartment on Fifth Avenue, a room purposefully decorated to give the impression that it must surely open out onto a vast private park belonging to a noble Georgian manor house in deepest Devon. However, it occupied a space even more expensive than rolling English acres, a full half-floor of one of the most indisputably impeccable buildings in all Manhattan, an East Side apartment house that had a pedigree that virtually guaranteed the background of everyone who was permitted to dwell in it.

Maggy had determined that in order to properly bring up a baby whose adulterous as well as illegitimate origins had been so thoroughly documented by the press of the world, she must do it in the highest of styles, in the most open and grand of manners. Every impulse that had made her tuck Teddy away on the comparatively unfashionable West Side, which had caused her to send her daughter to the little-known Elm School, was to be reversed in the case of Fauve. She would *establish* her granddaughter from the beginning. Everyone knew everything there was to know about her. Good! Since Mistral was her father, let that become an asset. Daughter of one of the world's greatest artists, granddaughter and only heiress of Maggy Lunel of the Lunel Agency—Fauve would become a *personage* even in the cradle!

She could have saved herself the trouble, she often reflected. Unless she was more of a doting grandmother than she believed, Fauve was a child who could have brought herself up. When she waved her arms and laughed her surprisingly deep gurgle, things happened, people came running, even strangers did her bidding. She didn't like to be cuddled for long, her firm body would squirm out of Maggy's arms as she continued her never-ending exploration of her universe; she liked nothing so much as a new face bending over her or a foreign object, any foreign object. Had she been in the vicinity of a thick snake or a large and dangerous dog she would have launched herself straight at it, shrieking with pleasure.

She was utterly without any sense of fear and she detested boundaries. At fourteen months Fauve was often furious because she fell down whenever she tried to walk and impeded locomotion was the worst boundary of all. In her playpen she rattled the bars like an angry little gorilla, shouting every word she knew, for she had an extensive vocabulary. When she was put down on the floor she would crawl about with amazing speed and a striking lack of judgment, bringing tables, lamps, vases and ashtrays crashing down about her and laughing heartily at the lovely noises she'd made. Even when she was hit by a falling object she only cried for a second. Life was too interesting for tears, unless they were tears of rage, and even those only lasted until she found some new and fascinating thing to look at.

Fauve had a nurse. Fauve had had a number of nurses, who, one by one, had left, unable to keep up with her energy. They loved the baby, they explained to Maggy, in fact they adored her, but they were just so *tired*. Maggy sympathized and hired another nurse.

Again she was trying not to make one of the many mistakes she was convinced that she must have made with Teddy. She spent a great deal of time with Fauve, reorganizing the Lunel Agency in order to do so. She had hired three highly efficient people to do much of the work she had once been certain that she must oversee in person and the agency was prospering and growing as never before.

Saturday, today, was one of the nurse's regular days off and Maggy and Darcy had formed the habit of taking Fauve for a walk in the park in her stroller. Since "21" frowned on babies, even one connected to Darcy, their valued customer since Prohibition, they headed to the Russian Tea Room on Fifty-seventh Street. There they could have a drink in one of the little red leather booths opposite the long bar while Fauve gulped freshly squeezed orange juice. Every waiter in his red cossack tunic, every motherly old Russian waitress, competed to bring the glass of juice to that resplendent child who could call a half-dozen of them by name: "Katya!," "Rosa!," "Gregor!," she would cry imperiously. She demanded no one as often as Sidney Kaye, the owner of the Tea Room, who told her funny stories with Yiddish punch lines to which she listened intently, gazing up at him from her stroller, with her gray eyes opened wide in wonder and her red eyebrows lifted, chortling when he came to the end of the tale as if, in some mysterious way, she had understood him.

"Do I look like a grandmother?" Maggy asked Darcy suddenly, as they sat enjoying the rare quiet of the moment.

Maggy was forty-six now, and during some otherwise noticed week or month between the years of forty and forty-one, she had lost the look of being younger than she really was, that she had kept throughout her thirties. One day, she woke up and discovered a woman in her mirror who had arrived at that age from which it is never possible to retreat, that "*certaine âge*" as every Frenchman gallantly but depressingly puts it.

She was an astonishingly well-preserved woman, Maggy told herself. But once anything is described as "well-preserved" its original essence has obviously been lost. It was the difference, she thought, between a ball gown on the night that it is first worn by a waltzing Victorian maiden, and that same gown, in mint condition, displayed in a case in a costume museum.

In the following six years the changes had been gradual but unmistakable for anyone with Maggy's judgmental, unforgiving eye. She could never be one of those women who only looks at her best features when she confronts the mirror, avoiding, unconsciously and so cleverly, the areas that show age. Maggy knew exactly how often she had to have her red hair touched up so that a sprinkling of gray didn't show at her hairline. She looked at her mouth, that still lush and forward-thrusting flower, and saw clearly that there were a few faint vertical lines above her upper lip. Her jaw line had relaxed and blurred ever so slightly. Oh, she was middle-aged and no good night's sleep, no vacation, no plastic surgeon could ever give her back again that unconditional freshness, that film of newness that announces youth. It was, she decided, as inevitable, and as little worth railing against, as the sunrise, or the fact that every apricot that isn't eaten will one day lose its bloom.

She didn't see the other changes that had taken place in her in the year since Teddy's death. Maggy's beauty was still bone deep, her surface was brilliantly maintained yet she had, from time to time, acquired an air of vulnerability. She never knew that the grief she lived with could be seen in an expression of bitter regret that veiled her eyes when, fleetingly abstracted, she seemed to be peering into a far and fearsome distance.

Her business manner, which had never been easygoing, was more terse, more quick to impatience than it had ever been. Her new assistants knew that while The Boss would not be unfair or unreasonable they had better have a sound and defensible reason for every decision they made. Most of the Lunel models were frankly petrified by her. Maggy knew this and sometimes it annoyed her, sometimes it amused her and, more often than not, she considered it a healthy state for them to be in. Better that than slackness.

"Do I look like a grandmother?" she repeated.

"You can never look like a grandmother," Darcy replied. He cared nothing about any of the changes in her—he didn't see them. Maggy's golden-green eyes that had first captured him had never let him go. She was still the magnificent woman whom he'd never been able to make completely his own from the very first night he'd seen her at Lally Longbridge's scavenger hunt. In a way that he had gradually grown to value, rather than to fight against, she had retained an inner enigmatic core. There were things about Maggy that were unaccountable: riddles, puzzlements, areas of her life about which she had never confided in him, no matter how close they became, and every year they grew closer. Finally Darcy was content not to even try to guess at them. Although she would never be his wife, she was his lover and his best friend and that had come to be enough.

He knew that their long affair irked many people. If Maggy and Darcy are going to be together—and so damned faithful, so devoted—they grumbled to each other, why don't they just get married like everybody else? Because we're not like everybody else, Darcy would have told them if they had dared to ask him directly. He wasn't sure what he meant by that but he knew that he possessed as much of Maggy as any man could ever have had. Unless he'd known her *before* Julien Mistral. She had left something essential in that long past relationship, something that remained only on canvas—or perhaps in her memory—although he tried never to contemplate that possibility—and almost succeeded.

Maggy shot him a quick glance. No, he meant what he said. He had answered her question with that hard gray flash, that bladelike look that had first attracted her notice. His thin face was even more distinguished than it had been so long ago, his hair was beginning to go distinctly gray, but his questioning philosopher's look had only sharpened, not grown more mellow with maturity and the unmistakable authority of his expression had settled more firmly on his lips. She put out her hand to him, lovingly. How *right* she had been never to marry this man.

A cascade of books slid to the floor behind them with a loud, long series of thumps. They jumped and looked around. Fauve came tottering toward them on her little fat feet, as unsteadily as if she were dancing on bubbles, her arms open wide for balance, a look of ecstatic achievement on her face. "Panda," the new pedestrian yelled in self-congratulation, heading for Darcy, who had provided the means for her jailbreak. "Climb panda!"

Venice, London, Alexandria, Oslo, Budapest—cities were no damn good. The country was no better: the Swiss Alps, Tuscany, Guatemala. Nor were islands possible: Ischia, the Cyclades of Greece, Fiji—all of them were empty of whatever it was he sought and finally Julien Mistral understood that he might as well go home.

He had painted nothing in the last three years but he had drunk an enormous amount of whatever was the strongest alcohol available in each place he had settled in for a week or a month or a day. Sometimes he had checked into a hotel and left an hour later, without any reason. Sometimes, he'd stayed on in a city long past the time when it had any novelty for him, out of an immobility that was as deep as his restlessness. Now he was too tired to go anywhere but *back*. Félice was a better place than any he had found.

The gates of *La Tourrello* were closed as Mistral drove up. He pulled to one side of the meadow and parked without honking or ringing the bell that sounded in the kitchen. It was lunchtime: all the household would be gathered inside and he wanted to avoid the inevitable moment of greeting. He took the path, now almost overgrown, that led beside the tall, protecting walls of the *mas*, around to the side until it reached as far as the small back door of his studio. One key existed for that door and it was still in his pocket. It was the only thing he had taken with him, besides the clothes on his back and the car he drove in, when he had gone to meet Teddy Lunel for dinner at Hiely in Avignon on a September night four years before.

He opened the door and went inside. The studio was dark except for a few stray rays of sun that came through the cracks in the shutters. Mistral pulled on the ropes that controlled the heavy canvas that covered the glass and in a minute the studio was drenched in the full light of high noon. Nothing had been touched since he left. The empty canvas with which he had posed with Teddy still stood on the easel. On a cluttered table lay the palette he had held, crusted with dry paint.

Slowly Mistral looked around the walls. There were those paintings, so thickly hung that some of them all but obscured a corner of others, that had so silenced the visitors from *Mode*. He looked long from one painting to another, not moving an inch toward any of them. For as far back as he could remember having had rational thoughts about the act of painting he had considered that he was trying to put on canvas what he *saw* in the most direct way he could, without letting an intellectual process come between his eye and the canvas. Now, in a growing swell of realization, he understood he had painted what he had *felt* at the time that he was seeing. The paintings were a visual equivalent of his emotions. Not the activity of the brain but the tides of the heart had been recorded here.

This comprehension gave him the first comfort he had permitted himself since he had knelt on the deck of *The Baron* and realized that the body that he held so tightly in his arms was dead, that Teddy had abandoned him. The paintings were proof that Julien Mistral had lived, that he once cared, once felt. He swayed, overcome by fatigue and the shock of allowing a feeling to touch him. Mistral had fled feeling with such absolute concentration for the last three years that any emotion, even a kind one, made him dizzy with the fear that it might be followed by pain so annihilating that he would kill himself to escape it.

There was an old mahogany and leather chair in the corner of the studio. Made long ago for a tobacco planter in Martinique, it unfolded ingeniously so that a man could recline at full length in it. Mistral sat down in it and gave a great sigh of relief. Within minutes he was asleep.

Hours later Kate went to the pool for her afternoon swim and noticed that the sun was shining directly through the glass of the studio roof. Otherwise the studio was as completely shuttered and closed as it had been for four years. Either the canvas had fallen or a vandal or a thief had broken in through the door on the side of the house. Moving soundlessly she walked alongside the length of the pool and approached the studio. One of the thick wooden shutters sagged slightly at its hinge and she had a hairline view into the studio. She saw only a part of a man's hand, motionless, dangling. Immediately Kate turned, went quietly back to the house and entered the kitchen.

"Marte, tell the cook to go out and kill another chicken for dinner," she commanded. "Send the gardener for more lettuce and tomatoes and grapes. You go yourself and open Monsieur's room, put fresh sheets on the bed. Make sure there's no dust, plenty of towels in the bathroom, a new cake of soap on the sink and tub . . . why are you standing there?"

"You didn't tell me you were expecting a guest, Madame," Marte Pollison answered with dignity. She disliked hurried, last-minute preparations.

"Monsieur has returned."

"*Oh, Madame!*"

"There is no reason for surprise," Kate said. She turned quickly so that Marte wouldn't see her small, calm, triumphant smile. "I've been expecting him."

On a late spring afternoon, four years later, in 1961, Maggy was dressing for dinner when Fauve burst into her room without knocking. She turned from her mirror but her intended remonstrances faded on her lips as she watched her splendiferous granddaughter skip across the pale carpet.

Fauve was almost eight, dressed, as always after a trip to the park, in tatters, her knees skinned, her shoes covered with dust, her ripped shirt pulled out of her cotton skirt, on which one of the pockets hung by a thread. At least she didn't have a black eye today, Maggy thought, or a bloody nose. Fauve, as all the boys in her class complained, "didn't fight like a girl." There wasn't one of them she hadn't punched out at one time or another, but still they wouldn't leave her alone. Irresistibly attracted to her, they manifested their fascination with eight-year-old pestering and sneaky tricks. If she'd had pigtails they would have found inkwells in which to dip them.

She had a disquieting, imprudent beauty, that sprang partly from an elation that soared so high that adults feared the tears that such a mood would have produced in an ordinary child. However, Fauve only wept, as she explained to Maggy one day, if there was a happy ending to a book she was reading or a movie she'd seen, but she didn't know why she cried and so she tried to hide those tears.

Her coloring bedazzled, the carrot fluff she had been born with had deepened into a red that had no name because it was so many reds, and it sprang out from her head in a thick tumble that mesmerized the eye with its electric energy, its meshed colors that in some lights made patterns that were more pink than bronze, in others more copper than gold. The light gray irises of her eyes were rimmed in a circle of the darkest gray. When she was serious, her glance was grave and level, and if Maggy searched her eyes she felt as if she were looking into heavy mist that parted only to reveal another curtain of mist behind which there was yet more mist. But today Fauve's eyes were so hectically bright that Maggy thought she seemed on the verge of something like hysteria.

"What have you been up to?" she asked anxiously. Unruly, more active than ten children, inquisitive, rebellious and strong-willed as Fauve was—all normal characteristics Maggy often reminded herself to be expected from a gifted child—there was never any way to predict what she would do next.

Fauve held one hand teasingly behind her back.

"I have a surprise, the most marvelous surprise, the best surprise in the world, Magali, Magali!" Fauve's voice cracked with the effort of not telling it right away. Maggy had refused to be called any variation on grandmother, yet Maggy seemed too informal, so Fauve called her by the real first name that no one had used since her own grandmother died. Maggy reached for her hidden hand but Fauve stepped back.

"No animals?" Maggy asked. It was an old battle.

"I promised, didn't I?"

"Vegetables or minerals?"

"Not that either," she sang out, bursting with information.

"Then I give up."

"*My father!*" Fauve exploded and whipped out a sheet of sketch paper and thrust it into Maggy's hand. On it was an unmistakable sketch of Fauve sitting on a park bench, her chin leaning on her hand.

As Maggy stared at it in mute shock, Fauve's words spilled out so fast that she could scarcely follow them. "We were all playing in the park and an old man with a beard came up and introduced himself to Mrs. Bailey and Mrs. Summer—they got all surprised and excited—and then he came over to me and said I must be Fauve Lunel and I said yes and he asked . . . he asked did I *know* who my father was? I said that I was Mistral's daughter of course, everybody knows that, and then, Magali, he said he was my father, he was Julien Mistral! For a second I didn't believe him because in the picture I have he's so much younger and doesn't have a beard, but then I *knew*, I felt it and I gave him a big hug, Magali, just the *biggest* hug, as hard as I can hug, and he said I looked exactly the way he thought I would look and he held my hands and kissed them and he didn't seem to know what else to say . . . that's when Mrs. Bailey and Mrs. Summer came over to talk to him, but he didn't want to talk to them, so he asked me to sit still for a minute while he drew my picture. He did it so quickly, even more quickly than I do, Magali, and you know how quickly I draw, and then he wrote you a letter and made me promise to give it to you. *My father*! Oh, Magali, I'm so *happy!* I wanted him to come back home with me but he said he couldn't, not yet . . . oh, here's the letter." She took a folded piece of sketch paper out of the one remaining pocket of her shirt.

"Fauve, go to your room now and wash your hands and face and put on something clean," Maggy said softly.

"But I want to watch you read the letter."

"Go on, darling, and come back in ten minutes. Remember, tonight's the Sabbath and I'm going to light the candles soon—you can't look a mess for that."

So it had happened, Maggy thought, not unfolding the paper. Had there been a single day during the past eight years when she had been free of the expectation of this minute? At first she had told herself it was only a question of time before he came, no matter what he had promised. Then as Fauve grew older, she almost persuaded herself that perhaps she had been wrong; perhaps this man who obeyed no laws but his own had decided to ignore an inconvenient child. But now she felt no surprise. She unfolded the paper.

Dear Maggy,

I thought I could see her just once and go away. I had to come to New York and once here I couldn't resist. Now I must see you and talk to you. I'll telephone you at your office tomorrow—or at home if the office is closed. Forgive me but I know you will understand.

Julien

Forgive him? It would be as impossible to forgive him, Maggy told herself, as it would be not to understand. *As he well knew.*

Julien Mistral never comprehended that it wasn't any of his reasonable arguments that persuaded Maggy to let Fauve spend the summer at *La Tourrello*, he never knew that he could have spared himself the interview with her.

During the years after Teddy's death she had been attacked over and over again by a wretched, fruitless monologue that replayed history in her brain. Wouldn't Teddy's life have followed a different course if she'd had a father? Mistral was so much older than Teddy—wasn't it merely a search for a father that had attracted her to him? What if Maggy had been able to talk about Perry Kilkullen—wouldn't that have made Teddy *feel* that she had had a father who was more real than those few childhood memories, like wisps of happy dreams? Worst of all, if Teddy had known all about Maggy's relationship with Mistral, known how heartlessly he had taken everything she had to give; her virginity, her whole heart, even her money, and then just dropped her without a thought or a scruple for a rich American—wouldn't that have caused Teddy to hate him from the cradle? How many chances had she missed to change the course of events? How *guilty* was she?

Eventually Maggy would make herself turn away from this tormenting litany of mistakes and busy herself with practical ways in which to guarantee that, whatever else happened, on a practical level Fauve's life would be different from Teddy's. Fauve must have traditions she determined as she bought a menorah to replace the battered brass one that she had left behind long ago in Paris. From the time Fauve could remember anything, she carried an image of Maggy lighting the Sabbath candles—it was the first fire the baby saw and she clamored for it, fascinated by its magic. Every one of the eight days of Chanukah was commemorated by its gift, and the lighting of first one and then an additional candle for each night of the holiday. From the time she was old enough to memorize them, if not to read, Fauve always asked the four questions at the festive Passover seder Maggy now gave each year, making sure that there were never any younger children present to claim that privilege.

She spent hours with Fauve every day and long before the little girl could understand what it meant, Maggy told her that she was her most beloved illegitimate granddaughter, in the way parents of adopted children use the word "adopted" to create an acceptance from the earliest moments of the child's comprehension. As Fauve grew old enough to understand, Maggy told her of her own family's history, from the highly embroidered scraps her grandmother Cecile had told her of the ancient history of the Jews of Provence right down to the tragedy of Teddy and

Julien Mistral. Before Fauve was four she had heard about Maggy and Perry Kilkullen, she knew the sad tale of the dashing David Astruc, Maggy's own father, and of Maggy's mother who had died in childbirth.

She had even been thoroughly introduced to the admonitions of Rabbi Taradash. Sometimes Maggy would wonder if she was right to fill the child's head with so much Jewish family lore—a child who had only one Jewish grandparent out of four—but what else did she have to give her? She knew nothing of the Kilkullens, nothing of the Mistrals, but on the Lunel women she was, alas, something of a specialist.

"Why doesn't my father ever come to see me?" Fauve would ask and it was the only question Maggy could never answer satisfactorily. "He's married . . . he lives far, far away, he's working very hard, he's a man who never travels . . ." What kind of answers were those? She had even considered writing to Mistral to remind him of his daughter's existence but she had never been quite ready to do it, reasoning that Fauve was such a happy child this single sadness would just have to be endured. But now that Julien had finally brought himself to see Fauve, Maggy set her teeth and gave her consent to Fauve's visiting for the summer in Provence. Only the thought of Kate Mistral made her uneasy.

"Maggy, I assure you, Kate wants whatever I want," Julien had said impatiently. "She accepts me as I am, she always has. A child of eight won't threaten her—think, Maggy, I'm sixty-one, she's almost sixty, we've been married thirty-four years . . . you don't imagine that she would be jealous of a little girl, do you?"

"I think she'd be jealous of a canary if you decided to make a pet of one."

"Maggy, you've never been rational on the subject of Kate."

"Kate is not a woman about whom it's possible for me to be rational. If she had agreed to a divorce so that you could marry Teddy . . ."

"We might have gone out on that boat anyway, Maggy. Who can look back and determine what combination of circumstances gives fate its chance?"

"I never believed I'd hear you talk about fate."

"It's the only explanation I can endure."

"You don't wake up at night and ask yourself what you did that made things go wrong? You don't *blame* yourself?"

"I will *always* blame myself. I *live* with blame, but does it help? Any tiny change in events could have changed what happened. If the fishing boat had passed a minute later, if I hadn't waved at Teddy, if she hadn't let go of the line when she did, if the Americans hadn't come to St. Tropez, if we hadn't been sitting at the Sennequier, if . . . there is no end to the ifs. All I can do is to paint, Maggy. That, at least, is something, but blaming myself is worth nothing at all. Am I wrong?"

"No." Maggy fell silent. To entrust Fauve to Julien even for the short summer months was dangerous. To entrust anyone to him was dangerous. But did she really have a choice? "No," Maggy repeated out loud, but it was not to Mistral that she spoke. It was even more dangerous not to allow Fauve a father.

22

On a June day in 1969, at the Gare de Lyon, Julien Mistral and his sixteen-year-old daughter Fauve boarded the deluxe express train that runs from Paris to Marseilles. Each June for the past eight years Mistral had traveled up to Paris from Félice to meet Fauve at the airport, spend a night in Paris with her and then travel down to Provence for the entire summer. During all those years it had never failed to thrill Fauve that the train was called *Le Mistral.*

She had assumed, that first time she traveled on it, that the train was named in honor of her father and she still wasn't quite sure when she had finally had to acknowledge that the train was named for the dominating wind of Provence. The mistral, that infernal cold dry wind, blows only when the sky is bright, bright blue and the sun is blazing, or, depending on whom you discuss it with, turns the sky white and hides the sun, this wind—again depending on individual opinion—that blows for a period of three days or six days or nine days without stopping; a wind that forces every last tree in Provence to bend toward the south; that causes every house to be built without windows on its northern wall, a wind like a dragon that hides quietly until the countryside has almost forgotten about it and then springs, screaming down from the Alps to the Mediterranean at fifty miles an hour, entering the most tightly closed rooms and giving the inhabitants of Provence an excuse for every ailment from a headache to a murder.

Fauve loved the mistral, to her it was an intensely personal wind, and she was its intimate She called it by its Provençal names *Le Mistrau* or *Le Vent Terrau*, and she grew madly exhilarated and elated when she heard the rushing, softly roaring noise it made in the branches of the trees around *La Tourrello.* To Fauve it was the spirit of the land.

Le Mistral's first-class carriages are divided into compartments holding two rows of three seats that face each other. Fauve quickly claimed two window seats, covered in a particularly nasty shade of moss green, while her father busied himself with the headwaiter of the dining car, buying the pink tickets that would reserve their seats at lunch. "Lyon, Dijon, Valence, *Avignon*," she murmured softly, wondering as she always wondered, how she would find the patience to wait the six hours it would take until they arrived. The period of time between Valence and Avignon was the most frustrating because she could see the countryside change dramatically as they drew near. Oh, the leap of her heart with the first welcoming stand of dark, jagged-branched cypress, the intoxication of the sight of the first groves of olive trees, the first long, low lines of grapevines!

"Fauve, don't you want an *apéritif* before lunch?" Mistral broke into her thoughts, standing before her as the train glided out of the station. She jumped up and followed him through the heavy doors that opened by an electric eye, into the dining car where waiters in their white coats were already pulling the corks of bottles of wine and serving whiskey and Perrier to the first-class passengers. This prelunch drink was another tradition that had started with her first trip down to Félice. She always had two bottles of sweet pineapple juice and then, after a little urging, a third, for they were very small bottles indeed.

"A sherry, please," Fauve said.

"Oh, so you drink now, do you?" Mistral put his hand over hers.

"Only on special occasions." She laughed at him, delighting in the passion of love she felt transmitted from his hand to hers. He was, she estimated, the most undomesticated man who had ever existed, yet she knew that anything that concerned her mattered to him more than anything else in his life.

"A sherry for my daughter," he said, "and bring me a *pastis*." Mistral searched her face, seeking as always with a painful mixture of hope and fear, traces of Teddy's classic, catastrophic beauty. But as Fauve grew older, it seemed to him that she possessed a loveliness that owed nothing to her mother but her height and the color of her hair. It was, he reflected, searching for the right word to adequately describe this child he so adored, an *intelligent* beauty. There was always something fascinatingly thoughtful in Fauve's expression, something that made him long to know exactly what was going through her mind at every minute, something that prevented him from ever being quite satisfied with a single one of the many portraits he had made of her. There was a brave and absorbing mystery about her almost unpaintable gray eyes—what would Leonardo have made of her?—there was a seriousness that lurked at the corners of her bewitching mouth up until the instant that it curved into a sorceress's smile.

Mistral had never found it possible to concentrate his gaze for long on Fauve's eyes or her mouth; he had to look at her face as a whole because to him it was like a landscape on a changeable day in the springtime. No one mood lasted for long, each moment brought a new enchantment, a new perception. No, he had never quite captured her on canvas.

As Fauve sipped her sherry she was aware of Mistral watching her carefully. It was always the same during the first week of each visit as he pored over the changes that a year had made in her. She submitted to his inspection with the cheerful resignation that came of growing up under Maggy's all-seeing eye. Did any other teenaged girl have to be scrutinized daily by the most knowledgeable woman in the world on the subject of the female face and then, on her summer vacation, be the object of the minute attention of a father who saw *everything*?

"Mascara," Mistral observed in a neutral tone.

"I thought you'd never notice."

"I suppose it goes with your drinking sherry?"

"Precisely. Magali says that it's perfectly proper at sixteen if I put it on right. She taught me how herself. Do you like it?"

"Not excessively, but, on the other hand, since you are otherwise fairly agreeable looking, why should I complain, particularly when I know it would avail me nothing? I've survived four years of miniskirts, which seem to be getting shorter each year, I lived through the era of the tiny white plastic boots, I scarcely blinked when you gave yourself a geometric haircut—Sassoon, was it not?—half of one anyway, so why should I worry about a bit of black on your lashes that will undoubtedly come off before the day is over?"

"What a philosophical, patient, dear little papa I have."

"You always made fun of me, even when you were a little girl. You're the only person who ever makes fun of me, do you know that?"

"And lived to tell the tale?"

"Who even tried."

"What about my mother? Surely she saw how droll you are?"

"No, no . . . or perhaps yes, but she never mocked me—she wasn't like you, Fauve. No one has your nerve."

"*Chutzpa*, Papa, that's what Magali says it is. And it's not supposed to be a compliment. It means audacity in Hebrew."

"What's wrong with audacity? You'll get nowhere in the world without it."

"Well, it also means brazen effrontery and outrageous gall—I think Magali'd like my audacity to be a little more ladylike. Still, I'm getting better. This year I didn't have a single fistfight and I went to lots of awful dances in pretty dresses and made dumb conversation with terrible, dreadful boring boys . . ."

"Nobody who interested you, not even one?"

"I would have said in my letters, you know that. No, Papa, you have a daughter who finds the male sex much less interesting than she has been led to hope they would be."

"But you're only sixteen! Why should you find them interesting at your age? There's plenty of time for that when you're grown up."

"Sixteen is supposed to be grown up," Fauve said earnestly but Mistral only shook his head at her. Sixteen was a child. Sixteen was a baby. He was sixty-nine and sixteen was so young that he couldn't remember anything of what it felt like, and certainly he didn't choose to remember that Fauve's grandmother had only been a year older than Fauve when he'd first set eyes on her naked body.

He thought as rarely as possible of Maggy. He wanted Fauve to belong to him alone, to be just his, Mistral's daughter, and nothing else, yet there was Maggy, so beloved of Fauve, to whom he now found himself linked forever, linked by blood. His grandchildren would be Maggy's great-grandchildren and who among them would make any distinction between generations in that unimaginable future? He resented Fauve's use of an occasional Hebrew or Yiddish word, he resented her observation of Jewish holidays about which she wrote him, he resented the way Maggy had indoctrinated her with Jewish family history—what had Fauve to do with all that? She wasn't Jewish!

Yet he dared not criticize Maggy, for it was the one way in which to make Fauve turn on him in anger. Last year she had discovered a poem in Provençal by the poet Frédéric Mistral—a song really—meant to be sung to a Neapolitan melody and he never told her how maddening it was when she sang it:

Mai, o Magali,
Douco Magali,
Gaio Magali,
Es tu que m'as fa trefouli.

"Wait till she hears it—'But oh, Magali, sweet Magali, lively Magali, it's you who made me shudder with joy'—how about that for sexy, Papa?"

"It should please her," he'd said carefully.

"Don't overwhelm me with compliments—oh, okay, so I can't carry a tune but at least I'm learning Provençal."

"And how useful is that?"

"In Provence at least, it's a lot more useful than any other language I could learn.

I'm planning to use it to keep on working on old Monsieur Hugonne and Monsieur Piano to let me organize a girls' boules team . . ."

"What!"

"That's what they all say, as if I'd asked to belly-up to the bar and take a swig out of the bottle of Pernod! Félice is not exactly a beachhead for female team sports but I'm not giving up. The biggest problem is the girls—they still look so shocked when I even mention it. What's so sacred about a ball of metal anyway?"

"Fauve, don't try to change customs that are hundreds of years old. Do girls play football in the United States?"

"Pops, girls do everything in the United States."

"Don't call me Pops," was the only response he'd been able to make to her shocking suggestion, he reflected, bending toward the *prix-fixe* menu the waiter had just placed in front of them.

The first-class dining car of *Le Mistral* has a kitchen at one end in which two white-capped chefs turn out surprisingly good food on the superior-bistro level. Fauve and Mistral both ordered the *lotte*, that fish that can only be found in France, and the rabbit stew with new potatoes and salad, followed by the assorted cheeses and the *bombe glacée*, an ice cream dessert Fauve looked forward to from one year to the next.

"What are you painting now?" Fauve asked. As the years went by Mistral painted more and more slowly, becoming more self-critical, finishing fewer canvases and destroying a larger percentage of those he completed.

"Never mind me—what are you working on? Still taking that life class?"

"Of course. Oh, Papa, there's so much to learn. Doesn't the day ever come when you feel that you *absolutely* learned something, just one single thing for good and all?"

"It's never come for me—not for 'good and all,' so why should it come for you? Each canvas must lead into a new problem, you must wake up every day wondering what you are going to discover, what you are going to teach yourself, what new things you didn't know this morning you will know by this evening . . . but how often have I said this to you, my Fauve? Will you ever start to believe me?"

"I keep thinking I should be better," Fauve muttered. Her painting was the only area in which she found herself increasingly baffled, unable to make progress because of a growing insecurity and frustration.

When she was little—and now, looking back it seemed like an innocent's paradise—she had had such daring, she had known no limitations to what she would try to draw or paint, but every year the burden of being Mistral's daughter had become heavier. She sometimes wished she had no artistic talent at all—it would make life so much simpler, not to want to work in the same field as her father.

As Fauve demolished her fish she remembered that first summer at *La Tourrello* when, after a day or two of consideration, Mistral had allowed her into his studio on the condition that she stay perfectly quiet while he worked. He'd given her sticks of charcoal, paper and then, as an afterthought, some old, almost used-up tubes of paint, and a few worn-out brushes and a canvas, and installed her in a corner.

At first she had just watched him, but he walked about the studio for so long between each lightning attack of his brush that she soon lost interest in his odd movements and turned to the materials he'd given her.

At home in New York she'd had only pencils, sticky crayons and pastels, which promptly broke, and sets of watercolors, with which she had tried, over the years, to copy the illustrations in some of her favorite storybooks, but no one had ever thought of letting her near oil paints.

The smell of the tubes was immediately inebriating, she could clearly remember that instant when she had rubbed the paint on her fingers and sniffed with rapture. Then, imitating what she had watched Mistral do before he started work, she squeezed a dollop of paint out of each tube and arranged them in a semicircle on the wooden board he'd handed her. What next? she had wondered, confronting the first blank canvas of her life. She wanted to ask her father but didn't dare to interrupt him. There were no books around for her to search for pictures to copy, no flowers in a vase or fruit in a bowl. The immense paintings on the walls all around her were too confusing, too complex for her to dream of trying to copy them, so eventually Fauve dipped her brush into the darkest of the paints, a deep, rich blue, and started to outline the most central object in the studio, her father's easel.

She pulled her red eyebrows together in a straight line as she concentrated on it, freely and boldly, undaunted by the problem in perspective since she didn't know what perspective was, and saw only what was literally before her eyes. She worked steadily and so quietly that it was an hour before Mistral remembered her. She was so engrossed that she didn't notice when he came up behind her and took a look at what she was up to. His hair rose on his arms and the back of his neck in a shock of recognition. *She sees the way an artist sees*, he thought, not needing to explain to himself what he meant. He made no comment that day but the next day he gave her a sprig of grass in a vase to work from, and the following day he gave her an apple.

"*Regard! Regard*, Fauve . . . use your eyes, my little one, you must learn to *see* . . . see that apple . . . it looks round, doesn't it? But if you look—if you truly look—you'll see that the top is higher on the left . . . it isn't round at all, is it? And why doesn't it roll like a ball, this apple? Because it's almost flat on the bottom—do you *see* that with your own eyes, little one? And that little scar on the skin of the apple . . . can you tell me where it starts and where it finishes? What color is the scar, Fauve? Is it almost white? *Regard*! Do you see how the red of the apple is touched by yellow? And do you see where the yellow becomes brighter, just at the side? Now—tell me, can you *see* where, on your board, you have placed these colors, this red, this yellow? It's all there, Fauve, if you only use your eyes."

Then, as he had been aching to do from the first day, in a moment that would never be forgotten by either of them, he had finally reached out and put his huge hand right on top of Fauve's hand and guided it with his powerful fingers so that her brush moved under his direction, his force passing into her own fingers. She relaxed her small hand but kept a firm grip on her brush and allowed her wrist and bones and tendons to *lean* into his, the way a good dancer follows a strong partner, neither too yieldingly nor too stiffly, and as she saw and felt her brush make stroke after stroke, she drank in knowledge with her muscles as well as with her mind.

This was what it should feel like, his hand was informing her hand, *this is the way it goes*. No matter how original an artist must become, Mistral believed that in art, as in language, there was a basic grammar that has to be learned before true speech is possible and it was in this grammar that he trained Fauve.

That summer of Fauve's eighth year, the summer when her art lessons began, was also the year that Mistral started to frequent the café in Félice again. After an absence of twenty years he began taking Fauve there with him before dinner every day merely to be able to order a drink "for my daughter, Fauve." Little by little the men of the town, who had almost never set eyes on him since the war had interrupted all of their lives, began to gather around and admire the little girl while he offered them round after round with a joviality he couldn't contain, a friendliness they began to accept, slowly at first and suspiciously, but won over by the lively, curious, friendly child.

Mistral had never taken his daughter Nadine into Félice with him. Even if he'd wanted to, Kate would have discouraged it. When he returned from his wanderings in 1956 he discovered, without any regret, that from the time she was eight Nadine had been sent to boarding school in England.

In spite of Nadine's first four years at the village school, Kate had always considered it unthinkable that her daughter should be brought up for long in the countryside, for she was to be a citizen of the great world in which Kate had lived before she met Mistral.

Nadine was very young when she had learned to consider Félice as a rather inconsequential and old-fashioned oddity in her own important life. It existed, like a backdrop, painted in a whimsically naïve style, a living Brueghel, that set off the qualities of Mademoiselle Nadine Mistral in a valuable way. Kate allowed her daughter to consider *La Tourrello* itself merely a charmingly unconventional choice of residence, dictated by the whim of a famous, therefore permissibly eccentric father.

As she grew older, Nadine discovered for herself that *La Tourrello* had great usefulness in her scheme of things, for it was famous all over the world, and when she spoke of it to her friends, its name was received with the same reverence as if it had been a castle. The *mas* became a showplace that she displayed from time to time to especially favored friends before she rushed off to stay with them at the more civilized and desirable spots where they spent their summers.

Nadine, exquisite Nadine, with her cool, aquatic green eyes, her straight, shoulder-length blond hair and that eternal little smile that was not a smile at all but the shape of the upper lip of her delicate pink mouth, was exceedingly unpopular in Félice.

When Mistral first brought Fauve to the café in the summer of 1961, no one worried overmuch about what Mademoiselle Nadine's reactions might be to the arrival of a little half-sister who had appeared out of nowhere, or rather out of the superb scandal they knew very well, for had it not been in every newspaper and magazine, and was it not the sort of story one could scarcely forget?

Nor were Kate's emotions treated tenderly in the torrent of gossip that inundated Félice at Fauve's arrival, another chapter in the endlessly chewy, delectably juicy explorations of Mistral's home life that occupied the villagers for many a pleasant hour over the years. Kate Mistral did all her shopping in Apt or in Avignon, ignoring the village stores, a detestable and unforgivable trait in anyone who lived in the vicinity, and one which guaranteed her an ever-mounting degree of enmity. Kate barely deigned to stop at the village gas station to fill up her car. But what could you expect of a woman who thought she was better than her neighbors?

None of the other rich families who had bought homes in the Lubéron were the object of anything like the speculation directed at Mistral. The others' homes were used for summer vacations, they were visitors only, clearly not *of* the countryside. But Mistral's position was ambiguous from the day he had settled in Félice in 1926. He had become almost, but not truly, a part of the village in those years when he was the chief stalwart of the boules team, those years before the war when Kate had been content to live in relative tranquillity, entertaining too often, it was true, but then she was American, after all.

After the war the climate of the village itself changed; eight men from Félice had been killed and a dozen had spent years in Germany doing forced labor, while many of the younger men had been in the *Maquis*.

At the café, where once the most animated discussions had concerned the relative merits of the boules grounds of other villages, politics were now argued seriously and the talk had a way of turning ugly; the supporters of de Gaulle refused to drink with the men who voted Communist. Mistral, with his loathing of politics, avoided the café, and his absence was perceived as a feeling of superiority, a belief clearly substantiated when Kate ordered the construction of the swimming pool. No one single thing she might have done would have more alienated her from her neighbors whose incomes depended, in the most basic way, on the amount of rainfall every year.

The distance that both Mistral and Kate put between themselves and the life of the village after the war did nothing to stem the gossip about them; quite the contrary, for were they not still *there*, as if defying their neighbors?

Nor did it help when Marte Pollison couldn't resist dropping certain details about life at *La Tourrello* into the ears of her cousins who owned the hardware store in Félice. Soon every housewife in the town knew precisely how much Madame Mistral spent on champagne for those parties she gave, how many kilos of pâté de foie gras and smoked salmon were delivered from the finest grocery store in Avignon before a grand reception, how many extra servants Marte supervised during the busy summer season.

Nothing could surprise them, they said to each other, about this woman who had actually installed five bathrooms with hot water and tubs in *La Tourrello* when she had first come to live there, at a time when many of the richest farmers of the valley had not yet installed running water in their homes. What folly! Did the Mistrals not realize that the tax inspector could not fail to notice them?

It would not have made any difference if the people of Félice had known that, in 1960 at Parke-Bernet in New York, an early Mistral had sold for half a million dollars. They had enough trouble crediting the details of the decoration of the room that was installed for Fauve during the six weeks that passed from the time Maggy agreed to let her visit for the summer in 1961, and the day she arrived.

A stonemason who was employed on the project of restoring the circular upper tower room in the *pigeonnier* was able to reduce them to silence by his account of its decoration.

"But yes I assure you, the walls are covered in fabric, from the floor to the ceiling, in deep folds like a curtain but running around from one window to another, hundreds and hundreds of meters of it, printed in lavender and white flowers. The housekeeper told me that it came from the factory of Monsieur Demary in Tarascon." He paused to make sure everyone was paying close attention. "And the bed," he continued, satisfied with his audience, "has a canopy of the same material and a headboard carved like one of the old chests in the Hôtel de Ville, fit for a princess. Tiles on the floor, of course, but also a white rug that Marte Pollison said came from Spain, and a white birdcage with lovebirds in it. Yes, I saw them myself. You know that bathroom Mistral made the plumber put in so quickly? Well, the bathroom walls are also covered in fabric!"

It was this final detail that made most of the housewives of Félice disbelieve his account for not even Madame Mistral could be foolish enough to do such a thing.

They were quite right. It had not been Kate, but Mistral himself who had feverishly harried the workmen; he who had decided to convert the dovecote, because he knew that a romantic tower room would delight a little girl; he who had thought of how to employ the traditionally patterned fabric to make sure that the occasional cold mistral of summer wouldn't come whistling through the old stones, replastered though they were; he who had accomplished the impossible by getting Provençal craftsmen to finish the work they had promised to do by the time they had agreed to do it, with an efficiency unheard of throughout the Midi.

When Fauve arrived in *La Tourrello* that first summer she had fallen in love with her room from the moment she entered it, yet, as the summer started, she spent many a sad hour there pondering the reasons for the hatred she felt emanating from Nadine and from Kate.

Was it, she wondered, the fact that her father was teaching her how to paint that made Nadine treat her with an enmity so remote, so totally rejecting, that she couldn't seize and wrestle with it? Would her half-sister have detested her under any circumstances?

Was it the fact that she was a bastard that made Kate regard her with an animosity that was sensed by no one but Fauve, for Kate was much too clever not to know that anything unpleasant she could say or do to the little girl would cost her far more grief from her husband than it would be worth. She was careful to seem ungrudging and generous, yet her loathing existed in the very way she pressed Fauve to have more homemade apricot jam, in the gesture she made to fill Fauve's glass of milk, in the smile that went with her suggestion that Fauve might enjoy having a bicycle so that she could go to the village.

Finally Fauve's pride asserted itself. If Kate and Nadine hated her she would ignore them and go her own way. She would seek out the children of her own age in Félice and set about making friends of them.

She never suspected how united the tightly knit community of eight-year-olds had been in their suspicions of her, a tall, oddly dressed American girl with flying red hair who bicycled up from *le château*, as they called *La Tourrello*, a girl whose fancy room they had heard too much about. Fauve spoke to them in citified Northern French but yet she made so many babyish mistakes in grammar, she didn't understand that she must shake hands all around or that she must not play the "Babyfoot" pinball machine with the boys, this girl with a most uncivilized name who did not even have her own saint's day to celebrate.

They envied the way Fauve's father promenaded her around the café as if she were a baby just able to take her first steps instead of a gawky girl as old as they were; they envied the shiny new bicycle and her pretty clothes. Who was she to descend on their little group and try to get in?

But none of them could resist Fauve for long, none of them could turn away from her brimming, open and ardent *intention* to love them. She offered to help them cut grass to feed the rabbits they raised for market and she volunteered to take care of their little brothers and sisters while they played tag. Fauve taught them how to throw a baseball, and she invited them all home for many a sumptuous *goûter* the afternoon snack of bread and brioche and chocolate and three kinds of jam that is the French child's favorite meal. Afterward she took them up to her room, to lie sprawled all over her astonishing canopied bed while she told them about her school in New York where, evidently, nobody really did any work at all, in comparison to what was expected of them in the village school. Then, during the winters, she wrote letters to each of them, so that when she came back each summer it was as if an old friend had returned.

Two of the girls in particular, dark, pretty Sophie Borel, whom Fauve nicknamed Pomme because of her apple-red cheeks, and Louise Gordin, called Épinette, or thorn, because of her hot temper that contrasted so strangely with her angelic little face, had become Fauve's two best friends. Pomme, a humorist and born trouble-maker, was a tremendous source of information since her father was the local post-man. Fiery Épinerte was one of Fauve's first champions. Almost from the beginning, she defended Fauve to other girls who had not yet been won over to the stranger's presence in their insulated and chauvinistic community.

She could hardly wait to see Pomme and Épinette again, Fauve thought, as lunch proceeded, and the waiters, as agile as acrobats, balanced the platters of spicy rabbit *ragoût*, serving everyone in the dining car with swiftly graceful motions, as the train, traveling at a high speed, swayed constantly from side to side of the sinuous road-bed.

Neither Pomme nor Épinette was a good correspondent and while Fauve was away from Félice she always worried that something might happen to change the village she loved so much. What if someone had built a supermarket or a Monoprix or a movie house?

Félice was utterly beautiful to her just as it was. It was as quaint, Fauve thought, as any town on this planet could be, but quaint was not the right word for anything so modestly, so naturally and utterly itself, a human dwelling place that put on no show to attract the casual visitor, a private world in which the way of life hadn't changed in basic ways for hundreds of years.

Often Fauve reflected on the difference between attitudes in New York and Félice toward her illegitimate birth. In Manhattan, as she grew older and more noticeable, she often was aware of an undercurrent of unwelcome and malicious attention whenever she went out in public with Maggy and Darcy or with Melvin Allenberg, who had become her guide to the art world. There was a certain type of alert, overly curious glance that moved too quickly away from her face; an unmis-takable nuance in voices discreetly lowered at a nearby restaurant table, an unnat-urally blank kind of impersonal look that managed to scrape over her entire surface and take in every detail of her appearance; all signs of recognition that told her unmistakably that someone had just whispered to someone else, "Look, there's that girl, Mistral's illegitimate daughter."

At such moments, without knowing that she did it, Fauve straightened up to her full five feet ten inches, threw her slim shoulders back and opened her eyes wide, without blinking, and faced the people who had noticed her with a look of such stern and frank pride that it would not have been inappropriate on her father's face, a look that could startle people into silence.

"Illegitimate," Fauve had once said to Maggy. "Why don't people bother to be original? I looked it up in Webster's *Thesaurus* and I could be called so many other things—by-blow, catch colt, *nullius filius*, whoreson and woods colt—I'd prefer woods colt, wouldn't you?"

"Yes indeed . . . pity more people don't have better vocabularies," Maggy had responded dryly.

But in Félice, when there were consequences of premarital sex, popular opinion held that the only fault lay in the parents not having been careful enough. No finger was pointed at a child who grew up illegitimate. In Félice, Fauve felt that she was fully Mistral's daughter, in a perfectly down-to-earth and natural way, accepted as the guiltless result of guilty passion, but *accepted.*

She looked impatiently out of the train window. They still hadn't reached Lyon and lunch was almost over. "Is there any news from the village?" she asked her father. "Nothing new since your last letter?"

"New? Not unless you count that accursed, tasteless rabble, that unspeakably foul pack of decorators from Paris who are buying up old houses all over the valley—painting them green and lemon yellow and even mauve, by Christ, against all tradition, doing them over inside and selling them to foreigners or filthy, decadent Parisians for ten times what they cost—it's a plague!" Mistral growled.

"In Félice?" Fauve asked, alarmed.

"Not more than before, only a few outsiders have discovered us, but in Gordes and in Roussillon it gets worse and worse. The villages have lost all their atmosphere, they look the way your Disneyland must look, sickeningly picturesque, with old houses tarted up like whores at a wedding, and swarms of hundreds of foreigners, God knows what kind of barbarians, arriving in tour buses, drinking Coca-Cola in the cafés, buying postcards by the dozen, ignoring the village itself, getting back on the bus and going on to the next place—one day to see the whole Lubéron!"

He looks more like a gallant, heroic conquistador than ever, Fauve thought, as Mistral fulminated. As she grew older he seemed to grow younger to her, perhaps because she had learned to really look at him, perhaps because he had shaved off the beard that had kept her from first recognizing him. His big nose was more prominent than ever, and his mouth more tightly set, unless he was looking at her, but the bold, arrogant adventurous set of his handsome head hadn't changed; he seemed, as always, stronger, more upright, so much bigger than any man she'd ever seen. He's prodigious, she thought, using her newest favorite word. I have a prodigious father.

23

"*Pervert!*" shrieked Pomme, "depraved . . . debauched . . . corrupted—you're *sick*, Fauve Lunel, that's what you are!"

"Backwoods . . . medieval . . ." Fauve gasped through tears of laughter as Pomme shook her as hard as she could. "You're living in another century, poor girl." When she'd put on her record of Three Dog Night singing "Easy to Be Hard" she'd known that her friends were far from ready for it. In the past she'd won them over to Johnny Cash and Engelbert Humperdinck although their hearts were really still with the Bee Gees. But she hadn't been able to resist bedeviling them. They enjoyed it as much as she did.

The teenagers of Provence were dance mad in spite of the fact that their taste in music lagged behind that of New York. Each village held two public dances every year so that in the Lubéron there was almost never a Saturday night on which it wasn't possible to go to a dance within an area that could be reached by car or by bus.

At fourteen and fifteen Fauve had been allowed to go to the dances with a group of girls chaperoned by one of their fathers, but now, at sixteen, they had all reached the age at which they were permitted—in fact, expected—to go to a dance with a date.

After Pomme and Épinette left reluctantly to go home for dinner, Fauve thoughtfully put away her records. It hadn't escaped her that there had been a basic change in her friends since last summer. Today they had talked of little else but the dance that was planned in Uzès for next Saturday to which they had each been invited by a boy from the district. They assured Fauve that she was invited to go to the dance with the four of them in a car belonging to the father of one of the boys, but once there, Fauve asked herself, what then?

Last year it had been perfectly honorable to stand in the "girls' corner" with a bunch of giggling friends and, if no boy presented himself, to dance with one of them. Indeed, because of her unusual height she was much in demand as a partner. But this year she was aware it would be something of a disgrace to dance with another girl. Most of the young females of Félice were going with dates, according to Pomme's information which was as official as any engraved announcement.

Morosely, Fauve considered Provençal dances. At the *Salle des Fêtes* girls and boys migrated to their separate corners as soon as they entered, eying each other as slyly and secretly as possible but otherwise not communicating, even if they had arrived together. The first dancers were always couples who didn't care what anyone thought: the cheerful grocer with his five-year-old daughter; a nine-year-old girl who had trapped her six-year-old brother in a grip he couldn't wriggle out of; two cousins who had formed a jocular alliance; perhaps a newly married couple or two, showing off for the neighbors.

Eventually each boy claimed his date, if he had one, but without any air of grace or pleasure. Why were they all so crazy about dancing, she groaned to herself, when they seemed so miserable when they were doing it? In Provence people danced like marionettes whose legs moved in independence from their stiff upper bodies. The proper expression during a dance was of frozen despair. Conversation, or even a smile between partners, was out of the question. When the dance was over the couple darted apart, as brusquely as if they had been locked together in a prizefight and returned to their respective corners, where, at last, they could communicate happily with members of their own sex. And they called that a dance!

Why did she have to subject herself to it? She could stay home Saturday night without any comment from anyone. Some English friends of Kate's were expected for the weekend, and no one at *La Tourrello* would know about the dance at Uzès and wonder why she wasn't there. Yet, she reminded herself, she had chosen to make herself a part of the village of Félice and if she missed a dance it would be interpreted, and rightly so, as turning away from her friends. Lack of a date was not the slightest excuse. Every girl from every village kilometers around who could get transportation to the dance would be there, because this network of dances provided the only means through which they would eventually find mates.

Oh, if it were only *last* summer Fauve thought with a rush of nostalgia, if only the whole business of pairing off hadn't already started! Pomme and Épinette, who once had thought of nothing but eluding their mothers and getting into mischief with her, were so excited about their dates for Saturday night.

Within two years they'd probably be engaged or married and then, before she knew it, they'd be young mothers, proudly displaying their babies to her, their freedom utterly surrendered, freedom that would be almost forgotten and probably not even regretted except for a moment or two of memory.

In the most basic way Pomme and Épinette were already gone forever, she thought, with a premonitory shudder. Her summer friendships, which had seemed eternal last year, now revealed themselves as ephemeral—they had been replaced, in the passage of a single winter, by the shadow, as unmistakable as it was unwelcome, of the end of adolescence. *Why did it have to end?*

Fauve flung herself on her bed with an impulse of passionate purity. *Who needed boys?* Why did Pomme and Épinette have to give a damn about them? Couldn't they have waited just one more year? But she knew it was too late. They had both set sail on the sea of romance judging by the certain note of inhabitual tenderness that Pomme, normally a fountain of mockery, had used when she mentioned Raymond Binard, the young electrician from Apt. And where was Épinette's predictable, delightful crustiness when she proudly announced that Paul Alouette, her "friend," who was on leave from his military service, had borrowed his father's new Citroën for the occasion? What sort of accomplishment was borrowing a car?

In New York Fauve was part of a group of classmates at the Dalton School, boys and girls, who had gone to the same dancing school and now got together for rock concerts and parties. They were, she knew, considered the late bloomers in a class where others smoked pot and experimented with sex, but none of her friends were in any rush to launch themselves into the complicated game of man-woman that they saw beginning to be played out all around them.

If only the time could stand still! If only nothing ever had to change!

Startled to find herself close to tears, she sighed deeply with a sigh that she didn't understand was her first sigh of adulthood, a sigh of recognition of the passage of time and the bitter, useless knowledge that there is nothing that can be done about it.

Slowly, Fauve began to feel comforted by her room. It, at least, was something she could always count on not to change. The tower room waited for her to come home to it each year, it possessed an interior life of its own that she knew yielded only to her. Before it had been used as a dovecote it had been a windmill, and she could all but see the great sails that had made their slow circles outside the windows a century ago; she could practically hear the whirring of the wings of generations of doves that had nested where her bed now stood.

In the last eight years Fauve had added to her room until it was a museum of her growing-up. Generations of dolls sat primly against the walls, photographs of Fauve and Mistral together, which had been taken each summer, hung on the walls along with old-fashioned postcards she had found in local antique shops, and flowers she had pressed and framed, as well as posters announcing past village fêtes, the volunteer firemen's balls and other occasions dear to her heart. She never subtracted anything from these collections of memories, nor did she ever bring anything home to New York from Félice. Instinctively she kept her two worlds apart from each other, just as they were in reality.

As Fauve lay, half dreaming, she suddenly heard Kate's voice in the courtyard. How much like Nadine she sounded, Nadine who, thank God, only visited *La Tourrello* once or twice every summer now that she was married to Phillipe Dalmas and living in Paris.

Had Nadine ever experienced regret, even a second of it, when she slipped from being a cool, composed, superior fifteen to a poised and worldly sixteen? Fauve doubted it. If Nadine and any of her crowd had ever dropped in at a village dance it would have been to stand on the sidelines and stare with open amusement as if it were a particularly droll folklorique spectacle. Had they condescended to join in the dancing it would only have been to turn it into a clever story that showed how quaint the locals were.

At the thought of her half-sister Fauve clenched her fists and bounded up from her bed, her gloom vanished in a rush of combat, which translated itself into the one eternal question which can make any female creature forget even such profound questions as the brevity of youth, the fleetingness of time.

What was she going to wear?

Five days later Fauve stood in the girls' corner of the *Salle des Fêtes* in Uzès, a bustling market town of many medieval towers which is the seat of the Duke d'Uzès, the Premier Duke of France. The year 1969 was a particularly confusing year for personal adornment, but even in the Lubéron the miniskirt had made its presence felt. Fauve had spent hours all week trying on and discarding one dress after another. They all looked, to her suddenly self-conscious eyes, either too dressed up, as if she were expecting some occasion more grand than a village dance, or too casual, as if she hadn't bothered to put on her best, as she knew the other girls would. She had still been standing indecisively, clad only in a pair of bright tangerine tights, when Marte Pollison tapped on her door to say that her friends were waiting outside in the car.

In a sudden rush of defiance Fauve jumped into a shocking pink minidress trimmed with a long, wide, geometric slash of purple ribbon. She gave one more lick of the brush to her red hair. Each long and lively strand flirted with the air. She thrust her feet into a pair of bright green Capezio ballet slippers and ran down the staircase of her private tower without going into the salon to say goodbye. If Kate disapproved of her sense of color she really didn't care to know about it. Not ever—and particularly not right now.

The girls' corner of the room was buzzing, but Fauve was not listening to the conversation. She could see two young men approaching her from the boys' corner; each seemed to have clear-cut intentions of asking her to dance. One of them was Lucien Gromet, whose bad breath she still remembered from last year and the other, Henri Savati, was the kind of dancer who could only trudge to the music. Wildly she wondered if she should ask one of the younger girls to dance and avoid them both?

The two boys were approaching at the same rate of speed, neither one of them willing to seem to be in a contest with the other. They were no more than a few feet away when suddenly they were pushed brusquely aside by a third male figure who skidded to a stop before Fauve. He turned to the two others with a flourish. "A thousand apologies, my dear friends, but Mademoiselle has promised me all the dances on her card this evening." Lucien's and Henri's jaws dropped at these words. The accepted way in which to invite a girl to dance was to mumble to her, hook a thumb in the direction of the dance floor and amble off without even looking to see if she was following. Dance card!

Fauve blinked twice. "Ah, Roland, I was beginning to wonder what had happened to you," she said, and put her arm through his. "I thought perhaps you had had to stop to feed the nightingales."

"No, tonight it was the peacocks—the peahen is in heat and they engaged in an unseemly tussle. Shall we waltz?"

"I would like nothing better—but alas, the orchestra is not in agreement."

"Then shall we sit this one out?"

"Perhaps it would be wise, Roland."

"My name is Eric," he said, "but you can call me Roland if for any reason you'd prefer it."

"My name is Fauve." Usually the young men of the neighborhood, who heard her name for the first time, made some silly remark. She waited but he said nothing, inspecting her openly with a look of frankest fascination. She thought that she couldn't remember if she had ever seen a man—for he *was* a man, not a boy—who looked so comfortably at home in his skin. Eric was well over six feet tall and there was some one outstanding quality to him that Fauve was intensely conscious of, yet she couldn't manage to put a name to it as she looked at him. It wasn't just good looks although he was exceptionally handsome, with strong, blunt, well-formed features, deeply tanned skin and thick brown hair that sprang up in an unruly way from a cowlick over his right eye and fell down over his forehead on both sides. His lower lip was full and indented in the center, the focus of his face, giving him a humorous and generous expression. But just what was it, Fauve wondered, that struck her as an unusual and important aspect of this stranger?

"You're staring at me," he said, and grinned.

"You're staring at *me*," she said indignantly.

"Would you rather dance?"

"Perhaps we should."

The orchestra had just begun to play "La Vie en Rose" when Eric took her in his arms. Fauve, who had stood braced in the normal dancing posture of the region, found herself being held close to his chest and masterfully led into what was, to her instantly responding feet, most decidedly a waltz. Perhaps the orchestra wasn't playing the requisite *one*, two, three, *one*, two, three of a Viennese waltz but, nevertheless, they were waltzing magically, and so gracefully that the orchestra leader, watching them, signaled his men to play "The Blue Danube" next. When that waltz was over they stopped suddenly, both of them amazed to find themselves in the center of a circle of other dancers who were watching them with as much curiosity as if Ginger Rogers and Fred Astaire had materialized on the dance floor.

"That was wonderful!" they each said at the same moment, their words colliding in midsentence.

"Come on, let's get something cold to drink. I've discovered three important things about you and I intend to impress you with my intelligence," Eric said, leading her out of the circle. There was a café next door to the *Salle des Fêtes* where the chaperones gathered to play cards. Fauve and Eric found a table and ordered Cokes.

"First," he said, "you are a foreigner, second you're an artist and third, you smell better than any girl in the world."

"But I don't use perfume," Fauve protested.

"That's just what I said."

"Oh." She thought about it for an instant and discovered that she was blushing, that disastrous blush that had been passed down in a direct line from one Lunel woman to another. "How do you know I'm a foreigner?" Fauve said hastily, slipping easily into the accent of the Midi.

"Too late to try that trick, and anyway I can do it too. You waltz like a foreigner—divinely, to be blunt—the only girl in Provence who could have taken Archduke Rudolf away from Marie Vetsera. You didn't learn that here."

"Oh!" Fauve had seen a revival of *Mayerling* on television and her blush deepened. "How do you know I'm an artist?" she demanded nervously.

"Because only an artist would deliberately wear those colors—the dress with your hair could be just to be noticed but then to add orange tights and those shoes . . ."

"I'm interested in art," Fauve said evasively. She never told people that she painted herself. Only her family and Melvin Allenberg and a few close friends knew that she painted and, of them, no one had any true idea of how deeply she felt about her work.

" 'Interested in art'?" he said. "Is that all—just interest?"

"I go to a lot of galleries and museums—New York is the art capital of the world, after all."

"So the New Yorkers would like to think," Eric said defensively. No Frenchman would admit that after the war the center of the art world had indeed shifted to the United States.

"Oh, come on, you know it is. Every Saturday afternoon you can see more new art just walking in and out of the galleries of Madison Avenue than you possibly could in Paris—not to speak of the museums. My friend Melvin and I go out looking two or three times a month," Fauve answered.

"Your friend Melvin? Is he some sort of expert?" Eric bristled.

"Melvin is absolutely brilliant! It's amazing how much he knows . . . and he's such a darling."

"This paragon—no doubt he's handsome too?"

"Well, perhaps not in the obvious way, but it's extraordinary how many girls fall in love with him. They get hooked by his brains and his talent first and then they realize how very attractive he is and how sweet. Sometimes I think that there's nobody in the world I can talk to the way I can talk to Melvin—it's as if I can tell him everything and count on his understanding me."

"That sounds to me as if you're in love with him yourself," Eric said grimly.

"In love'? Oh, Eric, what a marvelous idea!" Fauve chortled.

"What the hell's so marvelous about it? I think it's in terrible taste for you to sit here with me droning on and on about brilliant, handsome, sweet Melvin with whom you share so many artistic afternoons."

"And evenings too, Eric—there are all the gallery openings, you know, and my grandmother lets me go to the really important ones with him," Fauve said, with a wicked grin.

"Oh, that's too much!" Eric drained his Coke and slammed the glass down on the table. "I'm going back inside."

"Eric!"

"What?" he snapped, glaring at her.

"Melvin is an *old* man—ancient—he must be at least forty-three or four—he's like my uncle or something—he used to go out with my mother, for heaven's sake."

"How old are you, anyway?" he asked, sitting back in his chair, barely hiding his relief.

"Sixteen," Fauve answered. Sixteen suddenly sounded absurdly young. Her nostalgia for her fifteenth year had vanished, not to reappear for decades.

"I'm twenty."

They smiled at each other for no reason and for every reason. Fauve realized what it was in Eric's face that had struck her from the moment she'd seen him. She trusted him. She had trusted him overwhelmingly and instantly. It seemed like a strange thing to have picked out as the dominant quality in that face. How could she trust a complete stranger at first sight? And such a handsome one? Pomme and Épinette said men like that were spoiled and full of themselves, and to be avoided at all costs. Well, Pomme and Épinette didn't understand as much as they thought they did.

"Besides knowing all about art, thanks to doddering, kindly, antique Melvin, I suppose you know everything about architecture too?" Eric asked.

"Nothing, except the things you pick up just walking around. I'm genuinely uninformed."

"Well, thank God for that," Eric said delightedly. "I'm an architect, or rather I soon will be . . . I'm at the Beaux-Arts."

"Why are you so pleased that I'm ignorant?"

"I want to have something to teach you," he answered.

"Okay. Start."

"I don't mean now, I mean tomorrow, the day after tomorrow, next week, all summer long . . . don't you have any romance in you?"

"I'm not sure . . . I mean, how do you tell?" Fauve asked seriously, drawing her eyebrows together in concentration.

"So you're a romantic illiterate too? That's even better. Come on, Fauve, let's go and waltz some more and then will you let me drive you home? Or did you come with somebody? It's impossible to figure out at these dances." He sounded suddenly unsure.

"I came with some friends but they won't mind if you take me home."

"Where do you live?"

"Near Félice."

"That's not exactly around the corner." He sounded jubilant.

"It's about sixty kilometers," she said apologetically.

"That's what I like about it. Now Fauve, you've got to stop blushing when I compliment you. I'm going to train you, just like a dog. A compliment every ten minutes for a couple of hours and you'll forget how to blush . . . no, perhaps that's not a good idea after all. I think I like your blush . . . it adds such an interesting shade of pink to all the others."

Dances in Provence never start before nine and rarely end before two o'clock, but Fauve insisted on leaving soon after midnight since the drive was so long and her father always waited up for her safe return.

Near Remoulins, where they picked up the National Route 100 that led almost due east to Félice, Eric tried to persuade her to make a quick detour to see the Pont du Gard by moonlight. "It's one of the supreme wonders of antiquity, almost intact after two thousand years—you'll never understand the Romans until you see that aqueduct, it's . . . no, you're sure? You can really live another day without an aqueduct? Well . . . we'll have to come back."

At Villeneuve-les-Avignon, he had another suggestion. "Let's just go up to my parents' place and say hello—they're never asleep this early and the view from their terrace of the Fort St. André is the best you'll ever see—it may well be the best example of a fortification with twin towers . . . not that either? Don't you *like* a good fortress? All right, all right . . . I'll go straight across the river, looking neither to the left nor to the right although you're making a mistake not just taking a peep at the Popes' Palace tonight—it's never as good by daylight."

"Home, Eric," Fauve insisted, and once past Avignon they sped across the flat, rich plain, Eric proposing and rejecting a dozen projects for the next day. He felt a heavy responsibility for choosing Fauve's first experience with architecture. Since the nearby countryside possessed the ruins of a Phoenician city founded six centuries before Jesus Christ and a hundred other wonders from every era since, what should he pick as a starting point? How much of a ruin should a ruin be? What was her tolerance level for stones?

Fauve found herself scarcely listening to him as they got closer to Félice. Her father had never seen her with any special boy before tonight, she reflected with apprehension. What would he think of her leaving for the evening with a group of old friends and coming back home with an unknown young man she'd picked up at the dance? Surely it must happen to other girls all the time? He *should* be delighted that she hadn't been a wallflower, she thought as she indicated the road to *La Tourrello* to Eric. He *should* be pleased that she'd met somebody who was studying something as interesting as architecture, shouldn't he?

The great gates of the *La Tourrello* stood wide open and the lights of the salon were blazing on the far side of the courtyard. "Just drive right in," Fauve said absently. Eric parked the car in the courtyard.

"Well, you'd better come meet my father . . ." Fauve mumbled and nervously led the way to the salon where she knew he always sat, listening for her.

As they entered the room Mistral rose from his chair near the fireplace and walked toward them, looking from Fauve to Eric in surprise. Only surprise, thought Fauve, immensely relieved, not irritation.

"This is my father," she said, not daring to look at Eric. She should have told him she was Mistral's daughter, she knew she should, but there just hadn't been an appropriate time, or rather the time at which it would have been natural had come and gone so quickly that she hadn't had the wit to seize it, and anyway he hadn't asked and in any case, what of it? He didn't like her because she was Mistral's daughter and he wouldn't not like her for it either, but now, when it was too late, she desperately wished it hadn't come as a surprise. Eric might think she'd planned it to impress him.

"Papa, this is Eric," she said faintly.

"I can see that," said Mistral, shaking hands with a smile. "But, what is this strange tribal custom of the young never to know each other's last names? Eric what, may I ask?"

"Good evening, Monsieur Mistral." Why, Fauve wondered, did Eric sound so strange? Was he angry at her after all?

"The name of my family," Eric continued, "is Avigdor. And the name of my father, Monsieur Mistral, is Adrien Avigdor."

"But you can't possibly forbid Fauve to go out with this young man," Kate said evenly. "That's really out of the question, Julien, in this day and age. Think about it. You have absolutely no reason that she could understand or accept. All that would happen is that you'd encourage her to ask questions you don't particularly care to answer, isn't that so? If I were you, I'd just let the whole mess alone—it'll disappear of its own accord unless you meddle."

"You didn't see his face, Kate. You didn't hear his voice."

"Did he say anything unusual?"

"No, he was perfectly correct as far as that went, but there was *something*—I know I'm not wrong about that."

"Julien, all he could know is that his father was once your dealer. Naturally Avigdor must resent having lost you, what dealer wouldn't? It's unquestionably a famous family horror story—how Julien Mistral got his start from Papa Avigdor and then was so thoroughly ungrateful that he changed dealers—you know how those people talk business all the time. Losing you was probably the biggest event in Avigdor's life—next to getting you."

"I don't want Fauve mixed up with him."

"She's just a child—she's not old enough to 'get mixed up' with a boy at sixteen, not seriously anyway. What harm could come of it? An artist has the right to change dealers, after all. Fauve said that this boy is only twenty years old, didn't she? Well, you haven't seen Avigdor since before the war—it was sometime in 1938 I think that he came here the last time . . . or perhaps even as long ago as 1937—I don't remember. That's more than thirty years ago! Be reasonable! I think you're taking this all much too seriously, just because it's Fauve. You never made this kind of fuss about anyone Nadine went out with and God knows she brought home a lot of young men in her day."

There was no reason, Kate had realized long ago, for Julien to realize that Marte Pollison had told her exactly what had taken place between him and Avigdor during the war, and that her visit to Avigdor had confirmed that, and other facts as well.

There were many pieces of information about her husband that she had stored away in her memory. One never knew when they would become useful . . . they were a form of capital, perhaps in their own way as valuable as any of the canvases in the storeroom.

Meanwhile she relished the look of anxiety on Julien's face. She had so few weapons and he had so many. Strange. Once Fauve had seemed to be another of his weapons, a danger to her, a threat to Nadine. Now, as Fauve grew older and more precious to Mistral every year, more dear to him than anything—for Kate was too clear-eyed to ignore that—Fauve became a weapon she herself might find a way to use.

Some day, at some time in the future, repayment had to be made for the suffering Julien had caused her. Kate believed in the inevitability of revenge. Life could not, *must not* be allowed to treat her unfairly . . . not in the long run, not if she were patient. How deeply interesting it was that Fauve had met this young Avigdor. "What did he look like?" she asked lightly. "Was there much of his father in him?"

"Something . . . perhaps . . . but I didn't pay much attention. He's far better looking, taller, I would never have guessed they were related."

"You mean he didn't look Jewish?"

"That wasn't what I meant! Neither did Avigdor, as you know very well."

"Good heavens, Julien, there's no reason to lash out at me—do try to be less touchy. In two weeks Fauve'll be tired of visiting old buildings with this student and there will be ten other boys for you to worry about. So he was better looking, was he? How much better? Avigdor wasn't a beauty, after all."

"Very, very much better. Too much better."

"Try to get some, sleep, Julien," Kate said sweetly. "You're seeing ghosts."

24

"What were you thinking of, Eric, to begin this cultural project by going to the Popes' Palace?" Beth Avigdor said with mild, amused indignation. "Such a great barracks of a place, without even any furniture to make it look less inhospitable—and full of tourists as well? No wonder you're exhausted, Mademoiselle Lunel. I've avoided setting a foot in there for years."

"I enjoyed it . . . for almost the first hour . . . and by that time we'd passed the point of no return," Fauve answered, wriggling her sore toes, grateful for the umbrella that cast a cool shadow over the lunch table in the garden of Le Prieuré.

Eric's mother was a woman to reckon with, she realized, forthright and statuesque, with fine dark eyes and hair only beginning to show a thread of gray here and there. She looked as if she must be at least twenty years younger than Eric's father who sat, looking as much at ease as any man has ever looked, judiciously considering the fourteen-page wine list, which was wittily decorated by seven, full-page, ink drawings by Ronald Searle. Adrien Avigdor had never seemed particularly young even as a young man, and now he was pleasantly bald, pleasantly stocky, and pleasantly wrinkled, mellow, sturdy and as unremarkable as ever. His mien had always been so simple, so independent of any outstanding feature, so dominated by his expression of rustic goodness, that age had only enhanced it.

In 1945 he had married beautiful Beth Levi, who had fought beside him for three years in the Resistance. Their only son, Eric, who had inherited his mother's looks, and his father's mien, had been born in 1949. The Avigdors had a fine and harmonious marriage, and his gallery on the rue du Faubourg St. Honoré was one of the most successful and respected in France.

Many years ago, when he had bought a vacation house in Provence, he had chosen to live in the urbane, elegant little city of Villeneuve-les-Avignon, which was so different in topography and atmosphere from those savage hill villages of the Lubéron that still held memories he didn't care to resurrect. And now, by God, here was Eric turning up with Mistral's daughter, Avigdor mused, as he weighed the possibility of a potentially interesting Nuits-St.-Georges, Clos de la Maréchale against a highly promising Romanée-St.-Vivant.

It had been impossible to prevent Beth, her maternal curiosity immediately aroused by Eric's enthusiasm, from arranging this lunch. His wife had never known anything more about Mistral than the simple fact that her husband had once been the artist's dealer. "We didn't get along but it's too unimportant to discuss," he had told her years ago. Eric had grown curious, in the last year, to know the reason for his quarrel with the painter, but he'd resisted being drawn into an explanation with his son. "Just call it a mutual disagreement," he'd said, with such an uncharacteristic frown that it had only served to convince Eric that there had been a serious rupture between them.

There could not be anyone Avigdor was less anxious to see his son interested in than Mistral's daughter, but he resolved that he would be as pleasant to her as he would be to any other girl. Indeed, what man could not be, once he'd laid eyes on her?

The years had taught Adrien Avigdor certain things, and one of them was how lucky he had been to survive when so many had perished. It was important to him to be grateful for life, important not to dwell on old wounds. He asked only to live with dignity, and with decency toward others, but the hard-earned lessons of self-preservation he had learned during the Occupation made him turn his back whenever he heard people speak of religion or politics. If only, he thought often, those two forces that so violently and persistently divided humanity had been left out of the scheme of things, how sweet life could be for everyone. He wanted nothing to do with certain memories that, in spite of his philosophy, had never faded, and Fauve Mistral brought them back to life.

"So, Mademoiselle," he said, turning deliberately to Fauve with his benign air, "you go to school in the United States, do you?"

"Oh, please call me Fauve—yes, I live in New York but I come to visit my father every summer."

"Of course, of course, how pleasant. Ah, Jacques," Adrien Avigdor turned to Jacques Mille, director of the hotel, son of the proprietor of Le Prieuré, who had bought it from Madame Blé, "what do you think of the Nuits-St. Georges as compared to the Romanée-St.-Vivant? Your personal opinion mind you, among friends."

"If it were my palate, Monsieur Avigdor, I'd pick the Beaune Vignes Franches, 1955." Young Jacques Mille, dressed in a casual, distinctly English manner, possessing an open, upright charm, and brought up to preside over a masterpiece of a hotel and restaurant, was a man whose advice could be relied on in all things.

"Then that's decided," Avigdor said comfortably. The rest of the meal could now revolve around the wine rather than have the wine chosen to accommodate the food—he preferred it that way.

The garden of Le Prieuré was filled, as always, with festive groups: celebrating families and tables of serious gourmets, seated at round tables on bright blue cushions under red sun umbrellas. Waiters and busboys bustled about under the vigilant eye of vivacious Marie-France Mille, Jacques's soft-voiced wife who embodied that idealized brunette Provençal beauty that the Italian poet, Petrarch, had immortalized in his Laura.

What would the ghost of pious Cardinal Arnaud de Via, nephew of Pope John XXII, who had given his palace to twelve canons in 1333 to turn into a priory, have made of the merry lunchtime scene? What would the ghost of Madame Blé, who had run such a quiet *pension*, have thought of the Olympic-sized swimming pool and the two tennis courts that lay on the other side of the old rose garden, out of sight of the diners? What exclamations would she have made if she could have seen the splendid addition that had recently been built and perfectly integrated into the old buildings, with its air-conditioned suites and luxurious baths? And what would the ghost of Teddy Lunel have thought if she could have looked down from the room in which she had decided her fate and seen her tall, lovely young daughter sitting there about to have lunch with Adrien Avigdor, a man Julien Mistral never mentioned to her during their short life together?

"I'm so happy to meet you, Monsieur Avigdor," Fauve said. "My grandmother has told me of you."

"So Maggy hasn't forgotten me?" asked Avigdor, pleased.

"Of course not. Magali has always told me absolutely everything about her past. She believes that it's important for children to know as much as possible about their parents and grandparents—particularly when they're illegitimate."

Fauve chose her words deliberately. She wanted Eric's parents to know from the beginning that no matter what was in their minds about her birth they didn't have to treat her with cautious tact.

"I wish you'd tell me about my father, when he was a young man," she went on. "I've only really known him for the last eight years. Perfect as my father is, he refuses to reminisce. But you gave him his first show so you must have known him for—oh, more than forty years! What was he like then?" The most lively curiosity was fervent on her face.

Mistral as a young man? Quickly Avigdor searched for a pleasant memory. He could hardly tell this devoted daughter that her father had always been an accursed, bad-tempered, arrogant, selfish man. A man who had sent more than one Jew to his death. But he must find something to say.

"Well, now let me see . . . it's hard to describe him exactly. He was always impressive, always the most noticeable person in any room." He paused, searched a second and then found inspiration. "What I'll never forget, no never, is that very first time I met him. Kate Browning, that is to say your stepmother of course, brought me to your father's little studio in Montparnasse where he was living with your grandmother—why, I can still see Maggy walking out of the kitchen in her bare feet with the wine and the glasses—it's amazing how vividly I remember her, but, of course, she was so magnificently beautiful, such a superb girl and not much older than you are now, Fauve . . . just eighteen I think, and so much in love, so loyal . . ."

"Loyal," Fauve echoed in a small voice.

"But, of course loyal, that above all. I admired her a great deal, you know, supporting your father by her modeling before he began to sell—but, naturally when a woman is truly in love she will make any sacrifice, is that not so? Ah, they were a striking couple, both so tall, both with red hair, his so dark, hers so bright, they were the legend of the *quartier* . . . ah, yes, Julien Mistral and Maggy, *La Rouquinne*—they must have been together for quite a while before he met Kate. By the way, how is Kate now? I've totally lost track of her."

"She's . . . fine," Fauve said out of a confusion so deep that she spoke vaguely.

"Her health is good?" Avigdor asked.

"Perfect, as far as I know," Fauve said, forcing herself to smile politely. Adrien Avigdor spoke a moment longer before the arrival of the Dover sole turned the conversation to food but Fauve heard nothing more.

Her father and *her grandmother? They* had loved? *They* had lived together? But it had been her *mother* and her father who had loved, who had lived together! A wave of troubled confusion so strong and complicated that it prevented her from moving swept over her and only the anxious pressure of Eric's hand on hers under the tablecloth brought her back and enabled her to pick up her fork.

With a few nostalgic, well-meant words Adrien Avigdor had taken the design she had made to explain her own life and changed it forever, as irrevocably as someone giving a twist to a pattern in a kaleidoscope. The familiar shapes were lost, destroyed. Why did you never tell me *this*, Magali? I knew only that you posed for my father, nothing more. *What kind of man is he*? What really happened between you? What can I trust now of anything you've ever told me?

"Is your sole not good, Fauve?" Beth Avigdor asked gently. She would have kicked her husband soundly if she had had any warning that he was going to ramble on in that fatuous way, but to be fair, Fauve had brought it on herself, when she proclaimed that her grandmother had told her "absolutely everything"—did any parent or grandparent ever tell the young "everything"? This would have had to be the first instance in recorded history. For whatever reason, the girl was clearly lost in her own thoughts. "Fauve," she repeated, "is the fish not good?"

"Oh! No, it's excellent, thank you, Madame Avigdor."

"Fauve, I promise, no more architecture for twenty-four hours," Eric said contritely. "Two days? . . . a week? Whatever you say. We'll do whatever you like this afternoon."

"Let's go to the Pont du Gard," said Fauve, giving him a resolute smile.

"You're crazy—you look knocked out."

"I'm perfectly fine, and I'm panting to truly understand the Romans."

"Eric has this notion that you can't comprehend a civilization until you understand how they feel about water," Adrien Avigdor grumbled. "Why about water and not about wine? I ask you that. Ah ha! No one can give me an answer. They never can."

"You could probably get one from a Talmudic scholar," Fauve suggested, "if you really want to know."

"That's not the sort of thing they discuss in the Bible," Eric protested.

"The Bible?" Fauve laughed. "What has the Bible to do with dozens and dozens of books of debates and commentaries on the Torah, the Five Books of Moses?"

"Dozens and dozens of what?" Eric said, bewildered.

"Oh, stop kidding me. Monsieur Avigdor, there are bound to be at least two opinions in the Talmud, or maybe even a dozen, so you wouldn't ever really get an answer, but at least they'd give you a good argument. At least that's what Rabbi Taradash would have said, according to my grandmother."

Avigdor's jaw dropped in astonishment.

"Drink some wine, darling," Beth Avigdor said hastily to her husband. In her opinion it was a perfectly reasonable suggestion; old-fashioned, unexpected and quaint coming from such a young girl, but certainly not a reason for such gaping amazement. Mistral's daughter or not, wasn't Lunel a Jewish name, and a fine old one at that? What had come over the man?

By the time she went to bed that night, Fauve had drawn a self-protective shell of rationalization around the revelations of Adrien Avigdor. She no longer felt betrayed by her grandmother. Now that she could think over what he'd said without the element of surprise, it made perfect sense that Magali had not told her the whole story, had kept some part secret. When she was younger she simply wouldn't have been able to understand it. God knows, the family history of the Lunel women and all those star-crossed lovers of theirs was complicated enough. It was really rather romantic—love across two generations—she thought sleepily, but somehow she thought that she wouldn't ask her father anything about Monsieur Avigdor's memories . . . she'd wait to question Magali about it when she got home. No one had hidden things from her . . . no one had betrayed her . . . she could trust them . . . everything was as it had always been . . . there was just one layer of mystery . . . unimportant . . . so far in the past . . . so long ago . . .

"Fauve, hurry up and finish your breakfast," Mistral said. "It's time for your painting lesson."

"I promised to spend the day with Eric," Fauve said. "He's taking me to the Roman Arena in Arles."

"I assume you're teasing. I've put aside that time for you every morning."

"No, I'm serious."

"But, Fauve, you have your whole life to spend in looking at Roman arenas—what are your priorities? With your talent you can't waste time sightseeing! It's simply not possible! How many days are there in the summer? Don't you know how much you still have to learn?"

"I know, Father. But I promised."

"Julien," said Kate, "aren't you being unreasonable? Why should Fauve want to spend the morning shut up in a studio with you when she can be out with such an irresistible young man? I know that at her age I certainly would have preferred to flirt than paint . . . don't be insensitive."

"Kate, this has nothing to do with you. Fauve, come along. When that boy shows up, Kate, tell him to wait until Fauve's through for the day. If he's interested, he'll still be here at noon."

"No, Father."

"No? What does that mean?"

"I'm not going to paint with you this summer—not at all. I can't anymore."

"What are you talking about?" Now Mistral was too astonished to be angry. "Can't? Can't what? You're not trying to say that you are *unable* to paint? How many times have I told you that you have a serious natural talent? What's this all about?"

"I've thought about it all winter." Fauve faltered at first but her voice steadied quickly. "Last summer, you remember, when I wanted to do some experimental work, you said that I'd been contaminated by all the vulgarity and chichi of the shows I'd seen in New York and we went back to painting figures and landscapes and still lifes—well, I wanted to tell you then that I couldn't keep on trying to paint like Mistral, that I wasn't Mistral and never would be Mistral and there was no reason for you to keep hoping that I could ever be anything like you—but I didn't dare. I promised myself that I'd have the courage to do it this summer . . . well, that's it, that's why I'm not coming to the studio with you."

"Fauve," Mistral said, struggling to keep calm, "you live in the center of a whirlpool of all the filth of the entire world of art, if you can dignify that money machine, that total anarchy that reigns in New York by calling it art at all. I can understand why you aren't completely able to avoid some infection. It's a kind of Broadway-Hollywood interior decorator's insanity, a bunch of talentless exhibitionists—but surely you don't take people seriously who make 'art' from fluorescent light tubes and modular shelving and Styrofoam and comic strips and things they find in garbage cans—Jesus Christ, Fauve, if you want to be amused by art go study Marcel Duchamp—at least he did it with style and he did everything first!"

"You simply don't understand what I'm trying to say. I don't want to do Pop or Op or Minimal—or any of the others—I don't want to do what anybody else is doing—and I *can't* do what you do—I don't want to paint at all!"

"You can't possibly not want to paint, Fauve. You *are* a painter, you have no choice." Mistral's voice was gentle, patient, as if he were speaking to an unexpectedly stubborn thoroughbred horse. "I've never asked you to imitate me, not that I'm aware of. I've simply tried to keep you from being swept away into a cesspool of so-called new ideas—they'll only distort and corrupt your natural gifts. You know what I've always said: that you can't fly until you've developed wings strong enough to lift you off the ground and into the heavens. You *must* have all the essential equipment—afterward you can do *anything*—why, even Picasso, worn out and obsessed by erotica as he is, can still draw like a thousand angels when he chooses to. He had to have the classic training *in order to leave it behind him*. I'm telling you only that you don't yet—don't quite yet—have all that necessary background, all those skills. Fauve, let's go on up to the studio. You do anything you like this morning—no lessons—we'll just paint together quietly, no criticism, no suggestions, just paint."

"No, Father."

Mistral's lips tightened. He looked at Fauve and he saw something in her face that made him reflect for a second, and decide to meet her on her ground. "All right, then, if it's a Roman arena you feel you must visit this morning, go and have a good time. We'll talk more about this later, eh? It's not something we have to settle right now, after all."

The kitchen bell sounded. "That's Eric," Fauve said, jumping up from the table. "I'll be back for dinner . . . or if I'm not, I'll call." She kissed Mistral on his cheek. "See you later." She picked her shoulder bag off a chair and walked quickly out of the room.

"Well, Julien," Kate said, in her flat, uninflected way, "I must say I'm stunned. I had no idea that she resented your lessons so much—hasn't she any idea of the privilege it is to be taught by you?"

"Oh, don't talk rubbish, Kate. She's my daughter, and privilege has nothing to do with it. It's that New York world she lives in, all sense of values disappeared there long ago. It's the people she's permitted, God knows why, to associate with, that photographer, Falk, who's allowed to drag her to those disgusting new galleries, it's a contagion, it's a sickness . . ."

"Hasn't it occurred to you, Julien, that she may simply not be interested anymore? Why do you expect Fauve to be different from most other sixteen-year-old girls? They live and breathe horses or ice skating or ballet and then one day they discover a boy—like Avigdor's son—and they lose interest overnight in that one thing to which they've devoted years of their lives—it's a well-known phenomenon."

Kate stood up, shopping list in hand. Then, as if having a second thought, she continued. "After all, how many great women painters are there? How many times have you said that their energies go into childbearing? And how many children of famous parents manage to achieve anything important in the same field as their parents did, eh? Has there *ever* been a great—even a well-known—woman painter who was the daughter of an artist of your stature?" She put her hand on Mistral's shoulder. "Don't take it so hard . . . it was bound to happen sooner or later . . . young Avigdor just provided the spark that made the mixture explode . . . and I must say I can certainly see why now that I've met him. What an extraordinarily good-looking young man! And how hospitable his parents were to Fauve yesterday . . . they seem to have been in quite a hurry to take her to the bosom of their family."

"What an absurd thing to say about one lunch," Mistral said, his face red with rage.

Kate made a philosophic face. "That's what happens with children," she said, watching Mistral carefully. "You spend your life worrying about them and doing everything you can for them and then, just when they get to their most interesting age, they dash off with the first person who comes along and leave you waving goodbye. Do I complain that Nadine practically never comes here? Since she married Phillipe they spend all their vacations in Sardinia or Marrakesh or wherever their friends are—it's all quite normal. You accepted it with Nadine—the same thing is happening with Fauve, my dear, that's all." She gave a shrug of resignation.

"It seems hard to believe that you used to be an intelligent woman, Kate." Mistral was so enraged that his voice lost all of its color. "Fauve and Nadine have nothing in common. Fauve is gifted, enormously gifted . . . she was born to paint. She's simply going through a moment of rebellion. Tomorrow or the next day she'll be back at work." He stood up and left the room without another word.

Kate sat down at the breakfast table alone, listening to the sounds of the countryside. A brief smile crossed her finely molded lips as she thought of the stricken look on Julien's face, at the fury she had watched him conceal from Fauve. Ah, Julien, she said to herself. Don't you know that this is only the beginning? You've just started to lose her. You . . . you who used to be an intelligent man?

"Why Cavaillon?" asked Eric as he drove the car. "I know that's where they grow the best melons in France, but I thought that we were set for Arles? Cavaillon is basically without architectural interest."

"Because a Roman arena will wait one more day but in Cavaillon there's something I want to see. Anyway, didn't you say I could do anything I wanted to yesterday? And didn't I go to that old aqueduct and listen to all your explanations?"

"And I thought you were really interested."

"I was, I was incredibly fascinated. Roman water systems have a mysterious allure all their own," Fauve drawled provokingly.

"I think you need to be kissed," Eric said sternly.

"Oh, no, I don't!" Fauve cried, alarmed.

"Oh, yes, you do." Eric turned the car into a little side road and stopped the motor. He reached across the seat and pulled Fauve toward him easily in spite of her attempts at resistance, but once she was securely pinned in his arms he didn't try to raise the chin that she held firmly tucked into her neck but instead he kissed the warm, silky top of her head. Slowly she relaxed and they sat pressed together listening to the sound of their breathing and communicating a wordless secret of which they each possessed a half. Long, sweet dreaming minutes went by and finally Fauve said, in a small, shy voice with her chin still lowered, "You may kiss me if that's what you want."

"Isn't it what you want?" Eric asked, smiling at her youth.

"If you have to ask . . ." Fauve raised her head and drew a finger across the indented twin pillows of his lower lip. With a groan he pressed his lips on hers, feeling a jolt in his soul as he received the innocence of her full-hearted kiss. "Oh!" she whispered in incandescent surprise. "Oh, *how nice!*" She opened her arms wide and laced them tightly around his neck. They clung together kissing each other over and over, each kiss complete in itself, not leading to anything except another kiss, each kiss a miniature cosmos in which they lost all sense of the existence of any other world. Utterly captured by the moment as she was, Fauve was aware that deep in her chest a new pulse had announced itself, beating for the first time, as if it were a drum heralding the birth of something that had been waiting within her, waiting for this particular man to kiss her.

Suddenly the little car began to rock from side to side. Fauve and Eric stiffened in alarm and looked around them. The windows of the car were blocked halfway up by fat, dusty gray shapes, a noisy, indifferent succession of strong, mindless bodies that buffeted the Renault as if it were an inconvenient bush.

"I didn't even hear the sheep coming," Fauve said in amazement.

"Neither did I . . . oh, Fauve . . . my darling Fauve . . . oh, damn, here come the shepherds—look in the rear-view mirror." Eric moved away from her to a respectable distance.

"Shepherds?" Fauve scoffed breathlessly, taking refuge from her new emotion in teasing. "They're used to nature in all its manifestations. Come back here at once!"

Cavaillon, some fifteen kilometers southwest of Félice, in the direction of Avignon, is a calm prosperous market town of eighteen thousand inhabitants. Fauve and Eric sat outside the café in which they'd had lunch, holding hands silently, looking on to a drowsy, unimportant square. Finally Eric said, "I truly don't care that there's nothing to see in Cavaillon, though I do still wonder what we're doing here."

"We're waiting for the guide to show up."

"The guide? There's nothing here to merit a guided tour—just us and the waiter—even the shops are closed till four."

"Wait," Fauve said in a superior voice.

"Whatever you say, shepherd's delight."

"We did rather make their day, don't you agree?"

"I didn't think to ask, but possibly they've seen people kissing before."

"Oh, come on, Eric, I see him!" Fauve jumped up and started to cross the square toward a flight of steps in front of an unremarkable three-story building where a young man in his shirt sleeves had just stationed himself. Eric followed her, shaking his head in bewilderment.

As they approached the young man, people seemed to spring out around the corner of every street leading to the square, popping from parked automobiles and pouring from doorways, almost out of the very ground itself. By the time they had reached the base of the staircase they were part of a group of some twenty-five people, all of whom, to Eric's amazed eyes, seemed to know perfectly well where they were heading. He tried to keep as close to Fauve as possible but it was difficult since everyone was eagerly trying to climb the narrow staircase at the same time. At the top there was a balcony and a tall pair of handsomely carved, closed wooden doors set into a massive stone archway.

"What . . . ?" Eric began, but Fauve motioned him to be silent. The crowd finally arranged itself in place around the guide and waited in an expectant silence. The young man flung open the doors with a certain grave ceremony.

"Welcome to the Synagogue of Cavaillon," he said.

"I don't believe it!" Eric muttered to her.

"I figured you wouldn't—yesterday when you got the Talmud mixed up with the Bible," Fauve said, delighted with her surprise. "I discovered this when I was reading the green Michelin guide to Provence last winter, they've got it listed under 'Other Curiosities' in Cavaillon along with the old cathedral and the archeological museum. I'd planned to come here when I got back."

"Well, what are we supposed to do now?" Eric asked.

"Visit it, of course. Don't you want to?"

"Well, sure . . . I guess . . . why not?"

"You amaze me, you really do. I mean, you *are* Jewish, aren't you?"

"Naturally—my parents are, so I am—but what does that have to do with it? They aren't religious at all, neither of them, and I've never even been to a service—oh, wait, once a cousin got married, when I was a little kid, and they took me to the wedding in Paris, but I hardly remember it. To me being Jewish doesn't have a connection with going to a synagogue unless you feel like it, and I've never had the urge. Anyway, why are you so interested? Is it some kind of hobby?"

"Yesterday, your father was talking about my grandmother, Magali, remember? She's Jewish, born in France, and *her* daughter, my mother, was half-Jewish and half-Irish Catholic. My father is French Catholic so that makes me one-quarter Jewish—more than enough to fascinate me because it's part of my history, my *personal* history, and it's the *only* part I have any information about. My father doesn't know a thing about his grandparents—he frankly doesn't care and he's not even sure if they're originally from Provence in spite of his name. All I know about the other side of the family is that my mother's father was an American named Kilkullen—that and two dollars will buy you a shot of Irish whiskey on St. Patrick's Day. I'm curious enough to want to visit the synagogue, got it?"

"Anything you say, little nut. I just can't believe all these tourists—they've got to be speaking fifteen foreign languages—where did they all come from?"

"Fifteen foreign countries. This is a place of pilgrimage, Eric. What's more, it's even got a water system inside somewhere according to the Michelin, even if it's not a Roman aqueduct."

"What is it?"

"A ritual bath," Fauve pronounced, her eyes dancing with mischief.

"Oh, no! That's where I draw the line."

"It's only for women, you ignorant idiot, and anyway this synagogue is a monument, it isn't used for anything anymore. Look, the guide has a book for sale. Let's buy one so we can look around by ourselves without following this crowd. I hate being trapped in a herd."

Eric bought the entrance tickets and paid for a thin book by André Dumoulin, conservator of the museums and monuments of Cavaillon. It contained a short history of the Jewish community of Cavaillon, as well as photographs and descriptions of the synagogue.

Fauve and Eric left the group of tourists all listening intently to the guide, and wandered alone into the central part of the temple. Neither of them had any idea of what to expect and they stopped abruptly after they crossed the threshold, taken utterly by surprise. They found themselves in an almost empty room that nevertheless gave an immediate impression of the most gracious harmony of spirit. It could have been a perfect small salon from some abandoned palace built in the style and at the time of Versailles. The synagogue had been constructed in 1774, on the site of an older temple that dated back to 1499, and the architect and craftsmen of Cavaillon who had worked on its interior had been trained in the unsurpassably delicate formality of Louis XV.

The walls of the tall, balconied room were painted a soft white and entirely paneled. Each panel was adorned with wood that had been carved and gilded in motifs of roses, garlands of palm leaves, baskets of flowers, seashells and musical instruments—all the fantasies and fancies so dear to the taste of the Marquise de Pompadour. A number of chandeliers hung from the high ceiling, some of them dripping fragile pendants of old rock crystal, while others, more solid, were made of well-polished copper, all carrying gay clusters of tall yellow candles. A pale golden, muted light drifted in from high windows.

Both Fauve and Eric found themselves irresistibly drawn forward to stand before a railing, some four feet tall, made of intricately detailed wrought iron. It stood protectively around a pair of superbly carved and decorated doors that were the unquestioned focus of the entire temple. The doors, which looked as if they must open into a noble space, were flanked by tall Corinthian columns supporting an elaborate series of pediments crowned by a basket from which burst a profusion of sprays of roses.

Fauve, searching in the guidebook, realized that they were the doors behind which the scrolls of the Torah, the Hebrew Bible, had been kept when the temple had still functioned as a house of worship. She stood in awe, trying to imagine what she would see if she were to be allowed to penetrate the enclosure, to open the closed doors of the tabernacle, but she failed. It was beyond her.

Eric heard her sigh wistfully and pulled her gently away, leading her to the opposite side of the gemlike temple where they climbed one of the two semicircular staircases to the paneled, garlanded balcony that stretched the entire width of the room.

Fauve leaned carefully on the balustrade, as delicately fashioned as lace, and thought that from this vantage point the temple looked like a ballroom in which she could imagine ladies in powdered hair and men in brocaded vests dancing. But the guidebook, again consulted, informed her that she was standing on what had been the rostrum of whoever conducted the service. Her vision of dancers faded as she looked down and tried to imagine the sumptuous little temple filled with benches, and the benches crowded by people dressed as they used to be dressed throughout Provence, in costumes that were now only worn by folksingers performing for festivals.

The past seemed close, as if it were lying just behind a curtain of light; so powerful, so palpable was the atmosphere of the lovely deserted place that it was as impossible to realize that it was empty as it was to know what it had truly been like when it had been in use. Like all abandoned holy places, in which once the human soul has poured out its deepest emotions, it hummed with a complex energy and silenced the visitor.

As the horde of other visitors started to enter the main part of the synagogue, Fauve and Eric hastily descended the staircase and penetrated to the basement of the building, where, in the former bakery of the Jewish community, the city of Cavaillon and the Beaux-Arts had installed a small museum.

There, again alone, they found themselves in a long, low-ceilinged room with a stone floor. Two glass cases, full of photographs and documents, filled the center of the room and on both walls stood illuminated cabinets that contained all manner of ceremonial objects used in the performance of the service. It even contained the tabernacle doors of the temple of 1499, Renaissance in style, adorned with a bas-relief of vases, holding branches of fruit and flowers and painted with the Hebrew letters of the tablets Moses brought down from Sinai. Fauve was contemplating these doors that had been new almost five hundred years before, trying to pierce the veil of time, when Eric pulled her away to another of the cabinets.

"Look!" he said excitedly. "Here's a Roman oil lamp from the first century before

Christ. See the two menorahs on its base? It says here in the book that it's one of the oldest representations of the menorah ever found on French soil—it's a hundred years *older* than the Pont du Gard."

Fauve found herself abruptly appalled at the sight of the humble little object. "Oh, Eric, think of the earth under which it must have been found—so *many* feet of earth—too much history—too many years ago—how many generations are there in two thousand years, how many births and deaths? I can't bear to think about it—I'm having trouble going back two hundred years, much less two thousand." She turned away to the cases with relief. Photographs, no matter how old, were somehow of today.

She walked slowly up and down, almost weary, gazing with diminishing interest at old letters and proclamations. Suddenly she stood transfixed before a photograph, taken in 1913, of a dignified, handsome old gentleman with a trim white mustache, a double-breasted black suit and a black hat with an upturned brim of a typically Provençal style. He stood to one side of the railing that encircled the doors of the tabernacle in the synagogue above them and, standing on the other side, was a dark-eyed, stately woman in a long, tiny-waisted black dress with a wisp of veiling on her gray hair. "Eric," she cried, "come and look at this. Look, just look! It says that they were two of the last representatives of the Jewish community in Cavaillon."

"They're certainly very impressive," Eric said, puzzled by her emotion.

"Their names! Monsieur and Madame Achille *Astruc*—Astruc, my great-grandfather's name! Oh Eric, I haven't told you about him—David Astruc was Magali's father—these people might have been relatives of mine! They were old when Magali was a little girl—they could have been cousins, or great-aunt and uncle or—oh, I don't know . . . something—" Fauve had tears in her eyes as she pored over the photograph of the fine, serene old people. Eric stood quietly, rocking her gently with his arms clasped around her waist as she studied the picture, lost in speculation and wonder.

It was minutes before the other tourists started to trickle into the museum.

"I think we've had the best of it," Eric whispered to her and Fauve quickly agreed, casting one last glance at the photograph before she followed him up the stairs and outside.

"I need a Coke . . . don't you?" Eric asked.

"Something cold with a lot of sugar in it," Fauve agreed, and they returned to the café and almost collapsed at a table, with that peculiar, drained, but high-hearted exhaustion known only to sightseers who have somehow been allowed to travel in time and not been forced to merely observe.

Eric picked up the guidebook and riffled through its pages with curiosity. "I wonder how many Jews lived in Cavaillon—let's see . . . it says here that it was always a small number, never more than three hundred people at the most. This is interesting, Fauve, the municipal archives mention that there was a rabbi in Cavaillon as early as the eleventh century but when the Revolution came in 1790 the Jews began to leave Provence and spread out all over France and after 1793 there isn't even a *trace* of community activity. Look, here's a list of the names of the last members of the community—it's from the archives of Cavaillon and they've broken the names into groups to show their origins."

Fauve took the book. "There are more French names than any other," she said, "all taking their names from the various localities they came from . . . Carcassonne,

Cavaillon, of course, and Digne, and Monteux . . . all place-names . . . and . . . and Lunel."

"Lunel?" he echoed.

"Lunel! Then there must be a *place* called Lunel! I never knew that! It never even occurred to me that it might be a place-name. Oh, Eric, we *have* to be able to find it on the map if it still exists! Eric, when can we go looking for Lunel?" Her fatigue forgotten, Fauve looked as if she were ready to set out on the search at once. Eric smiled at the sight of her eager, open-hearted impatient beauty.

"It's got to be somewhere, Fauve, and I'll dig it up for you . . . places just don't disappear. But not today." He took the guidebook away from her and looked at the page from which she'd been reading.

"There are some other names with a Hebrew origin like Cohen and Jehuda and a few from the Latin—that's where your Astruc comes from, darling, from *astrum* meaning star. The last group are foreign, people from Cavaillon who came here from other countries . . . Lisbonne and Lubin . . . a Pole . . . and . . ."

"And . . ." Fauve asked, puzzled at his stopping.

"Damn *time!* It takes everything with it," he muttered. People named Astruc and Lunel had *belonged* to that temple he had just visited as if it were only a larger than ordinary curiosity from another civilization. The past, tantalizing, elusive, always just beyond reach, had rapped him smartly on his shoulder, and he shivered in wonder. If he knew enough, if there were documents—which there weren't—why couldn't he trace Fauve's family back before the Romans had built the Pont du Gard? Why had so much knowledge been lost? How had it come to be forgotten?

"Ah, don't be upset," Fauve said, understanding his emotion. "It just isn't fair, not being able to know, it's so frustrating . . . Eric, we're both so miserably uninformed and ignorant, aren't we? We're a disgrace."

"We certainly are."

"But imagine . . ." Fauve continued, her eyes bigger than ever with speculation, "just imagine . . . Lunels and Astrucs and Lubins and Carcassonnes all going to temple together . . . knowing each other . . . their families living right here for hundreds and hundreds of years . . . maybe one of them was that rabbi in the eleventh century—I can almost see them, can't you?"

Eric was silent, looking at her lovely, thoughtful face, so animated by the visions she saw. He found himself swooping back from the past and totally, marvelously alive in the present.

"It's impossible to see anyone but you."

"Eric," Fauve said chidingly. "What a lack of imagination."

"Because I'm in love with you."

"What?"

"I'm in love with you. Do you love me? Do you, my darling?"

"I don't know . . . I've never been in love before," she murmured.

"Look at me," he commanded. Slowly she raised her lids and what he saw in her eyes was so unmistakable that he almost cried out in joy.

"But I didn't *intend* to fall in love!" Fauve protested.

"It's too late now," he said triumphantly.

25

The writer who complains of the loneliness of his work, the artist who speaks ruefully of the solitude of his studio, the composer who announces that he is condemned to shut himself away to write music in a secluded room all share one trait: they lie. Were they to admit the unfashionable truth they would have to say that there are few places less lonely than that privileged space in which the mind is free to concentrate on its work, no privacy more jealously guarded from intrusion.

The vast studio in which Julien Mistral worked at *La Tourrello* had been his only true home for forty years. As he opened the doors he breathed in deeply, relishing the complex aroma composed by the smell of the poppy-seed oil-based paints, the prepared canvases, the seasoned pine used as stretchers, the agreeably rancid paint-smeared rags that lay about, all mixed into a pungent necromantic brew. Mistral found himself greeted by a population of images that represented everything he had ever cared about. In this studio he had expended his heroic resources. Brush stroke by brush stroke he had distilled his life itself and the release of this essence of each hour's work had left an imprint on the very air. The paintings that he had sold over the years seemed to him to be as constant in their presence as those he had kept for himself, as if they had refused to leave. He had never experienced a minute's loneliness in his densely peopled studio.

What then, Mistral asked himself savagely, was the feeling that plucked so insistently at his consciousness that he found himself looking blankly at a half-finished canvas for an hour at a time? What was this restlessness, this irritation, this sense of something not accomplished, something incomplete?

It was a month before he was willing to admit to himself that it was Fauve's absence, a month before he reached a point at which he could no longer tell himself that tomorrow she would be back, a month before he was able to isolate and define the realization that in the course of the past eight years the painting lessons he gave her every morning during her summer stay with him had become essential to him.

He needed her.

After Teddy's death Julien Mistral had resolved never to need another human being. He had given Fauve up without a moment's hesitation, he had stayed away from her for eight years because he was afraid that she would remind him of Teddy. When he saw no resemblance to her mother in her face, he had been relieved; no man could love twice as he had loved Teddy, and survive. He could not afford to give another such hostage to fortune. The nine months of the year that Fauve spent in New York passed without too much pain, although much too slowly, in the certain knowledge that every June she would come home to him, and they would be together all summer long.

Never would he have believed that she could desert him. There had been no sign, on the last trip down from Paris, only five weeks before, of any basic change in her. A new maturity, yes certainly, and a hint of dissatisfaction with her own work, now that he thought about it, but what true artist was ever satisfied? No, it had nothing to do with his disapproval of her ventures into Abstraction . . . surely Fauve must know that if she had really insisted on it she was free to paint with a broom instead of a brush, free to paint archery targets or jigsaw puzzles, free to make mudpies and plaster casts. All that was just a convenient excuse. The reason she'd left him was Eric Avigdor. Fauve had been his daughter until the night she met that boy.

It was so simple an explanation, and so obvious that Mistral didn't understand how he had failed to see it sooner. Kate had been right, entirely right—perhaps if she had said nothing he would have understood immediately, but whenever Fauve was concerned, he discounted any opinion Kate had.

Where, after all, had Fauve been all these past days? Arles, she said, and Cavaillon and Nîmes and Orange, Carpentras and Tarascon and St. Rémy and Aix-en-Provence. Oh, how banally touristic! What was her conversation about on those few evenings that she favored them with her company at dinner? An infuriating mixture of architectural wonders—not one of which Mistral thought was worth looking at as much as the sight of a single cherry tree in bloom—and the discoveries she was making, little by little, of that most confusing of all subjects, the history of the Jews of Provence.

Did she think that he gave a damn for one word of it? He had nothing against Jews, they simply didn't interest him, any more than Mohammedans or Hindus. Why was she fascinated by a past that had nothing to do with her, so little relevance to the modern world? Did she have any idea how farfetched the topic was?

Maggy, who had, after all, been Jewish, had never given it a thought as far as he could remember, and Teddy cared only for the present they had lived in together, and yet here was his own daughter, poking about in synagogues, in Avignon, in Aix, in Carpentras. Synagogues!

Only last night, irritated beyond endurance, he had asked her why, since she was going through a religious phase, and since three out of four of her grandparents had been Catholics, why didn't she visit cathedrals? "Cathedrals are just too accessible," she'd said, maddeningly pleased with herself. "They're everywhere, there isn't a town without one or two—they're old, but without mystery."

Mistral put down his palette and gave up any attempt to continue work. He paced the floor of his studio in a rising panic. It was almost mid-July. In six more weeks, Fauve's summer visit would be over and she was on the verge of drifting away from him. When she came back next year she'd be seventeen—no longer a child—and he would be seventy. Seventy—bah! It was just a number. He had more energy, more curiosity than he'd had when he was fifty.

It was the behavior of his teenaged daughter that bothered him, not the weight of his years. Exposed to the attention of the first young man who'd noticed her, she had turned flighty, giddy and filled with overblown, momentary enthusiasms. She needed to be brought down to earth, that was all.

During each of the past summers Fauve had posed for a portrait, but this year she'd been out gadding so much that he hadn't had a chance to claim her time. Everything they had been accustomed to do together—the painting lessons and the posing, the visits to the café in Félice, had been changed by the entrance of that abominable boy into Fauve's life.

Mistral took down the canvas on his easel and propped it carelessly against the wall. Moving as eagerly as a young man going to a rendezvous with a woman he loved, he went to the corner where his blank canvases were stacked and picked out the largest one he could find. Yes! A full-length picture, an ode, a hymn to Fauve Lunel and her miniskirt—she'd like that.

"I've found out why Avigdor means 'the judge,' " Eric said to Fauve. "It seems that in the Book of Chronicles the name is used twice and later interpretation says that it's one of the names of Moses. I told my father and he said not to get too exalted about it—there weren't any lawgivers in the family, he informed me, but only antique dealers until he came along, and now a budding architect."

"It's marvelous!" Fauve said proudly. The two of them were in a secondhand bookshop in Avignon, looking for volumes that might lead them somewhere in their quest for historical knowledge. So far they had had little real luck, finding only some minor references in books, but Eric was undiscouraged. "How did you find out?"

"I made a phone call. It was a wild guess but I knew that there had to be a rabbi in a big city like Marseilles so I just looked him up in the phone book, called him and asked. He said to call back in two days—give him time to look it up—and when I did, he told me. He didn't even sound surprised at the request. Maybe he gets a lot of phone calls like that."

"Hmmm . . . probably," she said, losing interest.

"Fauve, what's wrong?"

"It's my father."

"What about him? Look, I know he doesn't like me. Nobody could accuse Julien Mistral of being much of an actor. He hovers just at the very outer limits of tolerance when I come to pick you up, but I feel that as long as he allows me in the door, that's enough."

"No, it's not about you." Fauve sat down on the staircase that led to the upper floor of the bookshop, and folded her arms around her long legs. She was wearing a sleeveless, frilled, batiste camisole with a tiny peplum. It laced up in front like the underwear of an actress in an old Western movie and it was the latest rage in all the boutiques in Midi. Her sheaves of hair, bronze now in the watery light of the staircase, fell in heavy waves over her breasts. If she'd worn a petticoat instead of blue jeans she would have seemed like a Victorian maiden getting ready for bed. There was a richness of suggestion in her beauty, Eric thought as he looked at her, that would bring out the poet in the most mundane of men.

"He's always painted a picture of me every summer," Fauve went on. "He wants me to pose for him, starting tomorrow. I can't refuse, Eric, it's impossible, he'd be too hurt. It's a tradition with us. I feel guilty enough about not letting him give me painting lessons. He hasn't said another word about them, but when I see him at breakfast I know it's on his mind and he's just controlling himself. Oh, Lord . . ."

"I think it's remarkable that you've had the strength of mind to keep on resisting," Eric said.

"I have to," Fauve said simply. "It's a question of self-preservation. Father doesn't consciously understand that he *does* want me to imitate him. It's implicit in everything he shows me, everything he tells me, although he'd deny it and believe he was speaking the truth. You see, my father thinks that his way is the *only* way . . . he hasn't a good word to say for another living painter . . . the only ones he admires are dead. But his work comes from him, it comes out of whatever is inside of him, and that's not *teachable*."

"Then all these years of lessons . . ." Eric asked.

"Oh, they haven't been wasted—I do have technical ability—I'm not going to be modest about that—but so do a lot of other painters. If I have anything more I'll only know it when I start to work in my own style and I'll never find that style if I keep learning from him."

"Why did you wait so long to decide?"

"Until last year I was happy to paint 'little' Mistrals. I go to an art school in New York and the teachers are afraid to really criticize me because of who I am and because I've been doing work in his manner—they're so knocked out by who *he* is that I can't get an honest word out of them. It took me a long time to figure it out—I was dumb, I guess."

"Not dumb, darling, just young," Eric said.

"Father's always praised me too much," Fauve added thoughtfully. "I don't know if I'm ever going to be really good but I know damn well I can't be as good as he says I am. He's probably only doing it to encourage me, but it works in the opposite way—since I know my work isn't worth such extravagant praise, I wonder—is it worth any praise at all? If I truly couldn't paint he'd say so, but I'm in an in-between position. I *can* paint, like a very much lesser Mistral, and I don't want that! If I'm ever to do anything of my own it would be fatal to study with him anymore."

"Couldn't you tell him all this and make him understand?"

"I don't think I could get more than halfway through the first sentence. You've never heard him argue, or rather pontificate. And even if he heard me out and managed to understand what I was saying, working there in that studio isn't possible. It casts such a spell that you can't imagine seeing things in any other way than his. It overwhelms my own imagination, such as it is. But I do have to pose for him, there's no way out."

Eric sat down at her feet. "What does that mean as far as time is concerned?"

"He wanted to work for a few hours in the morning and a few after lunch but I said that I could only sit for him in the mornings. He said that we had only six weeks left, that mornings wouldn't be enough, but I insisted. I feel torn in two, Eric. I've never felt disloyal before, and now I feel disloyal to both of you."

"Not so. You're being loyal to both of us. Darling, darling Fauve, don't torment yourself. I know how much of your time I've been taking and I can't blame your father. We still have the afternoons and evenings. Look, I was saving this for later but you need to be cheered up." Eric took out an old, leather bound book from his knapsack and gave it to Fauve.

"Believe it or not my mother gave it to me just yesterday. She finally remembered that she had it put away somewhere—it was published in 1934 and when my grandmother died, it was in her house. Apparently no one in the family ever bothered to read it."

"*Histoire des Juifs d'Avignon et du Comtat Venaissin* by Armand Mossé." Fauve read the title of the book in a voice that rose in excitement. "That's it! That's got to have it all! The Comtat includes all the countryside around here. Oh, how terrific! Have you started it yet?"

"No, I thought we'd read it together, but now that we don't have as much time, you take it and read it whenever you get a chance. Maybe you can read while you're posing."

"Not with my father, I don't—no distractions, no eye movements, I hardly dare swallow." Fauve leaned down and took the book in her arms and cradled it against her breasts. "I'll take good care of it, I promise. I wonder how far back it goes?"

"I took a look at the first page and apparently Jews were being exiled from Rome and moving to France when Tiberius was Emperor—somewhere about twenty years after Christ—so if it's antiquity you're looking for, it's there."

"Oh—I had expected something a little more contemporary."

"A Jewish *Gone With the Wind?*"

"Well—why not, after all?"

Fauve stood by the model stand in the shocking pink mini-dress she had worn the night she met Eric at Uzès. Since she couldn't be with him while she was posing, at least she could wear what she'd had on the first time she'd seen him. She felt a need to be in some sort of contact with him at every moment of the day.

Now that she had resigned herself to the morning hours of posing, she found that they were welcome in a way she hadn't expected. They gave her time to really think about Eric that she hadn't had before. They'd spent almost every day of the summer together and when she came home she was too muddled with the slow, sweet momentum of his kisses to have any rational thoughts except an almost vertiginous astonishment that such happiness could exist. What a world of wonders in which an Eric could be alive, wandering around loose just as if he were like other people, a world in which he would *love* her. The amazement of it was so great that it was indecipherable, it changed everything, it turned all her past years into a faroff country that she had sailed away from without a backward glance.

She thought of the firm symmetry of his skull under her fingers when she ran her hands through that brown hair that was so clean and so thick that it resisted her fingers. She could actually feel the solid roundness of the bone in the tips of her fingers. She stood in her ballet slippers, her feet at right angles to each other, her weight resting on one leg, the other one slightly bent, her hands turned outward and her arms hanging loosely behind her back. It was a pose that Mistral had chosen as a tribute to Degas, saying that her pink skirt was shorter than any tutu and might even have brought a smile to the mouth of that vile-tempered, great old man.

To Fauve, posing patiently, the image of a small triangular scar on Eric's face, just below his right eye, the souvenir of a fall when he was five, was more real to her than the sound of Mistral's footsteps as he stepped backward from the easel.

On her lips she could feel how smooth the warm skin was when she kissed Eric at the edge of his ear and then, lowering her lips a quarter-inch at a time, kissed him lightly and softly down the side of his closely shaven cheek and along his jaw and finally, slowly, reached her lips up to his longing mouth.

He'd said that she had the softest lips in the world but Fauve told him that she couldn't make any similar comparisons because none of the other men she'd kissed in her life had had memorable lips. She smiled, remembering how he'd drawn back when she said that and demanded to know just how many men she *had* kissed before. A few, she'd answered, only a few, just a few, a miserable, pathetic few, knowing that nothing could be more calculated to infuriate him. She was unable to keep from making him jealous, because he was four years older than she was and, of course, she understood, although he never referred to it, that he must be experienced and she was not.

He was so infernally protective of her sixteen years, Fauve thought, frowning, unaware that Mistral was noticing every change of expression on her face. She wished fiercely now that she had lied to Eric when he'd asked her age. If only she'd said she was eighteen! With her height she could have made him believe it, especially since he had no way to compare her to an American eighteen and guess the truth. But he knew she was just barely out of her fifteenth year and he had a gallant, idealistic determination not to take advantage of her.

Last night they'd had an early dinner at a good, inexpensive little Italian restaurant called La Mamma in Villeneuve-les-Avignon, and afterward they had gone exploring in the garden of Le Prieuré, not the formal rose garden bordered by santolina and ancient urns trailing geraniums, but the hidden cutting garden, in which grew the fresh flowers that were placed in the guest rooms every day.

Because all the personnel of the hotel were concentrated on the busy arrival of the evening's guests for the restaurant, they'd been able to duck unseen through the garage and the boiler room of the hotel and emerge into the walled cutting garden, a paradise of blooms all bordered by those little hollow, elfin, red objects called Chinese lanterns.

They had wandered there—arms laced tightly around each other's waist, and finally come to rest leaning up against an old, overgrown, unpruned pear tree that stood in the far reaches of the garden.

Fauve and Eric were entirely alone and protected from sight by the branches of the tree and Fauve had flung herself on Eric, thrusting herself against him and rubbing up and down. She didn't care if she was awkward or clumsy or aggressive, whatever she didn't know about making love she could learn, she *would* learn, but he pushed her away, first gently and then with determination, holding her at arm's length.

No, he'd said, it was clearly impossible and she had to realize it herself. If he let her go on like that it must lead further and then even further and then they wouldn't be able to stop, wouldn't want to stop, didn't she understand? She was too young, it wouldn't be right, wouldn't be fair . . . Fauve sighed deeply, wondering if he was right, suspecting that perhaps he was, but oh, how she wanted him.

"Fauve! I can't work if you're going to make one grimace after another! Now will you try to keep your face quiet for a minute or shall we stop?"

Fauve blew her hair off her forehead with an exaggerated moue. "I'm not making a grimace, I'm thinking. Do you want to paint a picture of a mindless doll or a thinking woman?"

"Ha! You make a point, even if it's a bit premature. All right, let's take a break."

Fauve stepped out of her pose and uncoiled her body like a long piece of rope and stretched every joint. Then she walked over to the planter's chair in the corner of the studio and sat down, picking up the old book Eric had given her, and, within a few seconds, she was engrossed.

Mistral knew far too much about the book. When they had started on the painting she had brought it with her and, during every break, she had returned to it, often pausing to read bits and pieces of it out loud to him. Finally, exasperated, he had told her that it broke his concentration to listen to her, that it was bad enough for a painter to have to give the model a rest every so often without being forced to absorb a history lesson in addition.

"Well," she'd said mildly, "all right, but this is incredible stuff. I'll tell you about it later," and she'd gone back to her reading. Only last year, whenever it was time for her break, they'd talked about their painting, or she'd amused him with stories about those two friends of hers, Pomme and Épinette, who were, impossible though it seemed, the granddaughters of two of the members of his original boules team from the café in the village.

Sometimes, he remembered bitterly, they'd go to sit in the sun just outside the studio and discuss the status of the Union Sportif of Félice, the feisty soccer team that was engaged in a protracted and perpetual struggle with the other soccer teams of the neighboring villages. Often, in those precious minutes, he'd explained to her why art was the only thing worth doing in a world of chaos, the only thing that had any possibility of enduring. History, he had told her, was merely stories of what people think happened or want you to believe happened. History can't be trusted.

And now, there she was, obliviously plunged into history as if it were a revelation of an immutable truth. What would he give to have his daughter back again, to have the Fauve of last year in the place of this self-described "thinking woman"? Almost anything, Mistral thought, almost anything, but what was there that he had to give that a girl of sixteen could want?

"Ready to continue?" he asked.

"Oh . . . sure. But, Father, would you mind terribly if we stopped a half-hour early today? Eric's parents are spending a few days in Aix for the music festival and they've invited us down to lunch at the Vendôme—it's an hour-and-a-half trip and I don't want to be late. Is that all right, just for today?"

What could he say? Could he insist that she stay? That she make the time up tomorrow? This wasn't the first time the sitting had been cut short for one reason or another. To be fair, he told himself frowningly, it wasn't the first time he'd realized that in order to pose for him she was giving up some excursion that required an early start and a late return. When he painted her during all those other summers, their time together had been filled with a deep communion, the melody of which he only fully appreciated now that it had disappeared, to be replaced by duty and an abstracted fondness.

"Of course, Fauve, go ahead. We can stop now if you like."

"Oh, Father! You're a darling! Thank you!" Released, she gave him a quick hug and bounded out of the studio not even thinking to conceal her sense of relief.

Yet, he noticed, his jaw set in a grim, tight anger, a line of pain, and hurt pride, she hadn't forgotten to take that miserable book with her.

If style is achieved when your outer surface corresponds perfectly with your real personality, when you look like what you are, then Nadine was ultimately stylish, Fauve reflected as she joined her father, her stepmother and her half-sister for a rare family dinner. Nadine had just arrived from Paris for a few days at *La Tourrello*, leaving her husband engaged on the details of a business deal. Mistral detested the man she had married and a tacit arrangement existed between Nadine and Kate not to remind Mistral of Phillipe Dalmas's existence any more than was necessary.

When Fauve had come to Provence for the first summer, Nadine had been fifteen and a half, actually a half-year younger than Fauve now was herself, yet even then she had seemed more sophisticated than anyone Fauve had ever known before.

That early impression had only been confirmed by the passage of time. Today, at twenty-three, Nadine was all brilliant cutting edges. Her blond hair swung in two bright polished arcs under her chin as if it were a truncated wimple, her straight, long bangs looked as if they could slice into her forehead, her eyes were edged in sharply drawn lines of dark green, with an Egyptian precision.

The planes of her nose were whittled to a degree that just escaped being pointed, her teeth were so white and regular that they reminded Fauve that their primary purpose was to bite. There was a knifelike line to her jaw but her upper lip still curved in its eternal smile. She was compelling, Fauve admitted. It was all but impossible not to stare at Nadine. Wherever she sat or stood was, always, center stage.

Nadine Mistral presented herself as she was, with no attempt to mask her own high self-esteem. Superiority was manifest in the absolute perfection of her immaculately well-cut white linen slacks, in the starkly elegant lines of her black silk blouse that wrapped and knotted at her slim waist, in the splendid pair of onyx earrings rimmed in flashing diamonds that hung from the lobes of her ears.

She permitted herself no flaws, not so much as a single fingernail was shorter than the others. How many hours each week it took to maintain this ruthlessly gleaming exterior no one knew, but Fauve was sure that there were women who could spend their lives trying to emulate Nadine's glacial and insolent elegance without achieving it, because, at the last minute, they would be tempted to add a rope of pearls or brush a little softness into their hair or tuck a flower into a sash. Nadine was, in her own way, a Minimalist, who made her statement with the fewest possible elements.

Kate Browning's determination to devote herself to Julien Mistral, which had seized her on the day she first saw him and his work, had been largely transferred to her daughter Nadine. The four years during which Mistral had left her for Teddy Lunel and then, after her death, roamed the earth, had locked Kate into the most passionate of maternal connections. No matter how all-important being Madame Julien Mistral was and always would be to her, her second concern now was her daughter's happiness and her position in life.

Since Nadine's marriage, Kate had lived in a state of impotent fury against Mistral, who stood between Nadine and her rightful status as one of the great heiresses of France. In time, Nadine would inherit everything Julien owned, the treasure of paintings in the storage room, the rich, income-producing property of *La Tourrello*, their bank accounts, their investments; all this vast fortune would be hers by French law, but meanwhile, Nadine actually had been forced to take a job to maintain her style of life.

Two years ago she had married a man, Phillipe Dalmas, who, for want of a more specific description, was always referred to in the press as "an investor." He had been celebrated in the social and gossip pages of the media for many years before he met Nadine because of the liaisons he had enjoyed with a number of the most sought-after women of the day. Phillipe was often dubbed "the most elusive man in Paris" for, at thirty-nine, he had never been married.

By profession he was a deal maker, bringing together people who needed money and those who had it to invest. Somehow only a few of his deals ever came to pass, and his commissions on those that did amounted to just enough to support himself in great style as a bachelor.

Phillipe could afford to employ a houseman-valet, he had enough money to order suits made to measure at Larsen, where he could choose from the seven hundred bolts of wool that lined the walls like rare books, and his collection of cashmere scarves—for he never wore an overcoat—came from the great house of Hilditch and Key. His small apartment was in an irreproachable building near the Arc de Triomphe, and it was handsomely furnished with some good Empire pieces, but his only real capital was his charm.

Phillipe Dalmas was the World's Best Guest. Amusing, handsome and splendidly heterosexual, he was the subject of every hostess's reverie.

When Nadine met this sensual man, devoted to pleasure, given and received, a man enveloped in an immense glamour of unavailability, she was immediately determined to catch him. For his part, as Phillipe saw his fortieth birthday approach, he decided that it was a sensible moment to terminate his triumphant bachelorhood. He had no intention of spending a middle age visiting in other people's houses, no matter how agreeably.

Nadine succeeded in marrying him, where so many others had failed, by the simple, banal means of appearing at the right moment in his life. Her twenty-one radiant years, her flashing flawlessness and, of course, her. incontestable prospects as the daughter of Julien Mistral, made her an almost inevitable choice, for while Phillipe Dalmas would never have married only for money, he certainly could not afford to marry someone without it.

Nadine Mistral and Phillipe Dalmas shared the kind of profound, bred-in-the-bone superficiality that can become, when superbly mounted, a certain kind of meaningfulness. Their deep attention to façades gave each of them a high gloss and together they made an unforgettably decorative couple, like a pair of rare art objects, burnished to an enviable degree. Once all the hostesses in Paris had resigned themselves to the loss of Phillipe as a single man, they began to compete with each other for the presence of the Dalmases, who had one of those marriages in which the husband and the wife together become the single star of an evening.

Kate would have put away certain loftier ambitions she had long nourished for her daughter, for she couldn't deny that Nadine adored her husband, had it not been for Julien Mistral, who spent a half-hour with Phillipe Dalmas and decided that the man was essentially worthless. There would be no dowry, he declared, and his wedding gift to the couple was only a medium-sized apartment on the avenue Montaigne, the very least, Kate had managed to persuade him, they could decently offer.

Since then, the allowance he could so easily have made them, had not been paid—and never would be, as long as he was alive, he assured Kate. Nor was it possible now for her to give them lavish gifts. Mistral, who had allowed his wife to make all the financial decisions for him during their long marriage, suddenly insisted on carrying on his own correspondence with his dealers and his bankers.

Kate was effectively prevented from secretly handling any substantial sum and the only money she could still spend freely was that needed to maintain *La Tourrello*. She was reduced to little more than a housekeeper and estate manager, she thought venomously. But Nadine took the disappointment with the philosophy of one whose father is almost seventy years old. It was only temporary, after all, and in the meanwhile it was chic and amusing to say that she had to work for a living, more droll than if she had just been another rich girl, particularly since no one could doubt how immensely rich she would be.

Nadine had created a job for herself that displayed her to perfection. She worked with Jean François Albin, the only other French couturier who enjoyed the level of international importance of Yves Saint Laurent.

Her work was without specific title, its boundaries hard to define. She wasn't head of public relations, because that job, with its technical details of dealing with the world press, was handled by Lily de Mar, who had been trained at Dior; nor was she involved in the actual design of the clothes or the selling of them, or any of the business of the House of Albin. Yet, in a way that was as clear as if it had been official, Nadine was employed to be Jean François Albin's Best Friend.

She was the one human being in the world without whom he simply could not function. She acted as a buffer between him and the entire world that he saw as full of enemies, or, at the very best, brutes, people lacking in sensitivity. He believed that Nadine alone would never lie to him. He was convinced that she was the only person who did not seek some sort of advancement through her association with him, for what could the daughter of Julien Mistral gain from closeness to any couturier, no matter how famous?

To Albin, Nadine Dalmas was the idealized incarnation of the woman he designed for. He invested her with almost mystical powers to comfort and inspire and refresh him. He now needed her by his side at all times of crisis. Henri Gros, the solid businessman who was Albin's partner in a couture house that was swollen with profits from three perfumes and a number of worldwide licensing agreements, was delighted to pay Nadine a pleasantly handsome salary for her devotion, no matter how vague her role seemed to be. The fragile, creative machine that was Jean François Albin must be, at all costs, nourished, comforted and comprehended so that he could continue to turn out two collections a year.

As Nadine talked about her job at dinner with her parents and Fauve, her proud, cool, jaunty manner that was not an affectation but her natural form of expression, didn't change. Yet clearly, she was engrossed in her life. She spoke, as always, in even and assured tones that were pitched just a bit lower than anyone else's, so that people found themselves stopping their own conversations in order to listen to her.

"You see, Father, Jean François was at the breaking point. The new collection is all finished down to the last button, but last Wednesday he telephoned in despair in the middle of the night and I rushed over to the *atelier* to find him about to take a pair of scissors to every single garment. I led him away as gently as if he were a sleepwalker, and told him that we were going to the very best clinic in St. Cloud, where he would give himself over to a sleep cure until Monday and I stayed with him holding his hand, until he was actually sleeping peacefully. On Monday, when I return, he'll be a new man."

"Does that happen often?" asked Kate.

"He's had nothing but trouble these past months," Nadine explained. "All five of our new black manikins deserted to go to work for Givenchy, and that vacation house in Sardinia I told you about is driving him mad with worry. Quite naturally, Jean François insists that the interior decorator take the most precious old brocades and drape them like muslin and use inlaid woods with the same ease as if it were raw lumber but the man just can't seem to follow orders."

Gee whiz! Fauve whispered—to herself.

"Fortunately," Nadine continued, "I've been able to take a lot of this off his hands and leave him free to concentrate on his art, but no matter what I accomplish, in the end it's his decision that is vital, and this is just the worst of years. After all, he can hardly be unaware that he has become a cult object—nothing makes a person more vulnerable than to be elevated to that sort of worship—yet what can he do? He *must* expose himself time and time again—he must risk, he must change."

"Change what?" Mistral asked, pushing away his plate.

"The length, Father, Jean François feels that it's time to impose the maximum length—the mini is dead—but how can those cows of the public possibly be subtle and daring enough to follow? Can they rise to his level? He had such a horror of the buyers and the press—I don't know if he'll be able to face them after the collection is over—"

"Then why does he?" Mistral growled.

"If he doesn't come out and take a bow, Father, the rumors will start again—they'll say he's dead or drugged or shut up in a madhouse—I can't imagine how he endures it. The temptation, of course, is to compromise, to create a length that is not revolutionary but merely evolutionary—but Jean François is too great an artist not to be faithful to himself."

"Tell me," Mistral asked, "just how old is Jean François?"

"No one is sure, not even I, but I think he must be close to forty."

"He sounds like a child. And if you live in a child's world, you descend to his level," Mistral said scornfully.

"Enough of Jean François," Kate said abruptly, rushing protectively into the conversation. She was all too familiar with Mistral's opinions about the value of the haute couture and she knew how icy Nadine would turn if Jean François were criticized. "Nadine, you must ask Fauve to tell you about her summer—it's been an absolute revelation."

Nadine looked at her mother and caught a purposeful spark in her eye. They had never needed words to communicate. She shrugged lightly and turned to Fauve.

"You've been uncharacteristically silent tonight, now that I think about it. And yet it seems to me that I've heard something about you and a rather attractive young architect. So, little Fauve has finally deigned to recognize the masculine sex? And how do you find first love, eh?"

Nadine spoke with a cold curiosity so penetrating that Fauve almost flinched. Instinctively she sought a way to deflect that curiosity, for Nadine, like a tomcat, with a small animal in its jaws, wouldn't release the object of her attention until she was satisfied.

"I find the masculine sex marvelously useful, thank you. How have I spent all my summers here without any other transportation than my bicycle? This fellow has his own car so I've been able to convince him to drive me around—I've seen more of the countryside in six weeks than I saw in the last eight years."

"Your interest is only touristic? Fauve, do you expect me to believe that?"

"Believe what you want—I'm investigating the history of the Jews of Provence."

"Good Lord, how utterly bizarre . . . I thought they were all in Paris!"

"So do most people," Fauve said, almost laughing at the success of her gambit. Nadine hadn't even asked Eric's name. "There have been Jews living right here for two thousand years."

"Two thousand years . . . are you sure, Fauve?" Nadine drawled. Her hard glance, the green of malachite, was distinctly dubious.

"Absolutely! And until the Crusades they were treated more or less like everyone else. Even the Vandals and the Visigoths and the Barbarians left them alone when they invaded the countryside—it wasn't until the twelfth century, when the kings of France went chasing off to recapture the Holy Land, that they really began to persecute the Jews."

Fauve had put down her fork, excited by a chance to talk about the revelations she had come across every day in Armand Mossé's book, to which both her father and Kate seemed callously indifferent. She grasped this opportunity eagerly although she was perfectly aware that it had only come about because Kate wanted to head off an argument.

Fauve was literally on fire with names and dates and statistics; she felt as if Pope Alexandre VI and Jules II, who had both employed Jews as their physicians, were her personal friends. Just as heartily she loathed Jules III who had ordered the burning of the Talmud.

She was too involved in her subject to notice the veiled disdain that passed from Nadine to Kate as Fauve grew increasingly indignant over the more than five hundred years, ending only with the Revolution, during which all the Jews of Provence had had to submit, from childhood on, to the wearing of a distinctive yellow patch on their clothes. Mistral listened without expression while she described the horrors of the old ghettoes, locked and barred every night, in which countless generations dwelled in miserable, jam-packed airless hovels while all other men were free to live at liberty in the vast and rich valley of the Vaucluse. The rules, cruel and restrictive and arbitrary, that the authorities imposed on all aspects of Jewish life, came spilling out of her in one long, fervent monologue. Mistral stopped eating and his lips tightened angrily yet Fauve didn't notice. She had no idea how long and how passionately she had talked until Nadine finished her cheese, and said lightly, "Aren't you being a bit of a bleeding heart, Fauve? Those people have all been dead for a long time—it's so morbid to talk as if this still matters today—I find it distinctly odd of you."

"Not that odd, Nadine. Everywhere in Mossé's book I find the names of Lunel and Astruc—names of my family . . . my name in fact."

"Isn't that pushing what's probably a very distant connection?"

"Distant! No, damn it, I don't think there's anything distant about it . . ." Fauve responded furiously, when Mistral finally broke his brooding silence.

"*Enough!* When you came back from that place in Cavaillon you described it in a way that convinced me that the local Jews must have been well off and well treated and now you submit us to this endless catalog of misery. This is becoming a mania with you!"

"I was being an uninformed romantic, Father, living in an illusion." Fauve spoke up boldly, unintimidated by his disapproval. "That building isn't even two hundred years old and I was fool enough to think that it indicated an idyllic past. Now I know that it's a deceptive remnant of one of the brief periods in which the Jews were permitted to live in relative tranquillity—and even so, it used to be surrounded by a dreadful ghetto that's been torn down. There are still people, well-meaning people, who boast that Provence was 'The Paradise of the Jews'—well, it was, if you compare it to the dozens of other places in France where the Jews were all burned alive! Provence was a paradise in the most limited and ironic sense of the word, like saying it was the best of all possible prisons for people who had committed no crime."

"Prison?" Kate said, carefully watching Mistral's expression as Fauve defied him. She was the only person at the table who was aware of how deeply he resented Fauve's interest in anything Jewish, the only person who had enjoyed his reaction to every word Fauve had said. "Why 'prison,' Fauve? *We* weren't the people who were responsible for what happened to those people, *we* never were cruel to Jews, *we* never treated Jews as if they'd committed a crime. Really, Fauve, I'm surprised you haven't accused us all of sending them to concentration camps."

26

Kate Mistral had acted a role with Julien Mistral from the moment she met him. The closest he had come to awareness of her real self was in that moment she had asked him to marry her. Now, after forty-two years of marriage she was locked into a part that had evolved with the years, a part in which she had never revealed all her emotions to this most necessary of opponents. When she admired an actress on the stage or in a film it never occurred to her that in her own domestic life she had long been a habitual and consummate performer. All of her human relationships took place in an intimate theater in which she assumed that everyone was acting much of the time. The moments in which her dramatic mask could be partially dropped were rare. Sometimes she approached the truth—and a genuine inner moment of contact—with Nadine. Never with her husband.

Kate sat placidly in front of her dressing table, taking off her pearls while Mistral stood angrily in the door of her bedroom, unwilling to come in and sit down, yet unable to go off to his own room and try to sleep.

"What on earth are you so disturbed about, Julien?" she inquired mildly. "I'll agree that it's irritating that Fauve insists on boring us at the dinner table but why treat it like a major problem? All girls go through difficult phases in their teens."

"You deliberately encouraged her."

"Nonsense. You can't say a single polite word to Fauve these days without unleashing her obsession. You know yourself that if you just say good morning you risk a lecture about a thousand years at the Wailing Wall. There's no stopping her—whenever she eats with us I'm afraid we're in for it, unless you want to forbid it entirely."

"You can't forbid Fauve to talk about the things that interest her, she's not that kind of girl," he said grimly. "Goddamn that Avigdor brat! He's behind all this."

"You're being very unfair. Of course the boy adds fuel to the fire, but in my opinion it goes way beyond him. If you want to blame anybody, Maggy Lunel is the guilty one."

"What the hell does that mean?"

"The Jesuits say that if you give them a child for the first seven years they can form him for life. You gave Fauve to her grandmother and she lost no time in imposing her own identity on your daughter. After all, Fauve does have that Jewish streak no matter how little you like it. Don't underestimate its power, Julien. Every child needs a feeling of identity . . . or so they say."

"She's my daughter—she's a painter. Isn't that enough identity for her, by Christ? What more does a sixteen-year-old expect, for the love of God! But no—instead of taking advantage of this summer she's wasting her time chasing around imagining she's found a so-called tradition that has nothing to do with her. She's mad to imagine that the Lunels and the Astrucs in that cursed book are her family. She can't possibly find out anything—even if there were some sort of vague relationship, it's too unimportant to matter!"

"Perhaps just knowing that she's your illegitimate daughter isn't enough for Fauve." Kate put her bracelets away, closed her jewelry box and began to brush the fine hair that fell so neatly around her face. "Do go to sleep, Julien. You make me nervous standing there."

A minute later Mistral was on the way to his studio in a darkness that was illuminated by that light night sky of Provence in which the stars have moved in from space until they seemed as if they must sing to man as they do in the other great open lands of the earth, in the desert or in the great polar reaches. He didn't flick on the work lights but walked directly to the easel on which the half-finished picture of Fauve stood. He looked at the rectangle of canvas, an almost solid gray under the skylight, lost in thought. Kate's words repeated themselves in his mind. "Every child needs a feeling of identity." How could he deny that she was right? From the day Fauve was born he had been powerless to give her his own name. Under French law, he could not recognize her as his daughter, she could not call herself Fauve Mistral, so naturally she thought of herself as a Lunel—as one of them. All summer long she had been slipping away from him, eluding him more each day, and although he had captured her image on the canvas he knew that he had not, as in other years, come close to catching her spirit, for even as he painted her she was somewhere else.

Scornfully, Mistral turned his back on the painting—why even bother to finish that daub?—and prowled around the shadowy studio. How do you catch a sixteen-year-old girl and pin her down and make her see reason? It would be easier to talk sense to a hummingbird. If only she were French, brought up right here in Félice, under his eye. If only she didn't escape him every year, if only she could be frozen in time!

Restlessly he sought the only comfort he had ever found effective—the presence of his own work. He unlocked the door of the storage room, switched on the overhead lights and roamed the brightly illuminated aisles, pulling out a rack here and there, and contemplating the painting on it as if it were a strange object, as if he had never spent many weeks, often many months, of the most intense effort of which he was capable on each one of them. After a long while he began to reach out and run his hand over an occasional painted surface, feeling the rough textures of the canvas as if it were a sentient being. Little by little he allowed himself to be eased, slowly he accepted solace. *These lived.* He was as sure of that as he was of the fact that he was Julien Mistral. They lived now and they would live as long as they existed. This room was not full of finished paintings but of speaking, breathing creatures. Here was *his* identity, here in this windowless room was all that would ever need to be said about Julien Mistral.

There was a section of the room that he never visited. The paintings he had made of Teddy when she was pregnant and of Teddy and Fauve during the first two months of Fauve's life, during which he had worked more rapidly than he ever had before or since, were all kept on several dozen racks in the back of the large room. He had abandoned them in his apartment in Avignon after Teddy's death where they had been carefully guarded by the married couple who had worked for them. After his return to *La Tourrello*, Mistral had arranged for the paintings to be picked up and brought to the storage room, but he had never looked at them again.

Now he walked slowly to one of the racks and pulled it into the wide aisle. The rack held only one large unfinished canvas, the last picture he had painted of Teddy in St. Tropez. She sat in a garden on a blue-and-white-striped swing, holding Fauve close to her breast, her head bent as she studied the baby.

Even in his most tormented, longing dreams she had never been as beautiful. He had painted his love so clearly that the canvas seemed to cry out on one high, clear, wordless note of joy. Quickly, he shoved the rack away, out of sight, and rushed out of the storage room, locking it behind him. He took the back door out of the studio and hurried down the path that led around the walls of *La Tourrello*, stopping only when he found himself deep in the forest of live oaks. He sat down on the ground, his back to a tree, breathing deeply, as if he'd been running for his life. Why had he done that? Why had he risked such certain pain?

As instinctively as if he were jumping away from a stream of boiling water he preserved himself from feeling the wound by shutting out the image of Teddy and bringing into the focus of his mind the patch of canvas on which he had painted that scrap of a being, the baby Fauve. Even then she had possessed a burning vitality. He remembered her at the moment of her birth, wrapped in the pink blanket, only just out of the womb, but already so distinct that he had known her rightful name at once. The anger toward her, that had been building up in him all summer as she wandered out of his grip, evaporated as he thought of her as she had been at dinner tonight. Fauve's face had reflected every emotion she felt; she could no more restrain her idealistic, volatile nature than she was able to be hypocritical or diplomatic.

Julien Mistral was not a man capable of abstract compassion. Not only did he not empathize with people, alone or in groups, he lacked the slightest desire to do so. His art was totally personal; it embraced only those things that came within the dominion he claimed for himself; certain aspects of nature, certain elements of the human life of Provence, and the few—very few—people he loved. Without the motivation of love he was a stone—a stone who painted.

As he sat against the tree, his love for Fauve allowed him to enter into her mind, permitted him access to her spirit, and he became slowly aware of the questions she must be asking herself. Who am I? What is life all about? Where am I going? Who went before me? Is there a connection?

Of course she was searching for something that would answer those questions, for was she not a romantic, as romantic as Teddy had been? No wonder Fauve was confused, no wonder she was thrashing about with silly concern. For the space of a few seconds Julien Mistral allowed himself to imagine the glory of a life in which Fauve could have grown up, watched over and cared for under Teddy's eyes, a child who had both a mother and a father, safe, secure, beloved. He grunted under the blow of a useless despair and pushed the picture away, but, for the first time in his life he fully realized that he was not the only person in the world who had been bitterly deprived of the love of Teddy Lunel. And he had never even shown that painting of Fauve and Teddy to anyone. *Not even to Fauve.*

He sat perfectly still, so stunned with the idea that now came to him that he kept turning it over and over in his mind, searching for flaws, unable to believe that it had never occurred to him before. His stern chieftain's face expanded into an irresistible grimace of fierce joy before it hardened into a look of resolution so intense that he seemed to be enduring, even embracing, some deep hurt. He *knew* how to give Fauve the sense of identity that would bind her to him forever, that would imprint him on her life in a way that would make it impossible for her ever to seek out a heritage that had nothing to do with him. She was so desperate that she was reduced to skimming some sense of belonging from the shell of a

Louis XV synagogue. Yet he alone on the face of the great wide earth had the power to give her an identity, a heritage, a feeling of belonging that would make her realize that her most basic, most important tie in the world was, and always would be, to him.

Julien Mistral had never made a will, but, when his parents had died, he had been involved with the details of inheritance. His mother had astonished and displeased him by leaving one-third of her tiny estate to a friend with whom she often worked on her needlework, a woman to whom she wasn't related in any way. When Mistral had questioned the lawyer about the legality of this, he had been told that everyone is permitted to leave one-third of his estate to a stranger. The remaining two-thirds must be distributed among his legitimate descendants whether he wishes it or not.

Fauve was legally a stranger to him. Nothing in French law allowed them any official connection. She had no legal status. As an *enfante adulterine* she could inherit nothing—but as a stranger, one-third! Oh, how carefully, how intimately, how intensely they would go over all the paintings in the storage room, how many hours they would spend in the joyously complicated, thoughtful process of putting aside the one-third that would become Fauve's very own property, separating them from those that must, of necessity, belong to Nadine, and to Kate, of course, if she outlived him.

Fauve would be locked into his life forever. What dusty history book could bind her more closely to him than the possession of the very best of the work of his lifetime? What architectural bagatelle, what book, what list of names of people long dead, could make her feel a greater sense of identity than to know that, while he was alive, her father had given her as much as he could of the treasure for which he had lived? The work that was *him*.

He stood up and brushed the debris of the forest floor off his trousers. As he walked back to *La Tourrello*, Julien Mistral's silhouette in the starlight looked as eager and young as it had on the day he had first approached the gates of the vast farmhouse that was to determine the course of his future.

"Kate, please make arrangements for two of the guest rooms to be prepared," Mistral said to his wife the next morning as she sat alone by the pool.

"Have you invited visitors?" she asked, surprised. He left their social life entirely to her.

"Two men are coming, who'll have to take their meals with us since there's nowhere around here for them to eat. They'll probably stay for a week or ten days."

"Julien, what are you talking about—that's absurd."

"I've decided to make a will. The paintings must be appraised. This morning I telephoned to Étienne Delage for advice. As a dealer he knows all the tricks. He told me that I shouldn't make a will until I've established the value of each of my works. Otherwise the government will do it for me after I'm dead and, naturally, they'll put the highest value on them so that my estate will have to pay the biggest possible tax. But if it's done while I'm alive, I have the right to appoint one of the appraisers, and the government sends another—those are the two gentlemen who are coming—and between them they reach a fair compromise. Étienne has found me a man who will put the lowest realistic value on the paintings that he can—it's his specialty."

"How very thoughtful of Étienne. May I ask why you've decided to make a will?"

"I'm leaving Fauve one-third of my estate, the part that may go to a stranger." He looked at Kate for signs of distress but her dark glasses covered her eyes and her expression didn't change. "Last night I remembered that it was possible and I kept hearing your words—'every child needs a feeling of identity'—and I knew that it was what I must do. Of course you and Nadine will get the other two-thirds—I'm going to leave Fauve her share entirely in the form of paintings, since it would be useless to leave her one-third of a farm, or of investments in a country in which she doesn't live. That means that I must establish the total value of *La Tourrello* and of our bank accounts and other investments as well as that of the paintings in order to make sure that she gets her fair third."

"I see," Kate said tonelessly.

"All that will take time to establish—probably the details won't all be down in black and white until long after Fauve goes home, but Étienne says that paintings—like furniture or silver or jewels—can be left individually. In other words, a painting that's worth a particular amount will be left to Fauve, one worth the same amount to Nadine, and one to you, and so on."

"And so you're going to leave them all by name and description?"

"Yes. Oh, I haven't forgotten that you own all of the *Rouquinne* series, never fear. That was an intelligent investment you made, Kate."

"So it was."

"I intend to buy them back from you."

"Do you?"

"Yes—they should go to Fauve—after all, they're family portraits, so to speak." He grinned in a way she hadn't seen in years.

"Indeed—they are indeed. Have you any idea what they're worth?"

"Whatever it is, I'll pay."

"Good."

"Well." Mistral stood up, relieved. "It's settled then. You'll tell the servants whatever's necessary? The appraisers arrive in two days."

"Of course," said Kate. "Have you informed Fauve yet?"

"No, not yet. I'll speak to her tonight, when she gets back to dress—there's some sort of a party she's going to this evening." He disappeared into his studio, thinking that Fauve might as well run around all day today, for tomorrow she wouldn't be able to tear herself away from the discoveries of the storage room.

Kate sat perfectly still, wondering if she was going to be able to endure the slicing, writhing rage that cut into her flesh like engine-driven iron drills grinding into a piece of wood. So it wasn't enough to beggar Nadine, to force her to work for a living until he died, was it? Now he was stripping her, despoiling her, robbing her, lowering his own daughter to the level of his bastard.

Did he think that she was such a fool as to believe his explanation of the "fairness" of the process of choosing the paintings he would leave Fauve? Didn't he realize that she knew as well as he that between two paintings that are appraised for the same amount there will be an enormous difference in *importance* that the artist alone can assign? Didn't he even suspect that she knew perfectly well that he would give Fauve only the paintings that he was sure were his greatest? The masterpieces of his masterpieces? If Fauve received all of her one-third share in paintings, leaving out his land, his money, his investments, it might well be possible to give her at least *half* of the contents of the storage room—the image of that room made her suck in her breath and bend over, grasping her stomach in both hands.

How dare he do this to her? She, Kate Browning, had taken up an unknown artist and made him into Julien Mistral and goddamn him to hell everlasting, he *belonged* to her. He had no rights on the face of the earth unless she granted them. How could he prattle like an old fool about "sharing" his work, when everything, every last bit of canvas he had ever smeared paint on, was rightfully hers?

He was her creature. What would he be if she hadn't become his wife? *Nothing*! He would be nothing, an embittered old man, living in some shabby Paris studio, wondering why the world had not come to his door. He would have missed his moment and some other painter would have had the glory. And yet he dared, he actually *dared* to speak of giving his work to Fauve?

What was his work but what she had enabled him to create? If he gave his work he would be giving away the one thing in the world—the only thing—that belonged absolutely to her. That he could not do. That he must not do. Paralyzed by an onslaught of fury greater than she had ever known in her life, greater than the emotion she had felt when Julien left her for Teddy Lunel, Kate sat sightlessly in the sun while bubbling, bursting coils of violence grew in her belly until finally she had to jerk herself out of her immobility and dash into the pool pavilion in order to throw up the loathsomeness into the bathroom toilet.

When she was finished she felt steady, calm and very sure of what she had to do.

"Will you come into my room and shut the door for a minute, Fauve?" Kate asked as soon as she heard her come upstairs that afternoon.

"Sure—but I'm a mess and Eric's coming back to pick me up by six—do you want me for long?"

"No, not long. Fauve, I don't think you realize how much you're upsetting your father with the sort of discussion we were all treated to last night."

"Oh, I know I went on talking too long, Kate. I thought about it today and I realized that I'd sort of taken over the conversation. It won't happen again. I'm truly sorry."

"It's not how long you talked, Fauve, it's the subject matter. You never got off the topic of Jewish suffering."

"What?"

"I hoped I'd never have to tell you this but I see that you're really deeply involved in your maternal heritage—it's completely understandable and I find it quite touching and fascinating—but you see, your father . . . when you speak of Jews like that it opens old wounds."

"I suppose you mean that it reminds him of my grandmother? I know about that, Kate, and I can't believe that whatever I said would necessarily make him think of her. Maggy's not the only Jew in the world."

"I don't mean that at all. It had never even occurred to me. No, Fauve, it's something that's much more difficult for me to explain."

"What are you driving at, Kate?" Fauve asked, puzzled by the intent, concerned expression on Kate's normally controlled face.

"Fauve, you're only sixteen. You've always lived in a safe world, yet only ten years before you were born World War Two was going on, and catastrophes that you can't even begin to imagine were everyday events."

"Oh, my God," Fauve said slowly, "last night, when you said what you did about concentration camps, you were thinking of what happened to the Jews in the war, weren't you? You were trying to warn me off—oh, Lord, Kate, I'm so sorry! I didn't realize that it would upset him . . . I never thought . . ."

"Fauve, I haven't made myself clear. I'm talking about the Occupation of France and what happened to life here during that time. When I got back to Félice after the war Marte Pollison, who was here at *La Tourrello* the whole time, told me things that I thought I'd never have to speak of to anybody." Avidly, Kate watched Fauve's bewildered face, which had already been drained of the carefree, excited radiance with which she had walked into the bedroom. "Fauve, for weeks you've been fascinated by the Jews who lived in Provence and I've been a wet blanket about it. There was a reason for that—I thought you might finally lose your interest. But you haven't and now, before I tell you why you must stop bringing this subject up, I want to be sure that you truly understand your father. He lives only to paint. You realize what his work means to him, don't you? You know that his art is everything, his reason for being?"

"He's also a person, a man," Fauve said slowly.

"But not like the others. No genius ever is. I've had to learn it over the years, it's certainly not something I expect you to grasp fully, but there's a certain dimension that genius lacks, a dimension of ordinary humanity that is denied genius precisely because it *is* genius."

"I guess I don't 'fully' understand, Kate."

"No, I was afraid you wouldn't. An example can show you what I mean better than words alone. In those last years of the war there were Germans everywhere, no place was so remote that they didn't know what was going on, not even here in Félice. They took almost all of the able-bodied men away for forced labor in Germany . . ." Kate paused and shook her head sadly.

"And . . . ?"

"Your father would have been sent away too except for the protection of a high-ranking German officer with whom he became—very friendly, very close."

"I don't believe that."

"No, Fauve, of course you don't. That's exactly what I meant about the difficulty of making you understand, even such a little thing as that."

"A little thing?" Fauve's face had turned white, Kate noted with a thrill of satisfaction. And what had she told her yet? Nothing important, nothing at all. How wise she had been to stay in Marte Pollison's good graces over these many years. The woman was a tyrant but eventually she couldn't resist gossip.

"That officer was an art lover. He supplied your father with precious paints so that he could continue to work in spite of all the shortages and he took him off the list of those who were destined to be sent to factories in Germany. Some of his best work was done in those years, and yet if people knew about it they'd be quick to call him a collaborator."

"Why are you telling me this?"

"To make you grasp fully what your father's genius demands of him. When he told the German about the bunch of young good-for-nothings who stole his precious sheets—for years he had nothing else to use as canvas—how could he know that they were members of the *Maquis*? It was a terrible misunderstanding and he's never forgiven himself for it—twenty of them, all caught and executed on the spot. Why, he'd never even have known what had happened to them if the German hadn't returned the sheets."

"I don't believe a single word you're saying," Fauve said furiously. "It's a contemptible lie, and what the hell does it have to do with last night? I was talking about the way Jews lived in Provence before the Revolution, not about the war!"

Kate sighed and put her hands over her face for a brief moment. Now! She thought, *now!* "Oh, Fauve," she said wearily, her voice gentle, in supplication, as if willing the girl to make a leap of intelligence. "It was only an example of the sort of thing, the sort of horrible, tragic thing that can happen in time of war. It was to give you an insight into the situation with those Jews who came to him for help during the Occupation."

"*Jews*—what Jews?"

"Jews from Paris, trying to get out of Occupied France. They came and kept coming—people who had just presumed on the fact that they were old friends of his from the days he had lived in Paris, or from the fact that they'd been invited here before the war. Why, sometimes they were only friends of friends. Marte told me about it . . . oh, Fauve . . . this is just too hard to explain to anyone of your generation . . . what do you know about the war?" Kate slumped in her chair, her expression closed and guarded.

"What is too hard to explain?" Fauve said faintly, her heart beating so hard that she felt as if she must run away, as if the house were on fire and she was in mortal danger. Kate took a breath of resolution and spoke quietly, looking at the carpet.

"Your father ordered Marte and Jean to build a barrier to hide the entrance to *La Tourrello* down at the main road so that no refugees, Jews, any others, Jewish or not, would come up here to disturb him, to interrupt his work. Of course he had to close the big gates too because some of them actually infiltrated right through the woods—naturally they knew the house was here, if they'd been here before. But your father knew that if he weakened and let some Jew spend even one single night under his roof he could be in serious danger. Any Frenchman who helped a Jew was putting his own life in jeopardy."

"But what about all the French who did help Jews, who fought in the Resistance, who bombed German trains, who fought back?" Fauve asked tightly.

"Little people, Fauve, little people with less to lose than your father. He had to choose between painting and risking his life and I believe absolutely that he made the right choice and I pray you'll think so too—he decided that his only loyalty had to be to his work, not to sheltering people for whom he'd never had any responsibility. You must be grown up enough to understand that."

"Grown up," Fauve repeated, "grown up?"

"But Fauve, they simply had to be *made* to go away! Nobody invited them but they just kept coming. They would have destroyed his *peace of mind*. Why do you think it took him *eight years* to go to see you? He was afraid for his peace of mind, for his powers of concentration. Those Jews would have prevented him from painting, even if they'd never been caught, even if no one had known. *La Tourrello* is remote, I admit, but in the village everything gets talked about sooner or later and someone might have denounced him to the authorities. And that, Fauve, is why your keeping on about the Jews is upsetting him . . . it makes him remember all the people who got past the fence at the road and kept on ringing and ringing the bell in the kitchen."

"How do you know any of this! You weren't here! Is it Marte again, because I wouldn't believe one single goddamned lie she told you!"

"You still truly don't understand. Ah, Fauve, why would I bother to lie to you? Your father's *work* was at stake, don't you know what that means? Nothing could be more important."

"*Liar!*"

"Ask Adrien Avigdor since you don't believe me."

"What?"

"You heard me. He was your father's best friend before the war. But your father had to turn him away too, had to refuse him entrance. Avigdor told me so himself in 1946 in Paris and all the time that you've been seeing Eric I've been terrified that the old man might have said something to you. He was horribly bitter about it when I saw him last. It seems that he actually kept track of the people who came here . . . artists mostly of course. His personal animosity was frightening. He acted as if it were all your father's fault that there was a war going on in Europe and many of those unfortunate people were caught and deported—they probably would have died no matter what your father had done."

"Deported . . . died . . . caught . . ."

"Fauve, I simply had to tell you. We must *not* have any more of your history lessons during meals. Will you give me your word . . ."

Kate's words trailed off as she watched Fauve run out of the bedroom. No, she thought, no, she didn't think she'd left out anything important.

As Fauve pushed open the door into the studio Mistral was working on Fauve's picture, alive in every pore with energy and insight. His ability to participate in Fauve's quest for a sense of herself had provided the element that had been missing from his work these past few weeks and in one day he'd conquered the picture.

"Thank God you're back! I have so much to tell you." He threw down his brush and started forward to kiss her. She stopped, just inside the doorway, and held up one hand, warding him off.

"Father, did you refuse to give shelter to Jewish refugees during the war—did you listen to the bell ringing and not come to the gate to let them in?"

Mistral fought back. The shock of Fauve's challenge left him with only a single thought. "*Avigdor,*" he roared. "What the hell has he been telling you?"

"So it's true!" Fauve cried. All her desperate hope had died as soon as he'd said Avigdor's name. "Do you ever *think* about them—the Jews who died because of you?"

She turned, but not quickly enough to avoid seeing the truth that was branded so clearly on his face. He reached toward her but she was gone. *And he did not dare to go after her*. He stood, trembling, in the center of the empty studio, irresolutely, and then he began, with the haste of a man in danger of his life, to lock every door and window of his studio from the inside so that he would be safe from the hatred he'd seen in his daughter's eyes.

Eric Avigdor, arriving there three-quarters of an hour later, found Fauve waiting outside the walls of *La Tourrello*. Her suitcases were on the gravel driveway beside her and she carried her raincoat.

"Are we going somewhere, darling?" he said gaily. He was ready for all of Fauve's caprices.

"Please, Eric, take me to the train station in Avignon."

"I certainly won't. If you've had a fight with that so-called sister of yours I'll go right on inside and break one of her fingernails."

"Eric, don't, don't joke . . ." Fauve bowed her head and, with a pang of fear he turned to part the curtain of hair that almost hid her face. At his touch she gasped with a single rending sob and he saw that she must have been weeping long before he came, for her face was raw with tears that had run into her mouth and down her chin.

"My God, what's happened to you?" he cried, but she shook her head blindly and climbed into the car and huddled in the seat. He threw the suitcases in the back and tried to hold her in his arms and comfort her but she shook him off. "Get me away from here," she said in a way that made him start the car without another word. They drove off in the direction of Avignon. They had been speeding along the main road for five minutes before he tried again. "Fauve, tell me what's wrong. Please, darling, let me help. I know I can."

"No, Eric." Her voice seemed to have no home in her body.

"Fauve, don't you trust me? Nothing can be that bad."

"I can't talk about it." She had stopped weeping but there was a blotched, hopeless, creased look to her young face that terrified him when he glanced at her. He stopped the car and pulled off the road.

"Fauve, I won't drive you any farther until you tell me what this is about. I've never seen anyone in the state you're in."

She opened the door of the car and jumped out. Then she reached for one of her suitcases. He clenched his hand around her arm and dragged her back into the car. "What do you think you're doing? Are you crazy? Fauve!"

"If you keep asking me questions I'll hitch a ride to Avignon. Someone will come along and give me a ride."

"All right, all right. You win. But *why* won't you talk to me? Don't you know how much I love you?"

At that promise of tenderness, at that sweet watchfulness, she lost control of herself and abandoned herself to a tempest of wild grief, spasms of gulping, childish sobs mixed with a keening sound of such violent loss that Eric could scarcely prevent himself from stopping the car again. He felt as if the countryside around him had disintegrated. By the time they approached the outskirts of Avignon she had calmed down into a blurred, scattered emptiness.

"Please, let me off at the station. I'll wait there for the evening train."

"I'll stay with you."

"I wish you wouldn't."

"You can't stop me."

They sat on a bench outside the station, Fauve staring straight ahead of her as mute and barred-off from any contact as if she were in a concrete box. Eric tried to hold her hand but she drew quickly away from his touch and folded her arms tightly around her body, tucking her hands under her arms. Only her hair, burning with its inextinguishable flame, reassured him that this was Fauve, his teasing, blithe girl with her festival heart and mirthful impulses. Even when she'd been serious or sorrowful, she'd always been ready to explore difficult feelings without holding back, but now she was locked in a kind of a glacial trance that all his immense love could not penetrate. If only he were really grown up, if only he knew what to do, he thought in anguish, hating himself for being only twenty. He was not able to understand that she could no more tell him what she had learned than if she had been responsible herself for what Mistral had done. She felt extinguished by a weight of shame so great that it was no different from guilt itself. She felt contaminated by being her father's daughter, his monstrous love made her feel as if she must be tainted with his evil, and Kate's revealing words, one filthy secret after another, filled her head like grinding rocks that would rub against each other for a vile eternity.

"Where are you going?" Eric asked.

"New York."

"Do you have your plane ticket?" She nodded. "Your train ticket?"

"I'll buy it on the train."

"I'm going to get it for you now."

"No."

"Fauve, you must let me do something for you or I'll go mad!"

She shrugged her acceptance and he went off to buy the ticket and a supply of sandwiches and mineral water for the trip, and in an impulse of helpless grief, every magazine he could find, although he knew already that she would sit without moving all the way to Paris. Something frightful had been done to her and his passionate intuition told him that nothing on earth would ever give him back the same girl he had left at the gates of *La Tourrello* only a few hours ago.

"Thank you," Fauve said in a white voice when he came back with his purchases. "I'm sorry, Eric."

"Will you answer my letters?"

"Yes."

"Fauve, will you stop once in a while and remember that I love you, that I'll love you *forever* and I'll never stop? If you were only a few years older I'd never let you go, no matter what, you know that, don't you?"

"Yes, Eric," she answered but his heart shriveled as he heard the passive, faraway tone of her voice. She was just saying yes to everything to get rid of him, or make him let her get on the train that he could hear hooting in the distance. All around them people were standing and picking up their luggage and moving purposefully toward the platform.

The train came to a stop and Eric went ahead of Fauve, putting her suitcases on the rack over her head in a first-class carriage, finding her a seat and stowing away her provisions.

She slumped in her seat as limp as a dead animal and he stood over her irresolutely for a few seconds until he heard the guard's whistle blowing to announce the departure of the train. He took her by her elbows and made her stand up and face him.

"We never did get to Lunel," he said.

"No."

The train began to move slowly as he kissed her. It picked up speed and Eric released her. "I promised we'd go and we will. You're my one and only love, Fauve. Never forget me." He ran down the corridor and jumped off at the very edge of the platform, and stood there with tears running down his cheeks as he watched the train disappear to the north, taking his heart away.

On another late summer day, a year later, Kate Mistral sat alone after breakfast, waiting until Mistral left the house. For months he had been gone from morning to evening. He didn't tell her where his roaming took him, but she knew enough to guess that he was searching the countryside for a fresh idea. He had been in a long nonproductive period and for months he had spent no time in his studio. Kate was too realistic not to know that it was no coincidence that this dry spell had started when Fauve left *La Tourrello.* Since then, Mistral had written to Fauve six times. Marte Pollison, who collected the mail from the postman at the gate, reported to Kate when each of the letters was returned unopened. What lies, what attempts at explanations could Julien have concocted? Kate wondered. When Fauve had decamped he had told her only that it had been over a teenaged misunderstanding, a stupid fight about her spending so much time with that Avigdor boy and getting too involved with the Avigdor family.

Several weeks ago he had finally brought himself to write to Maggy and since then, Kate had waited with dread for a response that would reveal her part in Fauve's departure. Yesterday Maggy's answer had finally come, just before Kate left for an appointment in Apt, and Mistral had thrust it unopened into his pocket.

Last night, all through dinner, which was silent and gloomy as it had been for the past year, Mistral's expression had been angry and weary and bitter. It seemed to encompass everything; the fine meal he had been offered, the perfectly laid table, the deft service, even the deliciously scented night air. What could Maggy have written? She had to know.

As soon as Kate heard Mistral drive off she went upstairs to his bedroom and locked herself in. The room was, as always, tidy, impersonal, for his real life was not lived here. There was no letter on the night table where he kept that book on the Jews of Avignon which Fauve had left behind. Kate had seen it there before when, as she occasionally did, she checked his room in his absence and she could still not understand why he kept it around. It wasn't like Julien to torture himself. The top of his desk was bare as well. Deftly she went through its drawers and finally, tucked under a pile of unanswered mail from admirers from all over the world, she found the envelope she had seen him put in his pocket yesterday. It had been torn open. Quickly she read the short note it contained.

Julien,

No, I don't have any idea of why Fauve won't answer your letters, or even read them. I've tried to talk to her about last summer but she absolutely refuses to tell me anything except that she doesn't want to talk about it. She's been very sad and disturbed, more than I can say, and each time you write her it only makes her feel worse. When she saw that you had written to me, she said that I should answer your letter in any way I pleased but that in the future, if you wrote to her again, she didn't want to even know about it. From now on she has asked me to return any letters that you send without telling her that they have come.

I know nothing about this situation between the two of you and I do not intend to enter into it in any way. Whatever you did to make Fauve turn against you, is done and too late to be undone. My own experience with you is such that I have no inclination to grant you the benefit of any doubt.

Maggy

Twice Kate read the letter, replaced it and slipped out of the room, hurrying down to sit in the sun beside the pool.

She was safe now, quite safe, she thought. There would be no more letters to worry about, no possibility of Fauve writing to her father to tell him who had told her all that she had learned on that afternoon a year ago. Safe—all of his paintings, the land, the investments, the bank accounts, all safe from division, saved intact for Nadine to inherit. Her daughter's future would not be compromised, and she herself had nothing left to fear from Fauve.

Kate had never been without a sense of irony and it was that, and that alone, that now kept her sitting so quietly in the sun.

She had been on time for her appointment in Apt with Dr. Elbert yesterday. Elbert was the doctor who delivered Nadine and she preferred him to other specialists in Avignon. When she had begun bleeding again last week, fifteen years after she had gone through menopause, she had reluctantly visited the doctor whom she hadn't bothered to see for years. Cancer of the uterus, he had told her, and so far advanced that it had spread to her liver. How long did she have? A year, perhaps, a little more or a little less, but Madame Mistral, there is nothing that can be done at this stage of the disease. If anything could have been done I would have had to see you long before this . . . and even then, who knows?

Who knew indeed? Who ever knew? Kate asked herself. She looked around her. All was in order, a rich empire, magnificent, secure and absolutely intact. For the first time since Teddy Lunel had walked through the doors of *La Tourrello*, Kate finally could feel certain that she was in full possession again . . . for a year—or a little more or a little less.

27

It was Fauve Lunel's twenty-first birthday, in the middle of June 1974, and the second floor of the Russian Tea Room was crowded with two hundred people, each of them glowing with the unspoken satisfaction of knowing that their importance was validated by their having been bidden to this particular coming-of-age, a pleasure that is such a basic component of human nature that it must have been experienced by cave dwellers gathered around a particularly prestigious fire.

From behind his big glasses, Falk, whose closest friends still called him Melvin, scanned the horde that palpitated with noise at the decible level only achieved in New York; his eyes dilated with the intensity of an observation that was as profound as it was swift. Here, right here, he thought, were gathered together all the people who had the power to decide how the American woman would hope to look each morning when she woke up.

He kissed Diana Vreeland and Cheryl Tiegs, reaching up to do so with no more self-consciousness than that with which a short woman kisses a tall man, and, as he hugged Lauren Hutton, pleased by her particular conformation of features, he reflected that women believed that they made their own choices about their physical aspirations, yet it was photographers like himself who were responsible for the wind of change that sent women to hairdressers and cosmetic counters and department stores. Yet he realized that even he was not as influential as Maggy Lunel, who, by picking out new models and sending them to see the right people, could determine the way everybody in the world would eventually come to think about ideal female beauty.

But did the *ultimate* power really rest in the hands of the fashion or beauty editor who made the decision to use one girl rather than another, or, he wondered as he gave Christina Ferrare a kiss on each glowing cheek, did the power ultimately rest in the hands of these splendorous girls who offered themselves to the camera? Where would the entire establishment of fashion magazines, advertising agencies, cosmetic companies, photographers and model agencies find itself without a never-ending supply of beauties willing to devote their young lives to becoming icons for all other women? In any case, Falk didn't have to come to any hard and fast philosophical conclusions tonight since everyone involved in creating the standards to which women all over the country would find themselves responding was right there in this room. Everyone, that is, but Fauve. Where *was* Fauve?

In the last five years Falk had seen less of her than he would have liked. While she was growing up they had spent most Saturday afternoons making the rounds of the galleries, but in the early fall of 1969 she had, and there was no other way he could find to describe the change in her, quite simply turned her back on art. She had blamed this abrupt, and to Falk, shocking loss of interest on the experience of going to the landmark exhibition called "New York Painting and Sculpture: 1940–1970," which Henry Geldzahler had mounted at the Metropolitan Museum.

God knows, it *had* been enough to give anyone visual indigestion, that overrich slumgullion in which thirty-five different galleries had been used to give thirty-five retrospective exhibitions to thirty-five of the greatest contemporary artists, but Falk would have thought a sixteen-year-old appetite equal to such esthetic burn-out. Even he, veteran of the art spectacular, had found himself battered by the unheard-of gaudiness of the evening, bewildered by its excesses, deafened by the barbaric rock band and footworn from the sheer size of the show, but Fauve had responded with something close to hysteria, saying that she never wanted to look at another piece of art or sculpture again. He'd been sure that she meant only until the next interesting show. How could anyone with Fauve's passion for art become indifferent to the complex set of experiences that looking at new work must give her?

Yet as time went on, he found that her disgust not only endured but deepened into a kind of sadness, as if she were mourning the death of art. She had insisted that all the great men had already painted, all the innovations had been made, all the great themes used up, all graphic possibilities discovered, so that new artists were only using the sweepings of the studio floors of past masters.

Falk had laughed at Fauve's notions until he realized that she had stopped working on her own painting. When he questioned her about it she was direct. She didn't intend ever to paint again. How could she keep on going when she had nothing new to add? Although Falk had always recognized the unmistakable influence of Mistral on her work he had also seen a true and original talent struggling to emerge. He knew that it was merely a question of time before she came into her own, before all that was personal and fresh in her work grew strong enough to make her break away from her father and strike out on her own. But instead of making progress, she had quit, quit flat and by now, he was sure, quit for good and all.

Falk bit into a *pirojok*, savoring the hot, flaky puff pastry made from sour-cream dough, and, munching, reflected that what was, to his certain knowledge a real loss for the world of art had been a gain for the model agency business.

Who would have imagined that Fauve, graduating from high school at seventeen, would have decided to go to work for Maggy rather than go to college? And who would have expected her to be so astonishingly good at it? In the last four years she had not just learned the business through and through, but she had made innovations that had kept the Lunel Agency ahead of its competition, so that she had become Maggy's second-in-command. She had worked so hard, with so much ambition and energy and determination that her youth and inexperience had been overcome by the time she was nineteen and since then "Lunel" had come more and more to refer equally to Fauve as it did to Maggy.

Falk found himself standing with Dick Avedon and Irving Penn, the only other photographers who had remained at the very top for as long as he had, the only others to whom every new talent was inevitably compared. As he talked to them he reflected on the rareness of longevity, staying power and endless excellence in this world where change was the rule. Yet Maggy Lunel still moved in an aura of supremacy.

Now she was at that age that could best be described as "ageless," enigmatically, flamboyantly, triumphantly ageless. And ageless she would remain, he decided, saluting her in his mind, for at least another two decades, until she moved on, gracefully, into a period in which she would be known, no doubt to her vast annoyance, as a "living legend."

When he had greeted her tonight there had been an exchange of sad recognition beneath their smiles. Each had known the other's thoughts and shared an unspoken word of never-fading grief. *If only Teddy were here.*

Falk pushed away the thought, as he had done so many thousands of times, through three marriages to fashion models, through the birth of four children, all inheriting the genes of their mothers and now all taller than he was—thank heaven for great big girls—and looked around for the one person he sought in this crowded room. He was fond, very fond indeed of his own children, but Fauve had come into his heart before he had married for the first time, and by some process of wishful thinking that he never chose to examine, she had always seemed like the daughter he should have had with Teddy Lunel. But where *was* Fauve?

Maggy Lunel took a final look of self-appraisal in her floor-to-ceiling three-way mirror before she left her apartment to go to Fauve's birthday party. So she was a woman with a twenty-one-year-old granddaughter, was she? Well, so much the better! She pivoted, checking the back of her jacket, made of several layers of thin, drifting, black silk crêpe de chine printed with oversized flowers in melting Oriental shades of plum, lavender and deeper violet shading into purple. Did all women, she wondered, as she passed her hand over the back of her hair where it curved inward gracefully in a smooth pageboy at the nape of her neck, feel the same way she did? As if she had stopped growing older at some undefined age that never changed except on certain bad days? An age that hovered at some agreeably mellow yet fresh moment of time between twenty-six and thirty-two?

She picked up the edge of the jacket and inspected its leaf-printed lining. Now there was a refinement indeed, since the lining would never be noticed, but one that Karl Lagerfeld of Chloé, who had designed the vaguely kimono-shaped garment, and the small-scaled printed tunic dress that went underneath it, must have loved working out, for was he not the man who had quite seriously asked his mother to give him his own valet as a present for his fourth birthday? Yes, the costume was successful because the long, firm lines of the body under it had withstood the test of time, but when Maggy clasped the Van Cleef and Arpels diamond necklace around her throat she had to concede that her interior age level did not quite match the evidence presented by her neck. Why was it that most women who owned the kind of necklace that a jeweler, with an air that categorized the words as having an exact technical significance, could refer to as "important," were not likely to have unlined necks? Damn necks! If only all heads rested directly on shoulders how much more delightful the world would be. Her shoulders still could compete in any company.

As Maggy caught the fleeting, boastful thought she asked herself in a combination of amusement and irritation if she were growing vain? She could have sworn that any vanity she must once have had, had been absolutely knocked out of her by daily dealing with the youngest and loveliest of all the millions of girls in the world. Her neck must only be a stand-in for the milestone that was marked by Fauve's birthday.

Yet, in Fauve's case, twenty-one certainly didn't mean the beginning of maturity or adulthood. No, that change had taken place five years before and Maggy knew no more of what had caused it today than she did then, when Fauve had come home unexpectedly early from her summer in France. At first Maggy had bombarded her with questions, but Fauve had refused to discuss what had happened with a stubbornness, a leaden and inflexible tenacity that Maggy had been sure she couldn't maintain. But, as the weeks passed and she saw the differences in Fauve, the loss of her young girl's illusions, the disappearance of her innocent playfulness, she began to understand that once again she had sent a beloved child to Europe and once again that child had been changed, terribly changed, by Julien Mistral. But at least this child had returned.

After a year had passed, Maggy simply accepted the fact that she would probably never know what had taken place. Fauve, so spontaneous, so open, so alive that every enthusiasm that crossed her heart showed in her face, had somehow learned to keep a secret. It had been a deeply distressing year, that year between sixteen and seventeen, Fauve's last year in high school, Maggy reflected, secure now in the knowledge that it was long past. The mysterious hurt had never been resolved. Fauve never returned to France. After Maggy had answered the letter Mistral sent her, all communication between him and his daughter had ceased as completely as if those eight summers in Félice had never happened.

Fauve, so flexible, so loving and quick to forgive, had been utterly implacable on the subject of her father. She had cast him out of her life. At first Maggy had had to admit to an intense curiosity to know what had caused the rupture but, where Julien Mistral was concerned, it was unwise to think too long or too deeply.

For the first few years Fauve had received and answered frequent letters from that boy she'd met over there, old Avigdor's son of all people, but now the letters had almost stopped coming—Maggy couldn't even be sure if they still wrote each other now or not. But eventually, Fauve had pulled herself out of the depression in which she had been enveloped.

Time . . . it was partly the passage of time, Maggy decided, partly the blessed elasticity of youth and most of all it had been the remedy of work. When Fauve first announced that she didn't intend to apply to college but wanted to work, Maggy had thought for one despairing moment that Fauve intended to become a model. She wouldn't have been able to prevent it. Fauve had had the unassailable, mesmerizing quality that would have made her into the face that personified her era as clearly as Suzy Parker and Teddy had personified the fifties and as Jean Shrimpton had dominated the mid-sixties. But, thank God, Fauve had wanted to follow her into the business. She had turned her back on using the privileges of beauty as a source of identity just as resolutely as she had turned her back on her talent for painting. Fauve had no interest in becoming the vigilant caretaker of her façade, no wish to be obliged to deal in merchandising her own surface, and she had taken to the agency business as if she had absorbed it all of her life.

Fauve had immersed herself in work with an efficiency and a diligence that had amazed Maggy, and during those first two years she was given an opportunity to learn every job in the agency. By the time Fauve was nineteen, in the spring of 1972, Maggy grew accustomed to being able to count on Fauve to make decisions she had never allowed anyone else to make but herself. In action Fauve was crisp, forceful and effective in a way that demonstrated a solidity greater than her years.

It was then that Maggy dared to take a vacation, her first in a long time, and when she and Darcy returned from two weeks in London she found her agency flourishing and Fauve secure and serene. Maggy was invaded by elation, a giddy feeling, an intoxication of relief, glorious relief, that lightened her limbs and made her thirst for activities she hadn't allowed herself much time for in all those years since she'd started her own business, those years in which she'd supported herself and her daughter, vowing never again to be weak and foolish enough to depend on a man for anything but affection, and even to do without that if necessary.

She gave herself permission to sleep deliciously late in the morning, arriving at the office only two hours before it was time to go out to lunch with a friend, where she sat talking until the middle of the afternoon as heedlessly as if she had been doing it all of her life. She threw away all her hats and gloves—what were they doing in her wardrobe? She had her hair restyled and even changed its color, from the determined auburn that was appropriate for her office persona, to a softer color, artfully blended with titian and light brown into which a few stray strands of silver were allowed to wander as if by mistake. Maggy spent many hours shopping for new, less tailored clothes and she hired Susie Frankfort to give her grand, almost too dignified, apartment a whimsical and original charm. Oh, but it was bliss to begin to lay down the burden she had carried alone for so long, Maggy thought, but why had no one noticed? Everyone treated her just as they always had, she realized with increasing pique. She had been The Boss, that old reliable, a work-horse with business on her mind for so long that people saw her only in that light. She didn't expect them to act as if she had just been elected Queen of the May but surely someone might have noticed!

One night, late in that spring season that was like a rebirth, Maggy and Darcy went out to dinner. At "21," the headwaiter, Walter Weiss, led them to their table, the same table at which they had sat that first time they had been there together in 1931 when it had been the best speakeasy in New York.

Darcy, as was his unalterable, almost sacred habit of forty-two years, sat at table 7 in the first section of the bar, to the left of the entrance and in the center of the side wall. It was a prime, strategic, highly visible and much coveted banquette to which many other powerful men had aspired in vain.

Any table in the first two sections of the bar was utterly desirable, for "21" was the only dining place in New York that had retained the glory and the glamour of its legend, the only restaurant whose imperial status remained undiminished as it rode out the decades with the steadiness of a great ocean liner on which nothing could possibly go wrong; a world unto itself as no other restaurant in the United States has ever succeeded in being or ever will be again. The assurance of always being led to a certain specific and distinguished table in the bar at "21" was something mere money had never been able to buy, a symbol more valued than a membership in the most exclusive club or a seat on the most important board of directors since it signified a high and continued place in the power structure of the country. Darcy's lien on table 7 was part of the innermost organization of his life, and he sighed in visible contentment as they settled down on the banquette.

"Why," complained Maggy, "do we *always* have to sit in this bar? Do you realize that we've never eaten in the main dining room upstairs?" Darcy looked as astonished as if he'd found table 7 occupied by a rock star. "I understand," Maggy continued with a wistful air that verged on petulance, "that it's very agreeable upstairs. I hear it's less noisy and more spacious. Onassis always eats there and Dr. Armand Hammer and Mrs. Douglas MacArthur and Nelson Rockefeller . . . and we're always *stuck* down here. It does seem too bad."

"But you've never wanted to eat upstairs, you've never even seen it as far as I know." Darcy was outraged. The upstairs was all right, he supposed, solid and corporate and formal, but a man with any juice left in his bones would always prefer to eat in the bar, in which he fancied he could still feel and hear and smell those great days of Prohibition, when Jack and Charlie's served the best booze in town.

"That's no reason for you to make such assumptions," Maggy said plaintively. She plucked disdainfully at the distinctively checked red-and-white tablecloth. "On the tables upstairs there's lovely plain white linen, the heavy old-fashioned kind, all slippery and starched, at least that's what Lally said. And there are flowers on the tables instead of these ugly red match holders." She sighed with the resigned sadness of a penniless little girl pressing her nose against a candy store window and pensively adjusted the bow of the navy blouse that went with her new, dashingly nautical, white Adolfo suit.

"Damn it, if you're so unhappy here, why the hell didn't you tell me sooner!" Darcy said furiously. "Let's go upstairs . . . come on."

"Oh, no, it's too much trouble. It was just a thought, something that wandered through my mind," Maggy murmured. "Anyway I'm not exactly unhappy here, I'm just restless." She sipped the glass of champagne from the bottle of Bollinger Brut 1947 the waiter had opened as soon as he saw Maggy and Darcy sit down at the table at which they dined two or three times a week. "I wonder what tequila tastes like," she said in a forlorn, diminished voice.

"I'll order you some," Darcy snorted, raising his eyebrows.

"Oh, no, never mind, don't bother, I don't really care, it was just a passing fancy." She looked pitifully sorry for herself as she rejected the mere idea of tequila. "Champagne is quite good enough for me . . . or so you've always assumed . . . just pay no attention."

"What the devil is this all about actually?" Darcy asked, twisting around so that he faced her as she sat, as upright and slender as she had ever been and in so many infuriating ways as unexaminable a siren as she'd been on the first night he'd taken her here and looked into her great eyes of that color that was still just as much green as it was gold, and wondered who the hell *was* Maggy Lunel?

"I'm tired . . ." she almost whispered.

"We'll go home," he said, alarmed. Maggy was never tired unless she was sick.

"I'm tired of your thinking that I'm not open to new experiences, I'm tired of being treated as if any change in routine would be unwelcome," she murmured. "I'm tired of . . . of . . . your lack of attention, Darcy. You take me for granted," she said, broodingly.

"What absolute rot!"

"So you deny it, do you?" Suddenly she quivered with energy. Her words came pouring out. "I thought you would, an insensitive, thoughtless, unromantic man like you . . . a woman might as well go out for dinner with her old uncle . . . her grandfather . . . her *great*-grandfather."

"What!" he roared.

"Don't shout at me! Just how long has it been since the last time you asked me to marry you?" Her face was flushed with accusation and indignation.

"*How long?* As long as it's been since I decided to stop making a goddamned fool out of myself! That's how long . . ." he sputtered, with the injustice of her words.

"You haven't answered my question." She was implacable.

"Fifteen years—no, I think I asked you on Valentine's Day once, about a dozen years ago, like an utter ass. Yes—I remember it now . . . you seemed particularly loving that night and I just gave it another shot, just like poor, bloody, old faithful that I am, even though I knew perfectly well that there wasn't a chance. You'd think I'd have learned."

"Ah ha!" Maggy's anger was triumphant. "So now I know why you kept asking. Because you were *safe* and it cost you absolutely nothing to make the gesture. I've always thought so, I always knew you were just like the others, I've always seen through your act. I've had quite enough of this neglect, thank you! I despise your low tactics and I don't intend to put up with them for another minute. It's shameful, a disgrace!"

"You . . . you . . . ungrateful bitch!"

"Is that a proposal?" she demanded, eyes flashing fury.

"Absolutely not!"

"So! When it comes down to it you're unwilling to make a commitment, aren't you? Too big a decision, isn't it?" she sneered. "Okay, Darcy, you have exactly one minute to get your priorities straight."

"Is *that* a proposal?"

"Only a man who lacked gallantry to his very *soul* would ask a woman to answer such a question. How dare you?"

"Captain!" Darcy beckoned him over. "We're moving upstairs for dinner. Send up two double tequilas on the rocks. Madame and I have some arrangements to make and there's just too damn much noise in this saloon."

And so, Maggy remembered, they had been married two years ago, and high time too as Lally Longbridge had said, taking all the credit as usual. She was still standing in front of the mirror, almost in a trance, when Darcy came in, dressed to go to Fauve's birthday party. As she looked at their double reflection she felt a little, irrepressible jump of blithesome joy. How *right* she had been to marry this man.

Darcy ate another tiny potato stuffed with fresh caviar and dotted with sour cream and decided that Henry McIlheeny, that bon vivant who had once said, "Caviar should never be served with cocktails. You have to be seated to enjoy it," had been entirely too pompous. He took another and popped it into his mouth, making the most of a momentary lull at the top of the staircase where he and Maggy stood greeting their guests while behind them the party was approaching that moment at which it could be said to be in orbit. Yet *where* was Fauve?

Polly Mellen, of *Vogue*, who knew more about putting the absolutely right model in the absolutely right dress—and most important of all—in absolutely the right *way*, was there, with most of her staff members, and so was Tony Mazzola, who had been editor-in-chief of *Harper's Bazaar* forever, accompanied by his upper echelon, and so was Tom Hogan of Clairol and Estée Lauder with her entire family and Gilbert Shawn, president of Warshaw, the catalog producers and perhaps the most prolific employer of models in the world, and to Darcy's utter astonishment, so were Eileen and Jerry Ford, whose model agency had been Maggy's chief—and formidable—competition since the late 1940s.

The fact that Maggy had invited her only major rival was the most significant indication that the woman he had loved for so long had truly changed, Darcy mused. Three years ago, if he had been asked whether it was more likely that Maggy would marry him or that she'd ask the Fords to a party, he would have picked marriage, as impossible as it had then seemed. The competition between the two agencies had escalated with the years and with the steady raise in the hourly rates paid to the models.

Maggy's income, before expenses, on the fees earned by her girls, came to close to two million dollars a year and the Fords were not far behind. Each agency had, among its several hundred models, a group of a half-dozen or so top models, who would, while earning more than almost any man in America, always be called "girls" and never "women." These girls were property, as real as if each of them were a fully rented office building whose tenants always paid their rent on time.

For over twenty years Maggy Lunel and Eileen Ford had vied for these same precious pieces of property, and since neither woman took kindly to losing, and since one of them lost each time the other won, a truce, however momentary, amazed Darcy.

"We're like the oil-producing countries," Maggy had explained to him. "Eileen and I, and now Wilhelmina in the last seven years and even Zoli, since 1970, run the only games in town worth mentioning. We can't fix prices or form a monopoly because it's against those ridiculous antitrust laws. But we're responsible to our girls to maintain standards so that they don't get unfairly treated by the advertising agencies and the photographers—after all, they only have a few good earning years before they're over the hill—so, as their representatives I've always thought we should be on reasonably good terms with each other." Now Darcy understood her motivation; she was thinking about Fauve's future.

One day Fauve would be alone running the agency and Maggy wanted her to be as secure as possible, free of long standing feuds. Darcy didn't believe it was an idea whose time would *ever* come but he enjoyed watching Maggy struggling with her attempt to be pragmatic. Basically, he thought, as he studied her now, she was the most splendid woman in the room, even though it also contained Karen Graham and Renee Russo, but sweet reasonableness wasn't her style. He enjoyed her most when she was her feisty, fiery, everyday self, but organizing this party had brought out Maggy's mother-hen side, and she had, for the event, managed to gloss over the viciously competitive spirit that existed, had always existed and would always exist in the model agency business. Her very inconsistency delighted him.

Jason Darcy knew he was a lucky man. He'd dragged Maggy before a judge before she had a chance to change her mind but even as the ceremony progressed he'd wondered what differences a legal tie could make to a union that had lasted for so long. While he was repeating his vows he'd been remembering case histories without end of people who had had long and loving relationships until they made the mistake of indulging in marriage. What then about the example set by novelist Fanny Hurst, who had lived in great happiness with her husband for many years during which they occupied two different apartments and made appointments whenever they wanted to be together? Might that not be the ideal way to conduct such an unnatural, inhuman, artificial arrangement as marriage? But Maggy, this ardent, wistful, girlish, springtime Maggy who had popped out one night at "21," apparently intended to become his wife and he hadn't dared to entertain too many second thoughts.

And it *was* different. It was, quite simply, *better*. Better to know that she finally trusted him, better to know that after all she was willing to depend on him a little, better not to wake up in the morning in another room on another street and not know what his beloved was doing or feeling until he reached her by telephone. He decided that marriage was such a lovely treat that it should be reserved only for the middle-aged. Young people should be forbidden by law to regularize any of their romances until they had passed fifty because they couldn't possibly appreciate the charms of matrimony as long as they thought of it as a right rather than a privilege. It should be a *reward* for being faithful and loving, reserved for those who had been true to each other. He did, however, have the good sense to keep these opinions to himself. His reputation for crusty toughness would be destroyed if they ever became public and, since Darcy still published one of the most successful groups of magazines in the country, he didn't want to sound uxorious.

"Where the hell is Fauve?" said a man's voice behind him.

"I thought she might be with you," Darcy said, turning to Ben Litchfield, his one-time *protégé* whom he had watched rise from a space-salesman's job in the advertising department of *Woman's Journal*, the biggest and most successful women's magazine in the country, to editor-in-chief, bewildering the world of women's magazines by reaching the top just before he turned thirty.

"I wish she were," he said, "but I haven't seen her since Monday."

Benjamin Franklin Litchfield was the most fervent, and seemingly the most successful of Fauve's many suitors, although she kept her own council and Maggy and Darcy could only speculate. Darcy felt a proprietary interest in the man's case for he had introduced them himself a year ago.

Fauve and Ben should know each other he decided one day when he had tried to telephone each of them on a Sunday morning and discovered them both in their respective offices, hard at work on matters they had put aside for the weekend when they wouldn't be interrupted. He had insisted that they both finish up in an hour and join him and Maggy for lunch. It had taken all his authority to persuade the industrious pair to agree to such a reckless waste of time but, since that first meeting, Darcy had reason to suggest that they were moving toward spending Sunday mornings in bed together, an arrangement he favored as much more humane, and better for the circulation, the complexion and the psyche.

Maggy, too, approved of young Litchfield. In some ways he reminded her of Darcy when she'd first met him: he had that intensity that masked a capacity to be amused by the major absurdities of life, he had Darcy's curiosity and much, she sensed, of Darcy's generosity, but physically he had none of the lean and philosophic, almost ascetic distinction that had first attracted her to her love.

Handsome Ben Litchfield was a habitually rumpled man. He started out each day with the best of intentions, tall, muscular, conventionally clad in a well-pressed suit, a clean shirt, and freshly shined shoes, but by lunch he was a disgrace to the world of *Gentleman's Quarterly*. He had pulled at his thick sandy hair in despair so many times that it stood up on end where it wasn't falling into his eyes, he had tugged impatiently at the knot of his tie until it reached the third, by-now-unbuttoned button of the shirt that was peeping out between his vest and his trousers, his pockets were stuffed with papers and stubs of other people's pencils and he'd usually lost all of the three pairs of horn-rimmed glasses he needed in order to see layouts or read manuscripts.

But when Ben Litchfield took off his glasses his enormous, myopic blue eyes were as startled and happy as those of a baby waking up to the sight of his first elephant. He greeted everything in life with that same look of surprise and acceptance, although his associates had been heard to mutter that he was about as innocent as a vice squad cop in Detroit. He had the sudden, sweet, half-astonished smile of a man who's doing what he likes best and doing it better than anyone else. He'd been so busy getting to the top that he'd never paused and looked around for a serious girl until he'd met Fauve.

"Not since Monday?" Darcy asked. "I thought you two were seeing a lot of each other . . . that's three days."

"I know," Litchfield groaned. "Listen, Darcy. You've taught me everything I know as you've reminded me on innumerable occasions, usually in public. How do you get a girl to marry you?"

"Exercise patience, my boy, patience."

"Thanks a heap. That's a big help."

"Lunel women do not take to marriage easily, if ever." In fact, Darcy thought with complacency, he was the only man to have managed to marry one of them, the only man to have actually lured one of the line of three, lovely, redheaded Lunel women into matrimony. One of the three illegitimate Lunel women, he mused, for Maggy had told him the whole story on their honeymoon and he was, he believed, the only person on earth besides Fauve who knew that Maggy and Teddy had been as illegitimate as Fauve herself. "I won't have a minute's peace of mind until I see Fauve safely married," Maggy had told him. "Three bastards in a row are more than enough."

"Come on, Ben, let me buy you a *blini*, and we'll talk this over seriously. I may be able to give you some good advice—I don't think, after all, that too much patience is such a good idea," Darcy said. Perhaps it wasn't altogether fair to corner the market on Lunels. He owed it to Maggy to be more helpful. But where *was* Fauve?

He looked down the staircase again. At last! There she came, as flagrantly gorgeous as he'd ever seen her, long red hair flying, dressed in a streak of silver sequins, cut like a short slip, her cheeks bright with a flush of excitement, bounding up the staircase two steps at a time calling, "Magali, Magali, I'm sorry I'm so late!" A succulent girl like a salamander whose natural element is fire, Fauve Lunel arrived at her birthday party, but not alone. She had her hand firmly locked around the wrist of another girl—at least Darcy supposed it was a girl—a six-foot-tall scarecrow of a creature, in overalls and sneakers, with her flaxen hair cropped almost to a crew cut and a bewildered look on her face as she loped after Fauve.

"Magali—look what I brought you! She's just off the bus from Arkansas—do you think what I think?"

Maggy inspected the girl. The look of top models of the day was elegant, sophisticated, sculptured, with flowing hair. The girl was all bold bones and ever-so-slightly buck teeth, freckles and winged eyebrows. She had stupefying promise. So the look was about to change. Trust Fauve.

"Is she why you're late?"

"Yep. I was upstairs at the office, just checking out a few things before the party started and she wandered in off the street. Her friends, the ones she came on the bus with, had dared her to come up. So, naturally, that meant talking to them and then phoning her parents and telling them why she wasn't coming home and convincing them that I wasn't a white slaver and finding a place for her to stay . . . you know."

"What's your name?" Maggy asked the girl.

"Ida Clegg."

"Hmm . . . well, welcome to the Lunel Agency. Do you drink vodka?"

"Darned if this isn't a day for firsts," the girl said in a soft southern voice. "Yes, Ma'am, I believe I will."

Magali turned to Fauve and kissed her, whispering, "But why didn't you leave all those details till tomorrow?"

"Magali, she *also* had Eileen's address on a piece of paper—her friends had dared her to go there too," Fauve whispered back.

"Why didn't you say so right away, for heaven's sake? I was worried."

"Because look behind you."

Maggy turned and found Eileen Ford standing there, looking, as always, like the girl who will inevitably be elected president of any class she's in.

"Happy birthday, Fauve," Eileen said with a warm smile.

"Thank you, Eileen."

"You must be very proud, Maggy."

"Oh, I am!"

"And who is this?"

"A new girl we've just discovered—Arkansas."

Eileen gave Ida Clegg a quick, piercing look that saw everything, knew everything, understood everything. "Arkansas?" she asked. "Arkansas what?"

"Just Arkansas," Fauve replied.

"I see. How patriotic. Well, Arkansas, welcome to New York." Eileen walked away thoughtfully. She did not look happy.

"Who was that nice lady?" Arkansas asked.

"Ahh . . . that was . . ." Maggy began.

"Nobody you'll ever need to know," Fauve assured her hastily.

28

Fauve Lunel almost sprinted through the doors of the old elevator that opened so slowly on the tenth floor of the Carnegie Hall office building where the Lunel Agency was located. She was late for her regular Friday meeting with Casey d'Augustino, but Benjamin Franklin Litchfield had been exceedingly persistent last night and she'd overslept this morning. Fauve whisked through the reception room where the walls were hung with six framed magazine covers of former Lunel models.

"Only six," Maggy had once said, "out of all our hundreds and hundreds because when anyone waits to be interviewed in that room and looks at those covers she'll leave if she doesn't have enough self-confidence to make it. Then, when I have to turn her down, on her way out she'll find comfort in the same pictures because after all how could anybody be expected to be as beautiful as those girls were?"

The agency, as it had grown over the years, occupied more and more space in the fine old building and still it was crowded. All model agencies are crowded the way restaurant kitchens and army camps and backstages are crowded. There is never enough room for all the items needed to properly perform the functions for which the space is intended, and if by some miracle of design, enough room were provided, the work would suffer because of lack of communication between the necessary personnel.

Maggy's own office was large and comfortable but Fauve and Casey shared two small offices next to one of the three booking rooms which were the heart of the agency. The bookers all seemed to be busy on the phones, Fauve noted automatically as she sat down at her desk and buzzed Casey to come in. The Men's Division, supervised by Joe O'Donnel, who had once been a male model himself, was across the hall, and occupied even more cramped and less elegant space.

Casey d'Augustino had been working at the agency for only a year but she and Fauve functioned as a team. She was a graduate of Hunter, the public high school that accepts only the best and the brightest of New York's students, and smart, *smart* Casey, born with what she considered the unimaginatively ethnic name of Anna-Maria to a large Brooklyn family two generations removed from Palermo, was Fauve's closest friend. She sat down in one of the two chairs opposite the desk and groaned, cautiously patting her curly, short hair down over her forehead as if searching for bumps or bruises.

"What's wrong?" Fauve inquired cheerfully.

"Champagne hangover. The worst kind. Everybody has one. The whole staff. It was drinking all those toasts."

"I feel fine," Fauve said, surprised.

"You can't drink a toast to yourself, so don't look so virtuous, it was only because it was your birthday and not mine. On mine I promise you a lethal hangover."

"I brought you a present."

"Nothing will make it better."

"It's a counterirritant."

"I don't like it already."

"It's the new issue of *Cosmo*. Article on Lauren Hutton by Guy Flatley. Listen to this. She's talking about a 'go-see' with Diana Vreeland, her first venture into high fashion.

"A dozen models were parading all about her. And there I sat like a toad, taking in the whole scene. Suddenly—in the middle of a sentence—D.V. stopped and pointed a long, white-gloved finger at me. '*You!*' she said.

'Me.'

'Yes, you . . . you have a great presence,' she said, her great eagle eyes piercing me.

'Thank you,' I said. 'So do *you*.'

She gave me a tiny smile and went back to finishing her sentence. And that afternoon I got a call to report to Richard Avedon's studio and have some pictures taken."

"Oh, *shit!*" Casey jumped up. "No, tell me it isn't true! Tell me you're making it up! Tell me that this is just a vicious practical joke and you did it to show how much you love me, to take my mind off my physical paralysis, to force my blood to try and irrigate my liver once again."

"Feel better already, don't you?" Fauve said, pleased.

"God, yes. I feel like I could tear out a lioness's throat with my bare hands. Oh, how can they do that to us? Do you realize that *millions* of women read every issue of *Cosmo* religiously and when they see that little story they're all going to think that it could happen to them? 'Sitting there like a toad,' my ass! Lauren never looked like a toad on the worst day she ever had. Anyway *Eileen*, for the love of God, sent her to see Vreeland, she didn't just drop by! And where are all those *Cosmo* readers going to end up? Right here in our hallway waiting on line for the open auditions Tuesday morning. We'd better put on an extra girl to process them."

"Yep. But, Casey, you know it can happen and you know it must have happened just like that because Lauren's so straight she wouldn't make it up."

"Sure. 'Lightning' has to strike once in a while—but that doesn't mean that if you go out in Central Park and wait for ten years it's gonna strike you. Anyway, what's this I hear about you and Miss Texarkana? Faith's out with her buying her some clothes—what's up?"

"More 'lightning.' "

The two girls exchanged a smile of anticipation and cautious excitement, like two miners panning for gold who just may have hit pay dirt. Modeling was a business built on an occasional flash of lightning and many long hours of sheer hard work, but without the lightning, the sudden arrival on the scene of a new and singular type of beauty, it wouldn't be the business that had grown more and more fascinating over the last few decades, until it rivaled moviemaking in its appeal to the public.

Like everyone else who works in a field that trafficks in the flimflam business of glamour, they knew the truths behind that elusive illusion; the vital importance of being equal to the daily grind; the incredible persistence and the unending discipline, to say nothing of the absolutely crucial need to be in the right place at the right time. And yet they knew that glamour *did* exist and that certain faces had it, a quality no more to be explained than charm could be explained. They understood that some faces inspired *emotion*, and they were trained to recognize those faces amid a sea of girls who were just plain beautiful. The difference was so small that in most cases it had to be a subjective decision.

Every year thousands and thousands of girls were seen by the Lunel Agency; those who wrote and enclosed photographs; those who won the dozens of regional modeling competitions that were held all over the world; and those who came in person to the agency. And out of all of them they selected no more than thirty to represent. Why did they take on those particular thirty? Neither Maggy nor Fauve nor Casey could have written it out in words or made a diagram. All the basic rules were well known, all other physical requirements for a model could be met by a large number of the hopeful girls they turned down. They saw so many applicants that only someone who was blatantly special caused them to take a second look. Casey called it "something *behind* the eyes" and Fauve called it a sense of "heightened reality" but they both meant the same thing—lightning.

"First on my agenda," said Casey, "there's the case of Miss Day O'Daniel who called me again this morning. She's ready to jump ship and come over here but she wants her own booker."

"How negotiable is that?" Fauve asked briskly.

"It's her own booker or no go."

Day O'Daniel was one of the top half-dozen girls at another agency. Recently she'd become restless in the fretful ways models occasionally did for reasons no one could truly fathom, and had let it be known that she'd consider changing to Lunel. Her contract, like all contracts in 1974, required only thirty days' notice by either party for termination, and Fauve and Casey were eager to represent the exquisitely fine-boned brunette whose range was one of the greatest in the business. Range, the ability to inhabit a Galanos dress with careless authority and yet to look unthreateningly lovely in a mass-market magazine ad, was one of the qualities necessary before any girl who was already a top model could aspire to superstar status—and Day had it. However, Lunel had a policy, laid down by Maggy, of not permitting any model her own booker.

"Day said that she wouldn't feel she'd really come into her own until she had her own booker, she said that she wanted someone with whom she could feel totally secure and comfortable, someone who would know all her needs, someone who would give her the feeling that she was being taken care of. I quote."

"Maybe she should go home to mother," Fauve said broodingly. "It's such a mistaken and naïve idea that having your own booker is the only way to prove that you've made it. Doesn't she realize that if I give her her own booker every other booker in the agency will mentally click her off and forget about her? What if her booker is out to lunch? What if her booker's sick for the week or gets another job—Day would never be properly protected. It's a crazy way to run a career. I hope you told her."

"Gee, no, Fauve. I thought I'd let you do that yourself because you do it so well."

"Droll. I see you're feeling better. It's frightening how nice you can be when you're really sick. I'm always reassured when you revert to your truly rotten self. So our Big Board isn't enough for Day O'Daniel?"

Fauve's eyes wandered to the activity she could oversee through the half-glassed wall of her office. She had a view into all three booking areas: the smallish Test Board room, where all new girls, whose careers were just starting, were handled by four bookers; the huge Center Board room, where fourteen bookers arranged the schedules for the majority of the Lunel models, and the legendary Big Board room, in which three top bookers handled calls for a mere twenty girls, the stars of the agency. "Did she actually come right out and insist that it wouldn't be enough to be on the Big Board?" Fauve persisted.

"I thought I'd let you find that out."

"I think I'll let Magali ask her," Fauve said.

"She's gone to the country for the weekend, remember, and Ms. O'Daniel wants to get an answer today. Day left her home number—you can call her tonight."

"Okay, next." Once again Fauve was reminded that from Thursday evening till sometime late on Monday, Maggy now spent her time in the country place she and Darcy had bought outside of Bedford Village. It was still difficult to realize that Maggy had actually brought herself to leave her agency entirely in Fauve's hands for two out of five days a week. But Darcy had trained his various editors to claim only three days of his time each week, finding in the process that they became more efficient and self-reliant. He had always maintained that work contracted to fit comfortably into the least amount of time you were willing to devote to it, and when he and Maggy married he decided to fulfill his dream of spending long weekends in the country.

"Next," said Casey, "Miss Nebula, Miss Cosmos, Miss Super Nova, Miss Milky Way or whatever it was she won, declines to go through the Program. She says she doesn't need it—she's been through enough training for a lifetime. No, do not *dare* to ask me. I've already told her that everybody goes through the Program, without exception, unless she's a top model who comes over to us from another agency, and even then we make the decision on an individual basis, but she's Swedish, highly outer-galactic, and very stubborn."

The Lunel Agency conducted an evaluation, called the Program, of all new models they accepted, in which Maggy, Fauve, Casey and three of the most experienced bookers participated. The agency paid to send the girls to a photographer for an exhaustive series of pictures expressly designed to show how she worked in front of the camera in her own clothes and makeup. Every detail about her was then analyzed and the six of them decided how best to polish their new model. They asked each other if she needed help with her posture; whether her hair was the perfect length, style and color; what more must she learn to do with makeup to widen her range; whether she needed to have extra coaching on her expressions to gain flexibility and camera presence; or dance classes for ease of movement and poise. If she had come to them from a modeling school they asked, what did she have to unlearn?

"There's never been a Swede as stubborn as I am," Fauve remarked. "Unless she has her own flying saucer, Miss Sweden will go through the Program even if Revlon calls today and wants to sign her to an exclusive contract for the rest of her life. We made one mistake with Jane, when we decided she didn't need the Program—and that taught me a lesson I'll never forget."

"These top beauty contest winners do put in a lot of time before they make it," Casey said, in an attempt to be fair.

"None of which has anything to do with modeling."

"As I well know."

"I'll see Miss Truly Magnificent—I think it *was* the Universe, Casey, when I have a minute. Meanwhile, let's get Loulou in here." Fauve picked up the phone intercom and dialed the Big Board room and asked Loulou, the booker with the most seniority in the agency, to come into her office.

A half-minute later Loulou strolled in, flopping gratefully down into a chair. She was thirty, a plump, fair, pleasant-looking woman whose expression invariably combined deep worry and absolute optimism, so that she looked as if she were going down in the *Titanic* with firm faith in the existence of Paradise. Loulou, like a great racehorse trainer or a wise ballet mistress, had developed to an art that special equilibrium that enabled her to deal with a different race from herself. The model, highly strung, highly priced, highly vulnerable, a natural aristocracy, separated by the class system of beauty from ever being quite like other women.

"Hi, guys," she said. "Well, let's see. Betty won't pierce her ears for the diamond studs for the De Beers ad. She says she's not a coward, but she can't stand needles; Hillary booked out for the entire month of October. She's going to the Himalayas to meditate whatever with that guru of hers, whoever. *Glamour* gave me their budget for the Tangiers trip and it will only cover two and a half girls and they need three so I said I'd ask the girls if they'd take less to see the Casbah. That new Canadian girl keeps telling me she only wants to do catalog when I know she's ready for editorial . . . somebody has to talk to her about her image problem. Nine phones are out as usual but Pete, our semipermanent phone repair man, is on vacation and since nobody else really understands our setup, we're just lucky it's Friday. One of you is going to have to resign Cindy because I haven't had a request for her for two weeks and you know that means it's over for her here but, what the hell, she's twenty-six and she knows this has been coming for a year or more so maybe it'll be a relief. There's a sale in the Anne Klein showroom; Halston is giving a party and Linda didn't get an invitation—I can't be responsible for what she might do—keep her away from razor blades. I hocked and hocked Fabergé to use Jessica and now they're in love with her, they don't want anybody else, they need her tomorrow, but she's in Mexico; Dawn's father is in from Syracuse and she picked this weekend to skip town with her guy, what'll I tell old Dads? Doyle Dane suddenly called to remind me that Patsy has to drive a stick shift in that Alfa Romeo ad—she's halfway to the location and as far as I know she doesn't drive period; one of the booker trainees forgot to give Lani her wake-up call this morning so she overslept and kept ten people waiting for an hour and they want to charge her for it; Patsy just called and asked us to make dentist, doctor, facial and waxing appointments for her but we don't even know *what* she wants waxed . . . anyway, if you guys have nothing else to do but sit around and yak and complain that's grand, but I've a lot of work to do so if you'll just excuse me—oh, did you want to see me? What's up?"

"It's gracious of you to ask," Fauve said.

"Kind of you to make time for us," Casey muttered.

"Day O'Daniel will be joining our happy group," Fauve announced.

"Why not?" Loulou never showed surprise. Just as her expression never changed, her composure couldn't be shaken. If Fauve had decided to get rid of every single one of the twenty models on the Big Board, Loulou would have shrugged. Her philosophy was that every three months a new generation of models arrived from the vast reaches of that mysterious, unimportant world outside of Manhattan and her job was simply to put them to work as profitably as possible. The models on Lunel's Big Board earned seven hundred and fifty dollars a day, although a few among them had the notion that they were worth more, as much as a thousand dollars daily. No one, not Maggy, not Eileen Ford, not Fauve, and certainly not Loulou, had any idea that within a half-dozen years all the top girls at all the agencies would be getting three thousand dollars for a day's work.

Loulou had trained both Fauve and Casey and they knew that while Loulou had her favorite models, as did every booker, the agency was always more important to her than any individual girl.

"I'll set up a chart for her," Loulou sighed, stretching and yawning. "My *head*," she groaned.

"Loulou, don't you wonder why she's coming here?" Casey demanded.

"I *know* why. I've just won five bucks on it. Wish I'd bet more. Oh, God, why do I drink? Nothing's enough fun to feel like this for. Listen, guys, I have to get back to the board. It may only be a lousy job for you but it's life and death out there for me." She shut the door behind her as she left.

"One day," said Casey morosely, "I'm gonna surprise her."

"No, you're not."

"No, I'm not," Casey agreed. "*Bookers.*"

Surely, thought Nadine Mistral Dalmas, the bills from Arene must be wrong. How could she possibly have spent twelve thousand francs on flowers in the last few months? Arene was the most expensive florist in Paris and it was the most prestigious. It showed a lack of intelligence, in Nadine's opinion, to send a hostess flowers from any other shop, for no matter how much you spent elsewhere, they didn't make quite the same impression. Sending flowers, the right flowers, in the right way, from the right place, was one of the carefully calculated nuances Nadine had perfected in the course of seven years of being Madame Phillipe Dalmas.

They had been called the most envied couple in Paris, Nadine reminded herself as she sat at the desk in her modern salon and confronted the pile of bills with which she had finally brought herself to deal. Most of them were three or four months old, and many of them were from people who didn't care whether she was the daughter of the Comte de Paris, the legitimate Pretender to the throne of France, or the daughter of Julien Mistral, whose estate would make her so immensely rich when he died. *When* he died. Her father, damn him to hell, showed every sign of living to a hundred, and Parisian tradesmen had nothing in common with British tradesmen of a century before who would keep an heir supplied with money on the basis of his expectations.

Nadine inspected the Arene bill carefully. Two miniature cymbidium orchid plants planted in porcelain cachepots for the Princess Édouard de Lobkowicz. How could they have charged so much when she had provided the cachepots herself? She had been rather proud of that particular offering for she had invented the notion of buying the most charming of cachepots at Le Grenier de la Marquise, a fascinating old gift shop, on the rue de Sévigné, and taking them to Arene to be planted. Of course it did make the flowers far more expensive but how could anyone with the slightest claim to taste just send a banal bouquet to thank a lady who had been born Princess Françoise de Bourbon-Parme? A lady who had included Nadine and Phillipe with the Duke and Duchess d'Uzès and the Duke and Duchess of Torlonia at a dinner for twelve, served by four butlers on Meissen plates, a dinner at which the menu card before each plate had borne the crown of the Holy Roman Empire? She didn't send flowers each time they accepted the Lobkowiczes' hospitality, but when she did, they had to be extraordinary.

Lilies of the valley to the Vicomtesse de Ribes, sent only after invitations to two intimate dinners followed by film screenings and one seated, black-tie dinner party for forty. Nadine had hesitated as long as she could before settling on the flowers to send to the most elegant woman in Paris. Finally she had realized that only the simplest blooms would do. Of course, in that case it had been self-evident that there must be four dozen bunches . . . any less a gesture would have been skimpy, attracting no attention. Flowers to Helene Rochas, flowers to São Schlumberger, flowers to the Princess Ghislaine de Polignac . . . she put the Arene bill aside. She had no doubt that it was as exact as it was necessary, one of the obligations she accepted in order to keep her place in the inner circle of Paris society.

While it might seem to outsiders that the society of Paris was loosely organized, for it included certain dressmakers and a few writers and one or two decorators and even the Borys, who owned the huge grocery chain Fauchon, Nadine was keenly aware, with the delicate attunement to every vibration of a tightrope walker working without a net, that in fact it was a world in which, were it not for her ceaseless vigilance, even "the most envied couple in Paris" could quickly disappear from sight.

Discrimination had always been an art in French society where standing is so finely calibrated that even among dukes, three—Brissac, Uzès and Luynes—are more ducal than others. It is a society still based on titles. It is a tiny section of Parisians, but they were the only people on earth who mattered at all to Nadine. A few outrageously rich foreigners were always permitted entry since they didn't count—how could they when they weren't French? They were permitted to spend money on entertainment to buy their way into a purely temporary place in society, a place that depended entirely on the extravagant and tasteful quality of their largesse. A well-mannered, attractive extra man with highly placed mistresses, as Phillipe had been, before his marriage, was often admitted, as were certain foreign diplomats for the length of the time they kept their posts, as well as a tiny handful of powerful politicians.

But the great hostesses never invited people simply because they had asked them before. Each invitation, no matter how big the party, was considered, scrutinized, weighed, measured and then carefully reconsidered. Why, Nadine could imagine a hostess asking herself, do I ask the Dalmases to my table? Are they still good value? He adds nothing by way of status, for he's been around forever, and has no historic name, no accomplishment, and now, not even the virtue of being unattached. But she is closer to Jean François Albin than anyone else . . . his last collection was a marvel . . . and they're both still terribly decorative . . . yes, I'll ask them again this time. She is, after all, Mistral's daughter.

Three years ago Nadine had asked herself how long would the period of tolerance continue to be extended for the Dalmases, that amusingly poor married couple? Another year perhaps . . . or less? It was then that she had realized that they could no longer permit themselves to seem impoverished, how ever temporarily, without slipping socially. If she had not made the decision that they *must* entertain, they would soon be tainted with the deadly stamp of people who only accepted hospitality, and never extended it.

This would have been followed by gradual social oblivion, until they would have found themselves as far outside of authentic society as those members of Café Society who buy tickets to every big charity ball and overtip the headwaiter at the Relais Plaza to get a table near the bar, all to bask in the delusion that they have established themselves in Paris, when actually they have simply been permitted to fill up a little unused space.

What do they *do?* those people who aren't invited to the right parties, Nadine wondered, her entire body stiffened with scorn and contempt. How could they endure their lives when they had to live outside the only world that mattered? Didn't they know how low they were, how little they counted, how abject their position? Didn't they realize that they inhabited a wasteland as empty and as void of meaning as outer space? As she watched them, the outsiders, ordering splendid gowns at Albin's, she was repeatedly struck by the incomprehensible fact that these clothes were being bought to be worn *nowhere.* The dinners they were asked to were beneath contempt, their gala restaurant evenings were despicable. They existed only to make Albin rich. She might even find them pathetic if they weren't so abhorrent to her, if their inferiority did not make them, as far as she was concerned, less than human.

Nadine bent over the bill from Lenotre, the outstanding caterer of Paris. Since she and Phillipe had no staff except for a cleaning woman, Lenotre's bill was the largest she had to pay. Every three months they gave a "cocktail," astutely planned to occur just before an important first night or a big ball, so that people were content to serve themselves from a superb buffet of hors d'oeuvres, knowing that they would eat again later in the evening. As Nadine wrote the enormous check she thought that nothing would be more stupid than to employ a second-rate caterer. Better a Lenotre cocktail than a seated dinner of less quality, she assured herself, yet remembering with a pang of envy so pure that it felt like a cold wind, the recent wedding anniversary celebration they had been invited to by the Duchess de La Rochefoucauld. Jeanne-Marie had asked a hundred and forty people for a seated dinner and another two hundred were invited to come and dance afterward. The only way you could tell that the hostess was half-American was in her witty choice of food: Virginia ham and potato salad among all the other delicacies—ah, to be so enormously, unimaginably secure that you could serve such food to King Umberto of Italy and Prince Charles of Luxembourg, Nadine thought, still rigid with envy. Jeanne-Marie was the luckiest woman—did she know how lucky she was? Did she appreciate it?

Nadine pulled herself away from her reverie, reminding herself that she was far more exacting, more careful, more selective in her choice of guests than the busy Duchess who gave so many parties that she received people Nadine would never ask to her home. No, Nadine Dalmas's little cocktails had become famous for their relentless exclusion of anyone not absolutely of the first quality.

Frequently she and Phillipe accepted invitations from people whose social rank was ever so slightly dubious, simply so that she could fail to invite them. They were always so ridiculously hurt, expecting no doubt that a cocktail had to become a catch-all for all sorts of people, believing that reciprocity was due them. There was no question that her formula was right. Four cocktails a year for only the best people gave a hostess an infinitely greater allure than if she gave dozens of sumptuous but less discriminating dinners. And it was so very much cheaper.

Who would dream that they were not rich? The best florist, the best caterer, the best clubs short of the Jockey—Phillipe's family, though good, did not entitle him to belong to the Jockey. Here were the bills from the Polo Club and the Golf de St. Cloud. Phillipe had belonged to them as a bachelor, one of his few expenses in that period of his life, and to have dropped them was unthinkable. His bill for rented polo ponies in the last two months, during which he played on the Aga Khan's team, was over four thousand francs, she noted, but it was acceptable to rent your ponies if you played well and at least it wasn't as expensive as his heavy gambling losses during the winter when the Polo was filled with gin-rummy players.

Nadine wrote out the checks as quickly as she could to finish the chore, and as she wrote, she meditated on the things for which they didn't have to pay. These bills, no matter how high, represented only a tiny percentage of the scale on which they lived. Nadine's enormous wardrobe constantly renewed, was made entirely by the House of Jean François Albin; the apartment cost them nothing, they traveled in their friends' private jets, skied from their chalets in Haute Savoie or St. Moritz, sailed on their yachts in the Aegean, spent weeks in the private palaces of St.-Jean-Cap-Ferrat, Porto-Cervo and Bavaria. She had charge accounts at the Relais Plaza and Maxim's for lunches, again paid by the House of Albin; and, of course, they dined out every night during the season in Paris.

Nadine spent little cash and only where it would be noticed. At Édouard and Frédéric, the most in-vogue of the hairdressers of Paris, where she went on an almost daily basis, she tipped lavishly. The man who kept her blond, the boy who shampooed her hair, the man who blew it dry, the woman who did her nails and toenails—they would always be the first to gossip. If a princess or a Greek shipowner's wife could afford to be stingy, plain Madame Dalmas could not.

Plain Madame Dalmas. Nadine left her desk and prowled around her salon. Why, she thought, and wondered why she even bothered to ask herself the bitter question once again, *why* had she ever married a poor man? Why hadn't her mother prevented her? Why had she been allowed to commit the folly of a lifetime? Dazzled as she had been, surely someone could have, *should* have stopped her. And not just a poor man but an ineffectual ass as well who had put together only a few of his nebulous deals in the seven years of their marriage?

She must have loved him once, incredible as that now seemed to her. But what else could explain how she had spent the money her mother had left her when she died? Kate had died of cancer four years earlier, leaving far more money than she had told Nadine to expect. Apparently she had owned some paintings that she'd been able to sell at a vast profit. In any case, the money was gone now. Nadine had become a partner in Phillipe's dream, his stupid determination to have a home in the country. Half of her inheritance had been spent on buying a château in Normandy. Since then he had refused to give it up although they had never had the means to restore it properly, and make it livable. He'd yearned for a home of his own far too long, he insisted, and anyway, soon they'd have all the money in the world.

Love for Phillipe. It must have existed or why had she allowed him to invest the rest of her mother's legacy? There had been enough to buy a partnership in a new nightclub that was intended to rival Castel's, with its membership of three thousand. Jean Castel turned away hundreds of customers each night, so obviously another *boîte* was necessary.

Together, as Phillipe and his other partner believed, they knew everybody who mattered in that rarefied circle of the children of the night, those famous bored people, so bored that even their fame bored them, permanently displaced people who began at eleven each evening to look for a substitute for sleep. What they had failed to realize was that those people neither wanted, needed nor welcomed any place to go other than their own, dear, familiar Castel's on the rue Princesse. After a year Phillipe had had to abandon the horribly expensive undertaking at a total loss.

Yes, she must have loved him or else she was as criminally lacking in judgment as he had been. After the failure of the nightclub, Phillipe acted as if it had been her fault. He grew petulant and sulky with disappointment, punishing Nadine for not being able to provide him with fresh funds. He became too lazy to charm her any longer.

Was there any sourness to compare to that of living with a man who had nothing but charm when he let his charm drop away as if he were a fat woman releasing herself from a tight corset? Yet, should the phone ring, he sprang into charm even as he answered it. She could watch him at a party as dispassionately as if he were behind glass, observe how he was responded to by men and women both, this man who asked irresistible questions, who bestowed the most imaginative flattery, who listened with art and when he spoke of himself, did so modestly and only with humor. A coat of charm encased him like a matador's suit of tights. Every one of his tricks was nauseatingly familiar to her. Even his good looks were repellent. She cared so little about him that she was indifferent to his affairs. Fortunately he had the good taste to confine them to women of riches and power who were unfailingly hospitable. It was the only thing he did with any cleverness.

Nadine stacked the envelopes in which she had put the checks and carried them into her bedroom. She would take them to Albin's to be sent off on Monday. Why buy stamps when her secretary would put them in the mail? She opened the three sets of doors on one wall of her bedroom and appraised her wardrobe. A million francs' worth of clothes, shoes, hats, furs, lingerie; every single item but the lingerie made to measure, all at a cost to her of only dry cleaning and her pride.

It had been years since she realized she hated Jean François Albin. She didn't know when it had started, the recognition that she was no more than a glorified, dressed-up nursemaid to a whining, weak, utterly self-centered, frequently cruel little boy who had one single talent that the world accepted as enormously valuable. His best friend, his muse!

What a farce it was, a farce they both still played out; Nadine, because she could not afford to lose the free clothes and the prestige the association gave her; Albin, because once his brief enchantment with her had run its usual hectic and always disillusioning course, found that chic, superior Nadine Mistral had become useful to him. He now required her to take his neurasthenic Afghans to the vet, fire and hire his domestics, write his thank-you notes, lunch with the most tedious and wealthy of his customers, get rid of any overnight lovers who gave themselves pretensions, buy his hashish, and be at his service twenty-four hours a day.

Tonight Nadine would have to push and wheedle him through his own birthday party to which he insisted he wouldn't go after she had spent weeks planning it. Too many lobsters, he had complained, too many duchesses. Why had she not arranged something amusing, a picnic, for example, with sauerkraut and pickled pig's feet and lots of cheap red wine? Why had she been so conventional, so bourgeois? Nadine had laughed and told him to remember that red wine made him sick, but she was jagged with outrage. He was intolerable, she loathed the very sound of his voice, yet her job with Albin represented the only regular source of income that the enviable Dalmases possessed. It was only enough to meet a few of their needs, not quite enough to cover the florist's bill she had just paid. Since the time the nightclub venture had failed they had lived almost entirely on money Nadine borrowed from Étienne Delage, Mistral's dealer. She hated going to him because each time she did she felt more in his power, but who else would lend her money against the day her father died?

Nadine flung herself down on her bed and lost herself in her eternally comforting daydream. He would die. She would inherit. The estate must be worth . . . so much . . . so much! She couldn't imagine how much. Of course she couldn't sell so quickly that she depressed the market but she would realize at least many millions of francs at once, enough to pay all her bills, enough to provide her with every franc she could spend. She would leave Albin at the worst possible moment, crippling him emotionally right before a collection when he was most vulnerable. She would throw Phillipe out in a manner so humiliating that he could never discuss it with any of his friends. She would buy a vast private house on the Left Bank—on the rue de Lille perhaps—and have it decorated by Didier Aaron with classical refinement that owed nothing, absolutely nothing to mere fashion. And she would begin her life. Nadine Mistral the great heiress would take her *own* rightful place in the heart of the inner circle of Parisian society.

But until that day she would do absolutely nothing to disturb the status quo. She could not possibly get divorced as long as her social position depended on the charm and friendships of her husband and the magic of her employer's name. She still needed to be Madame Phillipe Dalmas, the best friend of Jean François Albin—no amount of orchids in cachepots could keep her on the invitation lists if she were without those protections. She could triumph as a single woman only as a rich single woman. She would wait. *Christ, how much longer could that old man live?*

29

Fauve stretched. Oh, it felt so good. Stretching, she thought sleepily, was right up there with eating and listening to music and kissing. Thank God nobody was too poor to stretch. She yawned. A great yawn was almost as good as a great stretch. She yawned and stretched at the same time. No, they lost something in combination. With so many agreeable sensations going she couldn't concentrate properly.

She rolled over in bed and reached for Ben to tell him about it but he wasn't there. She opened her eyes and looked around the dark bedroom, an unfamiliar place since this was the first time she had awakened in his apartment. Was it still night? Where could he have gone to? She waited awhile, almost falling asleep again, but when he didn't appear she slid out of bed, groped her way toward the windows and opened the curtains.

The thin, grudging sunlight of a March morning in New York made her flinch. Small clouds, high above the city, looked crunchy and little fingers of cold air seeped in from the edges of the windowpanes. She dove back into bed and considered her alternatives. She could call out and he'd come running from wherever he was. She could go back to sleep or she could try to find something to wear, since she was naked, and go brush her teeth. Teeth first, she decided, picking the bedspread off the floor and draping herself in it, since there didn't seem to be any of her clothes in the room.

In the bathroom she found a note impaled on a tube of toothpaste.

Darling,

I've just gone out to buy some stuff for breakfast. I'll be back as soon as I can. I love you.

Ben

Now that is thoughtful, she told herself, as she looked around for a toothbrush. A really magnificent breakfast—a regal, voluptuous, erotic breakfast—was the only way to start Sunday morning in New York. More important, it proved that he hadn't expected her to be here this morning or he would have stocked his fridge the day before. As she failed to discover any toothbrush other than Ben Litchfield's, she noted that he obviously didn't take the presence of a lady for granted or he would have had a spare. Well, a soggy and secondhand toothbrush was better than nothing. She took a quick shower, dried herself on one of his slightly damp towels and put on the clean but rather threadbare terry robe he'd left hanging on the hook of the bathroom door. Definitely a bachelor establishment.

Fauve padded out into the living room and knew immediately that there was no one in the kitchen making something marvelous. The room was not just empty, it had such a glacial impersonality that she was sure the decorator who had decorated Ben's office had done the apartment too. It had the same Barcelona chairs—did anyone ever have more than that predictable pair or was there a law against it?—

and identical glass and chrome coffee tables. The rug, like the chairs, was obviously expensive and carefully coordinated with the tweedy draperies, but the unlovable plants looked as if they'd been chosen for their ability to survive under neglect, and the lithographs on the walls betrayed no indication of personal taste.

The only sign of humanity in Ben's living room were the copies of the Sunday *New York Times* and *Sunday News* that he had stopped to pick up at the stand at Fifty-eighth and Madison last night before they came back. She looked at the eviscerated papers lying all over the coffee table and rejected the idea of picking them up. Somehow they didn't fit into her cheerful mood. Her body felt tender all over and well used, as indeed it had been. How much *good* news could she reasonably expect to find in the *Times* anyway? Certainly nothing that was fit to print, she reflected, and tried to curl up on the unsensuous couch.

Why did bachelors invariably own furniture that was stuffed with foam rubber? Should she go into the kitchen, wherever it was, and hunt around for a teabag? No, she'd wait for Ben to come back. After last night, a lonely cup of tea seemed an unworthy way to begin this lovely, lazy Sunday . . . this necessarily brief Sunday as he knew, since she had to leave for Rome later in the afternoon with the five girls Valentino had chosen to show his clothes on the runway at the opening of his spring collection. They'd all be gone for two weeks, on to Milan and Paris after Rome.

Without success, Fauve attempted to snuggle into a bouncy pile of foam rubber cushions. Benjamin Franklin Litchfield, where are you? Last night had been the first time she'd spent the entire night with him, or with anybody for that matter, Fauve thought, considering the brief list of her lovers. She knew it was unfashionable but there had only been two besides Ben.

Fauve supposed, when she had time to think about it, which was seldom, that the way she had lived was odd for the liberated 1970s. Although she worked long and hard and late at her job and had established her financial independence in a way that many other girls of her age had not, she'd been content to live at home until two years ago. She'd been pursued by many men, but, for at least three years after her last visit to Provence, Fauve had been too haunted by the memory of Eric Avigdor to respond to anyone else.

Finally there had come a time when mere letters hadn't been able to sustain that love. Eric had had to do two obligatory years of military service after he graduated from the Beaux-Arts, and that had stood in the way of any opportunity for him to visit her in the United States. She had taken brief vacations but they'd never come at a period when he was free.

After a while Fauve began to sense that both of them were being unrealistic about their intention to meet again. As the years went by those brief weeks together, when she was sixteen, became more fragmented as they receded further and further into memory. Certain moments were fixed, so vivid and clear in memory that she could scarcely bear to examine them, but the connective tissue between those moments faded. She couldn't call back the whole fabric of an entire day with Eric, only bits and pieces.

Had they not been equal to their feelings, she had asked herself sadly, or had they simply misunderstood the strength of those feelings? Surely he too must have gone through the same dimming of the past?

Fauve immersed herself in the world of modeling, and eventually it became increasingly difficult to write to Eric. She would reread her letters and ask herself how he could possibly be interested in the tradition-breaking action of high-fashion Lauren Hutton agreeing to pose for Avedon in nothing more than a black lace bra, a pair of black bikini underpants and a prankish hat? How could it matter to him that the major decision of her week had been to promote one girl from the Central Board to the Big Board? There was no way to adequately explain to him that it was important, because once a model made this crucial career move she couldn't go backward and if the move proved to be unsuccessful or premature, her career would be largely destroyed.

The details that filled her days, the preoccupations that seemed so crucial, because they concerned people she liked and because they had true business and personal repercussions, dwindled down to such triviality when she put them down on paper that she tore up five letters for each one that she finally sent.

If it hadn't been for the surprise of Magali's marriage, Fauve guessed, she'd probably still be living at home, happily joining Magali and Darcy for dinner several times a week. She'd been so comfortable and happy there that nothing could have pushed her out of the apartment except her determination to give them a chance to be alone together. Magali had protested that it was ridiculous to treat them like honeymooners, but Fauve had known her instinct and timing were right.

She'd found a cozy little duplex for herself in a narrow, old-fashioned brownstone in the East Seventies, near Third Avenue, and there, just before she turned twenty, she'd had her first love affair. And her second. Neither of them had been a particularly fulfilling experience, Fauve admitted to herself. Something, some essential element, had been missing, and if she had to put a name on it, damn it, there was only one word she could think of—romance.

Was she being absurdly nostalgic, was she looking for something that could only happen once in a lifetime? The physical experiences had been satisfactory, the men had both been intelligent and amusing, but that other dimension, that blithe thread of melody, that sense of poetry underlining the most ordinary undertaking, that transformation of the world, that she had once known sitting in a little car on a road near Félice surrounded by sheep, no, it hadn't happened.

Fauve had never let either of her two lovers spend the whole night with her although there was no question that her bed was big enough for two, that four-poster with billowing draperies of rosebud-sprigged gauze, so long that they trailed on the flowered, Victorian rug. It was just that she couldn't imagine *waking up* with either of them—waking up with someone seemed more intimate than making love in some ways.

Last night she had thought, as she fell asleep, that waking up with Ben Litchfield might be a revelation. Romance had seemed to be in the air, not quite close enough to capture, but definitely lurking, waiting to happen. He had tried to speak of marriage but she hadn't let him—it was the wrong time. She had felt as if she were listening to an orchestra tune up, an uncoordinated assortment of sounds that promised the arrival of music.

Right now, Fauve thought, conscious that her feet were freezing, she'd settle for food and let romance go wherever it went when it wasn't operating. Country farm sausage—the small, spicy kind, all brown and crisp—with pancakes, dripping with maple syrup, for instance. Perhaps that was what Ben was bringing back? Or waffles with melted butter and strawberry jam? Maybe he'd gone out for a brioche and croissants and thin slices of sugar-cured Virginia ham or even a Pepperidge Farm coffee cake, ready to heat, the kind with the *lovely*, sticky white icing and raisins? Or had he simply gotten stuck waiting on line to buy bagels? Pumpernickel bagels with sweet butter and slices of sturgeon, juicy white sturgeon from the Great Lakes? Oh, Lord, she wasn't asking for much—she didn't expect eggs Benedict with extra Hollandaise sauce; she wasn't insisting on a tall, frosty glass of freshly squeezed orange juice without the pulp; she only needed breakfast, not brunch, for God's sake, brunch with tender crêpes stuffed with chicken and covered with mushroom sauce or even . . . even oyster stew.

Fauve tucked her legs under her in the lotus position for warmth and in the hope that it might lead to meditation and that meditation would stop her from thinking about food. No matter what, she didn't intend to go poking about in the kitchen and spoil his surprise.

She had heard a great deal about Ben Litchfield before she started to go out with him, for his staff was full of wistful editors who yearned for him without success. She had observed him closely for signs that he took women for granted but found no sign of it in his courtship. He had a prickly mind, quirky and questioning and he understood her shop talk and her late hours. She liked his edges. He had an insistent energy and she felt at ease with his preoccupations, accustomed as she had become to the world of publishing through Darcy. Ben Litchfield had pursued her steadily and single-mindedly for a long time before she finally allowed him to make love to her several months ago. He was a most . . . comforting . . . lover, Fauve thought, searching for precisely the right word. She felt secure with him, safe and quiet and warm and . . . comfortable.

Fauve's stomach growled and she considered reading the newspapers after all . . . anything to pass the time without thinking about doughnuts, jelly doughnuts with powdered sugar on them, gingerbread doughnuts, whole-wheat doughnuts, chocolate-covered doughnuts—she didn't even *like* doughnuts, for the love of God. When on earth had Ben had time to go through the *Times* and the *News?* she wondered. Dimly she remembered half waking up in the middle of the night and seeing the light on in the bathroom and hearing the crackle of newsprint. Had he had an attack of insomnia and tried to read himself to sleep?

Ben Litchfield's key scraped in the door and he came in with his arms so laden that Fauve jumped up to relieve him of some of his burden.

"Two Kellogg's Snack-Paks, milk, eggs . . . *that's it?*" She wanted to whimper but pride prevented her.

"I didn't know if you preferred Corn Flakes or Rice Krispies," he said, "so I got plenty of both. There's butter in the kitchen, and some Wonder Bread." He kissed her on her nose, over a three-foot-high pile of newspapers.

"You've been gone for hours!"

"I thought you'd still be asleep . . . I had to go down to Hotaling's in Times Square and, wouldn't you just know it, the *Philadelphia Inquirer* was late this morning so naturally I had to wait," he said as he carefully put down the Sunday editions of the *Boston Globe*, the *Pittsburgh Press*, the *Washington Post*, the *Cleveland Plain Dealer*, the *Los Angeles Times*, *Newsday*, the *Houston Chronicle*, the *Atlanta Journal-Constitution*, and the *San Francisco Examiner & Chronicle*. "But on the other hand, I got lucky—look, a *Miami Herald*! You usually can't get one on Sunday . . . it almost makes up for not being able to get the *Chicago Trib*—that's never available till tomorrow. Give me another kiss."

"Isn't there any bacon?" Fauve asked carefully. "To go with the eggs?"

"Bacon crossed my mind, but I only have one frying pan so there's no way to cook bacon *and* eggs."

"Did you ever think of cooking the bacon first and then frying eggs in the bacon fat?" she asked in a hunger-inspired leap of her imagination.

"My clever darling—women know so many things. Let's try that some other time," he said absently as he started quickly going through the papers and putting certain sections to one side and flinging the rest on the floor.

"What are you looking for?" Fauve sputtered. "Has something terribly important happened?"

"Hmmm . . . no . . . nothing special . . . I have to read the Sunday magazine sections and the women's sections—Style, or View or Home or Leisure or whatever they call it . . ."

"You *have* to read them?"

"You'd be amazed at what fresh new ideas the out-of-town papers come up with on Sunday—they're very useful . . ." he muttered, searching feverishly through the *Cleveland Plain Dealer*. "Damn, *damn*, that bastard, he sold me a bummer! The magazine section isn't here! You can't trust those guys . . . it's a crime . . . well, what the hell, it's not the newsstand's fault . . . it's the people who bundle them up to get them on the plane on Saturday . . . oh, shit!"

"*Ben!*"

"Yes, darling?" He looked up.

"Let's go back to bed."

"*Now?*"

"Right now," she said, putting her arms around him and taking off his glasses.

"Before breakfast?"

"It's better on an empty stomach. Dangerous on a full one."

"Well . . ." he said, looking with an infinitude of regret and reluctance at his newspapers. "Well . . ."

"Or," Fauve suggested softly, "would you rather read your papers while I make breakfast—and then go back to bed?"

"What a marvelous idea! Oh, darling, I do love you."

"Ben, what's happened to my clothes?"

"Aren't you comfortable?"

"The bathrobe's too big and I don't have anything for my feet."

"I hung up everything in my closet while you were asleep . . . I hate to wake up in a messy room."

"Thank you," she said to him as he pounced on the View section of the *Los Angeles Times* with a junkie's avidity.

Five minutes later she let herself out of the apartment so quietly that Ben Litchfield didn't notice she was gone until it was too late. "Out to Lunch" read the message she had scribbled in lipstick on his bathroom mirror.

Maggy was sprawled on the floor of the big living room of the converted farmhouse, wearing brown tweed slacks and a toast-colored cashmere sweater. On the plaid rug was a long roll of graph paper, an array of colored crayons and the White Flower Farm catalog. Darcy, a book in his lap, sat looking into the flames of the fine fire he had built from the stack of wood next to the fireplace.

He sipped his martini and considered his happiness. Was there anything better than knowing that it was Sunday night and you didn't have to drive back into the city until late tomorrow? He and Maggy had gone for a long walk in the barely budding woods this afternoon, proving once again his theory that a martini never tasted better than after prolonged exposure to a large dose of oxygen and the brisk development of all the muscles. There was really no point in exercise if you didn't follow it with a drink.

"What are you doing, sweetheart?" he asked Maggy.

"I'm ordering some new plants for the day lily garden."

"But why the graph paper?"

"I don't just shove plants into the ground any old way, baby face. I measure my garden space and I work it out on paper, six squares to a foot, and I color in the outlines of the shapes of the patches of lilies so that they'll drift into each other naturally. Then I look in the catalog and pick out colors that harmonize with what I planted last year—and then I order them by mail. Actually I should have done this last month but I was too busy thinking out the new herbaceous English border."

"Oh, God, why did I *ever* say it?" he asked the whitewashed ceiling beams. "Why didn't I know better, why didn't anyone *warn* me?"

"What are you talking about?"

"The day I said you didn't know anything about gardening. I could curse myself. That was the day you fired the gardener, remember?"

"It was a turning point in my life, darling. You made me so angry that I decided to prove to you that anyone, even a city girl like me, could learn how to garden from books. It's no harder than cooking."

"But, Maggy, you're *obsessed!* I understand that theory about the wisdom of planting a three-dollar rosebush in a six-dollar hole but, my God, you made sixty-dollar holes all last summer! You ate up half the lawn with those holes. Each one took you a full day to dig and prepare."

"I only wanted to be sure that my bushes had all the room they needed in which to spread their roots, and all the nutriments at the bottom of the holes to help them grow for the next hundred years."

"But what about those nights you used to go out weeding and I had to hold the flashlight so you could see what you were doing? Do you call that normal?"

"When you only have weekends you have to take advantage of every minute," Maggy said serenely.

"And last fall when you spent six days mulching everything three inches deep with dried cow manure? You were in it up to your elbows!"

"When you put your garden to bed in the fall, cutie pie," Maggy said with a learned look, "you don't just wave goodbye . . . you *mulch!* I'll get my reward next month when things start to bloom. Gardening has taught me patience. You should be pleased."

"I'm enchanted. It's a whole new Maggy, the queen of the potting bench. I think you could carry double your own weight as long as it's wet dirt in a clay pot. But what I don't understand is why you're determined to go into the office tomorrow. So what if Fauve won't be there? It breaks up our weekend," he grumbled, suddenly remembering the flaw in the next day that he had forgotten.

"Darling, you don't have to drive back till evening and I'll be waiting for you then, but I don't like to leave the agency without anyone in charge."

"Casey can be in charge for one day, can't she? You're always telling me how reliable she is, and what good judgment she has."

"It's not the same thing. Fauve has the business in her blood. When she's not there, I should be," Maggy said.

"Always a Lunel at the helm? 'O Captain my Captain'? That sort of thing?"

"Lunel stands for something and I just can't let them all run around without some sort of final authority who's instantly available." Maggy was firm.

"You know best. Actually I never believed you'd be able to stick to your plan to spend these long weekends here . . . I shouldn't complain."

"No, you certainly shouldn't," Maggy said, thinking, as she turned back to her graph paper, of how quickly she had grown to hate these four-day weekends, one after another, all year long.

When Darcy had bought this house his plan for their life had seemed to promise the ideal combination of work and leisure. But after a few months she had realized that she wasn't built for four days of relaxed country living every week. Maggy took golf and tennis lessons and loathed every minute of them. She prepared far too elaborate meals for lunch and dinner, and she had begun to look hopefully under the beds for nonexistent dust when the challenge of gardening had come along and given her something that absorbed her energy.

If it hadn't been for gardening . . . she could almost understand how the Duke of Windsor, without his role of monarch to play, had been able to fill his years in creating a marvelous garden. But it was only a substitute for real work as far as she was concerned. It wasn't *enough*, even during growing weather and from late October till late March, while the garden slept, she was reduced to planning for the following spring. Maggy would have had to tell Darcy that the plan wasn't working, that it made her too unhappy to be idle, that she simply wasn't ready for this form of semiretirement, if it hadn't been for Fauve, and the need to prepare her to take complete charge whenever the business became hers.

The Lunel Agency had never stopped growing since its inconspicuous beginning in 1931. John Robert Powers had closed up shop in 1948 and even with the emergence of Eileen and Jerry Ford, now, in 1975, Lunel remained the biggest and most established agency in the world. But model agencies depend on the people who run them for their success, so Maggy forced herself to stay in the country on Fridays and Mondays as firmly as she forced herself to accept the decisions Fauve made on those days. She made herself give Fauve the freedom to run the business on her own, to make mistakes, to learn the hard way.

And the plan had worked. All too well, Maggy admitted to herself ruefully. You can't *half* abdicate, Maggy thought, realizing that this knowledge came too late. Fauve had earned the right to exercise power and if Maggy tried to nibble away at that power, tried to gather it back to herself, she would undermine the capable, self-reliant businesswoman Fauve had become.

At least tomorrow, with Fauve off to Europe, she had a reason to be at her desk on Monday—lovely Monday on which there might just be some sort of emergency resulting from the weekend activities of two hundred high-spirited girls, to say nothing of eighty healthy boys, Maggy thought with glee. Trouble. She was in the mood for trouble. Maybe, she told herself hopefully, there would be the sort of really nasty mess that everyone thought went on all the time in the model business but, in reality, rarely occurred. Or, if nothing happened on this particular Monday, during the next two weeks that Fauve would be away, something must surely go wrong. She'd take Loulou to lunch. They hadn't had a good juicy talk in weeks. But as usual, the first order of business was to smuggle the mail back without anyone noticing, Maggy thought, remembering the suitcase she had stashed away upstairs in her little sitting room, a suitcase jammed as full as possible with a random selection of the hundreds of pieces of mail that arrived every week, from hopeful would-be models.

At Lunel, as at the other agencies, this mail was routinely opened and examined by a booker-trainee or even by the receptionist, both of whom were perfectly well qualified to pick out any picture that should be referred to someone with more experience. Maggy managed to get her hands on some of these lowly communications, from which, in the history of the agency, only a few models had ever been found, and she brought them up to the country every Thursday night. Over the weekend, at odd times, when Darcy was busy elsewhere, she'd dart off to this treasure trove and, with a busy letter opener, she'd go through every last piece of mail. There was always that chance . . . always the possibility of . . . lightning . . . she thought as she cut open each and every envelope as eagerly as if it had been the most tempting of surprise packages. She hadn't discovered her last model yet. You never knew!

Fauve shepherded her five tall charges, as different from the hurrying Romans all around them as if they were a wandering band of wild gazelles, toward an empty table that she had miraculously spotted on the sidewalk terrace of the Pasticceria Rosati.

"Sit!" she commanded briskly, knowing from past experience that the successful capture of a table at Rosati's was like winning at musical chairs. Except for Fauve, who had visited Rome once, none of the group had ever been to Rome before. They all had the day free to get over jet lag before the models were due to start work and Fauve had chosen Rosati's for their prelunch drink because of its location on the Piazza del Popolo, that swooningly baroque ensemble of twin domed churches, the Bernini Fountain, the Rameses obelisk and the ceremonial gate of the Via Flaminia.

The piazza had been designed three hundred years earlier to impress the traveler as he first entered the Eternal City and it had succeeded so brilliantly that it almost seemed sacrilegious to sit and order a campari in a setting of such imperial pomp and ceremony. Yet that *was* Rome, the distillation of Rome, the unequaled theatricality of daily life in which laundry was hung out to dry on palaces designed by Michelangelo, a simple restaurant occupied the house in which Lucrezia Borgia was born, and children played tag in the gardens of the Villa Medici.

Nothing can surprise the citizens of Rome, nothing can impress them. They are a race that keeps itself aloof, reserved and private, notably taciturn toward tourists. They have had to share their city with pilgrims since the days of the Caesars. To Romans everyone else on the face of the earth is a mere provincial and they turn a deaf ear and a blind eye to the never lessening flood of visitors who surround them. There is only one exception, only one kind of stranger for whom the Roman will turn his head.

"Lordy," said Arkansas, "don't all these folks just look so friendly?"

Without surprise Fauve scanned the fascinated faces all around them, not even bothering to hide their interest. Never, in the history of modeling, had there been such a worldwide passion for American girls, tall, skinny, dashing girls with acres of hair in which the wind always seemed to be moving, with a strong yet innocent sensuality, brandishing excessive beauty and new-coined youth. The Old World couldn't seem to produce anything like these superb creatures with their laughing ease and their raging glamour who stormed Europe.

American photographic models now presented the new collection of fashion designers who, only a few years ago, would not have considered showing their clothes on anyone but the house models on whom they had been fitted, European girls who knew how to walk on a runway ten times more professionally than any American who normally worked in front of a camera. But now the business of haute couture was like a tiny, luxuriously kept pet poodle that drew behind it a great freight train of mass-produced products that were sold under the name of each designer. Dresses were still made by hand in Paris, in London and in Rome, but the few rich customers who bought them, no matter how young, were referred to as "dinosaurs" because they were members of a breed that had all but vanished from the earth.

Yet, fashion shows had never been so theatrical, nor so spectacular. Models were hired at great expense from every major model agency in New York and flown to Europe for the collections because the vast amount of publicity they generated was immediately reflected in sales of licensed goods in stores from Indiana to Oslo, from Tokyo to Hamburg.

The hectic fever, the mounting craze for American models, had spread to European fashion magazines and it had become routine for Maggy and Wilhelmina and Eileen Ford to send their most promising new models to live in Paris or Rome for three months at a time. Once there, the unknown girl would immediately be booked by the best photographers, all of whom were avid for the gloriously fresh American faces. She'd learn how to wear clothes that were more expensive and intricate than anything made in the United States; top-flight hairdressers and makeup artists would experiment with her looks until she knew the furthest limits of her potential; and she'd be able to build up her book with dozens of pictures from Italian *Bazaar* and French *Vogue* as well as from the many other fashion magazines published abroad. When this relatively raw, high school beauty queen came home, burnished, exotic, glossy and no longer wide-eyed, from the finishing school of Paris or Rome, she was more firmly launched in the business than if she'd spent two or three years of steady growth in New York.

If she came home.

Maggy and Fauve were well aware of the hazards of sending their models to Europe. Although most of them lived in private homes and all of them were booked by local agencies who kept in close contact with Lunel, there was a list without limit of things that could go wrong with young girls far from home. Someone from the Lunel Agency went to Europe every few months to make sure that all was well with them and, on this trip, Fauve was charged with looking in on all the Lunel models working in Europe as well as to make sure that Arkansas and the four other models who had been hired to do the shows for Valentino in Rome, for Armani and Versace in Milan, and Saint Laurent and Dior in Paris, kept to their demanding schedules.

"What did I tell you about Roman men?" she asked Arkansas, who was smiling shyly at the next table.

"Not to trust them worth a damn," Arkansas said, her smile widening.

"And who do you suppose are those men you are grinning at?"

"Well, Lord knows, they *might* be foreigners like us. They aren't wearing name tags, Fauve. You know why you're so suspicious? It's because you're a city person. Why, you're positively unfriendly. They look just perfectly fine to me."

"And you look just fine to them. Oh, dear God, is it going to be like this for two whole weeks? No, don't answer. It's going to get worse. This is only the beginning."

"But, Fauve," protested Angel, one of the latest crop from South Carolina, the state that mysteriously provided more high-fashion models than any other, "my mama told me that if a girl doesn't get her fanny pinched in Rome it's positively an insult. She said it's the custom of the country and I'll look like a hick if I get all uptight about it."

"The latest on Italian pickpockets is while that one pinches you the other grabs your wallet—so much for Roman admiration. Tell your mama that times have changed," Fauve said ominously.

"Are we supposed to spend the entire next two weeks working? What about dinner? We all need nourishment," remonstrated Ivy Columbo in her Boston accent. Intelligent Ivy had been accepted by Radcliffe and Lunel in the same week. Higher education never stood a chance.

"Look," said Fauve, "in Milan the men are different, more businesslike, slightly less dangerous. When we get to Milan you can go out to dinner if you still have the strength to leave the hotel after the day's work, which I doubt. But in Rome, stick with me. I promised to take you all to the best restaurants, didn't I?"

Fauve looked around at the circle of rebellious faces. A waiter approached bringing a bottle of wine.

"The gentlemen at the next table wish to offer the ladies a glass of wine," he said.

Fauve waved him away. "Thank the gentlemen but tell them the ladies' religion requires them to pay for their own drinks."

"Aw, shucks," Arkansas said.

"Meanie!" muttered Angel. "Spoilsport. Killjoy."

"It wouldn't hurt to be just a trifle more gracious," Ivy chimed in, shaking out her curly black hair in a manner calculated to attract every eye on the terrace. Even Bambi One and Bambi Two, who had said nothing until now, looked sadly at Fauve from their marvelous eyes.

"Listen, girls," Fauve said sternly, "this is the first morning of the first day of this trip and you're giving me trouble already. That's simply not fair, and I won't permit it. If I let anyone at all buy us a drink, it's going to be interpreted as an invitation to join us and then we'll have the trouble of getting rid of them, whoever they are. There's just no such thing as a *merely* friendly gesture from any man in Rome . . . not only can't you accept a drink but you can't return a smile, you can't even show that you've noticed them noticing you. Their whole lives are wrapped up in seducing women—Roman men are the most outrageous, untrustworthy Casanovas in the world—you wouldn't want to get involved with one under any circumstance. Do you all understand? Have I made myself plain? Not a word, not a look, not a smile . . ." she said, staring at them all earnestly as she spoke, for this was the first time that Maggy had felt she was mature enough to be entrusted alone with the taxing job of model-wrangler. She was in sole charge of this group and she didn't want them to have any doubts about her authority. Fauve was so absorbed in what she was saying that she didn't notice the man who was threading his way to a table on the other side of the terrace, a man who stopped, glanced at her, looked again and turned and began to move as swiftly as possible toward her.

" . . . not even a gesture of a little finger," she finished, glaring at her charges. As she spoke the last words the man reached her, unnoticed. He stood behind her for a moment, gazing down at her incredulously and then as all five models raised wondering eyes at him, bent down and kissed the top of her head. Fauve's mouth opened in outrage. She swatted at her hair and stood up furiously, prepared for battle.

"How . . . dare . . . *you!*" she squeaked as Eric Avigdor took her in his arms.

The girls burst into applause but Fauve didn't hear them.

30

"I've been timing her," said Ivy quietly, "and it's been a good five minutes since she's given us a single suspicious look." She sat, with the four other models, Arkansas, Angel, and Bambi One and Bambi Two, at a table in Dal Bolognese, a boisterous restaurant next to Rosati's. They were eating lunch at one table while Eric and Fauve sat together at another from which Fauve could see everything they did, although she was too far away to hear what they were saying.

"I'm so sick of pretending to maintain eye contact with you, Arkansas," Angel whined. "It's a good thing I can't see but halfway across this table without my glasses. Will somebody with good eyesight please tell me if that friend of Fauve's is as heavily into irresistible as I think he is?"

"My old high school teacher would say you're damning him with faint praise," Arkansas grumbled. "And why pick on me? Do your eye contact stuff with Bambi One or Bambi Two. It makes me downright nervous."

"It's easiest with you. You're the tallest shape I can make out," Angel explained. "I think Fauve is the meanest! It's all right for her to have lunch with a male person because he's an old friend, or so she says, and to prove that he's not one of those sinister Roman types he's got a French accent. So what? I say she's a big, fat fraud."

"If you weren't practically blind you'd know he's got to be an old friend," Bambi Two objected. "You should have seen the way he looked at her. He's a bit more than just an acquaintance if you ask me." She sighed longingly.

"Spare me!" Angel said, annoyed.

"Don't start to bicker, lovers," Ivy warned the four other girls. "We're doing brilliantly. She's forgotten about us. Don't slouch, don't turn around, don't get silly. Who's got the guidebook?"

"I have," said Bambi One, arching her long neck in a manner that had caused havoc since she was twelve.

"Well, open it and read out loud to us," Ivy said.

"But I'm eating," Bambi One protested. "And don't call me Bambi One anymore. I've just decided to change my name. My poor mom tried so hard to be original but there are five Bambis in the business, four Dawns, seven Kellys, a dozen Kims, seventeen Lisas, nine Heidis—from now on, call me . . . Harold."

"Harold, lover, open the guidebook. You can eat later. We'll all take turns reading," Ivy promised. "Even Angel will put her glasses on when her turn comes, won't you, Angel?"

The table of models fell to forking up their pasta in sweet seriousness listening intently as Harold read out of a copy of Fielding's *Europe.*

" 'Dal Bolognese,' " she intoned plaintively, " 'is a favorite meeting place of lovely budding movie stars, gal painters and gals in the Creative Arts'—hot spit! Wouldn't you just know? If I'm not budding, who the hell is? And I haven't met anybody but the waiter and the busboy—not even another creative arty gal, not that I'd be interested."

"Shut up and keep reading, Harold," Ivy commanded. "Fauve just glanced in our direction."

Harold bent her lovely ash-blond head even closer to the fat red book and continued to read rapidly as the girls ate with single-minded concentration, eyes held straight, not noticing that their table was the focus of the entire restaurant. Had such a sight ever been seen in the history of Rome? Five divinities, undoubtedly American, with eyes only for each other and some sort of book? Could they be a new kind of religious order? Could they be a cult of lesbians? And that unimaginably tall one with the shortest flaxen hair ever seen . . . was *that* the coming style, the Roman women asked themselves in anguish? If so, they were in for evil days for only the greatest beauty could get away with a cropped head. Yankees go home!

"They're spying on us, I can feel it," Fauve said, sitting up self-consciously.

"Not at all. They're fascinated by the guidebook like all good tourists. They seem like a charming, serious-minded group of girls," Eric said.

After the first minutes of wild excitement in which he and Fauve had been too surprised and flustered to say anything coherent, he had felt a totally unexpected shyness paralyze him. She had become a woman, a disciplined, experienced, polished woman, so much in charge of her life. What had happened to his Fauve? She looked so . . . so businesslike in her man-tailored black cashmere blazer, her gray flannel skirt, her low-heeled, expensive shoes and her impeccable white silk shirt. Only a plaid scarf reminded him of the deliciously crazy way she used to dress and even the plaid was subdued in shades of gray and rust. Her beauty, in this severe garb, was only emphasized. Her head was like one amazing great flower poised on a perfect stem. She seemed so much more grown up than that tangle of pretty girls who had surrounded her. No wonder she had never answered his last letter . . . she wasn't the same person to whom he'd written it.

"What are you doing in Rome?" Fauve asked with composure.

"I've joined an architectural firm in Avignon and I'm here for a conference on housing. It doesn't start for a few days but I came early. An architect should visit Rome at least once a year, no matter what his esthetic theories are . . . don't you agree?"

"Oh, of course. So many . . . ruins."

"Not just that, so many buildings from so many eras that are still in good condition," Eric agreed, unsmilingly.

He's forgotten about the ruins, thought Fauve miserably. No wonder he never answered her last letter. But what could she have expected? She had been writing to a twenty-year-old enthusiastic, impulsive young man, in love with ruined aqueducts and Fauve Lunel, but now he was so grown up, so totally a man. His hair still jumped up in that intractable cowlick she had smoothed down so many times, his lower lip was as full and she still couldn't take her eyes away from the indentation in the middle, but he spoke with a kind of self-containedness and ease that distanced him from her. His handsomeness was fully finished and formed, almost intimidating.

"What a coincidence that we should both be here today," she said.

"It's the sort of thing that happens in Rome," Eric answered casually.

"To which all roads lead?" Fauve asked, thinking that they were making, actually making conversation. And what did he mean by "the sort of thing"? Wasn't it *more* than a *sort* of thing?

"Fauve . . ." Eric began when a voice interrupted him. Ivy had materialized next to their table.

"Sorry, Fauve, hate to break in on you and your friend like this, but we all thought that since we have only one free afternoon to see the city the best thing to do was to take one of those glass-topped bus tours with an English-speaking guide and cram it all in." Ivy had the copy of Fielding tucked under her arm.

"This is Ivy Columbo, Eric," Fauve said, glaring at Ivy. "Eric Avigdor."

"You're absolutely right, Miss Columbo," Eric assured her quickly. "There's also a Rome by Night Tour—unless you're too tired from the trip over."

"Oh, no, we're all too excited to sleep. So whenever you're ready to leave, Fauve, we'd like to get going. Nobody is awfully hungry."

"Well . . ." Fauve hesitated. She couldn't just get up and walk away from Eric, even if he wasn't *her* Eric. Blast those girls, why couldn't they just eat their lunch peacefully? What the hell was their hurry?

"Whatever you say." Ivy stood by the table, clearly expecting a decision. "We could all go to the Via Condotti if you think the bus thing is a bore, and see the Gucci store—maybe they'll have something on sale? Just let me know what you've decided and I'll tell the others so we can look it up and read about it while you finish up here."

"But surely, Miss Columbo, you don't want to miss the Vatican?" Eric said. He and Ivy exchanged a quick look of instant understanding.

"Neat! Terrific idea! Fauve, you want to go to the Vatican, don't you?"

"Well . . ."

"Aw, gee, Fauve, make up your mind. We're wasting precious time. We're all dying to send postcards home from the Vatican."

"Oh, damn it, Ivy, go on! I'll meet you back at the hotel. I've *seen* the Vatican."

Ivy moved off to the other table, quivering with self-satisfaction. She'd always known that it wasn't enough just to be beautiful. When she'd insisted on reciting a poem she'd written about the heritage of Thomas Jefferson instead of tap dancing, and won the Miss Teen America Contest, it hadn't been because she couldn't tap dance up a storm. Bossy old Fauve Lunel wasn't going to stop Ivy Columbo from doing whatever it was that Romans do while in Rome, with tall, dark, dangerous, curly-haired Roman men with their shirts unbuttoned to the navel.

"Let's go, lovers," she murmured as she returned to the four other girls, "before she changes her mind. That guy is hip. But no stampede. I want to see a dignified, ladylike exit. Arkansas, stop snickering. Bambi Two, don't you dare look back at Fauve's table, Harold, stop winking at that man . . ."

"Lordy," complained Arkansas, "some folks just can't seem to get into *La Dolce Vita*."

"Don't bet on it," snapped Ivy.

"Shall we walk?" asked Eric as they emerged from the restaurant into the fluid pageantry of the Piazza del Popolo where the marble cascades of the balustrades leading up to the Pincio Hill seemed no less in movement than the swaying pines in the high garden of the Villa Borghese.

"Which way?" Fauve wondered, bewildered by the need to choose.

"No fixed destination," Eric said, taking her arm.

"That's my favorite place. Oh, I feel as if I'm playing hooky. I should be guilty, allowing them to go alone, but I just couldn't endure the thought of the Vatican.

I've only been in Rome once before and of course I thought I had to see it—by the time I finally reached the Sistine Chapel I was almost crawling. But how can you go to the Vatican and miss the chapel? It's a must. Obviously it would mean a lot to Ivy, but I just couldn't face it."

"Remember the Popes' Palace in Avignon?" Eric asked. "Ever since then I've known you weren't the Vatican type. It was a totally safe suggestion."

"Oh."

"You didn't think I was going to let you go off with those girls, did you?"

"I . . . wasn't sure."

"I have a lot of things to ask you. First, did you ever go back to Félice?"

"No."

"And you still won't tell me why?"

"No," Fauve said abruptly. "How are your parents?"

"Both of them are very well. Flourishing. My father has retired to Villeneuve so he's delighted that I've decided to live in Avignon. What about your grandmother? Is her marriage a success?"

"She and Darcy bought a place in the country and she's absolutely blissfully busy doing all the things she never had time for before. Magali loves her life—she only comes in to the agency three days a week now—she feels enough confidence in me so that finally she can live for herself a little . . . heaven knows she deserves it," Fauve said thoughtfully.

They were walking down the crowded, narrow Via Margutta in the direction of the Spanish Steps, blindly passing by dozens of art galleries, when suddenly Eric steered Fauve through a pair of double doors in an old and badly kept building. Inside there was a spacious courtyard and, at the rear of the courtyard, there was the verdant plunge of the Pincio Hill that descended steeply, covered in thick, plumy foliage, all the way down into the heart of Rome.

"This is it . . . no fixed destination," he said and looked at her for her reaction to his surprise. On his face she saw that special rare quality of trustworthiness that had first struck her in the *Salle des Fêtes* at Uzès and suddenly the years that had separated them dissolved, faded, disappeared as if they had never existed. She faced him and looked him in the eye.

"Why didn't you answer my last letter?" Fauve demanded, finally able to ask the question she hadn't been able to put out of her mind.

"But I did! You were the one who stopped writing."

"That's just not possible."

"I *know* I wrote you last," Eric insisted.

"I *know* I did."

"We can't both be right," Eric said.

"We can't both be wrong either!"

"Perhaps we're both—both right, both wrong?" he suggested.

"I thought—I thought that my letters were too petty, that you'd grown in such a different direction from me that you'd just lost interest in what I had to say."

"I thought my letters were too dull compared to your life. All I could tell you about was the Beaux-Arts and the army. I cherished your letters . . . I kept every one. I have them at home in my desk."

"I decided that you must have fallen in love . . . and you just didn't want to write me about it," Fauve said in a muffled voice.

"I imagined that every man in New York was after you."

"Oh, they were. In fact they still are. Half of them anyway. I beat them off with sticks."

"And that you were probably involved with somebody . . . in love with somebody."

"I wasn't."

"Not even a little bit?"

"What I call love doesn't come in little bits. But you . . . in almost six years?"

"Oh, I tried. I tried all the traditional specifics against a broken heart, hard work, drink and other women. But they didn't help."

"What broken heart?" she demanded, her eyes the color of a rising river mist at the end of a perfect spring day.

"Mine. I never fell out of love with you and you never came back to me. So it broke."

"Oh, my darling." Fauve rocked against him, the world wheeling around her in a vast, giddy, glorious circle. "How far is your hotel?"

"Five minutes if . . ."

"But the traffic—nothing's moving."

" . . . if we walk. Three minutes if we run."

It was a big bed with a mattress that sloped into a cozy valley in the center, and rose around them in soft, billowing puffs. It was like being lost in a warm snowbank, Fauve thought, as they lay so intertwined that she didn't know where her body stopped and his began. Her mind drifted through layers of feeling and emotion. So much had happened to her in the last hours that she was drunk, dazed and ripe and plump with discovery. Details were all mixed together; the astonishing silkiness of the hair under Eric's arms, the pang of acute modesty she'd felt when he'd faced her for the first time in his nakedness, the breathless quiet minutes when he'd suckled at her nipples and she'd looked down at the top of his dark head and knew that she had never experienced true tenderness before, and then the moment at which tenderness had shifted to a specific wanting so transcendent that it abolished tenderness; the burst of pure passion in which the two halves of the secret they had first shared in a little car on a road in Félice had finally been joined into a many-petaled flowering of surpassing joy—past and present mingled; they were waltzing together to the sound of a village orchestra, they were sheltered by the branches of an old pear tree in a walled garden, they were lying in that pellucid, honeyed, red-gold warmth that only the time-gilded bricks and stucco of Rome can distill from the sun. His eyelids moved, fluttering under her lips.

"I'm not asleep," he said, "just closed my eyes for a minute."

"Never, ever in my whole life have I been so exactly where I want to be," Fauve thought and then realized that she had said it out loud.

"Rome?" he muttered into her neck.

"This bed. The world is this bed. I never want to leave it."

"Ah, love, you don't have to. I'll keep you here forever. I'll bring you lovely food and wonderful things to drink and once in a while I'll change the sheets even though they smell so good from the two of us loving each other that I won't want to . . . I'll never let you go. I should have made you marry me when you were sixteen."

"You are a dreamer—to think that," she sighed.

"No, it didn't have to be a dream. I *could* have made it happen if I'd had any sense, any foresight." Eric slid out from under her arm and propped his head up on his hand and looked down at her seriously. "You don't know how many times I replayed the scene at the station in my head. Instead of taking you to the station I should have driven you straight home to my parents' house and taken care of you until you were getting over that strange, terrible state you were in, and afterward we could have been married and all these years wouldn't have been wasted. But I was too young to know what to do and like a childish, helpless idiot I let you leave. I've never forgiven myself."

"But, Eric!" Fauve sat up laughing, teasing—her small, tender nipples half covered by the veil of her hair. "That's just like babes in the woods covering each other up in autumn leaves. We were just kids—kids don't get married and go to live in a small cottage by a waterfall—you didn't really imagine all that, did you?"

He looked down and didn't respond.

"Why, I could no more have gotten married then!" Fauve continued. "I didn't know anything, I didn't have any experience, I hadn't learned what it's like to make a living, to run a business—I would never have been satisfied to be a child bride . . . you're, you're just joking, aren't you?" She scoffed at him, but there was a question in her voice.

With his finger Eric traced the high, rounded little apples that jumped into being high in her cheeks when she smiled—the *pommettes*, that curved sweet shape that he had remembered so often. A silence fell between them, a waiting silence like that in an audience between the end of one movement of a piano sonata and the beginning of the next movement, a silence tense with awareness that somebody who doesn't know the music might think that the piece had ended and applaud at the wrong time.

"Of course I was joking," he answered her finally. "Soldiers have some very wild fantasies in the middle of the night and that was the least lurid of mine. I had too much common sense and so did you—even then."

"Ah, darling, sometimes I wish I didn't have so much common sense. I get so tired of being grounded in reality. Have you ever read books by all those people who keep on and on about how you should live your life as if each day was going to be your last? I think they're just a bunch of sadists, promoting universal dissatisfaction."

"I wonder what the world would be like if everyone really did live as if there would be no tomorrow?" Eric asked.

"I can't speak for other people, but if there wasn't going to be a tomorrow for me, I know what I'd do."

"What?" Eric asked.

"I'll show you," she said and slid back down into the valley of the mattress and imprisoned his strong shoulders in her slim arms, and bent her head so that her lips fell directly on the warm skin between his collarbones where a pulse beat strongly. "I'll show you exactly . . . I won't leave anything out . . ."

Outside the sun withdrew slowly but neither Fauve nor Eric paid attention. It wasn't until a light was turned on in a window in a room across the courtyard of Eric's hotel that Fauve sat up with a violent start. "Oh, my God, what time is it?"

Eric reached to the bed table and looked at his watch. "About ten to six."

"Oh, no. Oh, no." She jumped out of the bed and ran to the bathroom, turned on the light and faced herself in the mirror. She was bedazzled, rosy, disheveled.

"Oh, no! They'd only have to take one look at me to know where and how I've spent the afternoon," she cried, panic in her voice. "I have to take a shower and put on fresh makeup and do something about my hair and even then they'll be able to guess. Eric, when does the Vatican close? Do you have any idea? Oh, I don't know where to start! What a mess!"

"Wait a minute, darling. Don't go crazy, let's just think."

"Think? Who has time to think? I just have to get back to the Grand as fast as possible and pray that they're there waiting for me. What if they're not?" Fauve raced around the bathroom stark naked, trying to adjust the strange shower, looking frantically and unsuccessfully through her handbag for a small hairbrush, splashing cold water on her burning face, turning around in circles, her wits scattered, appalled by the way she'd let the time get away from her.

"Darling, you're hyperventilating. And you're freezing, you're covered with gooseflesh." Eric trapped her inside of a quilt, wrapped it around her, picked her up and carried her, kicking, and protesting, back to the bed. "Now shut up and let me telephone. Did you say the Grand?" He spoke to the hotel's phone operator in rapid Italian.

"But, what on earth am I going to say? Hang up, for God's sake. I have to figure this out." She tried to wrestle the phone out of his hand but he held her down with one arm.

"*La Signorina* Ivy Columbo, *per favore*," he said.

"No! Not Ivy. She's the smartest one. Call . . . call Bambi Two."

Eric paid no attention. "Hello, Miss Columbo? This is Eric Avigdor, yes . . . how was the Vatican? Inspirational? I suspected that it might be. Fauve? She's resting on a bench and she asked me to call and check in with you. No, she's all right but she's feeling faint—it's a combination of jet lag and claustrophobia—we just got out of the Catacombs—yes, the Catacombs of St. Callisto . . . all the way outside of Rome on the Via Appia Antica. Miles and miles . . . it's all my fault, I'm afraid. It was my idea—I'd forgotten how dark and narrow they are and once you get down inside you have to stay with the guide or you could get lost and never find your way out—the visit goes on and on—but the Catacombs can't be missed—if you're interested in early Christian martyrs . . . you didn't know Fauve cared? She doesn't—it's one of my hobbies—I'm afraid I was very selfish. The thing is, my car seems to have broken down and this is the rush hour and the gas station attendant wants to close up—that's where I'm calling from—so I just don't know when we'll be back. Very late I'm afraid—impossible to say when. She's upset about abandoning you . . . no problem? Oh, you're all going to have room service and an early bedtime? You're absolutely right—it's the smartest thing to do. Everybody's exhausted? Well, why don't you put the 'Do Not Disturb' sign on all your doors when you finish dinner and I'll tell Fauve not to worry."

"Wake-up calls!" Fauve hissed at him.

"Don't forget to tell the operator when to wake you tomorrow . . . no, don't rely on travel alarm clocks, they never work. Right, I'll tell her. Good night, Miss Columbo—what? Ivy? . . . good night, Ivy. Thank you for being so sensible. Fauve will be relieved." He hung up the phone.

"Catacombs!" Fauve said. "There's no way she believed you."

"I thought I was very convincing."

"You were—I didn't know you could lie so well—but who on earth would be so absurd as to go visit Catacombs on a marvelous early spring afternoon in Rome?"

"The same sort of people who'd go to the Vatican."

"Oh."

"I believe it's what's called a Mexican standoff," Eric said tenderly, relaxing the arm that had pinioned her to the bed.

"And what's that?"

"It just means that nobody has the advantage, a stalemate."

"You mean I've lost my moral authority?"

"You're merely holding it in abeyance. Tomorrow you can put on that impressively severe jacket and your sensible shoes and round up your little flock . . ."

"But what do you suppose they're really up to? Did you believe her?"

"Why not? She did sound tired."

"Ivy? No way . . . she's probably tap dancing around the room," Fauve said grimly.

"I'm positive about the room service," Eric said, kissing her neck, and ending the discussion. How else could he have heard the distinctive sound of a champagne cork popping in Ivy's room?

The next morning Fauve was sitting in the lobby of the Grand reading the *Daily American* with the angelic and faintly put-upon air of someone who has been waiting patiently when the models drifted out of the elevator on time, and, as she was deeply relieved to see, obviously refreshed. She accompanied them to Valentino's, where they were to stay until evening being fitted into the clothes for Thursday's collection.

The day was, she thought, inevitably perfect, although March in Rome can be wet and cold. Already the outdoor cafés were filling up, the smell of espresso spiked the soft air, trees thrust their blooming branches from behind every wall, there seemed to be a flower stall, banked high with blossoms, on every street corner.

Fauve bought hundreds of tiny, pungent, dark-red carnations, filling both her arms and her shoulder bag with as many as she could carry. Her heart was full of an unruly, intoxicating tenderness. She felt like a pink balloon, filled with helium, that had been released into the turquoise sky, its string dancing gaily in the breeze. Why did she have so many flowers, she wondered for a minute, coming back to earth, and remembered that she was on her way to visit the three Lunel models who had been working in Rome for the past six weeks. She found them in high spirits and she gave them each a heap of carnations and a hasty kiss before she was finally free to dash away to meet Eric.

Until it was time to pick up Ivy and company at Valentino's the day was hers, to spend with Eric—time outside of time, time that had no connection to real life, time to be grasped and lived minute by minute, not touched by any thought of tomorrow. It was only Wednesday morning and she didn't have to fly to Florence until Thursday night—it was an eternity if she just thought of it as a string of miraculous moments, each complete in itself.

As they ate lunch in a little restaurant near the Forum, Eric couldn't stop gazing at Fauve. She looked fifteen, her face bare of makeup except for mascara and her hair brushed out so that its brightness had become a vermilion cloud. She wore a soft turtleneck sweater the color of pistachio ice cream and off-white corduroy trousers that she had stuffed into low, honey-colored boots. With the bright blue cotton poncho she carried, and her shoulder bag, she looked ready for the first day of school, he thought, his heart so nearly unmanageable with love that he felt witless. After lunch they walked to the Forum and paid their entrance fees at that little ticket booth that is so extraordinarily ordinary, as if a mere ticket is all that is needed to travel backward into history.

"I came here the last time too," Fauve said, "the day after the Vatican, and I promised myself I'd always return if ever I was in Rome again. You don't mind, do you? There's not much here for an architect, I'm afraid."

"Broken columns, a couple of arches, some headless statues?" Eric said, looking about. "A wilderness of fragments—everything tumbling over everything else, the debris of centuries fallen in on top of each other, and the whole lot covered with ivy and vines and holly—plenty here for an archaeologist anyway." He laughed. "What draws you to it?"

"It's the only place I found in Rome that seemed to give me a real feeling of how old the city is. Everywhere else the monuments are so kept up and restored that I lose that sense of the past—but here . . . well, there's so little left that I can dream, I can just surrender to its mood and let my imagination loose."

Fauve and Eric picked their way upward under the cypresses toward the crest of the Palatine Hill, where once the monarchs of all the known world had their palaces. No other tourists and certainly no Romans were anywhere in sight.

"This must be the most peaceful place in Rome," Fauve said in a low voice. The poetic hush of the Forum delighted her. There was something almost supernatural that came from being in possession of this mysteriously abandoned space where once crowds from all over the Roman Empire had jostled each other for room to see the fortunate citizens as they walked by in their splendor. She felt a thrilling sense of vainglory, as if she were stepping over millennia in seven-league boots. She picked a spray of dark green acanthus leaves and studied its classic form. She wished she knew how to make it into a wreath, she thought, looking up at Eric. She imagined that some young Roman consul, returning to report on conditions on the edge of the Empire, might have had the same look of adventure and strength that was stamped on Eric's blunt, bronzed features. His head demanded a garland.

They reached the top of the hill and climbed up the steep steps into the greenness of the small, overgrown boxwood garden that was all that remained of the once-great hanging gardens of the Farnese.

"How I love it here!" Fauve exclaimed. "Doesn't it smell marvelous? What *is* that smell?"

"The boxwood—or is it the centuries?" Eric asked, looking down over the entire littered Forum spread beneath them.

"I feel more alive here than anywhere in Rome," Fauve said in a wondering voice. "Even the ghosts are friendly."

"Yes . . . I feel it too . . . how did you know?"

"It was like that the last time . . . I was sure you'd feel the same way." They sat down on a stone bench and fell silent, enriched and comforted by the tangible vibrations of a past that had disappeared, yet would never die.

Eric was the first to break the silence. "Tell me about your painting . . . you haven't said a word about it yet."

"I don't paint anymore—I haven't since the summer I met you."

"You let it go?" he said in astonishment. "How could that happen . . . how was it *possible* when it meant so much to you?"

"Eric, darling," Fauve said in a voice that struck him by its deep note of puzzled regret, "don't ask me about it . . . I can't really explain, not even to myself. Tell me more about you. This conference thing, what's it all about?"

"It's thrilling, Fauve. Really truly important." He got up from the bench and walked back and forth on the gravel path, gesturing vigorously with his large, beautifully shaped hands as he spoke, his eyes full of fervor. "Do you remember all those hideous apartment buildings they put up outside the industrialized zone of Cortine on the outskirts of Avignon?"

"How could I forget them? They were the only ugly thing in the landscape."

"And they didn't *have* to be! The conference is about humanizing low-cost housing, making it good instead of bad for the same price—or less—than it costs now . . . it's a question of design, of *caring*. I'll never accept the idea that public housing can't be beautiful . . . and neither do a lot of other architects from all over the world. We're meeting to exchange ideas and techniques."

"Is that the only sort of buildings you're interested in?"

"Not a bit—just the most necessary, I think, but not necessarily the most fun. My specialty is restoring old farmhouses all over Provence. You wouldn't believe how many people manage to buy an old *mas* and then want to turn it into a Tyrolean cottage or a Grecian villa. I give them a comfortable house that works for modern life and still doesn't ruin the beauty of the original. But my biggest excitement is when I get a chance to build a new house. There I don't just copy an old *mas*—that would be easy, but where's the challenge? To design a new house for the Provençal landscape, a modern house that gives the pleasure to the eye and shelter to the body and respects the demands of the horizon and the hills—and the neighbors—ah, now *there's* an architect's dream! I want to *show* them to you—will you come and see some of my houses? Don't go back to New York after Paris—look, it's easy to plan . . ."

Fauve drew back immediately from his impetuousness. She held up her hand, warding him off. "No plans! The most I can go into the future now is to figure out what we're going to do about those girls of mine tonight. I have the strong impression that they have a hidden agenda. I can't leave them unattended, but I can't bear to be away from you for a minute."

"Why don't I dig up some other architects? We can all go out to dinner together," Eric proposed.

"Architects? *Roman* architects?"

"This conference is like the Olympics, all nationalities are represented. Lots of them like me are in Rome already."

"Hmmm . . ." Fauve considered deeply. "Latins of all kinds are absolutely out. Swedes are dubious—there's got to be some sort of reason why so many porno movies have the word 'Swedish' in their titles—Englishmen—Englishmen . . . no, there's that ancient French theory that no woman is as highly sexed as a supposedly frigid Englishwoman. What if it holds true for Englishmen too? I can't take that risk."

"Finns," Eric suggested. "Why don't we take a chance on Finns? They don't seem to reproduce much."

That night, after a dinner that would live in the annals of Lunel history, Fauve made sure that all her charges were safely deposited in their rooms before she slipped back to Eric's hotel. The big meadow of a bed, in which they had only spent one night, welcomed them. It had already begun to take on a mythic quality, Eric thought, as he counted the hours left to them. So aware was he of the passage of time that the texture of the sheets, the rolling terrain of the mattress, the amber glow of the little bedside lamp seemed to have become as much a part of the past as they were of the moment.

"There's only tonight," he said, cradling her head between his hands. "Tomorrow you can't be with me except while the collection is going on and then you get on that infernal plane for Florence. Why, oh why, do you have to leave Thursday night?"

"Don't count hours. Don't count minutes—you'll spoil *now*. Don't make me sad—don't make me sadder than I am," Fauve pleaded. "The girls have to be up bright and early Friday morning, you know it as well as I do. The fittings will be going on all weekend long—Versace, Armani—I thought you understood."

"Unfortunately it's as plain and logical as a blueprint. The thing I don't understand is why you've eluded me every time. I've tried to talk at all seriously to you since we met. I haven't pressed it because I figured that maybe the time wasn't right, but now . . ."

"Oh—let me elude you some more. I elude so delightfully," Fauve whispered, covering his chest with kisses.

"I will if you'll answer one single very simple question—do you love me, Fauve?"

"Oh, *yes*."

"Then we *must* make plans, we have to talk about the future . . ."

"You said that if I answered, you'd let me elude you," Fauve protested, breaking into his immoderate rush of words. " 'Plans . . . the future'—that's not the stuff that elusions are made of."

"If you'd said that you didn't love me I would just shut up and make love to you. But, you *do*—don't you see how that changes everything?" Relief transfigured his voice.

Fauve pulled away from his arms, left the bed and stood by the window, naked and white in the darkness that fell outside of the lamplight. She clasped her hands behind her bowed head and shook it from side to side in a barely perceptible gesture of confusion and negation. "Please, oh, please, Eric, not tonight."

"But *when?* You can't be planning to leave without . . . that can't *be!* Fauve, how many more second chances do you think we're going to have?"

"Eric, I just haven't wanted to think," she said slowly with her face turned away from him. "I've been living without reckoning or wondering about possibilities . . . I've been living—just drifting in the wind. I've been so happy just bobbing along like a soap bubble, but if we keep talking my lovely bubble will burst. *Please?*"

Eric came to stand behind her at the window and put his arms around her, holding the soft weight of her breasts cupped in his hands. He rested his chin on the top of her head and protected her with his big warm body.

"You're shivering. Don't stay here, it's too cold. Come to bed, my little love. And bring your bubble with you—it's such a bright bubble and you wear it so beautifully."

"Tomorrow, Eric, I promise."

"Tomorrow."

On Thursday, after lunch, Eric sat waiting for Fauve at Rosati's. He looked at his watch impatiently. The Valentino collection must have started by now. He and Fauve would have almost two hours in which to make their plans before she had to leave to pick up the girls and the luggage and drive out to Fumicito in time for the plane.

He saw her approaching and jumped up. She came toward him, wearing a sweeping travel coat. The spring wind was brisk in the piazza.

"Let's go and sit inside," he said, tipping her head up for his kiss. "Thank God you didn't get held up."

"Once that show started nothing but a bomb in the dressing room could stop my girls from performing—and probably they'd just walk around the rubble. I sneaked out. I have to be back in time to congratulate Valentino, but it's a long collection."

"Espresso?" he offered.

"What I'd really like is a big pot of tea. Do you have that in Italy?"

"There's a long tradition of eccentric Englishmen and women who came to Rome and never left it . . . I'm sure they make tea. Fauve . . . when will you marry me?"

"I was afraid you were going to say that," she said in a strange muted voice. Eric looked at her and it didn't seem possible that this pale girl, dressed again in black and white, with only her hair to give color to her face, could be the spirit of fire and abandon with whom he'd spent the night until she had left him just before dawn.

"Why afraid?"

"Because I can't."

"Why not, my darling? What reason is there why two people who love each other the way we do can't get married?" He spoke calmly and quietly. He'd been sure that she'd put up some sort of resistance, it had been evident in her evasiveness, in her insistence on never looking beyond the present. "You're not sixteen anymore . . . I know that was just a crazy idea—but now everything's different—there's nothing to stop us."

"I'm not ready to get married. How can you expect me to spend two days with you—only two days—and make a decision like that? It's been *perfect* and nothing *is* that perfect in real life, nothing! It couldn't keep on being like this—this was an *interlude*, Eric. But that's not the only reason." Fauve's voice was strong, sure of what she had to say. "I have a responsibility to Magali that I can't ignore. If I left the agency she'd have to come back and work five days a week or else give it up—sell it probably. She spent her whole life building that business and I've spent five years learning it and she counts on me—she has every right to. Oh, she'd never stand in my way, but I know that if I had to leave New York it would change the whole pattern of her life—just wouldn't be fair! She'd be miserable giving up the agency, and she'd be just as miserable working full-time again at her age. And anyway what would I do with myself living in Avignon?"

"Wait a minute! That's three reasons—could you just stop for a second and catch your breath? Drink your tea. Milk? Lemon? Okay, marriage wouldn't be like two days in Rome. *Nothing* is like two days in Rome. Nothing is like a week in Florence. Nothing is like a month in the country. Marriage is marriage and each one is different—and ours would be wonderful; from time to time it probably wouldn't be perfect, but only children expect marriage to be perfect—and you're not a child. That's one. Two. From everything you've told me about Magali, she can take care of herself. She'd be outraged if she thought you were sacrificing yourself for her . . . I can't imagine that she couldn't work it out one way or another . . . she's managed to do just splendidly on her own for most of her life, hasn't she? Three—now there's a real problem, but not one that we can't find an answer to. I could move to Paris, for instance, join a firm there and you could find a job, or you could open a model agency if that's, what you want . . . living in Avignon isn't essential to me . . ."

"Stop it, Eric! You're being so goddamned rational about this, you sound like a train schedule."

"But you're giving me reasons and I'm giving you the reasons why your reasons are wrong. If you want to give me irrational, I'll be quiet and listen."

"Oh—oh . . ." Fauve flung up her hands, speechless.

"Come on—give me irrational," he insisted.

"I'm frightened, I'm terrified, I'm scared shitless," she blurted. "I'm *paralyzed* at the idea of making such a big decision. It's too much for me—it makes my blood run cold just thinking about it—oh, Eric, I'm a natural-born late bloomer. I give up each stage of my life as slowly as I can, looking backward the whole time—I need old habits, security, familiarity—I'm petrified at the notion of spending the rest of my life with you—or with anybody, for that matter. I don't really know you, not the grown-up you. I don't even know *me*. I haven't had enough time to myself, I'm not ready to be a wife, I don't *want* to plan my future . . . it's easy for you, you're twenty-six, you've had time to discover yourself, to experiment. I feel rushed, pressured . . . how can you expect me to be ready?"

"That's not irrational, that's natural." He took her hands in both of his. "I understand that it's too soon to make a decision. Just come and live with me—just see how it is for us together. That's not too big a step to take, is it? No strings—only an interlude if that's all you want. Don't go back to New York after Paris . . . come and spend the spring in Avignon with me."

Fauve looked into her teacup, as addled as she'd been in her life. I can't make him understand . . . how can I say, after all, that I don't trust him, no, not in spite of thinking I did? I trusted my father, and look what he did . . . how can I trust any man, ever, ever? An "interlude" . . . only an interlude he says . . . it's always an interlude when it starts—before it does something terrible to you. It was just an interlude for Magali in Paris so long ago, just an interlude for my mother . . . interludes turn into preludes and then? What then, oh, God? *Springtime in Avignon*? No! It's dangerous, too dangerous. I'm right to feel the danger. There's always danger when you trust, when you depend on somebody else, when you put your life into his hands. Oh, I want the life I *know*, I want the life where I have a place, where I have an office, where people need me, a life where I grew up, where I'm safe. *Safe*.

"No," she said, looking into her teacup. "No, I can't. I have to go back to New York. Maybe when I have my vacation," she faltered, "the next vacation I have . . . maybe then . . ."

"Don't bother." Eric stood up. "I didn't realize that you really hated the idea," he said tightly. "I wouldn't have kept bothering you about it for so long if I'd known. You said you loved me but you don't—not enough. Not nearly enough. Sorry—my mistake."

He put some money on the table and walked away.

"I knew he wouldn't understand," Fauve whispered to herself.

"Is something wrong, *Signorina*?" asked the waiter.

"No," said Fauve, "nothing's wrong. It's just the end . . ."

"The end . . ."

"Of an interlude."

31

Falk was accustomed to the flattery of beautiful women and discounted it. He was so steeped in flattery that he believed he no longer knew what it was like to have the feeling of being flattered, but when Fauve Lunel invited him to have dinner with her alone in her apartment, the first dinner she'd actually ever cooked by herself, he felt . . . flattered.

"I'm probably not a good cook," she had warned him.

"Who said so?"

"Nobody, I've never cooked for anybody else before, so how could I be a good cook?"

"I'll take that chance."

As Falk waited for Fauve to come out of the kitchen where she was mixing drinks, he glanced around her living room. It was like looking into the attic of a family homestead, he thought, or through a pile of old scrapbooks. Hadn't Fauve ever thrown *anything* out? He could see only two examples of restraint; she had painted the floor emerald green and left it bare and the fabric she had used on her keenly overstuffed, exuberantly Victorian furniture actually matched; a pattern of giant cabbage roses on glazed chintz that, now that he looked at it closely, had surely been used as curtains in Maggy's Fifth Avenue apartment before she redecorated.

He could remember the genesis of so many of the objects he saw; there was the huge wire birdcage he had bought Fauve on Third Avenue one Saturday afternoon. It seemed to have spawned seven other birdcages that were artfully piled around it, making a complex structure through which no bird sang. And there was the giant straw hat he'd bought her back from a location trip to Yucatán now joined by dozens of others in every shape and size, all hung on hooks on the walls. The graceful old lyre he'd given her for Christmas when she was twelve was suspended from another wall, surrounded by a number of antique musical instruments; flutes, violins, oboes and even a battered clarinet that had been restored to a high polish. Fauve had baskets everywhere, baskets on top of baskets, some of them filled with growing plants, some of them with pencils, others crammed with notebooks and bolts of fabric and balls of yarn.

Pillows! Fauve seemed to have cornered the pillow market, he thought with the connoisseur's salute of a man who considers himself an expert on the cluttered look. This went beyond clutter—this was historical. The books in her jammed bookcases included a complete set of the *Oz* books, the many adventures of *Mary Poppins*, and the works of E. Nesbitt, as well as all the books she had read since she was a child, none of which she ever seemed to have considered allowing to escape her possession. A pair of draped stone sphinxes, life-sized, it seemed to him, although he'd never seen a sphinx while it was still in good health, guarded the fireplace, inside of which stood a polished brass grate.

There was no fire—it was a mild September day in 1975—but Fauve had lit a galaxy of white votive candles in little clear tumblers and distributed them on the grate so that the fireplace didn't look empty and dark. There was a round table that was set next to tall windows that looked out on a flourishing acanthus tree. It was covered with three different tablecloths. The first one, flounced widely to the ground, was crisp, bright red taffeta, the second was a small silky old flowered carpet in every shade of pink, and the top cloth was made of delicate white linen with a wide border of embroidered organdy.

On Fauve's desk, in ornate old frames, stood the only three photographs in the room; a snapshot of Maggy and Darcy sitting on the lawn in front of their house, a picture from a 1951 issue of *Life* showing Maggy surrounded by her ten most famous models, and an enlargement of one of the test shots Falk had made of Teddy in 1947. Teddy Lunel when she was twenty.

He turned away, unable to look at it for more than a moment, and his eye was caught by an extraordinary object, a gigantic stuffed panda that had seen better days, sitting in a place of honor on a rocking chair in a corner. Startled, he looked around for other animals. A fleet of ship's figureheads, an army of small statues, a collection of music boxes, a forest of unmatched candlesticks, and, on each table, clusters of bud vases of every height, each holding a single flower or a spray of tiny leaves or a few wild grasses—yes, all of that, but, he was relieved to see, no other stuffed animals.

"Very cozy," he said to Fauve as she handed him a glass.

"I haven't really done much to it," she said, "but little by little it's taking shape."

"What shape did you have in mind?"

"I don't know exactly. I'll know when I get there—probably when I can't walk across the room without tripping over something. That's why I don't have a rug. It cuts down on the confusion. If I had a rug I'd want to put another little carpet on top of it, and I'd need a hearth rug of course—something in pattern—I seem to keep finding things."

"I love things," Falk said. "There is *nothing* like a thing."

"I knew you'd understand." They smiled at each other in the most mutual possible pleasure. "You'd never ask me if it doesn't collect a lot of dust or what sort of neurosis it all represents, or comment meaningfully on my nest-building instinct."

"Never. But I do wonder . . . ?"

"What about?"

"No pictures?"

"Nope, I don't have any room for pictures. There's too much stuff on the walls and anyway, to do pictures justice you have to subordinate the room to them."

"This room is definitely insubordinate."

"Exactly. Oh, the chicken! Excuse me for a minute."

She came hack, a plain white chef's apron wrapped over her bare-armed, bare-backed dress of bright saffron cotton. "It's cooking, that's all I can say in its favor at the moment."

"What sort of chicken is it?" he asked hungrily.

"Hungarian. Chicken Paprika. I'm counting on the fact that there isn't anything in the world that can't be improved by a great deal of sour cream. I know it's cheating but I need all the help I can get."

"When did you start cooking? Did it just come over you all of a sudden?"

"I think it must be a maturation thing or maybe an unnatural craving like in *Rosemary's Baby*. Ever since I moved here if I'm not invited out to dinner I've picked up something at the Dover Deli. A few weeks ago, I was passing the butcher shop and I found myself just marching in and buying two lamb chops. I thought that I'd put them in a pan and cook them. Well, I'm still not sure what I did wrong but the kitchen filled with smoke, and lots of hot fat started to pop out at me. I got so frightened that I grabbed the pan off the fire and threw the whole thing out the back window. But that started me thinking that if Maggy could learn to garden from books, I could probably learn to cook. So I bought *The Joy of Cooking.* History will be made tonight." She began to set the table.

"Maggy thinks you're working too hard," Falk said. "She told me that you're letting the business dominate your life."

"She's got her nerve! Do you know what she did last weekend? She ordered five thousand daffodil bulbs. Five thousand! She's going to plant them herself on those low hills behind the house and next spring they'll come up as if they had been growing wild for years, in drifts. *Drifts*—she's constantly raving on about drifts. And once she's got the daffodils established she intends to make a shade garden in the woods, the way it would be in nature if nature had her sense of style. Can you imagine anyone who plans to dig five thousand holes telling me *I* work too hard?"

"You don't dig individual holes, you dig up a whole lot of dirt and sort of dribble the bulbs around, or so she said. Like sowing grain or something."

"Well, however you do it, it's work. You know, I feel that maybe Maggy's more interested in her garden than in the agency now," Fauve said, putting plates down on the linen cloth.

"What makes you say that?"

"It's something really weird about Thursdays. Every Thursday as the afternoon goes by, she gets more and more irritable, as if she just can't *wait* to get away, but refuses to admit it. She finds nonexistent mistakes everywhere, she walks around the booking rooms and double checks everybody's cards to make sure that nobody screwed up Friday and Monday, she starts worrying about models who are doing just fine, she goes into the bookkeeping department to talk about whether they're prepared for payday as if, after all these years, they didn't know that every model will be in for her check on Friday, rain or shine. She's driving everybody a little crazy. The new bookers are terrified of her. Then she keeps finding little things 'she has' to do as the afternoon goes on, so that we can't close on time . . . unnecessary things that Casey or Loulou or I could take care of on Friday perfectly well. It's as if she's forcing herself to work late because she feels guilty about taking so much time off, which is *totally* insane."

"Have you talked to her about it?" Falk asked.

"No, I guess I just don't want to say anything that might sound critical. I figure that the day will come when she'll figure out for herself that she just doesn't want to work three days a week and then she'll let me know," Fauve said, appraising her table and judging it complete.

"How would you feel about running the agency if she weren't around?"

"It's what I'm trained for, it's what I know. We have really reliable people working for us in every department. Casey can do anything I can do, Loulou has the booking side of things as much in control as booking can ever be—I know it's a big business for anybody my age to run, but I've been in it for five years and I think I could manage. Still . . . Maggy *is* Lunel. Every aspiring model in the world wants to get in to see Maggy Lunel, not Fauve Lunel. The magazine editors trust her judgment as they won't trust mine for years and years, the agency would *never* be the same again . . . but . . . if she really is fed up, I understand. I'd have to . . . oh, my chicken!"

When Fauve came back from the kitchen she looked relieved. "I tasted it and I do believe it's going to be vaguely Hungarian."

"Haven't you ever cooked anything for Ben Litchfield?" Falk asked.

"Ben Litchfield doesn't have any damn taste buds."

"I thought..."

"I know what you thought. That's all anybody thinks. Honestly, Melvin, all of Manhattan could be two blocks square the way everybody is involved in everybody else's private business." Fauve sat down next to Falk and drank half of her glass of wine. "I don't mean you, obviously."

"I know you didn't. So tell me all your private business."

"He wants to get married."

"What else is new?"

"No, I mean he *really* wants to get married. He used to mention it every fifth or sixth time I saw him, now it's every time. Pressure, pressure," Fauve brooded.

"Most girls," Falk said.

"Exactly. Most girls. All girls probably. He's a wonderful guy, he's brilliant, he's good, he's successful, he's serious, he's very, very attractive, he's somebody I can talk to, we have a lot in common, he's sweet, he's everything you could ask for."

"Oh, I don't think I like the sound of *that*."

"I think Ben and I are what people call good for each other," Fauve said with a wicked smile.

"If you'd said he was impossible, crazy, unpredictable, and you couldn't understand why you were so wildly in love with him... maybe."

"Maybe... maybe not. Even that wouldn't guarantee anything."

"Nothing guarantees anything, Fauve," Falk said gently. "It's all a crapshoot."

"Isn't there any way to be sure, any way to nail things down so that they happen under your control? If you're very, *very* careful?" Fauve asked wistfully.

"Not if you're going to risk making a change. Change just can't be shaped and organized and molded *before* it happens. The nature of change is that it takes you somewhere else than where you are now. You grow, that's the only thing you can really be sure of, growth. But any change has its share of surprises."

"I've never been all that fond of surprises," Fauve said with a shadowy look of such sadness on her face that Falk's heart contracted.

"Do you think the chicken is ready?" he asked. "It smells ready."

"I'll investigate. How will I know if it's ready?"

"When—the leg moves easily in the socket. Also, take a long cooking fork, stick it in and see if the juice that comes out is clear—stick it into the thigh, not the breast."

"How do you know?"

"How many wives have I had?"

"Only three."

"One of them must have taught me, but I can't remember which. It's good to know that sort of thing even if it's wrong. It's called folk wisdom."

Carrying a platter, Fauve emerged from the kitchen, beaming.

"It looks quite good, if looks mean anything."

The chicken was good, the rice was good, the string beans, French-cut and flash-frozen, were good, and the paprika-laced sour cream lifted everything into a realm in which sheer greed became a virtue, for not to eat it ravenously would have been a sin of omission.

When dinner was over, Fauve and Falk sat drinking brandy in front of the fireplace where the votive lights still winked. Fauve fell silent, pensive. After a long, comfortable silence she looked up and said, "All the most important people in my life, Magali, Darcy—and even Lally Longbridge, who's like an aunt really, and you, especially you, Melvin, with whom I can speak with more freedom than with anyone else—none of you will talk to me about my mother. I wonder why?"

"I've always thought . . . that Maggy had told you all about her . . . nothing's been hidden," Melvin answered, uneasily.

"Oh, the outline of her life, yes. The basic details, the things I have to be told. I've looked at so many photos for so many hours—there's a complete library of old magazines at the office and between 1947 and 1952 there are literally thousands of pictures of Teddy Lunel, but they can't tell me the things I want to know, no matter how long I stare into her eyes."

"What sort of things?" Falk asked, his heart beating heavily.

"I'm only a few years younger than she was when she died. Would I have loved her? What would she have told me to do about Ben? What did she care about most in the world? Why didn't she marry you?"

"You know about that? Who told you?" He put his brandy snifter down with a sudden, startled movement.

"Oh, I guessed a long time ago. There's something about your face when you look at me. I know—you were in love with her. Were you lovers, the two of you?" Fauve asked softly, seriously.

"I was . . . I was the first boy who ever told her she was beautiful, I asked her out on her first date, I gave her her first kiss, I was the first man who ever made love to her—the only thing I wasn't, was the first man whose heart she broke."

"I'm sorry . . . I'm so sorry, Melvin, I wish she hadn't broken your heart."

"She didn't want to, she couldn't help it, she just couldn't *quite* fall in love with me . . . she was looking for something else, something . . . some *other* thing."

"Did she have many lovers?"

Falk hesitated. Did he have a right to answer? Did Fauve have a right to ask?

"You see?" Fauve said. "That's exactly what I mean. If she were alive I'd say, 'Mother, did you have a lot of lovers when you were my age?' and she'd have to tell me something, even if it was just to mind my own business. But I can't ask Magali, obviously, and now you get all closed off. What *would* she have told me?"

"I think she'd have told you anything you wanted to know. I'm not sure that she would have given you sensible advice, being sensible wasn't a priority with Teddy—but I think she would have been frank with you."

"Well?"

"I told you she was looking for some *other* thing. She looked for a long time and whenever she realized that she hadn't found what she wanted . . . whatever it was . . . she looked somewhere else . . . so, she had a number of lovers. I don't know what 'many' means exactly, but perhaps she had one lover for every hundred men who wanted her—every two hundred—"

"But she cared about them?"

"Each one, until she stopped caring and started looking again. And then, she found your father and he was what she wanted, God help her."

"Am I being unfair to you?" Fauve asked suddenly. "Luring you up here with my divine chicken and then asking you about things you don't want to discuss?"

"No! God, no. I think we've all been terribly unfair to you, not telling you more, not talking about Teddy because it was too painful. Her death changed all the people who were left behind. None of us has ever been the same since."

"Isn't that true whenever somebody young dies?"

"Perhaps. But your mother was . . . she was . . ."

"Different? Special?" Fauve's voice trembled in its yearning need to know.

"I wish I could even begin to explain her charm—I used to read e. e. cummings—everyone my age read e. e. cummings—and I'd always think of her—'the musical white spring'—no, I'd have to be a poet to convey even a tenth of Teddy. And yes, you would have loved her so very, very much and she would have loved you more than anything in the world . . . that's the saddest part of it all." He stood up and went to where Fauve sat curled up in her chair and hugged her.

"Just remember one thing, your mother finally did find what she'd wanted for so long and she was marvelously happy until the very last second of her life."

"Can I give you a little more brandy, Melvin?" Fauve asked, standing up so abruptly that she knocked over a big folder that lay on a table next to her chair. It fell on the floor and papers scattered all over. Fauve darted to pick them up and Falk bent to help her. The papers slid around on the varnished surface and after he'd accumulated a small pile of them he stopped to see what they were. He looked casually, peered again through his glasses, and then took the papers away from the dimness in which they had been sitting, and thrust them under the light of a lamp.

"They're nothing," said Fauve. "Just give them to me."

"Like hell I will. Like *hell* I will."

"They're just doodles, Melvin. Come on, don't make me mad. That's private." She stuffed the papers she had picked up back into the folder and tried to pull the rest of the papers out of his grasp.

"Don't tear them!" he threatened, backing away.

"So? What if I do?"

"Fauve, you've been drawing, you've been working . . . how long has this been going on? Do you have any idea of how good you are, you dumb, *dumb* girl?"

"I just . . . I get a kind of nervous need to draw things . . . it's like a tic—*please* don't make a big number out of it, Melvin. You know how I feel about art—this is just a minor little, unimportant thing, not even a hobby. Everybody doodles, show me one person who doesn't doodle."

"Jesus, Fauve, who do you think you're talking to? Somebody who doesn't know the difference? These are fucking superb! Are you painting too? Fauve, tell me!"

"There's absolutely nothing to tell. Okay—so I draw a little—I admit it—I don't paint at all . . . I'm telling the truth . . . no paints, you'd smell them if they were in the apartment." Fauve flung her arms out in a gesture of innocence. "There's no law against drawing, it's never been considered a vice. Come on, Melvin, stop looking at me like that. It's embarrassing. And give me back my drawings."

He handed them back to her and shrugged. "If that's the way you want to go, baby, there's nothing I can say. If you should ever decide that you'd like to give me a birthday present or a Valentine's Day present or just a present . . . give me one of your doodles. Don't even bother to frame it. You've found your *line*—your own distinctive style, and it has nothing to do with your father or any other artist! Do you understand what that means? No? Never mind, stupid. I think I'll take that brandy you offered. I never needed it more."

Marte Pollison, in her seventies now, had never wavered in her long devotion to Nadine. In her eyes Nadine was still the miraculously beautiful little daughter she could never have had. Nadine, who knew that Marte adored her blindly, had always shamelessly and instinctively appealed to the sentimental side of the crusty peasant woman, running to her for sympathy when she had a bump or scratch that was so minor that Kate would have laughed it away; sitting with her in the kitchen listening to her chatter about the village life for hours at a time, waiting for the delicious sweets that Marte made especially for her. After Nadine left home for boarding school, she forgot about Marte entirely until she came home for vacations and then the old, satisfying relationship was immediately resumed, Marte growing more worshipful every year. After Kate's death, Marte became Nadine's only contact with the world of *La Tourrello* for Mistral had been blunt about not welcoming her.

"Your life is a farce, your husband is worthless and I'm too busy to be interrupted. You're not welcome here, Madame Dalmas," he had said unpleasantly the last time she had suggested coming to Félice for a weekend and from that time on, a period of almost four years, Nadine had prudently decided to remain in touch with Mistral through an occasional phone call to Marte.

Oh, how many times had she heard that dreary, unvarying, infuriating report, given in Marte's cracked old voice. "He's just the same, *ma petite chérie*. He gets up, he has breakfast, he shuts himself up in his studio all day, he has dinner and goes to bed. No, he's in good health, he never says anything to me except to warn me to keep strangers away, as if I didn't know. What does he do all day? He keeps the studio locked and I've never been one to pry. It's been a quiet, lonely time since your mother died. He's let the land go, he fired the men, the machinery has all rusted, the vineyards and the olive groves are the shame of the neighborhood, but he doesn't care, not he. If it weren't for me, he'd probably starve to death, and not even notice. I only stay on because of you and in memory of your poor mother."

In the middle of September 1975, Marte Pollison called Nadine to tell her that her father had been coughing for days. He had worked steadily, refusing to change his routine, but that evening he had been unable to get out of bed. "He won't let me call the doctor, *ma petite*, but I believe he may have bronchitis—what must I do?"

"Nothing, Marte, I'll be there in the morning. You know how he is about doctors—don't upset him."

Phillipe Dalmas made a perfunctory offer to fly to Marseilles with Nadine and drive up with her to Félice, a matter of little more than an hour and a half, but Nadine spurned it. As she drove up to the gates, she was shocked. *La Tourrello* looked abandoned, a stone pile from which the life had drained. In the kitchen she submitted gracefully to Marte's hugs. "You are more beautiful than ever—how gay it must be in Paris," Marte exclaimed, as she fussed happily over Nadine.

"Why is the house shut up, Marte? Why are the shutters closed, the furniture all covered?"

"Oh, don't blame me, it's not my fault. The pool is empty too and the garden's overgrown, but there's no one here but me to do all the work. I've kept the house dusted and swept and the tiles on the roof are repaired when they need it, but you know Monsieur fired all the domestics after Madame died, and my arthritis gets worse every time the mistral blows."

"Poor Marte—of course I understand," Nadine said.

"For a long while I offered to make up a fire for him in the salon so he could sit there at night but he never wanted one. I gave your room a good cleaning and airing this morning, and I'll serve you dinner in the dining room if you like, or in the kitchen with me. How long can you stay?"

"Until I'm sure he's better," Nadine had answered, and mounted the stairs to Mistral's room.

"I don't know why the devil you're here," Mistral barked at her as she entered. "It was too late to stop you when Marte, damn her, told me you were coming."

"Marte is concerned about you."

"She's an old busybody. Senile! I have a bad cold. All I need is a few days in bed."

"Don't you think you should call the doctor?"

"Don't be ridiculous. I've never seen a doctor in my life. I don't need a doctor, I need a little peace and quiet."

"Marte thinks it's bronchitis."

"She doesn't know what she's talking about. Is she qualified to make a diagnosis? Just leave me alone."

"Have you been working too hard?" Nadine asked.

"Working too hard? Do you have any idea of what that means? I work, that's all. Work is work." He coughed, an explosive, unexpected, uncontrollable cough.

"Get out of here," he said when he regained his breath. "You'll catch my cold." He sipped water from a glass by his bed.

"No, Father, I'll keep you company a little longer. Don't pay any attention to me. I'll just sit here."

Mistral closed his eyes in indifference and after a minute he fell into a light sleep, snoring at intervals. Nadine couldn't stop staring at him. Was this the man Marte described as in good health? Perhaps it was simply that Marte hadn't noticed, living with him every day, but Mistral was so thin that his body made only a long lumpy ridge under the bedclothes. From the chair by his bed in which she sat, his body smelled musty and rank with sweat. She shook with disgust.

He was a tough old man and only seventy-five. He had been able to work as usual until yesterday. Who knew what reserves of strength were left in that body? When she was a little girl he had been the strongest man in the world. Great painters, like great orchestra conductors, lived forever if they didn't manage to kill themselves in one way or another in their youth. Certainly his manner was not that of a man who believed himself to be in any danger.

Nadine bit her lips in a passion of impotent temper. It was probably a false alarm, a fever, a cough, a sweat, nothing she hadn't had herself a dozen times. Still there was no question that he had lost a great deal of weight. But thin people live longer than fat ones, she thought angrily, and tiptoed closer to the bed to gaze into his face. His nose seemed twice as large as it ever had for now it stood out from a face from which the flesh had fallen away, a harsh mask, somber and archaic.

"Damn it, Nadine, leave me alone! I want to sleep!" Mistral rasped, without opening his eyes.

Her heart jumped and she fled down to the kitchen.

"Marte, I don't think there's any reason to worry about him. He's too bad tempered to be really sick."

"I couldn't take the responsibility, I had to telephone you," Marte muttered.

"Of course you did. Anyway, I'm glad I came if only to see you. Father's kept me away for so long. You know I would have come as often as possible but he refused to see me. I've never understood it, but what could I do? It's his house, after all."

"If only your mother were still alive. Do you remember the parties? And how beautiful the house was, filled with flowers, servants everywhere, the kitchen full of food? And all the famous people? Oh, Madame was the queen of the countryside," she said sadly.

"You look tired, my poor Marte," Nadine consoled her.

"I kept looking in on him last night, climbing up and down those stairs. I didn't get much sleep, but you mustn't worry about me."

"I think we should both go to bed early tonight. I'm just down the hall from his room so I'll keep his door and my door open and if Father needs anything I'll hear him . . . I sleep lightly. You *mustn't* climb stairs like that with your arthritis. And tomorrow, if I think it's necessary, I'll call the doctor no matter what he says."

"I'm glad you came, *petite chérie*. I feel much better with you in charge. It's all too much for an old woman like me."

As Nadine lay in bed that night she was too alert to sleep. She imagined herself taking a candle and creeping down to the kitchen and finding the key to the studio on the big key ring that hung there. She imagined walking through the silent rooms of the shuttered house and going out the back, past the empty pool, to the great wooden doors of the studio. She saw herself unlocking the doors and snapping on the work lights and walking through the studio to the storage room where the supreme works of France's greatest living artist lay on their racks, hundreds of canvases, more valuable than any jewels. In her mind she counted them, she estimated their value—yes, in the hundreds of millions of francs, if Mistral's dealer was correct, and there was no reason to believe he was not. A fortune too great, too vast to understand. In that studio was her brilliant, triumphant future, Nadine told herself, hugging her body with impatience. Not mere paintings—no, so much more. The houses she would own all over the world, the marvelous objects she would buy and buy and buy, the receptions she would give; the inherited glory that would finally, conclusively descend on her, the allure that would allow her to know everyone. The world would be at the feet of Mistral's daughter. Soon. Very soon. *How* soon?

She got out of bed and walked softly into Mistral's room. His breathing was ugly to hear, so much more labored than it had been earlier. He struggled horribly to produce each strangulated snore. She observed him carefully for a long time, far enough from the bed so that he couldn't see her if he opened his eyes. Finally Nadine went back to her room and slept soundly until morning. She dressed hastily and returned to Mistral's bedside. He was half awake and the water glass next to his bed was empty. The chamber pot that Marte had put on the bedside table was half full. Nadine emptied it, sickened and rigid. She poured some water for him and held it to his lips.

"How do you feel?" she asked.

"Like yesterday," he said but his voice was a whisper and, even without touching his skin, Nadine could feel the hectic fever that was baking him reach its hot fingers out to her. She busied herself with a washcloth and warm water, dabbing away, concealing her revulsion. "I don't think I should try to shave you. I've never done it before," she said lightly. "Shall I ask Marte to make you breakfast?"

"Not hungry . . . more water," he muttered, coughing again in that savage, gasping way that seemed so deep that it might have come from his bowels, a cough that jerked him up in bed and bent him in half.

Nadine went down to the kitchen to find Marte just coming in, a worried look on her face.

"He spent a very good night," Nadine said cheerfully. "I've given him a sponge bath and made him nice and comfortable. He's gone back to sleep. That's the very best thing for him. I tried to get him to eat but he refused. I know exactly how he feels—when I have that kind of cold I don't want to even smell food, only sip liquids. My Paris doctor says that they still haven't invented anything to equal bedrest and liquids."

"Oh, I feel guilty about letting you do all this," Marte said unhappily.

"Marte, my old Marte, if I can't take care of my own father . . . ? Look, you make some good strong soup, a beef broth, and perhaps later I'll be able to get him to drink some."

"Don't you think we should telephone the doctor in Apt who took care of Madame?"

"That would put Father into such a rage that he'd get worse. You know how he prides himself on never being sick. I wouldn't want to be responsible for bringing a doctor to the house unless I thought he truly wasn't well. It would make him as mad as seeing a priest walk in! All he needs is good, plain nursing. Marte, I know what you can do to make yourself useful! Make me a beautiful roast chicken the way only you can make it. I'm starving! And one of your apricot tarts and a big platter of cheeses, just for me. I dream of the cheeses from Félice. And country butter."

"I'll have to go into the village, there isn't much in the house."

"Then go, go. I'll be here, don't worry."

During all that long, hot September day Nadine guarded the sickroom. She stood in the corridor outside of the half-opened door and listened avidly. Mistral coughed constantly and violently. Sometimes he moaned and called her name in a pleading, desperate voice that was so weak that it could barely be heard. He whispered harshly for Marte, over and over, and coughed again, more rendingly every hour and yet, it seemed to her, without as much force as before. Occasionally, he seemed to fall asleep but never for long. Downstairs, Marte, relieved and comforted, busied herself in cooking and making the house look welcoming.

"Open all the shutters, Marte, take those awful covers off the furniture, pick some flowers, build a fire in the grate—at night it's too depressing like this," Nadine had commanded, and Marte, delighted at the new life in the house, had been glad to obey. When Monsieur was well enough to come down to complain, it would be time enough to close the shutters again.

In the middle of the night Nadine woke up with a start, as if someone had called her name, but the house was quiet. Marte, she knew, was sleeping in her room behind the kitchen downstairs. Yet . . . something . . . there *was* something. She threw on a robe and went into Mistral's room. The second she entered the room she knew that he was dying. Death filled the space, a primeval presence, a thickness of the air, a withering that nothing could reverse. At last. *At last.*

He was drowning in the liquid in his lungs. She could hear it. She had never heard that hideous noise before but she recognized it. What else could it be, that choking, desperate gurgle? If only the stench in the room wasn't so revolting—but she didn't intend to leave, not until she was sure.

Nadine went to the window and opened it so that a breeze could enter and push away some of the loathsome vileness that emanated from the bed. She pulled a chair as close to the window as possible and turned on a standing lamp just above her head. Intently she inspected her fingernails. The polish on one of them was chipped. Oh, on two. She would have to find a manicurist in Félice before the funeral.

There was a faint new sound from the bed, a begging sound, a pleading sound. Water? Could he want water when he was drowning? Impossible. He was struggling to speak. Gibberish. Meaningless syllables. She didn't listen.

Soon there were no more sounds from the bed. None at all. Still Nadine sat quietly in the fragile pool of light. She waited until she was absolutely certain that she had won before she walked quickly back to her own room.

She needed sleep. The morning light would wake her. These things were so sudden.

32

It was still raining. It hadn't stopped all day, Fauve thought as she peered out of the window of Maggy's apartment, to which they had both retreated after hearing the news of the death of Julien Mistral.

"How long," Darcy asked Fauve gently, "do you think I'm going to be able to say that you can't talk to all those reporters? Aside from the *New York Times*, and the *Daily News* and the *Post*, there are wire service guys and half a dozen stringers from out of town, a bunch of photographers, and two TV news crews right outside the house. They haven't been allowed in the lobby but they're not going away, rain or no rain."

"Why can't they leave me out of it?" Fauve asked miserably.

"Unfortunately you're the juiciest part of the story, sweetheart. When all the media people went to their morgues to put Mistral's bio together, the most newsworthy angle, from their point of view, is Mistral's daughter, Fauve Lunel—unfortunately it's the part of the story with the most human interest and you're right here where they can get at you. His death would get enormous attention just by itself, but add your mother's story . . . well, you can see why they want you."

"Do I really have to talk to them and answer questions?"

"I don't see why Fauve has to do that, do you, Darcy?" Maggy asked. "Is it necessary?"

"It would be the simplest way to get it over with," Darcy answered. "Just bite the bullet."

"What sort of things will they want to know?" Fauve asked, utterly at a loss.

"First of all, they've all been asking me if you're going to the funeral. After that, I just don't know. When did you last see him, what's your reaction to the tragic event . . . you know the sort of stuff they ask family members."

"I never expected this," Fauve said slowly.

"I did," Maggy said bitterly. "I remember the way it was when your mother died . . . there's nothing they won't ask and nothing they won't print. Darcy, can't you write down a statement and read it to them—tell them Fauve is too upset to talk."

"It's worth a try," he said, dubiously.

"Just don't say I'm going to the funeral," Fauve warned, "because I'm not."

There was a silence in the sitting room, unbroken until Maggy and Darcy exchanged a quick look and, in response, he got up to leave. "I'll be in the library, writing the statement," he explained.

Maggy moved over to the sofa on which Fauve was sitting and took her hand. "Look, Fauve, assuming that you really don't go to the funeral, don't you see that it will just arouse ten times the amount of curiosity there is already? Whatever the personal problems you had with him, your father was a major figure to the whole world—not just to art collectors—and besides Nadine Dalmas you're the only other child he ever had. You *must* go." Maggy's tone was reasonable but confident. Since that morning they had avoided discussing Fauve's refusal to go to the funeral and

Maggy had had time in which to consider the situation.

"It has nothing to do with personal problems, Magali," Fauve murmured.

"Darling, I don't understand you. There's going to be a big funeral in Félice in three days . . . we know that from the news conference that Nadine gave. You can't *not* be there. I'll go with you if you like. It will attract even more attention, but that's not important."

"No, Magali. That's not necessary. Thank you—but I'm still not going."

"Look, Fauve, every day thousands of people go to funerals and nobody asks them how they felt in their heart of hearts about the person who died—it's enough that they make an appearance. It may only be a formality but it's a deeply significant one, a gesture of respect if nothing else. Particularly in the case of a father."

"I can't make that gesture," Fauve said in a voice so low that Maggy could barely hear her. She moved closer and put her arm around her granddaughter.

"Surely you can find enough in his work to respect him—no matter what went wrong between you. The work remains, Fauve. Don't forget that. You really *must* do this . . . it's a responsibility that you have as his daughter."

"No. Let's not talk about it anymore," Fauve said, standing up.

"I simply don't understand," Maggy cried in distress and bewilderment. Fauve was never unreachable by reason.

"I swore I'd never tell you—about what he did, about why I never could bear to see him again . . . but I guess I must now—or you'll just never understand." Fauve knelt by the sofa on which Maggy sat and looked up into her face with a look compounded of a mixture of regret and misery and reluctance and some other emotion that Maggy couldn't identify, some emotion that made her draw back in fear.

"The work you talk about, the work I should respect, Magali, he sacrificed many people to that work."

"*Sacrificed?*"

"During the war he chose to paint while the rest of the world was fighting. Others did that . . . he wasn't alone. He collaborated with the Germans . . . he wasn't alone in that either. When a group of Resistance fighters—*Maquis*—stole the sheets he painted on, he denounced them to a friend, a German officer. They were all murdered—all those boys—but he got his sheets back so his work wasn't *interrupted.* But that wasn't the worst, Magali, not even that. Throughout the war whenever refugees tried to spend the night at *La Tourrello* he refused to admit them—people on the run for their lives—mostly Jews. They were friends from Paris, Magali, probably many of them were friends of yours. He even turned away Adrien Avigdor. He could have saved some of those people but they might have *disturbed* his work. Jews—no one can say how many—went to concentration camps because of his work. *And they died there.* Nothing, no human decency was allowed to come in the way of his work."

"How . . . who . . . ?" Maggy gasped.

"Kate told me, but he admitted it."

"He *admitted* it?"

"Yes. To me. That was the day I left. I never wanted you to know, Magali."

"My God . . . my God . . . why were you so afraid to say anything? . . . you were only a child . . . you should have told me," Maggy said, brokenly.

"I was too ashamed. Later, there was no reason to say anything, it was all over. He knew that he'd never see me again."

"*Ashamed?*"

"Ashamed that he was my father, a man who could do such things. Ashamed *for* him, most of all, ashamed to know what he was worth as a man. That's why I can't make a gesture of respect, Magali, not to him, not to his work. What work can be more important than human lives?"

Nadine Mistral Dalmas did not feel quite the degree of gratification she believed should be hers. As always, she told herself, trying to put things into perspective, no human event was without some flaw. The funeral had been almost all that she had intended it should be. The minister of the Beaux-Arts had arrived from Paris with an entourage, and the windswept old cemetery, at the very top of Félice, had made a most photogenic background for the long procession of people who had followed the coffin after the high requiem mass.

All the adult villagers of Félice had been there of course, as they would be in the case of any death in the community, but the crowd had been swelled by a crowd of art lovers from all over Provence who wanted to be able to say that they had seen Mistral buried. A fine turn-out, she thought, in spite of the fact that aside from Phillipe and a few rather unimportant friends of his, no one from Paris had been able to come down. Of course everybody she would have cared to see was still away on vacation. Quite naturally it had been impossible for them to fly from wherever they were to such an inconvenient place. If only the old man had died in October, in Paris, it would have been quite different, Nadine thought. Still it *had* been a perfect ceremony. Even in this provincial village the Catholic church could be trusted for its sense of style. Quite unerring. There was nothing she would have changed about the taste in which everything had been executed.

She felt a bit bereft now that the press had departed so unceremoniously, withdrawing their attention as soon as the coffin had been lowered into the grave. Still, it gave her a chance to relax for the first time since the death.

It was this business of the tax man that really irked her, Nadine thought. It was unquestionably the major flaw. How *dared* that little functionary forbid her to open the studio? Did he expect her to *steal* her own property, she had asked him as he sealed the front and back doors? He had grunted in a way that was too noncommittal to be actually impertinent—just routine in a case like this, he'd said, only until the gentlemen from Paris arrived, merely a formality. But when she had complained to Étienne Delage, Mistral's dealer—her dealer now, she reminded herself—he had told her that there was nothing she could do. The state must establish its share of the estate before anything could be moved, much less sold. It was infuriating to have to wait one more minute after she had waited for so long, maddening to have to admit the claims of the government, but she had no choice.

"And now," Nadine asked Marte, who had appeared at the door of the salon, "what is it?"

"*Maître* Banette, a notary from Apt, has just arrived. He asked to see you."

"I've never heard of the man. Tell him I'm sleeping, get rid of him."

"I tried to, *ma petite*, but he insisted. He says that it's important."

"Oh, all right." Nadine sighed. Everyone knew there was no way to avoid a notary. She had already dealt with death and taxes, how could a notary not follow?

The man who entered, plump and red-faced, dressed in a formal dark blue, had the pretension to give himself an air of importance, Nadine noticed in a surge of temper.

"You pick a bad moment to intrude, Monsieur."

"May I offer my deepest sympathies, Madame Dalmas? But of course you will appreciate that I had to come as soon as I could."

"I don't know why—*Maître* Banette, is it? Why are you here?"

"Madame," he said with reproach, "only my professional obligations could bring me to disturb you in your grief. But this matter of Monsieur Mistral's will must, of course, be brought to your attention. It is on file at the Fichier Centrale des Dernières Volontés in Aix, as is proper, but I brought you my copy. I realized you would wish it."

"His will?" Nadine sat up with a jerk. "He made a will! I never knew." In alarm she asked herself if the old man could have possibly left some money to charity. No, that would not be like him. Most certainly not.

"He came to consult me three years ago, Madame," *Maître* Banette continued. "There was the question of the Law of the Third of January 1972 . . ."

"What law? 1972? I don't remember anything about a law then that affected property. My own lawyer in Paris would have informed me."

"Ah, no, Madame. It has nothing to do with property as such." *Maître* Banette bristled. "In 1972 the Parliament of France made it possible for the first time to legally recognize the children of adulterous unions. Monsieur Mistral made out an act of recognition of Mademoiselle Fauve Lunel."

Nadine sat speechless. *Maître* Banette continued. "Then there is his will, a very strange document. I found him a most difficult person to advise, Madame. At first he wanted to leave his entire estate to Mademoiselle Fauve Lunel. I explained to him that it was impossible under the laws of France. The most that he could do was to divide the estate between his two children . . ."

"Divide!"

"Madame, rest assured, it was not possible to divide in half, no, Article 760 of the law of *Les Successions* makes that plain. Mademoiselle Fauve Lunel is only entitled to one-half of what she would inherit if she had been legitimate, that is to say twenty-five percent of the estate, rather than fifty percent. You, Madame, retain seventy-five percent of what remains after taxes." He paused and waited for Nadine to say something but when she did not, he continued, warming to his task. "The will, Madame, is written in a way of which I do not approve. I informed Monsieur Mistral of my opinion but I regret to say that he did not choose to take my advice."

"Fauve," Nadine said in a venomous voice. "Always Fauve."

"Precisely, Madame. There seems to have been a . . . a leaning toward this particular child."

"What did he say?" Nadine demanded. "Here, give me those papers."

"Madame!" He held the papers protectively close to his portly chest. "It is only because Mademoiselle Fauve Lunel is not in Félice—I made inquiries—that I came to you without waiting for her presence. She will have to be notified, sent for, but meanwhile I thought it proper to inform you of the contents of the will since I have no way to know where to find her."

"Read the thing, damn it," Nadine spat out.

"Madame, that is precisely what I intend to do," he said reprovingly, clearing his throat.

> " 'I, Julien Mistral, wish to leave all my work to my most dearly loved and cherished daughter, Fauve Lunel. However, since the law prevents me from doing this, I wish her to have the series, *La Rouquinne*, that I bought back from my wife, Katherine Browning Mistral, the deed of sale to which is attached to this document. I wish my daughter Fauve to have all the paintings I made

of her and of her mother, Théodora Lunel, who was the only woman I ever loved. In particular, I leave to Fauve the *Cavaillon* series, which she inspired me to paint. Because of Fauve, I learned at last, but to my eternal regret, too late, the most important lessons of my life. I hope that one day she will understand that I listened to her and changed. If my beloved daughter Fauve wishes, I would like her to have the domain of *La Tourrello* and all the land that belongs to it. If she does not want to accept the domain, I direct that it be sold and the proceeds added to my estate.'

" 'Under no circumstances do I wish *La Tourrello* and the studio in which I have worked to become the property of Madame Nadine Dalmas. To my certain knowledge she has never appreciated or understood either the beauty of any land or the nature of any art. The rest of my estate, up to an appraised value of twenty-five percent, I also leave to my daughter Fauve. I would be honored if she would call herself Fauve Mistral but I will understand if she does not choose to do so.'

" 'Whatever is left must, according to law, go to Madame Nadine Dalmas who will, I feel assured, sell it as quickly as she can to buy herself a continuation of the shallow, unworthy, valueless, and utterly vain life she has always chosen to lead.'

"That's all there is, Madame."

"That bastard! That slut, filth, rotten bitch! No! Never! She'll not have a thing, not one franc's worth, not while I live! He must have been totally insane! I'll contest the will, it won't go through!" Nadine's face, a Japanese mask of evil, spewed forth a voice that made the notary rise abruptly and back away, disgust frank on his face. He made an effort to pull his dignity around him.

"I must tell you, Madame," he managed to quaver, "there can be no question of insanity. If I had doubted Monsieur Mistral's sanity I would never have drawn this will. It is perfectly valid."

"Get out! What the hell do you know? I'll call my lawyer in Paris. You pompous little ass, you provincial, stupid fool—of course this crazy will can be contested. *Out!*" Nadine advanced on the notary so viciously that the man picked up his hat and fled the room without another word, taking the will with him.

No question but it was the best story they'd had in a long time, newspapermen agreed as they learned the details. "*Inconduite notoire de la mère*," Code Civile, Act 339—they hadn't heard of that one in a long time. "Notorious misconduct" on the part of Teddy Lunel, still the greatest cover girl who'd ever lived—not easy grounds to prove, the experts among them said, but without doubt the only way to attack that extraordinary will Julien Mistral had made, the text of which had been sought out in the files in Aix as soon as the news of the suit broke, a text that had given them one hell of a grand story too. All in all quite a windfall for an item that they had thought had ended in a graveyard high on the north side of the Lubéron. It should run for weeks, said one junior reporter in excitement. Months, you young ignoramus, months, corrected his senior, rubbing his hands together in pleasure.

"It doesn't matter if Nadine Dalmas can't prove anything," Darcy said. "She'll still have her revenge, she'll still drag Teddy's name through the mud."

"She's free to dig up anything about my mother that she can find, even if it doesn't apply, isn't she?" Fauve asked violently.

"I'm afraid so. That's got to be just what she intends to do. Why else would she have taken a step that made the words of the will public? If she hadn't sued to break the will no one would ever have known what contempt Mistral had for her."

Fauve was prowling about Maggy's sitting room, her hands balled into fists. Every muscle in her body was so tightly clenched that she was bent, stoop-shouldered, as she shuttled back and forth, unable to stop and sit still for even a minute. She was caught up in the grip of a rage such as she had never known could exist. It was like a rogue wave that had suddenly appeared out of the calm sea, towering over a small boat, lifting it fifty feet into the air. Nothing she had experienced in all of her life now seemed to matter compared to Nadine's attack on her mother's memory. She would kill Nadine right here, right now, if it were possible, Fauve realized, and felt no shock.

"I'm going to Avignon tomorrow. I'm going to prevent this from happening. My mother's not going to be called a whore! I don't give a damn about the pictures but Nadine *cannot do this*—I will not allow it."

"Fauve . . ." said Maggy, and stopped. She began again. "All of this happened before you were born . . ."

"I'm going to pack," Fauve said, ignoring her.

"Isn't there anybody you can call?" Maggy pleaded. "Somebody who could help from all those summers you spent in France? Can't you think of a single person?"

"Yes," said Fauve slowly, stopping on her way to the door, "yes, there is somebody. How could I have forgotten?"

Eric Avigdor was waiting at the airport in Marseilles. He was constrained as he expressed his sympathy to Fauve, remembering the manner in which they had parted six months before.

"Papa was delighted that you called him," he said as they sped up toward Avignon on the Autoroute du Sud.

"He must have been astonished—I just asked overseas information for his number and we were connected within minutes. I'm afraid it was almost midnight. I hadn't thought about the time difference."

"He never goes to bed early."

"That's what he said but I thought he was only being polite."

"Papa? He gave up being polite when he retired."

"Has he found a lawyer for me?" Fauve asked anxiously.

"The best man in Avignon. He's waiting for you at my parents' house. His name is *Maître* Jean Perrin. He fought with Papa in the Resistance."

"It's so kind of your father."

"He's very fond of you." Eric smiled at her for the first time, and Fauve smiled a little. Just thinking of Adrien Avigdor made her feel better.

They lapsed into silence again but it was less formal than the stiff words they had exchanged during the wait for Fauve's suitcase. She had flown down to Marseilles directly after getting off the plane in Paris and she was exhausted and crumpled, but the afternoon light of Provence in early October, the sight of the eternally renewed olive trees and the sentinel, pointed cypresses worked their familiar miracle on her and a sheer animal pleasure in being back quickened in her blood.

For the first time since she was sixteen Fauve permitted herself to remember how much she loved this countryside. They turned off the Autoroute where it crossed over the main east-west road, and instead of going east, which would have brought them to Félice, they turned west and within a half-hour they arrived at the Avigdors' house on the rue de la Montée St. André in Villeneuve-les-Avignon.

Fauve was immediately disappointed and concerned at the sight of the lawyer. She had expected Jean Perrin to be the age of Adrien Avigdor but how could this man be more than thirty-eight or nine? He was slender, short, almost boyish in his looks. However, at second glance, he had gray eyes that made her stand up very straight, for Jean Perrin was one of the breed of men who take in everything with one rapid, comprehensive, commanding glance.

Adrien Avigdor, unchanged, was wearing a sweater and an open-necked shirt but *Maître* Perrin was dressed in a double-breasted suit with the rosette of the Legion of Honor in his buttonhole. His elegant, citified attire gave him, Fauve thought uneasily, something of the look of an urchin dressed in his best.

Beth Avigdor hugged Fauve as warmly as if she were a favorite niece.

"You must be so tired, my poor Fauve. The guest room is waiting for you. Would you like to lie down for an hour before we dine?"

"No, thank you, Madame Avigdor. I'd prefer to talk to *Maître* Perrin right away."

Fauve and the lawyer went to sit on the wide balcony of the house, high above the city, with the Rhône in the near distance and the silhouettes of the palaces of Avignon beyond, steeples and towers like an immense sailing ship riding the turbulent river.

"Eric told me that you were in the Resistance with Monsieur Avigdor?" Fauve probed, still troubled by his youth.

"Well, you see I hated school. It was more fun to run away to the mountains of Aix and play at games of good-guys-bad-guys. I was thirteen when the war ended. Alas, there was still time to make me go back in school, and so as you can tell, I became, relatively speaking, a respectable citizen."

"How old were you when you ran away from school?"

"Ten." He shrugged with a grin. "But as tall as I am now." As he smiled, Fauve caught a glimpse of the reckless, preteenaged patriot he had been and she felt all lack of confidence drop away from her.

"*Maître* Perrin, can you help me?"

"It is all I have been thinking about since Adrien called me yesterday night. In fact, Mademoiselle, I have spent the day working on it, a more interesting day than those I usually spend in my chambers, I must tell you."

"You've been at work already? But we haven't even talked."

"The question evidently reduces itself to the question of character witnesses, does it not? Therefore I looked for them. And I have found one, I am pleased to tell you."

"One? *One character witness?*" Fauve cried protestingly. "What good can that do against a charge of 'notorious misconduct'? My mother was twenty-four when she met my father . . . obviously she had lived, she wasn't a nun—and now she's in the hands of my half-sister who's out to ruin her . . . oh, my mother is so *vulnerable*."

Fauve's confidence in Jean Perrin vanished as quickly as it had come. How could this man, who now again seemed naïve and inexperienced, begin to guess what could be discovered and distorted about Teddy Lunel who had captured the hearts of so many men who were alive today? "A number of lovers," Melvin had told her, and she'd known that he was being tactful.

How many of them would boast? How many of them would be able to resist talking about their affairs with the most beautiful girl in the world?

"Mademoiselle, what does your mother's age have to do with this charge?"

"Everything, I should imagine," she said in distraction. He just didn't understand.

"You have not talked to a French lawyer, not even to a notary?"

"My grandmother spoke to the French counsel in New York and I got on the plane the next morning."

"Ah, a diplomat. A pity. Yet how could he have been expected to know, after all? You see, Mademoiselle, the law of France is most explicit and firm on this question, it does not permit of any doubt, it does not allow malicious charges to be brought idly. The charge of misconduct would only apply to the period during which your parents actually knew each other, during which your paternity might be questioned. From what I have learned, they were never apart from the day they met until the day she died. This fact I intend to see established beyond a doubt."

He looked away from Fauve's face. It was indecent to watch such relief. When Jean Perrin heard her begin to sob he got up quietly and went back into the house.

"What's wrong?" asked Beth Avigdor. "Shall I go out to her?"

"No, I'd leave her alone for a while," Jean Perrin advised.

Eric ignored him and rushed out to the balcony. Fauve was huddled in a deck chair weeping uncontrollably, shaking in a way that frightened him. He scooped her up and held her tightly in his arms, letting her cry until his chest was running with her tears. He comforted her with soft noises, rocking her like a baby until, finally, she lifted her wet, swollen, flushed face and gasped, "Handkerchief." He fished in his pocket and found nothing. "Wipe your nose on my sleeve," he said.

"Oh, I can't," Fauve wailed. "Not on your sleeve."

"Then I'll do it for you." He laughed, as he unbuttoned a cuff with one hand. "Now, *blow!*"

Half an hour later, Fauve, with her face washed and her hair brushed, sat in the salon with the three Avigdors as *Maître* Perrin recounted the details of his day with such well-contained pride that only Adrien Avigdor knew how he felt. Jean's eyes had shone like that, Avigdor thought, when he had come back from one of his forays during the Resistance. He looked as shyly pleased as on the night on which he'd blown up that freight train that was carrying arms to the Battle of the Bulge.

"I started by asking myself what it is that two people, who have, so to speak, vanished from their customary worlds, would still do that ordinary people do. That is to say, people who are not living for love alone," Jean Perrin began. "And to that there is only one answer, is there not?" He paused but none of them ventured a guess. "They eat."

"They drink wine," Adrien Avigdor corrected him.

"Both, *mon vieux*, both. And where do they eat? In restaurants, at least from time to time, for two people, no matter how much in love, will never be content with home cooking for an entire year. And where in Avignon would the greatest painter in France eat?" Again he paused, and this time Fauve answered, shouting.

"Hiely!"

"How did you know, Mademoiselle?"

"My father used to take me there as a special treat," she exclaimed, and then stopped, astonished. She flushed deeply. She hadn't said the words "my father" in so many years that she couldn't believe how naturally they had jumped out of her mouth.

"Of course, at Hiely, the only two-star restaurant in Avignon. It was not difficult to guess. So I went there this morning and spoke to Monsieur Hiely. He was learning his *métier* in his father's kitchen in 1953 but he had often crept to the door and peeked out to admire your mother. He remembered her well. I asked to see their *Livre d'Or* because I knew that they would have asked Julien Mistral to sign it. And there, on one of the pages, I found his signature. More than a signature, a charming sketch of Papa Hiely. And, at the bottom, your mother had signed it as well."

"But . . . but . . . that doesn't prove anything," Fauve faltered.

"Indeed no. However, the family Hiely sends Christmas cards to their good clients, and they have a record of their addresses. With a little searching through their files, I was able to find out where your parents lived while they were in Avignon, and there I went, without, as Adrien would be amazed to note, stopping first for lunch. The house is still standing and the same concierge who was there then is there now. I imagine that Madame Bette will still be there in the year 2000. In any case, she was most helpful . . ."

"The concierge?" Fauve interrupted.

"No, Mademoiselle, do not look so dubious, it is not the concierge who is your character witness, although she could well serve if we needed more than one. Madame Bette told me that your parents had become friendly with a doctor who still lives on the ground floor of the house. Not more than two hours ago I managed to find this doctor at home. He told me that he and his wife knew your parents from the day they moved in—indeed they helped move some of the furniture your father had bought. The two couples used to have drinks together from time to time and go out to dinner as well, to Hiely, to the Prieuré, to places in the country. They loved your mother very much, very much indeed. They never saw your father again, after your mother's death, but they have always understood why he disappeared from their lives. They spoke of your parents' total devotion to each other. The doctor, Professor Daniel . . ."

"Dr. Daniel!" exclaimed Beth Avigdor. "But I know him!"

"Naturally, Beth. He is one of the most distinguished men in all Avignon, a professor at the University of Aix, Mademoiselle Lunel," Jean Perrin explained, hurrying on. "Professor Daniel felt the most lively indignation at this odious and disgusting charge that has been made . . . he became quite outraged—indeed, one would have to say that he took it personally. Of course both he and his wife are ready to testify that your mother never had anything to do with any man other than your father during all the time she lived in Avignon. The attack on the will will be stopped before it starts. There can be no question of any further trouble from the quarter of Madame Dalmas." Jean Perrin gave his shy, rapscallion's grin of triumph.

"*Personally?*" Fauve asked. "Why did the doctor take it so personally? Was it just because of being so friendly with my parents?"

"It was he, Mademoiselle, who delivered you into the world."

33

"Madame Dalmas, what a pleasure to see you." Madame Violette, the senior *vendeuse* at the salon of Yves Saint Laurent was too highly trained to betray her astonishment as Nadine strolled in, but there was a perceptible rustle of startled interest from the group of lesser *vendeuses* who stood waiting to lead clients to their seats before the collection. As Madame Violette escorted Nadine to the most advantageously placed chair in the room she asked, "Is there anything in particular that might interest you, Madame?"

"A new wardrobe, entirely new," Nadine said with an indifferent air. "I've lived in Albin for so long that it has become utterly boring, too predictable."

"Ah, but Madame is superbly turned out. However, I must agree that a change is always amusing. Monsieur Saint Laurent will be sorry to learn that you came while he was out of town."

Nadine picked up the traditional stub of a gold pencil and the little white pad on which she would write the numbers of the clothes that interested her enough to try on. It was disorienting to sit, like any ordinary client waiting to see a new collection. And wildly exciting as well. There would be none of the overfamiliarity that existed when she had watched Jean François's designs evolve over a period of months, so that each time she put on a new garment she felt that she had worn it for years.

Saint Laurent was the best designer in the world, but it would have been unthinkable for her to admit it to herself before yesterday. Today she was free, finally free of the tyranny of that overrated, whimpering infant, Jean François Albin, with his sulks and his tantrums. Today she was in a position in which she could not imagine any other woman in the world being in: she had all the money she could conceivably spend, and a great deal more, and in her rows of closets there was not one dress, not one blouse, not even one handbag, that she intended to keep a day longer than necessary. Even a new bride of the richest man in the world, she mused, must have something in her old wardrobe that she didn't want to part with, something she intended to wear again. But since her interview—if that was what you could call it—with Jean François yesterday, Nadine intended to jettison the lot. It had not been anything that he had said, indeed, very few words had passed between them. Nadine had simply walked into his office and told him that from now on he would have to do without her.

"Ah, I see," he had replied, so expressionless that he must have been too stunned to begin his habitual complaining.

"You do understand, Jean François, that now . . ." She had lifted her shoulders in a gesture that said to perfection what words could not: now I have no more time to waste with your tiny, petulant needs, now you are going to have to struggle along without me, now you will find your silly little life falling apart because I cannot be bothered with you any longer.

"I do understand, Nadine. I shall have to make the best of it. Forgive me, Nadine, but Princess Grace is in the fitting room and I promised to go to her. Will I see you at her dinner tonight? No? Of course, you must still be in mourning. Well then, *à bientôt*?" He had kissed her on the cheek in the dry way he kissed everyone, and had rushed off busily, humming, shouting for his favorite fitter to attend him, instructing a secretary to send coffee down to the Princess's fitting room, pausing only once, to pet the Afghans that lay at the entrance to his workroom. "Yes, my beauties, yes, you are the most beautiful creatures God ever made, yes, my babies, yes," he had crooned to the dogs, and disappeared down the corridor.

A good act, thought Nadine, and one that might have fooled anybody. She knew, of course, that she had dealt him a severe blow, one which might well send him into one of his nervous depressions.

Nevertheless there had been something—something she hadn't missed—that had made her decide to come to Saint Laurent today. If she hadn't known Albin so well, she would have had to say that it was a look of . . . amusement? Was it possible? Certainly not, she thought, as she stared with only half-hidden contempt at the women surrounding her. This was not the right time of year to order new clothes; these were women from the provinces or foreigners who were thrilled to find themselves here. She didn't like finding herself watching the collection with them, but she chose not to wear Albin's clothes any longer. What could Jean François possibly have been amused *about*? The first manikins passed in a quick-stepping flurry of suits for early day, designed for fall and winter, clothes which had first been shown earlier in the summer. By now, Nadine thought, all her friends who dressed at Saint Laurent had already received their new autumn suits, and were wearing them.

If she asked Madame Violette, she was certain that the time required to make her clothes could be reduced to a minimum. She would have to be treated as if she were a tourist with only two weeks to spend on fittings, she thought grimly. Never mind, she would see next spring's collection at the press opening, decorating the front row of chairs with Saint Laurent's other favored customers, as much a part of the ritual as the clothes themselves and, in certain ways, more significant.

She scribbled numbers on her pad while she tried not to reflect on the conversation she had had this morning with her lawyer. She had gone back to him in one last effort to persuade him to make a further investigation of the life of that whore, Fauve's mother. When he had learned of the testimony of Dr. Daniel in Avignon, the lawyer had told Nadine that her case against her father's will was over, finished. She'd gone to other lawyers and they had all told her the same thing: one and only one "*action en reduction*" of a will may be brought. She must accept the will as final: nothing could now prevent Fauve from receiving 25 percent of the estate in precisely the way in which the will had been written. She would have to satisfy herself with 75 percent, they had told her, as if that would prevent her from knowing that she had been irrevocably cheated, *stolen from!*

How typical it was of her lawyer to insist on having the last word, even in failure, Nadine thought. He was criminally unprofessional, she'd told him, to which he had merely retorted that he had advised her against attacking the will in the first place. As she remembered his smugness Nadine's pencil broke in half with the pressure she put on it. Madame Violette, who had been standing at the back of the room, observing her clients, immediately brought her another.

Now a group of pant suits appeared on the runway, man-tailored with that special Saint Laurent exaggeration that Albin had never been able to achieve. Very much her style. Precisely what she liked best, thought Nadine, as she turned over her paper and began a fresh sheet.

The women on both sides of her were watching her write numbers with such obvious envy that she could have laughed in their faces. What must it be like to come here and know that you could only afford to buy a single ensemble? Unimaginable, a life in which you would look in your closet and find only one custom-made garment? It would be like having one meal a year and living on bread and water the rest of the time. Why did they even bother? Nadine wrote more numbers, quickly, greedily, knowledgeably. She could hardly wait to get into the dressing room and see herself in these clothes.

She blamed her lawyer for more than the ruinous testimony of that doctor in Avignon. Why had he not properly warned her that the text of her father's will would be made public? Why had he not told her that reporters would swarm to Aix, to read the copy that was filed there? Could that sickening, self-satisfied excuse for a man not have foreseen that the will would be translated into every foreign language, would become news in every foreign city? At least, that was what Phillipe had said. Perhaps Phillipe was wrong, perhaps it was only in Paris that it had appeared? She didn't intend to investigate.

Phillipe's opinions were nothing to her now, not even minor annoyances. She had kicked him out the same day that the will had been printed in *Le Monde* and *Le Figaro*. Told him to get out within the hour. It had been amazing, even admirable in its own way, the speed with which he packed, and with what little protest.

He must have seen it coming, Nadine concluded, must have braced himself for it. A man with his experience could not help but know that once she had her money she would get rid of him. He had probably been planning how to put a good face on it from the day Mistral died. Phillipe wasn't stupid about things like that, she had to admit. About everything else, yes, but not about other people's money. A man who could sponge for an entire lifetime had to have some shrewdness.

In any case, she told herself with relief, she need never be burdened with his bills again, neither his debts nor his opinions. The only opinions she valued were those of her friends. They would realize that Mistral had been senile—mad, sick, senile. The others, those nobodies who made up the rest of the world, would have forgotten within the hour even if they had bothered to read those headlines, that story. So Monsieur Phillipe Dalmas thought that she had poured a bucket of ordure over her own head, did he? Typical words of a bitter man on his way down and out. How could he explain that no one, not one single person, had even mentioned the will to her?

What an absurd idea to have . . . that no one had mentioned it because they had not wanted to embarrass her. Yesterday, when she had run into Hélène and Peggy outside of Hermès, neither one of them had said anything about the will. But they had not expressed the conventional condolences. They had acted as if nothing whatsoever had happened to her, since they had last seen her, before her father had died. They had seemed—well, a touch offhand perhaps.

Sometimes it was difficult for even the most well brought up people to speak of death. Wasn't that why they usually wrote notes of sympathy instead of phoning? Hélène and Peggy. Had there been something . . . amused . . . about their glances? If one of their fathers had written a will so self-evidently insane, she might well have had the chic, the tact, to make a joke of it, but she would have made the joke out loud, so that they knew that she understood how ridiculous, how meaningless it was, how little it reflected reality. Nadine took out a tiny handkerchief and touched her forehead, under her bangs. It was much too hot in Saint Laurent.

Ah, the short dinner dresses. She had always particularly admired the way he did them, his flamenco bravura. She had always resented having to wear Albin's dinner dresses with their classically muted sex appeal. He overdid subtlety, Albin, as he overdid everything else.

As Nadine inspected the dresses, her trained eyes gloating over each detail, she wondered idly what the *Cavaillon* series could be. It was a joke, disinheriting her from ownership of a house in which she wouldn't dream of living, and a group of portraits of three generations of sluts, as if they could possibly be more important than the vast body of his work that would come to her. Cavaillon? A market town, a place of no interest whatsoever.

Her curiosity didn't extend to the point that she was willing to be there when the tax authorities opened the studio tomorrow. Étienne Delage, her dealer, would represent her. He would make enough in commissions on her, God knows, to go and stay put for as long as was necessary, keeping a close eye on the tax men while they made their infernal inventory.

As the first manikin came out in an evening dress she simply had to have, Nadine ran out of paper on which to write its number. She had completely filled her tiny pad, jotting down all the wonderful clothes she was itching to order. She raised her head to signal Madame Violette for another pad and caught her, whispering behind her hand to two other *vendeuses*. All three of them were staring straight at Nadine. They averted their eyes the instant she spied them, but, on each of their faces she caught the same look of amusement that she had glimpsed on Jean François's face, on Peggy's face, on Hélène's face. They were laughing at her. Sneering? No, *laughing*.

Nadine got up, walking down the row without regard for the legs of the women she passed. She walked faster and yet faster as she approached the exit to the showroom.

"Madame Dalmas? Is there something wrong? May I assist you?" whispered Madame Violette, catching up with her just as she reached the door.

"It's stifling here. You can't expect anyone to sit for hours without air conditioning on such a day."

"Ah, Madame Dalmas, you are absolutely right. I am desolate. Monsieur Saint Laurent will be desolate. If you will permit me, Madame, let me take your pad. When you return I promise you the air conditioning will be on and all the numbers you've picked out will be assembled in our largest fitting room."

"I saw nothing I wanted."

"Nothing?" Madame Violette echoed, disbelieving.

"Not even a blouse. A disappointing collection. Albin has spoiled me for anyone else."

Fauve Lunel could be, if such a thing were possible, almost as stubborn as her father had been, Adrien Avigdor told himself, as he sat in discussion with her in the library of his house.

"I still intend to go straight back to New York," Fauve repeated, gently because she had deep fondness for Adrien Avigdor, but with a resolution whose wisdom she refused to question.

"Of course you do, but not now, not until the studio has been opened, not until you have seen the pictures that your father left you."

"Can't you just accept the fact that I don't want to have anything to do with them?" she pleaded again. "That I *refuse?* I've asked *Maître* Perrin to handle everything for me and he accepted."

"I have complete faith in Jean but there are some things you can't ask—can't expect—somebody else to do for you."

"I'm needed back in New York," Fauve said, trying another argument. "You don't fully understand, dearest Monsieur Avigdor. Imagine hundreds of beautiful girls and three thousand prospective clients, all craving their services. How can I abandon them?"

"These beautiful girls, you're selling them?"

"I think you know what I do." She laughed at his grave attempt to tease.

"I also know that there are people who can manage the agency while you're here. My old friend Maggy, I presume, has not grown idle with the passage of time? I have every faith that she will not let even one of those girls wither on the vine."

Fauve hesitated while she studied his face. He certainly didn't look immovable, impossible and intractable. He looked as placid and relaxed as a man milking a cow, almost asleep in the sun, but she still hadn't been able to convince him that she was right. Now that the question of Nadine's suit had been settled, now that her mother's memory was safe, *why* was Adrien Avigdor so intent on using the full force of his authority to make her stay longer? She felt too much gratitude for his help to simply ignore his determination, but on the other hand he had not been swayed by anything she said.

"There's nothing left to decide," Fauve replied, summoning her resolve. "What would I want with *La Tourrello?* I only have a few weeks' vacation every year and I wouldn't always want to spend them there, would I? Well, what happens when a house is left unoccupied? What about fire, what about pipes that burst, what about the mistral that blows a hole in the tiles and lets in the rain? I'd have to rent it or hire a caretaker who'd live there full-time. It's just too complicated. I'm going to sell it, of course."

"Your father's will said clearly that you should do as you wished."

"Well then?" Fauve asked.

"Nevertheless, I believe that you must, at least, *see* your legacy, the *Cavaillon* series. It's your duty."

"Monsieur Avigdor," Fauve said with finality, "we could go on like this for days. But that's not the point. I know . . . I know how my father behaved during the war."

"Ah." He managed not to show the alarming leap of surprise and shock that he felt.

"I also know that you know, that you are aware of what he did, not just to you, but to many others—no, don't say anything! Now, just tell me, if you still think I have a 'duty,' as you put it, to see my legacy."

"I do," he answered firmly.

"But why—how can you?"

"Because whatever else he was or did, you cannot deny that Julien Mistral loved your mother and that she loved him. And he loved you most dearly. That was made very plain in his will. The *Cavaillon* series, whatever it may be, was painted for you, Fauve, painted *because* of you. You cannot turn your back on it."

"Have *you* forgiven him then?"

"Yes, I hope I have."

"Why?" she asked again, leaning forward to try to understand.

"Why? In part, of course, because he was a genius. I know, genius is no excuse, but surely it is an explanation, a partial explanation. In the Book of Job, if I remember correctly, my father used to tell me that somewhere it says that 'Great men are not always wise.' Nor are they always kind or always brave, Fauve. But there is something more than that. I forgave him because he was a man and I too am a man—*merely a man*—not his judge." As he spoke this last word, Eric walked into the library and stood, listening to them. Fauve looked at Eric as she answered his father.

"Perhaps you are right, but still I want no part of the past."

"One visit, Fauve, that's all I ask," Avigdor insisted. "After that, do whatever you wish."

"I think," Eric said, "that the two of you could be said to have reached a Mexican standoff."

Adrien Avigdor looked with interest at the dark blush that mounted from Fauve's shoulders to her hairline as she nodded her reluctant assent. What made that rascal of a son of his think that he, Adrien Avigdor, needed to be told that he had reached a Mexican standoff, whatever bizarre thing that might be? He had merely won the negotiation, as he had always fully intended to, as he had always been certain he would. He was not in the habit of losing such matters.

Several days later, in the second week of October, the three appraisers who had been appointed by the Bureau of Estate Taxes were finally able to gather at *La Tourrello.* The government had waited until the top art experts in France were all available since the contents of Mistral's studio were too important a source of revenue to be evaluated by any but the most knowledgeable.

Fauve's anxiety mounted steadily as she drove toward Félice with Eric and his parents. She found it difficult to accept the fact that she had let herself be persuaded to come back even one last time to the house that contained the two rooms she had once loved most in the world: her father's studio and her *pigeonnier* bedroom, the house she had been trying to forget since she was sixteen.

The horror she had felt, the scalding bitterness, the hopeless pity for those unknowns who had been denied shelter, the abiding shame, all the emotions she had been battered by as she left *La Tourrello* so many years ago came flooding back as the car continued past Mènerbes and drew closer to Félice. She felt chilled to the bone, apprehension and tension made her conscious of her spine as if each individual vertebra were a tooth that had been attacked by a sense of intense discomfort. Not pain but an almost unbearable *uneasiness.*

Fauve's senses were too vivid. The colors of the countryside seemed so bright that even her sunglasses gave her little relief, she was aware of the voices of Eric and his parents as if they had been exaggerated, distorted slightly, tuned up to a higher pitch than normal. And their gestures seemed to be fragmented, jerky, flickering. She struggled to touch reality but everything had the quality of a hallucination that grew steadily more unendurable as they mounted the narrow road through the forest of live oaks and she saw the ancient walls of *La Tourrello* rise beyond the avenue of whirling cypresses.

They parked outside on the meadow, covered with tangles of thistles and spiky grasses, that had been drying all summer long. Fauve slid reluctantly, slowly, out of the car. The odor of honeysuckle hit her like a blow. She had managed to forget so many details. She had managed to forget that the *mas* was covered in honeysuckle. She had managed to forget how she could never breathe in its sweetness deeply enough, how it never cloyed, never grew less tantalizingly fragrant, with a scent that contained a mystery she had never captured, a scent that was the very memory of happiness distilled.

"Look, cars are here already. The appraisers must be inside waiting," said Adrien Avigdor, to try to get Fauve to move forward. She stood rigidly, unwillingness plain in every tense line of her body, and something more. Something that he could only call fear. He felt deep and painful emotion himself. He had not stood on this spot since the summer of 1942 when he had been refused entrance by Marte Pollison and had looked back to see Julien Mistral letting him leave.

"Let's go," said Eric, taking Fauve's hand unceremoniously. He pulled her along, through the open doors, into the courtyard.

A group of five men stood smoking and chatting in the courtyard. One of them was Étienne Delage, Mistral's dealer who now represented Nadine Dalmas, three of them were the appraisers and one a supervisor from the Department of Taxes in Avignon. They all introduced themselves solemnly shaking hands with Fauve, Eric and his parents.

"There doesn't seem to be anyone to open the door," said one of the experts, a bearded Parisian, tall and elegant.

"I have the key," said the dealer. "I've been informed that the old servant has retired. The house is empty. All the keys were left with the notary of Apt, *Mâitre* Banette. He asked me to give them to Mademoiselle Lunel since he was unable to be here today. He also asked me to say that he is at her service should she need him on estate matters." He took a ring of keys and handed them to Fauve.

"If you please, Monsieur," she said, drawing back abruptly, "would you unlock the door?"

Étienne Delage nodded and led the way. Although he was less familiar with the house than Fauve, she hung behind the others, every step she took an unwilling one, as he directed the group through the dimly lit *mas*, across rooms where an occasional shutter still stood open and finally out the back toward the studio wing. Finally they all stood in front of the doors to the studio of Julien Mistral.

The tax inspector from Avignon removed the seals that had been placed on the doors only hours after Mistral's death had been announced.

"Mademoiselle?" he asked Fauve, indicating the door. She shook her head in negation and again it was Delage who unlocked the studio doors.

Now, with one gesture, everyone stood back and Fauve was impelled, by their politeness and sense of occasion, to go first. She squared her shoulders and took half a dozen rapid, determined steps into the shadowy studio before she came to a sudden halt. The shock she had received from the scent of the honeysuckle was nothing compared to the assault made on her senses by the well-beloved, deeply familiar aroma of this dominion, in which her father had painted for almost fifty years. She almost cried out as she collided with the most important hours of her past.

The studio was not dark although all the shutters had been closed. Part of the skylight was open and the work lights were still on, as Mistral had left them. Shafts of morning sun, swirling with a billion universes of dust motes, seemed like columns from which the pungency of oil paint was released into the air.

Fauve closed her eyes for an instant, assailed by memories and then, recovering herself, stood stiffly, looking at the floor. Finally she raised her eyes and faced the studio.

What was this? What was this leaping symphony of flying paint? What were these huge canvases breathing life, this feeling of creation so glad, so generous that it had wings stronger than an eagle's? From what place came the rhythm that charged through the studio with majestic thunder?

There was nothing in all that vast space but some enormous paintings, larger than Mistral had ever painted, each hung with an exactitude of placement that spoke of much thought. The only sign of his presence was a sturdy, movable stepladder in one corner, his worktable and the old easel on which was placed an empty, fresh canvas.

As Fauve looked at the walls she gasped, bewildered, dazzled, stunned by the complex imagery that swept dancing out at her. Her eyes darted to one canvas and found crowned lions rearing into the air, lambs cavorting, gazelles prancing and doves swooping about, all against a tangled brilliance of jewel-bright wild flowers and apple trees, the green of peridot and celadon. She looked further, at the next canvas, her eyes captured by the majestic weight of piled sheaves of wheat and barley, heaping plenitudes of pomegranate and date, grape, olive and fig. Here, Mistral's lambent colors were the deep, opulent greens and golds of full summer, grains waving as splendidly as banners. The next canvas exploded with surging ripeness, the deepness, the intensity of the hues of the autumnal equinox: amethyst, wine, pumpkin and ruby, vibrating with the fulfillment of the harvest. Palm branches wreathed in willow and myrtle were flung aloft as in a glorious procession that took place beneath a full red moon and many stars.

Singing birds . . . the rose of Sharon . . . the cedars of Lebanon . . . what did it mean?

Then, on the far wall she saw the largest painting of all and was immediately claimed by its magnetism. All the brilliant profusion of other images faded around her and she narrowed her vision, approaching the gigantic canvas on which a sevenbranched candelabra blazed with a crescendo of essential light, a monumental menorah that radiated glory of thousands of years of faith against a background of triumphant crimson. Fauve stood there speechless, looking upward, her heart leaping, her mind empty of everything but awe.

Out loud, from behind her, Eric said the words that Julien Mistral had painted in tall, bold letters underneath the base of the menorah.

"*La Lumière Qui Vit Toujours. La Synagogue de Cavaillon, 1774*—the light that lives forever . . ."

"He . . . he went to Cavaillon!" Fauve cried out in wonder and joy.

"The *Cavaillon* series—that's what it means," Eric said slowly, with reverence.

"But the other paintings? What . . . ?"

"There's an inscription on each one of them," Eric answered. Throughout the studio the group of other visitors were spreading out, forgetting themselves in the adventure of discovery, exclaiming out loud, speaking as much to themselves as to each other, experiencing the uncharted seas of Mistral's genius.

Fauve didn't turn but continued to look searchingly at the great candelabra that commemorated the sacred vessel that had stood in the desert sanctuary and in the two Temples in Jerusalem. Finally she turned and took Eric's hand. Together they walked back the length of the studio and stopped in front of the first huge painting.

There two tall candles were set in polished candlesticks, a twisted loaf of bread and a silver goblet brimming with wine stood on a white tablecloth. Each of the simple, elemental forms passionately spoke of gratitude for the gifts of the Creator to man. A peace, a gàiety, a joyful solemnity poured forth from the painting and Fauve nodded her head in the beginnings of comprehension.

"*Shabbat*," said the bearded art expert from Paris, translating the inscription that was written not in French now but in the letters of the Hebrew alphabet. "The Sabbath." Fauve searched the strong, unfamiliar, evocative shapes of the letters and saw in them the brushwork that was distinctively Mistral's, vivid and fierce, yet contained within a discipline to which he had never bowed before.

She moved eagerly toward the next paintings and she realized that the three canvases, those on which gazelles were leaping and branches were growing, the first canvases to catch her eyes, had been hung so that they were clearly set apart from the others. She stepped back so that she could see them as a group.

Puzzled, yet raised to another peak of visual delight, she looked in excited confusion from one to another. What was the key to these passionate rhythms, the wealth of images?

At her right shoulder she heard Adrien Avigdor's voice, pausing between each word as he translated the meaning of the words of the Hebrew inscriptions, composed of letters that he had studied for a few years, a lifetime ago, letters that he discovered had never disappeared from his recollection.

"*Pesach*," he said in his resonant voice as he gazed at the first canvas.

"The Feast of Exodus," added the art expert from Paris. "The anniversary of the revelation at Sinai—he used the symbols of the Song of Songs."

"*Shavous*," Avigdor said, turning to the next canvas, and again the expert's explanation came. "The Summer Festival—the bringing of fruits and grains to the Temple."

"*Sukos*," Avigdor read from the third painting and paused. "The Autumn Feast," said the Parisian's voice. "The tabernacles made of boughs and reeds in which everyone slept for a week, seeing the sky above."

Fauve swayed and around her the immense shapes of the pictures seemed to reach higher and higher until they touched the roof of the studio, until they reached beyond it into a firmament filled with moonlight. The walls receded, the colors burned brighter and brighter, she heard the stars singing and the palm fronds laugh, she felt the wings of the wind as the images appeared to move, to lift off the canvases and to whirl around her in a towering, glowing, incandescent hymn of praise, a victorious hosanna of color.

Something deep in Fauve opened and finally understood; Julien Mistral had crossed the green fields of time and lived in old Jerusalem; his pagan brush had been transported and he had expanded his last and greatest forces on painting these celebrations of a people who had—who still—worshipped an invisible God.

He had respected the invisibility of their God. He had not tried the impossible; he had not attempted to paint the voice from the Burning Bush, but he had reached into the heart of their festivals and painted the spirit in which they commemorated their God, and painted it in a way that all the other peoples of the earth could understand, for all men lived by the ever-turned wheel of nature.

She closed her eyes and leaned on Eric's arm.

"Are you all right?" he asked anxiously.

"Let's go outside for a minute . . . I'll look at the other pictures later."

As they started toward the door Adrien Avigdor approached Fauve and put out his hand, a question on his face which was answered by one look at Fauve's transfigured eyes, He dropped his hand, satisfied, and let them continue. Fauve had passed Mistral's easel when she turned back, caught by the sight of a scrap of paper that was tacked into the wood. On it, in her father's familiar handwriting, was just one line. She paused. The bit of paper was worn, yellowed and smudged by a rainbow of fading colors, as if it had been much handled, yet it flew from the easel like a flag bearing a motto.

"Hear O Israel, the Lord our God, the Lord is One," she said, reading out loud. "That's all it says."

"Isn't that enough?"

34

"It's so maddeningly inadequate trying to describe them on the phone like this—can't you fly over and see them for yourself, Magali?" Fauve pleaded.

"I will, but right now it's impossible. Things have never been crazier and I don't dare leave the agency to run itself with both of us away. The most important thing is that we know that your father was moved to make those paintings, we know that he wanted to create something that could be balanced against the past. I guess the only thing to call it is redemption . . . not a word I normally find myself using, my darling. I thank God that he had the time to do it."

"It's more than his having the time, Magali. You'll understand when you see them. He painted with the last drop of his blood. Monsieur Avigdor says that sometimes this type of overwhelming vision visits an artist in his old age, but only the greatest of them—Donatello, Rembrandt—something totally fresh that soars above anything they've ever achieved. Like everyone else Monsieur Avigdor had thought, because father hadn't produced any new work in eight years, that he'd lost it, that he was hiding out because he didn't want to admit that he couldn't paint anymore."

"Were they all as stunned as you?"

"Yes, although, except for the Avigdors, they didn't have the extra shock of knowing how father had felt before about anything to do with Jews. The experts were stunned—just knocked out—even though they deal with great art all the time. The person who touched me most was the man from the Department of Taxes. He doesn't have any background in painting but he wandered around in a kind of speechless rapture, purely enjoying himself—so carried away by the *Cavaillon* series that he completely forgot about all the other paintings in the storage room. I wanted to call you right away but luckily I remembered that it was still the middle of the night in New York, so I waited till I knew you'd be at the office."

"Oh, I'm here all right," said Magali. "After all, it's almost nine o'clock."

"The thing is, I just can't leave Provence right away, Magali. There's going to be incredible interest in the series and since it belongs to me I have to stick around. I'm not at all sure exactly how soon I'll be able to get away. I hate to leave you up in the air like this . . ."

"Don't worry about me for a second. Everything's under control."

"But your weekends," Fauve protested.

"Never mind about them. The garden has almost finished blooming for the year and until you come back we'll go up to the country only for Saturday and Sunday. Darcy will understand . . . when did Darcy ever not understand?"

"Oh, Magali, thank you, and thank Darcy. I'll call every few days or so. Give everyone a kiss for me, especially to Casey and Loulou and . . . I love you, Magali. I'm so very *glad*."

"I can hear it in your voice, darling. Take your time, make wise decisions, just don't rush into anything. I love you, Fauve."

Maggy hung up and sat back in her desk chair. Like Fauve she was in a shock of euphoria. The description of the *Cavaillon* series, although Fauve had considered it inadequate, had lasted for more than twenty minutes of excited, rapturous details. So that man had finally used his God-given talent to make a greater contribution to the world than beauty alone. Maggy discovered that as overwhelmingly happy as she felt for her granddaughter, she was also happy for Julien Mistral, the Julien Mistral she had loved and hated for so many years. They had accounts between them that could never be settled, no, not if he'd illustrated every last line of the Old Testament, but now, at least, she could think, "Rest in peace," and mean it. She sat thoughtfully for a long while. Then, startled out of her meditations by a glance at her desk clock, she buzzed Casey and Loulou to come into her office.

"I've just talked to Fauve, ladies. She sends you both very special kisses and says that she's going to have to stay over in France for a while. There are things she has to take care of."

"How is everything with her?" asked Casey, anxiously.

"Absolutely wonderful! Never better. Now! There are a few matters I've been planning to talk to Fauve about that can't wait till she gets back. Casey, I've been looking over the test shots of that girl you found at the Southwest Regional Modeling Competition. No way, Casey, no way." Maggy shook her elegant head in firm negation.

"Maggy, she was clearly the most gorgeous girl in the competition," Casey protested.

"You fell into a trap. You went and saw hundreds of girls and you picked out the best one. But did you remember to take some pictures of our own girls to compare her to?"

"Well, no, I forgot. But I spent three whole, long, long days judging those girls."

"That's the problem. After three days of seeing one girl after another you jumped at the best of the lot. It's incredibly easy to fool your eye, to compromise, to forget how supremely good a girl has to be. I've done it plenty of times myself. She is a very pretty girl, Casey, but not pretty enough for Lunel." Maggy shoved the series of test shots over to Casey who looked at them carefully and sighed in agreement.

"Point made," Casey said. "Ah well, she's engaged to a boy back home anyway. Maybe she'll be relieved. Certainly he will be."

"Loulou," Maggy said, "I've been listening in on the open interviews. I notice that our reception room never seems to empty out. Are you aware that Bobbie-Ann has developed a Pygmalion complex?"

"Oh, Lord, she's been in charge of the auditions for a couple of months and I've been too busy to pay much attention. What's up?"

"Loulou, there are a million ways to turn people down nicely. But Bobbie-Ann doesn't say 'sorry' and keep it short and sweet. This morning she spent seven minutes showing one girl how to use blusher before she turned her down and another eight minutes with a different applicant talking about changing her hairstyle—then she turned her down too. It's not fair to give anyone false hope, not even for a few minutes," Maggy snapped. "Talk to her, Loulou. If Bobbie-Ann doesn't shape up she can always run a beauty school. If an applicant has to experience rejection, it should come with a minimum of personal contact, *before* she starts to feel that she's made a new friend. It doesn't hurt as much that way, I promise."

"Yes, Ma'am! I'll pass the word. Listen, Maggy, Bambi Two is worrying me. She says she's homesick and she's eating like mad. I caught her at it yesterday."

"I'll talk to her. Maybe if you all just stopped calling her Bambi *Two* it might help for a start. Try it. Let's see, she's had three *Glamour* covers and *Vogue* is considering her. I suppose she knows that?"

"Yup."

"Well, of course she's homesick, naturally she's eating all the junk she can get her hands on . . . maybe she can gain enough weight to stay *off* the cover of *Vogue* if she gobbles fast enough. It's just your everyday, ordinary, reasonable and understandable insecurity surfacing. Who wouldn't be having a little identity crisis—she was overdue for it." Maggy beamed at the girls. She'd helped half a hundred Bambis over this particular hurdle.

"Anything else?" asked Casey warily.

"No, not right now anyway. Have I remembered to tell you that as far as I'm concerned both of you are absolutely indispensable? No? Well, consider yourselves officially notified. Oh, and will you send someone out to buy me a red carnation—just one, for my buttonhole?" She picked up the phone to call Darcy as they left her office.

"Hmmm," hummed Casey when they reached the corridor.

"What does that sound signify?" asked Loulou, still delightfully rosy from Maggy's unprecedented compliment.

"It feels kind of good to have Marie Antoinette on the rampage again."

"Didn't we just get our asses kicked?"

"Just enough," Casey grinned. "Just *comme il faut*, Loulou, if you follow my meaning."

Nadine Dalmas had decided to change hairdressers, to try Alexandre. As always, when one is nice to people, they tend to creep toward familiarity, forgetting that the line between those who are waited on and those who wait on them may be invisible but it is real, and must never be bridged.

When she had gone to have her roots touched up last week, Monsieur Christophe, whose job it was to do her color, had actually presumed to regale her with an account of how his grandfather had died without a will. He had had three sons, one of whom, it seemed to be her destiny to learn, had been Monsieur Christophe's father. The heirs had fought so stubbornly over the division of the family farm that the property had eventually been sold at auction. Nadine hadn't been able to simply get up and walk away from this sordid account since the man was actually in the act of applying the bleach, nor had she dared to indicate that she was outraged at being treated as a captive audience. When a colorist has his hands in your hair you take good care not to antagonize him, no matter who you are.

"So, you see, Madame Dalmas, he was wrong, my grandfather, to expect his sons to come to an amiable agreement. He should have made a will, but since he failed to, the property passed out of the family forever. A great pity, don't you think?" Her face perfectly calm and remote, Nadine had had to incline her head to show that she was listening. Why on earth was she being subjected to this family history? What gave Monsieur Christophe the right to inflict his personal experience on her? "Yes, Madame, even a bad will is better than no will at all," he had said before turning her over to be shampooed.

The astonishing impudence of the man, to speak to her in a *consoling* tone of voice. Was he her equal that he dared to permit himself this intimacy? To offer her *his* understanding, *his* allegiance? On what grounds did he believe that she needed comfort, fidelity? His effrontery took her breath away. Yet if she returned next week Monsieur Christophe might have more to say on this odious subject, which he had obviously seized upon to give himself airs of being on a level with her.

No, here at Alexandre's, which she had never patronized before, she would be treated in the way that was due her and, now that she was rich, she wouldn't have to be as generous with her tips as she had been, Nadine reflected as she sat on the circular, haremlike, oversized piece of furniture, covered with leopard skin, on which everyone but queens had to wait their turn.

It was horribly crowded, even granted that it was a Friday. One of the advantages of her former salon was that everyone there was on her schedule, Tuesdays and Fridays for a wash and blow-dry, Mondays, Thursdays and Saturday mornings for a comb-out. It would take awhile to break in the staff of any new salon, Nadine reminded herself, determined to stick with Alexandre until she had worked out her maintenance routine to her satisfaction. She had no more worries about being late to the office, thank heaven. It was really astonishing how quickly Albin had been able to find one of the little Montesquiou girls to take over her job, thankless task that it was. She wouldn't stay with him long, that silly young creature. She'd be temporarily taken in by the chichi until she found out what a cesspool Albin's was.

Nadine waved away a pile of magazines that a young assistant in a smock presented to her. No, she did not want *Match* or *Jours de France* or *Marie Claire* or *Elle.* Thank you but no.

Indeed, she had already seen them. She had bought a pile of brightly colored weekly magazines at a kiosk yesterday and taken them quickly home to read in private; for each of them treated the *Cavaillon* series as its main story. What incomprehensible fit of madness had caused the old man to paint those monstrous things with Hebrew lettering on them? Nadine had asked herself in aversion and disgust. She couldn't endure looking at them—the inscriptions alone made her shut her eyes. How typical of the press it was to make such a fuss over them, such an inordinate fuss, as if Julien Mistral had been a new discovery, an overnight sensation, a revelation. She couldn't understand the amount of space, the covers and full-page photographs, that had been devoted to this mere handful of canvases. And, God knows, it wasn't sour grapes, she told herself. She wouldn't want them herself for anything in the world. "Immortal," one critic had actually said. "The final proof of his boundless genius," another. "A legacy for which the entire human race is richer" had announced a third. They were all equally ludicrous, each baying together like a pack of dogs, just as they always did, attempting to outdo each other, like the fashion writers after a successful collection. Their words could be about a new style as easily as about paint on canvas.

Yet, all it did, in the end, was to make her own pictures the more valuable. She couldn't really object if they wanted to rediscover Mistral, Nadine thought. Naturally they had all pounced on the *Cavaillon* series, when the old man had singled it out in his will, and naturally they had all insisted on treating Fauve as if she were the star of the whole sideshow. She didn't begrudge Fauve her cheap little moment in the limelight. It would dim quickly.

Nadine was so lost in her thoughts that she was surprised to find the coiffeur had presented her with a mirror so that she could inspect his work. She checked the back of her head carefully. She could see that it was perfectly acceptable but it wouldn't do to let him think that she was too easily pleased. "Perhaps you've made it a bit too tight at the side," she said, smoothing her hand under the shimmering hair that curved under her chin.

As he worked she looked around her. There must be a dozen women here she knew, Nadine realized as she exchanged nods and smiles around the big room. She had had no idea that so many of her friends came to Alexandre, that so many of his clients were the women she was accustomed to dining and lunching with. They all looked, in her opinion, overdone. Why had the Comtesse d'Ornano added that twist of false braids to her lovely black hair? And the Princesse Laure de Beauveau-Craon had chosen, for some strange reason, to wear sprigs of tiny purple orchids in her chignon. Quite odd. As for Baronne Guy, her long blond locks were imprisoned in a sort of gilded net. Madame Patiño, Princess Alexander of Yugoslavia, the young Baronne Olimpia de Rothschild—all of them with highly decorated hair. Didn't they know how fussy it looked, how unsuited to real life? If this was what Alexandre's stylists did to women whose taste was normally good, she had better be on her guard.

"If I might suggest, Madame," the coiffeur said, "perhaps we might try something a bit more formal?"

"Don't touch it," Nadine snapped. "It's fine."

"As you wish. I thought that for the ball tonight . . ."

"I'm in mourning," Nadine said quickly.

"My regrets, Madame." He was plainly relieved that he had not been tactless.

"I couldn't possibly go to a ball."

"Of course not, Madame. It is painful, is it not," he murmured. "Particularly painful to miss this ball, the first time that the Princesse Marie-Blanche has opened her château since her husband died. That's why we're so crowded this afternoon. They say it will be the greatest ball since the last one of the Baron de Rédé's."

"Yes, that was a beautiful evening," Nadine said mechanically. *Princesse Marie-Blanche?* So her affair with Phillipe had continued even while the Prince lay dying, even after his death, *even now*. Otherwise, why would she not have invited as close a friend as Nadine to her ball? The only possible explanation was that Phillipe was, in some way, going to be the unofficial host. Strange, that she had not heard any gossip about Marie-Blanche and Phillipe, for Marie-Blanche *led* Parisian society. When Marie-Blanche said dance, they danced; when she said drive fifty miles out to the country for a ball, they drove the fifty miles and counted themselves among the blessed. What would Marie-Blanche *want* with Phillipe Dalmas, for God's sake?

As Nadine stared into her own sharply outlined eyes in the mirror she tallied up in her mind the number of unattached middle-aged men in Paris who were charming, good-looking, well-dressed and heterosexual, who danced well, played cards well, played polo well and were adored by every hostess. Besides Phillipe she knew of three—no four, counting Omar Sharif. And how many women were there who were rich—many of them far richer than she—unattached, and desperate for an escort, let alone such a man? *Dozens.* Dozens and dozens. Her heart shriveled, a foul and evil dust filled her mouth, and a pain she would not have believed existed, ignited in her abdomen, a pain that seemed to be a burning rat eating at her insides, a rat on fire running wild with feet of hot lead.

No, she had not heard any gossip about Phillipe and Marie-Blanche. She had not heard any gossip because she had no invitations . . . no invitations worth speaking of, only a few unquestionably third-rate invitations that she hadn't deigned to decline. Faced with the choice between Princesse Marie-Blanche and Nadine Dalmas, people would, of course, choose Princesse Marie-Blanche. She would make that choice herself. There was no contest.

As she tipped Monsieur Christophe, so much that he actually looked surprised, Nadine had only one thought. By chance she had worn a black suit today. She must wear only black from now on. She would find a small hairdresser in her neighborhood, where she wouldn't run into her friends. Acquaintances. She had no friends. She would wear black for her father and she would decide what to do with the rest of her life, a life in which she would, no doubt, often be described as Jean François Albin's ex-employee, as Phillipe Dalmas's ex-wife, for who was Nadine Dalmas? *Who cared?*

She walked down the street looking for a taxi to take her home. An empty taxi passed as she stood, transfixed, staring at a headline in *France Soir* displayed on the wall of a kiosk. "*Fauve Lunel—Prendra-t-elle le nom de Mistral, son père?*" Would Fauve take her father's name? Who gave a damn what she did, that tawdry bastard, that interloper, that cunning tramp? Why was she being treated as if she were Julien Mistral's *only* daughter? "I," Nadine wanted to scream out loud at everyone passing by, "*I am Mistral's daughter!*"

When she decided to stay on for a few weeks in Provence, Fauve had taken a room at Le Prieuré, and then, when it closed for the season in November, she had moved into the Hotel Europe in Avignon.

One morning near the end of November, she drove her rented Peugeot toward Félice, determined to make a decision about *La Tourrello* before the day was over. The house had been full of people since the *Cavaillon* series had been revealed. She had had to act as hostess to a great variety of guests; journalists, art historians and museum curators. But now the question of what to do with the *Cavaillon* series had been settled. Yesterday the last canvas had been carefully crated and loaded into the padded trucks that would take them to Amsterdam, where they would begin their slow progress from continent to continent, from major city to major city, to every last one of the museums that had asked for them, carrying their festive message of brotherhood throughout the world. If she had kept them in *La Tourrello* only a relatively few people would have ever seen them except in reproduction. Someday the transcendent canvases would come back to her, but for many years to come, the *Cavaillon* series would belong to mankind.

Now that the studio was empty, now that the storeroom had also been cleared out of all but the family portraits that Fauve intended to keep for herself, she would be able to make a reasonable and leisurely judgment about the house. Except for the future of the *Cavaillon* series she felt as if nothing she had decided on since she left New York in October had been based on firmly collected thought. She'd had to dash into things, she'd been pulled along by events, and by the end of every day she'd been so exhausted that she'd fallen into bed with nothing on her mind but the appointments she had the next morning. She'd hired a young widow, Lucette Albion, from Lacoste, to come in every day and keep the house clean, and make lunch and coffee for all the visitors. Today the last of them had gone home, and *La Tourrello* would be completely empty, since it was Sunday and Lucette had gone to a wedding in Bonnieux, in which her two small children were going to be bridal attendants.

A mistral had been blowing for the past few days and Fauve was bundled up in a warm plaid jacket over loden-green wool pants and a creamy, cable-stitched, Irish fisherman's sweater, but that morning the wind had left the Lubéron as capriciously as it had arrived. The too-bright sky had turned an ordinary soft blue again, and frilly curls of clouds were draped like ribbons here and there, the party decorations of heaven. The only sign of true winter was the bareness of the fields. The wind-break borders of cypresses were green and alert, and in the olive trees, the leaves of the trees were so much like a silver stream that Fauve almost expected to see fish swimming in them. As she drove along she could hear the sound of shotguns in the hills as the farmers went looking for game birds; children's shrill, excited laughter rang out as they played Sunday games, liberated from their perpetual homework, and at the entrance to many a *mas* stood a table on which ripe fruit was displayed for sale. Fauve stopped at one of them, and bought a pear and an apple for her lunch.

She was getting roundish—well, a little anyway, she thought as she drove past Les Baumettes. Everyone she'd met had been so hospitable that, no matter how tired she'd been by the end of the day, she had often found herself eating a large dinner with Jean and Félice Perrin or with Dr. Lucien Daniel and his wife, Céline, or with some of the other new friends she'd made in Avignon, in Apt, in Bonnieux. In Félice she often shared a meal with Pomme and Épinette, both of them as tart and irreverent as ever, in spite of their married dignity. And, of course, she saw Adrien and Beth Avigdor.

Eric hadn't been around much, she reflected, feeling, against all common sense, that he should have been. But he had two important new houses under construction on the other side of the Lubéron mountains, in Les Baux, and it was a curiously long and complicated drive over little country roads from there to Avignon, since the Autoroute bypassed Les Baux entirely. He had designed the large vacation houses for a pair of Swedish industrialists and Eric had to supervise much of the building himself since the master workmen of Provence had not become less unpredictable as the demand for their services escalated. This part of France was a paradise for masons, carpenters and stonecutters. They could pick and choose their jobs. Eric intended to have those houses ready for their owners by spring, if he had to stay in Les Baux and watch them go up inch by inch.

Naturally he was as busy as she was, Fauve explained to herself. It was not by design that they had met so seldom. No, not by design perhaps, but couldn't he have *made* more time for her? Couldn't he have, damn it, been a little more desperate to see her? Nine months ago that man had wanted her to leave everything that made up her world and marry him. Now, his father and mother, for God's sake, treated her with more loving kindness than he did. To hell with Eric Avigdor! Let him spend his life nipping at the heels of hod carriers, she thought scornfully, as she opened the front door of *La Tourrello* with a key picked from that heavy ring that had become as familiar and unremarkable as her lipstick.

Fauve wandered around the salon of *La Tourrello* checking to make sure that Lucette had emptied all the ashtrays and removed all the wineglasses from the table where, yesterday, with Adrien Avigdor and Jean Perrin and varied gentlemen from the Amsterdam museum, she had toasted the departure of the *Cavaillon* series. The salon looked too neat, with all the pillows plumped up, all the surfaces of the tables clear. She hadn't bothered to buy any flowers for the house since she wasn't living in it. It felt like an office on Sunday, a place that wasn't meant to be opened up and lived in, Fauve decided, and retreated to the kitchen, where she discovered the leftovers from yesterday's big celebration lunch neatly put away in the refrigerator. Cold chicken, a half of a liver pâté, cheeses, the last bottle of white wine, still almost full.

As she set the food out on the kitchen table, she decided to start to diet seriously tomorrow. In a week, by the time she got back to New York, she'd have lost the five pounds she must have gained. She'd be home before the Christmas decorations were put up in the stores on Fifth Avenue, home for all the parties, home for the first big snow of the season. No, Fauve corrected herself, the decorations were already in place; they appeared before Thanksgiving. The first snow had come a week ago Maggy had told her the last time they'd talked, so now it must be already covered with grime; black flakes falling on white snow from the solid gray New York skies. Off-duty taxis; puddles of slush at every street corner so wide that you had to wade right through them to crowd into an overheated bus if it didn't rush right past your stop; the constant wail of sirens as if the city were perpetually on fire somewhere or other—but parties, perhaps a welcome-home party, the annual Lunel Christmas party, dancing at Doubles where she had a membership, the Horowitz concert for which Melvin had written he had tickets, the Avedon exhibition, Bobby Short at the Café Carlyle and Baryshnikov and bagels: Where else but in New York?

Fauve looked for the tomatoes Lucette had brought in yesterday. Good, there were enough left for a salad with the chicken. Or perhaps she'd only eat the tomatoes and fruit when it was time for lunch. It wouldn't do to return to the agency an ounce heavier than she'd left it . . . the models would be only too delighted to jump on her for the lack of discipline she preached to them. Somehow it was all right for the personnel of the agency to be as cozily plump as they liked, but Maggy and Fauve Lunel were supposed to be model-thin.

Fauve's mind fell into a reverie in which the treats of Provence were mixed and jumbled; the *tapenade*, that relish made of black olives that was spread on bread like butter; the stars that fell so low to earth through the night sky that a walk after dinner felt like flight; the café in Félice where she could sit watching the whole village pass by, knowing more people by name every day; the color of the light, the color of the sky, the color of the stones—the color of the light, the light. Sighing, she blew her hair out of her eyes and resolutely turned her mind to the problem of *La Tourrello*.

She could rent it as she had first planned, or sell it. Jean Perrin had assured her that either choice would present no problems; there was an enormous demand for properties all over the South of France and the luxuriously appointed home of Julien Mistral would command a huge price. It was as famous as it was unique, with its marvelously restored buildings, its swimming pool, its central heating, its comfortable bathrooms. She would rather sell it outright, Fauve realized suddenly. The apricot trees, the vines, the asparagus fields, the olive groves—all the fertile land of *La Tourrello* was in a shameful condition of neglect. How could she trust a tenant to oversee the work that had to be done? No one who merely rented a house would want to make the effort that was necessary to bring the domain back to its former productivity. On the other hand, anyone who bought the property would do so with the knowledge that the farm would bring in a steady and substantial income when it was again worked as it should be.

Yes, the ideal buyer would be a rich family man from somewhere in the sunless north of Europe, a man who had always wanted wide abundant hectares in Provence—didn't everybody dream of just that?—who would hire a local farmer and his wife to come and live here full-time, a man who would be able to spend his summers in Provence, and to fly down from Munich or Copenhagen or Brussels for the sun in the winter, two weeks at Christmas, a week at Easter; bringing the children of course; perhaps in a private plane that could land at the airport outside of Avignon. They could keep a car at the airport and be at *La Tourrello* within a half-hour after landing.

Fauve thoughtfully provided herself with the pear and the apple she'd bought on the road, as she walked through the rooms of *La Tourrello*, imagining herself the wife of the prospective buyer. She'd keep a few of the gleaming wooden antique chests and tables, she decided, but she'd change the carpets and the draperies and get rid of all the upholstered pieces—the place was *underfurnished*. The house cried out for bigger couches, deeper chairs, less pointedly simple fabrics—it needed color, it needed warmth, it needed, above all, *things*. Strange, she had never minded the artful austerity of the decor before, but then she had always thought of it as Kate's house and it had suited Kate. Well, it didn't suit her—still, who knew—perhaps it would be perfect, just as it stood, for the wife of that rich Belgian? She was almost certain it would be a Belgian. They endured some of the worst winters in Europe.

Her own bedroom in the tower? It would probably become a guest room, unless they had a teenaged daughter who fancied it for herself. Fauve hoped that they would have a daughter, someone who would lie on the bed and dream with her eyes wide open.

What would happen to the studio? Fauve asked, as she found herself in front of its doors. Perhaps they'd use it as a game room, even put in a ping-pong table? Yesterday, she had been too busy making the final arrangements with the people from Amsterdam to lock up the studio herself after the *Cavaillon* series had been carried out, so Jean Perrin had done it and given her the key before he left. She had never seen the studio empty of paintings, she realized, as she hesitated outside the doors. Did she want to go in? Did she need to go in? Did she dare to go in?

She told herself not to be absurd and unlocked the studio. The room she had always thought of as huge, vast, enormous—was just an ordinary size. A big studio, to be sure, but with Mistral's paintings gone, not that intimidating after all. A human size. Fauve understood that it was because the walls were bare. Her father's work had always opened up into another dimension; no matter what its subject it had led the eye beyond the borders of the canvas. Now there were just the walls and the high ceiling and the glass and the beams. The only reminders that Mistral had worked there were the worktable, the ladder and the easel with the blank canvas on it.

She put her pear and apple, both still uneaten, down on the least paint-stained corner of the worktable and automatically, without a thought, she set about gathering up the many brushes that lay scattered about. It had always been her special task after a day's work, picking up these brushes and cleaning them in the sink in the small room off the side of the studio where Mistral kept his painting supplies. Her father had always cared for his own brushes as meticulously as any good craftsman. In spite of the disorder there always was in his studio he started the day's work with clean brushes, and when he taught Fauve how to paint he had also taught her how to tidy up after herself.

She saw that it wouldn't be an easy or quick task. Both of her hands were filled with the brushes that he had put down on the last night he had ever painted, flung down hastily, she realized as she looked at them in dismay. They were matted, caked, stiffened with dried paint. Probably they should just be thrown out. It would be more work than she had realized to bring any life back to these mistreated tools. Yet Fauve found herself moving toward the sink on which stood the covered jars of turpentine and thinner.

Slowly, lovingly, painstakingly she began the slow job of cleaning Julien Mistral's brushes. Finally she left all but one, which hadn't been used, to soak overnight. She went back out to the worktable with the clean, single brush and stood irresolutely in front of the blank canvas, her mind blank, her hands still. She lingered there, with nothing left to decide, with no thought of what she intended to do next, until she found herself gliding backward in time, as, caught in a slow tumble of memory, she felt Julien Mistral's large hand cover her own, she felt it press down, communicating power to her, guiding her fingers as he had done so many times after the first day, that day when she was eight years old. She heard him give her those familiar orders. "*Regard*," she heard his voice say to her. "Do you *see*, Fauve? *Regard*, always *Regard*. You must learn to see."

And she did see, in a moment of complete definition, what she was going to do. It was more than just a knowing, it was a sudden admission of a long denied but total need, pure and assertive, without any complications, an absolute order.

Try. She was a painter. She had always been a painter. She had rejected the painter in herself when she had rejected her father but now . . . now . . . all she was sure of was that she must try. Walls had been torn down, doors had been flung open, a vast open meadow lay before her, a meadow she could not cross without risk, a meadow that, once crossed, would lead her into changes unguessed at, into tasks and trials she could only begin to imagine. But she had to try.

Fauve knew that she was at the very beginning of a long voyage of discovery, an adventure that beckoned her on irresistibly. On the other side of the meadow was a mystery, an unknown world that must be explored. She felt full of marvelously imprudent impulses, eager to meet the mystery, ready to dare, ready to try, ready to change.

A pulse that had never stopped beating quickened in Fauve's wrists and fingers. Powers and faculties that she had suppressed and turned away from began pushing themselves forward and upward with the power of young buds opening in the spring sun.

She would have to begin over again. Not at the beginning, but nevertheless, again. She must have lost technique, facility, ease—the machinery of an artist had probably rusted like the Tin Woodsman of Oz, left out in the rain. Paint and she would have to become intimate once more. But she'd known the language before . . . it wasn't all that easy to forget, particularly since she had never lost that nervous habit that made her hand pick up any available pen or pencil and draw lines on paper.

Fauve found herself sitting on the worktable looking at the canvas, a brush in one hand and the apple in the other. Would she eat it or paint it? She laughed out loud and bit into the apple. She'd paint the pear.

35

If she telephoned right now she would find Maggy and Darcy reading the Sunday papers after breakfast up in the country, Fauve calculated, counting the five hours' time difference. She jumped off the table, snatched up her pear and rushed from the studio to the phone in the library of *La Tourrello*.

She dialed the long-distance operator and then, before there was an answer, she put the receiver down hastily, overcome by belated second thoughts. This abrupt decision, this change of direction that she'd made so suddenly—how would it affect Maggy and the life she and Darcy had so carefully constructed for themselves, a life in which they were so well organized, so comfortable and so happy together?

Was this not precisely the sort of selfishness Fauve asked herself, within which her father had lived? He took any action that was best for him, regardless of its consequences. Was she now about to put her work ahead of all other obligations in life? Was her sense of purpose, her physical and spiritual need to paint, the very same feeling that he had known? Was this not the urgency that had driven him? *And blinded him?*

Fauve sat very still and tried to imagine herself putting this morning behind her and going back to the Lunel Agency. She could save her weekends for painting, after all. She would spend her days overseeing the fortunes of the two hundred best models in the world, trying to care again, as she had before, about everything that happened in the competitive hothouse of fashion. She'd been brought up to do that, hadn't she?

Not really. Not at all, now that she stopped and gave it serious consideration. When she graduated from high school, Magali had never indicated to her that she had a secret hope of one day renaming the agency Lunel and Granddaughter. It had been her own notion to plunge into learning her job as if that were the answer to all her problems. If Fauve knew one thing about the modeling business it was that you shouldn't work in it unless it *mattered* to you. When it stopped being a genuinely sickening disappointment to see a Wilhelmina girl instead of a Lunel girl on the cover of *Vogue*, it was time to get out.

As Fauve picked up the phone again she told herself that she knew one thing for certain; Maggy would want her to be honest even if she wouldn't be happy with the truth. To put painting ahead of many things was what every painter had to do. She must remember not to put it ahead of everything. At least not all of the time.

Fauve asked Darcy to get on another extension and she told both of them what had happened to her that morning. She was as direct and clear as she knew how to be. There was no point in trying to tiptoe around the facts or pretend that she hadn't made up her mind.

"Well," said Maggy, after a pause, in a voice that sounded either far away or very muffled, Fauve wasn't sure. "Well, I must say, Fauve . . . I'm not sure exactly how surprised I am."

"Magali, it isn't that I haven't thought what this will mean to you," Fauve said earnestly. "I know what a stickler you are about one of us being at the agency every day and I realize that either you're going to have to work full-time now—or somehow compromise and rely more on Casey and Loulou."

"I was beginning to wonder what was taking you so long, it's not as if it's been absolutely necessary for you to stay on in Félice all winter . . . you could have found people to handle your business there for you. Darcy, how many times have I told you that something strange was going on with Fauve?" Maggy asked, like someone who has won a bet.

"Magali! Don't you realize what I've been saying? I don't want to run a model agency, for God's sake."

"Well, *that's* understandable. Not everyone has the calling," Maggy said with a trace of smugness in her voice.

"You don't care?" Fauve cried incredulously.

"Not that I want to interfere in this career talk," Darcy interrupted, "but, Maggy, I just thought I'd better tell you that I've made up my mind that I'm absolutely opposed to your building that greenhouse onto the dining room."

"Damn it, Darcy, you know perfectly well that I've been planning to grow orchids all winter long after Fauve came back," Maggy said in irritation. "You can't do that without a greenhouse."

"But she's not coming back, the dirt under your fingernails doesn't come out from spring till fall . . . I didn't marry a female Nero Wolfe . . . I married Maggy Lunel. I know you're bored to death with four-day weekends. You've been ten times more fun to live with since Fauve left for France. No greenhouse."

"Darcy! How long have you known . . . about the weekends?" Maggy demanded.

"Let's say that I prefer to remain inscrutable."

"Are you two talking to me or to each other?" Fauve asked. "Is this a private discussion? After all, I'm paying for this call." Jean Perrin had told her that she would eventually inherit at least twenty-five million dollars but none of that sounded real to Fauve. However, long distance was long distance.

"You should have called collect," Maggy said. "We would have accepted it. Now listen, Darcy, does this mean that you *refuse* to let me build the greenhouse?"

"I thought I'd made that plain."

"In that case," said Maggy, "I *refuse* to give up my Fridays at the agency."

"What about Mondays?" Darcy countered quickly.

"On one condition. I'll spend Mondays in the country with you if I can buy that little bit of swamp just on the border of our place."

" 'Bit of swamp'? It's about seven acres! What do you want it for?"

"A water lily garden, like Monet's at Giverny," said Maggy in a visionary tone.

"That'll mean bulldozers," Darcy grumbled.

"But only for a few weeks. And just think, darling, we could have a rowboat and a little summer house and you'd row me out there for martinis in the summer before dinner."

"We're agreeing on three days, right?" he bargained. "Friday night through Monday?"

"It's a deal. On Monday I'll let Casey and Loulou and Ivy take over for me—it's usually a day that starts slowly anyway."

"Ivy?" Fauve asked, astonished.

"Ivy Columbo. Is there more than one Ivy? She decided modeling was too short-term for a career so she's starting as a booker. As a trainee supposedly, but that girl's so bossy that the word hardly applies. She reminds me of—me. It's a shame to retire the best pair of runway knees in the business but on the other hand she's engaged to some gorgeous Italian she met in the Sistine Chapel when she was in Rome with you last March. I like her, she'll do," Maggy said with satisfaction. "But, Fauve, naturally, if you come back, if you change your mind, your job is always open. You know that."

"Thanks," Fauve said absently—in the Sistine Chapel?—as she imagined the tugs-of-war that would take place on Mondays. Loulou had more seniority, Casey had more brains, but Ivy had . . . more of everything.

"Now, where are you going to live?" Maggy said in a practical voice.

"I thought you understood. Out here, in *La Tourrello*, of course."

"Live there alone!" Maggy became every inch a grandmother. "I don't think that's a good idea at all."

"You!" Fauve sputtered. "You who used to dance till dawn every night and were carried around stark naked on a platter and lived in some dive in Montparnasse with God knows whom—and probably smoked opium . . . you're a fine one to talk!"

"I see Adrien Avigdor has been reminiscing. He must be getting senile . . . I never, ever smoked opium. Not that it wasn't offered, mind you. Anyway, all that happened when I was young and foolish. By the time I was your age I was earning an excellent living and very respectably too."

"With an illegitimate child and probably carrying on like crazy with Darcy," Fauve suggested softly.

"I don't think I'd met Darcy yet, had I, darling? When was Lally's treasure hunt exactly . . . was it . . . ?"

"Magali, never mind the exact date," Fauve interrupted. "Anyway, I won't be here all alone. I'll ask Lucette if she wants to come and live here with her kids. She's sharing a house with her in-laws and hates it, so I'm sure she'll jump at the chance. And the place will be full of men working on the land. *La Tourrello* will never be empty again," Fauve said joyously.

"By the way, Fauve, I thought you should know that I saw Ben Litchfield in '21' last Thursday," Darcy said, with the air of one who feels obliged to add every last item to the scales. "By God, Pete Kriendler's given him table 9 and he's only thirty. Anyway, he asked when you'd be back as he left."

"Who was he with?" Fauve said automatically.

"An exceptionally pretty girl. She must be a model."

"Who's *she* with?" Fauve asked, sitting up in genuine interest.

"Us," Maggy replied dryly. "It was Arkansas, as Darcy knows perfectly well."

"Arkansas! Now why didn't I think of that? But that's perfect! She learns fast and it keeps Ben in the family. Just be sure to tell Arkansas that he does this really odd thing every Sunday morning, but not to pay any attention, it doesn't last long."

"I'll tell her no such thing," Maggy said, outraged.

"Then she'll just have to find out the hard way. I imagine she has already. Give her a hug for me. Oh, Magali, I've sent you that picture Father gave you, the one Kate gypped you out of . . . you know, lying on the green pillows, remember?"

"Hardly a picture that anyone could forget," Darcy said. "Just where do you think we can hang it?"

"You'll find a place," Fauve said blithely. "I've kept the other six for my great-grandchildren."

"Great-grandchildren? Fauve . . . you're not . . . you aren't . . ." Maggy stammered.

"Really, Magali, how could I possibly be? I'm not married, after all," Fauve reproved her. "But if I were pregnant, it'd be a clear case of genetic predisposition. Darcy, do you remember that panda you gave me once?"

"Vividly."

"Well, would you think I was being silly and childish if I asked you to send it over to me? He's sitting on a rocking chair in the living room of my apartment."

"Certainly not. Everybody needs a panda. Is there anything else you want from your place?"

"Actually . . . this house is bare as a bone. Maybe you could get a moving company just to pack it up and send it over?"

"Pack what up?"

"Everything in the whole apartment. Oh, I know it'll only be a drop in the bucket but it'll give me a start on filling these rooms."

"Why not?"

"Oh, Darcy, you are such an understanding darling. I'm so glad you made Magali marry you."

"She made me marry her, actually."

"I never knew that," Fauve said, fascinated. "How did it happen? Tell me all about it?"

"I think this conversation has gone on quite long enough," Maggy broke in. "Fauve, darling, you're doing the only thing you should do—I'm deeply happy for you, I'm happy for me, and I'm happy for Darcy although I'm not sure he deserves it. A man who breaks promises about a greenhouse . . ."

"There's somebody at the front door. I hear the kitchen bell ringing," Fauve said hastily. "I have to hang up. I'll call again in a few days. I love you both."

Lighthearted and lightheaded, she ran to the front door and discovered Eric Avigdor standing there, leaning on the door jamb, a jacket slung over one shoulder.

"Ah ha. The master builder. Come on in."

"I got home from Les Baux late last night and I went looking for you this morning. When you weren't in the hotel I thought you might be here so I just drove on out and dropped in . . . that all right?"

"Of course, I'm delighted to receive any son of my dear friends the Avigdors."

"You sound awfully . . ."

"How do I sound?" she asked, twirling around, her flaming mantle of hair flaring out combatively, her beauty focused and dazzling, as she well knew.

"I can't quite identify the tone," he said cautiously.

"I'll take that as a compliment. How are your houses?"

"Coming beautifully. The most important part of the construction is over, they'll be ready on time. I'll be back to my normal schedule soon. Listen, Fauve, I really came to tell you that I was sorry I haven't been around much but you've been so busy that it didn't seem as if you'd have any extra time anyway—and now Papa tells me that you're going back to New York next week."

"Duty calls," she said, giving him a wicked darting glance out of the sides of her great, misty-gray eyes. This, she thought, was the way her mother must have treated the men who couldn't help falling in love with her. She felt purely Lunel, for which she couldn't be blamed, could she?

"I guess it does," he said expressionlessly.

"Would you like some lunch?" Fauve asked hospitably.

"I don't want you to bother—look, come on, I'll take you to that little hotel, the Hostellerie in Bonnieux that has such good food."

"I'm too hungry to wait and I've got a kitchen full of leftovers that we might just as well finish. All I've had to eat since breakfast is an apple, and that was a lifetime ago."

She led the way to the kitchen where the table was already laden with the food she'd taken out earlier. The cheeses were properly runny now, the pâté and chicken had lost their refrigerated chill, and while Eric sat drinking a glass of white wine, Fauve set the table and sliced tomatoes for a salad.

"I've never seen you looking so domestic," he said broodingly.

"This is nothing. I'm a demon cook. My specialty is Chicken Paprika with lots of sour cream."

"Sour cream? What's that?"

"*Crème fraîche*, only better," answered Fauve, who had long considered this insoluble gastronomic problem and didn't believe she was committing blasphemy.

"Somehow I've never thought of you as a cook."

"*If* you thought of me at all," she murmured, measuring olive oil.

"That's not fair!" he almost shouted, putting down his wine.

"Oh, all right. I apologize. Cheap shot. Come on, lunch is ready."

They both ate hungrily, almost in silence. Fauve bent her head and her eyebrows pulled together in a straight orange line as she concentrated mightily on not looking at Eric's hands or the way his wrists emerged from the sleeves of his sweater, or at his throat or his face, not at his face, particularly not at his face.

"You know," she said finally, in a thoughtful, reportorial tone of voice, "I never would have taken you for a person who'd forget a sacred promise. Darcy promised Magali a greenhouse and he's taken it back, but that's different, I can understand that. It was a question of checks and balances. You, on the other hand, *seemed* very sincere."

"What the hell are you talking about?"

"You promised to take me to Lunel, remember? I always hoped that I'd find a clue there, an illumination that would tell me something about my identity. How many years ago did you promise me? You still haven't done it and I don't see that you have any intention of taking me there," she said calmly, remorselessly keeping any note of reproach out of her voice.

"Goddamn it, Fauve, that's just too much! You go away without a word, you disappear for years, you reappear in Rome for only two days, you disappear again, you show up out of the blue six months later because of something that has nothing to do with me, you spend all your time surrounded by lawyers and dealers and new friends and newspapermen and photographers, now you're about to disappear again, and you have the incredible, breathtaking nerve to accuse *me* of breaking a promise!"

"You don't deny that you promised?" she repeated calmly, with a sweetly innocent smile that ignored his outburst as if she hadn't heard it.

"Of course I promised. I have the maps in the car to prove it. God, you're *rotten*! Lunel is south of Nîmes and north of Montpellier—it's just a little off route A9. If we got in the car now we could be there in just over an hour—taking the shortcut through St. Rémy and Tarascon . . . it's not far from the ocean, it's on the edge of the Camargue, actually it's just a few miles off the map of Provence, it's in Languedoc, properly speaking."

"You've been there without me!" she cried accusingly.

"Of course not. I'd never do that."

"Then how come you're so sure where it is? Eric, where's my pear?"

"Pear? . . . I just ate it . . . I'm sorry, I should have asked if you wanted half. What's wrong with you?"

"You ate . . . you ate . . ." Fauve squeaked, hardly able to articulate the words, ". . . my first . . . *subject!*"

" 'Subject'? It was only a pear . . . I swear to you, Fauve, I never went near Lunel but I wanted to know exactly where it was . . ."

"Why?" she asked, recovering with difficulty from her fit of laughter.

"Just in case," he said, "you ever came back and remembered that you wanted to go there."

"How long have you had those maps in your car?"

"Ever since you left . . . when you were sixteen. When I got a new car I just took them out of one glove compartment and put them in another."

"Then I think I'll decide to forgive you. At least you meant well, even if you show a lamentable lack of follow-through. Good intentions count for something, I suppose . . ."

"I'd call it a hell of a lot more than good intentions."

"What *would* you call it?" Fauve leaned on her hands and looked directly at him across the kitchen table. "Would you call it sentimental? Would you call it nostalgic? Would you call it a romantic gesture in the direction of a way you used to feel?"

"*You little bitch!*"

"Oh?" She managed to raise her eyebrows in polite inquiry while her heart turned cartwheels of jubilation.

"Don't try that game with me again! You've already had your fun in Rome, remember? Letting me think you still loved me, letting me stay hopelessly in love with you, slipping away at the last minute, teasing, sadistic, heartless—just as you're doing now . . . there aren't words to tell you what I think of you." He rose to his feet.

Fauve, too, stood up and walked rapidly around the table, transfigured, certain, so certain, as certain as she had been in the empty studio, welcoming life.

Eric looked at her and his world was reinvented. The one love of his life, her face blushing and prodigal with love that equaled his own, was holding out her arms to him in a gesture that encompassed all their shining, unequivocal future.

"Are you trying to say, in your original way, that you still love me?" Fauve asked as she put her arms around his neck. "Are you trying to ask me to marry you? Because I warn you, I'm in the mood to take any kind of risk this afternoon, this is the time to pin me down if you want me, I'm feeling astonishingly reckless, I'm flying high."

"There's never been a second when I didn't want you—I thought you didn't want me," he murmured as he looked into the mystery of her eyes and penetrated to its heart. "But," Eric added, drawing back, suddenly troubled, "I don't want to take advantage of your mood . . . you've led me a hell of a dance . . . what if you change your mind tomorrow?"

"Eric, it's not a mood. Nothing has ever been less a mood. I was just teasing, I couldn't help it, I had to make you mad to get through to you. I've wanted to marry you all these years—remember your dream about running off together when I was sixteen? I had that dream too, over and over, but I was afraid to admit it because I knew what it would have to mean, where it would have to take us. I've never had an intermittent heart but I did have a lack of faith—oh, not in you but in the possibility of absolute trust—that's over now. There are two things I hope for in life and neither one of them will be right without the other. I want to be your wife and I want to try to paint . . ."

"Paint? How did that happen? When—no, never mind—tell me later—it's perfect—I've always known you had to go back to it."

"Would you live here, at *La Tourrello*, Eric?"

"This house has been waiting for us, don't you know that?"

"I'm a slow study . . . but yes, I know now."

He traced her lips with his finger, feeling his heart pounding in his chest. "Do you still want to go to Lunel? I don't want to keep breaking that promise," he said gravely.

"Not now, not today," she answered.

"Don't you want to see it for yourself?"

"I'm not in any hurry," Fauve said pensively. "I don't seem to need to anymore. But Eric, I would like to take a drive—not far—just down the road—I *have* to buy another pear."

Princess Daisy

For Steve—
my husband, my love, my best friend—always.

Special thanks go to these good friends who answered questions with the gift of their experience:

Bernie Owett

Steve Elliot

Dan Dorman

Aaron Shikler

and, particularly, to Rosemary de Courcy

and her lurcher, Jake.

1

We could always shoot this on top of the RCA Building," Daisy said, walking past the parapet, above which rose a high, metal railing designed to forestall would-be suicides. "They're not nearly as paranoid as you Empire State people." She gestured scornfully at the ledge behind her. "But, Mr. Jones, if it's not the view from precisely here, the message just won't be New York."

The man in uniform watched, motionless in surprise, as Daisy suddenly leapt high and held on to a rung of the railing with one strong hand. With her other hand she took off the sailor hat under which she had tucked her hair and let it blow free. The silver-gilt tumble was caught by the breeze that separated it into a million brave and dazzling threads.

"Come down, Miss," the man in charge of the Observation Deck begged. "I told you it's just not allowed."

"Look, I'm trying to show you what we're after," Daisy persisted. "It's a hairspray commercial, and artistically, what's a hairspray commercial without wind blowing in the hair—can you tell me that? Just hanks of hair, all chunky and boring—wind is *essential*, Mr. Jones."

The uniformed official looked up at Daisy with perplexed admiration and dismay. He didn't understand anything about her. She was young and more beautiful than anyone he'd ever seen but she wore a man's moldy baseball jacket which bore the now mournful legend BROOKLYN DODGERS on its back, a pair of United States Navy sailor pants and dirty tennis shoes. He was far from a romantic man, but everything about her stung his imagination with an unaccustomed fascination. He found himself curiously unable to look away from her. She was as tall as he, at least five feet, seven inches, and something about the way she walked had suggested the balance of the trained athlete even before she had jumped up to the perch from which she now gestured, intrepid, high-hearted, as if she were trying to catch a beam of the sun itself. The roof supervisor was aware of a particular clarity and cadence in her speech that made him think that perhaps she wasn't American, yet who but an American would dress like that? When she'd first appeared all she'd asked was for permission to film a commercial on his roof and now she was hanging up there like a goddamned angel on a Christmas tree. Thank heaven the place was closed for the day.

"You can't go up there. You didn't tell me you wanted to the last time you came," he reproached her, circling cautiously closer. "It's never permitted. It could be dangerous."

"But all great art has to break rules," Daisy called down to him gaily, remembering that when she had first checked out this location, a week ago, two twenty-dollar bills had ensured Mr. Jones's cooperation. She had many more twenties in her pocket. Several years as a producer of commercials had taught her to travel strictly on folding money.

Daisy scrambled a little higher and took a deep breath. It was a fresh, glinting spring day in 1975 and the wind had blown all the soot away from the city; the rivers that circled the island were as blue and as lively as the ocean itself, and Central Park was a great Oriental rug flung at the feet of the gray apartment buildings of Fifth Avenue.

She smiled down at the worried man looking up at her. "Listen, Mr. Jones, I know all three models we're going to use; one of them lives on raw veggies and is working on her black belt in Karate, the second has just been signed for her first movie and the third is an est trainer who's engaged to marry a man with oil wells—now, would three wholesome American girls like that have any intention of jumping? We're going to build a strong, absolutely safe platform for them to stand on. I guarantee it personally."

"A platform! You never said . . ."

Daisy jumped down and stood close to him. Her dark eyes, not quite black, but the color of the innermost heart of a giant purple pansy, caught the late afternoon light and held it fast, as she deftly pressed two folded bills into his hand. "Mr. Jones, I'm sorry if I alarmed you. Honestly, it's safe as houses up there—you ought to try it."

"I just don't know, Miss."

"Ah, come on," Daisy cajoled him. "Didn't you promise me you'd be all ready for us on Monday? Didn't you promise me a special freight elevator open for business at six . . .?"

"But you never said anything about going *above* the roof level," he grumbled.

"Roof level!" Daisy said indignantly. "If all we wanted was a simple high view there must be a dozen buildings in this city we could use—but we want yours, Mr. Jones, no one else's." The story board for the commercial had specifically stated the Empire State Building. Leave it to Revlon to complicate her life. As Daisy reached into her reserve pocket for an additional twenty, she remembered that, three years before, when she had started working as a production assistant, she had first seen a taxi-cab driver cheerfully accept forty dollars to turn off his meter to allow his taxi to be used for six hours in the background of a street scene. "But that's bribing people," Daisy had objected. "Think of it as rent, if you want to stay in the business." She'd been warned, and she'd taken the advice. Now, as the experienced producer of many of the best commercials ever filmed—if you like commercials—Daisy was hardened to the objections of civilians, and if Mr. Jones was more difficult than many, he was easier than some. Her next gambit was the one that usually clinched matters.

"Oh, I forgot to tell you," she said, coming closer to him. "The director wanted to know if you'd be in the commercial, standing there in the background, like the keeper of the keys to the kingdom. We only pay Screen Actors' Guild minimum, so you don't have to do it if you don't want to—we could hire an actor to play you, but it wouldn't be nearly as authentic."

"Well . . ."

"And, of course, you'd have to have make-up," she said, playing her best card.

"Oh. I guess it'll be all right. Yeah, without wind in the hair why would you need hairspray? I see your point. Make-up, huh? And would I have to wear a costume?"

"Your uniform will be perfect, just as it is. Goodbye, Mr. Jones—I'll see you first thing Monday morning." Daisy waved cheerfully at him as she walked toward the covered center core of the building. As she waited for the elevator to reach the eighty-sixth floor, the blonde girl in the baseball jacket, born Princess Marguerite

Alexandrovna Valensky, reflected that it was truly fortunate that there was one thing you could count on in this world: *everybody* wanted to be in show biz.

Mr. Jones was only one in a long line of men who had been fascinated by something in Daisy Valensky. Among the first of them had been the famed photographer, Philippe Halsman, the man who would take more *Life* cover photographs than any other in the history of the magazine. In the late summer of 1952 he had been assigned to take Daisy's first official photographs for a *Life* cover, since absolutely everyone, or so it seemed to the editors of the magazine, wanted to know what the child of Prince Stash Valensky and Francesca Vernon looked like. The sudden marriage of the great war hero and incomparable polo player to the matchless romantic American movie star had intrigued the world and inspired rumors which were only expanded and exaggerated by the seclusion in which Prince and Princess Valensky had lived with their first child since her birth in April.

Now, in August, Francesca Vernon Valensky sat in a field of long grass, in a Swiss meadow, with Daisy in her arms. Halsman found the actress faintly pensive, even remote, although he had photographed her twice before, the second time after she had won an Oscar for her Juliet. But it was the laughing child who interested him even more than the mystery of her mother's mood. The tiny girl was like a new hybrid rose in the inconsistency of her coloring. By rights, he thought, only generations of selective breeding should have produced a child who had the classically Italian dark eyes of her mother, and skin that had a Tuscan warmth to it, like the particular part of a peach into which you bite first, knowing that it will be the ripest spot on the fruit. Yet her little head was covered with Saxon-white curls that blew around her vivid face like the corolla of a flower.

Stash Valensky's old wet nurse, Masha, who still formed part of his household, had, with her characteristic self-importance, informed the photographer that Princess Daisy's hair was exactly like that of her father when he was a child. It was true blonde hair, she explained proudly, which may become gold in time but never changes to ash brown with age. She boasted of this Valensky hair, which was found somewhere in each generation as far back as the family could be traced, yes, back to the days of the earliest hereditary Russian nobility, the *boyars*, who were the companions of the Tsars for almost a thousand years before Peter the Great. After all, she asked, almost indignantly, was not her master a direct descendant of Rurik, the Scandinavian Prince who had founded the Russian monarchy in the 800s? Halsman quickly agreed with her that little Daisy's hair would always remain blonde. Remembering Masha's imperious ways, and realizing that she would soon be coming to take the infant back for her supper, he worked quickly to make the most of the time left to him.

Tactfully, he decided not to ask Francesca to jump in the air for a picture, his favorite ploy after a sitting, and a trick he had practiced with success on many celebrities and dignitaries of the highest order. Instead, the photographer used his charm to cajole Stash Valensky, who had been standing behind him, observing the scene, into posing with his wife and daughter.

But for all his poise and pulsing authority, Valensky was not at ease in front of a camera. He had lived for much of his forty-one years with two phrases somewhere in the back of his mind. One of them came from Tolstoy: ". . . living like a nobleman is a nobleman's business, only the nobility can do it." The other phrase came from a tattered text on the beliefs of Hinduism which had fallen into his hands during a brief period of hospital convalescence after he had bailed out of his first Hurricane fighter plane during the Battle of Britain. "Be like the eagle when it soars above the abyss. The eagle does not think about flying, it simply feels that it flies."

Neither of these two guiding principles permitted him to feel comfortable while holding still for a photograph. He was so stiff that Halsman, in a flash of inspiration, suggested that they go to the stables where the Prince's nine polo ponies were kept in loose-boxes, attended to by three grooms.

Francesca cradled Daisy in her arms while Valensky indicated the fine points of the animals. Carried away by his enthusiasm, Valensky had just invited the photographer to inspect the mouth of his favorite pony, Merlin, when Halsman wondered out loud if the pony would allow the Prince to lift Daisy on his back.

"Why not? Merlin has a contented mind."

"But he isn't saddled," Francesca objected.

"So much the better. Daisy will have to learn to ride bareback some day."

"She still can't sit up by herself," Francesca said nervously.

"I don't intend to let go of her." The Prince laughed, firmly taking the baby and setting her astride the low curve of the pony's back between loins and withers. Francesca reached up to steady her child and Halsman finally got his cover picture; the magnificent man and the magnificent women, their hands clasped around the little body, faces uplifted eagerly toward the sprite in a flowered lawn dress whose hands fluttered the air in jubilation.

"She has no fear, Francesca," Stash exclaimed proudly. "I knew she wouldn't have. Valensky women have ridden hard for hundreds of years—haven't I told you?"

"More than once, darling," Francesca answered with a laugh that held a wisp of sadness in its loving mockery, a laugh that only sounded for a brief moment. It was at that instant Halsman decided that the timing was right to get a jumping picture of the Prince. When he proposed the idea Valensky barely hesitated. Then, lifting Daisy from Merlin's back, he grasped her under her arms, held her high above his head, and jumped straight up into the air, with a wild and ferocious leap. The child screamed with delight and Francesca Valensky shuddered, she who had once been so dangerously reckless. What had this marriage done to her, Halsman wondered?

2

Normally the *Queen Mary* makes the New York to Southampton crossing without a stop. On this particular trip, in June of 1951, the great engines came to a full halt as the ship arrived at Cherbourg. It lay just outside the harbor while a barge approached the ocean liner and tied up at a baggage port. A dozen sailors wheeled large carts piled with luggage down the gangplank and deposited it in two heaps, one mountainous and one relatively modest. By the time all the trunks and suitcases were arranged, thousands of curious passengers crowded the railings to discover the reason for the unexplained delay. After a brief wait, three people walked down the gangplank, a slender man, arm in arm with a trim woman, preceded by four small excitable dogs, and finally another woman whom the college students in third class immediately recognized and greeted with cheers and applause. While Francesca Vernon sat on one of her suitcases and waved merrily at her admirers, the Duke and Duchess of Windsor, standing with dignity near the dozens of steamer trunks which held their summer wardrobes, saw no reason to respond to the democratic hullabaloo, nor did they deign to even nod to the actress whose face was as famous as theirs. Since they never set foot in England, yet always traveled by Cunard, their yearly arrival on the Continent was made in this unfortunately public fashion. While on board the *Queen* they invariably ate in their suite and only emerged to walk their band of cairns. Inured by habit, resolutely they paid no attention to the spectators, but to Francesca the audience only increased the swelling thrill she felt as the barge approached the customs shed where her agent, Matty Firestone, and his wife, Margo, were waiting for her.

The Firestones had been in Europe for several weeks before her arrival. They had rented a huge, prewar Delahaye touring car and engaged an English-speaking chauffeur. Francesca sat mute with expectation as the car sped along the poplar-lined roads leading to Paris. Her dark beauty, which spoke of fifteenth-century Italy in its uncontemporary cut and fashion, was lit by most unclassic anticipation as she leaned forward on the cushions of the car. She possessed a combination of tranquility and pure sensuality in the composition of the essential triangle of eyes and mouth. Her black eyes were long and widely spaced, her mouth, even in repose, was made meaningful by the grace of its shape: the gentle arc of her upper lip dipped in the center to meet the lovely pillow of her lower lip in a line that had the power of an embrace. Margo watched her with maternal emotion. She thought that Francesca had never been quite as touching in any of her roles as she was now, her whole being ignited with the excitement of her first hours on European soil. Few people besides Margo, who had been her friend, confidante and protector for six years, knew just how influenced by the stuff of fairy tales and stories of high romance the twenty-four-year-old movie star still was.

"We'll do Paris for a week, honey," Matty told his client, "and then the grand tour. Straight down France to the Riviera, then along the coast until we get to Italy.

We'll hit Florence, Rome and Venice and go back to Paris through Switzerland. Two months of it. Sound good to you?"

Francesca was too moved to answer.

By late August the Firestones and Francesca returned to Paris, where Margo had serious shopping to finish before their ship sailed at the end of the month. They stayed at the George V, then and now the hotel for rich tourists who don't care that the hotel is full of other rich tourists, but who do care about good beds, room service and efficient plumbing.

In the hotel bar, on the first evening of their return, Matty was greeted by David Fox, a studio vice-president he lunched with at least once a month back in Hollywood.

"You all have to come to Deauville for the polo match next week," David insisted. "It's the first important one since the war."

"Polo?" asked Matty indignantly. "A bunch of fancy no-goods on nervous little ponies? Who needs it?"

"But they've reached the finals—everyone will be there," David persisted.

"How do they dress in Deauville?" Margo interrupted curiously.

"Exactly the same way you'd dress for a cruise on the largest yacht in the world," the man replied knowingly. "And, of course, everyone changes three times a day."

Margo barely prevented herself from licking her lips. The semi-marine mode had always been particularly kind to her.

"Matty, darling, I *need* to go to Deauville," she announced, with an inflection that told Matty there was no use in further discussion.

Deauville, that timelessly chic resort, was established on the coast of Normandy by the Duc de Morny in 1866. From its inception it was intended to be a paradise for moneyed aristocrats, deeply involved in racing, gambling and golf. Because the grass of Normandy is the richest in France, its cows produce the best cheese, cream and butter. This same grass inevitably attracts Horse People, and the breeding and raising of horses takes place on the great stud farms of the surrounding countryside. The city of Deauville itself consists almost entirely of hotels, shops, cafés and restaurants, but the fresh sea air provides the illusion that enables the briskly strolling crowd on the boardwalk, the Edwardian *Promenade des Planches*, to imagine that the previous night, spent at the casino, must have been, in some way, good for their health.

The Hotel Normandy, in which Matty had been able to secure last-minute accommodations, is built in the English half-timbered style, rather as if someone had taken a normal country manor house and turned it into a seaside giant. In August, the Normandy, the Royal and the Hotel du Golf shelter a large portion of the people who will, inevitably, be in Paris in October, in St. Moritz in February and in London in June.

In 1951 these people were called the International Set. For lack of an engine the term "Jet Set" didn't exist, but even then newspapers and magazines, although less preoccupied than they are now, were fascinated by the comings and goings of the gilded mob who had, somehow, escaped the mundane, workaday world.

It was all fueled by money, although money alone didn't guarantee entry. Charm, beauty, talent—none of these attributes, even added to money, could make a person part of the International Set. What was essential was the willingness, the wholehearted intention to spend a life of a certain *kind;* a life in which the pursuit of pleasure and leisure could go on and on for years on end without causing any guilt, a life in which work had little meaning, and accomplishment, except in sports and gambling, had no place of honor. It was a life in which one's best efforts were expended on the exteriors and décors of life; grooming, fashion, luxurious and exotic interiors, constant travel, entertainment and wide acquaintance, rather than deep friendships.

Integral to the life of the International Set was the man then called a playboy. The true playboy did not usually have a great deal of money himself, but he was only to be found where the money was. He had good humor, reliable charm, the capacity to acquit himself well at almost any game, the tact to drink like a gentleman, to avoid gambling debts and to give women so much pleasure that they inevitably told their friends about him.

Prince Alexander Vassilivitch Valensky was not a playboy. But since he could so often be found where playboys clustered, the press had dubbed Stash Valensky a playboy as a careless point of reference.

Stash Valensky's vast personal fortune separated him completely from the playboy ranks. It was a fortune he had never had to question, even in his periods of wildest extravagance. Indeed, he never had to consider himself extravagant since he could afford to spend whatever he chose. The easeful relationship to wealth had been common to his ancestors, right down to his father, the late Prince Vasily Alexandrovitch Valensky. Nevertheless, Stash Valensky could never have been called a businessman. Until 1939, when polo stopped for the duration of World War II, he had devoted most of his adult life to the game. He had carried a nine-goal handicap since 1935, which made him one of the top ten players in a sport in which it was so expensive to participate that only nine thousand men in the world ever played it at any one time.

Valensky had the physical presence of a great athlete who has punished his body without pity throughout his life and the watchful, fighting eyes of a natural predator. His glance was bold and his thick brows were many shades darker than his blond hair, cropped short and as coarse as the coat of a hastily brushed dog. Valensky had never had to ask for anything. Either it had been given to him or he had taken it. His nose, broken many times, gave him the air of a roughneck. He had well-weathered, outdoorsman's skin and strong, blunt, almost brutal features, but he walked with the gait, rapid and graceful, of a man who was in control wherever he found himself. He was considered to have the best "hands" in the world of international polo. Not only did Valensky never employ unnecessary force on the bit and reins but he had been born, as some men are, with an instinct for establishing a communication between himself and his pony which made it seem as if the animal was merely an extension of his mind, rather than a beast with a will of its own.

Nevertheless, Prince Valensky owned nine ponies, rather than the more usual five or six, because he rode like a barbarian. It is not safe to ride a polo pony, galloping and turning at top speed, for more than two chukkers in any single game. Stash rode so aggressively that he preferred to have a fresh pony for each of the six chukkers and he chose never to have fewer than three animals in reserve. According to the rules of the Hurlingham Polo Association, under which he played, no man is allowed to "Ride at an opponent in such a manner as to intimidate and cause him to pull out." Stash stopped just short of that ambiguous distinction, but he never rode at an adversary without the clear mental intention of unhorsing him. There were many players who thought that the HPA Field Rules should have contained some special penalty which would disqualify Valensky, although no umpire had ever yet ordered him off the field.

It was a gala day in Deauville as the crowds pressed politely into the stands for the polo finals. When the Mayor of the city had been informed by the management of the Hotel Normandy that Francesca Vernon was their guest, he had called at the hotel in person and, with great formality, asked if she would present the cup to the winner of the day's match.

"The honor was to have been mine, Mademoiselle," he told her, "but it would be a great day for Deauville if you would consent." The Mayor understood perfectly that with the participation of a film star the outcome of the play would be covered more prominently than if it were a mere sporting event.

"Well . . . ," Francesca said, hesitating for form's sake, but already she saw herself clearly at the center of the competition.

"She'd love to," Margo assured the Mayor. She owned a white silk suit trimmed with touches of navy that she hadn't worn yet on this trip. She had suspected that it might be too formal for polo, but if Francesca had a place in the proceedings it would look entirely suitable. Margo was a great fan of pictures of royal personages presenting things to natives, something she would never have admitted, even to Matty. Sometimes Margo saw herself standing, gracious, smiling and about five inches taller than she was, being handed a huge bouquet of roses by a small curtsying child. It would never happen to her, but why shouldn't it happen to Francesca?

The Firestones and Francesca watched the match with interest which soon turned into confusion. The play was really too fast to follow without some familiarity with its intricate rules. However, the atmosphere of the match was electric. Polo spectators are elegantly dressed, superbly perfumed and given to a kind of upper-class hysteria which balances the intense knowledgeability of the bullring crowd in Madrid with the polite, dandified excitement of Ascot. All three of them soon gave up trying to figure out what had triggered the moments of applause or groans and gave themselves up to the spectacle of eight great athletes riding fast horses. What ballet is to dance, what chess is to board games, polo is to sport.

A burst of cheering signaled the end of the match. The Mayor of Deauville approached their seats and held out his hand to Francesca. "Quickly, Mademoiselle Vernon," he said. "The ponies are hot—we must not keep them out on the field."

Francesca, holding the Mayor's arm, picked her way across the polo grounds, now marred by divots which had been kicked up by the ponies' hooves. The full skirt of her green silk dress, printed with tiny blue and white flowers, snapped like a sail in the stiff breeze. She wore a large white straw hat with an undulating brim, banded and ribboned in the silk of her dress. As she used one hand to keep it on her head, Francesca realized that at some time during the match she must have lost her hatpins. The actress and the Mayor approached the spot where the eight players, all still mounted, were waiting for her. The Mayor spoke briefly, first in French and then in English. Abruptly he handed Francesca a heavy silver trophy. Automatically, in order to receive the trophy, she took her hand off her hat. It blew off at once, and went skimming along the ground, bounding from one tuft of turf to another.

"Oh no!" she exclaimed in dismay, but as she spoke, Stash Valensky leaned down from his pony and scooped her up in one arm. Holding her easily, across his chest, he urged his mount after the wayward hat. It had come to rest two hundred yards away, and Valensky, still holding Francesca to him, bent down from his saddle, picked the hat up by its ribbons and carefully replaced it on her head. The stands rang with laughter and applause.

Francesca heard nothing of the noise the spectators made. Time, as she knew it, had stopped. By instinct, she remained silent and waiting, passive against Stash's soaking-wet polo shirt. She could smell his sweat and it confounded her with desire. Her mouth filled with saliva. She wanted to sink her teeth into his tan neck, to bite him until she could taste his blood, to lick up the rivulets of sweat which ran down to his open collar. She wanted him to fall to the ground with her in his arms, just as he was, flushed, steaming, still breathing heavily from the game, and grind himself into her.

Collecting himself, Stash trotted his pony back to the other horsemen. He slid to the ground, Francesca still in his arms, and placed her gently on her feet. Somehow she was still holding the trophy and she tottered in her high heels. He took the cup from her, let it drop to the turf and grabbed both of her hands to steady her. For an instant they stood facing each other, linked. Then he bent from the waist and kissed one of the hands he was holding. Not the formal kiss that barely brushes the air above the hand, but a hard, hot imprint of his mouth.

"Now," he said, looking right into her astonished eyes, "you're supposed to give me the cup." He reached down for it and handed it to her. She gave it back to him, silently. The crowd applauded again, and under that sound, she said, in a barely audible voice, "Hold me again."

"Later."

"When?" Francesca was shocked at her abrupt, naked voice.

"Tonight. Where are you staying?"

"The Normandy."

"Come on. I'll take you back to your seat." He offered her his arm. They didn't speak again until she had been restored to Matty and Margo. Everything essential had been said. Anything else was impossible to say.

"Eight?" he asked.

She nodded agreement. He didn't kiss her hand again, but just bowed slightly and strode out to the field.

"Jesus Christ, what was all that about?" Matty demanded. Francesca didn't answer him. Margo said nothing, because on Francesca's lovely and familiar face she saw a dazed expression which, to Margo, was instantly apparent as a *new* expression, one that had been created by something outside the borders of Francesca's previous experience.

"Come on, darling," she said to the actress, "everybody's leaving." Francesca merely stood where she was, not hearing. "What are you going to *wear?*" Margo said in her ear. This time Francesca heard her.

"It doesn't matter what I wear," she answered.

"What!" Margo was shocked, genuinely shocked, for the first time in twenty years. "Come on, Matty. We've got to get back to the hotel," she ordered, and, leaving him to escort Francesca, she led the way, muttering incredulously to herself. "Doesn't matter! Doesn't *matter?* Has she gone mad?"

Francesca Vernon was the only child of Professor Ricardo della Orso and his wife, Claudia. Her father was head of the Foreign Language Department at the University of California in Berkeley, to which he had immigrated from Florence in the 1920s.

Both of Francesca's parents had origins, centuries old, in the many-towered, once noble hill town of San Gimignano, near Florence. In each of their families there had been strikingly lovely women, too many of whom had come to dishonor or disgrace, according to the strict values of their times. For hundreds of years, many a noble Tuscan gentleman had ridden to San Gimignano, attracted by the legend of the glorious daughters of the della Orso and Veronese families. Often, too often, they had not been disappointed.

As soon as Ricardo and Claudia della Orso saw the hereditary features appear in their daughter they realized that she would, inevitably, be beautiful, perhaps unsuitably beautiful. They hoarded their one precious child, keeping her to themselves as much as possible, although Francesca needed the companionship of children her own age. Years in the battlefield of a playground sandbox, and more years in the rough and tumble of kindergarten, throwing things, building things, and playing with all manner of boys and girls, would have been far more healthy for this girl, who had inherited the wild blood of all those dark and captivating women of San Gimignano, than the hundreds of hours that were spent nourishing her fantasy life as, endlessly, her mother read fairy tales out loud.

In their effort to keep Francesca safe, her parents fed her growing mind on old stories of gallant deeds performed for love, of heroes and heroines whose lives were filled with risk and honor. They were a willing audience for the dozens of plays she soon began to perform for them with plots borrowed from the tales on which she had grown up. Her parents, innocent and proud, never understood that they had encouraged Francesca to view herself from the outside, to watch herself *being someone she was not* and take deep pleasure in it, to find role playing more real than anything else life had to offer.

When Francesca was six and went to school, she found her first wider audience. In the part of the crafty Morgiana in a first-grade production of *Ali Baba and the Forty Thieves*, the same "Open Sesame!" that revealed the treasure cave gave her a sure knowledge of her future. She would be an actress. From that moment on, although she seemed, to the outward eye, to be following a normal course through school, she acted in her head. When she wasn't actually involved in the yearly class play, she would come to school in the character of the heroine of the book she was currently reading, and such was her cleverness that she was able to go through an entire school day without betraying herself to her classmates. They found her full of unexpected responses and unexplained moods, but that was just Francesca, who had, by reason of her inaccessibility, come to occupy a high position in the pecking order of school. Everyone wanted to be her friend because so few were granted the privilege.

Year after year, Francesca was given the lead in the school plays, and no one, not even other mothers, ever complained that it was unfair, since she was so clearly better than anyone else. A production in which she played a lesser role than the central one would have been lopsided. She had only to walk out onto a stage to project an inescapable flash of aroused expectation. There was an inevitable quality in her smallest gestures. Francesca didn't learn how to act: she merely turned her roving fancy toward the character she was playing and became that person with such naturalness that it appeared as if all she had done was to unwrap her emotions and let them appear on her face.

"Of all the occupational hazards of an agent's life, high-school plays are my least favorite," complained Matty Firestone.

"What about actresses' love affairs?" asked his wife Margo. "Last week you said they were even worse than negotiating with Harry Cohn."

"Point well taken. At least a play is over quickly," Matty agreed, although he still felt deeply aggrieved at being condemned to seeing a Berkeley High presentation of *Milestones* by Arnold Bennett; a warhorse of a production much favored by graduating classes.

"Don't you dare fall asleep with your eyes open again," Margo warned him affectionately. "It makes me nervous . . . and anyway, the Hellmans are your old friends, not mine."

"But you're the one who had to let them know we were in San Francisco. You should have remembered that it's June—graduation month," Matty grumbled. He always expected Margo to have his private life as perfectly organized as her enormous wardrobe. She was the ideal agent's wife; cynical, but never without harmless illusions, warm-hearted unsurprisable and totally kind, just as Matty was the ideal agent; a man of audacity and loyalty, gifted with a keen sense of exactly how far to go in a negotiation; of how much was too much and how little was too little; added to a scrupulous disinclination ever to tell an actual lie, yet not cursed with a dangerous compulsion always to reveal the truth. Neither he nor Margo could ever become the victims of flattery, but they were incapable of resisting the seduction of talent.

In the first act of *Milestones*, Francesca della Orso appeared as a young woman about to be wed; the woman who would, in the last act, be seen celebrating her fiftieth wedding anniversary.

"*That brunette!*" Matty said in Margo's ear in a tone whose meaning she knew well. It heralded good tidings. It was a voice loaded with solid gold. They looked at Francesca together, exploring the exquisite oval of her face, the small, rounded slightly cleft chin, the straight nose, the eyebrows set high so that her eyelids were of a strange and touching importance. Matty had only seen one woman as beautiful as this girl before and she had started his career and made his fortune. Listening to Francesca speak her lines, he felt sweat suddenly beading his upper lip. The hairs on the back of his neck rose; he felt his sinuses constrict. Margo, for her part, was keenly aware of the dark promise in the girl's wide, calm, imperious eyes, of the passionate spirit that was evident in spite of her smooth forehead and long, docile neck. Neither of them yet could understand the force of Francesca's fantasy life, the intensity of her moods, the fury of uncompromising emotions into which she could fling herself.

As soon as it was decently possible after the curtain rang down, Matty and Margo deserted their friends' lackluster daughter and went in search of Francesca della Orso. They found her backstage, still in the make-up of a woman of almost seventy, surrounded by an admiring crowd. Matty didn't bother to introduce himself to her. It was her parents who were his target.

His siege of Claudia and Ricardo della Orso lasted for weeks. Although they had always been filled with quiet joy and wonder by their daughter's performances in school plays, they were bewildered and outraged at the agent's proposal that he sign Francesca to an exclusive personal contract and that she come to live in Los Angeles under his wife's strict supervision. But eventually, to their own astonishment, they overcame their deep mistrust of Hollywood, vanquished by their perception of Matty Firestone's excellent intentions and the satisfactory protective qualities they saw in Margo.

Although the events that followed the production of *Milestones* startled Ricardo and Claudia, Francesca was not surprised. She had long lived in the world of dreams in which wondrous happenings took place predictably, and her ranging imagination had always whispered to her that she was not destined to lead the life her friends would lead. Nothing could have prevented her from reaching out for everything life offered.

Francesca Vernon, née della Orso, became a star in her first picture. Her reputation grew with astonishing speed in those lush days when studios could use the same actress in three or four major pictures a year. From the age of eighteen to the age of twenty-four Francesca went directly from one film to another, for she had been born to play the great romantic roles. More than ten years younger than Ingrid Bergman, Bette Davis, Ava Gardner or Rita Hayworth, she reigned alongside them, capturing parts which might normally have gone to English actresses, because there was no one in Hollywood who could match her as a heroine on the grand scale; the noble, the star-crossed, the stuff of tragic legend.

Francesca lived with the Firestones for a year before she bought herself a small house next door to them. Although she went to San Francisco to visit her parents on her rare, brief vacations, by 1949 they both died. Since Francesca didn't plunge into the Hollywood social scene she was soon typed by movie magazines as a mystery woman, an approach which wily Matty encouraged, knowing how tantalizing it is to the press. The studio's publicity department cooperated completely in the screen of secrecy which surrounded Francesca, for they realized, as well as Matty, that the truth about her would have been totally unacceptable to the prudish public of the 1950s. Francesca fell dangerously in love with almost every one of her leading men, and her discreet but full-blown affairs only ended when the final scene of each picture was shot. This amorous habit of hers might have killed Matty from sheer weight of aggravation if he hadn't learned that each affair had a finite end. She had never loved a man, a real person. She had loved the Prince of Denmark and Romeo and Heathcliff and Marc Antony and Lord Nelson and a dozen others, but once the ordinary mortal actor stood before her, she grew cold. It was wild, theatrical passion or cold porridge when Francesca's emotions were involved.

Margo Firestone, concerned with Francesca's succession of intense affairs, often with married men, asked her finally why she didn't try to have more *fun*, like other young actresses of her age.

Francesca turned on her indignantly. "My God, Margo, what the hell do you think I am—a Janet Leigh, or a Debbie Reynolds, with their cute little movie-magazine romances? And who the hell wants to have *fun*—what a silly word that is. I insist on *more*—and I know perfectly well how corny that sounds, so you don't have to bother to lecture me. Oh, I'm fed up with actors! But they're all I ever meet."

She had just turned twenty-four when she said this, and that evening Margo Firestone decided that Francesca needed a change of scenery. She was too caught up in the artificial world of the sound stage, too restless, too vulnerable. And the deaths of her parents during the last few years had left her depressed.

"If she were my daughter," Margo said reflectively, "I'd be damn worried."

"Still, last year she won the Oscar," Matty mused.

"I'd worry even more. Remember Luise Rainer?"

"Please! Don't even say it." Matty knocked on wood to fend off the memory of what he considered the mishandled career of the fragile Austrian actress who had won two Oscars in a row and then virtually disappeared from film importance in the late 1930s. God forbid such a thing should happen to Francesca. Or to him.

"Let's ask her to go with us to Europe next month," Margo suggested.

"But I thought you wanted a second honeymoon," Matty objected.

"I don't really believe in honeymoons, first or second," Margo said firmly. "As soon as Francesca finishes *Anna Karenina* have your office arrange to put her on the next boat—we can meet her there."

By seven-thirty of the evening after the polo match, under Margo's feverish direction, Francesca was ready. She wore a floor-length rosy-white chiffon evening gown designed by Jean Louis. The strapless bodice was held up by tiny bones and draped softly over her bosom. The first layer of chiffon was a dark pink, the next a lighter shade of pink, until the fifth and final layer, which was pure white. Around her bare shoulders she flung a chiffon stole of five layers like the skirt. Yards long, it was ornamented here and there by delicate sprays of palest pink silk flowers. The entire effect was eighteenth century and as fanciful as if she had stepped from a portrait by Gainsborough. Francesca's long hair, which she had refused to sacrifice for the new poodle cut, was caught up in a huge chignon at the back of her neck, and tiny curls of hair escaped just in front of her ears and lay on her smooth forehead.

Margo surveyed her with admiration and envy. Matty had wandered into the sitting room of Francesca's suite to inspect his client. "I hope that guy's dressed up too, hon."

"Matty, in Deauville they won't even let you in the gambling rooms at the Casino unless you're in evening clothes," Margo said, dismissively. She knew what was proper for a first date with a prince. She'd been planning one for herself since she was fifteen.

"Listen, hon," Matty continued, undeterred, "this fellow is a genuine prince. I've checked up on that. But he's got quite a reputation as a ladies' man. He's been divorced once. So keep that in mind. You're a big girl now—I know, I know, so don't tell me again."

As they sat waiting, there was a knock on the door. Matty opened it to find the hotel bell captain standing with a stiff white pasteboard box in his hands.

"Flowers for Miss Vernon," he announced. Matty took the box and tipped the man. "At least he knows all the gimmicks," he observed sourly. Francesca opened the box and found that it contained a triple circle of white rosebuds that she could twine around her wrist. Then, sharp-eyed Margo spied another smaller, black velvet box, tied in blue ribbon, which had been tucked under the roses. Francesca opened it quickly and drew in her breath in amazement. Fitted precisely into the velvet interior of the box lay a crystal pot, three-quarters filled with water. In the pot were three sprigs of thickly clustered flowers on stems of gold. Each flower was made of five round petals of turquoise with rose-cut diamond centers and leaves of jade. She took it out and set it on the table. The entire magical object was three inches high and the illusion of water was due to the clarity of the rock crystal.

"What . . . ? What is it?" she asked.

"Artificial flowers," said Matty.

"Fabergé . . . that's Fabergé . . . it couldn't be anything else," Margo breathed. "Read the card!"

Only then did Francesca tear open the card concealed in the old velvet box which bore the double-headed eagle, mark of the Royal Warrant.

These forget-me-nots belonged to my mother. Until this afternoon I had lost hope of finding someone to whom they should belong.

Stash Valensky

"He knows gimmicks they haven't even invented yet," Matty said, his face dour. But even to his unsentimental eyes the little vase was an extraordinarily precious object. Whatever else this bozo was, he certainly wasn't handing those out by the gross.

As Francesca finished twining the rosebuds around her wrist, the front desk rang announcing Prince Valensky. "Listen, hon, just remember that pumpkin can turn into a coach," Matty said hastily, but Francesca had left the room so quickly that she didn't hear him. He turned to Margo with an expression of dismay. "Hell, I meant the coach into a pumpkin—do you think she got it?"

"You might as well have been speaking Chinese," said Margo.

Valensky and Francesca Vernon, by unspoken accord, moved quickly through the crowded lobby of the Normandy where people had stopped to look at them the minute she stepped out of the lift, her beauty unfurled above the great float of chiffon. His open, white Rolls-Royce convertible was waiting at the door, and within seconds they were driving through the almost deserted streets of a city in which most people were either drinking or still dressing for the evening.

"Do you realize that this is unfashionably early?" he asked.

"But you did say eight."

"I don't think my nerves could last till nine."

"So you suffer from nerves?" Her famous voice, deep and gentle, came with difficulty, through lips that were suddenly dry.

"Since this afternoon, yes." Her tone of badinage had evaporated. He took one hand off the wheel and laid it over hers. The sudden, simple contact left her incapable of responding. None of her many lovers had, even in their most intimate moments, touched her in such a way. There was ownership in his fingers.

After a minute he continued. "I had planned to take you to the Casino for dinner . . . there's the polo ball tonight . . . it's the peak of the Season. Would you mind missing it? We could go to a restaurant I know on the way to Honfleur—Chez Mahu. It's good and it's quiet, or at least it will be tonight with everyone in Deauville."

"Oh, yes—please."

They drove in renewed silence through the lambent evening of Normandy, an evening of vast gray-blue skies covering a landscape cosily patterned by fields, orchards and farmhouses, seen in that last light of day, which for ten minutes makes everything look greener than it really is.

At Chez Mahu they found that they were able only to talk of unimportant things. Stash tried to explain polo to Francesca but she scarcely listened, mesmerized as she was with the abrupt movements of his tanned hands on which light blond hair grew, the hands of a great male animal. For his part, Stash hardly knew what he was saying. Francesca played straight into the heart of his deepest, most thoroughly concealed dream. For years he had had as many women as he chose to reach out for, sophisticated, clever, practiced and decorative women of great beauty, women of the International Set. He was a hardened man of the world who was, at last, experiencing the *coup de foudre*, the thunderclap of unreasoning, instant infatuation.

She was so young, he thought, and luminous in her majesty. Her dark and blushing beauty could have been as Russian as it was Italian. She reminded him of the miniatures of young princesses, framed in jewels and gold, the princesses of St. Petersburg that he had seen, when he was a child, in dozens of frames set in a nostalgic profusion on the tables around his mother's fireplace. The flesh of her shoulders, when she threw back her stole, had an almost impossible polish and freshness. The curve of her jaw where it approached her ear was of such a heartbreaking purity that he knew it would remain in his memory forever.

Francesca listened to Valensky's low voice, which had traces of an English accent, a brutal man's voice which seemed to vibrate with an underlying tenderness, as if he were talking to a newborn foal, and thought that this man was as far from the sort of man she knew as if he had sprung from another species. Every time she dared to look directly into the fighting gleam of his gray eyes she felt as if she had taken another step into a foreign land. He told her that he was forty but about him there clung an air of strength and purpose which made youth seem an awkward dream. Matty was forty-five. Stash made him seem seventy-five.

As they finished their coffee he asked her if she would go with him to visit his horses.

"I never turn in without checking the stables," he explained. "They expect to see me."

"And do they like female visitors?"

"They have never seen any before."

"Ah!" She shivered at the stern simplicity of the compliment. "Yes, I'll come."

They drove back toward Deauville, and, just outside of Trouville, took a road which branched off into a country lane which wandered through half a mile of ancient apple trees until it stopped at a gate set into a wall of irregular stones. At the sound of the horn a man appeared quickly and opened the gate so that they could drive through. Inside the courtyard was a substantial stone farmhouse and a number of farm buildings.

"My manager, Jean, lives here with his family," Valensky said. "The stableboys live in the village and ride their bikes over every morning."

He took Francesca's arm and led her toward the stables which were at some distance from the farmhouse. At the sound of their footsteps some of the ponies immediately whinnied and started to move around in their boxes.

"They don't get much to look at, poor beasts," Valensky laughed. "I'm their nightly floor show." He walked slowly from box to box, stopping to name each pony to Francesca, to tell her something of the animal's peculiarities while he observed, with a quick, keen eye, the health and mental condition of each one of them.

"Tiger Moth here is spending the week out to grass. He has a cut mouth—nothing serious, but I won't ride him until it's completely healed. Gloster Gladiator has a bad habit of eating his bed so I've had it changed from straw to peat moss. Good; Bristol Beaufighter is sleeping. He had a hard afternoon."

"Bristol Beaufighter, Gloster Gladiator?"

"I know they're odd names for horses. They're the names of planes . . . great planes. Some day I'll tell you more about them."

"Tell me now," she demanded, not really caring. His careless phrase, "some day I'll tell you" was all she'd heard.

"The Tiger Moth was a trainer . . . de Havilland. The Gladiator was a fighter, the Bristol a night fighter . . . there were many, now forgotten, unless you've flown one. Then you can never forget."

His voice trailed off as he saw she wasn't listening. The moonlight on her ball gown turned it into a sculptural mass of white marble.

"Come," he said reluctantly, "I should take you back. The gala isn't over yet and we can be at the Casino in less than fifteen minutes."

"The Casino? Certainly not. I want to hear more about the Tiger Moth."

"No, you don't."

"Oh, but I do." Francesca entered an empty box in which blankets and tack were stored and sat down on a bale of clean straw that stood against one wall. She tilted her head back against the wall and let her wrap fall carelessly away from her shoulders, knowing exactly how the promise of the movement would affect him. He saw immediately that she was not playing the coquette or the tease. The look she gave him was so profound that it gathered together her entire ardent nature and offered it to him with artful purpose. In one stride, Valensky followed her, put his arm around her waist and turned her to him. He whispered into her ear, "The Tiger Moth was a basic training plane for the RAF."

"Basic . . ." Francesca breathed.

"Very, very basic . . ." Valensky kissed the curve of her jaw, near her ear, moving his mouth softly until their lips found each other. At that instant something changed forever in both of them. They had crossed an invisible barrier and discovered themselves firmly planted on the other side of their lives. They knew almost nothing of each other but they were already beyond questions, reassurances or preconditions. It was as if they, two separate beings, had, in coming together, formed a third, quite different entity, that would never, now, be resolved back into the originals.

Francesca pulled away from his lips and, reaching up with both arms, unpinned her chignon so that all her dark hair fell down over her shoulders. She shook it loose impatiently and then, looking full into his eyes, she adroitly managed to unfasten her strapless dress and her crinolines, throwing them as hastily aside as if they were made of hopsacking. Recklessly she flung herself out of her clouds of chiffon plumage only to appear in her resplendent flesh, lying totally naked on a pile of horse blankets, laughing softly as she watched Stash Valensky, momentarily bewildered and taken by surprise, struggle out of his dinner jacket. Soon, very soon, he was as naked as she. He savaged her abandoned flesh with an urgency, almost a cannibalism, he hadn't known in years. This creature of roses and pearls had become, in a flash of magic, a demanding mortal who begged him, in hungry, hoarse tones, to take her as quickly as possible. She would not let him linger at any point; considerations of her own pleasure melted before her craving to have him inside her; deeply, fully, to possess him. When he mounted her and she opened for him, a queen joyfully squandering all her treasures, it was a primeval act. As he gave himself, shatteringly, to his climax, Francesca looked up at his face in the moonlight, his eyes tightly closed, an expression of intense concentration, almost of agony, furrowing his features, and smiled in a way she had never smiled before. Afterward they clung together under the horse blankets, their bodies radiating a triumphant heat, able now to touch each other with tenderness, to explore rather than plunder, to caress rather than raven. Again they made love and this time Stash would not permit Francesca to set the pace, but brought her with infinite skill to an orgasm so stabbing, so victorious, that it frightened her. They slept awhile and awoke to see the change of light, the unmistakable signs of approaching dawn in that fraction of the sky visible from their corner of the horse box.

"Your friends—my God, what will they think?" said Stash, suddenly remembering the Firestones.

"Matty will be making noises like an outraged father in a Victorian melodrama and Margo will be excited and curious and pleased with herself. Or they went to bed early and don't even know I'm still out . . . which would be most unlikely. In two hours Matty will start to think about going to the police, but he won't because he doesn't want publicity."

"I'd better let them know you're safe."

"But, it's too early to phone . . . look, the sun is just rising."

"I'll just go and tell Jean to ring up the hotel and say you're fine and will be back soon. Don't move."

He was back in minutes. "That's done. Now we'll make our plans and then we'll find some breakfast."

"Plans?"

"The wedding. As soon as possible and no fuss . . . or all kinds of fuss, if that's what you'd like. Just so it's soon."

Francesca rose halfway out of the pile of blankets in astonishment, her nipples still tender and sore from the assault of his lips and teeth, bits of straw in her wildly disordered hair. She gaped in astonishment at this man who was looking down at her with utter conviction.

"Married?"

"Is there any alternative?" He sat down and took her in his arms, pressing her forehead to the place where the tan of his neck turned into the rosy-white skin of his chest. She lifted her head and asked again, "Married?"

Stash pulled a blanket over her shoulders against the morning damp. His strong hands, accustomed to obedience, grasped the top of her arms and when he spoke his voice, though low, had the ring of a cavalry charge.

"I'm old enough to know that this sort of thing doesn't happen twice in a lifetime. At my age there's no such thing as infatuation. It's love and, damn it, I'm *no good* at love—I don't know the right words, I can't tell you what I feel because I've never done it before. I haven't used the real words, just other words, play-love words, seduction words—"

"But I have used *all* the real words, the most beautiful ever written—and *never* been good at love either—so we're equal," Francesca replied slowly, realizing a truth she had not said out loud before.

"Have you ever felt like this? Can you imagine feeling like this again?" Stash demanded.

Francesca shook her head. It was easier to turn her back on everything that had made up her life until yesterday than it was to think of life apart from Stash in any way.

"But . . . shouldn't we get to know each other?" she said, and then laughed deeply at the conventionality of the question.

"Know each other? Oh, God—we'd just end up in the same place. No, we will tell them we've decided to get married and that's that. Francesca, say yes!"

All of Francesca's romantic nature rose up within her. She didn't say yes but she inclined her queen's head and passionately kissed his hands in a fury of submission and possession. She wept and he kissed her wet eyes.

The sun was up and all the noises of the farm suddenly burst into their consciousness.

"You'd better dress," Stash grinned like a boy.

"Dress? Have you any idea . . . ?" Francesca pointed to a heap of crumpled chiffon and silk flowers lying on the dirt floor of the stable. "To say nothing of this!" She flourished a white lace undergarment which had worked its way under the horse blankets. It was called a Merry Widow, a corselette which started at a strapless bra, continued to form a fashionably tiny waist and reached halfway down the hips where garters were attached to hold up her stockings.

"I'll help you—but you got out of it so quickly."

"There are ways and ways—but getting back in is another story. No, Stash, I just can't put this all back on," she implored. "Look, my fingers are shaking."

They both froze, startled by the whistle of an approaching stable hand.

"I'll head him off," Stash whispered, trying not to laugh. "Get back in there." Francesca dove into the blankets giggling. The transition from high romance to farce was complete, as, with one eye, she could see the pony in the next box stretch his head in her direction and snort as if in shocked indignation, no doubt she thought wildly, trying to alert the entire stable to their carryings on. Before long Stash was back, holding a pile of clothes.

"I made a deal with that boy," he said, handing her a pair of well-polished old riding boots, a frayed blue shirt, and a pair of shabby riding breeches. "He's about your size and I think he had a bath this morning—but I don't guarantee it."

While Francesca managed to dress in the boy's clothes, mercifully clean and only two sizes too big for her, Stash brought her evening bag from the car. She peered into the mirror of her compact and saw that no trace of make-up remained on her face. She decided not to bother with repairs. Francesca loved her scraped and reddened skin, her bruised lips, her unfamiliar, excited eyes.

"I need a belt," she discovered.

Stash inspected the variety of tack hanging on the wall. "Martingale's too long. The bridle? No, it won't work, nor the curb chain. I'd give you my bow tie if I could find it, but it'd be too short. Here, this should do." He handed her a long length of material, doubled over.

"What's that?"

"Tail bandage—keeps the pony's tail from catching on the polo stick."

"Who said romance was dead?" she asked.

"Tell them it was an Act of God." Francesca laughed at a stupefied Matty.

"You'd have to be pregnant for that!" the agent exploded. "You don't even have a decent excuse! You're throwing away a great career to marry some Russian polo player out of nowhere and you're as fucking light-hearted as ten thousand goddamned angels dancing on the head of a pin."

Francesca flung clean defiance in the teeth of his logic.

"Matty, how many years does a person have to live at the peak? The sky-rocket years, Matty? The firework years? I'm in love with a real man for the first time, so be happy for me!" She made her demands with an infuriatingly carefree smile. "We want everything, Matty—all—all there is, and we want it now. Why shouldn't we have it? Can you give me a single reason that will mean anything—even in ten years?" she challenged him.

"All right, I'm happy, I'm thrilled, I'm overjoyed—my best client, like a daughter to me, is getting married to some bozo she met yesterday—who could ask for a better reason for feeling happy? And what does she say when I ask her why it has to be so sudden, why she can't go home and just do *Robin Hood* first and then get married? What does she say when I tell her that nobody wants to stop her from marrying her prince, but maybe she should get to know him better?"

"I said," Francesca answered dreamily, "that it *felt right.* I said I'd never been really sure of anything before—that I'd been waiting for him all my life and now that I'd found him I'll never leave him."

Margo heard a note in Francesca's voice that told her that whatever the girl was doing, it could not be delayed nor denied.

Matty threw up his hands. "I give up. I never had a chance anyway. All right, you're going to do it, so that's that and I'll cable the studio. So they'll sue—they have every right. And they'll win, too. I knew we shouldn't have come to Europe. It makes people *crazy!*"

3

Francesca had lapsed from Catholicism years before, but, like all Catholics she remained familiar with the rites of the church. In contrast to her Berkeley Sunday-school days, the marriage service in the Russian Orthodox Cathedral in Paris seemed like a phantasmagoric Hollywood production, Byzantine and bizarre. She almost expected to hear the director's voice calling "Cut" as, after an interminable service, she and Stash drank three times from a cup of red wine and were led by the priest three times around the lectern. Clouds of incense billowed around them in the light of hundreds of candles, and the unreality was underscored by the majestic, deep bass notes of the male choir singing without instruments, their only counterpoint the celestial sound of a choir of children. Two of Stash's friends held golden crowns over their heads as they walked and it seemed to Francesca that the circle of fascinated spectators was a crowd of dress extras.

Although they had tried to keep the date of the service secret and had invited only a small group of friends, word of their intentions had spread and the entire cathedral was jammed with the curious, standing, as was the custom, throughout the wedding and barely keeping order, so great was their desire to catch a glimpse of the ceremony.

Stash, for all his early talk of no fuss, had wanted this service, in all its grandeur and lengthy ritual, remembering the hasty insignificance of his first marriage in wartime London, at a Registry Office. He wanted to see Francesca doubly crowned, first with flowers in her hair, then with the heavy nuptial crown, held in the air over her head. He, who had only spent the first forgotten year of his life in Russia, wanted all the rich symbolism of the noble public service, atavistic, but still fully alive. He had even asked the superbly bearded and solemn priest wearing a silver chasuble and a sacerdotal head dress to link his hand with Francesca's in a silk handkerchief as he led them around the altar, rather than merely taking their hands in his.

Francesca consented to everything. No detail seemed of the slightest importance to her from the time she had made her decision in the stable. She existed on a plane of sublime indifference to everything but her concentration on Stash and her inner vision of the two of them together forever.

Margo was in her element, making arrangements which no one else could have managed. She gloried in Francesca's triumphant marriage and she made the most of the occasion, admitting to herself that at heart she thoroughly detested and mistrusted tasteful simplicity.

The wedding reception at the Ritz was certainly the greatest Margo Firestone production ever recorded. Afterward, Prince Stash Valensky and his new princess disappeared. Not even the Firestones knew that they were staying in Stash's large villa in the countryside outside of Lausanne where, at last, they could begin the never-to-end, not-to-be-rushed exploration of each other. As they rode or walked or lay together they told each other long tales of their childhoods and marveled that, but for the chance remark of a man neither of them knew, in the bar of a Paris hotel, they might never have met.

Francesca often stayed awake at night, although her body, bathed in the halcyon weather of satisfied passion, told her to sleep. She preferred to watch over Stash, brooding over his features in the flickering light of the tiny lamp lit beneath an icon that hung on the far wall of their bedroom. He was the hero, she told herself, of all the stories she had ever read. Bold, gallant, fearless . . . he was all that and something more. She searched for the word and finally found it. Imperishable.

Had he lived long enough for her to know him, Francesca might have used the same word to describe Stash's father, Prince Vasily Alexandrovitch Valensky. That man of dauntless presence, high rank and great physical strength had been the veteran of half a hundred affairs with the exquisite ballerinas of the Marinsky Theater, when, at the age of forty, he decided that it was time to take a wife. Quite dispassionately, he had chosen to propose to Princess Titiana Nikolaevna Stargardova because, of all the debutantes of 1909, she was most suited by birth to his own position. Now, incredulously, in the winter of 1910, he realized that in the most unexpected, undignified and irreversible way he had fallen totally in love with his own wife.

Before their engagement, Titiana was alluringly pretty though she had always kept her large blue eyes downcast whenever they met at a party or the opera. She had worn demure, rather high-necked ball gowns and she spoke in the softest voice which nothing more seductive than a pure gaiety was allowed to animate. From her simply dressed blonde hair and her habit of blushing when she spoke to him, Vasily Valensky had expected a wife who would be placid, correct, certainly conservative. And almost surely as boring as the wives of most of his acquaintances. But before their honeymoon was over, Titiana, who was as hot-blooded as she was clever, had utterly captivated her husband and he discovered that he had married an imperious and demanding mistress.

Today, less than a year after his marriage, as Prince Valensky left his marble-columned palace on the Moika Canal, he noted with amusement, barely touched with resignation, that once again everything and everyone in the palace was being turned upside down and inside out as Titiana prepared for another of her balls. She was reveling in her new position as one of the leading hostesses of St. Petersburg. Freed by marriage from the splendid, but chaperoned, decorum of the *bals Blanc*, at which young girls danced a sedate cotillion, the newly vivacious nineteen-year-old princess lost no time in placing herself near the center of the sumptuous society of the Imperial city.

"To Denisov-Uralski's," Prince Vasily commanded the bemedaled and uniformed doorman who guarded the entrance to the seething palace. Two footmen closed the heavy doors behind him and he stepped lightly into the back seat of the magnificent sledge, carved from ebony and lined with quilted glove leather.

Boris, the coachman, was wearing his winter uniform, a dark ruby-red velvet coat, completely doubled inside with thick fur and belted in gold, with a matching three-cornered hat. In common with all the coachmen of the nobility, he was an immense bearded man who enjoyed nothing more than driving his team of four huge black horses as fast as if there were no one else on the crowded streets of St. Petersburg. Indeed, Boris, who discounted the Grand Dukes as merely decorative, was convinced that his master, who wore the decorations of the Alexander Nevsky, the Vladimir and the St. Andrew, was next in importance only to the Tsar himself. He prided himself that he had traversed the distance between the palace and the shop of Denisov-Uralski without stopping or even slowing for another sledge. To have done so would have insulted the Prince.

On that December day Vasily Valensky's errand was to purchase a veritable menagerie. His wife still had a childish love of animal figurines and he had determined to overwhelm her this Christmas—if, he thought to himself with an inward smile of memory, she could ever be satisfied. Within a half-hour he had selected a number of precious animals, two of each so that Titiana would have a Noah's ark to play with. There were elephants carved from imperial jade with Ceylon sapphire eyes, lions of topaz with ruby eyes and tails of diamonds threaded on gold and giraffes made of amethyst whose eyes were cabochon emeralds with diamond pupils. Next the Prince went on foot to Fabergé and added smaller animals to the collection: turtles fashioned of pink agate with heads, feet and tails of silver and gold, their backs studded with pearls; parrots of white coral; and an entire school of goldfish carved in green, pink, mauve and brown jade, all with eyes of rose-cut diamonds.

This pleasant business done, he directed Boris to drive him to his offices. In the eleven hundred years his family had been noble, their estates had spread over the vastness of Russia and it was only with the aid of a corps of managers, many of them German and Swiss, that Prince Vasily was able to keep his affairs in order. In the Urals his estates produced one quarter of the world's output of platinum. In Kursk he owned the hundreds of miles of sugar plantations and dozens of sawmills, fed by still another hundred miles of forests. In the Ukraine he was the proprietor of immense tobacco plantations. But it was in the fertile province of Kashin that he had his favorite estate. There, on land blooming with orchards and dotted by dairy farms, he raised his winning race horses and invited parties of a hundred noblemen to shoot his fat deer, his wild boar and his thousands of game birds.

There, too, he and his wife rode together through the forest pathways and, as Prince Vasily was still astonished to remember, there they had made love often last summer, hiding in secret places deep in the woods, just like the peasants. It was hard to reconcile the tumbled, eager girl he took so urgently in the nest they had made of moss and leaves, with the great lady, crowned with his mother's diamond-and-emerald tiara, who would receive eight hundred guests tonight, all of them noble and all of them dressed to her command in cloth of gold or silver. They would dance to the music of six orchestras and be served a midnight supper from gold and silver dishes presented by a hundred uniformed footmen while they were serenaded by both Colombo's and Goulesko's gypsy bands. As he had left the palace, Valensky had seen the heated carts arriving with the flowers Titiana had ordered from the Riviera. Their private train had been dispatched to Nice to be loaded with flowers still in bud. They were sped through the winter of Europe, unloaded at the station in St. Petersburg as they were beginning to flower. Half the blossoms of France, lilacs, roses, hyacinths, daffodils and Parma violets, opened for just one night in this city on the Gulf of Finland where the winters were endless and the winds were damp and freezing.

In November of the following year, 1911, Vasily and Titiana's son was born. They named him Alexander after his paternal grandfather, and the young mother who had missed so many entertainments while she was pregnant was more determined than ever to dance every night. Valensky did nothing to dissuade his wife from her pursuit of pleasure as she graced the balls given by the Sherementevs and the Yousoupovs, the Saltykovs and the Vasilchikovs. She led all the other ladies of St. Petersburg in the élan of her waltzing, and she astonished them with her inventiveness at the costume balls of Countess Marie Kleinmichel.

The approach of Lent, which began on the Sunday before Ash Wednesday, signaled the end of dancing. During Lent, concerts and dinner parties replaced balls and, in the private opinion of Masha, Alexander's wet nurse, it was a good thing that her mistress was going to be forced to go to bed earlier. Although the Princess only flitted in from time to time to watch Masha as she nursed the baby, the peasant girl, stout, plain and sensible, thought to herself that in spite of her prettiness the Princess looked tired and too thin. Masha was only seventeen. She had spent all her life on the Valenskys' Kashin estate where she had been unlucky enough to bear an illegitimate child the day before Alexander's birth. However, Masha's baby had not lived and the estate manager immediately sent her to St. Petersburg to nourish the newborn heir. Her homesickness had disappeared as soon as little Prince Alexander had claimed her milk.

On that last Sunday the Valenskys went to a lunch party on a country estate. Afterward they joined in a parade of galloping troikas and finished the afternoon with an especially boisterous snowball fight. When the last dance of the season stopped at the sound of the great clock in the hall striking midnight, Vasily found Titiana strangely willing to drive home. He had expected her to be in despair at the prospect of a temporary end to merrymaking, but instead she felt so tired that she went to sleep in his arms in their heated carriage and the next morning she slept late and woke up no more rested than she had been the night before. She complained, in petulant tones, that she must be getting old.

Vasily immediately sent for the doctor. He had never seen Titiana listless and fretful before, and he was frightened. The doctor spent an endless amount of time in Titiana's pink and silver damask bedroom. When at length he emerged, he spoke of a minor congestion of the bronchi, of a tendency to overstrain the nerves, of a febrile condition.

"What is the treatment?" Vasily demanded impatiently, interrupting the man's interminable medical obfuscation.

"Why, Prince, I thought you understood at once. It may be an inflammation of the lungs, in effect, although I am not a specialist, you must understand, in effect, it may be tuberculosis."

Valensky stood as if he had been shot and was waiting to fall. Titiana and *tuberculosis?* Titiana, who galloped in breeches as in the time of Catherine the Great; Titiana, who only laughed when she was thrown into a snowbank from an overturned troika during a race; Titiana, who tobogganed fearlessly down the dangerous twisting slopes of the ice hills; who had given birth to their son in six hours without a whimper; Titiana, who would let him take her even in a field where the harvesters might have found them?

"Impossible!" he cried.

"Prince, I am not an expert. You must call Dr. Zevgod and Dr. Kouskof. I cannot be responsible." The doctor edged toward the door, anxious to escape before the Prince realized that he had pronounced what, at that time, often amounted to a death sentence.

Zevgod and Kouskof agreed on the necessary steps to be taken. Princess Valensky had admitted to them that, for the last months, she had been troubled by night sweats and a loss of appetite, but she had refused, foolishly, to worry about them. Her lack of caution and her strenuous life had aggravated the condition and now no time could be lost. The Princess must go directly to Davos, in Switzerland, where the treatment of the disease was clearly superior to that found elsewhere.

"For how long?" Vasily asked sternly.

The two doctors hesitated, neither one willing to commit himself. Finally Zevgod spoke.

"There is no way of knowing. If the Princess responds to the treatment, she may be back within a year . . . or two. Perhaps a little more. But she must not return to this damp city until she is perfectly well. As you know, it is built on marsh and swamp. To come back would be suicide for anyone with a weakness of the chest."

"A year!"

"That would be a miracle," Kouskof said gravely.

"Then you really mean that it could be for many years—is that not what you are trying to tell me, gentlemen?"

"Unfortunately, Prince, yes. But the Princess is young and strong. . . . We must hope for an early recovery."

Valensky dismissed the doctors and went to his study and closed the door. He could not possibly tell his sparkling, brave, treasured wife that she had to go away for even as long as three months or three weeks. There was nothing on earth which would make him sentence her to live in a sanatorium. The very word filled him with horror. No! She would go to Davos, that was essential, but they would take Russia with them.

Prince Vasily dispatched his chief male secretary to Davos to rent the largest available chalet. Three French lady's maids were immediately put to work filling Titiana's trunks. There was one which contained nothing but gloves and fans, three which held only narrow embroidered satin slippers, twelve for her dresses, four for her furs and five for her underclothes. Pouting enchantingly over the clothes she had to leave behind, she told Vasily that it was a good thing that she was not overfond of her wardrobe, like the Empress Elizabeth who had owned fifteen thousand dresses.

Meanwhile, the other servants were packing the finest furnishings of the palace, under the direction of another of the Prince's private secretaries, who chose only the best French pieces from the period of Louis XV and XVI. Valensky himself made the decisions about which works of art to take. He was an avid collector but since he didn't know the dimensions of the chalet they were to inhabit, he took only easel paintings by Rembrandt, Boucher, Watteau, Greuze and Fragonard, leaving behind the vast canvases by Raphael, Rubens, Delacroix and Van Eyck.

In spite of the modern way in which they lived, the Valenskys, like all Russians, had never stopped venerating icons and the Prince stripped the separate rooms which had been kept as an oratory. There, rows and rows of icons, many of them so adorned with gold and jewels that they were literally priceless, stood with lamps burning before them day and night. Their protective curtains were drawn, they were laid in their own velvet-covered boxes, after which they were carefully placed in special crates. Certain icons, particularly personal, that were considered to be protectors of the household, would travel in the train with the family in their own compartments.

Nothing that was needed to reproduce the palace on the Moika was left behind, from kitchen pots and pans to three rock-crystal chandeliers that had once belonged to Madame de Pompadour.

Ten days later, forty servants, an adequate if skeleton staff in Vasily's opinion, gathered at the station in St. Petersburg. Additional sleeping cars had been added to the Prince's train to accommodate them all. All the baggage cars were fully loaded, and the two kitchen cars were so packed with food that the chefs had difficulty going about their tasks.

Prince and Princess Valensky, with Masha carrying little Alexander, drove to the station in a closed carriage accompanied by a most important servant, Zachary, the chasseur, in his dark blue uniform with gold epaulets and his formal cocked hat trimmed with white feathers. Zachary was in charge of the actual logistics of the journey; he was responsible for making sure that there would be no frontier delays, no lack of fresh provisions, no lost baggage or any other problem that might disturb the smooth progress of the train on its long southwest journey.

At Landquart, in Switzerland, the private train had to be abandoned since it could not run on the narrow-gauge Alpine tracks. The Valenskys remained in it for several days until all their servants and possessions had been laboriously transported by a smaller Alpine train up to the heights of Davos-Dorf. Then they, too, made the steep, winding, upward journey among frozen waterfalls and snow-smothered fir trees. Titiana shivered although the compartment was warm and she was covered with furs. Her glance recoiled from the vast drop into the abyss on one side of the train but could find no comfortable resting place on the peaks toward which they climbed. Her small, gloved hand clutched her husband's arm as they climbed higher and night began to fall. It was dark outside before they reached the point at which the valley began and the roadbed became level.

"We're almost there, my darling," Vasily said. "Boris will be waiting at the station with the Rolls-Royce."

"What?" Titiana asked, her strange terror momentarily canceled by surprise.

"Certainly. Did you think we were going to drive in some hired cabriolet like a good bourgeois couple on their way to a christening? I ordered the new Silver Ghost last year as a present for you. It was ready two weeks ago so I merely telegraphed Mr. Royce in Manchester and requested that he send it on here instead."

"But Boris can't drive an automobile," Titiana protested.

"I instructed Royce to send one of his English driver-mechanics with the car. He can teach Boris—or, if not, we'll keep the man on."

"Even the Tsar doesn't have one!" Titiana clapped her hands gleefully. "How fast will it go?"

"Last year a special model went one hundred and one miles an hour—but I think we'll stay well under that—I don't want to frighten Boris." Vasily was delighted with the success of his surprise. It was exactly the thing needed to take Titiana's mind off her arrival in a strange land where her disease would finally have to be faced. It had been worth all the effort and thousands of pounds expended to make sure that the automobile would be in Davos in time for their arrival.

It seemed perfectly natural to Titiana Valensky that her chalet in Davos should be a miniature of her palace in St. Petersburg, and that she should have the same quality of total service she had always taken for granted, service so complete that the same woman who risked her life on a horse without hesitation had never put on her own stockings. Women of her class never knew the price of anything, neither the price of their jewels, their shoes nor their furs. They would not recognize that piece of paper called a bill if they had ever chanced to see one. They chose everything they wanted without asking or thinking of cost. Expense did not exist for them, not even as an abstract concept, just as it never occurred to them to visit the kitchens of their own palaces.

Now that Titiana was confined to Davos, she set about regaining her health with as much blind determination as she had put into losing it.

Vasily, marooned as a mountaintop, kept in almost daily touch with events in Russia by means of mail and the telegraph, and Russian, French and English newspapers reached him twice weekly by a special courier from Zurich. In 1912, when five thousand workers in the Lena goldfields went on strike and incredibly held out for a month, he took note. This strike led to others, far more widespread until, in 1912, there were over two thousand strikes. The last time there had been such serious troubles in Russia had been in 1905 when troops had fired on workers in front of the Winter Palace, a day that would always be known as Bloody Sunday.

For long hours Vasily pondered in his library in Davos. It was evident to him, from the doctors' reports, that his family and his servants were not to leave Switzerland for many years. While his wife had not become dangerously worse, neither had she shown signs of improvement. Willpower was no match for fever, courage could not win a victory over a bacillus. Her nighttime temperature curve was slightly higher than it had been several months ago when they first arrived and the rales in the right lobe of her lung were as harsh as ever. The doctors never spoke of time; a question about the future was treated as if it hadn't been asked, as if it were the question of a fool.

Prince Vasily Valensky set his teeth and determined that if his family was to live in exile for years, they must certainly live without the bother of sending to St. Petersburg for money. He decided to sell his platinum mines in the Urals, and his sugar plantations, forests and sawmills in Kursk. He put the immense fortune thus realized into Swiss banks where it would be immediately available to him.

Tattersall, the Englishman from Manchester, who had failed utterly in instructing Boris in the mysteries of the Rolls-Royce, now taught Vasily to drive the Silver Ghost. The Prince discovered that while the great machine, the most famous model the firm of Rolls-Royce ever made, could negotiate any mountain road ever constructed, there were not enough roads around Davos for a good day's motoring. It was then that he sent to Russia for the great wooden troika. As soon as snow covered the ground, Vasily took the reins of three strong horses, and strapped little Alexander securely to the seat at his side. The father and son became a familiar and much admired sight in the shop-filled, festive streets of Davos, as they passed through the town on their way to the snow meadows.

There were other Russians of noble birth among the patients of Davos, as well as a good sprinkling of British and French aristocrats, and soon many of those who were ambulatory could be discovered at Princess Titiana's. It had never occurred to anyone in the family even to try to adapt themselves to this foreign country: cozy, quaint, comfortable, safe, dull, dull Switzerland. To enter the chalet was to walk into St. Petersburg where all things produced a distillation, profoundly nostalgic, of the profusion, the elaborate, careless abundance and warmth of their vanished home. Certain refugees who entered the chalet for the first time gazed about them, breathed in the scent of the dark, gold-tipped Russian cigarettes, listened to the sound of rapidly spoken French and burst into tears.

These elegantly dressed habitués, cheeks a shade too red, eyes a shade too bright, ate with unappeasable appetite. Here and there, throughout the reception rooms, stood long tables covered with food. The Valenskys kept open house, both at tea time and dinnertime, with dozens of Russian servants busy refilling glasses and plates and passing boxes of imported cigarettes and cigars. On those evenings when the Princess was not well enough to appear, none of her guests was so tactless as to remark on her absence. On the days when she felt strong enough, she was dressed by her maids in one or another of her two hundred tea gowns. Languidly Titiana decided whether to wear her rope of Burmese sapphires of the prized cornflower blue which matched her eyes or her triple string of matched black pearls, before she descended on Vasily's arm to reign over her guests.

The festive atmosphere of the Valensky chalet might have deceived a total stranger, but everyone in the huge house was trained to revolve around a sickroom. The inner weather of the family depended on whether the Princess had spent a quiet night or a restless one. The barometer of spirits, from the kitchen to Vasily's study, from the peasants' rooms to Alexander's nursery, rose or fell determined by Titiana's fever chart or the news that either she had been permitted out for a walk or was confined to her balcony. Every day two doctors attended her and, at all times, two trained nurses made up part of the permanent household.

From his earliest memories, the little boy, Alexander, never knew what it was like to have a healthy mother. His babyish play with her was always cut short by someone who was afraid that he was tiring her. When Titiana read out loud to him, a nurse would always close the book far too soon. When Alexander grew old enough to play simple games of cards with his mother, her chief doctor took him aside and gravely warned him of the dangerous excitement engendered by any games of chance. His love for her was imprinted, from earliest memory, by the terrible tension which lies between the sick and the well. From babyhood on he was crippled, permanently, with a resentment, a wordless hatred, and a deep and irrationally superstitious fear of any sign of illness. Even normal weakness was loathsome to him, although his frustrated child's love for his mother made him conceal his sense of horror.

From 1912 to 1914 this life, half enforced holiday, half devoted to the monotonous routine of the cure, endured. On that day of June 28, 1914, when the Austrian Archduke Francis Ferdinand was assassinated in Sarajevo, the Valensky family, attended by ten servants, was having a rare picnic in a green pasture from which they could clearly hear the sound of cowbells. Titiana was making the most of one of her brief and deceptive periods of well-being. Their world had just died although no one yet knew it.

Two months after that happy Alpine picnic, the defeat of Tannenberg took place, during which the finest and best of Russia's fighting men were lost. Within a year over a million Russian soldiers were dead, while in Davos, far from the sound of guns, Alexander received his first pony for his fourth birthday. In 1916, the year of Verdun, the year in which nineteen thousand British soldiers were killed in a single day in the Battle of the Somme, Alexander's chief interest was in the hours he spent in the garage, being surreptitiously introduced to the interior workings of a Rolls-Royce engine.

On March 12, 1917, after another long winter during which his father had rarely smiled, Alexander, six years old, and already an audacious skier, had gone to the slopes of spring snow with his school friends. On that day in St. Petersburg, now called Petrograd, and soon to be called Leningrad, a starving mob, waving the red flags of the revolution, was seen near the Alexandra Bridge. Opposing them, on the other side of the bridge, stood a regiment of guards, the nemesis of rioters. However, the mob continued to press forward and the guards held their fire. Then, in a moment which was to change the history of the world, the two groups merged. Like two drops of water, the masses and the army became one body. As Alexander climbed back up the shadowy slopes for the last run of the day, as Titiana poured hot water from the samovar and offered a cup of tea to a French count, as Vasily, haggard and sad from his years of involuntary internment in Switzerland, bent over newspapers that were three days old, the Russian Revolution began.

World War I had been over for almost three years when the decision was made to send Alexander away to school. He was only nine years old, and Titiana might possibly have allowed him to continue in the Davos school where he was the undisputed leader of the gang of village boys, self-willed, taller, rougher, stronger and more ready to take a reckless dare than any of them, but Vasily saw clearly that their son was running wild. He had been born a prince but he was in danger of becoming a peasant. Even in a world in which princes were considered obsolete—particularly Russian princes—if they had managed to survive at all, there was the Valensky tradition to honor, and the Valensky fortune to inherit. He must be educated like the noble gentleman he would become.

"We'll send him to Le Rosey," he told his wife. "I've already made inquiries. He can start in the fall, just before his next birthday. Now don't look sad, my dearest—it's only at Rolle, not far from here, and in the winter the whole school moves up to Gstaad. It's so near that Alexander will have no trouble coming home for holidays."

Eventually, Titiana accepted the idea as, with the necessary self-absorption of the chronic invalid, she had accepted the fact that her family was doomed to eternal exile, that the world of her girlhood no longer existed and that her disease never slept for long. Hope, in her soul, had been replaced with endurance.

Each time Alexander came home for vacations, his parents saw how he was being changed by his new life in the world's most exclusive and expensive boarding school. They noticed little by little how his manners, in the fashion of his international crowd of schoolmates—young potentates, heirs to dynasties—began to show that he was newly comfortable wherever he found himself. He was at ease in *their* way, a way which was based on a sense of hauteur that eventually turned into the special, superior kind of lofty amusement which clings to the elite of the Le Rosey students, a secret, inward smile. He even acquired a new name—Stash—to which both his parents objected because it was a Polish, not a Russian, diminutive, but which they had to admit suited him in a way that Alexander never had.

4

Stash had just turned fourteen when he came home, as usual, for the Christmas vacation of 1925. He had reached that age at which the outlines of the man he would become were unmistakably present to an attentive eye. His nose had been broken for the first time in a brawl with the heir to a French marquisate, his curls had been cut short and although he was still far from reaching his full muscular development, he was close to six feet tall. His lips were red with the turbulent vitality of youth and permanently chapped from outdoor sports. His eyes had exchanged their innocence for a gaze in which a hint of the relentlessness of his later years had already appeared.

As he always did, after a day of sport, Stash left his ski boots outside the chalet for one of the servants to clean. He put on a pair of after-ski boots and slipped into the salon in search of something to eat. He was an expert at moving among his mother's coterie with a kind of warding-off politeness which prevented them from detaining him with unwelcome questions. Privately he thought them all unworthy of his mother, this titled band of tuberculosis patients whose illness alone brought them together. His terror of disease expressed itself as contempt for the invalids themselves. With an arrogance which made an exception only of his mother, he even despised the courage and resignation with which they faced their lives and he told himself that he would rather die cleanly than live with rotted lungs.

Deftly he helped himself to a big cup of hot chocolate and a plate of pastries, and started to escape to his own room. However, a languid hand raised from a far corner indicated to him that this was one of the days on which his mother had joined her guests, and instantly he turned to cross the room and greet her.

Princess Titiana was sitting deep in conversation with her close friend, the Marquise Claire de Champery. The red-headed Frenchwoman kept her lush body tightly girdled, her bright hair was carefully restrained, but nothing could conceal the feline expression of her sulky, green eyes, her small, pouting avaricious mouth or her malicious half-smile. She used very little make-up and dressed almost entirely in black with an uncompromisingly severe chic. On meeting her, men felt an erotic shock.

Although the Marquise had lived in Davos for seven years, she had no trace of sickness. She had originally traveled to the Alps with her husband, Pierre de Champery, expecting that a few months of mountain air would cure him of the bothersome cough he had acquired during his distinguished military service. This accomplished and polished Parisienne had never contemplated spending seven years waiting to return to civilization, but she was a prisoner in Davos, linked to a man she had never loved, even before her marriage, by one of the strongest of bonds, that of prospective inheritance. In order to maintain her position in Princess Titiana's salon, she worked diligently and knowledgeably before her mirror to conceal that flamboyant spoor of her sexuality, to maintain her guise as a lady of the highest class of society.

Claire de Champery's husband clung to her with all the determination permitted to a man of wealth who had married a penniless woman twenty years younger than himself. He lived in a sanatorium because he was far too ill to live anywhere else, but he had rented a charming little chalet for his wife. The doctors told her it would not be long . . . yet they had told her that for years.

Stash approached the two women, kissed his mother's hair and bent to brush the air above the Marquise's hand.

"So, my little Stash is home from school," mocked the sleek red-headed woman, sitting with disciplined decorum in an armchair. "Do tell me, my dear child, did you manage finally to do well in your examinations? And are you still a member of that fascinating inner circle you spoke of last summer—the little jumped-up American millionaires and the little British lords with bad teeth and the naughty baby cattle barons from the Argentine, and all the other grandees of your school?"

Stash tightened his lips in rage. One day last summer, when he was only thirteen, he had made the mistake of describing his best friends to her. She seemed to be taking a genuine interest in his school life. Most of his mother's intimates, occupied with the myriad intrigues of their hermetically sealed world based on illness and gossip, had learned not to pay attention to the difficult, unfriendly boy, but the Marquise had drawn him out until he allowed her a rare glimpse into his school life.

"And you. Madame la Marquise," he shot at her, ignoring her questions, "are you still the notorious *femme fatale* of this vast and cosmopolitan center? Or have you been replaced by someone whom I have not yet met?"

"Alexander," flashed his mother. "That is quite enough! Claire, you must forgive him—he's just fourteen you know, that impossible age when you think it's amusing to be impudent. Alexander, apologize at once!"

"No, Titiana, darling, don't be silly . . . I was teasing him and the little one got angry." Claire de Champery was in the best of humors. She felt the congestion of blood rushing between her primly pressed together thighs, proof positive that she had been right to provoke the boy. From the moment she had seen him coming across the room, she had noticed that the childish beauty she had savored in secret for years had become that of a youth. She saw the faint beginnings of a mustache on his upper lip, she measured with her eyes the new physical development which had given a fourteen-year-old the muscle structure of a youth. No longer a boy, yet not a man—a most delectable, a most tantalizing, a most fleeting age. A moment in a man's life, she reminded herself, that did not last long. A youth—a pure and perfect youth—that most tasty morsel of all. He knew nothing yet, she was sure of that. Off at a boys' school all year long, what could he possibly have learned besides the little dirty games they might play with each other? But his fiery reaction to her mockery told her that he was ready to be taught.

"Claire," Titiana insisted, "he simply must apologize. I can't permit him to behave in such a manner."

"Let him do a penance instead, Titiana darling. An apology is too easily given. Ah, I have it—he shall take me for a troika ride—that is, if he is old enough to control the horses?"

"I have been driving the troika for over four years," Stash said with scorn.

"*Tant mieux.* Then I have nothing to fear. Be at my chalet at three tomorrow afternoon and I'll be ready to leave. Now, baby, go and eat your pastries . . . you look as if you're longing for them."

As the Marquise dismissed the sullen youth, she turned back to Titiana and resumed the conversation with the facile charm which had drawn the Princess to her in the first place.

The day after Stash's scene with the Marquise de Champery, he arrived on time to take the Frenchwoman for a troika ride, since his mother had continued to insist on it.

The maid who let him into the chalet told him that her mistress was not quite ready to leave. She took his coat and led the way to a little sitting room just off the Marquise's bedroom. A fire had been lit and the room was very warm. The maid pointed out a tray of bottles of different liquors and an assortment of boxes of various kinds of cigarettes, and left him. Stash tightened his lips in annoyance. He was not old enough to drink or smoke and he knew that the Marquise was aware of it. This was just more of her baiting, another reminder that he was still a child. He was still standing resentfully in the center of the luxurious nest of a room when the Marquise entered. She was dressed in a loose flowing tea gown of black chiffon trimmed with lace.

"Oh, so you're not coming driving then," Stash exclaimed in relief, at the sight of her unsuitable clothes.

"No, I have merely changed your penance, my boy."

"Penance! You mean charade! This whole thing is absurd. I'm not a child to be treated like this. I'm leaving . . . enough of this!"

"I think not," the Marquise said softly. "You spoke to me most rudely and your darling *maman* is still very angry with you." The woman knew well that the only influence to which Stash made himself subject was that of his mother.

"Come sit down on this couch with me and I shall tell you what it is."

The boy suppressed a sigh of anger and silently did as he was told.

"I have been thinking," she mused. "We've known each other a long time . . . is that not so? You were only seven when I first saw you . . . a little boy. And now you are almost a man. Do you have any idea how old I am?"

Stash was startled and deeply gratified at being told he was almost a man. His anger forgotten, he answered shyly. "You're not as old as my mother . . . certainly, but I can't guess women's ages."

"I am twenty-nine," she said, lying by only three years. "Does that seem very old to you? Of course it must. No . . . don't protest, don't be polite, it doesn't become you. When I was your age, twenty-nine was unimaginably old. So I have decided, as your penance, to teach you a lesson . . . a lesson in relativity."

The Marquise's small and swollen mouth was fresh as a fruit and she licked her lips thoughtfully. She moved closer to where Stash sat stiffly on the rose satin upholstery she knew was in bad taste but nevertheless permitted herself in private apartments. One of her plump white arms reached out, the black lace falling away from it, and she placed her hand on his head. "I miss your curls," she said softly, rumpling his thick hair. He sat straight and motionless, his nostrils drinking in the unfamiliar scent of a woman in a low-cut gown. By the light of the fire, out of the corner of his eye, he could see the blue shadow where her breasts began. Her hand left his hair and began to caress his neck with the most neutral of touches, as if she were absent-mindedly stroking a pet. Stash felt, with horrified embarrassment, that his penis had become rigid inside his trousers. He did not notice Claire's glance at his crotch, her eyebrows lifting only slightly as her practiced eye told her what had happened. Idly, she played with his earlobe, not moving any closer to him.

"So, what is relativity? Can you tell me? No . . . I thought not. The lesson in relativity begins with the realization that my hand and your neck have no age at all. They are only flesh meeting flesh. But to appreciate the true meaning of relativity, we must go further . . . much further." She allowed her wandering fingers to touch the soft hollow at the base of his throat, exposed in his open-necked shirt, and then she slipped her entire hand into his shirt and found one of his nipples and started to circle it with one finger. Stash groaned aloud and she drank in the sound with gourmandise—that was his first groan as a man, she thought, feeling his nipple harden. Now he would never forget her. "Ah, little man, you are beginning to understand relativity," she whispered to the boy who still looked ahead, his mind spinning. What was she doing . . . his mother's friend . . . impossible . . . another mockery. In confusion he thought—but he couldn't be certain—that her hand, which she had withdrawn from his shirt, had, for an instant, fallen lower, to his crotch, and brushed like a feather over the stiff lump of his penis. But then this same hand, quickly raised, now gently unbuttoned his shirt, revealing his strong youth's chest down the center of which fine blond hair made a straight, faint shadow. She moved closer to him, threw back his shirt, and ran the fingers of both her hands down his half-naked, already well-muscled arms and murmured to herself, "How very grown-up you are, after all, my Stash." The boy was stunned into immobility even when she caressed him under his arms, fingering the scant, silky tufts of hair that had so recently sprouted there. The painful tumescence of his penis seemed shameful to him, a confession of weakness before this dominant woman. He knew her, the sly one, she wanted to make him try to touch her and then she would remind him of what a child he was. He gripped the pillows he was sitting on in order not to move, not to give her that satisfaction.

Then he felt her unbuckle his belt and unbutton his fly. For a moment she seemed to hesitate, her head lowered in the firelight, riveted at the sight of the outline that reared under his restraining undershorts. The size of it seemed to make her decide. She slid to the thick carpet and looked up at him as he sat on the edge of the couch, his teeth biting into his lower lip in a grimace which hardened his face into a look it would not naturally wear for ten more years.

"Now . . . now we come to the penance, Stash. You must stand up." She remained still, waiting patiently, steadily watching him, not repeating her command. Slowly he stood up, his trousers falling to his feet. Controlling her breathing with difficulty the woman looked at the slender youth who stood before her, not daring to meet her eyes. Through the opening of his undershorts the thick, jutting shaft of his penis was clearly visible.

"Pull down your shorts," she whispered. He obeyed. His body was marvelously made, pale except where the winter sun had touched his big hands and strong neck. All his joints and tendons were tender-skinned, yet firm and defined. A little blond hair grew on the legs and a deeper shadow of coarser hair curled at the base of his testicles.

"Step out of your pants and lie down on the sofa," she ordered. "Don't touch me, Stash, or I will stop what I'm going to do to you. I am the teacher here and you are doing your penance, so be obedient. If you move, even one little inch, I'll stop the lesson. I swear it." The threat in her voice was real. She pulled at her gown so that it dropped from her shoulders. Her breasts sprang out from the confining lace. She cupped each of them in a hand, leaning over him so that he could see how sumptuously heavy they were, tipped with the light brown nipples of a true redhead. He lay still on the rose satin, not daring to arch his back and thrust his agonizingly hard penis upward. She brushed her nipples tantalizingly over his chapped lips. "Don't move!" she warned again, adoring the sensation of the roughness of his young open mouth on her flesh. When he moaned in fearful desire and tried to touch them with his tongue, she moved away at once. "Ah! No! I've only begun . . ." Very delicately, with the lightest possible touch, she moved her full, succulent mouth down this body which had just emerged from boyhood, stopping to anoint each of his nipples with her pointed, flicking tongue. Finally she hovered over his penis for a long moment while he held his breath. Her sleek head hung, almost in meditation, as she observed how it strained upward, jerking toward her mouth. But, without even touching it, she passed on and went lower, tonguing the insides of his strong thighs. As she knelt on the sofa she had gradually slipped out of her gown so that her full body, with its rich bounty of lush perfumed flesh, was entirely exposed, but from his position on the sofa, he could not see her nakedness clearly without raising his head. She had not yet touched him with anything but her nipples and her mouth, nor had he touched her at all. He ground his teeth and clenched his fists in frantic frustration and heard her low, satisfied laugh, the laugh of the true gourmet.

"Oh, yes, indeed, yes, you are making progress. You are beginning to appreciate relativity. You are almost prepared for the end of the lesson."

The Marquise's tongue traveled leisurely from Stash's thighs back to his testicles. She blew on his pubic hair very lightly, and again, he couldn't prevent a groan from escaping his dry lips. Like a line of fire, the tip of her experienced tongue ran up the base of his straining penis and then rested for one whirling moment on its tip.

"No," she said, pensively. "No, you cannot control yourself well enough." With a little movement she positioned herself until she was straddling Stash's body, one knee on either side of his tensed thighs. Slowly, with the leisurely care of a woman of thirty-two, she parted her thick, red pubic hair and opened the lips of her vagina with the fingers of one hand and, with the other, she gently pulled Stash's penis back from his stomach until it was pointed straight up into the air. He was so hard that she had to hold it back firmly while, taking an infinite amount of time, she gradually lowered herself onto the swollen tip. She gathered her ripe body into a soft pillar of flesh and slid down on him. When he was completely enclosed within her, she leaned forward and whispered into his contorted lips, "Now, now . . ."

Stash, released from his bondage, grasped the kneeling woman around her waist with both his arms and, without removing his penis from her tight sheath, lifted her up and turned her so that she was under him. With one gigantic thrust he poured himself out into her while he bit her lips mercilessly and crushed her breasts in both hands. As soon as he could breathe again, he said, "Don't you ever dare to ride me again! I'll do the riding from now on!"

"Oh, ho," she muttered in a harsh whisper, "so now it's you who gives the orders? But, my friend, only one of us is satisfied . . . so relatively speaking, the lesson has not been learned."

"No?" She realized that his penis had never left her vagina. It was growing again, growing bigger than before. He ground it into her waiting body with unsteady strokes, until she reached a violent orgasm. And still he rode her, swollen with blood, pausing only once to wipe his sperm from her wet pubic hair with her black lace gown. This second time he had already learned much he needed to know and he took his time in pleasing himself, ignoring her protests that he was hurting her, that he must stop a minute, that he was too big. His second orgasm was much more intense than the first, coming, it seemed, not just from his penis and his testicles, but from his whole spinal column. The fourteen-year-old boy lay, momentarily exhausted, beside the voluptuous, satiated form of the woman. Neither spoke as the fire crackled in the fireplace. It was dark outside.

"Claire," Stash said. "I'm going to take a bath in your tub. Ring the maid for hot chocolate and bring it to me there. And then . . ."

"Then . . . ?" she interrupted, astonished at the voice of command which came from the youth to whom she had just given his first lesson in love.

"And then we'll have another lesson in relativity. In the bedroom. This couch of yours is too slippery for me." His voice was rough with new authority.

"But . . . you're crazy!"

He took her hand and put it on his penis. The hot sticky organ was already beginning to rise and fill. It moved under her touch like an animal. "Don't you want me to bathe?" he asked. "Shall we just go to the bedroom now?"

"No, Stash—no—go take your bath. I'll ring for the chocolate." She hastily covered herself with the bedraggled gown.

"Don't forget the pastries."

Every day of that Christmas vacation, Stash cut short his skiing and spent all afternoon in the rose-red sitting room or the lavender bedroom of the Marquise de Champery, leaving only when it was time to go home for dinner. She wrote a note to Titiana to say that a head cold prevented her from joining the usual gathering at the chalet and gladly gave up her dinner engagements to preserve the fiction.

Stash became familiar with the long slow strokes, the quick jabs, the excruciatingly disciplined pauses which only made them both more eager, the quiver, the holding back, the pulses beating together—all the ebb and flow of making love. The Frenchwoman taught him how to please her, and all the other women he would possess, with a sensuality that explored every detail. She taught him to be shameless, as she was, so that all the prohibitions of conventional sexuality never had a chance to make an impression on him. She taught him the many delicate uses of his mouth, his tongue, his teeth and his fingers moving urgently between her legs. She taught him the importance of patience and stealthy gentleness. She taught him nothing of tenderness or sentiment . . . between them there was none of that . . . she was not false, whatever else she was. When they parted, as he left to go back to school, there were no promises exchanged or backward looks. He was a youth, she a woman who did not permit herself the luxury of believing for an instant that he would come back to her for anything except her body . . . and then only if he did not find another he preferred. But she knew that in the entire lifetime which stretched ahead of Stash Valensky, she would occupy a place that no other woman would ever fill. When he was an old man and had forgotten a hundred other women, he would still remember the rose satin and the firelight and the lesson in relativity.

After the boy's departure, the head cold of Madame la Marquise vanished. However, she decided not to return every day to the claustrophobic tea-time group at the Princess Titiana's. Instead, she took up skiing. In the next decade, as her husband persistently, unforgivably lingered on the verge of death, Claire de Champery deserved credit for having been the instructor of an entire legion of naive village youths, those Alpine ski instructors who are, today, legendary animals of pleasure. Even if they have never heard of her, they owe much to her teaching, lessons which have been handed down from one generation of ski-school heroes to another.

In 1929 Stash Valensky graduated from Le Rosey. He spent that summer on a vast ranch in Argentina, owned by the father of one of his classmates. The finest polo ponies of the world were bred in South America and many of the best players lived there. They came up from Argentina to compete with the American or British teams, often bringing a string of forty ponies which they sold after the season for great prices. The golden age of polo lasted from 1929 to 1939, those years during which Tommy Hitchcock, Winston Guest, Cecil Smith, Pat and Aiden Rourk, the brothers from Ireland, Jai, the Maharajah of Jaipur, Eric Pedley from Santa Barbara and other equally great players were all in competition, all marvelously mounted, all devoting their lives to the game.

At Rolle, the spring and fall campus of Le Rosey, and during his summer vacations in Davos, Stash had become a consummate horseman. Now, in the Argentine, he discovered why. Polo might have been invented for him. Had he another life to live, he would have chosen to be Akbar, the Mogul ruler of India in the 1500s who loved polo so much that he played it in the dark, with balls of smoldering wood, galloping after the trail of sparks they left behind them. After three months of constant practice, in the "pit" and on the field, his hosts felt it safe to pay Stash the honor of asking him to play in a practice match. Filled with jubilation he wrote home and explained that it was absolutely necessary for him to extend his visit for another three months, since the South American polo season was just beginning.

Princess Titiana was desolate that her son was staying away for so long, but Prince Vasily took the request with equanimity. What else was there for a boy to do, after all?

"My dearest, had there not been the Russian Revolution or the Great War, your Alexander would have made a splendid cavalry officer. At least polo is becoming to a prince." He deposited a large sum of money in Stash's Buenos Aires bank account and wrote to him that he must buy his own ponies and no longer depend on borrowed mounts.

The essential element in a great polo player, once he has established the perfection of his horsemanship and his coordination, is raw courage. Stash Valensky, who had now reached his full height of six feet, two inches, was perfectly trained for the sport, but more importantly, his warrior spirit *needed* it.

Beginning in that summer of 1929 when he was eighteen, Stash roamed the world, following the polo seasons: England in the summer, Deauville in August, autumn in South America, winter in India, spring in the United States. With him went his household: his valet, an Englishman called Mump, his grooms, his trainer and, of course, most important of all, his ponies.

Mump's duties extended beyond the care of the Prince's wardrobe. He spent as much time at the florist's and delivering notes by hand as he did on his master's boots. Stash, who had been so precociously indoctrinated into carnal love, spent no time laying siege to marriageable virgins or even young ladies of good reputation, virgin or not. He had early learned a taste for another kind of woman, and such women were inevitably the wives of other men. A complication, but not one which couldn't be managed, particularly with the participation of Mump—who made sure that letters were discreetly delivered and received; that flowers only arrived before or after a party, so as not to arouse suspicion; that no lady who found herself alone for a minute in Stash's apartments would ever stumble upon evidence of another.

Stash discovered that polo had a way of confining him to a single love affair at a time, since the lady in question invariably considered it her precious prerogative to drive out to the field and watch the teams practice. Decency demanded that two women were not observed, each parked in a great open car, cheering him on at the same time. However, the teams never lingered long in any one country, and the glowing general's wife in Brazil never knew about the young maharanee in Delhi; the exquisite English countess had never heard rumors of the lovely San Franciscan who came out every day to the Old Monterey Polo Club.

The only interruption in the gilded years of pleasure Stash led after his graduation from Le Rosey came when Princess Titiana, worn and wasted, yet struggling to the end, died in 1934. Stash had always visited his parents in Davos twice a year and neither of them ever brought themselves to comment on the dash and heedlessness with which he lived. It made them too happy to see him full of health, brio and the joy of the chase. Now Stash paused long enough to realize that his father was sixty-five, a devastated man whose reason for living had vanished. For the next few months Stash remained in Davos with Prince Vasily, curbing his impatience to resume his life. Soon he saw that his father was slipping away, giving up, coming to an end of the exile that he had imposed on himself, an exile that had preserved his fortune yet left him only half a man, able only to watch, but never to participate in the great events of history, self-marooned, on the heights of Davos-Dorf.

After the death of Prince Vasily Valensky, the new heir found that besides the diminished but still great amount of Russian gold that had been deposited in Swiss banks twenty-two years before, he had inherited a huge houseful of terrified servants, all of whom had come from Russia with his parents and were now well into middle age. None of them knew anything but service to the Valenskys. Their greatest fear was of what was to become of them. Stash was their feudal lord as far as it was possible in the modern world. They neither accepted nor aspired to any other point of view. Their children had been brought up as Swiss citizens, but nothing could shake the need these old Russians had to cling together in an atmosphere that reminded them of a country as remote as drowned Atlantis.

They were his responsibility now, Stash realized, with a grimace of astonishment. He had never considered what he would do with them if his parents weren't alive, never once thought realistically about the future. Now he called their leaders, Zachary, the former chasseur, and Boris, the former sledge driver, to him.

"I dislike Davos," he told them. "It has too many sad memories. Yet some of you have children in Swiss schools. What would you think if I were to move to a lower part of Switzerland—and take you all with me? Would you want to come or would you prefer to stay on here? In either case you all will continue to be paid during my lifetime."

"Prince Alexander," answered Zachary, "we have no home that is not your home. We are not too old to move, but we are far too old to change."

Soon Stash found the villa outside of Lausanne and, within a short time he had reproduced there the interior of the palace he had never seen in St. Petersburg, just as his father had brought it intact to Davos. But the Lausanne establishment was free of any trace of the sickroom, empty of the chatter of invalids, swept bare of any nostalgia except that which might cling to the increasingly valuable paintings and furniture. The treasure of icons remained sleeping in their velvet boxes, with the exception of the one his mother had always loved best, which Stash kept in his bedroom, and the humble ones the servants hung in their own rooms. Stash spent only a month or two of every year in Lausanne, just enough to reassure the servants, but they maintained the great house as if he were expected home every night.

In 1934 polo and women were almost eclipsed by a new passion. The lure of flying caught him after the English summer polo season had ended. A badly broken leg, souvenir of a match in September, had kept Stash from going on to South America that year and, on the 20th of October, 1934, he was among those who gathered at dawn at Mildenhall, Suffolk, to watch the start of the MacRobertson Race, from England to Australia, the single greatest sporting event in the short history of aviation. He was immediately caught up in the thrilling, exultant tension of the crowd of sixteen thousand, as it watched twenty of the finest, most experimental aircraft of the period take off toward the East and the first checkpoint at Baghdad. That same day, still on crutches, Stash joined the London Aero Club, an offshoot of the Royal Aero Club. By the following week, he had convinced his doctor that he no longer needed crutches, and he immediately drove to the Aero Club for instructions. He soloed after six hours in a little training biplane, the de Havilland Moth, and after another three hours of solo flying, followed by an examination, he earned his pilot's license.

Stash bought a monoplane, the Miles Hawk, and began the pursuit of speed which was to obsess him for the next six years. He entered his first race in France the next year, the Coupe Deutsch de la Meurthe, flying a Caudron racer, small-winged, slim and built of wood, with a supercharged Renault engine, a plane which could, at its peak, reach a record-breaking 314 miles per hour. In 1937 he went to the United States to compete in the Bendix Trophy race and returned to try again in 1938, to become one of the ten men to lose to Jacqueline Cochrane, a woman who set the coast-to-coast endurance record in ten hours, twenty-seven minutes, fifty-five seconds. He flew Severskys; he flew the madly dangerous, tiny Mignet Pou-du-Ciel or Sky Louse. He flew anything with wings, and he always flew alone, a predilection which prevented him from entering many of the distance competitions which required a flying partner. But being alone in the air was more than half of the joy of flying to Stash. It provided such a total contrast to the team play of polo. The sky meant solitude, a solitude which had become almost impossible to find on the ground. The next four years, spent in headlong pursuit, chasing almost mindlessly after speed records in the sky and women and polo balls on the ground, were scarcely interrupted when Stash read, one day at the end of September 1938, of Chamberlain's return from Munich with the promise of "peace in our time."

However, the following March, in 1939, as soon as he read of the German seizure of Czechoslovakia, Stash saw clearly that war was inevitable, and, immediately, he left Bombay for England. On his arrival he went directly to the headquarters of the Royal Air Force Volunteer Reserve and made his application for a commission. By June, Flight Officer A. V. Valensky was involved in full-time training of young pilots at Duxford in Cambridgeshire, most of them young university squadron members.

When Britain and France declared war on Germany on the 3rd of September, 1939, almost a month short of Stash's twenty-eighth birthday, he had been trained as a fighter pilot and was a member of the 249 Squadron, flying a Hurricane, powered, he saw to his delight, with a Rolls-Royce Merlin engine. But when his squadron was declared operational in July and qualified for night fighting, Stash, to his inutterably violent and bitter rage, was promoted to Flight Lieutenant and ordered to Aston Down where he was doomed to remain for one entire year, teaching young pilots the techniques of fighter flying.

Nothing he had ever experienced in his life of action had prepared him for those twelve maddening months in which men he had trained were sent off in batches, to "clobber bandits" as they cheerfully put it, leaving him behind to teach, not fight. Whenever he could, Stash went down to London to besiege RAF officials in his grim efforts to get posted to a fighter squadron.

"Be reasonable, Valensky," he was told with cold regularity. "You're a damn sight more useful to us right where you are than if you were busy getting shot up somewhere—*someone* has to teach the kiddies, after all."

Filled with pent-up frustration and feeling utterly worthless, Stash drank heavily for the first time in his life. When he met Victoria Woodhill, a WAAF, he put all his pent-up frustration into conquering the rather curt and aloof young woman whose chief attraction was that she was not interested in him. Anything he could batter, beat against and overcome was a target for Stash during those months that saw the Germans push deeper into the body of Europe. They were married in June of 1940 and almost immediately afterward lost sight of each other as Victoria was posted to Scotland.

Officially the Battle of Britain lasted almost four months, from the 10th of July, 1940, through the 31st of October. It was actually a series of battles, fought by six hundred RAF planes against the mighty *Luftwaffe* flying to dominate Britain with its three thousand bombers and twelve hundred fighter planes. Had the RAF lost, England would almost certainly have been invaded.

For Stash, the Battle of Britain lasted only three months, beginning in August 1940, when the powers that decided such things finally reached the last-ditch conclusion that they could no longer afford the luxury of Training Units, but sent their newly hatched airmen out to operational squadrons to be trained between and during actual combat.

At last Stash was posted to Westhampnett, near Portsmouth, where he arrived on a day which would be known as "Black Thursday," the day of August 15, 1940, the day on which Göring unleashed his "eagles" from all the flanks under his command in an all-out air assault. A vast armada of Dornier 17s and Junker 88s, escorted by fighter planes, had crossed the coast of England when Stash's new squadron was scrambled. In the blue English sky his first air battle was a maelstrom of diving, swerving, spinning, firing planes, thrusting and striking even as they died.

By the time the battle was over, Intelligence had confirmed that Valensky had bagged two German bombers and three German fighters. He had never even heard the shouting which filled his earphones as the other pilots warned each other of an attacker or screamed in jubilation when they'd made a hit—the cold, concentrated, lethal rage of his own flying made them inaudible to him. Nor did he realize that each time he shot down an enemy he uttered a harsh war cry which rang in the ears of the other members of his flight. After they'd driven off the Germans, with their tails between their legs, the air was full of comment.

"Christ, what in bloody hell was *that*?"

"The new chap—can't be anyone else—no one here but us chickens."

"Well, it sounded like a bloody condor to me!"

It was as Condor Valensky that Stash fought the Battle of Britain; and later, transferred to the Western Desert Air Force, he flew by day and by night in operation "Crusader" to relieve the port of Tobruk in November of 1941. It was as

Condor Valensky that he flew a Hurricane "tank-buster" against Rommel at El Alamein; as Condor Valensky that he won the DFC and the DFO and became Squadron Commander in 1942. He was not called Stash again until the war had ended. And been won.

5

As autumn approached, Francesca and Stash, still deep in the first weeks of their honeymoon, began to plan for the future. They discussed the idea of traveling to India toward the end of November, in order to be in Calcutta for the December and January polo season which would be followed by the matches in Delhi in February and March. But, one day in the middle of October, Francesca became certain that she was pregnant.

"It must have happened that first night in the stables," she told Stash. "I suspected it three weeks after we were married but I wanted to be absolutely sure before I told you." She was resplendent.

"Then? In the stables? You're sure?" he demanded, transported by the sudden joy.

"Yes, then. I know it. I don't know how I know, but I do."

"And do you also know that it will be a boy? Because that *I* know."

Francesca merely murmured. "Perhaps." She knew why Stash wanted a boy so badly. He had a son by his brief first marriage, a boy who was now almost six years old. The boy had been born after Stash and Victoria Woodhill had separated. That hasty marriage, product of Stash's frustrated warrior spirit, had not lasted long into peacetime. They had waited only until after the child's birth to get divorced. The boy's mother had no intention of saddling her son with more foreign a name than the one he had been born with, so he was called George Edward Woodhill Valensky. However, as a baby, she had dubbed him Ram, because of his habit of butting his head against the side of his crib, and Ram he had remained. He lived with his mother and stepfather in Scotland and only visited Stash on infrequent occasions. Stash's hope, so strong that it was expressed as a certainty, that Francesca's baby would be a boy, was a way of ensuring himself another son, one who would not be taken from him.

Francesca had seen photos of Ram, a straight dart of a boy, with brows knitted together as he stared defiantly into the camera with a stern and unchildlike expression on his handsome face. She recognized little of Stash in this son who had an air of aristocratic coldness, a high-strung, almost bitter expression that already indicated that he would never allow himself to relax into the rough and confident stance of his father.

"He's a regular horseman, even now, even at this age," Stash said. "Ram's a perfect physical specimen, brought up like a little soldier—that damned British upper-class tradition." He looked at the photograph again, shaking his head. "However, he's intelligent and as tough as they make them. There's something . . . closed off . . . in him . . . like all his mother's family. Or perhaps it was the divorce. In any case, it couldn't be helped." He shrugged, put away the photos with the gesture of a man who doesn't intend to look at them again for a long time, and held Francesca close to him. His eyes searched her face and, just for a moment, his predator's gaze softened and she felt that it was she who was his rock in a stormy sea.

The villa outside Lausanne was so comfortable and spacious that the Valenskys decided to remain there until their child was born. Lausanne itself, with its excellent doctors, was only a short ride away, and, since there was no longer any question of going to India, Stash sent his string of ponies to be put out to grass in England. After the war, he had taken the larger part of his fortune out of Switzerland and invested it in the Rolls-Royce Company. Born in Russia, brought up in the Alps, a nomad of the polo seasons, he found that his nationality was emotional, dedicated not to a country but to an engine, the Rolls-Royce engine that had, to his way of thinking, surely saved England and determined the course of the war.

In the summer of the following year, when the baby would be a few months old, Stash assured Francesca that they would move to London, buy a house, get properly settled in and make that their home base for the future, but meanwhile they lived those first months of their marriage in a state of such incredulous adoration of each other, such passionate absorption in each other's body, that neither of them wanted to travel any farther than to Evian, just across Lac Leman, where they went from time to time to gamble at the casino. The trip by lake steamer in the early evening was a dream of pleasure as they stood together at the rail and watched the small boats, their yellow, red and blue sails like huge butterflies, heading for the harbor in the sunset. When they took the midnight steamer home to the Ouchy landing stage, they were never sure if they had won or lost at *chemin de fer*, nor did they care.

To mark the passage of the weeks, Stash gave Francesca more of the Fabergé rock-crystal vases from his mother's collection. Each one held a few sprays of flowers or branches of fruit worked in precious stones, diamonds and enamel: flowering quince, cranberry, and raspberries, lily of the valley, daffodils, wild roses and violets, all fashioned with the most imaginative and delicate workmanship, so that the rich materials never overwhelmed the reality of the flower and fruit forms. Soon Francesca had a flowering Fabergé garden growing by her bedside, and, when he learned of the coming child, Stash gave her a Fabergé egg made of lapis lazuli mounted in gold. The egg contained a yolk of deep yellow enamel. When this yolk was opened it activated a mechanism that caused a miniature crown to rise up out of the heart of the egg, a perfect replica of the dome-shaped crown of Catherine the Great, paved with diamonds and topped by a cabochon ruby. Inside the crown still another egg was suspended, formed from a large cabochon ruby, hanging on a tiny gold chain.

"My mother never knew if this was an Imperial Easter egg or not," Stash told her as she wondered at it. "My father bought it from a refugee after the Revolution who swore that it was one of those presented to the Dowager Tsarina Marie but he couldn't account for how he happened to have it and my father knew too much to insist . . . however, it bears the Fabergé mark."

"I've never seen anything so perfect," Francesca said, holding it on the palm of one hand.

"I have," Stash answered, running his hands down the length of her neck until they found her breasts which were growing fuller and riper with each passing day. The egg fell to the carpet as he fastened his lips on her darkening nipples and suckled as demandingly as any child.

In Lausanne, as winter closed in on the great villa, Stash exercised the large bays in his stable during the afternoon, and Francesca napped under a light, mauve silk eiderdown, waking only when she could tell, from the subtle smell of snow that invaded their room, that he had returned.

After tea, if the early evening was not too windy, Stash took Francesca for a horse-drawn sleigh ride, and often, seeing the moon rise as they returned to the huge villa, as welcoming, cheerful and brightly lit as an ocean liner, listening to the snuffling of the horses and tender music of the sleigh bells, warm under the fur-lined lap robe, with the hood of her full-length sable coat drawn up over her chin, Francesca felt tears on her cheeks. Not tears of happiness, but rather tears of that sudden sadness that comes at those rare moments of perfect joy that are fully realized at the exact instant at which they are being experienced. Such knowledge always carries in it a premonition of loss, a premonition which needs no reason or explanation.

Just as Francesca grew expert in the ways of the great silver samovar that occupied its traditional place of honor on a round, lace-covered table in the salon, she became accustomed to the ways of Stash's crowd of servants who treated Francesca with a mixture of irrepressibly loving concern and overbearing curiosity. She found herself virtually engulfed in—not "staff" she thought, nothing that starchy, not "help," nothing that casual, certainly not "domestics," nothing that removed, but rather a tribe of what she could only think of as semi-in-laws.

She had married into a way of life, a life which included Masha, who, as a matter of course, invaded Francesca's lingerie drawers in order to fold each object with exquisite care, Masha who hung up her bathrobes and then tied the sashes and buttoned the buttons, so that it was no longer possible to put on a robe quickly, Masha who had her own way with scarfs, arranging them according to color rather than according to utility or size, so that old favorites had a way of disappearing into the spectrum, Masha who appeared in Francesca's bathroom as she got out of her tub, with an enormous warm towel unfolded and ready to wrap around her.

Within a few weeks Francesca felt entirely comfortable with Masha's ministrations and allowed her to brush her hair and even help her into her underwear, quite, Masha told her, as she had been allowed to do for Stash's mother, Princess Titiana, when the Princess's own maids were unavailable for one reason or another.

"Is that so, Masha," said Francesca with lazy interest, but as she relaxed and gave herself over to the gentle brushing, she *saw* herself vividly, lying there on the heap of lace-covered pillows in a velvet dressing gown with her hair being tended devotedly. She had only to ask for a luxury in order to have it brought to her immediately—or, in the case of the men who came from Cartier to show Prince Valensky jewels for his wife, she had only to indicate which of the jewels pleased her, to own it. Yes, now when she walked, she walked like a princess, Francesca thought, and didn't even ask herself what she meant.

The inquiries Stash had made among his friends in Lausanne had indicated that Dr. Henri Allard was the most highly considered specialist in the city. He ran a private clinic which was, in effect, a small, extremely well-run, modern hospital, much favored by wealthy women from all parts of the world.

Dr. Allard himself was a compact, beaming, competent and energetic man who grew tulips almost as well as he grew babies. He told Francesca that she could expect her child sometime at the end of May. Her monthly visits to Allard were a small and mildly annoying interruption of the great dialogue on which she and Stash were embarked until February. That day Dr. Allard bent over Francesca's belly with his stethoscope for an unusually long time. Afterward, in his consulting room, he was more cheerful than this perpetually jovial man had yet been.

"I believe we have a surprise for the Prince," he announced, almost bouncing in his chair. "Last month I was not completely certain so I said nothing, but now I am. There are two distinct heartbeats, with a difference of ten beats a minute. You are carrying twins, my dear Princess!"

"A surprise for the *Prince?*" Francesca's voice rose in astonishment.

"Is there no history of twins in your family then?" he asked.

"History? I don't . . . no, no history. Doctor, is there anything special . . . is it harder to have twins . . . I can't believe . . . twins . . . you're *sure?* Don't you have to make an X ray to be sure?"

"I would prefer not to do so yet. Perhaps next month. But both heartbeats are there, each quite separate, so there can be no doubt." He beamed at her as if she had just won a gold medal. Francesca was unable to sort out her feelings. It was almost impossible to imagine the reality of one baby, let alone two. Lately she had been dreaming of a baby, always a boy, who lay in her arms looking a great deal like Charlie McCarthy, and spoke to her as if he were an adult—happy, funny dreams. But two!

"So, my dear Madame," the doctor continued, "you will now come to see me every two weeks for the next month and then, just to be on the safe side, once a week until the babies begin to manifest a desire to enter the world. Yes?"

"Of course." Francesca hardly knew what she was saying. Suddenly the bewitched dream of her world had been destroyed as easily as an iridescent soap bubble. She wanted only to leave and drive back to the villa and try to absorb this invasion, this new reality.

The entire chalet beat rapturously to the rhythm of the news. Twins! Stash, in his incredulous delight, hadn't been able to resist telling his valet, Mump, almost immediately. Mump had told the housekeeper, the housekeeper had told the chef, the chef had told Masha, who, bursting with excitement, ran to find Francesca in the library and reproached her mistress for not having announced the news herself.

"I should have been the first to know, Princess. After all . . . and now everyone knows about it, right down to the old laundry women and the men in the stable."

"Oh, for heaven's sake, Masha, *I* didn't even know it myself until yesterday. Why, oh why, do you all gossip so much?"

"Gossip? Why, Princess, we never gossip. We only say what we have happened to overhear or observed or have been told. . . . That's not gossip!"

"Of course not. Now Masha, we're going to need twice as much of everything now. Two layettes, dear God, even one seems too much! Bring me some paper please, and I'll start making lists."

"I think the Princess should lie down," Masha insisted.

"Masha, the Princess has work to do!"

February and March passed gaily, except for Francesca's ever increasing discomfort. At night she could lie only on her side, Stash behind her. Often, for hours, he stayed pressing closely the fragrant length of her body, his arms around her so that he could feel the movements of her swollen belly.

"They push you like two little horses," Stash murmured proudly. "When I was a baby Masha used to tell my mother that she had never heard of a child who suckled with such strength. She said no man had dared to treat her with such impudence, not even the one who gave her a bastard. My God, imagine two like me!" He gave a lofty chuckle.

Francesca smiled to herself at his absolute conviction that he was simply going to be reproduced in miniature, not just once but twice.

He took it for granted that the babies would be no less than extensions of himself. Already he had made plans to teach them to ride and ski, as if they would be born at the age of four, each a precocious Hercules.

One day, during the third week of April, Francesca's back ached particularly badly. That night she woke up as if she had been tapped on the shoulder in the dark. "Who . . . ?" she said, not really awake, and then she knew. "Well . . . well . . . what do you know?" she asked herself in a whisper and lay quietly, waiting. Half an hour later, after two more contractions had gripped her, she woke Stash gently.

"It's probably nothing, darling, but Doctor Allard said to phone him if anything happened at all. This must be false labor, nothing to get excited about, but would you call him for me, please?" She felt shy about waking the doctor in the middle of the night.

Woken from depths of sleep, Stash jumped out of bed with the instant reactions that had become second nature in the RAF.

"Wait, it's not a scramble—take it easy," Francesca said, basking in a feeling of heightened well-being.

Stash returned from the phone in a minute.

"The doctor said to come to the clinic immediately. Here's your coat and your handbag . . . oh, your boots."

"I'll brush my teeth and pack a nightgown and . . ."

"No," Stash ordered, bundling her into her coat and bending down to put her bare feet into her fur-lined boots.

"At least wake somebody and tell them we've gone," Francesca gasped.

"Why? They'll figure it out in the morning."

"I feel as if we're eloping." Francesca's laugh spilled out as she watched Stash plunge into his clothes. She continued laughing quietly as he led her through the quiet villa to the garage, clumsy as he tried to support her weight when she was perfectly capable of walking by herself.

By the time they reached the clinic Dr. Allard and his chief assistant, Dr. Rombais, were waiting for them right inside the door. Francesca was surprised to see her dapper obstetrician dressed in loose white pants and a matching smocklike top. She had never seen Dr. Allard without a vest immaculately piped in white under his excellently tailored jacket.

"So, Princess, we may have less time to wait than we thought," he greeted her, with his usual cheer.

"But it's too soon, Doctor. It must be false labor. You said not till May," she cried.

"Perhaps that is all it is," he agreed, "but we must make sure, must we not?"

From then on everything else was forgotten as Francesca was settled into a bed with side rails on it. As soon as she was comfortable Allard entered and closed the door behind him.

Allard knew his statistics. Any woman faced with the delivery of twins faces a twofold or threefold increase in the possibility that the birth will be fatal to her. However, this remote chance was not his chief concern, although his operating-room staff was prepared for all possibilities. Francesca was not exhibiting high blood pressure or any signs of a toxic condition. However, by his calculations, labor was five, perhaps even six weeks premature, and under such circumstances, particularly with twins, he had every reason to be cautious.

"Well, *Maman*," he said after he had examined her. "The great day is here." Allard always called women in labor "*Maman*," feeling that it focused their minds on the future rather than the present.

"So it's not false labor?"

"Indeed, no. You are well on your way, but we must expect a certain number of hours to pass. After all, this is your first delivery, even if you are a bit early."

After the next half-hour of contractions, Francesca's calm acceptance of her physical discomfort began to disintegrate. Fun was fun, she told herself, but this was really hurting. There was no way in which she could visualize herself playing the role of a woman in labor. She was *in* it for real and she wanted to be out of it, and fast.

"Doctor Allard, could I please have something for the pain? I'm afraid I need it now."

"Alas, no, *Maman*, in your case we must avoid giving you any drugs."

"What!"

Beaming as if he were giving her good news he continued. "Anything I gave you now would affect the unborn babies adversely. It would be passed along to the babies through your bloodstream. Because you are more than a month early, they still have not reached their proper weight. To be frank, I can give you nothing at all . . ."

"*No drugs!*" Francesca was pale with terror. Like generations of American women, her idea of childbirth without drugs was firmly based on the long and fatal agony of Melanie Wilkes in *Gone With the Wind.*

"It is for the best, *Maman*, much for the best."

"But, my God, for how long?" she asked.

"Until you are ready to deliver the little ones. Then I can give you a saddle block and from then on you will feel no pain at all."

"A saddle block? My God, what's that?" she gasped in horrified apprehension.

"Merely a painkilling injection," he explained, thinking it best not to add that it was administered into the fourth lumbar interspace of the spinal column. The Princess was agitated as it was, without exact explanations.

"But Doctor, can't you use a saddle block now?" Francesca implored him.

"Alas no. It might stop the labor and your babies want to be born, *Maman*." He was kind, but she knew then that absolutely nothing she could say would move him.

"Doctor, why didn't you tell me about this before? It just seems incredible that with modern medicine . . ." Francesca stopped, unable to adequately express her outraged, fearful disbelief.

"But you are having premature twins, *Maman*. Modern medicine calls for precisely these measures." The doctor took her hand and stroked it paternally. "I will leave my head obstetrical nurse with you now, but I will be in the next room. If you need me or want me for anything, just tell her and I will come at once."

"The next room? Why can't you stay here?" Francesca begged, terrified at the idea of his leaving her for any length of time.

"For my catnap, *Maman*. Tonight I have already delivered two babies. You must try to relax completely between contractions—I strongly advise that you take a catnap, too."

The next eight hours passed in a kaleidoscope of emotions: physical anguish of a kind never experienced or dreamed of, which left no time for thought; anger that this was so much worse than she had expected; raging euphoria tinged with the knowledge that it would only last until the next contraction; fear, like that of a swimmer realizing that the tide is too strong and all hope of fighting it is gone and, above all the other emotions, *triumph* which painted those hours in their single unforgettable light; triumph at being fully alive, totally involved with every atom of her mental, moral and physical resources engaged in the most important work of her life.

Francesca endured without medication, helped only by the constant encouragement of the two doctors and the many nurses who came and went, busy with examinations which she soon disregarded entirely. When she saw the two orderlies appear with the cart on which they were to roll her into the delivery room, she was too dazed to realize what they had come for.

On the delivery table, Dr. Allard waited until Francesca was between contractions. Then he helped her to a sitting position for the saddle block. Afterward, she was placed flat on her back with a pillow under her head. The complete relief of pain, as astonishing as a clap of thunder, was so extraordinary that Francesca was startled and alarmed.

"I'm not paralyzed, am I, Doctor—it's not that, is it?"

"Of course not, *Maman*—you are doing wonderfully. Everything is going just as it should. Relax, relax . . . we are all here for you." He bent over her for the hundredth time with his stethoscope, listening for the fetal heartbeats.

"Oh, this is heaven . . ." Francesca sighed.

Although the delivery room contained Allard and Dr. Rombais, as well as three nurses and an anesthesiologist, silence was the rule for the next forty minutes except for Allard's instructions to Francesca. Allard's team were trained to work together without speaking, by eye and hand signals, since it was his belief that women giving birth were more than normally alert to any spoken words and almost certain to misinterpret them. "Remember," he would say to his staff, "a *Maman* may look unconscious under anesthetic but the sense of hearing is the last to go—say nothing."

After forty minutes Francesca was once again conscious of pain, but of a greatly diminished degree.

"Doctor, Doctor," she murmured, "I think the injection is wearing off."

"No, indeed—we are merely coming to the end," he reassured her in the most jocund of tones. "Now, when I say push, bear down as hard as you can. You won't feel the contractions but I can see them, so you must obey my instructions."

In another ten minutes Francesca heard him grunt in satisfaction. Almost immediately she heard the cry of a baby.

"Is it a boy?" she whispered.

"You have a ravishing daughter, *Maman*," answered Allard, hastily handing the baby to Dr. Rombais who carefully clamped its umbilical cord. Allard plunged back to his position between Francesca's thighs. The nurse who was monitoring the fetal heartbeats had just indicated urgently to him that the heartbeat of the unborn child was becoming slower. He saw, to his consternation, that the amniotic fluid which still appeared was yellow green in color instead of clear. The heartbeat of the second twin was growing slower every second. Allard palpated Francesca's uterus and discovered that it had gone completely rigid. All contractions had stopped. He signaled vehemently at Dr. Rombais to put immediate pressure on Francesca's fundus, the uppermost part of the uterus, while Dr. Allard squeezed with all his might on her now boardlike uterus. Using all the force at his command, he manipulated the second twin down the open birth canal into a position from which he could deliver it with forceps.

Within a matter of minutes, no less than four and no more than five, the second twin was delivered. She did not start to breathe spontaneously as the first one had, but had to be roughed up in a towel with considerable friction before a weak cry came from her mouth. As Dr. Allard cut her umbilical cord, he carefully noted that although the child appeared perfectly formed, she could not weigh much more than four pounds, a guess confirmed by the delivery-room scale. Worse, as he had feared, because of the sign of the yellow green amniotic meconium in the amniotic fluid, Francesca had suffered a massive internal hemorrhage due to an abrupt separation of the placenta from the walls of the uterus minutes before the delivery of the second twin.

"Doctor?" Francesca's voice implored. "What's happening—is it a boy or a girl?"

"Another daughter," he answered briefly. The terseness of his answer, the neutral quality of his normally merry voice, indicated to the others in the delivery room that their chief was deeply concerned about the second child. Something was gravely wrong.

Even as he spoke, the anesthesiologist who was watching Francesca's vital signs saw that her blood pressure had suddenly dropped and her heartbeat had risen markedly. Her pang of bitterest disappointment at Dr. Allard's announcement was forgotten as she became aware of feeling suddenly nauseated and dizzy. Sweat began to pour from her body. Still she persisted. "Show them to me . . . please show them."

"In just one minute, *Maman*. You must try to relax now." Allard motioned for two nurses to start simultaneous transfusions in each of Francesca's arms. She was beginning to go into shock, but within a short while the transfusions and the administration of fibrinogen brought her pulse rate and her blood pressure back to safe levels. As soon as he saw that his patient was stabilized, Allard told Dr. Rombais to bring the babies to the delivery table. Both infants' eyes were tightly closed, both of them had their fists firmly curled. On one twin the Saxon-white hair, which had just been gently dried, had already started to curl. On the other, the pale hair was still a bit damp.

Both of the babies were wrapped in soft white flannel cloths and as Francesca, weak but alert, studied them, she felt a burst of astonishment such as she had never known before. The transition from the creatures with whom she felt a total connection and communication as she carried them inside her, to the sight of these two separate human beings who each possessed the individual authority to close their eyes and curl their fists and thus reject the brightly lit world in which they found themselves, was such a stunning and incomprehensible change that she couldn't grasp it intellectually, but only feel it emotionally.

"Are they identical, Doctor?"

"Yes, but your second daughter weighs less than the first. This one," he said, pointing to the smaller baby, "must go directly into an incubator until she gains some weight. But rest assured, we have counted and they both have all their fingers and toes."

"Thank God," Francesca whispered.

"Now, *Maman*, you must rest."

"Tell my husband."

"He must wait for just a while." The doctor had no intention of leaving Francesca until he was completely satisfied that the new blood running into her arms had done all its work. He didn't leave her until she was ready to be transferred to the recovery room. Then he left the empty delivery room untying the strings of his white cap wearily.

When the tired doctor entered the room in which Stash had been waiting, he saw that he had fallen asleep sitting up, his forehead pressed to the window out of which he had been peering, sightlessly, during all the long night. Dr. Allard stood behind the sleeping man for a long minute. Then he sighed and lightly pressed Stash's shoulder. The Prince woke instantly.

"Tell me!"

"You have twin daughters. Madame is well but very tired."

Stash stared wildly at the doctor as if there might be other information. The assault on his rigid expectations was so ruinous that he could say nothing. The doctor, after a short pause, continued blandly to answer the unasked questions with which other men would have bombarded him.

"One of your daughters is in excellent condition, Sir. As for the other . . ."

Stash finally found his voice. "*What* about the other. . . . Tell me!"

"There was a problem, a clinical condition, before the second child was born. The placenta separated from the womb just before birth and Madame suffered an internal, concealed hemorrhage."

Stash slumped against the wall. "So the child is dead. You can tell me, Doctor."

"No, the child is alive, but I must warn you that she is in grave difficulty. She is very small, only four pounds, two ounces, and because of the *placentae abruptio*—the separation—and the presence of meconium in the amniotic fluid, we know that there was a period during which no oxygen reached her brain. We acted as quickly as possible, Prince, but it was four minutes, perhaps four and a half, before we were able to deliver the baby safely."

"What are you trying to tell me? Just say it, Doctor!"

"There is the probability—no, the certainty—of brain damage."

"Brain damage? What the hell does that mean—what are you saying?" Stash took the doctor by the shoulders as if to shake him and then lowered his hands. "Forgive me."

"It is much too soon to tell. The extent of the damage cannot be foreseen until I have had an opportunity to examine the baby closely."

"How soon will you know—when will you examine the—the other?"

"As soon as I think she is strong enough. Meanwhile, as a precaution, she should be baptized. What name shall she be given, Prince?"

"I don't give a damn!"

"Prince Valensky! Calm yourself. There is absolutely no need to give up hope. And you have one healthy, perfect little daughter. Don't you want to see her? She's in the nursery. She weighed five pounds, ten ounces, so there was no need for an incubator. Would you like to visit her now?"

"No!" Stash spoke without thinking. All he knew was that it would be impossible to look at any baby. The doctor observed him shrewdly. This was far from the first time he had received such a response.

"My advice," he said kindly, "is that you go home and sleep and then return to visit the Princess. You have been up all night under great stress. And when you come back, no doubt the little princesses will also be awake."

"No doubt." Stash turned to go, turned back and said in a tone which contained a hidden question, "I'm sure you did the best you could."

"Indeed, yes, Prince. But there are some things about which we can do nothing."

Still Stash glared at him. The little doctor drew himself up, offended in his art. "Accidents happen in nature, against which the utmost skill of man can do nothing except salvage as best it can."

"*Salvage?*" Stash said the word as if he had never heard it before. What had he to do with salvage? There had never been any allowance in his life for loss, so what room could there be for salvage? "Goodbye, Doctor."

He drove home at a dangerous speed, ignoring the servants gathered at the front door. He didn't stop at the villa but sped on farther to the stables. There he hurled himself out of his car, ran inside the stable and jumped on the back of the first horse he saw. As the groom saw his master about to ride off bareback, he ran up to Stash and shouted, "Prince? How are the twins—and the Princess?"

"The Princess is well. One child. A girl. Now get the hell out of my way!" Stash drove his heels into his bay's side and buried his hands in the beast's mane, with a command that was more a howl than a word. The animal, suddenly as savage as its master, reared with a great whinny and galloped off into the hillside with Stash kicking him on as if the devil were riding behind him.

6

In Dr. Henri Allard's clinic in Lausanne the month of April 1952 passed. The month of May passed too, and Francesca Valensky and her twin daughters had not left the clinic since the premature birth. It was on a June day, rather late in the month, that a nurse brought Marguerite, the firstborn of the twins, into her mother's room for the earliest of her two daily visits. The nurse, Soeur Anni, barely glanced at the passive woman with an extinguished face who sat, motionless as always, in an armchair. Soeur Anni had long ago become bored with the monotony of these useless, routine visits. All the other nurses in the clinic who had, at first, bulged with cautious gossip about this glamorous patient had become equally accustomed to the facts of the case. Princess Valensky never spoke and had not shown a minute's interest in her babies; she would not take the slightest care of herself although she wasn't physically sick, and she only left her bed if two nurses held her by the elbows and guided her, unprotestingly, around the little enclosed garden outside her bright, sunny room.

Postpartum depression in all its sad guises was nothing new to them. Poor thing, they agreed, but then even the doctors didn't know what to do. Sometimes they got better by themselves, sometimes they just never recovered—each nurse had some particularly lurid tale to tell about such cases—but they were careful not to indulge in them within earshot of the special round-the-clock psychiatric nurses who were in permanent attendance on this patient who must never be left alone, even while she slept.

Soeur Anni nodded to the special nurse who was knitting in a corner. "You might as well take your break now. I'll be here with the baby—no need for two of us to be hanging about, is there?"

"Not really. She's been quiet—as usual."

It was a particularly warm and sunny day. Holding Marguerite expertly in the crook of her arm, Soeur Anni opened the windows wide and drew aside the curtains to let in the fresh, flower-touched air. Then she sat down in the chair next to Francesca and after ten minutes, which passed in the customary silence, she began to doze off.

A ladybug flew inside the room and settled on the baby's forehead, right between her eyes, like a Hindu caste mark. The nurse, her eyes half-closed, paid no attention. Francesca glanced at the drowsy nurse and child without a flicker of interest. But, in one tiny part of her mind she waited, without knowing it, for the nurse to notice the insect. After a few minutes the nurse's faint snore still showed no sign of stopping. The ladybug promenaded around on the baby's face and finally lit on one delicate eyelid, close to the fine line of lashes. Too close, perilously close. Francesca reached out a tentative finger to brush away the bug. As she did so she touched her child for the first time, touched the baby skin and found it shockingly soft, shockingly *alive.* The child's eyes opened wide, looking straight at her, and she saw that they were black, as black as her own. She ran one finger over the almost imperceptible blonde eyebrows and then timidly curled a lock of the child's flaxen hair between her fingers.

"Could I . . . could I hold her?" she whispered to the half-slumbering nurse. The nurse slept on, unhearing.

"Nurse?" Francesca said in a low tone. Only a snore answered her. *"Nurse?"* This time her voice was stronger. At its sound something heavy shifted inside of her, some mass blew apart as she rediscovered her own voice. "My God, my God," she said out loud, stroking the baby's hair with fingers to which life and joy had returned.

"NURSE, GIVE ME MY BABY!"

The nurse woke up abruptly, disoriented and flustered. She held onto the infant firmly.

"What? What?" she stumbled. "Wait—stop—I'll call the doctor . . ." She scrambled to her feet, backing away.

"Come here," Francesca ordered peremptorily. "I want to hold her. Now. Give me my baby immediately. There was a bug on her eye!" she added, accusingly. Francesca rose from her chair and drew herself up with all the vivid authority with which she had once faced the cameras. As suddenly as if she had materialized out of a bottle, Francesca Vernon, the great star, stood in front of the nurse, holding out her arms with an imperious gesture.

The nurse was thoroughly startled but not daunted. "Forgive me, Madame, but I can't permit it. I have firm instructions to hold the baby at all times."

Now the woman changed again. Without lowering her arms she became, unmistakably, Princess Francesca Valensky, a princess who was never disobeyed, never questioned—a princess to whom all was allowed.

"Call Doctor Allard at once!" Francesca's voice was rusty but its power filled the room. "We'll see about this nonsense!"

Allard took only a few minutes to reach Francesca's room. He entered running, stopping abruptly as he faced the suddenly beautiful woman, as dark and passionate as a puma, who gazed hungrily at the baby. Charged with adrenaline, she stalked around the bewildered but still defiant nurse.

Mildly, but hiding as much excitement as he ever permitted himself, the doctor spoke. "Well, *Maman*, so we are beginning to feel better? We are making friends?"

"Doctor Allard, what the hell is going on? This crazy woman won't give me my baby."

"Soeur Anni, you may give Marguerite to her mother. Perhaps you might leave us for a moment." Without a word the nurse passed the baby to her mother. Marguerite was wearing a light shift from which her delicate arms and legs, just beginning to show signs of plumpness, wriggled freely in pleasure at the sunshine and the light breeze. She was an inexhaustible treasure of pink and gold, so tiny and yet so definite that even jaded doctors and nurses hung over her crib.

Allard watched carefully while Francesca gazed into the baby's eyes. "Who *are* you?" she asked. Hearing the human voice, Marguerite stopped wriggling for a second and looked at her mother's face. Then, to Francesca's stunned disbelief, she smiled.

"She smiled at me, Doctor!"

"Of course she did."

Francesca ignored the remark. "Doctor, what's this nonsense about not leaving me alone with the baby? I simply don't understand."

"You have not been well, Princess. Until today you didn't want to hold her."

"But that's impossible! Ridiculous . . . simply ridiculous. I've never heard anything so absurd in my whole life!" Francesca looked at the doctor as if she had never properly seen him before. "Where's my other baby?" she asked. "I don't understand what's been going on around here and I don't like it one bit. Where's my husband? Doctor, call Prince Valensky and tell him to come here at once," she commanded. "And tell me where my other baby is . . . I want to hold her, too."

"Your smaller daughter is still in the incubator," the doctor said quickly. There could be no question, no question at all of his patient visiting the other child. The infant had had a convulsion only that morning, the second since her birth. The sight of the sick, piteous mite could well upset the mother to such an extent that she would relapse into the depression in which she had been plunged for so long. Nothing could make him risk that.

"Where's the incubator, Doctor?" asked Francesca, starting to walk toward the door with Marguerite in her arms.

"No! *Maman*, I forbid you! You are not yet well, not as strong as you think. Do you have any idea how long you have been here, my dear lady?"

Francesca stopped, puzzled. "A while? I'm not exactly sure—perhaps—two weeks?"

"Almost nine weeks . . . yes, nine weeks . . . It's been what you Americans call a long haul," the doctor said gently, seeing that his patient had given up her idea of going to the incubator.

Francesca sat down, still gathering her child close. She had the impression that she had been some sad place far away, locked in a world as dismal and colorless as rain in winter; some place lost, in which dim events passed before her eyes like a remote shadow play glimpsed through a distant window. But nine weeks! Suddenly in every bone and muscle, she felt her force drain away. Mutely, she held the baby out to the doctor.

Allard took advantage of the moment. "We must regain our strength, *Maman*, before we start to go visiting." Francesca nodded tiredly in agreement. "In a week, perhaps even less if you do not overtire yourself. You have a long way to go, my dear, before you get back to normal. Now, we have talked enough for the moment. You must try to sleep, heh?" He brought the baby close to her. Francesca brushed her lips over the choicest part of any baby, the fragrant, silky little folds that will one day become a neck. "She will come back to you this afternoon—you can give her the next bottle," the doctor promised, opening the door so the waiting nurse could come in. He carried Marguerite back to the nursery, saying over and over to himself, "Thank God! Thank God!"

As soon as the doctor telephoned, Stash raced to the clinic at ninety-five miles an hour. During the past weeks he had spent hours every day with Francesca, trying vainly to penetrate her withdrawn silence, her fathomless misery, so thick that it seemed to come from without, like a cloud which had enveloped her and made her invisible. His vigil had been made bearable by the visits Marguerite made to her mother, visits ordered by Dr. Allard whether Francesca responded or not.

Stash had fallen passionately in love with his daughter. He played with her for as long as they would let him. He insisted on unwrapping her completely so that he could see her naked. He displayed her enchanting little body to Francesca, hoping that the sight of this newborn perfection must move her as much as it did him, but to no avail. He had had long conferences with Allard, demanding constant reassurances that every precaution had been taken to prevent Francesca from doing herself harm.

When he wasn't with Francesca, Stash shut himself up in the villa, seeing no one from the outside world. Just as he and Francesca had managed to escape, undetected by reporters, on their honeymoon, so he was able to prevent news of the birth of his children from appearing in the press. Dr. Allard's clinic offered complete privacy and the only people who had known that Francesca was pregnant were Matty and Margo Firestone. Stash had written them during the first week after the premature births, telling them only of Marguerite and of Francesca's postpartum depression. He had asked, and obtained, their silence on behalf of the sick woman.

But now . . . now! he thought to himself, as he waited impatiently in Dr. Allard's consultation room, at last life could begin again. He had known, from the beginning, that he must *win* this cruel game. He had promised himself a thousand times that it was only a matter of time before he could take Francesca and Marguerite home with him. Stash had never permitted himself the slightest doubt.

At length Allard appeared, fairly waltzing in satisfaction.

"Can they come home with me now?" Stash demanded, without even greeting the doctor.

"Soon, soon, when the Princess is stronger. But first, my friend, we must talk about the other baby, about Danielle." Even the doctor had not been able, during the time of Francesca's depression, to force Stash to discuss his second child. Good Catholic that he was, Dr. Allard had seen to it that she was baptized the day after her birth, since he was not sure she would survive another twenty-four hours. He himself had chosen the name, that of his own mother, hoping that it might bring some good luck to the unfortunate infant.

"Danielle." Stash said the name as if it were a foreign word which had absolutely no meaning for him. "I do not expect her to live." His voice carried a tone of finality, of utter dismissal.

"But if she lives, and she *may*, you will have to deal with the neurological complications . . ."

"Doctor, not now!"

The doctor continued imperturbably, with emphatic gestures and formal intonation. "I have examined both of your children, Prince. There is a precise set of tests used to determine the extent of nerve development in newborn babies. Doctor Rombais and I have examined them together in order to compare their reactions and . . ."

Stash interrupted him with the savagery with which he confronted any obstacle in his path. His neck and head became the hunting beak of an angry, vicious bird as he spoke.

"Just give me the results!"

"Prince," the doctor replied, without changing his measured lecturing tone, "you must become aware of what we have to deal with, no matter how little you wish to know about it. I assure you that there is no way in which I can give you the results, as you put it, in two words. Now! If you will permit me to continue—Marguerite responds in all ways like a normal, strong infant. She sucks vigorously, her rooting inflex is strong and the Moro reflex was normal. To obtain it I put her on her back and slammed my hand down loudly near her. She extended her arms and legs abruptly and fanned her fingers and toes. When I held her up with her feet touching the examination table, she made stepping movements, and when I pulled her to a sitting position for the Traction Response, her shoulder and neck muscles contracted. All in all, it was a lively session."

Stash followed every word the doctor said with painfully reined-in attention. He needed no doctor to tell him Marguerite was perfect. There was a slight pause while Allard collected his words for what he had to say next. He sighed heavily, but resolutely.

"Danielle showed very little reaction to all of these tests. I repeated the examination twice at a three-week interval and the results obtained were no different. There is a paucity of movements, she rarely cries, she has not yet held up her head and she has put on only a little weight . . . what we call a failure to thrive."

"Failure to thrive! You mean she's a vegetable!" Stash could contain himself no longer.

"Certainly not, Prince! She is only nine weeks old and there is still positive hope that her body will, with the best of care, develop along normal lines. If she should continue to gain weight at the rate she is gaining, slow though it is, there is nothing to stop her from eventually becoming a physically active child. She is not deformed in any way, merely weak, very weak."

"And mentally?"

"Mentally? Mentally, she will never be normal. We have known that from the beginning."

"But what are you telling me *exactly*, Doctor? How far from normal will she be?"

"She will be retarded, that much is certain. The exact degree of retardation is something which I can not possibly estimate at this time. We cannot even give your daughter an I.Q. test until she is three years old and even then the judgment may not be final—in this problem, Prince, there are so many, many variations, from mild to moderate to severe . . ." Dr. Allard paused abruptly and lapsed into silence.

"Could it be . . . mild?" Stash finally forced himself to ask, in a low, disbelieving voice, each reluctant word acid on his lips.

"Prince, there is so much room for possibility in these cases. Sometimes only a few percentage points of I.Q. can make the difference between a child who is only barely trainable and a child who can develop certain skills—no one can predict where the strengths might be . . ."

"Spare me these vague generalities!" Stash bit out. *"What is her future, damn it!"*

There was a short silence. Dr. Allard finally answered with the most precise information available to him.

"The most we can hope for is that little Danielle will be somewhere on the borderline from low-mild to high-moderate retardation, that she will manage some personal care, that she can form some social relationships, that she can express some simple phrases on a prereading level—perhaps that of a four-year-old . . ."

"A four-year-old—Doctor, you're talking about a *kindergarten mentality!* And you call that 'moderate'—no matter *how* old she gets to be?"

"Prince," answered the doctor, facing the question squarely, "that is probably the best, the very best you can hope for. Because of the little one's lack of oxygen before and during birth, the poor response to the tests—the convulsions—no, Prince, we cannot possibly hope for more than that."

There was total silence in the room for minutes. Finally Stash spoke again. "What if you're wrong, what if she's severely retarded? What then?"

"Don't borrow trouble. There will be, in any case, the question of constant care, even with moderate retardation. With severe retardation the problem becomes enormous. Great watchfulness is necessary in all cases, throughout the child's life. Once the child can walk, there will always be danger. As puberty approaches, the problem becomes aggravated. Often an institution is the only answer."

"If . . . if she lives, Doctor, how long can she remain here in your clinic?" Stash asked.

"Until she gains enough weight to go into the nursery with the others. Not until she weighs five pounds, eight ounces, Prince, which is a question of only a few months, in my opinion, if there are no complications. While she is still in the incubator, of course, we are in complete charge. But once she grows large enough for the nursery, we can't continue to keep her. At that point you should make preparations to take her home."

At the word "home" Stash's face hardened. "Doctor Allard, I don't intend to speak of this to my wife until she's stronger."

"I agree. In fact, I advise great caution at the moment. There has been massive denial, on the part of the Princess, of either child. However, now she has made normal contact with Marguerite and the prognosis is extremely good. However, her depression was severe, most severe, and in such a case she must not have any further shocks. If the Princess continues to do well, you can take her and Marguerite home in a few days. I shall see to it that she doesn't see Danielle until the baby is, as you put it, 'out of the woods.' Nature will decide the timetable."

It was on a brilliant day, almost the last in June, when Dr. Allard declared Francesca well enough to go home. From the instant that Stash had hired a baby nurse from a Lausanne agency, it seemed as if every international newspaper correspondent in Switzerland had been alerted to the news. A crowd of reporters and photographers waited with increasing impatience outside the impenetrable gates of the private clinic. They had been keeping vigil since early morning, and now, seven hours later, when Stash and Francesca Valensky appeared at last, carrying their baby, there was an uproar in a dozen languages, demanding that the child be held up for the cameras.

In spite of the protective scowl of her husband, the pale woman, whose prodigal beauty had vanished from print many months ago, carefully tilted the white lace cocoon so that the infant's sleeping face could be seen. A quilted, white silk cap covered the tiny head but wisps of hair escaped and flared silver in the breeze like delicate petals. Although the child had been christened Marguerite Alexandrovna, she seemed in her mother's arms so much like a flower in human form that the imagination of the press was fired. In every one of the pictures that appeared of that moment she was crowned Princess Daisy.

The convoy of photographers and reporters followed Francesca and Stash all the way back to their villa. They besieged the great house, standing outside the locked gates in a large group and shouting, over and over, "We want Daisy." When, at last, they left, persuaded only after a long wait that there was no chance of getting any stories or even any more pictures than those they had snapped on the steps of the clinic, everyone had forgotten that the baby had ever been named Marguerite, even her parents.

She was Daisy to Stash and Francesca, and Princess Daisy to most of the servants who still clung to the old ways.

She was a circus of a baby when she was awake, distributing smiles to all her hovering adorers, lifting her head halfway off the mattress of her crib if she spied a butterfly or a flower or a friendly finger, making music with the collection of rattles which hung on the side of her crib, kicking her legs for joy when she was touched. She slept almost eighteen hours a day, by Francesca's reckoning, and ate for two hours, but the remaining four hours in every day she held a royal court.

For several days all of Francesca's attention was focused on Daisy. Each morning she asked to be driven into Lausanne to see her other daughter, but Stash managed easily to convince her that she wasn't strong enough yet to make the trip. Indeed, her vitality was exceptionally slow in returning. She was so weary by late morning that she spent most of each day on the chaise longue in her room. But finally, after a week, exhausted though she still was, Francesca fretfully demanded to be taken to visit Danielle at once. The moment Stash was dreading had arrived. He had prepared his words over and over.

"Darling, the doctor and I have agreed that it is a very bad idea for you to visit Danielle yet."

"Why not?" she asked in quick alarm.

"The baby is . . . very small, extremely weak . . . in fact, my darling, she's ill, very ill."

"But that's all the more reason. . . . I might be able to *do* something, maybe I can help . . . why . . . *why* didn't you tell me before that she was *sick?*" Her face was contorted, her eyes jagged with shock.

"Christ! Look at you!" he cried in fear and anger. "I knew I shouldn't have told you! You're much too upset. You haven't been well enough to be told, and damn it, you aren't well enough now."

"Stash. *What's wrong with her?* Tell me! You're only making it worse!"

Stash took Francesca in his arms. "She's too small, darling. You wouldn't be even allowed to touch her. Now, listen to me, my dearest, since you know she's not well, I'm going to tell you the whole thing. That's the only way you'll understand why you shouldn't see her yet. The chances that the baby will survive are almost nonexistent. Allard feels, and I totally agree, that for you to become attached to the baby now might plunge you right back into your depression . . . when . . . if . . . anything happens to her."

"But, Stash, my own child . . . my BABY."

"No, Francesca! No! Don't you realize how sick you were? It's absolutely out of the question to risk anything like that again. You just can't be the judge—you're not well enough yet, no matter what you believe. Think of Daisy if you won't think of yourself, think of Daisy and think of me."

He had found the magic argument. He felt Francesca stop struggling in his arms, saw her relax her fight, watched with relief as she gave in to her grief. Let her cry, cry and cry, for it was just no good, no bloody good and no way to make it better.

Week after week passed. Stash went faithfully to the clinic and reported to Dr. Allard that Francesca was making a very slow recovery and that, in his opinion, she was still too close to her long depression to allow her to chance a visit to a baby who was visibly not well. "She's too fragile, Doctor," he said. "It would be the worst thing for her."

When he returned from these excursions he told Francesca that the baby was still in the same condition as before, holding on to life only by each breath she took and that the doctor refused to hold out any false hope. Her misery was such that after a few weeks she merely looked at his somber face and forebore to ask about

Danielle. She knew that if the news was better he'd tell her immediately.

At the clinic Stash never once went into the incubator room to look at Danielle. After what the doctor had told him about her future he had discarded her. She did not exist for him. She could not exist. *She must not exist.* He had never seen her and he had no intention of ever seeing her. Nature was cruel, accidents happen, but a strong man could override the blows of fate. The mere idea of a child of his—a child of *his*—in *his* home, growing up, yet *never* growing up, growing into something he refused to contemplate—*no!* When that thought touched his mind he rejected it with all the power of his warrior's nature. After his childhood, so distorted by the overwhelming concentration on his mother's slow dying, compassion, that most human emotion, had died totally within him. The fate that awaited the child he never saw was so dreadful that he determined to eliminate it from his life. It was the one thing in the world of which he was in fear.

With ease Stash concealed these emotions from Dr. Allard and, little by little, he asked the subtle questions which brought him the answers he needed to keep him to his resolve. Yes, it was most possible that the Princess would become enormously devoted to Danielle; yes, the mothers of retarded children often spent much less time with their normal children in favor of the sick one; yes, it was not at all impossible that the Princess would refuse to have the child institutionalized no matter how necessary it was. Indeed, there were many such cases. The maternal instinct was often strengthened beyond the imagination of man by the care of a sick or retarded child and there was no force as strong as that instinct. Nature was indeed marvelous. Mothers were self-sacrificing, the Prince was right. Yes, even beyond the point where it was reasonable or even wise. But that was the way of life—what could man do in the face of it?

Grimly, Stash received news of Danielle. She had begun to put on weight. She had had no further convulsions. In Dr. Allard's opinion it was perfectly safe for the Princess to come and visit the little one. In fact, he had expected that the Princess would have come sooner, in spite of her weakness, knowing her determination as he did.

"My wife does not *intend* to see her, Doctor." For many days Stash had rehearsed various replies for the inevitable moment which had now arrived.

"*Indeed?*" The little doctor expressed his astonishment only by that one word. He had, in the course of practicing his profession for many years, almost learned not to show surprise.

Stash turned his back on the doctor and went to stand by a window, looking out as he spoke. "We've been talking it over, and over, from every angle. We've agreed that it would be a serious mistake to try to bring up—Danielle—in our own home, and that the time to make this decision is now, not later. A clean cut, Doctor." Stash sat down solidly, relieved to have met the charge head on.

"But what do you intend to do?" the doctor asked. "Danielle weighs over five pounds now. Soon she'll be able to leave the clinic."

"I've made thorough inquiries, of course. As soon as she's old enough, she'll be sent to live in the finest of institutions for children in her condition. I understand that excellent ones exist when money is no problem. Until then I believe she should be boarded with a foster mother. In fact, I've heard of several right here in Lausanne. Could you just look at this list of names and tell me if there is anyone here you particularly recommend?"

"And this is what you are *resolved* to do about Danielle?" the doctor asked intently. "And the Princess agrees?"

"Absolutely," Stash said, handing the doctor the sheet of paper. "We always agree with each other in family matters."

Madame Louise Goudron, the foster mother most highly recommended by Dr. Allard, had been available to take over the care of Danielle. As long as the banker's check for the child's care that arrived each week continued to come, she required no further information than Dr. Allard's request. Danielle was far from the first imperfect baby she had sheltered in her home, which was both comfortable and cheerful, but would have been neither if this childless widow had not discovered that some people, whose names were no concern of hers, preferred not to be burdened by their own children.

Only a few weeks after Madame Goudron had fetched Danielle home from the clinic, Francesca reached a decision. She was feeling so much stronger physically, so much more able to cope with her emotions, that she knew she had to see her second daughter, no matter what Dr. Allard or Stash thought. Neither of them had any idea of what she could endure. They were both sheltering her too much and she'd had enough of it. She must see Danielle whether or not the baby's life was in danger, whether she could touch her or not. It would be far worse if her child died and she'd never even seen her alive again since her birth—why couldn't they understand?

"But it's impossible, my poor love," Stash said.

"Impossible? I tell you I'm *ready*—you don't have to worry—I can take anything—except this awful limbo, Stash. Don't you realize it's been over five months and she's still alive?"

Stash didn't falter. The expression on his face was the expression he had worn in a battle in the sky when he pressed the button of the machine gun that would shoot the enemy out of the sky. He took Francesca's hands in his and pulled her toward him.

"Darling, darling—the baby is dead."

She screamed just once, waiting in the fearful anguish of someone who has cut herself deeply, to the bone, but who has not yet seen the blood begin to flow. Her eyes flashed and then dimmed as if the last candle had been extinguished in a dark room. Stash held her so tightly that she couldn't see his face.

"She died soon after we brought Daisy home," he continued. "I waited to tell you until you were able to hear it. . . . She was far worse off than you ever knew . . . . She would never have been well, darling, never, never in all the world." He spoke rapidly, tenderly caressing her hair. "She was seriously ill from the minute she was born. We didn't want you to know but there was no future for her, she would never have been normal—brain damage during birth—nobody's fault—but you might not have recovered if I'd told you while you were still so emotionally disturbed."

"I *knew*," Francesca whispered.

"Impossible."

"No . . . there was always a feeling . . . I knew something was wrong, something was being kept from me . . . but I was too cowardly to find out . . . I didn't want to find out . . . I was afraid . . . a coward . . ."

"Oh, my love, don't blame yourself, your instincts were right, you were saving yourself . . . and saving the rest of us. What would Daisy do without her mother? What would I do without you?"

"But I *knew!* I must have known all along." She was sobbing frantically, pulling herself away from him, kneeling on the rug, doubled up in the cramp of her grief. It might be hours, he thought, before she could be persuaded to allow him to comfort her, to press her to him again, but already Stash could anticipate the gradual acceptance of the child's death—to him a reality—which would eventually enter her body and make her cling to him as she had from the moment they had met. He waited patiently, this man who so rarely waited for anything.

Within several weeks Stash, who had been observing Francesca closely, judged that the worst of her grief and shock were over. He allowed *Life* to send Philippe Halsman to come and take pictures for their cover. Francesca now spent almost all of her time with Daisy, who had progressed from shaking her rattles to an insatiable interest in her mother's glittering, tinkling charm bracelet. The baby had developed a genuine belly laugh and nothing pleased her as much as being allowed to grab at the dangled bracelet. It was a game, a real game, and she squealed with rapture every time she caught it and tugged almost hard enough to pull it off. Stash and Francesca watched, holding their breath, while the fat, fair bundle actually rolled over from her back to her stomach. Wonder of wonders, she seemed to talk to her tiny stuffed animals, although it was no language known to man. Her enormous eyes were alert and happy from the instant she woke, and when she slept on her stomach, her minute heels drawn up under her diapered bottom, Francesca decided that she looked like a heavenly jumping frog. They put her on a heap of Francesca's furs, naked except for her diaper, and she lifted her head up with her chest high and crowed in surprise.

"She might as well know what sable feels like," said Stash.

"You'll spoil her rotten."

"Of course I will."

"But why not start her on the mink? Show a little restraint?"

"Nonsense. She's a Valensky, and don't you ever forget it. And speaking of that," Stash said, suddenly serious, "I really think we've had enough of country life, don't you? I'm bloody sick and tired of Switzerland. What would you say to moving to London? I know damn near everybody there who's much good. We could get back into the swing of things, go to the theater, entertain, see friends . . ."

"Oh, yes! Yes! I've been wanting to get away. And now . . ." Francesca stopped, thinking that she never wanted to see Switzerland again.

"Now it's time for London, now it's time for that house I promised you. And then we'll go adventuring—all three of us!"

"They warned me about you, the playboy prince! Don't think I don't know the way you used to roam the world. Oh, the stories I've heard . . ."

"All true."

"But over now? You're not restless in domesticity?" She teased him, more beautiful than she had been in many months.

"All over. I have everything I want." He was staggered again at the pleasure she was able to give him, the way every angle and every curve of her face was illuminated for him as no other face had ever been. Again, the lawlessness in him met the lawlessness in her and they joined in outrageous delight. The sooner they left Lausanne and the clinic of Dr. Allard, the better, he thought, as he plucked Daisy off the sable coat and tickled her stomach.

"Let's go to London and buy a house. Can you be packed by tomorrow?" he asked.

"No, you go alone, darling. I don't want to leave Daisy by herself, not even with Masha and the servants—I just wouldn't have a second's peace of mind."

"Right. But if you don't like the house I choose, you'll be stuck with it."

"Spoken like a true prince," she laughed. "The last man in the world without servant problems. I'm sure you'll pick the best house in London—they expect it of you."

"What the devil are you complaining about? I know some women who would have killed to be in your position," he grumbled.

"Don't get so indignant—at least the silver is always polished." She threw a cushion at his head. "Give me my baby. You've had her long enough. Poor baby—six months old and jaded already."

The day Stash left for London, Francesca sent Masha into Lausanne with a precisely detailed list of shopping to do for her. She should really have gone herself, she thought, for without doubt Masha would manage to buy the wrong shade of nylons, but she had plotted to arrange this afternoon completely alone with Daisy. Although the trained baby nurse had been discharged weeks before, Masha, with her position of former wet nurse to Stash, with her decades of devoted service to all the Valenskys, had never learned to properly knock at a door. She kept coming in and hovering over them when Francesca was tending Daisy, making well-meant but vaguely critical comments all the while. It would have been impossible to ask her to leave without hurting her proprietary, grandmotherly feelings, and Francesca, so recently returned to the world of everyday joys, was reluctant to cause anyone pain.

She looked up in annoyance when Masha returned, an hour before she was expected. The Russian woman clumped into Daisy's room, her broad, kind face flushed with anger, her mouth working silently, every inch of her sturdy, reliable body conveying an imminent explosion.

"Masha—what's wrong with you?" Francesca whispered. "Daisy's just gone to sleep—hush, now."

Masha was so disturbed that she could only keep her voice low with difficulty.

"She—that nurse—Soeur Anni—I saw her in the store—that, that *creature* had the nerve to say to me—I've known her for years, mind you, and she, oh, it's not to be endured . . . to *me* . . . ach, I can't even say it myself, it's disgusting, the gossip, the things people will say . . ." Masha stopped abruptly and sat down squarely in the yellow rocking chair, unable to continue for sheer anger.

"Masha, what exactly did Soeur Anni say?" Francesca asked quietly. She knew that in the nine weeks of her depression she must have been worse than bizarre, strange in ways of which Masha couldn't be aware. It was unprofessional of the nurse, to say the least, to discuss a former patient, but her years in Hollywood had hardened her to the blows of gossip mongers.

"She told me . . . she said . . . she . . . *ach*—the things these crazy people believe! She said that our poor little baby who died—that the baby wasn't dead at all!"

Francesca went gray. Gossip was one thing, but this was of such vileness, such palpable evil, to speak of her tragedy as if it hadn't happened, to use her grief as material for a rumor. One look at Masha's face told her there was more.

"I want every single word Soeur Anni said. She's a dangerous woman—the whole story, Masha, out with it!"

"She said that little Danielle, that our baby, was in the clinic for months—months—after you left, until she got big enough and then they sent her away to be boarded at that Madame Louise Goudron's, a woman who takes in children . . ."

" 'They?' Did she say who 'they' were?"

"No, she didn't know, but the worst of it, Madame, the worst was what she said to me when I told her it was the foulest lie I'd ever heard. She said I could say what I liked but she knew some people who are so rich and high and mighty that if they don't like the baby they have, if something's wrong with it, they just get rid of it! I damned her to burn in hell, Princess, right to her face!"

"Masha! Now just calm down . . . you'll wake Daisy . . . . It's not possible that Soeur Anni—of course, I was rude to her, but still, to be so vicious, to dream up a story like that. . . . She's mad, utterly mad. I've got to do something about her. She must *never* be allowed around sick people again. She's crazy, Masha, don't you see, really and truly insane."

"Oh, Princess, Princess . . . the wickedness of it. What if she's told other people, what if they believe her?"

"Nonsense. No one in his right mind would listen to her. The Prince would strangle the woman if he even heard—is that everything she told you?"

"Yes, every word. I left the store and came right back to tell you."

"I'm going to call Doctor Allard right away. . . . No . . . wait. I'll sound as mad as Soeur Anni. You'll have to be my witness. We'll go into town and see him tomorrow morning, first thing. That way she can't deny what she told you. That bitch. That utter bitch!"

Stash's valet knocked at the door.

"What is it?" Francesca said, angrily.

"Princess, you're wanted on the telephone. It's the Prince, from London."

"I'll be right down, Mump."

The telephone was in the library of the villa. Francesca rushed down the stairs and picked up the receiver.

"Darling, I'm so glad to hear your voice! Why? Oh, I was just feeling terribly lonely for you, that's all. It's been a whole day." As she spoke she thought that there was no reason to tell Stash about Soeur Anni. He would go into one of the cold, devil-sent rages she had seen overcome him when someone or something challenged his power over his life, and heaven knows what he would do to that crazy woman. She was perfectly capable of handling this nasty incident herself. "Daisy?" she continued. "She just went to sleep. We had a wonderful afternoon, all alone together. No, darling, nothing new . . . two more days . . . maybe three? So, it's not that easy to find the perfect princely residence. Just don't rush it . . . . I'm being well taken care of. Goodnight, my dearest heart. I love you."

The next morning Francesca and Masha were driven by the chauffeur into Lausanne. Francesca told Masha to stay in Dr. Allard's waiting room while she went into his consultation room. As the receptionist ushered her in, the little doctor bounced up from behind his desk at the sight of her.

"Ah, ha, *Maman*, you've had a change of heart! I was sure of it! I knew it! I knew it! I was certain you'd never really give up your baby, not a woman like you! Of course, at the time—but, my dear, what's wrong?" Dr. Allard caught Francesca just as she stumbled to a chair. He busied himself reviving her from her faint, murmuring, "Naturally, the emotion, the emotion . . ."

As she came back to herself, the horror was all around her, a sick whirl, yet without a name, without specifics, generalized, surrounding, stifling. She knew nothing except that something very bad had been done, something criminal. Every ounce of acting ability Francesca possessed was mustered as she slowly realized where she was and the full implications of what Dr. Allard had said. Instincts of cunning she hadn't known she possessed took over.

"I'm sorry, Doctor . . . it must be the reaction to coming back to the clinic. I'm perfectly all right now. No thank you, no water, I'm fine. Well! How are you?" She was gaining time settling down into a natural rhythm, her words coming from her numb lips as if she really were in full command of herself.

"I? I am a happy man today, Princess. When the Prince told me that you had decided never to see Danielle, that you refused to bring her up, I must confess that I was deeply disappointed. But I do not consider it my business to comment on such decisions, you understand, that is always a matter the parents must decide. But somehow, something told me, yes, even at the time, that when you were quite well again you would reconsider."

"Doctor, I went through a very difficult time. I'm not sure that I really understand now, even though I've recovered, exactly what happened. Could you straighten it out for me, tell me just what occurred? I didn't pay enough attention to the whole thing and I'm ashamed of myself. . . . I don't want my husband to know how little I listened to him." She smiled at him, composed, charmingly helpless.

When the doctor had finished the long recital, filling in every detail with Swiss precision, remembering with no trouble all of his interviews with Stash and all the details of Danielle's condition, Francesca sat numbly. Every word was a heavy spiked object that fell straight on her heart, blow after blow. The foreknowledge of approaching doom was as palpable as an open casket. She wanted to scream, to scream and never stop screaming, so that she would never have to think about what the little doctor had told her. Instead, calmly, out of a cave on the dark side of the moon, she heard her voice asking, "You still haven't told me exactly what sort of special care Danielle will need."

"Only what you've given Daisy—I see that is what the newspapers call her now, our little Marguerite. At the moment, before Daisy starts to walk, the differences between them will be less than they will be in the future. Danielle will, of course, be slow and late to develop in every way, and a good deal less active than her sister, but, as I have assured you, she will look normal. Soon, very soon, it will be time for speech . . . the first major problem. Then, in a few years, Danielle can be tested. With luck there are many, many things the little one can be taught to do for herself, but all that's in the future. For now it's only love and attention that she requires."

"Doctor Allard, I foolishly gave away her crib and all her clothes . . . everything that might have reminded me. . . . I'll need just one more day to get ready for her."

"But of course . . . one day, two days, what do they matter now?" The doctor looked at her keenly, thinking that perhaps what she really needed was time to get used to the idea, now that her difficult decision had finally been made.

When Francesca came out of the doctor's consulting room, Masha was waiting with fiery impatience to be summoned as a witness against Soeur Anni. Francesca intercepted her before she could say anything.

"Masha, it's all settled, our business. Come on, right away, we've got a lot of things to do." She grasped the older woman's arm and tugged her out of the door, hurrying down the clinic corridor into the street.

"Princess, did you get that woman thrown out? Why didn't you let me tell him? You were in there so long I was worried."

"Masha," Francesca began and then stopped. In the space of an hour everything on which she had based her beliefs had vanished. Nothing was as it seemed. Deception, lies, cruelty, impossible hurts, a vast, confused landscape surrounded her.

"Masha, she didn't lie to you. Danielle—she's alive!" The strong peasant woman tottered. Francesca held her up with all her strength. "Masha, come, we'll sit in the park. I'll explain it all."

At the end of Francesca's recital, broken as it was by incredulous cries of denial from Masha, the two women sat silently on the park bench, eyed with mild curiosity by the chauffeur who was still parked in front of the clinic.

Slowly Masha turned to Francesca. "You must understand, Princess, even as a little boy he was in terror of weakness, sickness, only that, no other failings. I've watched him over the years—oh, I know he pays no attention to me, but I've watched and watched. He has to have everything his way. He always wins, always. There is no hope, Princess. He'll never admit the poor baby to his heart."

"He won't have to," Francesca said in a voice that was almost a howl of potent, rending rage. "He's lost every chance."

Masha's subservient reaction to Stash's point of view had mobilized her as nothing else could have. The old woman was actually trying to explain what he had done, as if his actions could be accepted, *had* to be accepted.

"I'm going away, Masha. I'm taking my children with me. Nobody can stop me, I warn you. He *lied* to me. He let me think she was dead! He *stole* my baby. If I don't protect her, who knows what evil thing he might do next? Think what he did, Masha. Think what he *is*. I never want to see him again. I'll be gone before he gets back from London. All I ask from you is to say nothing until I've left."

Masha's eyes filled. "What do you take me for? Once I had a baby . . . but he died. Still, I have always had a mother's heart, Princess. Anyway, you can't manage without me. Just how do you think you are going to take care of two babies all by yourself? I'm going with you."

"Oh, Masha, Masha!" Francesca cried. "I hoped you'd say that—but I would never have asked you to leave him."

"He doesn't need me. You do," Masha said with stately finality.

Francesca spent one day at the U.S. Embassy in Geneva making emergency passport arrangements, assisted by a bored and incurious clerk, bought airline tickets in a Geneva travel agency, returned to Lausanne to cash a large check at their bank and hurried back to the villa to pack. For herself she took almost nothing but her travelling clothes, but she filled two big suitcases with all of Daisy's clothes and necessary temporary supplies. She took out all her jewels and looked at them speculatively. No, she was no longer the wife of the man who had given them to her. Her garden of Fabergé crystal vases, filled with jeweled flowers? Yes, somehow they belonged to another life—a life before the lies—and they rightfully could go with her. The lapis lazuli egg with the diamond crown of Catherine the Great inside, bearing a ruby at its heart? Yes! That was undeniably hers, hers for bearing the twins. She shut the vases and the egg into their boxes and put the small packets in the bottom of her vanity case. Each of her actions, all day long, had been executed with precision, perfection and perfect ease. She had been taken over by a molten core of anger which powered her like an enormous engine. Her strength knew no limits, her brain worked at ten times its normal efficiency, she was a living fire, burning, burning toward the moment when she would take her children to safety. Should she cable Matty Firestone to meet her in Los Angeles? No. Absolutely no one must know she was leaving until she'd gone.

She answered Stash's next phone call that evening with such a perfect imitation of the tone of the night before that, from the observing part of herself, she was astonished. But all that night she prowled back and forth in her bedroom, hurling words of loathing and bitter blame at him. A man should die for what he had tried to do—had done. How frighteningly little she had really known him, how trusting she had been, how easily she had been duped, used as if she were a figure on a chessboard. How she hated him!

The next morning she telephoned Dr. Allard. She would be sending a nurse to Madame Goudron's to pick up the baby in two hours, she told him. Would he have the kindness to telephone the lady and ask her to have Danielle ready, and warmly dressed? It was such a chilly day. Yes, yes, she was happy, very happy and very excited. The doctor was perfectly right. It was a wonderful day. Yes, she would give the Prince his best wishes for them all . . . how very kind.

Precisely two hours later Francesca sat hidden in the back of a taxi, holding Daisy, while Masha went into the neat little house. No one would have recognized the woman in a bulky travel coat, wearing dark glasses and a deep-brimmed hat, a woman without make-up, her hair pulled back into a tight bun, as that lyric, famous beauty, her long hair flying, who responded in such carefree, innocent delight to the cheers of her fans on her arrival at Cherbourg, just a little less than a year and a half ago.

Five minutes passed before Masha emerged, waving at the woman at the door who lifted a wistful hand. As the taxi started toward the airport, Masha and Francesca exchanged babies. Francesca lifted the hood of the carrying blanket which almost covered the child's face. How small she was. How incredibly sweet. Silver blonde hair, curly and fine. A grave face, a bit sad, but so marvelously familiar. And the eyes—the same velvety black, the black of a purple pansy, Daisy's eyes. But dull. Just a little dull. Perhaps only dull if you compared her to Daisy . . . and that was something you must never, never do, never again.

In one glance she committed herself irrevocably to protect and cherish her child, knowing that whatever happiness this attachment would bring, it would always be linked to shadows and a vast sadness that she rejected even as it was stitched tightly into her soul.

7

None of the servants dared to say a single word to their master. Stash Valensky's face, as he went about the business of selling the huge Lausanne villa and moving them all to London, was set in lines of pain which made him almost unrecognizable. Even among themselves they only whispered a few words of speculation. The unexplained disappearance of the Princess, with Daisy and Masha, was so threatening to their sense of security that they tried to ignore it. They closed their minds to the mystery. A family quarrel, they prayed, that would be resolved as suddenly, as mysteriously, as it had sprung up.

Stash could do nothing. Any legal action to recover Daisy would instantly become public knowledge, and then the whole story would have to be revealed. He had entirely justified his actions to himself, but, armored with scorn, he accepted the fact that the great majority of people, people who allowed unfortunate accidents to control their little lives, would never understand what he'd had to do about Danielle.

They would never understand how right he had been. How right he *was*. He reasoned that the situation couldn't last long. Francesca had acted emotionally, out of the shock of the moment, but she'd come to her senses soon and realize that he had merely *shaped* events for her sake and for Daisy's sake, that he had taken the only rational, the only right course to ensure a happy life for the three of them.

Yet Stash had no idea where Francesca was. By the time he had returned from London and discovered that she was gone, he could only trace her as far as Los Angeles. He called Matty Firestone. Whatever further information existed, her former agent was the obvious first source.

Matty expressed his almost incredulous contempt for Stash by informing him that *both* of his daughters were very well; in fact, Danielle was beginning to hold her head up nicely for a second or two. Daisy? Oh, yeah, Daisy. She was sitting up and saying mama, but that little Danielle, now she was amazing. He could almost swear she'd smiled at him the third time she saw him.

Stash spoke as coldly as possible. There was nothing to be gained by rising to the bait. Would Francesca see him? Could he write to her? There had been a misunderstanding which could be worked out.

"Well," said Matty, enjoying himself viciously, "there's no way on earth that I'm going to let you know where they are. They're safe and they're well and they're not starving and that's all you get out of me. And it's more than you deserve."

Months passed. Stash went to California, but Matty was obdurate. He was acting under orders from his client. Mr. Valensky would get nothing from him. Of course, he could sue for divorce if that's what he wanted. The newspapers would bless him. There hadn't been any juicy scandals lately.

Stash spent New Year's Day of 1953 alone in his great house in London. His wife and child had been gone for just over four months. He was a prisoner in his own home. He knew that if he appeared in public without Francesca the rumors would start. Already he had received telephone calls from the British press requesting interviews with Francesca. Everyone, they assured him, wanted to know how the movie-star-turned-princess was enjoying London. They all clamored to photograph her with Daisy again. The *Life* cover picture was many months out of date. He ran out of credible excuses. He knew that soon his postponements would be futile and that any day now the press would be watching outside the house to see if they could spot a nanny with a pram.

Stash fled to India, where the polo season was in full swing, but this year he didn't play. There were palaces into which no reporters had ever dreamed of being allowed to penetrate, a dozen maharajas who were delighted to have their old friend as a houseguest. Calcutta was safe during all of January; February and March could be spent in Delhi, Bombay and Jaipur. But in the spring where would he go?

By April he had had enough. Stash announced that he and Francesca had separated and that she had returned to the United States. He had no plans for a divorce. And he had nothing else to add. In a week, for lack of details, the story faded, disappeared and was soon forgotten.

That summer of 1953 Stash played polo again. The thin line between riding fairly and riding to intimidate grew even more questionable than it had been before, but he still kept on the right side of it. He flung himself into the purchase of new ponies and the establishment of a stable in Kent, within an easy drive of London. He sold the British fighter jets, both the Gloster Meteor and the de Havilland Vampire, which he had bought after the war. He acquired an Argentinian plane, the Pulqui, another fighter jet of a later vintage, which was powered by a Rolls-Royce Derwent engine. He tracked down and bought the most recent model available of the Lockheed XP-80, known as the Shooting Star, a jet which for many years could outmaneuver and outperform almost every other aircraft in the world. He invented excuses to fly these warplanes: keeping his pilot's license current, recreation and relaxation. What he never admitted to himself in the years after Francesca left him was that he would welcome another war. Only an aerial duel with an enemy, with death the inevitable outcome for one of them, would have given him the terrible release he sought. Girls, fresh desirable girls, at the peak of their youth, were everywhere he looked. There was so little struggle and even less pleasure in their capture that he sometimes wondered why he bothered.

Anabel de Fourment was a member of a unique, little-known breed of woman, the great modern courtesan. Few women other than her own kind ever managed to comprehend her ruinous charm. She was not a great beauty, she lacked chic and she was close to forty. Yet, stretching from her nineteenth year there existed a history of notable men who had spent fortunes for her favors. One brief, youthful marriage had convinced her that the role of lover was far more agreeable than the role of wife. Ravishing young women anxiously asked each other what her secret was, but only a man who had lived with her could have told them.

Anabel wrapped a climate of utter comfort around the man who possessed her. With her possession—and it could belong only to the very rich—came entry into a hitherto unknown country of harmony, ease and a level of good humor which seemed Edwardian in its mellow patina. She made it her business to find and keep the best cook in London. Her home was arranged with such art that no man ever managed to analyze why it was so supremely relaxing: all they felt was that the problems of their world stopped at her door. Anabel didn't know what a neurosis was. She had no complexes, no phobias, no obsessions. She was never depressed or out of sorts or annoyed or short-tempered. She had iron health and no one had ever heard her complain of so much as a broken fingernail. In fact, she had never been known to speak in anger, yet she managed her domestic affairs with absolute dispatch. Below Stairs she was a benevolent dictator who maintained absolute rule.

She was never, never boring. She was rarely witty, but she was often just plain funny, with a fresh felicity of phrase. She couldn't remember the punch lines of even a single joke, so she laughed as much the tenth time as the first time she had heard the same man tell one—a laugh that might alone have ensured her fortune, a laugh so generous, so full-bodied, so *admiring* that to hear it was to sit at a fireside and expand in its welcoming warmth. She was not shrewd but she understood instinctively why people acted as they did. Anabel was not outstandingly clever nor particularly intellectual, but she had a way of looking at people as she spoke to them which invested the straightforward, uncontrived things she said with significance and grace. She always asked precisely the questions a man was most anxious to answer. Perhaps it was her intensely personal voice, perhaps the rhythm of the words themselves, that explained the sense of utter agreeableness men found in the way she expressed herself. They looked forward to a peaceful chat with Anabel as they never looked forward to a *tête à tête* with women known to be far more brilliant and sparkling.

Anabel de Fourment had a *bounty* which made her only average prettiness seem like beauty. Her skin was flawless, and so were her teeth. Her hair was straight and Titian red and always incredibly clean. She had a wide, happy mouth, a rather long nose and nice gray green eyes, remarkable only for their kindness. Her body was so soft and supple, so subtly perfumed, so well-tended, that it was unimportant that she was always just a little too plump. Her breasts were sumptuous and her bottom was full and dimpled and no man ever noticed that she was short-waisted and just a bit dumpy.

Anabel had been born to an improvident French portrait painter, Albert de Fourment, the black sheep of a good, old provincial family of minor nobility. Her mother, a fey, rebellious daughter of a stuffy English lord, was an art student at the Slade who had hung around the fringes of Bloomsbury, trying wildly to be let into that feverish, incestuously tangled circle, but found herself only marginally accepted as an artist's model, valued for her beauty but judged of little talent. She married the first real artist who asked her, only to discover that his was merely a small talent, too, scarcely greater than her own.

Their only masterpiece was their daughter Anabel, whom they brought up on a diet of crusts and caviar. Anabel's earliest memories combined, in a confusing mixture of place, delicious, improvised meals in a shabby Paris studio where there was always enough wine for the multitude of guests, even if the food ran out, and Christmas visits to a grand English country house. There the little girl was allowed up for Boxing Day dinner, and looked with wonder at the grownups wearing evening gowns and funny paper hats, pulling snapping crackers and blowing horns at each other as if they were as young as she. As she grew older she decided, very quickly, that she liked the ease of her parents' bohemian life but didn't like being poor: that she liked the wealth of her grandparents, but didn't like doing what was expected of her.

Her only marriage, at sixteen, was a mistake. No amount of money could compensate for being as bored as she had been, Anabel decided. After her divorce at nineteen, she had been discovered by the first of the men who would be able to afford the enormous private extravagance of keeping Anabel. He was a member of the House of Lords, a friend of her grandfather's, a distinguished man in his sixties to whom she remained faithful for the last ten years of his life, years that were the best he'd ever known. It was he who introduced her to the succulent details of her true career, he who patiently educated her in the complex expertise of wine and food and cigars, he who hired a clever Frenchwoman to "maid" her, he who took her to Phillips of Bond Street and trained her to recognize and use only the best Georgian silver, he who explained why the banked fires of old, rose-cut diamonds were so much more becoming to her than anything from Cartier no matter how sumptuous. It was during those years with him that she learned that old money, aristocratic money, was the kind of money she understood. She hated all that was flashy and modern and obvious. The ambience she created always had, lingering in its perfumed leisure, the honeyed graciousness of some other better time than the present.

Anabel was not a daytime woman. She slept very late, lunched alone and spent much of every afternoon regulating the perfect functioning of her household and arranging large bunches of flowers in great, seemingly careless bouquets which gave all her rooms the feeling of being inside a Renoir. To her cook's jealous dismay, she particularly enjoyed marketing, personally picking out the ripest fruit, the best meat, the most aromatic cheeses. The merchants who enjoyed her custom saved their finest produce for her because Anabel de Fourment not only paid for quality but she made the transaction a pleasure in itself. She entertained frequently; small dinner parties of an interesting composition. The men were always invited by her protector, the women by Anabel. These women were wellborn—or at least always seemed to be—but either they were not English or they were not members of London society. They were a worldly, raffish, reckless, amusing lot and they set Anabel off as a collection of costume jewelry would set off one perfect gem. Her dinner parties became a delightful club to which only a few important men belonged, a club whose very existence was a secret. When Anabel needed a woman friend for woman talk, which wasn't often, she could always count on the members of her loyal, if unconventional coterie.

Somehow Anabel never looked chic or even elegant in her expensive day clothes. She knew it and didn't care in the slightest. She was at her best at twilight, in her own house. There she was superb. She spent a fortune on what her lingerie maker called "at-home garments," long robes of velvet, silk, chiffon and lace, of no particular period or style, brilliantly designed to expose the wonderful skin of her bosom with a flattery so subtle that it was never recognized. Her underclothes and nightgowns were custom-made for her with equal skills from a treasury of fabrics. Her bed linens were those of a queen and on them occurred an astounding number of what Anabel called, but only to herself, "nice, comfy fucks." She didn't much care about sex. She was a courtesan, not a full-blown *grande amoureuse*, a type who could be so showy and drearily full of troublesome passion, always getting involved and making messes. The worst thing that could happen to her, she knew, would be to fall profoundly in love. That was not at all her line of country. Young, ardent men were as schoolchildren to her, schoolchildren on whom she had no time to waste. Oh, she loved the sensuality of being made love to, but sexuality was another story—hardly worth the trouble it took. She purred and sighed and moaned softly and thought that really it *was* rather nice.

After the death of her first protector, Anabel found herself, at twenty-nine, in possession of a private income which, though generous, was not quite enough for her needs. The way she lived, unostentatious as it seemed to her, cost an astonishing amount of money. She also owned the leasehold, good for another eighty years, of a good-sized house in Eaton Square which presented to its neighbors a columned façade precisely like those of all the others in that grandest part of Belgravia, but, on the inside, was decorated with a concentration of comfort that few of them could boast. Although Anabel's quintessentially feminine presence was central to it, the house was, for all its greens and grays and taupe tones, for all its flowers and silver, profoundly a man's house.

She made plans for her future. She had no desire to ever marry again because marriage had been so excessively boring. She would have rather enjoyed a child or two, she thought, but babies were even more boring, if such a thing were possible, than marriage. She knew the limitations of her looks, just as well as any of the women who lunched together and picked her to pieces in irritation at not being able to understand why all their husbands and lovers found her so attractive. But she knew that simple truth that they could never comprehend: she could give the most complicated men simple happiness. A great courtesan in a day when courtesans were no longer in style? Bosh, thought Anabel. I'm a classic type—good forever. She had not the slightest doubt that the day when her kind of women went out of fashion would be the last day of civilization as she knew it. And after that, who cared?

Placidly, enjoying the privilege of selection, she waited for her next protector to identify himself, rejecting any homage which didn't please her fastidious tastes. In the following ten years she belonged to three men, one following the other, each in his own right as worthy as the lucky old lord who had formed her. Her private income did not grow, for none of them died, and the only gifts she ever accepted were of jewels or pictures, but she continued, in a time of inflation and rising taxation, to live as well as ever in utter disregard of money. In the late fall of 1955, she was thirty-nine and, for the moment, without anyone who could say she belonged to him.

"Anabel?"

"Sally, sweet Sally—how are you?" Anabel recognized the anxious American voice immediately. Sally Sands, scatty, droll Sally, was the London editor of an American fashion magazine and she was usually anxious, frequently over the nasty necessity of breaking a solemn engagement to be married. She had been engaged six times in the past two years.

"Anabel, would you do me an enormous favor?"

"If I can, but first tell me what it is. . . . Oh, well, all right, why not, after all?"

"Thank God. Then you'll be my maid of honor."

"Now, Sally, you've gone too far—that's utterly ridiculous." Anabel laughed her valuable laugh.

"Be serious . . . I need you, Anabel. *Please.* He's terribly British and I adore him and his family'll be there, but mine won't be, so you'll lend me class, darling—there's nobody else I know who would do at all."

"It's most unsuitable—maid of honor, indeed, when the bride's a mere twenty-six! But every year I do go to *some* sort of wedding just to reaffirm my belief that holy wedlock isn't for me—and your wedding will do as well—in fact, probably better—than any."

"Oh, but Anabel, this is the real thing." Sally reproached her.

"Of course, poppet, for you, but I just don't believe in the drill myself. It's not going to be a big do, is it? I don't have to carry your train or something?"

"Just a Registry Office for now. We'll have a church wedding back home. He's a viscount and I couldn't cheat mother of that. Afterward, I'm planning a little, simple reception at the Savoy."

"Oh, no, Sally, I don't think a hotel is ever really much good. The walls reek of too many other parties. I'll give the reception here—it'll be my wedding present to you."

"Oh, I was hoping you'd say that! Anabel, thank you!"

"I know you were." Anabel laughed again. She liked to be generous in anticipation of being asked a favor.

"Just don't change your mind again, Sally. I've never given a wedding reception before and I don't want to have to cancel it at the last minute and drink all the champagne myself."

"I promise, Anabel, *honestly*. Oh, you're an angel!"

"Sally, one thing . . ."

"Yes?"

"Relax."

"Relax? My God, you're amazing. How can I relax at a time like this?" Sally's voice scaled new peaks of anxiety.

"Sit down in a chair and say 'viscountess' over and over for a half-hour . . . that should be very relaxing indeed."

The Registry Office had been as unromantic a place as you could find for a wedding, Anabel thought, surveying with satisfaction the success of the reception she had arranged. The groom's entire entourage had brightened visibly as they had entered her flower-filled house and now, hours later, stuffed with caviar and pâté and an elaborate cold buffet, they were making a real party out of it. The bride and groom as well as the tall, grand parade of the groom's relatives had long since left, but the remaining guests had passed into the stage of singing old songs.

Apparently, the men had all served in the war together, Anabel decided, since her drawing room now was filled with musical sounds from an airforce film of the late 1940s. Fortunately, she didn't have the kind of breakable objects around with which many women filled their homes.

She had been too busy being a maid of honor, a duty which had finally boiled down, as she had fully expected, into forcing a recalcitrant, hysterical Sally to show up for the wedding, to pay much attention to the other members of the wedding party. She kept a stern eye on Sally until the final vows were said and then raced home to change and be ready to greet the reception guests. The small, simple reception Sally had spoken of had ballooned, once she knew that Anabel was giving it, to a party of over a hundred guests, and now Anabel patiently waited until the last song had been sung and the last bottle drained, to usher her guests out.

Finally, after midnight, she went upstairs to her bedroom. As usual, her maid had taken off the heavy, yellow damask bedspread and turned back the lace-trimmed sheets, made of linen so smooth that it felt like silk. As usual, her chiffon nightgown was spread on the bed and her embroidered slippers were on the carpet. But, not as usual, there was a man asleep in her bed, face down on the mattress, his naked shoulders burrowed snugly under her white wool blankets.

The next time Sally gets married she can jolly well have her reception at the Savoy, Anabel thought. Helplessly she looked at the morning coat, one sleeve inside out, the striped trousers, the shirt, the four-in-hand, the shiny black shoes, even socks, and God save us, undershorts, all strewn on her carpet. She started to ring for the maid and decided against it. No point in waking the butler either. He and the cook had had a busy day, even with the caterers doing most of the work. She went to the bed and inspected the usurper. From the color of his hair she realized it was the best man. Their only exchange had been one vivid flash, an ironic look they had exchanged during the ceremony which conveyed that they both shared an equally dim view of the entire performance.

Well, she thought, he *had* seemed a gentleman, and she was damned if she was going to make up a bed in one of the guest rooms at this hour. She undressed in the bathroom, put on her nightgown and slipped into the other side of the big bed. At least he doesn't snore, she thought, and went to sleep.

Sometime during the night Stash woke and realized he was in bed with a sleeping woman whose identity was unclear . . . in fact, unknown. Since this was no novelty he went back to sleep.

Both Stash and Anabel woke late, within a few seconds of each other. She leaned on her elbow, her dark red hair spread loose on her shoulders, and said, "Shall I ring for breakfast, Prince Valensky, or don't you feel up to anything but an Alka-Seltzer?"

"Breakfast, please, Miss de Fourment."

"Eggs? Coddled in cream? Freshly-baked croissants? Irish ham? And honey? In the comb?"

"Please."

"Tea or coffee?"

"Tea, please."

"You're very polite this morning. I'll say that for you."

Anabel spoke on the bedside phone which was connected to the kitchen and ordered.

"You wouldn't happen to have a bathrobe handy . . . a man's robe?"

"Certainly not. I live alone."

Stash got out of bed, stalked naked to the bathroom, and closed the door behind him. Anabel rocked with laughter in the bed. The test would be what he wore when he came back. She had huge towels piled in heaps by the tub. The bathroom door opened and he returned to bed, as naked as before. He'd passed one test, at least, and very, very handsomely indeed, she thought.

"Good morning, Marie," she said to the maid who entered with one tray. Landon, the butler, stood behind her carrying the other.

"Good morning, Madame."

"Marie, give that tray to the Prince. Landon, that's for me. Yes, here, thank you. Is the sun out?"

"Lovely day, Madame. Shall I open the curtains?"

"No, thank you, Landon. I'll ring if I need you." She poured herself a cup of tea. Stash ate with concentration.

"Wonderful eggs," he said.

"My dairy man keeps chickens and lets me have them the day they're laid."

"Really."

"Really."

"Stop laughing at me," he said fiercely.

"You're so terribly funny. Why shouldn't I laugh?"

"I'm not used to it. I don't like it."

"Oh, God. You do take yourself seriously." She laughed harder than ever.

"Look, the morning after you've slept with a man, you don't treat him as if he's the new comic from the Palladium. It's simply bad manners, if nothing else."

Now it looked as if her laughter was going to pitch over the tray, if not cause her to fall out of bed. Stash put their trays on the floor, grabbed her and shook her. Anabel subsided enough to gasp out three words.

"But we *didn't* . . ."

"Well, that was a mistake. Set that right in no time."

"Damned if you will. You're not my type."

"Try and stop me."

She couldn't. In fact, she reflected, hours later, she probably, in all fairness, hadn't tried as hard as she might have. Although he had made her miss breakfast—and lunch as well.

Anabel de Fourment, Stash realized, was exactly, precisely, positively what he needed. And what he needed, he got.

It wasn't that easy. It took him another month of proper courtship before she would allow him more than a goodnight kiss. And still another month before she allowed him back in her bed. Anabel could be taken by surprise only once . . . after that the game was played on her terms. There were practicalities which had to be settled first . . . certain financial understandings which had to be reached, provisions made. Once all of her exceptionally stringent conditions had been met, and properly, she permitted herself to wonder if perhaps she would have taken him on for nothing. Just for fun. No, probably not—she couldn't afford that sort of luxury. But there had been a moment of temptation, about which she'd never tell him. Stash didn't want to be responsible for a woman's emotions, and, from the very little he'd told her, she could understand why.

With Stash came an occasional bonus; infrequent visits from his son, Ram, who was now eleven, and in school at Eton. There was something irreducibly stubborn and unreachable in his dark, slim face, that troubled Anabel's kind heart.

Ram's mother, Stash's wartime bride, had remarried and lived in a half-tumbled-down castle in Scotland. Occasionally the boy spent a rare school holiday with his father, whenever Stash was in London. The relationship between the boy and the man was as strained as such arrangements were bound to make them. Stash hadn't seen Ram grow up, he hardly knew how to communicate with him. The boy already bore him animus because of the small, malicious remarks his mother had made for as long as he could remember; he felt neglected when, as often happened, his father was away playing polo during those times when he could have visited him; he felt cast off from his rightful heritage when he compared the way in which Stash lived with the shabby, faded, ramshackle Scottish life which he had to share with three half-sisters and a stepfather he didn't like.

And yet he had such towering pride in being a Prince Valensky! He had cultivated this pride as one cultivates an ultimate, only possession. During his three years at Eton, he had had the bad luck to fall in with a crowd where the choice was clearly to bully or be bullied. Of course he had become a bully, strong as he was, with his father's soldier's temper. He had lessened the disadvantage of a foreign name by stressing the fact that he was a prince, rubbing their noses in it, making up tales about his ancestors when the real ones would have been more than impressive enough, had he but known them.

At eleven he was well grown, but with a tightness, a withheld quality in his approach to people which didn't go with his age. A diffuse, generalized, but biting envy of happy people—all happy people—made him shy and guarded, quick to amass grudges and hoard bitterness. He knew, without articulating the exact words, that he had been cheated—cheated since he was born, and he chewed over that fact endlessly. It was a constant, dark rhythm which went with him everywhere.

And yet his face betrayed nothing. He was an exceptionally beautiful boy with none of the Valensky blondness except for his gray eyes which looked so much like Stash's eyes that Anabel was drawn to Ram immediately. He was dark, like everyone in his mother's family, with skin so olive and a nose already so aquiline and haughty that he could almost have passed for one of those young Hindu maharajas whose labyrinthian genealogies stretched back thousands of years and were known only to the Brahman priests in the sacred town of Nasik. He was a boy of mystery, Anabel decided, an unhappy boy, and it went against everything in her nature to have an unhappy male of any age in her vicinity. She bent all her arts and wisdom to making a friend of Ram. Soon he loved her, as much as he was able to love, and he found, when she invited him to special private lunches alone with her in her house, a spontaneity and well-being he hadn't known before. Only with Anabel could he stop envying happy people because with her, he became—for a short while—one of them.

8

When Francesca had fled Lausanne with the twins and Masha, her only clear intention had been to get away from Stash. But, as she flew westward, to New York, she realized that the only people in the world who could help her now were the Firestones. As soon as they had passed through customs at Idlewild she telephoned Matty in Hollywood and asked her former agent to meet her at the airport in Los Angeles.

"Please, Matty, don't ask me any questions. I'll tell you everything when I get there," she begged.

"But hon . . . never mind . . . we'll be there, don't worry." I knew she'd be back, he thought, as he hung up the phone. I knew that shit would make her miserable. But none of his premonitions prepared either Matty or Margo for the sight of two babies. Their astonishment went beyond questions, particularly since Francesca and Masha were both so exhausted by the hours of travel that they were too tired to make sense. The Firestones drove the huddle of women and infants back to their home as fast as they could and fed them and put them all to bed at once.

"Now sleep! We'll talk about it in the morning," Margo ordered.

As soon as she woke up, Francesca told the Firestones the whole story, pouring out the words with fresh incredulity. During the achingly long trip, in order to shepherd her band to safety, she had had to concentrate on practical details and prevent herself from dwelling on the facts she had discovered so recently, but now, as she put the words together for Matty and Margo, she became hysterical. Only Margo's assurance that there existed a safe place for her and her children kept her from breaking down.

"We'll go there tomorrow," Matty said.

"No, *now!* I can't stay here—he'll find me here!"

"But it's a six-hour drive, hon."

"Can we make it if we leave in fifteen minutes? We haven't even unpacked."

Matty glanced at Margo, and then turned back to Francesca. "Sure—so we'll arrive after dark—no big deal, we'll turn on the lights."

In Matty's big Cadillac they drove up Route 101 to Carmel. There Matty turned back down the coast, taking Route 1, the narrow, twisting, dangerous coast road, and drove thirty miles to a vacation cabin he and Margo owned in the Ventana Wilderness of Big Sur.

The cabin, almost invisible from the steeply rising dirt road which climbed up to it, was built of weathered, local redwood. It had running water, electricity and heat since the Firestones had discovered that even in the summer Big Sur can be bitterly cold at night. Margo had furnished it with sturdy American antiques from Carmel and had used old quilts for bed covers and upholstery. From the small clearing of wild grasses in front of the cabin, which was tucked among redwoods, aspens and sycamores, there was a view straight out over the Pacific Ocean, a thousand feet below. At that height the wild waves and breakers flattened out and the ocean looked calm and harmless.

When Francesca gazed down at the sea on the following morning, she saw a coastline that is not equaled for elemental beauty anywhere on earth. She sensed that gods and goddesses had walked there and she felt an intimation of safety beginning to grow in her. She had never been to Greece but something about the absolute serenity of the steep wooded knolls that rose directly from the water made Francesca feel that this was a place protected by forces of which she knew nothing. The cabin was part of nature. After the Firestones went back to Los Angeles, black-tail deer began to appear at the edge of the clearing and the coast jays soon learned to join them when Francesca and Masha fed the babies outdoors, stealing food from their plates.

There, in the Ventana Wilderness, Francesca held her little household together. Sometimes in the all but overwhelming remoteness of the Big Sur country, Francesca thought that she had bitten right out into the very edge of her soul and that the next day would find her with no more courage, no more patience, no more strength to give to her children, but she never broke. *Intact.* That was the word that was always on her mind. Year after year she kept them intact; Daisy, who crackled so with energy that when Francesca managed to capture one of her busy hands she expected to receive an electric shock, and Dani, who, at three and a half, could walk upstairs only if she held on to the railing, and then only by putting one foot on each tread and then the other so that it took her an eternity to creep to her bedroom; Daisy who sang long, rhyming songs to anyone who would listen and could name every animal in the picture books and every flower in the woods and could put away every object in the kitchen in its proper place and take her own bath and brush her own teeth; and Dani who built towers only two blocks high, who knew how to turn three or four pages of a book at once, but never managed one page at a time, and who understood only the simplest of verbal instructions.

Yet it was with Dani that Francesca found her most peaceful and harmonious moments. Dani's eyes, like a baby's eyes, seemed to remember something of a previous life which couldn't be communicated, but which reassured and comforted her. Dani's vulnerability was her strength, since no one saw her without feeling the impulse to protect her. Dani was never unhappy because she was never frustrated. If she couldn't do something, she didn't bang furiously on the table the way Daisy did when she first discovered that she didn't know how to read. Dani didn't ask endless questions, didn't plague Francesca with demands to climb a tree, catch an earthworm, make cookies, train a hummingbird, take a walk in the woods and collect pebbles on the beach—all in the same breath, as Daisy did.

Every week Margo or Matty Firestone would telephone to find out how they were faring, and Francesca was able, with honesty, to tell them that all was well with her. She was so caught up in the intensity of her maternal feelings that she had no time to regret the years during which she had been a movie star or the months during which she had been a princess. Love for Daisy and Danielle—and fear for them—isolated her more than any other emotion she had ever known. She, who had had within her something as powerful as a huge magnet that had irresistibly attracted many, many men into her field of force, now allowed that magnet to become just another piece of inert material. Occasionally she would consider briefly her solitary life, hidden from the world, and remember the days when she had loved Stash. She would murmur a few lines from Hamlet—

There lies within the very flame of love
A kind of wick or snuff that will abate it,

—and return to the present, remembering only that Ophelia had always been a part she had disliked.

"I don't understand her," Matty said to Margo. "How can a woman like that not go totally bananas stuck up there all alone with only Masha and the kids to keep her company? What kind of life is it for her, I ask you? It doesn't make sense."

"She's playing the greatest role of her life," Margo answered.

"Bullshit. That's what you said when she was doing the princess number."

"Matty, you really still don't get it, do you? That whole princess thing was a lightweight farce compared to being the tigress mother. Now she has those two precious babies to protect and bring up and she doesn't *need* anything else—not men or acting or even friends. It'll change as they get older, I guess, but right now she's absorbed in them to the exclusion of everything. Nothing, *nothing* has any other meaning for her."

"That was some great idea you had, to take her to Europe," Matty sighed in incurable despair. "If it hadn't been for that trip she'd still be the greatest star in the business . . ."

"Don't look back, Matty. It doesn't help."

Daisy had started to talk a steady stream of jargon at about fifteen months, spaced with clear-cut, well-pronounced names and a few demands. By the age of two she was spontaneously combining words into short sentences, using pronouns and verbalizing her immediate experience. "Daisy not afraid of thunder," she would announce, grabbing Masha's hand and squeezing it hard. Anxiously, Francesca waited for signs of speech development in Dani, who could say "Mama," "Asha" for Masha and "Day" for Daisy, but instead she heard only occasional sounds which were utterly without meaning, gibberish composed of distorted and unarticulated syllables. She waited and patiently tried to teach Dani, but the little girl added only a few basic words—like "yes" and "no" and "bird" and "hot"—to her vocabulary. However, to Francesca's horror, Daisy started to use Dani's gibberish. She listened, fear cold in her bones, as the twins communicated with each other in the way of idiots. She was afraid to say anything about it to Daisy, hoping that if she didn't mention the strange phenomenon it would go away. Instead, it got worse. Finally, when they had passed their third birthday, Francesca asked, as casually as possible, "Daisy, what are you and Dani talking about?"

"She wanted to play with my dolly but when I gave it to her she didn't want it anymore."

"Why do you talk to Dani that way, Daisy?"

"What way?"

"The way you just did—all those funny noises. Not the way you talk to me."

"But that's just the way she talks, Mama."

"Can you understand everything she says?"

"Of course."

"What else do you talk about?"

"I don't know." Daisy looked puzzled. "We just talk."

That night, as she was putting the twins to bed, Francesca heard the strange sounds start up again.

"What did she say just now, Daisy?"

"Dani said, more kiss. That means she wants you to give her another goodnight kiss."

"Couldn't you teach her to say kiss, Daisy, the way you say it?"

"I don't know. I don't think so."

"Will you try?"

"Yes, Mama. More kiss for me, too?"

That night Francesca spoke to Masha about the twins' strange form of communication.

"Yes, I've noticed it many, many times, Madame," Masha answered slowly. "It reminds me of something from Russia—something I heard when I was growing up—it must have been about fifty years ago. There were twins—boys they were—who lived in the village nearest to ours and I still remember my mother and my aunt whispering to each other about them. The twins talked to each other all the time in a language nobody could understand. People thought perhaps they were . . . they didn't know—"

"Were they normal, Masha?"

"Oh, yes, Madame. They stopped doing it when they got older and by the time they were six or so everyone thought they had just forgotten it. They talked just like everyone else. But then I left, to go to St. Petersburg, and that's all I can tell you—about them or about anyone else in that village," she finished sadly.

Francesca knew few other people to consult about this problem, or any other problem in her life. She was living in the most isolated way possible, except for the phone calls from Matty and Margo. Francesca understood that if reporters were to come across the fact that Francesca Vernon Valensky lived in Big Sur with two identical twin children, she would be hounded to the ends of the earth, until the whole evil story was discovered. She was not protecting Stash, but protecting Daisy from ever knowing what her father had done.

Whenever she had to drive into Carmel for supplies that couldn't be found in the tiny general store that supplied the few, scattered permanent residents of the area, she left both children at home with Masha and wore such concealing clothes and head scarfs and sunglasses that she was never recognized. She dared not make friends. No friends, old or new, could be trusted except Matty and Margo. She lived frugally, accepting the cabin without shame, for her children's sake. One by one, through Margo, she sold the jeweled flowers in the crystal vases. Each object was worth only some fifteen hundred dollars to a Beverly Hills dealer, but fifteen hundred dollars could keep the four of them for six months. She guarded the lapis egg for last, when the flowers would be gone. Margo had described it to a salesman at *A la Vieille Russie* in New York, who said that if it were genuine Fabergé it might be worth up to twenty or thirty thousand dollars to them. That it was genuine Francesca didn't doubt—it was her only security. She cursed herself to sleep night after night thinking of the jewels she had so proudly and foolishly left behind, thinking of the money she had made in Hollywood and casually spent, every penny of it, on clothes and cars and books and extravagant presents to her parents and friends.

From time to time Matty would send her a script some hopeful producer had given him to "pass on if you can." For the first three years Francesca refused all these offers without thinking about it because she couldn't dream of leaving Masha alone to cope with the two children for months at a time.

Two years after Francesca's flight, Stash had a letter from Matty Firestone. He was informed that Francesca believed that Daisy, now three years old, needed to know her father. She would permit him to visit the child four times a year, for three consecutive days, four hours at a time, provided that he do so without making any attempt to see Francesca or discover where she lived. He was told to go to the Highlands Inn in Carmel and wait.

Stash left London that same morning. A few hours after he arrived, the desk clerk told him that he had visitors. In the rustic lobby Masha was waiting for him with Daisy holding her hand tightly.

There was no sign of Francesca or Danielle. Stash asked Masha no questions, none at all, and she volunteered nothing but a quiet greeting to the man she had once suckled at her breast.

At the end of the first hours with his strong, brave and beautiful daughter, Stash drew pictures for her, stick figures of a man and a little girl adorned with big red hearts. He explained to her that whenever she received one of these in the mail it would mean that he had been thinking about her every day. He mailed one every two or three days until his next visit. The minute he was alone with her he asked her if she had received them.

"Yes, Daddy."

"Do you like to get them?"

"Yes."

"Do you remember what they mean?"

"That you think about me."

"Do you keep them?"

"Oh, yes, Daddy, I keep them."

"Where do you keep them, Daisy darling?"

"I give them to Dani."

"Oh."

"She likes to play with them."

"Daisy, let's go and look at the kitten."

Each time that he returned to London from California, Stash willed himself not to start counting the weeks until he could see Daisy again. He failed utterly. He was unable to resist the temptation of consulting a judge he knew personally, telling him nothing of the existence of Danielle, but merely explaining that after his separation, his wife had restricted his access to his child. The only remedies open to him, he soon was made to understand, would have to involve publicity. Stash was advised to wait. Often, in cases such as his, as a child grows older, access is made easier, particularly as the child herself can be influenced more strongly as she gains in maturity. So he waited, with the same wolfish, undefeated yet helplessly impotent fury that he had known during his first year in the RAF; yet he never contemplated anything but victory. If not now, then soon.

By the time Daisy was five, the child was providing real help around the cabin, making both her bed and Dani's, cleaning the room they shared, drying dishes, watering and expertly weeding the vegetable garden. Francesca, who had just received a letter from Matty enclosing yet another script, a good one, explained to Daisy that she might have to go away for a short time to do some work which would earn some money for all of them, but that she would be back very, very soon. "How long?" Daisy asked fearfully.

"Only six weeks," Francesca answered and Daisy burst into tears.

"Daisy," Francesca reproached her, "you're old enough to understand now. Six weeks isn't very long and I'll come home as soon as they're over. Just six Sundays and six Mondays . . . it's not so much."

"And six Tuesdays and six Wednesdays," Daisy said sadly. "Would you make a lot of money, Mama?"

"Yes, darling."

"And then you'd come right home?"

"Yes, darling, the minute the work is finished."

"All right, Mama, I understand," Daisy said reluctantly.

Later, Daisy and Dani exchanged a long stream of sibilant babble, with Daisy saying almost everything and Dani asking what obviously were questions. At the end of the conversation Dani, who could walk perfectly well by now, went down on all fours, like a baby, crawled into a corner of the room, pulled up a rag rug, and lay under it, her silent, wretched little face turned toward the wall.

"Daisy? What did you say?" Francesca demanded, alarmed.

"I told her what you explained to me, Mama. She didn't understand. I couldn't make her understand. I tried and tried, really I tried. She doesn't know what coming back *means*—she doesn't understand about earning money."

"Try again!"

"I tried . . . now she won't listen to me. Oh, Mama, I tried so hard."

"All right . . . it's all right, Daisy darling. I don't really have to go away. It was just an idea. Would you tell Dani that I'm not leaving, that I'm not going anywhere?"

Daisy put her arms around her mother's neck and pressed her warm, soft face into Francesca's cheek. "Don't be sad, Mama. Please don't be sad. I'll help you work. I'll help you make some money. I promise I will."

Francesca looked at the courageous little figure with the eyes like flowers, her white-blonde hair in one long braid which reached halfway to her waist, her tan knees scratched from adventurous rambles in the deep forest, her hands beginning to lose their baby fat, to become capable, caring and strong.

"I know you will." She smiled without a trace of sadness. "We'll figure out something . . . something fun."

"Can't we ask Daddy?"

"No! Daisy, that's the one thing we can never, never do."

"Why not?"

"I'll explain—when you're older."

"Oh," said Daisy, with an air of resignation. "That's one more thing I have to remember, for you to explain when I'm older."

"Do I say that a lot?"

"Yes, Mama. But it's all right. Don't be sad again."

Suddenly Daisy changed the subject. "Mama, am I really and truly a princess? Daddy said I was."

"Yes, you are."

"Is Danielle a princess?"

"Of course she is—how could you be a princess if Dani weren't a princess too?"

"But you, Mama, are you a queen?"

"No, Daisy, I'm not a queen."

"But in stories the mother of a princess is always queen," she said stubbornly.

"Once—I was a princess, too, Daisy," Francesca murmured.

" 'Once'. . . . Aren't you a princess anymore?"

"Daisy, Daisy, it's too complicated for you to understand right now. And anyway, it's just a word, it doesn't mean anything really, nothing important, nothing for you to bother about. We don't live in a world of princesses here—just the two of us and Masha and Dani and the deer and the birds—Isn't that good enough for you, my Daisy?"

Something about Francesca's face told Daisy to agree with her mother. But it wasn't good enough for her, she didn't understand it at all and no one seemed to ever give her an answer to her most important questions, particularly the ones she had never dared to bring up: why did her father only come to see her at long intervals? Why did he never see Dani? And most important of all, what had she, Daisy, *done wrong* to make him go away each time after only a few days? It was never discussed, never even hinted at, and somehow she understood that she must never ask, never.

"Masha, look, I've shelled all the peas."

"How many did you eat, little one?"

"Only six. Eight. Maybe ten."

"I know, they are better raw. I always thought so, too."

"Oh, Masha, you know everything!"

"Ah, will you tell me that in ten years?"

"Masha, Masha . . . why is Dani different from me?"

"What . . . what do you mean?"

"She's my twin sister. That means we were born at the same time. Mama told me that. That's what twins are, two babies in the same mother. But Dani doesn't talk like me and she can't really run like me—not as fast—and she can't climb trees and she's afraid of thunder and rain and birds and she doesn't draw pictures like me or cut her own meat, and she can't count like me, or tie her own shoes. Why, Masha?"

"Oh, Daisy, I don't know."

"Yes, you do, Masha, you know. Mama won't tell me but you will. You always tell me everything."

"Daisy, you were born first, that's all I know."

"*Born first?*" Daisy was astonished. "Twins are born together, that's what makes them twins. You're silly, Masha."

"No, Daisy, one twin is born after the other. You are both in the same mother, the way your Mama told you, but one has to come out of the mother first and then the other. You were born first."

"So it is my fault." She spoke slowly, as if something she had long suspected had, at last, been confirmed by adult authority.

"Don't be silly, little one, it's God's will, not anybody's fault. You should know better than to talk like that! Daisy?"

"Yes, Masha?"

"You understand, don't you?"

"I understand, Masha." Yes, she understood. She *had* been born first so it *was* her fault. Masha always talked about God's will, but Daisy knew that when Masha said that it meant that Masha didn't understand either.

As 1957 wore on, the winter storms brought driftwood to the hidden beaches of Big Sur, wild, windswept beaches where sandpipers jittered and great waves carved strange bridges out of giant rocks; where sea lions often roared; beaches from which migrating whales could be sometimes seen in their benign, silent flotillas.

Francesca had found a craftsman in Carmel who made lamps out of driftwood and she made a little money collecting it from the beaches, polishing the best pieces and bringing them in to him from time to time. She usually went alone to the beach, but one early spring day in 1958, she took Daisy and Dani with her. She left Dani in Daisy's charge and wandered along the beach, one piece of driftwood luring her to another, until she suddenly realized that the children were out of sight.

"Dear God!" She ran back the way she'd come and stopped suddenly. Daisy was sitting on the warm sand out of range of even the farthest lapping wave. She held Dani in her little lap, awkwardly since they were almost the same size. Their sixth birthday was only a week away. Daisy was rocking Dani back and forth and from the shape of her mouth, Francesca could see that she was singing to her sister. From time to time Daisy patted her hand over Dani's hair and kissed her cheek, with a maternal gesture. Dani's beautiful face wore its usual sweet, contented expression. A great inner peace descended on Francesca, a feeling of joy so simple and so deep that she almost fell on her knees. She had been right. She had done the only possible thing. She had been blessed.

One week later Stash received a long-distance call from Matty Firestone in California. The agent was sobbing unashamedly.

"You get here as quickly as you can. Francesca's gone . . . she's dead. She was driving back from Carmel, on the ocean side, Route One, I always warned her—some madman in a pickup truck swung wide, she went off the road . . . into the sea."

"*Daisy!*" Stash screamed.

"Francesca was alone. I went up and brought Masha and the kids back. They're here at our house. Come and get them, Valensky. . . . You're all they've got left, God help them."

9

On a spring Sunday in London in 1963, Stash Valensky and Daisy, who was now eleven, entered the Connaught Hotel for their regular Sunday lunch alone together.

Lunch at the Connaught is one of the premiere experiences of Western civilization, the Uffizi Gallery of dining, and Stash, still absorbed in taming his invincible child, thought that the Connaught, with its richly subdued air of comfy pomp, its air of being not a hotel but a lordly private house, in which one always feels the subliminal ticking of a soberly friendly Victorian grandfather clock, provided the best atmosphere for his purpose. The doorman greeted them as old friends; they walked through the small, deeply carpeted, russet-toned lobby dominated by a sweeping, prodigiously polished flight of mahogany stairs, and turned right to pass through the corridor which led to the restaurant, recognized as one of three finest in England. As usual, Stash had to keep a firm hand on Daisy's elbow, for the passageway was lined with a series of tables bearing silver platters laden with a dozen different kinds of cold hors d'oeuvres, melons, salads, lobsters, stuffed crab and a selection of game pies. The tables laden with food were crowded in that wide corridor, which also held a little mirrored bar and tall vases of spring flowers, in a way that suggested an overflowing abundance that caused Daisy to linger inquiringly over each dish, trying to decide, even before she read the menu, what looked most interesting today.

The restaurant had walls of highly waxed, dark honey-colored wood, on which glowed crystal sconces with apricot shades. The chairs and banquettes were covered with burgundy-striped velvet and large screens broke the restaurant up into sections, at the same time imparting an Alice in Wonderland feeling to the substantial room since the bases of the screens were carved wood to the height of a seated diner, but above they were made of engraved glass, so that standing up, one could see through them. Stash and Daisy's favorite table was in the center of the restaurant rather than at one of the banquettes because it provided a vantage point from which they could see all their fellow gourmets and speculate on them.

Many people looked up from their plates as they entered. Stash had changed almost not at all. At fifty-two, his hair was as blond, as thick and as close cropped as ever; his features as strongly marked with an air of valor and resolution. Alone, he would have attracted attention, but with Daisy he aroused the most lively inspection, even in this sanctuary of solid, upper-class lack of curiosity, for she was a child out of fairyland. Daisy was five feet tall now and possessed the slim roundness of prepuberty which is so tender, so free of the slightest fault, so pristine and yet so full of rushing life, that it causes the most hardened adults to give a sigh for a vanquished vulnerability and strength they must have once possessed. She wore an ivory dress of the thinnest wool challis printed with clusters of pale pink flowers and pale green leaves. It was pleated down the front, with a sash that tied in the back, and the collar was like a little garland around her neck, where the flowers of the dress had been cut out and thickly appliquéd.

Her gilt-blonde hair almost reached her waist and it was brushed back and held by a simple band, but nothing could restrain the individual curls that sprang from her forehead and escaped above her ears. The light coming from the great Victorian windows of Carlos Place seemed to attack Daisy's hair, snatching and catching it with a rollicking freedom, all the planes and shafts of the watery spring sun finding an object worthy of their focus. It was the hair of an old-fashioned heroine, tresses that looked as if they had been lovingly brushed by a mother and admired and envied by aunts and sisters; hair precious enough to be kept in lockets and treasured for decades.

Stash guided her to their table with an air of possession that he couldn't conceal. He cherished Daisy in a way that deeply frightened him. He had long ago learned that it was unbearably dangerous to invest so much emotional capital in another human being, but he was helpless in the face of the mere existence of this daughter of his, this treasure he had almost lost, this obstinate, bold-hearted, loving female creature he had worshiped from the first, never-to-be-forgotten sight of her, as he had never worshiped another female in all his life.

Now, in Daisy, he saw himself as a young boy, the forever lost, forever innocent, forever hopeful self which can only be recaptured in a dream, the forgotten self that vanishes as one wakes, leaving only a feeling of impossible brightness and unreasoning happiness, a feeling that rarely lingers for more than a few seconds.

As the tail-coated waiter handed Daisy the white menu bordered in brown and gold, with the date printed at the bottom, she gave a sign of anticipation, although she knew it nearly by heart now, after almost three years of such lunches. She had long since passed the stage of chicken pie, of lamb chops, even of roast sirloin of Scottish beef, the three favorites on which she had first settled. Stash had, in the beginning, tried to lead her carefully through the menu, but he quickly found out that there was no way he could convince or cajole her into ordering something new. She had no interest in "training her taste buds," she said to him, repeating his pedantic phrase with a teasing look. He often wondered where his nimble girl, who never faltered in her attempts to make her own decisions, had learned to be so adamant in those backwoods in which she had spent those early years of her life. But even when she was first confronted by the grandeur of the service of the Connaught, Daisy's smile informed the maître d'hôtel that she represented no one on earth but herself and that since she had wanted chicken pie every Sunday for a year, that was what she would order.

"Well, Princess Daisy," the maître d'hôtel greeted her with relish, "what is your choice today?"

"What," she asked, "is the '*croustade d'oeufs de caille Maintenon*' besides eggs?"

"Tiny quail eggs, served with creamed mushrooms and hollandaise on little pastry *barquettes*."

"Daisy, you had eggs for breakfast. Why don't you start with some smoked Scotch salmon?" Stash asked.

"That's listed under the 'extras,' Father," Daisy rebuked him gravely.

Stash sighed inwardly. No matter how often he explained to her that she was permitted to order from the extras, she never would. Her habits of thrift, learned so young, couldn't be forgotten even in this restaurant in which the final bill would represent such an astonishing total that one or two extra dishes wouldn't be noticed. She went to the Connaught because he took her there, but nothing he could say had ever convinced her to order an extra, not even the *Salade Caprice des Années Folles*, surely the most delightfully named dish in the world.

"If I might suggest," said the maître d'hôtel, "the trolley of hors d'oeuvres so that you have your choice, and then, perhaps, the lobster grilled with herbs—we have just received a superb shipment from France—"

"Are they still alive?" asked Daisy.

"But of course! They *must* be alive before we cook them."

"I'll have a Lancashire hot pot then," announced Daisy, not knowing what on earth it was but determined not to directly cause the immediate death of a single lobster.

Ah, thought the headwaiter, Prince Valensky must take care. If the little girl should become, disaster of disasters, a vegetarian, we might not see her every Sunday.

Lunch finally ordered, Daisy and Stash settled into the easy conversations he enjoyed now more than any other single thing in his life. He was teaching her his world, little by little, and she, in turn, brought him all the excitements of her life at school and acquainted him with the small adventures of her friends. But today she had something special on her mind.

"Father, in your opinion, do I have to do maths?" asked Daisy.

"Naturally—they teach it in school, don't they?"

"Yes, but I hate it and I can't study my maths and do a proper job on my new pony. How can I ride Merlin every afternoon after school and then muck out her stall and turn over her bedding, groom her with the curry comb and vacuum her all over and use the body brush and the rub rag and the hoof pick and . . ."

"All that takes exactly one half-hour and you know it," Stash said, laughing at the dramatically detailed list she'd presented him in the hope that he'd be impressed. "You still have time for maths."

Daisy, a seasoned strategist, abandoned Merlin instantly. "Anabel says she doesn't see why I have to do maths—she never did and she says she never missed it. Anabel says she's never balanced a checkbook in her life and the only reason for maths is to balance checkbooks or find out if the fishmonger is cheating you and if you tell him he is, you won't get the best fish so you might as well resign yourself."

"So Anabel has become your authority on education?"

"Anabel is my authority on many things," said Daisy with dignity. "However, if you gave me three good reasons why I have to do maths, I'd try, even though I think there's something missing in the place in my brain where most people have maths."

"I'll give you only one good reason because I don't need another—Lady Alden *requires* that all girls at her school do maths."

"I think it's most unreasonable of Lady Alden . . . most unreasonable," Daisy grumbled.

"Did Anabel teach you to say things are unreasonable?"

"No, you did. You said it was most unreasonable of me to want to jump Merlin over the railings in Wilton Crescent." Daisy's face crinkled in mischief. She changed her moods so rapidly that Stash sometimes wondered if he was talking to a child, a grown woman, a scruffy farmboy or a sage member of Parliament.

"I'm afraid you're a pagan, Daisy."

"I wouldn't mind. Don't they dance around trees and do strange things when the moon is full?"

"I believe those were Druids. Pagans are like the ancient Greeks or Romans, people who worshiped many gods, not just one."

"Oh, good, I think I'd like to be one. Like you are, Father."

Heading her off this unpromising subject Stash asked quickly, "How's Merlin getting used to the stable?" Merlin, the latest in a series of ponies, each taller than the last, was named after Stash's old favorite, now retired from the fray. Daisy's horse was stabled in Grosvenor Crescent Mews, a few minutes away from Wilton Row, where the Valensky house was located. The stable had been run by Mrs. Leila Blum for twenty years. It was dark, with cobbled floors, and Merlin occupied one of the four loose-boxes rather than a less spacious stall where she would have to be tied up.

"She's as happy as the day is long," Daisy said importantly. "There're a few black cats hanging about and she gets along very well with them, but Merlin really and *truly* wants a dog. She *craves* a dog, passionately."

"She does, does she? Did she say what kind of dog?"

"Just a dog."

"She 'craves' it passionately?"

"Absolutely."

"Something tells me that Merlin's been talking to Anabel."

"No, Father, she communicates with me. You know horses can, if they like."

"Hmmm. Daisy, isn't it time for a sweet?"

Daisy inspected her father's face closely. For three years she had been trying to get him to buy her a dog. He wasn't a man who loved dogs, he wasn't a man who even liked dogs, and he had resisted her successfully. Today, by the light in his eyes, she realized it was hopeless to pursue the subject.

"I'd love a sweet," Daisy said. The matter was not yet settled, but it was only a question of time. She had no intention of giving up.

Stash signaled the waiter who wheeled over one of the dessert trolleys, shining objects of solid mahogany on four silent ball bearings, with several levels of trays, each covered in an array of desserts: chocolate, lemon and raspberry mousse, bread-and-butter pudding, rice pudding, apple tarts, assorted pastries, poached fruit in port, fresh fruit salad served with thick cream from Normandy, large, rich cakes and *mille feuilles aux fraises*. The doting waiter, worthy inheritor of the Connaught tradition, never waited for Daisy to make the agonizing choice but simply filled a plate with small samples of every dessert on the trolley, except for the rice pudding. After dessert, while Stash had his coffee, the waiter, as he did at each table, brought a silver compote on which lay a variety of miniature sweets: fresh strawberries dipped in chocolate, tiny eclairs and cherries iced in frosting. Each one of them lay in a fluted paper cup. While Stash stared fixedly at the floor, Daisy deftly swept every single one of these delicacies into her small handbag, which she had lined with her best handkerchiefs in anticipation of this loot. The first time she had done it Stash had been horrified.

"Daisy! A lady can eat as many of those as she likes *at* the table, but she doesn't take them away with her!"

"They're not for me."

"Oh." Stash knew immediately for whom they were intended. She was taking them to the other. He never mentioned them again but endured in silence the humiliation of the weekly incident. Daisy would not have allowed him to order a box of the candied treats for her, he knew, because then they would be "extra" and he couldn't bring himself to deprive her of the pleasure she took in her gift to her sister.

When Stash had received the telephoned news of Francesca's death from Matty Firestone, he had started to consider his options even as he booked the flight to Los Angeles. Almost immediately he realized that someone had to be told the story which had been, until now, kept absolutely secret from all the world. He needed help in managing the future and Anabel was the only person he trusted. During the few days that Stash was away in California, Anabel managed to find Queen Anne's School, the best home for retarded children in England, and make arrangements for Danielle to live there.

She drove Stash's big car to the airport to meet the little band since he had been adamant about the need to keep the arrival of the children hidden, even from his chauffeur. As they came through customs she saw Stash, walking ahead, with Daisy's hand in his. The little girl was as confused by the rapidly changing events of the last week as she was grief-stricken. She still didn't quite understand how it was possible that her mother had driven off one afternoon and had not come home. How could she be dead? Neither Matty nor Margo nor Stash himself had yet been able to bring themselves to explain the details of the accident to her, and Daisy was engulfed in the reality of her childish fears of abandonment. Behind Stash walked Masha, carrying Danielle who had retreated into a world of silence and immobility. Quickly, without asking questions, Anabel drove them to the school which was located in the country outside of London.

When they arrived at the large building which had once been the main house of a great private estate, and was still surrounded by wide lawns, fine old trees and flower gardens, Stash told Masha, Daisy and Anabel to wait in the car for him. He picked Danielle up, the first and last time he ever touched her, and stepped out of the car, putting Danielle's feet firmly on the driveway. Daisy jumped out and followed him, hanging on to his leg as he started up the steps, Danielle silently trailing behind.

"Daddy, where are we going? Is this where you live? Why isn't Masha coming, too?"

Stash kept climbing the wide steps. "Daisy darling, your sister's going to live here for a while. It's a wonderful place, a school for her. You're coming to live with me in my house in London."

"*NO!*"

He stopped, bent down and spoke earnestly to the disbelieving and defiant child. "Now, listen to me, Daisy, this is very important. All the things you know how to do that she can't—like telling time and reading the cards I send you and jumping rope? Well, if she lives at this school for a while she'll learn how to do all those things from the best teachers in the world and then you'll be able to play together the way you've always wanted to . . ."

"I *love* to play with her exactly the way she is—oh, *don't make her, Daddy, don't*—she'll miss me so much. I'll miss her—please, please, Daddy!" As she began to understand the implacable extent of his intentions, Daisy's defiance turned to terrible fear.

"Daisy, I understand that it's hard, but you're thinking only of yourself. Danielle will get to like it here very quickly and there are many other children for her to play with. But if she doesn't live in a special place like this, she won't learn. Now, you don't want that to happen to her, do you . . . you don't want to keep her from learning all the grown-up things that you can do? It wouldn't be *fair*, you know that. Now, *would that be fair, Daisy?*"

"No," she sobbed, tears running down her face, down her neck and disappearing down the front of her dress.

"Come along and you can see her lovely room and meet some of the teachers."

"I can't stop crying . . . I'll make her cry, too."

"You *have to stop*. I want you to tell her all the things I said. You've always said that she understands you, best."

"She won't understand now, Daddy."

"Go ahead and try."

Finally Daisy controlled herself enough to communicate with her sister in their private language. After only a short while Danielle was weeping huge tears and howling like a small animal.

"She said: 'Day, no go!' "

"But didn't you tell her about all the things she'd learn?" Stash said impatiently.

"She didn't know what I meant."

"Well, that just shows I'm right. If she learns the things they can teach her here, she *will* understand. Now come on, Daisy, get her to stop that terrible noise she's making and we'll both take her to her nice room and she'll be fine, just fine, before you know it."

The dedicated professionals who ran the institution were accustomed to, as they put it, "unfortunate scenes" when a child was finally left in their excellent care, but nothing had prepared them for the parting of Daisy and Danielle. All of them who were unlucky enough to be present found themselves in despair and some of them were reduced to unprofessional tears by the time Stash finally pried Daisy away, as gently as he could, although he eventually had to use brute force.

After Daisy, shrieking and struggling and kicking, had been bodily carried down the corridor from Dani's room and bundled into the car, Stash determined that such emotional traumas could only be bad for her. The following Sunday, when he had promised Daisy that she could visit her sister, he refused to take her, carefully explaining that it was for her own good and for Danielle's good, too. The little girl listened intently to every word he said and, deigning no reply, merely turned away and went to her own room.

After one day Masha knocked on his door.

"Prince, little Daisy won't eat."

"She must be sick. I'll call the doctor."

"There's nothing wrong with her body."

"Then what is wrong? Come on, Masha, stop giving me that disapproving look of yours . . . it hasn't had any bloody effect on me since I was seven."

"She won't eat until she can visit Dani."

"Ridiculous. I'm not going to be dictated to by a six-year-old child. I've decided what's best for her. Now, go and tell her it didn't work. She'll eat when she gets hungry."

Masha left the room silently. She didn't return. Another day passed, and Stash sought her out.

"Well?"

"She still won't eat. I warned you. You just don't know Daisy." Masha looked at him grimly until he looked away, still resolute.

It took still another day of the hunger strike before Daisy brought her father to terms. Not one bit of food entered her mouth until she had his sworn promise that she could visit Danielle every Sunday afternoon. Stash had learned, once and for all, not to thwart her in anything to do with Danielle.

For several months after Francesca's death, Stash had received letters from Matty Firestone, asking about the children and how they were settling down in London.

This was a complication that Stash decided to put behind him. He could not contemplate the possibility of a continued correspondence with the agent and his wife, whom he regarded as his sworn enemies. Eventually he composed a letter in which he demanded to be spared any further inquiries into his private affairs, a letter that was so curt, so profoundly unpleasant, so thoroughly nasty and peremptory, that both Matty and Margo decided that there was no further reason to write Valensky. Daisy and Danielle were his children, he had every legal right to them and, as Margo asked Matty sadly, realistically, what could they do about it? It was best to forget now; forget Francesca, forget the twins, put the whole tragic chapter in their lives behind them. It was over, gone, lost and they had done the best they could. Now it should be left alone.

"You mean *try* to forget," Matty said bitterly.

"Exactly. The only alternative is to sue for custody and you know we'd never get it."

"But those little girls—they were *family*, Margo."

"For me too, darling, but not legally. And that's what counts."

The Firestones stopped writing, and Daisy, in London, continued to visit Dani every Sunday. Stash never took her to Queen Anne's School himself. Rather than risk having to see the other, he sent Daisy, accompanied by Masha, on the hour-long trip, by train and cab.

During the summer months of the following years, when Daisy was on vacation from school, Stash took her with him to the house in Normandy, *La Marée*, that he had bought as a gift for Anabel soon after she had come into his life. However, every two weeks Daisy insisted that she must go back to England for the weekend so that she could visit Dani. His lips pressed together in an unwilling line, Stash saw his daughter and Masha off at the Deauville airport on a Saturday morning and returned on Sunday evening to greet them, never asking any questions about the time they had been away.

Stash received monthly reports on Danielle from Queen Anne's School, reports which he often left lying about for weeks before he brought himself to open them. They would all be the same, he told himself, and indeed they were. She was well, she was happy and well-behaved. She had learned to do a few simple things, she enjoyed music and played with some of the other children and she was particularly attached to several of the teachers. She knew a few new words and communicated with the teachers she liked, but it was only with her sister that she seemed to have any sort of conversation.

Curiously, Daisy never spoke to Stash about her twin, after she had forced him to capitulate in the matter of the visits. There was no one in her life except Masha with whom she had the slightest impulse to discuss Dani. She never spoke of her to Anabel although she knew that Anabel was aware of Dani's existence. Nor did she ever try to tell any of her school friends that she had a twin sister. She did not dare. It was a prohibition so strong that it had nothing to do with an ordinary secret. It was taboo in the most primordial sense. *Her father did not want it.* In some mysterious way Daisy was convinced that her *survival*—and Dani's too—depended on her silence. It defied her comprehension but she *knew*. She could not risk losing her father's love, that love that had been given and then withdrawn so inexplicably for the first years of her life. He was wrong about Dani, but Daisy was aware of the limits of her powers. She could tease Stash about some things, she could act the playful tyrant, but only within certain well-defined borders. Motherless, she had to cling to her father and accept the way he felt about her sister without discussion, or be totally orphaned.

The compromise they had reached in that first week, that enabled Daisy to visit Danielle, slowly became more and more acceptable to her as her sister's pliable nature adjusted happily to the teachers and the other children at Queen Anne's School. Daisy couldn't help but realize that she couldn't go to Dani's school and Dani certainly couldn't go to Lady Alden's.

The five years of seclusion in Big Sur grew ever more remote and far away as her new life in London unfolded itself, a life she found constantly less possible to even attempt to explain to Dani. Their conversations were limited to Dani's small circle of comprehension and, every year, Daisy felt more like an adult talking to a child, than one child talking to another. Daisy often drew pictures for Dani, until the walls of her room were almost papered with them.

"Do pony" was one of Dani's constant requests, because of the old horses that grazed in a meadow near Queen Anne's School. At a time when Daisy's peers at Lady Alden's were struggling to draw presentable apples and bananas, Daisy was already able to do a lively sketch of one of the most difficult of all objects to draw well, a horse.

When Daisy had first appeared in London, Ram had been a precociously alert thirteen. He had always rejected the existence of this half-sister, a product of a marriage made after his own birth. He did not accept the fact that this usurper had any rights. She was nonvalid. Worse, far worse, she was a *rival*.

Ram was preoccupied, even more than most of his friends, all upper-class, public-school boys, by the importance of being an "heir."

At Eton, enormously important distinctions concerning inheritance had been made since the school was founded by Henry VI in 1442. In 1750 the lists of pupils at Eton still appearing in order of rank, with dukes' sons coming first. Titled boys wore special clothes, had special seats and special privileges of all kinds. In the supposedly democratic 1950s and 1960s, certain of these out-of-date marks of a rigid caste system had been abolished, but the orderly passage of property and titles from one generation to another was deeply ingrained in the collective unconsciousness of Eton and the other great schools of Britain. They were as much in the air as the importance of cricket or the bad form of "showing off."

Ram couldn't remember a time when he hadn't looked forward to inheriting Stash's property, *all of it*. He didn't consciously wish his father dead, he didn't even consciously realize that only his father's death could make that property his, he simply lusted after it without any of the complications of guilt. He believed, in his heart of hearts, that the acid feelings of injustice from which he suffered—and which he never recognized were envy of happiness—would disappear when he was the possessor, the undisputed owner, *the* Prince Valensky.

The fact of Daisy meant that he would never have it *all*. No matter how many times he reassured himself that even if she got something, there was more than enough for both of them, still she had destroyed the splendid fullness of his prospects. However, he was too crafty and too wise to ever allow any of these feelings to surface and reveal themselves to grown-up eyes.

As for Daisy, from the first moment she saw Ram, he filled a great place in her imagination. He was like the young heroes in the tales that her mother used to read to her, someone who could leap across dangerous rivers and tame the wildest horses, climb up sheer mountains of glass, ride on the wind and battle with giants. To the little girl who had lived for as long as she could remember in the solitude of far-off Big Sur, this straight, tall, darkly handsome boy with his slim, stern face, his dark eyebrows and haughty Etonian air, was the most fascinating person in her new life, particularly since he had an offhand manner with her which lacked the indulgence she received from everyone else.

She could never have imagined the worm of obsessive envy that ate at Ram. At Christmas, while they were each opening their presents, he watched, behind lowered eyes, and saw that although both he and Daisy received equally expensive presents, Stash's eyes were only on Daisy as she opened the gifts, waiting to drink in *her* pleasure. Immediately Ram's own presents lost all meaning for him. When he received Daisy's letters at Eton, and she innocently wrote describing a Sunday Connaught lunch, Ram thought bitterly that the only times Stash had taken him to the Connaught had been on his birthday or to celebrate a school holiday. Twice, at Christmas, his mother insisted that he come home to that cold, drafty castle near Edinburgh instead of staying with his father, and those were the two times that Stash chose to take Daisy away to Barbados for a month of sun . . . a deliberate choice, without doubt, Ram told himself, feeling the pain of being left out burn deep, although he never said anything to anyone.

As Daisy grew older, every time he went to London he hoped to find that she had finally broken out in adolescent pimples or started to get fat. He received the admiring looks she gave him without any flattery and when she asked him questions about his life at school, he answered as briefly as possible. He watched, missing nothing, as she stole all the attention that should have been his, took the place by his father's side that was Ram's by right. And all the while, Daisy, who never had any idea of how he felt, was impelled by his manner to continue to try to form a connection with him, inspired by a deeply feminine impulse that was so strong it positively tugged at its moorings in search of his love. She drew his face so often that Dani began to say, "Do Ram" although she hadn't the glimmer of an idea who Ram might be.

Stash had bought a house that was not typical of London houses, the finest of which tend to have those identical classic exteriors which are the cause of the remarkable architectural unity of London's squares and crescents. He had discovered a house in Wilton Row, a small cul-de-sac off Wilton Crescent, a street within a short distance of Hyde Park on the left and the gardens of Buckingham Palace on the right, that, nevertheless, had a quality of remoteness, an almost secret existence.

In that sedate, supremely aristocratic part of London, with its concentration of imposing foreign embassies, Stash had managed to find an exceptionally large house, low and rather wide, painted a pale yellow with gray shutters. It had a distinctly foreign look about it, this house that might have fit easily into many parts of the European countryside. The three sides of Wilton Row surrounded a cobbled space with a pale blue lamppost at its center, where no cars were allowed to park unless they belonged to the other homeowners, all of whom had painted their houses in pastel, altogether un-British colors.

There were bow windows on the ground floor of Stash Valensky's home and the rooms inside had fine proportions. He had filled them with the contents of the Lausanne villa; those rare and valuable French rugs, furniture, paintings and jeweled bibelots which had once made the journey from St. Petersburg to Davos with his parents. It never occurred to Stash to decorate his home in any way but the one he had been used to as a child.

The noise of London was extinguished in Wilton Row, and an air of rustic peace prevailed. At the corner, where Wilton Row joined a tiny alley called Old Barrack Yard, stood a pub, the Grenadier, bravely painted in red and gold, with benches in front, sheltered by a twisted, venerable wisteria vine. A sign announced that only customers who had entered Wilton Row by taxi or on foot were allowed to be served. All in all, there was scarcely a more private dwelling place in all that great, gray city than the Valensky home.

For many years Stash and Daisy spent a large part of Saturday in Kent, where he owned stables in which he kept many of his horses. It was after one of their companionable rides through the country, on a day when Daisy was almost twelve, that father and daughter spied two gypsy caravans. They were parked close to Stash's property and, mistrustfully, he eyed the wagons with their painted canvas tops stretched over hooped ribs. They hadn't been there last week. Stash went over to investigate.

"Daisy," he ordered, "you go back to the stable. I'll just be a minute."

"Oh, Father, you wouldn't deprive me of seeing gypsies?!" she cried in dismay.

"They're just tinkers, Daisy, but I don't want them around my ponies. They can always use an extra horse or two or five."

"Please, Father," she said longingly.

"All right," he sighed, not in the mood for discipline. "Just don't let anyone tell your fortune—I detest that."

The gypsies were friendly, overfriendly, thought Stash, and easy about answering his questions in their accented English.

They would move on if he liked but they were only planning to stay another day or two anyway. Just the time to do a bit of tinkering in the local village.

Not really reassured, but not able to order them off a field he didn't own, Stash turned to leave, but Daisy was no longer at his side. She was on her knees in front of a box crooning a love song and both hands were full of a puppy which looked to Stash like a beanbag. The puppy's bottom and hind legs drooped down from one of Daisy's hands, his head and front legs flopped from the other. In the center of Daisy's palms he rested his bulging belly. The puppy's color was at one and the same time gray, brown and blue, with white paws and white ears. He looked as if he could be any kind of dog at all except some recognizable breed.

Damn and bloody blast, thought Stash, puppies! I should have guessed.

Stash was not a sporting man, not for him the joys of the turf or the pleasures of the hunt, both of which seemed so inferior compared to polo. He hadn't the faintest interest in animals other than horses and he had no knowledge of the part that hunting game on foot plays in the lives of many country people.

"He's a good lurcher," said the gypsy. "And for sale."

Had Stash any knowledge of dogs or the hunt this statement would have caused him to take Daisy by the arm and leave on the instant. No gypsy can sell you a "good" lurcher puppy. It is a definition without meaning since no lurcher can be called "good" until it is old enough to hunt, for that is a lurcher's role in life. It is a poacher's dog, a gypsy's dog, a tramp's dog, silent, swift, deadly. A good lurcher can catch a low-flying seagull in one jump; a good lurcher can support a family in its deadly nightly raids on the countryside, can leap high barbed-wire fences, gallop miles over frozen ground and kill a deer by itself.

"Looks like a mutt to me," said Stash.

"No, a lurcher. Dam's half Irish wolfhound crossed with greyhound, and his dad's a cross of deerhound and greyhound with whippet and sheepdog both in there one generation back. Can't ask finer than that."

"That's just a mongrel."

"No, sir, lurcher. You won't find them in dog shows, but you can't ask for a better dog."

"If he's such a prize, why are you selling him?"

"Got eight in the litter. Can't take them all traveling, now, can we? Still, a bargain for the man who buys him." The gypsy knew that the puppy Daisy was holding with such adoration had one hind leg shorter than the other. Such a lurcher probably couldn't outrun a hare and wouldn't be worth feeding. The gypsy had planned on abandoning him when he moved on, but the puppy's ancestry was exactly as he had reported it and had it not been for that short leg, he wouldn't have sold him for a hundred pounds.

"Come on, Daisy, let's get back."

Daisy didn't have to say anything. The appeal in her eyes was enough to make Stash suspect that he had postponed the dog question too long.

"All right," he said hastily, "I promise I'll get you a dog. Next weekend, Daisy. We'll go visit some good kennels and you can pick any dog you want. That's a mutt, some kind of hound and God knows what else. You don't want him. You want a purebred puppy."

"I want Theseus."

"Theseus?"

"Father, you *know*, the boy who went to fight the minotaur in the labyrinth—we're doing the Greek myths this term with Lady Ellen."

"And *that* is Theseus?"

"I knew the minute I saw him."

"Funny name for a lurcher," said the gypsy.

"Never mind about that," snapped Stash. "How much are you asking for him?"

"Twenty pounds."

"I'll give you five."

"I'll give you the other fifteen. I've got it from my Christmas money, Father." Daisy rushed into the bargaining, shocking both men who had been ready to settle for ten pounds right from the beginning.

And so Theseus the lurcher, for whom Stash eventually had to give twelve pounds, came to live in London, where Daisy now added the duties of feeding him and training him and exercising him to her other activities, managing somehow to get over the first few difficult weeks when Theseus often collapsed on the floor from the weight of his full stomach and wasn't able to get up without assistance. However, with enough minced beef and raw eggs and milk and honey he soon grew stronger and finally came into his lurcher heritage on the day he slipped like a shadow into the big kitchen larder and without a sound which might have betrayed him, snatched clean a platter of stuffed, boneless chicken breasts, leaving a raging cook with suspicions but no proof.

He soon accommodated himself to his shorter rear leg which only showed up in a rolling gait, like that of a hard-drinking man who's had three martinis but is still good for a few more. He slept in a basket next to Daisy's bed, often on his back with all four legs up in the air, and quickly was on the most intimate and friendly terms with Daisy's pony, sniffing Merlin's nose like an ardent lover and curling up at her hooves.

However, he divided the Valensky's servants into two camps: those who wooed and spoiled him, victims of his con-man tactics of wild affection combined with a certain morose look of incredible pathos he knew how to give them that melted their hearts, and those who detested him on the solid grounds that nothing was sacred to Theseus, not their roasts of beef nor their blinis, nor their rashers of bacon, nor their piroshki nor their fondue, and certainly not their mugs of stout.

Stash's Russian servants were now all in their seventies, many of them had died and others retired, but those who remained, those who had left Russia as very young people in 1912, now enjoyed a diet that combined English, Swiss and Russian culinary delights. Age had only improved their hearty appetites.

Theseus seemed to eat his weight every day, and in a short time the floppy puppy became a lean dog, the size of a large, strong greyhound, two and a half feet tall at the shoulder. Short of locking and barring the doors to the kitchen and larder, it was impossible to keep out the crouching, sidling, slinking, all-but-invisible animal who pounced silently, consumed his prey in a gulp, and disappeared before the theft could be discovered. He was merely performing his function in life, but few of them were sympathetic to this inborn criminality, a lawlessness which had been carefully bred into him throughout centuries.

Yet lurchers, for all their stealthy ways, are noble dogs. Many hundreds of years ago the ownership of these rough-coated, mixed-blood greyhounds was confined to princes. They wore collars of gold, they were indispensable at court, where hunting was the principal pastime, and many an antique tapestry is adorned by their royal presence.

Daisy's school, Lady Alden's, was the most fashionable in all of London. It operated on two principles which, extraordinarily enough, turned out well-educated young women. The teachers all were required to come from aristocratic backgrounds; Lady Alden had a decided preference for the daughters of impoverished earls—Lady Janes and Lady Marys abounded. The girls, from six to sixteen, did not need to fill such requirements. All they needed was parental money, preferably on a monarchical scale. That many of the parents were also wellborn was merely a happy coincidence.

During all the nine years that she was a pupil at Lady Alden's, Daisy wore the expensive uniforms bought in different sizes every year at Harrods, but always exactly the same design: navy blue sailor dresses with white collars and piping, covered by pale blue pinafores that buttoned down the back.

She arrived every day before nine o'clock at the entrance to the school's three adjoining buildings on a quiet street not far from Kensington Gardens and the Albert Memorial. After prayers Daisy and all the other students, some hundred girls in all, filed out past Lady Alden, dropping her a curtsy and saying good morning in a voice which had to be clear, audible and well-articulated. Lady Alden, a former beauty, was a firm disciplinarian, and when her attention turned toward any individual girl a heart palpitated instantly. She wielded a formidable ruler which she never hesitated to use on the knuckles of her pupils, and even the titled teachers quailed before her.

When Daisy left for school one fall day, shortly after Theseus had come to live in her room, the cook and the ancient butler carried out a plot to get rid of Theseus. The cook lured the dog to the front door by holding a chicken high in the air. She flung the chicken outside, onto the cobbles, and when Theseus flashed through the open door she closed it behind him and locked it. The two conspirators waited for sounds of the dog's paws on the front door, determined to ignore him until he wandered away. Theseus merely engulfed the chicken, briskly shook his coat of longish hair that was rough to the touch, perked up his white ears, and followed Daisy to Lady Alden's by smell. When she emerged that afternoon she found him there, patiently curled up outside the entrance to the guard box from which Sam, the porter, protected the school and its precious young ladies from contact with the world.

"So that's your dog, Miss," said Sam, who called all the students Miss because he couldn't be bothered to remember the great variety of titles they bore. "Well, he can't stay here every day, if that's what you're thinking. Against the rules. Lady Alden'd have a proper fit if she knew." Theseus, in a delirium of delight, was hurling himself at Daisy, putting his front paws on her shoulders and passionately nuzzling her face, all in proper lurcher silence.

"No, Sam, of course not," said Daisy thoughtfully.

Had a dog ever gone to Lady Alden's school before? No one knew. Such a violation was beyond the realm of imagination, rather like the possibility of the art students having a naked man to pose for them, or for that matter, a naked woman. But go to school Theseus did for three years; smuggled in through a tiny door at the back of the shed that was reserved for the gardener. Tactfully, he slept all day on a bed of cushions Daisy brought, one at a time, from her own room, so totally hidden in one dark corner that he went unnoticed except for the cooperative gardener who loathed Lady Alden as much as he loved dogs and never asked any questions, but made sure he carried his own lunch in a buttoned pocket, having had much experience with lurchers before he came to the City.

Daisy was fifteen. It was April of 1967 and London was at its peak, the center of all that was new and vital. Daisy was equally in love with all the Beatles, Vidal Sassoon, Rudolf Nureyev, Twiggy, Mary Quant, Jean Shrimpton and Harold Pinter. She was not in love with Andy Warhol or Baby Jane Holzer or even Mick Jagger.

Yet in a year in which any shopgirl could choose between dressing like an American Indian in leather and beads and headbands, or like a romantic trollop in *Viva Maria*-inspired lacy, tucked bloomers and frilly blouses, in a year in which the miniskirt became a micro-skirt and eventually turned into shorts, she was still confined to a navy sailor dress and a pinafore.

"I'd have to wear my school uniform all the time, if it were up to Father and Masha," she exploded to Anabel after lunch in Eaton Square one Saturday, tucking her long slender legs up under her on one of Anabel's gray green couches.

"Hmmm. You don't look so terribly underprivileged to me," Anabel answered, surveying her from top to bottom. Daisy was wearing black velvet knee breeches and a matching jacket trimmed with gold buttons and black braid, over a ruffled blouse of white silk. She had on white ribbed tights and flat black slippers with a rosette on the front. Today she had dressed her incomparable hair in curly bangs and tied it back on each side of her face with bunches of shiny black ribbons. She had darkened her blonde eyebrows a little and wore a hint of mascara, but no other make-up.

From the time Anabel had first seen Daisy, a six-year-old whose mother had just died, a six-year-old who was about to be separated from her twin sister, and who had come to live in a strange country with a father she knew only from fleeting visits, Anabel had been fascinated by the little girl's indomitable sense of what was right. She could scarcely believe that a child was capable of the absolute loyalty that had enabled her to force even Stash, that man of hard metal who, in Anabel's opinion, had never quite gotten the hang of life, to give in to her insistence that she visit her sister every week. She had watched Daisy grow up with intense interest, missing nothing. Often Anabel wondered how Daisy managed to slip, seemingly without too much difficulty, into a life that must have been utterly foreign to her. Anabel was too wise to think that she understood everything about Daisy—she was not a child who confided, who poured out her troubles. She was not a child without secrets. She *must* have paid a price.

Would Daisy, Anabel wondered, burn out this early promise and become just another pretty teenager? Now at fifteen, Daisy had not only retained the purity and fire she had always possessed but approaching adulthood could be clearly read on her face. There, thought Anabel, is a girl who is going to cause all kinds of perfectly wonderful trouble. Even another woman was forced to imagine the pulse of curiosity which must beat in the hearts of the men who saw her . . . that full, enigmatic mouth, so ripe with promise and yet so innocent, and those eyes that, no matter how frank they were, contained unfathomable, never to be analyzed depths in their velvety blackness . . . and, oh, a body, a faultless body, strong and slim, and lucky child, she came naturally by the romantic and wild look which was the fashion of the day. Yet here Daisy was, suddenly painfully full of the pent-up turmoil and ferocious misery of adolescence, now focused on clothes, which had never meant anything to her before.

Indignantly, Daisy continued, "You just don't know how I had to fight like a mad thing to get Father to let me go shop at Annacat—can you imagine it, Anabel, Father wanted me to go to Harrods' young ladies' department and buy plaid skirts and twin sets. *Twin sets!*"

"That's what English girls are still wearing, some of them anyway," Anabel observed mildly.

"Only in the country, only if they're parsons' daughters, and *then* only with jeans," Daisy said rebelliously. "He doesn't realize I've grown up. I'm not allowed to go out with boys yet, not that I know any! It's just impossible!"

She was at the rebellious age, no doubt about it, Anabel thought. Trouble in sight for Stash with his old-fashioned ideas. At fifty-six he had become as conservative where Daisy was concerned as he was unconventional for himself. Not an uncommon fix for the fathers of beautiful daughters to find themselves in, she ruminated with a touch of inward glee. Why, when she was only a year older than Daisy was now she'd run away and married that awful bore, what's his name. He'd died last year . . . yet if she'd stayed married to him, she'd be the Dowager Marchioness now. At the thought Anabel couldn't help but smile, although she was trying to be as serious as possible since she truly loved the girl and knew how adolescents hate it if they aren't treated with appropriate solemnity. Anabel had arranged their intimate lunch on purpose for just such conversation, because she sensed the essential, the irremediable loneliness of the age Daisy was going through.

Both the girl and the woman were surprised at the sound of the doorbell on the floor below. Anabel expected no visitors until Stash that evening. In a minute Ram entered the drawing room and Daisy rose to her feet in delight. Now that he had his own flat and was working in the City she rarely saw this twenty-two-year-old half-brother.

"What's that God-awful fancy dress you've got on?" he asked. He looked annoyed. He'd dropped by unannounced, hoping to find Anabel alone, so that they could have a chat, and here she was closeted with Daisy. He didn't even notice that Daisy's expectant look of joy, her open smile at the sight of him, a smile that had such completeness to it, faded and shrank with hurt at his careless words.

"You don't know one damn thing about fashion, Ram," Anabel snapped in an irritated voice he'd rarely heard her use. "Daisy looks divine, as any fool would know."

"Only if you say so, Anabel darling," he said absently, ignoring Daisy. "I've got to get home," Daisy said hastily. She couldn't wait to take off the velvet knee breeches and ruffled shirt she'd been so proud of. Now this ravishing pageboy, this festival of a girl felt ashamed of the way she looked. Ram's approval, which she had sought so fruitlessly for the last nine years, meant almost everything to her, no matter how often she told herself that for reasons she couldn't understand he didn't like her and would never like her. He had the power to hurt her as no one else could. Ram, unattainable, detached, withdrawn, undemonstrative Ram, who showed so little emotion on his dark, haughty face, made her helpless with love and passionate with the desire to please.

At Lady Alden's, where Daisy was in her next to last year, she was the acknowledged leader of her class, the champion jacks player of the school, one of the only girls who had never been reduced to tears by the application of Lady Alden's ruler, and the center of a group of special friends who were as physically daring and as horse-mad as she. They formed a potentially revolutionary society within the docile body of the school, which, had Lady Alden known of it, would have caused the dreaded ruler to fly as it had never flown before.

Now Daisy, still smarting with the reception her first venture into grown-up clothes had drawn from Ram, contemplated taking out her feelings with a devilment which would exceed anything in the annals of the school. Her emotions were almost adult but she still only knew childish ways to relieve them.

Even her best friends were aghast at her proposition.

"A gymkhana! Daisy, you're bonkers. You know as well as I do a proper gymkhana's got to be a field day, with horsemanship, exhibitions and all sorts of pageantry. Lady A would never hear of it."

"Lady A doesn't own Belgrave Square."

"Oh, Daisy! Oh, how perfectly awful! Oh—could we really do it?"

"Why not? If you're all with me, that is. It's merely a question of organization."

The Metropolitan Police were never able to explain the Great Belgrave Square Gymkhana to their superiors. How were they to know of the cunning resources of two dozen fiery young equestrians, who stole into that august park in the early morning hours and set up jumps and flags and brilliantly colored pennants and all matter of gates and fences? By the light of dawn in their beige breeches and polished boots and stocks and tweed jackets, looking like all the other proper young ladies who ride in London, these she-devils quietly collected their horses from various stables all over Mayfair and assembled at the entrance to that beautifully groomed square of turf and trees onto which face the embassies of Portugal, Mexico, Turkey, Norway, Germany, Austria and, appropriately enough, the Royal College of Veterinary Surgeons and the Imperial Defense College.

One of the fearless number lived on the Square and had a key to the high iron entrance, and before the police had collected their wits not only had the Gymkhana started, but the entrances to all the main streets which led to the Square—Upper Belgrave Street, Belgrave Place, Wilton Terrace, Wilton Crescent and Grosvenor Crescent—were blocked with cars, abandoned by their passengers who had flocked out to see what was going on. And what were a handful of policemen to do with a horde of whooping, hurrahing wild teenagers, veterans of dozens of horse shows, as tough as cavalry and twice as tenacious, all mounted on swift horses, galloping madly about in the vernal sunshine as if a troop of Amazons had suddenly materialized from another time in history? Led by Daisy, her bright braids flying behind her, they jumped fence after fence in a bacchanalian circle, holding their pennants high in the air and brandishing them at the London sky with no lack of pageantry. Yet there was discipline in their ranks and Daisy's whistle could make them all slow to a canter or form into a double line at a trot. The police could no more have arrested them than if they'd been a Guards' Regiment, coming to Troop the Colors. Nor could they be caught. The Gymkhana ended only when the sound of police sirens started to get close to Belgrave Square. At that moment, Daisy raised her arm and shouted—and all her inspired band scattered, jumping their horses over the railings and fleeing into the friendly, cheering carnival crowds who had surrounded the square.

It was perfectly true, as Daisy had said, that Lady Alden didn't own Belgrave Square. The Earl of Grosvenor did, just as he owned almost every square inch of Mayfair and Belgravia. The Grosvenor family is the wealthiest private landlord in England, with these three hundred acres in the heart of London representing only one of their holdings all over the world. The Earl of Grosvenor most certainly owned Wilton Row . . . Stash only leased his house from the Grosvenor Trust.

In the offices of the trustees of the Grosvenor Trust there was little amusement concerning Daisy's Gymkhana. The gardeners of Belgrave Square had reported that the turf was damaged to the tune of hundreds of pounds. However, that wasn't their chief objection . . . it was the principle of the thing. A typical sign on a typical park in Grosvenor territory reads like the one which adorns the entrance to Wilton Crescent's semi-oval green space. Some of the injuctions written thereon forbid any game involving noise, prohibit any children under the age of nine who are unaccompanied by adults and outlaw all dogs. Although tricycles and scooters may be used by accompanied children, they must be ridden only on the paths, no flower beds may be trodden upon or dug, and, in particular, organized groups of children cannot be admitted to the park at all.

The tradition of these sedate and quiet parks had been violated—shaken to its depths—by Daisy, who had been recognized and identified by one of the Grosvenor traffic wardens who had helplessly observed the Great Gymkhana. She was, he reported in an outraged voice, a young lady who owned . . . a lurcher! That news alone was enough to cause a hush and raise the eyebrows of the trustees, landowners all and therefore victims, down to their last remembered ancestor, of poachers and their dogs. A lurcher indeed! Just what kind of young lady could possibly own a lurcher?

It was not, as one of the trustees soon explained to Stash, that they wished to punish his daughter, but if she was capable of such insurrection, what might she do next? Stash thought about his lease, which had only three years to run before it would revert to the Grosvenor estate, and agreed with the trustee that certainly he would have to do something serious about the discipline of his daughter. In addition, Stash was genuinely shocked at Daisy's behavior. It was more daring than anything he remembered ever having done himself, at her age, even making allowances for the fact that she was a female.

After the trustee had left, with a check for the damages and Stash's assurances that the matter of Daisy would be attended to, he sat alone for a long time, thinking about his foolhardy daughter. How was she to grow up properly with, as adult examples, only himself and Anabel? Neither of them was immoral, it was true, but they were certainly amoral, both of them heedless of the laws of ordinary society. Eton had turned Ram into a sober, unemotional, hard-working young man, but Lady Alden's had missed having a salutory taming effect on Daisy. What would happen to Daisy when she no longer lived under his roof? This matter of the Gymkhana went far beyond an irresponsible childish prank, Stash thought, feeling every one of his fifty-six years. He blamed himself. There was no doubt in his mind that he had spoiled Daisy. But what to do about the future? He would not always be there to get her out of trouble.

During the rest of April and May Stash considered the problem of Daisy as he attended to his affairs. Eventually, he sent for his solicitor and made certain thoughtful changes in his will, and then forgot about the matter, satisfied that he had acted prudently. A great deal of his fortune was now invested in Rolls-Royce and Stash watched with deep interest as the company attempted to break into the American-dominated manufacturing of airplane engines. In 1963 his faith in Rolls had been bolstered as their Spey turbofan engine was being widely bought and now in 1967 they were going after a contract with Lockheed to produce the engine for its TriStar Airbus, the RB. 211. His investments had always been made on an emotional basis rather than on that of cold financial judgment, and Stash poured even more capital into the company he loved.

However, the training of his stable of polo ponies occupied most of Stash's time. He flew less and less now, having lost the need for the release from fury he had found in the air after Francesca had left him, fourteen years ago. All that seemed very far away and unimportant. Still he kept his jet license current and occasionally he flew aerobatic exhibitions in the many air shows which were so popular all over the country, returning for a few nostalgic hours to the cockpit of a lovingly preserved relic of a Spitfire or a Hurricane, with their Rolls-Royce Merlin engines, still as trustworthy as ever.

On a fine Sunday in May, there was no fault in the engine of the Spitfire he was flying at the Essex Air Show. The undercarriage of the twenty-seven-year-old plane stuck and the landing gear could not be released. Stash headed for the woods beyond the runway, hoping that the trees might cushion the crash. Many a fighter pilot had crash-landed in these planes and lived to tell the tale. He did not.

10

In the weeks right after Stash's death, Anabel, who grieved for Stash in her own way as she had never grieved for anyone before, Anabel, who had a premonition that Stash would be the last man in her life, pulled what was left of the family together.

She insisted that Daisy and Ram spend the summer at the house near Honfleur that Stash had bought for her seven years before. Seeing Ram so unlike himself, functioning without his usual effectiveness, she persuaded him to take a leave of absence from his job in the City for all of June, July and August. However, with her great virtue of good sense, Anabel realized that three mourning people should never be alone together and she arranged for a constant stream of houseguests to come and stay in the large house; friends from both her London life and her French summer world, people who would distract and beguile the sad household.

Daisy, Anabel realized, was feeling the loss much more than Ram. It was she who was absolutely orphaned now—even Masha had died two years ago. When Daisy went to visit Dani for comfort, her twin, with uncanny intuition, seemed to smell her grief even though Daisy smiled as she hugged and petted her. Dani became so upset that she was reduced to silent tears. "Day, no *do*," she said, drawing away, and finally Daisy sent her running gladly back through the gardens to her own friends.

Ram was *the* Prince Valensky at last. Not only had he inherited the London house and its valuable antique contents, with the exception of the Fabergé animals which had been left to Anabel, along with a certain amount of Rolls-Royce stock, but he had inherited all the polo ponies and the stables in Trouville and Kent and one half of Stash's fortune, both in Rolls-Royce stock and all that remained of the Swiss gold. Stash had left Daisy the other half of his fortune, all of it invested in Rolls stock. Several weeks after the Belgrave Square Gymkhana had convinced him that Daisy shouldn't be in charge of her affairs until she turned thirty, he had made Ram, that dependable, clever boy, co-trustee of her inheritance, along with the Bank of England.

Ram was rich and he was in charge. Yet he had a nagging sense of incompletion, as if his father, in dying so suddenly, had remained intact, as if Stash were still *the* Prince Valensky. There was a sense of unfinished business about the whole thing—something not done, something not finished, something not *won*.

That summer, at Anabel's house, *La Marée*, there were never fewer than eight people at any meal, and often more than a dozen. Anabel's invitations were eagerly accepted by everyone she knew. As she had grown older—she was now almost forty-eight—she collected around herself an atmosphere more filled with intimacy than ever before, as more and more people found her the perfect confidante. She wore their secrets like priceless pearls tucked inside the neckline of a thin dress so that only a faint glimmer of them showed that they were there, but they added constant new depth to her ageless charm and the comfort of her presence. One of her friends, a recently lapsed Catholic, had told her that he felt as cleansed of sin after he'd talked to her as if he'd been to confession, only—and this was the best of all—he had not had to promise never to sin again.

La Marée was a house which could be described by no other word in the language except *enchanted.* There must be in the world many great houses on the top of thickly wooded hills overlooking the sea, but no one who had ever spent any time at *La Marée* had failed to be marked for life by its strange, poetic, nostalgic, tenderly mysterious atmosphere.

It stood behind high walls and acres of overgrown gardens, on the Côte de Grace, the thickly shaded, narrow road that mounts up steeply from Honfleur in the direction of Deauville. From the windows of the house, on all but the front façade, there was a high view over the entire estuary of the Seine, with Le Havre clearly visible in the opalescent distance. Behind the house was a wide gravel terrace from which tangled, fragrant woods led steeply down to the boundaries of two small farms. These woods were crisscrossed by a maze of hidden paths. Beyond the farms was the sea and on the sea was constantly changing, gay armada of fishing and pleasure boats going in and out of the port of Honfleur. Farther out, great ocean liners and cargo ships passed back and forth. The terrace faced due west, and in the evening, when the sun was finally eaten by the horizon and the lights of Le Havre became visible, there was an almost unbearable poignancy about the moment which caused people to speak in lowered voices, or not at all.

La Marée itself proved that magic still existed. It had grown out of an ancient farmhouse, little by little over the centuries, and by the time Anabel became its owner it possessed thirteen different levels of roof, each covered with thatch, from which, in the spring, seeds left in the straw would sprout and send up wild flowers. Some parts of the house were three stories high; the kitchen wing, which was the oldest part of the house, was a single story; but all the various parts of the structure were unified by being built from exposed wooden beams and plaster, most of which wore a rippling mantle of the big-leaved ivy called *la vigne vierge,* which turned bright red in the autumn. The enormous house looked more like a growing thing than a building, and the feeling inside of it was that of being part of a living, breathing space which belonged as much to the outdoors as the indoors. All day long the tall windows were thrown open to the sun and Anabel went out early to gather the baskets full of columbine, coreopsis, roses, asters, lupines, delphinium, dahlias, heather, baby's breath and the *pied d'alouettes,* an old-fashioned flower that appeared in Breugel's paintings, from which she filled vases even more imaginatively and abundantly than she did in London where she was dependent on her florist's stock to choose her blossoms.

Although Anabel expected her guests to live at *La Marée* in an informal, holiday way, the house itself was well-staffed and decorated with a certain formality. Each bedroom had walls of finely pleated damask, color on color, woven in flower motifs and hanging from floor to ceiling. The same fabric that covered the walls was draped on the four-poster beds and at the tall windows. Daisy's room was all sea-green, Anabel's rose and cream and Ram had the blue bedroom. The main salon of the house was enormously high and, in one corner, a circular staircase led up fourteen feet to the balcony that surrounded the room on three sides. The back of the balcony was lined with bookshelves and there were many recesses, invisible from below, in which one could spend all day on comfortable loveseats, reading from the slightly musty volumes which had been there when Stash acquired the house as a surprise for Anabel. It had suited him well because of its nearness to Trouville, where he had still owned the stables to which he had once taken Francesca. He had also been attracted by the legend of the house in which, as everyone in Honfleur knew, its former owner, Madame Colette de Joinville, had hidden eleven British soldiers after Dunkirk. Unable to reach the evacuation beach, they had been guided to her by the Resistance, of which she was a member. At great personal risk, she kept them safe in her attic for nine months until they were all able, one by one, to make their way to Spain, through the Underground, and return to England to fight again.

Soon the routine life of *La Marée* established itself: late breakfast at the long wooden table in the big kitchen, to which they all drifted when they pleased, dressed in bathrobes or peignoirs, after which, Daisy and Anabel, with sturdy market baskets on their arms, went shopping for fresh produce in the port of Honfleur. Lunch was preceded by sherry on the terrace, lasted for two hours and was followed by coffee, again on the terrace. After coffee each followed his own pursuit: antique hunting, sightseeing, napping or rambling in the countryside. Finally cocktails, dinner, a few games of poker or liar's dice, and an early bedtime ended the lazy day.

Daisy found that she was least unhappy when she was alone with her sketch pad, drawing the unforgivably picturesque houses of Le Vieux Bassin in Honfleur, a favorite painter's subject for the last hundred and fifty years, or in trying to capture on paper the three umbrella pines that guarded the ocean side of *La Marée*.

When Daisy took her bath she saw that day after day in the open air had tanned her to the color of a freshly baked croissant. She was not used to looking at herself naked she realized, as she studied with fascination the interesting contrast between her white breasts and her tan shoulders, marked with white only where the straps of her jerseys covered them. Then she was white again right down to the place where her tennis shorts ended and from then on, her legs were even tanner than the rest of her. She turned around and around in front of the mirror, half amused by the comic effect of being colored like a piebald horse, and half admiring the new high fullness of her well-separated breasts and the sleek, long curve of her flanks. Daisy was sexually backward for her age of fifteen and a few months. She had led a severely protected life dominated by a father who had not allowed her contact with boys of her own age. Her friends at school had been those whose sexuality was still invested in horses and dogs. She had often been restlessly aware of physical desires but they had been either suppressed or released in sports. She rubbed her hand questioningly over her white-blonde pubic hair and hastily removed it when she saw what she was doing in the mirror. It was softer than the hair on her head, Daisy thought, oddly embarrassed, and she quickly dressed herself in her summer uniform: worn, tight tennis shorts from the year before that she hadn't bothered to replace and one of the sleeveless striped fishermen's jerseys she had bought in Honfleur. She wore her hair loose, and often, after one of her rambles in the woods, a twig or a bud would be caught in the tangled excess of her curls.

Ram was violently critical of the way she looked. "Christ, Anabel, can't you speak to her about the way she goes about? She's like some sort of savage. It's not only disgraceful, it's damned near indecent. I can't stand to look at her! You're not doing the job you should be with that girl—I'm surprised at you letting her get away with being such a pig!"

"Ram, come on, relax. Honfleur's a resort—everyone dresses like Daisy," Anabel chided him gently. "You're the one who should let down a bit and get into the spirit of things—do I see the playing fields of Eton around your neck, my dear?" Ram refused to even smile but stalked off, stiff with outrage. Hurt, Anabel shook her head sadly as he disappeared. Every time Daisy tried to talk to him, she thought, Ram found something about her to comment on in an unpleasant way, until the girl had almost stopped trying to include him in her conversations. Still, there was nothing Anabel could do except try to reach Ram through gentleness . . . she thought that this was probably his own strange way of reacting to Stash's death, this anger, this . . . almost . . . cruelty.

A few days later, at breakfast, as Ram unwisely tried to take a glance at the newspaper before he'd started his bacon and eggs, Theseus gobbled down everything on his plate. Ram lashed out at the dog with his fist but Theseus was long gone. "Damn it to hell, Daisy, that goddamned verminous mongrel of yours has got to go!" Ram's face was knit in thundering fury. "I'll kill that creature when I catch him!"

"If you touch him, I'll kill you!" Daisy shouted.

"Children, children," Anabel murmured ineffectively.

"I'm warning you, Daisy—I won't stand for that filthy animal," Ram continued. "He's not a joke anymore."

Daisy held out her own plate at him. "Look, take my breakfast, it's just the same as the one Theseus had—Ram, you put temptation in his way—you ought to know him by now. And he's *not* dirty! Here. Don't be mad."

Ram thrust away the proffered plate. "I'm not hungry anymore. And I'm sick of your excuses for that filthy beast. Just keep him away from me." Abruptly he got up from the table and went to his room.

"Oh, dear, oh, dear," sighed Anabel. If only people would be kinder to each other. Of all human sins, the only one Anabel really found unforgivable was unkindness.

Toward the end of the first week in July, Anabel awaited with particular anticipation the arrival of her friends Guy and Isabelle de Luciny, who were bringing their children; Valerie, who was a little over a year younger than Daisy, and Jean-Marc, who was almost eighteen. She hoped that their company might entice Daisy away from her solitary expeditions. She remembered Jean-Marc as a sturdy lad of fifteen, rather short and plump, but pleasant and well-spoken.

She scarcely recognized the tall, attractive Frenchman with fine brown eyes who got out of the car and came toward her as she stood, welcomingly, in the circular entrance hall of the house. His manners were as polished and suave as only those of an almost adult, well-bred French youth can be, and it amused Anabel wickedly to see this self-possessed and rather lordly young sprig fall for Daisy as acrobatically, as dramatically as if he'd been hit over the head in a silent movie. He followed her around more closely than Theseus; he literally couldn't move his eyes away from her, which made him difficult at meals since he ate without looking at his food and he never heard a word anyone else said, not even a request to pass the salt. At first Daisy seemed more interested in his sister Valerie than in Jean-Marc, who insisted on accompanying them into Honfleur each morning for their shopping, carrying Daisy's basket, but eventually she began to respond to the smitten youth, with a kind of mischievous pleasure, the first she'd shown in many weeks.

"Honestly, Jean-Marc, I think I'm going to have to take legal measures. There's something curiously adoptable about you," she told him after lunch one day as the whole houseful of guests lay lazily on the terrace, except for the young man who was busily dragging his striped canvas deck chair closer to Daisy's. Her clear voice was heard by all the others, and Isabelle de Luciny and Anabel exchanged hopeful glances.

Under the influence of Jean-Marc's admiration, a new Daisy appeared at dinner, a Daisy who had taken the time to change into a mini-skirt and a thin summer sweater and offered to pour the coffee after dinner, a grown-up duty which she had occasionally attempted with a lack of interest, but which she now accomplished with finished grace. When this new Daisy was complimented by Guy de Luciny she received his words with the poise of a much older woman, sliding her black eyes toward Jean-Marc with a look that seemed both insolent and alluring, as if to ask why he had left it to his father to say the things he was thinking.

Now Daisy permitted Jean-Marc to go with her on her trips into Honfleur to sketch, and several times the two of them were late for lunch, returning flushed with the sun and still trembling with laughter over jokes they assured the others they wouldn't understand.

On the night of Bastille Day, the *Quatorze Juillet*, there is dancing in the streets in every city in France. In Honfleur the square in front of the town hall is turned into an outdoor ballroom and everyone, townspeople, tourists and the owners of the houses in the surrounding countryside, all come and dance with anyone who asks them, stranger or not. Daisy wore her best dress, from a London boutique called Mexicana, a long, demure, fragile white dress. The closely fitted bodice and full milkmaid sleeves were both made of bands of lace alternating with bands of finely tucked cotton. The lace and cotton formed a high, frilled collar. A hot pink satin sash with a big bow at the side was tightly clasped about her waist and below it fell a tucked cotton skirt with a wide lace hem which swept the floor. She had taken just the top layer of her hair, divided it into six sections and braided each section with white silk ribbons which ended in bows at the end of each braid.

The innocence of the covered-up white dress and the beribboned braids contrasted strongly with Daisy's straight, thick brows and excited pansy-centered eyes. Her full mouth was endowed with a new maturity as she felt for the first time in her life the intoxicating bone-deep assurance that tonight she was the unquestioned center of the group, the key to the romance of the evening. She had become an enchantress; in one stroke, she had absorbed and embodied the spirit of *La Marée*. None of the guests could stop looking at her. It was, thought Anabel gleefully, as if they had all turned into a band of besotted Jean-Marcs—all but Ram, whose disapproval of his half-sister seemed to have been accentuated by her success. He stood aside, an unpleasant expression crossing his aquiline features, his gray eyes colder than those of his father had ever been.

Anabel was glad that Daisy had always had courage. It takes courage to be a beautiful woman, she thought. Beauty, in Anabel's estimation, is the female equivalent of going to war, bound, as beauty is, to put a woman in hundreds of unwanted situations that otherwise she could have avoided. And Daisy was almost a beautiful woman—she had only a year or two of girlhood left, Anabel thought, with pity . . . and a little envy.

The entire house party, some fourteen people, drove down to town to dance and watch the fireworks. Daisy, as conspicuous as a bride, and as lively as the traditional *guinguette* music which demands no other knowledge of dancing than whirling, passed rapidly from the arms of a fisherman to a local painter to the Mayor of Honfleur to Jean-Marc; from the arms of the butcher to the arms of the sailors from the French Navy vessels moored in the port and then back to Jean-Marc again. She held herself as proudly as a young tree in its first season of spring bloom, her silvery hair flew and flew and even the braids couldn't prevent it from getting tangled as she danced. Her lips were parted in a smile of pure, unthinking, undirected pleasure. Her cheeks were flushed a deeper pink and the punctuation of her black eyes made the vivid, flying figure in its white dress elementally alluring. As the music went on and on far into the night, Daisy danced with every man in Honfleur except Ram, who had danced not at all, preferring to stand aloof on the edge of the crowded circle of jostling figures, arms crossed, eyes baleful, watching the merrymaking with an oddly malevolent expression on his face. Finally, Anabel and Isabelle de Luciny persuaded everyone that it was time to drive home, if only out of pity for the band, which was starting to look as if they would be glad to stumble back straight into the Bastille if only they didn't have to play another tune.

The next morning everyone was late for breakfast. Jean-Marc missed the meal completely. It wasn't until after he'd also been absent for lunch that his mother finally went to his room to wake him. She found his bed empty and a note addressed to her on the pillow.

Dear Maman,

I had a discussion with Ram last night which makes it impossible for me to remain here one minute more. I'll be back in Paris by this afternoon. I have a key to the apartment so don't worry. Please make my apologies to Anabel and thank her for the time I've spent here. I'd rather not explain any further, but I couldn't stay. Don't be upset.

Love,
Jean-Marc

Astonished, Isabelle took the note to Anabel.

"*Ma chérie*, does this make the slightest bit of sense to you?"

"Ram? I don't understand it at all. What on earth could Ram have had to do with it? If he'd had a fight with Daisy I wouldn't be a bit surprised if poor Jean-Marc disappeared—but Ram?"

"I'm going to ask him," said Isabelle, with serious maternal irritation. She and Anabel began to search the house.

Before lunch that day, Daisy had taken her sketch pad and gone to one of her favorite, secret places in the woods, a sweet-smelling eucalyptus grove thickly carpeted with aromatic leaves, from which there was a clear view of a small farmhouse. She often spent long hours drawing there, listening to the faint sounds of the barnyard far below, completely hidden from the world. Her triumph of the night before had left her languid, too lazy to get down to work, and she had stretched out on the leaves and slept for hours. She woke to hear footsteps crashing through the wooded trails. Curious, she peered out from her hiding place and saw Ram walking at a fast pace.

"Ram, I'm here," she called, sleepily.

Ram entered the grove and stood directly in front of her, without a greeting. Daisy looked up at him and laughed. "If you've come to see my view, you happen to be blocking it."

He threw himself down at her side, on the leaves, and roughly, silently, knocked the sketch book out of her hands. Then he took all her precious pencils and broke them in two and threw the pieces away furiously. Daisy watched him, speechless, incredulous.

"I've gotten rid of Jean-Marc so you needn't bother to go dangling yourself in front of him like a slut anymore!" he burst out in a strangled voice. "That exhibition last night was the last straw—I've never seen anything so disgusting, so degrading in my life—the way you slobbered over every sailor, every fisherman, every damned farmer—they must be calling you the cock tease of Honfleur!"

"*What?*" Daisy didn't know what he was talking about.

"Don't pretend that you don't understand exactly what I mean—all dressed up, pressing yourself against the local idiots—everything for everybody! And as for your love, your precious Jean-Marc, I told him that maybe it's done in France to come to visit and seduce the daughter of the house, but only a filthy, rotten swine would be such a shit."

"*Seduce?* But you're insane. Oh, Ram, I only let him kiss me on the cheek—he's fun, that's all, I swear it. How could he be my love? You've got it all wrong," Daisy said, gazing indignantly at Ram, her voice ringing with truth and surprise. He kept his eyes fixed on the ground, stubbornly holding on to his jealous anger, his face set in disbelief. "Ram, look at me," Daisy commanded. "Do I look as if I'm lying to you?" She put out her hand and tried to turn his head toward her, but, at her touch, he flinched away, making an animal sound of protest. "No, no, Ram, that's just not fair!" Daisy cried out. And innocently, out of her lack of sophistication, moved by an impulse to heal the hurt she saw on his beloved, sullen face, with fatal simplicity, she kissed him full on his stern mouth.

The gesture obliterated sanity for Ram. Groaning, he took her into his arms and buried his face in her hair. He kissed her hair over and over again, shaking in every limb with repressed emotion, half-rage, half-desire. He tried, for one brief moment, not to kiss her lips but a red wind of passion drew him to them.

He gave up the struggle and devoured her lips with his own, kissing her as if he were dying of thirst and her mouth were a moist fruit. Daisy, amazed, innocently and awkwardly returned his kisses giving herself up to the joy of realizing that Ram, whom she had never stopped loving since she first saw him, Ram who had always been the secret hero of her dreams, Ram from whom she had hopelessly begged a smile or even a mere word, was holding her tight, being kind to her, good to her, kissing her.

She abandoned herself to the comfort of this fulfillment of years of yearning, all thoughts blotted out. Daisy, who had never been kissed on the lips before, made the discovery of the mouth of another, of the roughness of his shaven cheeks, of the hardness of teeth, the wetness of his tongue. She kissed him back as if each kiss could bring back the life she had carelessly romped and reveled in, bring back happiness, kiss it into returning.

Daisy gave herself so completely to the happiness of being—after so many years—held and kissed by Ram, that she didn't realize that he had opened the buttons of her thin shirt until she felt his mouth move down to the nipples of her breasts. The feeling was the most exquisite she'd ever known—his beloved mouth tugging on the tender, sensitive buds—a feeling too new, so rapturously new and good that tears stung her eyes. In a flash Daisy felt all the intimations of physical passion she had never localized before, this girl to whom a gallop on a bright morning had been the height of pleasure of the body. Her pale, pale pink nipples grew firm and pinker as he kissed them, holding her breasts in each of his hands, and her head fell back on her willing neck as she surrendered to his lips and his fingers, feeling his hair against her shoulder, unhearing, unthinking, a creature of feeling only. She was dazed, almost paralyzed by the electric flashes of desire which were whipping through her body, when suddenly she returned to reality. Ram was fumbling at the waistband of her shorts, trying to take them off. She pushed him away as hard as she could, but he used all his strength against her sudden panic, her belated realization. She struggled with him, her mind a jungle of confusion. What had happened? How had it happened? What was going to happen? Soon, in spite of all her efforts, she was naked, her brown and white body revealed in all its terrified beauty.

"No! No!" she panted, "please, no!" But Ram was deaf to her pleas, deaf to her sobs. His face was as inhuman as a spear as he bent over her body. Nothing, no one could stop him now. In an ecstasy of lust he pried open her thighs and quickly, pouncing, found the opening he had to find, and drove himself into her, pounding brutally through the tender flesh because she was a virgin and he had to have her or die of anger and need.

Daisy's mind stopped working. Spangles of red and white and black exploded in her brain like the fireworks of the night before. Even as she groaned, even as she grunted in violent protest, she clung to his plunging body because, more than anything, she was desperate for reassurance that this cruel stranger was Ram, her Ram—only that knowledge would prevent her from being annihilated.

Afterward it was the man who sobbed and the girl who held and comforted him, kissing his dark hair and whispering, "It's all right, it's all right," clinging to him like the survivor of a vast tempest, eucalyptus leaves sticking to her back, the mingled smell of sweat and sperm rising to her nostrils for the first time in her life, her thighs stained with blood which she blotted away with pages of the broken sketch pad. When Daisy looked at Ram, his head hidden in her arms, prodigal flares of dark light came from her eyes. Although, instinctively, she tried to reassure him, she was herself drowning in a murky pool of feelings, totally foreign in a life in which she had always seen her way clearly and cleanly. Daisy was filled with her awakened knowledge of physical desire but it was mixed with a kind of shame she had never known before. Her whole mind and body ached with acute conflict and resentment. She wanted to bite, to kick, to shriek to high heaven, to faint, to run away. She wanted to go back to where she had been only an hour ago, but she knew already that there was no return. Deep within her something sounded, as if the string of a great cello had been plucked, a note of remote, mysterious but unmistakable warning.

When they finally returned to the house, the sunset was so brilliant that it partially blinded the eyes of anyone looking toward the woods which lay between the house and the horizon. The rest of the de Luciny family, having been unable to find Ram or come to any satisfactory explanation of the mystery of Jean-Marc's departure, had hastily packed and left for Paris. Anabel was in the salon, as Ram and Daisy materialized out of the woods, several feet separating them from each other. Daisy turned quickly and disappeared, entering the house, almost running, but Anabel was able to collar Ram before he started up the stairs.

"Ram! We've been looking everywhere for you. For God's sake, what happened with Jean-Marc?" she demanded.

"It's not something I want to talk about."

"What nerve—you drove him away somehow—you'd better have a good reason."

"Anabel, I'm telling you that it's best left alone."

She stood up, moved to unusual anger. "Now, just what the hell happened?"

"Since you insist—Jean-Marc made some disgustingly improper remarks about Daisy and I told him he wasn't a gentleman."

"Oh, for heaven's sake, Ram, you sound like something out of the eighteenth century. Improper remarks? What on earth are you talking about? Just what did he say?"

"Look, I refuse to have Daisy insulted, that's all. Jean-Marc apparently thinks English girls are pretty hot stuff, Daisy in particular."

"He never said that!" Anabel eried.

"You weren't there. You would have been as revolted with him as I was," Ram insisted coldly.

"Oh, what a total mess! He probably didn't mean what you thought at all. And since when have you been Daisy's champion? And now they've all gone off three days before they were supposed to leave and there's been *such* an unnecessary scene. I do wish, Ram, that you'd try to develop a sense of humor," Anabel said with unaccustomed asperity.

"The fact that he ran off with his tail between his legs speaks for itself," Ram answered, obdurate.

Anabel looked at her watch and was startled. "Ram, don't you realize that we still have a houseful of guests and that it's time for drinks? At least make yourself useful and run down into town for me and get some ice—the fridge is acting up, as if we hadn't had enough confusion today . . . quite seriously, Ram, I'm fed up!" As he left on his errand, Anabel thought that difficult as he had been since she'd known him, she had never been quite as angry at Ram as she was now. Nor had he ever seemed more indifferent to how she felt, now that she thought about it.

Nevertheless, as she surveyed her dinner table an hour and a half later, Anabel had to admit to herself that whatever it was that had been changed in the atmosphere of *La Marée* by the departure of Jean-Marc and his family, only good had come of it, unpleasant as the preceding day had been. It was the most agreeable evening she could remember of the entire summer. Everyone seemed touched with kindness and good will and jovial spirits and they were not caused just by the four bottles of champagne Ram had brought back from his errand to buy ice. Perhaps, she mused, it was because Ram himself had finally relaxed and lost that cruel, unforgiving look she was so sadly accustomed to seeing on his face. He played the host with charm and a grace which Anabel, herself the consummate hostess, could thoroughly appreciate. Although only his gray eyes physically reminded her of Stash, there was something of Stash in the way he dominated the table, yet refrained from taking over, allowing each guest to shine. He had a special air of being at home that Stash had always adopted unthinkingly wherever he went; he was gracious and gallant to all the ladies and with the men he seemed more mature than his twenty-two years, almost their equal, yet he retained a flashing, youthful gaiety that she was touched to see in him, in spite of her fading anger. It was so unlike Ram to express easy happiness that she couldn't begrudge it. As for Daisy, although her cheeks were red and her eyes almost feverish, she was subdued. Anabel made a mental note to have a serious talk with the child about getting too much sun: did she want that skin of hers to be tanned like a piece of leather by the time she was thirty? Tonight Daisy didn't offer to pour the coffee but gladly left it to Anabel, and the capriciousness which she'd been practicing on poor Jean-Marc was absent.

She seemed disoriented and far away, as if she had been sapped of her usual energy, and no wonder, Anabel decided. That riotous, nonstop night of dancing yesterday would be bound to cause a reaction in such a young girl. She wasn't surprised when Daisy decided to go to bed almost as soon as the late dinner was over.

Once she had shut herself into her sea-green refuge, Daisy collapsed on her bed. She was in such confusion of mind and body and spirit that it had taken all her resources to get through dinner. Too much had happened for her to think about it coherently. In her mind she was still lying in that eucalyptus grove, still hearing Ram's voice saying her name. Uncontrollable vibrations swept over her newly awakened body. She quivered from her toes to her scalp. She unbraided her hair and brushed it hard, she took off her dress and flung open the windows, hoping that the sight of Le Havre gleaming in the far distance might calm her, but the slightly misty air was too soft and the stars over the sea hung too low and the crickets were chirping in a way which she had never noticed before, a way that she could barely endure. She had never understood why adults asked each other how they had slept. That night Daisy was initiated into the great company of those who have passed sleepless nights. "White nights" the French call them, a night filled with thoughts she couldn't escape. The thing that had happened—Ram hadn't *meant* to do it! He was sorry—had he not wept, had he not said he was sorry, over and over? Of course it would never happen again. Of course they must never let anyone know. These tormented thoughts mixed and whirled with thoughts of Ram's lips, Ram's words of love, above all his words of love. He had told her he loved her. *He had said he had always loved her.* First one thought attacked her, then another, then they twined painfully round and round in her brain until, blessedly, at last the sun rose and touched the tops of the umbrella pines in front of her window, and she knew she could get up and find Theseus, who now slept outside, and take him for a good long run before breakfast.

Ram had never been so happy in his life. He felt as if only today had he become himself. He had come into his full heritage. He finally was *the* Prince Valensky with all the prerogatives that title implied. Of course, Daisy was *meant* to belong to him, just as everything his father had had was meant to belong to him. He looked back at the past weeks and realized what a fool he'd been, how he'd been angry and cold and unkind to her when it was only the simple injustice of not possessing Daisy that was the cause of his feelings of incompleteness, of unsecured happiness.

As for Daisy being his half-sister, it simply didn't matter. There could be no barrier, when two people are not brought up together, Ram told himself. Why, he hadn't even given a thought to Daisy's existence until he was fourteen. Not for them the shared family warmth, the well-worn jokes, the cloying familiarity of ordinary people. They had seen each other only on scattered holidays, almost totally separated by age and interests. In fact, he smiled to himself, they had been the closest thing to born enemies that two children of the same father could be. No. Ordinary rules for ordinary people did not apply to him and he most certainly wasn't going to concern himself with them, just as his father never had. Of course, he would make sure that other people—particularly Anabel who was basically conventional, in his opinion, in spite of the fact that she'd been his father's mistress—didn't meddle in business that didn't concern them—his business. He was so grandly happy, so sublimely conscious of everything he was and would become, of everything that, at last, he owned, that he, too, spent a sleepless night.

"Let's go to the stables and decide what to do about the polo ponies," Ram said to Daisy the next morning. They were the only ones in the kitchen. Even the cook was still asleep and they had made breakfast for themselves, each unexpectedly shy and glad of the business of frying eggs and looking for the wild strawberry jam the cook always hid.

"I thought you didn't want to make any decisions about them—That's what you said to Anabel."

"That was the other day—but I can't have that whole lot, not just the horses but the men, too, eating their heads off in Trouville and not do something about it. Either I'll keep them or I'll sell them—but first we'll go take a look."

"I'll be ready in fifteen minutes. Will you leave a note for Anabel?" Daisy ran upstairs to get into her riding clothes, her heart beating lawlessly.

They were gone all day, like truants, riding for hours in the green fields, changing from one pony to another, and finally, worn out, they flung themselves under a tree to eat a picnic lunch of long, mild, buttered radishes and a crusty loaf filled with ham and cheese that had been provided by the wife of the stable manager.

Eventually Ram decided that since he didn't play polo he'd put all the ponies up for auction at the first opportunity. There was no point in keeping even the best of them for ordinary riding; they were too finely bred, too nervous for his taste; he liked a larger horse, a good jumper, and Daisy had just acquired a fine pale bay with a black mane and tail who was stabled back in London, so she didn't need another mount.

During the long day and the drive back neither Ram nor Daisy referred to what had happened in the woods. Then, just as they turned into the driveway of *La Marée*, Ram took one hand off the steering wheel and laid it, heavy with authority, on top of her thigh.

"I'm going to kiss you there, right there, tonight," he said brusquely. She didn't dare look at him. Her whole body was blushing. Emotions spilled over which had been trembling near the surface all day, held in check only by the constant exercise into which they had thrown themselves.

"No, Ram!" she said in a low tone of prohibition which blotted out everything else, even the sight of some of the guests playing badminton in the garden.

"Be quiet," he ordered her, and she was quiet, finding, from somewhere, a smile with which to greet the others, an expert smile she didn't know she owned, a social smile and a social voice.

That night, after all the lights of the house were off, Ram tapped on the door of Daisy's bedroom and came in without waiting for her answer. He locked it behind him. Daisy was on the window seat, her knees drawn up under her, her arms circling her legs, her chin on her knees, as if she'd been sitting there thinking for a long time. He walked over to her and swept back the pale curtain of hair which fell over the near side of her face. She didn't move as she tilted her face so that he could see her eyes.

"We must *not*, Ram," she said.

"Daisy, you're still a baby. There aren't any stuffy musts or must nots for us—except that we must love each other."

"But not like . . . *not* what you did yesterday . . . Ram, just . . . sweetness, just being together," she said, hope and supplication mingled in her voice.

"Darling Daisy," he said, "just being together." He put both his arms around the entire slim circle of her body and carried her over to her bed. She lay there, hugging herself, stiff, silently resisting, abashed. When he kissed her the first time she pressed her lips tightly together and tried to turn her head away, but he wouldn't allow it. Very gently, very tenderly, but with absolute conviction, he parted her lips with the tip of his tongue. Now that he owned her he could take her slowly, surely. Her breath caught in her throat as she felt his tongue press on her clenched teeth and then felt it retreat to circle her lips, until she felt that her mouth was a ring of fire. Gradually, in spite of herself, she uncoiled her limbs as his lips traveled up her neck to her ear lobe. "Daisy, my Daisy," he whispered into her ear in a voice so soft that she could barely hear him. With a plaintive sigh she threw her arms around his neck and held him with all her strength. Oh, how content she was with this, nothing more, just this closeness, this dear affection. She felt sheltered, protected, safe from everything and everyone, a security she had thought she had lost forever when she was told of her father's death.

"Hug me tight," she asked. "Just hug me tight, only hold me, Ram, promise me, promise me . . ."

"Yes, Daisy, yes," Ram answered, while his fingers stealthily untied the ribbons of her long peignoir. "Yes, I'll hug you, my darling, I'll hug you." And he felt the outline of her small, firm breasts with careful, traitorous hands, brushing lightly over the tips of her nipples again and again until they rose to his touch and became so singingly sensitive that he knew he could bend his head and suck them and she wouldn't beg to be hugged anymore. He filled his mouth with the delicate rosettes, remembering their pale pinkness, still gently, still tenderly, until she lay back on the pillow giving herself in fresh astonishment to the darts which shot throughout her body from each nipple to her vulva, as if some crucial nerves had been activated, connections she'd never known existed.

Ram had been erect from the second he'd touched Daisy on the window seat but instinctively he had known to keep his rigid penis from touching any part of her, until she was led, step by step, into desire. Now he took one of her hands in his. "Daisy, feel how much I love you." He guided her hand to his penis and closed her hand around the quivering organ. She jerked her hand away immediately, shocked, struck with fearful alarm. He didn't try to make her touch him again but covered her lips with deep, slow, hot kisses, until he felt her mouth open of its own accord, until he felt her tongue tentatively reach out to touch his.

For half an hour he kissed her mouth and sucked her nipples until he could feel her beginning, just beginning, to stir her hips, unconsciously rotating them in a rhythm as old as time. Then he whispered again, "Daisy, touch me, touch me . . . you'll feel how much I love you . . . please touch me," and he took her hand again. This time she was too deeply bemused by her own aroused passion to resist. He took her hot fingers and tried to show them how to clasp his painfully engorged penis, but he had reckoned without his own towering desire. At the touch of Daisy's hand he realized that he was about to come to orgasm. Ram clutched his penis in one hand and shoved it roughly into the girl, just as the spasms overtook him. He bit his tongue to keep from crying out in the silent house. Bewildered, and hurting, she felt him quake in great, silent tremors.

After a brief time in which he lay panting, he kissed her once more. "Now, I'll hold you, my little Daisy," he muttered, and he lay, half asleep, clasping her in his arms for long, quiet, motionless minutes. Daisy didn't dare to move or speak. She was an accomplice. She had *let* him do it to her. If she protested he would fall into one of his sudden rages, or even worse, turn away from her and leave her all alone. But she could not be alone again. She had believed that all she wanted in Ram's arms was protection, security and the feeling that someone loved her but now, painfully excited, and shipwrecked anew, she wanted . . . she didn't know what she wanted. Furtively she pressed her lips to his bare shoulder, and as she did so they heard someone open, and a minute later, shut a door along the corridor.

"I'd better leave," Ram whispered.

"Yes."

He left her with a hurried kiss, left her high and dry, burning, burning, sickened with desire, sickened with shame, burning, burning.

The next day, after lunch, Anabel told Daisy that so many of the guests she had invited for the next week had announced that they were coming that Daisy would have to share her room, since it had two beds in it.

"I never dreamed they'd all say yes, but it's too late now. You'll like your roommate, I hope—she's an American girl, Kiki Kavanaugh, the daughter of an old friend of mine. Her mother is American too—she was Eleanor Williams when I first met her. She married a man who's in the motor business in Detroit."

"I'm half an American girl, too, Anabel—although I don't feel it."

"Do you remember much of it, Daisy?" asked Anabel, struck by some note of pathos in the girl's voice she didn't remember ever having heard before.

"So little. Mostly this feeling of having *been* with Mother and Dani and Masha—and sort of a dream memory of the way things looked, the big waves on the beaches, the forests, the light—I've never seen such light in England. I wish I could remember more. It seems as if my life was just split in half." There was a wistfulness in her voice like the residue of sugar in an empty cup, the memory of uncomplicated sweetness. Anabel wished sharply that she hadn't asked if Daisy remembered her American years—the girl looked even more weary than she had at dinner the night before, although at her age it was difficult to detect signs of fatigue.

Ah well, the death of Stash was a period they all had to live through, no way of skipping it and just carrying on as if nothing had happened. Anabel herself had had to strain every emotional resource she possessed to keep the house full and lively. Her own impulse was to crawl into a quiet room and just let desolation wash over her, but she couldn't permit herself to do that, mainly for the sake of Daisy. There were no more words between them as they sat on the striped canvas deck chairs on the terrace, their backs turned to the sea which, at this hour, was too bright to look at. Anabel had the gift of reposeful silence and she never asked what anyone else was thinking, a simple combination which had been only one of the many things men loved, that few other women had ever understood.

11

In the course of the following week, Ram came to Daisy's room every night. Now that he possessed her the feelings he had repressed for longer than he realized had been freed. They burst, full blown, into obsessive madness. He could think of nothing else but Daisy. At last he had her to himself, at last his father didn't come first with her, at last he could do as he wished with her.

At night he waited only until the corridor was clear before he slipped through her door. He no longer cared if other lights were on in the house once he had locked the door. As soon as he saw the secret, tender whiteness of her breasts and her belly, as soon as he smelled the smoky, sweet wine of her hair, as soon as he felt her amber arms around him, he became so inflamed with the need to take her that all consideration, all caution, all vestiges of reason left him. And she was dominated by him, totally suffused with a strange mixture of wanting, still wanting, his kisses and yet dreading what she now knew he would eventually do to her. Each night, in torment, she waited for him, thinking that this time she would have the will to prevent him, and each night she failed.

There was never any physical release for Daisy, and she was so naive, so untutored that she had no clear idea of what there might have been. Even if she had known, she would have been too ashamed to ask for it, because to ask for it would have been to participate even more than he forced her to in the thing he did to her. She concentrated only on the minutes of kissing and holding and being held and blocked the rest out of her mind as best she could. And afterward, there was her punishment; the dizzy fog of misery and sticky, blood-heavy frustration that enveloped her throughout the long, hot days.

Unlike Ram, Daisy felt intolerable guilt, although she was too innocent to identify the emotion clearly, experiencing it as crushing fatigue and a black sadness. But she was torn by her continuing need for Ram, a need as strong as her guilt. She had loved him since she was six and she didn't know how to break away from his hold on her. Guilt and her fear of having no one to hold on to, no one to belong to her, fought inside of her daily and she grew more unhappy and confused and unable to think things through . . . to think at all.

"Daisy, let's go into Deauville for the day, just the two of us, and do some shopping. The boutiques are full of fall clothes—we could see what's going on at Dior and St. Laurent and Courrèges—you've grown so much that you need new things," Anabel said, looking anxiously at the signs of something very wrong on Daisy's face.

"I'm not in the mood to buy anything, Anabel—I'm so worn out I don't think I could stand to try on clothes."

"Then I have a great notion. I've always wanted to try that spa near the boardwalk—it's supposed to make you feel marvelous—rejuvenation therapy. First they pound you with sea water from a giant hose and whip up your circulation, then you soak in a hot tub full of bubbling sea water, then a long massage and finally they wrap you up in towels like a baby and make you rest in a deck chair for half an hour. It's all over by tea time, and, afterward, we'd go directly out to tea and chocolate eclairs. Why don't we try it?"

"It sounds like water torture to me," Daisy said indifferently.

Anabel, not defeated, proposed a drive to Pont-l'Evêque to buy the cheese that has been prized since the thirteenth century, or even just lunch at the Ferme St. Siméon, at the bottom of their hill, where the Impressionists used to meet, a favorite treat for Daisy in former years. But Daisy refused all of Anabel's suggestions, on one pretext or another. She didn't want to be alone with her secret and Anabel. She was afraid that Anabel, always so sensitive to mood, might divine the truth. She was even more afraid that she might *tell* Anabel. And then—what would Ram do to her?

One afternoon, disconsolate and restless, Daisy secluded herself in one of the deep recesses of the balcony of the salon, intending to attempt to read Balzac in French, something the honorable Miss West, French mistress at Lady Alden's, had suggested for all the girls' summer vacations. Before she was more than three pages into the dusty volume, barely understanding a word of what she read, Ram discovered her hiding place.

"I looked for you in the woods," he said, with reproach in his voice. "Why are you stuck away up here—it's gorgeous out."

"I wanted to be alone."

"Well, I want to talk to you. I've decided what to do with the house in London. It's far too big for us—Father never needed all that space—and the real-estate market's never been better. I'm going to sell it and buy a house that makes sense; one that doesn't need more than three or four servants to run. I think we should live in Mayfair, Upper Brook Street or South Audley Street—somewhere in that general area."

"You mean—live together?" She gaped at him.

"Obviously. You have to live somewhere. Do you think you're old enough to live alone?"

"But, I thought, I assumed—I'd be living with Anabel, Ram, not with you," Daisy said with all the grown-up dignity at her command.

"Impossible. I won't permit it. Anabel will have found another man to keep her within a few months and you can't be exposed to that sort of thing."

"Ram! That's a beastly, stinking thing to say—Anabel's like my mother!"

"That only proves I'm right—you're too much of a baby to understand that Anabel lives off rich men—always has and always will."

"It's not true! How can you be so awful?"

"Then why did Father never marry her?"

Daisy faltered, unable to answer his question. Frantically she turned to another objection. "What about the servants? What are you going to do with them?"

"Pension them off, of course," Ram said in an indifferent voice. "They're far too old—every last, decrepit one of them—and there's no good in thinking that we're doomed to keep them doddering about until they drop dead one by one in the pantry—they were all just another of Father's crazy extravagances, like putting all his money into Rolls-Royce for sentimental reasons. I'm getting out of Rolls, Daisy, and I'm taking your money out, too. It's high time we put that money to work—and time to get as much of it out of England as possible!"

"Ram, no! You can't sell my stock . . . Father left it to me and I'm not going to sell."

"Daisy," Ram said reasonably, "the market's no place for emotional attachments. I'm the legal trustee of your money and if I want to sell your stock I can."

"Would you do that to me? Against my will?" she blazed at him. The stock in Rolls-Royce suddenly seemed all she had left to cling to, a real and tangible relic of her father's concern, of his caring protection, of the fact that she still possessed a link to the past that Ram was so abruptly dismantling.

"Oh, to hell with that," he barked. "Keep the stock if it means so much to you."

"And my horse? Where will I keep her?" Daisy asked, struggling to find another fixed element of her life that Ram couldn't wipe away with a word.

"We'll find another stable, nearby our new house—don't worry. You can have two dozen white horses if you want, Daisy, and a kennel full of lurchers," Ram said, relieved that Daisy seemed to be running out of reasons why they could not live together.

"But your flat," she said feebly, "you were so pleased with it."

"It's far too small for the two of us. I can get rid of it in a flash, and at a profit. Father's pictures will fetch a fortune at Sotheby's, even though I'm going to keep at least two Rembrandts and the furniture—my God, do you have any idea what signed French pieces like that are going for these days? To say nothing of the icons—that will be a major sale just in itself."

"So you're going to sell *everything*—everything I love, everything I grew up with," she gasped, with stricken eyes. She wanted to writhe and tear at Ram, but she knew he could do whatever he wanted with his own property. He took her in his arms and crushed her body to him.

"We'll be together, just the two of us, and no old servants around to poke and pry and treat you like a child—you want that, don't you?" She didn't answer, gasping in outrage, and taking her silence for agreement, he thrust his hand under her shirt and cupped one of her breasts firmly, his thumb making circles around her nipple. Furious as she was, her nipple hardened and he pulled her shirt higher and fastened his mouth on it, sucking with a desperate, hasty need. His other hand was reaching under her shorts, searching for the downy hair, fingertips blindly reaching for her special warmth. Daisy froze as she heard a light footstep mounting the staircase to the balcony, but deaf to everything, Ram pulled on her nipple harder than ever, as if he wanted to inhale her all in one mouthful. Daisy, with a terrified force she didn't know she possessed, pulled away and flung herself as far from him as she could on the loveseat, pointing frantically in the direction of the footsteps while she pulled down her shirt. Dazed, Ram finally understood, and when Anabel appeared with a vase of flowers, she found the two of them sitting several feet apart, Daisy apparently engrossed in Balzac.

"Children! Oh, you frightened me! I thought I was alone up here. Just look—aren't these Queen Elizabeth roses marvelous? Daisy, they're for your room. The Kavanaughs are coming tomorrow early and I'm filling the house with flowers for them."

"Christ! Not more people. This is becoming a boarding-house," Ram said in disgust.

"You'll like them," Anabel said lightly, not, at the moment, really caring if he did or he didn't. She supposed they'd been fighting again from the way they looked. Well, they'd have to work it out between them, whatever it was.

That night, as soon after dinner as possible, Daisy went upstairs to her room and locked herself in. Later Ram knocked several times, each time a little louder, and whispered her name. Defiantly she glared at the door and neither opened it nor answered him. Only when she heard him stride off did she allow herself to whimper in fear.

Daisy fled *La Marée* at dawn the next morning, putting a big chunk of bread and an orange in her pocket. She roamed the country lanes of Honfleur with Theseus, keeping him firmly attached to a leash so that he didn't take off for any of the kitchens or farmyards of the neighborhood.

She felt that she could somehow, in solitary companionship with her dog, retreat into a time when life was simple, when rules were made for her, when she knew the guidelines and lived within them happily. But as hours passed and the sun rose high overhead she realized that Anabel would be expecting her back for lunch. This was the day of the arrival of the new guests, Eleanor Kavanaugh and her daughter, with some sort of silly name, the one Anabel thought she'd like. The idea of meeting new people was an almost unbearable complication right now, yet the girl would be sharing her bedroom, and that was a profound relief to Daisy, a respite she couldn't have arranged herself.

The Kavanaughs' arrival at *La Marée* was announced from the driveway by an enormous, dark burgundy Daimler, parked in front of the door, with a dozen suitcases still being carried inside by their uniformed chauffeur. "Oh, bloody hell!" said Daisy to herself, as she contemplated the scene. It was the most violent expression of disgust she knew. Anabel hadn't said they were on an official tour of the native islands. Did they think they were royalty? She looked down at her dusty tennis shoes, her outgrown shorts, and her worn jersey. Her hair, she imagined, must look like a vulture's nest. With luck, she judged, they might all be outside drinking sherry and she'd have time to make herself presentable before she met them.

Seeing no one, Daisy slipped up the staircase and quietly approached her room. She heard no noise inside, no sounds of unpacking, so she entered briskly, and then stopped, almost falling over her feet, at the sight of a girl curled up on her window seat, looking out at the sea. Too late. The girl turned and looked at Daisy with an expression of amazement.

"You can't be Daisy!"

"Why not?"

"Daisy's a little girl—fifteen or something."

"How old are you?"

"I'm almost seventeen."

"Huh—you don't look it."

Kiki Kavanaugh drew herself up impressively. Five feet, two and three quarters of an inch of audacious female. She had frolicsome eyebrows, the face of a kitten who knows she's the pick of the litter and a short, fluttering mop of once brown hair which she had just had streaked in Kelly green, à la Zandra Rhodes. Her big eyes were umber, a dark, dusky brown with yellow lights in them—the eyes of a waif—spawn of a devil—and her beautifully shaped head was adorned with a pair of small, perfect, almost pointed ears. She was wearing what might have been either a Ukrainian wedding dress or something invented by a newly rich Afghanistani princess, made of red pleated linen, largely embroidered, appliqued in gold lace, fringed, wrapped, and tied here and there with multicolored beads. She lacked only anklets of bells.

"You're absolutely sublime, whoever you are," this apparition told Daisy. "I tried to convince Mother it was time to get back to classics but she never listens—after all, what could *I* know compared to the Queen of Grosse Pointe? Wait till she sees you—will she be sorry she let me keep this hair."

"Can't you have it, ah . . . put back?" Daisy suggested.

"Try that and it falls out—I'll just have to wait till it grows. Oh, balls! I can't go out there and meet all those people like this. Will you lend me something to wear—shorts and a shirt? And some of your hair?" Kiki circled Daisy in rapt admiration. Even Daisy's old shoes seemed to her to be the ultimate in throw-away chic.

"But they'd be way too big . . . of course, I would, but you'd swim in them," answered Daisy, enthralled by this gypsy who had camped in her bedroom.

"Oh, never mind, I'm always like this when I see someone divinely tall and naturally silver-blonde and absolutely, incredibly beautiful—it gives me a swift rush of shit to the heart but I'll be okay in a few minutes. I mean, I actually have a fairly healthy ego but bugger it all, wood nymphs set me back to square one. Do you like 'bugger'? I just learned it in England and I think it's an awfully useful word." She looked at Daisy, her raffish smile inquiring.

"Lady Alden disapproved of 'bugger'—very strongly—so it must be a good word. We got the ruler if we ever used it."

"The ruler! Capital punishment? No, corporal punishment—or whatever. They'd do that to you? How dare they? But then . . . you *must* be Daisy."

"Well, what would I be doing in this room if I weren't?"

"I thought . . . well . . . never mind. No, scratch that. I made a resolution never to say 'never mind' again. It drives people crazy and they always get it out of you anyway. I thought Daisy was a perfectly dumb name, so sickeningly pristine, an anachronism. But now it's just right for you, since you're she . . . or her?"

"She."

"Lord have mercy, I just guess at grammar. You realize, I had this mental picture of a little girl called Daisy, a princess no less, and what do I find but a fucking goddess—I tell you, it's enough to make me try to be mean—but who could be mean to you? Listen, do you know what I hate most in the world?" Daisy never took her eyes off Kiki. She had just realized that Kiki had on green nail polish, green mascara, and green eyeshadow. "It's those frantically well-dressed people in *Vogue* who say they live in only three wonderful old skirts they had made to order fifteen years ago—by Main, of course, who else?—and just two plain black cashmere sweaters and then they add one perfect jewel of an accessory every year, like a pair of priceless, antique Chinese slippers—you know it's a filthy lie but how can you prove it? Shit, I'll never get it right." She slumped despondently in the middle of her elaborate costume.

"Don't change, don't move, don't despair," said Daisy, suddenly restored to her role as the leader of Lady Alden's. "I'm coming right back."

She returned in five minutes, her hair all pulled up on the top of her head, skewered by pins into which she'd tucked some of the purple bougainvilla which grew on the walls of the house. She wore a mini-dress of flashing silver paper which she'd bought for three pounds at Biba. It could only be worn once and she hadn't dared to take it out of her wardrobe until today.

"Do you have any Paco Rabanne jewelry?" she asked Kiki.

"Doesn't everyone? Just a minute." Kiki rummaged in one of her seven suitcases and pulled out a space age, cast-metal neck sculpture which looked like a large, elaborately framed mirror, a chastity belt for the upper body. She clasped it around Daisy's neck. "Earrings?"

"No—I think that might be too much. I'll just wear bare feet—same effect but less fuss."

"You can't be fifteen," said Kiki flatly, admiringly.

"I'm wise beyond my years. Come on—let's give the old people a shock they won't forget."

During the week of the Kavanaughs' visit, Ram, for the first time in his life, found his generalized bitterness against the world turning to actual fantasies of murder—Kiki's murder.

Her mother could have told him that it couldn't have been done without a silver bullet. Kiki, a brisk, practiced and roguish prankster, stood for having fun in a way which, in spite of her intelligence, had caused four of the best girls' boarding schools in the United States to fail to "invite" her to reregister for the following year. She had survived the inestimable damage of immunity enjoyed from earliest childhood, the damage which might have been caused by knowing, almost from the playpen, that she was a member of the only local aristocracy worth belonging to in Grosse Pointe, that of the motor industry; as well as the damage which could have occurred as a result of being the longed-for daughter in a family of three older brothers—she had survived because of a stern, inborn, incorruptible honesty. Kiki told the truth, to herself and to others, a trait so rare as to make her seem eccentric. Her honesty went hand in hand with her impulsiveness, and she and Daisy, separated in age by little more than a year and a half, fell into instant complicity. They were a match in their love of a dare, their fancy for the improbable project. If Kiki was far more worldly and sophisticated, Daisy was the braver and more stalwart of the two; where Kiki was spoiled—or as she liked to put it, "divinely rotten"—Daisy was merely stubborn. The greatest difference in the two girls was in their emotional attachments. Kiki admitted to many, none of which troubled her—she took her father, her brothers and especially her mother for granted and found them, all of them, *amusing*—an attitude which puzzled and entranced Daisy.

However, during the week Kiki and her mother spent at *La Marée*, the two girls spent little time in serious discussions. Like fillies let loose in a pasture, they were busy exploiting their new camaraderie. Daisy, after a long night of uninterrupted sleep, suddenly felt full of her old laughing vitality, as if she'd had her youth returned to her, an unquestioning, untormented youth which led the two of them on expeditions into Honfleur to banter with the fishermen, to fill themselves with Coca-Colas Anabel wouldn't have in the house, to buy coarse garlic sausages that they ate on the street, taking huge bites and talking with their mouths full. They hired a taxi and went to Deauville at teatime and paraded slowly through the lobbies of the great hotels, like strolling players in their rich-hippie rig-outs, enjoying the outraged looks of the middle-aged women in their safe, laughably expensive Chanel suits. They kept a score of how many women they could stare down in any given lobby on any given day. They exchanged clothes avidly, finding that Daisy's shorts and shirts would fit Kiki if she hitched them up with a belt and folded over the waist bands. Dressed alike, they ran up and down the beach at Trouville treating placid family groups to rude shouts. From a rented cabana they swam in the cold, northern waters, often arriving back late for meals at *La Marée*, with barely an excuse except to Anabel who didn't need one, since she was so delighted with the success of her hopes for a friend for Daisy.

Kiki had only one complaint. "That brother of yours must simply loathe me," she said to Daisy. "I've been flirting with him like crazy. I've invited him to come with us and I've been getting absolutely nowhere with him—and that, I promise you, is something that doesn't happen to me a whole lot. If at all! Does he have something against Americans? Or is it my green hair? Is he queer? I just don't get it."

"Oh, Ram's hopeless—forget him, it's that Etonian superiority of his. He doesn't mean to be rude . . . it's just his way," Daisy answered evasively. Couldn't Kiki see how jealous he was, she wondered? Of course not—how could Kiki imagine that she, Daisy, was clutching at her companionship in an effort never to be alone with Ram. She watched him at the dinner table staring at her, his eyelids hooded like those of a sculpture of a knight, killed long ago on a Crusade. Just the thin slivers of pupils peered out from his closed face, but she could feel Ram pulling at her across the table.

Several times he'd trapped her alone on the staircase, and had been about to fall on her with kisses but the sound of Kiki, faithfully following her, had forced him to let go. Ram was both malignant and reckless in his powerlessness but Daisy managed to never be far from Kiki, admitting to herself that this shield couldn't last for long, but using it to the full while it did. She needed this time apart from Ram, she needed it so much that she was willing to risk the punishment she knew she'd have to face when it was over. Every night, for long after Kiki had fallen asleep, Daisy lay awake thinking, trying to put her emotions in some sort of order, but not succeeding. She sorted over and over the facts of her long love for Ram, her need for Ram, and her conviction, which grew every day, that what Ram did to her was utterly bad, utterly wrong, no matter what he thought. She once toyed with the idea of consulting Kiki, but the mere realization of the words she'd have to use convinced her that it was impossible. The burden was one she had to bear alone, in shame. Dreadful, inescapable shame, shame unending.

Finally the day came when the Kavanaughs had to leave for the Côte d'Azur, where they were to meet Kiki's father, who was flying there from Detroit, via Paris. They planned to break the trip at Limoges and drive the distance in two long days on the roads. In a few weeks Kiki was going to enter the freshman class at the University of California at Santa Cruz. Although she hadn't officially graduated from any of her various schools, her college boards had been good enough for Santa Cruz and she had been welcomed by that most liberal and free-spirited of universities. Her parents had carefully coordinated this summer's trip so that they could spend time with their daughter before, as Eleanor Kavanaugh almost tearfully put it, "we lose her to higher education." There was no question of her disappointing her father and staying on at *La Marée* as Daisy and Anabel had asked her to do.

"Daisy, I promise you that, at Christmas, you can go visit Kiki in the United States," Anabel told the miserable girls.

"Christmas is a million years away. Why can't Daisy come to Santa Cruz, too?" Kiki asked rebelliously.

"She has another year at Lady Alden's before she even takes her university examinations," Anabel said, patiently.

"Oh, balls, balls and bugger! Excuse me, Anabel. I feel like a star-crossed lover or something," said Kiki.

"You don't quite sound like one," Anabel laughed kindly. She had taken a great liking to this unlikely creature, such a strange daughter for her old friend Eleanor, who had been, before her great automotive marriage, a conservative and well-bred American miss.

That night, when Ram rapped on her door, Daisy opened it immediately. The departure of Kiki had made her realize that, in the course of their tomboy week, she had made a decision about her future she wasn't conscious of having reached. But now she felt a need, as sharp as thirst after a long day on an empty boat, to return to her lost girlhood, to become again as chaste as she had been on the *Quatorze Juillet.* She was calm, determined and possessed by the certainty that everything must be sacrificed to that end. Her confusions had fallen away. She could do without Ram. His protection was infinitely worse than being alone in the world. All the corners of her mind seemed clear and in focus for the first time since her father had died.

Ram came in and locked the door behind him. Hurriedly, he tried to take Daisy in his arms but she retreated to the window seat. She hadn't changed from the yellow cotton dress she wore at dinner and the lights in her room were all on.

"Sit down, Ram. I have something to say."

"It can wait."

"No. Not another second. Ram, what we've been doing is over—finished. I'm your sister. You're my brother. I won't do it ever again because it's wrong and I don't like it."

"It's that bitch, Kiki—you told her, didn't you?" he said in a voice of white revenge.

"Not a word. No one knows and no one will ever know, I promise you. But it's over."

"Daisy, you sound like some little bourgeoise—'it's over'—how can it ever be over? We love each other. You *belong* to me, little idiot, and you know it."

"I belong to no one but myself. You can do whatever you like, you can sell everything Father ever loved, you can live any way you choose to live, but I intend to stay with Anabel in Eaton Square—I'm sure she'll have me—and that's the end of it. I don't need you anymore!"

Ram came closer and put one large hand around the top of her arm, just below the shoulder, hurting her with his fingers. She sat as silent as a marble girl. There was enough light for him to look right into the velvet centers of her eyes and what he saw there, utter, indomitable conviction, clear and hard, maddened him.

"Ram, take your hand off my arm," she ordered him.

Her words, still delivered with the calm and composure she was hanging on to desperately, only acted as goads. He fastened both his strong, bony hands on her arms and jerked her sharply to her feet, as if she were a mere beast who had to be taught a lesson in discipline. Still she stood fearlessly in his grip, looking him straight in the eye. With relentless force he pulled Daisy close to him and kissed her lips. Her mouth didn't move under his. She scarcely breathed. He appropriated her mouth, consuming it with calculated skill, and held back his anger. He gave her the long, delicious, unthreatening kisses she had craved only a week ago. But she remained passive and detached, her lips closed and cool under his skillful mouth. He stroked her hair with a hard, possessive, demanding hand and whispered in her ear, "Daisy, Daisy, if you don't want more than this I won't do anything else . . . just kissing and being close—I promise . . . I swear." Yet, as he clutched her to him and battered her cheeks with scorching kisses, she felt his penis rise and press dangerously against her belly. With a violent summoning of her energy Daisy flung herself away from him.

"No good, Ram. I don't trust you. *I don't want you!* Nothing of you—no kisses, no hugs, no more lying words. Just get out of my room." Her voice was low, because of the others in the house, but tense with a wounding distaste.

She had backed away until she reached the far wall of her room and now he came at her, his features blunted and swollen with lust, his eyes dulled by the intensity of his need to possess her. Ram was out of control. He pressed Daisy against the wall with all of his weight, lifted her skirt with a brutal hand and ground the hard butt of his penis against her underpants. With his other hand he snatched at her breasts in a frenzy, viciously bruising the young nipples.

"You wouldn't *dare* if Father were alive, you filthy coward!" Daisy gasped.

Ram hit her on the face with his open hand. She felt her teeth cut into the inside of her cheek. She felt the blood begin to flow onto her tongue. He hit her again and then again, and while she was trying, in a panic, to get the breath to scream, he put a hand over her mouth and dragged her to the bed. With every bit of force she possessed, Daisy wasn't able to pull his hand away from her mouth during the brief, hideous minutes which followed. As she swallowed her own blood to keep from choking, Daisy felt him rip off her underpants. He had to hit her twice again before he could wrench her legs apart with his knees and then there was the searing, rasping eternity of a nightmare as he stabbed his penis into her, again and again, with the inhumanity of a madman, dry and closed as she was. Then he was finished, and gone. Daisy lay inert, blood seeping from her mouth, so extinguished, so obliterated, that it was many minutes before the tears she longed for finally came. After the tears, painfully, resolutely, Daisy got off the bed and went to wake up Anabel.

Anabel gave Daisy warm water and soft towels and stopped the bleeding and listened, holding her close, as Daisy told her the entire story, again and again, until she had finally calmed down enough to fall asleep on Anabel's bed. Only then did Anabel give way to the sobs which were more piteous, more tormented and far more furious than those Daisy had shed. She had failed Stash, she had failed Daisy. Ram's crime had to remain secret, depriving her of the revenge she would have taken. She would never speak to him again—he was dead to her forever—but there was no way to bring him to justice. What was done was done—she cursed herself, her blindness, her assumptions, her trust.

As soon as daylight appeared, Anabel telephoned to the hotel in Limoges where the Kavanaughs were spending the night on their trip south.

"Eleanor, it's Anabel. Don't ask me any questions but do you think that Daisy could possibly get into Santa Cruz?"

"This year? Isn't she too young?" Eleanor Kavanaugh answered with her habitual direct approach to the fundamentals.

"Age isn't the question now—it's whether she could pass the exams. It's *very* important, Eleanor, or I wouldn't let her go so soon."

"I'm sure she could pass the college boards, Anabel. Her education is already beyond an American girl's of seventeen, thanks to our atrocious high-school system. Look, I'll find out if there's still room and where she can take the exam—all right?"

"Could you do it tomorrow—today, I mean. Don't wait till you get home," Anabel pleaded.

"Count on me." Eleanor had never been a person who asked unnecessary questions. "Whenever that admissions office is open in California I'll telephone them—and then I'll call you, and you can send them Daisy's records."

"Bless you, Eleanor."

"Anabel, we're old friends, remember? I haven't forgotten . . . and don't worry.

Daisy'll get into Santa Cruz, I guarantee it. After all, I made them take Kiki, didn't I? Just realize, it's not exactly Harvard."

But it is six thousand miles away from Ram, thought Anabel, as she hung up the phone.

12

Handwoven!" Kiki proclaimed excitedly.

"What?" Daisy looked up from the catalogue of courses offered at the University of California at Santa Cruz. Kiki had been ruminating for a good half-hour as she cast a disgusted eye on her still-unpacked suitcases sitting in one corner of their dormitory room.

"But that's it! That's the key! Handmade, homespun, second-hand, third-hand, stolen or bartered for—but above and before all else, *handwoven*. I mean, we don't want to stand out like a couple of nerds, do we?"

"I thought I'd gotten away from uniforms once I was freed from Lady Alden's—don't tell me I've got to get back into another one here? And anyway, why is how we dress so important?" Daisy inquired. "I thought this place was casual."

"Daisy, you just don't understand yet," Kiki sighed patiently. "Once you know how to dress for a place or an event—once that's figured out, the rest takes care of itself. You spend too much time at the same school so you never had to worry, but if you'd been to as many schools as I had, you'd realize that you can only survive and be yourself if you *blend* into the surroundings. Now neither of us is exactly inconspicuous and we both want to spend the next four years sort of incognito—no princess for you, no Miss Grosse Pointe Automotive Heiress shit for me—so we've got to get into handwoven right away, even if it itches."

"Done. Now how about deciding what courses you're going to take? That won't take care of itself," Daisy said, waving the catalogue at her meaningfully.

"There's a course in surfing that sounds intensely interesting. Also kayak handling, bike maintenance and jazz dancing. But the only one I'm absolutely definite about is trampoline."

"Kiki—you're impossible. There's no credit given for any of those."

"Bugger."

"I'm taking pottery, drawing, print making and painting—all necessary for an art major," said Daisy smugly. "And, since we have to satisfy something called the Social Sciences requirement, let's both take Dreaming S. Oh, hell, it says here that we have to take Western Civilization too—a must for Freshmen."

"I'll sign up for anything to stay here. I think we've landed in Camelot," Kiki said, looking out of the window blissfully.

"Look, take trail riding with me. We've got to get some phys. ed.—oh, blast, no credit for that."

"Give me that catalogue," Kiki demanded. "Ah ha! Workshop in Theater Production satisfies the Humanities requirement—how about that? We get to be in a play—I think I'll major in Drama."

"Good. Our education's settled," Daisy said in satisfaction. "Now let's go shopping. Or should we just buy our own loom?"

Daisy had given an entirely adequate performance on the College Board Examinations—Lady Alden's ruler had not been plied without a purpose—and Santa Cruz had been glad to welcome the fifteen-and-a-half-year-old student from London.

Kiki and Daisy were roommates at Cowell, the first of the largely self-contained residential colleges to open in Santa Cruz which was, itself, the most beautiful baby of a great university system. It had been founded in 1965, just two years before Daisy and Kiki entered this experimental school built on two thousand dreamingly lovely acres overlooking Monterey Bay, seventy-five miles south of San Francisco.

A visitor, driving toward the university from the Victorian seaside city of Santa Cruz, grows dizzy with the rich, lazy, untouched sweep of open fields and deep forests of a former working ranch, still guarded by old fences, dotted with limestone kilns and graced by a few ancient farm buildings. The university is made up of separate residential colleges, modeled after Oxford or Cambridge in their conception of community but designed by some of the greatest modern architects in the United States. The colleges are so cleverly hidden in the trees that they can almost be overlooked entirely, although the students, who could be dress extras in a lumberjack movie, contrive to stay visible as they lope from class to class, bearded genial boys and gilded, if messy, girls.

Daisy and Kiki romped through Santa Cruz, taking courses that always sounded easier than they turned out to be, and working much harder than they had planned to, but, in the course of it, becoming increasingly drawn into the worlds of art and the theater which opened up to them.

Daisy discovered that her talent for drawing, which she had reserved for the sketches she made for Dani and her moments of solitude, was a substantial talent, a far greater gift than she had realized, a serious potential. She immersed herself in drawing and painting, watercolor, pastel and oil, never tempted by the abstract-expressionist mode, but rather sticking to what she did best: realistic and sensitive portraits, studies of nature, and, of course drawings of horses. Kiki found an outlet for her randy, inquisitive and honest self in the theater where nothing she could do or say aroused any surprise form her peers. They were all "into self-expression" which suited Kiki very well. This was finally the "fun" she had always searched for everywhere, and at Santa Cruz she could get academic credit for it.

Kiki was a spendthrift with her small delicate body. She had many love affairs, caring nothing for her Grosse Pointe indoctrination into the nature of virtue, her good name or public opinion. She cared for no opinion of her actions but her own, and her strict code was satisfied by personal generosity and absolute sincerity. She had a talent for falling for the wrong men, but she reveled in her errors, getting out before she hurt anyone but herself. She observed, in sinful amusement, the efforts of others to try to make her feel guilty. Fun came first—why couldn't people just admit it—take their fun, take their lumps and go on to the next adventure? Why did you have to *learn* from your mistakes? You'd only find a different one to make the next time anyway.

Daisy and Kiki roomed together during all their years at Santa Cruz, often talking far into the night and sharing their experiences, yet Kiki, whose many antennae seemed to sprout like a network from her whimsical head, knew that there were large areas in her friend that she didn't understand. Daisy was, even in their senior year, still something of an enigma and Kiki had little patience for enigmas.

"Daisy," she suggested one day in 1971, the winter of their senior year, "think about the clitoris."

"Before lunch?"

"Why, I ask you *why*, is it where it is? All tucked away, practically invisible, impossible to find without directions that I, for one, am fed up with having to provide."

"I thought you just told them what you wanted them to do and they did it," Daisy said, incuriously. Her friend's complaint was not an unfamiliar one.

"Why should I have to give them a goddamned roadmap? A man doesn't have to show a woman where his cock is! It's not fair!"

"Just where do you think it should be moved to?" Daisy inquired reasonably. "The tip of your nose?"

"I'm not giving up sex," Kiki answered her quickly, "but there's a real need for reform."

"Hmmm." Daisy waited patiently for the real purpose of this conversation. Whenever Kiki talked about the clitoris she was leading up to something.

"While we're on the subject, Daisy, there's one thing I really don't understand about you," Kiki continued.

"Only one?"

"Yup—how come you're still a virgin? Everyone's talking about you—did you realize that? They call you Peck-on-the-Cheek-Valensky."

"I know. It's un-American . . . I'm an embarrassment to you, aren't I?" Daisy laughed.

"It's getting that way. Do you realize that you're going to be nineteen on your next birthday? In a few months? And still a virgin? Forget un-American—it's unhealthy and unwholesome. Really, Daisy—I'm serious."

"I'm waiting for Mr. Right," Daisy said annoyingly.

"Bullshit. You go square dancing with Mark Horowitz who's having a mad thing with Janet except she hates square dancing; you go riding with Gene, the Gay Caballero; you go to the movies with absolutely anybody so long as it's a mob; you let Tim Ross buy you pizza and he's so in love with you that he's happy just for the honor of paying for your pepperoni; you go into San Francisco for Chinese food with three *girls*, for God's sake, and yet every *one* of the most attractive guys at school has been after you! And I'm not even counting the men you've met when you come home with me for vacations—the most eligible bachelors in Grosse Pointe have all been spurned by you, kid, including my poor brothers, those sweet assholes, and what about the men you meet when you go to Anabel's for the summers? I've seen the letters they write which you don't even bother to answer. What's with you?" Kiki finished, her arms akimbo under her tattered poncho, her pointed ears pink with indignation.

Daisy looked at her, suddenly serious. Kiki had been sounding this note for well over two years now and evidently it really bothered her enough to make an issue over it. And when Kiki made an issue she was capable of bringing Napoleon back from Elba.

"Okay, you're right. I don't want to get involved with a man, not at all. I don't want anyone to have any power over me. I don't want anyone to think he is entitled to any part of me. I don't want any man to get that close. I can't stand it when they think they have a right to kiss me just because we've spent an evening together—who the hell asked them to—who gave them any permission, how *dare* they act as if I owed them anything?"

"Hey, take it easy—calm down—we're not talking about the same thing. You're supposed to *like* getting close to a guy—or didn't they ever tell you when you were growing up? Haven't I gotten through to you, ever?"

"But I *do not* like it—I don't want to try it—and that's the way it is. You should be able to accept that about me by now," Daisy said with finality.

"You're right, I should. But I don't."

"Well, keep trying," Daisy advised her.

Since Daisy had arrived at Santa Cruz she had been plagued by the romantic passions she inspired in various young men and, as far as she was concerned, their romantic passions gave her less sympathy for them than if they'd lost a shirt in the laundry. No one, *no one* was to be allowed to have the faintest hope of possession—she stamped out their feelings without the slightest remorse. She wasn't responsible for them and if they wanted to be miserable because of her, let them. The minute anyone she went out with started to try to turn the neutral peck on the cheek into a larger embrace was the minute her relationship with him ended. There were always others to take his place.

At almost nineteen, Daisy had consolidated her early beauty. Her spun silver-gilt hair, which she rarely cut except to have a quarter of an inch trimmed off the ends from time to time, reached almost to her waist. No matter how she tried to control it, to braid it or bunch it or tie it in neat clusters, it was impossible to do anything to keep her nape, her temples and her ears from being tickled by wisps, cowlicks and curls of shorter hair which escaped her firm hand and created a halo around her face. Her skin still held the warmth, that of a ripe peach, that she had inherited from Francesca and those generations of beautiful women of San Gimignano, and men found themselves impaled on her eyes. Eyes as large, with pupils of such a blackness as Daisy's, were almost impossible to penetrate . . . yet the men of Santa Cruz never gave up trying. The touch of strangeness, which lent her beauty the necessary counterpoint, was her eyebrows, which were so straight and determined above the mystery of her eyes. As she grew older, her full, Slavic mouth, the one feature, aside from the color of her hair, that she had inherited most noticeably from Stash, became more firmly marked. At Santa Cruz she had grown taller until she reached her full height of five feet, seven inches, but her body had not succumbed to institutional food. She was as slim and limber as ever: she rode every day in every kind of weather, and she had the firm, graceful arms, thighs, calves and shoulders of a horsewoman. Her breasts were fuller than they had been four years before but were still high and pointed.

Both Daisy and Kiki wore the uniform they had settled on in their freshman year—jeans and handwoven tops, the jeans as battered as possible, the tops as ethnic. The two of them, known as Valensky and the Kav, were a legend on a campus where almost everyone was eccentric, because of the contrast in their personalities and their looks, to say nothing of Theseus who slept in their room and accompanied Daisy to all her classes. The only place from which he was barred was the eating commons, by demand of the other students.

In spite of the intimate friendship between them, Daisy had never told Kiki about Dani, to whom she mailed, twice each week, a detailed drawing, sometimes showing a scene from her own life, sometimes a scene from Dani's life, drawings which included those teachers and friends of Dani's she had come to know so well. Sometimes Daisy asked herself if there might have been a time when she should have told Kiki about the existence of her twin sister, but, year after year, that moment had never presented itself. She still felt the power of the absolute prohibition which had been imposed by her father, that prohibition which she had been under since she was six, a prohibition she understood to be total, without knowing or questioning why it should exist. The longer it lasted, the more binding it became, and it was all the stronger for never having been discussed or explained—a terrifying taboo, that *must* be served because of consequences that were unthinkable, irrational, but entirely real.

The only person left alive in the world who knew about Dani was Anabel, but Daisy never discussed Dani even with her. After Stash's sudden death, Anabel had assured Daisy that Danielle had been provided for. Nevertheless, Daisy knew, in the deepest part of herself, that Dani was a secret she was under a compulsion to bear by herself. *She had been born first*—nothing had changed that fact, and her deepest loyalties and sense of responsibility still went to Dani. Often, when she was in the midst of some special enjoyment, she would imagine Dani, her double, her other self, more her child than her sister, playing in the garden or singing the simple songs she had been taught, and hot tears would fill her eyes at the realization of all her twin was missing, all the new knowledge and experience she would never have. Her only comfort was the realization that Dani was as happy as she could possibly be, that Queen Anne's School was truly home to her and that the staff and other patients had become her family.

Daisy had not, of course, been able to visit Dani from Santa Cruz, but during the long breaks at Christmas and Easter she always flew to England to see her, and every summer was spent with Anabel at *La Marée* so that she could be within a few hours of Dani by plane. The staff at Queen Anne's School took photographs of the two sisters together whenever Daisy visited, and these photos, which covered a period of thirteen years, were pinned up on a special cork board in Dani's room. Often she pointed it out to her friends and teachers with great pride. "See Day? See Dani? Pretty?" she would ask, time after time, knowing that their answer would always be, "Yes, yes, pretty Dani, pretty Day!"

During her years at college, Daisy had received letters from Ram, since all her school bills, all her travel bills and clothing bills were sent to him for payment, and her allowance checks had to come from him, too. Daisy could not tear up the letters and throw them away unread. Unfortunately money matters still gave Ram a hold on her and she could barely wait to graduate to get a job and become completely self-supporting.

During 1967 and 1968, Ram's letters had been totally impersonal, noting only that he had paid the various bills she had sent him out of her income from her stock. Then he had started dropping disquietingly intimate sentences into his communications. The first time this happened he had written, after disposing of business, "I hope that my actions of the past won't be held against me for the rest of my life. I've never stopped condemning myself for what could only have been a case of temporary insanity." The second quarterly letter was even more upsetting. "Daisy, I've never forgiven myself for what I did to you. I can't stop thinking of how much I loved you and how much I still love you. If you would only write to say you forgive me—and that you are now able to understand that you *literally* drove me crazy, you would relieve me of a great burden." This letter had struck a chord of terror into Daisy. It was as if Ram had reached out and tried to touch her. She looked around the room she shared with Kiki, trembling at the thought that her only safe refuge was here, and yet even here he was able to enter, if only in a letter.

When she opened the first letter Ram sent her in 1969, she hoped that her lack of any answer to his last two letters would have caused him to return to simple business matters. But instead, he wrote, "I understand why you don't feel ready to answer me yet, Daisy, but that doesn't change the way I feel about you or the fact that I feel I *must* have, some day, a chance to gain your forgiveness *in person.* No matter what you think, I am still your brother and I always will be and nothing can change that—just as nothing can change my memories. Can you really forget the eucalyptus grove? Have you really no feelings toward someone who loves you so much?"

The next time a letter came from Ram, and every time thereafter, Daisy dropped them, unopened, into the big trash basket in the coffee shop, unwilling to put them into the wastebasket near her desk. The arrival of one of them in her mail cubbyhole was like the sight of a curled-up snake. Her fear and loathing of Ram had grown stronger every year and his pleading words were vomitous, somehow menacing even in their humility.

Long hours of introspection had permitted Daisy to understand that her premature sexual experience had been possible only because of an incompleted mourning process for her father that had catapulted her into a state in which she felt that she had lost a part of her own *self*, and so had fled to Ram to become whole again. She could never stop blaming him, never stop reassuring herself that *it had not been her fault*, but his. And yet, somehow, the guilt lingered, the guilt she knew she had no reason to feel, and she was angrily unwilling to venture into sexuality again. Daisy walled off and defended herself against sexual feelings—they caused pain, confusion, shame. She knew that she wasn't being rational, but her emotions could not be reached by logic.

Instead, she threw herself into a schedule of activities so full that her energy was consumed. Besides her regular classes and her daily trail ride, she became a member of the crew responsible for the stage sets of the many performances put on in the various Santa Cruz University theaters. She was so eager and ready a volunteer that more and more of the work fell on her shoulders until, by the fall of senior year, she was in full charge of all scenic design, and leader of a crew of scenery painters and builders called "Valensky's Vassals" because of their devotion to their demanding chief. During her time at college Daisy created many stage sets which combined ingenuity with illusion in a highly professional manner. She also became familiar with all the varied crafts of stage décor: lighting, set dressing and costume design, as well as her own speciality of scenic design. She loved the stage of a theater as much as Kiki did; Kiki, who had become such an iridescent personality, as she acted in play after play, that to most people but Daisy, she seemed a splashy, spangled creature, so colorful that the details of her real self were overlooked in the glitter. But while Kiki appeared in front of an audience, Daisy's feelings for the stage were based on the handling and working of actual materials and seeing what could be made of them. She took rich pleasure in seeing a freshly painted backdrop laid out on the grass of the sculpture garden of College 5, and later transforming it, with furniture and props, into a startling reality, as much as she loved creating a set for a dance group, using nothing but a curtain of long ropes of Christmas tree ornaments and spotlights. Daisy didn't know what kind of job she would eventually get in the theater, but that was her ambition, and, until graduation, she planned to cram as much of stagecraft into her life as possible.

Early in the fall of her senior year at college, Daisy was engrossed in sketching costumes for a futuristic version of *The Tempest* when an excited Kiki, shouting,

"Hey, Daisy, where are you?" burst into their room at a run. "Oh, great—you're here. Listen to this, I just got a letter from Zip Simon, head of advertising at old Dad's company and he's coming out next week and we're invited!"

"What does an executive of United Motors want with our humble, but admittedly lovely selves? And by the way, you've interrupted me. How do you think Prospero would dress on a spaceship?"

"In a spacesuit—just leave that alone for a sec—I told you ages ago that Zip promised me that the next time they shot a TV commercial anywhere near here, he'd let us watch—and they're going to do one in Monterey next week. It's to introduce the new model of the Skyhawk. You know, the car that's been such a secret."

"A television commercial! Oh, really, how *gross!* Stop kidding, Kiki," Daisy said disdainfully.

Students at Santa Cruz made it a fetish not to watch television except for an eccentric few who followed "As the World Turns" and insisted on being proud of their addiction. As far as commercials—all commercials—went, their contempt knew no bounds. Kiki, as an heiress to a vulgar Detroit fortune, was often hard-put to swallow her thoughts when she heard the lofty, utterly impractical ideas of her fellow students on American industry in general, and television advertising in particular.

"Daisy Valensky!" she said indignantly. "Don't you know that Marshall McLuhan said that historians and archaeologists will one day discover that the ads of our time are the richest and most faithful daily reflections any society ever made of its entire range of activities?"

"You're making that up!"

"I am not! I memorized it because I'm just so sick and tired of the way everyone goes on around here—talk about ivory towers—wait till they try to get jobs, they'll find out. Oh, come off it, Daisy, maybe you'd learn something from seeing them do the commercial."

"I suppose one can always learn something—like how not to do things."

"Oh, you're so fucking condescending! You've been at Santa Cruz so long your brain's decayed."

"Spoken like a true daughter of noble Detroit."

"Elitist swine!"

"Capitalist pig!"

"I got to say swine first, so I won," Kiki said, delighted at her victory in their long-playing game of insults.

A week later, on historic Cannery Row in Monterey, less than an hour's drive from Santa Cruz, the two girls approached a roped-off section of the street where a small crowd of spectators had already collected. A gigantic truck, with the word "Cinemobile" printed on its side, was parked close by. There was also a large Winnebago, and a truck carrying the new Skyhawk that was draped in heavy canvas. A vintage Skyhawk that was draped in heavy canvas. A vintage Skyhawk, in perfect condition, stood on the street.

Kiki and Daisy edged cautiously through the crowd up to the ropes and inspected the scene of the commercial shoot.

"Nothing's going on," Daisy observed.

"Weird," Kiki whispered, looking at the crowd of people inside the ropes who were frozen in widely separated groups. Two of the groups were made up of conservatively dressed men in dark suits and ties muttering together in low tones. She pointed to them with knowledgeability. "Our gang's from the agency, the other's from the client—my old dad's guys."

"Those must be the crew," Daisy said, indicating a tangle of men and women in jeans so shabby that they wouldn't have looked out of place on campus, all of whom were drinking coffee from plastic cups and munching leisurely on doughnuts as if they were on vacation. Both girls looked with more interest at two people, isolated from everyone else who, at least, showed signs of animation. One was a tall red-haired man and the other a young, plump, severely tailored woman.

"This doesn't look right to me," Kiki said snappishly. "I've seen them shoot commercials before and they're not supposed to be just *standing* there."

"Look, you're not in charge here," Daisy reminded her.

"Yeah, but Zip Simon is. Hey, Zip! Over here!" Kiki called boldly, with all the assurance of the client's daughter, which is second only to the assurance of the client's wife.

A short, bald man broke away from one of the groups in business suits and came over to escort them through the ropes which were being guarded by policemen.

"Kiki, how are you, kid?" He hugged her. "Who's your friend?"

"Daisy Valensky."

Zip Simon sighed gloomily. "Well, gals, it looks like you're not going to see a commercial made after all. We've got big, big trouble. And I still can't believe it. North is the best damn commercial director in the business and he can't shoot. It's a disaster."

"What's the disaster? Is someone sick?" Kiki asked.

"Unfortunately not—that we could ignore. We've had this fucking commercial—sorry, Kiki—planned for months and now we've blown the location."

"What's wrong with it?" Kiki asked.

"It's been fucking *renovated*—that's what. North used a location scouting service and the bastards showed us perfect photos—Cannery Row in its prime. When we got here we found it'd been turned into a Design Research store, and there isn't a building left in this whole lousy town that looks old anymore. Oh, shit! Sorry, Kiki. Excuse my language, Kiki's friend."

"Why does it have to look old?" Daisy ventured.

"Because of the story board," he said, as if that would tell them everything they wanted to know.

"What's a story board?" Daisy asked. He looked at her incredulously. Such ignorance was not possible. On the other hand, she was another person he could complain to.

"The story board, Kiki's friend, is a big piece of paper with cartoon figures drawn on it and balloons coming out of people's mouths with words written on them. Got it? It's like the Bible to us simple folk in advertising. And in this story board you see an old Skyhawk convertible parked in front of a restaurant on Cannery Row forty years ago, see, and then a couple in period costume come out and drive off, and then you have another funny picture and you dissolve into the new model Skyhawk, in front of the same old place, and a couple in modern clothes walk out and drive off and voice-over you hear—now get this: 'The United Motors Skyhawk—*still* the best car you can drive!' "

"I love it," Kiki squealed.

"It's a gem—simple but eloquent . . . and we're going to shoot the same scene all over the country in historic, picturesque locations—or, at least, we were. . . . Now, who knows?"

"But, why can't you un-renovate the building—build a set?" Daisy wondered.

"Because we don't have time. Tomorrow the new car has to be on a plane headed back to the factory in Detroit for the unveiling at a stockholders' party—a gigantic affair—don't even ask how many people are invited. And if we don't get this shot done today, we'll blow our first air date. Does it hurt to commit hara-kiri?"

"Oh, Zip, don't be so hard on yourself—you didn't screw up the location," Kiki said fondly.

"I was going to do the hara-kiri on North, not me."

"Which one is North?" Daisy asked curiously. Zip Simon pointed to the red-headed man. "That's the son-of-a-bitch, and the gal with him is his producer, Bootsie Jacobs."

Forty feet away from Simon, North was speaking so quietly that no one could overhear.

"Bootsie, this is as careless as expecting an ear, nose and throat man to look up your ass with a flashlight and tell you why you've got a sore throat."

"That location scouting service will be out of business next week," she said, struggling for her usual taut composure. "Palming off pictures that were two years old—*two years!* Okay, okay, North, it was my fault for not double-checking. There's no one you can trust—I know it, it never fails—especially when you have the client and his whole mob and the agency and their shitheads all watching this little road show. Wonderful! They outnumber us two to one, even counting all the models and hairdressers and make-up people—I told that lot not to set foot out of the Winnebago. It looks bad enough already." Panic was seeping through her crisp tone. "If they'd only let us keep that new Skyhawk for a couple of days, we could go to EUE's big Burbank studio and shoot down there—but that's absolutely not possible."

"You'd better think of something to pull this one out, Bootsie," North said angrily. "That's your job, not mine."

Frederick Gordon North was the best director of television commercials in the United States. He knew he was. Everyone in the business knew he was. What's more, he charged a thousand dollars a day more than any of the other top directors in the business and got it, as many days a year as he wanted to work. While the likes of Avedon, Steve Horn and Bob Giraldi all charged four to five thousand dollars a day as their personal directorial fee, North got six thousand. Even Howard Zeiff had never charged as much in the days before he became a film director, during which he was the undisputed king of commercial directors.

Why were they willing to pay so much? Why would advertising-agency creative directors pay North a thousand dollars a day more than directors *almost* equally good? Everyone had a different answer. Some talked about his "eye"—the way he *saw* things as they would appear on film with just a little more originality, a little more visual interest than anyone else saw them. Others talked about the way he worked with actors, bringing out more than they knew they had to give. There were those who insisted it was his matchlessly innovative use of lighting, and still others spoke of the way he managed to telegraph more of a message in thirty seconds than other directors could in a full-length motion picture.

The truth lay in the blood he spilled. North would do anything to make a good commercial, and he put his blood and that of everyone else he worked with on the line. He didn't secretly want to make "real" movies, like the majority of commercial directors, nor did he hanker to do the most marvelously artistic still photography. To Frederick Gordon North *THE perfect art form* was the television commercial, whether it was thirty seconds, sixty seconds, or even only ten seconds long, and that quality of utter commitment made clients slaver for him. Of course, it was essential that his work was technically superior, but that wasn't the real lure—the hook was, had always been, the smell and sight of blood.

Daisy turned away from her inspection of North and his producer to speak to Zip Simon.

"Excuse me, but do you have other problems besides the set?"

"No, just that minor detail," Simon said bitterly. "But we can't get a set built by tomorrow, and the car leaves in the morning, even if we could work all night."

"I can get it done," Daisy said.

"Sure you could. Two minutes ago you didn't even know what a story board was, Kiki's friend."

"My name's Daisy Valensky and I'm the head of Scenic Design at the University of California at Santa Cruz," Daisy said with dignity. "I have a crew of forty top workers who will be here in an hour if I make just one phone call. They'll work all night."

"Is she for real?" Simon asked Kiki.

"Of course! They're professionals, for God's sake, Zip," Kiki said, quivering with the unmistakable imperiousness of her old dad's daughter, an unfamiliar guise to Daisy, but one which Kiki knew precisely when and how to assume.

"So, what the hell, Daisy, let's talk to North. It's worth trying—at this point anything's worth trying." Zip Simon was so disgusted that he didn't mind confronting even Frederick Gordon North with this absurd idea. The shoot couldn't get more fucked up than it was.

North and Bootsie Jacobs watched them approach with lively suspicion. Zip Simon, Vice-President in Charge of Advertising at United Motors, did not communicate with the director of his commercials casually. And, at a moment like this, accompanied by two hippie girls, he was particularly unwelcome.

"North, this is Kiki Kavanaugh, daughter of my boss and your client, and her friend, Daisy—ah—Valensky."

North frowned. If there was anything worse than having a client on the set it was having the client's daughter, and after that came the client's daughter's friend.

"Hi. Sorry we don't have time to chat today. Nice to see you." He turned away, leaving them with the impression of supreme indifference and wrathful blue eyes.

Daisy tapped him on the arm. "Mr. North, I can have this place looking any way you want it by tomorrow or sooner."

He turned and gave her a look of freezing irony. "Who let you on the set?"

"Listen," said Simon, "this kid's head of stage sets or something at Kiki's college. She's got a thousand willing nuts who want to build you a set."

"Kids?" North asked Daisy.

"People. Good people. They like to work."

"I don't care who they are. Do you seriously believe that you can take this building and make it look exactly like the outside of Cannery Row fifty years ago, before eight tomorrow morning?" He gestured in disgust at the spanking-new brick, the gleaming paint, the huge, modern windows.

"We can certainly try," Daisy said resolutely. She looked boldly at North as she spoke. He had shockingly red hair, a fox of a man with a long, pointed nose, lots of freckles and blue eyes which told her that no matter how bad this moment was, it could not possibly end in failure. He was a man of sharp, clear edges. There was nothing indistinct or rounded or even comfortable about his clever features. He turned to Bootsie Jacobs and asked calmly, "What do you think?"

"We'd be breaking about sixteen union rules I can think of and about sixteen I don't know about yet. Using nonunion labor would be the least of it, and that's big trouble. Anyway, how can it work? They've got to be strictly amateur time. I think I'll kill myself," Bootsie said grimly.

"Why not let us get to work?" Daisy said eagerly.

"North," Zip Simon said angrily, "you've come up empty. Now here's a chance to get something on film before I put the new Skyhawk on that plane tomorrow. I don't care if you shoot the damn thing upside down, sideways or hanging from a tree—it's up to you to *do it!* That's why we hired you. I don't plan to go back to Detroit and have to tell my boss that the location just 'happened' to be renovated and we couldn't do a single thing about it. Miss Kavanaugh says that this young lady can help—so let her! Unless, of course, you have a better idea." His bald head had gone almost purple with aggravation.

Bootsie glanced briefly at North. "Go call your crew," she said to Daisy. If Zip Simon thought he'd be in trouble if they didn't get the film, what did he think would happen to *her* if she couldn't make this shoot happen? She'd begged and begged the agency to let her build a Cannery Row set at the automobile plant just to avoid trouble, but no, they had to be authentic—fuck authentic—and fly the prototype all over the country for historic streets to shoot on. What an utterly corny idea—but how many clients did sixty-second spots these days? And now here was the client's bossy daughter with her helpful suggestions—well, if this long shot didn't work, wouldn't it be partly the client's daughter's fault, instead of hers alone? And who knew, with the right lighting and the right filters and a stiff breeze . . . who knew?

Daisy was already headed toward the phone.

Santa Cruz didn't have a football team, but it had one hell of a Theater Arts department. And, as Daisy knew well, they had stored backdrops and props and varied other bits and pieces from past performances of *Camino Real* and *Streetcar Named Desire* and *Petrified Forest.* She told her people to bring everything, whether they thought they'd need it or not, and bring it fast. She ordered them out in full strength, not just the scenery painters, carpenters and prop people, but the stage hands, the lighting crew and even the costume and make-up teams. They could all help, including Kiki.

They swarmed to the location loaded with all the stuff that had been stashed away in the storeroom, including paints and tools, as thrilled to get their hands on an honest-to-God, real live television commercial as if they'd never looked down their idealistic noses on the entire medium.

An hour and a half after Daisy's phone call, they reported to their chief ready for a night of work. The art director from the advertising agency handed over the photos of the demolished location to Daisy who snapped her orders and deployed her forces throughout the long hours before dawn. Zip Simon, the art director and Bootsie stayed up all night watching, while the cast and crew drifted away to sleep. North coolly went to his hotel to have dinner and get a night's rest. The catering service was on duty all night long, and by sunrise the set was ready. A Monterey which had long vanished had reappeared, if not absolutely authentic in every detail, still echoing the period and the mood of the old photos. It was jerry-built and a strong breeze might have destroyed it—but, somehow, it existed. It was usable.

Exahusted, but too delighted with her success, and, by now, too interested in what was going on to leave, Daisy stayed throughout the shoot, understanding very little of what was happening. It was as different from a stage production as a stage production is from a basketball game. She watched the coffee-drinking rabble of yesterday become a crew such as she had never seen before, intimately connected to one another as members of a primitive clan, working together with the precision only enormous discipline can bring, more quietly expert than she had ever imagined technicians could be. They were all satellites of North, who controlled the set by the force of a hypnotic power, pleasure and displeasure shooting out from him as he rehearsed the actors to the constant accompaniment of asides to a girl who sat on a box seemingly chained to an enormous stopwatch which she wore around her neck.

"We have four seconds here," he said to her. "How many have I used?"

"Three and a half."

"Yell when I've got four."

As Daisy watched him, she realized that this man in his early thirties, tall, lean and tense, was a battered lion tamer of diehard toughness. He wouldn't be daunted by a cage of mixed rattlesnakes, porcupines and polar bears, to say nothing of lions. No matter what problems circled, prowling and growling, around him, North never put down his whip and chair, invisible though they might be, and once he began directing, every person on the set was convinced that his eye was on them at all times, even when he was looking through the camera.

The client group and the agency group stood at a respectful distance, glancing constantly at their watches, but drinking in the electric tension of the curses, the frenzy, the lightning flashes of temperament, the freely opened veins. They were in show biz, they thought, not realizing that as far as North was concerned, this had nothing to do with show biz and everything to do with advertising.

The crew combined alertness and stillness in equal combinations, as people do who are sure of their skills and aware of when they are needed and when not. The technical jargon Daisy heard was strange to her in spite of her knowledge of stagecraft, and many of North's directions to the actors sounded odd.

"Four seconds," Daisy muttered to Kiki, "what can you do in four seconds?"

"Sell cars," said Kiki smugly.

Over and over and over she heard North say, "Stand by . . . and . . . action!" The word "and" was drawn out almost unbearably. Many times it seemed to her that everything had gone perfectly, but he never seemed satisfied until, abruptly, he was. He coaxed, he warned, he encouraged, he grew taller, he grew shorter, he got violently angry, he became suddenly gentle and calm, he screamed for quiet in a terrifying voice and, seconds later, looking through the lens and talking to his cameraman, he was as loose as if he had been alone on the street. Once he caught her eye with a raking glance, unexpected and startling.

Pointing to the couple in modern dress about to get into the new Skyhawk, he said to them, "Now the intention here is that you're going to take her home and give her a zatch—I haven't been out myself since 1965, but am I wrong about the intention here?" Odd direction or not, the actors immediately grew into a couple in love when before they had only been a couple.

Everyone worked without a break, not even for lunch, because of the pressure to send the new Skyhawk back to Detroit. The auto carrier that would take the car to the cargo plane was delayed until the last possible second before the automobile, again hidden in its canvas covering, was carried away. Only then did North call a break.

Daisy expected that after lunch the set would become more relaxed, since they had the use of the vintage Skyhawk for as long as they needed it, but the tense time pressure was as strict as before. Time, on a commercial shoot, is always the enemy—there is never enough of it, and both North and Bootsie had to be back in New York for a production meeting with another client on the following afternoon.

Finally North said quietly, "Right, it's a wrap," and the technicians began to dismantle their equipment, the models vanished into the Winnebago with their attendants, and the large lights, cameras, sound equipment and other tools of the trade were quickly stowed away in the Cinemobile. It was like the dismantling of a circus and Daisy felt sad as time turned back into an everyday beat, time which had been counted in seconds and half-seconds, all day long.

"Hey, they're leaving without saying goodbye," Kiki said with astonishment.

"No, they're coming over here," Daisy said. "How could they not say thank you?"

North and Bootsie, almost running, approached the two girls.

"Be sure to strike the set and make certain everything is back exactly as it was," North ordered.

"Uh—sure," said Daisy.

"Sorry, but we have a plane to catch," Bootsie said rapidly. "You were really great—Daisy, you'd make a terrific production assistant if you ever want a job."

"Thanks—but no thanks," Daisy answered.

"Come on, Boot, we haven't got time to talk," North snapped impatiently. "So long, ladies." He took Bootsie by the arm and turned her toward the waiting car. As they drove off Bootsie Jacobs said, "You could have been a little nicer to them—they really helped, for Christ's sake!"

"They wouldn't have been necessary if you'd done your job," North answered absently.

No one, but no one impresses him unless they get in the way of his blasted parade, Bootsie thought wrathfully, and then . . . watch out!

Four months later, in February of 1971, with graduation only four months away, Daisy received a letter from Anabel.

Daisy dearest,

Isn't it frightful! I'm in such a state of shock at the news. Honestly, I know just how the Minister of Aviation felt when he spoke in the House last week—"never in my wildest dreams or nightmares did I dream it was as bad as all this." I can imagine how you feel, too—Rolls-Royce in receivership! It simply does <u>not</u> seem possible—only three <u>months</u> ago the government said that they were going to simply <u>pour</u> money into the company—but when they saw the books! I've been wiped out, of course, financial idiot that I am—but I assume that Ram got your money out ages ago. I hate to say it but when he told me to sell I thought he was too young to change Stash's investments, but it's no good even thinking that way. Do you know what he put your money into? I detest asking a question like that but, darling Daisy, there's a reason. Although your father and I never married, I considered myself responsible for Danielle's upkeep and, *from the income of the stock he left me, I've been paying her bills since he died. When the stock became worthless I went to see Ram. Daisy, I know what you're thinking but it was the only possible thing for me to do. I had to tell him . . . after all, she's his half-sister too. It was almost impossible to convince him that she existed. And then he refused to do anything! He said that if Stash had never seen fit to bother him with Dani he must not have wanted him to know about her . . . he even said that as far as he was concerned she simply wasn't real. She was no responsibility of his. And he's rolling in money . . . simply rolling! He categorically rejected contributing a shilling to her school bills. Forgive me for telling him, Daisy, but I was sure he'd help, fool that I was. I should have known how he'd react, but I had to try.*

Anyway, I'm going to have to retrench severely. I'm selling Eaton Square and moving permanently to La Marée. With the few investments I still have and the sale of my paintings and the Fabergé animals there should be enough of a nest egg so that I can invest it in something safe and live off it for the rest of my life. Even a modest income would be enough, particularly if some of the friends who used to visit me will want to come and stay as paying guests. Well, darling, next summer I'll find out.

The problem isn't what's to become of me—of course I'll manage one way or another—but what will happen to Danielle?

The school has sent in their quarterly bill for what amounts to almost five thousand dollars in American money and I find that I simply can't put my hands on that sum. I just can't believe it! It's no more that I used to spend on underclothes without thinking twice. How our vanities catch up with us. But, oh, it was glorious while it lasted. Never forget that.

Now, to business. Can you take over some—in fact most—of the Queen Anne's bill? I do hope that Ram invested wisely for you? But enough of this. I've never thought for so long or written so much about money in my life. It makes me fairly lightheaded—how can people stand to be bankers? And to think that I still must spend a whole afternoon with an estate agent about Eaton Square! I find I don't mind selling this house as much as I thought I would—the idea of living all year in La Marée is so appealing. You'll be coming at Easter, of course, my pet, won't you? Perhaps all the apple trees will be in bloom as they were last year . . . but that was an early spring.

My dearest love always. Je t'embrasse très fort!

Anabel

Daisy read the letter over three times before it made complete sense to her. She hadn't bothered to look at a daily newspaper in weeks, and this was the first she had heard of the bankruptcy of the Rolls-Royce Company. Ram had never, in the letters she had read before she started throwing them away, again suggested that she sell her stock, but she had always assumed that she possessed more or less what the stock had been worth right after her father's death, when it had amounted to roughly ten million dollars.

Daisy realized with wonderment that she had not the faintest idea of where her money was. Even though she had cut off communications with Ram, she had remained in his power financially. What had he said in the letters she had found too distasteful to open?

Daisy went to her desk and wrote Ram a brief note asking for a complete statement of her financial position, and then wrote a much longer letter to Anabel saying how unhappy she was about the changes Anabel was going to have to make in her life, but assuring her that she must not worry about Danielle's future expenses. From now on, Daisy wrote, she would be responsible for her sister. It was out of the question that Anabel should beggar herself for Dani—her generosity had been already enormous. She'd had no idea where the money for Dani's bills was coming from or she would have taken them over long ago. And of course she understood why Anabel had told Ram. As for *La Marée* at Easter, she wouldn't dream of missing it.

She posted the two letters and rushed off to the playhouse where she was already a little late for a dress rehearsal of *Hamlet* performed entirely in mime and jazz dancing. All the parts were being played by females, and Elsinore had been relocated to the island of Lesbos.

Daisy felt a persistent uneasiness as she waited for Ram's reply, but she dismissed it and immersed herself in work. Five days later she received a cablegram.

HAVE WRITTEN THREE TIMES IN LAST YEAR FOR PERMISSION TO SELL YOUR STOCK. HAD NO REPLY SO ASSUMED YOU INSISTED ON HOLDING. UNFORTUNATELY, COMPANY IS NOW NATIONALIZED. STOCK WORTHLESS UNLESS GOVERNMEMT REIMBURSES BUT DOUBTFUL SINCE YOU HELD COMMON STOCK NOT PREFERRED. HAVE ADVANCED FROM PERSONAL FUNDS MONIES FOR ALL YOUR EXPENSES FOR PAST FOURTEEN MONTHS SINCE ROLLS INCOME NOT SUFFICIENT. INTEND TO CONTINUE TO SUPPORT YOU. CONSIDER IT APPROPRIATE IN VIEW OF OUR RELATIONSHIP. R.A.M.

Daisy dropped the cable on the floor and ran to the communal bathroom. She felt as if someone had come upon her in her sleep and hit her head with tremendous blows. She reached a toilet stall just in time before she started to vomit. She hugged the chill bowl as if it were the last refuge on earth. After the final dry heaves had stopped she remained kneeling in the bathroom, mercifully empty of students, clutching the friendly porcelain. She felt that there was still an unexpelled mass in the back of her throat, a solid ball of disgust and panic, like some monstrous embryo clinging to her breathing passages as it might cling to a womb. Her aching stomach muscles tried to clench again but failed to dislodge the mass. There was nothing left, not even bile, to throw up. Her sense of life being safe and good had evaporated in the lethal gas of Ram's message. She felt as if she had fallen far down into one of those dark places, unbearably sad, filled with danger and threat and fear of the unknown, the places she had lived in for so long after her mother had disappeared, after Dani had been taken from her, when her father had died—all the great and sudden losses of her life seemed concentrated again in the news she had just received. All the victories she had won, all her stubborn refusals to be controlled, felt hollow and tawdry now that she knew Ram had been giving her everything she thought she had paid for with her own money. She was in his debt now, God help her, and her stock was worthless. Why hadn't he simply sold without her permission? As her trustee he could have done so and he must have known what was happening to Rolls-Royce. Was it possible that he had *let this happen* just to put her where she was now? She would never know, Daisy realized, and it really didn't matter. She *had to manage* somehow. With this thought her fighting spirit began to return. She stood up, her flesh and bones so sore that they seemed to be in conflict, and went to one of a row of washbasins to brush her teeth and splash her face with cold water. She met her eyes in the mirror and willed them to be undefeated, and they were. She left the bathroom and went to her room to think.

There were four more months until graduation and the chance to get a job. That meant, Daisy told herself, that she just wouldn't graduate—she didn't have the luxury of time. She had one asset and one only, the lapis egg which still sat in its box in the bottom of her chest of drawers, the egg Masha had given to her as she lay dying six years before, the egg Masha said that her father had given her mother when she found out she was pregnant. The time to sell the egg had come—it would buy at least a year, perhaps a little more, for Danielle.

A job. She knew enough about the theater to know that she stood almost no chance of finding employment except in an experimental playhouse which would pay almost nothing. The only time in the last four years that anyone had mentioned any other form of employment was last fall, when that woman commercial producer, Bootsie somebody, had told her she'd make a good production assistant. Whatever that was, precisely, it had to pay more than the theater. Get the name of the commercial company from Kiki or that nice fat man, Zip Simon, who worked for Mr. Kavanaugh, call what's-her-name, and ask for a job. What do I have to lose? thought Daisy. The worst they can say is no. And maybe they'll say yes. Even if they never did say thanks.

13

"The catfood people called again," Arnie Greene, business manager of Frederick Gordon North's commercial studio, said hopefully.

"And?" North asked.

"This time it's for six spots, thirty seconds each, big, *big* budget. Easy to do—no way we couldn't make lots of very pretty money."

"How many times have I told you, Arnie? *No catfood!* There's no budget big enough to make me shoot that stuff. I can't stand the way it looks."

"And what should I tell Weight Watchers? They want us to bid on their new business."

"You can tell them to stuff it. I saw the story board they're going with—spaghetti, cheeseburgers and strawberry shortcake in drippingly edible closeups with a voice track saying that if you join Weight Watchers you can enjoy your favorite treats and *still* break the habit of eating fattening foods—and those sadistic bastards are going to run the spots at night, *after* dinner, just when fridge orgy time starts. I'm not against it on humanitarian grounds—I think the concept's basically bad and while I can choose, I choose not to do Weight Watchers."

Arnie Greene sighed mournfully. He was in charge of all financial transactions at the studio, and he turned down more work than North could possibly turn out without expanding his operation from its present size, but he still hated to send a potential client packing.

"Where's Daisy?" he asked, looking around the conference room.

"She's out nailing down the Empire State Building for the Revlon hairspray spot—then she's through for the week—it's Friday, remember?" North answered. "Why do you want her?"

"She's got the bills from the catering service. She took them home last night to check them, said we were being overcharged. Won't let me pay them until she found out where. Honestly, North, I think she's paranoid—she always says they're ripping us off on Jewish fish. I told her we *have* to give the clients smoked salmon for lunch—they come all the way in from Chicago, they *expect* smoked salmon. Four years now and she's still checking the bills."

"It keeps her off the streets," North said curtly. It irritated him, for no rational reason, to think that Daisy still had the determination and willingness to spend her free time worrying about bills after the exhausting days she put in on the job . . . it irritated him almost as much as the weekends she frequently managed to spend in the countryside enclaves of the horsy set. Leave it to Bootsie Jacobs to hire a production assistant who turned out to be some kind of White Russian princess with revoltingly classy friends. If she weren't so fucking good at her work, he'd never have given her Bootsie's job when it became available. But then, who would have thought Bootsie had it in her to get knocked up? And want to keep the brat? Of course she had been married ten years, so he guessed she was entitled.

"North," Arnie said, handing over two checks, "sign these please and just don't bother to look at them." North signed the two alimony checks grimly. Arnie went through the don't-bother-to-look-routine every month.

"Can you tell me why I married the two most beautiful models in New York and why they both turned out to be raving neurotics in less than a year and why I have to support them?"

"Why ask me, do I look like a shrink?"

"You look so much like the shrink I went to with the same questions that you could be his brother—probably are for all I know."

"Well—what'd he say?"

"I didn't wait around to find out."

"Why not?"

"He asked too many personal questions."

"Yeah, that would do it."

Frederick Gordon North was known simply as North because he wouldn't permit the use of his first two names, foisted on him by family-proud parents from old and comfortable Connecticut families, and Fred, Freddy, Rick, Ricky, and Gordy had all been ruled out as well. A timid movement at Yale to dub him Flash—which would have suited him best—had only lasted one day. His parents still called him Frederick, but he was North even to his brothers and sisters, who, in any case, only had occasion to use the name at Christmas and Thanksgiving since they were an unclannish family, of which he was the most unclannish member.

He had been a loner almost from birth, and throughout Andover and Yale he had been persuaded to perform only a minimum of the obligatory extracurricular activities. The first thing he ever set his solitary heart on belonging to was the Yale Graduate School of Drama. His goal was clear to him—he wanted to direct: Shakespeare, O'Neill, Ibsen, maybe even a little Tennessee Williams. But he had set his course without understanding his own inner pace. The mounting of a theatrical production takes many months, and North's viciously concentrated attention span demanded quicker results.

Soon after graduation he met a third-rate veteran commercial cameraman who was willing to try him out as director on a commercial with a budget so low that any profit that could be wrung out of it would have to come from using a nonunion crew and director, all at bargain-basement rates.

That first commercial, a thirty-second local spot for a chain of discount clothing stores, caught North as firmly as if it had been a chance to work with Lord Olivier at the Old Vic. He had found his métier, a medium that throbbed with a beat that matched his pulse, his heart and his inner eye. Now that he knew what he really wanted to do, remorselessly North jettisoned his baggage of the world's greatest playwrights and headed straight for Madison Avenue where he spent four years learning all the technical ropes at the knew of Steve Elliot, the dean of commercial directors, a violin-playing, bulldozer-driving, Renaissance man who, with his brother Mike, had been among the first commercial directors to get their cherished cameraman's cards back in the early 1950s. The Elliot brothers had founded Elliot, Unger and Elliot, a firm which later became EUE/Screen Gems, then and now the giant of the commercial-making industry.

At twenty-five, North went out on his own, living for the first six months on money he'd saved, hustling every contact he'd made at EUE, until a few small accounts came his way. By the time he reached the top he was only thirty. When Daisy went to work for him, she was barely nineteen and he was thirty-two, a scratchy, cantankerous, impatient perfectionist of extraordinary talent and equally astonishing charm, which he saved for the rare times he had unavoidable social contact with his most important clients, and the frequent times he had deliberate carnal contact with a long and lovely parade of women, two of whom he had had the bad judgment to marry. He was no more of a joiner in a marriage than he had been when his father had tried to get him to become a Boy Scout, but, fortunately, he had avoided having children, as Arnie Greene frequently reminded him when it came time to sign the alimony checks. "At least there's no child support, you should knock on wood."

Daisy, once she was assured that there would be no further problems with Mr. Jones, supervisor of the Deck of the Empire State Building, headed downtown to the SoHo apartment she shared with Kiki.

Something about the arrival of spring had put her in a reminiscent mood that even the subway ride couldn't modulate. She found it hard to believe that four years had passed since she had left Santa Cruz.

Bootsie Jacobs had answered her letter immediately. They not only needed another production assistant, they were desperate for one. When Daisy found out what the job entailed she realized that their desperation was permanent and well-deserved, since few people lasted more than two months in the incredibly demanding and underpaid job. However, she had had no choice. She was paid one hundred seventy-five dollars a week for the nonunion job at which she worked at least twelve hours a day, but it was enough to live on and still save money for Danielle's bills, provided that she lived on next to nothing, a style of life she had perfected until it had almost become an art form. Of course, without the thirty thousand dollars that she had received for the lapis lazuli Fabergé egg she could never have met the bills until she developed another source of income aside from her job. Thank God, thought Daisy, for kids on ponies.

She remembered how it had started. Jock Middleton, who had played polo with her father, had received a letter from Anabel asking him to keep an eye on Daisy in New York. He'd invited her out for a weekend with his family in Far Hills, a horse-crazed part of New Jersey which rightfully belongs in the Bluegrass country. Daisy had packed her riding clothes, just in case they had a mount for her, and spent a happy Saturday riding with a flock of Middleton grandchildren. At an elaborate dinner party that night, Mrs. Middleton had introduced her to everyone as Princess Daisy Valensky. On Sunday, when Daisy had made a sketch of the oldest Middleton grandson on his pony, as a thank-you present, she signed it as she had always signed her work, with a simple "Daisy."

A few weeks later she'd had a letter from Mrs. Middleton. The sketch had been so much admired that she wondered if Princess Daisy would consider doing one of a neighbor's ten-year-old-daughter, Penny Davis? Mrs. Davis was willing to pay five hundred dollars for a sketch, or six hundred and fifty for a watercolor. Mrs. Middleton made it plain that she was embarrassed to mention money to Prince Stash Valensky's daughter, but Mrs. Davis had insisted. Mrs. Middleton blushed to make such a commercial proposition, but her neighbor had just not given her a second's peace. Daisy had only to say no and she wouldn't be bothered again.

Daisy rushed to the phone to accept, wishing she could suggest doing it in oil and charging another hundred dollars. No, better not—she didn't have the money to buy oils and canvas.

Any well-trained, competent artist should be able to draw a horse, but there are special abilities involved in understanding the movements, the stance, the anatomical differences and the variations of color necessary to make one horse look entirely different from another. Daisy had been drawing and riding horses most of her life. As for the children, she'd drawn them too, by the thousands, during all those years of making drawings for Dani, and she'd taken advanced courses in portraiture at Santa Cruz. Her sketch of the Middleton grandson had revealed an innate and pronounced knack which was to give her equestrian portraits a lively quality of sympathy and immediacy.

When she arrived at the Davises, a larger and more luxurious Monticello, Daisy was introduced to Penny Davis, who was already dressed in her best riding clothes. Daisy took one look at the child's rigidly set face and apprehensive eyes.

"I thought we'd all have lunch together before you get started, Princess Valensky," Mrs. Davis said. "And you must be ready for a Bloody Mary after the trip out."

"That's awfully thoughtful, but what I'd really like to do first is ride with Penny," Daisy answered. She wasn't about to work with a model who not only was miserably shy but didn't want to have her portrait painted under any circumstances.

"But what about lunch?"

"We'll manage. Penny, why don't you put on some jeans and show me the stable?"

When the girl returned, looking a tiny bit less uncomfortable, Daisy whispered to her, "Is there a McDonald's near here?" Penny looked around quickly to see if her mother could hear. Out of the corner of her mouth, she confided, "It's only five miles if you ride across country. But I'm not allowed to go there."

"But I am. And you're my guest. Let's just git!" The little girl's eyes lit up as she glanced with surprise at Daisy.

"Are you really a princess?"

"Sure. But to you I'm Daisy."

"Do Princesses like McDonald's?"

"*Kings* like McDonald's. Come on, Penny, I'm having a Big Mac fit."

Penny led the way over fields and fences. Within ten minutes and double Big Macs, Daisy discovered that Penny thought portraits were dumb. Worse than that, who would want to have a picture of herself with braces on hanging around for the rest of her life?

"Penny, I promise, cross my heart, I won't paint your braces. In fact, if you want, I'll paint you the way you're going to look when they come off—with a gorgeous smile. But think of it this way: an equestrian portrait is as much a portrait of the horse as it is of the person. You'll have to sell Pinto in a year or two, the way you're growing, and now you'll always have a picture of her to remember her by. Hey, could you eat another of these—I'm having one. Good—maybe I can get them to give us extra sauce."

"They're all having trout in aspic for lunch at home."

"Ugh, ugh, ugh! Wonder what's for dinner?"

"Roast duck—it's going to be very fancy—she's invited practically everyone we know."

"Oh, well," said Daisy philosophically. "Duck's better than trout."

That afternoon, as the young girl posed, relaxed and willing, Daisy made dozens of sketches to pin down the natural, spontaneous gestures and characteristic expressions of Penny Davis. She also took many pictures with the Polaroid she'd borrowed from the studio. They would be used as visual aids for the watercolor she planned to complete at home. She blessed the classes in anatomy she'd taken as she carefully sketched Penny's hands holding the reins, and further blessed the natural limitations which surrounded an equestrian portrait, since they ruled out too great a variety of pose or attitude. She sketched lightly, without any tightness or stiffness, not trying for perfection, but for a feeling of the child in relationship to her pony.

On Sunday, as Daisy traveled back from the Davises' estate, driven home by their chauffeur, she reflected on the fact that Mrs. Davis, like Mrs. Middleton, had ceremoniously and importantly introduced her as Princess Daisy Valensky at the big, formal dinner party last night. After her four years as Valensky at Santa Cruz, Daisy had almost forgotten that she had a title. Obviously it was a business asset—in Horse Country, anyway. Since painting kids on ponies was probably the most commercial way in which she could use her talents, Daisy ground her teeth and resolved to milk the princess routine for every penny it was worth. When she had finished the watercolor of Penny Davis, she signed it in clear, careful lettering, "Princess Daisy Valensky." It meant six hundred and fifty dollars for Danielle.

Slowly, through word of mouth, after the Middleton sketch and Davis commission, Daisy got requests to paint other kids on ponies. Her prices rose steadily. Now, not quite four years later, Daisy was able to ask and get two thousand, five hundred dollars for a watercolor. These commissions, which had started to come just before the Fabergé money ran out, represented the difference between being able to support Danielle and being forced to try to get Ram to pay, any way she could. Daisy had never told Anabel where her money came from, because she didn't want her to know that she had been left penniless after the bankruptcy of Rolls-Royce. Nor did Daisy tell anyone at the studio why she spent so many weekends flying to Upperville, Virginia; Unionville, Pennsylvania; and estates near Keeneland, Kentucky. She knew they considered her to be a full-fledged member of the social, horsy set, but as long as she did her job, she didn't see that it was any business of theirs what she did with her own time. Of course, Kiki, who saw her working night after night to finish the watercolors, knew about her work, and in certain circles a portrait of one's child on a pony by Princess Daisy Valensky was quickly becoming a status symbol.

When Daisy had had to leave Santa Cruz to get a job, she finally told Kiki about Danielle. There was no other possible way to explain her leaving college a mere four months before graduation except by telling the truth—or part of it.

She remembered the scene as she had told the strange, sad story, the variety of expressions that crossed Kiki's winsome, urchin's face; disbelief, astonishment, sympathy, indignation and wonder replacing each other in quick succession. Daisy had anticipated the two questions she knew her friend would eventually ask when the reality of what Daisy was telling her finally struck home.

"But why *won't* Ram support Danielle?"

"It's a way to get at me. We had a serious and permanent quarrel over a family matter, and nothing can change that or make us friends. Believe me, it's final. He doesn't consider Dani his sister anyway—he's never even met her. It's out of the question."

"Then why won't you let me help?" Kiki asked, warned by Daisy's tone not to pry into the nature of the family quarrel.

"I knew you'd get around to that. First of all, I have to do it alone because it's going to be a permanent thing—even you, generous as you are, can't take on someone else's relative for an indefinite period. But I'm not too proud to borrow a couple of hundred dollars just until I get my first paycheck."

She hadn't expected Kiki's last reaction. "I'm leaving school, too—we'll go together," she proclaimed, when Daisy had finally managed to convince her that she wouldn't let Kiki support Dani on a regular basis.

"Never. No way. That's out! I refuse to be the reason why you don't get a diploma from *somewhere.* Your mother'd never forgive me. But I'll rent someplace that's big enough for the two of us and the minute you graduate I'll be waiting for you with open arms and half the rent bill—retroactive. It's only four months. Do we have a deal?"

"Christ, you're bossy," Kiki complained. "Can I pay for the furniture? At least?"

"Half of it."

"I assume it'll be Salvation Army."

"Unless you can get your mother to ship us some of her extra stuff—anyone who redecorates once a year must have leftovers. The idea is that we'll accept donations of *things*, just like any other deserving organization, but we won't take money—because that gives people a right to say what we *do*. Got it?"

"Can we take money on Christmas and birthdays?" Kiki asked wistfully.

"Definitely. And we never go out with anyone who doesn't pay for dinner. Dutch treat is out. Together, we'll bring back the fifties."

As Daisy climbed up the steps to their third-floor apartment in a shabby building on the corner of Prince and Greene Streets she sniffed the pervasive smell of fresh baking in the air. Cinnamon rolls today, she decided. SoHo, only fifteen years before, had been declared the city's number-one commercial slum. Now it was the boiling, self-conscious main outpost of Bohemia, a boom town for artists where the current dress code called for paint-encrusted overalls, whether, as Kiki remarked disdainfully, you had ever held a paintbrush or not.

But then Kiki had finally discovered how to cope with her preoccupation about the right way to dress in any given locale. Thanks to the timely death of her grandmother, she was rich enough in her own right to become the owner, producer, and permanent leading lady of her very own off-off-off Broadway theater, The Hash House. She was, in fact, the recognized Ethel Barrymore-Sarah Bernhardt of SoHo, and she dressed to suit whatever play she was currently mounting. Her latest production, *The Lament of the Pale Purple Faggot*, was keeping the theater comfortably full, especially on weekends when the uptowners came down to see what was going on in playland. Casting herself as the protagonist's only female confidante, Kiki had been drifting around for the last few weeks in an arrangement of a lavender leotard, pink tights, purple suede boots and a mauve feather boa, all of which suited her admirably.

Daisy unlocked the door and looked around. The apartment was empty. That meant that Kiki was probably still at the theater and Theseus was with her. He consented to spend the day lying on a bean-bag pillow at Kiki's feet or following her around the theater. He was only totally happy when Daisy came home, but it was impossible to have a lurcher on a set. The caterer's table would have been denuded before the first sleepy grip asked for a cheese Danish in the morning.

Kiki and Daisy's place in SoHo wasn't one of those enormous lofts that many artists had carved out of former cast-iron, palazzo-styled, industrial buildings. It was an apartment on a human scale in a shabby building that boasted a small art gallery on the first floor. But it was large: big enough to contain a rambling living room, three bedrooms, a studio for Daisy, a fairly large kitchen and two bathrooms which unfortunately seemed to still have their original plumbing. The style could only be called free-floating. At various times their apartment contained bits and pieces from the sets of Kiki's plays; odds and ends from the junk dealers of the neighborhood, and much fine furniture from Grosse Pointe. The only constants were a fireplace, Daisy's working materials, decent-enough beds and the mural with which one of their friends had been inspired to decorate a living-room wall: a pastoral scene featuring Theseus engaging in various criminal acts in a series of farmyards. Neither Daisy nor Kiki had the instincts of a homemaker, and when they weren't invited out to eat—a rare situation—they bought something from a local delicatessen for dinner. When they bothered about breakfast, they snatched it at a little street stand right around the corner which sold a doughnut and coffee for fifty-five cents, and, mysteriously, featured fresh coconut.

Daisy flopped down with a sigh of relief on the latest couch, brown satin and agreeably overstuffed, that had recently arrived from Kiki's mother. Every time she sent them a new shipment they promptly sold their old furniture. Eleanor Kavanaugh found it strange that they'd been able to absorb such *quantities* of objects, but she said, sniffing in disapproval, she supposed Kiki needed them for *that* theater .... Thank heaven Grandmother Lewis hadn't lived to know what had happened to her money. Although, of course, if she *had* lived, there wouldn't have been—oh, never mind, just don't tell her all the ghastly details.

"She's actually thrilled," Kiki declared. "I know that she boasts about me at the country club—she calls me a patroness of the arts."

Daisy roused herself from her comfortable place on the couch long enough to take off her baseball jacket. She'd bought it right after going to work as a production assistant for North. She'd appeared on that first morning in her newest jeans, freshly pressed, her best beige cashmere turtleneck sweater and a checked hacking jacket that had been made for her in London years before.

"Oh no!" hissed Bootsie, when she saw Daisy arrive.

"What's wrong?" Daisy asked, alarmed.

"Christ—do you have to look so much like old money?"

"But it's my oldest jacket."

"That's the point, dummy. It reeks of that good green stuff. And besides doing your job, you have to spend as much time as possible getting friendly with the crew so that they'll tell you everything you need to know, something I positively do not have the time to do. You're going to be pestering them with questions from morning to night and you're going to be dependent on their good will. They're the sweetest guys in the world if they think you need help, but no way do you look like a working girl who needs a job. That jacket says that you ride, you've ridden for years, you have better riding clothes somewhere else, and you're probably still using them. And they're hip to that. So get rid of it!"

"But *you* look very put together and expensive," Daisy objected.

"I'm the producer, kiddo. I can wear whatever I want."

Now that Daisy had Bootsie's job, which paid four hundred dollars a week, she still wore the baseball jacket from time to time. It reminded her of those first frantic, panicked months when, just as Bootsie predicted, she floundered around from grip to gaffer, from the sound man to the assistant cameraman, from the hair stylist to the set designer, from the prop man to the script supervisor, asking what now she realized must have been incredibly stupid questions, and writing down all the answers in a little notebook. Her jacket had won her friends by its mere existence, developed dialogues, created innumerable opportunities to join in mutual nostalgia for the lost team. It had made her one of the boys at a time when she desperately needed to be one of them.

She looked at her watch. In one hour she would be picked up for dinner at La Grenouille, followed by the opening of the new Hal Prince musical. Her hostess, Mrs. Hamilton Short, lived on a large estate in Middleburg, and she had three children, none of whom Daisy had been asked to paint . . . yet. Cinderella time, she thought, and reluctantly got up and went to her room to start the transformation from working stiff to princess. Or rather, from working stiff to working stiff, if the truth were known.

Ram was thirty. He lived in a perfect house on Hill Street, only a step away from Berkeley Square, a house decorated by David Hicks in severe bachelor sumptuousness. He was a member of White's Club, far and away the most exclusive and difficult to enter of British gentlemen's clubs, and he was a member of Mark's Club, that private restaurant which is the haunt of the most languid and most privileged of the young elite of London. His suits, which cost nine hundred dollars each, were made at H. Huntsman and Sons, the best tailor in England, as were all his riding clothes. He was counted as one of the best shots in the British Isles and owned a pair of shotguns, made to his measurements, from James Purdey and Sons, a firm that had existed in the time of George III. It had taken three years before they were completed, at fifteen thousand dollars the pair, and they were, Ram thought, well worth waiting for. His shoes and boots came, of course, from Lobb's and cost from two hundred and fifty-five dollars a pair upward, depending on the style and the leather. He collected rare books in a major way and avant-garde sculpture in a minor way. He wore white silk pajamas piped in a sober burgundy, heavy silk dressing gowns and shirts made from the finest Sea Island cotton, all made to order at Turnbull and Asser. He considered Sulka vulgar. He never left the house without his umbrella from Swaine, Adeney, Brigg and Sons. It was made of black silk and the handle and shaft were carved out of a single piece of exceptional hickory. He drew the line at a hat—perhaps in ten years, but not now, except for fishing, riding and yachting, and his dark hair was cut in the privacy of one of the ancient wooden rooms at Trumper on Curzon Street. He dined out every night, except on Sunday.

Ram's name appeared with frequency in those sugary columns about society written by "Jennifer" for *Harper's* and *Queen* magazine. Jennifer invariably described him as "the notably handsome and totally charming Prince George Edward Woodhill Valensky." He also often was mentioned in Nigel Dempster's purposefully bitchy column in the *Daily Mail*, where he was sometimes called "the last, dare we hope, of the White Russians," although Ram had made it a point not to join the

Monarchist League run by the Marquess of Bristol. He had no interest in a group he considered fundamentally frivolous, nor did he care to rub elbows with archdukes in exile, who, even if they might be cousins, would almost surely prove to be needy. His business sense had led him to multiply his fortune many times. Ram was a full partner in an investment trust, Lion Management, Ltd., which had had impressive success in supervising the placement of large amounts of money from the pension funds of trade unions and corporations in highly imaginative and productive international investments.

If he had wanted to spend a weekend at one of the country estates which still, in spite of taxes, exist in Great Britain, Ram had but to pick up a phone and call any one of dozens of the young lordlings he had known at Eton. An equal number of the most spirited and desirable young beauties of 1975 would have invited him to their beds with enthusiasm, for Ram was one of that small group of rich and wellborn young men whose name appeared on every list of the Most Eligible Bachelors in England.

However, his status in British society had nothing to do with his money or his title. It rested on the one indispensable thing he had never even bothered to covet during his youth—land. And the land came through his mother's family, the family he had barely considered as he grew up. His mother was the only child of an untitled family, the Woodhills of Woodhill Manor, in Devon; quiet squires who had lived in one spot since before the Norman Conquest, looking down their noses, with pastoral certainty, at all parvenus, whether they were recently created earls whose titles didn't go back further than the eighteenth century, or merely merchant princes whose businesses had made England great in the Victorian era. As far as the Woodhills were concerned, they were all "fearfully recent" people.

The important thing about Valensky, everyone agreed, was that, when his grandfather died, he had inherited Woodhill Manor and the nine hundred acres of farmland that went with it. It was the ownership of this small piece of England that put Ram on the same lists as H.R.H. Prince Michael of Kent; Nicholas Soames, grandson of Sir Winston Churchill; the Marquess of Blandford, who would one day become the twelfth Duke of Marlborough; and Harry Somerset, heir to the Duke of Beaufort. Without Woodhill Manor and its pleasant fields, Ram's fortune and title would have always been just a bit *foreign*, but with Woodhill backing them up with the reassuring solidity of county status, they could be appreciated fully.

Ram went to his office in the City every day and worked hard. He returned home on foot, considering the walk as necessary exercise, changed for dinner, went to the entertainment of that particular evening, drank little, came home at a reasonable hour and went to bed. He rarely picked up his phone to arrange a country weekend, nor did he often ask for admittance to any young woman's bed. When he did it, he never asked a second time, not wishing to encourage bothersome attachments or raise false hopes. If he had had a cat, he would have kicked it.

When he reached his thirtieth birthday, Ram decided he must consider the idea of marriage to someone suitable. Not immediately but eventually. Looking around White's one night, when he'd taken a partner there for dinner, he'd noticed how different the club's atmosphere was from the busy, cheerful lunchtime scene. Only a handful of tables were occupied, many of them by solitary, older men who were far more interested in their wine and food than struck him as entirely decent. Ram didn't care for that fate. He began to consider the available crop of possible wives in the intense, humorless, practical manner that fit his outward demeanor.

Ram knew perfectly well that eligible as he was, he was not really liked. He didn't know why and he considered it of little importance. Some men spent their time being liked, others had better things to do. He was, however, highly and widely *respected,* and that, he felt, was the important thing, the *major* thing.

When Daisy's picture appeared in *Vogue* or any of the other publications, English, French and American, which kept an occasional eye on her horsy weekend parties, Ram looked at them with bitter disapproval. He felt absolute disgust at her job with North, working in a field he considered low, common and contemptible. Her social life seemed, to him, to be devoid of discrimination. Whenever any of the people he knew questioned him about her, he took pains to inform them that she was only a half-sister, with no English blood, and that he knew nothing and cared less about her private life. If it were not for the dreams about Daisy, dreams of love; hopeless, endless, devouring, destroying, never diminishing love, that tormented him ceaselessly, week after week, year after year, he might almost have managed to believe what he told his acquaintances. How he wished she were dead!

14

Conference rooms are, almost by definition, designed to impress, but few of them were as explicit, Daisy thought, as that of the Frederick Gordon North Studio. It always amused her to look around and appreciate its purposefully spare and unornamented severity, its deliberately unemphatic and austere whitewashed brick wall and bare wooden floors lacquered in shining black. No one of any sensitivity could fail to be susceptible to the astringent luxury of the chrome Knoll chairs covered in pewter suede and the ascetic sweep of the huge, bare, oval conference table of white marble. From his place at the table, North could operate a concealed console of pushbuttons that signaled to the projectionist in the booth outside, telling him when to darken the room, when to lower the screen from the ceiling and when to roll film, a device which rarely failed to make even the most sophisticated clients sit up and pay attention. The conference room was on the top floor of a three-story building which had once been an abandoned music school in the East 80s, between First and Second avenues. Seven years ago North had bought it and converted it into one of the few privately owned commercial studios in the city. The first and second floors formed one huge sound stage which could be arranged in a thousand ways. Only the top floor was used for offices. North also owned his own cameras, lights and equipment. Since the vast majority of commercial directors had to include the cost of rental of studio space and equipment when they bid on a job—and most advertising agencies ask for at least three bids on each assignment they award—North was able to underbid on almost every commercial he went after, and still make a larger profit than his competitors despite his high fee.

Now, in the fall of 1975, six months after the hairspray commercial had been shot, an important meeting was being held in the conference room. Before the average commercial job, North usually met only with Daisy and Arnie Greene, but today he had insisted that all of his key employees be present for the first planning session of the Coca-Cola Christmas commercial.

By now Daisy knew the people gathered around the table so well that they felt almost like extensions of herself. There was Hubie Troy, the free-lance scenic designer with whom North worked so often that he might just as well have been on staff; Daisy's two young male production assistants, both recent Princeton graduates who would learn, or try to learn the business, and then go on to something which paid better; Alix Updike, her assistant for wardrobe and casting, a tall, quietly dressed and reserved girl, who used to be the lingerie editor at *Glamour;* and Wingo Sparks, the twenty-nine-year-old, full-time cameraman, in his Ivy League, unpressed duck trousers and splotched tennis sweater which was unraveling in six places. Daisy was sure he'd plucked out the threads himself.

Wingo was a Harvard graduate, the son of one top cameraman and the nephew of another. Had it not been for these family connections he wouldn't have been able to enter the cameraman's union, as tightly controlled as any medieval guild. He'd served as an assistant cameraman to his uncle for the necessary five years before getting his own union card. North infinitely preferred working with young men because they were receptive to even the wildest of his innovative ideas, and although, as the owner of his own business, he was entitled to operate a camera himself, without a union card, he disliked being responsible for all technical considerations in the heat of filming, while he had to concentrate on the actors and an overview of the entire set.

Daisy's eyes rested with affection on Arnie Greene, the business manager, who still found it hard to believe that after working most of his life for EUE with its four hundred employees he was now part of a "boutique" operation like North's. However, many of the top directors in the business preferred to work in small, compact shops, and although Daisy knew that Arnie hated the term "boutique," a word that was totally inappropriate for what was a mini-movie studio, it was used by the entire industry.

Finally, Daisy considered the flamboyantly elegant figure of Nick-the-Greek, North's full time "rep" who worked on commission getting new business. Nick was, to Daisy's knowledge, the only rep in the city who had found his way into the advertising business via a spitball. In the mid-1960s, when the big advertising agencies were each fielding a baseball team, and competing ferociously against each other, a copy writer at Doyle, Dane Bernbach had heard of a Puerto Rican high-school kid from the Barrio who was the best pitcher north of 125th Street. He'd given him a token job at the agency after school just to secure him for the team. But Manuel took one shrewd look at the agency business and liked it a lot better than any possible future in Spanish Harlem. The tall, flashingly handsome teenager baptized himself Nick-the-Greek and here he was now, earning over one hundred thousand dollars a year, wearing seven-hundred-dollar suits and drifting over to "21" for lunch every day, catching top jobs as easily as a lizard catches flies on his tongue. He could handle clients as carefully as any mahout ever handled a royal elephant during a lion hunt in India.

Now, just as North was about to call them all to order, Nick took the floor.

"*Compañeros* all—I have here the results of a new Gallup poll," he said, taking out a clipping from the *New York Times* and brandishing it at them.

"Can it, Nick," Arnie begged, knowing that when Nick-the-Greek got started, time got wasted.

"Wait! You don't understand. This concerns all of us, Arnie. Those of you who suffer from Jewish Guilt or Italian Shame or Wasp Resignation—come to order, *por favor,* and pay close attention. This poll concerns honesty and ethics in various professions as perceived by a cross section of the American people."

"That has *nothing* to do with Coke, Nick," said North, impatiently. "So why don't you just go away and hustle? Haven't you got some hungry, rich, potentially profitable client to take to lunch? *Vámonos*—we've got work to do."

"Not until I give you good tidings" said Nick, who, like all reps, made it a point of honor to be far more grandiose than the working stiffs for whom they labored. The reps of New York, a mafia of superslick, ultra-fashionable salesmen, consider themselves to be to the actual commercial makers as Russian wolfhounds are to a pack of mongrels.

"Here it is—clergymen, you'll be thrilled to hear, rate highest in the poll. Doctors and engineers come next. Out of twenty professions, *twenty,* the *next to last* rating is given to something called 'advertising practitioners.' That means us, *compañeros,* boys and girls included. Forty-three percent of the whole, fucking American public gave us a very low, repeat, *very low* rating for, and I quote, 'honesty and ethical standards.' The only people they rate lower than us are *car salesmen!* We even rate lower than state officeholders! Don't any of you guys feel we should protest? March on Washington, take out ads to say how clean, upstanding, patriotic and plain, down-home good we are? I don't think we should sit here and let them dump on us. Have you people no pride? Nor moral indignation? Don't you give at least a little, tiny shit? This can't be allowed to go unchallenged." His faultless teeth gleamed in his swarthy face, as he stood there, mockingly listening to the burst of hooting, catcalls and derisive whistles that filled the room.

"Nick, for a man who suffers from Greek Fire, when he's never been to Athens, you'll have to muster the indignation for all the rest of us. Out! The headwaiters of the world are waiting eagerly for you," North said firmly.

As the rep left, Arnie Greene said aggrievedly, "If doctors rate so high, how come there are so many malpractice suits?"

"Nobody pays attention to Gallup polls anyway." For a second North's wily grin appeared. "Forget it Arnie. Now that Mr. Wonderful has boogied off, let's talk advertising for a change. And I'm warning you, anyone who isn't taking notes will regret it. This is a ninety-second commercial, and the story board makes a Max Rhinehardt production look like batshit. Not only that, Luke Hammerstein is going for humor, and they're not even going to show the product—which makes the whole thing different from what anyone else is doing."

"Not show the product?" Arnie Greene asked, in such astonishment that he squeaked.

"Nope—not show it and not *mention* it for one whole incredible *minute and a half!* Then, at the very end, we'll hear Helen Hayes saying, 'No matter how your family spent the night before Christmas, Coca-Cola wishes you wonderful holidays all year round.' "

"Did you say humor?" Daisy asked.

"Yup—Luke calls this the 'Flip Side of Christmas,' and he is seriously nervous about his idea. Luke talked Coke out of going with a big montage of Christmas dinners all over America, very mixed ethnic, your standard Mid-American big-yawn time, but Luke managed to sell them this—haven't I always said he was the best creative director in the world?"

"Yeah—but the two of you don't usually work together. You fight all the time," Daisy murmured, still dubious.

"True." North gave her a disapproving look for her interruption. "Luke *is* my close friend, but he has the conviction, unfortunately shared by most agency people, that the *concept* is what sells the product and that the concept begins and ends with the agency. As far as they're concerned, all a director does is bring the concept to life. I say it's both the concept *and* the way I make it make it work—my taste level, if you'll excuse the expression. That's why we fight. I want my share of the credit, Luke wants his share, and unfortunately together they add up to a hell of a lot more than a hundred percent. However, this commercial is a clear-cut case. He needs my help. And he knows it! With the story board they've got here it's either going to be a mild giggle or a fucking classic." The sharp planes and angles of North's face, his nose which ended so abruptly, even his freckles, all seemed to quiver with eagerness. North could hear the roar of the crowd under the circus tent, he was getting ready for the moment when he'd go into the cage and show the monsters who was boss. Daisy had seen him like this before, many times, but rarely had she seen him so excited by a challenge.

"May one ask what the 'Flip Side of Christmas' is?" asked Wingo, in his usual cheeky drawl.

"It's the shit that really goes down—thirty seconds backstage at a grade-school Nativity play, thirty seconds of a family of eight trying to get into a car meant for five small people, loaded with bulky presents, skis, what-have-you, all on their way to Christmas dinner at grandmother's, and last, thirty seconds of the sheer, hideous trauma of decorating the goddamned tree and everything that can go wrong—beginning to get the picture? And soft, soft sell—Coke doesn't want to be hustling during the CBS Christmas special, so that, Arnie, is why we don't show the product."

"Is any of this location?" asked Hubie, who was already sketching rapidly on the pad he always carried.

"No, thank God, we're doing it all in the studio. Hubie, you've got not one, not two, but three—count them—*three-walled* sets to build. Nobody's seen three-walled sets used in a year, so get lost, you know what you have to do—here's Xerox of the story board. I want everything middle-class but nice, and authentic, so fucking authentic you can smell the Christmas tree, smell the kids backstage, even smell that car with too many people in it."

As Hubie left, North fixed what was left of his audience with a stern eye and continued. "Daisy, you and Alix pay attention. Casting is of major, major importance in this—you know what the Coke commercials usually look like—everybody totally all-American, too many teeth, so much blond hair you could repopulate half of Scandinavia with the models—I don't want that. This is going to be different—we're not selling Coke to make you popular or happy, we're selling all that funny-awful crap that happens at Christmas, and telling everybody that maybe they should just laugh at it. So don't cast all-American Prom Queen. Most people get depressed enough at Christmas just seeing too much gorgeousness. For the kids' Nativity-play scene, I don't want little Jamie from Ivory soap or little Rusty from Crest toothpaste, I want real kids, nearsighted, fat, pimply, snot-nosed—cast sideways, not straight ahead, cast *bent,* as bent as you can get. Don't give me those looks. You think I don't know how much harder it's going to make the job? Shit, ladies, if a kid can't sit still, concentrate and follow directions, it's home-movie time. That's a chance I'm willing to take because this has to look like a real Christmas play in a real place—not TV-commercial heaven."

"North," Daisy asked suspiciously, "is this *all* in the story board—you're sure the client wants bent kids? Coke *always* goes for more-beautiful-than-life people."

"Daisy, just do me one small favor? Stop trying to second-guess me," he snapped, thoroughly annoyed. "This story board calls for a dozen kids, good mix, three black, five white, all colors of hair, two Oriental and two Chicano. On the other thirty-second scenes you need nine people for the tree-trimming episode and eight for the family in the car, plus a dog, a really big, awful-looking one—a crummy, slobbery, hairy dog . . . not a cute one . . . also a baby, nine months old. Get me the quietest babies in the world—remember we can't keep them under lights for long, so we may need a dozen in reserve. Check it out. But bring me just one familiar face and I'll tear your heads off! This is going to be the Dickens *Christmas Carol* of Christmas commercials."

Arnie Greene rolled his eyes to heaven. He knew what could happen when North got really excited about a job. No matter how he insisted that he was in advertising, not show business, they might go over budget to get just exactly what he wanted and he wouldn't be satisfied with a millimeter less. He didn't know what the words "good enough" meant. Well, he owned the business and this year they'd net enough so he was entitled to play a little.

"Wingo," North turned to the young cameraman. "There're three Hollywood studios in town now shooting movies. You may have trouble getting the crew we want, so get off your ass and start phoning. Tell 'em it's four days work, starting ten days from today."

"Four days—since when can't we do ninety seconds in three?" Wingo objected.

"With kids and dogs and babies? We'll run over—it's inevitable. And if you say three days they might have other jobs on the fourth—how'd you like to lose your crew before you finish?"

"The thought," said Wingo, "is not attractive."

"So why are you still here?"

"Excellent question," he said cheerfully, rising from his seat. "It all sounds easier than it's going to be, North, but at least Luke didn't ask us for the 'Robert Altman look'—not, of course, that you couldn't give it to him."

Before Wingo reached the door, North caught him with a last goad. "Wingo, young man, I hear from my secretaries that that lady of yours named Maureen has been calling you every ten minutes. Why don't you just throw it into her and get her off our back?"

"Sorry, but no time for social chatter this morning, boss," said Wingo, closing the door quietly behind him.

"That boy will go far," North said in satisfaction. "I like his fucking nerve."

Sure you do, Daisy thought balefully, in a man. But let a woman try it and you wouldn't merely threaten to tear her head off, you'd cut her heart out and eat it for breakfast.

"Daisy," North said, "tomorrow, we go to the agency for a meeting with Luke and his people. Do you think you could try to look like a lady, or at least a female?" He shot an unmistakable glance of disapproval at Daisy's habitual working costume.

"I'll make every effort, but I can't guarantee it—not on what you pay me," Daisy retorted. It was a never failing source of irritation that although she was the "producer" of the commercials, and in charge of coordinating every detail of every shoot, her job was nonunion and she was paid less for working more hours than anyone else in the studio. North ignored her remark, as he always did, refusing to acknowledge the fact that Daisy's clothes made good sense.

Soon after she had learned her trade she discovered that since someone was always looking for her to solve a problem, her jeans and work shirt made her difficult to spot in the denim-clad multitude of the crew. She had worked out an outfit that had three virtues: it was cheap, practical and highly visible. In cold weather she wore U.S. Navy, World War II, ordinary seaman's pants with their complicated set of thirteen buttons and their sturdy fabric. In summer she wore white Navy bell-bottoms. To go with these basic trousers she had a dozen boys' Rugby jerseys in the boldest stripes and brightest colors she could find. In the huge, grubby confused studio she always wore tennis shoes and thick white socks, and braided her hair into one fat pigtail that fell over one shoulder, but at least it stayed out of her face.

If it's ladylike you want, North, she thought, I'll give you ladylike till your fillings fall out. The meeting ended while Daisy was planning her look for tomorrow—the 1934 Mainbocher suit, she thought, high heels, a tight chignon and *gloves*, you rotten bastard.

No matter how she railed at North in her mind, Daisy never failed to be astonished as he unpacked one fresh idea after another from the inexhaustible stock he seemed to possess, closely folded in his mind. His highest praise after a complicated, difficult commercial had been completed was to say to her, "It'll probably work," yet, for these three words, like a horsewoman trying out for the Olympic jumping team, she was game to attempt any fence, no matter how high. She could understand, she told herself in an attempt at fairness, why so many models insisted on telling her how devastatingly, divinely attractive her boss was, but then they didn't know him as she did. How could they begin to imagine the hardness of the man, the lack of warm humanity? His brilliance gleamed, but with a cold light. Nevertheless Daisy was unable to keep herself from trying to please him in her dedication to her job. As she had mastered her skills over the past years she took a craftsman's pleasure in her work, in each full, clean, well-organized day of shooting, the details of which, without her, would never have come together. She gloried in the flashes of inspiration that enabled her to solve the inevitable emergencies that plagued any shoot. With all modesty, she knew she was very, very good at what she did. Damn him, if only, just once, he'd *admit* it!

It is not often that the creative people who make television commercials have a chance to break the rules. Normally they are limited, almost entirely, to working in a world in which moldy grout can ruin a woman's life, while at the same time, perfectly white teeth can guarantee her love and happiness; a world in which her husband's morning is destroyed by a weak cup of coffee yet his virility can be validated by the brand of beer he drinks; they inhabit a cosmos in which thick, bouncy hair is life's dearest treasure and moist underarms are a constantly lurking menace; a territory in which best friends exist only to make critical remarks, and the choice between one kind of tampon or another is the difference between a carefree, athletic existence or being haunted by relentless anxiety. It's a threatening world in which the only real hope is the right kind of life insurance or a new set of steel-belted radials; a world of unending physical effort in which perfectly nice women are given life sentences in which they must produce immaculate floors, pristine toilet bowls, and even impeccable laundry; a world in which the people who depend on iron supplements to give them vitality barely look old enough to vote, in which the best filled medicine cabinet is certain to lack that one particular preparation which will make pain and head colds not just bearable but almost enjoyable. When this world isn't scary, it is frustratingly filled with too-healthy people having impossibly delightful fun in far away places, all thanks to an after-shave lotion or the right eye make-up. In advertising land it's quite all right to use obscenity to sell cigarette lighters—they couldn't dare mean anything dirty by "Flick my Bic," could they? But bra ads can't show women wearing bras, navels don't exist, and a pregnant woman may never seem to have the desire for physical contact with a man, not even her husband. There is even a regulation preventing a woman from sucking her own forefinger on camera. Singing cats can sell cat food better than any other commercial in history and creative advertising men write their copy in a cold sweat of fear and angst, not knowing whether a new idea will make them a hero or get them fired. With ten-second commercials becoming more and more popular, with research showing that viewers don't remember commercials that contain more than one single message, and with prime *seconds* on television costing hundreds of thousands of dollars, the opportunity to make expensive mistakes continues to multiply and the pressure to play it safe grows.

Luke Hammerstein had persuaded his bosses to go with his intuition on the Coca-Cola Christmas commercial, and intuition could mean disaster. If anyone had ever told Luke Hammerstein, when he was a wild, brilliant graduate of the wild, brilliant School of Visual Arts on 23rd Street in New York City that one day he would routinely send his most original ideas off to be tested in front of a carefully chosen target audience at Audience Survey, Inc., *before* he elected to use them or not, he would have sneered in outrage. But that was in the early 1960s when boy wonders in Edwardian clothes were grabbed up by the big agencies and started as assistant art directors when they were just out of school, the free-spending, innovative, let's-build-an-igloo-in-the-Mojave-Desert-and-see-if-it-melts days of commercials. Many of the other boy wonders didn't survive into the tighter-money, harder-sell days of the 1970s, but just as Luke had seen the change in the spirit of commercials coming long before it happened, he had traded in the poetically dandified elaborations of his attire for severely tailored suits with matching vests, started to wear solid blue shirts with starched white collars and French cuffs, begun to sport a stickpin in his dark, plain tie, and grown the perfectly trimmed Van Dyke beard which lent the final touch of authority to his aesthetic features. The distinguished aura of a young Oxford don replaced the graces he had cultivated in his early days as he progressed, in an amazing ten years, from assistant art director to art director to art supervisor and finally to creative director, with fifty people working under him, and eighty million dollars of annual billing under his supervision. Luke Hammerstein, only son of a conservative German-Jewish investment-banking family, was a superstar on Madison Avenue, even if his mother—who thought all advertising unnecessary and common—would never believe it.

Luke knew, from the beginning, that if an art director is ever going to advance in the agency business he has to be more than an art director; he has to also be a source of original ideas, a copy writer, a salesman and an expert on media and research.

Luke was in the center of the creative revolution when the power in the agencies passed from the people who created the words to the people who created the pictures. He had risen to a position of enormous power. But no power on Madison Avenue can survive unless it sells the product. The chance to do a Coca-Cola commercial without having to sell the product left Luke light-headed with the sheer freedom of it, and as antsy as he'd ever been.

Luke was almost never present at the shoot of one of his ordinary commercials, but during the four long days it took to finish the Christmas commercial, he showed up at North's studio every day, accompanied by the account supervisor, the assistant account supervisor, the copy writer and the art director, all of whom had been involved in the working out of Luke's commercial before he ever truly believed he could get the client to go for it. His agency group arrived no earlier than 10:45 A.M. although the cast and crew's call was for 8:00. Wise to the ways of commercial makers, Luke knew that the first take couldn't possibly take place before 11:00. In the words of one advertising immortal discussing the first three hours of every working day, "We shoot a commercial the way we used to build pyramids . . . everything is improved except the equipment . . . it's two guys carrying things on their backs, like over the Burma Road . . . you pull and you push."

The clients, the men from Coke, were there in force, too. Sometimes as few as six, invariably, just before lunch, as many as twelve. Although Daisy had been involved in dozens of shoots where the agency and client contingents—the "hungry worriers" as North called them—outnumbered the commercial makers, this time the cast, crew and observers were so numerous that the big studio was strained as it had never been strained before.

Looking back, after it was all over, Daisy couldn't be sure what had been, for her, the high point of the whole enterprise. Was it her canny method of casting kids who looked "real" but were actually professional models? She and Alix had spent four days searching out those unfortunate child models who'd had to stop work because of broken limbs, the early onset of acne, acute obesity problems, missing teeth, braces, growing out of their cuteness—even a month could do it—and just plain discipline difficulties, kids who were considered troublemakers. She winnowed out a gang of authentic misfits, none of whom could have sold a single box of cereal, no matter how sugar coated. These rejects provided enough difficulty on the set to convince North that they were normal, but without their foundation of professional training, the Nativity scene could never have been shot, not just in the agonizing day and a half it eventually took, but not in a week or perhaps not in a month.

Or was the best part, she asked herself, the satisfaction she had in casting Theseus as the dog in the car scene? Since North had wanted a difficult dog, Daisy reasoned there was no reason why she shouldn't make the money which would otherwise have gone to a recognized dog model. It came to her share of two months rent and, as usual, Dani's expenses had left her with no money to spare. She enlisted Kiki as dog wrangler for a day, with strict instructions.

"Keep him on the leash at all times until North signals for him. That'll be when the family's finally all stuffed into the car—one of the kids is going to whine, 'We forgot my dog.' Then let him go."

North inspected Theseus superciliously. "Where did you find that beast, Daisy? I've never seen anything like him before."

"Not to worry, he comes highly recommended."

"But I wanted a more *annoying* dog, something really shaggy. Something sloppier," he complained.

"This dog is guaranteed to be annoying," Daisy assured him. Since she had carefully hidden tiny bits of raw sirloin in various pockets of the clothes worn by all the actors in the scene, clothes she had chosen for the fact that they had pockets that buttoned, she had total confidence in Theseus's performance. With his hunting blood at boil he'd be all over those unfortunate people, loose in a lurcher's potential paradise.

Theseus didn't let her down. Take after take, he bounded into the packed car and wormed his way around the eight "family" members, poking his nose into their most private places, wagging his tail in their outraged faces and amorously pawing all over them in an unceremonious delirium of confusion and quest. All around was the smell of meat—but where was it? At the end of each take, Kiki dashed in with the leash to lead him out, slipping him a piece of meat from a Baggie full of beef tidbits which Daisy had given her, so that Theseus wouldn't get too frustrated—never enough to satisfy him but just enough to keep his appetite at its height.

By the middle of the day North said in admiration, "That's the worst behaved mutt I've ever seen in my life. He's driving them up the wall—perfect, Alix, perfect!" Naturally, thought Daisy, he doesn't even give me credit for casting my own dog, the son-of-a-bitch! North was even more pleased when the model playing the mother of the family developed a violent allergy to Theseus and couldn't stop sneezing.

"Write it in," he told the hovering copy writer. And for the next twenty-nine takes, between constant sneezes, the woman had to say, "You *know* that dog makes me sneeze!" and the impossible teenage son had to reply, scornfully, "Oh, *Mom!* It's just psychosomatic!" There was no question that Theseus was the star of the thirty seconds which everyone called "Over the Hill to Granny's Pad."

By the last day of the shoot, when they reached the tree-decorating scene, a childish spirit of fun had overtaken even the hungry worriers. They started to suggest lines and situations which weren't on the story board.

"This is getting like the Yiddish Art Theater," North told them. "Fellows, we have enough problems right here—nothing is going to go right, I promise you, so could I bother you guys for some fucking quiet?" He was prophetic. Nothing did go right. It took forty-five takes before the gaffers could manage to get the tree lights to blow all the fuses inside the set without having them blow all the lights outside the set as well, plunging the studio into total darkness each time.

Long after the Coca-Cola commercial had won a Clio, the commercial world's Oscar; long after it had won the New York Art Director's Club coveted annual award; long after it had been exhibited at commercial film festivals all over the world and brought back awards from Venice and Cork and Tokyo and Paris, Kiki had no doubts at all about the high point of those four days. What were the awards compared to the moment she had met Luke Hammerstein?

Kiki had felt so sorry for poor Theseus, after he'd spent all day sniffing for hidden meat, that as soon as the scene was declared a wrap, she'd let him off the leash.

"Excuse me, dog handler," Luke said to her, "are you aware that your animal is on top of the caterer's table, creating consternation and famine?"

"Don't worry about that food," Kiki said. "If you're hungry, I'll take you out to dinner. If you're not hungry, we can go to my place and just talk." Luke Hammerstein was sinewy and of medium height. He had green eyes which were both audacious and dreamy, insolent and kind. His eyelids were melancholy and his manner detached.

"Jesus," said Luke. "Is that a pass?"

"You'd be wise to consider it as such. I don't just kid around," Kiki said, with open admiration in her umber eyes.

"But what about the dog?"

"Forget him—I was just babysitting him for a friend. Coming?" Kiki was still the diabolic tatterdemalion, the elfin gypsy she had been when she and Daisy met eight years ago, but now she was far more aggressive and self-assured. Her excesses were harmless, her frivolity and self-indulgence basically benign, but she avoided the serious moment as if even one might turn her into a pillar of salt. In all her unsheltered years she couldn't remember meeting a man like Luke. She reached up and stroked his pointed, silky beard. What possibilities, what fantasies, what lubricious potentials it presented!

"Well . . ." Luke hesitated. All day long he'd seen Kiki on the set until she'd become part of the scenery, and suddenly, she had transformed herself into a peremptory female who seemed to have a specific intention regarding him and no problem about showing it. In fact, in the black pants tucked into the black boots and the severe black shirt Kiki had decided were right for her background role today, she seemed to him to be an apprentice highwayman, or rather, highwaywoman.

Every poll he'd read recently indicated that when women made the first approach it had a desirably erotic effect on men.

"Do I have a choice?" he wondered.

"Not really," Kiki said in a voice of despotic allure.

"I guess I don't at that . . . anyway, what do I have to lose?"

"Nothing you want to keep," Kiki assured him with her low laugh which was as fresh and aphrodisiac as a puff of spring air. At a distance Daisy was trying to decide who was doing the most damage, Theseus or Kiki. From the look on Luke Hammerstein's face, she decided it was too late to save him . . . anyway, he was a grown man and should be able to look out for himself . . . but she still might salvage enough from the caterer's table to feed the crew who had worked long over their normal quitting hour and would be expecting their dinner, as well as their extra money. She collared Theseus with one practiced gesture, pulling him from his perch on top of the platters of roast beef, corned beef and ham.

"Christ, Daisy, don't you have the sense to keep your hands off that wretched animal?" North said, as he passed by.

"Theseus, my own precious," Daisy said, with a hand signal she'd taught him ten years ago, "go give your Uncle North a nice big kiss."

Daisy had been invited to Middleburg, to Hamilton and Topsy Short's, for the weekend following the Coca-Cola shoot. As she considered what to pack she realized how important it could be—*must be*—to her. Daisy needed money badly. The Horse People had been scattered all over the world the past summer and she hadn't had a commission for a kid on a pony in months. Mrs. Short had hinted, in that dangling way in which certain rich, prospective patrons torment artists, that if the small sketch she had asked Daisy to do of her eldest daughter was satisfactory, she would consider commissioning an oil painting of all three of her children as a birthday present for her husband. That, Daisy calculated, would be at least a six-thousand-dollar job, although it would take several months to complete in what little spare time she had.

But there was no doubt about the utter necessity for earning some money. The quarterly payment for Danielle's care was due in a month. The prices at Queen Anne's School had gone up gradually, over the years, more than keeping up with the sums Daisy made through her painting as well as whatever was left over from her salary. Danielle's continual care now cost Daisy almost twenty-three thousand dollars a year and she hadn't been able to afford to fly to England to see her twin in the past eight months. Although she still faithfully made drawings to send Dani, sometimes she had so much work that she had to substitute one of the postcards she bought at a store in SoHo called "Untitled Art Postcards," postcards she knew Dani would like: the original illustrations from *Alice in Wonderland*, Odilon Redon butterflies, the carousel figure of an ostrich from the Philadelphia Museum of Art, three Edward Lear cartoons of Foss the Cat from Lear's *Nonsense Songs and Stories*, the strange fairy painting by Anne Anderson which illustrated Charles Kingsley's *The Water Babies*.

And now, just when she needed advice, Kiki wasn't exactly being helpful. Ever since she'd met Luke Hammerstein yesterday she'd been acting as if she were a moonstruck female satyr.

"Kiki," she'd objected, "I saw you coming on to Luke Hammerstein yesterday—you just can't behave like that . . . it isn't ladylike."

"My dear Daisy," Kiki answered loftily. "It worked and that's what counts. And, in any case, your language shows the deplorable effect of association with that person you call Nick-the-Greek, if I may say so."

"What does that mean, 'worked'?" said Daisy suspiciously. "Where did the two of you go last night?"

"Out to dinner." Kiki's face was a circle of merriment and secret humor.

"And?"

"Princess Valensky, the fact that at the advanced age of almost twenty-four you only have had two unimportant love affairs with shy, undemanding, easily handled, and essentially passive men hardly makes you a person to consult on romantic matters. I'll answer your question when there is more to report."

During her years in New York, Daisy had, by dint of persuading herself that it was necessary to overcome her feelings about sexual involvement, allowed a few of her most persistent suitors to make love to her. She found that she could respond to them physically but not emotionally, and the relationships had not been important or lasting.

"I've had *three* love affairs," Daisy said angrily. "And one was with your own cousin."

"But did I describe the gentlemen properly?" Kiki demanded.

"You didn't say that they were all very attractive."

"I stand corrected. They were, but not my type. Now Luke Hammerstein on the other hand . . ."

"Spare me. Kiki, come on. Help me out. I've only got an hour to pack. The car's coming to take me out to the airport at six—the Shorts' jet leaves promptly at seven. Now, what do you think I should wear on Saturday night? It's that usual nonsense of 'Don't bother to dress, dear, because we're only having sixty for dinner.' In Middleburg they think dressing for dinner is 'pretentious' so they compromise—you know, silk blouses, long tweedy skirts, granny's pearls, everything fabulously expensive and just the right amount of dowdiness. You know I don't have that sort of drag—I wouldn't even if I could afford it," she said in a worried tone.

When she had first started spending weekends with the Horse People, Daisy had been forced to carve out a unique style for herself. She couldn't possibly buy fashionable dinner clothes so she became an old-clothes aficionado, avoiding the antique-clothing boutiques with their exquisite garments which only a Bette Midler or a Streisand could afford; avoiding the almost-new shops which were crammed with last year's couture clothes, already dated; and avoiding as well the flea markets at which only a miracle could uncover a garment in good condition.

Her buys all came from London jumble sales in church halls that she found time to go to each time she visited Dani. There she specialized in unearthing English and French couture originals, preferably over forty years old, clothes that had been made in the great dressmaking decades of the twenties and thirties. She researched them after she brought them back in triumph, for nothing she owned had cost over thirty-five dollars.

Daisy led Kiki into the third bedroom of their apartment in which she kept her nonworking clothes hanging on a horizontal pipe which crossed one end of the room.

The two girls stood and contemplated the garments that hung there. "It wouldn't be so hard if you only had regular clothes, like other people," Kiki sighed.

"Ah . . . that . . . how right you are. But it's simply too expensive and too dull, although I admit it would make life easier," Daisy replied.

"The Vionnet?" Kiki suggested.

"Too dressy," Daisy said regretfully, fingering the pale violet satin dress, cut on the bias and dating from 1926. "What do you think about the striped Lucien Lelong?"

"To be honest, I've never really liked it on you. Your essential wood nymphishness is not enhanced by zebra stripes, no matter how well done. How about the black velvet Chanel suit? It may be forty years old, but it looks as if it had been born yesterday," Kiki answered.

"It's not the right time of year for black velvet, especially in bluegrass country."

"Wait, *wait*, I see those Dove tea pajamas—you said they were around 1925? Just look, Daisy, cyclamen brocade and green satin with a black satin jacket—it's a smash!"

"They're Locust Valley maybe or Saratoga, but definitely not Middleburg."

"So that lets out the white satin pajama suit from Revillon too?"

"Afraid so. Oh, rot!"

Kiki carefully pushed the hangers aside, sighing wistfully over Daisy's treasures—they were all too long for her, but she itched after them.

"Ah ha!" Daisy pounced. "How could I have forgotten? Schiaparelli to the rescue, as usual." Triumphantly she held up an ensemble from the late 1930s when the daring Schiaparelli was doing clothes which were four decades ahead of their time. There was a jacket in lettuce green tweed touched with sequins at the lapels, worn with a pair of corduroy pants in a darker shade of green. "Just right, don't you think?"

"It's heaven—really a fuck-you number, as in 'fuck you, Mrs. Short, I know it's tweed and I know it's sequins and I know you didn't think they can be worn together, but now you do.' "

"In a nutshell. I really need this commission, so it's important to look as if I didn't."

"Then you'd better take my fake emeralds again."

"Emeralds with green sequins?"

"*Especially* with green sequins!"

15

Of all the potential differences in human tastes, habits, interest and predilections, among the strongest is that which divides people who care about horses from people who don't. People can love cats or dogs and not feel as if they exist on an entirely different plane from those who are indifferent to these animals, but Horse People not only do not care to understand people who don't give a damn about horses, but the mere idea that such people exist—and are the vast majority—makes them wonder about the future of the human race. Horse People may be heads of state or professionally unemployed in their ordinary lives, but horses are their passion, as Jerusalem was the passion of a soldier in some ancient Crusade. The cult of the horse as their idol is as central to their lives as cocaine is to some and applause is to others. Perhaps not all of them know that the earliest work of art known to archaeology is a two-and-a-half-inch sculpture of a horse, made from the ivory tusk of a woolly mammoth, a masterpiece of supple grace which is thirty-two thousand years old—but this fact would seem only fitting and right to any Horse Person. It is only normal that the Cro-Magnon people of the Ice Age appreciated the horse twenty-five thousand years before the dawn of our civilization—normal and to be expected, since they believe that the horse is nature's finest achievement, not excluding man.

"Stupid, *dumb*, moronic beast!" Patrick Shannon told his horse quietly. He didn't want to be overheard. He was taking a private riding lesson in an outdoor ring at a stable in Peapack, New Jersey, only an hour and fifteen minutes from Manhattan. During the last month his chauffeur had driven him out to the school every night, right after he finished his heavy schedule of work as president and chief operating officer of Supracorp, a two-billion-dollar corporation. This had meant giving up all social life and the after-work squash games at the University Club that were one of the only chances he ever had to release his tensions, a cherished respite that he had now abandoned, in favor of this enraging, ridiculous, humiliating pursuit of something at which he would never be really good. At thirty-eight, Patrick Shannon was a natural athlete who had a way with a ball, any ball . . . but growing up in an orphan asylum had given him lots of ability with balls and none, none whatsoever with horses. He hated the things! They drooled and they snorted and they huffed, they turned their heads and tried to nip at his legs with their ugly, big teeth, they reared like silly girls if they saw something they didn't like, they walked sideways when they were supposed to go forward, they stopped to eat the grass when you hadn't pulled on the reins and wouldn't start when you kicked them.

They smelled good—that was all he would say for them. Horseshit was the best smelling shit he'd ever come across, oh, he'd grant them that.

The trail of events that had put Patrick Shannon on the back of a horse was clear. He had set his heart on acquiring for Supracorp another real-estate company, one solely owned by Hamilton Short. Ham Short had suggested that Shannon come next month to spend a weekend in Middleburg, Virginia, while the wooing of his business was going on. Short, assuming that Shannon rode, had spoken of "a little hacking about." Shannon, after committing himself to the weekend, had realized too late that he hadn't said he didn't ride. He didn't know just how crazy Horse People were, but he certainly knew enough about them to guess that the only excuse they would find understandable for an able-bodied man who did not mount a horse was a broken leg. He assumed that many of them rode even with broken legs, and he was perfectly right. Horsemanship, from the moment he accepted Short's invitation, became a challenge, which was next best to the thing he loved most—risk.

Pat Shannon was a born risk taker who understood that the ability to cope with an occasional failure was a vital part of successful risk taking. But his failures, few as they were, had been business failures, and they had never been due to lack of effort or preparation. Since it was clearly possible to learn to ride, ride he would.

Short had said that he had some "fairly pleasant trails" on his place. Shannon had had one of his secretaries check the place out and discovered that it was called Fairfax Plantation, covered eighteen hundred acres, boasted a private jet airstrip, housed twenty servants and was worth, conservatively, four million dollars.

Shannon didn't have to be very clever to realize that if he were to go hacking about on almost two thousand acres, he had to count on fairly long hours in the saddle. And Shannon was clever, indeed exceptionally so. And a clever Irishman can be counted among the cleverest kind of man the human race produces. Hadn't Shannon's favorite Irishman, George Bernard Shaw, said, "A lifetime of happiness! No man alive could bear it; it would be hell on Earth." Pat Shannon grimly reminded himself of these words as he gave his horse the signal to canter for the fiftieth time that evening.

"You're making progress," Chuck Byers said drily, in a tone of voice which took any approval out of the remark. He had never had such a pupil before. He hoped never to have such a one again. Shannon had told him he wanted to learn to ride. Fair enough—lots of people did. But no one else had ever demanded that he be able to trot at the end of the first lesson, canter at the end of the second, and gallop at the end of the third.

Byers had told him it was impossible. Byers had said he'd break a bone at the least and he had made Shannon sign a paper saying that the stable wasn't responsible for any injuries to the man and that Shannon was responsible for all injuries to the horse. But the bastard had galloped after three lessons although Byers could tell by the way he walked back to his car that every muscle in his body was killing him.

The man was a demon, Byers thought. After the third lesson Shannon had sent out a crew of electricians to rig up lights around the ring so that he could ride late into the night, and he had insisted on a three-hour lesson every single night, paying so much that Byers had had to accommodate him in spite of his family's objections. He hadn't spent any time with his wife and kids since Shannon had started this nonsense.

Something about the single-minded way in which Shannon tackled the business of learning to ride made Byers feel downright vindictive toward the man. To Byers riding was the last vestige of chivalry in the world, a realm of magic which linked the past to the present as nothing else did, a sport that was both his religion and his romance. He grew more and more disgruntled as he watched Shannon make incredible progress of a mechanical kind, but without falling in any way under the spell of horses—the son-of-a-bitch acted as if mastering horsemanship was simply another form of locomotion. And not for him the ritual, pleasant half-hour of discussion after the lesson was over. No, the man just said a brief goodnight and disappeared into that big black Cadillac in which his bored driver had been reading all the while, and sped off to the city. Byers was a proud, sensitive man, and he knew he was being treated as a mere convenience. If a robot could teach riding, he was convinced that Shannon would have preferred it. He never realized, nor did Shannon tell him, that Pat Shannon didn't think of learning to ride as a human occupation which made human contact with his instructor necessary. It was merely a challenge he had chosen to confront, an obstacle which he had to conquer, a necessary nuisance which he had to put behind him. He went at it with total concentration, as if he were breaking rocks on a chain gang with an overseer watching him. He resented having to spend these hours in the ring just as much as Byers resented teaching him.

They had only one moment of non-instructional discourse in the past month. Shannon was limping badly, Byers noticed, in his new boots from M. J. Knoud, Inc., the venerable firm which had also made his handsome riding clothes.

"Trouble with the boots, Mr. Shannon?" Byers remarked, not without malice.

"My ankle bones are bleeding," said Shannon in a matter-of-fact fashion. "I suppose it's always like that when you break in new boots."

"Not necessarily—people don't all go at it the way you do."

"What size foot do you have, Byers?"

"Twelve-C."

"That's my size. Will you sell me your boots?"

"What? No, Mr. Shannon, you don't want these boots"

"It happens that I do—they're exactly what I want. Beautiful leather and well-broken in. We wear the same size and you certainly have other pairs."

"I do indeed."

"I'm willing to pay whatever you ask, but I want your boots, Byers. I'll give twice what you paid for them, hell, make it three times."

"You're absolutely sure about that, Mr. Shannon?" Byers didn't show he was offended.

"My God, they're not sacred objects, man, just boots. What's all the fuss about?" Patrick demanded, more harshly than he realized. He'd been in considerable pain for three hours, although he would never have admitted it.

"They're yours," said Byers curtly. "No charge." He had been many things in his life but never had he bargained over second-hand boots.

"Thanks, Byers," Patrick said. "I really appreciate it." As far as he was concerned, it was the least the man could do, although he would not have grudged him any profit he cared to take. Business was business. He had no conception of the cult of tack, the preoccupation with all the leather appurtenances which belong to the equestrian world.

As Byers handed over the worn pair of boots he thought to himself, screw you, Pat Shannon. Who the fuck do you think you are?

It was a thought many people had had about Shannon in the course of his life, and all of them had eventually realized that whoever Shannon thought he was, he turned out to be. This had not endeared him to a rather large group—and if he'd bothered to consider this he would not have been astonished. Particularly since he'd forgotten all their names in the course of his climb to the top. A dedicated nonconformist, a maverick by deepest instinct, his success had depended on his following no one's plans but those he chose for himself, without consultation.

There were only a few men Patrick Shannon considered his equals in the corporate world. No man, no matter how powerful, who had inherited his business, belonged in his peer group. They had to have made it on their own. God knows he had.

From the orphanage in which he'd grown up he had won a scholarship to St. Anthony's, a minor Catholic boys' prep school. The scholarship had been established by a former student, now an elderly and childless millionaire, for a parentless boy who showed equal excellence in academics and athletics.

At St. Anthony's, Patrick saw immediately that he had found his first world to conquer. Nothing about the upper-middle-class East Coast boys he found himself among was familiar; their points of reference and the things they took for granted were all unknown territory to him.

For the first two years, he watched, listened and learned, always more comfortable with the adults in the school constellation than with boys of his own age. His speech had always been correct, taught, as he had been all his life, by nuns, and fortunately, the school required a uniform so that all the boys dressed alike. He learned that his black hair had always been cut too short, that his aggressiveness on the football field and the baseball diamond was acceptable, and as much as he relished the exercise of his brain, it was preferable to save demonstrations of intelligence for exams and term papers rather than display it in the classroom.

By junior year he was ready to emerge from the unobtrusive place he had taken everywhere except in sports. Pat Shannon had carefully marked out the boys he wanted to become friends with, singling out from the herd of his classmates the half dozen who displayed excellence, not merely in their achievements but in their character. By the end of his four years at St. Anthony's, he had made six friends he would never lose. Loyalty was his religion. If any of his friends had asked Pat to meet him in Singapore by noon on the day after tomorrow, with no explanation given, he would have been there. And they would have been there for him. Lacking a family of his own, he had created a family from strangers. The flavor of his soul had always been tough but loving. However, his strength concealed that love from all but a few.

He was a tall boy, big boned, and fast as a leopard. His coloring left no question about his ethnic origins: it was classically Black Irish, blue black hair, dark blue eyes and white skin that flushed easily. His forehead was broad, his eyes set wide apart under heavy brows, and his open smile was so winning that it was easy—though dangerous—to forget how bright he was.

By senior year he was president of the class, captain of the football team and first in all his classes. He won a full scholarship to Tulane from which he graduated in three years by taking an extra class load, going to summer school every summer, and restricting his sports activity to football. At twenty-three, Patrick Shannon was a graduate of the Harvard Business School and ready to conquer the world.

A week before graduation he had been hired by Nat Temple, the man who had founded Supracorp many decades before. Shannon gave himself ten years to make it to a position close to the top in the corporate structure. He allotted the first three years to absolutely unrelenting work. Pat Shannon was perfectly aware, from visiting his friends, that living *well* took time and money and he would have neither to spare, by his calculations, until he was twenty-six. Although he felt an impatience to enjoy the good things in life, his self-discipline and bred-in-the-bone motivation were strong enough to make him keep to his plan. He never considered marrying money—he had met many of his classmates' sisters who would have provided it—but everything about the idea displeased him. He *had* to do it on his own—that need to prove himself was stronger than any other he had ever experienced, and each victory only led to new challenges which had to be met. In Shannon's life there were no plateaus, no resting places from which to look back and contentedly relish the victory gained, the game won, the achievement completed.

Now, at thirty-eight, he was saturated with success. Nat Temple, the man who had first seen his potential, had retired as president of Supracorp three years before, retaining the title of chairman of the board, leaving Shannon to run a conglomerate that, from the time he was put in charge, started the expansion that had recently doubled its earning per share. His own salary and bonuses were in excess of three quarters of a million dollars a year.

A fair number of the powerful and conservative men among the major Supracorp stockholders were still not at all sure they approved of him. He had his enemies, watchful ones, who resented the firmness with which Nat Temple had backed Shannon and given him his head, who envied him his youth and his achievements, men who didn't like to take chances of any sort. These enemies were quiet for the moment but they were waiting and watching, ready to push Shannon out if he ever gave them the opportunity.

Shannon had acquired all the material things that go with this sort of success: an apartment high up in the United Nations Plaza, decorated by John Saladino in what he told Shannon was a style of "elegant alienation," a style that Shannon found out—too late—that he didn't enjoy although he admired it in the abstract; memberships in the Century, River and University clubs; the house in East Hampton which he almost never had time to use; and the inevitable divorce from a woman he should have known better than to marry: a socialite and beauty who had one of those dark, sensuous, syrupy, knowing voices which other women dislike and mistrust instantly and for good reason.

There had been no children. If there had been, perhaps there would have been no divorce, for Shannon, although not a religious man, never forgot the loneliness of being brought up without parents. After his brief marriage was over, he permitted himself only a series of second-string girls whom he took with such intense, entire, purely physical thoroughness that it was as if they had been consumed by a brush fire set by a carelessly flung match in late autumn. The finality of falling truly in love, the possible pain of it, was something he avoided with ease. Love, he sensed, was a greater risk than even he cared to take.

Supracorp, with its web of companies—cosmetics, perfumes, foods, magazines, liquors, television stations and real estate—was his baby. His children were the boys of the Police Athletic League, with whom, unknown to anyone in his world, he spent as much of every weekend as he could. With these boys, an observer would have seen uncritical, undemanding, extravagant love pouring from him. To his boys, being with him was like being in a brisk sea breeze on a day of blue sky. He made them aware of life's possibilities, and he tried to give them as much as he could of any knowledge he possessed, whether it was how to hit a ball, how to fly a kite, or how to do long division. The years had not changed his smile; it was still open, still winning, and his eyes were still of that blue which proclaims a victory, but now he had deep vertical lines on either side of his mouth and deep horizontal lines on his broad forehead over which his dark hair always fell no matter how often he pushed it back.

Patrick Shannon had propelled himself right past and through his youth, and he would never be able to recapture a time—not even in memory—that simply hadn't existed for him. He had never been really young. He had never played. He had never had time for irresponsibility or carefree freedom. It was quite enough, he told himself, that he had accumulated success, power, money, information and a small group of friends, without also having reaped a harvest of nostalgia for fun and games.

And what's more, now he could—more or less—ride a goddamned fucking horse.

When Hamilton Short, a shrewd, tough real-estate manipulator, made his first, second and third million he put them in treasury bonds and forgot about them. At forty-two, already paunchy and bald, his tenth million safely behind him, he had little trouble in convincing Topsy Mullins, a timidly luscious eighteen-year-old from an ancient but impoverished Virginia family, to marry him. During the next eight years, as business took the Shorts to Dallas, Miami and Chicago to live, Topsy produced three children, all girls, and Ham produced more millions; by his estimate he was worth twenty-five million, and the real-estate business had never been better.

Topsy had gone to a famous horsy finishing school on the last remnants of her family's money, and there she had met many New York and Long Island girls from rich, social families. She had followed their careers in fashion magazines and society columns with biting envy. She had married for money and all it had brought her was three pregnancies and fleeting acquaintances in three, to her, provincial cities. The only way to really be a part of the fashionable world was to be considered fashionable in New York City—other places didn't exist on Topsy's narrow horizon.

However, she had a clear-eyed idea of just how difficult it was for strangers to be launched in New York life, particularly a stranger who could claim only a few schoolgirl friendships, long faded, and whose husband was hardly an asset to a dinner party. She resolved to make her assault on New York from her home territory, from Virginia where her family was known and respected. She decided that an estate in the heart of the thousand square miles that make up Northern Virginia's Hunt Country was the answer; it would take the curse off new money. When Ham was informed by Topsy that it was time for them to buy a place in Middleburg, a town of 833 people, lopsidedly, if conveniently, divided into two groups, millionaires and servants, there was more than restlessness in her words. He heard the unmistakable indication that only a considerable, a *very* considerable establishment in Middleburg, would guarantee that Ham Short's marriage would continue to run in the comfortable, well-ordered and convenient way he had learned to take for granted.

At twenty-five, Topsy's early promise had ripened into decided beauty. Seven years of marriage, with only the birth of children to disturb her concentration on herself, had polished her chestnut-haired, hazel-eyed prettiness until it gleamed. The large breasts, wide hips, and tiny waist that had first caught Ham Short's eyes were as appealing as ever. Even if he rarely bothered to appreciate them now, he certainly didn't want any domestic problems. He was not a sensual man, a quick fuck every week or two was all he asked, but he insisted on peace and quiet at home while he worked on more millions. Middleburg or Miami, it made no difference to him, as long as Topsy would stop complaining about their lack of social life.

Fortunately Ham Short continued to increase his millions in the next two years, because the restoration of Fairfax Plantation consumed money as greedily as if it had been a whale swallowing plankton.

Fairfax, a late Colonial mansion, had been built in the 1750s by master craftsmen brought over from England by the first Oliver Fairfax who, like other wealthy Virginians of the time, had a fine taste for architecture and enough knowledge to realize that only in England could he find the workmanship he demanded. Unfortunately, the last Oliver Fairfax had long outlived his family's fortune and when the Shorts bought Fairfax Plantation, it was close to a ruin. But nothing, short of fire, could disguise the glorious wood carving throughout the house, which the legendary William Buckland had fashioned out of clear, mellow white pine and perfectly seasoned walnut and poplar, all of which came from the plantation's own forests, as did the bricks which were baked from clay dug from the broad fields. Buckland's Palladian woodwork, equal to that of any great home in England, had been set off by a collection of Chinese Chippendale, Hepplewhite and Sheraton furniture, covered in reproductions of the richest fabrics of the late Colonial period. The marvels of the interior—Topsy Short's decorator specialized in Instant Museum Quality—were quite overshadowed by the gardens which no amount of neglect could affect, depending as they did on a severely classic plan of slow growing boxwood hedges which had taken a full two hundred and twenty years to reach their current majestic proportions. Topsy Short had to be content with letting her horses graze in the great fields behind the house although she would have preferred to be able to see them from the front rooms of the mansion—as did many of her neighbors.

"Lordy," she would say enviously. "That old Liz Whitney Tippett's horses can just about poke their noses into her drawing room."

"Well, dig up the boxwood," Ham suggested absently.

"What? My landscape architect would kill me. They're historic. There's nothing like them, not even in Upperville or Warrenton or Leesburg. He told me that even Bunny Mellon doesn't have older boxwood," she said, invoking the name of the largely invisible queen of the Hunt Country.

"Then don't dig up the goddamned boxwood."

Ham Short, master of all he surveyed, had more on his mind than hedges. The offer from Supracorp was interesting, highly interesting. If he consented to the marriage of his healthy real-estate company to Supracorp's even healthier two-billion-dollar operation, the stock he would receive would rise to a point where, instead of working on his thirtieth million, he could start thinking in terms of his sixtieth. Not only that, it would get him out from under the day-to-day operation of what was essentially a one-man show. His children were all girls, he had no one to bring into a family business, and it would give him the time to start living the life of the gentleman Topsy had always tried to pretend he was. But on the other hand, did he want to give up control? Wasn't it more satisfying to have his own company and be free to run it as he chose? Why become another acquisition of Supracorp, why become another division head under Patrick Shannon? Did he really want to live like a gentleman and take an interest in the Middleburg Hunt and give an honest damn about horses? Perhaps the coming weekend, with the chance to see Shannon as his guest, would provide the answers to some of the questions he asked himself, as he wavered between selling and not selling. He'd asked Topsy to keep the guest list small for exactly that reason.

"Who's coming this weekend?" Ham asked abruptly.

"The Hemmings and the Stantons from Charlottesville, the Dempseys from Keeneland and Princess Daisy Valensky, to do a sketch of Cindy. That Shannon of yours, of course, and . . . some people from New York." Ham Short knew the first three couples, Horse People all. "What people from New York?" he asked idly.

Eyes wide with a mixture of terrified anticipation and excitement, Topsy answered, "Robin and Vanessa Valarian."

"The dressmaker? Now what the hell do you want with them?" Ham asked the question casually, not noticing his wife's flustered air.

"Oh, Ham, I don't know how I stand it," Topsy wailed plaintively. "You're a disgrace. The Valarians are—oh, how can I make *you* understand—they're the chicest people in New York! They go absolutely *everywhere* and know absolutely *everybody*. I knew Vanessa Valarian a little at school—she was three years ahead of me—I bumped into her last time I went to New York for shopping, and we had a drink together, but I wasn't sure they'd come when I asked them."

"Why not, aren't we good enough for a dressmaker and his wife?" Ham demanded.

"We're not chic, Ham, we're just rich, and not as rich as *really* rich people either!" she said with an accusing note in her voice. "No use your snorting like that . . . you have to be worth over two hundred million to be really rich—I read all the lists—and you know as well as I do that we're just small potatoes compared to—oh, never mind!" She flounced off the chair in which she'd been sitting and started to finger a Chinese Export bowl her decorator had insisted she buy—a steal at twenty-eight hundred dollars.

"Not chic? Well, who the hell said we had to be chic? Who the hell gives a shit? What the hell does it mean anyway—who elected the Valarians to decide?" Now Ham was injured. He was proud of his money and he didn't like being reminded of the fact that, rich as he was, he still couldn't play with the big boys.

"Oh, Ham, honestly! It merely means that they're in—*in*, damn it, the way we'll never be! They're invited to every good party, and they get pages and pages in *Vogue* and *House and Garden* and *Architectural Digest* on their apartment and their table settings—oh, and they fly all over the world to be with people like Cristina Brandolini and Helene Rochas and André Oliver and Fleur Cowles Meyer and Jacqueline Machado-Macedo—people you wouldn't *ever* know! Unless the Valarians are there a party doesn't have cachet!"

"Cachet? Christ, Topsy, you've got another bug up your ass, that's all it is. First we had to have this museum and enough horses for the Charge of the Light Brigade. Now you've finally become best buddies with our neighbors and you still need a stamp of approval from a dressmaker? I don't understand you."

If Ham Short hadn't been so offended he might have realized that there was something a little overdone in Topsy's insistence on the chic of the Valarians . . . something a little overdone in her display of pique.

"Robin Valarian is one of the most famous dress designers in the country," Topsy answered loftily, "and, as for Vanessa, she happens to be considered the most elegant woman in New York."

"I've seen his picture enough to know what he does—if you ask me, he looks like a fruit—full-blown."

"Don't be disgusting, Ham! They've been married almost as long as we have. Men like you always think other men, who don't happen to be interested in merely making money, have to be gay."

"Oh, so now it's 'gay'—I suppose that's the only possible word to use?"

"Yes, as a matter of fact, it is," Topsy retorted, in a voice she decided to make conciliating. This argument was driving her wild with nerves.

As Ham Short's irritation cooled, Topsy found herself replaying, for the thousandth time, the scene in the Valarians' library a few weeks ago in New York. Vanessa had poured her a Dubonnet and flattered Topsy with questions.

"Tell me about your life," she'd asked with unmistakable interest. "What's it like living in Middleburg most of the year? Divine or drear?"

"If I couldn't get up to New York every few weeks I don't think I could stand it," Topsy had admitted. "I'm Virginia born but I think I have New York soul. It's simply too quiet . . . but Ham loves it."

"And what Ham loves, Ham gets?"

"More or less."

Vanessa got up and closed the door of the library. "I think it's a crime that anyone as deliciously pretty as you is wasted in Horse Country," she told Topsy, coming to sit next to her on the loveseat. Topsy blushed in embarrassment and surprise. In school Vanessa had been the leader on whom half the girls in Topsy's class had had a crush—Vanessa, even then, had been sophisticated beyond their teenage dreams.

"Thank you," she murmured, sipping her Dubonnet.

"It's the simple truth. Do you know that way back at school I noticed you? I'll never forget how you looked with all that wonderful red brown hair—it's only a little darker now—and even those frightful uniforms we had to wear couldn't hide the fact that you were going to have a perfect figure. I envy you—I'm so damn skinny—I'd give anything for a few curves. Didn't you ever notice me watching you, young Topsy?"

Topsy could only shake her head in denial.

"Well, you must have had other things on your mind—I used to look at you at meals—just a peek, mind you." Vanessa laughed and casually took one of Topsy's hands in hers, gazing at it as calmly as if she were a fortuneteller. Suddenly she bent and kissed Topsy's palm with a warm, open mouth, laughed, and released the hand as if nothing at all had happened. That had been all, but again and again, from that afternoon until now, Topsy's mind had returned to the scene, wondering what might have happened next, and then telling herself that nothing, absolutely nothing could possibly have happened next—she was just being silly.

"Ham," she said, returning to the present, "let's not fight, please. I'm nervous enough about the weekend without having a fight."

"Okay, honey—I don't know what the whole thing's about anyway, but so long as it makes you happy, that's fine. And, if you want my opinion, those Valarians will be more than enough impressed by the Hemmings and the Stantons and the Dempseys and Patrick Shannon—and what's her name, that princess, so will you, for Christ's sake, just stop wandering around like you're about to break that bowl? Sure, it's insured, but I'd hate to try to collect!"

On mid-Saturday morning all of Topsy Short's house guests assembled at the stables. Topsy supervised the matching of horse to rider and only her lifetime of riding enabled her to fulfill this task with an outward show of calm. She was in the grip of an emotion she avoided examining, but she felt more ill-at-ease, more electrically anticipatory than she had in years. She was staying behind to keep Vanessa Valarian company since Vanessa had announced, at breakfast, with a laugh that was delighted with itself, that she had always been terrified of horses, even at school. She made the confession sound like an asset.

Patrick Shannon was firmly in the saddle of a large black gelding, but he was too intent to take in much of the busy, cheerful scene around him. This was the first time he'd actually been on a horse in the company of riders other than his instructor. He was absorbed in remembering every detail of every lesson he'd taken, blocking out the distraction of the stomping and blowing of the other horses, the maddening way they persisted in getting in each other's way. He tried to keep his lively mount to one side of the milling crowd of horses and riders, hoping that the brute wasn't as nervous as he was, and wondering if it was true that the horse knew how he felt just from his touch on the reins.

Young Cindy Short was mounted on a handsome pony, and Daisy had been allotted a grand chestnut mare who had fetched a healthy forty thousand dollars two years ago at the world famous Keeneland July auction of yearlings. After sharing Cindy's breakfast and spending the early hours of the day with her in the stable, she and Cindy were fast friends. When she rode, Daisy dressed with severe correctness. She braided her hair tightly and then hid it under the regulation protective hat, covered in black velvet, that is to riders what a hardhat is to construction workers. She wore a snood into which she tucked the ends of her braids so that they wouldn't catch on branches.

Ham Short wanted to demonstrate his daughter's equestrian achievements to his guests.

"Cindy," he called, "you go first and we'll follow."

Cindy, who was patient in her familiar role as a show-and-tell child, kicked her pony into a trot and then into a canter. Daisy, who wanted to observe her as she rode, waited until Cindy had had ample time to be admired and then followed the roly-poly figure. Daisy sat her thoroughbred with such beautiful calm that she made a noble and gallant sight in the crisp Virginia morning . . . in spite of the fact that Theseus followed closely behind the heels of her horse with his rolling half-drunken gait.

As Patrick Shannon watched Daisy disappear over a slight rise he had a sudden perception of what riding could be. Whoever that is, he thought, *she's the real thing.* All of his life spent in conquering new worlds had sharpened his eye to the look of those who do effortlessly what it is supremely difficult to do at all. He knew little about ballet but he could always tell a great dancer by the way the hair rose on the back of his neck at the sight of certain, apparently effortless gestures. Daisy's slender, straight back, her perfectly relaxed shoulders and arms, the carelessly confident poise of her head as she rode away, filled him with admiration . . . and bitterness. He was acutely aware of the splendid economy of her movements, movements over which he'd spent the last month sweating and cursing and bleeding. To be able to command a horse, with an imperceptible pressure of the hands and knees and calves, so that the damn fool beast sprang forward, not at a walk, or a trot, or a slow canter, but at a fast canter and no nonsense about it . . . shit, you had to be born to it, he thought, it has to be *given* to you, handed over as just another of the accomplishments people like you are expected to master.

Patrick Shannon never allowed himself to compare his grim and lonely childhood with the lives of the people who lived in the world in which he was now such a potent force, but every once in a while, taken unaware, in a situation he hadn't yet conquered, he would become briefly, but stunningly, conscious of early deprivation; relive in a flash the late and difficult transition from the gauche boy who entered prep school on a scholarship to the man he was today. The others—his friends at St. Anthony's, at Tulane, at Harvard—most of them had had it good, so good—and it showed—perhaps not to them, but to him because he wasn't one of them and never would be.

The ease of it, he said to himself, the momentary bitterness fading, that's the secret. As he ordered himself to relax, Ham Short walked his horse over to Patrick's.

"Do you mind if we don't try to keep up with the others?" Ham asked. "I ride Western—kinda like a rocking chair—never had time to learn English—a bunch of nonsense if you ask me." Patrick looked down at his host, incredibly attired in cowboy boots and chaps, slumped in a Western saddle on a comfortable looking cow pony.

"Whatever you say," he answered. Ham Short wondered why Shannon was looking so stunned. Didn't a man have a right to ride any way he chose, for Christ's sake?

Vanessa Valarian and Topsy walked back to the house in silence, broken only by Vanessa's vague comments on the weather, the location of the house, the landscape; comments which Topsy barely heard. As they walked up the driveway, Vanessa grasped Topsy by the wrist.

"Show me the house," she demanded in the low, ardent voice that was her chief beauty. She was supple as a piece of silk, so lean and slender that her husband's dresses never looked as right on a professional model as they did on her. She had made the most of looks which depended on absolutely white skin contrasting with the blackness of her hair, which she wore in a pageboy style with straight bangs right down to her eyebrows. This unfashionable Prince Valiant hair style, "signature hair" as a fashion magazine called it, was only one of the marks of personal style which made her unmistakable. Others were the wide, angular jaw, the heavily made-up, almost Oriental eyes, the bright red lipstick on her wide mouth, the big, unabashed grin she wore in every photograph ever published of her. She had curiously beautiful hands, long and slim, as supple and strong as if she were a sculptress or a pianist, yet her nails were always cut short and she wore no rings on those elegant fingers. Vanessa never compromised or changed her looks. She wore her long nose as if it were the mark of royal birth. For this mild, Virginia morning she had chosen a thin, far-from-simple dress of black cashmere, huge gold earrings and eight David Webb bracelets, a costume she had picked deliberately for its incongruence, the way it jarred with her surroundings; an effect she enjoyed creating.

Topsy flutteringly led the way through several excessively fine rooms in which the Hepplewhite hunting boards, the Sheraton barrel chairs and the Sully portraits had been assembled for just such a display. She found herself forgetting which period pieces of furniture belonged to, fumbling over the simplest names, actually trembling at the entrance to each room, not because she had any doubt of its correctness, but because she was so intensely conscious of Vanessa's elegant, dark presence at her side, never touching her, but never as far away as people normally kept from each other. She felt as jittery as she had before her first dance.

"It's enchanting," Vanessa pronounced, "and it suits you . . . it makes New York look terribly raw. But now, my young Topsy, don't you think it's time to show me the upstairs? I'm curious to see your bedroom—the reception rooms of a house are never as revealing as the private rooms, don't you think? Or am I being too nosy? It's just that I've already seen so many marvels that I'm quite ill with envy. Next time that you come to visit us in the city—and I hope it'll be soon—you'll understand."

Topsy caught her breath in leaping joy. Magic words—a promise, a visit!

In Topsy's bedroom Vanessa sat down on the edge of the wide canopied four poster that Topsy had prevailed on her unwilling decorator to swathe in three hundred yards of peach silk.

"And is this the *letto matrimoniale?*" asked Vanessa, indicating the four poster with a languid wave.

"*Letto* . . . oh . . . I see. No, Ham sleeps in his own room. He likes to work late and start telephoning early."

"And does he come to visit his wife in her bed, or does she go to his?" Vanessa continued, imperturbably.

"Why . . . ah . . ."

"Oh, Topsy, what a darling you are . . . you're blushing again, the way you did in New York. Oh, I know, when people tell you that, it only makes you blush more—but I couldn't resist. Sit here . . . I can't talk to you when you're a mile away." Vanessa patted the coverlet, until Topsy, almost unwillingly, sat down next to her. Vanessa took her hand and circled Topsy's palm with one of her talented, Gothic fingers. "I wondered if you were going to invite us . . . after what happened in New York I was worried that you might be afraid of me . . . no? I'm glad . . . so glad. I've been thinking of you everyday . . . thinking that we could so easily become very, very close friends . . . would that please you, young Topsy?" Idly she licked the tip of her forefinger and with a rapid movement touched the wet finger gently to the center of Topsy's outstretched palm. When Topsy gasped at the unmistakably explicit signal but didn't draw back, she raised the hand to her lips and took one of Topsy's fingers in her mouth, sucking on it gently from the base of the finger to the tip of the nail. Topsy moaned. "You like that—don't you? Remember the first time I kissed your hand—remember how surprised you were? And do you still remember what I told you—that I'd had my eye on you years ago?"

Mutely Topsy nodded.

As strong and fast as a man, Vanessa put one arm around Topsy's waist while she bent and brushed her neck with a feathery kiss, just above her collar bone. "Darling, I won't do anything to you that you don't like . . . don't be afraid of me . . . you're not, are you? Good." Swiftly, on stocking feet, Vanessa locked the bedroom door and returned to the bed where Topsy half sat, half lay back with eyes wide and wild with reluctant temptation. "How adorable you are—you still have your shoes on." Vanessa gave her low laugh. "Let's get rid of your shoes, at least . . ." She bent and took off Topsy's shoes. "Close your eyes," Vanessa whispered, "and let me be good to you—you need someone to be good to you, don't you, young one—someone who just wants to make you feel all the things you've always dreamed of feeling but haven't really ever felt . . . oh, yes, I thought so . . . I could tell just by looking at you that you were ready for me." As she spoke she deftly unbuttoned Topsy's blouse and released the hook which held her brassiere together in the front. Topsy had magnificent, soft round breasts, with prominent brown nipples, surprisingly dark on her white, abundant flesh. "Oh, but you're beautiful! You're superb . . . I knew you would be," Vanessa whispered, lightly tracing the outline of Topsy's half open mouth with one dark red fingertip. She glanced carefully at her prey, not wanting to do anything too suddenly. With her warm, agile fingers she traced a line from the girl's throat down under and around each heavy breast, creating a circle of exquisite lightning, but holding herself back from the nipples that she could see were becoming tight and hard. A voluptuary of the most accomplished kind, she was infinitely willing to wait for her pleasures and nothing excited her as much as the initiation of a woman she knew had never experienced the excruciating pleasure she could give her.

"Topsy, this is all for you . . . I don't want anything . . . you don't have to move an inch . . . just lie back and let me look at you . . ." As she unbuttoned the waistband of the woman's skirt and slipped it off in a gentle movement, she sucked again on Topsy's fingers, taking two of them in her wide mouth and fluttering them with her practiced tongue. Topsy shuddered, unable to believe that she was becoming so excited by nothing more than being touched on her breasts and on her fingers. She relaxed when Vanessa told her that nothing was expected of her . . . she wouldn't have known what to do. Now Vanessa surrounded each nipple with five adept, caressing, gentle fingers which delicately teased them up into two hard points. Only when Topsy began to sigh, unable to remain silent, did Vanessa finally fasten her mouth on one nipple with luxurious leisure, flicking the point of her tongue over first one hot, hard nubbin and then the other. She spent long, long minutes without ever leaving those wide, brown nipples, pulling on them, bathing them with swift strokes of her entire tongue, until they were stimulated to a point just below pain. Only then did she stretch down her arms and take off the rest of Topsy's clothes.

The girl's eyes were still closed, Vanessa noted as she rapidly took off her own clothes. Good, it was easier that way . . . the first time. She cradled Topsy's head in one slender, strong arm and with the other reached down and ran her fingers as lightly as possible, so that their touch was barely perceptible, yet maddeningly arousing, over the delicate swell of her, down to just above the chestnut tangle of thick pubic hair. When Topsy made no indication of protest, Vanessa moved, with the grace she was famous for, and straddled the woman's body, one knee on either side of Topsy's full hips. She sat back on her heels and devoted herself to gliding her fingertips down Topsy's beautiful white thighs and calves all the way to the tip of her rosy toes and then back again, avoiding the pubic curls with absolute discipline. She saw Topsy's hand come to life; one of them reached down and captured one of hers and pulled it toward the mound of Venus that the girl was lifting up toward her. Vanessa freed her hand and whispered, "No, no, you can't have it yet . . . you're not ready . . ." and she began to caress the soft skin inside of Topsy's thighs, her fingers reaching higher and higher until they were fluttering just at the rim of the pubic tangle. Topsy moaned imploringly and opened her legs. Vanessa saw the slick glisten of wetness on the offered lips. Her own vulva was so heavy and congested that she could scarcely restrain herself from grinding it into the girl, but she held back, crouching low to blow gently on Topsy's thick hairs, parting the curls with her breath, until she could see the girl's swollen clitoris. Then she reached out again with her tongue and, making it into a point, darted and darted it again and again at the tiny organ, sometimes sucking it with her whole mouth, sometimes just licking it with a light, flickering touch.

"*Fuck me*, for God's sake—fuck me!" Topsy muttered, unable to endure any more.

Vanessa knit the three middle fingers of her right hand together, and worked them several inches up between those eager lips. Topsy strained upward frantically, and Vanessa, kneeling, bent again and took the girl's vulva entirely into her hot, avid, wide mouth, sucking rhythmically on the clitoris at the same time that she slid her three fingers firmly in and out of Topsy's vagina, sometimes only an inch or two up, sometimes as far as they could go. Topsy was aware only of the most intense delight; the fingers in her vagina produced a hardness and knobbiness of stimulation that a smooth penis never had, and the sucking, oh, the teasing sucking, was like nothing she had ever believed possible. She felt herself pausing on the edge of orgasm, pausing, pausing and then coming into Vanessa's mouth with a bursting rush and a widening pool of spasms which made her scream in incredulous abandon.

While she was still throbbing and jerking her hips forward, Vanessa threw herself on the other woman, kissing her for the first time on her dry, open mouth, pressing her own vulva, lightly covered with dark hair, into Topsy's curly mound, cupping Topsy's full, round bottom in both her hands and rubbing, relentlessly, until she came quickly into the masterful orgasm she had been holding back for so long.

Minutes, many minutes passed before Topsy sat up, dizzy but still aware of the passage of time. "They'll be back for lunch in ten minutes . . . and Ham'll be calling for me. What must I look like?"

"You look glorious," Vanessa said, slithering quickly into her clothes. "Do you have a garter belt and stockings around somewhere?"

"I bought them once . . . for Ham . . . but they didn't work any great wonders. Why?"

"Would you wear them, for me? Without panties? All day long, all evening, all day tomorrow? So I can look at you and think of just how I could be touching you under your clothes . . . so you can look at me and see me thinking?"

"Oh!"

"Will you?"

"Yes, God, yes!"

As the members of the Shorts' house party gathered for drinks before lunch, Robin Valarian approached his wife and put his arm around her.

"Did you have a good ride, my angel?" she asked him, tilting up her proud nose and widening her Oriental eyes.

"Marvelous—it's really a shame you've become afraid of horses, my poor pet. You used to ride so well. And you, was the hunting good?"

"Superb, quite simply superb."

"I hoped it would be. I almost envy you."

Daisy lunched with Cindy and her sisters in their playroom and then spent the afternoon sketching the little girl on her pony. The younger girls, who were seven and five, equestrians both, watched respectfully for a while and finally, bored, wandered off. After she'd worked until Cindy would pose no longer, Daisy indulged in the great gift the weekends with the Horse People could provide: a solitary ride accompanied only by Theseus. These hours alone, galloping, free, abandoned, mindlessly happy, as if she moved in a wind of vernal delight, were a luxury she could never have afforded otherwise, and she'd become adept at snatching them when she could, without taking time she could have used for work. Reluctantly, in the last afternoon light, she trotted back to the stables and went to her room to bathe and dress for dinner.

It was the thing she liked least about these weekends, she thought, as she carefully put away her riding clothes, the obligatory dinner with the assembled guests, the obligatory conversations, the obligatory princess image her hostess expected from her, *exacted* from her actually. Kiki often wondered why she disliked it so, why she endured it only to help sell her work. "*I* would adore to be a princess," she said, shaking her head at Daisy severely. She'd never been able to explain, not even to Kiki, what she could barely begin to work out for herself, that she felt, in some deep way, like an impostor in the persona of Princess Daisy Valensky, as if she had no right to the title. Granted, titles were out of date in the modern world, except for those few countries still ruled by monarchs, but many people in many other countries still used them without the malaise she felt.

As Daisy lowered herself into her hot bath, she realized, because of the sudden shock of comfort she experienced from the embrace of the water, that she was sad, with a familiar sadness which overcame her from time to time, a sadness against which she battled without understanding its origin. She had periods of depression that she could see coming like the first hint of a sea fog dimming the light, a tendril drawn across the back of her mind that soon turned the furnishings of her life into dismal heaps. In such a mood, if she were home, she would creep under all the blankets she could find, thrust her feet into heavy wool socks and lie shivering for hours, wondering why the future held no delight, trying to imagine a situation, a place, a happening which could tempt her back to reality. She would hold Theseus close, ruffling him over and over, and cuddling him tightly.

Whenever she tried to trap this despairing sadness, lay it bare and examine it, Daisy was immediately caught up in a web of unwelcome questions that no one left alive could answer for her.

What if, for instance, she had two parents like most people? What if her mother, like other women who are separated from their husbands, had managed to explain to Daisy, when she was a child, why they lived hidden in Big Sur, seeing no strangers, having no contact with the outside world? Even if the explanation hadn't made too much sense it might have satisfied her for a while, until she was old enough to understand. What if her father had ever told her *why* he could only spend such a short time with her and had to leave so abruptly, year after year, keeping her in constant fear that he'd never return, in spite of the letters he sent her? What if her mother—that all-too-vague memory of absolute security and love—hadn't gone without a farewell, vanishing into the sea on a sunny afternoon? What if her father had allowed Dani to stay with her instead of imposing a rigorous, hermetic seal of silence on her very existence? And what if Stash hadn't died when she was fifteen; what if he were still alive, protecting her by his very existence? What if Ram had been a real older brother, concerned and kind, someone to whom she could go with her problems, instead of the sick madman only she and Anabel knew he was?

Daisy got out of the tub and started to dress. As she brushed her hair she looked at Kiki's fake emeralds that lay on the dressing table. The necklace and bracelets would be perfection loaded onto the green tweed jacket with its ruffled lapels, but the earrings would be wasted, hidden by her hair. She found some hairpins and twisted them through the great oval pendant drops, rimmed with rhinestones. She was wearing her hair down naturally this evening, after having kept it braided all day, and the gorgeous, heavy, silver-gilt stuff, in which she deftly fastened the earrings, fell in little ripples. Her Schiaparelli trouser suit made her look like a young Robin Hood, a Robin Hood who'd gone all the way to Paris to rob the rich, and, as she finished dressing, she stared at herself in the mirror as firmly as if she were dealing with a skittish horse and said out loud, "Daisy Valensky, it's no good wondering 'what if?' What is—*is!*"

Patrick Shannon recognized Daisy as the girl he'd seen riding that morning only from the set of her head as she entered the drawing room. Otherwise he would have thought she was a new arrival, since he had not seen her at either breakfast or lunch. As she entered the room, in which the other guests were already assembled, a small piece of time seemed to be frozen, a split second in which the hum of conversation hesitated, fragmented and then resumed.

Daisy knew no one in the room, and Topsy guided her around, making introductions. As she approached Patrick, he thought, so that's who she is, he might have guessed. Although he spent no time at all keeping up with celebrity news, like everyone else he had been aware of Daisy's existence. He could vaguely remember the cover of her as a baby in *Life* when he'd been a teenager.

They shook hands with perfunctory smiles, Daisy preoccupied with remembering all the new names—these people were her possible future customers—and Shannon trying to fit her into a slot. He was a man who liked to place new people immediately, get a fix on them, so that he knew where they stood in relation to him. He had already dismissed the Horse People as utterly unimportant in his scheme of things, tagged Vanessa and Robin Valarian as people he would never do business with and become convinced that Ham Short was a man with whom he could work profitably and well—he liked his style. As Daisy turned to be introduced to the Dempseys, he thought, another butterfly, pampered, petted, indulged, flattered and vain. The lesson of his ex-wife had been well learned . . . he knew the type.

At dinner his judgment was confirmed as he listened to the conversation between Daisy, who was seated on his right, and Dave Hemming and Charlie Dempsey.

"I'll never forget seeing your father playing in a high goal tournament in Monterey in the thirties," Charlie Dempsey said to Daisy. "I don't remember the exact year but he was playing at three with Eric Pedley from Santa Barbara playing one, Tommy Hitchcock at two and Winston Guest at four—greatest team ever mounted in my opinion."

"Nonsense, Charlie," Dave Hemming interrupted from across the table. "The greatest team ever mounted was Guest, *Cecil Smith,* and Pedley, with Hitchcock at three—with all due respect to Stash."

"I'm sure you're both right," Daisy smiled. "But nobody, not even Cecil Smith, could ride like my father." She had grown accustomed to these conversations in the last few years. Almost every Horse Person over fifty had his own memories of her father, and she liked to hear them discuss him . . . it brought him back for a moment, even though they were talking of memories of very long ago, before she'd been born.

While the familiar argument went on, Daisy turned to Shannon.

"Are you a polo aficionado, Mr. Shannon?" she asked politely.

"I don't know a thing about it," he answered.

"That's refreshing."

He thought she was mocking him. "And what do you do, Princess Valensky, when you're not arbitrating arcane disputes about a game that took place forty-five years ago?"

"Oh—this and that. I'm sketching young Cindy this weekend, on her pony."

"For fun?"

"More or less." Daisy considered it necessary at all times to hide the true commercial nature of her presence at these house parties. The fact that she was there to make money she had to have, the fact that she spent the evening carefully and casually finding out if any of her fellow guests had children who might be prospective subjects for her, the fact that she was doing nothing more or less than commission hunting, was best concealed by the mask of the dilettante. Her profession was well served by word of mouth rather than self-advertisement.

"Do you hunt in the neighborhood, Mr. Shannon?"

"Hunt? Here? No." My God, Patrick thought. After one month of riding school how could anyone expect him to be jumping fences?

"Then where *do* you hunt?" Daisy continued, confidently.

"I don't hunt at all," Patrick said shortly.

"But of course you do—or did—no? Oh, then why have you given it up?"

Shannon looked for malice in her eyes and found nothing but the gleam of candlelight on black velvet. The flames, the chrysanthemums on the table, the reflections from the heavy silver and Irish cut glass—all had become accomplices in illuminating her beauty which met and outmatched every brightness in the room. But he thought he heard a sardonic note in her amused interrogation.

"I assure you that I don't hunt, have never hunted and have no intention of ever hunting," he answered her with a coldly reined-in courtesy.

"But . . . your boots . . ." Daisy murmured, confused.

"What about them?" he snapped.

"Nothing," she said hastily.

"No—I insist. What about my boots?" Now he was certain that she was making fun of him.

"Well, only . . . oh, it's not important, really, it's just silly of me to have noticed . . ." Daisy babbled, trying to avoid his eyes.

"The boots?" Patrick asked, implacably.

Now Daisy got angry. If this man was going to treat her like a witness in a murder trial, she'd jolly well speak up.

"Mr. Shannon, your boots are black with brown tops. Only a Servant of the Hunt, that is a Hunt official, like a Whipper-In or the Master of the Hounds or the Master of the Hunt himself is *entitled* to wear boots like that. If you don't hunt, your boots should be one solid color."

"The devil!"

"Someone should have told you," she hastened to add.

"Aren't you saying that it's one of the things which everyone is expected to know?"

"It's really not important," Daisy answered as coolly as possible.

"You mean it's not the 'done thing'?" he said, stingingly, venting his fury at Chuck Byers who had given him the boots without an explanation.

"It's unheard of," she said, her temper rising.

"Then why hasn't anyone else said anything—I've been out riding all day," he accused her in a hard voice.

"They assumed, as I did, that you hunted. It's as simple as that."

"I don't ride well enough for any rational person to imagine that I hunt," he replied furiously.

"Then perhaps they were being tactful, perhaps they guessed that you'd get upset and they didn't want to risk your mighty wrath? Why get angry at me, Mr.

Shannon? I didn't sell you those boots." Daisy turned to Charlie Dempsey and started to talk polo to him.

Patrick Shannon was left simmering in the suspicion that all of the people he'd ridden with today must have been curious about his boots and been too polite to question him—and, no doubt, had been laughing at him behind his back.

Shannon did not enjoy feeling like a horse's ass.

16

There was only one private room in the Valarians' apartment, only one room which had never been photographed in the course of Robin's never-ending redecorations, which totally renewed the look of their Park Avenue duplex every two years. This was the room in which they spent their rare time together, in which they indulged in a cherished ritual before dressing to go out or to entertain at home as they did virtually every night of the week. Each evening at six o'clock Robin and Vanessa met in their private room which had walls and floors covered in thick carpeting the color of vicuna and a domed copper ceiling, from which warm light, glowing from hidden recesses, spread over the many orchids that grew in hanging baskets. In the center of the room, which was otherwise entirely empty, was a carpeted platform on which rested a gigantic oval hot tub—a tub as large as most ordinary bathrooms—made of black fiberglass. Six inches deeper than tubs generally are, it had four adjustable water jets of brushed chrome that created whirlpools of water that could reach 110 degrees. Naked in the soothing water, their marvelously taut, superbly kept bodies glimmering, they lay and sipped cold, dry white wine, gossiping about their days and their doings. There they reaffirmed the deep bonds which held them together.

Like many married homosexual couples they formed a stronger, more solid and durable relationship than almost any of the heterosexual couples they knew. There is no team so committed to their joint and individual successes as the homosexual husband happily married to a lesbian wife, no love match as tight and protective and close-knit. Together they received immense benefits they could never have obtained outside of marriage, the most important of which was that protection from being single which leads, in the case of any attractive male or female over thirty, to lively speculation about their sexual preferences on the part of almost everybody who meets them. Together they formed that unit, "the married couple," that is far more easily absorbed into social life anywhere than any single homosexual or a homosexual couple of the same sex: they provided their hostesses with that most desirable addition to any party, a perfectly matched pair.

Together they made a traditional, infinitely secure home for each other, in which Robin was free to indulge his talent for creating resplendently baroque surroundings and ever more sumptuous flower arrangements. It was he who found and trained perfect servants, and Vanessa who planned the exquisitely thought-out parties she had used so effectively to promote Robin's career. Finally, since they had no jealousy of each other, as lovers might have, each was free to indulge his sexual tastes with the added pleasure of knowing that the other was eagerly waiting to hear about it, to advise, to assist, to smooth the path, even to entrap, and if necessary, to comfort and console.

Their marriage gave them an entrée into the mainstream of the establishment of society and wealth which would not have been possible on the same level had they remained single. As "the Valarians" they dined at the White House, sailed on the largest yachts, stayed in the most historic English and Irish country houses, an impeccable couple, above scandal, if not entirely above rumor—but who paid attention to rumors in these days?

As "the Valarians" they were forever free of the taint of the homosexual; as a married couple they moved with impunity in the widest world of celebrity, while, in their own inner circle, they were not only recognized as brilliantly successful deceivers, but applauded for their cleverness in finding each other and using each other so well. They had understood the secret, so rarely brought out in its raw and naked state; the fact that among the successful of the world, there is *no gender*—there is only success or lack of success. The only important question is: *are you or are you not one of us?*

Homosexual married couples come in a variety of combinations: the bisexual husband, the kind Robin always called "a Jazz-Tango," who in the first years of marriage occasionally enjoyed his wife and almost always produced astonishingly beautiful children; the true homosexual man and the wife who is terrified of sex of any kind; and the lesbian with the passive, almost neuter husband. The Valarians were of the variety that most certainly has the best stories to tell each other, since Robin was as active sexually as his wife.

Robin Valarian truly loved Vanessa and she truly loved him, both with anxious tenderness. If he had a cold she brought him vitamin C every hour and watched while he swallowed it. If she had a tiring day, he would rub her back for an hour until she purred with relaxation and then he'd go into the kitchen, tell the cook exactly what to put on a tray and bring it in himself, settling her among the cushions on the bed and insisting that she eat. The life they had made together was a living, growing, deeply rooted thing, totally dependent on their joint contributions. Vanessa often quoted Rilke: "The love that consists in this, that two solitudes protect, and border and salute each other."

Beyond love, they were each other's best friends. Robin admired her nerve, her savage pursuit of what she wanted and he was particularly grateful for her role in his career. She had so much style, which leapt out directly from her personality, that she imparted it to his merely fashionable clothes. His abilities as a designer were limited: he knew how to make women look pretty and feminine—he specialized in cocktail and dinner dresses, leaning heavily on the allure of ruffles and the rustle of taffeta, but never in his life had he had an original design idea. Yet, year after year, rich women all over the country bought Robin Valarian's expensive couture clothes. This came about only partly because of the exceptionally friendly way in which he was treated by the fashion press, whose members enjoyed being included in the parties given by this most exclusive of couples. Essentially his clothes sold because Vanessa was so frequently photographed wearing his dresses with her swaggering, devil-be-damned flair, surrounded by people of taste and status, that "a Valarian" had come to mean a safely pretty dress in which an upper-class woman could feel almost as if she were Vanessa Valarian herself, rising to the challenge of being dashingly, ruthlessly, clashingly chic.

Their duplex reflected the strength of their bond. It was not cupidity that made them load every table with precious bibelots, but the nesting instinct gone wild, castle building on a domestic scale. Every object they chose and bought together reaffirmed their commitment, a set of Pyrex mixing bowls as strongly as a costly silver mermaid fashioned by Tony Duquette. There was to them a sacredness about their table linen, their silver and china such as only newlyweds know. Long before it became fashionable for a man to be interested in domestic detail, Robin Valarian prided himself on his abilities as a homemaker. Unlike the goddess of interior design, Sister Parish, whose two watchwords were luxury and discipline, the Valarians believed in luxury *and* luxury. Every one of their down pillows was piped, or tasseled, every lampshade lined in pink silk, every curtain double-lined, looped and caparisoned, every wall rich with at least twelve costly coats of lacquer, when it wasn't covered with rare fabric, every sofa overstuffed and oversized and totally comfortable, so that their guests felt as comforted and cocooned as if they were babies in their cribs, an illusion which caused them to gossip more freely than they ever did in less cushioned settings. The Valarians never gave a party at which at least one reputation was not made and another reputation ruined.

This couple, who defended the fortress of their marriage with the rigorous loyalty of blood brothers, was spared the ambiguous changeable moods of lovers, escaped the predictable limits imposed by monogamy and enjoyed all of the privileges granted to matrimony.

Vanessa Valarian was a subtle and devoted practitioner of the art of doing favors. She had long nourished a private theory that a favor done for the right person at the right time, done without planned motive or direct expectation of reciprocity, would eventually prove to be a useful, even an essential piece of the superb mosaic of her life . . . caviar flung on the waters. The right time was, in her experience, when the person for whom she did the favor had no reason to expect anything of her, when the favor seemed to come straight from good-hearted openhandedness and appreciation of that person's rare qualities. She almost never did favors for anyone who came to her for one; her favors had to appear as unhoped-for and unforgettable. The person for whom she did a favor needed no recommendation aside from Vanessa's keen intuition that told her who was coming up and who was going down, who would make it, who had potential that hadn't been detected, and who wasn't worth bothering with. Like an expert surfer, she was able to detect the big waves before they gathered momentum, able to hop on board before the other women in her world had spotted the swelling and the power.

When Topsy Short had mentioned that Daisy Valensky was sketching Cindy as a sort of trial before Topsy made up her mind about commissioning an oil of all three girls on their ponies, Vanessa felt the tingle of opportunity. She had observed Daisy the evening before at dinner. She had known instantly, as no one else did, that the green Schiaparelli suit was almost forty years old and that the emeralds were false and that the girl was, in some way or another, *vulnerable.* How she could possibly be vulnerable in light of her title, her share of her father's presumably fabulous fortune and her beauty was inexplicable, but Vanessa *knew.*

"Why don't we look at her sketches before she goes back to New York," she suggested.

"Oh, I don't think she'd like it," Topsy answered. "She told me when I asked her to come that they'd just be rough studies, like shorthand notes. She'll send me the finished sketch in a few weeks."

"What does it matter what she likes, young Topsy? Let's have a peek—it might be amusing."

Reluctantly Daisy allowed the two women to see her sketch pad. There were dozens of rapid, bold line drawings but none of them could convey to a nonprofessional what the finished sketch would be like.

Topsy was silent, her disappointment visible on her face, but Vanessa instantly grasped the extent of Daisy's talent.

"You're good—but of course you know that," she said to Daisy. "Topsy, you'd be making the mistake of the year if you don't have Princess Daisy paint all three of your girls. In a few years you'll have to pay twice the price for anything she does—if she even has the time for you."

"Well . . . I'm just not sure—what if Ham doesn't like it?" Topsy looked at Vanessa adoringly. How could she be interested in making decisions about paintings when, under her skirt, she could feel her naked thighs rubbing softly together, aching, trembling for the touch of Vanessa's marvelous hands?

"I can't imagine anything he'd like more, and if you don't do it now—Topsy, pay attention!—you won't have a record of the girls before they start to grow up—they're just at that perfect age. If I were you I wouldn't hesitate for a second. I'd have a really big oil, an heirloom . . . that is," she said, looking at Daisy, "if you have time to take on such a job?"

"I could make time," Daisy said, thinking that she'd paint all night for a month if necessary to get it done before the next bill came from England.

"Well, then, that's settled. I've done you a great favor, Topsy, and I don't want you to forget it. You'll bless me someday."

"Thank you, Mrs. Valarian," Daisy said hastily.

Vanessa spied the hidden relief on Daisy's face. So, she needed money after all. *Curious.*

"Thank me? Topsy's the one who should thank me—she's damn lucky to get you," Vanessa answered with the guileless, great, open smile that accompanied the execution of a promising favor that every instinct told her to grant. Daisy Valensky was now in her debt. "The next time we're in England, I'm going to tell Ram just how talented I think you are. He's a great friend of ours—we're devoted to your brother."

"Thank you, Mrs. Valarian," Daisy said again, automatically. She felt a chill like a stain spreading over her heart.

"What you need, Luke Hammerstein," Kiki announced sweetly, "is someone to wreak havoc with your life."

"That last exhibition just about did it for me," Luke answered as they found a table in The Ballroom.

"I thought you'd like it—how many people have ever seen Quebec manhole-cover rubbings?"

"It was a definite first. I've been curious about them as far back as grade school. And I like the fact that the group who did them is making rubbings from the manhole covers in SoHo to show in Quebec. It's that kind of cultural exchange that may do something to help the uncertain relationship we've always had with Canada."

"Yeah—I worry about Canada a lot."

"Do you?"

"Naturally. There's a tunnel in the heart of downtown Detroit which takes you right into Canada. When my brothers and I were kids we used to pester our father to take us. It sounded so romantic."

"Was it?"

"Of course not—that just proves that you know nothing about Detroit . . . or Canada."

"We can't all get lucky."

"You're making fun of me again," said Kiki, her eyebrows, with their jubilant angles, rising toward her ruffle of hair which was temporarily its natural brown.

"I'm sorry but I can't help it. You're like Beatrice in *Much Ado About Nothing*—remember, she was 'born in a merry hour'?"

"Well, did she get the guy in the end?"

"You never stop, do you?" Luke Hammerstein had been pursued by females since he was twelve, but never had he met one as frank about her intentions as Kiki Kavanaugh. Was she a compendium of every craft and guile known to women, or was she was she presented herself to be, an innocent sensualist out to have a thoroughly good time—with him as a partner? Luke was used to the new breed of women, but Kiki was a Green Beret in the battle of the sexes. It put him off balance, he admitted to himself. He was actually playing hard to get, like a woman was supposed to do—this role-reversal stuff was kind of fun.

"Get me a drink, for God's sake—I'm beat," he said. They were both carrying baskets loaded with the afternoon's purchases.

"Have you ever had hard cider?" Kiki asked. It was her favorite next to the iced Irish Coffee.

"Not yet, but why don't you order it since you're obviously going to anyway."

He looked in mild exasperation at the baskets they'd deposited on the white tiled floor. Kiki had bought, if he remembered correctly, an appliqued apricot satin cover for a hot-water bottle at a store called Harriet Love, a sculpture of a green frog, done entirely in neon tubing at a gallery called Let There Be Neon, two black satin garments, ambiguously called "guest kimonos," two bottles of Soave Bolla and one of Wild Turkey bourbon at a liquor store which had, in its window, a sign announcing WE DO NOT HAVE PINT BOTTLES OF WINE, and a piece of jewelry which made him nervous, an ivory heart with a red stone hanging from it like a drop of blood. Even the jewelry in SoHo had names, he thought—this one was called "They've Been Kicking My Heart Around." And that wasn't counting what she'd bought at Dean and Deluca, the great gourmet grocery store, where overflowing baskets of garlic buds, apples, lemons, black radishes, walnuts and plummy dried yuccas stood decoratively in the doorway and expensive pots and pans hung from the skylight two stories above. There she'd gone wild. Slabs of pâté en croute and duck gallantine, both at over twelve dollars a pound, from a counter on which two dozen different pâtés were displayed; a jar of heather honey from Holland; whipped cream cheese and a Petit St. Marcellin, the small cheese wrapped in chestnut leaves; three different kinds of salami, one from Spain, one from Italy and one from France; a pound of smoked Scotch salmon; a jar of hot okra pickles; a pound of Black Forest Ham; a dozen freshly baked croissants; half of a perfect brie; and, from the baskets of bread which hung all over the store, she'd picked one twisted challah, four bagels and one loaf of dark pumpernickel. Then she'd added a box of Dovedale Butter Shortbread from an English company which had been established in 1707, and several bars of bittersweet chocolate from the Ghirardelli Chocolate Company in San Leandro, California. There was something about the combination of foods she'd bought which struck him as highly suggestive.

Luke had been to SoHo a number of times before, since no advertising man he knew would miss the opportunity to see the big new works that were displayed in the galleries; but mainly he'd stuck to quick visits to 420 Broadway, where the major uptown dealers had their downtown branches: Leo Castelli, Sonnabend and André Emmerich.

Today he'd seen a SoHo he'd overlooked, the SoHo of people who actually lived here, a SoHo in which the Porcelli Brothers displayed fresh honeycomb tripe in the window of their butcher shop; in which a little kid walking a bike had stopped Kiki at a corner and asked, "Miss, could you cross me, please?"; in which a sign proclaiming PERSIAN CAT FOUND was displayed in the window of the M and D Grocery, a shabby, old-fashioned store which nevertheless had a freezer full of expensive Häagen-Dazs ice cream and shelves on which salted nuts shared the space with religious pictures and ten kinds of yogurt; a SoHo where, in the Mandala Workshop, you could buy a symbol representing the Jungian effort to reunify the self, made of hand crochet and stained glass. This SoHo was one of exotic contrasts. J. Volpe, General Machinist, was next door to a gallery which offered prints of "erotic food"; stores selling plumbing supplies and the A and P Cordage Co. existed cheek to jowl with the Jack Gallery with its Erté and Jean Cocteau watercolors.

Kiki looked at Luke shrewdly. He was in SoHo shock . . . she knew the signs. She had planned to have dinner at The Ballroom but the enormous mural on the wall opposite their table would only intensify his discomfort, showing as it did, in vivid photo-realist fashion, nineteen of SoHo's most famous artists and citizens, including Larry Rivers and Robert Indiana.

"I know what you need," she told Luke.

"Now what?"

"Chinese food."

"By God, you're right! It's the only thing I could eat. How did you know?"

"You're Jewish—it's simple—when Jews go into culture shock the only thing that brings them back is deli or Chinese. We gentiles feel better right away if we just sit around and watch white bread burning."

"Don't you mean toasting?" he asked limply.

"No, burning, like a Yule log. Come on, we'll go to the Oh-Ho-So. It's right across the street."

Since no one had yet taken their order they unceremoniously picked up their baskets, left The Ballroom, crossed the street and staggered into the bar at the Chinese restaurant: a most welcoming bar crowded with worn, green velvet loveseats and chairs of carved wood, no two alike, all pulled up around tables which were made from a clutter of Victorian leftovers and, when the Victoriana failed, battered sewing-machine tables.

In the light of the jukebox, Kiki's umber eyes were shot with sparks of opals, yellow diamonds and glee.

"The gentleman will have a double Wild Turkey on the rocks," she told the waiter, "and I'll have some hard cider. Now let's talk about the other night. Why didn't you want to make love? Were you really too tired?" she asked Luke, with her bawdiest smile.

"Shit—just when you start to coddle me, like a real woman, you turn all aggressive. Wait till after the egg roll, won't you?"

"All I meant was *I* wasn't too tired—and I'd had to handle Theseus all day. So how come? Are you shy . . . do you wait till the third date—have you religious scruples?"

"*After* the egg roll," he reminded her mildly. He had the equilibrium of strength. Luke was fully aware of his forces, so he didn't mind revealing his weaknesses.

He'd never met the woman who was a match for him—it was his secret pride. Three older sisters had taught him more about women than he needed to know, he had once liked to say, although he was aware that those had become fighting words in recent years. He saw Kiki sizing him up with the skill of a Monte Carlo croupier, no, make that a pit boss in Vegas. He smiled at her faintly, tauntingly.

"You know what you remind me of?" she said heatedly. "Those crypto-Greek heads in the Met from five hundred B.C.—they all have the same smug, superior, secretive smile—not even the decency to *pretend* to be honest—total conceit that has lasted for three thousand years."

"*After* the egg roll."

"All right—but then—watch out!"

"Do you always warn your intended victims?"

"I try to be fair. Men are, in many ways, more fragile than women."

Luke sighed, looking, giving Kiki the feeling that he was like nothing so much as a whole pile of presents that she was itching to unwrap.

"Okay, we'll talk about other people. Tell me about your mother," Kiki suggested.

"My mother is an arch-conservative. She never redecorates. We still have art deco."

"My mother redecorates every year. We're just getting art deco."

"My mother warned me that if I ever marry a beautiful gentile girl, one day she'll turn out to be just another old *shiksa—shiksa* is the only Yiddish word she knows."

"My mother believes that the way to break in a sable coat is to wear it to a Japanese restaurant the first day it comes form the furrier. She orders sukiyaki cooked at the table, and sits in the coat during the whole meal. It takes about a week to air it out, but after that the coat knows that she's the boss. Also I think she's an anti-Semite."

"My mother is such an anti-Semite that when her club started letting in Russian Jews, instead of only German Jews, she left it."

"My mother's worse than that. She took a course in mouth-to-mouth resuscitation in case my father ever got a heart attack and then, when she was in a bank, a man had a heart attack right in front of her and she didn't try to save him because he was so repulsive looking she was afraid of catching whatever he might have had . . . and he died right there in front of her."

"Jesus! Did she really?" Luke said, fascinated. Kiki was winning the mother-game.

"No, but it did happen to her real-estate lady," Kiki admitted.

"My mother doesn't have real-estate ladies," Luke said with a cool smile.

"Don't you ever move? You have to have a real-estate lady to buy a house."

"My mother doesn't believe in moving—it's nouveau. She just has . . ."

"The apartment on Park Avenue and the house in . . . Pound Ridge . . . and the place in Westhampton—no, East Hampton—right?"

"Almost—how'd you get so close?"

"It figured. I think we have the same mother only they don't know it."

"Do you realize," Luke said moodily, "that five times more people buy pet food than buy baby food? Isn't that horrifying?"

"No, dummy. It's because babies grow up and start to eat like people but pets eat pet food all of their lives."

"You're not entirely stupid," Luke said, reluctantly. Most people reacted to the pet-food statistics with dependable indignation.

"Do you want to hold hands?" Kiki asked hopefully.

"Not during lobster Cantonese!" he said scandalized.

"You lack passion," Kiki warned, looking yearningly at his mouth—there was something about a man's mouth, presented between a mustache and a beard, which made it so much more edible looking than if it just sat there on his face surrounded by skin.

"You're just saying that to make me prove to you that I'm not boring. It won't work." Luke applied himself to his lobster with calm relish. Kiki looked at him in dismay. This wasn't going right at all. Most men, in her large experience, had no defenses against a well-mounted, absolutely shameless attack. Bewildered, confused, flattered, they fell for it, and once they'd fallen for the idea they were only a step away from falling for her. Luke made her uneasy . . . she had the feeling that somewhere she'd gotten her act wrong, but she'd started out with him as she had with dozens of others and now the pattern had been set. Maybe he *was* just hungry. Maybe he *had* just been tired. With Daisy away for the weekend, and the provisions she bought for breakfast and lunch tomorrow, she still had lots of time to work on this unexpectedly stubborn customer. She really *had* to have him.

"Could you please bring us some hot tea," she asked a passing waiter, "and some optimistic fortune cookies?"

The Friday following her weekend in Middlebury, Daisy found the studio unexpectedly peaceful. North had gone off for a week's vacation, the first in over a year, so there was no production meeting scheduled until the middle of the next week. There were myriad details for her to check in the office, but she was pleased when Nick-the-Greek and Wingo Sparks invited her to have lunch with them. Normally she ate lunch at her desk, with a sandwich in one hand and the phone in another.

Once the waiter had brought them their food, Nick said casually, "So how's the job going, kid? You holding up all right? I mean, we all know it isn't easy working for North. Sometimes I get the idea that he doesn't realize what you're worth."

"He's not exactly given to praise, but when he doesn't foam at the mouth, I know I've done a good job," Daisy shrugged.

"So you're willing to settle for that kind of validation?" Wingo asked.

"Why not? Is there something wrong with that?" Daisy wasn't about to complain to her coworkers.

"Lots wrong," said Nick. "It's like being satisfied with crumbs from a rich man's table, *campesina*, and I, Nick-the-Greek, am here to tell you that in no way is it enough."

"What are you trying to start, Nick?" Daisy asked curiously. "You get your commissions and they're hardly crumbs."

"You want to tell her, Wingo?" Nick asked the young cameraman.

"You bet I do. Listen, Daisy, Nick and I have been talking. We both think that we could go into business for ourselves. Nick's the best rep in the city—he knows where all the accounts are who want the North look but don't want to pay North's prices. North thinks of me as just a cameraman, but I can do his stuff, too—lots of guys are director-cameramen. It took me five years to get my cameraman's card—but I could be a director tomorrow just by saying I'm one. And I'm good—"

"How do you know?" Daisy challenged.

"I've been watching him long enough—I'm on to his tricks . . . and face it, how hard is it to direct a commercial?"

"This is what we have in mind," Nick interrupted Wingo. "We want to start our own shop but we want you with us . . . as a partner and producer. You wouldn't have to invest a dime, but you'd get a third share in the profits. Once I'm free of North, I could go out and sell Wingo—I've got a piss pot of prospects lined up. The reason we want you is because you happen to be the best producer anywhere—you work harder, you can talk people into doing anything for you, you watch the money as if it were your own, you double check everything—so, lucky lady, you get a free ride on this deal."

"You and Wingo and I would just up and leave—taking the store with us?" Daisy asked.

"It wouldn't be exactly that," Wingo protested. "North could replace each of us . . . eventually . . . nobody's indispensable."

"Yes, eventually—but meanwhile, he'd be crippled for how long? You're talking rip-off, Nick," Daisy said, in growing anger.

"Tough shit," Nick said, carelessly. "This is a rip-off business."

"Nick," Daisy asked, "who gave you your first chance at repping—who took you out of that ad agency and taught you the ropes? Who showed you where to dress and encouraged you to let loose your natural chutzpah and okayed your expense accounts for those first months, when you were getting nowhere? North, right? And Wingo, just who the hell hired you on a regular basis instead of using a free-lance cameraman like almost everyone else? How many days a year would you be working if you were merely another free lance? And who was the only person willing to take a chance on a kid who had *just* gotten his card? Most directors go for experience—they don't want to touch a raw kid . . . too much trouble. And how come you think you're such a hot-shot director when all you know is what you've *seen* North do? Don't you understand that you don't know *why* he does it, or *how* he gets his ideas? Perfect proof is that you think it's *easy* to direct a commercial—maybe it is—a bad commercial or even a fair commercial. But a *good* commercial? A commercial you don't absolutely hate when it interrupts your favorite television show? A commercial that doesn't make you want to vomit with the sheer banality of it? A commercial that looks so good you remember it a week later? Or even a month later, when you've seen thousands of others since? What's more, you don't know word one about casting. Alix and I only make a selection of possibilities, North does all the final casting and that's essential to the success of a commercial."

"Shit, Daisy, if you're going to talk about loyalty . . ." Nick interrupted in disgust.

"You're goddamned right I'm talking about loyalty. I remember the time you got drunk and came on so crudely with that gal art director from BBD and O that we lost the job, and I remember the time you were so anxious to get those big beer spots that you gave them a Y and R firm bid without checking with Arnie and we lost money every day we worked, and I remember the time—or rather the times—when North was going crazy on shoots because of client interference and you showed up too late to take them to lunch and get them out of his hair for a few hours, and I remember . . ."

"Shut the fuck up, Daisy," Nick said, looking sick.

"The hell I will—My point is that all those times North got furious, but he *didn't* go looking for another rep—he stuck to you because he had a commitment to you and you're more good than you are bad—but when you're bad, you're *horrid!*"

"But North's so rude to you . . ." Wingo started, defensively.

"That's my problem," she snapped, "and I don't need your sympathy. He's rude because he never works any way but under tension. There isn't a minute that the time pressure isn't getting to him. If somebody can screw up, somebody *will* screw up . . . And he knows it. It's my business to keep the confusion to a minimum. There's nothing personal in his rudeness—I'm an extension of his work and he doesn't need to play Sir Walter Raleigh with me. As a matter of fact, you two are only extensions of his work, too. Nick, if you weren't selling North, you just might have to work for a living. Wingo, if you didn't have North checking each shot before you roll a foot of film, I wonder just what your work would be like? You've both had a good ride on his back. I'm not saying you don't have talent, Wingo—just that you aren't ready to be a director-cameraman yet, and that for you and Nick to get together behind his back and try to steal off with everything he's given you both in terms of learning and experience and confidence—and to try to get me to go with you—that's the lowest kind of ingratitude!"

"Nick," Wingo said nastily, "we've obviously made a big mistake about the princess here . . . she just hasn't got what it takes to go out on her own. Daisy, you won't get a chance like this again."

"Maybe next time somebody will ask me to rob a bank . . . who knows, I could get lucky. Now listen, you two masterminds, I haven't had one bite yet of this lunch you invited me to and I'm not hungry anymore. I'm going back to the studio and work. As far as I'm concerned this is perfectly splendid meeting never took place. You didn't ask me about anything and I didn't tell you how I felt. Whatever you decide to do is up to you. I've forgotten the whole thing. Personally I hope we'll be together for a long time. We're not a bad team—*all* of us. Or, on the other hand, if you do leave, good luck! I predict many wonderful days for the two of you shooting the attack of the fifty-foot hemorrhoid. See you later."

As Daisy left, Nick looked at Wingo. "I wish I could say she's a bitch."

Wingo's face was that of a man who had just missed being run over by a bus. "You can't and neither can I. I just wish I could say she was *wrong*."

When Daisy got back to her apartment that night she found Kiki thumbing through an issue of the *Soho Weekly News*. "Daisy, do you have a date tomorrow night?"

"You know I do—your cousin is coming to town to take me out for dinner."

"Oh, right, I'd forgotten . . . So he hasn't given up on you yet, huh?"

"Henry? I don't think he understands English. I've said no so many times it's boring, but, my God, he's persistent. He's so sweet I don't want to hurt his feelings. I keep telling him he shouldn't see me because it's like cutting off a dog's tail in little pieces—it would be kinder to whack it off with one quick stroke—sorry, Theseus darling—but he won't pay any attention. Why'd you ask?"

"Oh, I just thought we might do something—there's a tap dance epic at the Performing Garage and a poetry reading at St. Mark's Church and La Mama is doing Brecht for a change and there's Microwave Music at Three Mercer—all kinds of things," Kiki said glumly.

"Christ! What's the matter? Have you taken your temperature? Where does it hurt?" Daisy said, looking at her friend with concern. Kiki was curled up on the couch in an old caftan, surrounded by scripts, letters and magazines.

"Don't be an ass—there's nothing wrong with me—I just thought we should seriously invest in a little cultural enrichment, that's all. I have my theater, even if it is temporarily dark, but *you*, what do you do all day but think about things that are directed at making millions of women have anxiety attacks?" Kiki asked waspishly. "That, plus those Horse People will make you a cultural idiot if you're not careful."

"Let's just stick to the facts," Daisy said, ignoring her words. "You've never gone in for cultural enrichment since Santa Cruz misguidedly gave you a diploma. That means you don't have a date for Friday night for the first time in something like eight years, and you're in a panic. Now that's absurd and you know it. There are a dozen guys you could call who'd jump . . ."

"I don't want *them*!" Kiki said, sounding more confused than adamant.

"Who do you want?"

Kiki remained stubbornly mute.

"Shall we play guessing games? Who is it my Kiki wants? Who did she fill the fridge for last Saturday so that we had to eat pâté and cheese for breakfast all week long to get rid of it, who was unkind enough . . ."

"Oh, stop it, Daisy! You're getting so rotten," Kiki snarled.

"Luke still hasn't called," Daisy said flatly.

"No, he hasn't. I'd like to kill him. How dare he do this to me? I simply don't understand it! Nobody does this to me, nobody!" Kiki's whole little body was huddled and shivering under the caftan as if she were preventing herself from springing forward and pounding her fists on the floor like a baby in a tantrum.

"Nobody but Luke Hammerstein."

"That's right, rub it in," Kiki said bitterly.

"Kiki, come on, I'm sympathetic! But you have to face facts if you want to change them."

"Oh, spare me—Miss Lonely Hearts rides again."

"Do you know somebody else you can talk about it with?"

"Daisy Valensky, you have the makings of a first-class bitch somewhere inside that glorious exterior. You know I don't," Kiki said, seizing Theseus in a despairing embrace.

"I think you're right," Daisy said with a pleased smile. "This is my day for telling it like it is or some such slogan left over from—was it the fifties or the sixties?—never mind . . . but you're not the first person who isn't happy with me today. And guess what—I don't give a shit."

"Oh, be quiet and listen. That son-of-a-bitch has refused my advances, not once but *twice*. How can there be any *possible excuse* for that? Do you think he's impotent? Do you think maybe he has an incurable form of some kind of V.D. and doesn't want to tell me? Do you think . . . oh, God . . . do you think he's in love with somebody? Oh, Jesus . . . I bet *that's* what it is—that's the only thing it could be!" Kiki's hands flew up and covered her mouth as she contemplated this worst of all possibilities.

"If he were, I'd know it. He and North are tight—I'd have picked up something, somehow—that studio is like a commune, gossip like that would have zipped around by now. Kiki, it's simple, and you brought it all on yourself."

The phone rang and Daisy picked it up. "Hi. Oh, hi, Luke, it's Daisy." Kiki lunged for the phone but Daisy backed away holding it firmly on its long cord. "Nope, sorry, she's not here. No idea . . . could be any one of a dozen places . . . I haven't really seen her all week, to tell you the truth, except running in and running out . . . but I'll take a message." Kiki signaled frantically but Daisy made horrible grimaces and ferocious eyes at her while she shook her free hand menacingly back and forth. "All right—I'll ask her to try to call you when she gets a chance. I'll leave it on the top of her other messages . . . I'm beginning to feel like a switchboard. I don't know why Kiki doesn't get a service or something. No, that's all right . . . I don't really mind . . . at least you're a client which is more than I can say for all of the others. Bye, Luke."

"Daisy! How could you?" Kiki cried as soon as she'd hung up.

"*That's* how you do it!"

"You've got to be joking. That's the oldest game in the book. Nobody does that anymore."

"*Everybody* does that who has the sense she's born with. Too bad you didn't know Anabel better."

"But I've never played hard-to-get in my life," Kiki sputtered, "and I've had more men than anyone I've ever known."

"Men you were not really after. It's easy to get a guy if you genuinely don't want him. I've seen you in operation for years; everything made easy for the poor sucker, and he walks right into your big, beautiful spiderwebs, thinking how he's made a conquest, and before he knows what's happened, he's a goner because right at the *heart* of your whole number is the fact that you simply couldn't care less—you're just doing it for kicks, a slap and a tickle, and he senses this, subconsciously anyway, and *that's* what drives him crazy, not your availability but your essential *unavailability*. I defy you to name just one man you've had whom you didn't give up if someone more attractive came along . . . I defy you to tell me the name of one guy who made you suffer . . . up till now."

"Why should I let a man make me suffer? What's so good about that?" sniffed Kiki rebelliously.

"Nothing. Suffering isn't noble. But the fact that you have steadily refused to put yourself in a position where you might have had to suffer is what I'm talking about. You've always gone in for basically unimportant relationships; good sex, lots of laughs, but not 'meaningful,' if you can overlook that cliché. Sorry, *sorry*, but it's true and you know it, too. Now, along comes a man who could be important to you and you haven't got any idea how to approach him. You're putting on your old act with a new cast and it just isn't working. So try a new script. Luke is smarter than you are, hard as that may be for you to believe. He's got you figured out, he can tell that you're used to having your way with men, and he isn't going to let that happen to him. What else is he doing but playing hard to get with you? He waited five days to call? Well, you're not going to return his call for a week . . . maybe more. And when you do see him again, you're going to be a whole new Kiki,"

"It's too late, I've already blown it," Kiki said dismally. "I mean I really let him know I could be had . . . and all that food! I could cut my throat! And, Daisy I do adore him so . . ."

"First impressions can be changed. You're an actress, aren't you? It's simple—you threw yourself at him because you had nothing better to do *that* particular week. *But*, since then, things have changed. Don't *ever* be specific about what has changed—he'll imagine them. *Now*, you're not interested in getting involved. You're cool, restrained and maddeningly off-hand. You can't accept the first two times he asks you out but you leave the door open—you're friendly—in fact, it's as if the two first encounters had just never taken place. But don't overdo it. Be yourself, but *don't come on*. Let him try to figure that one out! I think they call it 'bait and switch.' "

"I think they call it entrapment," Kiki murmured, radiant with admiration. "Daisy—I can do it—I know I can. But what if it doesn't work?"

"Then you'll just have to resign yourself. It's better to know right away than to find out after you've turned yourself inside out for months over the guy. 'Men have died from time to time, and worms have eaten them, but not for love.' "

"Betty Friedan?"

"Shakespeare—*As You Like It*."

"Oh, what did *he* know. 'Dost thou think, because thou art virtuous, there shall be no more cakes and ale?' "

"I knew you didn't need cultural enrichment."

"I put on *Twelfth Night* last year—don't you remember—on skateboards?"

"Could anyone who had the good luck to be there forget that immortal evening? Listen, I can't stand eating any more of last Saturday's gourmet leftovers. Let's go get a pizza as soon as I've cleaned up a bit. All right?"

"You're on." Kiki was already pacing the room like an oversized elf, holding herself tall, with an elusive, faintly amused, slightly preoccupied expression on her face and her body clearly expressing "touch-me-not." Daisy flung her a fond look and left the living room quietly. When Kiki was getting into a character she liked to be alone. Daisy deliberately took her time washing her hands and suddenly she found herself plummeted from the peaks of the day into another of those strange pockets of sadness she had experienced only a week before, in Middleburg, at the Shorts. She'd been flying high all day today, telling Wingo and Nick-the-Greek what she thought of their sneaky plan and now straightening out Kiki.

But abruptly, face to face with herself, her life seemed, in a frightening way, to be composed of a patchwork of odd bits and pieces which didn't form anything as substantial as a quilt. Her work at the studio, difficult though it was, didn't have the virtue of continuity; with every new commercial the achievements, the triumphant struggle of the week before were immediately replaced by today's crisis. North's lack of anger was not really a substitute for genuine appreciation, no matter what she'd told the others at lunch. She felt that she was forever playing catch-up on the job, always having to prove herself, over and over. As for her painting: her scramble after commissions was at the whim of capricious patrons who often treated her sketches and watercolors as just one step higher than a professional photographer's studio portrait. And her raggedly excuse for a love life was even more unfulfilling than she'd admitted to Kiki. The reason she could sound so wise on the matter of Kiki's refusal to be vulnerable was because it was a trait she knew all too well, an element that was far more deeply established in her own sensibility than in Kiki's prankster emotions. The idea of spending another evening fending off poor, dear, damp-minded Henry Kavanaugh was dreary. She should never have let him make love to her in the first place. She had never been in love—it was simple and bare as that, and a constant source of uneasiness and depression, like a low-grade fever which would not go down. She thought of Kiki, practicing being hard-to-get in the other room—that was the one constant in her life, her friendship with that great, good loony. Nothing she could ever do for Kiki would pay her back for all the emotional support and unswerving affection she'd given Daisy in the ten years since her father had died.

Theseus padded into the bathroom and sensed her mood. He put his front paws on her shoulders, just as he used to do when she was little, and licked her nose. "You lovely lurcher, you," Daisy told him and realized that she was crying. He was licking up her tears. Damn it, Daisy, she told herself, you go around as if you have the answers for the whole world, so just stop feeling sorry for yourself. Enough! You're doing fine . . . just keep on truckin'.

17

Hello, Ham?"

"Yup?"

"It's Pat Shannon—how's it going?"

"Couldn't be better," Ham Short grinned. The one who phones first in the mating dance of companies and corporations has put his cards on the table. And he likes a man who made his own phone calls. Nothing offended him as much as having another man's secretary get him on the line and keep him waiting until she put him through to her boss. He invariably hung up on her, unless, of course, he wanted something.

"How about coming up to New York, whenever it's convenient, and spending the day with me at Supracorp? I'd like you to know more about us."

"How's tomorrow?"

"Fine. We'll send one of the company's Gulfstreams for you."

"The hell you will—I only fly in my own Aero-Commander . . . got it fixed up the way I like it."

"Western?"

"Damn right—the thing's got everything but it's own still and an outside crapper."

"A car and driver will be waiting for you. When will you get in?"

"Nine sharp, give or take an hour waiting for landing clearance."

"See you tomorrow. I'm looking forward to it."

"You bet."

Supracorp's New York offices occupied five full floors at 630 Fifth Avenue, where the great bronze statue of Atlas, bearing the globe on his shoulders, guards the enormous doors. Ham Short stepped out of the elevator on the tenth floor to find himself in a world designed by Everett Brown to combine drama with rich spaciousness. The receptionist sat behind a twenty-foot semicircular desk made from glowing white oak which curved in front of a wall of bronze mirrors. On either side of the huge reception room were floor-to-ceiling, free-standing columns of stainless and Plexiglas steel in which were displayed examples of Supracorp's products.

Ham gave his name to the receptionist and turned to inspect the columns. Before two minutes had passed, he was gratified and surprised to see Pat Shannon, in shirtsleeves, the knot of his tie off center and the top button of his shirt undone, appear to greet him. They passed through wide corridors carpeted in deep brown, so well lit and humming with invisible energy that Ham felt as if he were on a spaceship. Shannon ushered him through a large room with yellow linen walls in which three women were busily telephoning or typing, each at her own large rosewood desk, and on into his own office. Ham, anticipating an expansion of the refined, subdued, but unembarrassed opulence he had just glimpsed, was astonished to find himself in a room which could have been in a ranch house in Sante Fe. Shannon gestured toward a pair of deeply tufted, pleasantly worn leather chairs and poured Ham a cup of coffee from a large thermos which stood on a low pine table.

"What's this? Shirtsleeves to shirtsleeves in three generations?" Short asked.

The lines on either side of Shannon's mouth deepened in amusement. "Beats the hell out of me how a man can get a day's work done in a jacket. As for the three generations—I'll never know. You're looking at a genuine orphan, Ham."

"Don't look to me for a drop of sympathy. I left home at twelve—always wished I'd been an orphan. Still do—I'm supporting two dozen no-goods back in Arkansas," Ham said, still inspecting the room. The walls were simply painted in a calm, pale gray. It was sparely furnished with a few mellow, not exceptional pieces of pine furniture, and several Navaho rugs were hung on the walls. The door was covered with adobe tile. It was so clearly a room that had been designed by the man who used it, and only for his comfort, that even Ham Short was impressed. This lack of pretension was more meaningful than the most magnificent office would have been. There wasn't even any art—only a few large chunks of quartz and a number of American Indian blankets. Ham, looking through three big, uncurtained windows at a startling view of the spires of St. Patrick's Cathedral directly across the street, thought that this had to be one of the most expensive pieces of office space in the world.

"How much do you know about Supracorp, Ham?" Pat Shannon looked even younger than he had in Middleburg. The informality of his open shirt, the obvious comfort he took in his old chair, the lack of any attempt to disguise his intensity, his focus on Ham Short, the glint of playfulness in his eyes, all made Ham feel as if he were meeting a good friend rather than someone with whom he was merely having an exploratory business discussion. He remembered, looking at Patrick's muscular neck and the big, hearty Irish smile of the man, that he'd been one hell of a linebacker when he'd played for Tulane. Ham Short felt very much at ease.

"Only what I read in *The Wall Street Journal.* Not a tenth of what you fellas must have found out about my little outfit."

"You and your outfit interest us a lot, Ham."

"I gather so. How come you picked on me?" Short was quite as wary as he was flattered.

"Obviously we want to get into shopping malls. We already have a real-estate division and it's healthy and growing. There are many real-estate operations we could be interested in besides yours. But it's Ham Short we want to acquire, as much, and, in fact, more than your property. We admire the way you've built your business, we like your brains, we like your methods, we like the way you operate and we like your results. We need a man like you."

"Don't beat about the bush much, do you?"

"It takes too much time. A lengthy courtship isn't necessary when two people want the same thing. But there's no point in talking specifics unless you're interested as well, and that's why I asked you up to visit—to show you what we're about. If we bought your company, Ham, you'd not only double your net worth within a few years, as one of the largest single stockholders in Supracorp, but you'd be on our board of directors and we'd be able to get the benefit of your thinking in operating all of our various divisions. Hell, Ham, we'd pick your brains like a bunch of vultures. And, of course, you'd continue to run your own show with the advantage of our lines of credit and the profits we're sitting on, ready to invest."

"Reporting to you?" Short said flatly.

"Yes. And I report to the stockholders. I don't believe you and I would have problems getting along."

"Hmmm." Ham Short liked Shannon, but he had never reported to anyone in his life. Still, he had always been intrigued by the activities of the large, varied conglomerates. He felt he was ready to spread his wings over a great deal more space than that covered by mere shopping malls.

"Come on—let's take a walk around." Pat Shannon knew just how bitter a pill he'd just given Short to chew on and he didn't want to leave him too much time to taste it. On the other hand, it had to be said, and the sooner the better. There was only room for one man at the top. He led Ham out of his office, this time stopping briefly to introduce Short to his three secretaries.

"Some of our divisions are based here," Shannon explained as they walked on down the corridor. "Lexington Pharmaceuticals, which was Nat Temple's first baby, has its main office on the next floor up—did you ever hear the story of how this whole company was founded on a cough drop? Nat Temple cooked it up on his mother's wood-burning stove and was the first person to give the Smith Brothers real competition. Now Lexington makes everything from miracle drugs to . . . Hi, Jim." Shannon stopped a man passing in the hall. "Ham, this is Jim Golden, one of the vice-presidents of Lexington Pharmaceuticals. Jim, Hamilton Short."

"Mr. Short, it's a pleasure. Pat, how was Paris? When'd you get back?"

"Yesterday. And Paris was as usual—two full days of meetings. Choiseul and O'Hara, our wine and liquor importing division, is based there," he explained to Ham. "For every one taste of the new vintages I must have had a bottle of water. We're looking to buy a big natural source water but the one I liked best wasn't for sale—belongs to the government."

"No jet lag?" Ham asked, with curiosity.

"No, almost none. I have them put all their watches on New York time when I get there and stay on New York time until I leave, so it doesn't hit me. It's a necessity. Yesterday, only hours after I got back, I was the guest speaker at the New York Society of Security Analysts, and last night was the opening of a Broadway musical to which we own the movie rights, and I'd invited a few senators and their wives up from Washington, so I had to be awake."

"But what about meals? Don't your French people get mixed up?"

"They're used to it by now. They don't complain so I assume they don't mind. When I fly to Japan—we have four hundred people in the office there—I do the same thing."

"And they don't complain either?" Ham asked, looking suspicious.

"Not so you'd notice. But I don't stay more than three days at a time—they manage. Now, let's take a look at Troy Communications. It's our entertainment division. The film studio and the television production company are both based on the Coast, of course, but the paperback publishing house is right here, two floors up, and the main offices for our seven radio stations and our TV stations are in this building too. Next year we're thinking of getting into hardcover publishing."

"I thought publishing was strictly a gentleman's business, and a dying one at that," Ham said.

"Not anymore, Ham." Both Shannon and Jim Golden laughed. "If it were, you can be sure Supracorp wouldn't be in it. We've only got one division that's doing badly: Elstree Cosmetics."

"Elstree? The English firm? Seems to me my mother used Elstree."

"That's the problem. It's even more ancient and venerable and respectable than Yardley or Roger et Gallet. Everybody's mother used it, but nobody's *daughter* is using it. We bought them almost two years ago and we haven't been able to turn them around yet. Elstree lost over thirty million last year. I'm going to get involved personally in the new advertising campaign. The whole line is being redesigned—again."

"Pat," Jim Golden said, "I know you're busy, but when you get a chance, would you drop into Dan's office?"

"Problem?"

"Big, big problem."

"Why didn't you call me sooner? Let's do it now," Shannon said impatiently. Walking quickly, he guided Ham and Golden straight past the bank of elevators and took the fire stairs, two at a time, to the floor above. Quickly he threaded his way through the maze of handsome corridors and went straight into the offices of Dan Camden, president of Lexington Pharmaceuticals. Ham Short was fascinated to note that the large office, which had the same view as Shannon's, was furnished in an all but overpowering mixture of jewel-hued damask and eighteenth-century antiques. He felt so strongly that he could have been at home at Fairfax Plantation that he knew the antiques were genuine. Stepping from behind an enormous Chippendale desk, a small, bespectacled man welcomed them with a worried and preoccupied air. Almost immediately he directed their attention to a large white square that lay on top of his desk.

"Pat, this is one of the first completed samples. In my opinion the last layer simply isn't as good as the lab boys thought it was. Six months of testing and they haven't got it right! Now these first five layers here are all right, they perform to specifications perfectly. So far, so good. We could wipe the competition off the map, except that the last and crucial layer doesn't work. Or, let me put it this way, it works, but just not well enough to justify the claims we plan to make."

"Got any water?" Pat asked quietly.

"Right here—I've been working with it all morning." The three men stood dripping water, drop by drop, onto the first layer of the white square. They all watched a large desk clock as, patiently, carefully, with intense concentration, they bent over the desk for long minutes. Ham Short sat down and watched the utter intensity on the faces of each of the three men. Patrick Shannon's gaze never left his task. Ham felt himself dozing off.

"*There!*" Dan Camden exclaimed at last. Ham sat up with a jerk to see the man pointing an accusing finger at a tiny bead of moisture on the highly polished wood of his desk. "It's at least two or two and a half minutes too soon."

"Shit," Shannon said in a soft voice. "Dan, you assured me only ten days ago that the tests looked good and you know that I went before the stockholders at the meeting last week and told them that we were planning to grab a large chunk of the market with this new product. We're not just looking at three million dollars of lab work that doesn't come up to the mark, and we're not just talking about a well-plotted media campaign to test the market in twenty cities which will now have to be postponed, we're talking about the expectations you let me present to our stockholders, not one of whom will forget them." He spoke quietly and calmly, but the flush which Ham Short noticed on his neck gave away his controlled anger.

"Pat, I'm just as upset about this you are," Camden protested, wiping his glasses in agitation.

"Not really. You only have me to contend with and I'm perfectly capable of understanding how the lab could fuck up—which, as it happens, I do. But I've got those bloodthirsty stockholders to deal with and I relied on *your* advice and *your* documentation. Next time, don't give me a green light until you're absolutely sure.

Personally sure. Don't take anyone's word for it."

"The chief chemist . . ."

"Not even the chief witch doctor's. Understood? Now I want those lab people over here from Jersey and in my office at four sharp this afternoon, so make sure they're all present and accounted for, Dan. We'll go into this then. See you later."

He turned away from the president of the giant pharmaceutical company who was, once again, absorbed in the white square on his desk.

"Come on, Ham, we've still got a lot of touring to do."

"What was all that about?" Ham asked, once they were out of earshot of the secretaries working in the outer office. "Some sort of new invention?"

"When it works, and it *has to*, it'll be the softest disposable diaper on the market. But it'll never sell if the mother has to change her baby too often. We have to have a minimum of another three minutes of resistance in the outer layer and we can give Pampers a run for their money." Pat's jaw was set in determination as he talked.

"Hmmm," grunted Ham Short.

"Now, let's go up to Troy Communications. I'll give you a quick tour before lunch."

"Sure." Lunch sounded like a good idea and the sooner the better. Later that afternoon Ham had an appointment at his investment banker's and he planned to ask the man what he thought of Shannon . . . personally.

"He's a damn *privateer!*" Reginald Stein said.

"Didn't strike me that way," Ham Short commented.

"Listen, Ham, he's a damned riverboat gambler, or halfway to it. He's too bold, takes too many risks for my taste and I've got too much Supracorp stock not to be worried about him."

"But look at the growth of the corporation," Ham protested.

"I know, I know, you can't fault that, but everybody's growing, Ham. These are fat years for certain kinds of businesses and Supracorp's in a lot of them. What worries me so much is the downside risk, and Ham, you know as well as I do that there is *always* a downside risk. Shannon takes chances he doesn't *have* to take—and I don't like that. He's not involved in safety and I am. And so should you be, my friend." The banker paused. "Ham, just why do you ask?"

"No real reason, Reggie, just curiosity."

By now Ham Short knew for certain that he wasn't going to have anything to do with a business that not only had a downside risk but was a business in which the seepage rate of baby piss was treated as a matter of life or death. He had enough plumbing problems in his life as it was . . . and sewage disposal problems as well—to get involved with dirty diapers. He was too old and he was too rich. He didn't need these complications. Maybe Pat Shannon could live with the shadow of the stockholders hovering over his daily life, but Ham Short didn't intend to ever have to report to anybody. Not even to Topsy.

"And please give me only brown eggs with breakfast tomorrow, Mrs. Gibbons," Ram instructed his housekeeper after dinner late on Friday night at Woodhill Manor.

"Certainly, Sir," the stout, self-respecting lady replied. Queen Elizabeth, too, would eat only brown eggs from a farm in Windsor. Mrs. Gibbons, to her relief, had seen few changes in forty years at Woodhill but she was beginning, albeit reluctantly, to approve of her late master's grandson and heir.

This rare weekend alone in Devon was a necessary respite for Ram. Recuperation and meditation were on his agenda. All winter he had been working particularly hard and staying out much later than was usual for him. His decision to set about a search for a wife had led him to accept invitations to a number of weekends and parties he normally would have refused, but the candidates had to be surveyed before he could make a logical and reasonable choice.

Now, at least, he was able to define what he did *not* want, although he still hadn't found anyone remotely suitable. As he methodically got ready for bed he reviewed the possibilities he had rejected. They included any number of that group known as the "Sloane Rangers"—after fashionable Sloane Square in Chelsea. They were clever young society women who spent their days shopping and having their hair done and trading secrets over lunch at San Lorenzo in Beauchamp Place, a close-knit clique who dressed in an informal uniform of checked or plaid blazers, silk shirts, wool skirts from St. Laurent and highly polished boots. Ram found them highly antipathetic. They knew each other far too well, they told each other far too much, they had, quite simply, been around too long to attract him. And having thoroughly looked over the current debutante crop of last spring's beauties who had just been hatched, he hadn't been charmed by a single one of the worldly herd of Amandas, Samanthas, Alexandras, Arabellas, Tabithas, Melissas, Clarissas, Sabrinas, Victorias and Mirandas, who at only eighteen already "knew everybody." He fell asleep while he was mentally rejecting every girl he had met in the last four months.

The next morning Ram took one of his Purdey shotguns and set out on foot. He intended to inspect his fences, at least symbolically, since nine hundred acres of fields could hardly be covered except by his bailiff and his men. However, Ram liked the idea of walking on his own land.

There was something in the air, even now, as early as the beginning of February, which if it was not quite green, somehow smelled of approaching greenness, but it went unnoticed by Ram, who was thinking of an article he had recently read by Quentin Crewe, who pointed out that if a man had earned 250 pounds a week since the Crucifixion and saved every shilling of it, he still would not be as rich as the Dukes of Westminster or Buccleuch or Earl Cadogan. There were nineteen dukes, thought Ram, who each possessed over ten thousand acres—yes, land was still where the money was in England. But only as long as it wasn't taken away by the government in the form of taxation. Private British wealth might only last out his lifetime—perhaps not as long as that. Ram had foreseen that possibility long ago and invested so heavily in other countries that even if he had to leave England and all he owned, including these ancient acres, he would always be excessively rich.

Did he require a wife to be rich? Not necessarily, thanks to his foresight. Did he require her to be of absolutely impeccable birth? Yes . . . sheer self-respect demanded that minimum. A virgin? Again yes. It was perhaps, in fact, unquestionably, an old-fashioned notion in these days, but firmly in Ram's mind was a need to find a girl of innocence, someone who hadn't been exposed prematurely to the taint of the London Season, a girl not quite formed, who would adore and admire him. A proper wife.

He turned to look back at Woodhill Manor, a dwelling dating from the Elizabethan period, added onto in the time of Queen Anne, and boasting a new wing of Edwardian origin, which, because of the fairly uniform use of gray limestone and stone-tiled roof, formed a charming harmonious whole. It was not a truly grand house in the tradition of the great English country estates, but it had something new money could not buy: tranquility, grace, timelessness.

He had sensed that same quality—to a much higher degree—on a trip he had recently made to Germany, in connection with investments in a large ball-bearing factory. There, he had been invited to spend the weekend at a Bavarian castle, a *schloss* which had belonged to the family of his hosts since the thirteenth century, in which twenty-two generations had managed to live without interruption in spite of wars, pestilence and other nastiness of history. This Germany, the Germany of the Furstenburgs and the Windisch-Graetzs, the Hohenlohe-Langenbergs, and Hohenzollern-Sigmarigans and von Matternichs, this Germany of Serene Highnesses and Royal Highnesses and Illustrious Highnesses, called to something elemental in Ram. Not only did he appreciate the straightforward, unabashed richness of his hosts, he also approved of the emphasis he found everywhere among the nobility on serious, sensible application to the *business* of life. These were practical, stern, proud people who did not let the antiquity of their names deter them from extracting the maximum from their forests and their vineyards, from expanding their family businesses and investing in foreign countries. As he had sat at lunch with his host and hostess, Ram had seen, outside on a path on the other side of the lawn, two young girls, perhaps not more than eleven or thirteen, accompanied by a groom, riding past.

"Our daughters," the Prince had said with a casual wave toward the window which did not conceal the pride he took in them, even as he returned to an explanation of why anyone listed in Part One of the *Almanach de Gotha* cannot marry somebody who is not listed in either Part One or Part Two without losing his royal prerogative. This discourse was largely lost on Ram, as, in his mind's eye, he contemplated the momentary vision of the two blonde children as pure and untouched as if they were figures in a tapestry.

Still, he could not look to any young German girl for a wife. It was out of the question, for no matter how perfectly brought up and carefully protected she might be, no matter how flawless her English, how ancient her lineage, how splendid her accomplishments, she would still be foreign. To people like the Fulfords of Great Fulford Devon, and the Crasters of Craster West House, Craster, Northumberland, to others of the great untitled families of England, the Monsons, the Elwes, the Henages, the Dymokes—he, a direct descendant of Rurik, Grand Duke of Novgorod and Kiev, founder of Imperial Russia—he, Prince George Edward Woodhill Valensky, was still something of a foreigner.

Ram shrugged and resumed his walk. He faced without rancor the fact that he felt that his own Englishness was not firmly enough established for him to take a non-English wife. In his own opinion, even Queen Victoria had never quite lived down the stigma of Prince Albert's nationality.

As he cast a last backward thought at the memory of his glimpse of the two young German princesses he realized that he had been wasting his time prospecting in London, evaluating the harvest of young women. Although they told anyone who would ask that they were *not* officially entered in the marriage stakes, although "having" a London Season was now emphatically dismissed as merely a chance to "widen one's circle of friends," Ram was not fooled. A rich husband was even more avidly sought after in tax-poor England today than he had been in England of yesterday. Granted, the time was past when the first thing openly asked about any prospective mate, male or female, was the extent of that person's wealth or expectations. Such healthy honesty had gone underground since the days, not so long ago at that, when Jane Austen would cite the precise number of pounds of income per year as an absolutely essential part of her description of any of her characters.

Ram had always known the importance of money. There had never been a time he could remember when he was too childish to realize that his father was rich and his mother and her second husband were not. Nor did he believe that other people weren't as involved with money as he was. It was merely that they hid their fascination, as indeed he did, except at work. It was all very fashionable and up-to-date for a girl to protest that the worst thing that could happen to her was to be considered a prominent debutante, that what she really longed for was to become a student of Russian or Chinese history or travel around the world in a sailboat, that all she wanted was to be young and carefree and never think of things like income. Ram knew better. Her career, such as it was, would be abandoned gladly when the proper young man with the proper amount of money came along. That's what they were after, all of them, except for a few rare, odd females who had always been out of step with their world, a world that was certainly dying but nevertheless, as far as the English upper classes were concerned, the best world that had ever been.

As Ram moodily considered the case of certain eighteen-year-old eligible beauties—Jane Bonham Carter, great-granddaughter of Prime Minister Herbert Asquith, who was already ensconced in the study of economics and philosophy at London University; Sabrina Guinness, working for a living and in a frightfully unsuitable way if what Ram heard was true, as a governess for Tatum O'Neal—he suddenly realized that he should be searching in the world of seventeen-year-old girls. Eighteen was just too sophisticated, too headstrong, too stubborn, too self-oriented an age for a wife. By eighteen, a girl was ruined, Ram decided, breaking off a branch from a young oak and inspecting the buds without really seeing them.

Sarah Fane, Sarah Fane? The name swam into his mind, and it took a minute for him to remember that last week over a business lunch, her father, Lord John Fane, had grumbled to him about his daughter. Had he been complaining because she insisted on coming out at Queen Charlotte's Birthday Ball next May or because she had refused to be presented at the ball? Ram couldn't recall—he hadn't paid attention—but he did remember that he'd been surprised that the subject was even raised. It seemed a short time ago that he had seen her, a child of fourteen, when he'd gone to spend a weekend in Yorkshire at Lord John's—it must have been mid-August because they'd been gathered for the opening of the grouse-shooting season.

Could it have been three years ago? He had a memory of a tall, shy silent girl with blue, clear eyes and long, straight blonde hair that kept falling over her face, but with something of an air about her. She had held herself with none of the stoop-shouldered attempts at invisibility one might have expected of an adolescent, but walked well, her steps firmly planted on the Fane moors as she followed the shooting party at a discreet distance. Well, whatever her plans for the London Season, it didn't traditionally start until the Private View at the Royal Academy on the first Friday in May. Ram decided to investigate Sarah Fane—the Honorable Sarah Fane, to be exact. She'd probably prove to be another of many disappointments, determined to become a photographer's model or a cordon bleu chef—but she had carried herself well, and by all calculations she must still be under eighteen. He'd write himself a memo when he went back to the house. It was worth looking into. And after all, her grandfather *was* an earl.

18

I just don't like it, Kiki, can't you understand?" Daisy went to the window and looked out at Prince Street, already busy with tourists from uptown spending this early fall day of 1976 wandering about SoHo. The air was still warm and the potholes of the winter of 1975 were twice the size they had been, and half the size they would be by next spring, but there was no sign that the city intended to repair them. Perhaps, she thought, they were already considered historic landmarks.

"Daisy, look at it this way," Kiki implored her. "You're doing them a favor by wearing his dress to their party—you'll probably be photographed and that's good publicity for Robin Valarian."

"I don't trust the whole thing," Daisy repeated stubbornly.

"The dress? But it's so pretty," Kiki protested.

"No, I admit the dress is nice, even if it's not my style. I mean, you don't think that a wisp of chiffon and feathers like this, stolen practically line for line from St. Laurent's last collection, will still look great in thirty-five years, do you? But that's not what I mean. I get this feeling of spider webs, spun from pure gold—but still webs. You think I'm being paranoid, don't you?" she accused Kiki.

"Maybe a little. In the last year you've got Vanessa to thank for two major commissions, that big oil of the three Short girls and the other oil you did last Christmas of the two Hemmingway boys. She persuaded you to raise your price for watercolors by five hundred dollars, she's insisted on giving you a couple of dresses, she's invited you to a lot of parties—I grant you that. But look at what she's had in return."

"What *has* she had in return? That's precisely why I don't trust her. She is simply not the kind of woman who does nice things for the pure joy of it. I know her better than you do, Kiki, love—tell me what she's getting from me?"

"Ah . . ." Kiki was momentarily wordless.

"Another party guest? You don't really think that's enough, do you?"

"Well—*yes*, if you're a people collector, and she is."

"Come on, Kiki. I'm not all *that* important or that glamorous or that anything."

"You underestimate yourself—will you never stop! Look, you don't do the New York social scene because you're too busy during the week and on weekends you're usually away working at your portraits, so you have a definite *scarcity value.* That means something to Vanessa!" Kiki's eyebrows shot up to their most demonic heights. She thought it only normal and right that the Valarians should be generous to Daisy. It infuriated her that Daisy had never taken advantage of the collateral she possessed merely by being who she was, that she didn't milk her beauty and her title for all they were worth, that she hadn't jumped on board the great American celebrity train that was just waiting for her to ride it. "Daisy, you're not Cinderella, you know, you're legit."

"And you're a romantic—you still believe in fairy tales—no, take that back, you're a terrible cynic who wants me to cash in on an accident of birth. Even Serge Obolensky doesn't use his title anymore."

"Well, he doesn't have to sell portraits to Horse People—and plenty of other Obolenskys are still called prince and princess."

"Kiki, do you think we could stop splitting imperial hairs and get started on figuring out what I'm going to take to Venice? What do you suppose the weather is like in Venice in September?"

"Changeable," Kiki answered authoritatively.

"Luke should take a stick to you."

"He doesn't go in for kinky sex," said Kiki smugly.

"Oh? And just what does he go in for?"

"Hugging and kissing and touching . . . giving pleasure and caressing and . . ."

"Fucking?"

"Really, Daisy, how crude! As a matter of fact . . . since you insist, he definitely goes in for . . . making love," Kiki said, prim as a mid-Victorian clergyman's daughter.

"Mercy, mercy! Aren't you ever so pure now that you've got him . . . you *do* have him, don't you?" Daisy asked with a touch of anxiety.

"I just don't know." Kiki's small, pointed face suddenly looked like that of a baffled kitten. "I did everything you told me. I only accept dates with him every other time he asks—sometimes not even that often—I've worked up a whole fantasy world of other men that's so real I believe in it myself, and I'm more and more in love with that son-of-a-bitch every day. But he *eludes* me!" She pounded her small fists on Theseus who licked her hand. He liked pounding. "Do you think I shouldn't have gone to bed with him . . . was that a mistake?"

"Of course not. The day is over when a girl can get a man by withholding sex. That wasn't my point at all when I told you to be essentially unavailable. 'Essentially' doesn't mean sexually, dumbbell—it means somewhere way down deep. In your soul."

"I think my soul *is* available," Kiki said despondently, "and he knows it. Can you harden your soul the way you harden your heart?"

"Do you have a spiritual adviser?"

"Of course not."

"Perhaps you'd better start looking for one. Now, come on! What do you have that I can borrow?"

Arnie Greene, North's business manager, was unhappy. He'd advised North against taking the Pan Am job. It was a top account, but a Venice location meant that North and Daisy and Wingo would all be out of the studio for almost a week, unable to attend production meetings with other clients during the entire period, a fact that might cause a few days gap in their work schedule when they got back.

"Isn't it going to take more time than it could possibly be worth?" he asked North when Nick-the-Greek first brought in the job and asked him to bid on it.

"Probably," North had answered. "But for some reason or other, I've never been to Venice, and I want to get there before it sinks."

Arnie sighed. If he had his way, North would never shoot on location farther from the office than Central Park. He reluctantly accepted the fact that when a story board called for flocks of pigeons, the Piazza San Marco and gondolas, you couldn't do it in Central Park Lake . . . the pigeons maybe, but not the piazza. With melancholy, he wondered if gondolas were as unpredictable to work with as kids or animals. Well, he'd made damn sure that there was enough padding in the bid to absorb the overtime of even the most incompetent gondolier. Hell, he'd even taken out insurance in case a gondolier *drowned*. Arnie had also taken into account everything he'd always darkly suspected about *La Dolce Vita*, assumed that local technicians, wardrobe and make-up people, all brought in from Rome, would insist on two-hour lunches, counted on problems of crowd control and pigeon shit, figured out what it would cost to transport North, Daisy, Wingo and six models to Venice and back, first class all the way, added in a per diem living cost for all of them at the Gritti Palace which would pay the rent on his apartment for almost a year, made sure that every single item on the five-page list every commercial producer has to submit to the agency was as exact as he and Daisy could estimate, *plus*. They'd done their job. Even if something went wrong and North had trouble, they could handle the extra expenses out of the padding of the bid—standard procedure. Fortunately they weren't financially responsible for the delays caused by weather. If he'd had to worry about the weather he'd have three more ulcers than the two he already had.

"All right, but for Christ's sake, North, don't fall in a canal. The water will give you, at the least, hepatitis."

"Arnie, have I ever fallen into a canal?"

"You just said you'd never been to Venice. And don't eat raw shellfish . . . also causes hepatitis."

"Is it all right to look at the sunsets, or will they give me eyestrain?"

"Nobody appreciates me."

"Not true." North gave Arnie a friendly glance. "But you worry too much."

"Well, something always does go wrong, doesn't it?"

"Sure—if it didn't we might as well be making buttonholes. But you know Daisy will take care of it, whatever it is. That's what we pay her for, isn't it?"

By the time the luggage was retrieved at the Marco Polo Airport and they'd gone through customs and piled everything into a *vaporetto*, the Venetian equivalent of a bus, it was too dark and too late for either Daisy or North to see much of Venice. Wingo and the six models, three male and three female, were due to arrive the following day, but North had decided that he would leave a day early in order to see the sights of Venice undisturbed. Daisy could use that extra day to make a last-minute survey of the locations, check with the local police about crowd control and make sure that the accommodations were ready for the technical crew, wardrobe people, make-up people and hairdressers who were due in from Rome the next afternoon.

Venice was an audible shock, Daisy thought, looking out of the window of her room directly onto the Grand Canal, still hearing the slap of little waves against the side of the *vaporetto*. It didn't matter how much one had read about Venice or how far back in memory one had known that it was built on water, the reality came as a total surprise. It was impossible, she realized, to *imagine* Venice. In spite of the thousands of paintings it had inspired, it had to be experienced to become real, and even as a reality, it seemed improbable, as if she had, like Alice, gone through the looking glass into a land of wonders, a play world, insubstantial, so romantic that it was almost ridiculous, a city that was one vast composition of great art, presumably dying and crumbling for hundreds of years, yet still vital, the inexhaustible subject of so much prose that there was nothing left to be said about it, yet millions of words had not drained one drop of magic from it. What ambitious creatures men were, after all, to have even attempted such a city!

Across the canal, in the middle of the moonlit night, she could plainly see the dome of Santa Maria della Salute, that supreme masterpiece of Venetian Baroque. The fact that it was actually exactly where it should be was somehow miraculous and unexpected. . . . Daisy wouldn't be surprised if it had vanished by morning, nor if it remained standing long after New York and London had been reduced to rubble.

Tomorrow, at 7:00, she had to be up to start work, Daisy realized with a start, turning back to her high-ceilinged room, gay with striped blue-and-white satin walls and pink brocade draperies. That meant five hours sleep at the most. Luckily she had been able to nap a little on the trip over. North had sat in the front aisle seat of the first-class compartment, where he had room to stretch out his legs, and Daisy had taken a vacant seat several rows behind, so that she wouldn't disturb him. She knew that before a shoot as complicated as this one promised to be, he liked to withdraw into himself even more than usual, in preparation for the energy he would be pouring out during the next few days. As she got ready for bed Daisy wondered if, as she had plotted, she was going to be able to return to New York by way of London so that she could see Dani. She hadn't been able to go to Europe at Christmas this year. The two large oils and six watercolors she had done had just covered Danielle's expenses, so Daisy had been forced to choose to make the money rather than to make the trip. It had been too long, oh, really much too long, she thought, since she'd seen either Danielle or Anabel. She had decided not to ask North about taking the extra days off until the shoot was almost over. Then, with London so near, it would be difficult for him to refuse and her ticket could be rewritten at a minimum of expense.

Wearily, Daisy pulled off the ancient jeans, T-shirt and British Army Commando jacket—fifty cents at a church jumble sale in London five years ago—that she'd worn on the plane and hadn't had off since they left New York. She took a shower, a long, languorous shower, very different from the brief "working" shower she was used to at home, which, dictated by the inadequate plumbing, she told Kiki was as much fun as bathing with a Water Pik.™ Her nightwear was ordered from the Montgomery Ward catalogue, an old-fashioned straight-top vest in pink cotton with a drawstring around the top of the camisole and ribbon straps. Instead of the matching bloomers, Daisy wore purple satin basketball shorts, and her man's dressing gown was from Sulka, a dark-red, figured silk with a shawl collar, still in excellent condition after twenty-five years, even if it swept the floor in a way it had never been intended to. Her mind jumbled with practical considerations and the waiting excitement of Venice, Daisy fell into a light and confused sleep, full of fragmentary dreams.

When her traveling alarm clock went off, she was glad to jump out of bed and run to the window, the dreams disappearing in the promising, water-refracted light of morning. Dazzled, almost paralyzed with wonder, she stared at the view until she shook herself out of her reverie. It was really insane, she thought, to be expected to work here. They should have come a week earlier just to get acclimated to the beauty. But perhaps even a month wouldn't have been enough. Bitterly she envied North his day of sightseeing and promised herself as she dressed rapidly that she'd get everything checked out so efficiently and quickly today that she'd have a few hours, at least, to roam around by herself before the others arrived.

Late that afternoon, when North finally wandered back to the hotel, he found Daisy waiting for him right inside the entrance, curled up in a chair.

"All set?" he asked her.

"Not exactly."

"What d'ya mean? If everything isn't buttoned down, why are you hanging around the lobby? Isn't there something you have to do?"

Daisy stood up, her hands on her hips, her feet apart, her energy restored.

"North, hold it." She put up a hand like a traffic cop. "It seems we have a small problem."

"You and your problems," he said indifferently. "My feet hurt." He started for the desk to get his room key. She followed and tapped him on the shoulder.

"North?"

"Oh, what the hell is it? Honestly, Daisy, isn't it your job to worry about the little things? Oh, all right, tell me . . . there's a permit missing, the gondola's painted the wrong color, one of the models has a pimple? Improvise—how many times have I told you? *Improvise*, Daisy. If I've said it once I've said it a thousand times—you take care of the little things and I'll make it come out all right once I start working."

"Do you think you could get Alitalia to go back to work?"

"Why worry about Alitalia—we're working for Pan Am. Christ, Daisy, you have no sense of proportion," he said, turning away in exasperation.

Behind him she said softly, "None of the other airlines is landing in Italy, North. Sympathy strike." He spun around. "Wingo and the models can't get here."

"So what?" he said in renewed irritation. "Worse things have happened. Haven't you contacted models from Rome? If I can't use the girls I picked I'll use others, and I'll manage without Wingo. Rome is full of cameramen—and beautiful women."

"The trains are on strike too," Daisy said softly.

"Tell them to *drive*, damn it! If they start now they'll be here by tomorrow. If they'd started when you found out about the strike, I bet they could have been here by now," he added accusingly.

"The technicians are out on strike too. No crew, North. There's nobody in Italy to handle the equipment, which, incidentally, is sitting somewhere between Rome and here. No camera, no brutes, no fey lights, no clapboard, no dolly, not even a stopwatch—*nada!* And that's why I didn't book models from Rome."

"All right, very funny, very clever. Didn't it occur to you that we could drive to France or Switzerland and shoot there? Get ready to leave," North snapped.

"Shoot the Piazza San Marco and the pigeons and gondolas in France or Switzerland?" Daisy asked sweetly.

"But, damn it to hell, call New York! You know that the agency can rewrite the story board in an hour if they have to—"

"The strike," said Daisy slowing, lingering delightedly on every word, "has most unfortunately spread to the telephone system and the telegraph system. If some of those birds outside are carrier pigeons . . . Otherwise we're stuck here."

"That's insane! Daisy, you're not trying! Call up and rent a car. We'll take a motorboat to dry land and drive to the nearest border and call New York from there. Let them pick out an alternative location—Pan Am goes everywhere. Why the hell did you have to wait for me to get back to figure out something as simple as that? Why aren't you packed? What's the matter with you—you're slipping badly!"

"The car-rental people are out on strike. So is the gondoliers cooperative, and the *vaporettos* as well," Daisy said, her black eyes so dark that the dance of joy and amusement in the depths of her pupils was almost concealed.

"Shit! Daisy, they can't *do* this to *me!*"

"I'll tell them you said so," Daisy said, "when they've gone back to work."

"It's . . . it's . . . uncivilized!" shouted North, waving his arms around the princely lobby of the hotel which had been the residence of a doge in the sixteenth century.

"Why don't we try to be philosophical, North? It's not as if we can do anything about it," Daisy suggested calmly.

Daisy had been thoroughly enchanted by the events of the day. As each avenue of escape closed, as, finding her phone useless, she went down to the lobby to keep in touch with news of the spreading strikes that the reception desk relayed from the radio, every moment became more pleasurable. She felt something invading her which she had difficulty in recognizing until she finally identified it as a sense of leisure . . . she remembered how leisure felt from college vacations. The charmingly attentive hotel employees, of whom there were two to every one of the hotel's hundred guests, joined in her holiday mood—for tomorrow, who knew, might they not be out on strike too? It was just the right weather for a strike, one of them had pointed out to Daisy. She agreed with him completely. If there was one thing in the world she could have wished for in Venice it would be a few days outside of time. And the hall porter assured her that no guests at the Gritti Palace had ever starved. Even if they had to eat buffet style, the management was prepared. At the worst, the *principessa* might have to make her own bed.

"Philosophical?" North was outraged. Events did not do things to him, he did things to them. "We're locked up here as if this were the Middle Ages and you talk *philosophical?*"

"There is still one way out," Daisy said faintly.

"*What*, for Christ's sake!" he roared.

"We could . . . swim."

North swung around wrathfully and looked at his demented producer. At his gaze Daisy squeaked with suppressed laughter until she sounded like a whistling teapot about to come to a boil.

"Arnie's . . ." she sputtered before she was shaken by great outright howls of mirth, "Arnie's . . . *face!*"

The vision of Arnie Greene's mournful visage prophesying his inevitable hepatitis appeared before North's eyes and his face splintered slowly, reluctantly, but unconditionally, with laughter.

The hall porter and the doorman looked at the two Americans, shaken by spasms of hilarity, and shrugged smilingly at each other. The young *principessa*, the concierge thought, dressed rather unsuitably for the daughter of Prince Stash Valensky, who had been a faithful guest before his death, always coming to Venice for a week or two in September after the polo was over in Deauville. Only this morning she had come downstairs in a man's white pants and a striped purple-and-white soccer jersey. But perhaps it was a new fashion?

"You planned this whole thing, didn't you?" North gasped, getting control of himself.

"It wasn't easy," Daisy admitted modestly.

"A whole country shut down so you could get a day off—nothing to it."

"I'm efficient, I grant you, but I couldn't have pulled it off in New York—too many gypsy cabs."

"Have you checked our gypsy gondolas?"

"A boy in a rowboat is the best I could find."

"Where to? I've got to have a drink before the bartenders go on strike." North felt giddy. The combination of a day in Venice with the complete collapse of the support system he took for granted, made him feel like a kid let out of school just before an exam.

"Harry's Bar?" Daisy suggested.

"You mean like tourists?"

"Of course . . . but I have to change first. And you need a bath. I'll meet you down here in an hour. Actually, I think we can walk there—I've got a map."

"I've been walking all day. Tell the rowboat boy to wait."

"Yes, boss." North found himself smiling at Daisy. He supposed there really wasn't anything *specific* he could fault her with . . . at least not until he found out more about this strike for himself.

Back in her room, Daisy hesitated among the dresses she had packed, just in case something came up that she couldn't do in her work clothes. She felt entirely feckless, as weightless as an astronaut. She picked the most elaborate dress she owned, a Vionnet gown from the mid-1920s. Kiki had insisted that she take the bare-armed chemise, skimpier than a slip, cut on the bias from black velvet. It had the deepest possible rounded neckline held up only by shoulder straps of crystal beads. The same beads were embroidered on the velvet in wide, fantastic circles, in a descending oval, so that it looked like a long necklace and the hem hung in two rippling points on either side of Daisy's body, showing a flick of knees in front. It was a dress that must once have caused a major scandal. Black velvet in September? Why not? thought Daisy as she unbraided her hair. The style of the dress indicated a sophisticated hairdo, but she didn't have sophisticated hair, Daisy realized, as the Venetian light tangled in the blonde strands. She lifted it in both hands, extended her arms at full length still holding onto her hair and whirled around and around. What to do, what to do? She wasn't in a chignon mood or in a braid mood—she was in a crystal mood. Finally she parted her hair in the middle, took several yards of silver ribbon she'd saved from a Hallmark commercial and twined it around so that some of the most flighty locks were held back from her face, the rest flowing loose. She flung on the cape of green and silver-shot lamé made in the same period as the dress by a now unknown firm called Cheruit and went down to the lobby, more romantic than any heroine ever painted by Tiepolo or Giovanni Bellini.

North was waiting, ready to leave. Not much of a drinker, he was unusually anxious for a drink. Alcohol was supposed to be a depressant, wasn't it? A depressant might help counteract the dangerously free-floating feeling in the atmosphere tonight. He needed to be brought back to earth, and there was no damn earth here—only the rippling reflections on the canal which made everything tipsy to start with. Where the hell was Daisy? Why was she keeping him waiting? He couldn't remember ever having to wait for Daisy since he'd started employing her.

"*Dio! Che bellissima! Bellissima!*" the hall porter said behind him.

"*Bellissima!*" echoed the doorman and the passing waiter and two men lounging about the lobby.

"Well," said North, looking at Daisy. Now he really needed a drink.

"A Mimosa, Signorina, or perhaps a Bellini?" the waiter suggested. North looked around at the long, narrow, famous room.

"Do you make a martini? I mean a *dry* martini?" he asked, dubiously.

"Fifteen to one, Sir. On the rocks?"

"A double. Daisy?"

"What's a Mimosa?" she asked the waiter.

"Champagne and fresh orange juice, Signorina."

"Oh, yes, please." The waiter showed no signs of leaving. He simply stood there looking at Daisy, expressing the most pure admiration with every inch of his wrinkled face.

"We'll have our drinks now," North said flatly, breaking the spell and sending the waiter hurrying off.

"So," North said in a voice which invested the syllable with discovery, mistrust and surprise and belligerence.

" 'So'?" asked Daisy with slightly fake innocence. "What does that mean? Do you think just because it looks as if nobody in Venice is worried, there isn't really any strike?"

"*So* this is what you look like when you're not working, and *so* you must be putting on quite an act at the studio, and *so* I really don't know a hell of a lot about you, and *so* this is what you get up as soon as you have a chance."

"So?" Daisy shrugged blithely. "What's wrong with that?"

"That's exactly what I'm trying to figure out. I know there's *something*."

"North, North, go with the flow."

"What the hell is that supposed to mean?"

"I'm not sure, but it sounds just right for this time and this place. How's your martini?"

"Adequate," he said grudgingly. It was the best martini he'd ever had in his life. "How's your orange juice?"

"Pure heaven, absolute bliss, total delight, a dream, a vision, a revelation . . ."

"You mean you'd like another?"

"How could you tell?"

"There was something . . . just a touch . . . almost but not quite a hint . . . an intimation."

"Very good, North," Daisy approved. "When you start with intimations you're getting there."

"Where, getting where?"

"Into the flow."

"I see."

"I thought you would. I've always considered you a fairly quick study," Daisy said airily, whirling her champagne glass between her fingers.

"Calm affrontery—that's your game after hours. Damning with faint praise."

"I think flattery is tacky."

"I'm just surprised that you didn't say that when other people said I was stupid, you defended me."

"Wrong. When other people say you're an absolute shit, I defend you." Daisy smiled angelically.

"Christ! Wait till we get back to the mainland! Waiter, a butterfly net for the lady please, and two more drinks."

"I'm having fun," Daisy announced.

"So am I," said North, startled and newly suspicious.

"Feels odd, doesn't it?"

"Very. But I don't think it will do any permanent damage. Unless we got used to it, of course," North said thoughtfully.

"You mean that fun's fun but real life isn't supposed to be fun, at least not this much?"

"Absolutely. You're not utterly devoid of a sense of values. That's what I tell people when I defend you. They say that Daisy Valensky is nothing but a hard-working drone who never has any fun, and I defend you. I say that for all they know you may have fun sometimes—they shouldn't judge by appearances."

"You really *are* a shit, North," Daisy said, in a lilting voice.

"I *knew* you were shining me on."

"Why don't you fire me?" Daisy suggested.

"I'm too lazy. And anyway I am a shit, sort of. I mean, I'm not your ordinary good-natured slob."

"You're not even an ordinary bad-natured slob."

"No use trying to provoke me . . . you said to be philosophical so I'm being philosophical."

"How long can this last?"

"Go with the flow, Daisy."

"That's my line," Daisy said possessively.

"I'm a creative borrower," North loftily proclaimed.

"Get your own line," Daisy insisted.

"That's stingy. You must be hungry. Should we eat?"

"I didn't have lunch," said Daisy plaintively.

"Why not?"

"I was too busy finding out about the strike." She looked at him virtuously.

"Which strike?" wondered North.

"We *should* eat."

"That's my line," said North. "But I'll let you have it. I'm feeling generous. Where shall we go?"

"We can stay and eat here," Daisy suggested.

"Thank God. I can't get up. Waiter, bring us everything."

"Everything, Signor?"

"Everything." North gestured broadly.

"Certainly, Signor." The waiter appreciated the signor's dilemma. How could he order sensibly in the presence of such glorious, fresh, young beauty? How could he even eat? Still, they must be properly nourished. To begin, naturally the famous *filetto Carpaccio* and then the green *tagliarini gratinati*, the noodles blended so suavely with cream and cheese and after, perhaps the calves liver in tiny strips *alla veneziana* served of course with polenta and for dessert—he would wait to decide on their dessert until after they had started on the liver. Sometimes tourists skipped dessert.

"Thank you so much for a lovely evening," said Daisy in a small, precise voice, outside the door to her room at the Gritti Palace.

"Ah . . . I enjoyed it, too," North answered. "That's the right response, isn't it?" He willed her to look directly at him, to meet his gaze, but she kept her eyes demurely downcast.

"No, you should have said that you hoped you'd see me again and asked if you might telephone when we get back to the city."

"Can I?"

"*May* I," Daisy corrected him.

"May I come in?" asked North.

"No, you may call me."

"But I said, 'May I come in?' " North repeated.

"Oh, well, yes, in that case do call."

Impatiently, he put one finger under her chin and tipped her head up toward him, but she lowered her lids and continued to avoid his glance. "There's a phone strike—so how can I call you?" North asked.

"True. But you could knock on my door," Daisy said, vamping for time.

"I said, 'May I come in?' " he repeated urgently.

"Why?"

"Just because . . ." His face had lost its sharpness in the dim light of the corridor. His stance retained its swagger, his toughness still proclaimed itself in the set of his shoulders, but the familiar North air of indomitable willfulness, of battle readiness had softened, as if the moonlight had begun to wash it away.

"Oh, well . . . in that case . . . I guess so," Daisy said, opening the door with her key.

"It's only reasonable," he assured her.

"Reasonable?"

"Stop questioning everything I say."

"Stop telling me what to do," Daisy countered.

"Right." North took her in his arms and bent down to her lips. "From now on I'll order you."

"How will I know the difference?" Daisy asked in a panic, leaning away from him.

"You'll figure it out."

"Wait!"

"Why?"

"I'm not sure that this is a good idea."

"I'm the one who has the ideas . . . and this is a natural." He picked her up and carried her to the bed as wide as a barge. "You, Daisy, are the detail person—I'm involved in the larger creative effort." He kissed her, holding her head between both of his hands.

"North?" she said, pushing herself up on the pillows.

"Huh?" he answered, busily coaxing the crystal straps from her shoulders.

"Is this a mistake?"

"I don't think so, but we have to make it to find out . . . oh, oh you never told me you tasted so good."

"You never asked."

"My mistake."

There was awe in his voice as he murmured. "Where have you been hiding all these years?" a note Daisy had never heard from this man whose terse, rapid commands had been the whip that drove her on. He, who had always crackled with combative directions, touched the tips of her breasts as carefully and reverently as an archaeologist, amazed and moved by the discovery of a long buried statue of Venus. His sharp features were blunted by the light reflected from the Grand Canal, and through her half-closed eyes she searched for the harsh and contained fire of the man she knew. But all his hard edges seemed to have melted as he was transformed into a tender, laughing, unknown lover, who covered her with long, sweet, almost thoughtful kisses as he slid his hands down to her waist and took possession of the warm, supple curve where her hips began and pulled her closer to him so that they lay face to face.

"May I?" he murmured, waiting until she nodded before he undressed her and then took off his own clothes and stood looking down at her with a smile of revelation on his lips, his naked body finer than she would have imagined it . . . and now she knew that she *had* imagined it, perhaps since she had first seen him. The turmoil of this sudden knowledge made her pull him down to her and finally dare to kiss his pointed nose and his eyes and his ears and his cheeks, all the surfaces she had watched so anxiously for years, trying to anticipate his orders, always tense with the necessity of keeping up with his frenzied pace, of being ready to supply whatever he needed. Abruptly, in their nakedness, they were equal, and under her lips there was only a warmth and this new, dear proximity. In a rush of prodigious pleasure Daisy thought, but he *likes* me, he approves of me, I'm a human being to him, he must truly care. She opened her arms wide with surprise and flung them around his neck, pressing herself close, as close as possible, trying to keep him there in the compass of her arms so that he wouldn't change back to the North she had known. Little by little she became convinced that this unknown lover would not vanish. As he sensed Daisy gradually yielding up her fears and her hesitations North's caresses became more firm and more insistent. He allowed himself to learn her body an inch at a time and when all protest, all holding back was long past, he parted her willing thighs, but before he entered her, he whispered again, "May I?"

"Yes, yes, yes."

"Still no change?" North asked the hall porter.

"No, Signor, I regret, nothing is happening, but we have learned that these strikes do not end as quickly as they begin. However, they do not occur often, a major strike like this, most positively, I assure you."

"Well, that's show biz," North smiled, his lean body relaxed. "Did you notice where Miss Valensky went? She's not in her room."

"Ah, the *principessa*, yes, she just left, Signor. She said she had to pay a boy who was waiting with a gypsy rowboat. At least that's what I think she said. Perhaps it was a gypsy boy. In any case, I offered to do it for her but she insisted."

"My God!" North's mouth quivered with laughter. "She really had one lined up . . . I should have known."

"Signor?"

"Nothing. I'll go find her." He walked quickly toward the entrance to the hotel and bumped into Daisy who was hurrying back in.

"You weren't trying to escape, were you?" he asked.

"Merely cutting off the last route to civilization."

"I overslept," he told her.

"So I noticed. You're very interesting to watch when you sleep. You don't look at all the way you do when you're awake."

"How do I look?" he asked, warily.

"It's how you *don't* look—no turbulence, no truculence, no irascibility, no sound and fury, no invulnerability, no . . ."

"You're taking advantage of me," he said, trying to cut her off.

"Oh, I hope so! I've always wanted to—it's been one of my heart's desires. In matters of this sort I find that it's always best to be the first one awake."

"How much do you know about matters of this sort?" he barked.

"I don't know you nearly well enough to tell you," she said airily, smiling at him at the same time with an insolent light in her eyes. He seized her by the scruff of the neck, to the discreet delight of the entire lobby staff, and dragged her over to a window.

"Let me get a look at you, damn you. How can I see into your eyes when they're so black?"

"You can't possibly," she said triumphantly, her dark gold eyebrows forming a straight line. "But as for you, you poor, transparent, red-headed, blue-eyed man, I can look right straight into your brain and out the other side!"

"Bullshit. Nobody looks into my brain."

"Wanna bet?"

"Not before breakfast," he said hastily. "Anyway, haven't you got better things to think about? Do you realize you haven't done any sightseeing yet, outside of Harry's Bar?"

"And the ceiling of Room Fifteen at the Gritti Palace . . . dimly," she added with a reminiscent grin that made him shake her again.

"Let's grab breakfast and go walking."

"I've had breakfast, but I'll watch you eat," Daisy announced graciously.

"Why do I have this strange feeling that you think you're smarter than I am?" North grumbled.

"That's the sort of question you must search your soul to answer." Daisy laughed.

"See, you're doing it again!"

Daisy and North felt as if the fabric of the world had been whisked aside and another, alternative world presented in a sumptuously tarnished cornucopia of unforeseen pleasures, as if, during the march of centuries, Venice had been waiting confidently just for them. They found themselves miraculously stripped of those defensive postures that had passed for character, and turned into wondering children. Everyone, from the shopkeepers to the cats in the narrow *calles*, was an accomplice, locked willingly together into this sea-bound relic, this most sensuous city on earth. Their sense of life, strong, blood-hot and buoyant, had never been so focused on each individual moment as it was in this generously proffered world in which the familiar concepts of time and space and light had all been washed by the patient sorcery of centuries into something better than either of them had ever known.

A dark church, illuminated in an unexpected corner by a masterpiece, a wicker table at a café, an arched bridge over a canal, a barking dog, the rose-orange-lavender façades of faded, still-regal palazzos, the regular tolling of the bells in the Campanile at dusk, a hamburger of Florentine beef, the Viennese waltzes played at Quadri's, or the glimpse of a courtyard garden in which old roses still bloomed in the Campo San Barnaba, all mingled together in one blissful dream as they walked and ate and talked and made love, waking each morning with the fear that the strike might be over, a fear immediately banished by the sight of the Grand Canal on which only private boats and market barges could be seen.

Making love with North had finally taught Daisy what it meant to truly desire a man and be fulfilled physically by him. But, as the nights passed, drugged with pleasure, Daisy realized that in a way he seemed to be unaware of, she was still holding back. That caged *thing* in her heart that begged to be liberated, that thing that craved and yearned to be dissolved, to achieve a release beyond the physical, still held tight, taut and unbending even when they were closest to each other. She ached for it—whatever *it* was—to burst into flame within her, and still it remained solidly locked behind bars of reserve. North, she thought, had yielded up to her his cantankerous, difficult and abrupt exterior and brought forth moments of incandescence, yet, try as she would, Daisy still knew him, as she had always known him, as an opponent, beloved now, but an opponent, even during these days carved out of time.

Was it North's essential nature, his essential apartness that did not yet permit her to sense the full merging with another that she had always sought? She asked herself what it was in him or in her that wouldn't permit her to surrender to absolute intimacy. Just as Daisy had somehow felt an impostor when she was being treated as a princess, she wondered if she and North were, in some way, impostors when they treated each other as lovers? Perhaps, she told herself, it was just too soon, perhaps the leap they had made had been too quick, jumping from a working relationship of many years to becoming lovers after only a few hours of unexpected flirtation.

Daisy was troubled by something indefinable in the new way they acted with each other, something that rang with a note of the illusory, the temporary, something that might be dissipated by a minor incident. As she drifted off to sleep she thought that perhaps it was always this way at first. Perhaps, later, there would be more. But if there were not more, was this enough?

Yet, as one day followed another, Daisy felt herself like a field of flowers on a summer afternoon, buzzing and humming with the busy sound of happiness. She wondered what she and North were creating together. Was it just a few days in another time frame? She had known him so well in his movements of command, and of watchfulness, known his favorite words and catch phrases, his gestures and expressions. Now she knew him as the first man who taught her body true passion. But what did they know of each other on a more profound level, a level of deep and continuous connection? Did he want that knowledge? Did she?

In their conversations there was a hint of expectation, of restless waiting, as during the chatter that precedes the raising of the curtain at the theater. Yet, it was clear to her that the time hadn't come to speak of any of her closely kept secrets . . . perhaps it would come tomorrow, or the day after . . . or never. Perhaps it should not be something she longed for, perhaps these secrets were meant to stay hidden—she didn't know. She couldn't judge, and present joys prevented her from giving the subject more than a thought or two, before sleeping.

It always seemed, in their private weather, to be either the first best day of spring, that day on which people finally realize that spring really *is* in the air, or else that day just before they say with a disappointed sigh, "Oh, but it's summer already." They were living an idyll trembling on the brink of becoming—Daisy couldn't complete the idea, nor could she share it with North. The fragility, the evanescence of passion had become evident to her almost as soon as she first experienced it.

There were, during that week, an infinite number of harmonies in her beauty. Venice inspired her to meet its fantasy with her own, to finally wear the Norman Hartnell dress designed during the last years of the twenties, a dress that she had never quite dared to put on in New York, a "picture frock" as it had been called, with a pink chiffon bodice under an orchid taffeta surplice above a skirt of pale blue taffeta with a hem thickly bordered with hand-painted flowers. During the day in her sailor pants and rugby shirts, she weighted her wrists with barbaric bracelets, bought for three dollars, but at night her hair was entwined with fresh flowers.

As the sun, constantly reflected from the water, turned North's freckles darker and his blue eyes bluer, it tinted Daisy's warm color with a light copper glaze that contrasted so strongly with her hair that people openly pointed to her in the streets.

Although Daisy and North ate lunch in any convenient trattoria during their daytime rambles, they always had dinner at Harry's Bar, which instantly becomes a club to anyone who has been there twice. There were other tourists, of course, but they were far outnumbered by true Venetians who, since 1931, have stopped by Harry's at least once a day to find out what is new in the world, that, to them, is simply and entirely Venice, Venetians who possessed a cool lacquered elegance which belongs to an ancient race who have learned that everything must be treated as a surface.

One night, a week after they had arrived, Daisy spilled the salt on the pink tablecloth. Both she and North reached for it and simultaneously flung a pinch over their shoulders.

"You realize that's just superstition?" North asked.

"Of course. It's not as if anything bad would happen if we didn't." They both knocked on the wood of their chairs quickly and automatically.

"A pure atavism," North assured her.

"A primitive ritual," Daisy agreed.

"If there isn't any wood around, you're allowed to knock on your head—it counts," he offered. "Or use mine."

"Oh, I know. But you mustn't wait longer than three seconds."

"I walk under ladders," North said, with the air of one who knows more than he tells.

"I never even *think* about broken mirrors," Daisy countered. "Or hats on the bed or whistling in dressing rooms or black cats."

"*Only* salt and wood?" he asked skeptically.

"And wishing on the first star at night. You can wish on the new moon too, but only if you happen to see it over your left shoulder without planning to."

"I didn't know that."

"It's a very important one," Daisy said wisely, tweaking a lock of his red hair. "And you can wish on a plane, too, if you really think it's a star, but only as long as you're in a car moving in the same direction as the plane."

"I'll remember that," North said with rue in his voice, the wistfulness of falling leaves, a sad, autumnal tone he'd never used before.

"What's wrong?" she asked.

"Absolutely nothing. Everything's perfect."

"Yes . . . I know what you mean." Daisy was thoughtful. "It is a problem."

The next morning while they were still asleep, the phone by the bed rang.

"You didn't leave a wake-up call, babe, did you?" North muttered, confusedly, after the phone had rung several times, dragging them both from their dreams.

"No, no," Daisy sighed, reaching with acrid resignation for the insistent phone.

"Don't answer it!" He put his hand tightly over hers.

"North . . . you know what it must mean," Daisy said urgently.

"Leave it! We can have one more day." She listened carefully to his voice, torn between the honest urge to shut out the world and his instant inescapable response to the continuing summons of the phone. Daisy evaluated what she heard and picked up the receiver while she smiled at him with love, regret and understanding, so mingled that they formed one cloud of feeling, so bittersweet that her voice trembled.

"Hello Arnie. No, no, you didn't wake me—I had to get up to answer the phone."

19

Sarah Fane, in Ram's considered opinion, was both more and less than he had hoped she would be when he had acted on his decision to investigate her as a candidate for marriage, months ago in the early spring of 1976. She pleased him rather better than he thought she had any right to, since she did not fulfill all his requirements for a wife. True, she had been most carefully brought up and she was accustomed to holding her own in the great world as she had seen it, as a future debutante, in its country hunting-fishing-shooting manifestations. In this he found her irreproachable, neither too sophisticated nor too provincial. Yet, according to Ram's calculations, according to any reasonable analysis of what any woman, much less a young girl, could hope for from the attentions of an excessively eligible bachelor such as he, she should have been prepared to adore him, as Miss Fane, the Honorable Miss Fane, did not. At least not visibly.

She was a flirt. A damned hard, cold, calculating flirt. And she was a beauty, a damned hard, cold, ravishing blonde beauty of the kind that has always been known as the "English Rose," a kind whose unblemished perfection of feature, whose dainty pink-and-white coloring, whose lovely lips and candid eyes, has caused many a man to curse the falseness of the sweet exterior that concealed a temperament and a will worthy of Queen Victoria. Ram wondered how he could ever have suspected that Sarah Fane had intended to skip the Season. She was going to have it *all*, not just Queen Charlotte's Birthday Ball, dressed in her long white gown and long white gloves, but Royal Ascot and Henley as well. She was invited to every important private dance that would be given from May to July, and there would be six hundred guests at her own dinner dance in July. After the dancing season was over, she had planned to go to Goodwood for Race Week, Cowes for the Regatta, and Dublin for the International Horse Show. When Ram pointed out that Cowes Week and the Dublin Show overlapped by several days, she only smiled beautifully and explained how she intended to attend almost three-quarters of each celebration by leaving the Isle of Wight for Ireland right after the Royal Yacht Squadron's Ball. "It would be a pity to miss Dublin, Ram, now that my parents have finally admitted that I'm old enough to go," she said with a ravishing smile which Ram only wished he could say was too practiced, a smile he had to admit was both innocent and unspoiled. Her prettiness was of the kind which would never slide into mere decorativeness but rather would grow greatly distinguished as she aged—and she even knew *that*.

Sarah Fane's last three years had been spent at the Villa Brillantmont, the Lausanne finishing school which still provides a rapidly vanishing minority of upper-class girls with a polished education, excellent French and friends culled from the richest families around the world. As far as Ram was concerned, its chief function had been to serve as a quarantine that kept Sarah from being overexposed to London.

Brillantmont had confirmed Sarah's opinion that almost all girls fell into two categories: those who wanted to get out of school and find some exciting, glamorous job, and those who wanted only to free themselves of chaperones as soon as possible and enter into a giddy whirl of romantic adventure. Both categories she judged were equally self-deluding. However, she was delighted that they didn't understand, as clearly as she did, that the first step in any future life was the right marriage. For some it could be merely an acceptable marriage, for others a good marriage. For herself she contemplated only the *exceptional* marriage, even taking into account the fact that in any given year only a few exceptional marriages were made. She added up her assets, without false modesty, and decided that she was entitled to the very best.

Sarah Fane despised the relative poverty she saw gradually enveloping the English upper classes. She felt personally offended by the fact that she'd been born into a society that had virtually undergone a bloodless revolution, a socialist society with the name of a monarchy.

But, she reminded herself, there was no point in being petulant. The 1970s wouldn't go away because she found them odious. The trick was to evade them, to escape them, to ensure a life that would come as close as possible to being the life she *should* have led by right.

From Brillantmont, Sarah had closely observed the elaborate cotillion of each London Season as she waited for her year to come. She had concluded that the best marriages were those made during a girl's first year out, while she was still a novelty. The expression "post-deb" actually made her feel a pang of revulsion—could there be anything more bedraggled? *Timing.* Timing was the secret, she thought as she sat at her desk, going over the guest list for her ball. She put down her pen to add up the months. She had the entire spring and summer of 1976, lasting through September if she went north for the great Scottish balls. Then, of course, to London for the Little Season which continued until Christmas. After that came the exodus to country houses. With the coming of the spring of 1977, the focus of the year would change and it would begin to belong to the next crop of girls who would be coming out. So a mere nine or ten months, in reality, were all that existed of the best part of her debutante year.

That increasingly rare and elusive species, the eligible English bachelor, with great wealth and solid background, often waited until they were well into their early forties before they were brought to the altar. Some, too many, never married. No fools they, she thought, tightening her dainty pink lips over her faultless teeth in a momentary grimace. They never went out of style: a man could be sixty-five, ugly, bad tempered and boring and he was still a catch if he had a good position in the world. As for the bachelors who were distinguished chiefly by the fact that they were someone's heir, they wouldn't do for her at all, living, as they did, on overdrafts and expectations. Nor was she attracted by those possessors of ancient names who formed syndicates to open flashy new restaurants or discotheques. The young lord as a saloon keeper struck Sarah Fane as an unacceptable prospect, quite as bad as those who, for financial reasons, became photographers or film producers and pretended it was merely a whimsical lark. In her eyes this substantially diminished their value, even if they enjoyed worldly success. Nor would she be happy as the chatelaine of a great house who had to allow the public to come in and look around, at so much a head, in order to keep the roof in repair. A mug's game, that. Why be a Marchioness if you had to run a roadside attraction?

How did she feel about Ram Valensky, Sarah asked herself, pushing the list aside? Ever since he had invited himself to visit for a weekend, he had shown certain signs of becoming attached, although never quite enough for her to consider him as a declared suitor. He had been one of the great catches of the country for seven or eight years now, and, so far, he had easily resisted capture. He was certainly handsome, in his steely, slim, aristocratic way, with those intelligent gray eyes which looked at her with keen interest yet cool appraisal.

She couldn't help but enjoy seeing herself reflected in all her immaculate prettiness in the expression of measured approbation on his dark, aquiline face. He had just enough grave, quiet distinction; he approached life in a way she shared—he, too, felt a desire to get the best out of what was left to people of their kind. She liked the way he held his shotgun, at a lazily alert angle, neither too tensely nor too casually. He danced adequately for a man who didn't like to dance, and he rode superbly. And he was a great gentleman. Of course he didn't have a sense of humor, but humorless people were easier to deal with in the long run. Sarah Fane had little tolerance or need for humor.

From a purely objective point of view, and Sarah Fane was nothing if not objective, there were a great many things right about Ram. His age was ideal: at thirty-two a man was ready to settle down. From her father's grunts and offhand remarks, she judged that his fortune, the vastness of which was so often the subject of speculation and rumor, must be remarkably solid. Sarah had great respect for her father's money sense, and he was as closely informed as it was possible to be about Ram's financial position since they did a great deal of business together. Her mother was the genealogical expert in the family and she had indicated in her vague but fully conversant way that Valensky, while not an English name, was quite good enough, joined as it was to the Woodhill side of the family. A trifle unorthodox perhaps, but quite sound, and indeed one mustn't be stuffy, especially since his father Stash Valensky had flown with her father during the war. Her mother wouldn't have said anything more approving if she had been discussing the heir to the throne. In fact, she had even been known to sniff at the House of Windsor, when she had a genealogical rampage going. And how fortunate it was that his father was dead. With Ram, one knew exactly where one stood in respect to those death duties which could hang over other eligible prospects indefinitely.

She didn't know about Ram's sensuality, Sarah Fane reflected absently. She had always reserved sensuality for some time in the future. She feared and respected the powers of sensuality, thinking of it as a priceless coin in the game of life which should never be played unless it were the very last coin you spent in order to ensure the future. Sensuality, poorly handled, was clearly responsible for bad marriages. Thank God her sensuality was no problem and never had been. In her opinion, uncontrolled sensuality was for people who couldn't afford luxuries.

Ram Valensky was quite possibly her best shot, Sarah Fane decided. Hers and that of every other girl who was hoping to marry as well as she intended to. But he was far from a sitting duck. He behaved more like an inquisitive, measure-taking eagle. As she thought that, she decided definitely not to ask him to be her escort at Queen Charlotte's Ball. She knew that he expected to be asked, as he had been asked year after year by other hopeful girls. A marvelously guileless expression spread over her pure features and lit her lovely, clear blue eyes as she imagined Ram's reaction to being excluded from the first important event of her year. It was the best idea she'd had all morning, she told herself, and returned to her guest lists with renewed zest.

Reluctantly, in spite of his well-concealed rage, Ram began to respect Sarah Fane. He suspected every move she made, but nothing she did or said ever betrayed the glacier-hard calculation of her maneuvers.

Her manner toward him was admirable. Instead of the melting and preening he had every right to expect from a young and inexperienced girl to whom attention was being paid by a man of his stature and desirability, she presented an unwavering picture of placid, sunny charm. She almost, but not quite, treated him as just a friend of her father's, younger than the others but still not inordinately interesting to her. She thanked him for his flowers on a note of gratitude that indicated precisely that they were far from the only flowers she had received that day, yet her thanks never dipped into the perfunctory. She let him take her to the theater and to restaurants almost as often as he asked, but somehow other couples always joined them so that he was never alone with her. "But Ram, dear, it's always like this during the Season—you know that," she lightly reproached him on the solitary occasion on which he protested that he did not enjoy being part of an eternal crowd. After that, he accepted the flock of young people with whom she was surrounded without any sign of impatience. I know her game, he thought, as she teased some young man with one of her classic smiles or delicious pouts, but he found himself wondering more and more if he really did. Ram decided it was advisable to be seen with other young women: there were many he took out or served as escort to during the months of the Season, treating them with the same, exactly the same, careful, restrained, lordly gallantry as he did Sarah.

The Honorable Sarah Fane was having a splendid Season. All the magazines and newspapers agreed that she was among the most beautiful debutantes of the year and her name was proposed as a possible bride for Prince Charles, despite the fact that he favored her with no more—and no less—notice than he did other young ladies. However, finding brides for Prince Charles was a permanent national pastime. April and May passed and June came, with no change in Sarah's bright, serene attitude, as she continued to float through a series of parties and dances, always faultlessly dressed in clothes chosen to play against her pink-and-white beauty. Rather than the obvious pastels, that were almost mandatory for debs, she leaned toward deep dusty blues and rich emerald greens, severely cut, never too sophisticated gowns above which white shoulders gleamed with a special distinction. She never mentioned to Ram the almost unending parties to which she was invited, unless, as she did occasionally, she asked him to go with her. Her bland reticence was more infuriating than any amount of information would have been. He waited for her to boast and he waited in vain. He waited for her to mention the other girls he saw, and again he waited in vain. She was a formidable adversary, he finally admitted to himself. He would have preferred to have found the proper wife embodied in someone less sure of herself, and yet he was flattered to think that his choice, now that it had been made, was of an exceptional young woman. It began to seem inevitable that, rather than some unformed girl who would have fallen automatically into his hands, he should have picked a girl who knew her own worth and disdained to sell herself cheaply.

Fane Hall was the scene of Sarah's own dance, catered by the venerable firm of Searcy Tansley, a dinner dance under a series of elaborate tents, flung out from all sides of the rosy, Tudor grandeur of the great house. A number of young people had been invited to spend the night at Fane Hall and the other guests, unless they drove back to London, were all to be accommodated at the homes of various neighbors. The entire proceedings were almost as complicated and detailed as in the planning of a coronation, Sarah observed with a merry laugh, as if they had nothing to do with her. Hers was to be the sort of party that was rarely held in the straitened, stingy 1970s, a party that was a comforting throwback to the good old days. The Fanes could afford it, people thought to themselves, and added another layer of respect for Sarah to her already glowing aura.

The date was the first weekend in July, 1976, after all the university and university-entrance exams were over, and it would mark the beginning of the very height of the Season, as all of England's wellborn youths were freed from the prison of academia.

Sarah ruled over her ball in a strapless gown of white silk, tied with satin ribbons below her breasts, at her waist, with more ribbons twice restraining the enormously full skirt, so that it fell in three billowing tiers. She wore her grandmother's tiara on her neat, lovely head; she wore a smile that was as kind and pleased and unaffected for a duke as it was for another debutante; she wore an air of being a living part of a great tradition of aristocracy without stiffness or self-consciousness; she wore her flawless prettiness as if she were so accustomed to it that nothing could ever fade or diminish it. As any debutante is, she was the queen of her own ball, but there was something in the air which tipped her reign over into the realm of the legendary, something that told everyone there that Sarah Fane's ball would go down in the history of great debuts. She reached a summit that night as she danced with more than two hundred men, whirling and whirling with tireless grace, never faltering in her command of the occasion. Ram was able only to capture her for a moment or two and he spent the evening dancing with many other girls, observed favorably by mothers and daughters alike. He was almost tempted, that night, to propose to her, but he held back. On a night of such victory, such self-importance, he estimated that his proposal would not be accorded the total value it should be given. It would be just too much icing on the cake for Sarah Fane . . . he'd let her have the run of her Season. It would do her good to wonder for a few months more why he continued to favor her with his attention and still said nothing.

"Just give me a for-instance," Kiki invited. It was a Sunday morning in Luke's apartment, specifically in Luke's bed, and she really didn't want a for-instance, she wanted Luke to kiss her again. Luke kissed her again.

"For instance," he said, "Christ, you're never as delicious as you are in the morning *before* you've brushed your teeth . . . 'morning mouth,' I *love* it! And then you look at the camera with those big pussycat eyes and that foxy focused sensuality around your nose and lips, and we hear your voice off camera saying, 'What man wants to kiss the smell of mint the minute he wakes up? A little Scope the night before . . . that's *my* secret.' And then I kiss you again, like this, and I say, 'Yum, yum . . . don't you dare get out of bed.' "

"But that's terrific! Why can't you use it?" Kiki asked. "It even makes *me* want to buy Scope so it must be a good idea."

"It's a great idea but it could never get on the air. The sponsor doesn't want animal sexuality, the network won't allow it, the public would be shocked. Also it probably isn't true and we have to worry about truth in advertising."

"Do you mean I should brush my teeth?" Kiki said, worried.

"No, darling idiot, only that not every man may be queer for morning mouth, the way I am." He kissed her again. "You can't claim that Scope works all night long, and if you have two people in bed, one of them must be suffering from acid indigestion or stuffed sinuses and the other should be Florence Nightingale, not a couple of happy lovers who obviously just woke up—America's not ready for that."

"But it's real," Kiki protested.

" 'Real' isn't why we make commercials. If we wanted 'real' we'd do documentaries," he mumbled, kissing her under her arm. "I think I like morning armpit more than even morning mouth."

"Give me another for-instance," Kiki purred.

"There's this one woman and she says, straight to camera, 'I *hate* Howard Cosell!' And then there's another and another until you have the screen split sixteen ways, all types of women all saying, with increasing hysteria, 'I hate Howard Cosell!' And then you hear a voice over—a calm woman's voice saying, 'Monday-Night Football getting to you? Try Bufferin. It won't make *him* shut up, but *you'll* feel better.' "

"Now, what's wrong with that? You're not saying anything that isn't true."

"No, but Howard Cosell just might have grounds for legal action, and the network wouldn't run it during the game which is the only time it could play to maximum effectiveness, and all the Howard Cosell fans would never buy Bufferin again."

"Are there Howard Cosell fans?"

"I've never met one, but it figures," Luke said morosely.

"But what if you hired Howard Cosell to say, 'Try Bufferin—it won't make *me* shut up but *you'll* feel better'?" Kiki wondered. "I bet he'd do it—he's probably dying to be a spokesperson like Don Meredith and Frank what's-his-name."

"Kiki," Luke said, almost sitting up in excitement, "I think we've just stolen the Bufferin account!"

"Come back here," Kiki ordered. "It's Sunday—you can't snatch accounts on Sunday." Luke settled back under the covers and continued his list of dream commercials.

"I've also got a great one for Tampax. You get someone like Katharine Hepburn or Bette Davis, an authority figure with total moxie, and you just shoot her straight, and she's saying something like, 'If women didn't menstruate there wouldn't be any human race at all so why don't we stop being so coy about it and realize what a marvelous thing it is that women have ovaries that release an egg each month and that since they do, it's only sensible to use Tampax when the egg isn't fertilized, because Tampax is comfortable and does the job.' "

"Hmmm," said Kiki.

"Yeah, you see, even *you're* shocked. Women don't have menstrual periods or ovaries or vaginas or any of their equipment on television—except in the soap operas when they're always taking out everything in the hospital—hysterectomy city—it's the biggest fucking taboo—even if you can discuss it in detail on a soap, you have to use little hints like 'difficult days' in a commercial. We're the last bastion of the Puritan fathers."

"Poor sweetheart—you must be so frustrated."

"Sometimes I am, but generally I just forget what I'd like to do and do what I can as well as possible. It's a living," he grumbled.

Kiki flung her arms around Luke and held him as tightly as she could. "Listen, it's more than just a living, you dope. Don't you ever realize that without advertising there wouldn't be any newspapers or magazines or televisions except whatever the government paid for? Advertising is what supports all that information and entertainment, so don't get all snooty about it. You do a job that has to be done and you do it better than anyone else!"

"I'd forgotten that I was talking to a native-born capitalist," Luke laughed. "I'm so used to girls who put down advertising that it's a pleasure to hear from the delegate from Grosse Pointe."

Kiki, who already had him firmly in her grasp, tried to shake him, but he was too big for her to move satisfactorily, so she contented herself with hissing, "No gratitude. No class. No taste. To even *mention* other girls at a time like this—I'm getting out of bed, Luke Hammerstein, you goat."

"Ah, don't—I'm sorry, I was just kidding, honest."

"I have to pee," she said haughtily.

"How about this? This great-looking girl, beautifully dressed in the height of fashion, says, 'Excuse me, but I really have to pee,' and the other beautiful girl—they're having lunch at La Grenouille—says, 'What toilet paper do you prefer?' and the first one says, 'Lady Scott of course, because even the best people have to pee—so you might as well do it in style.' "

"Brilliant," Kiki sneered, "I think you should be teaching English at Harvard. Your mind is sick, Luke Hammerstein, *sick*."

"Just because I mentioned Grosse Pointe?" he said wickedly.

"Go fuck yourself!" Kiki said angrily.

"Not while you're around."

"I suppose I'm to take that as a compliment?" she huffed.

"Damn right. Now will you go pee and make it snappy. And don't brush your teeth while you're in there!" He stretched lazily and happily in bed. There was only one problem on his mind. Bagels, cream cheese and smoked salmon first and fucking later, or fucking first and bagels after? Even Maimonides wouldn't be able to decide that one.

"What's it all about, Theseus?" Daisy asked her dog, scratching his ears in a way which he particularly enjoyed. "Just tell me what's it's all about."

"If I weren't here," said Kiki, "I'd understand your asking him, but since this great wisewoman is available, I'm rather offended."

"I thought you were too busy changing your nail polish to talk."

"One thing has nothing to do with another." Kiki bent over her hands rapidly, using polish remover on the deep red, almost brown polish she had been affecting recently. "How many manicurists are tongue-tied?"

"I've never been to one—how would I know? I thought maybe they operated in holy silence."

"Wash your own hair, do your own nails—no wonder you have to ask a dog for advice," Kiki snorted.

"How can I talk to you?" Daisy said reasonably. "You're so happy and excited that you can't possibly be intelligent. You see everything through the eyes of true love, than which there is nothing so distorted . . . your perceptual apparatus is anesthetized, your judgmental functioning is paralyzed, your free will has been taken away from you and you're operating on a set of premises which no one in this world understands but you—at least Theseus isn't in love."

"Ever since you came back from Venice," Kiki said, thinking out loud, "—it's November now, so that means two months ago—you haven't been yourself. My perceptual apparatus, as you see, is as sharp as ever, as long as you don't ask me about Luke. You're semi-miserable, semi-demi-tormented, mini-pleased with yourself, major-mini-yearning of a somewhat sentimental nature toward North. Why didn't you ask me before you got involved with the man you work for?"

"There was a phone strike," Daisy reminded her.

"Excuses, excuses. What is the exact status of the relationship, if I may use such a word about something so sacred?"

"Shifty," said Daisy.

"A *shifty* relationship? You mean there's something not kosher about it, something sinister?"

"Oh, God, Kiki, you've missed the point again. Shifty like the wind blowing from the east and then blowing from the west, shifty like the mist forming and then dissipating and then coming back, shifty like I don't know which way is up, quick-sand-type shifty."

Kiki glanced sharply at Daisy. She had lost weight, Kiki thought, which she certainly didn't need to lose, and her temper had suffered, not that she was ever bitchy, but she was strung very tightly these days, and she spent too much time grooming Theseus and taking him for runs around the neighborhood and too little time with North, in Kiki's opinion.

"Could you be more specific?" Kiki asked, unwrapping a new bottle of pale pink polish and beginning to apply it.

"It's hard to point to any one particular thing. When we got back, I knew that everything had to change. After all, the circumstances in Venice were totally abnormal—I don't think North's had that much time off in his life before. And, of course, I was right—everything piled up afterward and we had to work twice as hard as usual to make up for the week we'd lost, but I understand that—I'm part of it, hell, without me they couldn't have done it. And the working together felt good. He treated me the same as he always had in front of the others—I certainly don't want Nick and Wingo and the rest to be leering at us—and when we were alone he's . . . fun . . . and he wants me physically . . . and he's loving . . . I guess . . ."

"But . . ." Kiki prodded.

"But . . . that's as far as it's gone."

"I don't see how that makes it shifty."

"It's something in the *way* he's loving, something that doesn't firm up, something that isn't going anywhere, something hanging, incomplete, something unconsolidated, something tentative . . ."

"Is it in you or is it in him?" Kiki asked shrewdly. Daisy stopped fluffing up an unfluffable Theseus and considered the question as if it hadn't occurred to her before.

"I think—in both of us, now that you ask," she said slowly, sounding surprised.

"Then you really can't complain. No, I take that back, you *can* complain! If you can't complain to me, what kind of friend am I? So go on, complain!"

Daisy cocked a loving eye at Kiki who, now that she noticed, was looking very strange. Her ruffle of hair was brushed neatly down around her face and even her bangs had been arranged to fall quite calmly across her forehead. Her eyes looked two sizes smaller without the exaggerated make-up she always used on them. She had on just a touch of mascara, and her lipstick matched her nails. Her gypsy quality was minimal, replaced by a subdued, quiet, well-kept, and somehow diminished manner, as she sat there in her underwear waiting for her nails to dry. Which was also strange. Since when had Kiki taken to wearing half-slips and bras?

"Go on. I won't be satisfied, if you don't complain now," Kiki urged again.

"I have this feeling inside . . ."

"Yes? Oh, come on Daisy. I'm good with feelings."

"It's—I keep wondering if there hadn't been that strike, would anything have ever happened? Wasn't it maybe just the circumstances? We'd never even flirted before and I've worked for North for more than four years—If there *was* anything there before Venice I would have known it, wouldn't I? Maybe it's just one of those things?"

"That's not a complaint and that's not a feeling—that's just a quibble. It *did* happen and it's still going on. If he'd been stuck in Venice with someone he didn't care for, nothing would have happened at all—right?"

"I suppose. On the other hand, in that magical atmosphere almost anyone might have looked good to him."

"Daisy! Stop that at once!" Kiki was outraged at her friend. Even after years of experience, she still couldn't believe that anyone so beautiful could poor-mouth herself like Daisy Valensky.

"You're right—I'm doing it again, shit! But there was something just the other day that I can't get out of my mind. We were lying around North's place, we'd just made love and I was lying there, just wanting to be petted and hugged, you know—held—and he moved away, restlessly, and he said in this sort of remote, lazy voice—not bored exactly—well maybe just a little—and he said, 'Daisy, amuse me.' "

"That *asshole!*"

"That's exactly what I thought! I don't plan to see him again, except at work."

The two girls' eyes met, each understanding the other perfectly.

"But what did you say next?" Kiki asked hotly.

"Nothing . . . I felt sick. I just got up and put on my clothes and came right home."

"Why didn't you tell me right away?"

"First I thought I was making too much out of it, being oversensitive or humorless about it—it was just a *little* thing," Daisy said broodingly.

"Yeah, and it's the little things like that you have to pay close attention to—those little things get you where you live and they show you where *he* lives," Kiki said, smearing her polish in agitation. "Making 'too much' out of his talking to you as if you were some sort of amusing convenience? A harem girl, a popsie, a toy doll you can wind up and have it play a funny little tune? No wonder North's been divorced twice—that son-of-a-bitch doesn't know shit about women." Kiki's heart sank for Daisy.

"Listen, not to change the subject, but isn't Luke coming for you in five minutes? You don't even have all your make-up on yet, or even your dress. You'll be late."

Startled, Kiki reached into her closet and came out with a plastic garment bag from Saks. She opened it and deftly slipped into a simple, conservative and expensive dress in creamy off-white flannel with a belt of braided navy and cream-colored leather. She put her stockinged feet into demure navy pumps, closed at the heel and toe, and clasped a modest strand of pearls around her neck. She turned and looked defiantly at Daisy.

"What's *that?*" Daisy said, in disbelief.

"Mollie Parnis," Kiki rapped out.

"You're not ready to go out?" Daisy asked. She'd seen Kiki in every possible variety of costumes, but this one was the most impossible to credit.

"Yes."

"Somebody died? It's a funeral?"

"No."

"It's a girl who's entering a convent and you're invited to watch?"

"No."

"You've been asked to the White House?"

"Not that either."

"A costume party and you're going as a nice girl."

"Close. Luke's taking me out to Pound Ridge . . . to meet his mother," Kiki said with a little grin.

"Praise the Lord!" Daisy shouted, jumping up so excitedly that Theseus, half-asleep, was spilled to the floor.

"And sing hallelujah!" Kiki shrieked, breaking into a triumphant little dance.

"But you can't, you simply *can't* go like that!"

"Why not? It's perfect—his mother is ultraconservative."

"Because you'll tip your hand. Who do you want to impress the most, Luke or his mother? If you dress like that, he'll know you're trying to get his mother's approval and that's *fatal* with a guy as cool and hip as Luke. You've got to look as if this isn't any big deal. Don't disguise yourself as a fiancée before he's even asked you to marry him, for heaven's sake. Oh, dumb, dumb . . . the Grosse Pointe has surfaced. He'll laugh himself sick."

"Oh fuck—you're absolutely right," Kiki wailed. "But what *am* I going to wear? I haven't got anything even vaguely appropriate." She was a study in dismay, plunging clumsily into her closet and throwing one outrageous get-up after another onto the floor in a panic.

"Pants? What about your good black crepe Holly Harp pants?" Daisy asked.

"They're covered with paint. I forgot I had them on and painted scenery in them yesterday."

"The other ones? The wools?"

"They're all at the dry cleaners. Oh, Daisy, why am I such a mess? Why does this always happen to me? He'll be here in a minute," Kiki lamented.

"Just stand still for a second." Daisy surveyed Kiki closely. "All right. Take off those pearls and your bra and your pantyhose and put the dress back on. Good, now put on your wedgies, the ones with the glitz all over and the twelve-inch cork soles. Lucky thing your legs are still tan. Now unbutton the dress to the waist. No, that's too far . . . go up two buttons. Fine—I still see tits, but only a little. Here's a belt . . ."

"Daisy, that's Theseus's collar," Kiki protested.

"Shut up and see if it goes around your waist," Daisy snapped. "Damn, too short, and it would have been perfect. Belt, belt . . ." she muttered, scrabbling through her drawers and finally pulling out a length of bright red chiffon onto which she had stitched a large 1920s diamanté buckle she'd unearthed in a thrift shop. She looked further and came up with a small red silk flower.

The doorbell rang. "Go do your eyes," Daisy ordered. "I'll entertain Luke. Don't hurry it, stay calm, keep a steady hand for God's sake," Daisy fretted, pushing Kiki into the bathroom and closing the door behind her.

Luke darted into the living room spouting greetings to Daisy and Theseus. To Daisy, who was accustomed to his usual absent-minded, dreamily remote manner, he seemed unquestionably nervous. Even his eyelids were too jumpy to be melancholy and he kept tugging at his beard and picking invisible lint off his sleeves.

"Where's Kiki?"

"Just getting ready," Daisy said with dignity.

"I suppose she's got on one of her acid-green body stockings and some sort of Mayan serape?" Luke asked.

"Something like that I imagine."

He turned away and looked out of the window, tapping his foot on the floor and drumming his fingers on the wall. "My mother hates it when I'm late," he remarked.

"She won't be long. What's happening tonight?"

"Sort of a family dinner actually. In fact, my grandmother is going to be there," he said moodily.

"A three-generation dinner, hmm?" Daisy probed.

"Also a couple of aunts and uncles who invited themselves when they heard I was coming with a girl."

"Haven't you ever brought a girl home for dinner before?" she asked, astonished.

"Not since high school." Luke gave Daisy a swift, terrified, feverishly determined glance which told her everything she needed to know.

"Excuse me for a minute, Luke, I'll just go in and see if I can persuade Kiki to hurry up," she said. On the way to the bathroom she stopped in Kiki's closet and retrieved the navy Ferragamo pumps and the navy and cream belt that Kiki had had on before. She looked consideringly at the bra and pantyhose which lay in a heap on the floor. She took the pantyhose and left the bra. No point in going overboard. She opened the bathroom door quietly. Kiki had put her eyes back on. "Take off those atrocious wedgies," said Daisy, busy unclasping the red chiffon belt and retrieving the flower.

"*What?*"

"Change of procedure. Don't ask me to explain. You don't have time. Here's your belt. Were those real pearls?"

"Of course—my mother's."

"Okay, put them back, too. Do up one more button and let me look at you. Here, brush your hair a little so it doesn't look too meek. You'll do—divinely. Here's a heavy sweater you can borrow—you don't own a decent fall coat."

"A white cashmere cardigan? Daisy, that's from before we went to college, it's from when you were a kid in London!"

"Anyone can buy a sweater, but ancient, definitely yellowing cashmere—they'll understand that."

" 'They' who?"

"Never mind. Luke's impatient to get going. No, wait . . . you still need something . . ." Daisy tucked the red silk flower in the belt. She stood back to inspect the effect. "Refined, elegant, expensive, quietly sexy and *patriotic* . . . could they ask for more?"

"I could be Jewish," Kiki said gloomily.

"They can't expect miracles."

" 'They' again—you're making me nervous," Kiki jittered, while she admired herself in the mirror.

"That's all right, too, they'll like it if you're nervous—it's only decent. Get going." Daisy pulled Kiki away from the mirror and pushed her in the direction of the living room. She heard rapid, muffled greetings and then the front door slammed behind Luke and Kiki. Slowly she walked into the empty room. Theseus was standing there with a questioning tilt to his head, one white ear up, the other down.

"You may well wonder what's going on," she told him, with a catch in her voice. "But can you answer this question? Why, oh why, can't I do for myself?"

20

What the fuck do you mean, the sponsor's coming!" North screamed into the phone. "Luke, you know as well as I do that that's impossible. The campaign's all set—why should he come now? Why should he come *ever?*"

"Listen, North, don't you get angry at me. The last person I want in any meeting is anyone from the account's side of the table, you know that," Luke said heatedly. "But it's unheard of that the man himself should insist on coming. On a small account I could begin to believe it, but the president of Supracorp? He should be a thousand miles above this sort of thing, damn it."

"Who cares if he's above or below—the point is he's taking away our freedom!" North shouted.

"North, you just think you have freedom because that's what you like to believe. Basically ain't none of us got freedom—the money is there for the sponsor to decide how to spend it. He's the one with freedom. All the freedom I have is to suggest clever ways for him to spread it around, and all the freedom you have is to make the commercials the best way you know how."

"Spare me the deep-thinking bullshit. My point is that he's gonna poke around in things he doesn't know fuck-all about and he's gonna think he's smarter than we are and even if he likes what we've got he's gonna change it just for the pleasure of meddling in something that's none of his damn business. The bastard is going slumming! Probably he's already given nervous breakdowns to everyone who works for him, so he's looking for someone new to do in—I know the type."

"You don't know Patrick Shannon."

"Do *you?*"

"No—but I've heard he's tough, rough and smart as hell."

"Perfect," North said bitterly. "Just the kind of trouble I don't want hanging around my production meetings. It's bad enough with just the two of us. More rough, tough and smart is unnecessary."

"Listen, I'm on your side. But I can't tell him he isn't welcome, can I?"

"You could try."

"You try, North. You're the one who's so free."

"I'll see you tomorrow." North hung up the phone and sat thinking about this new development. That an actual real live sponsor, that legendary hangover from the early days of radio and television, should come down from his place on Olympus and attend a commercial production meeting was an atrocity! North knew exactly where sponsors were supposed to be: they were disembodied, invisible entities, probably groups of people rather than one man, who sat somewhere up in the clouds of vast corporations, in enormous boardrooms, overlooking huge views of the Hudson and nodded yes or nodded no to advertising campaigns proposed, prepared and carried out by lesser beings.

They didn't mess with the way the machine worked, they weren't the mechanics who tended the Cadillac, but just the aloof, super-rich passengers. Somehow they managed to convey to the chauffeur the direction they wanted to take, but aside from this they had nothing to do with the running of the car. Or that's the way it should be, by God! All the sponsor had to do was decide if a program "paused" for his message, or was "presented" by him, or was made "possible" by him or merely received a "word" from him.

The idea that the sponsor should choose to reveal himself in the person of Patrick Shannon was monstrous. What abomination could it lead to? Maybe he'd like to deliver the "message" himself like those homemade used-car commercials . . . maybe Pat Shannon was another Cal Worthington. So what if the Elstree campaign was going to be a multi-million-dollar media buy—this joker, Shannon, should have the grace to let his highly paid professionals worry about it. It followed that there was no telling how deeply he'd want to be involved. He'd already broken all the rules by proposing to attend the meeting, just when Luke and the Elstree ad boys had finally agreed on a decent campaign. Nobody coming in at this point could spell anything but trouble. Major trouble.

"Daisy," he snapped into the interoffice phone. "Come in here right away." If Shannon was coming to the meeting, North wanted everyone in his organization to be there, too. Daisy'd have to be responsible for that. He had important things to attend to.

Daisy made a last survey of the large conference room. The most irregular meeting that was scheduled to begin in minutes had already caused such consternation and high irascibility that she had decided to make sure that, even if nothing else went smoothly, at least the people who would be gathered together would have enough ashtrays, pencils and carafes of ice water. It was a fortunate decision since somebody had forgotten to put out scratch paper. If people couldn't doodle in preproduction meetings they would quickly take to using their nails on each other, Daisy thought, as she rushed to tell North's secretary to provide piles of fresh white pads.

There was still a minute to spare, and Daisy went to her own office to make a final check before the mirror. All seemed to be in order. She had managed to make herself nearly invisible. Her hair had been gathered ruthlessly into one thick plait that she hid by tucking it into the roomy neck of her white work shirt and letting it hang down her back. Over the shirt she had a deliberately baggy pair of white carpenter's overalls and she had pulled a white canvas sailor hat well down over her forehead so that it effectively hid her eyes. She was satisfied that against the white bricks of the conference room, she would fade into the background.

There had been no possible way for Daisy to avoid being at the meeting, but at least she felt reasonably certain that Patrick Shannon could not possibly spot her as the woman he had met at the Shorts' dinner party in Middleburg, a woman who had, in a way that must have seemed malicious, made him very angry, so angry that she was concerned that her mere presence might add considerably to the high tempers she knew everyone else was bringing to the studio today.

Now the sound of the rising elevator told Daisy that the meeting was about to begin. Luke Hammerstein, accompanied by five of his subordinates, was the first to arrive. Daisy stood to one side as the room started to fill up. North had excused nobody from today's summit conference and Arnie Greene, Nick-the-Greek, Hubie Troy, Wingo Sparks, Daisy's two assistants and Alix Updike were all there. Full-dress parade today, Daisy thought as she saw a perfect place for her to sit—in the lee of Nick, whose peacock figure was clad in a particularly lively glen plaid. Every eye, she judged, would stop at Nick and, wildly wondering, go no farther.

Precisely on time Patrick Shannon entered, followed by five people whom he introduced quickly: Hilly Bijur, president of the Elstree Division of Supracorp, Jared Turner, head of marketing, Candice Bloom, head of publicity for Elstree, Helen Strauss, head of advertising, and Patsy Jacobson, product-line manager.

In the time it took for them to all find chairs, Daisy was able to peek out from her strategic position and briefly study Patrick Shannon, who had seated himself without hesitation at the opposite end of the table from North. It was the first time she had seen North with a man who was clearly his equal. She could feel, even without looking, how Shannon dominated the room. Everyone, no matter how they were placed, seemed to be leaning toward him as if he were a magnet. Perhaps it was the weight of all their ears cocked in his direction that gave her that impression, she thought, restraining a giggle at the absurdity of this whole solemn occasion. Shannon's appearance in the room was so unnecessary that she couldn't believe that Luke and North had taken it all so seriously . . . and with such vehemence. If that pompous man wanted to get the impression that he was doing something "creative" about his company's commercials, why not humor him, she wondered. He was no different from all the other people who employed North. Invariably, on a shoot, they asked to look into the viewfinder of the camera before a take. North always let them go ahead—once—although they didn't know what they were seeing or what it would mean on film, and all they ever did was nod wisely and approve of whatever he had been planning to do in the first place.

Still . . . Shannon *had* entered the room with the firm, possessive step of a ship's captain strolling on his own deck, a ship, Daisy suspected, that would raise a flag bearing a skull and crossbones just as soon as it was safely out to sea. He was a pirate, a rumple-haired, blue-eyed, Black Irish brigand, improbably disguised as a prince of industry.

The meeting opened as Luke rose to his feet. He was privately, but thoroughly, annoyed at having to recapitulate the story of work that had already been through weeks of discussion, work that had been finalized, but Shannon had phoned him and asked him to fill everyone in on the entire picture at the start of the conference.

In a voice that brought them all to immediate attention, Luke began abruptly. One of the requirements of all the jobs he'd had in the past, which had led to his present position, had been the ability to "talk" a commercial so dramatically that you could see it without pictures.

"Elstree suffers from an image problem. Fuddy-duddy, old-world, your grandma's favorite. We knew that was the trouble going in. Last year another agency took off on a losing basis, using the purity of the ingredients as their main selling point. It didn't work—that's why Elstree changed to our agency. Purity isn't enough in a world in which there are a number of lines of cosmetics making similar claims with as much justification." He paused and checked his audience. They were all listening intently.

"Faded gentility and purity are *out!* We are going to capture today's most lucrative market: the working woman—dynamic, adventurous and *with her own paycheck.*" Luke picked up a large, glossy blow-up of a girl's face and displayed it to the listening crowd. "This is Pat Stephens, the new Elstree girl. The commercials will present her in a number of situations that have never been done before in the cosmetics-fragrance field . . . she'll be doing aerobatics in a small plane, we'll see her weightless, in a pressurized chamber taking training for space flight and racing in the Indy 500 in a special car G.M. is making for us. Pat will always wear some sort of uniform and a helmet. In the last thirteen seconds of each commercial, as she talks Elstree, she'll fling off her helmet and we'll finally see her face, conveying a tremendous impression of vitality and strength—driving, exciting, dashing and above all, *young*—not just the woman of today but also the woman of *tomorrow*."

Daisy contemplated the blow-up as objectively as possible. The girl was splendidly clean-featured, but her sleekly cropped head and screechingly All-American look rendered her devoid of nuance, Daisy thought. Teeth and cheekbones she had in abundance . . . but appeal?

"We intend to sign Pat up for two years so that no one else will be able to use her," Luke continued. "She'll become the living symbol of the utter now-ness of Elstree. Within months, maybe less, everyone will forget that Elstree has been in business for a hundred years because they'll associate it with Pat Stephens, functioning confidently in the present and on into the future."

He sat down to a round of applause led by Nick, who had received his instructions before the meeting. Then silence fell.

Patrick Shannon nodded in the direction of the people from Supracorp. "Ladies, Hilly, Jared—and the rest of you—first of all I want to apologize for butting in here. I know it's irregular to have this mass meeting with everyone involved but I've no time to go through channels and no time to spare anybody's feelings. As you know, although Mr. Hammerstein and Mr. North may not, I've been away for months, off and on, and I have to leave for Tokyo today." He waited, pausing just long enough to receive the expected nods from the men and women whose positions he was preempting.

"When I got back to the office a few days ago I found this campaign on my desk, ready to go. It was the first time I'd seen a photo of the Elstree girl."

"We were waiting for Danillo to photograph her with her new haircut, and he took longer than expected," Helen Strauss explained quickly.

Shannon slammed his hand down on the huge blow-up. "She looks like a tight end for the Dallas Cowboys." Nervous laughter greeted his remark. Sponsors were entitled to a sense of humor.

"It's not funny, ladies and gentlemen. I'm not joking. She's a good-looking kid, but unfortunately you picked a jock. This campaign can't work." The sound of shock, an absence of breathing or moving, filled the conference room. Shannon continued evenly.

"I'm sure I don't have to emphasize that Elstree lost thirty million dollars last year—it's the talk of the fragrance industry. My competitors dine out on it. I'm going to spend many millions more to turn the company around—launching a new fragrance, new packaging, a new advertising campaign. Big as Supracorp is, Elstree cannot afford to lose any more money because my stockholders will not—I repeat, will not—understand. They have a hell of a lot less patience than I do."

Shannon paused, but no one in the room showed any inclination toward speech. He picked up the blow-up of Pat Stephens and held it up. "This girl and Mr. Hammerstein's campaign will certainly *change* Elstree's image, but they will not sell, and I repeat the word *sell*, cosmetics or fragrance. I simply don't believe that women will identify themselves with this girl or the situations you plan to put her in. It must have sounded original and fresh when you all decided on it, but do you think it remotely *believable* that this tough cookie would be using blusher and mascara under all those helmets? I'm damn sure that she wouldn't be wearing perfume inside that space capsule or whatever the hell it is." Shannon let the glossy fall to the floor before he went on. "I think that the time has come to return to a romantic sell in fragrance, a classy, feminine sell. The working woman hasn't become any less womanly because she earns money. This tomboy you want to sign for the Elstree girl may well be somebody's fantasy of today's woman, but, sorry gentlemen, she's not mine."

Luke finally had to protest. "Look at the Charlie campaign, Mr. Shannon," he said calmly. "It's been a fabulous success for Revlon and their entire selling point is that girl with her extra-long legs taking huge strides all over the world—clean-cut, not especially pretty, but putting over that to-hell-with-everything-folks-I-can-take-care-of-myself image."

"That's one of my objections, Mr. Hammerstein," Patrick Shannon countered. "Charlie is three years old now—soon that campaign will be dated. And I don't intend to imitate Charlie . . . not even Charlie in the year two thousand." His wide mouth tightened in a way his employees knew well.

"Pat . . ." Helen Strauss began. Advertising, after all, was her responsibility, or, at least, it was *supposed* to be.

"No, Helen, I don't buy this campaign. Not any of it."

"Did you have something else in mind, Mr. Shannon?" North asked with politeness. His face quivered with impatience at the whole windy proceedings, but he knew he wasn't nearly as disturbed as the agency and the Supracorp people. He only had to make the commercials, not create them.

"I don't throw things out unless I have a notion of how to replace them, Mr. North," Shannon said. He took off the jacket of his suit, rolled up his shirt sleeves with deliberation and stretched; a big man thoroughly at ease in a roomful of people who had just seen months of carefully made plans laid waste. Daisy heard Nick-the-Greek whispering, "Shee-it" in admiration. She could almost feel him wondering if he should stop wearing the vests he adored.

"I've done a little homework since I first saw this photo," Shannon continued. "The natural look is still the most important one; the natural-looking blonde is still the model who will sell more than the brunette. I want you to find me a natural blonde and put her in natural situations. I want her to have class, warmth and a kind of glow that seems achievable. I want a real woman, not just the Elstree Girl—but someone who will become known by her own name. If Candy Bergen weren't already committed to work for Shulton and that new fragrance of theirs, I'd say she's the girl for us, but it's too late to get her now."

"You mean you're looking for a celebrity endorsement?" Luke asked, keeping the incredulity out of his voice. It just might be the oldest idea in advertising. They had actually used it in the days of Queen Victoria, for Christ's sake.

"Why the hell not? Remember 'She's engaged, she's lovely, she uses Ponds'? Nothing basic has changed since then, Mr. Hammerstein. Nothing in human nature. I didn't promise to be original—just different." Shannon grinned, with a larky bandit's look in his eyes, that freebooter gleam that told everyone from Supracorp that his mind was made up.

For a few seconds Luke was stunned into silence as he pictured his wonderful girl of the future being watered down into a simpering deb with white satin draped around her privileged shoulders, selling drugstore cold cream to the masses. His voice stayed reasonable but it demanded an effort. "Don't you think that there's a danger in an approach that might be perceived as snobbish—and out-moded?"

"I'm not talking debutantes, Hammerstein—Ponds was merely an example. I'm talking *star*. People still love stars, today more than ever. I want you to make a star or find a star to be the Elstree Girl. Just remember—she *cannot* be one of the boys."

Until this minute, Hilly Bijur had refrained from interrupting, although he was president of Elstree. Let Helen Strauss take the heat. But now he sought to regain the control he had lost by Patrick Shannon's intervention.

"You're on the money about natural blondes," he said to his boss, overriding Luke who was about to speak. "I managed to sneak a look at the new, top-secret Clairol report that says the trend toward blondes is hotter than ever—not the streaked blonde but the total blonde, the blonder-than-ever blonde."

Luke and North looked at each other in disgust. The meeting was being taken over by report-quoting, image-crazy civilians, and there wasn't a damn thing they could do about it. Nick-the-Greek sat squirming in frustration in his seat. Everybody was putting his two cents in and he hadn't said a word yet. He didn't like being ignored. Since North had insisted that he come to this asshole hassle, he was going to add something to it. In spite of his tailored-to-the-eyeballs exterior, Nick had never abandoned one habit that he'd learned in his childhood in Spanish Harlem. In each of his startling suits there was a special pocket in which he always kept a sharp knife which, had he cared to give it its precise name, was a switchblade. It kept him from feeling nervous. Now he reached for his dangerous security blanket and quietly snapped it open. All this pissant talk about blondes . . . They wanted blonde, they'd get blonde—from Nick-the-Greek.

In one fast movement, he turned his powerful body, snatched off Daisy's sailor cap, pulled her braid out from its hiding place and cut the ribbon which bound it so tightly. Before she could move, using both hands he rapidly unplaited the braid until her masses of hair were firmly held in his hands. Daisy struggled and gasped in disbelief, but he'd moved so quickly that she wasn't even sure of what was happening. Nick stood up, bringing Daisy with him since he had grabbed her by every hair on her head, and said loudly, "This what you mean, Mr. Shannon?" He waved Daisy's hair triumphantly, as if he were raising the flag on Iwo Jima.

"Damn it!" Daisy sputtered. "Nick! Let go! Stop it!"

"What the hell do you think you're doing?" North snapped.

"What's going on?" asked Hilly Bijur, while Wingo Sparks was doubled up in malicious laughter.

"You guys don't know shit from a real blonde, that's all," Nick insisted loudly, without releasing Daisy. "You think they're so easy to find?"

"Nick, put her *down!*" Luke said, crisply cutting through the confusion. Nick looked around with indignant righteousness, but let Daisy loose so that she could regain her seat. She kicked as hard as she could at his ankles, wishing she were wearing pointed shoes instead of sneakers. "You *bugger!*" she hissed at him, looking for her sailor hat without success.

"Excuse me, but could I just see the young lady again?" Patrick Shannon asked as the tumult died down.

"*No!*" said Daisy.

"Mr. Shannon, the young lady is my producer, Daisy Valensky. She works here, she works for me and she happens to be blonde. Could we just go on with this discussion and get something settled before you have to leave for Japan?" North said impatiently.

"I want another look at her, North," Shannon demanded.

"Daisy?" North asked. "Would you mind?"

"Yes, I *would,*" she said wrathfully. "Get yourself some other blondes to look at—call the model agencies, leave me alone."

"Daisy, cool it. Take it easy, it's no big deal. Mr. Shannon just wants to *see* you again—a look won't kill you," North insisted in annoyance. Sponsors—all clients when it came to that—were a law unto themselves—idiots one and all—but there were times when you had to humor them.

"See *what*, damn it!" Daisy muttered, trying to make her hair less conspicuous by pushing it behind her ears. She glared at Shannon, her skin flushed as much with fury as embarrassment.

"I remember you," he said flatly.

"How nice," she said, forcing herself to speak with cool politeness. Even in her anger, the incident of their meeting had been enough to warn her that this high-flying, risk-taking, master builder of the world of big business did not take kindly to what he might perceive as an affront.

"She has an unforgettable face," Shannon said to the room at large, in an uninflected voice.

"Very pretty," Hilly Bijur said busily. "Very pretty . . . thank you, Miss . . . ah . . . thank you very much."

"I said," Patrick Shannon repeated quietly, but in a way that brought every one of them to instant attention, "that she has an *unforgettable* face."

"Of course, Pat, you're absolutely right," Hilly Bijur, flurried, hastened to agree. "Now that we know what you have in mind, it won't take Helen more than a day or two to find a dozen girls who are suitable. She'll contact every agency in town, won't you, Helen? Or Luke will be in charge of it . . . or . . ." He floundered and subsided, not entirely sure into whose department casting fell.

"Wait a minute—just wait a minute—she's *also* a princess." Now Shannon spoke rapidly, his face concentrated in sudden excitement.

"You can forget it, Shannon. I've just told you, she works for *me*," North burst out, popping like a dry log on a brisk fire. He had become a bad-tempered redhead, his above-the-battle manner quite abandoned.

"A blonde . . . a face . . . a title," Shannon repeated to himself. "Princess Daisy . . . yes . . . yes . . . I like the sound of that."

"Mr. Shannon, this is not another remake of *A Star Is Born*," North said with escalating asperity.

"She might just do—might do very well," Shannon said, as if he were alone in the room

"Hey, that's not fair—it was my idea!" Nick-the-Greek exploded harmlessly into preoccupied ears.

"Helen," Shannon directed, "send her to be photographed immediately so that this time we know what we have. She looks like what I want but I won't be sure till I see the actual pictures." He rose, ready to leave the meeting.

Hilly Bijur hastened to join himself to Shannon's point of view before his employer could leave. As Shannon put on his jacket, Bijur spoke quickly. "I like it, Pat, you're absolutely right. Princess Daisy? . . . Didn't North say Daisy Valensky? Valensky? Wait a minute! That means her mother was Francesca Vernon. And for Christ's sake, her father was Stash Valensky—doesn't anyone here remember? Holy shit, but this little lady's going to move merchandise!" He subsided, pleased at a chance to exhibit his memory even as he dissociated himself from the unfortunate ad campaign he had approved.

"Tell them you want a hundred grand a year," Nick whispered to Daisy, who still sat speechless in her chair. "And don't say I never did anything for you . . . plus, you bruised my socks."

"We'll have to change the packaging," worried Jared Turner, obsessed, as usual, by marketing considerations. "Princess Daisy doesn't sound like a modern line."

"It's going to postpone out distribution date by almost a year!" Patsy Jacobson complained. "Meanwhile, what do I tell the stores?" This was a product-line manager's nightmare.

"Could I have some quiet!" North shouted and then stopped as he saw Daisy jump out of her seat and stride rapidly around the table. She stood just behind Luke's art director, who had already lettered in the words "Princess Daisy" with Magic Markers on a piece of paper. She snatched the paper from the table, tore it in four pieces, and jammed them in one of her pockets. "Mr. Shannon," she said in a voice which rang with clear outrage, "I am not for sale! I have absolutely no intention of letting you use my hair or my face or my name to sell your products. How dare you treat me as if you own me? You're crazy, rude and totally insensitive—all of you—and . . . and . . ." Swiftly, she gathered up the battery of Magic Markers the art director had arranged in a neat row and flung them on the marble table where they scattered loudly like small firecrackers. "I suggest that each of you goons take one of these and—stick it where the sun don't shine!" She slammed the door behind her.

"I didn't know Daisy even knew that expression," Arnie Greene marveled.

"She doesn't usually talk that way unless something goes wrong on location," Nick agreed, still aggrieved at the theft of his inspiration.

"She's awfully touchy," brooded Candice Bloom. If she were going to have to work with *that* girl, public relations were not going to be easy.

North sat back, smiling nastily at Shannon. He enjoyed vindication. "I told you that Daisy was just a working girl. She doesn't seem to want to be a model, does she? You'll have to excuse her."

"I have absolutely no intention of excusing her," Shannon answered with confidence. "She'll be the Elstree Girl."

"Daisy's not in the habit of changing her mind. You'd better not count on it," North retorted smugly.

"Oh, but I do," said Shannon. "Hilly, hold all Elstree decisions until I get back from Japan. We're going to get it right this time."

"Daisy's invaluable at my studio, Shannon," North said hotly. "You can't try this."

Patrick Shannon gave North his buccaneer's smile, that big, reckless Irish grin that everyone in Supracorp had learned to watch out for.

"Would you care to bet?"

Just before Christmas of 1976, Ram decided that it was time to get the matter of Sarah Fane settled. She'd had her fill of the Season by now and was not yet engaged to be married, but soon she'd be leaving for a round of country house visits and, just to be on the safe side, he judged it a good idea to arrive at an understanding before she left.

"I want you to dine with me tomorrow," he said on the phone. "But alone, none of your friends coming along."

"But Ram, I'm invited to Lucinda Curzon's little cocktail tomorrow."

"It's one or the other, Sarah," he said in a level voice.

Her sense of timing whispered urgently in her ear. "Since you put it that way, ıd since I can, after all, go to Lucinda's first, before meeting you, why not?" she 'd with a tiny hint of delicate reluctance.

'Why not indeed?" he said, admitting to himself that one had to admire her ·e.

They dined the next night at Mark's Club on Charles Street in Mayfair. Behind the tall unmarked door of the thin townhouse which houses Mark's, lie several dining rooms. Ram had reserved a table in the first and largest dining room from which they could see everyone who came and went. He had deliberately not chosen a quieter corner of this supremely exclusive dining club, owned by Mark Birley. Ram preferred to spend the first part of the evening in the richly appointed candle-lit room with its turquoise cut-velvet banquettes and deep terra-cotta walls whimsically covered by realistic Victorian paintings of animals, framed in gold scrollwork, square, oval and round, which almost hid the walls entirely.

Although Sarah had heeded him and arranged for them not to be joined by any of her friends, between them they knew almost everyone who was at Mark's that night, and their dinner was interrupted dozens of times by greetings, something Ram had anticipated. After they had finished their coffee, he asked, "If one more person comes by to tell you that you are the deb of the year, what will you do?"

"I shall howl," she announced, managing to look both fragile and charmingly modest. "I shall get up from my seat and howl until they have to send for the police to take me away."

"Then shall we go to my house for a brandy?" There had been the strain of a balanced, formal minuet tinkling in their ears all evening, a minuet to which they had both been dancing for many months. Abruptly, with Ram's invitation, the music came to a stop. Something wavered, hesitated in the air between them. Sarah's mind jumped to memories of the many beautiful and courted girls she knew he went out with. Whenever she saw him with them he looked as seriously watchful of them as he had ever been of her. She looked at him thoughtfully. If she went to his house with him now, she had no question of what he would expect.

"I'd love a brandy but . . ."

"Does that mean yes or no, my dear Sarah?"

"Well . . . we can't stay here forever . . . so I suppose . . . again, why not?"

"It's an absolutely marvelous house, Ram," she said, after he had shown her the first floor.

"Let me show you the upper floors."

"No, I don't think so," she said sharply, drawing inviolability quickly around her shoulders like an invisible cape.

He smiled somberly. "Are you playing the prude?"

She was stung. "How ridiculous! I'm just tired, Ram. Will you take me home please? It was lovely brandy."

"No, Sarah, darling, I won't take you home. I love you, Sarah."

She stood quietly by the fireplace, watching him, without responding to his words.

"I want to marry you," he continued. Still she was silent. There was, she thought, something inaccessible about his mouth. "Sarah," he repeated, coming close but not touching her. "Will you marry me?"

It had taken him long enough to get to the point, she said to herself. Should she put him off and wait until the next time he asked? No, it was best to cap her Season with the engagement of the year. Next year another debutante would be in the spotlight—but if she were Princess Valensky, what difference would a mere debutante make to her? She curved her perfect lips in her perfect meaningless smile and inclined her perfect head. She didn't move toward him until he leaned down to her.

As he kissed her he sighed, "The first time . . ." She well knew that indeed it was the first time they had kissed like this alone and on the lips. Only occasionally had she given him the smooth skin of her cheeks before, in impersonal public thanks. She had played a hard, long relentless championship game.

He kissed her again and again, with increasing hunger, and the Honorable Sarah Fane couldn't tell whether what she was feeling was excitement because she had achieved her victory and caught Ram Valensky, or whether the excitement was that sensuality she had never had any trouble dismissing.

"Come upstairs with me now, my darling, come with me," he urged against her mouth.

"No . . . Ram, please . . . I can't . . . I never have . . ."

"Of course you haven't, Sarah, my lovely Sarah . . . but you're going to be my wife—it's all right now."

"Ram, no. I couldn't . . . I couldn't *possibly* . . ."

He let her go so abruptly that she teetered slightly and had to catch the mantel. He backed away from her and stood frowning at her with scornful eyes.

"You haven't even said you love me, Sarah . . . did you realize that? Perhaps you don't love me, perhaps you're not yet ready to make up your mind? I've been watching you, my dear—do you think I don't know the kind of flirt you are? Does it amuse you to make a man propose, and then not even give him an answer except a tiny *gracious* nod of your head? I've rather enjoyed seeing you play the innocent coquette, the untouchable and pure aristocrat, every single calculating second of it, everything you do orchestrated to the greatest glory of Sarah Fane." His accusing, sardonic eyes began to frighten her a little, but at the same time, she felt a thrill at seeing Ram lose his composure. Oh, yes, it *was* exciting to be able to do this to a man. She could not prevent a shadow of a complacent smile from touching her mouth. Ram saw it and took a swift, angry step forward and grasped her arm.

"So you *do* think you can make a fool out of me," he said, suddenly furious in a way that took her by surprise. "So that's your little plan, so that's what goes on inside that manipulative, self-centered mind of yours—another conquest for Sarah, another contest you've won—probably you'll be boasting about it tomorrow." His fingers tightened on her arm and the triumph that had been hers a moment ago seemed about to disappear. She knew she had to play her last coin. Still, wasn't it for exactly this moment that she'd guarded it?

"Ram, stop it! You didn't even give me a chance to say I love you. You're not being fair, you're wrong about me . . ."

"Am I? Am I?" he whispered, in a hot, maddened voice, as if her words had meant nothing to him. "A common tease, that's what you've been all along . . . a common tease, right out of the schoolroom . . . ." He let go of her arm and stood wrathfully in front of her. Everything she would get if she married Ram Valensky formed one great ball in Sarah's mind, a great golden ball studded with precious jewels. She stretched out her hands to it and to him.

"Upstairs . . ." she whispered, in a faltering voice. Ram grasped her in strong hands and led her stumbling toward the staircase. He was hurting her arms again, but in her mixture of greed and confusion and dread and excitement, all Sarah could remember was an American friend at school who used to say, "Always pour cement over a bargain." Suddenly Sarah knew exactly what that meant.

Oh, God, why did it take him so long, Sarah Fane wondered in agony. No one had ever told her it would be like this, long and painful—so disgustingly painful—and labored and utterly ignominious. And so silent, so wordless. Where was the romance she had expected, where the pleasure? There was only shame. She was plunged into a revolting dream, the kind that went senselessly on and on, captured under the weight of a man who was so far out of control that there was nothing she could possibly do about it. His hard lips and hard hands never allowed her a second's respite, but all she could hear above her was the sound of his tormented breathing. In her hideous misery she tried again and again to protest but he didn't, *wouldn't* hear her. His breathing grew louder and louder until it seemed to her that it must finally burst into a shout, but then it would start all over again, on a lower note, and rise to another crescendo. His eyes were tightly closed in the low light of the room, but he had his hands in her hair and was pulling at its golden strands until he made her cry out in pain. Oh . . . oh, now it was surely going to end . . . no one could gasp and labor like that for long and live. Please, please, let it happen quickly, quickly . . .

"*Daisy! Daisy!*" Ram screamed into the dimness, "*Daisy, I love you!*"

Finding strength in her violent outrage, Sarah Fane flung herself away from Ram and stood, huddled in a mixture of humiliation, growing rage and incredulous, but certain knowledge, looking at the creature on the bed, a mad, sobbing loathsome creature who had buried his disgraced head in the pillow, a creature she would have to destroy for what he had done to her, done to Sarah Fane.

21

When the Valarians had invited Daisy to join them on their chartered yacht in early January of 1977, she had refused. The idea of spending five days cooped up with Robin and Vanessa and their cronies, cruising the Caribbean, sounded like going to a very expensive jail. She could almost hear the worldly, self-important exchanges of gossip and hidden spitefulness, count the never-ending games of backgammon, imagine the cases of white wine and Perrier that would be consumed, estimate the number of changes of costume and jewels that each woman would be making during the day. It was everything she hated, but Vanessa had been relentlessly insistent and Daisy had finally not known how to get out of it without becoming truly offensive. Vanessa had come as close to anger as Daisy had ever seen her.

"I won't take no for an answer again," she'd finally said. "I've invited Topsy and Ham Short—he happens to be a fan of yours, and there will be several other people aboard who have children who need painting—among the other guests—but I don't see why the devil I have to lure you with the possibility of commissions. Really, Daisy, you're making me feel very much as if you've been *using* me. When I say that Robin and I are counting on the pleasure of your company don't you feel that's enough of a reason to accept?"

Remembering what she indeed now owed Vanessa, Daisy had hastily agreed. The studio could get along without her for a few days, in fact her last vacation had been so long ago that she couldn't remember it. Most important of all, she couldn't risk allowing a source of income to disappear, as Vanessa was clearly threatening.

Now, as she sat with Ham and Topsy in their Aero Commander, on the flight to Nassau, where they would all join the yacht the Valarians had chartered for the holidays, transforming it with their own possessions into a floating approximation of their New York apartment, Daisy reflected that it was, after all, a good time to get away. Since that scene when she had rebelled against the idea of becoming the Elstree Girl, she had felt at odds with almost everyone in the studio. North seemed to think that she had gone out of her way to insult an important client, and the atmosphere at work was tense and heavy. As the plane began to descend, Daisy thought that it was no longer anger she felt, nor even genuine annoyance at the way the men from Supracorp had treated her, at the cavalier way in which they had simply assumed that she was a blonde *thing* for them to use to sell products. After all, without her consent they were powerless and they knew it. No, what still made her feel a deep stab of warning, a warning that still reverberated throughout her, was the idea of *becoming* Princess Daisy in that horrifyingly exposed position called the "public eye"; a profound fear of being perceived as a particular personality who was called Princess Daisy and who would be photographed and manipulated to sell Elstree in commercials, in ads and on display counters, until her Princess Daisyness would be burned permanently into the consciousness of the consumers of the

Western world. So far, in her adult lifetime, she had managed to slip by, to soft pedal, to hide out.

No one at Santa Cruz had ever thought of her as anyone but a girl named Valensky; at North's studio any vague interest anyone might have had in her title or her background had long ago vanished and only occasionally reappeared as a joke. To all her coworkers she was Daisy-the-producer who knew where everyone was supposed to be and when—and why—and raised hell if they didn't perform as expected. Only in the well-guarded enclaves of the Horse People was she Princess Daisy, and there she was protected by their associations with her father, whose name was still well remembered and honored. Horse People were safe.

Patrick Shannon's proposal to make her a public figure, to exploit her as Princess Daisy, touched on a vital nerve—it aroused terrors she had fought in the shadow, year after year, without being able to explain to herself why they had such a hold over her. All she knew was that they planned to tag her, to label her something called *A Princess Daisy*, and if she allowed them to do it, she would be giving up something more precious than the relative anonymity she had preserved for so long. As well as privacy, she would be giving up something Daisy could only think of as *safety*. The public eye was a dangerous place in which to conduct her life—she didn't need to search for any logical explanations to be certain that she was right.

A launch brought Topsy, Ham and Daisy out to the yacht where Vanessa was waiting for them all. After she had had the Shorts shown to their quarters, she led Daisy to a medium-sized stateroom done in yellow-and-white striped canvas. Vanessa's mood was cheerful.

"Everyone's one board now, thank heaven. I'll tell the captain he can get underway as soon as he's ready," she said. "We're all getting some sun on deck—no? Too sleepy? Well, then, drinks in the main saloon at seven o'clock. Good to have you aboard, love bug." Vanessa squeezed Daisy in an impersonal way. Like all accomplished lesbians, she had never in her life committed the mistake of making the slightest sexual gesture toward another woman unless she was convinced that it would be welcomed. Daisy wouldn't have been importuned by Vanessa if they'd been cast away together on a desert island . . . at least not until a month had passed without rescue.

The gently rocking motion of the ship, the escape from New York, the subtle freshening of air in the room as the yacht's distance from the shore grew greater, all combined to make Daisy's nap as relaxing and refreshing as a short voyage in itself. She woke to the reddening light of a tropical sun, a light so pure in its clarity and the intensity that came from its refraction on open, blue water, that it seemed to be actively resisting the approach of twilight. She lay on her bed, a mock four-poster, with the bed clamped to the floor and the curtains firmly anchored to the ceiling, and, in a ruminative mood, decided that she was well off here, away from the city where she would have been alone all week. Kiki was spending two weeks of winter vacation with Luke, at his little place in northern Connecticut. She had looked like an untamed powder puff as she flung clothes into her suitcase with the abandon of one who knows that a possible potential mother-in-law will not be around to observe her. Theseus, impossible on a yacht, had been left for these few days with Daisy's landlady, whom he had grown to accept peevishly.

Daisy showered and dressed, but it was still too early to join the others. Thank heaven they'd all be in their staterooms, intently adjusting their resort dinner clothes, caparisoned for the delectation of each other.

She made her way to the prow of the yacht and stood there alone, blending and losing herself in a breeze that danced with her. The rays of the sun crystallized her hair, turning it into a spun-sugar forest, like some treat from a children's Christmas. The large ship rose and fell comfortingly as it chopped through the water, already many marine miles from the harbor in Nassau. The thought of Patrick Shannon, that presumptuous, impossible man, touched Daisy's mind and she found that it barely annoyed her. She had, after all, shown him that he couldn't command her life, no matter how everyone else deferred to him. And what about North, who, as surely as Shannon, had treated her as if she had no more humanity than a chess piece in his confrontation with the sponsor—a piece of property that belonged to the studio, a parcel he wasn't inclined to part with? Daisy shrugged and smiled. She found that she didn't care about North either. To hell with all of them. Her eyes filled with the sea and the sky, Daisy was at peace.

She stayed on deck until she knew she was unquestionably late for cocktails, and then, as reluctantly as she had done her Maths at Lady Alden's, but knowing that there was no way to avoid them, she went in search of the main saloon. She passed one large room in which crew members were laying tables for dinner. Next to it was an even larger room in which Daisy could see the silhouettes of more than a dozen people. On the opposite side of the yacht, a wall had been opened up with great glass windows, and the gory, blinding pyrotechnics of the sunset backlit the guests so that Daisy couldn't make out their faces. As she pushed open the door, Vanessa materialized out of the glare and took her by the hand, leading her, blinded, into the room. A man's figure walked toward them and Vanessa put Daisy's hand in his, and immediately drifted away.

"Hello, Daisy."

Ram's voice.

She staggered backward. Ram steadied her swiftly, catching her by the arms as he tried to kiss the top of her head, but even as Ram's lips reached for her, she had lunged backward. She was beyond words, beyond screams, beyond any movement except retreat. She stepped back again, turning to run, but as she did so a strong arm grabbed her around her waist. Vanessa, clutching her in a jailer's grip, pressed her forward insistently. The pulse of time, like a power line struck by lightning, dimmed, lurched, flickered until it almost went out and then, as Vanessa's voice began, time began to beat again, but slowly, without assurance. The other guests were watching, not understanding, but suddenly curious and listening. Vanessa's voice, that charmingly ardent voice, was raised to address them all, covering Daisy's silence, distracting attention away from the brute fear in her eyes.

"See, Ram, I told you she'd come," Vanessa said triumphantly. "I've always said family quarrels are utterly silly, haven't I, Robin, darling—and when Ram told us he hadn't even seen his little sister in years I just said to myself, well, that's too ridiculous—just totally absurd. I knew my Daisy would never carry a childish grudge that long, no matter what the spat was about, and Ram certainly has no hard feelings, so we all planned this surprise together, this family reunion, when Robin and I were in London for New Year's Eve. And now, love bug, aren't you pleased that I did? After all, how many brothers does one have in a lifetime? You and Ram are all that's left of the Valenskys, and I promised myself I'd make you friends again. Everybody! Let's all drink to the end of misunderstandings and to all good things—come on, Ham, Topsy, Jim, Sally, the rest of you . . . a toast!" Releasing Daisy, she raised her glass and moved toward the others. The hearty clinking of their glasses broke the circle, like an evil enchantment, in which Daisy had been locked in frozen black terror.

"Why?" she hissed under the sound of the toast.

"Just a reunion," Ram answered, his gaze, set and hungry, denying his social smile.

"How? What does that bitch *owe* you?"

"Nothing," he lied easily. Ram had persuaded his partners to loan the Valarians the money to launch an entirely new dress line, priced for the average woman, an expensive undertaking on a large scale.

"I don't believe you!"

"It just doesn't matter what you believe. You're here . . . you can hardly run away." His eyes scavenged her face. He was as quiveringly rapacious as a miser alone in King Solomon's mine. He spoke without knowing what he said and without caring. He didn't have to placate her. She was weak, weaker than she yet knew, and he was strong, and that was all that mattered.

Swiftly Daisy turned to walk away. He put a restraining hand on her arm. She turned back in a frenzy of disgust. Pure contempt flooded her as she looked straight into his avaricious eyes.

"Never, never touch me, Ram. I warn you," she spat at him. Acid black hatred poured from her eyes. She went rigid in a passion of revulsion. Slowly he released her arm, but his eyes refused to let her go. For an instant they stood locked in the intensity of their emotions.

"Daisy! Ram! Dinner's served . . . didn't you two hear the steward?" Vanessa gestured toward the general surge in the direction of the next room. Automatically Daisy found herself following the others.

Two round tables had been laid, not in Robin's marine manner, all silver-mounted conch shell, chunks of rare coral and blue and white Chinese Export ware, that he reserved for particularly snowy winter nights in the city, but in his grandest Chinese form. At each place was a round red lacquer tray set with a rare K'ang Hsi plate, inlaid black and silver chopsticks and a single green and white orchid in a black porcelain bud vase. Between the trays were artfully scattered a collection of ancient Oriental weapons, dirks and daggers, mixed fetchingly with eighteenth-century *Famille Noire* cats in various sizes. In the center of each table was a low *Famille Noire* bowl filled with the heads of enormous orange tiger lilies from the pistils of which Robin had carefully cut the dark rust pollen heads that, if touched, left a stain that was almost impossible to remove.

Vanessa had not pushed her audacity so far as to seat Daisy and Ram at the same table. Daisy's dinner partner on her left was Ham Short. Stunned into immobility by shock and growing panic, she found she couldn't begin to eat the first course of ginger-flavored minced squab. Ham attempted to distract her with an account of his own worthless passel of relatives back in Arkansas, but he might as well have been talking to a dead girl, propped up beside him. She sat with her eyes fastened on the bowl of tiger lilies, until Ham, in embarrassment, turned to the woman on his left. When the second course was served, Daisy made a half-hearted attempt to pick up her chopsticks, but before her hand touched them she realized that she wouldn't have the coordination to be able to use them, and that even if she could, the taste of any food would make her vomit. Her dinner companions, who had been forced into a general conversation by her silent presence, tacitly agreed to pretend to ignore this fascinating phenomenon even as they covertly watched her, storing away all their deliciously scandalized impressions for the stories they'd tell once they got off the yacht. As course after course of exquisite food was presented, prepared by the chef the Valarians had hired for the cruise, who cooked in five different cuisines, Daisy touched nothing and talked to no one. Ham Short, who admired her, dominated the conversation and kept it flowing, so that no one turned to her with any questions. At one point he sought her hand, as it lay still on the table, and squeezed it to show his support. Although she returned a tiny pressure, she didn't remove her unseeing eyes from the tiger lilies.

Vanessa had certainly gone too far tonight, more than one of the women in the room managed to signal delightedly to another during the endless dinner, which proceeded as if Daisy were invisible. Ram, habitual diner-out that he was, presented to them all his normal, handsome, unendingly correct, indisputably gentlemanly surface. He ate with polite relish and discussed Henry Moore with the lady on his right and the merits of various saddle makers with Topsy, on his left. There was well-concealed malevolence as, from time to time, he scanned the room for a split second, searching for his prey like a carrion bird, but no one noticed. To Daisy, the walls of the dining saloon pressed in like those of an echo chamber. The voices of memory, ugly and dangerous, clamored at a distance, sometimes louder, sometimes softer, and the other guests seemed as distant and indistinct as large fish languidly waving their fins behind the wall of an aquarium.

After dinner, Vanessa led the way back to the main saloon. Daisy had been waiting for this moment, and, as soon as Vanessa rose, she flew up from her chair and darted out of the door which led to the deck. Although she moved quickly she felt as if her body were numb and incapacitated, with that helplessness, that slowing down and impairment of all the faculties that appear in a nightmare. She had passed the main saloon, running in the direction of her own stateroom, when Ram caught up with her.

"Stop! We have to talk. It's important!" he shouted, but he didn't try to touch her.

Daisy stopped. It was so impossible that he could imagine that they had anything to say to each other that sheer incredulity overcame her other emotions. She felt safe enough, with a steward in sight, carrying a tray of brandy and glasses, and the door to the main saloon only feet away. She could see people inside, buzzing away like flies in a bottle, but on deck it was quiet and the breeze was warm. She held on to the railing of the yacht with both hands and turned to face Ram, creating a distance between them merely by the way she stood.

"Nothing is important enough for us to discuss, ever again," she said through dry lips.

"Anabel," he said quietly, with vulturine watchfulness, "Anabel."

"Anabel? She has nothing to do with you. Do you ever stop lying? I had a letter from her only a week ago."

"And of course she didn't tell you." Ram was sure of his ground. It wasn't even a question.

Daisy went white and clutched the rail. He knew something she didn't know. She recognized the unmistakable expression of repressed pleasure on his face.

"What about Anabel?" she whispered, as if a whisper could soften his answer.

"She has leukemia."

"I don't believe you!"

"Yes, you do. You know I'm telling the truth."

"Why didn't she tell me? Why should she tell you?" Daisy demanded automatically while the shock of his words went inward, surrounded her heart like an explosion of fragments of pointed glass.

"Because she thought that you have enough problems of your own, supporting your sister. She had to have money for the treatments and she simply didn't want you to know she was in need. She knows you're stretched as far as you can go, so she came to me."

"Oh, dear God, *not* Anabel," Daisy moaned. Anabel, who'd come closer to being a mother to her than anyone, Anabel, the dear friend and counselor and confidante of her youth, Anabel, whose presence in her life warmed it with generous laughing love and still lent it a quality that even today was almost like having a home, Anabel who kept her from feeling utterly orphaned.

"The doctors have told her that with luck and care and she can expect to live for many years. It's chronic leukemia, not acute. She's not sixty yet—she can still live the rest of her life in comparative comfort and security but . . . it's a question of money."

"*You* have money!"

"Anabel threw me out of her house ten years ago and told me she never wanted to see or hear from me again. She's never changed that position—except now, to ask for money. I don't feel I have any reason to give her anything unless I choose, *choose* to be generous. Anabel is merely a former mistress of my father's. He left her a sizable estate which, since she declined to take advantage of my advice, she let slip through her fingers. She held on to her Rolls stock as long as you did. I have no sympathy for people who can't take care of their money."

"Anabel was so good to you!" Daisy almost shouted, but he ignored her words.

"If I should choose to help her it means taking on heavy and unforeseeable expenses for an unknown amount of time—hardly the act of a prudent man. Obviously, she can't keep *La Marée* any longer by taking in paying guests—she won't have the energy. When she sells it she'll have some money, but it won't last long since she has few other sources of income. After that's gone, it's a question of finding a place to live, either a nursing home or an apartment, depending on her physical condition. She'll need help, later if not immediately. And there will be constant doctor bills. It could last ten years, fifteen years—even twenty. There's no way for Anabel to pay for these things . . . the expenses will have to be met as they arise."

Daisy struggled to keep to practicalities while the points of glass pressed deeper into her heart with every word he spoke.

"Why should she sell *La Marée*? You know as well as I do that if Anabel can live for years there is no other place in the world she would be as happy. You have the money to support her without thinking twice about it . . . and she'll have to live somewhere . . . since she's come to you for help, *why* should she be forced to sell? You are going to help, aren't you . . ." Her voice faded as she looked at his face, locked in brooding righteousness.

"I feel no moral obligation at all to become financially responsible for Anabel. None. However I have a proposal which can solve the problem. I've been disturbed for years by reports from my friends who visit the United States for the hunting that you go about visiting at their hosts' houses trying to drum up commissions for your little paintings. I know, of course, although they don't, why you need the money. The only way I would undertake the support of Anabel for as long as she lives is with the absolute understanding that you give up your shoddy job and your hand-to-mouth sideline of portraits and come back to London."

"*You really are insane*," Daisy whispered slowly.

"Nonsense. I'm asking nothing in return for what will prove to be many years of heavy expenses except that you live in a way in which an unmarried sister of mine should live, properly and respectably. I'm even prepared to let Anabel keep *La Marée* since you feel so sentimental about it. And naturally I'll take over your sister's support as well."

"*I'd be your prisoner!*"

"How absurd. Don't be so melodramatic. I simply want you to fill your normal place in society in a country in which society still means something. Your life in New York is disgusting—a vulgar world full of vulgar people. It happens to embarrass me among my friends. I offer you protection and security. I want nothing from you—I have my own life to live." His voice was cool and reasonable, but Daisy saw that his eyes had never ceased their urgent assault on her face and body. Like furtive cat burglars, they snatched and grabbed. Lust lay like a dry powder on his thin, fine lips. She had been in the presence of his madness before and nothing had changed except that this time she knew him for what he was.

"Every word is a lie! You'd be after me again the way you were before—*I smell it on you*! You say my life in New York is disgusting—I say if my father weren't dead, he would have *killed* you and you know it!" Her voice rose dangerously.

"Shut up, shut up! People will hear you!"

"Why should I? So that you won't be embarrassed? Do you think I give a damn . . . do you still think I'd ever let you force me to do anything against my will?"

"Anabel . . ." he began again.

"Blackmail!" she raged at him. "How can you live with the filth you are?" She turned and strode rapidly back in the direction of the main saloon. She opened the door and stood there for a second, panting, open-mouthed, searching for Vanessa. When Daisy saw her, sitting at the backgammon table, she walked straight toward her and put a hurting hand on Vanessa's shoulder.

"I want to talk to you."

"Daisy, love bug, wait till the game's over, hmmm?"

"Now." The pounding, molten emphasis in Daisy's voice summoned Vanessa to her feet. "Outside," Daisy ordered. Vanessa followed, smiling broadly and flittering her hands as several inquiring looks were directed at her.

"Daisy, just what is it—how dare you?"

"Vanessa, tell the captain to turn this boat around and put me ashore."

"That's impossible. Now just calm down . . ."

"You've collected on your debt. Whatever I owed you, I've paid. Vanessa—I'm *warning* you."

Vanessa, experienced, astute Vanessa, didn't have to think twice. The menace, almost out of control, that she saw on Daisy's face could only lead to trouble. And, in Vanessa's brilliantly balanced life, that life of so many delicious but dangerous secrets, risk and consequences had to be eliminated as quickly as possible.

What could Ram *have done* to her, she wondered to herself, as she hurried to the bridge to speak to the captain. Oh, how she'd love to find out.

"What's all this?" Patrick Shannon demanded of his executive secretary as he sat down behind his desk. He had just come back from Tokyo and he expected, as usual, to find the clean desk he'd left. Each of his three secretaries would have compiled dossiers of matters to be attended to, but he hadn't sent for the folders yet.

"Mr. Bijur asked me to put them where you'd see them first thing."

Shannon lifted the six photographs, each of which had a sheet of paper attached to it. "They're all princesses, Mr. Shannon. Mr. Bijur thought you'd like their family trees, too. There are two Belgians, one French and three Germans. He said to tell you that he'd gone over every white princess in the world and these were the only really beautiful ones. Princess Caroline and Princess Yasmin won't return his calls, but he's still trying, through channels."

Shannon roared with laughter as he looked over the photographs.

"Oh God, oh God," he groaned as he laughed, "he must have worked like a son-of-a-bitch—poor Hilly—doesn't he know when I say unforgettable I don't mean merely beautiful? Miss Bridy, will you put me through to Daisy Valensky at North's studio? If she's not there, find out where she is and get her before you try any other calls."

Daisy was standing with her arms akimbo, eyeing both of her production assistants severely.

"Do you mean to tell me that the grip just walked into Central Park and sawed a limb off a tree without either of you telling him to do it? It couldn't possibly have been his own idea. Don't you creeps realize that there were five people trying to make citizen's arrests following him? We almost had a riot."

"It was just a little branch."

"It isn't as if there were leaves on it."

"We needed it in a hurry—the tree on the street was too puny."

"No excuses," Daisy said. "If it ever, *ever* happens again, you both go back to robbing graves."

"Daisy, phone," one of them said, grateful for the interruption.

"Studio," Daisy answered, as she always did.

"Princess Valensky, this is Patrick Shannon."

"How was Tokyo?" she said in a neutral tone, watching her two assistants slink off as inconspicuously as they could.

"Too far. Listen, I didn't get a chance to apologize to you for the way I talked to you the last time we met."

"Or the first time we met either."

"That's exactly what I was about to say . . . I feel that somehow we've gotten off to a bad start—all right, two bad starts—and I'd like to do something about it. Is there a chance that I could persuade you to have dinner with me? I promise not to say a word about Elstree. This is not an attempt to get you to change your mind. I wouldn't be that obvious—or devious."

"Just a friendly meal?"

"Right, I don't like leaving the impression that I'm a heavy."

"Would you admit that you're aggressive?" Daisy asked sweetly.

"Aggressive—sure, but not a heavy. Will you be free for dinner sometime this week?"

"I think I might manage dinner," Daisy said.

"What's a good night for you? I haven't made any plans for the rest of the week so you pick the day."

"Tonight," she said without a second's hesitation. There was a moment of blank silence.

"Oh. Of course. Tonight."

"It's the corner of Prince and Greene. The southeast corner, third flight up. I'll expect you at eight o'clock. Ignore the sign that says 'Fierce Guard Dog'—he doesn't bite unless I tell him to . . . as a rule."

Daisy hung up before he had a chance to say goodbye. "Ginger," she said to North's secretary. "If North comes in, tell him I've taken the afternoon off. If he wants to know why, tell him I didn't say. If any of the others need me, tell them to figure it out for themselves. If anyone calls, tell them I can't be found. If anyone asks you what the hell is going on, tell them you don't know."

"It'll be a pleasure," Ginger assured her. "Got a date, huh?"

"Not exactly," said Daisy.

Daisy knew exactly what she was looking for. There has never been a season, in spite of the programmed fluctuations of fashion, in spite of swings in taste from classic to kinky, in which Bill Blass has not quietly made a group of sublime black dresses, the witty, wily discretion of which combines the ultimate in rich-lady good taste with the ultimate in naughty-lady sexiness. Sometimes he does it with net and chiffon, sometimes with lace and silk, mixed with such supreme distillation of the tactile advantages of each fabric that it is impossible to say just where one melts into the other. Daisy finally found the Bill Blass she sought on Bendel's second floor and, on her way out, she stopped at Jerry Miller's first-floor shoe department, Shoe Biz, and bought a pair of thin, high-heeled black silk sandals with tiny rhinestone buckles. A pair of sheer taupe pantyhose were found on another counter and Daisy left the store on West 57th Street having spent just a dollar or two more than three weeks salary.

Recklessly she took a cab home instead of the subway, and, as soon as she'd hung up the dress, she washed her hair in the shower. Even with a powerful blow dryer it took almost an hour to get it all dry, and by the time she finished her arms ached. Theseus, back from his brief stay with the landlady, cowered under a sofa. The only thing in the world he was afraid of was the hideous whine of the blow dryer. Fortunately Kiki was still out of town with Luke. Daisy would not have liked to answer questions about her extraordinary preparations for the evening ahead. She would not have liked inquisitive Kiki to wonder why she was cleaning up the living room, throwing dozens of extraneous objects in closets with abandon, until the room presented a perfectly neat and, in fact, elegant appearance—thanks to Eleanor Kavanaugh's latest shipment of expensive white wicker furniture covered in a flowered Woodson print which cost forty dollars a yard and looked like the surface of a lily pond painted by Monet. She burrowed anxiously into Kiki's chest of drawers until she eventually found the black silk evening bag she had counted on using. Kiki really should take better care of her things, Daisy thought, as, nervously, she started to dress.

At precisely eight o'clock the doorbell rang. As Daisy opened the door the smile on Patrick Shannon's face froze.

Daisy had put herself together tonight with the most meticulous attention to each part of her self-presentation, but she hadn't been able to assess the total and get an objective view of herself. All she was sure of was that she had made a desperate investment in the Blass dress and done her hair in the most classic way she knew. It was a roll of the dice, risking so much money, but the stakes were too high to leave anything to chance. Any one of her jumble-sale costumes, no matter how exquisitely made, might make her look eccentric. She had to look *solidly rich.* It was as simple as that.

How many times had she heard Nick-the-Greek explain that the reason North could charge a higher fee than any other director in the business was because he had more clients than he had time for—all, of course, thanks to Nick's own efforts—and so, not needing the money, he commanded it? If she were to become the Elstree Girl, and now Daisy knew she had to take that job at whatever cost to herself, she had to make it pay enough so that she could take care of both Anabel and Danielle for a long time into the future. She couldn't settle for model fees, not even the thousand dollars a day that certain top models were commanding. It must be more money, much, much more. Against the spiritual threat which emanated like a stench from Ram, money was her only protection. It was the only shield solid enough to trust.

The woman who greeted Shannon was not the fantastic girl he'd met dressed in green sequins and corduroy with fake emeralds pinned in her long hair, nor the disheveled, furious, funny figure in carpenter's overalls, but the most unreasonably beautiful creature he'd ever seen. He literally gaped as he looked at her. The heavy, low braided chignon into which all of Daisy's hair was caught, emphasized the length and molding of her neck, and the proud, high carriage of her head. With her hair pulled back from her face, the particular ripe peach bloom of Daisy's skin, her thick, straight brows over her dark purple, pansy-centered eyes and full, strongly marked mouth, all stood out in the kind of relief which the wonder of her unbound hair would have diminished. Her dress had a halter top of dotted black net which dissolved at the slender, wrapped waist into a swoosh of full, rustling black skirts, and from it her arms and shoulders, quite unornamented by any jewels, rose in simple majesty.

"Aren't you going to come in?" Daisy said, with a gracious smile, which she had sternly prevented from turning into a satisfied grin. Apparently she'd managed to achieve the effect she was trying for, if the test was rendering Pat Shannon unable to function normally. And he was.

Silently he walked into the apartment and stood in the center of the living room.

As gently as if she were talking to a sleepwalker, Daisy asked, "Won't you sit down and have a drink?" Shannon sat.

"Vodka, whiskey, white wine?" Shannon nodded agreement, to all her suggestions, his eyes never leaving her. Rather than disturb his concentration, she poured wine for both of them, brought the drinks and sat down near him. Finally he spoke, automatically saying the first thing that entered his bedazzles mind.

"I like your apartment."

Demurely she answered, "My roommate and I have lived here for four years. It's rather an amusing part of town."

Daisy could tell from the faint tightening of the lines around his mouth that he was aware of how many different kinds of romantic relationships were tucked into the convenient, ubiquitous title of roommate.

"She's Kiki Kavanaugh," Daisy continued, composedly. "Perhaps you know her father—he's president of United Motors? No? She's back home this week," Daisy said. "I was supposed to go, too—Uncle Jerry, Kiki's father, is having a birthday and I'm considered part of the family, but I didn't think it was quite fair to leave the studio. My assistants aren't as dependable as I'd like and I've just been away in Nassau."

"Your work," Shannon asked tentatively, "is it something recent? When we met in Middleburg somebody said that you were a painter . . . at least that was the impression I got."

"Oh, that—it's just my hobby. I love children and I love horses and I love to paint, so sometimes I treat myself to all three of them together," Daisy said with a fine carelessness. "Actually I've worked for North since school—it's so much more amusing to *do* something, don't you think? Otherwise, life tends to become self-indulgent . . . one simply must fight that dreadful tendency to drift. And the studio is the ideal solution. No week is the same as any other, we have new problems, new crises, new solutions and never a second to get bored."

She smiled as complacently as Marie Antoinette discussing her cows while she briefly batted her eyelashes in supplication to Kiki's patron saint, the deity of all those who told lies in a good cause and gave themselves airs and graces.

Shannon looked at her questioningly. "Funny, I've picked up the idea that a job like yours demands a high degree of efficiency and very long, hard hours . . ."

"Oh, of course it does," Daisy drawled. "But *that's* the joy of it . . . it's *such* a challenge! Would you enjoy doing something that wasn't a challenge?" Daisy leaned languidly back against the water-lily pillows in an attitude which persuaded Shannon that long, hard hours must be the inevitable choice of any rich girl with a brain in her head.

"I take it North is a good man to work for?"

"The day he stops being one is the day I'll quit," Daisy said lightly, thinking of North's sardonic snort if he could hear her. "Of course, you mustn't judge by Nick-the-Greek—the one who insisted on displaying my hair—he's a bit of a barbarian, lacks finesse, but I'm fond of him just the same . . . he just got carried away."

"So did you, rather."

"Oh that. I'm well known for my evil temper." She smiled with that particular smile of people who are proud of their defects, because they are themselves so important that no one dares to rebuke them. Actually, Daisy thought, it was North's smile she was borrowing.

There was a scratching at one of the doors of the apartment, followed by the sound of a body hurling itself against the door. Daisy murmured, "Excuse me," and she walked toward the door, her skirts swaying, her back naked almost to the waist under the dotted net. Patrick Shannon followed her with his eyes, marveling.

"Now stop it, Theseus," she called through the door.

"Is that your guard dog? I'd like to meet him, or her, as the case may be." He was intensely curious about everything about this rare creature, Daisy. He imagined her idea of a guard dog would be an overbred Afghan, or a yapping poodle.

"He's nervous with strangers," Daisy warned, but she opened the door.

Theseus appeared, ears perked up like flags, and silently padded into the room with his drunken-sailor gait. Shannon rose at the approach of the big, rough-coated animal, with the mixture of gray, brown and blue hair. Theseus gave Shannon a suspicious, furtive, sideways look and started to sidle past him to his favorite pillow on the floor. As he got closer to the visitor, to Daisy's astonishment, he changed directions, reared up on his hind legs and hurled himself on Shannon in a brazen display of sniffing, licking and searching. Shannon, laughing, started to calm him with a game of tickle, scratch, rough and tumble that left Theseus his slave for life.

"How very strange," Daisy said coldly. "He usually doesn't go near strangers. Are you sure there isn't anything to eat in your pockets?"

"Oh, dogs like me—dogs and children."

"And that, I suppose, is traditionally the sign of a man you can trust?" she asked, leading the dog out of the room with a most unusual firmness of touch of which only Theseus was aware, since it was accomplished with an imperceptible movement of her strong wrist.

"That's what they say," he called after her.

Daisy returned, walking with a dignity that made Shannon think confusedly of throne rooms and crown jewels and the Changing of the Guard. "You haven't touched your drink," she said. "Can I give you something else?"

"Why don't we go on to dinner?" he asked, looking down at his full glass in astonishment. How had it got there? An authentic guard dog. An authentic roommate. What more did she have hidden here? "The car and driver are just downstairs. At least, in this neighborhood, I hope they're still there."

"Oh, it's absolutely safe. The Mafia protects us—half their grandparents still live within blocks—SoHo is the most crime-free area in the city." Airily Daisy had converted her semi-slum street into a whimsically inhabited island paradise.

Le Cirque is the kind of grand and expensive New York restaurant that only certain New Yorkers really understand. It's not about food, as the great restaurants are, and it's not about décor, as so many others are, nor is it about beautiful or chic people. It is a restaurant about power. Only the powerful go there, to test their power by the table they are given and to enjoy their power in the company of other powerful people. Le Cirque is attractive enough, with its obviously costly décor of murals of costumed monkeys painted in a Watteau-Fragonard manner, its heavy linen tablecloths and flattering light coming from clusters of tulip-shaped fixtures. The food is firmly if unimpassionedly French. It could equally well be Spanish or Italian since most of the people who dine there order veal or fish, cooked as plainly as possible—the diet of thinness and ulcers—the diet of power. A visitor to New York might find himself lunching and dining at Le Cirque every day for a week if he were being treated to a display of the power of his hosts. On the other hand, if his hosts were true gourmets or devoted to amusing atmosphere, he might never even hear Le Cirque mentioned.

Daisy had never been there. It was not North's kind of restaurant, since he refused to dress in a suit and tie for any meal unless Nick-the-Greek had finally persuaded him to be pleasant to a big client. Nor had Henry Kavanaugh, Daisy's still languishing suitor, ever thought to take her there. Le Cirque at lunch was chiefly about publishing power, and at dinner it was about corporate power, but it had nothing to do with young-Grosse-Pointe-fortune power.

Tonight, as always, Patrick Shannon had one of the three best tables in the house, the banquettes just to the right of the entrance. Daisy sensed the power in the air as they walked into the restaurant. She glided to her seat perfectly aware that almost all the people in the room were watching her, although she seemed oblivious to them. Her memories of the heavily power-weighted atmosphere of the Connaught made her impervious to being impressed by a mere restaurant, and no amount of being looked at could intimidate the daughter of Stash Valensky, who had become blithely accustomed to the covert sensation she and her father had made whenever they went out together on those Sunday mornings so many, many years ago.

She looked around with calm approval. "How pleasant," she said in a casual lilt, breathing in the palpable atmosphere, compounded of smug self-satisfaction, of self-confidence, of frankly appraising glances from people who were secure enough not to think it rude to stare, and of the mutual congratulations—just on being there—that were beamed from one table to another until they formed an invisible tent in the scented air. Although Daisy was starving, she ordered with the unmistakable Spartan lightness of someone who is so often confronted by menus, one more elaborate than the next, that food has become almost, but not quite, boring.

Pat Shannon found himself, for the first time in years, at a loss for conversation. Daisy seemed to be utterly comfortable looking idly around the room, without making any attempt to talk to him. Why didn't she chatter, why didn't she flirt, why didn't she try to get him to talk about himself like any other decent, self-respecting woman?

As Daisy sipped her cold cream-of-cucumber soup, Shannon launched into an account of his trip to Tokyo. She asked just the right questions, he thought, but she seemed . . . was it reserved, or bored, or withdrawn? None of those words aptly described the faintly detached, although perfectly polite way in which she somehow indicated that there was perhaps something overly *mercantile* about conglomerate affairs in Japan.

As they were served their filet of sole Véronique, several men Shannon knew passed on their way to the street. They greeted him in a lingeringly hearty way that virtually demanded that he introduce them to Daisy. What the hell, Shannon asked himself, had inspired that ass Harmsworth to kiss her hand—a man who had been born and brought up in the great Midwest, even if he did own half of Chicago? And why did Zellerbach give him that meaningful parting look, as if Shannon had just won the decathlon?

Daisy sat back, not permitting the lure of the soft banquette to caress her shoulders. She sat in a straight-backed way that, although it was not stiff, indicated, by her example, that while others might lean over their plates or loll in their seats, she had been so trained in queenly posture that it was second nature. She blessed the example of an old Grace Kelly movie she'd seen on television a few nights ago.

Shannon turned the conversation to Daisy, asking her where she'd gone to college, but even as she told him the bare details she was unenthusiastic about reviving memories of her student days, nor did she find the topic of Ham and Topsy Short, their only mutual friends, particularly spellbinding, a judgment with which Shannon privately agreed. While Daisy thought about and wistfully rejected the idea of ordering cheese—she had made herself refuse dessert because rich women never eat dessert—two couples Shannon knew stopped by their table. The women, Shannon thought in disgust, literally fawned over Daisy. How else could you describe their asking her where she'd found her divine dress and who did her divine hair? People had an atrocious way of demanding information from strangers, he told himself, as Daisy answered their questions with every indication of the mild, automatic pleasure of someone who is accustomed to such admiring questions, consigning her homemade chignon to Suga without a blush.

As the waiter brought his floating island Shannon realized that he was about to burst. His promise not to talk business seemed, retrospectively, absurd. What were they doing here, the most looked-at couple in the room, the focus of curiosity of the whole damn place, if it didn't lead to a reopening of his Elstree proposition? He envisioned a dozen dinners during which, to keep from arousing Daisy's ire, he would allow the Elstree campaign to go down the drain, drop by expensive drop. In a last effort to keep from stirring up her evil temper again, he blurted out a question that had been on his mind since they'd left her apartment for dinner.

"Where did you get your lurcher?"

She turned toward him, black eyes filled with a disquieting gleam, a lively suspicion on her lips. "And just how did you know Theseus was a lurcher?" she demanded.

"Oh, shit!" Shannon groaned.

"*How*? I called him a guard dog."

"It's Lucy—" he started to sputter with laughter.

"Who's Lucy . . . your clairvoyant? Nobody in this city has ever recognized a lurcher," she said, the light of battle in her eyes.

"Lucy's my lurcher," he confessed.

"Ah-ha—the man dogs and children just naturally trust! So that's what he smelled on you, *eau-de*-lady-lurcher. Why didn't you tell me then?"

"I honestly don't know . . ."

"You don't? I've never met a lurcher owner who didn't ask me, *immediately*, what cross Theseus was."

"What cross is he?"

"Don't try to change the subject."

"I believe I was trying to impress you," Shannon said, his dark blue eyes under their black brows challenging her to a frolic, "but I blew it, didn't I?"

"Not necessarily," Daisy said with her first provocative smile of the evening. She had decided to let him off the hook. He was not a man who would enjoy being embarrassed again. "Since you ask, Theseus is Irish wolfhound crossed with a greyhound on one side of the family and deerhound on the other, with whippet and sheepdog thrown in. What's Lucy?"

"Brindle greyhound with Alsatian but I'm not positive about the rest—more greyhound certainly. She's a bit of a bastard."

"What lurcher isn't? Do you hunt on foot with her?"

"Lucy'll chase anything that moves, but she's anti-blood sport. She nearly died of fright one day when she killed a rabbit. She must have bumped into it."

"I've had to train poor Theseus to heel—or keep him on a lead—I can't let him hunt—he's the most frustrated lurcher in captivity," Daisy said sadly.

"Perhaps," Shannon said delicately, "they should . . . meet."

"And what," asked Daisy, "would you do with the pups?"

"I'd give you the pick of the litter, of course, and split whatever the rest of them went for." As soon as he said it he felt like a fool. Did one discuss money with this sovereign woman?

"That's generous of you," Daisy said, lifting her eyebrows in a tiny movement of disdain, "but I don't want the responsibility of a pup. You keep the best one and give the money to some charity or other." She was silent for a moment and then added, smiling, "I don't usually meddle in Theseus's romantic life—he manages quite well enough on his own—but since Lucy is a lurcher, too, I think a blind date might be a good idea."

Emboldened by her affability on matters canine, Shannon decided to take the risk of discussing Elstree with this proud and so easily offended creature. The more he looked at the pure felicity of her profile and observed the serene harmony of her gestures, the longer he listened to her low and charming voice, the more convinced he became that she could restore faith in hereditary aristocracy in any land, including Red China, and what was more important, sell important quantities of cosmetics and perfume to American women.

"Daisy," he started and then stopped. Her heart, which had been beating hard at the prospect of having to reopen the Elstree question herself, slowed to a slightly slower pulse. She could tell by the way he'd said her name that he was about to begin negotiations.

"Yes, Shannon?" she said invitingly, and the way she looked at him made him think of a shower of dark falling stars.

"Daisy, I know I promised not to talk about it, but I wish you'd reconsider the matter of doing the Elstree commercials. I promised not to put any pressure on you, but it occurred to me that you might not have thought of it as a challenge—you said you loved challenges when we were talking before—and perhaps if you could put your mind to the question in that light . . ."

"I already have. In fact, I've given it a great deal of serious consideration."

"And? . . ."

"Shannon, if I sign a contract to endorse a Princess Daisy line for Elstree, it would mean the loss of a number of things that are very precious to me: first, and most important of all, my privacy; then my reluctance to trade on my title; and almost certainly my job since I could never do justice to both. I'll have to give up my ability to come and go as I please without anyone looking at me and thinking, Oh, that's Princess Daisy, the Elstree Girl—and I detest being pointed out and stared at. I'd lose all the anonymity I've guarded so carefully for years." Her voice was almost harsh with this accurate picture of the future. "I'd become just another household word—if the campaign worked—and you can't go back from that."

"So it's no," he said.

"It's yes." She didn't wait for him to react. "I want one million dollars and a contract for three years, during which time you can use my face, my name and as much of my genuine blonde hair as you want to sell Elstree in everything from commercials to department stores. But the million dollars has to be paid in three installments, the first third on signing, and the rest to be paid over the next three years, *whether or not* the campaign is successful, whether or not you decide to drop the Princess Daisy line because it isn't selling, whether or not you change advertising agencies again and they want to try something else. Otherwise we don't have a deal."

A million dollars, said Shannon to himself, and I don't even know how she'll photograph.

"Or," said Daisy, "we can forget it."

"We have a deal," he said hastily. "What made you change your mind?"

"Private reasons," Daisy answered, with a small, secret smile and a great wave of terror and triumph lifting her heart.

22

North was amused for not quite three minutes. As amused as if a familiar, fluffy pussycat had taken it into its head to snarl at him. Why not let it exhaust itself while he fended it off with a touch of fancy footwork and the casual back of his gloved hand? Less than three minutes into Daisy's patient repetition of her plans he realized she was serious.

"Don't be absurd," he said severely, a frown settling on his face. "You can't do it, you don't know the first thing about modeling or promotion—you'd be rotten at it—the whole business is ridiculous. I thought you had more sense than to make a fool of yourself."

"Shannon doesn't think I'll be a fool," Daisy said sharply. She had enough inner doubts without fighting North's assessment of her value.

"Shannon! That meddling prick! Coming in here and junking a perfectly good campaign, going ape-shit over your gee-whiz hair and your classy look—he's nothing but another businessman-snob who imagines himself a star maker," he sneered.

"I don't want to get into a screaming match about Pat Shannon," Daisy said. "I just want you to realize that I have to leave the studio."

"Something that you haven't the slightest right to do! Who the hell took a chance on you when you came out of that crazy California college desperate for a job—a job I must have twenty applicants for a week?"

"Bootsie Jacobs hired me, as a matter of record."

"Only because I said she could. Do you have any idea of how much time and money it cost me to make you into a commercial producer? Your whole learning process has been at my expense. I don't care if you worked your ass off fourteen hours a day, you got invaluable training and not every director in town would have put up with you—eagerness isn't everything."

"I learned fast. You've had me working hard for five and a half years and even in the beginning I had talent, too," Daisy said defiantly. "Always."

"Talent isn't everything! Lots of people have talent. It's knowing the ropes—and now, now that you're useful, you choose to walk away. How you can do this with any decency is beyond me. I don't think anyone has ever been so ungrateful."

"I repeat, I need to make a lot of money, North."

"Money. *Money*—you know damn well you get paid as much as any other producer in the business."

"Then add a hundred dollars to what I make and you can try to hire Bob Giraldi's producer or Steve Horn's producer or Sally Safir—you've always admired her."

"But Sally's an equal partner with Richard Heimann! Who could afford that?" North cried in highest outrage.

Daisy surveyed him calmly. "Evidently Richard can."

"Is that what you're holding me up for—a piece of the action?"

"Of course not. I'm not holding you up for anything. I'm leaving to make as much money as I possibly can."

North's whole face sweetened into an expression of intimacy that she hadn't seen on his features in weeks.

"Okay—I admit that I can't compete with Elstree. I don't understand why you have to make all that money, but I respect the fact that it must be very important if it's led you to make this bizarre decision. All right—go in good health, Daisy. I wish you luck. But all I want to say is, have you considered what this will do to our relationship?"

"What will it do?" she asked in deceptively mild curiosity.

"Since you insist on leaving, it's got to change things." He looked at her narrowly, radiating all the valuable, disabling charm he knew how to project whenever he chose to.

"What things?" she asked innocently.

"Oh, shit, I loathe this sort of discussion," North flung at her. "It's typically female."

"And you started it. Listen, North, what went on in Venice should have stopped right there, the day the strike ended. You just can't stand inactivity and that's why it happened. It's been over for weeks now and you know it. Stop digging in the ashes. I'm quitting, and you'll manage without me."

"You're goddamned right I will!" He was outraged, this man who had almost never been thwarted and certainly not left. When there was leaving to be done, he did it, on his terms, just as easily as he did the plucking of the fruit when it was ripe. His tame beasts did not roar back at him and they never, ever left the cage without permission. "You're not fucking indispensable," he shouted at her.

"*I have no choice.*"

"The hell you don't!"

Daisy looked at him consideringly. She knew she was right not to tell him her reasons for taking the Elstree offer; the same instinct that had prevented her from talking about herself, except in a superficial way, when they had been together in Venice, still hummed deeply within her. North was too flinty, too harsh, too quick to discard anything that was less than perfect. He was like her father in that, she suddenly realized. Even during the hours of their lovemaking she had seen only minor signs of any change in him. There had been no deeply loving tenderness, no true softening of his taut exactingness, no greater allowance made for human vulnerability. He lacked some gift, some talent for loving and accepting. She would not use information about Anabel or Danielle as emotional blackmail to force him to be forgiving, she could not spread out her personal problems before him in order to bribe him to allow her to accept an opportunity she had every right and every reason to take. She stood still, facing North, patiently, undemandingly, yet so obdurate in all the power and dignity of her beauty, that he used his last ploy.

"I hope you realize that we could have meant a great deal to each other, Daisy. We could have had a wonderful relationship." His voice and expression would have caused ten cobras, a dozen pythons and at least three boa constrictors to lie down and coo.

Daisy listened to him in silence and put on her coat. As she reached the door, she turned back.

"North, if you found yourself stuck on a desert island with no phone service, you'd have a relationship with a coconut."

"I don't know what to be more excited about," said Kiki, "and I may have a nervous breakdown from indecision." She dallied with Luke's beard and asked, "Did you know your eyes are exactly the color of seedless green grapes?"

"You have problems, lady," Luke agreed. "Tell the doctor about them and I'll make you all well." He settled her more comfortably against his shoulder and pulled the covers up over them.

"Well, on one hand Daisy's going to be rich and famous and be a star in commercials, which is wonderful and thrilling and makes me very happy, and on the other hand my mother is coming to town and she wants to meet your mother and your mother wants to meet my mother, which is terrible and awful and makes me sick to my stomach."

"But it's only natural that they want to meet, poor baby—their children are going to get married. They are going to be *mishpocha* for the rest of their lives, so they're a touch curious about each other. Plus you've been hiding me from your mother long enough."

"What? What are they going to be? It sounds revolting. Oh, God, you never told me about that before!" wailed Kiki indignantly.

"It means, ah, sort of relatives, or maybe relatives by marriage—something like that, I can't be a hundred percent positive. You know my mother has always discouraged the use of a single Yiddish word—puts me at a hell of a disadvantage sometimes . . . maybe I should take lessons? But it's plenty serious, believe me. A *mishpocha* is a *mishpocha* forever!"

"But why do we have to *be* there when they meet? Couldn't we just make a lunch reservation for the two of them at some very nice restaurant and let them introduce themselves to each other?" Kiki suggested, nervousness making her sound like a ten-year-old.

"I'm not too sure about the protocol of getting engaged, but I know that your suggestion is strictly inadmissible. Don't even think about it. God—but it *would* be wonderful to miss it. Eleanor Kavanaugh, the queen of the Grosse Pointe Country Club, and Barbara Hammerstein, the queen of the Harmonie Club, neither of which will admit members of the other's religious persuasion—except as tokens, if at that—*mishpocha*!"

"Please stop saying that word," Kiki pleaded. "There must be some nicer way to put it."

"*Mishpocha* has nothing to do with niceness—it's a condition of life, visited upon you by your children, and if you're lucky it isn't quite as bad as any of Job's afflictions, but you have nothing to say about it—you take it as it comes and moan a lot in private. Try to think of this as an interesting episode in the joyful ongoing relationship between the Christians and the Jews."

"I think it's going to be more like the Six-Day War," Kiki said ominously. "Luke, do you have to . . . I mean, are you planning to? . . ."

"Go on—you can ask me anything," he encouraged her.

"Wear a . . . hat? At the wedding?"

"Good heavens, of course not. Why should I? Unless you think I look good in one. It might be rather chic with my beard, at that. Perhaps a homburg, or maybe a derby. After all, I am piss-elegant, or so they tell me."

"But I thought you *had* to," Kiki said, bewildered.

"Not when you're being married by a judge," Luke laughed. "But, of course, sweetheart, if you'd prefer a rabbi—no? Well then, we could always elope."

"What, and break my mother's heart? I'm the only daughter she has, you unspeakable cad. I've explained why we have to wait till summer for the wedding—there's the trousseau to get together, thousands of engagement parties *and* we have to wait for all my cousins to get out of school, or else someone would miss the wedding."

"God forbid!" sighed Luke with resignation.

"And then I have to have eight bridesmaids and Daisy as my maid of honor and my brothers for ushers—you'll have to dig up six more from somewhere—and now, of course, we can't have the bishop, but I never liked him anyway. Mother's taken the judge part very well, considering that she's been planning my wedding since I was confirmed."

"I doubt that she ever dreamed it would be a triumph for ecumenism," Luke laughed wickedly. "We must all take the broad view," he said as superciliously as possible, wondering where he could find six presentable ushers. He'd be laughed out of the Art Director's Club.

"Oh, fuck you, Luke Hammerstein!"

"Willingly. You just put your little hand right here and sort of slide it up and down . . ."

Two days later, at the stroke of one o'clock, a trembling, neatly dressed Kiki, her lips quivering with fright, guided her majestic and still-beautiful mother through the doors of La Grenouille. She and Luke had picked the most elegant restaurant in New York in the hopes that the atmosphere would soften the two dragon ladies. There would be at least ten minutes worth of conversation on the topic of the flowers on the table, Luke had pointed out, and another twenty in considering the menu. Luke was already seated with his mother, a fine and youthful-looking woman in a definitive hat, a hat that would inform Grosse Pointe exactly who Barbara Fishbach Hammerstein was. Luke and his mother rose at the approach of Kiki and Eleanor Kavanaugh who was standing tall and formidable.

"Mother," both Luke and Kiki said at the same time. Then they stopped and started over. "Mother, this is Luke's mother," Kiki babbled, having forgotten Luke's last name.

Eleanor Kavanaugh extended her hand, peering closely from the near-sighted eyes on which she refused to wear glasses, and then she slowly withdrew her hand, saying questioningly, "Bobbie? Could it possibly be you, Bobbie—Bobbie Fishbach?"

"Oh my God! Ellie! Ellie Williams—I'd know you anywhere—you haven't changed a bit!" cried Barbara Hammerstein in wonder and joy.

"Oh Bobbie!" Kiki's mother threw herself into the arms of Luke's mother, "Bobbie precious! I've always wondered what became of you."

"You never answered my letters," replied Barbara Hammerstein, bursting into tears.

"My parents moved so many times—I never got them. I thought you'd forgotten me."

"Forget my best friend?" Luke's mother said, still weeping. "Never."

"When did all this happen?" Luke asked wildly. "How come you didn't recognize each other's names?"

"It was in Scarsdale—we went all the way through tenth grade together," Eleanor Kavanaugh sniffed emotionally. "Then Grandfather went bankrupt and we had to sell the house and move—and, for heaven's sake, Luke, just never mind. Oh, Bobbie—isn't it wonderful? Now we'll be *mishpocha*!"

"How do you know *that* word?" asked Mrs. Hammerstein, recoiling.

"I've been practicing it for weeks, Bobbie darling. But let me kiss this son of yours . . . after all, he *is* going to be my *aydem*," said Mrs. Kavanaugh, proudly reeling off the newly learned Yiddish word for son-in-law.

"Your *what*?" asked Mrs. Hammerstein.

Patrick Shannon paced the adobe tile floor of his office. It was the day after he had obtained Daisy's agreement to represent Elstree, and he had taken the first possible opportunity to call together the people who would be involved in the new campaign, the same people from Elstree and the agency who had been at the meeting in North's studio.

Shannon seemed to thrive on the necessity to cut through red tape, Luke thought to himself, trying to count the number of essential meetings he was missing at this very moment, back at the agency.

"We haven't got a day to lose," Shannon told them all, looking as determined as an outlaw chieftain who has caught sight of a fully loaded wagon train innocently crossing the prairie. "The cosmetic and fragrance industry does ten billion dollars worth of business every year, and one third of that is done between Thanksgiving and Christmastime. We've got to be in the stores by Thanksgiving this year to even think about breaking even. That gives us just under seven months to launch the line next September."

"It's not enough time, Pat," said Hilly Bijur. "Look at what you're talking about: new packages, new commercials, new print ads, a whole new sales pitch to the buyers . . ."

"Hilly, look at what we've got," Pat interrupted him. "We have the basic cosmetics, a complete line. We don't have to change anything about them except the packages, because they're perfect—they just don't sell. Yet. We've got the doors—Elstree is already carried in five thousand class retail outlets. We've got the shipping and the billing and the cost accounting down to a science. It's not as if we have to start up from nothing—all we need are the trimmings, the icing on the cake. For Christ's sake . . ."

"Pat . . ."

"Now, listen, Hilly, that new fragrance the Elstree chemists came up with last year is a *winner*. It never even had a name—now it's called Princess Daisy and even my dog likes it. As well she should with oil of jasmine at four thousand dollars a pound. All we've got to do is get women to smell the perfume and try the cosmetics—they'll like them—they're good items."

"Pat," Jared Turner, the marketing director, asked, "considering that Elstree lost thirty million last year, what sort of figures have you projected for this year?"

"I'm looking for a volume of one hundred million in retail sales."

Oh, fuck and be damned, Turner thought to himself. Out loud he said reasonably, "But Avon's the biggest cosmetic business in the world and they do a billion. You're talking about ten percent of their business, and we're in the hole as of now."

"One of the things I like about this game is that you can turn it around fast," Shannon answered, pulling some thorns out of one of his cacti in excitement. "Really fast—if you just get the right handle."

"You haven't told us what your ad budget is going to be," Luke broke into the conversation. All this talk about handles meant nothing without the money to back it up.

"The industry average is to spend ten percent for advertising and promotion out of every dollar of retail sales—I'm planning to double that. Based on my estimated volume, we'll allocate twenty million dollars to Princess Daisy perfume and cosmetics."

There goes the ballgame, thought Hilly Bijur. I wonder if Norton Simon, Inc., isn't looking for someone to head up Max Factor for them. It's in trouble, but not as big trouble as Elstree is going to be in.

"Twenty million dollars," Luke said impassively, stroking his beard in a way that had Oscar Pattison and Kirbo Henry, his team of copy writer and art director, looking at each other in glee.

"And one third of it right before Christmas," Shannon added. "That means, of course, that I'm blowing our potential profit for this year, any way you look at it, but I'm thinking in long-range terms. In two years we'll be in good shape, in three years—the sky's the limit."

"But Pat," Turner persisted, with the reckless air of a man refusing a blindfold before a firing squad, "what if you just don't turn Elstree around? We'll lose another fucking fortune!"

"And the stockholders will roast my testicles for breakfast," Shannon said cheerfully. "In a hot chili sauce, over a slow fire, to loud applause."

"We could cut back in packaging," Hilly Bijur said helpfully. "We have a hell of a lot of money invested in last year's packages—maybe they could be used in some way so that they wouldn't be a total loss. . . . Maybe . . ."

"Hilly, we're introducing an absolutely new line—Princess Daisy—no *retreads*." Shannon cut him off. "I thank you for thinking about economy, but this is no time to cut corners. Get your packaging designers together and tell them to go all out, full throttle—it's got to be so classy it makes your hair stand on end. Electrify me! Spend whatever you need, but make sure the packaging reflects Daisy's personality—nothing too modern, nothing space age, no gimmicks."

"Right, Pat," Hilly Bijur said, thinking that, now that Charles Revson was safely dead, it would be a good time to take a shot at a job at Revlon. He'd even take a cut in salary if he had to. "Reflects Daisy's personality"—that girl in the carpenter's pants—where the fuck had he put his Rolaids?

"We've come up with a concept or two," Luke said, "since that last meeting with North. You were talking romance, warmth, glamour and star quality. Now that we've got Daisy to work with, we've been playing around with what Oscar here calls the Romanov approach—Princess Daisy as she would have looked back before the Revolution, dressed in period court costume, wearing the crown jewels or as close to them as we can find outside of a Russian museum . . ."

"Sorry, Luke, but that's too high and mighty for my taste—I want her to be closer to the customer than that," Shannon said instantly.

"I thought you'd feel that way," Luke smiled. He always gave them a plausible bummer to shoot down. He continued smoothly.

"Our next concept is contemporary and I think it taps into every woman's deep and constant desire to be attractive to men, which women's lib doesn't seem to have diminished by one jot or tittle, thank God. We'd film a ballroom full of dancers—or a disco full of dancers—any and all variations on dancing, panning in from above, and then cutting closer and closer to Daisy dancing, hair flying, absolutely radiant, sensually abandoned to the music, the spirit of the dance incarnate. Then . . ."

"Sorry, Luke," Shannon interrupted again, "but I don't buy that either. It might work with just any ordinary model but since we're dealing with a princess we've got to play up every inch of class, it seems to me, and that abandoned sensuality doesn't hit the right note." Shannon frowned. Since all the chairs in his office were taken, except the one behind his desk, which he never used unless he was alone, he was leaning against the wall. He looked like a studious boy, his black hair tumbling over his forehead down to his furrowed brows, his blue eyes concerned, the vertical lines around his wide mouth set in consideration of the problem which, for the moment, had replaced all the other business of Supracorp.

"We have a third concept, which I personally think the most appealing," Luke said without discomfiture. Not only did he have a third but, if need be, he'd come up with a thirtieth. Fifteen percent of twenty million was three million dollars; the advertising agency's commission. Shannon was entitled to a piss-pot full of concept for that.

"Let's have it."

"Daisy is a member of the aristocracy and there are two main ways in which Americans perceive aristocrats, foreign aristocrats, that is. They're either presiding at state functions—boring—or they're having fun because they're rich and go where the fun is. I'd like to send Daisy all over the world, to wherever the aristocracy of various nations gather—St. Moritz, for example, or the Aga Kahn's resort on the Costa Smerelda—and show her mingling with her own kind of man, dressed in whatever the newest outfits are for the particular place we'd be shooting—ski clothes and furs, bathing suits, French dresses and big hats—whatever—she'd be living a dream life, *but* because of who she *really* is, it would be believable. Here we'd tap into every woman's desire to lead a glamorous life . . . she could lead it through Daisy. And by association, when our potential customer uses Elstree, she'd have a little of that glamour rub off on her."

Everyone in the room waited for Shannon to receive this latest idea. Helen Strauss, although she was the advertising director of Elstree, had again realized that this decision was not hers to make. The silence lengthened as Shannon thought.

"Luke, it's a good idea, but it turns me off because I think that the Jet Set, which is really what you're talking about, is perceived as basically worthless—the old, idle rich. If Daisy is constantly shown as a part of that world, she'll be tainted with the same brush. I think you risk creating envy and a woman won't go and buy the products that are being touted by someone we're deliberately giving her every reason to envy. Our consumers, so far a non-existent group, will be drawn from a population in which over half the women work and the other half are housewives or students. We don't need to sell the idle rich because there aren't enough of them. But I like the idea of presenting Daisy as an aristocrat—that's what Supracorp's buying in her—but in another, more subtle way. I keep visualizing her in England, for some reason, and I'm not absolutely sure why."

"It's because she still has a tiny, almost unnoticeable trace of an English accent—she was brought up in England until she was fifteen," Luke informed him.

"How do you know so much about her?" Patrick asked with a sudden touch of suspicion which surprised him even as he heard it in his voice.

"I'm . . . ah . . . engaged to her roommate," Luke said sheepishly. Being engaged was as square a thing as original, unconventional Luke Hammerstein had ever done.

"The roommate from Grosse Pointe?"

Luke nodded.

"Kiki Kavanaugh—United Motors? Congratulations, Hammerstein, that's wonderful."

Everyone in the room looked at Like with new appreciation. Kavanaugh—Detroit—United Motors—well, well! Good for Luke! They'd known he was smart—but not *that* smart.

Luke, annoyed, hurried back to the subject. "You said England, Mr. Shannon?"

"Yes, and castles—I see her with castles in the background, *always castles*, and doing something like galloping up to the entrance—no model alive can ride like that girl, or maybe walking dogs in a garden with a castle behind her . . ."

"Corgis—that's the dog the Queen of England always has with her—they're the royal favorites," Candice Bloom said helpfully.

"A lurcher, maybe two," Shannon said in a visionary voice, confusing everybody.

"Eating strawberries and cream on a lawn, with the castle in the background," Oscar Pattison said.

"Good—that's a nice one," Shannon agreed, "yup, outdoors, England, castles—maybe a guy with her—*always* a guy with her—but no male models—real lords, young ones—but a gentle approach, simple things, so long as you have that castle . . . she'll supply all the rest, the glamour and the romance. Every woman would like to be a princess and live in a castle—maybe not for always but certainly once in a lifetime," Shannon said, finally satisfied. "And since she's American they can identify with her—by the time this campaign is ready to go the whole country *should know* that she's an American working girl who also happens to be a princess.

"Candice," he continued, turning to the publicity woman, "you're going to make sure of that. I want the biggest publicity push you've ever worked on for Daisy—a fabulous party to introduce her to the press right before we launch the perfume, and really *lean* on all your contacts for interviews and photos. It's a natural for the press, considering who her parents were and considering that she's pretty much of a mystery girl—but just because it's a natural, I don't want you to wait for them to come to you—be as aggressive as if you had an absolute unknown to work with. Of course we'll get *Women's Wear* and *Vogue* and *Bazaar* and the syndicated columnists, but I want the mass magazines too, *Good House* and the *Journal* and *Cosmo*—you know the drill. But more than anything else, I want *People*. I want a cover on *People* just before Thanksgiving—in fact I'm counting on it."

Candice Bloom merely nodded. She knew how good she was. She could probably deliver just about anything except covers on *Time*, *Newsweek* and *People*. If Daisy were a teenage rock singer, or the star of a weekly comedy sitcom—or a new pope—she could *maybe* get *People*—but what the hell, she had contacts over there she'd been saving for something crucial and it was worth a try, if she wanted to keep her job, and she did. P. R. was pure shit but she liked it—even her analyst didn't know why.

Luke thought that this was the first time he'd created a campaign with a sponsor in on it from the beginning and doing most of the talking, but it seemed to be working. He had heard of a "hands on" top-level manager, and now he understood what that meant. However, Shannon didn't know everything. Luke had a few cards still up his sleeve.

"Mr. Shannon, a major problem here, for Elstree as for any perfume sold in America, is that women tend to treat their perfume as an art object. They buy the bottle or get it as a gift and then they only use it for special occasions or let it sit on their dresser tops unopened—unlike the Europeans, who will wallow in the stuff and then buy more. American women really use the cosmetics, but they act as if perfume were champagne instead of Gallo white wine. We haven't talked yet about the copy line for the Princess Daisy campaign. We're trying to sell *two* things—an entire line of cosmetics, and an entire line of perfume and cologne. I'd like to use only one line in every commercial and on every piece of print advertising, a line which applies as well to the cosmetics as to the perfume—and a line which has the advantage of being one which Daisy can say convincingly, without having to be an actress." Luke rose to his feet. Only a loser presented the copy sitting down. He paused for exactly the right beat and then spoke. "I wear it *every* day—Princess Daisy—by Elstree."

"*Perfect!*" Shannon said. As soon as the word left his lips, the room was as clamoring with congratulations as it would have been full of silence if Shannon hadn't liked it.

"Simple but eloquent!"

"Easy to remember!"

"Great product identification!"

"Tremendous message! It's better than Western Union!"

Luke smiled modestly. He felt modest. Art it wasn't, but it sure as hell was a living.

Ram walked briskly along Old Bond Street toward his club on St. James Street. He was at least five minutes early for lunch, but he saw no temptation to stroll in the miserable London weather of late February 1977. He passed into the warmth of Whites quickly, swinging his umbrella and greeting a young man he knew who was leaving. The man neither returned his words nor seemed to have seen him. But surely, Ram thought, they had spent several evenings together last fall? Wasn't the fellow one of the group who had hung around Sarah Fane? Or perhaps he just looked like him? In any case, he was a nobody. Ram shrugged and went into one of the lounges to wait for Joe Polkingthorne of *The Financial Times.*

Ram had, in past years, made a habit of lunching with this journalist every three months or so. Although the great newspaper he worked for had correspondents all over the world, Polkingthorne was often sent abroad to write special reports. He had a shrewd flair for sniffing out areas that were ripe for financial development, and his advice had sometimes proven to be rewarding for Ram and his investment trust. Polkingthorne, for his part, thought of Ram as one of the two or three brightest and best informed men in the City, one who would surely become more powerful with each year, and it pleased him to exchange pieces of information and opinion that they both considered, quite rightly, as more valuable than any material gift they might have made each other.

Before Ram could order a drink from one of the stewards, he saw Lord Harry Fane and several other men he knew leaving the lounge on their way to lunch. Ram had not seen Henry Fane since he had stopped showing attention to the man's daughter, almost two months before, but he had prepared himself mentally for the inevitable time when they would resume their business relationship. As Fane came closer, Ram inclined his head at precisely the proper, impersonal, yet friendly angle which would, as no words could, indicate that he, Ram, did not intend to allow any hasty and shallow behavior on the part of Sarah Fane to make any difference to him. He held no foolish grudges.

Harry Fane stopped walking as he saw Ram. He looked at him incredulously and then turned an angry red from his collar to his hairline. The men with him hesitated. Then Lord Harry Fane started to walk again, scowling fiercely, his fists jammed into his pockets, passing by as if Ram were invisible, followed by his friends, none of whom greeted Ram, although they had all known him for years.

Ram sat down in a deep chair and heard his voice calmly requesting a whiskey and water from the steward. This was impossible, he said to himself, even as his body, which knew what had happened, felt as if he had received an all-but-killing blow in the gut. This was not the eighteenth century, his rupture with Sarah Fane was the sort that happened constantly among young men and women busily arranging and rearranging and generally sorting themselves out into couples. While he was telling himself this, Ram knew that there must be something more to explain his having been cut—*cut*, for God's sake, actually cut—by five men in the space of a few minutes. What had happened to destroy the respect that he had always prided himself on so intensely? He had spent an entire lifetime shoring up that respect against any attack, respect that had always been a thousand times more important to him than any amount of affection or good-fellowship.

Even as Ram asked himself this question, he simultaneously acknowledged that it had been over a month—perhaps more—since he had received any invitations, either to dinner or for the weekend. After his return to London, after that accursed trip to Nassau to try to reason with Daisy, he'd been too busy working to worry about his social life. In any case he'd had no desire to see anyone in London, and he had paid only faint attention to the fact that his mail consisted chiefly of bills and that his phone rang only for business calls.

Yet last year at this same time he'd been out six nights a week and refused twice as many invitations as he could accept. He sipped his whiskey and water as he added up the evidence that told him that he was a social outcast. At the very moment that he asked himself what had caused this to happen, he understood, with cold and complete horror, that he would never know.

Sarah Fane could not possibly have told anyone what had actually happened between them without ruining her own reputation. Therefore, she had invented something—some lie that was plausible enough for everyone to believe, some foul, degrading, disgusting lie that he would never hear repeated but that would follow him forever throughout the only world in which he cared to live.

Ram knew the rules and he knew he was finished. He could still work effectively; Sarah Fane's lie would not tarnish his placements of capital all over the world. Her words could not reach the ears of art dealers or the men from whom he bought rare books or custom suit makers or the men who sold him horses or who farmed his land. But, sooner or later, it would come to the attention of everyone who mattered in the world in which he had been one of the most sought-after bachelors in the land.

English society had a way of dealing with people it thrust out from itself; a silent, deadly, irrefutable method that Ram had seen at work before. There was no court of appeals because there was no one to whom an appeal could be addressed, no one to whom a question could be put, no one who would admit to having heard anything. If he had had friends . . . Ram realized that there was no man nor woman among the hundreds of people whose parties he had attended in the last years whom he could consider a close enough friend to go to in this moment. A lawyer? What was there to say? Could he imagine himself complaining that some men with whom he was acquainted had not greeted him? Could he claim damages because he had not been invited to dinner? It was nothing—and it was everything. And the shame could never be brought to light and reduced to the lie that it must be.

Whatever she had told people, this girl who was the reigning debutante of her year, this girl with her hundreds of years of aristocratic English blood, it would go no further than the members of a small group. Ram was free to make a new life among intellectuals, among artists, among businessmen without society connections, among foreigners who lived in London, among people of the theater or among people who cared for politics. He would be barred only from some country houses and certain parties, from shooting with a particular selection of men and from riding with others. He would lose—had lost—only the company of everyone in the world whose respect he valued.

"Well, there you are, Valensky!" Joe Polkingthorne thrust out his hand and Ram shook it as he rose from his chair. "Not going to finish your drink? Well, there's always wine . . . make up for it at lunch, eh?" As Ram found himself feeling *grateful* for the journalist's hearty, easy manner he first realized the full measure of his destruction. When the headwaiter led him to his usual table and informed him, deferentially, of the various specials of the day, when the wine steward waited attentively as he made his choice, when he looked around and realized with relief that the men at the next table were strangers, the great, yawning wound in his middle opened wider. Each attention by a paid servant, each new face cautiously observed, was another door shutting behind him as he walked into the jail in which he would spend the rest of his life.

He listened intently as Polkingthorne discussed South Africa and the impossibility of depending on the gold miners; he launched himself with more vivacity than he had ever displayed into a long account of the most recent doings at Lion Management, he ate avidly and drank more than his share, as he tried to do something to stem the seepage he felt in his center, but it was steady and relentless.

"Well, shit, what's the point of arguing about it ourselves? Let's call up and make sure that Shannon didn't really mean only castles—he was probably thinking of great houses and palaces, too," said Kirbo Henry.

"I wouldn't do that if I were you," Luke answered warningly.

"Damn it, Luke, a real castle, by definition, has to be defensible by a fucking army . . . most of them are in ruins, for Christ's sake—they haven't been built since feudal times, unless you're going for the fake ones the Victorians built which, in my opinion, look like backlotsville. Take Culzean Castle in Ayrshire—it even has palm tree in the foreground! I mean look at these pictures, will you—Hedingham Castle in Essex and Rochester Castle in Kent—they simply don't look lived in!" he said, handing Luke pictures of the ruins of great square twelfth-century towers, menacing Norman keeps, massive and square.

While Luke shook his head at them, Kirbo produced pictures of Stourhead, that meltingly lovely, enormous Palladian villa which was built during a period which lasted from 1727 to 1840. "I'm sure that's what he had in mind—it's where Kubrick filmed *Barry Lyndon*—it's absolutely gorgeous! Can't we check it out, at least?"

"Shannon said a castle and he meant a castle. Don't show me anything without a tower, a keep, a moat, a drawbridge, battlements, ramparts—some place where you can pour boiling oil down on the enemy, Kirbo. Just stop complaining and get back to the research. There have got to be castles in England that people still live in, or that look that way, because *that's the concept.*" Luke dismissed his grumpy art director, who was pissed off, in his opinion, because he hadn't thought up the castle idea himself.

"Gelatinous!" Daisy said rebelliously to Theseus. He looked at her questioningly. She had always talked to him, but this was not within the range of his understanding. "The way the time goes," she continued, "the hurry up and wait . . . it's driving me crazy." Daisy continued to complain to Theseus as she walked around the apartment looking without success for something to put in order, something that might be blessedly in need of mending or straightening or fixing. The months since she had signed the Elstree contract had passed in the most unexpectedly slow manner. Somehow, having made her decision, she had imagined that she would be caught up at once in a whirl of work, but she found out that instead she was a prisoner of Supracorp.

Although they didn't need her on a full-time basis until July when commercials would be shot, they wouldn't let her leave town either, because she was sporadically needed for public-relations opportunities. "I'm sorry," Candice Bloom had said firmly, "but you really *cannot* go to England, not even for just a few days. Leo Lerman's giving me a call about lunch and I'm not sure what day he'll be free, Trudy Owett at the *Journal* wants to see you for a possible fashion layout and I'm waiting to hear form her any minute . . . no, Daisy, I want you where I can get my hands on you in five minutes."

During the long, tedious spring and early summer Daisy's days were broken up, from time to time, by consultations and fittings with Bill Blass, who was doing a capsule Princess Daisy wardrobe both for her personal wear in public appearances and for use in store promotions. There were also occasional interviews, most of which had not yet appeared, as well as photographic sessions for the Elstree ads.

She huddled, disconsolate and wistful, in one of the wicker armchairs in the living room and wished that Kiki were there. Although Kiki still nominally shared the apartment with Daisy, in reality she spent most of her time at home, in Grosse Pointe, doing complicated, ritualistic things connected with her wedding. Whenever she was in New York, she stayed at Luke's, flying in and out of the apartment like a demented bee. Daisy felt as abandoned as a dog who had been left alone locked in a car, unexpectedly, with no reason given. She had not been fully aware of her need for Kiki's volatile, insouciant, brazen and consistently confused presence until her friend had disappeared into the busy world of premarital goings-on.

Kiki with monogrammed towels indeed, Daisy thought sadly, as she realized that the towels were only a tiny sign of the difference Kiki's marriage was going to make in her life. "I am suffering from separation anxiety," she announced to Theseus. It started as a joke, but as she said it she heard the catch in her voice. "Fool, silly fool—no, Theseus, not you, *me*," Daisy assured the dog, realizing that behind her feeling of impending loss at the thought of Kiki's getting married were other losses, ancient losses she could not afford to dwell on, lest she start to weep. She got up briskly and started to get dressed. In a mood like this, the only answer was to take to the streets with Theseus, avoiding butcher shops and other temptations, but, at all costs, getting out of the empty apartment.

As she dressed, Daisy admitted to herself that in spite of her impatience to finally get down to work, healthy consuming work, in spite of her feeling that once the whole Elstree business started, her boredom and restlessness would be cured, she was terrified of that future moment. I'm going to be such a big target, she thought, confusedly, not knowing precisely what she meant. All she was sure of was that she had kept a low profile for all of her adult life in the nebulous hope that it would prevent her from losing any more than she already had. Now, with her face and name soon to be exposed many hundreds of thousands of times in the most public way possible, she felt an almost superstitious fear of the future. Fool, she thought again, but didn't say out loud, to spare the feelings of her dog.

As Daisy roamed SoHo with Theseus, trying to keep busy, Luke found time to telephone North.

"All packed and ready to go?" he asked heartily.

"Fuck off, Luke."

"Thanks, North, but you haven't answered my question."

"I've decided that I decline to be any part of this absurd production. Get yourself another commercial maker."

"No way. Arnie bid on the job, we accepted the bid, and we're counting on you."

"It's not the same job—the conditions have all changed."

"However much money Arnie wants to tack on because we're shooting in England, is going to be all right with the agency—I can guarantee that. But we want a Frederick Gordon North commercial, my boy, we want your verve, your sense of design, your perception of volume and contrast, the nuances of your unique lighting, your inspiration and audacity, your inimitable taste and your technical integrity—or, to put it more bluntly, we won't let you off the hook because Shannon stole Daisy from you."

"That has absolutely *nothing* to do with it!" North shouted.

"Splendid! I'm relieved to hear it, because I admit that I certainly could have understood it if you were unable to do these commercials because you can't function without Daisy. Since that's not the case, as you've just assured me, you have a commitment to us, and, as one of your old and faithful friends, and occasional major customer, we certainly expect you to honor it. Gee—I'm sure glad to hear there are no hard feelings."

"Shitweasel!"

"Temper, temper." North was still his good pal, Luke thought, but he needed him, or rather Daisy would need North's skill to direct her. Of course, he had no legal hold on North, but sometimes a little arm twisting was in order, especially if you know how to use a man's failings against him—and North's was pride. Or rather, pride was *one* of his failings.

"We're waiting to get permission from the National Trust—they own the castles we're going to use," Luke told North. "I hope your new producer has settled on Daisy's wardrobe and decided who you're bringing to England and who you're going to hire over there and all the other little, petty, niggling details Daisy used to handle with such dispatch."

"You really *are* a first-class prick."

"How many times have I told you that compliments don't affect me? Oh, and by the way, North, will you be my best man? We're having the wedding after the shoot so you can't use that as an excuse. And I think you'll enjoy the ambiance of Grosse Pointe. It's shaping up into a fairly decent little wedding; unpretentious, impudent, almost, but not quite, petulant, and of a promising year."

"I'm not the best-man type," North snapped.

"I quite agree . . . but it happens to be one of the burdens of friendship. Why should you escape? I had to do it twice for you."

"Go shit in your hat, Luke,"

"I take it that means you accept? Knew you would."

Now, late in June, Daisy looked forward with a feeling of urgency to the next month when they would all leave for England, where a ten-day shoot was scheduled. Meanwhile, from her position of outsider, she watched in concealed anxiety as Mary-Lou Duke, North's new producer, coped with the job of getting the shoot organized. Daisy had, as a courtesy, offered to show her the ropes at the studio, but her offer had been coldly declined by the woman North had hired away from his closest competitor by dint of paying her one and a half times as much as Daisy had been getting.

Mary-Lou was a woman in her thirties, handsome, almost imposing and placid. Placidity, constant, indestructible, relentless, was her secret weapon. She was as sparkling as lead, as much fun as an empty beer barrel, as humorous as a plain pipe rack—but you could depend on her. While Luke's people were finishing their own preproduction work, she took Daisy on a tour of Seventh Avenue, selecting clothes for the shoot. Mary-Lou hailed the cabs, she held the elevator door open for Daisy, and led the way into the showrooms with Daisy, captive, at her side. Daisy, so used to being the fusser rather than the one fussed over, felt like a cop, accustomed to absolute charge of passing traffic, now reduced to watching a ten-car collision without raising a hand. But she resisted all her impulses to jump in and try to make decisions. She knew damn well, even as Mary-Lou was informing designers of just what she was looking for, that most, if not all, of the clothes they brought back to the studio for North's final approval would be rejected. She kept silent as North, increasingly impatient, sent them back for different clothes on three occasions. After the third time Daisy had to go through a wardrobe parade, and after North had again turned down the clothes, Daisy felt she had to say something. They had only seven days of preproduction time left. She took the new producer aside.

"Mary-Lou—may I make a suggestion?"

"If you feel it's that important," she said reluctantly.

"The reason North doesn't like the riding jackets and the shirts we've been bringing back is that I shouldn't be in a tailored jacket and shirt—I have to be in proper riding clothes from the waist down, but above the waist I should be wearing something dashing and unusual."

"But that wouldn't be *proper*," Mary-Lou said severely.

"No, not at all, but it'd work, for what they want."

"But if people don't ride dressed like that . . ."

"The number of people who'll know the difference will be tiny. It's the general effect that counts—don't you think?"

"If you don't mind breaking the rules . . ." Mary-Lou shrugged. Even her shrug was inexpressive, not an easy thing.

"And for the picnic on the lawn, the trouble is nobody is doing the right clothes for that this year . . . but I know a place, a special place I've never been able to afford, where we might find just the thing," Daisy said eagerly.

"Daisy, perhaps you'd better just run along and look for clothes without me," Mary-Lou decided. It went against her principles to delegate any authority but she had so many more important things to do.

Mary-Lou didn't care when people insisted on trying to contribute ideas, just as long as they didn't get in the way of her logistics. Ideas were like balloons children play with—let them have their fun being "creative"—logistics were serious business. Her mind was almost entirely occupied with the mechanical details of getting North and company to England, picking up the English technicians, conveying everyone to their locations, housing them, feeding them, and making sure that they had every last piece of equipment they needed. The only thing that bothered her was that the first-class section on British Airways seemed to be heavily booked on the day they were leaving. Now *that* was something she couldn't wait to get her teeth into.

Daisy, released, dashed out to costume herself, not forgetting that she had an appointment with the Elstree make-up people that afternoon. They were taking no chances on untested English make-up artists. A top commercial make-up expert would be part of the troupe that went to England, as would one of the highest paid hairdressers in commercial work. They were each getting fifteen hundred dollars a day plus all expenses for each day they'd be away from New York. "Hardship pay" they called it, although it was difficult to see where the hardship lay in England. However, they would have charged no more to go to the Sahara. Once out of Manhattan, it was "hardship," and let no producer forget it.

Since the make-up expert had her own prized collection of dozens and dozens of hard-to-find, *recherché* types of make-up she had discovered over the years, she was not at all happy about having to use only Elstree products, but truth-in-advertising laws forced her to do so, since Daisy was going to say, "I wear it every day."

"Luckily," she said, looking at Daisy, "you don't need much make-up—I'm not used to this muck."

The Elstree product-line manager flinched. "They're excellent products," Patsy Jacobson said in irritation.

"Yeah—but its not theatrical." The two women glared at each other.

Daisy, who was sitting in front of a mirror, as motionless as a mannequin, was seized by an urge to get into this conversation. Severely she stopped herself. Develop an *attitude*, she told herself. *Be a star!* Don't get into their act. If they're having problems, that's not something I should be worried about at this stage of the game. It'll put them in shock if I turn back into Daisy the Fixer. It'll get resolved faster and better without me and if it winds up being something I don't like, I'll simply tell them to start all over again, until I do like it. If I dare. If I dare? Of course, I'll dare, won't I? After all, I am the star.

She sat quietly, thinking of the check for three hundred and thirty-three thousand dollars, and thirty-three cents, she had received from Supracorp last January when she had signed her contract.

She had written Anabel as soon as she had made the deal with Patrick Shannon at Le Cirque, telling her the news of her riches, telling her she knew of Anabel's illness, telling her not to sell *La Marée* whatever she did, telling her that she, Daisy, could easily meet all of Anabel's expenses, in addition to Danielle's, and that Anabel was not to even think about money but just concentrate on getting better. She never mentioned Ram. Even as Daisy wrote the letter she knew that she wasn't being rash in making these promises before the contract was signed. Whatever kind of man Patrick Shannon was, he wouldn't change his word, once given. She knew that as surely as she knew that Columbus had not circumnavigated the globe.

There had been several other dinners with Shannon in the months between then and now, oddly formal dinners, Daisy thought, to which various members of the

Supracorp hierarchy were invited, almost as if she were being presented to them, or them to her. Shannon had been away a great deal, off and on, during the last months, on Supracorp business, and he had not renewed his suggestion about a rendezvous between his lurcher, Lucy, and Theseus. Daisy wondered if perhaps her princess act had been a little too convincing.

At last, it was July, and the shoot had officially begun, although filming would not start for another day.

Daisy was alone in her suite at Claridge's. Somehow, by means she preferred not to discuss, Mary-Lou had contrived to get them all first-class seats on the flight they wanted. Now she and North were conferring with the actors who had been chosen to be with Daisy in each commercial. Shannon's desire to show her with genuine lords had given way to North's absolute refusal to use more than one untried, non-professional in the shoot.

As Daisy wandered about her suite, so large that its closets could have been small bedrooms, she thought of all the things she might be doing in London, from riding in Hyde Park to hunting up a jumble sale. She had only a few hours before they all met the English location crew to leave in a procession of cars and equipment-filled trucks for their first location, in Sussex. Not enough time, she fretted, to visit Danielle and be sure to be back in time. But once the shoot was over a few days would belong to her. Then—ah, then she'd see Danielle, and go to visit Anabel.

As she waited, she felt absolutely alien in the city that had been her home for so many years. Who knew who now lived in the pale yellow house on Wilton Row in which she'd grown up? Who had bought Anabel's house in Eaton Square? The only places in which she might perhaps feel a sense of belonging were the stables in the Grosvenor Crescent Mews or at Lady Alden's School, and something kept her from revisiting these old haunts. Restlessly Daisy went down the great flight of stairs to buy some magazines to read in her sitting room, which was large enough for a cocktail party of sixty.

"Magazines, Madame?" the head hall porter said politely. "Oh, we don't *keep* magazines, Madame. However, if you will just tell me what you require, I'll send a lad to get them for you, immediately."

"Oh, never mind, it's perfectly all right." Daisy retreated to her room, furious with herself and furious with a hotel so uncommercial that it didn't even have a magazine stand. She realized why she hadn't gone out anywhere, why she had not chosen to leave the absolutely protective luxury of this monolithic hotel during these last free hours before work started. She was afraid of meeting Ram.

Herstmonceux Castle, in Sussex, had been chosen as the location of the first of three thirty-second commercials. The soft-rose brick building was surrounded by an exceptionally wide moat which could be crossed only by a long drawbridge, built on a series of graceful arches sunk into the deep waters of the moat. Its builder, Roger de Fiennes, Treasurer of the Household of Henry VI in the mid-fifteenth century, must have had good reason to suspect that someday he might need to defend himself, for he had built a strong and most beautiful fortress, with a gate-house protected by two powerful octagonal, crenelated towers, above which stood double fighting platforms. This castle had been chosen for the commercial in which Daisy would ride up to the entrance, since Kirbo, when he had finally found pictures of it, had suddenly seen that a gallop across a bridge was more visually interesting than a gallop up just any driveway. North planned on shooting at Herstmonceux first, since it involved horses and would demand less of Daisy's acting ability than the other commercials.

When North had first seen the pictures of the castle, he was disgusted. "That bridge is thirty feet above the surface of the moat, Luke. Even with a barge and a crane, I can't get high enough—it's a helicopter or nothing, for the approach and the gallop, and then as she rides closer and gets off the horse I'll only have the width of the bridge to work on."

"Old Roger didn't want to make it easy for strangers to walk in uninvited," said Luke, unmoved. If there was one thing he never let worry him, it was the technical problems of commercial makers. He had never met a good one who couldn't have humped a camera to the top of the Great Pyramid of Gizeh—all by himself if necessary. They wallowed in stories of technical impossibilities they'd conquered; their magazine, *Millimeter*, was full of harrowing tales of difficulties overcome, and while it was true that nine commercial makers *had* been killed in helicopter accidents, they'd still swim a river crawling with man-eating alligators for the right shot . . . or get out of the business. Even as Luke refused to react to North's niggling objections, North himself was thinking that the old bricks of Herstmonceux would look even lovelier through an amber filter and a few smoke bombs set off in the back-ground would make it seem to literally float on the surface of the moat, a trick he thought he might have invented even before David Dee.

As North stood just outside the great portcullis of Herstmonceux that first week in October, with Wingo just inside, riding the camera, watching Daisy, her hair flying like the standard of a great queen, galloping toward him on a huge black horse, followed by a white horse carrying an actor who looked more like a lord than any lord could have, he had to admit that she didn't look like an amateur. She didn't even *sound* like an amateur as she dismounted and spoke her one line, dressed in fawn breeches, black boots, and a soft, open-necked, full-sleeved, billowing white silk blouse such as one of the Three Musketeers might have worn. The changes of expression on North's face, flickering with quick emotions, sometimes crossed by a smile he didn't know was there, the descriptive pantomime gestures of his hands, as if he were engaged in hypnosis or legerdemain, led Daisy through her paces over and over, and still once more, and then again, and yet again, until he was satisfied. She had never, not even in Venice, felt so much closeness between them as during each take. She finally understood his particular genius in its very special manifestation and she knew, finally, why he had married his two best models—she knew already why they had divorced him.

Even before he looked at the rushes in London, less than three hours away by car, North was aware that he had something extraordinarily special on the film; he could tell by the way a chill had run down the back of his neck and upper arms each time Daisy galloped closer to the camera and he anticipated the lyrical moment when she pulled up her huge beast and leapt off, laughing. It had been years since he'd felt that chill, that promise of something inexpressibly *right*.

The mystery that had always engaged him, the deep unsolvable mystery of the human face and its ability to convey emotion—even if it was only an emotion that led the viewer to a certain counter in a supermarket—this mystery was charged with power by Daisy's features on film, North realized, as he watched the rushes. Why had he never even thought to film her before? He resented her excellence only a little less than he was relieved by it.

From Sussex, using cars, planes and trains, with admirable precision, Mary-Lou led the entire company far north, to Peeblesshire, in Scotland, where the castle called Traquair House was located. Totally different from stern Herstmonceux, it had evolved from a simple stone tower built in the middle of the thirteenth century. By the time of Charles I, the castle itself had grown into a tall, pale gray edifice guarded by a long expanse of delicate iron gates which had been shut by the owners until such a time as a Stuart was again crowned King of England, and, even for Frederick Gordon North, they could not be opened. However, right outside the gates was a flower-dappled meadow in which Daisy, and an actor, were to picnic on strawberries and cream.

Daisy was wearing a dress from Gene London's Gramercy Park Shop made of antique Victorian panels. It had cost four thousand dollars to rework the rare material into a dress that didn't look like a costume, a dress that floated almost transparently from her half-bare shoulders, with wide, long sleeves, like wings. The color of the frail, old ivory lace against her skin was entrancing, and the hair-dresser had pulled her hair up and away from her face with a twist of silk ribbons, as green as the color of the meadow, and then let it fall down simply at the back.

"No helicopter here," North decreed, when he saw the Traquair location. "The rotors would blow the grass and flowers flat. There's only one way to get this shot right. Mary-Lou, get me a Hovercraft."

"Who is she, when she's at home?" asked Wingo.

"Mary-Lou," North rapped out. "Hovercraft."

"As large as the ones that cross the English Channel or a smaller version?" she intoned, expressionlessly.

"As small as you can get. Since it rides on a cushion of air, a few feet above the ground, or above the water, as the case may be—are you listening, Wingo, you ignorant lout—it'll look as if we're lighter than air. What I want in this entire scene is the viewpoint of a *butterfly*, not a bird, not a bee, but a dipping, gliding, lazy, fucking butterfly."

"What keeps it up?" Wingo asked suspiciously.

"Keep your eyes open. Maybe you'll find out," North answered.

As Mary-Lou went off, looking quietly pleased with herself, to conjure up a Hovercraft, North said, loudly enough so that Wingo and Daisy could hear him, "Damn that broad."

"North, she's only being efficient," Daisy protested.

"Yeah. But why does she have to be so fucking surreptitious about it?"

"That's not fair. She's just doing her job."

"Daisy, do me a favor, will you? Try not to explain my prejudices to me?"

When Patrick Shannon made a deal, he liked to understand both sides of it. He always knew what he intended to gain, but the other man's motives, the reasons behind his agreement, were more fascinating. Shannon realized that he had no idea why Daisy Valensky, a rich society girl, who worked to keep from being bored, who insisted that she cherished her anonymity, would have consented to the ordeal of becoming the linchpin of an entire company's efforts to put themselves back on the map through exploitation of her personality and persona. "Private reasons," she had said when he'd asked. What private reasons? Why did she want a million dollars during the next three years? It didn't make sense if she was what she was, and he couldn't believe she was not.

For months, these questions occurred to him from time to time as he spent weeks in California, dealing in Supracorp's entertainment division, as he flew back and forth twice to Tokyo and once to France. This gap in his understanding bothered him like a grape skin stuck between his teeth. He suspected that he'd fallen into some sort of trap, that something was going on over which he was not quite in control, but the never ending pressures of running a conglomerate had prevented him from digging into the matter.

He had no trusted second-in-command with whom to discuss this unusual state of affairs, nor was he the kind of man who could speculate with a chosen cohort. At Supracorp, either the employees accepted the fact that, at any time, Shannon might step personally into their domains, or they quit. But they never had to worry about a court favorite screwing things up between themselves and the man at the top. Problems, pressures, tensions, the cat's cradle of thrust and counterthrust of corporate politics were pure joy to Shannon and he had no urge to share them. But he hated operating in an unclear area and, as Patrick Shannon inspected the folder of publicity material Candice Bloom had built up on Daisy, now a respectable pile of photographs and interviews, he decided to fly to England to see what the hell was going on.

As the chauffeur-driven Daimler carried him from Heathrow to Bath, where North and company were staying during the shoot of the final commercial at Berkeley Castle, Shannon realized that he was attaching a unique importance to the Elstree problem. He'd never visited the locations of any of the dozens of commercials which were made yearly for various Supracorp products. He paid people well to do just that. When had this begun, he asked himself. When had Elstree stopped becoming a worrying trouble spot on the conglomerate balance sheet and turned into something almost personal? Damned if he knew. But he'd soon find out. He instructed his chauffeur not to stop at the hotel in Bath, but to continue on to the location.

"Where are the commercials being shot?" he asked the man who sold him his three-shilling ticket in front of the gray stone keep which dated from 1153.

"Beg your pardon, Sir?"

"Americans, with cameras," he said.

"All over the place, Sir."

"No, I mean big cameras—lights—for *television*," he explained impatiently.

"Oh, them, Sir—yes, they'll be in the Bowling Alley, I believe."

"Could you tell me where it is and I'll . . ."

"Straight through the Castle, Sir. Here, Mildred, you attend to the tickets. I'll show this gentleman to the Bowling Alley," the man said, glad of a chance to get a glimpse of the goings-on. "Right up these stairs, Sir," he said, as Shannon followed him into the vast pile of stone. "Now here, Sir, you have the room in which Edward the Second was murdered," he said proudly, pausing for effect. "And that hole in the corner goes down to the dungeon!"

"Could we just keep going?" Shannon said, without hiding his impatience. His guide sniffed in surprise. *All* visitors like to linger in the infamous chamber and peep into the dungeon. However he went on, old and walking at his own pace, through a narrow door into the later parts of the huge savage building, leading Shannon as quickly as he could through the Picture Gallery and the Dining Room and the fourteenth-century Kitchen and Buttery—the only way to get to the other side of the Castle.

"Sinks of solid lead, Sir?" he said, hoping for a pause. Patrick Shannon groaned to himself as, silently, he navigated the Buttery, which led to the China Room, and the China Room led to the Housekeeper's Room and eventually to the Great Hall.

"Are we getting nearer?" he finally asked, surveying the unexpected immensity of the Great Hall.

"Ah, well, there's still the Grand Stairs, and the Long Drawing Room and the Morning Room and the Small Drawing Room—we're a bit more than halfway, Sir," said his guide encouragingly, beginning to walk the sixty-two feet of the Great Hall with an air of proud possession, wondering why this strangely uninquisitive visitor didn't want to know more of the history of this most famous of castles that had been and still was inhabited by the very same family that had built it eight hundred years ago. Why, he thought, indignantly, Berkeleys had lived at Berkeley since before the Magna Carta. Twenty-four generations of them.

Since his guide was obviously neither inclined nor able to hurry, Shannon resigned himself to following, feeling at each step a plucking in his chest that refused to go away, a queer, peevish, nervous twanging of some chord of impatient longing. Damnation, why couldn't the man walk faster?

Eventually, they came out on the south front of the Castle and there, below them, Shannon recognized the clutter of cables and equipment he had been waiting so expectantly to see. There it all was at one end of a long rectangle of close-cropped lawn flanked by a tall, creeper-covered wall on one side and great old yews on the other. But no people were visible. "Where are they?" he asked his guide.

"I should expect they're having tea, Sir."

"*Christ!* Oh, sorry—but I'm in a hurry."

"So I gathered, Sir."

"Well, then, where would they be having their tea?" Shannon asked, biting out each syllable politely.

The old man pointed out a charming country house at a little distance, surrounded by trees. "The Berkeley Hunt stables and kennels, Sir. That's where they parked those great lorries of theirs."

Pat wheeled on him. "Then I could have come the way they came?"

"Ah, certainly—but then you would have *missed* the Castle, Sir," the man reproached him.

Shannon left him standing without another word and strode hurriedly down the terraces which would lead to the stables. Below the deserted Bowling Alley lay a lily pond on the other side of which was a stone staircase that he hoped would open out onto the meadows and the trees. He was almost running as he crossed the lawn to the lily pond.

"Are you looking for someone, or just lolling about?"

He spun around. Daisy was sitting on a low stone wall, barefoot, a mug of tea on the grass beside her. She laughed at him with the lavishness of one who knows her beauty is inexhaustible. He stopped and looked at her.

"I was in the neighborhood . . ."

"So you thought you'd drop by," she finished. "Here, have my tea." She held the mug up to him and he took it, automatically sitting down on the wall. "Anyone who makes it through that Castle needs a stimulant—I wish I had some brandy for you."

He drank the entire mug of sweet, still-hot liquid. That strange, unnerving, nagging tugging in his chest had gone, dissolved into a feeling he couldn't identify or name, a feeling which brought with it a rush of pure gladness.

"Your tea's all gone," he said, struggling to repress what he knew would be an idiotic grin.

"Not a hundred yards from us is an entire trailer filled with people completely devoted to brewing tea, day and night, night and day—not to worry," she said.

"Okay—how's it going?"

"Very well. We should be finished by tomorrow. Today I was working with the dogs, walking them on that lawn you just came over—it might have been easier if the story board hadn't specified lurchers."

"Oh, damn—that was my fault."

"I *knew* it was—we had to send them back—too excited—and now we're waiting for some dogs who don't go crazy every time they smell a bird or a rabbit. They almost pulled my arm off. They just wouldn't *listen* to North." She started to laugh again and he joined in. The idea of two skulking, criminal lurchers daring to disobey North's commands struck them both as the most irresistibly agreeable thing they had heard of in their lives.

"Oh . . . oh . . ." Daisy gasped, "nobody else thought it was a joke, let me tell you . . . he kept saying, 'I'll *kill* the person who wrote that story board, *kill*.' But don't worry . . . I didn't tell."

Shannon suddenly stopped laughing. "Your arm . . . is it all right?"

"Of course."

He took her hand and turned it over. The palm was hot, red and swollen where she'd been gripping the leashes for hours. He stared at it for a moment and then lifted it and pressed her palm gently, remorsefully, to his cheek.

"Forgive me," he muttered.

"It doesn't matter . . . *really*," she said in a low voice. Her other hand reached out and touched his dark hair, lifting the lock which lay on his forehead. He raised his head and looked at her. He kissed her feverish palm. They drew apart, still looking at each other.

"And just what the fuck are *you* doing here?" North demanded in furious surprise, coming around the corner.

23

Five days later, North and Luke sat wordlessly in North's screening room. They had just finished seeing the rough cut of all three Elstree commercials.

"What can I say?" Luke asked finally, pushing his words through the wall of North's frosty, unfamiliar indifference.

"You'll think of something."

"I don't have to tell you it's the best work you've ever done?"

"Nope."

"I don't have to tell you these will be the best fragrance commercials ever made?"

"Nope."

"Can I just thank you?"

"I consider myself thanked. Could you just stop gushing, Luke? I'd take that as a favor."

"Right! Oh . . . Kiki wanted to ask you if you had any idea when Daisy'll be coming back—she hasn't heard a word."

"No idea."

"Well, I'm going to call Shannon." Luke turned away from the uncomfortable atmosphere his friend had created. "Christ, wait till he sees these!" he said eagerly, picking up the phone and dialing Supracorp's number. He spoke to one of Shannon's secretaries briefly and hung up, disappointed.

"Apparently he's in England on business—his secretary didn't have any idea when he'll be back."

"I could have told you that."

"Huh? Oh. OH! Oh, my God, wait till Kiki hears . . . so *that's* what's wrong with you . . . oh, *shit!* I'm sorry, North, that was totally stupid and tactless of me . . ."

"It could not possibly matter less," North said, spitting out each word venomously.

"No, no, of course not. I don't even know what made me say it." Luke was as close to dithering as he'd ever come. "I've got softening of the brain, probably coming down with Chinese flu, everyone in the office has it." Hastily he returned to business. "When will you have an answer print? Until these spots are completely edited and scored I don't want anyone to see them. The whole cosmetic industry is rip-off city."

"Two—two and a half weeks."

"Well, I've got to get back to the shop. Let me know the instant they're ready—okay? The sooner the better—put as many people on it as you have to. They've got to start to run well before Thanksgiving. And North—thank you again. There's no way anyone but you could have pulled it off."

"You can do me a favor, Luke. Next time you want a job done with a fucking amateur, give it to somebody else. I don't need the hassle," North said viciously.

"Right. You've got it. Talk to you soon? Take care of that flu," Luke said, getting out of the room as quickly as possible and ignoring North's roar that Luke was the one who was sick, not him. It just didn't seem like the appropriate time to remind North about being best man at the wedding. And he could hardly call Kiki and tell her how magnificent, how wonderful, how preposterously perfect Daisy had been, and he seriously doubted that North would have appreciated his using the studio phone for that. On second thought, wouldn't Kiki be more interested in the news about Daisy and Shannon in England? Where was the pay phone, damn it?

During the last day of the shoot at Berkeley Castle, Shannon had been unable to stay away. Although he removed himself as far as he could from the scene of the action, he kept edging closer and closer, without realizing it, until a look or a word from one of the crew, or a cable grazing his foot would remind him that he was in their way. He watched, in a trance, as Daisy and an actor walked the length of the Bowling Alley with two well-trained miniature collies, the gray-lavender walls of the great keep visible on their left.

He was in a most peculiar state, Shannon told himself. Most peculiar. It would seem, he thought, trying to analyze himself, that he felt something that could certainly be called a *decided preference* for Daisy. She seemed to be the person he most wanted to be with. All the time. Just why this was so, he didn't yet understand. It wasn't as if she'd *done* anything to make this so. She simply *was*. That was what puzzled him so mightily.

Patrick Shannon had, from the time he was a young man, been able to spot the inner truths of other people the way a stag could sense a doe in the forest. He moved on instinct, intuition and an inner knowledge based on a hundred perceived clues that had proven, time after time, to be reliable and valid. Ambition, talent, fear, goodness, pettiness, honesty—he could sniff them in the air. If he'd been a mystic he would have said he could see them like auras around people's heads. And because he so firmly believed in the accuracy of his senses, he used them. In the corporate power world this ability translated itself directly into action.

But today he felt as if his sense of the realistic had been switched off and his instincts were as unstable as King Arthur's had been when he'd wandered into the charmed circle of Morgan le Fay. What, after all, did he know about Daisy? He discarded as worthless evidence their meeting in Middleburg and the time he'd seen her in North's studio. Dinner at Le Cirque? The laughing girl he'd sat with on the wall yesterday just was not the same grandly reticent woman he'd dined with at Le Cirque nor the pleasant, proper, aloof young princess he'd introduced to the Supracorp division heads from time to time during the last few months. Last night, when everyone had eaten together at the Toad in the Hole in Bath, she'd been very silent, exhausted from the day perhaps, or just quiet. And now, today, she was different again.

Daisy was wearing the same dress she'd worn yesterday, a simple turtleneck dress made from the softest wool woven in shades from pale fawn to rich brown, with rust and bark and berry mixed into a subtle woodland conspiracy. It just brushed her high breasts and was lightly caught by a chain of woven gold at her waist. Daisy called it her Maid Marion dress and wore it with boots of thin, russet leather. Shannon thought it looked like a dress of spicy feathers. Each time she came to the line, "I wear it every day," she pulled the brown velvet ribbon off the one heavy braid which lay over her right shoulder and shook free the silver of her hair. As she did this, time and again, he could think of no other word to express what he saw: she was a star. Everyone there, every single person on the location, had no reason for existence except to record her walking on that centuries-old lawn. Yes, North told her what to do, but he couldn't tell her how to do it—that spirited, natural grace had to come from her. No one could make her up to look so virginal and yet so fruitful. No one could bestow on her that combination of gentle approachability just touched with an air that said, unmistakably, that she was far, very far, from the girl next door.

That afternoon North announced that it was a wrap. The plane back to New York would leave from London the next day at noon. As Mary-Lou dispatched the crew with the crispness of a NASA flight control officer, Patrick Shannon made his way to Daisy's make-up trailer.

"Are you going home tomorrow?" he asked her, his manner as gauche as if he were back in his first year at prep school.

"No, I have business to attend to in London. And then I'm going on to France to visit—family."

"I have business in London, too."

"Ah?"

"But you know the English—you just can't interrupt their weekends. So I'll be staying over till next week. Would you like . . . are you free for dinner tomorrow night? I suppose you're busy? . . ."

"No. I'm free. I'd like to have dinner."

"What time shall I pick you up?"

"Eight-thirty at Claridge's." She'd be back from spending the day with Dani by six-thirty. That would give her two hours in which to get ready. She wondered if they were going to be dining alone or would he produce yet another couple of Supracorp strangers for her to meet.

"Well . . . I'll see you then," Shannon said awkwardly as he backed out of the trailer.

That moment on the wall yesterday, interrupted by that total bastard, North, had left him in a condition he didn't have any reference points to explain. He was buffeted by shivers of crystalline delight, filled with impatient, precarious joy, conscious of an excess of something vital and valuable but yet unidentified that was invading his spirit. Altogether a most intemperate state to be in, and thoroughly disconcerting. He scarcely knew his own name. Damn, but he was happy!

Usually a reservation at the Connaught for Saturday night has to be made almost a week in advance. But, since Shannon stayed at the Connaught on his frequent business trips to England, he had no trouble getting a table. He had given a lot of thought to the question of where to take Daisy for dinner, and the honeyed hum of the Connaught dining room appealed to him more than the high-priced, hurried atmosphere of London's many fashionable Italian restaurants or the solemn elaborations of its best French restaurants.

Daisy was waiting in the lobby of Claridge's when he arrived, and they spoke only a word or two on the brief drive around the corner. She was emotionally drained by her reunion with her sister. It had been a difficult day, long, and both sad and happy as she saw that Dani had not changed, had remained eerily beautiful and untouched by time, a happy five-year-old in Daisy's body. She felt frail and vulnerable tonight, disconnected, muddled, at once very old and very young.

As the chauffeur stopped the car in front of the familiar entrance with its elaborate glass canopy, Daisy only said, "Oh," so quietly that Shannon didn't hear the note of shock in her voice. She stepped into the lobby in a dream, and walked the familiar route to the restaurant, not stopping as she used to, to inspect every dish on the laden trolleys, but looking straight before her, biting the inside of her lower lip so that it wouldn't tremble as the sounds and smells and light of a never forgotten paradise surrounded her again. As she and Shannon waited to be seated, standing for a moment in the entrance to the room, a headwaiter suddenly stopped taking an order at a table near the door. He looked only once. He left an astonished duke, who was inquiring about the family tree of the *fois gras*, and walked swiftly, much too swiftly for any self-respecting maître d'hôtel, to the door.

"Princess Daisy," he cried in astonished joy and then abandoned all professionalism entirely as he enfolded her in a great bear hug. "Princess Daisy—you're back! Where did you go? Everyone missed you so much—but no one knew what had happened—you disappeared!"

"Oh, darling Monsieur Henri, you're still here! I'm so glad to see you!" Daisy cried, returning his hug with all her might.

"We're all still here—you were the one who left," he said, rebuking her in his surprise, ignoring the fact that all the diners in sight of the door had abandoned their food to watch the unimaginable sight of a Connaught headwaiter hugging a Connaught customer, as if she were a long-lost daughter.

"I didn't want to, Monsieur Henri, but I've been living in America."

"But when you came back to visit? Why did you never come back to see us, Princess Daisy, during all those years and years?" he said reproachfully.

"I haven't been back to England," Daisy lied. "This is my first time home." She couldn't tell him that on her trips to see Danielle she didn't have the money to eat at the Connaught.

Shannon coughed. The maître d'hôtel abruptly re-entered the real world. Within seconds they were seated. He had, without thinking twice, given them the same table Stash Valensky had always requested, central yet private. Shannon looked at Daisy carefully. She was holding back tears, the struggle visible on her face.

"I'm sorry . . . I had no idea," he said. "Does it bother you to stay? Wouldn't you rather go somewhere else?" He took one of her hands and covered it protectively.

Daisy shook her head, and gave him the beginning of a smile. "No, I'll be fine. It's just . . . memories. I'm glad to be back, truly. Some of the happiest moments of my life were spent right here at this table."

"I don't know anything about you!" Shannon burst out. He felt overwhelmed by jealousy of her mysterious past. What a terrible way to start the evening—reunions, memories, tears. What next?

"It isn't fair, is it?" she asked, reading his mind.

"No, it isn't. Every time I see you, you're different, damn it. I just don't know what to make of you. Who the devil are you, anyway?"

"This from the man who's so sure of my identity that he's going to blazon it all over the world? If *you* don't know who I am, how can 'Princess Daisy' exist?"

"You're laughing at me again."

"Do you mind?"

"I like it. Anyway, you're right. 'Princess Daisy' has to do with Elstree, not you. And I still don't know who you are." Entreaty, as loud as trumpets, shone in his eyes.

"I used to come here with my father, for lunch, almost every Sunday from the time I was about nine until I was fifteen. Then he died and I went to college at Santa Cruz in California. After that I worked in New York for North."

"Except when you were painting pictures for fun on the weekends?"

"For *money*. I painted every single picture for the money," Daisy said gently, "and I worked for North for the money and I'm doing the commercials for the money. If you want to know me, you have to know that." As she heard herself speak, she realized that she had just told Shannon more about herself than she had told any man. Yet she wasn't surprised, nor was she dismayed at what she'd revealed. Perhaps it was the result of her day with Dani, but her emotions were close to the surface tonight and she knew, with a profound, bright certainty, that it was safe to tell this man things she had muffled in shrouds for so long.

"Why do you need the money?"

"To take care of my sister." As she spoke, Daisy felt a wave of relief so strong that it made her give a great shuddering sigh and slump back in her chair, but her hand didn't move from under his.

"Tell me about her," he asked softly.

"She's very, very sweet and good. She's called Danielle. Today, when I saw her, she remembered me perfectly even though it's been several years since I could come to visit her. The teachers there, at her school, told me that she talks about me often—she says, 'Where Day?' and she looks at all the photographs of us together," Daisy said in a dreamy voice.

"How old is she?" Shannon wondered, at sea.

"She's my twin."

Two hours later, dinner finished, they sat still talking over brandy in the restaurant which was now more than half-empty.

"Something went wrong way back in my life," Daisy said. "I've never been able to be sure what it was exactly."

"Was it when your mother died?"

"Nothing was ever right after that. But I think it went wrong long, long before that, perhaps even when I was born . . . born *first*."

"You can't remember back to when you were born," Shannon said, startled. "How do you know you were born first?"

Daisy looked at him in astonishment. "Did I say that? Did I really say 'born first'—say it out loud?"

"Whatever it means, you did."

"I didn't realize," she murmured. Since they had started talking, as with the first faint lilt of a waltz played at a distance, she had begun to feel a dancing pace lift her heart. It was as if that stubborn stone she had carried there for so long had begun to dissolve into music.

"Daisy, what are you talking about? Up till now you've made sense, but suddenly you've lost me. I don't understand."

He looked at her in bafflement. She seemed to be talking out of a deeper dream than the one she'd been in when she first told him about Danielle.

"All my life I've been trying to repair the damage, trying to make it unhappen, to solve it, to pay for it somehow, and, of course, it hasn't worked."

"Daisy, explain—what do you *mean?*" he begged. "You're still talking in riddles."

She hesitated. She had broken the taboo her father had placed on any word about Danielle, she'd told Shannon all about the way in which she'd been brought up, about Rolls-Royce and why she had no money, about Anabel's leukemia, about *La Marée*—she'd told him everything except about Ram. She never, never in her life would tell anyone about Ram.

"The only reason Danielle's retarded is because I was born first." Daisy took a deep breath before she continued. "She got less oxygen—I got everything I needed and she didn't. If it hadn't been for me, she would have been perfect."

"Jesus! *You've lived with that all your life!* My God, Daisy, that is the craziest thing I've ever heard! Nobody in the world, *nobody*, no doctor, no thinking person would agree with you. Daisy, you simply *cannot* really believe that."

"Of course I don't believe it logically—but emotionally . . . I've always felt . . . *guilty*. Tell me, Pat, how do you unthink something you *feel?* How do you forget something you heard when you were a little child, something that explained everything you didn't understand, something you couldn't tell a single other person about, something you lived by for so long that *whether it was right or wrong didn't matter*, because it has an inner truth for you that is stronger than any logic?"

"I don't know," he admitted slowly. "I'd give anything to know. Perhaps you have to replace the truth that is wrong with the truth that is right? Does that sound possible? Or am I getting too metaphysical? I'm not used to this sort of problem. I wish I were," he added humbly.

"Come on," she said, mirth changing her face, "the metaphysical Mr. Shannon—if they could only see you in the boardroom now."

"It would make a lot of people happy—Pat Shannon without an answer." He studied the sweeping line from Daisy's forehead to the tip of her straight, fine nose and thought that it had a particular determination he had not properly taken into account before. The furrow between her nose and upper lip was a deliciously shaped shadow, full, suddenly, of lurking laughter.

"I have a sneaky feeling that the waiters, adoring as they are, wouldn't be unhappy if we left now—there's no one here but us," he said.

"You may have to carry me out. I'm exhausted. I can't remember when I've been so tired," Daisy said. "But I feel, oh, I feel . . ."

"Yes?" he asked anxiously.

"Like the crazy title of a song Kiki picked up somewhere—it's called 'The Name of the Place Is I Like It Like That.' "

"I know what you mean. Now listen, I'm taking you back to your hotel so you can sleep. Tomorrow, are you going to see Danielle again?"

She nodded.

"And Monday? Will you be here Monday?" he asked.

"No, Monday I have to go to Honfleur to see Anabel."

"Let me go to France with you," he blurted.

"But you have business in London," she reminded him gravely.

"Did you really believe that?"

"That comes under the heading of leading questions."

"Well, can I come?" he asked again. He had never felt so much at risk.

"I think Anabel would like to meet you," Daisy said slowly. "She's always had an eye for men. Yes, that's a fine idea. And unless you've been to *La Marée*, you can't really understand when I talk about it. But what will Supracorp do without you?"

"Who?"

In the early days of July the ivy which covers *La Marée* begins to turn red in streaks. By the end of the month the entire sprawling *manoir* is hidden by rippling flames of shouting color and the huge-headed dahlias in the garden are in full flaunting bloom, each one of them worthy of a Fauve canvas all to itself.

Anabel was standing at the front door when Daisy and Shannon drove up. As she kissed her, Daisy inspected Anabel carefully for signs of change. There was an expression of resolution on her loving face which had never been there before. Perhaps it was a sign of the price she had paid for acceptance, for knowing the truth. And there was a new and unfamiliar shallowness in the color of her eyes. But her gaze with its supreme pragmatism had not changed, nor had her eternal amusement at life.

"What have we here?" she exclaimed, looking Shannon over. "A distinctly tall and rather gorgeous American? That does make for a pleasant change. Why is his hair so black and his eyes so blue? But, of course, it's Irish blood. I must be getting old not to see that immediately. Daisy, couldn't you find an American who looked like an American—rather blond and bland? I've always heard about them, but I've never seen a specimen. Perhaps they don't exist? Never mind—we'll make do with this nice, big, beautiful one. Come in, children, and have some sherry."

"You're a terrible flirt," said Shannon.

"Nonsense, I've never flirted in my life. I have always been dreadfully misunderstood," Anabel said, with that laugh that had half-seduced every man who heard it. The red of her shiny hair was fading and she had grown thinner but, as she led them through the salon out to the terrace overlooking the sea, it was uncanny to see with what gentle strokes time seemed to have touched *La Marée* and its owner. Daisy's heart leaped as she thought how this place, this haven, at least, could never be taken away from Anabel.

That evening, after dinner, Shannon took himself off to read in one of the balcony window seats above the salon while Daisy and Anabel sat together in the chairs around the dining-room fireplace. On this summer night there was no fire, but the memory of the many holiday fires of childhood still lingered there.

"How do you feel, *really?*" Daisy asked, at last.

"Now? Not really all that much different. The first few months were a bit nasty—drug therapy isn't much fun, but now I only have to see the doctor once a month and I'm over the sticky part. I've lost weight, which I rather like, but my energy is low . . . still, I can't complain, darling. It could have been much worse. I promise you I'm telling the truth."

"I know you are." Daisy bit her lip before she spoke again. She didn't want to use Ram's name. "Did you let him know you didn't need him?" she asked.

"The instant I got your letter. I told him that I wouldn't trouble him again, ever, and I told him why, or he'd never have believed me."

"What did you say?" Daisy asked anxiously.

"I simply said that you'd been picked to do some commercials and that you were going to make enough money to take care of both me and Dani."

"And thank God for that," Daisy said, gazing into the fire.

"Yes. Ram is truly evil. I wish I could have helped him, but it was too late when I met him. Yet he was only twelve or so."

"Who was to blame?" Daisy asked.

"I've often wondered. He was always unhappy, always envious, always an outsider, a child of divorce, of course, but that can never be the whole explanation. He was also your father's son and your father was a hard and selfish man. Often he was a cruel man. Perhaps Stash could have helped Ram, but he never even bothered to try."

"You've never said that to me before," Daisy said, astonished.

"You weren't mature enough to hear it . . . to hear it and understand it, and know that I still love your father even as I say it. Now I think it important that you know. That day Stash left Danielle at the school, I almost left him, too."

"Why didn't you?"

"Because he needed me to keep him human . . . and, as I said, I loved him . . . and perhaps, even then, a little bit, I stayed for you. At six you know, you were quite irresistible . . . before you grew so old and ugly."

"Flirting again, Anabel. I'll tell Shannon."

"Ah, that Shannon. Since you have finally asked me, I approve. You've begun to show a little sense. I've been worried about you, Daisy, for years. You have a truly incredible talent for staying out of trouble—it wasn't normal. Now, with Shannon—ah, well, I have to admit that I envy you . . . "

"Anabel! I hardly know him!"

"Indeed! Then, if I were only thirty years younger . . . or even twenty . . . you wouldn't have a chance! I'd take him right away from you."

"You would, too, wouldn't you, Anabel? You really would," Daisy marveled. "No sense of fair play at all?"

"Where a man like that is concerned? You must be joking. What does 'fair play' have to do with it? Your British education has given you some very odd notions. No wonder they lost India."

Soon afterward, Anabel declared that she felt tired and she was going to bed. She had given Daisy her old room, the walls still covered in green silk, now faded and even frayed in places, and she had put Shannon in the brown and white room, the most comfortable of her guest rooms, all the way at the other end of the house.

After they'd said their goodnights, Daisy sat on her window seat in the dark and looked out over the spangled estuary of the Seine to the lights of Le Havre. There must be ghosts here, she thought, watching the beloved silhouettes of the three umbrella pines, listening to the rustle of the long-leaved eucalyptus trees, smelling the wood-brown ivied fragrance of the walls of *La Marée*, hearing the occasional lowing of cows from the dairy farms at the bottom of the hill. There *are* ghosts, but tonight I'm free of them, tonight I'm safe from them, tonight nothing can hurt me . . . I could even walk in the woods and feel no fear. Abruptly, she remembered Ram, stretched out in a familiar pose in one of the striped deck chairs, looking at her intently through his half-closed eyes, beckoning to her with a careless, owning hand. No, you have no power over me, mad ghost, Daisy thought, none at all—and you know it.

Shall I walk in the woods, she wondered as she brushed her hair. Sparks of static electricity like a flock of indignant fireflies crackled in the night air. She wandered over to the chest of drawers in which she kept a store of old clothes for her visits to *La Marée*. She was wearing a pair of much-washed cotton pajamas which she'd owned since she was sixteen. The jacket had missing buttons and the pants had shrunk.

Or, Daisy asked herself, shall I go and see if Pat Shannon is quite comfortable in his room? Standing with the hairbrush still clasped in her hand, she thought of how he had looked rushing down the terraces of Berkeley Castle. What urgent errand had brought him there? She remembered how quickly he had brought her back to Claridge's last night, understanding that she was so tired that even an arm around her shoulders would have been a burden to her, of how tactfully he had left her alone to talk with Anabel earlier that evening. And yet I do believe he finds me attractive, she told herself, smiling in the dark, remembering the wordless moment when he had kissed the palm of her hand. Yes, unquestionably attractive. He's almost *too* considerate. Wouldn't it be hospitable to see if he's comfortable? Truly and deeply hospitable? Thoughtfully, Daisy took off her pajamas and searched rapidly in her suitcase for the good-luck present Kiki had given her before she'd left for England. Daisy pulled out of the tissue paper a nightgown such as she'd never owned, a slithery gown the color of apricots, made of two shining pieces of satin held together at the sides only by tiny bows which linked one piece to the other at eight-inch intervals. Daisy dropped it over her head, gasping as the fall of satin touched her naked skin with its coolness. Then she put on the matching robe that closed with a bow at the base of her throat. She considered looking in the mirror to see how she looked, but she didn't want to turn on the light.

Daisy opened her door as silently as a somnambulist, but there was nothing of the sleepwalker about her steps as she walked, on her hospitable mission, quietly, but with eager determination, down the entire length of the house to the door of Pat Shannon's room. She knocked at the door and waited, hardly breathing, for it to open. There was no response. She knocked again, rather louder this time. It was, of course, possible that he was asleep, she thought. But it was also entirely possible that he wasn't comfortable. There was only one way to make sure. Daisy opened the door and saw him, sound asleep in the wide, double bed. She padded silently across the room and knelt on the floor next to his dreaming form, throwing off the long robe as she leaned over him. There was enough moonlight for her to study his face. In sleep the lines on either side of Shannon's mouth softened and their relaxation lent his characteristic expression of purposeful banditry a youthfulness at which Daisy peered tenderly. His hair, always tousled, fell more carelessly than he would have permitted in a waking moment, adding to his unguarded look. He seemed trapped in a savage solitude, Daisy thought, wondering what he was dreaming about. Shannon, so often seen in action, swift, set apart, beyond self-doubt or failure, the powerful conductor of the great conglomerate orchestra, was sleeping the sleep of childhood, his wide mouth vulnerable, somehow beseeching, a look on his face as if he'd lost his way. She pressed her lips softly to his. He slept on. Again she kissed him and still he slept. This is not at all gallant of him, thought Daisy, and kissed him once more. He woke up gasping.

"Oh, the *best* kiss . . . " he mumbled, still half-asleep.

She kissed him again, fleetingly, before he could say more.

"The sweetest kiss . . . give me another . . ."

"You've already had four."

"No, impossible, I don't remember, they don't count," he insisted, finally awake.

"I just came by to see if you were comfortable. Now that I see you are, I'll go back to my room. I'm so sorry I woke you—go back to sleep."

"Oh, Lord, don't! I'm not! It's freezing here and the mattress is lumpy and the bed's too short and too narrow and I need another pillow," he grumbled of Anabel's luxurious guest accommodations, as he adroitly lifted Daisy from the floor where she was still kneeling and tucked her under his covers.

Shannon cradled her in his arms as gently as a cherished child and they nestled quietly, each tentatively experiencing the warmth of the other's body, the sound of the other's breathing and the beating of the other's many pulses—a communication without words, so full of a sense of the extraordinary that neither of them dared to speak. Little by little they sank deeper, and surrendered themselves, with their whole sentient beings, becoming immersed, enlaced in awareness of the life force of the other, until, without voices or motion they had attained a trust that had been waiting to be born.

It seemed a long time before Shannon began to imprint a blizzard of tiny kisses at the point where Daisy's jaw joined her throat, that particularly warm curve, spendthrift with beauty, that he had not allowed himself to realize had haunted him for weeks. Daisy felt fragile and rare to Shannon, as if he'd trapped a young unicorn, some strange, mythological creature. Her hair was the most intense source of light in the room since it reflected the moonlight creeping through the windows, and by its light he saw her eyes, open, rapt and glowing; twin dark stars.

It seemed to him now as if they had never kissed before. The kisses she had awakened him with were so chaste, so tentative that they were only the memory of a kiss. Now he pressed her mouth with a rain of kisses like blazing flowers.

Oh, yes! she thought, opening her lips to him, tumbled and craving and daring. She arched her body toward him, nudging his hands toward her breasts until they were clasped and claimed. It was she, not he, who raised her nightgown over her head in one swift impatient movement and tossed it on the floor. It was she who guided his hands down the length of her body, she who touched him wherever she could reach, as playfully as a dolphin, until he realized that her fragility was strength, and that she wanted him without reserve. He bent to the glorious task, dimly aware that never before had life flowed through him without the static and interferences of thought, never had he been so close to drinking the elemental wine of life. He tasted it on her lips and on her nipples and on her belly, his whole skin drank thirstily of her and when he thrust into her, he knew he had arrived at last at the source, the spring. Now, Daisy lay quietly, invaded, filled, utterly willing. She felt as if she were floating down a clean, clear river with birds singing in green trees on the bank. But there was more; more than this blissful peace and together they quickened, panted, quested as eagerly as two huntsmen after an elusive prey, plunging through the forests of each other until they came at last to their victories, Daisy with a sound that was at least as much a cry of astonishment as it was of joy. She had experienced fulfillment before, but never with this excellence, this plenitude.

Afterward, as they lay together, half asleep, but unwilling to drift apart into unconsciousness, Daisy farted, in a tiny series of absolutely irrepressible little pops that seemed to her to go on for a minute.

"Termites riveting," observed Shannon lazily. She lunged out from under the covers and almost managed to jump off the bed before his long arms pinned her on the mattress.

"Minuscule termites, midget Rosie the Riveters. You get an E for effort."

"Let me go!" she cried, humiliated.

"Not until you realize that if you fart, you fart—and that's fine . . . farting's part of life."

"Oh, please stop repeating that word!" Daisy begged, more embarrassed than ever.

"You've never lived with a man." He stated this rather than asking.

"What makes you think that?" she said quickly. Of course she hadn't, but at twenty-five, what woman would admit it?

"Because of how you reacted to . . . ah, giving a salute to the queen . . . does that sound better?"

"Yes, much," she murmured, pressing her face into his shoulder. "Is that your idea of a romantic declaration?"

"The circumstances were not of my choosing. I think I can do better."

"Go right ahead."

"Dearest, darling, adorable Daisy, how can I convince you of the profound chivalry and absolute tenderness and devotion which lie in my heart of hearts?"

"You just have." She trembled with laughter. "Now, go to sleep, Shannon, or it will be morning. I'm going back to my room and you'll have to make the best of the terrible lumpy bed."

"But why? Sleep with me. Don't go. You can't leave me here all alone," he protested.

"Yes, I can. Don't ask me why because I don't know." He sat up, watching as she wrapped her robe around her naked body, all shadows and secrets in the moonlight. "Goodnight, sleep tight, and don't let those termites bite," she whispered, kissing him on the lips with the speed of a hummingbird, and was gone.

At breakfast Anabel serenely offered Shannon a choice of five kinds of honey to go on his buttered brioche while she managed simultaneously to watch Daisy, incendiary with joy, yet limpid as dawn and dressed like a ruffian.

"And what are your plans for today, children?" she asked.

"Children?" Shannon grinned at her.

"A generic term," responded Anabel, "for anyone not of my generation."

"You don't have a generation," he assured her.

"And you grow more charming every day."

"We were going to walk into Honfleur to show Shannon the port, but perhaps I should just leave you two alone together," Daisy suggested. "You could spend the time doting on each other."

"No, much as I would like that, there's a long list of things for you two to pick up for dinner. When you're ready to go, it's on the kitchen table. I'm going to cut some flowers," Anabel said tranquilly.

"I'll go get it now—I'm all set," Daisy said.

"Like that?" Shannon asked.

"Naturally." Daisy looked down at her costume. When she woke that morning she had jumped into a pair of jeans with holes in the knees which dated from her freshman year at Santa Cruz, a sleeveless jersey equally dilapidated, and tennis shoes that had weathered almost a decade. Around her neck she'd slung a moth-eaten navy cardigan which had been part of the detested uniform at Lady Alden's School, worn when the girls had marched into the park to play rounders. She'd made two long, absolutely simple braids which hung down her back, and she wore no make-up at all. "Not chic enough for you?" she asked him with a grin which should have told him that she knew exactly what she was doing and that she had prepared this new metamorphosis of herself just to further enchant and befuddle him. However, she doubted that he was in any fit condition to figure it out—hers were hardly Supracorp tactics.

"I like you like that," Shannon said. "It makes another Princess Daisy for my collection. And quite a different one than the Princess Daisy I saw recently, just last night in fact."

She said nothing but she instantly noted his words. *Another* Princess Daisy? His *collection?* Her grin faded imperceptibly while Anabel's eyes brightened as she watched them. She supposed they thought she couldn't read their words and actions as clearly as if they'd made an announcement. Oh, but it was strange to watch old stories being acted out as if they were fresh and new, and had never happened before. Still, one never knew the endings, only the beginnings were the same.

"I'm trying to count how many people kissed you on both cheeks this morning," Shannon said when they had finally filled their shopping baskets and found a seat at a café looking out onto the arc of the old port with its motley collection of boats bobbing in front of the tall, narrow houses that edged the opposite side of the little harbor. "There was the butcher and the cheese man and the vegetable lady and the fruit man and the fish lady and the mayor and the policeman and the postman—who else?"

"The baker and his wife, the man who sells newspapers, the old fisherman who used to take me out in his boat and the two art-gallery owners."

"But the waiter here only shook hands. Why is he so unfriendly?"

"He's new here—It's been about eight years since he was hired, so I scarcely know him," Daisy answered, drinking her Cinzano.

"This is really home for you?"

"It's as close to a home as I've had since my father was killed. And remember, they watched me grow up, every summer from the time I was a child. Nothing changes here . . . only more tourists."

"You're lucky to have a place like this," he said wistfully.

"And you? What do you have? You complained that you didn't know anything about me. What do I know about you?" She touched his lower lip with one finger, the quirky lip which she found herself looking at so often, that expressive lip which could be thoughtful, humorous, decisive—she didn't doubt it could be disapproving, angry—perhaps even merciless?

"I have a few faint memories of being a little boy with a mother and father who loved each other and loved me very much—we were very poor, I realize now, and we didn't have any family in the mill town where my father worked—at least I don't remember any. He was a mechanic, and I think that he must have been out of work a lot because I remember that he was around the house much of the time—too much." He paused, shook his head and sipped his drink. "When I was five they were both killed in an accident—a streetcar—and I grew up in a Catholic orphanage—I was a miserable kid, suddenly all alone, not understanding anything and too much of a handful for anyone to want to adopt me. It wasn't until I realized that the only way out was working, working much harder than anyone else, getting better marks, being the best at everything, that I changed—and by that time I was too old to be adopted."

"How old was that?"

"Maybe eight—nine. The nuns put up with a hell of a lot from me."

"Do you ever go back?"

"The orphanage is closed now. They ran out of orphans—or maybe they relocated it, but I've lost track completely. I wouldn't want to go back anyway. My real life started when I got a scholarship to St. Anthony's at fourteen."

Daisy listened attentively, almost painfully, trying to extract the secret meaning of his bare recital. Nobody's "real" life could begin at fourteen, she thought, too much of what forms the personality of the adult has happened by then. Perhaps she would never know enough about him to be able to share his childhood as he had shared hers. Perhaps it didn't matter? In any case, they would soon be late for lunch, which would annoy Anabel.

As they walked back, up the steep hill of the Côte de Grace, Shannon was thoughtful. He'd never talked as much about his early years. He sensed that he'd left out something, missed some essential connections. But all he could find to explain himself to Daisy was his favorite quotation from his durable sage.

"Listen—this is the way I feel about life—George Bernard Shaw said it. 'People are always blaming their circumstances for what they are. I don't believe in circumstances. The people who get on in this world are the people who get up and look for the circumstances they want, and if they can't find them, they make them.' " He had stopped walking as he spoke.

"Is that your motto, too?" she asked.

"Yes. What do you think of it?"

"It's almost probably half true . . . which isn't at all bad for a motto," she said. "You might try to give me a kiss . . . there's no one to see us."

He kissed her for a long moment and Daisy felt that she was growing around him as a climbing rose grows around a sturdy arbor.

"Am I a 'circumstance'?" she murmured.

"*You* are a silly question." He pulled her braids. "I'll race you back."

As the three of them ate dinner Anabel asked, "How long can you stay, Patrick?"

"I'm leaving tomorrow," he said. There was regret in his voice but no touch of indecision.

"But can't you stay just one more day? You've just come," Anabel protested.

"Impossible. I've been out of the office and out of touch for days. The people at Supracorp will think I'm dead. It's never happened before."

"Don't you take vacations?" Anabel asked curiously.

"Not out-of-touch vacations? Not even out-of-touch long weekends. It makes them nervous or it makes me nervous; I'm not really sure which." He laughed, the buccaneer again.

"Daisy, you can stay a while, can't you?" Anabel inquired hopefully.

"No, she can't, Anabel," Shannon said firmly. "She has to get back to New York. There are dozens of things going on—interviews, photographs—my publicity people have been working on stuff that I don't know about yet. Remember, Supracorp has a ton of money tied up in Princess Daisy. The commercials were only the beginning."

Daisy bit the inside of her lip in vexation. She was perfectly aware that she had to return, but she bristled to hear Shannon answering a question Anabel had asked her. But there was a gulf between her responsibility to the corporation and being told by Shannon what she could or could not do. Did he, by any grotesque chance, think that now *he* owned her? Bugger that!

She turned to Anabel, ignoring Shannon's words. "Actually I really have to go back for Kiki's wedding. . . . Nothing Supracorp needs me for is more important."

"Well, thank heaven that wedding's taking place," Anabel said with that slightly condescending appreciation of respectability to which only the most successful of retired courtesans feels entitled. "From what you've written me, and what her poor mother has hinted at, I'd say it comes not a minute too soon."

Daisy giggled wickedly. She had a pretty shrewd idea of Anabel's life history.

Anabel looked at her sharply with the eternal, invaluable complicity of females. Although they were speaking of Kiki they were both thinking of Shannon. He's a good man, and you deserve this—go to it! Anabel's glance told Daisy. Don't jump to conclusions, Daisy's eyes warned Anabel, as clearly as if she had spoken.

24

What do you mean I 'tried so hard to get him'? I'd never sink so low," Kiki fulminated.

"Selective memory," Daisy marveled.

"You're the one who forgets. Who was a free agent? Footloose, jaunty, jolly, lighthearted, having the most wonderful time in the best of all possible worlds? ME! You never saw me go out with the same guy for two nights in a row," Kiki swaggered.

"Or in the same bed for more than three months at a time," Daisy replied.

"Oh, that. You know, Daisy, you have a sort of shit-eating grin now that I get a good look at you. And you used to be almost pretty." Kiki hunched her bare shoulders in a way which indicated clearly that she had given up on her friend. Dressed only in a pair of unqualifiedly indecent black lace underpants from Frederick's of Hollywood, she pawed in an idle way through a pile of spidery, suggestive garter belts, some black, some red. Around her neck she had draped a pair of thin black nylon stockings with seams down the back.

"Just answer some questions for me," Daisy said patiently. "Do you actually hate him?"

"I wouldn't go that far," Kiki answered in a disobliging voice. "Hate is too strong a word to use—indifferent might be more like it."

"Does he bore you?"

"Not totally—he just doesn't fascinate me. My God, Daisy, the world is full of men, absolutely crammed with them. Do you realize how many men there are out there? Each one different, each one with some particular kink or craziness or talent or charm or sweetness that *you'll* never know about because you're too lazy to investigate them? You really lack something—*tempérament* I think they call it in France—it's what makes great amorous women, the legendary lovers—George Sand, Ninon de Lenclos and *me*, damn it, only you won't admit it."

"I'll admit it," Daisy said in a conciliatory voice. "You were really something."

"I still am!" Kiki objected like a bad angel. She shook her head until her hair looked like a ball of tumbling tumbleweed, and her tanned naked breasts quivered in indignation.

"When you make love," Daisy asked, "can you tell him how it feels—you know—tell him that you like this or that, or do it more, or three inches farther to the left—can you tell him things like that just as easily and freely as if he were rubbing your back?"

"Well, naturally," Kiki said in a mean-spirited tone. "But so what?"

"Just asking, just indulging my prurient curiosity."

"Indulge mine—what about Patrick Shannon?" Kiki asked, suddenly fizzing with interest. "Just precisely what is going on with you two?"

"We're getting to know each other," Daisy answered with dignity.

"Oh-ho—so you won't answer the kind of questions you expect me to answer."

"I'll tell you anything you want to know."

"Is he in love with you?" Kiki pounced.

"He's very . . . attentive."

"You mean he hasn't said anything definite, hasn't asked you to marry him?" Kiki put aside her own troubles. She'd been so busy complaining that she just hadn't had time to interrogate Daisy.

"No, and that's the way I prefer it."

"Keeping him at a safe distance, like your other men, is that what's happening?"

"The distance is too narrow to be called safe. There's a confusion—he's so much *there*—I love to watch him dealing with the world, but he's so dominating that it scares me . . . a little anyway. Or maybe a lot. I find myself wondering if he doesn't intend to run everybody and everything, and yet I can tell him almost anything and count on him to understand. Still . . . I'm not absolutely sure that it isn't just another one of his many ways of getting what he wants. I just don't know. Sometimes—it's so right, so *honorable*—and then I'll find myself wondering if he doesn't think of me as just another *acquisition*, like having the Elstree company embodied in one person. One thing is clear—he's totally in love with that whole 'Princess Daisy' *idea.* And I don't like *that* one bit! Oh, shit, I'm mixed up."

"But is he a good lover?" Kiki probed. Daisy blushed. "Hmmm?" hummed Kiki encouragingly. "You promised you'd tell."

"The best—oh—better than that! But that's no reason to get a fix on the future. I'm not ready to even think about making decisions. I don't want to jump into anything prematurely. I want to stay the way I am, and I'm not going to get deeply emotionally involved . . ."

Kiki jumped on her like a hellcat. "But you're the one who's telling me to let myself be corralled, captured, rounded-up and branded and tied up in chains like a galley slave! Daisy Valensky, you have one hell of a nerve! How dare you give me advice when you're not ready to get involved! Of all the revolting clichés!"

"Well," said Daisy mildly, "it's not *my* wedding day, those three hundred people downstairs in your mother's living room aren't waiting to see me get married, I'm not the one with eight bridesmaids and eight ushers, to say nothing of a groom, all dithering around and wondering why you're locked in here with me and when you're coming out."

"It's all his fault!" Kiki cried, her slender body looking as forlorn as if she were a kitten who'd been left out in the wet all night. "That smooth-tongued advertising man, I should never ever have let him talk me into this. Oh, Christ, what a horrible mistake."

"You're the one who's a cliché, darling Kiki. You're just like all the others before they get married, don't you realize?" Daisy asked kindly.

"They're the clichés, I'm the *real thing!*" Kiki stormed. "What *am* I going to do? Is it too late to call it off? No, it's never too late. Who cares what people say? Daisy, look, I won't ask you ever again to do anything for me, but could you just go and find my mother and tell her to call it off? She can handle it, she's good at organizing things. I think she'd take it better coming from you." She looked at Daisy with low cunning.

Daisy shook her head. "Tergiversations. I should have known."

"What the hell are they? Don't change the subject!"

"Repeated changes of attitude or opinion—Kiki, you know perfectly well that your mother would never call it off. And even if she did, would that make you happy? How long would it take for you to change your mind again? Nope. You're going through this if I have to haul you down there myself. But you'd be more comfortable if you put on your wedding dress first."

"You're a cold hard bitch, Daisy Valensky, and I'll never forgive you as long as I live."

"Oh," said Daisy, looking out of the window of Kiki's bedroom, "I just saw Peter Spivak drive up. Here comes the judge! We're practically in business."

"No!" Kiki said frantically. "I *can't!*"

"Do it one day at a time, Kiki. The way AA tells people to give up drinking, just one day at a time. Don't sit around thinking about how you'll feel living with the same man for fifty years—just ask yourself if you could stand being married to Luke until tomorrow morning—or even just till midnight tonight. Could you possibly endure it? Just till midnight?"

"I suppose," Kiki said sulkily.

"Well, that's all you have to do. Tomorrow you can get divorced. Okay?"

"I see right through you—you know I won't want to get divorced tomorrow. *Nobody* ever got divorced the day after she got married. It's unheard of. That whole number is just more of the kind of scheming that got me into this!" Kiki accused her.

"Right, I admit it. But now get dressed! On the double!" Daisy sounded as menacing as if she were talking to Wingo.

Kiki chose a red lace garter belt and put on the black stockings, hooking them carefully into the red satin snaps and straightening the seams with gloomy attention.

"I love your underwear," said Daisy. "It's so suitable."

"Damn it, Daisy, if I have to wear white at least I'll know that what's on underneath isn't Miss Grosse Pointe Virgin of the Year," Kiki said, stepping defiantly into a pair of plain white satin pumps. "Fuck-me stockings without fuck-me shoes," she said sadly. Glaring at Daisy, she opened the closet where her white satin wedding dress was hanging, draped in plastic to keep it spotless.

"I think I'm supposed to be doing that," Daisy said, jumping up. Her chiffon dress was the color of spring grass and her hair was worn in plaited coils over her ears. She had on flat green slippers so she wouldn't tower over Kiki any more than was absolutely necessary. Daisy carefully slipped the wedding dress out of its protective wrappings and unzipped it so that Kiki could put it on. She held it by the shoulders and fluttered it temptingly at Kiki, the way a bullfighter attracts a fighting bull. "*Olé*, anybody?"

"Oh, shit . . . *olé* . . ." said Kiki grudgingly. "As if I had a choice."

"Girls? Girls? Aren't you ready yet?" Eleanor Kavanaugh's nervous voice was heard through the locked door. She'd been completely dressed for over an hour now. The wedding was unquestionably going to be late.

"We're getting there, Aunt Ellie," Daisy answered. Kiki pulled a horrible face but said nothing.

"Can I come in?"

"Ah—we'll be out in a sec," Daisy called.

"Do you need any help, Daisy darling?" she quavered. She couldn't have the vapors, Eleanor Kavanaugh told herself. They would wrinkle her dress.

"How about . . ." Kiki began, but Daisy put her hand over her mouth.

"No, we've got everything we need, Aunt Ellie," Daisy said. "Honestly. Why don't you just go downstairs for a minute."

"I was just going to ask for some Valium," Kiki whispered cantankerously.

"I've *got* Valium."

"You do?"

"Did you think I was going to let Theseus disgrace us?" Both girls looked at the lurcher, sitting calmly and happily on a pillow, with a woven satin basket full of baby's breath, white orchids and freesia tied under his chin, a leash of white velvet around his neck. "He's doped to the eyeballs," Daisy said, proudly.

"A stoned flower dog!"

"Couldn't take a chance."

"Oh, Daisy, darling, you'd do that for me?" Kiki wailed.

"Of course. Now why don't you put on that dress, for me? Hmmm?"

Slowly Kiki allowed Daisy to hook her into the full-skirted dress, the white of the best quality whipping cream, the white of a baked Alaska, the white of a meringue glacé. She finally looked at herself in the full-length mirror and a seraphic smile began to touch her lips. Daisy, encouraged by this sign, asked, "What are you thinking about?"

"All my old lovers. Just think if they could see me now—they'd be *sick* with envy."

"Is that any way for a bride to feel?"

"It's the *only* way . . . imagine, getting married if you didn't have any old lovers, what a bizarre idea!"

Jerry Kavanaugh, Kiki's father, in his morning coat and striped pants, now knocked on the door. "Kiki, for heaven's sake, when are you going to be ready? Everyone's waiting. My Lord, Kiki, don't just hang around in there, girl—get moving."

"We're coming right out, Uncle Jerry," Daisy assured him at the top of her voice. "Kiki, let me put on the veil, quickly now, no more kidding around. They're playing your song."

"What song?"

" 'Here Comes the Bride.' "

Kiki paled, kissed Daisy on the cheek and squared her shoulders. "It's all so fucking grown-up!" she murmured plaintively as she walked toward the door and the future.

Candice Bloom was thinking. She stood, as always, with her hands thrust deep into her pockets, leaning slightly backward, her sharp hipbones tilted prominently forward. Candice, who never let anyone call her Candy twice, squeaked with chic and had refused one excellent job in California on the grounds that there was simply nowhere there to shop for shoes. Her assistant, Jenny Antonio, waited patiently for her instructions.

"Call Grossinger's," she said, finally, "and the Concord. Find out the total capacity of their snow-making machines and how long it takes before the stuff will start to melt in mid-September, assuming that we don't have our usual heat wave, which, in itself, would be a miracle. And ask what it costs to rent them. *Tu comprends?* Oh, and get the Parks Department on the phone for me. Something tells me I have to get a permit for this. Where are the proofs for the invitation?"

"What if Grossinger's and the Concord are using their machines themselves? Don't they have skiing practically all year round?" Jenny asked, with the eager and bright-eyed intelligence of her twenty-three years.

Candice looked at her in stupefaction. "Jenny, you don't know much about how Supracorp works yet, do you? We're giving The Great Russian Winter Palace Party of this or any other year, we're taking over the entire Tavern on the Green in Central Park to launch the Princess Daisy line—and that means *snow*—even if we have to *buy* snow-making machines or build them. Just get on the phone and stop asking silly questions. *Vraiment!* I bet you don't even have the answers for me on the troikas?"

"Any carriage drawn by three horses can count as a troika, so we don't have to find actual sleds. Just the carriages and a hell of a lot of horses."

"One problem solved and ten thousand to go," Candice brooded. "When is my meeting with Warner Le Roy to discuss the menu?"

"He wanted to make it tomorrow at lunch, but that's when you and Daisy are having lunch with Leo Lerman for the 'People Are Talking About' column, so I said I'd call back."

"Good. This is really the ultimate crunch," Candice Bloom said with a gloomy relish. "It's all very well to run commercials and print ads—and thank God they're all done—but without P.R. you can forget your enormous impact because you don't get free editorial space, and without free space you might just as well not exist. Now get out that folder again and let's take another look at it. Okay—we have all the fashion magazines and *WWD*, but they had to give us the space—look at the advertising dollars they're getting. And *Cosmo's* promised us something, also Trudy Owett's spread will run next month in the *Journal*. Here are the clips from AP, UPI, Reuters and the Chicago Trib Syndicate. So far so good. But we haven't heard from the Los Angeles Times Syndicate and I want them. *Merde!* Where did you put my list of columnists? Why hasn't Shirley Eder called back, damn it? Try her in Vegas . . . or at the Beverly Hills Hotel. Has Liz Smith confirmed? Only a maybe? the 'Today Show' is still being negative and Mike Douglas and Dinah all want to know what Daisy can talk about. Merv, bless him, said yes—next month sometime. But the others insist on a theme, damn it, and they don't give a shit that she's a gorgeous princess." Candice prowled around her office in disgust. "*Shtick!* They want *shtick* from a princess, a hook, some peg to hang her on—it'd be easier if she were a stand-up comic on roller skates."

"You can't really blame them," Jenny ventured.

"I don't. I know their problems better than mine. But Shannon isn't going to give me brownie points for being turned down for even the best reasons. We've been trying—and not doing badly under the circumstances—to create an instant celebrity. But Daisy's not famous for being famous, like a Gabor, she's not a designer, she's not a major heiress, she's always avoided publicity like the plague—so we had to start from ground zero. Sure, her father was a hot-shot playboy and her mother was a legend in her time, only all that was over twenty years ago and who remembers? Francesca Vernon never made another movie after she married Stash Valensky; she just disappeared." Candice assumed her habitual expression of discouraged optimism as her secretary buzzed her for a phone call.

"Put her through." She put her hand over the mouthpiece and hissed excitedly. "It's Jane, my old, so-called friend from *People*. That bitch has been dodging my calls for practically half a year. *Now* she's decided to call! It's got to be bad news." Both Jenny and Candice waited galvanized.

"Hi, Jane—*pas mal*, and you? Good. Princess Daisy? No, we haven't definitely got a go-ahead from any other news magazine yet but it's all in the works. *Exclusively? Merde!* Jane, I'd give my all to say yes, but I just don't think my boss would agree. After all *Time* and *Newsweek* and *New York*, you should pardon the expression, all have departments she'll fit into perfectly. *A COVER STORY!* Are you sure? No, no, I didn't mean that . . . but it's just that I'd have to promise him and if it didn't work out I'd be looking for a job. *Definitely?* You said definitely? Ah ha. Ah ha. I see. He's absolutely right. I couldn't agree more. Ah ha. Got it. Look, let me check it out with the man and I'll get back to you within a half-hour. A quarter of an hour. Right. Bye."

She put down the phone with the stunned care of one who has just handled an artifact which has been buried for five thousand years, and that proves the existence of another civilization.

"It's *incroyable*," Candice said in a remote voice.

"I don't get it—you pitched them a story—but a *cover?*"

"She said that her boss is tired of having eight out of ten cover stories coming right out of Hollywood or the tube—he thinks the West Coast is trying to take over, in spite of the fact that the editorial department is here. He says *People*'s turning into nothing but a fan magazine. He wants something different, something high-fashion and elegant and New York—and he fell in love with the pictures of Daisy we sent over. Also he had a mad crush on Francesca Vernon when he was young—saw all her movies a dozen times—he says Daisy has her eyes."

"My God," Jenny said slowly.

"Jenny, this is fucking unreal and you may never see it happen twice so don't get big ideas, but now you understand the fatal fascination of public relations. And my analyst had the nerve to hint that I had a Snow White complex—he suspects that in my heart of hearts I'm waiting for my prince to come." She laughed shortly and gleefully. "Well the prince just did! Wait till I tell my doctor that!"

"What'll he say?" Jenny asked curiously.

"Nothing—Good Lord, Jenny, you are an innocent—it's the principle of the thing. It proves my analyst doesn't know *everything*. Oh, shit, if he doesn't know *everything* maybe he doesn't know *anything*." She opened her mouth in a grimace of worry.

"The other day you told me that analysts were only human," Jenny reminded her.

"Jenny, this whole thing is too deep for you. You're not neurotic enough. But you will be. *Je t'assure*. How long has it been since Jane called?"

"About a minute."

"Too soon to call back. I don't want to seem overeager."

"But you said you'd have to check with Shannon, and he's in Tokyo again."

"Check? On a *People* cover? Not while I'm alive! You don't think I need his permission for this?"

"Exactly two minutes," Jenny said helpfully.

"Balls! I may not last. Oh, wow!" Cynical, blasé Candice Bloom did a frenetic Irish jig in the center of her office carpet. She stopped and faced her astonished assistant. "Bet you didn't know the only four magazines you have to stock at any magazine stand in the whole United States—the must magazines?" Without waiting for a reply, she recited the four sacred names. "*Playboy*, *Penthouse*, *Cosmo* and *People*—as long as you have those four, you can pick and choose from among hundreds of others from *Field and Stream* to *Commentary*, but the big four are the ones that keep a newsstand going. Without them, you're dead. End of second lesson for today. What was your first?"

"If Shannon wants snow, we get snow."

"*Très bien, très bien!* You may make a P.R. person someday. Then you can afford your own analyst."

A week later Daisy hesitated rebelliously outside the ostentatiously discreet studio of Danillo, the world's most celebrated portrait photographer. She held Theseus's leash tightly as she studied the inconspicuous door behind which was a brownstone as narrow as any private house in Manhattan. The door itself was adorned only by a single push button and a small brass plate which bore the initial D.

The emotion with which Daisy faced the door was divided into equal parts of resolution and reluctance. Earlier that morning, as she was getting ready to leave, Kiki had telephoned and offered to take Theseus off her hands while she was sitting for this all-important photograph, but Daisy had refused. She knew perfectly well that clinging to Theseus was a sign of her precariously ambiguous feelings toward the process which would be put into high gear by today's session. She knew how childish it was, and she had also decided that she didn't give a good goddamn. The idea that *People* was actually going to do a cover story on her made the reality of the disappearance of her privacy seem far more palpable than had the making of the commercials, the interviews or posing for the ads. Nothing Candice Bloom had planned for her had quite seemed *real* until this moment, and now everything seemed focused on the inescapability of the next few hours. Yet her obligation to go through with the sitting was stronger than her premonitions, and she pushed firmly on the maliciously unimpressive button.

When the door clicked open, Daisy, closely followed by her dog, ambled into the small and crowded reception room which was already filled with people waiting for her. While they chirped greetings, Daisy surveyed her surroundings. They were remarkable chiefly for the absence of Danillo.

Daisy had expected this. She had overheard too many models gossiping not to know that Danillo would stage his entrance much later in the proceedings.

She felt the glances of sweeping appraisal from Alonzo, the make-up artist, and Robertson, the hairdresser. The two were veterans; they knew when Danillo booked them that they would have to put in at least three hours work on his subject before he started to shoot. His work depended on their talents. He needed them in order to achieve his trademark, the more-perfect-than-life face. His success was not based on his camera technique or communication with his subject or any depth of inspiration. All of his portraits had the same basic quality, an easily identifiable, inhumanly slick veneer, a spurious but convincing imitation of invention that resulted in a faultless, irresistible and dependable surface of resolute, just-short-of-plastic perfection that editors loved. They never worried about the results of a sitting with Danillo, and Alonzo and Robertson, who were paid seventy-five dollars an hour, with a minimum guarantee of five hours of work, were delighted to have been chosen today from his pool of fawning painters and crimpers.

"I won't need either of you," Daisy said, smiling at the two men. "I thought that had been settled."

Robertson glanced swiftly at Alonzo. Who did this one think she was?

Candice Bloom hurriedly intervened.

"Daisy, I told Danillo what you'd said, but he insisted *absolument*." She made a piteous face at Daisy to indicate that the people from *People* were not to be upset by any ructions—the cover story was simply too important. Alonzo tried to lure Daisy into the dressing room.

"Just come in here and sit down, dearie," he said, "and we'll get started. It's a bit late, you know."

"I think not," said Daisy. The magazine researcher, sensing a confrontation, automatically slipped out her pad and pencil.

"Get Danillo, Robbie," the make-up man commanded. "And what kind of nice doggie is that?" he asked Daisy while the hairdresser hurried up a flight of stairs.

"Theseus? You might say that his pedigree is unknown."

"Oh, I'm sure of *that*, dearie. Or should I call you Princess?"

"Daisy will do," she answered briefly. God, how tired she was of that question.

Danillo appeared, annoyed at being interrupted in his real art, that of retouching. The photographer was slender, unobtrusive, with close-cropped blond hair. In one keen quick glance he observed the inescapable power of Daisy's beauty and rejected it. She was a twenty-five-minute job, one of hundreds this year, and the adamant impersonality of the famous man in faded jeans and high-heeled boots had punished the egos of many women who had thought themselves tougher than he. He raised one indifferent, languid eyebrow at the crowd in the reception room. "We'll do it my way," he announced.

But Daisy persisted. Years of making commercials had taught her a great deal about make-up, although she used very little of it.

"I've done my eyes and lips, Danillo, and I never use a base," she insisted. "So why do I have to be made up?"

"Boys, you're running late," Danillo said, not in reply, but as if she hadn't spoken. With Candice Bloom grasping one arm and the senior of the *People* editors clutching at the other, Daisy realized that she was not only outnumbered but that nothing could be more ludicrous than a scuffle. She shook them off and walked into the narrow dressing room where she found a high, backless kitchen stool in front of a long table, behind which ran a mirror. Theseus settled himself on top of the red vinyl couch.

"Danillo, darling," she heard the senior *People* editor say anxiously, "you *are* going straight for the regal quality, aren't you?"

"I thought we were agreed to try for *ancien régime* nostalgia, Marcia," the junior editor said in surprise.

"I have nothing against nostalgia, Francie, so long as it's majestic," Marcia snapped.

"Try some fresh papaya juice," Danillo said and left them abruptly.

Daisy sat still and watched Alonzo deftly cover the warm blush of her skin with a thin, even layer of beige liquid that turned her into the blank page on which he intended to paint his own concept of what she should look like. He covered her face and neck completely. Even her lips lost their own deep rose and were wiped out by beige. Her golden eyebrows disappeared as the coat of base extended from her hairline, where the tiny tendrils of her silver-gilt hair sprang untamed, right down to the base of her throat.

"This gets a bit messy. Don't you want to put on a robe?" Alonzo asked, pleased at the obliteration he had wrought.

Daisy opened her mouth to speak.

"*Don't talk!*" he cried warningly. "I haven't got your lips on yet."

Danillo's stylist, Henri, a tawny boy, lounged in the doorway, carrying a King Charles Spaniel in his arms, and surveyed the scene disdainfully. However, he condescended to hand Daisy a terry robe and indicated a bathroom in which she could change. Then he saw Theseus.

"Who brought that *thing* in here?" she heard him ask indignantly. Daisy shook with laughter behind the door at the thought of anyone with intentions of evicting her animal. She hoped he'd try. As she emerged, the King Charles Spaniel, who rejoiced in the name of Yves St. Laurent, was yapping in high-bred protest at Theseus's existence, but a glance at her own dog told Daisy that he was maintaining his ruffian dignity, the saturnine yet convincing composure of a dexterous and unrepentant scoundrel.

"Doesn't anyone want to order *un petit* sandwich?" Candice Bloom asked eagerly. P.R., as she had so often told Jenny Antonio, was *merde*, but today things seemed even more tense than usual. However, there was no situation that couldn't be helped by food. This was lesson number one from the public-relations course Candice aspired to teach at a great university in the far future. Everyone, including the hair stylist and Alonzo, hungrily gave her complicated and detailed orders, and she sent Jenny off to the nearest delicatessen.

Daisy returned to her uncomfortable stool and looked on in resignation as Alonzo began to sculpt shadows on her beige mask with a stick of brown grease.

"Five different psychics told me that I was going to be called to Hollywood this year," he confided to her earnestly, dabbing away. She tried to signal polite curiosity with her looming eyes, the only thing left on her face that still showed any expression, but their very darkness was too intense to convey such pallid emotion.

"Do you know Hollywood? No! Don't talk! Close your eyes." Relieved, Daisy did as she was told, and the small room, crowded with watching people, faded behind her lids as she felt him doing things with brushes of various sizes. She felt hands on her hair and heard the angry admonition, "Get away, Robbie! You can have her when I'm finished and not before. You almost jiggled my arm!"

While the editors and Candice chattered, Daisy reflected on the fact that she had never been looked at the way Danillo had looked at her; not coldly but not warmly, neither approving nor disapproving, but with a simple and absolute lack of interest. He was bored, Danillo was, she decided, and she realized she didn't care. He had sittings like hers as often as twice a day, every day of the week, charging an average of three thousand dollars for the single shot that would be chosen. Even the best plastic surgeon, doing two face lifts a day, didn't make more money than this man. Four babies could be delivered by a Park Avenue gynecologist for one of Danillo's portraits, Daisy thought, trying to ignore the tickling of a brush inside her ear. "You can open now," Alonzo instructed her. Warily, she raised her lids and confronted her image. The beige mask still looked at her, embellished by deep, unfamiliar shadows that had settled on its cheekbones, its neck and its eyelids. "We're only getting started," Alonzo explained to Candice Bloom.

Robertson, the hairdresser, wearing an expression of exaggerated patience, slumped against the wall, his battery of curling irons and hot rollers unpacked in readiness for a job he wouldn't start for at least an hour and a half. Featherbedding. Daisy knew his expression well, from years of dealing with the unnecessary grips and gaffers on whom the union had insisted. She felt sharp, poignant regret for those days, so recently over, those hectic, harried days, so many of which had resulted in thirty or sixty seconds of the finest commercials ever made.

Jenny Antonio came into the dressing room bearing a platter of thick sandwiches which she had unwrapped and arranged in a tempting pile. She put the platter down on the couch and joined Candice and the *People* editors in their inspection of Daisy. Alonzo had started to fill in his new version of Daisy's mouth, and when she tried to say something he wagged a stern finger at her. Five women clustered around while he deftly redesigned Daisy's upper and lower lips to his satisfaction.

"Okay," he grunted, "you can talk now."

"I'm afraid it's too late," Daisy said, trying to sound regretful.

"Too late for what?" he asked.

"Lunch," said Daisy.

Seven pairs of eyes looked at the bare sandwich platter. Seven pairs of eyes accused Theseus but no one had seen him move, no one had heard him eat, he was sitting, as ceremoniously uninvolved as Al Pacino during a gangland murder, in the same position he'd been in since he first sat down.

"I fed him before we came, but . . ." Daisy tried to explain.

"My God, he's a monster," breathed Marcia, the senior *People* editor, but the researcher, who had grown to know Theseus while interviewing Daisy, said, "He can't help it."

"How *dare* he?" shrieked Marcia, deprived of her ham and swiss on rye with plenty of mustard and coleslaw.

"I'll tell you when we get back to the office. It's a long story," said the researcher with an informed smile.

"Jenny, *vite, vite!* More sandwiches!" Candice ordered urgently. Lesson number two in her public-relations course would be to never permit a *chien*, no matter to whom it belonged, on any job she was involved in, ever again.

Alonzo stolidly continued his handiwork. Daisy felt as if she'd been sitting on the stool forever, although only two hours had passed. If she'd had Alonzo on a location shoot he'd have been long dead by now, she told herself, with mounting irritation. She would have stabbed him herself with one of the many instruments he was using on her. But it was typical of the anointed necromancers of the glamour business to insist, as Danillo did, on subjecting his subjects to discomfort. For a sitting with Danillo one had to step within his magic circle, pay endless obeisance before this very mirror, showing an essential neediness by putting up with this transfiguring nonsense in order to be assured of the master's imprint.

Jenny returned with a new supply of sandwiches and Daisy was relieved as the room cleared. At length Alonzo decided that he'd done all he could do and he turned her over to Robertson.

She no longer recognized the painted person in the mirror, with the wrong mouth, the wrong brows and the wrong skin, who looked ten years older than she had this morning. The face in the mirror had nothing to do with her, and when Robertson began to build her hair into an elaborate, tall coronet, rather like that of Princess Grace at a Monaco Red Cross gala, Daisy didn't bother to object.

"I have to make a base for the tiara," he told her as his hands deftly reduced her hair to a solid package of complicated swirls and curls.

"Tiara?" she questioned with lips that moved in a strange and disquieting way.

"Henri's borrowed a tiara and pendant earrings and a dog-collar necklace from *A la Vieille Russie*," he told her. "We're going for a real pre-Revolutionary look, kind of Anastasia, you know, the whole Romanov bit."

"I didn't know," said Daisy, "and I wish you hadn't told me."

"Huh?"

"Never mind." Candice Bloom, with her little French phrases, dropped like a tic into every other sentence, had evidently made plans she hadn't seen fit to tell Daisy about. Daisy's visual indigestion was being joined by a feeling of actual nausea at the thought of being turned into a reincarnation of the long dead and pathetic Grand Duchess. But just as she was about to get up and speak to Candice, Henri sauntered in carrying several black velvet boxes. Without a word he clasped the dog collar of emeralds, rubies and diamonds around her neck, and he fastened the matching tiara in her hair.

"You don't have pierced ears!" he whined, accusingly.

"Would you care to try and pierce them?" Daisy asked softly. He backed away from the menace in her eyes.

Danillo's voice could be heard calling impatiently from the studio. He was finally in the mood to work, and if everyone was on schedule he'd be finished with this in less than a half-hour.

"Ready?" asked Robertson.

Daisy took one more look in the mirror. It was hopeless to make any objections. They'd done so much to her that she hadn't the faintest idea of where to start to make it less awful.

She got up gingerly. The stool had cut off the circulation in her legs and she felt stiff and weary. She didn't need to change from the terry robe since she would merely slip it off her shoulders for the head shot. She belted it more securely and turned to look at Theseus.

"Now you stay right here until I get back," she told him. Instead of his usual patient acceptance of her instructions, he stood up on the couch, bared his teeth at her and growled low in his throat, breaking his lurcher's silence. It was unthinkable. Daisy went closer to him and he suddenly cringed away, growling desperate protest all the while.

"Theseus!" she cried. He shivered all over at the sound of Daisy's voice coming from the stranger's face, and when she put out her hand to him, he flinched and refused to sniff it.

"*THAT DOES IT!*" Daisy said and turned back to the table, plunged her hand deep into a jar of cold cream and smeared it forcefully from one cheek to another. "Take off the jewels, take down my hair and call Alonzo in here to take off the rest of the make-up!" she ordered the hairdresser. Robertson, who could feel the room darkening and whirling around him, had retreated to a corner to get away from this madwoman.

"Alonzo," Daisy called out to the reception room, "I need you."

The make-up man hurried in as she was scrubbing the second handful of cold cream over her chin and forehead.

"Get me some towels," Daisy demanded. "And tell Danillo I'll be out in just a little while. It only takes me about three minutes to do my own make-up if I start with a clean face. Robertson! Hairbrush, please! Oh, for heaven's sake, Alonzo, just put your head between your legs and take a few deep breaths!"

"Could we just go over what we have so far, Warner?" asked Hugo Ralli, the general manager of the Tavern on the Green. Candice Bloom and Warner Le Roy had seen eye to eye so quickly that he wanted to make sure that they hadn't overlooked anything.

The secretary read from her notes. "The Elm Room is to be used for the receiving line. Both the Elm and Rafters rooms will have ten rolling tables circulating from the moment the party starts, with two waiters at each table. The tables will carry three ice sculptures of the Princess Daisy bottle, each three feet tall, one to contain ten pounds of caviar, one to hold a jeroboam of champagne, specified Louis Roederer Cristal, another a bottle of Stolichnaya vodka. The caviar will be served on small plates with whatever trimmings the guest chooses."

"You left out the gypsies," said Candice, adding a touch of lemon juice to the smoked trout she was eating. Warner Le Roy looked at her kindly from behind the glasses. As always, when he went over a party with someone who was taking over the entire restaurant, he dressed in his most conservative way. Today he had adorned his agreeably liberal girth with red trousers and a gray, red and white plaid jacket. He enjoyed clothes even as subdued as these. He enjoyed boyish, bossy Candice Bloom. He enjoyed owning Maxwell's Plum and the Tavern on the Green. He enjoyed life and life enjoyed him.

"I was just about to get to the gypsies," the secretary said. "During the arrival of the guests there will be a thirty-man gypsy band playing outside on both sides of the front entrance and another thirty gypsies strolling through the Rafters and Elm rooms, not, note *not*, playing loudly, or else they may drown out the introductions to Princess Daisy on the receiving line. There will be eight searchlights placed around the restaurant and an additional fifty parking attendants will be hired to supplement our regular staff because of the troikas. The men must be trained in handling horses."

"What did we finally decide about the buffet?" asked Candice, as she sat, finishing her trout, at a round table under an umbrella on the terrace of the restaurant.

"It's supposed to be set up in the Pavilion Room," the secretary said, consulting her notes.

"I'm not sure about that," Warner Le Roy said. "I think that with six hundred guests we've got to have two separate buffets."

"Agreed," said Walter Rauscher, the banquet manager, who made the fifth member of the lunch party.

The secretary made a note and continued. "During dinner there will be a waltz orchestra playing in the Crystal Room and waltzing will take place both in the Crystal Room and outside under the trees on the terrace. Both gypsy bands will play in the Pavilion Room. The disco band will play in the Terrace Room at the back of the restaurant, starting right after dinner."

"What if it rains?" asked Candice.

"We can put up a tent outside and have radiant heat but I think that so early in September, you don't really have to worry," Warner Le Roy reassured her.

"Warner," Candice said, in as waggish a tone as she'd ever permitted herself. "I'm still not *tout à fait* happy with the caviar. We just say 'caviar' but I'd like to get more precise. I take a personal interest in it."

"If you want to go all the way, I could try to order the golden Iranian, but I doubt that there'd be enough available," he told her. "And most people wouldn't know what it was, anyway."

"What's the next best?" she asked, finishing her trout. Public relations had its moments of compensation. She must remember to tell her analyst.

"The best beluga. No problem getting it. If you want to be reasonably lavish you provide two large scoops for each person, three ounces in all, so that makes one pound for every five people, considering that not everyone likes caviar."

"My orders are to be unreasonably lavish," Candice said with gusto. "How about four ounces per person? And let's figure that everyone wants caviar because I intend to put away two pounds myself and I expect a large doggie bag and a dogsled to take it home in."

"So, six hundred people at four ounces to a person . . . makes two thousand, four hundred ounces . . . of course the Russian pound is only fourteen ounces so that makes . . ."

"To be on the safe side, Warner, one hundred seventy-five pounds of the best beluga at a hundred and twenty-five dollars a pound, wholesale, and one large doggie bag," Walter Rauscher suggested.

"Done and done," Candice pronounced, her Tootsie Roll brown eyes sparkling with anticipatory greed.

"Shall I go on?" asked the secretary. Candice nodded.

"The buffet will feature whole cold sturgeon and salmon, roast quail, roast wild boar with sautéed apples and lingonberries . . ."

"Ah, look, Warner, I just don't know about that wild boar," Candice said. "I know it's Russian, but are you sure?"

"It's sensational. We marinate it for five days and do it in light bread crumbs with a Béarnaise sauce." He waved at the secretary to continue reading the long buffet list. Eventually she came to her last notes.

"The desserts will be served at the table. Mr. Ralli and the head chef will decide on the most appropriate ingredients for a variety of sculptured bombe desserts to be carried in, *en flambé.*"

"Not a flaming Princess Daisy bottle," Candice warned.

"Of course not!" Warner said, shocked. "Trust me."

"I do," said Candice wistfully, "but I just don't see why we can't have icicles on the trees on the terrace. We're going to have snow all around the Tavern, except on the outside dance floor, so *pourquoi* isn't there some sort of real dripless icicle?"

"We could do theatrical icicles, I suppose, or I could put up the winter lights," Warner said thoughtfully.

"Oh yes! That's it! The winter lights, all white and tiny and twinkling—I remember them from last Christmas, driving by. They were *incroyable!* Let's put them up," Candice said in excitement.

"There's just one problem. They'll have to come down the next day—I don't start winter until just after Thanksgiving."

"What's the problem?"

"There are sixty thousand lights. That's going to cost a lot for labor."

"Mr. Shannon wouldn't like to hear that I decided to draw the line at twinkle lights," the publicity woman told Warner. "Not with fifty thousand dollars worth of manmade snow."

Hugo Ralli coughed. "Did we say *only* candlelight?" he asked, thinking of places that demanded electricity.

"No, we said at least two thousand candles, in silver candelabra—candles everywhere they could possibly be, but electric light in the johns," Candice remembered. "And now, about the flowers, Mr. Ralli, they're terribly important. Millions of daisies. I don't know where you'll find that many in the city, but we've got to have them, no matter what. *C'est indispensable!*"

"I can get them, but they won't make the right effect unless I mix them with white roses and spider chrysanthemums in yellow and white," he insisted.

"Okay, just so long as you find the daisies." Candice turned to Warner Le Roy, grandson of Harry Warner, grand-nephew of Jack Warner, heir to a sense of the spectacular not possessed by any other restaurateur in the world. "Could you just give me a ballpark figure on how much this party is going to cost? Forget the snow and the troikas and the horses."

Warner thought for a minute, remembering the twenty-fifth anniversary party for the Klebergs of the King Ranch in Texas, who had flown 250 people to New York and taken over the restaurant. "Somewhere in the neighborhood of—well, with all the extras and the ice sculpture and all, somewhere in the neighborhood of two hundred thousand—it could go higher, depending on how much caviar you want in your doggie bag."

"Sounds reasonable," Candice said, judiciously, waiting for the next course to be served. Lunch, thank God, had only started.

When he woke from his first restless hours of sleep, Hilly Bijur, president of Elstree, often wondered what had ever lured him into the jungle of the fucking fragrance business. As soon as this question formed in his mind, he had trained himself to try to relax his muscles, grimly starting at the top of his scalp and working down to his toes, and then back up again, not neglecting his clenched teeth, as the hypnotherapist he had gone to for insomnia had taught him, but by the time his ears were relaxed and he started on his forehead, words started to whirl in his mind: Quadrille, Calèche, L'Air du Temps, Arpège, Cristalle, Jontue, Halston—damn Halston—why couldn't he have a French name like the others?—Aliage, Infini, Cabochard, Ecusson . . . when he got to Ecusson he usually was able to return his concentration to his forehead and sometimes he got down as far as relaxing his jaw muscles when another set of names would start dancing behind his eyes: first, Dick Johnson, perfume buyer for the Hess chain based in Allentown, Pennsylvania; then Mike Gannaway, merchandise manager at Dayton's in Minneapolis; swiftly followed by Verda Gaines, head of cosmetics at Steinfeld's in Tucson; Karol Kempster, buyer for Henri Bendel; Marjorie Cassell, buyer for Harvey's in Nashville; Melody Grim at Garfinkle's—the list could go on all night, but when Hilly Bijur reached Garfinkle's he gave up trying to work on his muscles, got out of bed and took a sleeping pill that his doctor had guaranteed to be nonaddictive, nonbarbiturate and without evil side effects which might cause it to build up in the body. This remarkable pill had only one drawback, Hilly Bijur reflected, it did not put him to sleep. However, just swallowing a pill made him feel calmer, even if it only acted as a placebo, he assured himself as he crept out of the bedroom so as not to wake his wife. He read a few more pages of Leon Edel's five-volume biography of Henry James. This great scholarly work, detailed, leisurely and undoubtedly good for him, had the virtue of not being a page turner. At about five in the morning, trying hard to think only about James churning out books in London, books Hilly Bijur had never read, he ventured back to bed and usually managed to sleep for several hours before he woke up to another day of the Princess Daisy project.

It was now early September of 1977, almost eight months since preparations had begun for the new line of perfume and cosmetics. The fragrance which Patrick Shannon had named Princess Daisy had actually been seven years in the creation, the work of a man who was considered the greatest "nose" in France. To Hilly Bijur's pragmatic judgment, it smelled good. As far as he was concerned, the world needed only one perfume, Arpège, the scent of the first woman he'd ever laid. Arpège turned him on in the way Youth Dew, his mother-in-law's perfume, turned him off. What, he wondered, if his first real fuck had worn Youth Dew and his mother-in-law used Arpège? Would his tastes be reversed? Did perfume smell like sex or did sex smell like perfume? What would sex smell like without any perfume at all? Better? He thought so—but business was business and if people wanted to describe a perfume as "irrepressible yet romantic" or "spirited yet reserved" or "endearing and joyously feminine" they had as much right as wine freaks. He didn't even give a good goddamn when they started talking about "single-note florals" or "ylang-ylang notes" or "little greenies" or throwing around phrases about a "serious perfume that goes with serious clothes" or the "musk revolution," and he was indifferent to whether a perfume was "created" or "designed," whether a claim was made that a woman didn't just "put on" Chloe, but "entered it" or any equally baroque fragrance-world bullshit.

It was a question of merchandising, that's all it was about, he thought to himself in the shower. Merchandising the sizzle, not the steak. Merchandising the fantasy, not the reality. Merchandising a luxury that had become increasingly a part of American life, a luxury that was sold in discount drugstores and continued to base its advertising on snob appeal.

He remembered, shudderingly, that first sales conference at which he had announced the new Princess Daisy concept to his sales staff, and told them of Shannon's one-hundred-million-dollars' sales expectation for the new line. Six of his top salesmen had resigned on the spot, and the ones who were left made the crew of H.M.S. *Bounty* look like the peaceful and contented seamen of the H.M.S. *Pinafore*. When he boiled it down, Hilly reflected, it simply amounted to the fact that no one was happy about being in on a launch. They'd have been more willing to go along with the old Elstree line, fading quietly into the back of consumers' minds, than to have to hustle their asses trying to get cosmetic buyers to place orders for anything new, no matter how good, no matter how it was going to be backed up by advertising and packaging.

Hilly Bijur, seasoned merchandising man, had not been picked by Shannon as president of Elstree by accident. Within a month, spending freely, he'd cleaned house and built a much stronger group of sales people, who, since they hadn't worked for the old Elstree, had nothing to prevent them from being enthusiastic about the new plans. He'd made the important decisions about how many items to offer in the new cosmetic line, knowing how store buyers detested being asked to order a great variety of stock they weren't sure they would sell. The Princess Daisy cosmetic collection was a full but strictly edited group of products: the essential moisturizing lotion, a cleansing cream, a body lotion, a liquid make-up base in the six most important shades, lipsticks and lip glosses in the basic groups of pinks, reds, raisins and plums, nail lacquer to match, four shades of blusher, four hues of face powder, roll-on mascaras in black and brown, eyeliner in four colors, eye shadow in eight shades (an area in which he congratulated himself on almost unheard-of self-restraint, since over twenty shades were average for most cosmetic companies) and, of course, the soap, the after-bath dusting powder, the spray cologne in three sizes, and finally the perfume, in the half-ounce, the one-ounce size and the two-ounce bottles. As he turned over and over in his mind the array of new products, Hilly Bijur was remembering the words of the voice of his conscience, the very same Dick Johnson of Allentown who woke him up at night.

"Yeah, you would not be exaggerating at all if you were to say we have too many products on the market today—the manufacturers are overdoing it completely." Oh, Dick Johnson of those eleven eastern Pennsylvania cities which shelter a Hess's, Inc., why were you not more like adventuresome Verda Gaines of Tucson who said, "Without new products, there is no progress." Why??

Eleven percent of every dollar cosmetic and fragrance manufacturers spend goes into packaging. It was this fact that made Hilly Bijur erase Dick Johnson from his mind as he plunged into delighted contemplation of the marvelous bottle that had been designed for the perfume. It was inspired, at Daisy's suggestion, by the Easter eggs which Peter Carl Fabergé had made for the Imperial Family—fifty-seven eggs in all, between 1884 and 1917. Now they were scattered in museums all over the world, although some had found their way into private collections. Marjorie Merriweather Post, the great heiress of the General Foods Corporation, had been one of the few private people in the world to possess several of the Imperial eggs, and even in her vast collection of Russian treasures, they were the rarest, most prized objects.

The Princess Daisy bottle was egg shaped, hand-blown crystal, bound from its base to its top with four slender, rippling vermeil ribbons which came together above the stopper to form a bow. It stood on a graceful three-legged vermeil stand surmounted by an oval hoop into which it fit snugly. In a year of ever more modern bottles, at a time dominated by the severity of Halston's packaging and the classicism of Chanel's, the Elstree bottle was jewel-like, unique. It was impossible to see it and not want to lift it from its stand and caress it. After all, Bijur reflected, was the egg not considered nature's most perfect form? *Take that,* Dick Johnson of Allentown! And take the rest of the packaging as well, jars and bottles and cases of deep, brilliant lapis lazuli blue, so highly glazed that they resembled Fabergé enamel itself, each one bearing a single white and gold daisy on a green stem, a highly stylized design which was the trademark for the entire line. They were so fucking *perfect* they could make you fucking cry, Bijur had told Patrick Shannon and, for once, Shannon had agreed without even trying to suggest a single improvement.

Princess Daisy perfume was going to sell at a hundred dollars an ounce. Justified? Bijur thought so. Unlike many perfumes that sold for less, it was made only from natural oils and essences, produced and bottled in France. Of course, it didn't cost anything close to one hundred dollars an ounce to make it or bottle it or merchandise it—my God, he thought, if it fucking did, where would the profit be? When cosmetics and perfumes start selling for anything even *near* the price they cost to produce, it'd be like fucking Russia.

As Hilly Bijur walked briskly down Park Avenue to the Supracorp building, he thought about the Christmas catalogues which major stores all over the country had sent out in August, almost all of them offering Princess Daisy perfume and gift boxes of various combinations of perfume, cologne, soap and bath powder. If they'd missed being in the Saks and Neiman-Marcus catalogues, to say nothing of the dozens of other catalogues in which they had been featured, Shannon's wild dream wouldn't have had a chance of being realized.

The Princess Daisy launch was being coordinated as if it were as important as D-Day. Shit, if you had a sense of perspective, it fucking *was* D-Day, Bijur ruminated. On the one hand there was Candice Bloom taking care of the fluff, building all that media excitement about Daisy herself which would finally flare into an explosion with the publication of the *People* cover story tomorrow, to say nothing of The Russian Winter Palace Ball, the launch party that should make every newsmagazine and newspaper women's page in the country. And Helen Strauss had the advertising well in hand, the commercials, the double trade magazine ads, the four color brochures. Hilly himself was complacent about his shipments of perfume in the New Jersey warehouse. Everything had arrived from France in good time and in good shape and the salesmen had taken spectacular orders. Even Saks Fifth Avenue, traditionally the one store to get a perfume before anyone in New York had been persuaded to share the launch with Bendel's and Bloomingdale's; the special Princess Daisy capsule collection of fall fashions by Bill Blass was one of the most opulent that consistently elegant designer had ever created, and the clothes had been shipped to major stores across the country to be shown in banks of display windows the week of the launch; the Elstree saleswomen were being given an extra bonus commission on top of their regular commission for the first three months of sales; the samples of Princess Daisy perfume had already arrived in the chosen stores by the tens of thousands, to be distributed with an open hand at special designer "outposts" on the stores' ground floors, and Daisy herself was scheduled to fly from one city to another on a whirlwind tour of thirty major markets during the weeks following the party to make personal appearances at the largest department stores and draw the winning number which would give one of the women at each store who had bought Princess Daisy perfume or cosmetics a gift certificate for a thousand dollars.

So what could go wrong? Christ—almost everything, Hilly Bijur thought, shuddering. In the crazy world of fragrance, who the fuck knew?

"Of course she's unimportant, a totally unimportant miserable little bitch. You don't have to tell me that . . . it only makes it worse, Robin, don't you understand?" Vanessa said furiously. "She was never worthy of our kindness. And no, I do not want a Miltown or a Valium or a sleeping pill, so will you please stop trying to make me take one?"

It was three in the morning and Vanessa had awakened, as she had so often in the last months, in a knotted fury. Although she tried not to disturb him, Robin always seemed to know when she couldn't sleep and woke, loyally prepared to listen as Vanessa poured once again over the rosary of her grievances. It made him sad to look at her. Although her long, slashingly elegant body was unchanged, her mouth was tightened in an unattractive line and her face looked thinner than it ever had, almost gaunt. But no matter how he tried to distract her with plans for vacations, new ideas for redecorating, no matter how often he held her tight and massaged her upper back where the worst of the tension was, she wouldn't forget Daisy and what Daisy had done to her.

"First and foremost, and you have to admit it, Robin, she was *never* properly grateful, not for a second. Oh, she said thank you, but only when it was absolutely necessary, when I persuaded Topsy to let her do the children in oil and when I got her that other commission. But how did she say thank you? As if she were doing *me* a favor! If there is one thing I can't forgive, it's ingratitude—she never had me fooled for a minute. And she owed us so much! How many parties I invited her to was she 'too busy' to come to? Who the hell does she think she is? No one—*no one*—is too busy to come here. Ever!"

"Vanessa, everyone who counts says you give the best parties in New York. What does she matter?" Robin said patiently for the hundredth time.

"That's not the point and you know it. It's her whole attitude! That high-and-mighty 'You can't touch me because I'm special,' and 'You don't impress me no matter what you do'—it's *that* I simply cannot endure. And what about those dresses you gave her? You practically had to force them on her, for Christ's sake—you'd think she preferred to wear those crazy, playacting castoffs of hers."

"She has to wear decent clothes now," Robin said, realizing an instant too late that he could hardly have been more tactless. Vanessa had been filled with wrath on the topic of Daisy ever since the unfortunate yacht incident last winter, but when the news of the Princess Daisy campaign was announced, when personal publicity started to appear about Daisy, when the story of the million-dollar contract was bruited about and, finally, now that she had heard that there was to be a *People* cover story, Vanessa's envious outrage grew until it consumed her.

"I notice she didn't come to you for them," she sneered at her husband spitefully. When he merely shrugged and refused to answer, she sighed and touched his arm tenderly. "Sorry, darling, I didn't mean that the way it sounded. Her taste is so outlandish that of course she wouldn't have the intelligence or the class to wear your things, that's all."

"It's all right," he assured her. "Would you like a little wine? It might make you sleepy." Vanessa shook her head again, sternly.

"Robin, I assure you that I'm indifferent to all those cheap advertising ploys—I'd say let her have her moment in the limelight and who cares—but what I can't forgive, what I'll never be able to forgive, is the way she ruined that yachting party. Don't you have any comprehension of what a fool she made me look? Do you have any understanding of the things people have been saying about us ever since? Yes, *ever* since, even now! Everyone on that boat must have blabbed to every last solitary soul they knew in the whole world. It's been months and months and people haven't stopped baiting me . . . 'Vanessa, love, so that little family reunion you planned backfired, did it?' 'Vanessa, I've heard the most fascinating story . . . what *really* happened, darling?' 'Vanessa, why on earth did you have to turn the yacht back—Why did Daisy Valensky sneak off in the middle of the night? What could have caused Ram Valensky to spend the rest of his trip in his cabin . . . so rude of him, poor sweet . . . do tell . . . I'm sure you know more than you're saying . . . how *could* they act that way toward you?' Oh, Robin, you just wouldn't believe the rumors—vindictive, mean, stupid, ugly—and all of them making me look like the biggest idiot alive. And it comes from everyone—people I thought were friends—I hardly dare to make a lunch date even now because I know there's going to be this inquisition. Don't you see what she's *done to me*, that pretentious bitch!"

"It was just a nine-day wonder, darling. I'm sure people can't still be talking about it," Robin said, without conviction. He had been the target of many questions himself.

"Bullshit—and you know it. It might have been all right if Ram hadn't acted the way he did. I could have just said that Daisy was seasick or had an allergic attack or something, but he had to go and shut himself up, for God's sake, and not even say goodbye to anybody—that's what really did it, that's what really made people talk. When I think how much trouble I went to for that bastard, talking Daisy into coming with us, I could die. Even if he did finance your new line, nothing entitled him to hold *me* up to ridicule," she raged.

"Vanessa, dearest, please, you're just eating yourself up about this. You can't go on . . . you've got to try and put it behind you."

"I damn well will!" Vanessa pulled herself up from her pillows and wrapped herself in a bathrobe.

"Robin, what time is it in England now?"

"Morning. Why?"

Without answering him she placed the call to London, waiting in their bedroom, that often photographed jungle of Victorian chintz and Edwardian lace, until she had Ram on the line.

"Hello, darling—it's Vanessa! Robin and I were just having a nightcap and suddenly we both realized how frightfully long it's been since we've had news of you. So I thought, why not just pick up a phone? We were so sorry you weren't well on the yacht—in fact we were rather concerned. But of course I understand, I get the most fearful migraines too. No, no, don't apologize. But you're fine now? I'm so glad. Yes, Robin and I are both in the pink. And I suppose you're up to date on all the good news about Daisy? She must have written you . . . such excitement, my dear, you can't imagine. They're making simply the most marvelous fuss about her—isn't it thrilling? To think that she just never seemed to have two dimes to rub together and now a million dollars! That old title of yours is worth something over here after all . . . democracy or no democracy, like the English, we dearly love a lord. Even *People* is doing a cover story on her now and if anything will put her on the map, that will. So you, my darling, had better get used to seeing your little sister simply plastered all over the billboards and magazines and television—even in England—hadn't you? Just imagine, a Valensky *touting* lipsticks and God knows what else. Still, I suppose there are just no lengths she won't go to for Patrick Shannon. What do you mean, what about Patrick Shannon? He's the head of . . . sorry, darling, obviously you know who he is. What I meant was that they're *madly* in love. Everyone in New York is gossiping about them ever since they came back from England together. They're having the most *glorious* affair! It's simply delicious to watch them . . . makes you believe in romance again. But didn't you see them when they were over there together? Oh, I see . . . in the Mideast . . . so you missed the lovebirds. Well now, *there* is where I think Daisy's been particularly clever. *People* covers are all well and good, but Patrick Shannon is the most divine man these old eyes have seen in years. And a man who gets *everything* he has ever wanted. Just yesterday there was an article about Elstree in *The New York Times* and they quoted him as saying that Daisy was 'one of a kind.' Pretty faint praise, considering—but, on the other hand, he was probably just being discreet—the last time I saw them at a restaurant together he could *barely* keep his hands off her. Now don't be old-fashioned, Ram! Daisy's hardly a teenager. She has a perfect right to a dozen lovers . . . but she only wants Shannon it seems, and who could quarrel with that?

"Well, listen sweetie, I won't keep you any longer. Just checking to make sure you were better—old friends shouldn't be out of touch for so long. Robin says to tell you he sends his best. Goodbye, love. See you in the funny papers, as they used to say."

With the first genuinely pleasant look he had seen on her face in months, Vanessa put down the phone very softly. "Robin, perhaps I'll have a little wine after all."

"Feeling better darling?" Robin asked anxiously.

"Infinitely!"

The pain Ram had felt ever since he had crept away from *La Marée*, leaving Daisy bleeding on her bed, had been a pain of such need, of a wanting so great that it lived in a place where no one knew about it but himself, a place so far inside that his sanity was unquestioned because his outward appearance was correct, impeccable. He was to continue to live and function without Daisy because no one else had her. But she had always lived on in his fatally obsessed mind as if she still belonged to him, lived on in a cage of hopeless, endless longing from which he had neither the will nor the desire nor the power to escape, a cage which contained no images but those of Daisy and himself. True, she turned away from him, in the cage, but she did not turn toward anyone else. How could she, since she was his possession?

Ram had not been jealous because there was no one to be jealous of, no actual threat, no embodiment of a third person between him and his fantasies.

Now, with a few insinuating words, chosen with her infallible instinct for weakness and vulnerability, Vanessa had aroused a literally unbearable sense of impotence, of mutilation. There was no place left for Ram to stand, no inner core in which to take refuge from the pain. Jealousy was born, ravening and gibbering, as old and as mad as if it had had a million years in which to reach hideous, unendurable, acid-drenched maturity.

He dressed quickly, and within half an hour after Vanessa's phone call he was at the mews garage in which he kept his Jaguar.

Ram had always known where Danielle was. The directors of the school were accustomed to his occasional phone calls as he checked up to find out if Daisy had been able to continue to pay for Danielle. For years he had waited for the day, the inevitable day on which she would be unable to shoulder the burden and would be forced to come to him for help.

Within twenty minutes Ram was headed out of London, speeding in the direction of Queen Anne's School, by a route that had been clearly mapped out in his mind for many, many years.

25

Oh, my God, NO!" Candice Bloom screamed. Jenny, her assistant, whirled around. Her boss had turned the color of a Kleenex and on her desk was an advance copy of *People* which had just arrived by messenger, a magazine that would be on every newstand in America twenty-four hours from now.

Jenny rushed over to Candice's desk, almost afraid to look at the cover. She was sure they'd been bumped for another story . . . Candice had been dreading that all along. She'd always said it was too good to be true. But no, there *was* Daisy . . . obviously rebellion was one way to inspire Danillo . . . it was a marvelous picture. On the side of the cover a copy line, in red, shouted "PRINCESS DAISY: Her life isn't just sweet scents; the strange, secret story of Francesca Vernon and Prince Stash Valensky's daughter." Jenny's hands fumbled as she tried to find the page on which the story appeared.

"Page thirty-four," Candice gasped.

Jenny finally found the double spread with which the cover story began. The entire right-hand page was one huge black-and-white photograph. She stared at it, read the caption and then looked again at the picture. The world was reduced to that page, that photograph, those two girls, two girls with blonde hair and black eyes, two girls with the same faces, two girls with their arms around each other, two smiling girls of about twenty-three, so alike, *so impossibly alike.* The caption read: "Princess Daisy on a recent visit to her identical twin sister, Danielle, in the home for permanently retarded children in which she has been secreted since she was six."

The two women stood frozen, staring, staring, unable to speak, struggling for comprehension of something that just could not be.

Finally, in a white voice, Candice said, "She . . . she's a little shorter."

"Her eyes . . . they're the same . . . but her look is . . . vague?" Jenny's words stumbled. She could only absorb the shock detail by detail.

"And her hair, it's just shoulder length and it's not as, not as . . . bright . . . but it grows in just the same way, exactly the same way." Candice sounded as if she were speaking from another room.

"Her features are different, no, not *different* really, but just not quite as . . . clear, not as fine. She looks, oh, younger, as if she doesn't have a sense of humor," Jenny said wonderingly. "But it *is* the same face . . . Daisy's face."

"No!" Candice said. "Not the *same*—you wouldn't look *twice* at her!"

"No, no . . . you would *not.*" Jenny agreed in horror. "My God, look at that other picture," she said, pointing with a finger that shook. It was a reproduction of the *Life* cover of twenty-five years before . . . Stash and Francesca, and the laughing baby on Merlin's back. She read the caption out loud. "No one knew, when Prince and Princess Valensky posed for *Life* that another child had been born to them, a child they hid away from the eyes of the world."

"Jesus God!" Jenny whispered. They both started to read the story, flipping through the five pages, skimming and reading out loud.

"In an exclusive interview with Prince George Edward Woodhill Valensky, half-brother of Princess Daisy, *People* learned of the existence of . . . sister . . . I.Q. of a four-year-old . . .' My God, Candice, a *four-year-old!*"

Candice stopped Jenny firmly. "Shut up, Jenny—there's more. Listen to this, just listen! 'Prince Valensky violently opposes the commercialization of his ancient family name by his half-sister whose endorsement of a new line of cosmetics he termed "a vulgar and unseemly action." ' That son-of-a-bitch!" She continued reading in a voice that grew progressively louder. " 'In his opinion, if Francesca Vernon had not abandoned his father and kidnapped the twins, they might have had a normal childhood, but by the time his father regained the children, it was too late to help Danielle . . . Prince Valensky, seven years older than Princess Daisy, is a highly respected investment adviser. Bitter toward his sister, who has been paid one million dollars for her endorsement, he said, "She inherited ten million dollars and let it slip through her fingers because she was too foolish to take any advice. She'll go through this money just as quickly." ' "

"My God," said Jenny, "do you think she did?"

"Wait! Here's the worst. 'Daisy Valensky has been called 'one of a kind' by Patrick Shannon, the sometimes controversial president of Supracorp'—Jesus, Jenny, '*one of a kind*'—'who is betting many millions that her face and name will lend prestige to the line of . . . Last year Elstree's losses were reported at over thirty million . . . unparalleled media blitz to promote the newest face in the beauty business including . . . ' That's it, I can't read one more word." Candice sat down. "Get Mr. Bijur on the intercom, Jenny, and tell him I've got to see him immediately."

In spite of the urgency of Candice's order, both she and Jenny stood for another minute looking at the photograph of Daisy and Danielle. Neither woman could take her eyes off the haunting picture of the twins. They were unable to stop comparing the slight but all-important differences in their faces which made of one a glorious beauty and left the other unformed, unfinished, uninteresting, with a muted little smile, pathos in her big black eyes.

" *'One of a kind,'* " Candice murmured. "God—we've had it—by tomorrow this picture will be seen all over the world."

"Do you think *People* knew about this stuff when they decided on the cover story?" Jenny asked.

"No way. They angle stories in a special way, but not as bad as this. I can tell by the way the text reads that it must have come in at the last minute—it's hasty, reads more like a newsmagazine piece than a *People* story."

"But then how could it have happened?" Jenny asked.

"God knows, and I don't care. When something this bad happens, 'how' just doesn't matter any more. Get me Bijur's secretary."

"May I make a suggestion?" Jenny asked.

"What?"

"Fix your eye make-up before you see him. You've been crying."

"So what? So have you. Oh, okay, okay."

Daisy woke late on the morning that Candice and Jenny were reading *People*, and considered her day. At lunch she was going to be interviewed by Jerry Tallmer of the *New York Post* for a feature article, at 2:30 she had another interview with Phyllis Battelle of King Features and at 5:00 a date for drinks and an interview with Lammy Johnstone of Gannett for their national wire service. Candice would be with her at all these interviews, some-how disappearing into the background as Daisy answered questions, yet listening carefully and sometimes stepping lightly into the conversation to amplify a statement or suggest a new line of discussion. Even though that skinny, swaggering, terse young publicity woman was only three years older than Daisy, she managed to convey a faintly maternal feeling; that of an accomplished and socially secure matron introducing her daughter to the ladies who run the debutante cotillion. She was able to gently point to Daisy's qualities in a way that Daisy would never have been able to do for herself.

Nevertheless, as a veteran now of at least a dozen interviews, Daisy realized that each reporter, no matter how pleasant or charming, was looking for an edge, waiting for her to say the one thing she shouldn't say, probing, in a seemingly random and innocent way, for the stray remark that would make news. Just the day before, one of them had actually asked her if she liked the way the new perfume smelled. My God, did he actually think she'd say no? But it was all part of doing his job, she realized—and if she had said no, it would have made a much better story.

She dressed carefully in one of her new things. That was another part of her job. Everytime she was interviewed, she was closely scrutinized; every detail of what she had on went into the reporter's notebook. The *image*, the absolutely essential image was being created day by day, interview by interview, dress by dress, question by question. Perhaps eventually, Daisy thought, she'd get hardened to it, accustomed to the process, but she still had to remind herself of that million dollars before she could get started on the morning metamorphosis. But it went with the job, and, by God, what went with the job, she did. Daisy brightened as she realized that she could save all the new clothes she was being given and then, thirty or forty years from now, bring them out again and really enjoy wearing them. She'd be the most originally dressed sixty-year-old in the world.

She looked at her watch. She just had time to feed Theseus, get him settled on his pillow, and rush down the street to the Café Borgia II for a quick cup of espresso before she had to start uptown for her lunch interview. It had taken her a full hour to dress, put on her make-up and do her hair. This patient triangulation of her obligations to the image had, in the past, taken only seven minutes, or less. Being a princess just took too much time, Daisy thought, as she grabbed her mail without looking at it and hurried out.

At the café on Prince Street, she found an outside table. She sat there and basked in the September sun while her sense of smell leaped in response to the odor of freshly made bread from the bakery across the street. But she wouldn't have anything to eat now. She'd learned it was important to eat heartily at lunch interviews because the excuse of a mouthful of food gave her time to consider her words, before she had to speak. She finished her espresso and ordered another. With Kiki gone, there was very little mail. Why had she brought along this manila envelope? Now she'd have to carry it around all day. She looked at it again. It had been delivered by hand and the name of the researcher from *People* was written on the left corner. In dismay, she thought that she hadn't planned on facing *that* until tomorrow. She supposed they meant to be nice, but an advance copy was the last thing she wanted. However, she might as well get it over with. She opened the envelope and drew out the magazine. A smile of pure delight spread over her face as she saw the cover photograph. She knew she'd been right to take off all that awful make-up. As she read the cover line, her smile stopped. "The strange, secret story? . . ." She turned to the inside pages in a sudden fright, the slippery paper evading her fingers. What editor could have turned the detailed, exhaustive, but resolutely cautious interviews she'd given the researcher into a "strange, secret story," she asked herself as the chill of what she still did not know, except in some part of her brain that had always, always, always, been alert to attack, began to creep over her.

She turned another page.

The cruelty exploded inside her heart and spilled into her entire chest cavity. She screamed and shut the magazine. A waiter approached and she waved him away, covering the copy of *People* with her handbag. A violent burst of pain, like steel knitting needles driving their points into her breasts, made her clasp her hands tightly to them in an incredulous attempt to protect herself. It couldn't continue to hurt like this for long or she wouldn't be able to breathe. A sharp, rippling feeling of breakage and rupture made her pull her head down to her hands as if to doubly protect her heart, yet it would not stop. She felt lacerated, attacked from all sides, by gratuitous evil, utterly exposed to the tearing and crushing of the teeth of nameless beasts.

The waiter came back, an expression of concern on his face. In another second he'd speak. Daisy got up, clutching the magazine and handbag and staggered, with the cautious, clumsy movements of an old woman, to a table inside in the corner of the empty café where she couldn't be seen from the street. Panting with savage pain, streaming with the sweat of utter panic, she hunched over the table and opened the magazine and read the entire article. Then she read it twice again. There were no tears, just as there were no words in her mind. Nothing existed except the article and the need to stop the feeling that she was being cut apart, opened up, her insides torn out. She could not believe that the floor wasn't covered with her blood. Daisy folded the magazine and hid it in her handbag. She wrapped her arms around her body and bowed her head, trying to become as small as possible.

"Another espresso?" the waiter asked softly.

She nodded.

She drank as if it might save her life. Slowly her brain began to work again. The evil fastened at her breast with metallic teeth, but she began to think. She had to get help. There was only one person who could help her. She put some money on the table, walked swiftly to the street and stopped a passing cab.

In Patrick Shannon's office three people sat silently: Shannon, Hilly Bijur and Candice Bloom. Only Candice knew what time it was and that Jerry Tallmer and Daisy were waiting for her at Le Perigord Park. Thank God Tallmer was a gentle, kind man and thank God Daisy knew where to meet him for lunch. They wouldn't miss her.

Bijur was the first to break the silence. "Pat, this doesn't have to be a disaster."

Shannon looked at him without comprehension. He had to find Daisy before she saw this. "Where's Daisy?" he asked urgently.

"Having lunch—she's okay," Candice reassured him.

"Pat, will you just listen! Look, for Christ's sake, just let me read some of this stuff back to you," Hilly insisted. He turned to the second page of the article. " 'Queen Anne's. A well known school for retarded children, is regarded as one of the finest institutions of its kind. The fees are high, averaging twenty-three thousand dollars a year for each child. Mrs. Joan Henderson, head of the school, said that four years after Prince Stash Valensky's death in 1967, Princess Daisy took over the entire financial burden of her sister's support.' And then they quote this Mrs. Henderson, 'It could not have been easy for her,' Mrs. Henderson said, 'since we sometimes had to wait for her checks, but eventually one always came. I don't believe that more than a few days in any week have gone by in the last ten years'—*the last ten fucking years*, Pat—'that Danielle hadn't received a letter containing a drawing or a picture postcard from her sister. Princess Daisy always visited every Sunday while she still lived in England, even though she and Danielle were only six when they were separated.' *Six*—only six, Pat! And, look, here she says, 'The twins are very close in spite of the difference in their intellectual capacities. Danielle certainly understands Daisy better than she understands any of her teachers—indeed, in a long lifetime, I have rarely seen devotion such as Princess Daisy's.' End quote. And then there's the picture of Daisy painting a kid on a pony, and just listen to this caption, 'Daisy's expert portraits paid for her twin's continued residence in the only home she's ever known, while Daisy herself lived in a low-rent SoHo walk-up and held down a full-time job as well.' "

"On the next page, right under the picture of Daisy on a set wearing her baseball jacket and her sailor hat, there's a quote from North. Let me read that one, Mr. Bijur," Candice said eagerly.

" 'Top commercial director, Frederick Gordon North, says that he was very disappointed when Princess Daisy decided to leave her job with him. "She was unquestionably the most creative and hardest working producer any director could hope to have. Everyone who ever worked with her loved her. She has a great talent for this business." When he was asked if he missed her collaboration on such widely admired commercials as those he directs for Dr Pepper, Downy, and Revlon, Mr. North said with a rueful smile, "She can have her old job back any time she wants. I wish her well." ' "

"Mr. Shannon," Candice said, "Daisy's a heroine."

"My point, my point exactly!" Hilly Bijur said in increasing excitement. "Look, Pat, yesterday we had just another pretty face going for us and today we have a candidate for Joan of Arc—she can fucking get the Helen Keller humanitarian award of the year—look at it that way, for Christ's sake."

"But," Candice said with a trace of timidity rarely heard in her, "how do you think Daisy's going to feel about having this all come out? Since she's kept it secret for so long, she couldn't possibly have wanted anyone to know."

"What the fuck does it matter how she *feels*?" Hilly Bijur gloated, fairly jumping up and down with glee. "It's probably the best fucking publicity break anybody ever got in the history of fucking fragrance. Holy shit, it'll make every paper in the country tomorrow. Ha! Just you tell me Candice baby, what Lauren Hutton or what's her name Hemingway or Catherine Deneuve or Candy Bergen have in their private lives that could be one-tenth as fascinating as this? Those stores are going to be mobbed when she makes her personal appearances! Every woman in the country will want to see Daisy with her very own eyes. She can get on Phil Donahue . . . a whole hour! Merv will love her, Mike Douglas, 'The Today Show' . . . maybe even Carson . . . sure, Carson, too . . ."

Patrick Shannon stood up. "Get the hell out of my office, Hilly, and don't come back," he shouted at the president of Elstree in a passion of disgust.

Shannon had told all his three secretaries to go to lunch and he was still sitting, his elbows on the desk, his head in his hands, a copy of *People* open before him, when Daisy silently opened the door of his office. She saw immediately what he was

"Pat, Pat, why are you doing this? I've been in advertising too long not to know what difference it's going to make. You can't fool me."

"Daisy, you know how to make commercials, but you're not an expert on Supracorp's business." He took her in his arms again and kissed her lips. "I am, and I say you are *not* going to do it."

"Why are you being so good to me?" she asked as relief began to creep over her.

"Would one reason be enough?" He kissed her again and she nodded in acquiescence. "I love you, I'm in love with you, I love you absolutely and completely. Three reasons, and I could go on and on . . . but they'd all be variations on the same theme. I love you. I think I forgot to tell you that at *La Marée*. That was a serious omission, and I'm going to spend a lot of time making up for it." He wanted desperately to ask her if she loved him, but he didn't think it was fair. She was too open, too raw, too wounded. She'd feel gratitude and she'd say yes and if she didn't really love him, she would never tell him. He felt tingles as if from a million injections of love. He was tatooed for life. He could wait.

"It was a bloodbath," Luke said, dropping wearily into a chair. "And that's just for openers." Kiki gave him the martini she had just made, her only domestic skill, and watched like a mother wolf to make sure he drank up every last medicinal drop. That's what wives were for.

"I called Daisy," she said when he'd drained the glass. "She knew already, she'd seen it. I'm having lunch with her tomorrow."

"Christ! What kind of shape is she in?"

"Weird, didn't want me to come down to be with her tonight. Kind of strange, far-away, detached, terribly tired."

"Maybe we should both go down anyway."

"No, I'm convinced that she wants to be alone. She just didn't want to go into it anymore."

"I've been talking for the last six hours—I have a faint notion of how she feels. Could you give me another of those splendid martinis, sweetheart? Did you know that a theory exists that it doesn't hurt if you put a tiny drop of vermouth in it?"

"Oh." Kiki's father, as his last piece of paternal advice, had told her that the secret of a dry martini was just to pour straight gin of an excellent quality. That way you couldn't possibly go wrong.

"Tell me what happened," Kiki said.

"When I got back from lunch, there was a message to get my body over to Supracorp right away. Hilly Bijur was there, in Shannon's office, and Candice Bloom and her assistant and a dozen other people from Elstree. Shannon told all of us that Daisy was going to be left absolutely alone from now on, that no one was going to bother her, and then he just simply dropped the bomb—no Princess Daisy line, no launch, no commercials, no nothing. Zip! Finished! Over! Like it had never happened. Everything—every fucking thing."

"*But why?*" Kiki cried in astonishment. "Can't they go on without Daisy in person for goodness sakes?"

"He's right, Kiki. The launch wouldn't get off the ground and the stores wouldn't promote the stuff the way they've planned to and there are a half-dozen other perfumes being launched this month which were going to mean stiff competition for attention, no matter what. Without Daisy, we've got only some print ads and commercials which we could keep running for a while, but after that—nothing.

Bubkis. See, the whole thing is based on *her*, on Daisy, her name, her face, and most of all, her personality. If Charlie lost that girl, they could replace her because the perfume isn't called by her name and most people don't even know who she is—just another pair of pants. If Lauren Hutton lost all her front teeth, instead of having that famous little space there, Revlon would find another girl or buy her new teeth. With Estée Lauder, it's not so much Karen Graham as it is Skrebneski's fantastic photographs that's the trademark. With Halston and Adolfo, Oscar de la Renta and Calvin Klein you've got four big-name designers, already enormously established, famous guys, all of whom are going to do store promotions like crazy, with their new fragrances—with Daisy we only had the romance of Daisy herself to *build* on. No, honey-bunch, Shannon knows that it's time to cut his losses. No matter how much Supracorp has spent on the Princess Daisy line now—something like forty million—it's better to lose that much than to pour in more millions and end up losing them too. We spent all afternoon canceling what could still be canceled. But just money isn't the biggest part of the loss anyway—not for Shannon."

"I guess it's just a lucky thing that Supracorp's such a big business," Kiki said, testing the waters.

"No business is so big that they can overlook this sort of disaster. Not when they have stockholders. Shannon's going to be eyeball-high in serious shit. He could perfectly well have held Daisy to her contract. However, he made the decision not to. Don't worry about Daisy though—according to her contract, she still gets paid. Worry about Shannon. Oh, baby, worry about them both."

"I am!" Kiki breathed.

"Yeah. Listen, should I console you or should you console me, since Daisy won't let us console her?"

Kiki sat in his lap, tickling her nose on the tip of his beard. "That sounds like six of one and half a dozen of another."

"Let's try it and find out. Those old sayings usually have some truth to them."

26

The following morning, shortly after *People* appeared on the newsstands, Joseph Willowby and Reginald Stein, two major stockholders in Supracorp and both members of the nine-man board of directors, telephoned Patrick Shannon's executive secretary and demanded an immediate meeting. They arrived within ten minutes, flushed with a combination of anger and triumph. Shannon had finally given them the ammunition they'd been waiting for.

"What do you intend to do about this mess?" boomed Willowby, brandishing a copy of *People.*

"I warned you a year ago that the best thing to do with Elstree was to sell it, but no, as usual, Patrick Shannon had one of his off-the-wall strokes of genius and he had to have it his way," Reginald Stein said in tones of vindictive satisfaction.

"Sit down, fellas. I'll tell you what I'm going to do," Shannon said cheerfully.

They sat down and he told them. When he'd finished, Willowby said in fury, "In other words, Elstree is a total loss for the third year in a row? And you call that a way to run a business? We'll have lost almost a hundred million on that one pet division of yours—Shannon's baby. Of course, you realize what this has done to our over-all profit picture?"

Shannon nodded calmly. There was no point in interrupting Willowby. And he also happened to be correct.

"To say nothing of our stock," Stein chimed in bitterly. "It went up in anticipation of this new move and all the excitement you spent so much money to create, but by the time the exchange closes today I don't even want to think about how far down it'll be. And when the news gets out that we're closing down the whole Princess Daisy operation—shit, Shannon, would you like to bet on how many points Supracorp will drop? Would you? How many points, Shannon?" he roared.

"I don't know, Reg, but this move isn't something I'm prepared to negotiate with you. I've told you what I intend to do. I made the decision and I'm standing by it."

"You cocky bastard, don't count on that!" shouted Willowby. "I'm going to call a special meeting of the board, Shannon, and throw your ass out of Supracorp if it's the last thing I do. I've had it with your so-called independence and high-rolling and flying by the seat of your pants. We'll get someone in here who doesn't throw away millions of dollars on a lousy whim. If you hadn't let the Valensky girl off the hook we could probably salvage this fuck-up—in part, anyway. It's your own fault and I'm going to nail you on it. You've made one high-handed decision too many, Shannon!"

"Call a meeting by all means," Shannon said. "I'm perfectly prepared to sit down with the board at any time. But now, gentlemen, if you'll excuse me? We do have seven other divisions and I've a number of matters to attend to."

After the two fuming men had left his office, Patrick Shannon sat and thought for a few minutes. Several other members of the board had leanings toward caution and conservatism quite as strong as those of Joe and Reg. He'd had constant trouble with their group in the few, short, exhilarating years during which he'd been head of Supracorp. They didn't know him well enough yet to be entirely convinced of his basic soundness, but as long as he'd been making money for them they'd been prepared to put up with him, little as they liked it. Supracorp was perfectly strong enough to withstand the Elstree problem in the long run, and they knew it as well as he did, but this was the best opportunity Joe and Reg and their gang had yet had, or probably would ever have in the future, to get rid of him. Yesterday, when he'd made the decision to protect Daisy from all the exposure necessary to ensure the success of the launch, it hadn't been a business decision. As a business decision it stank, Shannon admitted to himself. He'd taken losses before, but never for reasons he could control. He'd risked failure before, but never, *never* for anyone else. But he wasn't going to win at the expense of Daisy, not while he had a choice left. And without a choice he wouldn't want his job anyway. A good thing too, since it was entirely possible that he would be voted out of Supracorp.

"So . . . fuck *that* noise!" Shannon said out loud, grinning, and went back to work.

In North's studio the copy of *People* had been passed from one person to another all morning. A Planter's Peanut spot was being shot on a closed set while a football star did fifty-four consecutive takes which involved actually eating two nuts and delivering four lines on the virtue of "freshly roasted flavor," while simultaneously opening a fresh can and holding it up to the camera. This feat of hand-to-eye-to-mouth coordination had prevented anyone from exchanging their reactions until the lunch break. Wingo, Arnie Greene, Nick-the-Greek and North finally had a chance to meet over sandwiches in North's office with the door closed behind them.

"I should never have gotten her into this shitpot," Nick said, with an air of great gloom. "It's all my fault."

"Typical," Wingo said waspishly. "You'd take credit for everything, including pogroms, floods and stuffing ballot boxes."

Nick mournfully fingered his switchblade. "Be fair, Wingo, it all started with her hair, and that *was* my fault. Say, remember how cute and mad she was the day we tried to get her to join us in the new production company?"

"Nick," Wingo hissed, "could we be spared your reminiscences?"

"What are you talking about, Nick?" North asked, suddenly interested.

"Ah, balls, I couldn't care less if you know," Nick said. "Wingo and I were thinking of going out on our own if we could get Daisy as our producer, but she straightened us out good; loyalty, what we owed you and all that bullcrap, horse turds and eighteen other kinds of buffalo droppings. Wish you'd heard her."

"I don't want to be just a cameraman forever, North," Wingo said defensively. "I can direct—even if Daisy didn't think so."

"How long ago did this happen?" North demanded.

"Maybe a year, maybe more, and there was nothing cute about her that day," Wingo answered. "She was as angry as I've ever seen her, even worse than the time the Cinemobile people got lost in Arizona and we wasted the whole day sitting broiling under a tent like a bunch of fucking Bedouins."

"Nah," said Nick, "I think she was angrier the time that chimp she located down in Mexico took a piece of luggage into his cave and just played with it for six hours, instead of trying to tear it apart so we could show how tough it was. Remember the things she said to try and make it come out?"

"None of you ever heard Daisy really upset," said Arnie miserably. "Because you weren't there the day she found out that the caterer had charged us for ten pounds of smoked salmon on a shoot for Oscar Mayer where we only served the sponsor's products. Now *that* was angry! We'll never find another producer like her again."

"Listen, why don't you guys get out of my office?" North bit out the words. "If I want to go to a wake, I know a couple of Irish funeral parlors—at least the ethnic quality would be pure."

"Shove it, North," Wingo said. "You're more upset than any of us. You think you can kid us?" North looked at him and fell silent.

"I never realized why she worked so hard," Arnie said, compulsively turning to the pages of the *People* story again. "No wonder she didn't seem to have much of a private life. That poor kid."

"Listen," North said, "I want this whole subject dropped, permanently and forever. None of us really knew Daisy and none of us really understands her now, even with that magazine piece, so will you all just shut the fuck up about it and go back to work? And that's not a suggestion."

He watched the three men file out of his office and locked his door behind them. Systematically, methodically and quietly, he then proceeded to demolish a new Cooke zoom lens, a twenty-five-thousand-dollar piece of equipment that had just arrived from England. He didn't know any other way to mourn, he didn't even know he was mourning, and he certainly didn't admit for whom he was mourning, but never again in his life did Frederick Gordon North visit Venice.

Vanessa Valarian called Robin at his showroom the minute she read *People.*

"Send someone downstairs to buy you a copy and I'll meet you in a half-hour for lunch. I can't possibly wait till tonight to talk about it. Oh, Robin, darling, it's so thrilling!"

As soon as they were settled on their banquette at La Côte Basque, without preamble, Vanessa fixed Robin with her eyes. "Now, listen, sweetheart, the main thing to remember is that we knew her *when.* We were her very first friends, her first sponsors, the first people who held out a hand to her without knowing a single thing about how or why she had to struggle, that brave, wonderful little darling."

"We helped her first, before anybody cared," Robin repeated.

"Because," Vanessa went on, paying no attention to him, "we sensed a rare spirit in her, a beauty of spirit that others had overlooked. And we always knew that there was something marvelously worthwhile about her—her sensitivity, Robin, her enchantingly modest reluctance to accept gifts or invitations because she couldn't reciprocate—*as if we cared*!—but, thank God, we were able to help her with commissions and clothes—I don't know if she would have managed without us."

"It wouldn't have been possible, darling," Robin assured her. "I'm sure everyone who knows us will realize that."

"I can hardly wait for the Winter Palace party—she'll be so happy to see a few familiar faces in the mob—I feel so *protective* of her, Robin. Almost maternal. And now I'll be able to tell everyone about what *really* happened on the yacht—all those people who've been hounding me with their nasty questions—and vicious insinuations. At last I'll be free to reveal the truth without betraying Daisy."

"What *did* really happen, Vanessa?"

"Never mind about the details, dearest. I'll think of something."

It was a dreary, wet morning at Woodhill Manor, ugly weather for early September, which usually was fine in England. Ram, sitting down to breakfast, could think of nothing but the fact that, allowing for the difference in time zones, the issue of *People* with Daisy on the cover would be appearing on American newsstands by the time he ate lunch that same day. He contemplated, with a lack of interest, those choice brown eggs, boiled for exactly three and a half minutes, that faced him on the table. He rang for the manservant who attended his breakfast.

"Why are there no gooseberry preserves, Thompson?"

"I'll inquire, Sir." He returned within seconds. "The grocer had promised them for yesterday but he didn't deliver because his van broke down. The cook regrets the problem, Sir."

"All right, Thompson. It's not important." As Ram sat motionless in the dining room of his gracious dwelling, one of the most peaceful in all of plenteous, gentle Devon, he wondered how many people in the neighboring market town would eventually read that issue of the magazine. It was easily available in London, of course, with scarcely a day's difference in time. And in Paris, Rome, Madrid . . . within a week it would be everywhere. Leaving his breakfast untouched, Ram rose from the table and rang again. "I'm going out, Thompson. Tell the cook to make sure the grocer delivers today. If he can't, go into town and pick up the order yourself."

As Ram walked, carrying his shotgun, across his ancestral acres, as he opened the gates of fences and wandered across the meadows, he thought about the pictures and the interview he had given the correspondent for *People.* It would be an enormous story. It would destroy her. She would never recover from it. He had made sure of that.

And so her picture was going to be used on the cover? Was it indeed? Ram stared out across the wet fields, imagining her face, imagining it smashed, crushed, broken, punctured, blood running from her nostrils, from her ears, from her eyes. From moment to moment he was able to sustain himself with these images but then he would see her again and again as she had been on the night of the *Quatorze Juillet,* see her as she danced in her white lace dress, flying mirthfully from arm to arm, ardent and innocent, eyes alight with discovery and jubilation, hair flying, tangled . . . laughing, laughing, dancing—dancing with everyone but him . . . the night on which he had finally acknowledged that she must be his or he would die.

He didn't come back for lunch on that rainy day, nor did he return for tea. Mrs. Gibbons, the housekeeper, began to fret about her employer, who was always so gratifyingly precise in his habits.

"It's ever so windy out," she complained to Sally, the housemaid, "and not a day to go out shooting, not at all. There won't be any birds about. I thought so when I saw him leave the house, but of course it wasn't up to me to say anything."

"Gentlemen have to have their sport," the housemaid replied, philosophically.

"It's pneumonia weather, that's what it is, and cook had such a lovely bit of steak for his lunch," Mrs. Gibbons grumbled.

"Someone's knocking at the pantry door," Sally announced to the housekeeper, who had become increasingly deaf during her long years of service to the Woodhill family. "I'll go."

"Tell whoever it is to wipe his feet before he comes into the kitchen."

The housemaid's screams penetrated Mrs. Gibbon's deafness, penetrated into the most distant corners of Woodhill Manor, penetrated into the wing that had been built during the reign of Elizabeth I, into the wing that had been added in the days of Queen Anne, into the wing of Edwardian vintage. Every room in the time-blessed, lovely old house echoed for minutes with the screams of the woman who had opened the door to the farmers carrying Ram's body, his head half shot away, but washed so clean of blood, because of the hours during which the rain had fallen on his dead body, that they could see the half of the brain that remained.

That evening, when they sat huddled together over a glass of brandy, after the local mortician's men had finally taken the body away, Sally, her eyes red, said in bewildered tones, "Why aren't gentlemen more careful, Mrs. Gibbons? I never do like it, never, when I see someone walk out with a loaded gun, no, not ever, no mateer how good a shot he is. I don't care for the sporting life. Poor Prince Valensky."

"There'll be another Woodhill to take his place as soon as the lawyers get on the job, Sally. I wonder who it will be?" said Mrs. Gibbons, comfortingly. "Time will tell, I suppose. It always has."

No one studied the cover photograph of Daisy more thoroughly than the Honorable Sarah Fane. No one read the article more carefully, almost memorizing each word, than the Honorable Sarah Fane.

As she held the magazine up to her mirror and compared herself to the cover picture, an expression of pleasure and finally gratification dawned on her features, the features of that exquisite English rose that takes hundreds of years to breed.

She's a very, very good type—if one likes that type, thought Sarah Fane. Actually, one could hardly ask for anything more lovely. It could be considered to have been a compliment, a rather strange compliment . . . and one she could never repeat . . . nor forget . . . but nevertheless . . . yes, definitely a compliment.

She threw the magazine into a wastepaper basket and continued dressing. She was so punctual that she was able to linger a bit, admiring her thirty-two-carat engagement ring, far, far too big to be vulgar, thinking of the marvelous life that stretched in front of her as the future wife of the richest oil man in Houston. He was rich beyond comprehension, beyond passion. Nothing in the entire world would ever be out of her reach. His mother's family came from Springfield, Illinois, and it included two vice-presidents of the United States, one great senator and one signer of the Declaration of Independence. He had a pioneering robber baron as a paternal great-grandfather, a combination which, in America, melded neatly into the equivalent of royalty. Sarah Fane had always sworn to herself that anything was better than being an unmarried post-deb but there was no way to deny—although only to herself—that she had mismanaged her year. Still she'd made the best of it before it was over. Life in Houston, where she would, of course, reign as queen, was by all accounts remarkably civilized. They would travel a great deal. And he did worship her, she reminded herself. His worship was so palpable that she could smell it on her hair, feel it swirl around her like smoke burned before an idol. His worship created an image of herself which even she could not wish to be more faultless. And, whatever the future held, he would do exceptionally well as a first husband.

Daisy slept the deep sleep of complete emotional exhaustion. She woke early the next morning, filled with a profound, dream-induced joy. All specific memory of her dreams faded except for one fragment, a single glimpse, one bright image of running rapturously through a vast, flowered field, hand in hand with Danielle, who could run as lightly and as rapidly as Daisy herself. That was all there was to it. Daisy lay bathed in a transport of happiness so phosphorescent, so tangible that she did not dare move for fear of losing this vision, this completely mysterious visitation. Had it ever happened? Had they ever run so together? How old could they have been? She had no memory of such an experience, but she felt, deeply, that it must have occurred—or, if it had never happened, it had *now* happened in such a vivid dream that it had become a memory more real than reality. It was part of her existence, crystallized forever in light and color and the sensation of running—she and Danielle had run together during that night and they had both been happy. So happy. Together and equal.

The rapture of the dream lasted, the glorious vision persisted, even as the phone started to ring and Daisy realized she had to get out of the apartment in a hurry. She dressed quickly in jeans, sandals and a thin navy cotton turtleneck. She pulled all her hair tightly around her head and secured it firmly and impatiently. Then she wrapped a large navy and red scarf over her hair so that not a strand of it showed. She found the biggest pair of sunglasses she owned and, when she put them on and glanced in the mirror, she was satisfied that no one would recognize her. It was just past nine now and the phone kept ringing eight or nine times, then stopped and then started again.

Daisy put Theseus on his leash and hurried out, away from the phone, away from any contact with anyone who might be trying to reach her. She took a cab through the morning traffic from SoHo all the way up Park Avenue, then went west, crossing the park at 72nd Street. When the driver was near the Sheep Meadow, she got out, paid him and let Theseus loose to frolic. Around her swirled the other dog-walkers, the children playing with Frisbees, the perpetual volleyball games, the young couples necking on blankets under the sun of the morning, as settled in as if they had been there all night. Daisy sat cross-legged on the dubious grass and watched the towers of the city circle around her.

After a few minutes Daisy was aware of a feeling rising like a tide from her toes to the roots of her hair, a feeling she was unfamiliar with and couldn't identify although she knew it was important. She tried to capture its essence, but it wasn't until she had watched Theseus running loose and wild, ranging from one end of the vast field to another with the bounding energy of a dog who usually has to be kept under stern control, that she began to understand. *She felt free.* She felt as if a great clutter of debris of the past had been swept away, debris as caked in mud and sediment as objects brought up by a diver from a sunken ship, debris that had enchained her. It had demanded so much of her attention, that heavy, mucky load. She had needed to dismantle the past before she could dive into the sea of the future and, in one stroke, Ram had unfettered her, no matter how brutally, from a lifetime in which she'd been bound and gagged by irrational taboos, fears, secrets. She had been led out of the labyrinth, led, by cruel surprise, out into the fresh, clean air by an act that was meant to annihilate her. Again she saw Ram lying in the deck chair at *La Marée*, beckoning, always beckoning, and this time she began to forgive him and, in forgiving him, she made her first step toward forgetting him.

A grimy little boy stumbled over Daisy's legs and fell, crying, into her lap. She comforted him until his mother arrived, in no particular hurry. To collect him. Another baby hung in a sling on the woman's back. Daisy gave the child up without reluctance and returned to her thoughts.

In London she had asked Shannon how she could unthink her feelings of guilt for Dani's condition, just because mere logic told her it wasn't her fault. He had answered that perhaps it was necessary to replace a truth that is wrong with one that is right. But what if there was a third way? *What if she simply had to let it go?* It was not her problem to portion out blame. Why should she be limited forever by whatever it was her father and mother had done to each other—and to her and to Dani?

Ram's assertion that Dani might have had a normal childhood was disproved by dozens of memories Daisy had of the time in Big Sur, of the differences she had seen between herself and Dani from the earliest days she could remember. Her dream of running in a field of flowers—she knew now that it had never happened. Dani had never been able to run like that. But Ram's falsehoods had been printed and no amount of later retraction or clarification would ever change the public's idea of the truth. *But what did it matter?* Everyone concerned was dead now, and she was the only person left who cared. And it was all too long ago. Ram's series of ancient recriminations made Daisy realize how much she, too, had been caught up in the fatal net of the past.

Abruptly Daisy found herself in the line of fire between four leaping, shouting Frisbee players. She sat quietly while they threw the plastic disk harmlessly over her head. In a few minutes, their game moved to one side and their exhortations to each other faded, as her thoughts turned to feelings she had tried to cope with so often during her life, the feelings of being an impostor, not Princess Daisy, not someone with a right to that title. Suddenly it seemed so clear that she gasped. She hadn't been Princess Daisy because Dani had not been Princess Danielle. All the while that Danielle had been hidden away from everybody, the thought of her, closer than any sister could be, had always been carried within her. Her knowledge that Dani was doomed to never grow up had prevented her from really living her own life. She had always held back from taking happiness as her due, she had not felt *entitled* to enjoy to the fullest whatever joy had come her way. But now! Now she and Dani were rejoined. There in *People* she stood with her arm around the twin who had been taken away from her so long ago. Their separation was over. Their immemorial kinship had been avowed, once and for all. And now Daisy could admit that Dani was happy in her own way and that nothing that Daisy did *not* have would make Dani any happier. She couldn't solve the past. It was impossible. It had always been impossible.

And in the dream, in the dream . . . they had both been happy.

Theseus came loping up, a pigeon held gently in his mouth, and deposited the struggling bird in her lap. It was unharmed and indignant and Daisy, knowing the fearless gangster ways of New York pigeons, watched without surprise as it merely walked away with hasty dignity.

"No, Theseus. Naughty dog." Oh, why not, she thought, let him catch another if he can. It's not as if he ever kills them. "Go on, run, Theseus, run as much as you like. Good dog."

What was it she had always thought she wanted? The freedom to become herself? Well, by God, she'd become herself, willy-nilly, in full color and black and white and hundreds of words of text. In spite of Ram's inaccuracies, her double life, with the tiptoeing around the Horse People to make the money to keep Dani in Queen Anne's was now common knowledge. And so what? She'd never sold a portrait of which she was ashamed. And what difference did it make that she'd taken the Elstree contract to buy her freedom from Ram? She had the right to dispose of herself any way she chose, just as any other woman did. She didn't have to worry about the Valensky name—she *was* the Valensky name and she could do with it what she liked. What a pompous, stuffy fool Ram had sounded. Daisy knew exactly who she was and she knew why it was worth a million dollars to Supracorp to obtain the rights to an image that could be photographed and interviewed, an image that was a potentially profitable approximation of someone called Princess Daisy. But, since she was clear about the difference between the two, what harm was there in it? The people she cared about knew the difference: Kiki, Luke, Anabel—even Wingo and Nick-the-Greek. And North. To be fair, North had known the difference. Maybe that was what had made him so angry at her.

And Patrick Shannon. Daisy carefully inspected the shabby turf of the Sheep Meadow before she lay back on it. Patrick Shannon. Patrick Shannon. He loved her. He didn't love the *idea* of "Princess Daisy"—he loved Daisy. She had been so agonized yesterday that his words hadn't really hit her with their full impact, but now, as she lay staring up at the sky over Central Park, her heart, to which entirely too much had happened in the last twenty-four hours, leapt around like an unleashed lurcher surrounded by pheasants. How much of her fine new courage, Daisy wondered, how much of this feeling of glorious freedom, how much of her new wisdom, how much of this unmistakable intuition of permanent change, came from the knowledge that Patrick Shannon loved her? How much of it came from the realization that she loved him, as she had never loved a man before or ever would again?

Daisy jumped up. *That* was one more question that definitely didn't need answering. To hell with weighing, measuring, examining, testing, holding back, calculating, protecting herself, always protecting. Over! She looked at her watch.

There was still a half-hour before she had to meet Kiki at the zoo. She whistled for Theseus and dodged another Frisbee. As she bent down to attach his leash, she almost snarled her hair in the catch. Daisy straightened up in surprise. What had happened to her scarf? She pivoted and spotted it lying where she had been sitting and thinking. Evidently . . . apparently, unless you believe in ghosts who go around untying scarves and undoing hair, she must have done it herself. Daisy laughed in joy and reached into her shoulder bag for the little brush she carried there. She brushed out her silver-gilt hair, brushed and brushed it until it streamed down her back like a cape and danced in the wind like a thousand bright butterflies. She looked in her compact mirror and used a dab of powder on her nose and some pink gloss on her lips. She dropped her sunglasses into her bag, tucked in her pullover and threaded the scarf through the loops of her jeans and tied it with a huge bow in the front.

Daisy and Theseus strolled leisurely toward the zoo, both of them, the proud dog and the proud princess, holding their heads high. As she approached the zoo, the crowd began to grow thicker. The fine fall weather had brought out half of New York; not just the nannies and children and out-of-work and the elderly. As Daisy approached a bench, two middle-aged women who were sitting there, passing a copy of *People* back and forth, spotted her.

"Oh, look! It's just got to be her!" one of the women said to the other.

"I think—yes, you're right. Oh, I don't believe it, Sophie. I just don't believe it."

"I'm going to get her autograph," the first woman said excitedly.

"Oh, no, you wouldn't dare, oh, Sophie, don't."

"Just watch me." The woman snatched the magazine away from her friend and walked up to Daisy.

"Excuse me, but you're Princess Daisy, aren't you?" she asked.

Daisy stopped. So it was starting. She hadn't thought it would be so soon. She smiled at the woman.

"Yes, I am."

"Could I have your autograph—would you mind?"

"Oh, it's—it's okay—it's fine—but I don't have anything to write with."

"Here, here's a pen." Daisy took it and started to write her name on the cover.

"Oh, no," the woman protested, taking the magazine and turning to the photograph of Daisy and Danielle. "Here's where I want it. And could you write to Sophie Franklin? That's spelled S-o-p-h-i-e F-r-a-n-k-l-i-n," she added helpfully.

Daisy looked at the big black-and-white photo. Two girls, together, both smiling, both happy. She wrote quickly, gave the magazine back to the woman and walked on.

"Oh, look, just look what she wrote," Sophie Franklin said delightedly to her friend. "See—it says 'With best wishes to Sophie Franklin from Princess Daisy and Princess Danielle Valensky.' Well! And you didn't want me to ask her!"

Kiki was sitting grimly at a table outside the zoo cafeteria clutching an extra chair and snapping at people who tried to sit down and share the table with her as was the zoo custom.

"Are you keeping that chair for anyone, lady?"

"Daisy!"

"I'm sorry—am I late?" Daisy laughed, taking the chair.

"No—I got here early—but . . . my God, Daisy, you look gorgeous!"

"So, what else is new?"

"Daisy!"

"Kiki, do you think we could eliminate these exclamations of 'Daisy' every other sentence? I know I'm Daisy, you know I'm Daisy, we both know I'm Daisy, so why make such a point of it?"

"Daisy!"

"Really, Kiki, you're not getting the point again."

"You're goddamned right I'm not," Kiki said. "I was thinking of myself as a Saint Bernard dog or a knight in shining armor, or at least a friend in need, and what do I find but a blooming, downright glowing . . . no, more like delirious . . . what's come over you?"

"I've come over me."

"That makes no sense at all."

"Well it does to me and that's what counts. Poor darling Kiki, you must have been so worried. I'm sorry I gave you such a bad time."

"Me? I've had a wonderful time compared to everyone else involved in this shindy. Luke came home absolutely wrung out last night. And the whole media department spent the afternoon on the phones canceling the network commercials and the print ads—whatever wasn't too late to be stopped . . ."

"*Wait a minute!* The only things Pat said he was going to cancel were my interviews and the store appearances and maybe the party! What are you talking about?" Daisy asked in alarm.

"Oh, Christ. Maybe I shouldn't have told you . . . I just don't know . . . they had a meeting yesterday afternoon at Supracorp and Shannon told them he was going to give up the entire Princess Daisy line. Luke agrees with him that without you the whole thing just wouldn't work. Shannon decided to cut his losses before they spent any more money than they already have. Luke said it's got to be at least something like forty million down the drain what with one thing and another in the last eight months. He says they'll probably try to sell Elstree—*if* it's worth anything now."

"But Kiki, I am going to do the publicity and the stores. I'm going to do everything—everything I said I would."

"Daisy!" Kiki groaned. She wished her friend would be more consistent. All these changes were confusing, even to someone as poised as she.

"God, Kiki, where's the phone? What if it's too late?" Daisy said in a sudden frenzy of realization.

"They can cancel the cancellations!" Kiki shouted at Daisy, who was running rapidly into the cafeteria. "Don't worry!" She sat down and looked at Theseus. "Don't ask me why, kiddo," she told him, "but I'm going to get you eight hotdogs. No? Ten? Oh, all right then, I'll make it a dozen. We both know you're spoiled, so why fool around?"

In the phone booth Daisy fumbled frantically in her change purse. It bulged with infuriating pennies and unusable half dollars. No dimes. Finally she dredged out two quarters. She dialed Supracorp, got a wrong number and listened, appalled, as the first quarter dropped. The second time she dialed with the care of a scientist dealing with a dangerous bacteria culture.

"Mr. Shannon's office," trilled one of his secretaries after Daisy had been put through by the switchboard.

"Please, may I speak to him?" she asked, breathing so fast that she could hardly speak.

"I'm sorry, Mr. Shannon is in conference and he particularly asked not to be disturbed," the secretary said with the self-satisfied pleasure of the shoe clerk who tells you he has nothing at all in your size. "Would you like to leave a message?"

Daisy took a deep breath and found a voice of ringing metal. "This is Princess Daisy Valensky and I want to speak to Mr. Shannon immediately," she commanded.

"Just one minute, please."

"I'm in a pay phone, I've run out of change and if you don't put him on in two seconds, I'm going to . . ." Daisy realized she was talking to dead air. The secretary had put her on hold.

"Daisy?" Shannon said, with tense concern.

"Pat, is it too late?"

"Too late for what? Are you all right?"

"Yes," she said quickly. "I'm fine. But is it too late to put the Elstree thing back together, everything, the whole campaign, me included, media, stores, everything—is it too late to go back to yesterday where everything was before I saw you?"

"Wait a minute, how do you know what's been going on?"

"Kiki told me, but that's not important. Pat, Pat, it's too complicated to explain on the phone but I've . . . oh, I've come into my own *self* is the best way I can say it . . . it's . . ."

The operator's voice intoned, "Five cents for the next five minutes, please."

"Daisy, where are you?" Shannon shouted.

"Will you take five pennies, operator?" Daisy asked pleadingly.

"Daisy, what's the number there for Christ's sake?"

"Oh, Pat, just listen, I could have been one of quintuplets and I'd still be me, I could cut off all my hair or dye it black, I could never paint or ride again, or I could learn Speedwriting or sky diving, or I could become an interior decorator or a movie star or a bookbinder, and *I'd still be me*," she exalted.

"Where the hell are you calling from?"

"The zoo. Pat, Pat, don't you see? I'm the person you know, just her—or is it just she?—never mind, but I'm no one else, I'm me, Daisy Valensky, from the inside out, all the way through down to rock bottom and I like it, it feels good for the first time, really good, and *real*, Pat, real, as if I deserve it, the good of it and the bad of it—oh, I keep forgetting—it's not too late to go back to the plans for the Princess Daisy business, is it, to cancel the cancellations?"

"Hell, no, of course not, but Daisy, where are . . ."

His voice was cut off and the shrill of a nonfunctioning telephone replaced it.

Daisy looked in astonishment at the box on the wall. She, the utterly efficient organizer of a thousand complicated location shoots, had failed to follow the basic technique required of the lowliest production assistant: when calling from a public booth, give your number and wait to be called back. She hung up the phone and went to borrow some change from Kiki. She hadn't finished talking to Patrick Shannon, not by a long shot.

If a person lives in Manhattan long enough he gets to accept the fact that there are perhaps only a dozen perfect days in any given year; days during which New York City regains that sea-girt light that once was responsible for so much of the magic; days on which a breeze sweeps the city but does not blow so hard that it creates whirlpools of filth on the pavement; days on which it is possible to remember and understand that the city was once a pastoral island, surrounded by swift rivers; days on which the eye is able to see clear across town from the Hudson River to the East River; days during which New Yorkers congratulate themselves on sticking it out during the rest of the year.

It was on the night of such a day that The Russian Winter Palace Ball took place. An unexpected calm descended on the detail-burdened spirit of Candice Bloom as she woke up that morning, looked out of the window and sniffed the air. She knew immediately that there would be no last-minute illness in the ranks of Warner Le Roy's four hundred and fifty employees at the Tavern on the Green; no single one of the six hundred guests, carefully culled from the upper reaches of every segment of New York's overlapping worlds of society, the arts and power, would fail to appear; there would be no problem with the ice sculptures melting before they could be displayed; none of the horses hitched to the troikas would bolt and run off with their precious passengers; the night would be mild, the stars would be clearly visible in the plum-colored New York sky and there would be no need to put up a tent on the outside terrace of the restaurant, that, only yesterday, had been planted with seven hundred pots of tall daisy bushes flown in from California. No moon, but who needed a moon with two thousand candles and sixty thousand twinkle lights? In every bone of her lanky and skimpily fleshed frame she knew that Friday, September 16, 1977, was going to be her lucky day.

Daisy woke up early on that same morning with a moment of confusion before she realized that last night she had gotten into bed with Patrick Shannon and never left it. This was the first time she'd spent a whole night in his apartment and she blamed it entirely on Lucy, Shannon's lurcher, who, after first flirting and then spurning Theseus's affections for an absurdly long time—at one point tucking her tail resolutely between her legs and biting him on the nose—had finally, cautiously, changed her mind just as Daisy was about to take a crestfallen but still willing Theseus home to his own pillow. Lucy was not an easy customer, Daisy thought sleepily, but if there was ever to be a chance to breed true lurcher puppies so that she could give one to Kiki, she would have to put up with the bitch. She fell asleep again for a few minutes and woke up in Shannon's arms. Oh, but this was something outside the realm of past experience, this emotion of deep, sure gladness. From head to toe, her body was dancing with joy and welcome. There was a lack of any barrier between their two skins and their two minds and their two hearts, as, intertwined, they seemed to lie in a pool of golden light, pure, gay and penetrating, even though the sun itself had not yet entered the room. Daisy felt as if she were at the very center of the earth, like the pit of a great fruit, and at the same time she felt as if the two of them were flying together at the rim of the world, on the outer edge of experience.

"Is this bliss?" she whispered to him.

"This is love," he whispered back and when she reached up to put her arms around his neck, he felt the tears of happiness on her cheeks.

The snow-making machines had started on the bridle path where it coiled past the entrance to the park at 59th Street. They had spread a thick carpet of snow, one hundred feet wide, all the way to the Tavern at 67th Street. There the bridle path passes directly in front of the terrace of the restaurant and the snow makers continued to cover the path until the terrace was out of their sight. Then they doubled back and covered the entrance court of the Tavern and the street leading out to Central Park West, so that the guests, whether they came by limousine or by troika, all crossed into winter. From as far as Florida, Maine and Texas, Jenny Antonio had located thirty troikas and had them trucked to New York, but even she hadn't been able to get enough for all six hundred guests. Troikas are in short supply in the United States and, in spite of the dictionary-assured fact that any carriage drawn by three horses could be reasonably called a troika, Candice had insisted on picking only those that looked foreign, if not absolutely Russian. "I don't intend this to look like a *nouveau* version of 'Wagon Train,' " she told Jenny with asperity.

The Parks Department had given Supracorp permission to gather the troikas, their drivers and horses together and erect a temporary platform from which they would pick up their passengers and depart. Joseph Papp's chief set designer had been inspired by Supracorp's money to develop a healthy capitalistic outlook. The result was a daisy-bowered, latticed pavilion which managed to suggest what the Kremlin might look like if anyone with taste could get hold of it. Huge flags, in Princess Daisy lapis lazuli blue, with the stylized single daisy embroidered on them, blew from every corner of the pavilion, which was bathed in the footlights and spotlights, cunningly concealed in trees. All thirty of the troika drivers had been outfitted by a theatrical costumer in authentic greatcoats and three-cornered hats, some in red, some in green and still others in blue.

That night, as dusk fell, Candice Bloom and Jenny first took their hired limousine to the Tavern on the Green, where they made a final inspection of the arrangements, lingering a minute to watch the ten ice sculptors who were just finishing their work. The press photographers were already gathered at the entrance to the restaurant. Candice decided that she had hired more gypsy violinists than anyone needed, so she delegated a group of them to trudge down ten blocks to the pavilion where they could fiddle for the specially honored guests who had been invited to assemble there and arrive by troika.

As dozens of waiters started to light the two thousand candles in their silver candelabra, Candice and Jenny climbed back into their long, black car and were delivered to the empty pavilion. A few minutes remained before Daisy and Shannon were supposed to arrive so that they could be driven to the restaurant before the first guests were due. Candice, quivering with nerves, bent over her immaculate, thoughtful, quite possibly perfect list, a creation of the Art of Public Relations which, she now insisted, deserved its own graduate school.

Troika One: Princess Daisy and Patrick Shannon.
Troika Two: Mayor Koch, Governor Carey, Anne Ford and Bess Myerson.
Troika Three: Sinatra, Johnny Carson, Sulzberger and Grace Mirabella of *Vogue*.
Troika Four: John Fairchild, Woody Allen, Helen Gurley Brown, David Brown and Rona Barrett.
Troika Five: Streisand, Peters, Barbara Walters . . .

Something disturbed her in her devout contemplation, some movement that should not yet be there in that bright, waiting, flower-filled pavilion. No, Candice thought, no, that simply could not be Theseus. He was NOT ON HER LIST. Big, hairy and, for once, horribly frisky rather than sly, the terrifying beast bounded into the pavilion, hanging his head in a sinister manner and looking at her in a leering fashion that obviously preceded some sort of attack. Candice was frozen in bewitched abhorrence. The dreadful animal sidled up to Candice, nuzzling her crotch in a yearning way that, had she but known it, was a serious compliment. She shivered in outrage.

"He likes you," Daisy said.

It was only then that Candice realized that Theseus was firmly attached to a leash of silver sequined ribbons into which a bunch of daisies had been threaded. She was saved from whimpering out loud. Still not daring to raise her eyes, she quavered pitifully, "Daisy, exactly what breed of *chien* is that, for God's sake?"

"A noble lurcher," Daisy answered, settling the question forever.

As Daisy advanced, all the lights in the room broke into millions of sticks of splintering brilliance as they were reflected by her dress. It was paved with silver sequins and, at the narrow waist, bands of gold and bronze sequins had been woven into trompe l'oeil ribbons. The same bands formed a great bow at the high neck and defined a wide hem. The dress was a concentration of matchless theatricality such as no one had dared to wear in the last fifty years—a once-in-a-lifetime gown, fit only to be given to a museum after tonight.

Daisy and Patrick Shannon, with Theseus between them, crossed the pavilion and stepped outside where a silver-lacquered, flower-filled troika waited for them. The muscular driver looked at the three of them kindly.

"Let me know when you're ready and then sit back and brace yourselves," he announced.

"Please," said Daisy, "give me the reins. You can get down and drive the next troika."

"But you can't drive this thing, Miss," the man replied, shocked.

"If I can't," she laughed, "then there's no such thing as heredity."

"It's at your own risk," he warned her.

"Perhaps . . . but that's not going to stop me."

Recognizing defeat, the driver jumped out, muttering to himself.

Princess Daisy Valensky rose, in one fluid, untroubled motion, and placing her weight equally and firmly on both feet, her arms extended, gathered in the six reins with a movement that made the night sing. At her touch the three white horses quieted, gentled down, waiting. Shannon and Theseus both sat easily, looking up at her. She was strong, pliant, serene, joyous, mistress and servant of the moment.

"Well?" she asked questioningly to Shannon, "how do you feel about 'Tally-ho'? "

"I sort of prefer, 'Lafayette, we are here,' " he answered.

"But why not *en avant*?" Daisy asked, prolonging the delight.

"Perhaps even a simple giddy-up would do," he replied, feeling an instant's worth of pity for all the men in the world who were not Patrick Shannon.

The silver bells of the horses jingled sweetly in the night and, with one effortless gesture of authority, so flawless, so decisive that she needed no words of command, Daisy started the three white horses at a gallop, racing the troika over the snow toward the lights she knew were beckoning in the distance.

I'll Take Manhattan

For Steve, who knows why I keep dedicating books to him.
With all my love, always.

I am grateful to these friends who generously told me things I needed to know.

Helen Gurley Brown of *Cosmopolitan*
Alexandra Mayes Birnbaum of *Good Food*
Amy Gross of *Vogue*
Cathie Black of *USA Today*
Mark Miller of Hearst Magazines
Ellen Levine of *Woman's Day*

1

Maxi Amberville, with characteristic impatience and a lifelong disregard for regulations, sprang out of her seat in the moving Concorde that was taxiing to a stop, and raced along the narrow aisle toward the forward exit. Her fellow passengers sat in the aloof tranquility of those who have paid twice the price of a first-class ticket to travel from Paris to New York and felt no further pressure to hurry. As she flew by a few eyebrows were elegantly raised at the sight of such an unpardonably pretty girl in an undignified rush.

"What's taking so long?" she demanded of the stewardesses.

"We have not yet arrived, Madame."

"Arrived? Of course we've arrived. Damn these things—they spend more time on the ground than in the air." Maxi quivered in fury and every inch of her body, packed with nervous energy and intensity of purpose, expressed disapproval of Air France.

"If Madame will please return to her seat?"

"The hell I will. I'm in a hurry." Maxi stood her ground, feet planted in the flat boots she always wore for travel. Her short, dark hair was ruffled in seven different directions, here standing straight up and there covering part of her forehead with thick bangs that fell over her indignant face. She would have been riveting in a room full of beautiful women, for she made mere beauty seem not only irrelevant but uninteresting. In the subdued daylight of the cabin she was as alight with anticipation as if she were about to enter a ballroom. Maxi was wearing an old, tightly belted cognac-colored suede jacket and well-worn jeans tucked into her boots, a shoulder bag slung like a Sam Browne belt from one shoulder to the opposite hip, and as she pushed her bangs back impatiently she revealed the thick blaze of white hair with which she had been born, a streak that sprang out of her hairline over her right eye.

The Concorde whispered to its final stop and the stewardess, with dignified disdain, observed Maxi as she stomped through the exit door before it was fully open, clutching an American passport in her free hand.

Maxi came to a full halt at the closest Immigration booth and thrust her passport at the inspector. He opened it to her picture, studied it casually, and then looked at it intently.

"Maxime Emma Amberville?" he asked.

"Right. Isn't it a god-awful photo? Look, I'm in a hurry. Could you just stamp that thing and let me get out of here?"

The inspector looked at her with noncommittal scrutiny. He calmly punched up some keys on his computer.

"Who," he asked her finally, "is Maxime Emma Amberville Cipriani Brady Kirkgordon?"

"I know. I know. An unwieldy name at best. But it's not against the law."

"What I mean, miss, is why don't you have your full name on this passport?"

"My old passport expired during the summer and I renewed it at the Embassy in Paris . . . you can see that it's new."

"Did you change your name legally?"

"Legally?" Maxi said, offended. "All of my divorces were perfectly legal. I prefer my maiden name so I returned to it. Do you want to hear the whole story of my life? Everyone on that blasted plane is going to get ahead of me. Now I'll have to wait at customs!"

"The baggage isn't off the plane yet," he remarked reasonably.

"That's the whole point! I don't *have* any baggage. If we weren't haggling about my lurid past I'd be in a taxi right now. Oh, bloody, *bloody* hell!" she complained, ardent in her fury.

The inspector continued to study the passport. The photograph didn't manage to convey her quality of electric vitality and as accustomed as he was to bad pictures he had not, for a brief moment, been convinced that the snapshot was legitimate. It showed mostly bangs and a neutrally smiling mouth, but the woman standing wrathfully in front of him, her hair looking like the feathers of an outraged bird, had a boldness, an audacity, that would have forced him to notice her, as if a flare had been sent up in front of his nose. What's more she didn't look old enough to have had more than one husband, much less three, in spite of the date of her birth, twenty-nine years ago.

Reluctantly the inspector stamped her passport with the day's date, August 15, 1984, and gave it back to her, but not before he'd made a special illegible notation on the back of her customs declaration.

Moving with the tadpole agility of the born New Yorker Maxi slapped her shoulder bag down on a customs table and looked around impatiently for an inspector. At this early hour they were still gathered in one corner of the big room finishing their morning coffee, not anxious to start the day's work. Several of the customs men caught sight of Maxi at the same time and each of them put down his mug of coffee abruptly. One of them, young and redheaded, broke from the pack and started off toward Maxi.

"What's your hurry, O'Casey?" asked another inspector, catching him by the arm.

"Who's in a hurry?" he asked, shaking off the arm. "This pigeon just happens to be mine," he announced, walking quickly toward Maxi, outdistancing the closest of his fellows by several yards, in his determination.

"Welcome to New York," he said. "The Countess of Kirkgordon, unless my eyes deceive me."

"Oh, cut out the countess nonsense, O'Casey. You know I dumped poor Laddie a while ago." Maxi looked at him with a trace of unease, her hands on her hips. Just her bad luck to fall into the hands of cocky, freckled, far-from-unattractive Joseph O'Casey who fancied himself some kind of throwback to Sherlock Holmes. There should be a law about civil servants like him molesting decent citizens.

"How could I have forgotten?" he marveled. "You got divorced just before you came through with a major new wardrobe from Saint Laurent. . . . You never were much of a seamstress, Miss Amberville—those labels you sewed on from Saks were very unprofessional. Will you never learn that we study the European fashion lines as soon as they're photographed?"

"Good for you, O'Casey." Maxi gave him a solemn nod of approval. "I'll keep it in mind. Meanwhile, could you do me a favor and check out my shoulder bag? I'm in a desperate hurry today."

"The last time you were in a hurry it was a question of twenty bottles of Shalimar, the two-hundred-dollar size, and the time before that it was a new Patek Polo, the one you were wearing in plain sight on your wrist, thinking no doubt of the story of the purloined letter. It was carved out of solid gold and worth eight thousand dollars, no less. And then, let's see now, it wasn't too long ago that there was that little problem of a Fendi mink, the one dyed pink, that you told me was a fun fur from a flea market worth under three hundred dollars. Fifteen thousand bucks in Milan if I remember correctly." He smiled, pleased with himself. There was nothing like a memory for details.

"The Shalimar was a *gift*," Maxi objected, "for a friend. I don't even wear perfume."

"You're supposed to include gifts, it says so right here on the declaration," O'Casey said blankly.

Maxi looked up at him. There was no mercy in those Irish eyes. They were smiling, all right, but not harmlessly.

"O'Casey," she admitted, "you're perfectly right. I am a habitual smuggler. I have always been a smuggler and I'll probably always be a smuggler. I don't know why I do it and I wish I could stop. It's a neurosis. I'm sick. I need help. I'll *get* help, when I have a chance. But I swear to you that this time—this one single time—I haven't got anything with me. I'm just here on business and I have to get into the city fast. I should be there now, for pity's sake. Search my bag and let me through." She spoke imploringly. "Please."

O'Casey studied her intently. She was so pretty, this chance-taking dame, that he felt his toes curling right down into the soles of his shoes at the mere sight of her face. As for the rest of her, for like all customs inspectors he was trained in the meaning of body language, it betrayed nothing at the moment. God knows what she must be bringing in to be able to stand there so innocently.

"Can't do it, Miss Amberville," he said, shaking his head in regret. "Immigration knows about your record, he noted it right there on the declaration, and there is no way I can just wave you on. We'll have to do a body search."

"At least look through my bag, damn it!" Maxi demanded, no longer the supplicant.

"Obviously it wouldn't be there. It's got to be on you, whatever it is," O'Casey replied. "You'll have to wait till a female inspector comes on duty. There should be one here in an hour or two and I'll make sure she attends to you first."

"A body search? You're not serious!" Maxi cried in unpremeditated astonishment. Twenty-nine years of having her own way in almost everything had created a conviction that ordinary rules just did not apply to her life. And certainly nobody did anything to Maxi Amberville without her permission. Never. Never *ever!*

"I'm perfectly serious," O'Casey said calmly, with a hint of a grin on his lips. Maxi looked at him incredulously. He really meant it, this power-mad bastard. But every man has his price, even Joe O'Casey.

"Joe," she said, giving a deep sigh, "we've known each other for years, right? And I have never been a bad citizen, have I? The United States Treasury is much richer from my fines than if I'd just paid the duty."

"That's what I've told you, every time I've caught you, but you just won't listen."

"I've never brought in drugs or unpasteurized cheese or a salami with foot-and-mouth disease—Joe—can we make a deal?" Her voice traipsed the range from cajolery to delicate, yet unmistakable down-and-dirty.

"I don't take bribes," he snapped.

"I know," she sighed, "I know only too well. But that's your problem, Joe. You're neurotically honest. No, I want to make a trade."

"What kind of nonsense are you giving me, Miss Amberville?"

"Call me Maxi. I am suggesting the straightforward, honest surrender of a body in exchange for an unnecessary body search."

"A body?" he repeated blankly, although he had a clear notion of her intention and the very possibility of such an extravagant bounty was enough to make him forget the uniform he wore.

"A body, my very own, duty-free, welcoming, warm, and all of it, every inch, for you, Joe O'Casey," Maxi said, casually running one of her fingertips down between two of his fingers without taking her eyes off him. She gave him a look that Cleopatra had invented but Maxi had perfected. The man cracked. She could tell from the way he blushed so deeply that his freckles almost disappeared. "Eight tonight, at P. J. Clarke's?" she asked, almost casually.

He nodded speechlessly. Dreamily he put a chalk mark on her bag and waved her on.

"I'm always on time," Maxi flung over her shoulder as she took flight, "so don't keep me waiting."

Two minutes later she began to relax as she sat back in the long blue limousine that had been waiting for her, driven by her chauffeur Elie Franc, known as the canniest and swiftest in the city. There was no point in telling him to hurry for nothing on wheels could overtake Elie except a traffic cop and he was too smart to fall into their traps.

With a quick glance at her watch Maxi saw that, in spite of the impossible sluggishness at which airlines and arrival procedures operated, she would manage to reach her destination on time. Only yesterday morning she had been in Brittany, at Quiberon, subjecting herself to the hot seawater bubble-bath regime that was indicated after an unusually hectic summer, when she had received a telephone call from her brother Toby, telling her to get back to New York in a hurry for an unexpected board meeting of Amberville Publications.

Their father, Zachary Amberville, the founder of Amberville Publications, had died suddenly, as the result of an accident, just over a year ago. The company he had left behind was one of the giants of the American magazine business and board meetings were normally planned well in advance.

"Something about this rush makes me nervous, Goldilocks," Toby had said. "I smell trouble. I heard about it by chance. How come we weren't notified? Can you make it on such short notice?"

"Absolutely. As soon as I shower off the salt I can get the plane from Lorient back to Paris, spend the night and catch the Concorde while you people are still sleeping in New York. No problem," she'd answered. And indeed, except for the hitch almost imposed by O'Casey, she would have been early rather than just barely on time.

Now for the first time since the Concorde had landed, Maxi noticed that even though the day was cool for late August it was getting warmer minute by minute. As she took off her jacket she became conscious of something rubbing against her waist, under the belt of her jeans. With a perplexed look she fished inside and drew out a thin platinum chain that she had clasped there not more than six hours before in her favorite suite at the Paris Ritz. Dangling from the chain was an immense black pearl crowned by two plumes of diamonds from Van Cleef and Arpels. Well, bless my soul, Maxi thought as she hung the jewel around her neck. It was glowingly baroque, prodigally opulent and outrageously conspicuous. How could she have forgotten it so totally? Still, a penny saved is a penny earned, she gloated with the triumphant pleasure of someone who has won by cheating at Monopoly.

2

Elie slammed to a stop in front of the new Amberville Building at Fifty-fourth and Madison. Maxi didn't wait for him to come around and open the door. Again consulting her watch, she jumped out of the limo and tore through the four-story-tall glass atrium, not noticing the dozens of trees that had each cost the price of a small car, not glancing at any of the hundreds of pots of hanging orchids and ferns. Botany was not on Maxi's mind as she commandeered the express elevator up to the executive floor and her objective, the boardroom of the empire her father had started in 1947 with one small trade magazine. She pushed the heavy doors apart and stood stock still, surveying the assembled company with both hands on her hips, her booted legs spread two feet apart, a stance which she had often assumed since she had learned to stand upright. Frequently enough the world was up to something not entirely to Maxi's liking to justify a basic skepticism.

"Just why are we here?" she demanded of the group of senior editors, publishers, and business managers in the instant of silence that preceded their exclamations of surprise and greeting. But they were as ignorant as she and many of them had rushed into the city from interrupted summer vacations to attend the meeting. The difference was that they had been summoned back officially while Maxi had found out accidentally. Maxi had missed many an editorial board meeting, to all of which she was routinely invited, but it was unheard of that she should not have been informed.

A tiny, exquisite, white-haired man detached himself from the others and came toward her.

"Pavka!" Maxi exclaimed in delight, embracing Pavka Mayer, Artistic Director of all of the ten Amberville magazines.

"What's going on? Where's my mother and Toby?"

"I wish I knew. I don't appreciate rushed trips from Santa Fe, to say nothing of missing last night's opera. Your mother still hasn't arrived," Pavka replied.

He had known and loved Maxi since her birth, understanding that her complicated life was dedicated to extracting the greatest amount of fun that could still be found on the planet Earth. He had watched her as she grew up, and she reminded him of a miner panning for gold, moving feverishly from one claim to another, here hitting an ounce or two of ore, there finding only worthless pebbles and passing quickly on, but forever searching for that vein of pure gold—pure *fun*—that major strike which, so far as he knew, still eluded her. But she believed that it existed, and Pavka Mayer was sure that if anyone were to find it, Maxi would be that person.

"I find this all very strange," Maxi murmured.

"I too. But tell me, what have you been up to all summer, little girl?" he asked.

"Ah, all the usual—breaking hearts, cutting capers, playboy bashing, not playing by any fair rules, getting up to speed, keeping up with the golden lads. You know about them, Pavka darling; my normal summer games, sometimes winning on the swing and losing on the roundabout, a spot of seduction here and there . . . nothing serious."

Pavka inspected her in one experienced art director's glance. As well as he knew her he was always slightly amazed—and as if he had sustained a small electric shock—by her actual physical presence, for Maxi was, somehow, more real than other people, more *there*. She was only of medium height, somewhere around five feet six inches tall, and her beautifully boned body did not take up a lot of real room, yet she created a vibrating space around herself through sheer mesmerizing energy. Maxi was formed like a great courtesan of the Belle Epoque with a tiny waist, excellent deep breasts and sumptuous hips, yet she was not oppressively voluptuous and the masculine, piratical swagger of her garments only made her all the more feminine. Her surpassingly green eyes, the precise color of Imperial Jade—fresh, brilliant and pure—were unshadowed by any trouble.

Pavka knew that no photograph would ever capture the essence of Maxi because she lacked the ruthless bone structure that a woman needed for photography, but he never tired of looking at her dark straight eyebrows that were always raised in faint surprise over her wickedly undeviating gaze. Her delicately molded nose would have been classic if it hadn't turned up slightly at the tip, giving her a look of witty alertness, and the white streak in her hair only made her forever-tousled, capriciously falling mass of short thick hair seem darker by contrast. Yet to Pavka her mouth was her most compelling feature. Her lower lip was tenderly curved into a hint of a smile and her upper lip was unabashedly, undeniably bow-shaped, with a tiny beauty spot to the left of its deeply indented center, the mouth of a trueborn sorceress, he said to himself with the well-earned judgment of a man who had successfully loved women for more than fifty years.

Pavka was still admiring Maxi when the boardroom doors opened again and Toby Amberville walked in. Maxi ran toward him.

"Toby," she said softly just before she reached him and he stopped in mid-stride and opened his arms to her, pulling her close. For a long, quiet minute she remained clasped to him, lifting up her face to his bent head so that they could rub noses. "What's going on, Toby?" Maxi whispered to him.

"I don't know. I haven't been able to reach Mother for the last several days. It's a mystery, but I guess we're about to find out. You're looking great, babe," he added as he released her.

"Says who?" Maxi whispered.

"I do. I smell it in your hair. Your cheeks feel sunburned, high mountain sun, not Southampton. And you've put on weight, about three-quarters of a pound, give or take an ounce, right here on your butt. Very cozy." He pushed her gently away and she watched from the hallway as he continued on into the room, her older brother, by barely two years, a brother who could tell more about her from touching her palms or listening to her say three words, than anyone else in the world.

Toby Amberville was a tall, seemingly tireless man with an absorbed inward-listening manner that made him look older than his thirty-one years. At first glance he didn't have any particular physical feature in common with Maxi yet there was a similarity in the way in which they both fully occupied the space in which they found themselves. Toby's mouth, tender and full, seemed to contradict the strength of his chin, the obstinate determination that made him intimidating to many people, in spite of his easy laugh and his robust, healthy handsomeness. He had amberbrown eyes around which lines were beginning to show, lines which, to a casual observer would have been the sign of a man who squinted, a man who was possibly near-sighted and refused, out of vanity, to wear glasses.

Maxi hung back to scrutinize him as he walked easily and confidently ahead, sitting down in the chair that had been left empty for him by decree of his father since his twenty-first birthday, a chair that waited for him at each editorial board meeting, a chair he occupied more and more rarely, as the advance of his disease of retinitis pigmentosa made his eyesight increasingly limited. Was his tunnel vision still relatively stable? Maxi wondered. It was never easy to know what Toby saw or didn't see since one of the characteristics of his disease was that his vision varied from hour to hour, depending on the set of conditions in which he found himself, the distance and angle from which he looked at something, the brightness or dullness of the light, and a dozen other variables that had a maddening inconsistency so that at times he had moments of accurate seeing which only made the return of his condition of near-blindness more difficult to endure. But he *had* endured, he had made his peace with his condition as much as any man could, Maxi thought as she listened to him greet the various people in the room, immediately recognizing and turning to them at the sound of their voices. For a moment Maxi forgot why she was here in this large room, and lost herself in loving contemplation of her brother.

"Maxime." Her name was spoken in a voice that had a faint British accent, a silver voice whose beauty caused Maxi to shiver. Her mother's voice was the only one in the world that could make her jump and yet it sounded as if it had never been raised to give an order or ask a favor, much less express anger. It was a voice of such an assured and graceful pitch, of such cool, supple charm that it had obtained everything—or almost everything—that its possessor had ever wanted. Maxi turned to greet her mother, bracing herself.

"When did you get in, Maxime?" Lily Amberville asked betraying some surprise. "I thought you were still skiing in Peru. Or was it Chile?" She pushed her daughter's bangs to one side, a familiar caressing gesture that indicated permanent disapproval of the way Maxi wore her hair. Maxi felt a futile anger that she had stopped expressing years earlier. Why, she thought, can no one make me feel ugly except my mother?

Lily Amberville, who had lived the last three decades of her life in the aura of homage that surrounds a very few of the rich and powerful great beauties of the world, embraced her daughter with vice-regal dignity, an embrace to which Maxi submitted as she always had, with a mixture of resentment and longing.

"Hello, Mother, you're looking glorious," she said truthfully.

"I wish you'd let us know that you were coming," Lily replied, not returning or acknowledging the compliment. She almost seemed nervous, Maxi realized, although that wasn't a word she had ever thought of in relation to Lily. Nervous and a little tense.

"I think there's been some sort of mix-up, Mother. Nobody told me about today's meeting. I wouldn't have had any idea if Toby hadn't phoned. . . ."

"Obviously there's been some sort of communications problem—but hadn't we better sit down?" Lily Amberville said vaguely and drifted away, leaving Maxi standing in the doorway. Pavka Mayer came up to her.

"Sit next to me, you devil. How often do I get this opportunity?"

" 'Devil'? You haven't seen me for two months," Maxi protested, laughing again. "For all you know, I may have reformed."

"Devil," Pavka insisted as she followed him into the room. How else, he thought, to describe the quintessence she distilled, a nimble, feisty, inquisitive, wide-awake ability to cause trouble, fascinating trouble that he couldn't and wouldn't do anything to change?

"Reformed? *My* Maxi?" he quizzed her. "May I assume that the seven dwarfs gave you that amazing black pearl because you were so innocent, so untouchable, so pure, so much like Snow White?"

"There was only one of him, actually, and he was of a perfectly normal height," Maxi said, unblushingly, tucking the again-forgotten pearl quickly inside her blouse. It most certainly wasn't daytime jewelry.

Before she had settled into the chair next to Pavka a hand grasped her too firmly by the arm. She swung around, stiffening with displeasure. Her uncle, Cutter Dale Amberville, her father's younger brother, bent down and kissed her on her forehead. "Cutter," Maxi said coldly, "what are you doing here?"

"Lily asked me to come. I'm surprised to see you, as a matter of fact. I was convinced that you'd abandoned us for more interesting places. I'm so glad you're home, Maxime." His voice was warm and welcoming.

"Just where did you think I was, Cutter?" Only an effort at control kept the dislike she felt out of her voice.

"Everyone thought that you were skiing in Peru or Chile, somewhere quite unreachable. Something to do with helicopters and glaciers."

"Is that the reason that I wasn't notified of the meeting today?"

"Naturally, my dear. There didn't seem to be any point in trying. We didn't have a phone number. But I'm delighted to see I was wrong."

"You should never listen to rumors, Cutter. Toby knew where I was if you'd thought of making that most obvious inquiry. But apparently even he wasn't told. I find that very odd indeed. What's more, even if I'd been up the Amazon I don't like to be out of touch," she stated crisply.

"It must just be a simple mistake." Cutter Amberville smiled, a smile that reached the depths of his youthful blue eyes, a smile that redeemed his features from being impossibly distinguished, a smile so wide that it disarmingly revealed one crooked tooth and transformed his elegant head from that of an ambassador to that of a roustabout. He owed his fortune to the undeniable power of his smile and he had long forgotten the prep-school days when he used to practice it in front of a mirror, forcing warmth, and thus sincerity, to mount from his lips to his eyes by subtle alterations of his facial muscles.

Cutter Amberville had spent the last three years in Manhattan, returning in 1981 after an absence of more than twenty-five years punctuated only by a few brief visits. He had changed surprisingly little during all that time, never losing the spare fitness of the superb athlete he was. His still-blond hair was closely cut, his gaze a slash of blue, his manner never less than disarming. He was a compellingly alluring man who had bewitched many women, yet there was a darkness of some inner purpose in his manner, a hint of something hidden. He seemed to have little need for humor or for people whom he didn't find useful. During his entire lifetime Zachary Amberville had loved his brother deeply.

Cutter continued to beam down at Maxi with the unanswerable weapon of his smile. His hand still held her arm in a firm, even a protective way. Abruptly she jerked away, not caring if it looked rude, and popped herself down near Pavka. Cutter, unrebuffed, touched her hair with a small yet clearly intimate movement that made Maxi's nose twitch briefly in disgust. Just what the devil, she wondered, had brought Cutter to the meeting? He had never attended one before.

She watched as her mother, with the distinctive floating walk, the unshakable proud distinction of the ballerina she had once been, went to the head of the table. Lily sat down next to the chair that had remained empty since Zachary Amberville's death, a chair different from the others in the room, a worn, battered chair that achingly reminded everyone there of the laughing, daring, eager, gutsy, earthy man who had gone so suddenly.

She must not allow her tears to fall, Maxi told herself angrily. Every time she saw her father's chair she was so vividly aware of him that, try as she would, tears rushed to her eyes. God knows, she'd wept and wept during this last year for the father she had adored but she always tried to keep her outbursts private. People were always embarrassed by the outward expression of another's grief and such emotion had no place in a boardroom.

Holding her breath and concentrating fiercely, Maxi made herself retain her composure. Her eyes were bright but the tears did not fall. Safe now, from a public display of her deep loss, she watched as Cutter followed Lily. Just where was he planning to sit? Maxi asked herself. There didn't seem to be an extra chair for him. She watched, incredulously, as her mother made a gesture as precise as it was astonishing and with one slender hand indicated to Cutter that he should take the chair that had never been occupied by anyone but her husband.

How could she! How *dared* she let Cutter sit there? Maxi cried to herself, her heart thudding. Next to her she heard a muffled sound of disbelief escape Pavka's lips and all around the table there were hastily stifled sounds of shock. The atmosphere in the room quivered with the impact of this unexpected act of Lily's and people exchanged surreptitious, bewildered glances. However, Cutter seemed oblivious to them and sat down without any change in his expression.

Zachary Amberville had dominated his privately owned company, assisted by the group of people who were all in the room today. After his death his widow had started to appear at the board meetings that she had never attended during her husband's lifetime. She was now the majority shareholder of the company. Lily had been left seventy percent of the voting shares in the corporation; the other thirty percent had been divided among Maxi, Toby, and their younger brother, Justin.

Maxi and occasionally Toby had both tried to attend board meetings when they were in town. However, Maxi had never heard her mother express any opinion or take part in any decision, nor had she done so herself. The editors of each magazine, the publishers and the business managers, headed by Pavka Mayer, had continued to run the huge enterprise as they had done under Zachary, with devotion, competence, great expertise and no diminution of zeal.

There was a moment of silence. Since no one knew the agenda of this meeting, they waited for Lily Amberville to announce it to them. But Lily still said nothing, her eyes cast down toward the table. Maxi watched, dumbfounded, too amazed to take a breath, as Cutter pushed her father's chair a few inches out from the table, leaned back comfortably, perfectly at ease and took over the meeting.

"Mrs. Amberville has asked me to speak to you today," he began quietly. "First of all, she regrets that she had to bring some of you into the city on such short notice, but she has an announcement to make that she felt you should all know about as quickly as possible."

"What the devil . . . ?" Pavka said, in a low voice, turning to Maxi. She shook her head, tightened her lips and glared at Cutter. What had induced her mother to ask him to address the board? Why wasn't Lily speaking for herself, instead of this investment banker, this stranger to the group who had no right to be taking any part in the workings of Amberville Publications?

Cutter continued to sit calmly and speak in measured, authoritative tones.

"Mrs. Amberville has not, as you all know, made any changes in the structure of

Amberville Publications in the last year since my brother's unexpected and tragic death. But she has made a serious study of the future of this company, of its ten magazines and its real estate. Now, I think the time has come to face the fact that although six of the magazines are undisputed leaders in their field, four of them are in trouble." He stopped to take a sip of water and Maxi's heart beat even, more rapidly. Her devious uncle was giving himself the aura of a general. "I think," he had said, and all down the long table people were sitting without a sound, waiting for the announcement he had promised and had not yet made.

"We all know," Cutter continued, his manner leisurely, "that my brother took more pleasure in creating a magazine than in enjoying its success; more interest in curing the problems of a sick magazine than in exploiting to the maximum the potential of a well one. That was his great strength, but now that he is gone it has become a weakness. Only another Zachary Amberville could have the necessary stubbornness, the willingness to sustain years of losses, and, particularly, the faith in his own creativity, that is necessary to continue to pour the profits of our six successful magazines into the hungry mouths of our weak ones."

"*Our*," Maxi thought in outrage. *Since when*, Cutter, have you had a part of Amberville Publications? Since when do you have the right to say "our"? But she sat in antagonistic, apprehensive silence, waiting, her stomach sinking at his ominously dominating manner.

"Three of our newest magazines, *Wavelength*, *Garden*, and *Vacation*, have been losing money at a rate that is simply unacceptable. *Buttons and Bows* has a value that, for years, has been purely sentimental. . . ."

"Just a minute, Mr. Amberville," Pavka Mayer finally spoke, his voice slicing through Cutter's composed urbane tones. "I hear a businessman talking, not a magazine man. I know every detail of Zachary's future plans for *Wavelength* and *Garden* and *Vacation* and I can assure you that he didn't expect them to be showing profits yet. However, it's only a question of time before they do. As for *Buttons and Bows*, I feel . . ."

"Yes, what about *Buttons and Bows*, Cutter?" Maxi interrupted violently, suddenly finding herself on her feet. "You probably don't know, innocent as you are of the business, but Father always called it his baby. Why, he founded this whole damn company on it!"

"A luxury, my dear," Cutter answered, ignoring Pavka Mayer as if he hadn't spoken. "It was a luxury to keep a magazine going because it had been lucky for him a long time ago, a luxury your father could well afford."

"Then what the hell has changed?" Maxi cried. "If he could afford it, why can't we afford it? Who are you to tell us all what we can and can't afford?" She was shaking with pure, released anger.

"My dear Maxi, I'm speaking for your mother, not for myself. She *controls* Amberville—you seem to have forgotten that. Naturally it's a shock to you to have the brutal facts of business expressed by someone who is on the outside."

He looked at her expressionlessly yet he turned slightly toward her, focusing his words. "While your father was alive this corporation was a one-man show, as even you, my dear impetuous Maxi, would have to admit. But today Zachary Amberville isn't here to make the difficult decisions. Only your mother has that right, only your mother has that power. She feels that it is her duty to engage in sound business practice since we don't have the genius of your father to guide us. It's her duty to look at the profit-and-loss statement, to look at the bottom line."

"I look at the statement, Cutter. So do Toby and Justin. Last year our profits were many, many millions of dollars. You don't deny that, do you?" Maxi asked defiantly.

"Certainly not. But you aren't taking into account the fierce competition we face each month for our share of the magazine market. It's a little frivolous to ignore the fact that with one difficult, painful decision . . . one necessary decision, Maxi, that your mother has *decided to make*, Amberville's profits can be vastly increased."

"Frivolous! Wait a minute, Cutter, I refuse to allow that kind of . . . "

"Maxi, the word was ill-chosen. I apologize. But you are aware, are you not, that your mother is accountable to no one, to no one whomsoever?"

"I know that, but I tell you that Amberville is *not* in financial trouble," Maxi insisted, mutinously, stubbornly determined that nothing should change in the world her father had left.

Pavka Mayer, at her side, was gripped by an equally fierce resolution. As he had listened to Cutter Amberville's words he had been seized by memories of Zachary leading the editorial group with unfaltering courage and imagination over so many difficult periods in the magazine business. Zachary, his friend, who had never attempted to conceal his real motives or emotions as did his subtle brother; Zachary who had plunged into each meeting with a gusto that had made all his colleagues feel as if they were his equals, his companions in the challenges of publishing. Pavka knew far better than Maxi that Amberville Publications was in no difficulty but, unlike her, he didn't have the authority that stock ownership gave. He watched grimly as Cutter turned away from Maxi's protests as if she had become invisible and looked around the table, meeting the eyes of each member of the group briefly.

"Amberville Publications," he said, "is in a situation in which it is *intolerable* that certain, clearly predictable losses should be permitted to continue. Mrs. Amberville's decision is to *cease publication*, as quickly as possible, of the four magazines that have been losing money. She regrets the necessity of this decision but it is not open to discussion."

He leaned back easily, armored and impassive, knowing that the reaction to his words would, in spite of anything he had said, erupt in the room full of men and women, many of whom had just had their working lives demolished. Frightened and incredulous voices burst out all around him. Maxi had gone to Toby's side, whispering fiercely to him. Suddenly the room grew still as Lily Amberville, astonished at the opposition that came from all sides and finding herself, for one of the rare, almost unthinkable times in her life, on the defensive, held up both of her lovely hands, palms forward.

"Please! Please, there *is* something I realize I must say after all. I see now that I've done a disservice to Mr. Amberville in asking him to tell you this difficult news. I didn't anticipate . . . didn't quite understand how unsettling it would be . . . a business decision merely . . . but I should have tried to talk to each one of you separately. However, I'm afraid that was quite beyond my powers. Please don't blame Mr. Amberville for my decision and don't feel that he had no right to announce it to this group. I haven't even been able to tell my children the reason I asked him to speak for me until this minute . . . I . . . " Lily turned to Cutter imploringly and fell silent. He took her hand and again looked around the table with perfect self-possession, like a lion tamer in a cage establishing his supremacy.

Maxi watched them in a condition of incoherent insurrection. What possible excuse could Cutter have to speak for her mother? She remembered unwillingly, but unable to prevent the thought from surfacing, a night when she had been fifteen and Cutter had been on one of his rare visits to New York, staying in one of the guest rooms of her parents' house. She had been in bed, studying for an exam, when he had come into her room in his bathrobe, looking for something to read. He had asked her what she was working on and had approached her bed to inspect the textbook. Suddenly she had felt his hand darting under her pajama top, grasping her bare breast, fingering her nipple. She had pulled violently away, her mouth open in shock, ready to scream, and he had drawn back with a smiling, smooth, plausible apology. But Maxi had known, in that instant, what he had wanted, and he had known that she knew. The attempt had never been repeated, but she could never be with him in the same room without remembering that split second of evil contact. Why was Cutter holding her mother's hand?

"Yesterday," he announced, looking directly at Maxi, his triumph so certain, so absolute, that it seemed emotionless, "Mrs. Amberville and I were married."

3

Zachary Anderson Amberville had never looked anything like an Anderson, his mother, Sarah Cutter Anderson, of Andover, Massachusetts, had been heard to remark plaintively. The boy was obviously a throwback to one of the French Huguenot Ambervilles who had come over to fight for American independence with Lafayette, in the regiment of the Marquis de Biron, and decided to settle in New England. Every generation or so, a dark-haired, dark-eyed Amberville boy or girl would be born who would grow to only medium height and who would have a lamentable tendency toward a certain plumpness in middle age, and her oldest son was one of them, she complained, to mask the pride she felt in him which it would have been unbecoming to express.

Her own Anderson ancestors were stern Swedes and the Cutters were . . . well, the Cutters were Andover. No money anymore, of course, in either of the two branches of her family, but the Ambervilles hadn't done particularly well for themselves either, considering the head start they had had on the rest of the country. They might all have been considered a bit stick-in-the-mud, determinedly provincial, except that Zack had as much dynamism, as much ambition, as much get-up-and-go as you might hope to find in one entire large family of recent immigrants.

He was born in 1923, several years after Sarah Anderson's marriage to Henry Dale Amberville, the young editor of a small country newspaper near Andover. By the time Zack was seven he had his own paper route, delivering his father's paper every day at dawn. He tried valiantly to expand his sales to include the *Saturday Evening Post* but he had little luck, for the Depression had just started to settle over the United States and people were beginning to cut back on every unnecessary expense.

The Ambervilles' second child was a daughter named Emily, who became known as Minnie Mouse and finally just Minnie. By the time their last child, Cutter, was born in 1934, the Depression had almost wiped out the small income of Henry Amberville's newspaper. Zack went to the local public school instead of to Andover, which generations of Ambervilles had attended, and after school he always managed to hunt up some kind of paying job: jerking sodas, delivering groceries, chopping wood, running errands for the town's shopkeepers. He didn't care what he did as long as he could contribute to the family funds. His summers were spent working at the newspaper for his father, learning the business, trying to sell ads and taking over many of the tasks his father now had to do single-handedly, since Henry Amberville had eliminated his tiny staff as the Depression grew worse.

Zachary was a brilliant student who had skipped fifth and eighth grades and his sophomore year of high school. In the spring of his senior year of high school, when he was just barely fifteen, he applied for a scholarship to a number of colleges. His dream was to go to Harvard, for in Cambridge he could have stayed close to his family. His sense of responsibility toward his parents, toward Minnie, and particularly toward his four-year-old brother, Cutter, was so strong that he proposed to go to work after high school and forget about college, but the Ambervilles would not permit this. "We can manage, Zachary, so long as we don't have to contribute to your tuition, but if you think that I'm going to see a son of mine do without a college education . . . " His father's voice trailed off in horror at the enormity of such an idea.

The only university that offered Zachary Amberville a full scholarship, including books, room and board, was Columbia, in Morningside Heights. Ambervilles and Cutters and Andersons and Dales had visited Manhattan, of course, throughout the centuries, but never had one of them actually spent more than a night in the city that they found, unanimously, too loud, too crowded, too expensive, too full of foreigners, too commercial, in fact, as one of them finally put it to everyone's satisfaction, "Not, in point of fact, really American at all."

At fifteen, Zachary Amberville, strongly built but still growing, was a full two inches short of his final height of five-ten, and three years younger than most of his classmates, but he had the mind-set of someone not just bigger but also older. He had been independent for so many years, so driven by the need to take care of his family that he had an inner sense of authority that college freshmen almost never have. He inspired respect at first sight although he was, by nature, invariably rumpled, his black hair ruffled by his habit of running his hand through it and tugging on his white streak whenever he was temporarily puzzled by anything. He was carelessly dressed and obviously neither knew nor thought about how he looked. He was volatile, ready for any adventure, talkative, intensely curious about everyone and everything new, and had a belly laugh that could be heard from one end of the dorm to the other. He had never had a drink, never used profanity and never spent a night away from home, but there was a boldness and a largeness about this teenager that had nothing to do with the rules by which college boys usually judge each other. Zachary Amberville had a good, wide mouth and a pleasingly big, blunt nose and most lively, easily amused, animated green eyes under thick quirky eyebrows. He wasn't handsome, this dark Amberville, but he had a quality that made others like him at first sight and follow him in his many enthusiasms.

Zachary Amberville fell in love with New York City at first sight. " 'I'll take Manhattan, the Bronx and Staten Island too,' " he sang to himself as he studied in the stacks of the Low Library, the words of the immortal song that Rodgers and Hart had written in 1925, never far from his lips. I'll *take* Manhattan, oh yes I will, I'll *take* it and I'll *keep* it! he vowed to himself as he grabbed a subway downtown whenever he had a few free hours. He knew the city on foot from the Battery to Harlem, from river to river, he knew the bridges and the parks, the avenues and the sidestreets, and except for the museums, he knew it all, from the outside only, for the price of a subway ride and, once in a while, the best hot dog in the world bought at a pushcart on Delancey Street. Money for the subway, the hot dogs and all his other small needs came from his part-time job waiting on tables at the Lion's Den, the sandwich place on campus. Every extra penny he earned he sent back home, deciding that the luxury of abandoning the Lion's Den job to try out for the *Spectator*, the Columbia daily paper, was something he couldn't afford. In fact there was no element of reluctant choice in what he did. To assume responsibility for his family was a natural function of his personality.

Zachary Amberville had planned his future. When he graduated from Columbia he was going to get a job at the *New York Times* as a copyboy. Surely, he reasoned, as he spent his summers putting out a daily paper almost single-handedly, for his father's health was steadily failing, he would be able to persuade them to give him a job . . . he knew every aspect of the business, from printing through delivery. The

Columbia School of Journalism, he judged, would be a waste of precious time and he couldn't afford it in any case.

He had taken the tour offered by the *New York Times*, managing to join groups of schoolchildren who were welcomed into the infernal lower depths of the *Times* building and given a glimpse of the great presses at work. From copyboy to reporter, from reporter to . . . there his imagination stopped, stunned by the richness and varieties of opportunity offered by the best newspaper ever published.

The world had other plans for the members of Columbia's class of 1941. The day after war was declared, eighteen-year-old Zachary Amberville, a full-fledged senior, joined the Marines. He could have waited to be drafted and probably, almost certainly, he would have been allowed to graduate, but he was too impatient to get the war over with and get back to the *New York Times*. "Tell me what street compares to Mott Street in July," he sang, roaring out loud above the sound of the engines of his Marine Corsair fighter plane as he flew countless missions in the Pacific; a hero, a Major by his twenty-first birthday, a Lieutenant Colonel by V-J Day, and, six months later, in Hawaii, a violently angry full Colonel.

"What the fuck do you mean, I can't go home yet? I should have been out on points months ago, sir. Sorry, sir."

"Colonel, I'm sorry, but the General needs you."

"Damn it, sir, what about 'first in, first out'? The General has dozens of other officers, what the hell does he need me for?"

"It seems you have unusual organizational abilities, Colonel."

"I'm a fighter pilot, sir, not a pencil pusher. Sorry, sir."

"I know how you feel, Colonel. I'll talk to the General again about you, but it doesn't look good. He said, 'Tell Amberville that if he wanted out so badly he should have joined the Army Air Force.' "

"That's a fucking insult, sir!"

"I know, Colonel, I know."

World War II had been over for ten months when Colonel Zachary Amberville finally got back to New York City. His father had died in 1943 but Sarah Amberville was living in the family home near Andover. Her husband's life insurance had been meager but her son's flight pay, sent home regularly and saved carefully, was still helping to bring up the younger children.

J. Press was the new civilian's first stop. He couldn't show up at the *Times* in his uniform and medals. It would look ridiculous. Copyboys had to dress like copyboys, he reasoned as he knotted his first personally chosen tie in more than five years; a red one with white polka dots that expressed the jubilation that danced in his eyes. He didn't want to look too Ivy League either, though God knows, the only suit J. Press offered that he could afford was a stiff and hairy tweed that would have been perfectly at home in the Harvard Yard if it had only fit him and been twenty years older. The only thing that looks good, brand new, Zachary Amberville reflected, studying his barely recognizable self in a full-length mirror, is a toothbrush.

"I don't understand," he said to the *Times* receptionist. "I simply do not understand."

"We have as many copyboys as we can possibly use and we have a waiting list," she repeated patiently.

"But I have years of newspaper experience. I've run a newspaper. All I'm asking for is an entry-level job—I didn't ask to be city editor."

"Look, Mr. Amberville, the *Times* promised all its copyboys when they went into the service that their jobs would be waiting for them when they got back. God knows they didn't all get back, but those who did were the first ones to be hired. Then there were the former servicemen who were graduated from journalism schools. In fact we have copyboys who *taught* at journalism schools. It's too bad you never graduated from college. Then, of course, the other former officers . . ."

"Any Marine Colonels?"

"We have a former General, Mr. Amberville, only one, but he *was* a General."

"Air Force?"

"How did you know?"

"It figured. Those fuckers. *Sorry*, Miss!"

"I'd be glad to put you on the waiting list?" she offered, suppressing a giggle.

"I don't have the time to wait. But thanks anyway." As he left the *Times* Building, Zachary Amberville passed an eager group of schoolchildren about to start the tour. He turned aside, and, for the first time in his life, bought a copy of the *Daily News* and opened it to the pages of want ads.

The Five Star Button Company had prospered mightily through a war in which metal and fabric and leather were rationed, yet buttons could be made out of almost any nonessential material. "Change Your Buttons, Change Your Look," had been their slogan and they sold many millions of buttons made of feathers and pom-poms and sequins. They made a superior button, Mr. Nathan Landauer explained to Zachary, a button that you could count on, a button that you could be proud to wear.

"I'm sure of it, sir," Zachary answered, looking around the walls of the office on which cards hung, onto which models of hundreds of different buttons were pinned.

"It's just that the job seems a little, well, not exactly what I'd expect you to be looking for," Landauer continued, admiring the Marine Air Force Colonel's uniform, the four rows of medals, the military haircut.

"It's running a paper, isn't it, sir?"

"Yes . . . if you call a house organ for a button company a 'paper'—frankly I've never thought of it that way . . . just an extra service for our customers, Colonel, and a way to make our employees feel a part of one big family."

"But you publish it every month, you use a regular union printer in New Jersey, there's an office and a part-time secretary that goes with the job, and the salary is sixty-five dollars a week?"

"That's right."

"I'd like the job, sir. Very much."

"You've got it, Colonel."

"Call me Zack. I'll be back in an hour. Just going to change into something more comfortable. Change my buttons, change my luck." Nathan Landauer looked after him wistfully. Those were the best-looking buttons he'd seen in a long, long time. Nathan Junior, proud as he was of him, had spent three years in the Navy, as a simple seaman, and if he had a decent button on his uniform he'd never so much as showed it to his father.

"Nat," Zachary Amberville said to Nathan Landauer, Jr., between bites of pastrami on rye, "don't you want to do something more with your life than make buttons, even if it's more than a living? More than a very good living?"

"What else can I do? It's a family business and Pop expects me to take over for him when he retires in five years. I'm the only son in the family and he built that business up himself from absolutely nothing. It's the biggest button business on Seventh Avenue. I'm trapped, Zack. I just can't break his heart. He's a good guy."

"He's a great guy. But you're not trapped. You can run the business with one hand tied behind you, and with the other . . ."

"With the other?"

"You can become a partner in a magazine."

"Indian say, 'Never invest in show business.' "

"What's that got to do with it?"

"Didn't you see *Annie Get Your Gun*? Ethel Merman asks Chief Sitting Bull how he got so rich and he says, 'Indian never invest in show business' . . . magazines are show business as far as I'm concerned. I don't know fuckall about them."

"Do you know belts? Do you know about bows? Do you know braid? Do you know hooks and eyes and fake flowers and snaps and crochet trim and . . ."

"You can't walk down Forty-sixth Street without picking up a notion about notions, Zack, it's all part of Seventh Avenue . . . a garment has to have something besides buttons on it even if Pop would never admit it. Yeah, sure I know a little, but so what?"

"*Trimming Trades Monthly*. A new magazine."

"You leave me less than overwhelmed. Condé Nast you're not, my friend."

"It could serve a need. Thousands of garment manufacturers in this country making thousands of different kinds of garments, and none of them knows what's new, what's happening, what's available in the trimming trades."

"Somehow they seem to struggle along all right without being up to date, haven't you noticed?"

"Sure, and they didn't need the wheel either until someone thought of it."

"*Trimming Trades Monthly* . . . would it have color photos of pretty girls wearing nothing but little knitted pussy wigs?"

"No, Nathan Junior, with your filthy Navy mind, it would not. It would have information, ads, stories about what's happening on Seventh Avenue, where the trimming trades are going, what the designers are using this month, maybe even next month, what's happening in Paris, how the various companies are doing, who's changing jobs, who's getting promoted, ads and more ads. In black and white, on medium-quality paper so the print doesn't come off on your hands, but nothing too fancy, and a large, handsome picture of your father on the first cover."

"And, as the sun sets slowly over the beautiful downtown garment center, I begin to see what you want, Colonel, sir. And here I've always thought you loved me as a fascinating lunch date."

"You'd own half."

"How much would it cost?"

"We'd need at least fifteen thousand dollars, before we could begin to make money, according to my best estimates. I don't think we'd pick up enough subscribers for—oh, at least six months to begin to make a profit and, of course, I'd have to quit my job at Five Star to spend my time getting ads and writing the magazine, so I've included my salary in there."

"How much would you invest of this fifteen thousand dollars?"

"The idea and my salary. I wouldn't get paid until we made a profit."

"What would you live on?"

"There's plenty of room in your apartment, two can eat as cheaply as one, girls are willing to go Dutch, and I walk to work anyway."

"I'd put up *all* the money?"

"Who else?"

"*You'd* be editor?"

"Who else?"

"Christ, I know I'm an easy lay . . . but what am I supposed to get out of this? Besides half of the nonexistent profits?"

"You'd be publisher. Every magazine has one, God knows why. And you'd own half of the magazine, you'd be more than a button manufacturer, when you met a new girl and she asked you what you did for a living you could say, 'I'm a publisher, my pet.' "

"What if she asked the name of the magazine?"

"You'd be on your own . . . lie, say anything you like . . . and when you finally meet a girl who really loves you then you can tell her. But I can't change the name, Nat, it's got to tell you what the magazine's about or nobody will go for it."

"*Playboy*. I'll tell them it's called *Playboy*," Nathan Junior said dreamily.

"That's a *lousy* name for a magazine, Nat. But suit yourself. Let's go visit your bank before it closes."

Trimming Trades Monthly broke even in four months and soon Zack Amberville was able to pay himself a salary of a hundred dollars a week. Since he still lived at Nathan Junior's he sent most of it back to his mother.

Minnie was in her first year at Dana Hall Junior College and Cutter, at fourteen, was going to Andover. Sarah Amberville had found a job in a gift shop and between her modest wages and Zachary's earnings they were able to send the younger children to the best of schools, in spite of the fact that neither of them had won scholarships. In fact Minnie was lucky to get into Dana Hall, hardly a center of intellectual ferment, but she was so pretty and droll and happy that nobody minded that she never could better her C average, try as she would. Cutter, on the other hand, had a good, if lazy mind, but he chose not to work too hard at his studies, chose it coldbloodedly, because boys who were too bright were always menaced by unpopularity and he wanted popularity above all.

Cutter Dale Amberville, even in his cradle, had shown that he was going to take after the Andersons. He had grown quickly into a tall, exceptionally blond boy with the Swedish blue eyes of his ancestors, a fine-looking youth with an evil, ugly worm living and growing in his heart. He had despised growing up on the edge of poverty. As long as he could remember he had known that he was one of the poor Cutters, the poor Andersons, the poor Dales and the poor Ambervilles, in a small community in which the four families were all cousins to some degree and in which these distinctions of wealth were closely calculated and never mentioned.

Cutter looked down on his father's choice of career. Why pour your heart into a newspaper which obviously would never make any money? What kind of man would make such a choice? But the disregard he felt for his father was mild compared to the absolute repudiation he felt toward his brother whenever he was forced to realize that he was being supported by Zachary. However, he considered himself too far removed from the ordinary to go out and get a job himself. He was related to all of the best families in town; it was unthinkable that he should find himself delivering their groceries or standing behind a counter making sodas for them. Nor had his mother ever suggested such a thing, for she wanted Cutter not to know the struggle that Zachary had shouldered.

Sarah Amberville never suspected how Cutter felt about his brother, never knew that Zachary had always seemed sickeningly, terrifyingly all-powerful to her youngest child. Cutter judged him with contempt, mixed with baseless fear. Zachary was a violent, insufferable, potentially dangerous wind who swept into the quiet house whenever he could find time and filled it with his boisterous, laughing, uncouth presence, immediately becoming the center of his mother's and father's total attention. It seemed clear to Cutter that their pride in this almost stranger, this loud, brash, bold brother who hadn't lived at home since he, Cutter, was five, left his parents no room to remember that he was alive, much less be interested in him.

Bitterly he would return, time and time again, to dozens of memories of his childhood, telling them to himself like a rosary. There had been the time when he was eight and had the leading role in the school play but all his parents could concentrate on was the fact that his brother had gone off to fight in the war. For the next four years, no matter how popular he was in school, no matter that he became a junior tennis champion of Massachusetts, his parents were constantly waiting, every minute of every day, for news of their other son, the war hero, the fighter pilot. And when the war was finally over had his mother finally turned to him? No. Never. Not once. What could a teenaged boy bring home to show his mother that would compare to a letter from Zachary telling her of the new magazine he was creating in New York? To a copy of the magazine itself?

Cutter Amberville had always been so sure that Zachary had sucked up for himself all that was worth having that he turned secretive and bitter, not giving his parents a chance to become involved in his life. The heavy, omnipotent shadow of his brother had, Cutter *knew*, deprived him of the love and attention that would rightfully have been his. He'd been shoved aside, to the margin of his parents' life, and he interpreted his brother's generosity as bones thrown to a dog. The more Zachary gave him the more he owed him and the more Cutter owed his brother the more he hated him, with a passionate, permanent hatred that was deeper than any love he would ever know, the hatred that only early, unspeakable *envy* of one sibling for another can inspire.

At Andover, Cutter said as little as he could about his family. He certainly never intended to admit that his fees were paid by a mother who worked and a brother who edited a magazine with a name of which he was ashamed. He concentrated on developing his personal popularity within the school, using flattery as his weapon of choice. He cultivated the ability to ask those subtle questions that put other boys in the best possible light and, at an age when self-centered boasting was the rule, he learned the power of the person who would listen and admire. The worm in his heart was his teacher. He was excellent at sports but his marks were deliberately average. Quickly he became an accomplished courtier who bothered to cultivate only the boys whose parents were both rich and powerful. His good looks were highly finished, with strong, natural distinction, and a bred-in-the-bone strength. His well-cut hair covered a long, strongly shaped skull; Cutter's blue eyes could hold those of others with a steady, sincere expression, and he had trained himself not to use too often that practiced smile that seemed so charmingly natural.

Zachary was proud of the serious, striking teenager, although he found curiously little to talk to him about on the rare occasions when they were together, for now his brother's school holidays and weekends were invariably spent visiting in some home where young Cutter Amberville was regarded as a most welcome guest.

⅔

One autumn Monday of 1948, Nathan Landauer, Jr., walked into the offices Zachary had rented, with a combination of fearful joy and deep embarrassment on his pleasant face.

"Zack, I met a girl," he mumbled. "At a football game, on Saturday. She was with some guy who knows your family in Andover, nobody she cared about, so I persuaded him to get lost."

"There are a million girls in New York and you've met half of them. . . . What's so special about her?" Zachary asked, putting his feet up on his desk.

"Everything. She's perfect. I even told her the name of the magazine, the real name, I mean."

"And she didn't fall down shrieking with humiliating laughter?"

"No, not exactly. She thought it was very interesting, not just interesting but odd, considering that I'm the publisher of *Trimming Trades* and you're the editor and she and I had never met before. She said you must have been keeping us apart on purpose. Were you, Zack? Why didn't you ever introduce us, anyway?"

"Introduce you?"

"To Minnie?"

"Minnie? What Minnie?"

"Minnie your sister. The most beautiful, the most adorable, the . . . how come you never told me about her—I thought I was your best friend."

"It never crossed my mind. She's just a kid—eighteen—and you're a dirty-minded former Naval person who doesn't think about anything but getting laid."

"I'm an *ex*-dirty-minded former Naval person. I've reformed. Listen, Zack, buy my half of *Trimming Trades*. I'll practically give it to you."

"Are you crazy? Why would you want to sell? It's making a hell of a lot of dough between the ads, the new subscriptions and the low cost of production."

"I know, but I don't believe in doing business with family . . . it's the classic way to lose a friend."

"Family? Hold on now. Aren't you taking a lot for granted? Doesn't Minnie have anything to say about this?"

"After the football game we had drinks. After drinks we had dinner. At dinner we decided to get married. In two weeks you'll be my brother-in-law." Nathan Junior looked every one of his twenty-five years as he entered into manhood.

"My God, you're serious, Seaman Landauer."

"Some things you know right away. I knew about Minnie right away and she knew about me. That's the advantage of all my experience."

"You two were simply made for each other. Minnie never needed experience." Zachary stood up and grabbed his former partner in a giant hug. "How much do you want for your half?"

"Pay me what you figure is fair. I'll lend you the money to buy it."

"Love doth make suckers of us all," Zack yelled and waltzed Nat around the office. "Congratulations, sucker!"

⅔

Owning a magazine, becoming the sole proprietor, unleashed in Zachary Amberville all the ambitions he had not quite dared to entertain before. He had been marked by the Depression more than he realized and a certain natural caution had always restrained a devouring desire to create, to risk, to rule.

Soon after the marriage of his sister Minnie he launched his second magazine, *Style*. From everything he had learned about the garment industry and fashion magazines he knew that there was a place for a magazine that would appeal to women who couldn't afford to buy the clothes shown in *Vogue* and *Harper's Bazaar*, who were obviously too old for *Mademoiselle*, yet were too sophisticated for *Glamour*, with its rosy-cheeked, just-out-of-college models.

He went to banks for the money to start *Style* and they lent it to him, on the basis of the balance sheet of *Trimming Trades Monthly*. The late 1940s and early 1950s were prosperous ones for publishing, as the country entered a postwar boom economy and Americans, hungry for the material things of life, bought magazines with the same greed as they bought new cars.

Style made money almost from its first issue. Zachary Amberville had an invaluable knack for discovering and promoting new talent, and *Style* owed much of its immediate success to the talents of an unknown illustrator, Pavka Mayer, whom Zack had first hired to do black-and-white sketches for *Trimming Trades*.

Pavka had come to the United States in 1936, at the age of eighteen, a Berliner whose family had been wise enough to leave Germany. He had spent the war in the Army, landing on Utah Beach on D-Day, officially a translator and unofficially, as the Army fought its way up to Paris, a procurer of milk, hard cider, and fresh meat in return for blankets, soap, and sugar. Even an occasional entire jeep had been known to disappear along the route of Pavka's barter service.

"Go to it, Pavka," Zachary Amberville had told the diminutive, dapper man who was only five years older than he was. "Use any photographers you want, any models, any quality paper, any printer. We have too much competition. We can't hold back, we simply have to give the reader more than anybody else."

Pavka worked hand-in-hand with the fashion editor, another unknown named Zelda Powers. Zachary had spotted her toiling away in a back room at Norman Norell's—for even the great Norell could not design without buttons—and he had been struck by an immediate appreciation of her eccentric, brilliant, purely personal style. She was from Chicago, a passionate student of fashion who would work at anything as long as it kept her near the world in which clothes were created.

"Listen, Zelda, you don't know anything about being the editor of a fashion magazine," Zachary said to her. "That's why I want you. Give me the kind of magazine no one else has ever put out. The kind you'd want yourself. No imitations . . . strictly original. Do anything, *anything* you want, so long as you keep the advertisers happy and show their clothes the minimum amount of times you have to. Remember who's in your audience—and give them dreams they can *afford*, but give it to them your way."

Pavka and Powers, according to people who watched the progress of fashion magazines, were single-handedly responsible for the unexpected emergence of *Style* as a force and a presence. But people who had met Zachary Amberville knew otherwise.

By 1951 Zachary had made his fifth million. The first one had been due to *Trimming Trades* and *Style*, the others to *Style* and particularly *Seven Days*. He founded the weekly in 1950 with the large size and photo format of *Life* and *Look*. But with a difference. He had made his own studies of the reading habits of the American woman and he had become convinced that there wasn't a female so high-minded that she wouldn't read a dozen movie magazines in private if she were sure no one would see her doing it. He understood the deep appeal of gossip columns and the power of men, like Walter Winchell, who seemed to take the public behind the scenes. He realized that there would always be a society column in every newspaper, no matter how much some people deplored it.

Average people, who were almost everybody, wanted to know about non-average people, wanted to know *everything* about them, Zachary told himself as he walked the streets of Manhattan. He visualized a big shining weekly magazine with lots of color pictures; not heavy with text and letters and editorials, not concerned with farmers or football or Middle America, not anxious about the rest of the world and its miseries, not slightly to the right like *Life* or slightly to the left like *Look*, but completely apolitical and resolutely unserious. A magazine that would tell you what had been going on in the last seven days in the lives of glamorous, exciting, famous people, and tell it for an American audience in a way they'd never been told before, in a way that was irreverent, that didn't keep any secrets that its libel lawyers didn't say it had to keep, that held no man or woman sacred, yet realized that movie stars and royalty were more interesting than anyone else even if the United States was a democracy. *Especially* because it was a democracy.

Zachary hired as many of the best writers in America as he could find to craft the short articles that accompanied the many photographs. "Don't give me literature," he told them, "give me a first-rate blazing read and give it to me with guts . . . we're not a nation of intellectuals, as you may have noticed. It's too bad, but facts are facts. I want it fascinating, I want it red-hot and I want it yesterday."

Pavka Mayer took over the art direction of *Seven Days* and made it so piss-elegant that no one who read it noticed that it hardly appealed to their finer instincts. The world's best photographers were delighted to buzz off to all the corners of the world for higher prices than were paid by *Life* or its European rival, *Paris Match*. *Seven Days* was a wild, runaway, classic hit that became a national addiction almost overnight.

Late in 1951 Zachary Amberville decided to visit London. He'd been working too hard and as each of his European bureaus opened he'd missed the excitement of hiring bureau chiefs and seeing them get under way. London was his most important foreign bureau, except for the Paris office of *Style*, so he planned to stop there first. His executive secretary suggested that it might even be a good idea, while he was in England, to get a haircut and have some suits made.

"That's not even a hint, honeybunch."

"It wasn't meant to be, Mr. Amberville, it's not suitable for a man of your position to look the way you do. You're not even thirty and you could be a very handsome man if you cared to be," Miss Briny said with determination.

"I'm clean, aren't I? And so's my shirt. Even my shoes are polished. What's your problem?"

"A secretary is only as distinguished as the man she works for. You're undermining my position in the Executive Secretaries' Lunch Club, Mr. Amberville. Everyone else's boss has his suits made to order on Savile Row, he goes to the St. Regis for a haircut at least every ten days, his shoes are made by Lobb but you . . . you don't even go to Barney's," she complained tartly. "You don't belong to any exclusive clubs, you eat a sandwich at your desk instead of going to the best restaurants, you're never photographed in nightclubs with beautiful girls—I just don't know how to *explain* you."

"Did you ever tell them what you make?"

"Overpaying your secretary isn't what makes a man chic," Miss Briny sniffed.

"Honeybunch, your values are screwed up. But I'll think about that haircut."

Zachary refused to justify his private life to his secretary. It was none of her business. The occupations of a well-known bachelor around town were his idea of nothing to do. He didn't have the time or the interest. He knew a number of women, damned attractive ones, but somehow he'd never fallen in love. Too selfish? Too preoccupied with his magazines? Too cynical? No, why try to kid himself, he was too fucking romantic. Somewhere in the back of his mind there was a dream girl, and if that wasn't pure corn, what was? She was gentle, pure, idealistic; hardly a type who flourished in Manhattan. She was as unreal as she was beautiful and one day he'd get her out of his mind and settle for a gorgeous, sensible broad with a sense of humor. He needed a wife, if only to protect him from his secretary.

4

Nobody in her noble family could claim to understand the Honorable Lily Davina Adamsfield but they were as proud of her as if she'd been a rare portrait by Leonardo da Vinci, passed with reverence from one generation to another, the family treasure. She was the only child of the nineteenth Baronet and second Viscount Evelyn Gilbert Basil Adamsfield and Viscountess Maxime Emma Adamsfield, born the Honorable Maxime Emma Hazel. Her many cousins, male and female, were perfectly upstanding, healthy and appropriate, and they did the expected things. They cared for the family estates, they hunted, fished, collected, gardened, took an interest in good works and married the obviously appropriate young members of their own world with whom they would have quite satisfactory and appropriate children.

Ah, but Lily! Like so many of her friends, she had started to go to dancing school at the age of four. Miss Vacani's was and is the proper institution to which little aristocratic girls, and junior members of the Royal Family, are routinely sent to learn to waltz and polka. Almost all of them pass through Miss Vacani's as routinely as they learn to mount a horse. But Lily turned out to be one of the very few, the unpredictable yet constant few, who become utterly possessed by the ballet training from the very first moment. There is nothing any parent can do to quench this passion, as they learn in time, often to their regret.

At eight Lily had auditioned for the Royal Ballet School which she attended after school three times a week. She grasped ballet to her as if it were a vocation, as if she had had a visitation.

"If we were Catholics," her mother had said to her father, "that girl would be counting the days until she could enter a convent."

"She certainly isn't one for chatter," her father had grumbled. "You'd almost think she already belonged to one of those orders that take a vow of silence."

"Now darling, that's not entirely fair. Lily just has a problem expressing herself—she's never been an easy talker. Perhaps that's why dancing is so important to her," Lady Maxime had replied soothingly.

When she was eleven Lily was able to audition for and be accepted by the Royal Ballet Upper School where she could combine her academic and ballet studies. Her life was totally absorbed by her work and, racing from one class to another with her schoolmates, she never minded that she had to renounce all the traditional activities of other girls of her background. The only human contacts in her life besides her parents were with her teachers and her fellow students and even those were limited to a necessary minimum. Lily wasn't at the Royal to make friends with her rivals, for by the age of eight she had an almost adult understanding of the nature of the ferocious competition that rages in the world of ballet, a lifelong competition that is only interrupted when a dancer finally retires.

For years her greatest fear was that she might grow too tall to dance. If she had reached five feet seven and a half or, God help her, five feet eight, she would have outgrown her future. Her discussions with other dancers were limited to the obsessive issue of height and her second greatest fear, that she might "get an injury," a terrible, ever-present possibility they all shared equally.

When she had completed the Upper School Lily's teachers agreed that she had so much promise that she should study for yet another year at the school run by Sir Charles Forsythe, a great dancer and teacher who had been formed by Anthony Tudor and Frederick Aston. This additional year of training would give her the final polish that would enable her to audition most successfully for one of the great ballet companies of the world.

Lily Adamsfield had grown into a girl of exceptional beauty, with gray-blue-green eyes as changeable as opals; lunar eyes that she never stopped in front of a mirror to admire. They were there merely to be enlarged by the stylized black makeup that she wore on stage. Her lovely hands, her long fingers, existed only to extend those gestures of languor and fragility that require the strength of a stevedore to look effortless. She had tiny breasts, broad, well-defined shoulders, arms and legs that were almost too elongated in comparison to her torso but perfect for the demands of the ballet; no heaviness or extra flesh anywhere, a flat back and a neck of exceptional grace; a body that had no other function than to dance. Her naked feet, without toe shoes, looked a thousand years old.

It never occurred to Lily that she was missing the pleasures of being admired by young men, for the only males whom she thought about were her partners in class; the only criteria by which she judged them were their elevations, the number of their leaps, the security with which they gripped her waist when they lifted her. She came into occasional contact with boys of her own social world and she had difficulty in finding anything to say to them. Outside of the cloister of the world of dance she had a speaking voice that, for all its silver sweetness, was tremulous, even slightly timid.

When Lily wasn't dressed in her rehearsal clothes, the beloved, well-worn tights, leg warmers, leotards, and sweaters that turned her into a bundle of moving rags, she had no idea what to wear. Viscountess Adamsfield, a woman of taste, chose all her clothes for her. Lily had no conversational ability, no practice at banter, nothing to say about the world of sports, of films, of new cars or horses. Any boy of her own age who was attracted by her newmoon loveliness soon gave up trying to get her to respond, or at least to pay some attention to him, and wandered off in search of a girl with more animation.

However, her parents and Lily's many cousins had no concern about this strange swan they had nurtured. She was wonderfully different, what did it matter that she wouldn't have any quick, worldly success as an adolescent? She would, as a matter of course, be presented at Court. It would be simply *too* odd for her not to make that necessary curtsy, not to have her photograph taken by Lenare, not to enter the grown-up world, but Lily drew the line at a debut, a party, a season. She had no time for any of those rituals for she was destined for glory. Indeed all their world knew that the Adamsfields' youngest girl was going to become another Margot Fonteyn. Her devoted family was as convinced of Lily's future as Lily was herself.

She took no credit for the conformation of the body with which she had been born but she knew that without her unquestioning, willing slavery to the almost unendurably hard work of ballet, without her unswerving determination, the mere possession of a dancer's body would mean nothing. Her muscles and sinews and the articulations of her joints, the length of her limbs, were a lucky accident of birth. But the career of a prima ballerina was not made by a body alone, it depended on something else, something even more than talent, something in the spirit, and whatever that something was, she knew absolutely that she had it.

No one who observed the shy girl who used no makeup, who wore her long, fair hair falling carelessly around her face, who hesitated on entering a room, who avoided conversation, who walked with an unstudied, felicitous grace but kept her eyes fixed in the middle distance, could have guessed at the thirsty ambition that never was far from her thoughts. She was violently proud, viciously proud, and she carried this strong plant of pride within her as well concealed as if it were a newly conceived child.

"She's an exceptionally accomplished performer," the familiar voice said. "There's no doubt that they'll accept her at the Royal."

Lily, on her way out of the school building, and already late for dinner, hesitated in the corridor. Sir Charles was talking to someone behind his half-closed door. Who else, she asked herself in anguish, which other girl among her classmates, her competition, would have such an easy time getting into the Royal Ballet? She had been given the lion's share of leading female roles this past year, but evidently she must have a rival. Jane Broadhurst? Anita Hamilton? Were they good enough for Covent Garden? Both strong dancers, but *that* good? She stood perfectly still, waiting to hear more.

"She could try for other companies, too . . . even the New York City Center." Lily clenched her fists. The second voice was that of her ballet mistress, Alma Grey. "Or perhaps Copenhagen—they need new dancers there since Laura and the other two were lured away to New York."

The Royal Danish? Lily repeated to herself, unbelievingly. It simply was not possible. There was no one to whom such prizes should fall but her.

"Yes, Alma my dear," she heard Sir Charles say with finality, "there really isn't a first-rate company in the world that wouldn't jump at Lily. Fifteen years ago, even ten, I would have said she might be too tall, at five feet and seven inches, but now that's not a serious problem if she's stopped growing. My regret is that she should be as good as she is . . ."

"Ah," sighed the ballet mistress, "it's heartbreaking . . . to come so close, so very, very close. This year she almost . . . yes, Charles, yes . . . she almost crossed that barrier. I promise you that there were moments when I prayed for her, as I watched, and then . . . no, I said to myself, no, it just isn't going to happen. She has such beauty, and technically nothing is missing. Yet . . . somehow . . . that *other* thing, that thing we can't put a name to, that thing that the public recognizes immediately, that lifts them out of their seats, that something just is *not* there."

"I have often thought that it is a question, in some way, of personality," Sir Charles mused.

"As for me, I don't try to dissect it. I prefer to call it magic," Alec Grey replied.

"She can dance all the second roles, in any first-rate international company," Charles Forsythe said judiciously, "and principal roles in lesser companies."

"Prima ballerina? I disagree. Lily will never be a prima ballerina. My dear Charles, you have to admit that there are no *almost* prima ballerinas," Alma Grey said sharply.

"There are indisputable prima ballerinas and there are greater prima ballerinas who sometimes are given the 'Assoluta' to console them as they age, but I suppose that was wishful thinking. . . . There are no 'almost' prima ballerinas . . . with that I must reluctantly agree."

"A strange metier, Charles, when you get right down to it, an unnatural sort of thing, and desperately unfair, I often think. As hard as we teach, as hard as they work, no one can really be sure until they have *already* devoted their youth . . . oh, of course there are those exceptions, the ones you know about immediately, but Lily never was one of them."

"And just how many have you seen in your lifetime, my dear?"

"Only four, Charles, as you know perfectly well. I'm waiting for the fifth. There will always be another, one of these days."

"Perhaps next year? Or the year after?"

"One can hope."

Envious, Lily thought, fleeing into the street so blindly that she was almost hit by a taxi. Old, disgustingly old, dried out, vile, pitiful, ignorant and above all *envious*, pure pig envy of her youth, her talent, a talent neither of them had ever had, those two old people raving on about something they admitted they couldn't even find words to explain, faking crocodile tears, gloating to each other, presuming to judge her, only too thrilled to be able to say she wasn't good enough at the same time they had to admit, were literally forced to admit that any ballet company in the world would want her.

Envy. She'd known about envy since she started dancing, Lily raged as she walked home as quickly as possible. She knew well the envy of her classmates each time she was singled out, praised, given a principal role. Envy meant that she was the best, the infallible sign, the one emotion no one could conceal, the one tribute that reassured her absolutely. Envy was her ally. But it made her sick to find out that even Sir Charles and Alma Grey weren't immune . . . they were supposed to be teachers, guiding and caring, not competitive; beyond envy, but obviously that was too much to expect from human nature. They would go to their graves envying her, shriveled, wasted, wizened with *envy*, for what else could it be? They nauseated her, she could almost feel sorry for them if they weren't so completely revolting. She walked faster, almost running, trying to put the words she had overheard out of her mind. Why should she waste another minute thinking about something that couldn't possibly be true? She walked with her head high, her shoulders back, with the *portée* of a prima ballerina, the finest way a human body can move.

"Lily, you're so late. Is everything all right?" Lady Maxime called from the drawing room.

"Of course it is, Mother. I'm sorry if I've kept you waiting . . . I won't be a minute."

Damn Miss Briny, Zachary Amberville thought, he should either have brought her along or not listened to her sartorial jitters. He stood, jacketless, in front of a heavy wooden table on which were piled, in constantly sliding heaps, bolt after bolt of the finest silks and cottons in the world, solids, checks, stripes, plaids, a bewilderment of shirtings. The Bespoke Department of Turnbull and Asser was no place for a man who hated to shop and didn't have a clear idea of what he was looking for in the first place. The polite young salesman had finally left him alone, to meditate on a choice, after an hour of making fruitless suggestions and draping various lengths of fabric over Zachary's shoulder. He had brought over smaller swatches in little booklets, dozens of them, but the more choice there was, the more difficult it was to decide on anything.

Pale blue? That seemed to be the only sensible and safe idea but Zachary refused to be reduced to ordering custom-made shirts in the same solid color he'd been buying for years. Nor could he just leave quietly, not after having taken up so much of the salesman's time. Resolutely he started to eliminate the materials he couldn't imagine himself wearing, putting those bolts to one side. One thing he had learned about the British this Saturday morning, he reflected, was that loud shirtings were highly considered. Never had he seen so many perfectly outrageous candy-ass contrasts in stripes, bold checks and plaids so aggressive that only a gangster could even consider them.

Engrossed, determined, he finally picked out four possible fabrics and, as the salesman had shown him, released them from the bolts, in long lengths, and swathed himself in them. He studied himself in the mirror and shook his head in dismay. There was almost no light, either electric or natural, in the small room, and all the quiet stripes he had picked out seemed almost identical. He looked as if he were wearing a Bedouin tent.

"Excuse me, but would you mind giving me some advice?" he said, in the direction of a female figure he had vaguely noticed sitting for some time on a little couch, while an older man with whom she had entered the shop was deep in conference with his salesman.

"Forgive me?" she said, startled, as if aroused from a dream.

"Advice. I've got to have a woman's advice. Would you mind getting up and taking a look? Tell me what you think about these stripes. Don't be polite . . . if you don't like them, say so. I'd come over, but if I do these bolts will unwind all over the floor. I'm anchored to this table and I've lost my salesman's attention."

"I'll fetch him for you."

"Don't bother, he's given up on me. I need a fresh eye."

Reluctantly, Lily Adamsfield rose and approached him. Odd manners, but what could you expect of an American?

Hell, she's awfully young. Well, that just isn't going to matter, Zachary thought in a flash of absolute certainty that left no room for doubt. In one glance at Lily he fell in love, in love with her oval face framed with thick, straight sheaths of fair hair, in love with her eyes, their gray depths holding glints of the misty sea, with her mouth, vividly sweet in form, with a trace of delicious sadness, meant to be kissed away. He fell in love forever. She was his girl. And so vulnerable. If he'd known that the girl of his dreams really existed he would have come for her long ago. Zachary let the shirtings fall from his shoulders and took Lily's hand in his.

"We'll go now and have lunch," he told her.

The Honorable Lily Davina Adamsfield, just eighteen, a queen of the nymphs in her Norman Hartnell dress of priceless lace, and Zachary Anderson Amberville were married a month later, in January of 1952, with the bewildered blessings of Viscount and Viscountess Adamsfield, at St. Margaret's Westminster, in front of four hundred and fifty people, including the recently crowned Queen Elizabeth and Prince Philip, Miss Briny, Pavka Mayer, the entire Landauer family and Sarah Amberville. Only Cutter, who was in the middle of exams, was missing. Lily had seated Sir Charles, Alma Grey and all her fellow ballet students in the second row, directly behind the Queen and her parents.

Let them have a good look, a really good, long look, she mused as she carefully arranged their placement, at how happy she was, even as she sacrificed her career, her never-to-be-questioned future as a prima ballerina. She would always dance. Dance was essential but she wouldn't perform. The difficult, dedicated, single-minded existence demanded of a prima ballerina couldn't be included in the triumphant life that lay so radiantly, so securely before her as the wife of this amazingly forceful American, a man who worshipped her, who believed in her absolutely.

As she had told her astonished mother, if she had to give nightly performances it wouldn't be fair to Zachary. Joining the New York City Center Ballet was out of the question now. "I'll have the best of both worlds . . . all I'm giving up is a title, two words, 'prima ballerina.' What if I'd wasted my life on being those two little words, Mother? I can't marry Zachary and lead the life I thought I wanted. I have to grow up, and choice is part of growing. Yes, it is a sacrifice, you're not wrong, but it's a sacrifice I want to make. A sacrifice I must make. It's not a waste, I promise you. All those years haven't gone for nothing—I've just outgrown that life. Believe me, Mother, I know what I'm doing."

He'd taught her to kiss, Zachery thought in the state of light-headed euphoria that he seemed to have entered into permanently from the day he first saw Lily. She hadn't known how to kiss, she had never been kissed, he'd let everything he possessed that if he hadn't come to England he could have spent the rest of his life in the United States without finding a girl who looked like Lily and had never been kissed.

And now he had to teach her to make love. Oh Jesus, if only it were a year from now and they were all settled into the big house she would pick out for them on any New York street that pleased her, if only they were going up to bed in a familiar room filled with all the beautiful things she was going to buy, to a bed with sheets that didn't have the cold, immaculate, polished finish possessed by these sheets in the Bridal Suite at Claridge's. Friendly sheets, damn it, might help. Or even a French hotel. Claridge's was too majestically British. Tomorrow they'd be in Paris, but tomorrow wasn't tonight.

If only he were one of the Ambervilles from centuries past facing a traditional New England wedding night with a virgin bride, something that would have been the only possible and natural state of affairs, just what he had been brought up to expect. Tradition was what he needed. Some ordinary old-fashioned traditional values. Maybe next year he'd vote Republican.

He suddenly remembered his own first experience, with one of the student nurses from St. Luke's Hospital, whose residence window was opposite his dormitory windows in Columbia's Hamilton Hall. He'd been a fifteen-year-old freshman and she'd been young too, but not as young as he. Whatever her age, she'd known exactly where and when and particularly how. Know-how . . . that was all it took. Every girl he'd made love to since that memorable night had had some degree of know-how, and not a virgin among them.

But he hadn't fallen in love before. So, he was a sort of virgin too, a twenty-nine-year-old emotional virgin, a virgin Marine fighter pilot, a virgin owner of three magazines, a many-times-over-millionaire virgin, a virgin who had had dozens of women, more than he could count. "Stop thinking," Zachary said out loud to himself in his dressing room. "It ain't helping."

He was momentarily reassured by the first sight of Lily in front of the wood fire that was burning in their immense paneled bedroom. He never realized, when he took her in his arms and felt the chill of her skin, that she owed the supreme composure with which she stood so quietly in her white satin and lace peignoir to hundreds of rehearsals of *Giselle*, to muscle memory of *Coppelia*, to the nights on which she had danced Odette in *Swan Lake*. The posture developed for dancers during a hundred and fifty years of classical ballet will sustain any one of them in any situation for the raising of any curtain. But once Zachary and Lily lay together in the wide bed, once she had laid her peignoir on a chair and wore only a satin nightgown with thin shoulder straps, he became aware that in spite of the warmth of the room she was shivering.

"Come on, kid, this is all too damned silly," he announced, bundling her up, blankets and all, and carrying her over to sit in his lap in a deep chair in front of the fire. "I feel as if we should invite the room-service waiters and chambermaids in to watch . . . it's like those royal wedding nights I've read about in the old days where everyone stood around putting the poor bride and groom to bed, gaping and, no doubt, making bawdy jokes."

"Tell me a bawdy joke," Lily said, trying to smile.

"You probably wouldn't understand the ones I know. And I can never remember punch lines anyway. It's one of my failures in life, but it makes me a hell of a good audience because every joke's new to me."

"What are your other failures?" she asked seriously.

"I can't play golf, always lose money at the track, but I still love to bet, I can't remember vintage years of wine or even the difference between a Bordeaux and a Burgundy, I never got that job as a copyboy at the *New York Times*. . . ."

"I mean real failures, major ones, the kind you never recover from," she said, unsmiling.

"I don't think I've made any. And I don't intend to. Not ever."

"That's what I thought about you the day we met . . . you're not a man who fails at anything in life."

"Darling, you sound so fierce." He looked in astonishment at Lily, his mysterious, timorous, inexperienced bride, whose every gesture seemed at once a caress and a quest for nourishment, yet whose expression was suddenly intent in a way he'd never seen before.

"You don't really know me, Zachary. I am fierce," she said in a voice that was so naturally angelic that he simply laughed and kissed her lips. She responded with the still awkward willingness that he found so touching in her. He put his arms around Lily under the layers of blankets. She was warmer now, more relaxed, the shivering had stopped. He ran his blunt fingers over the column of her neck, touching with wonder the astonishing curve where her neck met her shoulder. His hand ventured to her collarbone, felt the strength, the power under the muscles of her slim shoulders. He could ring her upper arm with one of his large hands. There was a delicate tautness there that made him alarmingly aware of the difference in the stuff of which they were made. She was like steel covered with silk and he was just flesh, ordinary flesh.

Excitement flowed through his veins, moving like a forest fire that has been started by lightning in a dozen different places at once, but he kept himself under absolute control. There was only one single thing he knew about teaching Lily how to make love and that was to take it easy, to go as slowly and as tenderly as was humanly possible, or, if it weren't possible for a human, to become inhumanly controlled. Minutes passed, while Lily, her eyes tightly shut, became aware of Zachary's fingertips gliding with the faintest of pressure from her shoulder to her elbow. The strap of her nightgown was a thin roll of satin, and it slipped off a shoulder, exposing one of her small, saucer-shaped breasts with a tiny, flat nipple, of a pink so pale that it made almost no contrast to the whiteness of her skin. Zachary saw her breast by the light of the fire, caught his breath, squeezed his thighs together mercilessly, and kept his hand away from the ravishing little mound. She wasn't ready to be touched yet, he told himself, as he lightly brushed his lips along her neck, under her hair. Lily made no sound at all and sat motionless, almost weightless in his lap, but he could feel that she was holding herself together tightly, scarcely breathing.

"Relax my darling, my baby, I won't do anything you don't want me to do, there's no rush, we have all the time in the world," he whispered to her, but she gave no sign of hearing him. His fingers left her elbow and descended caressingly along her forearm, reached her wrist and then spread out to cover her hand with his. In a quick movement that surprised him she turned her palm toward his palm, grasped his hand and lifted it up so that it abruptly covered her breast. "No darling, no, you don't have to, it's all right," he said in a low voice and took his hand away. She was only doing what she imagined was expected of her, he thought. Mutely she kissed his mouth, pressing her cool lips on his, seeming more like a child in search of security than a woman. He ground his teeth together to keep himself from thrusting his tongue between her lips. In the last month he had taught her to kiss without keeping her lips tightly together but she had retreated from his tongue as often as she had accepted it, and he was unwilling to initiate anything she might not want, tonight of all nights.

Lily, with a quick shrug of her other shoulder, caused the second strap of her nightgown to fall away from her body. With the blankets still covering her legs she sat defiantly upright on Zachary's knees, naked from the waist, her eyes still closed but her torso entirely revealed, a torso in which the combination of the girlishness of her immature breasts and the almost boylike width of her shoulders created a furiously erotic counterpoint. From her breasts to her waist she could have been molded out of ivory, Zachary thought. He could count her ribs, he could see her heart beating, the veins of her chest made an eternally memorable design under her pale skin. Using the utmost deliberation he traveled the largest of the veins above her breasts with his index finger, careful not to wander between her breasts, not to risk boldness too soon. He had to cross one of his legs over the other to restrain his rearing penis from forcing itself out between his thighs, for no matter how he fought to keep them together, the thick tip had a life of its own and nothing could keep it from swelling upward.

Lily seemed to shudder. Was she still cold or was she finally impatient? he wondered, and he let himself touch the tip of a nipple with one finger, touch it lightly, just brushing it, watching to see if she had any reaction. She neither shrank back nor pressed forward, but it seemed to Zachary that the nipple had risen, that it was distinctly standing up from her breast, and when he touched her other nipple he saw, with joy, that it too responded to his caress. "Yes, yes, that's right, that's good, that feels good," he muttered between his teeth, willing himself not to frighten her now that she was just beginning to enjoy it. He teased her nipples for minutes more, tracing their small circles around and around, returning again and again to the points that were now distinctly firm, and finally he bent his head and took one of the hard buds into his mouth, circling it with his tongue for a long moment before he actually dared to suck on it. Lily seemed to tense herself when he started to suck and he stopped, thinking, with an emotion that was almost reverence, that it was the first time a man's mouth had ever been on her body, on her private places, but finally with another sudden and resolute movement she pulled his head back toward her breast with one hand and with the other she cupped her breast and offered it to him, put it in his mouth and mumbled, "Don't stop."

Soon both nipples were wet, lapped and tugged into small islands of engorged tissue, and when Zachary saw how big they had grown he picked Lily up, her nightgown slithering down the length of her body as he crossed the room. He put her down on the bed carefully and lay down next to her, preserving a distance between them so that she would not feel his rigid penis that lay straight up over his stomach, jerking in violent impatience. He rose on one elbow and with his other hand he tentatively smoothed her tiny waist, her elegantly narrow hips, her supple, firm, supremely developed thighs, learning the shape of the kind of body he had never seen on any other woman. Naked, Lily was a divinity, he knew, like the statue of a goddess from some other civilization, some finer civilization. His reverence grew, painfully mixed with the most maddened desire he'd ever felt when he saw Lily's pubic hair, blond and slightly curly and so much thicker than he had ever expected, over the rise of her mound of Venus, the pubic hair of a woman, not a girl. She quivered slightly under his hand, turning her head from side to side, her eyes still closed, but just as she didn't push him away she didn't put out her hands to touch him. It was almost as if she were asleep, he thought, almost as if she wanted him to take her in a dream.

After Zachary had touched as much of Lily's proffered body as he could, for as long as he could endure the giving of caress after caress, without moving closer, he pulled her to him and put one arm under her head. He took his free hand and put one of his fingers into his own mouth and wet it thoroughly. With that gentle finger he carefully parted her pubic hair and found the concealed entrance to her vagina. Slowly, a fraction of an inch at a time, he worked his finger into the passageway, anxiously searching her face for signs of pain or fear. Her expression didn't change although her lips were again firmly pressed together, her jaw set.

Zachary wet his finger again and again, each time returning cautiously to the warm tunnel, finding no resistance even when his finger was up inside as far as it could go. He couldn't tell if she had become wet by herself or because of all the wetness he had brought to her, but he knew that the moment had come to enter her. He straddled Lily on his knees and elbows and carefully lowered himself so that just the rounded, engorged tip of his penis nuzzled at the mouth of her delicate opening. Then he pushed into her, at first less than an inch and then a half-inch more. Slowly, oh so slowly, he moved, the sweat standing out on his forehead, always scanning her face for the moment when he would have to withdraw, when it would hurt her too much, but she was expressionless, although her breath came more quickly. She didn't move, she lay under him unflinchingly and let him fill her. Finally, after long minutes, she had accepted his entire penis, it throbbed within her at its full length, and Zachary lowered himself so that his legs were outstretched on the mattress, while his elbows kept him from crushing her. He could feel his penis swelling, growing larger and larger, although he didn't move a muscle. The soft, hot, tight inside of her was too much for him. Without a single thrust he came, his spasms so wrenching, so strong, so impossible to control after the frustration of the last hour that he poured his sperm into her with a rush, a flood, that was so quick that it was pure animal release.

For a minute Zachary, lost in the pounding of his heartbeat, forgot Lily, but as soon as he recovered himself he rolled off her body and gathered her in his arms, covering her face with kisses of wild gratitude, a hail of kisses mingled with the tears he couldn't keep from shedding. He hadn't expected her to become aroused. In the days to come, gradually, and with infinite care, he would teach her to enjoy sex, but now he was astonished at her courage, infinitely moved by her refusal to allow her innate modesty to make him feel as if he were brutal, touched to the heart by her willingness to permit him to enter her without any other sign of the effort she was making than her closed eyes.

"Did I hurt you, darling?" he asked at last.

"No, of course not." She opened her eyes and smiled at him. How could he know that her body had been trained to accept pain, to welcome it, to embrace it? How could he understand that the new set of feelings she had just encountered were as nothing compared to breaking in a pair of toe shoes? For many hours each day, from the age of eight, she had lived with constant pain, pain she was trained to smile through, pain that a dancer, like any other athlete, considers an inevitable part of life.

Lily had expected something different of her wedding night, something rough and exciting and unknown, something far wilder than the sensations she had when a strong partner lifted her farther than she had ever been lifted before. She had expected a duel of two bodies that would leave them both sore, aching, sweating and exhausted, as after a great performance. Not this long, drawn-out cuddling, not the stealthy exploration of a body she had long ago stopped thinking of as anything but an instrument, a body about which she had not the slightest self-consciousness. Oh, but how much she had wanted and needed to be *taken*, used, overcome, relentlessly plunged head over heels into a world she had never known, a world she sometimes heard the other students giggling about, a world that had fascinated her even as she rejected it.

She couldn't *do* more than she had, Lily thought, she didn't know the right movements, the right positions to take, but surely her immobility must have indicated clearly that she would permit him anything? She could not endure feeling awkward, ill at ease with her muscles, yet there was no one to teach her except Zachary. He was the one with the experience, she thought, as she drifted into sleep. He was the one who had to make it important to her. She had done her best. Now it was up to him to make it wonderful, yes wonderful, even more wonderful than applause.

The Ambervilles returned to Manhattan after a ten-day honeymoon in Paris. Zachary had never been away from his offices such a length of time, almost six weeks from the day he first left for London, and aside from fleeting visits to his London and Paris bureaus, he hadn't made the tour of inspection he'd planned. But he was much too happy to care.

Every night for ten nights he had made love to Lily, every night he had spent hours, hushed, halcyon hours, hours that were, to him, like the slow exploration, inch by inch, of a new, moonlit countryside. She was like a melody, he thought, an exquisite melody in a minor key that no one else could hear.

Lily never refused him anything except for one night, when he had first brushed his mouth between her thighs. She'd tentatively put her hands over her pubic hair and then taken them away. He'd immediately understood that she wasn't ready for that final intimacy and he had made no further attempt. He was certain that one day soon he would, by virtue of his patience and his tenderness, find the way to make her feel pleasure of her own. It was not that she had any distaste for sex, Zachary assured himself, but just that she hadn't yet learned to let herself go. It was a question of time and of never allowing himself to forget what it must be like for an eighteen-year-old girl—scarcely more than a child—who suddenly finds herself married to a man of twenty-nine. The foreknowledge that Lily always opened herself to him each night enabled him to moderate any roughness, any haste, any gesture that might, he suspected, seem animal, too rough, too frightening to a girl of her sensibilities.

After that first night he found that he always needed to take her a second time; her very immobility aroused him as if it were the most potent aphrodisiac, and after he had reached that first satisfaction he was able to stay inside her for a far longer period, lying motionless, hearing her breathe, kissing her gently while his penis grew and grew harder without friction, with just the smallest rocking motion of his pelvis against hers at his climax, so as not to bruise that infinitely delicate, silently accepting creature who was his bride.

5

Cutter Amberville decided to go to college in California rather than spend four years at an Eastern school. He wanted to put as much distance between himself and his brother as he could, to leave behind that part of the world in which the name Amberville immediately caused people to ask him if he were related to Zachary. At Stanford, or "the Farm" as Berkeley students, from their traditionally intellectual perch within sight of San Francisco, mockingly refer to their elite and non-egalitarian rival, he found companionship that wasn't different from that which he'd nourished at Andover; rich boys, boys who had something he wanted.

At Stanford Cutter had to work harder at his studies than he had done at Andover but he soon learned the art of doing only the necessary minimum, leaving himself as much time as he could to continue in his chosen fields of excellence: tennis, squash, sailing, polo and skiing. They were indisputably a gentleman's sports, they were a rich man's sports; they required years of practice to do well; they inspired admiration and confidence when a young man was able to master all of them. They demanded skill, coordination, endurance and, particularly in the case of polo and skiing, an acknowledged willingness to put himself on the line as far as physical courage was concerned. There was no risk—no reasonable risk—that Cutter wouldn't take on a horse or on skis, since physical courage, he deduced, with the measure of calculation he so carefully hid, was usually accepted as shorthand for courage, pure and simple. His brother, his enemy, had never learned to do any sport with skill.

Not the least of Cutter's abilities were devoted to tennis and squash. While his other chosen sports demanded that he compete against an animal or the elements, racket sports were man-to-man competition. Winning took an effort, but it was nothing compared to the skill and the technique with which Cutter eventually learned to lose a few crucial games, brilliantly contested games with a few carefully chosen fathers of his friends; men who played exceptionally well for men of their age; men who were in investment banking, men who would, someday in the future, be in a position to give him a job in a business in which contacts often meant commissions. Losing at tennis, losing with good temper, convincingly and without arousing any suspicion that he wasn't trying his hardest, became one of Cutter Amberville's particular assets, as important as his good manners and his good looks, even more important than his unquestioned courage.

"Yesterday I went shopping with the first Mrs. Amberville," Zelda Powers said acidly to Pavka Mayer as they had a drink together before lunch.

"Ah? You sound as mean as you look, my love. After all, Zelda, you have to remember that she's very young and very British and has been protected almost from the day she was born, or so I gather from Zachary, by her total immersion in the ballet. If she doesn't know how to dress, except in a tutu, that shouldn't be a surprise to you."

"But the Honorable Lily does know how to dress . . . now." Zelda said with a rancorous, sideways look at Pavka.

"Bad taste? Or just dull, ordinary provincial taste? The British aren't famous for their skill in self-adornment."

"We went to Bergdorf's, we went to Saks, we went to Bonwit's, we went to every fine shop in New York because Zachary wouldn't allow me to take her wholesale, and she looked at all our best designers' dresses with as much interest as if I'd taken her to see an exhibition of earthworms," Zelda said viciously. "There was just nothing she could even be bothered to try on, nothing at all. And she really needed clothes, Pavka, because her mother didn't have enough warning of the wedding to buy her a complete trousseau nor did either of them have any idea of what young married women wear in New York. She was all done up in pastel tweed that looked like a cross between Alice in Wonderland and a very young Crowned Head on a State Visit to somewhere unfriendly."

"But so very, very beautiful," Pavka said quietly.

"I don't deny that she's beautiful . . . I just wanted to be helpful . . . you know I'd do anything for Zachary. Anyway, as a last resort, I took her to Mainbocher and she perked up, showed some signs of animation and by the time we'd left she'd ordered thirty-seven different outfits, almost the entire collection. The first fittings are in a week."

"Well, what's wrong with that? It solves your problem, doesn't it?"

"It does something to my insides. Mainbocher at her age! Custom-made, *the* most expensive clothes in the entire United States . . . very quiet clothes, Pavka, very well-bred, absolutely perfect clothes that could be worn inside-out if you wanted to. The ladies who buy there are the richest women in New York, they're members of a particularly exclusive elite. You work your way *up* to Mainbocher, damn it! And I'll bet not one of them has ever ordered so many things in a single visit. That, that *teenager*—she didn't even ask what they cost . . . it just never occurred to her."

"So what? Zachary can afford it."

"It's not the money, it was her attitude I couldn't stand. Has he told you about the house he's buying? The only house in the whole town that she condescended to like?"

"He mentioned something about it but I didn't pay too much attention."

"She took me to see it. Pavka, you know what sort of a guy Zachary is. Simple, down to earth, couldn't care less about show? How do you think he's going to like living in a pale gray marble palace that takes up half a block, spread out over three stories, with a ballroom, my dear, and a huge garden at the back? For just two people? It's half the size of the Frick; it's not a home, it's an absolute mansion."

"He'll love it if it makes her happy," Pavka said, enjoying being the devil's advocate.

"But *why* should a kid like that need such a palace to make her happy, for God's sake? Who lives like that anymore? Just think of the renovations, the interior decorating, the staff to keep it up, someone to tell the staff what to do because she won't know, or want to be bothered. Think of the gardeners. Gardeners in New York! You really don't have the slightest idea of what it's going to cost, do you?"

"No. But we both know Zachary can afford it, a hundred times over. I don't believe in deciding how other people should spend their money, Zelda, and I don't think you do either . . . you never did before." He softened his words with a tender, well-placed pinch.

"You're trying to say I'm jealous, aren't you, Pavka, my darling?"

"Well?"

"Of course I am. I should be ashamed. But I'm not."

"Even Zelda Powers allows herself a perfectly normal female reaction. Careful, you may lose your uniquely original touch. This could mean bad news for the circulation department of *Style*."

"Don't bet on it."

"I won't. And you must have another drink. I insist. I will even pay."

In the days when they were young bachelors, right after the end of the war, Nat Landauer and Zachary Amberville spent many an afternoon at the track with Barney Shore, an amiable, carrot-haired young man in his middle twenties who had been Nat's roommate at Syracuse. Just as Nat was destined to run the Five Star Button Company, Barney was the heir apparent to the family business, something he referred to casually as "the racks."

"Dress racks?" Zack asked him one day.

"Nah, magazine racks."

"You make them?"

"Nah, we fill them," Barney said dismissively, not anxious to abandon his study of the *Racing Form*, a devout exercise which never did him any more good than it did Zachary. It was not until he began to publish *Style* that Zachary understood the importance of an institution called Crescent, founded by Joe Shore, Barney's father, which, along with Curtis, Warner, Select and NICD was one of the major national distributors of magazines.

Without these powerful distributors the business of publishing magazines could not possibly exist. While Zachary owned only *Trimming Trades Monthly* he sold his copies by subscription, but when he created *Style* he signed a three-year national distribution contract with Joe Shore, which established a pattern for the future. For the first year of *Style*'s existence he paid Crescent ten percent of the cover price of each copy sold, and for the second and third years, six percent. In return Crescent acted as *Style*'s banker, paying him against the number of copies printed.

Joe Shore, deceptively mild-mannered man that he was, could make or break a magazine by deciding how many copies he would send on to the various local wholesalers, who would then deliver them to individual retailers, who eventually—and sooner rather than later, the magazine publisher prayed—would put them out on the racks in prominent positions.

Zachary Amberville had instantly appealed to tough, quiet Joe Shore, whose approval was not easily gained, but, once gained, was never lost for any act short of not living up to a business deal. Murder, arson, loitering with intent to litter; none of these offenses would change Joe Shore's mind about a man he liked who kept his word.

"Joe," Zachary said to him one day in 1953, as they were having lunch together, "I want you to meet Lily. Would you and Mrs. Shore, and Barney and that new girl he's seeing, have dinner with us a week from next Tuesday?"

"We'd like that, Zack. Wait a minute, did you say Tuesday?"

"Right. Not this coming Tuesday, a week from Tuesday."

"Any other night, Zack, with pleasure, but not Tuesday, not *any* Tuesday. My wife would kill me."

"A pussycat like you? I thought you had the ideal marriage."

"Zack, don't kid a kidder."

"Come on. What's Tuesday night?"

"Milton Berle. Tuesday at eight o'clock."

"So what?"

"How many stories have you done on Milton Berle in *Seven Days*?"

"I'm not sure. . . . I keep seeing the damn things and wondering why, but my television editor tells me to trust him. Since I doubled his salary to get him to move over from *Life* I've tried not to second-guess the guy. Personally I've never had the time to watch much television, and Lily isn't interested in it at all. Maybe," Zachary grinned, "it's just her language problem."

"Hopeless. You just don't know what you're missing." Joe Shore shook his head in wonder. "I bet you don't even have your own set yet."

"I looked at Barney's once and all I saw was a bunch of midgets. They've got to do better than that. Give me a movie or a Broadway show anytime. Coffee?"

Imagine, Zachary thought, as he walked back along the busy streets, Joe Shore, a man who had as much tangible power as any man he'd ever personally known, couldn't make a dinner date on any Tuesday night because of Milton Berle. Did Eisenhower and Mamie watch? Did Senator Joseph McCarthy watch, and Estes Kefauver? Personally he was too restless to sit still for long, except for an occasional ballgame. Whatever importance television had, it was as a competitor for the advertiser's dollar, and not one to worry about nearly as much as he did about other magazines. He stopped abruptly at the corner of Fifth Avenue and Fifty-second Street. Did the whole country come to a stop on Tuesday at eight? Probably it did and probably it came to a stop for Lucille Ball and Sid Caesar and "The Honeymooners" and who the fuck knew what other shows? He, Zachary Amberville, was a shortsighted, ignorant horse's ass who had almost made the fatal mistake of thinking that he could judge the American public by his own tastes. But not too big a horse's ass to learn when he'd been one and to do something about it. *Television Week*? Too businesslike. *This Week on Television*? Too long. *Television Weekly*? There was something overtly intellectual about that, it smacked of *Harper*'s or *The Atlantic*. *Your T.V. Week*? Still too long. *T.V. Week*. That would do. He crossed the street, imagining the first issue clearly. A square book, eight by eight, on good-quality paper, crammed full of photos and text, and television schedules of course, with a large color picture of Milton Berle on the cover. As his pace quickened, Zachary Amberville returned to his office, already, although he did not yet realize it, worth tens of millions of dollars more than when he'd left for lunch.

Months before the plans for the redecorating of the great gray marble house on East Seventieth Street had been completed, Lily discovered she was pregnant. Her immediate reaction was fear: what would this do to her body? Then she smiled at herself. That was a typical dancer's reaction and she had given up her career for a normal life. This baby would be the proof, if one was needed, that she was free, her own woman, a double rejection of that hermetic little world she had put aside. She always did her barre exercises for an hour every morning in the large suite at the Waldorf Towers where the Ambervilles had settled temporarily, but she hadn't so much as been to the ballet since she'd come to Manhattan. The barre was a habit, a way of keeping in shape, nothing more.

Her marvelous new clothes! Her hands flew to her mouth in dismay. They wouldn't fit in a matter of weeks. Well, it simply couldn't be helped. She'd go to Mainbocher this afternoon and ask him to design a complete maternity wardrobe. Should she write her mother immediately, or even telephone? It wasn't a minute too soon for Mother to start looking for just the right nanny to come over from England and take charge. Doctor Wolfe had told her to watch her weight . . . a good doctor, she thought, but a silly remark. When in her life had she not watched her weight? Lily hugged herself in the beginnings of enjoyment. Inevitably her slight dancer's breasts would become voluptuous. How nice she'd look in a low-cut gown. She'd tell Mainbocher that she wanted deep necklines for evening; wonderful, wide-skirted dresses, tied under the breasts in the Empire style. She might as well enjoy having a bosom while it lasted, for of course she wouldn't nurse the child. Her cousins had all nursed their children and it had seemed to her to be a most appalling waste of time; hours and hours of sitting patiently, night and day, while some little thing used you as a human cow, a baby who couldn't possibly remember if it had been nursed or not and most certainly wouldn't be grateful one way or the other.

She made a mental note to tell her decorators where to put the nursery. It should be so far from her bedroom that under no circumstances would she be disturbed by the noise the baby would make, day or night. A baby's crying was unquestionably the single most irritating sound in all of nature and she didn't intend to endure it, any more than she would buy dresses off the rack.

A mother at her age? Well, she might as well get it over with while she was young, as the Royals always did, especially since she had no choice. But it was rather a pity really since she had so recently come to Manhattan, so recently begun to realize what it was like to be able to have everything she wanted, when she wanted it, at the slightest tug of desire. Still, a baby didn't mean postponing any satisfactions for more than a few hours. She'd known in London that Zachary was tremendously rich, but Lily now understood that he was far, far richer than she could have imagined, and far, far more generous than any man she'd ever known. Her father had been rather stingy, now that she came to think of it, he believed that children should be brought up with strict discipline about pocket money. She'd never needed pocket money, since she'd had no interests to spend it on, but since she had given up ballet, there seemed to be a multitude of things she did rather like buying. The shops of Manhattan were irresistibly tempting, and it was quite . . . cozy . . . to know that there wasn't anything in any of them that she couldn't buy, nothing Zachary didn't want to give her.

"Wealthy"—a disgusting word. Rich. The only way to say it was flat out. Rich. *Very, very rich.* Perhaps, when the baby was presentable, she'd let *Style* photograph her for its pages. The Honorable Mrs. Zachary Amberville, and her child. No, not *Style.* It wasn't designed for the very rich. Perhaps that was why it sold so well. *Vogue* then, or, better yet, *Town & Country.* There was a certain cachet, now that she reflected on the subject, to making her first appearance in the society magazines everyone in New York read every month, as a young mother rather than just as another young bride.

Of course New York society was one vast joke. In London you were either in society or not in society. If you were a viscount's daughter you would always be a viscount's daughter, no matter whom you married. You had your relatives, you had your ancestors, you had your place in the constellation. A girl could marry a title or into county society—or even an American—but everybody would always remember who you had been before your marriage. It would take generations before it didn't matter, or perhaps it would always matter, perhaps people would say hundreds of years from now, "Oh yes, Lady Melinda . . . her great-great-grandmother was some banker's daughter before she married the Earl of wherever." Snobbish, fearfully snobbish, she supposed. Nevertheless that was simply the way it was.

But New York! So many of their "great ladies" were three—or at the most four—generations removed from robber barons, and robber barons were simply successful thieves. Of course they had their *Mayflower* descendants and that Society of the Cincinnati, descendants of officers in Washington's army. In other words, Lily mused, they were descendants of colonials who had rebelled against a rather good sort of king, not even two hundred years ago. Apparently it was considered fearfully impressive to be a member, although Zachary, who could have joined, had never bothered. As her mother had told her in the few weeks before the wedding, although fifty families considered themselves to be historically "Old New York," there were only a handful of them who could claim really good Old World ancestors. The Van Rensselaers, whose coat of arms came from the Prince of Orange, had no land left. The Livingstons however were alive and prospering and they went back to the noble Scottish House of Callenders; the Pells too had been aristocrats in England and the Duers and Rutherfords had pedigrees with which anyone could be satisfied. Ancestor worship had its place, Lily thought mockingly, but shouldn't the ancestors have a bit more patina on their graves? Only a few years before the American Revolution, Louis XIV of France had sold titles for six thousand six hundred livres, whatever that might be in today's money, leaving blank the space in which the newly noble Frenchman would write his name. So little really stood up to the inspection of more than a few centuries. Even the Adamsfields had only been squires until the 1300s. No, being a title snob was quite nasty, and beneath her.

However. However, she was going to live in Manhattan and sheer self-respect demanded that she receive proper consideration. Once the baby was out of the way she'd meet the few really quite decent people, and know them. Invariably she'd be asked to join many charitable committees, or whatever they called good works here—it seemed to be a New York mania—and she'd pick several, choosing them very cautiously. It was so very unwise to make friends too quickly in a new place, her mother had always said. You spent the next ten years getting rid of them.

Lily stretched agreeably. The house, the superb antiques she was buying to fill it, endless new clothes, the reign over Manhattan that was hers for the taking, the servants, the trips they would make when New York grew too hot or too cold, the jewels that she was beginning to contemplate and compare at the great jewelers of Manhattan . . . it all seemed to merge into one comfortable and busy circle of pleasure. She must have been quite mad to have spent most of her life chained to a discipline that allowed for no pleasure except the fleeting enjoyment of an exceptional performance. Ballet dancers, especially prima ballerinas, were truly *slaves*, she reflected, shaking her head. Slaves to their own impossible set of standards, slaves to their teachers, slaves to their bodies; slaves, above all, to the public who, by possessing a ticket, demanded a perfection the price of which none of them could possibly understand. Dancers were like trained animals, brought out to go through the hoops and yet, unlike animals, they had chosen to be slaves. How fortunate she was to have escaped in time. For once she had become a prima ballerina, as of course she would have, it might have been far more difficult to abandon that obsessive life.

The phone rang, and Lily stirred, her reveries broken. "Oh. Yes, darling, I slept beautifully," she said to Zachary. "No, nothing particularly new, just another day of talking to upholsterers and decorators. . . . Don't be silly, dear, I *am* having fun." She supposed she could have called to tell him the minute she found out about the baby but it had slipped her mind. Well, tonight would be time enough. Of course he'd understand that soon they would have to stop going to bed together. Soon, quite soon. She put down the phone and then picked it up again. She'd phone Miss Varney, her saleslady at Mainbocher, and make an appointment for tomorrow. No . . . for this afternoon. Why wait?

"Not nurse *my son*? No, darling, I couldn't possibly have said that."

"Lily, darling, come on, don't you remember? I distinctly heard you telling Minnie that all the stuff about antibodies in mother's milk was some American fad and fresh air and a good nanny were what counted."

"Perhaps. I'm sure you're right. But what does it matter since I've changed my mind? Where is that nurse with my son? She should have been here five minutes ago. Zachary, could you please go and find her? I'm terrified the hospital and staff might give him a bottle of formula for their own convenience . . . they hate mothers who nurse. It makes more work for them."

While Zachary roamed the corridors of Doctors' Hospital looking for a nurse, any nurse, Lily fretted impatiently in her bed. Tobias had been born three days before, an easy birth, and as soon as she had seen him, with his little pointed cap of blond curls, his fat cheeks and perfect body, she realized that she had never loved before. Not her parents, not ballet, not Zachary, not herself The last thing she had expected was to be taken by surprise by a wave of maternal emotion but she had spent the entire day after the birth weeping because her son was not by her side but in the nursery with the other babies. He *was* her, he was *part of her body*, how could they take him away as if he didn't belong to her? It was simply too late to arrange for "rooming-in," keeping the baby in her own room in a little crib, her doctor explained. Every other mother in the hospital it seemed had opted for rooming-in and they didn't have the necessary equipment for half of them. If only she'd asked for it a few months ago, he had said, as if, a few months ago, she could possibly have known her baby would be Tobias?

Of *course* she'd had a boy. All that nonsense that people talk about not caring about the sex of a child so long as it's healthy! Everyone knew in the heart of hearts that the first child should be a boy. Cavemen knew it and so had all humans since then.

"Here he is!" Zachary said, pushing open the door for the nurse, "and he sounds hungry. I tracked him down by the noise."

"He needs to cry, it's good for his lungs," Lily said, sounding as expert as her mother before her, holding her arms out greedily.

"Shall I leave you and Father alone with the baby?" the nurse asked.

"I don't need you now, thank you, nurse. Zachary, darling, would you mind? I'm rather new at this . . . I think I'd like a little privacy. Come back in, oh, an hour or so. He does enjoy taking his time."

"You're sure?" Zachary tried not to sound as deeply disappointed as he felt.

"Won't you need anything?" He looked at her lovingly, propped up on half a dozen pillows, their silk cases thickly encrusted with fine old lace, as were the sheets and coverlet she had brought from home. Lily had never looked so angelic as she did at this minute with her hair spread over her shoulders. At her ears were the enormous sapphires set in diamonds he had just given her from Van Cleef and Arpels—sapphires for a boy. The box that had contained the necklace and the bracelets that completed the parure lay open on the table beside her and the jewels themselves were heaped near the lamp, captured dreams of a midsummer's night.

"If I do, darling, there's a perfectly good bell right here on the bed table and I'll ring it, I promise. Now go, both of you, before my son wakes everyone in the city."

While the argument over the influences of environment and heredity will rage forever, no one could possibly deny that Tobias Adamsfield Amberville was destined to grow up a monster. It was unthinkable that a child born to such an adoring father and a mother who regarded him as an extension of herself, a self to whom she denied nothing, could not be overindulged.

"It must be his Anderson blood," his grandmother, Sarah Amberville, remarked. "The Protestant work ethic, you know."

Lily, six months pregnant with her second child, laughed merrily. "He does precious little work yet, Sarah."

"Look at him digging up the garden so seriously and methodically. You'd think he was getting paid by the shovelful. He hasn't cried once since I've been visiting you, he goes quietly to bed when he's supposed to, and according to Nanny, he gives her no trouble at all. He eats all his vegetables, and even Zachary didn't do that. I hope your next baby will be as easy."

"The next baby is intended to be Tobias's playmate. It's bad for a child to be an only child, that's why I'm bothering to have one so quickly. Otherwise I'd be very happy just watching my son grow up."

Sarah Amberville said nothing. She still hadn't grown used to her daughter-in-law and she never would. Actually she was rather frightened of her because she knew that if she got on the wrong side of Lily she wouldn't get to see her grandson, or much of her son either for that matter. Minnie had been banished for months when she'd dared to comment on the fact that since perfectly good clothes for children were made in the United States it seemed a bit farfetched to have them sent from London, especially since Toby outgrew them so quickly.

"Look, he's coming back. He must be ready for lunch," she said to Lily.

"Wait till the gardener comes tomorrow," Lily chortled.

"Will he be surprised?"

"Tobias has just dug up all the tulips, every last one. They were due to bloom next week. The gardener planted four hundred bulbs last autumn."

"Dear, dear," Sarah Amberville murmured. She hadn't realized that Lily had known all along that Toby was harvesting tulips in full bud. She'd been sitting firmly on her hands for the last two hours, biting her lips and praying for courage to stay silent. Well, perhaps it was easy to find good gardeners in Manhattan. In Andover the problem didn't present itself. Being a grandmother wasn't somehow as much fun as she'd thought it would be. But what was?

Maxime Emma Amberville was about as unattractive a baby as Lily could imagine: something like a plucked chicken, without hair at all, a pair of bandy legs, and a heat rash that developed on the first day. She had colic, she screamed when she was hungry and she screamed when she wasn't hungry. She was apparently the most difficult child in the nursery as the supervisor of nurses confided in her.

"I hope you told that supervisor to go fuck herself," Zachary burst out when Lily reported the remark to him.

"Zachary! I most certainly did not. The poor woman was at her wits' end. I just assured her that the baby would be going home tomorrow. The thing I'm really worried about is Nanny. What if she leaves? She's so used to Tobias."

"Nanny is underworked and overpaid."

"I called the employment agency and hired a second nurse. They have a very well-recommended woman, a Miss Hemmings, who specializes in difficult cases. She'll be here when we leave the hospital, and take over immediately. Fortunately Maxime's room is not right next to Tobias's so she won't wake him."

"Jesus, Lily, the baby's got ordinary colic, not leprosy. I happen to think the kid's got a hell of a lot of spirit and I like the way she looks. She looks like me, damn it."

"Darling, you're too silly. You know you're madly attractive."

"You've never seen my baby pictures," he said grinning.

Vaguely, Lily murmured, "I assume she'll improve—with time. She could hardly get worse."

Maxime's colic and heat rash disappeared at the same time. Within six months she had put on enough weight so that her skinny little legs were dimpled and straight, her hair, once it started to grow, was straight and thick and, to Zachary's sweet and triumphant delight, she had a pure white streak exactly the same place as his. As for her spirit, she managed within twenty-two months to break that of the nurse who specialized in difficult cases.

"Madame," Miss Hemmings said, almost in tears, "I've had sick babies, babies so quiet that you knew there had to be something wrong; I've had hyperactive babies who got into everything, including the sewers; I've had babies who could and did climb a tree before they were a year old; I've had babies you couldn't toilet-train for four years, I've had every kind of baby I thought was possible, but Maxi . . . I just have to go away for a rest, Madame, or I'll have a nervous breakdown."

"Oh, no! Don't do that, Miss Hemmings. Please, please don't leave!" Lily begged.

"I must, Madame. I love Maxi too much. She's so adorable and she's so *naughty.* I can't bring myself to punish her and that's bad for the child."

"I thought you were supposed to be able to handle that sort of problem," Lily said coldly. The woman was obviously determined to leave. "I'm afraid that Maxi has been spoiled rotten. She wants what she wants when she wants it . . . surely you should have managed to do something about that."

"I've tried, Madame, but . . ."

"But you've failed; it's that simple, really, isn't it?"

"If you want to look at it that way, yes." Miss Hemmings's tone was that of someone who refused to be drawn out and Lily found herself intensely irritated.

"I hold you entirely responsible for Maxi's discipline problem, Miss Hemmings, and I'm afraid I can't give you a good reference."

"That's up to you, Madame. But I doubt that Maxi's problems can be solved just by finding another nurse."

"We'll see about that! I'm sure someone else will do quite well," Lily said furiously.

"I don't like to blame the parents," Miss Hemmings said, her professional pride wounded, "but there's only so much any nurse can achieve. Now if you'll excuse me, Madame . . ."

"Just a minute. Precisely what do you mean about blaming parents, Miss Hemmings?"

"Maxi is spoiled because her father gives her everything she wants and you spend all your available time with Toby. She's trying terribly hard to get her mother's attention and, since you asked me to speak out, she's using her father as a substitute." Before Lily could begin to reply Miss Hemmings left the room and went upstairs to pack. In a long and honorable career she had never spoken her mind so clearly, and as miserable as she felt about leaving Maxi she was rather pleased with herself.

Toby's English nanny, Mrs. Browne, was made of sterner stuff than Miss Hemmings. She took over Maxi, referring to her as "our two-year-old" in a way that explained away everything. Lily, unwillingly stung by Miss Hemmings's remarks, now made a point of reading to the little girl almost every evening before the child's dinner, and of letting Maxi play with her jewels for half an hour on Sunday mornings, perched shoeless in the middle of Lily's antique lace wedding cake of a bed. No one can ever accuse me of being a neglectful mother, she thought, raging with resentful boredom as she read aloud.

It was soon after Tobias's fourth birthday that he began falling out of bed. For two years he had occasionally awakened in the middle of the night and gone to the bathroom when he had to, treading carefully along the familiar route so as not to disturb anybody.

"Could I have a night light, Mother?" he asked Lily one day.

"Oh, my darling, you haven't had one since you were a tiny thing. Did you have a bad dream? Is that it?"

"No, it's just that when I wake up I can't see anything. I can't tell where I am in bed unless I feel around and if I'm near the edge I fall off. And I can't find the bed lamp in the dark. It's happened a few times and it hurts when I fall."

"Perhaps it is too dark in your room."

"It . . . it never has been. There used to be enough light on the street to see by . . . but, I don't know, I don't seem to see in the dark anymore."

"Well, I'm sure it's nothing to worry about," Lily said, her heart beating heavily, "but I'll take you for a checkup to Doctor Stevenson. You probably need to eat more carrots, my baby."

The pediatrician gave Toby a thorough going-over. "He's a fine young man, Mrs. Amberville. As for the falling out of bed, I'm sure it's not serious but, just to be on the safe side, I think you should have his eyes checked."

"But you just looked into his eyes," Lily cried.

"By a specialist. Merely to be on the safe side."

"To be on the *safe* side?"

"Please don't worry. Children have all sorts of passing symptoms, particularly when they're growing as quickly as this young man; but it's always a good idea to follow up on them, even if it proves unnecessary."

The famous ophthalmologist, Dr. David Ribin, to whom Dr. Stevenson sent Toby, gave him a complete eye examination. Lily sat in the waiting room trying to read a magazine as the time passed. Suddenly she looked up and saw Zachary standing by her chair.

"No!" she screamed. She knew, the instant she saw her husband, that the doctor had telephoned him to come.

"Lily, Lily." Zachary enfolded her in his arms. "Whatever it is, medicine can cure it. They can do anything with eyes, it's the most advanced field that exists, Lily, I'll take care of it, don't worry. Come on, the doctor is waiting to talk to us. A nurse is keeping Toby busy, I saw them as I came in."

"I'm deeply sorry to have to tell you this," Dr. Ribin said, as they sat before him. "But Toby has retinitis pigmentosa. We don't know the cause of this disease. Night blindness is often the first symptom."

"Disease—what sort of disease?" Zachary asked, taking Lily's hand.

"First of all, Mr. Amberville, I should explain that the retina is a thin membrane that lines the inner eye. It contains rods and cones, which are the structures that are sensitive to light. The rods are the receptors used in dim light, which is why an alteration in their functions, as in Toby's case, causes night blindness before anything else."

"Doctor Ribin, what's the treatment that's used in this sort of thing?" Lily asked, maddened by the length of the doctor's explanation.

"We have no treatment, Mrs. Amberville. The nerve cells of the retina cannot be replaced if they are damaged."

"No treatment? You mean no medicine?"

"I'm afraid not."

"Surgery then? Will he have to have surgery?" Lily cried.

"We have no surgical techniques for retinitis pigmentosa," Dr. Ribin said gravely.

"It's not possible! I won't believe it! Everybody can be treated! He's only four years old, a little boy, just a little boy," Lily said fiercely, refusal still stronger than grief.

"What's going to happen to Toby?" Zachary asked, holding her hand so tightly that it hurt.

"It's a progressive disease, Mr. Amberville. The sides of the retina are normally affected in the beginning, and although Toby's central vision may stay fairly stable for many years, there will be a progressive narrowing of his field of vision as he grows older. Eventually, we don't know exactly when, he will have only a pinpoint of vision left. But that may not happen for many years. He'll have a long time, I hope, until then, but I can't promise how long."

"Forgive me, Doctor, but couldn't it possibly be something else?" Zachary had to ask, although he knew the answer from the doctor's expression.

"I wish it could be. For your own sense of sureness I'd advise you to get another opinion, but unfortunately the disease, though rare, is unmistakable and quickly diagnosed. There are clumps of pigment scattered throughout the retina, and the vessels of the retina are narrowed. I hate to be so certain. I wish I thought I was wrong, Mr. Amberville."

"But how could he have caught it?" Lily cried in her anguish. "How, oh, tell me, how did it happen?"

"When children have retinitis pigmentosa, unlike its appearance in senile degeneration, it can only be hereditary, Mrs. Amberville."

6

Cutter Amberville was almost tempted to remain in California after graduation. At Stanford, he had made many influential friends and grown to agree with the local superstition that Harvard was second to Stanford in excellence. Sarah Amberville visited her youngest child several times a year but Cutter spent his holidays and summer vacations on the West Coast. He went on to Stanford Business School and, after graduation, worked for a few years at Booker, Smity and Jameston, the San Francisco investment banking firm, whose president was his roommate Jumbo Booker's father, a lean, fit, small man, a passionate tennis player who had delighted in taking a number of games off young Amberville.

However, in the early months of 1958, when he was twenty-four, Cutter decided to move to Manhattan. He had discovered that even in California, there was no one whom he was likely to meet who wouldn't ask him about his brother. Perhaps, Cutter thought, if he moved to China he could escape the inevitable question, but otherwise there was no avoiding the association. Since it existed, he might as well take advantage of it, for the center of all investment banking was in New York City, and to be an Amberville couldn't hurt his career. He intended to make a great deal of money. Zachary must not be the only rich Amberville.

Cutter had been steeped in the Stanford-San Francisco traditions of manners and culture and an aristocratic attitude that extended to the business world. He found it difficult to adjust to the collective frenzy of Manhattan. Who *were* all these people? Why did they run instead of walk? Why couldn't they conduct conversation at a civilized decibel level? Was there really not enough of anything to go around or did they just act as if there weren't?

Within a week he decided simply to ignore most of the city, not to begin to try to understand it in all of its distasteful manifestations. He had discovered that after all, on certain streets his kind of people lived, and his friends from Andover, Stanford and San Francisco had provided him with instant entry to the homes of the only people in Manhattan with whom he could feel at home.

Cutter Amberville was, indeed, more than welcome wherever he went. He was tall, six feet two inches, with a body molded by those sports which build the kind of long, elegant muscles that make a tailor purr. The distinctive looks that had made him outstanding as a boy had matured as he grew older, and now Cutter was an unusually handsome man. He was deeply tanned and his hair was bleached by the sun of California summers. His nose was large and perfectly shaped between eyes as blue as the sea in Sicily, as cold as the water of a fjord, and he had an ascetic, keenly etched mouth that no woman could ignore. He didn't have bulk but he had power, and there was a strong suggestion of what Byron called "the light-limb'd Matadore" when Cutter walked into a room. For all his blondness he had a bullkiller's sternness and dark purpose, he moved with an assurance and a self-esteem so ingrained that no one would ever believe that he had trained them into his stance, with as much will as he had trained warmth and sincerity into his smile.

His undeniable charm of manner was now completed, part of his core, his essence; that pleasing, flattering, *necessary* charm of an envious man whose life was dedicated to gaining the attention and affection he believed had been so unfairly denied him as a child.

The eleven years that separated Cutter from Zachary had come to seem like more than a generation to him. Although nothing could ever happen to make him give up the deep, gnawing hatred he felt toward his brother for overshadowing his youth; although no amount of personal success in his own world could ever compensate for the eternal loss of what he knew had been due to him, his hatred had become so familiar that, from time to time, he could almost put aside his litany of injustices, almost allow the worm in his heart to sleep.

Yet even if Zachary and Zachary's enormous success, success following success as if to torment Cutter, could be temporarily ignored, there was no possible way to simply take them for granted, to come to terms with being Zachary Amberville's younger brother. Cutter could never make himself feel, in his profound self, that Zachary's success did not *subtract* something essential from his own life. He was *diminished* forever, unfairly diminished, and it had to be Zachary's fault. Cutter, for all his singular appeal, a handsomeness that verged on beauty, was a man who wore invisible bitterness as permanently as if it had been tattooed onto his heart. He nourished and cherished his hatred; if it had disappeared he would have had to restructure his world, explain it in some other way. But there was no chance of that, not with the Amberville publications appearing weekly and monthly on the newsstands, their brilliant new covers beckoning, growing thicker with advertising month by month, not with *T.V. Week* an automatic purchase made by millions of Americans each week, visible next to the television set in every library into which Cutter walked.

When Cutter first arrived in New York it had been a year since Tobias's disease was diagnosed, yet except for his night blindness, he seemed to continue to see as well as ever, as far as Lily could tell. She and Zachary had told no one, not even Nanny, about their visit to Dr. Ribin. They had consulted another specialist who confirmed the diagnosis, but since there was nothing anybody could do, they kept their silence. They couldn't endure any discussion of Tobias's future, not even with each other. Particularly not with each other.

"Hereditary." Both doctors had agreed. There was no blindness in the Ambervilles' family history, nor in that of the Andersons, the Dales or the Cutters. But there had been a blind Marquis who had been Lily's maternal grandfather and a blind uncle, also on her mother's side of the family. No, they couldn't possibly discuss Toby, for the only words either of them could think were words they would never say. Her genes, thought Zachary. My fault, thought Lily. Unfair, utterly and absolutely unfair. They both knew those words were unfair, but they could not, not think them.

The enormous silence, the void that was created by this silence penetrated into the heart of their life together and they were as aware of the unspoken words as if they were palpable, a glacier that was inexorably creeping over their always fragile intimacy.

By the time Lily was twenty-four she was recognized as the most impressive woman to emerge in several generations of New York society. Women thirty years older than she, women of wealth, cultivation and immense standing, went to great lengths to meet her, for not only was she the daughter of Viscount and Viscountess Adamsfield, but she was Mrs. Zachary Amberville, wife of the man who had just given a million dollars to the Metropolitan Museum's collection of American paintings, and contributed two million dollars to Columbia University for its general scholarship fund; gifts he gave in Lily's name.

Lily entertained so discreetly and yet so lavishly, with piles of money exquisitely spent, that she stayed out of the newspapers, yet when she departed from New York for a trip to London or to France it was felt as a loss, a diminution of the luster of Manhattan. When she returned every fashionable florist had a dozen orders to send her baskets of welcoming blooms, the homage that was her due, and the pace of the life of the city's society took on a quickness that made her large circle feel that things were in place again, that a gala season had started.

Lily was a generous patroness of every ballet company, and took her hour at the barre every morning without fail. She led in all of the anointed cultural events that brought New Yorkers of a certain class together, yet she was rarely a member of any committee; her mere appearance at a benefit or opening night as delicately dominant as a rising moon, always dressed in Mainbocher, her hair worn back from her face in a heavy chignon, was enough to stamp an evening as significant.

Brisk New Yorkers, quick of speech, rapid in calculating social weights and measures, appreciated the quality of Lily's initial diffidence and understood, with their canny, native perception, that it represented the kind of superiority that they were willing, in fact pleased, to acknowledge. Her superiority only enhanced their own. The mere fact that she had decided never to use her "Honorable" gave them the delight of telling the uninitiated that she was a Viscount's daughter, a nineteenth Baronet's daughter. Soon not telling became a matter of pride to those who knew her—who *thought* that they knew her—best.

Long before Toby had shown any signs of disease, Lily had abandoned the notion that there existed some passionate physical pleasure that she would finally experience. She believed that she was made by nature so that she didn't need the kind of sex for which some women seemed to live. There were degrees of everything after all, and some women actually lived for chocolate and others for martinis. Lily wasn't rebellious about her lack of desire since life contained so many delectable and obtainable objects for which she had an endless appetite that never failed, no matter how much she acquired.

Zachary, for his part, had gradually come to think that Lily's coldness was incurable. He never lost his gentle patience, but nothing seemed to bring her to sensual life. She had never turned away from him, but his passion for her grew less as he understood that it couldn't be returned. His love only deepened as it was tinted with a pity for his wondrous girl who never complained.

"This one," said Maxi, pointing to a word on the *Racing Form*. The four men, seated with her in a box at Belmont Park, looked at the little girl questioningly.

"So the kid can read, Zack?" Barney Shore wondered in amusement.

"Can you read, Maxi?" her father asked. Anything was possible with a three-year-old. She might have taught herself.

"This one," she repeated.

"Maxi, why that one?" Nat Landauer wanted to know.

"I like that one, Uncle Nat," Maxi replied.

"*Why* do you like that one, young lady?" Joe Shore asked in a quiet voice. All four men fell silent, waiting.

"I just do, Uncle Joe," Maxi said imperturbably. "That one."

"What's its name, Maxi . . . can you tell Uncle Joe its name?" he persevered.

"No, but I like it."

"The young lady can't read," Joe Shore announced with authority.

"But maybe she can pick a horse . . . maybe she's a . . . you know, an idiot savant, like those guys who can tell you when it's going to be Thursday a thousand years from now," Barney Shore said in excitement.

"Please, a little respect for the young lady," his father commanded. "What kind of expression is that to use in front of a child?"

"Sorry, Dad. Maxi, do you like any of the others?"

"No, Uncle Barney, just that one."

"To win, place or show?" Barney persisted.

"To win," she responded immediately. She hadn't known that there were games where you could just choose to win.

"Come on, Barney, you're not taking this seriously, are you?" Zachary protested halfheartedly.

"It can't hurt to listen to Maxi. The four of us put together can't handicap a mouse. Maybe we just need a fresh point of view. Woman's intuition, Zack. You've always been a believer."

"And how much could it cost?" added Nat Landauer. "Two dollars each, that's not too much to lose . . . last year I figure I dropped ten thousand."

"Two dollars to win for each of us, my treat," Zachary proposed. After all, Maxi was his responsibility.

"I'll go buy the tickets," Barney volunteered.

"Can I have a hot dog, please, Daddy?" Maxi asked. Zachary looked at her perched composedly in her seat, a little like a Japanese doll with her straight black bangs and her thick hair neatly trimmed in a circle just at the nape of her neck. She wore a yellow dress with a white collar, smocked at the yoke and at the cuffs of its short sleeves, white socks and black patent leather Mary Janes. The piquant, droll deliciousness of her face astonished him no matter how often or how long he looked at her.

"Daddy? Please, a hot dog?"

Nanny would kill him if she found out. "No, darling. I'm sorry but the hot dogs here aren't good for little girls."

"They smell awfully good." She gave him a tentative smile.

"They don't taste as good as they smell."

"So many other kids are eating them." Maxi's smile grew more tentative and now it became gently pathetic, the smile of someone who understands why she cannot have a glass of water when she is dying of thirst, the smile of someone who forgives the person who denies it.

"Maxi, it's not safe to eat hot dogs at the track," Zachary pleaded.

Maxi took his hand in hers and nestled against him. "All right, Daddy. I wish . . . I wish . . ."

"What, darling?"

"I wish I'd had more lunch," she said with patient sadness.

"Are you hungry?"

"Yes, but it doesn't matter, Daddy. I don't mind." She looked up at Zachary, a tiny tear brimming in each eye. "Really, I don't mind at all."

"I can't stand this," Nat Landauer announced. "I can't take it, you inhuman, hard-hearted unpatriotic son of a bitch! Uncle Nat will get you a hot dog, Maxi."

"No thanks, Uncle Nat. Daddy says I shouldn't eat them."

There was a silence. Joe Shore looked pained and gave a deep sigh. Zachary Amberville glared at his brother-in-law. Nat Landauer glared back at him. Maxi looked from one to another, holding her breath. A tear crept down each of her cheeks.

"O.K., O.K.! But no mustard!" Zachary shouted.

"The mustard's the best part, you schmuck." Nat's teeth ground together in anger.

"Young lady, do you like mustard?" Joe Shore asked, a smile restored to his face.

"I like ketchup on hot dogs."

"Ketchup's perfect," Zachary said hastily. Kids lived off ketchup, even Nanny liked it.

He held Maxi up so that she could watch the race. She daintily ate her hot dog while her horse won.

Barney Shore went to cash in the tickets. He returned beaming and extracted an amazing amount of cash from his pocket. "I bet a hundred each to win and another hundred for Maxi. You guys are pikers. Somebody could say 'thank you Barney.' "

"Thank you, Uncle Barney," Maxi said. She really liked this game. She decided to give Uncle Barney a kiss, to reward him for being so nice.

"And of course, I don't have to introduce the two of you," said Pepper Delafield, moving away from Lily and Cutter to greet a new group of guests.

"It would look odd if we shook hands," Cutter said, taking Lily's hand in his and holding it. "I should kiss you on the cheek, but that would be odder still, from one stranger to another."

"The oddest thing of all is that we've never met before. Every time Zachary and I visited San Francisco you were on a trip out of town. And you never came to New York . . ." Lily's voice trailed off and she withdrew her hand. She had no idea that whenever Cutter had seen photographs of her in *Vogue* or *Town & Country* he had turned the page quickly and angrily, dismissing her with scorn as a typically bland little English face whom his brother had probably married for her title, like someone buys a particular cupcake because it has a cherry on top. He'd seen Zachary, of course, for his brother had paid all his bills until he started making a living, but he drew the line at playing the younger brother-in-law to the Honorable Lily.

"I'm here now," he said, "for good." Around them the large party had taken on that sound that reassures every hostess no matter how experienced, the sound of lively, laugh-punctuated, easy conversation, seamless and as constant as the bubbling of a big stew on just the right degree of fire, a sound that covered up the awkward pause that fell between Lily and Cutter. She stupefied him, this woman he could no more dismiss than the law of gravity. Until this minute he had known only American girls, debutantes or post-debutantes of the East and West Coast Establishments, girls, he understood immediately, who had patterned themselves, consciously or not, on an ideal, the ideal that was Lily. How glorious she was! She had a quality of consummate rarity: every detail of her face was heightened, as if he were looking at an enlarged photograph, yet the whole was simplified, as only the purest beauty is simple.

Necessary. This incandescent woman was necessary to him, this woman who, of all women in the world, was his brother's wife. She couldn't possibly love Zachary. He knew that fact instantly without a single doubt, because if she loved his brother she wouldn't, she *could not possibly* be looking at him as she was, with wild curiosity, with fear, a fear that made him hear a great tom-tom of triumph, a fear he could clearly see trembling on her lips, quenching her social smile, forcing her to lower her eyes, stiffening her posture so that she wouldn't shake. There could be only one reason for that fear, a reason Cutter understood perfectly, for he felt it himself. It was the fear of someone whose life has, in the space of a minute, changed forever and ever.

"Cutter, by God, Cutter! I've been looking all over for you. Pepper told me you were here. Damn it, Cutter, it's good to see you!" Zachary hugged him with a quick, embarrassed hug he couldn't restrain. He had long been wounded by the cold, distant stiffness his brother displayed toward him, but he couldn't seem to change it, try as he would. There had always been something strained in their relationship which he had never been able to understand. Finally, helplessly, he had decided to attribute it to the decade that separated them, to the cliché of the generation gap. But he was delighted to lay eyes on the boy. No, he corrected himself, the man, for Cutter was unquestionably a man now, twenty-four years old and, in all ways but age, the most commanding presence in the room.

"I'm glad to see you too, Zack," Cutter said smiling automatically. How had he *dared*, how had he had the monstrous effrontery to marry this girl? He had no right to her, didn't he know that? He could deck her out all over with diamonds and sapphires and call her what he would, but she had never belonged to him. He stared down at Zachary, noting the few extra pounds around Zachary's waist, the more obvious since he hadn't had time to have a new dinner jacket made for several years, seeing the strands of gray that had begun to invade his dark hair. There were lines on Zachary's face that were unfamiliar to Cutter, lines that had appeared during the last year, during the long nights that he stood outside of Toby's room where, now, a lamp always burned.

"You look wonderful, Cutter! Doesn't he look wonderful, darling? Listen, have you found an apartment yet? Because if you haven't, you can always stay with us while you look."

"Rented one today, Zack, on East Sixty-seventh, just a few blocks from your house. It's a furnished sublet, just temporary, until I find the place I want to settle in, but perfectly adequate."

"Great, that means that you have to come and see us—Lily, how about tomorrow . . . are we having dinner at home tomorrow night?"

"Yes."

"Is that good for you, Cutter?"

"I'd love it."

"Come early, so you can see the kids. We'll eat at eight but if you can get to our place by six-thirty you can see both of them before Nanny spirits them away."

"Terrific. I'll count on it."

"You're not all supposed to be standing around talking to your own family," Pepper Delafield said, sweeping up to the three of them, and scattering them strategically among her other guests as only she knew how to do.

Lily didn't sleep at all that night, and finally, at five, she got up and wandered around the great house, touching polished wood, picking up heavy silver boxes and putting them down, crushing velvet-covered pillows. When she found herself methodically destroying a bouquet of flowers, plucking petal after petal from the hearts of roses, rolling them in her hands until they grew limp and wet before she discarded them angrily on a table, she decided to go to the ballroom, which had been turned into her dance studio, and work at the barre. It was an infallible remedy for any kind of thought, an ingrained rhythm of body and mind that had never failed her. Yet, as dawn broke, so did her dancer's discipline, and for the first time in her life she did not finish her barre, nor did she care. She was waiting, listening, in the quiet house, for something to happen, something she could not put a name to, and she knew that she was in no condition to face her day's appointments. She would cancel them and stay at home.

She spent the morning flipping unseeingly through a pile of new magazines in her sitting room. For two years she and Zachary had had separate sets of rooms and the servants were accustomed to her taking an occasional day off from her exhausting schedule and, as now, ordering lunch on a tray. Lily sat looking at the untouched tray, counting the hours until six-thirty. Every few minutes she got up to look at herself in a mirror and each time she saw nothing except eyes that seemed strangely terrified, and burning cheeks. She tried to make a few phone calls but stopped in the act of dialing because she couldn't imagine what she would talk about to any of her friends.

Nothing seemed important, nothing meant anything anymore. It was as if she had had no past and possessed no future. She put her hand to her throat and felt the pulse beating furiously. She walked around and around the room, repeating the few words that she and Cutter had exchanged, such banal words, their only comfort offered by the fact that he had said he was in New York for good. She had seen photographs of him, of course, family photos that her mother-in-law had shown her, but nothing about the pictures of a blond boy with severe, regular features had led her to expect him to be a magnificent man who struck her dumb with mute, primal longing, helpless and quivering and mad with restlessness, bewildered by a feeling of unknown horizons opening before her unto wild and inevitable skies. Again and again she looked at her watch. Five and a half more hours.

There was a tap on the door and the houseman entered.

"Mr. Amberville, Madame," he announced and crossed the room to remove her lunch tray. Cutter stood still, just inside her door. She dared only to glance up once at his face but she couldn't bring herself to meet his gaze or to rise from the couch on which she was sitting. Both of them were motionless until the servant had left, closing the door behind him. Then Cutter came to the couch and picked her up easily until she stood against him, shaking, speechless yet without surprise, astonishingly without surprise. He put one hand on either side of her hot cheeks and, with the utmost deliberation and gravity, kissed her on the mouth, kissed her time after time until they both sank to their knees because they didn't have the strength to stand. They exchanged no words but soon they were both naked, their clothes ripped off in silence, lying on the carpet, panting with haste. He was hard and he had only one goal. She was unsmiling. She had the same goal. Flesh to flesh, sighing, gasping, they made each other whole. They had exchanged no salutations, and no promises, but they had exchanged their separate solitudes, their unrealized selves, their lonely, craving souls. Afterwards, almost immediately, he took her again and this time, now that the world had reformed itself for her, Lily discovered that secret of human passion that she had never known, discovered her own rhythm, a rhythm that had waited, hidden in her body, until this moment in time. What, oh what if he had not been alive? How had she endured so long without him?

"I don't know what to do," she said at last, uncaring, scarcely able to form the words.

"I have to leave you now, beloved. It's getting late and someone is sure to disturb you. Will you make my excuses about tonight? I couldn't stand to see you with him . . . you understand that, don't you? I'll be back tomorrow, at the same time, if you say so. Do you love me, Lily? Do you?"

"Oh, God, yes!"

Cutter put his fingers deeply into her. She was ready for him again; she hadn't closed up and tightened the way women did when they'd had enough. "Tomorrow," he repeated and left.

There were hours of that afternoon, after Cutter left, that Lily could never account for. She supposed that she must have taken a bath, that she must have read to the children and watched them have their supper, that she must have had dinner herself and explained why Cutter wasn't there. But for the rest of her life there were seconds of that first day that she would always remember; the smell of her hands after he had gone; the torn clothing she had hidden in the back of her closet; the way she had to leave the sitting room windows open so that the smell of their lovemaking wouldn't hang in the air; the cream she had slowly, dreamily smoothed on her cheeks where the bristles of his beard had scratched her slightly; the feeling of the carpet under her open legs; the hour she had spent locked in her bathroom, unable to stop sobbing, tears of terrible joy cascading from her eyes; sounds, like those of the newly born, escaping her lips.

After dinner, knowing that she would be unable to function normally without the children or the servants around, she told Zachary that she felt the need of a brisk walk. He nodded, deep in thought, and she left him working in his library on the papers he had brought home from the office with him. Twice, three times she walked around the block, wondering if she could manage to get through the evening without going to Cutter's door. Finally she realized that it was hopeless and she almost ran the three blocks to his apartment. She buzzed. If he weren't there what could she do? She held her breath until the door clicked open and she stumbled up the two flights to his apartment not knowing what she was going to say. He was standing in his doorway, dressed only in a bathrobe.

"I willed you to come here. I've been thinking about nothing else since I left you," he said. She walked into the room without noticing that it was furnished with the most nondescript of rented pieces, worn leather and mustard-colored chairs. He stopped her before she had advanced farther than three steps. "Have you ever done this before? With anyone in the world?" he demanded sternly.

"Of course not," she replied in amazement, her face flushed from the wind, rosy with daring.

"That's what I thought, that's what I knew you'd say," he told her, unbuttoning her coat and leading her into his small bedroom where the open bed waited for her. He pushed her skirt up to her waist and pulled down her brief underpants. She wore a garter belt and stockings and between the top of her pants and the lower edge of her garter belt her blond pubic tangle was framed. He bent down toward it, stuck out his tongue and licked her slowly between those delicately closed lips. She screamed. "Shut up, darling," he whispered, and licked her again, deeper this time, so that the lips parted and his tongue met wetness. Ruthlessly his tongue dragged back and forth, traveling over her clitoris every time it made its trip. Her legs spread as wide as the pants around her knees would permit, her back arched, her mouth opened, she breathed shallowly, concentrated entirely on the voyage of his tongue, knowing, in a delirium of passion, that nothing in the world could make him stop. She lifted her hips off the bed to offer herself more easily to him, she pushed her mound into his face and rubbed it around in a circle, but he wouldn't allow that. He was in charge, he was the boss, and he held her immobile between his elbows, withdrawing his tongue until she whimpered, until she pleaded, until she begged for it, begged out loud. Then he plunged his tongue as deeply into her as it could go, up to the root, in and out, flicking her clitoris every time and when she screamed and screamed he kept going until she was quiet at last.

"Do you *belong* to me?" he demanded.

"I belong to you."

"You have to, don't you, always? Nothing can change that, can it?"

"Never. Nothing. No one."

"Feel me," he commanded.

She put her hand on his penis. It was as hard as it had been when he had first undressed her in her room that afternoon.

"Last night, when I first saw you," he whispered harshly, "I got hard, right away. I was hard all the time we were talking so politely at the party. In my dreams, last night, I came in my sleep and this morning, when I woke up, thinking about you, I had to come again, in my hand, because I was so hard that it hurt. Now I want to come in your mouth."

"Yes," she said. "Yes. Oh, yes."

They took risks only madmen take. They stood up, fully clothed, in the phone booth at L'Aiglon, his hand holding the door closed, while Zachary and Cutter's date had another pre-dinner drink, and he rubbed her against his penis, rocklike under his trousers, until she came, biting back her cries. She went to his office, once he had started working on Wall Street, and while his secretary was out to lunch he knelt on the carpet and she sat on the couch, with her head thrown back and her eyes closed, and slowly, with just his fingers wet with her own juices, he worked her to a shuddering orgasm, watching her face every second.

Often, very often, when they weren't in his apartment, he would not let her touch him no matter how she begged. He experienced a violent joy in withholding his own pleasure, in creating situations in which she would come but he could not. Lily stopped wearing underpants. She never knew in advance when he would let her have his penis, and he never told her.

He would take her casually by the elbow at a crowded party and lead her with deliberate lack of haste to a bathroom, lock the door and tell her to lie on the bathmat. Fully dressed himself, he would raise her wide skirts to her waist and suck her ruthlessly until she came, and then leave her immediately. The next night, at another party, he would guide her away from the other guests and, once in the bathroom, unzip his fly, take out his naked penis and put it in her with total self-absorption, coming quickly and pulling out, deliberately not waiting until she had an orgasm. He would leave the bathroom first and observe her during the rest of the evening, watching her as she moved across the room, wet with his sperm under her gown, wet with her own wanting, but successfully maintaining her serenity by avoiding his eyes.

During intermissions of Broadway musicals, while Zachary waited in line to buy lemonade, they would stand in a corner, not looking at each other. "I want to suck you," he whispered, licking his thumb and pressing it into her palm. "I want to suck you slowly, for an hour, so slowly, so slowly, and not let you come." He reached under the flap of her evening coat, took out her breast from the low-cut bodice of her dress and held it in his hand, his wet thumb rubbing her nipple. She came, standing up, came in quick, shallow spasms that left her eyes brighter than before, came only halfway as he had known she would, so that she would spend the whole of the second act dying for more, unable to touch him.

Lily stopped wearing lipstick, saying that she had become allergic to it; she carried a tiny hairbrush in her handbag at all times and a small bottle of perfume and carefully folded wads of Kleenex. She kept a small traveling toothbrush and a miniature tube of toothpaste in the same bag, and they both used it when they could, but if they weren't near a bathroom they drank some brandy as soon as they joined any group of people. They were both mad with lust, but not so mad as not to realize that they must smell of sex.

Lily grew addicted to the postponed satisfactions; she gloried in not knowing what he was going to do to her. She refused herself any gratification no matter how he had frustrated her, so that she was melting, fluttering with desire at every hour, particularly as she was dressing to go to one of the many parties to which they were all invited, since Cutter had quickly become a part of the group of people the Ambervilles saw almost every evening of that New York spring season. Whenever she crossed her legs she had a short, quick orgasmic spasm.

Lily dropped out of almost all of her committee work with vague excuses, and refused all lunch dates so that she would always be free to meet Cutter at his apartment if he called. He could take the subway back and forth to Wall Street and still have time enough to spend a long half hour with her in the middle of the day, and that became the only time they would lie totally naked in bed together. But he rationed this pleasure unnecessarily, saying he had to go to business lunches, because he far preferred the chances they took in public places to the shelter of his bed; preferred the dominion over her that he had by merely touching her elbow, taking her away from a cluster of people, particularly when Zachary was part of that cluster. Sometimes Cutter would stand next to Lily, queenly silk-clad, Lily, Lily in her splendid jewels, with her sheaves of hair flowing down her back, for she would wear it no other way now, and talk business to Zachary for three-quarters of an hour, knowing that she was waiting for him to signal her. Then he would walk away with barely an excuse and talk to somebody else. Those were the best moments of all, those evenings when he would deny both of them, when he would merely brush her cheeks with his lips at the end of the party, knowing that at any minute during the past hours he could have had his brother's wife kneeling at his feet, her lips open to receive him.

7

Ever since Maxi was born, the Ambervilles had owned a summer house, a great shingled mansion that overlooked the Atlantic from its perch above the Southampton Dunes. Lily enjoyed those lazy summers. There was something almost English about the quality of utter leisure, the taking of tea, the cutting of roses, the croquet games, the daily visits to the Maidstone Club to play tennis in an atmosphere of protected, soft-voiced, well-mannered distance from the New York crowds. She found more time for her children during the summers and on the weekday evenings, when Zachary was rarely able to drive out for dinner, she often chose not to see anyone, but to eat alone. After dinner she would sometimes walk by herself on the beach, feeling the sand still warm under her bare feet, thinking about nothing at all, and find herself almost happy.

Now as she faced the summer of 1958, a July and August that would separate her from Cutter except for the weekends, Lily tried frantically to find a reason to stay in the city. But there simply wasn't one: she could hardly send Toby and Maxi and the servants out to the beach by themselves while she camped in the city house with a skeleton staff on the pretext of not wanting to leave Zachary alone . . . everyone would find that most unusual and unnecessary, Zachary above all.

It was still mid-June but she thought of little else than the impossible summer ahead. She went through the motions of her life without allowing her preoccupation to become visible, as once she had danced with bleeding feet and a brilliantly fixed smile, until, in the middle of one spring night, she woke up in a state of alarm from a nightmare that she couldn't remember a split second after she opened her eyes. Her heart was beating so heavily that Lily pressed her hands over her breasts bearing down on her fright, unable to sort out her thoughts. Her heart began to slow down as she tried to recollect the dream. What could have so terrified her? She lay still, searching, her hands still cupped comfortingly around her breasts, taking deep breaths, when suddenly a message passed from flesh to flesh and her heart lurched again into a violent rhythm. Only twice before in her life had her breasts felt like this: sensitive, warmer than usual, with a hint of the fullness to come.

There was no question of whose baby it was. She had allowed Zachary to make love to her a minimum of times in the last months, only often enough to prevent any possibility of a confrontation, and each time she had taken every precaution not to become pregnant. With Cutter she had forgotten the meaning of caution just as she had forgotten everything else in her recklessness.

Joy, a joy that accepted none of the problems of reality, invaded her. The fear she had awakened vanished totally as Lily, deeply happy as she had never known she could be, said over and over to herself, "Cutter's baby, *our* baby." She was too excited to stay in bed even though it was not yet dawn. She went to her window and looked out at a city which, for a few minutes, was as close-to-quiet, as close-to-dark, as it ever became in any twenty-four hours, no longer a strange and lonely citadel of hard, bright towers, a city now imbued with the color of her only love, her once and forever love. Here she had first met Cutter, here she had conceived his child, here she had become a woman.

Cutter sat on the edge of the bed and put his arm carefully, protectively, around her bare shoulders. Lily was like an undetonated bomb that might go off at any minute and blow his life sky-high. From the instant she had told him she was pregnant he had been seized by a cramp of such panic that he had barely been able to react. Wordless by necessity he let her bubble on in her lunatic joy as he scrambled in his mind, considering the import of her news.

At her first words he had withdrawn deep inside himself, understanding suddenly but absolutely that she and he were thinking and feeling on two planes that could never meet. Cutter loved Lily as much as he would ever be able to love a woman. She had all the qualities he admired and her inborn sense of superior aristocracy flattered his needy nature. She seemed to be made on purpose for his private pleasure. She was a marvelous sensual adventure, and his lust for her did not lie only in the fact that she was a means of taking hidden, gloating revenge on Zachary. But publicly she was taboo. Lily was his sister-in-law, a married woman with two children, and the fact that she was now pregnant by him was enough to make the past months of fascinated passion vanish from his mind. The only emotion he felt was utter fear and the determination to get out of this situation no matter what he had to do.

"Darling, what do you intend to do?" he asked calmly.

" 'Intend' . . . I don't have any intentions. I thought that you . . . that together we . . ."

"Would somehow get married and live happily ever after?" His words were gentle but his hands were balled into fists.

"Yes, I suppose that's more or less what I thought. Oh, Cutter, I can't think . . . I'm much too happy to think. I love you too much to even try."

"Darling, look, one of us has to be sensible. I want a child with you, Lily, I want lots of children with you—but, what about Toby and Maxi? Have you considered them?"

"Toby and Maxime? Well, naturally they'll be with me. We'll all be together—they won't suffer, Zachary would never let them down in any way and eventually things will sort themselves out, the way they seem to in this country." Lily gave a carefree shrug.

Cutter looked at her, his fear growing. This insanely romantic, infantile madwoman could ruin him unless he could control her. Still he controlled his voice.

"The Zachary you know is a doting indulgent husband, more than ten years older than you, who gives you everything you want, my darling. Nevertheless there's no way to predict how he'll act when he finds out what's been going on. If I were in his place I think I'd try to kill you. Certainly I'd try to take away the children. Do you imagine he got where he is because he lets people take things away from him? Do you believe that he lets anybody make a fool out of him? You don't really know your husband, beloved, but I do. . . . I've known the greedy bastard since I was born. He might, eventually, let you have a divorce, because he'd see that there was no way to keep you, but it would take a very long tough time."

Lily shook her head violently. Nothing Cutter said was right. Nobody could prevent her from having what she wanted. Cutter didn't understand Zachary as well as she did . . . he didn't know that Zachary had never been able to make her love him. It was *all Zachary's fault*... all those years and years without love—all those fruitless, arid, passionless nights. She'd been so patient, so innocent. She had given Zachary enough of herself, she thought bitterly, and now it was over.

"Lily, listen to me. There are only two ways we can make things work for us. Either you have to wait to get a divorce until after the baby is born or you have to have an abortion now... no, *stop* that, Lily, stop and listen! You can go to a good, perfectly legal clinic in Puerto Rico or Sweden, or to a dozen different Park Avenue doctors, the same ones your friends go to. God knows, sweetheart, I can't stand to think of you having to go through an abortion but there isn't any other alternative."

"I will not have an abortion," Lily declared, her face set in an expression of absolute disdain and defiance.

"I understand why you feel that way but..."

"No, you don't. If you did you couldn't possibly suggest it. It's utterly out of the question. Nobody can make me. I'm going to have our baby."

Abruptly Cutter got up and crossed the room and consulted his watch on his dresser. If he listened to her for another minute, laying down the law, so confident in her selfish, shortsighted, childlike stupidity, he'd hit her. There was no telling what she was capable of, what scandal she might unleash, but one thing he was sure of now was that she was fully capable of destroying his career without even realizing what she was doing. He'd be out on the street in five minutes if his firm heard about this, disgraced everywhere in his world, every man he'd ever known snickering at him, stuck with the responsibility for a married woman and her brat at twenty-four, when his life was just beginning, because this God damned bitch hadn't had the ordinary common sense to use a diaphragm.

"Darling," he said, "I'm late for work already. I have to rush. You go home and relax and leave this to me. I'll find a way for us to be together. It's as important to me as it is to you. Now get dressed... I've got five minutes to shave and shower."

"When will I see you?"

"Tonight there's that business dinner I told you about and tomorrow is my class reunion at the University Club. Hell... it all couldn't come at a worse time but I'm scheduled to make a speech. Look, I'll get away from the dinner as soon as I can and I'll meet you back here. Zachary will still be in Chicago so we can spend the whole night together. Just let yourself in with your key and wait for me."

Smiling, Lily slid out of bed. She didn't mind this enforced separation. It would be lovely to have a little time alone to gloat over her happiness. Men were so preoccupied with details.

A letter was waiting for her on Cutter's bedspread when she arrived the following night.

My darling,

If I didn't love you so much I might be able to destroy your life just so that we could be together, but I can't do that to you. You've been protected in a way you don't begin to comprehend. You went straight from your father's house to your husband's house without ever disappointing anybody or being disappointed yourself. You've led a life in which disgrace and scandal and particularly dishonor have had no place, and I can't put you in that position because of your love for me.

I could stand proud under the dishonor of having fallen in love with my own brother's wife because I know the deep truth about the way we feel about each other. But in the eyes of the world, in the eyes of all your friends in New York, you would be the one who would be blamed. You would have taken all your husband could give you and then turned around and betrayed him. Your parents, in particular, would be heartbroken. Women are always the ones who are considered to be at fault in this sort of thing unless the man is a well-known bastard—it's not fair but you know it's true. The men are considered lucky rascals and the lady is a whore. I can't let you be smeared by gossip and in your case it would be much worse than gossip, it would be headlines in the press, here and in England too.

I've done nothing but think since I left you. Toby will always need the most expensive kind of special education that only Zachary can give him. You know how devoted Toby is to his father. How can I ask you to take a child who's going blind away from his familiar life, his own house, his own father? Maxi could adapt to almost anything but Toby is a special case, and I can't allow myself to hurt him because of our love.

I know that you wouldn't mind living on what I make, I know you don't care about not having the houses and servants and all the other things that Zachary gives you, but I would mind, desperately, *seeing you reduced to cutting corners, taking care of three children, having to help with the housework, worrying about money. We've never talked about my economic situation but I'm really just beginning my career. Someday, and I know it will be soon, I'll be making enough to support you, but right now it would be impossible with three children unless we were able to depend on Zachary for our income which would mean a kind of sick dependency which would tear us apart.*

My beloved, my Lily, you re the only woman I'll ever love, but has it ever occurred to you that I'm only twenty-four years old?

God, I'd give anything to be older, established, able to take you away from him and give you everything and to hell with what people say. But we must wait. *If you have the courage to wait we can have a life together. You have to make the decision about the baby. Whatever you do will be the right thing to do, the only thing to do.*

I'm going back to San Francisco. By the time you read this I'll be on the plane. I'm too much of a coward to say all of this to your face, too ashamed that I can't make it right, couldn't find a way that we could be together. Please, beloved, don't hate me. I hate myself enough for the two of us. I'll always love you and one day we'll be together if you can be patient, strong, brave and forgive me. And wait, wait.

Cutter

Lily read the letter once. She folded it and put it in her handbag and proudly walked out of the empty room. How much, she thought, Cutter must love her, to have thought only of how the baby would change *her* life. If only he were here, so she could tell him that there was no reason for him to be ashamed. Hate him? How could she possibly hate him? Every word of his letter told her how much she meant to him. Didn't he realize that their child meant that they would be linked forever? And oh, how well she knew how to wait.

Every Wednesday afternoon there was a meeting of the people on whom Zachary Amberville relied to run his magazines. The group didn't have any formal name, since, as in many privately owned companies without stockholders, there was no board of directors, but Zachary gave a lot of thought to the invitations he tendered. It was understood that anyone who attended one meeting would, from then on, attend all of them. In a magazine business, where top editors are not infrequently wooed by the competition, and issues are planned five months in advance, secrecy about future plans is vital. Zachary waited a long time before asking any employee to come to the Wednesday planning session.

Zelda Powers, Editor-in-chief of *Style*, had some eighty people working for her of whom a handful had their own clearly defined areas of responsibility; among them: fashion, beauty, accessories, shoes—almighty shoes whose manufacturers advertise mightily—and features. Features included all the major articles in *Style* and a front-of-the-book catchall for whatever was new in the worlds of movies, art, television, music, and books, called "Have You Heard?" To have a job in the "Have You Heard?" section of *Style*, a job that paid less than that of any self-respecting saleslady at Macy's, was the equivalent of the honor bestowed on Jean Lannes, Duke of Montebello, the only one of Napoleon's twelve *Maréchals* who was allowed to address the Emperor in the familiar form as "thou."

No poor girl could afford to work for "Have You Heard?" nor would a rich but not terribly bright girl stand a chance. She had to be both well enough off to support herself from outside income, and enormously smart, for the competition for these three assistant editors' jobs started early on the campuses of the Seven Sisters, the Ivy League women's colleges. Young editors were hired by the features editor, John Hemingsway, who enjoyed every second of the power he wielded, for it was he who decided which personalities would have profiles written on them for the main section of the magazine; which American man or woman was ripe to be explored in color photos and three thousand words; it was he who decreed that any given human being merited merely a thousand words and a black-and-white photo, or determined that any particular topic had suddenly become worthy of notice by *Style* and should be assigned as an article.

For his three "Have You Heard?" assistants Hemingsway hired only unmarried women; only those who dressed well; only those who were shorter than he; only those under thirty; because if they were over thirty and still unmarried they were bound to be too neurotic to work as well as he expected them to; and only those who were willing to work nights because if they had too many boyfriends he knew they would be more interested in marriage than in "Have You Heard?" No matter how hard they worked, he hired only girls who were not ambitious enough to want his job, for he didn't trust women at all.

Dozens and dozens of girls managed to qualify for these three jobs at *Style*. Two of them who held the jobs were true to the Hemingsway mold, and the third, who was secretly ambitious and thus the cleverest of all, was able to work late and still keep a half-dozen boyfriends entangled in her web. Fortunately Nina Stern needed very little sleep and worked quickly.

Nina Stern was twenty-five and of all the beautiful, rich, *unmarried* Jewish girls anyone in 1958 had ever heard of, by far the oldest. People had even stopped trying to probe at this problem with her mother. It was taken for granted among the many friends of the Stern family that there was something invisibly but unquestionably wrong with Nina. Even a hint of a hint would be cruel and, what was worse, would have no result. The poor thing didn't even have a broken engagement to her credit. Why meddle if it couldn't help? It was more productive to meddle where there was still some hope.

Marriage, in Nina Stern's opinion, was the end of the line. She had probably flirted with the doctor who delivered her, and certainly with every living creature she had encountered after that minute. The only form of communication Nina knew was one form or another of flirtation; but accused of flirting she truly wouldn't have understood what people were talking about. She flirted with children, teenagers, all adults of both sexes, homosexuals of any persuasion, and any animal she came across. She had never flirted with a rock but she had flirted with many trees and flowers. Her flirtation wasn't specific, neither sexual nor romantic, but merely an instinctive approach to any situation in which she found herself, a general, permanent, immutable inclination toward courtship. Her flirtatiousness was not "correct" in the French sense, meaning proper; it was great, even noble. It was also essentially harmless and it explained why, like businesses that are depression-proof, Nina Stern at any age would always be proof against any shortage of males. Just as she knew her name was Nina she knew that there would always be men for her and she adored variety too much to even consider settling down with just one man.

She liked to meet her college friends for lunch and admire the photographs of their fast-growing families; she felt only sincere admiration when the much younger sisters of these friends displayed their engagement rings, but monogrammed towels reminded her of straitjackets, and new sheets of shrouds. The only shopping in New York she couldn't endure was on the second floor of Tiffany's, where she often was forced to buy yet another baby present. There, certain interior decorators were given a free hand with the vast stock of the store and vied with each other in arranging china, crystal and silver in ways that tables had never been laid before. When Nina confronted the glittering, fantastic tables as she left the gray-velvet-lined elevator, all that filled her mind were images of women standing in line for the butcher's personal attention at Gristede's, cluttered kitchens and dirty dishes. Otherwise she had no time for gruesome fantasies, unless it was to report on the newest horror film for *Style*.

She was, at first sight, the embodiment of the happy medium, although nothing about her was average. Her shoulder-length hair was light brown, but of the irresistible and indescribable shade called *marron glacé*, the color of candied chestnuts. Her height was five feet five and a half inches, mysteriously just the right height for every activity except professional basketball. Her face wasn't distinctively heart-shaped or round or oval, but its shape pleased every eye. It was simply the right shape and her features were the right features and her body was the right body, and her voice was the right voice, in the sense that the slightest alteration in them would have been *wrong*. Seven full pages in the *Oxford English Dictionary* are devoted to definitions of the word "right," but one close look at Nina defined rightness in a flash.

This great flirt, with her definition-defying rightness, sometimes had to work on Saturday if she'd had a particularly full week fending off all the men who wanted to marry her without driving them away for good. One particular Saturday in June of 1958 when the only possible activity for a self-respecting New Yorker was opening up the beach house or painting the shutters in Fairfield County, on a day on which no Manhattanite should have been caught in Manhattan, Nina Stern was forced to go to the office to finish a last column for "Have You Heard?" She took the newly automated elevator to the fifteenth floor. Somewhere between the tenth and eleventh floors the elevator stopped, with a particularly final grinding sound.

"Now what?" asked Nina of a male unknown to her, the only other passenger.

"There's a phone . . . I'll call for help," Zachary Amberville said.

Whoever was supposed to be on the other end of the phone was evidently out to lunch. The only sound was Muzak as Zachary tried repeatedly to get an answer.

"I wouldn't mind so much," Nina said surveying him, "if it weren't for that noise. Death by Muzak. They'll find us here on Monday morning, out of our minds, singing 'Rudolph the Red-Nosed Reindeer' for the rest of our lives."

"Do you like rye bread?" Zachary asked.

"Corn rye or regular rye with caraway seeds?"

"Regular. I stopped at Reuben's and picked up a sandwich before I came to the office." He unwrapped the enormous crusty oval-shaped sandwich, sliced on the diagonal in three sections, filled with thick layers of pastrami, Swiss cheese, corned beef, cold slaw, and Reuben's own mustard.

"You even have a pickle," Nina marveled.

"It stimulates the brain," Zachary said with authority. "Better than fish. Why don't we sit down?"

"If only there were some way to turn off the Muzak."

"There is. You have to climb on my shoulders and push that little switch on the top of the door to the left."

Nina surveyed the stranger. He couldn't be a mad rapist or he would have raped her by now. He obviously was kind-hearted since he was willing to share his perfect sandwich when they might have another day and a half before they were released. In spite of childhood conditioning she wasn't afraid that he was in the white slave trade. Her mother had never let her go to the movies on Saturday afternoon except to the Trans-Lux on Eighty-fifth Street, where a matron patrolled the aisles with a flashlight, because it was well known that any nice New York girl, alone in the movies, would be pricked with a hypodermic by any man who took the seat next to her, pass out and, a week later, wake up as a white slave in Tangiers. Nina thought she would be rather well treated in Tangiers, if it came to that, and anyway this man did not look like the type. He was wearing an expensive tweed jacket, even if it didn't fit him. He had very clean black hair, even if it needed a cut. His flexible, quirky mouth was kind, his dark eyes bright with amusement, and his shoes were handmade.

She nodded agreement to Zachary and he bent down, like a fullback, and she took off her shoes and hopped on his shoulders. "Get up very slowly. I've never done this before," she ordered. Zachary rose inch by inch, while Nina clutched his hair. She eliminated the Muzak with a quick flick of the switch and he carefully lowered her to the floor of the elevator. They both sat down. It was a clean elevator and the only one they had.

"That gave me an appetite," Nina said.

"You can have the middle piece," Zachary offered generously, spreading out the silver foil. The middle section of a Reuben sandwich was always the most succulent.

"Thank you," Nina said. All her life men had given her the best piece, just as she'd always been offered the white meat of every chicken and the crispest piece of bacon and the female lobster with the delicious coral in it, but although she was always grateful she was no more surprised than Morgan Le Fay would have been. She smiled at Zachary. Of all the utterly right things about Nina Stern, her smile was the rightest. Of all the flirtatious things about Nina Stern, her smile was the most flirtatious. What a nice girl, Zachary thought. "Where do you work?" he asked.

"At *Style*, in 'Have You Heard?' What about you?"

"Sales," he said dismissively, with a shrug.

"Unexciting? Horribly boring? Dreary and dull?" she sympathized.

"Necessary," Zachary said stoically. "But nothing you'd want to hear about. I've just spent three days in Chicago at a sales convention and enough is enough."

"Oh, go on, bore me. Tell me about dismal sales, all about pokey, stuffy old sales, everything about tedious, monotonous, unfortunately necessary sales. Stop when I go into a coma."

"I never bore a lady on purpose," he grinned. "Tell me about 'Have You Heard?' "

"If you won't bore me, I refuse to bore you . . . it's all just a lot of chat, basically unimportant. Anyway, wouldn't you rather eat than talk?" Nina's work was too vital to her to discuss with the many men in her life and she had just realized that this stranger was unquestionably going to be a man in her life. It usually did not take her more than a split second to make such a decision but until today she had been terrified of being trapped in elevators and her reflexes were slower than normal.

"We could do both," Zachary said, "at the same time."

"Should we try to make this last as long as possible in case they don't rescue us, or should we just . . . ?" Nina pondered.

"Big bites. You can't enjoy a sandwich and hold back at the same time."

'I'll remember that . . . you're so wise."

Really a bright girl, Zachary thought. Exceptionally bright. I think I'll invite her to the next Wednesday meeting. We can use her kind of brain. And there's something nice about her, can't exactly put my finger on it.

The elevator started just as they were finishing the sandwich. Nina got off at her floor. She held out her hand and smiled at him again.

"Nina Stern," she said.

"Zachary Amberville."

"That's not fair!" she laughed as the door closed. She was still laughing as she opened her office door. Nina, she told herself, you've just blown the chance of a lifetime.

For a smart girl she could sometimes be very dumb.

"This great big city's a wondrous toy," Zachary sang out loud as he walked home much later that day, his work done. "Just made for a girl and boy." As always he hit a false note on the word "boy." He jaywalked expertly across Madison as he reached the last lines of his song. " 'We'll turn Manhattan into an isle of joy.' " He hadn't felt like this in a long time, he realized. He hadn't sung his song in months, years. How did he feel exactly? he asked himself, his steps slowing. Was it the brisk, blowing spring evening with the promise of something brightly thrilling in the air that only New Yorkers feel as the days grow longer? Was it the satisfactory afternoon's work shaping a new magazine no one else knew about yet? Was it just New York, intoxicating center of the galaxy, where his ambitions were born and fulfilled? *Good.* He felt good. Why the hell *shouldn't* he feel good? What man wouldn't feel good who was worth so many millions he hadn't counted them lately, what man wouldn't feel good who had the power he had, who had the fun . . . "sales" he remembered, and laughed out loud. Sales, divine sales!

How old would a girl like Nina Stern be? Shit, but he felt *young*! He was thirty-five and he felt like his sixteen-year-old self at Columbia, waiting on tables for enough money for the subway and a hot dog . . . it hadn't been all that long ago, a war ago, a marriage ago, but still, only nineteen years ago. And only six of the nineteen years spent as a married man. He frowned, his mood suddenly almost punctured. If he felt so young, how come he hadn't made love to Lily in the last few weeks? How come they made love so rarely, now that he came to think about it? As Nat, his brother-in-law, would say, who's counting?

He was counting, that's who. Lily had never been passionate and he'd accepted that about her . . . that was just the way she was . . . but she'd always been so willing.

Sweet and delicate and docile. He'd had to make that be enough for him, although many and many a night he'd yearned for a wife who would match his hunger. But, in six years, he'd never played around. Funny about playing around: so many men did it, even when they loved their wives, even when their wives were, he imagined, available in a way that Lily, somehow, didn't seem to be anymore, except at increasingly rare intervals. It occurred to him that mentally, if not physically, she had recently turned away from him when he came to her room and indicated in a subtle, graceful, wordless way that she really didn't want him, not that night, not right now. Was there some inward drama, unguessed at, in her life?

Available. So many women were available in this town. But not all of them. A girl like Nina Stern for instance. She wouldn't be available. She was probably married or engaged or had a list of hopefuls an arm long. Girls like Nina, nice and bright, were spoken for, it stood to reason. And she had a healthy appetite too, always an attractive thing in a woman. " 'We'll go to Coney,' " he sang, " 'and eat baloney on a roll, through Central Park we'll stroll, da dum.' " Someone turned around to look at him and he realized he was singing out loud again. He'd make sure to tell Hemingsway to bring her to the next Wednesday meeting. Do the girl good to see how the magazines were run from some other point of view than that of "Have You Heard?" Better yet, he'd send her a personal memo, a special invitation. Motivated, of course, by her deep interest in sales. "That's not fair," she'd said . . . and it wasn't. He should make it up to her. Smiling he opened his front door and entered the gray marble house just as the butler finished crossing the hall. He had a flash of disbelief . . . could this be his own house, did it really belong to him? He felt so young again, so much the way he had felt when he ventured downtown from Columbia and walked all the streets of his city, not even wondering what lay beyond the doors of houses like this one, splendid beyond the limits of his imagination. He passed the butler with a cheerful greeting and mounted the stairs to his private library where he preferred to work, rather than in the big library downstairs.

"Lily?" he said, astonished. She was standing at the window, looking across the garden, and turned impatiently as he entered.

"I've been waiting for you to come home, darling. I do wish you didn't have to work on Saturday, especially after being away most of the week," she said in her silvery, most loving voice.

"It was something that I had to think through, and I think better at the office. Also my desk was piled high with things I won't have time for on Monday. But I love finding you here. What's that? Champagne? Did I forget something? It's not our anniversary, it's not a birthday, what are we celebrating?" He opened the bottle and deftly filled the tulip-shaped glasses standing on the silver tray she had put on his desk.

"A toast, darling,"—she said, as they touched the rims of the glasses together. "The best possible news . . . another baby."

"Another baby! I *knew* something wonderful was going to happen!" he shouted for joy and grabbed her in his arms, all other thoughts forgotten.

Lily submitted to his hug, her eyes filled with tears. Courage, Cutter had said, and bravery. She would do anything for him. The most difficult part was over. Now the waiting began.

8

Only the blankness of deep shock and the veneer of basic, automatic manners carried Maxi and Toby through the moments in which they had to congratulate Lily and Cutter on their marriage. Words were said, nods were exchanged but neither of them even tried to manage a smile. It was, Maxi thought, as if the four of them were engaged in trying to decently bury the nameless victim of a hit-and-run accident, a victim whose body was that of Zachary Amberville.

The consternation and astonishment that still filled the boardroom was actually welcome because it enabled the brother and sister to retreat quickly, clutching each other's hands and slipping into the express elevator while Lily and Cutter were still engaged with those members of the Amberville editorial group untouched by the death of four magazines, who were able to offer their own good wishes with a naturalness that neither Maxi nor Toby had been able to muster. Elie took them both back to Toby's town house on a quiet street in the East Seventies. Wordlessly Toby stalked to the bar beside his swimming pool which he had constructed out of the entire first floor and garden of the narrow but deep brownstone, and poured each of them a large drink.

"What is it?" Maxi asked.

"Brandy. I never drink it but if ever there was a time . . ."

"I simply don't believe . . . I just can't understand . . ." Maxi started to say but Toby cut her off.

"Shut up, drink it and have a swim. We can't talk about this yet." He stripped and dove into the pool with that fast, flat dive that had helped him become a swimming champion many times over. Maxi joined him, wearing only her black pearl, and they swam laps until she could feel some of the ball of emotions that filled her begin to dissolve into simple weariness. She stopped swimming and sat by the edge of the pool until Toby surfaced at last and easily hoisted himself up to sit beside her. He had splendid muscles and shoulders yet he was almost fragile at the waist, like many other great swimmers.

"Better?" he grunted.

"As much better as I'm going to get. Which is not a hell of a lot. I feel as if I've been hit by a hand grenade—all to pieces."

"I wonder if we haven't both been overlooking a lot about those two, if we aren't naive to be so surprised."

"Do you mean that obviously Mother had been lonely since . . . oh, God, since Dad's death . . . and so she turned to Cutter and obviously they are both about the same age and no matter how much I don't like or trust him, he's objectively an incredibly handsome man and after all life and sex don't stop in the late forties? And that it's natural that she'd be embarrassed about getting married to her own brother-in-law and sneak off and do it without telling us in advance? After all, Toby, it was no accident that she told us about it in public. . . . The one thing I can't imagine is that they just decided to elope on the spur of the moment. They're not Romeo and Juliet."

"Yes to all of that," Toby said, "but there's something else that I've noticed and haven't really paid enough attention to . . . there's a *complicity* between them . . . there always has been, to one degree or another, since Cutter came back from England. And when Dad went, so suddenly, last year, it's gotten steadily stronger."

"Complicity? What's that supposed to mean, exactly . . . that they are partners in crime?"

"No, a deep sort of *involvement*, an intense interest in each other's needs and wishes, an agreement that goes beyond agreement, so that it creates a bond that is stronger and more durable than the fact that he's good-looking or she needs a man in her life or any of those self-evident things."

"How come you're such an expert?" Maxi asked rebelliously.

"I *hear* it. You know I hear things in people's voices that you don't catch. I hear it in the way they move when they're together. When you're blind, Goldilocks, you learn to hear people moving in hundreds of different ways, and each means something different. They're deeply complicitous. I hear it and, by God, I *smell* it . . . under all the perfume and soap and after-shave in the world I can smell it on both of them."

Maxi squirmed in a primitive resistance to his words.

"Why do you persist in calling me Goldilocks?" she asked, trying to change the subject.

"Because I like the word. If your hair were all white I'd just see tiny bits of it, now and then, so I call you whatever I like. Just don't go bald. Now, back to Mother and Cutter. He's got her exactly where he wants her. It's the first time I've ever known her like this, so dominated, so dependent. While Dad was alive I felt a certain set of things when she was with him, something utterly different. They were kind to each other . . . I supposed they'd come to terms. They were friends, or at least not enemies, but no complicity."

"You're revolting."

He laughed and smacked her on her bare thigh. "Nice and fresh," he said appraisingly. "You should be good for another ten, maybe fifteen years, before you start to lose that special springiness in the muscles."

"Take your hands off me, you degenerate."

"Do you love me, Goldilocks?"

"I love you, Bat." It was their ritual. Tobias's earliest memory was of touching the cheeks of baby Maxi and her first memory was of his hand picking her up when she tripped on an icy street.

"Oh, if only you could have seen those poor bastards at the meeting, Toby. Some of them looked as if they'd just been sentenced by a hanging judge."

"I heard them. That was enough."

"But how can we accept the way he said that he spoke for her? You know that Mother couldn't possibly have made this decision on her own—she's never been involved in running the company. She doesn't think about profits, for heaven's sake! It's all Cutter's doing, God knows why. But he cannot be *allowed* to kill four magazines all at once! We can't let him do it! Our father would *never* have considered such a thing, not for any reason unless he were flat-out bankrupt. Toby, Toby! *Remember Dad!* It's not euthanasia, it's outright murder!" Maxi's voice grew louder with every word.

"But what can we do about it, babe? Mother has the power, clearly, to enforce her 'decision,' whoever influenced her. Whatever she wants to do with the company she has the absolute legal right to do."

"Moral suasion," Maxi said slowly in a voice midway between inquiry and the dawning of an idea.

"Moral suasion? Obviously you've been away from your native shores too long. This is New York City, babe, and moral suasion is found only on the op-ed page of the *Times*."

"A special kind of moral suasion, Toby. Manhattan style. If you feed me lunch I'll have the strength to pay our uncle a visit in his office."

"Damned if I know what you're up to."

"Damned if I do . . . yet. But dig we must . . ." she chortled.

"For a better New York," he added, joining in the line they both used to explain any and all inconveniences in the city that was, to them, the center of the universe.

"That would be most unwise, Maxi, and it wouldn't get you anywhere," Cutter said, sitting behind his desk in his Wall Street office. "Whatever you and Tobias feel, and believe me, I truly do understand your sentiments and I sympathize . . ."

"Leave out the hearts and flowers," Maxi snapped. "Let's go straight to the bottom line, since that seems to be your favorite place to operate." She hadn't been home to change since her arrival in New York, but the swim with Toby and the superb lunch he had cooked for her had restored her dauntless spirit, and during the ride downtown she had formed a clear idea of what to do, how to attack.

"I don't care if Amberville is a privately owned company or not, Cutter, it's still subject to public opinion. When Toby and I go to the press, as we plan to, with our minority shareholders' report, we are going to tell them that we are convinced that you have obviously exercised undue influence over our mother, your most amazingly recent bride, and put four magazines to death without prior consultation with Toby or Justin or me, all of us shareholders and highly concerned parties." Maxi stretched out her booted legs defiantly and slumped in her chair with every sign of confident relaxation.

"Perhaps your own skin is thick enough to ignore public opinion, but have you thought about your customers?" she went on. "What about your carefully low-profile partners? Have you thought about everyone in the magazine business, the Newhouses, the Hearsts, the Annenbergs and all the others? What attitude will they have, what will they say about you, Cutter? They all know you are not a publisher, never have been, never will be. It's going to be a juicy, big, *nasty* story for the media . . . four magazines folding at once, hundreds and hundreds of people thrown out of work, all based on the judgment of someone who's never spent five minutes in magazines, someone whose only tiny perch in the business was given to him by his wife?"

Cutter turned over a paper knife, rearranged an inkwell, adjusted his desk clock. There was a brief silence before Maxi continued, since he obviously intended to say nothing.

"I wouldn't want to be in your shoes when we hold our press conference, Cutter. I'm certain Pavka will join us. I know he doesn't have a piece of the company but the media adore him, they consider him a genius, which he is, and a grand old man. Remember the lines around the block for his retrospective at the Museum of Graphic Arts? He's an institution and my father gave him his first chance, to say nothing of the fact that *Wavelength* was Pavka's own idea. Zachary Amberville had faith in the future of those magazines, and people had faith in him—that's what you seem to forget. *My father was a legend. He still is.*"

"You're trying to blackmail me, Maxi, and it won't work. Those magazines are out of business as of this morning. The decision was your mother's to make and she made it."

"You," Maxi said slowly, "are a stinking, rotten, filthy liar. Mother didn't decide anything. But you did. I don't know why yet, but it's all your work, Cutter."

"*How dare you speak to me like that?*"

Maxi had never seen Cutter really angry before. She smiled right into his eyes, which were frozen and savage with fury. If it had been her mother's decision in any degree, he would never have let such words escape him, not Cutter, always so tightly, beautifully controlled, always urbane.

"And I deny the charge of blackmail," Maxi said, her smile widening, as insolent as a tomcat on its own turf. "Can't you even recognize moral suasion when you hear it?"

"*Moral* suasion—coming from you that's not funny, it's absurd. All right, just what do you want, Maxi?"

"A magazine. I want one of the four magazines and I want a year in which you leave me absolutely alone to do anything I like with it. No strings, no looking over my shoulder, no budget cutting. Particularly no budget cutting."

"Apparently you think you've inherited your father's touch. So you're going to save a whole magazine singlehanded? Why, you've barely done a single consecutive week's worth of honest work in your life, and the only time you did work was one summer when you were a teenager. But let's stop fighting," he said, regaining his temper, "it's unproductive. If Lily can be persuaded to give you a magazine, because she's the one who would have to agree, you and your brothers would have to guarantee not to bring the media into a family affair."

"Then we'd be giving you a free hand with the other three," Maxi said, suddenly glum.

"I don't need your free hand, I don't approve of giving in to blackmail, whatever you choose to call it, and I don't think that a press conference held by a well-known playgirl and a man who, because of his unfortunate handicap, can never so much as scan a magazine layout, would be taken very seriously. But, for the sake of family harmony, and because you undeniably have a certain amount of nuisance value, if Lily should approve, which magazine would you single out for your amazing resuscitation attempt?"

"*Buttons and Bows*," Maxi answered promptly. She hadn't the slightest doubt that if her father were still alive his first publication, his talisman, would be the magazine he would care about most of all.

"I'll do my best with your mother, Maxi, but I can't promise anything until I've talked to her."

"Bullshit." Maxi rose quickly and walked to the door. "I consider myself Editor-in-chief of *Buttons and Bows*," she said as she left his office, "as of this minute. No, don't bother to see me to the elevator."

Wearily, but with a sense of triumph percolating in her veins, Maxi arrived home at her apartment on the sixty-third floor of the Trump Tower. She hadn't been at all sure that she could crack Cutter, whose reputation as a sound, if not particularly successful investment banker, might have sustained an attack on his business judgment. Many magazines had died in the last decade, been briefly mourned and forgotten. As Maxi turned the key in her lock, she thought that if Cutter had ever been a member of the editorial board of Amberville Publications, she could never have gotten away with her threats of a press conference. Exactly how, she wondered, do you "call" a press conference?

"Yeow!"

Maxi collapsed to the floor under the weight of a lanky, barefoot, shrieking creature, burdened by a backpack and three tennis rackets, a creature that howled and hugged her until she screamed for mercy.

"Mother, my little mother, my very own tiny little mother," the creature yodeled for joy, "you're home! I just got in and looked in the fridge. There's absolutely nothing to eat in this place, but I know you won't let me starve, oh, little mother of all the Russias."

"Angelica, baby, please get off my bones," Maxi begged. Her eleven-year-old daughter had grown a yard at tennis camp. "What are you doing here? You weren't supposed to come back till next week."

"I split camp when I was eliminated in the eighths finals. It's so tacky to be eliminated in the eighths . . . it's O.K. if you don't get that far and O.K. if you're eliminated in the semis, but the eighths, no way, José."

"Angelica, how did you get back from Ojhi? You didn't . . . oh, my God, you didn't *hitch* did you?" Maxi asked, horrified.

"I called Dad for money. I flew, of course, and he met me at the airport. But he didn't have time to feed me . . . that is he didn't feed me *enough*, just a few hamburgers and a couple of chocolate milkshakes . . . did you see how I've grown? Isn't it great? I'm not going to be a dumb, normal-sized person like you. Maybe I can be a model. Do you think I need a nose job, everyone at camp is having a nose job, where are we going for dinner, did Dad call you in Europe to say I was coming back? I've got a nickname, you have to call me Chip from now on, and I'm going to call you Maxi, it's more mature."

"Call me anything," Maxi groaned as Angelica leaned on her lovingly, "but don't expect me to call you Chip. Somebody has to draw a line somewhere." Maxi put her hands on her daughter's shoulders, pushed her a few inches away and inspected her closely. What particular combination of genes, she wondered, had assembled to create this breathtaking, classic promise of exceptional beauty? The Ambervilles, the Adamsfields, the Andersons, the Dales, the Cutters, had contributed to the amazingly poetic, romantic mixture that was Angelica Amberville Cipriani, and yet the dominant traits in the girl's face were those of her father, Rocco Cipriani; magnificent Rocco, Renaissance Rocco, fascinatingly brooding, darkly luminous Rocco whose ancestors had left Venice—probably the only Venetians who had ever left Venice voluntarily—for the United States less than a hundred years ago.

"Are you also planning a nickname for your father?" she asked, making, as she always did, a point of being polite about her first ex-husband, with whom she shared custody of Angelica.

"Oh, Maxi, you gross me out, you really do. A person doesn't call her *father* by a nickname. Sometimes I wonder about you."

"I see the double standard still prevails," Maxi murmured in resignation. "And don't ask me what that means because you'll find out soon enough."

"Now about dinner . . ." Angelica said, strewing the contents of her backpack around the room. "I thought maybe Thai, or sushi. Tennis camp food was strictly for out-of-towners and you know what that means . . . horrendous squishy white bread, orange-yellow sliced plastic cheese, pale pink baloney . . . I haven't had a decent meal in two months."

"Angelica, we'll get back to your stomach in a second, but how about asking me how I am?"

"How are you, Ma?" Angelica said amiably, trying to find a pair of clean socks.

"I'm the new Editor-in-chief of *Buttons and Bows*."

"Come on . . . how are you? Did you meet some wonderful human being? I haven't had a stepfather recently."

"You will never, *ever* have another stepfather, Angelica. I've told you that a thousand times. I'm serious about *Buttons and Bows*. I'm taking it over."

"*Trimming Trades Monthly?*" Angelica stopped her fruitless quest in astonishment at Maxi's words. "What do you want with poor, old *Trimming Trades?*"

"What are you talking about?"

"*Buttons and Bows* . . . Grandpa always told me that its proper name was *Trimming Trades Monthly* . . . it says so right on the cover, in tiny little letters. *Buttons and Bows* is just the name some desperate editor slapped on it to try and jazz it up. Not that it helped. He said he only kept publishing it out of pity for the people who'd been there for so long . . . he didn't think they could get other jobs, and a lot of them had been there all of their working lives, but he'd lost interest in it ages and ages ago. Seriously, Ma, when was the last time you saw a copy? I think they're practically collector's items. It must have a circulation of at least two hundred and ten. Boring."

"Angelica, how do you know all of this?"

"Grandpa and I used to talk about the business . . . he said I was the only one of the whole family with a head for publishing. Do you happen to have any socks I can borrow, Maxi? . . . Hey, Ma, do you feel all right? You look a little funny. It can't be jet lag or did you fly a regular airline? Maybe you're just starving, like me. Listen, Ma, when do we leave for Venice?"

"Venice?" Maxi repeated vacantly.

"Ma, we are going to spend two weeks in *Venezia*—you know, the one in Italy—before my school starts," Angelica explained patiently and slowly as if to a very elderly person. "Don't say 'Venice?' as if you didn't have the tickets and the reservations because it was all planned months ago."

"We can't go."

"But you said!"

"No Venice. I'm sorry. I'll make it up to you. I have to go to work. At *Trimming Trades Monthly*."

"Jesus! You're serious. Have we lost all our money?"

"I've made a fool of myself."

"Is that worse or better?"

"Worse, much much worse, infinitely worse. Oh, fuck!"

"Ah, Ma, don't feel bad." Angelica enveloped her in a bone-crushing hug. "We can have dinner at Parioli Romanissimo—so what if I don't get to see the land of my ancestors—a restaurant's almost the same thing as Venice without the canals . . . the pigeons . . . the Piazza San Marco . . . the Gritti . . ." her voice trailed off with pitiful poignancy.

"I can't even have dinner with you tonight, Angelica. I'll call Toby and he'll take you anywhere you want to go," Maxi said, hating herself.

"You have a date?" Angelica brightened.

"A promise. And it's not one I can break. Call it a debt of honor. I have to be at

P. J. Clarke's at eight sharp." Maxi sank back into a chair and curled up into a ball of misery.

"Angelica, do you happen to like black pearls? Because if you do, I've brought you one back from Europe."

"Ah, give me a break, Maxi . . . come off the guilt trip. It's strictly not your style," Angelica said kindly.

A customs inspector certainly knows his way around the female human body, Maxi thought cheerfully as she tried to wake up the next morning. Was there a man on earth who could make love like a really straightforward Irishman at the peak of his form? And O'Casey was in the prime of his prime. Her second husband had been Australian but his ancestors had come from Ireland, sweet Bad Dennis Brady, a lovely boy as they would have said in the Old Country, but with an unfortunate habit of combining iced tequila and Buffalo Grass vodka in equal quantities and absorbing several generous glasses of the mixture before trying, without the captain's help, to berth his ship in the harbor of Monte Carlo. Perhaps the marriage might have worked if he hadn't been so otherwise bone-lazy or if the boat hadn't been an oceangoing eighty-meter yacht with its own helicopter pad. Perhaps if the helicopter had been properly fastened down the crash—or was it a shipwreck?—wouldn't have been as embarrassing. Maxi had jumped that particular ship of fools after six months, she remembered sleepily, sadder, but not much wiser.

WISER! The word echoed in her mind and brought her out of bed in panic. Wiser? Who was wiser? What time was it? She had to get to work immediately. The staff at *Buttons and Bows* must have heard all about yesterday's meeting, undoubtedly they were sitting around in doubt and tears waiting for the official ax to fall. She had to get there, wherever it was, and reassure them and take over and do . . . and do . . . whatever was necessary. Yes, *do*, take action, make decisions, take stock, take over, do something, do *anything*. She scampered around trying to draw the curtains open so that she could find a clock or a watch, but she was disoriented, not sure how the heavy draperies worked or where the light switches were.

Maxi had not slept in her new apartment before she had left for Europe two months earlier. At that time, like many of the apartments in Trump Tower, it hadn't yet been finished although Maxi had bought it from floor plans several years earlier from her pal, Donald Trump, when the apartment was no more than his vision of what to do with an all-but-priceless piece of New York airspace. Finally she located the right cords and opened the heavy, interlined, apricot silk draperies.

Maxi stood in front of the windows immobilized by surprise. Was this Manhattan, the familiar, loved and hated city or, while she slept, had her new apartment been dropped gently onto another planet? The sun, which was just rising in the East, behind her, cast its rays across Central Park, which was still in partial darkness, and lit the peaks and spires and towers of the city for as far as her eye could see; north to Harlem; west, across the Hudson River to New Jersey; south, down beyond the Trade Center, to the open Atlantic. Lord have mercy, she thought, it is Manhattan and I've *bought* the whole damn town! She was filled with glee, the kind known as unholy. Manhattan belonged to her! She must be the only person awake this early, the only person with this view, that had been carved out of sky. Perhaps there were taxis and buses and fire engines down there but Maxi couldn't hear them on the sixty-third floor. She was floating, but not adrift, anchored in a nest that had cost her more than four million dollars, a nest that was almost as high as the wispy white

Fragonard-like clouds that were turning pink over the park. As she watched the sun rise higher in the sky, flashing on windows which, one by one, sent messages directly to her, messages of a new day, tidings of a new morning, Maxi realized how lucky she was to possess a view that altered the spirit.

" 'I'll take Manhattan,' " she sang, " 'the Bronx and Staten Island too.' " And she danced and danced by herself to the song her father had taught her.

"Angelica, I have nothing of a publisher-nature to wear," Maxi realized at breakfast.

"I thought you were the new Editor-in-chief, Ma. Have you been promoted already?"

"In the middle of the night I woke up and suddenly realized that *Buttons and Bows* must already have an Editor-in-chief, and it would be an unpopular way to start by waltzing in and taking over somebody's job, so I made myself publisher. Since Grandpa died the publications haven't had a publisher."

"How should a publisher dress?" Angelica asked, eating four fried eggs heavily basted with butter, directly out of the pan, the way she liked them best.

"Like an authority figure, a leader, someone who inspires the troops, someone with unquestionable, impeccable, irrefutable judgment."

"So that lets you out." Angelica sprinkled the eggs with a judiciously thick layer of Tabasco.

"Right. But they don't know that, and if I dress in a dynamic way they'll respond to the image, or so I've been led to believe. However, my wardrobe seems not to start till lunch, a competitively chic Le Cirque lunch, a Côte Basque lunch, not a serious, businesslike publisher's morning. Then I have—too many clothes—for cocktails, dinners, balls, yachts, chalets and beaches. Plus the boots and pants I travel in."

"It sounds like some sort of character test. If you look in my closet you can tell me who I really am," her daughter observed.

"I wish you weren't so honest, Angelica. Couldn't you be a little more tactful?"

"You brought it up. Anyway, what about that double-breasted black Saint Laurent pantsuit you bought last year and never wore because it looked so awful on you?"

"It hasn't changed," Maxi said glumly. "It made me look like a short, dumpy man in drag. You can't tell that I have a waist and it eliminates my legs. I do, you have to admit, have the best legs in New York."

"We all know that, Ma. In the Saint Laurent, with spike heels you'd look like a medium-sized man in drag. And the shoulders are really intimidating."

"Maybe with a sensational blouse?" Maxi said, brightening.

"A severe blouse and a macho scarf flung carelessly over one shoulder. Viva Zapata."

"I loathe that look, and the scarf always falls off."

"You have no choice," Angelica said broodingly. "Listen, Ma, have you ever been seriously in love?"

"I don't answer questions like that this early in the morning."

"If I ever met him, do you think Woody Allen would be too old for me?"

"Not really. But I don't think he'd want to get involved."

"Nobody does," Angelica said sadly.

"It's the malaise of the age. Whatever that means," Maxi explained.

"Whatever," Angelica agreed. She *almost* knew what it meant. "So you really are going to the office this morning? Awesome. Well, good luck, Maxi."

"Thank you, darling. What are you doing today, shopping?"

"Yup, back to school. First I'll check out Armani, Krizia, Rykiel, Versace, Kamali, and end up buying Guess?"

"I wish I were as tall as you," sighed Maxi.

"I think you're cute just the way you are. I like a medium-sized mother. It makes me feel grown up."

"I didn't know you didn't," Maxi grumbled.

9

The offices of *Trimming Trades Monthly* were still located on Forty-sixth Street between Sixth and Seventh avenues, where Zachary Amberville had rented space for his first office. When the magazine had been founded the building was slightly run-down but no more so than the rest of the neighborhood, and within walking distance of the trimming trade industry. Nothing had changed except that run-down had slid into disrepair. Maxi noticed nothing of this as she located the offices and announced herself to the receptionist.

"I'm Miss Amberville. Could you please tell the Editor-in-chief that I'm here?"

"Does he expect you?"

"Just tell him. Maxime Amberville."

Seconds later Robert Frederick Fink arrived in the small reception area. He was round and rosy, some sturdy age between sixty-five and seventy, a natty dresser and absolutely delighted with her visit.

"Maxi!" he cried. "Give your Uncle Bob a kiss! I'll bet you've never forgotten the time we won twelve thousand bucks on the Exacta? Come on into my office and tell me about yourself . . . it's been years and years."

"About twenty," Maxi guessed, smothered by his embrace. She didn't remember Uncle Bob, but she still remembered that race.

"Seems like yesterday. Watch that door, it doesn't open very far."

Maxi squeezed into the editor's office and stopped abruptly. The medium-sized room held eight desks and on top of each desk were towering stacks of paper of all kinds, arranged carefully so that the piles somehow held together with no possible means of support. There was just enough space between the high walls of paper to walk, in single file, to Bob Fink's ninth desk on which the papers had only reached a height of some eight inches. He carefully eased her into the only visitor's chair in the room and then edged himself around his desk and sat down comfortably.

"I don't believe in filing cabinets, Maxi, never did. You put something in a file and you forget it's there and you never see it again. Might just as well burn it. Ask me for a document, any document."

"Huh?" Maxi clutched her serapelike plaid scarf around her with both hands and crossed her arms across her breasts. If she sneezed, she thought, it would take a week to dig her out.

"Ask me to find something for you . . . like a bill or a voucher or an expense account or anything at all."

"A copy of *Buttons and Bows* from, let's see, 1954."

"Nah. Too easy."

"A record of payment for . . . paper . . . from June of 1961."

Bob Fink got up, surveyed his domain severely for two minutes, threaded his way to one of the desks and, with the utmost delicacy, extracted several papers out of one of the minarets. "Here you go. Just look at that! Paper was a hell of a lot cheaper in sixty-one."

"Incredible," Maxi said, beaming at him. "Do you suppose I could see an issue of *Buttons and Bows*, the last one?"

Bob Fink's face fell. "It's right here, but I'm not proud of it. Nothing's been the same since 'Blouson Noir' was let loose."

"Who?"

"John Fairchild. The French designers called him 'Blouson Noir' meaning a motorcycle gang hood in a black leather jacket . . . because he was so tough on them. But what he did for the circulation of *Women's Wear*! A rocket, sweetheart. And when our advertisers saw that, naturally they decided to put all their ad money into *WWD* and if that weren't bad enough, Fairchild publishes *Footwear News* every week, which wiped up our buckle and strap advertisers. So between one thing and another . . . well, we have some subscriptions that still have a few years left to go, some small advertisers who get a kick out of seeing their photographs on the cover; but Maxi, let's face it, *Buttons and Bows* is . . . well, to say it was in trouble would be very kind. If you're in trouble you're still alive, *Buttons and Bows* is in intensive care but the hospital just closed."

"Could I see it anyway?" Maxi asked, not at all discouraged.

He gave her the thin magazine with a brave red cover. There was a photograph of John Robinson of the Robinson Braid Company on the cover and most of the text covered the career of Mr. Robinson. There were a few pages of news of the world of braid and trim and there was an article on the use of buttons on Adolfo suits, illustrated with a line drawing of a cuff with three buttons on it; and there were a few small ads. The two largest of these were from the Robinson Braid Company and the company that sold Adolfo his buttons.

"Uncle Bob, have you heard anything about the meeting yesterday?" Maxi asked, folding the copy of the pathetic scrap of a magazine in half and slipping it possessively into her handbag.

"A rumor, naturally. Well, maybe a dozen phone calls. All right, two dozen. I think it's damn nice of you to come here yourself and tell me the news. Your dad, may he rest in peace, would have done the same thing. I knew it was bound to happen."

"But it is *not* going to happen, Bob! I've been made the new publisher of *Buttons and Bows* and together we're going to make this magazine into a winner again, the way my father would have done!" Maxi almost brought a ton of paper down on her head as she rose in excitement.

"If that's the second prize, sweetheart, I wouldn't like to win the contest. Sit down, for God's sake!"

"I'm not kidding. I'm serious! Damn it, Bob, the sky's the limit, we can do anything that Fairchild can do. We'll turn this place upside down and inside out . . . not your office, of course, but . . ."

"Maxi," Bob Fink interrupted gently, "the garment industry doesn't *need* more than one major publication and what they need is a newspaper, *WWD*, not a monthly. You aren't planning to publish another daily, are you?"

"Well, no, actually not. But what about *W*? We could do something like *W* only better."

"The trouble is that *W* uses stuff that's already been photographed and written for *WWD* . . . sometimes they run the copy a little longer and they use color, but it doesn't cost them anything to lay their hands on it . . . money in the bank for Fairchild and only ten thousand subscribers. Most of *W* is ads, all those great big pretty pictures," he sighed. "I must be getting old . . . I'm not ready for those gorgeous girls wearing boy's underwear. Whatever happened to panties?"

Maxi squirmed in her Calvin Klein jockstrap. They'd added a new dimension to her sex life. Was she a pervert, did she only know perverts, or was Bob Fink old-fashioned?

"How can *W* only have ten thousand subscribers? Everybody I know reads it," she protested.

"That's the point . . . every issue is read by dozens of people and most of them have high incomes, which I guess explains the ads. Maxi, you can't go into competition with Fairchild. They founded that company in 1881 and they've specialized in trade papers before your dad was born, almost before *my* dad was born. And why the hell would you want to? You're an Amberville."

"Bob, I hear what you're saying but I'm convinced that I can turn *Buttons and Bows* around. With your help, of course." How, she wondered, could she get rid of such a dear old man? If only he weren't so pessimistic.

"My help? Maxi, I've been aching to retire for a long time. I just hung around here because I owed it to your dad's memory, but fortunately I invested in real estate at the right time. Most of the ex-presidents of the United States have built their houses on land I sold them in Palm Springs. Only big piece out there that I wanted but I never could get hold of is Annenberg's, golf course and all. Missed that one, but you can't win 'em all."

"Retire? You want to retire?"

"And move west. And watch my palms grow. Maybe learn to ride a horse."

"But . . . all your desks?" Maxi gestured carefully.

"Burn them. It'll cost a fortune to get the stuff out of here, but I'd definitely do that and burn it, if I were you."

"What about the rest of the staff?" Maxi asked wildly. "All those people my father didn't want to fire?"

"Let's see . . . there's Joe who thinks up the ideas and writes the articles, and Linda who buys all the artwork and does the layouts and handles production; and I've been my own ad manager. No circulation department, of course. The receptionist also handles the switchboard and the typing. I put Joe and Linda into real estate with me—and the receptionist could get a job anywhere. Very skillful young lady, hates it here. Have to overpay her to keep her."

"Three people? *Only three?* How can that be possible?" Her head felt light but she must not faint.

"Well, there's also a guy we hire from the building to empty the wastebaskets and dust off once in a while, there's a Xerox place downstairs for anything we want copied and the printer sends someone around once in a while to sell us paper; but otherwise, let's see, yup, three people. And we're still losing money. Rent, salaries, supplies, they all cost money. Of course there's lunch; everybody has to have lunch."

"The company pays for lunch?" Maxi squeaked incredulously.

"Your dad started it, back in the good old days. He insisted. Of course Lindy's was open then. Lunch hasn't been the same since they closed."

"When," asked Maxi faintly, "were you thinking of leaving? I don't want anyone to think I'm in a rush but . . ."

"Today's what? Thursday. We could all be out by Friday. Hate to leave you with this mess though. I'll arrange for the garbage guy to come and get it, don't worry, and Hank, from the building, doesn't mind working overtime so the place will be clean, more or less, by Monday, maybe Tuesday."

"You're sure you don't want to stay?" Politeness was all she had left, Maxi thought.

"Sweetheart, I'm on that plane already. And listen, if you don't mind an old admirer putting his two cents in, that outfit you've got on isn't . . . maybe something more . . . ah . . . *less* threatening? I'd be afraid to meet you in a dark alley, Maxi. Look, if you want, I'll take you wholesale . . . Beene maybe, or Ralph Lauren. There's nothing wrong with you that a change of image couldn't fix."

"You have the nerve to call that lump of mealy mush a Golden Delicious?" Toby roared. "Bite into it, you bastard, and tell me how many months ago it was picked and put in a cold room." With one hand, he grabbed the wholesaler by the back of his shirt and with the other he presented him with the apple. "Go on, bite!"

"I was robbed, mister," the man protested. "I just bought twenty cases from upstate and they swore they were picked this week, fresh off the trees."

Toby let the man go in disgust. "Sure you did. Well, it serves me right for trying a new supplier. Don't you realize I can tell everything about this fruit? All I had to do was touch its skin and I knew it was from last season, it doesn't smell the way a fresh apple smells and if I made myself taste it I'd puke. Go try to sell it to D'Agostino."

He turned away and spoke to Maxi. "Most of the guys here know me and they don't try to pull that sort of stuff; I've never bought from him, thought I'd give him a try."

"That's the last time he tries to rob a blind man," said Maxi. "At least one of us hasn't been robbed this week."

"Will you get your tail out from between your legs and stop complaining?" Tobias commanded, as he turned down the aisle of fruit wholesalers. As he always did in the dangerously cluttered Hunt's Point Market, Toby used his laser cane. Its three beams of invisible infared light made a pin vibrate that contacted his index finger, telling him if there were objects straight ahead of him, above his head or drop-offs below his feet. He swung it easily, in an arc, using the cane skills he had developed years before. Systematically Toby started choosing samples of apples from various cases, feeling, smelling, turning them over expertly in his long fingers as if each one were being considered for a still life, yet working with an astonishing speed.

"I'm not complaining," Maxi said bitterly. "I'm just so fucking mad at myself. Joan of Arc saving the skin of the man who owns Rancho Mirage . . . to say nothing of thirty years of free lunch. If only I thought Cutter were capable of laughing himself to death."

"Look, you've still got a magazine, an office, and a year to do anything you like. Only your pride is wounded, Goldilocks."

"It's not a magazine, it's pure vanity press. The office . . . well even *you* would have to see it to believe it. Your cane would blow its gasket. How many apples are you buying, for heaven's sake?"

"This is *Tarte Tatin* time, babe, and that means thousands."

"Why the hell didn't I at least have the sense to ask Pavka or Nina Stern before I picked the magazine I wanted? I could have had any one of them! Why did I have to rush into it?"

"Ah, the mystery of human personality. If you'd been slightly cautious you wouldn't be Maxi and if you weren't Maxi the whole world would be a sadder place."

"But wiser."

"Maybe. But wiser isn't all that it's touted as being. Wiser is like celibacy . . . put it off as long as you can." Tobias ordered his apples and led the way out of the huge, ugly complex that supplied at least half the food of Manhattan. He no longer did his daily buying himself, relying on assistants, but from time to time he visited Hunt's Point to check out new developments there for his three local restaurants. He owned two others in Chicago and four on the West Coast, all equally successful.

Tobias had discovered the kitchen sometime before he was eight. It was forbidden territory to him although his day vision was still relatively good. Lily was irrationally terrified at the idea of his being near any kind of fire, which only made him more determined to invade the mysterious room.

One night he waited until the entire household was asleep and then crept downstairs, along all the familiar passageways, and entered the big tempting space. Turning on the light, he began to explore, inch by inch, starting with the lower cabinet and drawers, subjecting every object to his five senses. Already, there had been enough deterioration in his sight so that he used all his senses to investigate strange objects. Each cooking utensil, each empty pot and pan, the chopping blocks and the cooking knives and forks and spoons were all applied to his nose and his fingertips. He smelled the knives, touched them with the tip of his tongue, licked their noncutting edges, ran their cutting edges gently over his hand, pressed them to his cheeks. He shook all the objects, and listened to the noise they made, he hefted their weights and compared them to each other, and, as he learned each one, put it back in its place. On the next night he ventured farther, to the refrigerator, and there, during the long quiet hours of the night, the overprotected little boy fell in love. An egg was a world to Tobias, an artichoke a galaxy, a chicken a universe.

Night after night he spent hours in the kitchen until every corner of it was utterly familiar, until there wasn't a wilted piece of parsley he hadn't tasted, although, obedient to his mother's interdiction, he had never lit the stove, but only swarmed all over it, inside and out, until it was imprinted on his sense memory.

One night he hadn't been able to forbid himself from cautiously cracking an egg into a bowl. If the outside of an egg was fascinating, the inside was utterly irresistible. Another egg followed the first until a dozen eggs swam in the large brown crock, their shells, stacked inside each other, neatly piled on the side of the kitchen table. Obviously they were meant to be mixed with a fork, Toby told himself. He had almost finished, mixing neatly, methodically and vigorously, when the kitchen door opened and he was discovered by the cook. His first cooking attempt proved only that it wasn't possible to mix eggs in complete silence.

Zachary insisted that Tobias be taught to cook and a chef from the Cordon Bleu School was engaged to work with him every afternoon after school.

Soon Tobias could tell if olive oil was pouring at the proper rate into a mayonnaise he was beating by listening to the noise the drops of oil made as they fell. He could hear that particular second when an omelette was ready to be rolled out of its pan, he could smell the exact moment when an onion had been properly browned, he didn't need a timer for boiling eggs or anything but a sharp knife for cutting the thinnest slices of any fruit or vegetable.

However, as he grew into his early teens Toby was having increasing problems with his vision. In spite of his natural grace he appeared awkward and clumsy, constantly bumping into people and objects he should have been able to see clearly.

Lily, who still refused to accept the fact that Toby would one day be almost, if not entirely, blind, somehow managed to make herself ignore these incidents, but Zachary, who frequently took the children to the movies on Saturday afternoon, realized that in a darkened movie theater Toby was helpless, lost until the house lights went up. Soon it was obvious that he couldn't play team sports, with his poor side vision, couldn't follow the path of a volleyball or a hockey puck, and in spite of Lily's determination not to warn Toby of what the future held—why should he know until it was absolutely necessary, she said—Zachary decided that his son had to be prepared.

Almost nothing was known about retinitis pigmentosa in the 1960s and Dr. Eliot Berson of the Harvard Medical School, to whom Zachary took Toby for an ERG exam to measure the strength of the signals given out by the nerve cells of the retina, couldn't tell him what the prognosis was, except to say that if Toby were lucky he would still have some functional vision after his late twenties.

Even Zachary couldn't bring himself to say these precise words to Toby but he did his best to explain why Toby should concentrate on nonteam sports like swimming and gymnastics, choosing to discuss sports rather than life, referring to the rods and retina rather than to tunnel vision.

"Am I going to go blind, Dad?" Toby asked, after the few minutes of silence that followed Zachary's confused exposition.

"*No!* No, Toby! Not completely, never completely, and not for many years." Zachary's heart broke as he said the words in a manner that he kept as unemotional as possible.

"Still I'd better learn Braille, hadn't I?" Toby asked after more silence. Zachary couldn't answer, couldn't say no. "Braille and touch-typing then," Toby said and rose and went to his room. What he suffered there, no one was ever to know, but he emerged with his whole young soul determined to make the most of his life even if he couldn't conquer his fate.

Braille, which he did not yet need, was best learned as young as possible, and soon he went regularly to Braille classes. He swam with a private instructor in the covered pool that was built for him in the Ambervilles' town garden, with the same energy as he continued his cooking lessons. Toby lived as if he had two lives, one sighted and the other in darkness, and for a dozen years the disease, as was often the case, seemed to grow no worse. By the time Toby had graduated from the Hotel School at Cornell, he had spent eight summers apprenticed to great chefs in France, Italy and Hong Kong and he was ready to open his first restaurant.

For years, like a knight sharpening his weapons and oiling his armor against a far-distant battle, he had investigated the myriad of kitchen aids for the visually impaired, and whenever he found one he liked, like the Magna Wonder Knife, he would adopt it, even though he didn't yet need it. The kitchen of his first restaurant was unique in its impeccable organization. No obsessively neat housewife would ever achieve the absolute rigidity with which Toby, using his common sense, arranged his tools. His trusty warhorse was a pair of bakers' balance scales from the Acme Scale Company, one of them fitted with an electronic detection device that could measure spices from zero to sixteen ounces, another that could measure up to one thousand pounds of other ingredients, both with weight indicators that had been brailled at half-inch intervals.

His gauntlets were a pair of oven mitts that were seventeen inches long and protected him from heat on the backs of his hands as well as on the palms and fingers; his swords were non-heat-conducting wooden spoons, his double spatulas, his nested measuring cups that could be monitored by his fingers, eliminating the line calibrations of glass. His jousting pole was a battery-operated "Say When" liquid level indicator and his helmets were mixing bowls from Dansk and Copco, all of which had rubber rings at their bases to stabilize them.

In his late twenties, with two restaurants operating successfully, Toby realized that the blank spaces in his view of the world were growing larger; people and objects swam in and out of them bewilderingly, in a faint, fragmented and increasingly colorless fashion. He had trained himself to make his problems as inconspicuous as possible but now he realized that he needed highly professional help.

For a period of four months Toby went for training to the St. Paul's Rehabilitation Center in Newtown, Massachusetts. There, all the students, no matter what degree of vision they had, were blindfolded for instruction which ranged from such mundane matters as table manners and counting money to more challenging cane technique. He took fencing lessons that helped in the location of sound, and "videation" or learning orientation and mobility through extravisual means such as judging the speed of wind, the feeling of sun on the face, the textures of whatever was underfoot and all other possible perceptions of the sounds of nature and man and automobiles. By the time he left St. Paul's Toby felt as well skilled as he could possibly be for the future.

He returned to New York and continued to experiment with the enormous variety of systems which had been developed for the blind who work in kitchens. Each time he opened a new restaurant he installed a kitchen that was an exact duplicate of the others. His corps of chefs, all sighted, were trained by him to cook in his way, using his weapons, and soon, if need be, they could all cook in the dark.

Now Toby still cooked from time to time in his first restaurant, inventing new dishes, but the others were run by his chefs, whom he visited, unannounced, on trips to Chicago or Los Angeles. Within twenty minutes of inspection he knew if the most insignificant compote dish had been misplaced. Woe to the *sous-chef* who had been skimping on the wild mushrooms; woe to whoever had misjudged the ripeness of a Brie; woe to the roast cook whose chicken was not moist to the wingtip; woe to the *saucier* who had used an eighth of a pinch too much salt. Woe, woe, to the restaurant manager if the tablecloths lacked a certain crisp finish, if the crystal wasn't like satin to his touch, if the candles were an inch too short or the flowers an hour too old. "Tobias the Terrible" they called him after one of his raids, but afterwards his teams worshipped him even more than before.

Toby nudged Maxi as she brooded. "I'd have had more fun taking Angelica shopping," he said. "Look, you've blown it but it's not the end of the world. Pick yourself up off the floor and pack it up. Don't piss into a violin. Forget the whole thing. Obviously you can't rescue *Trimming Trades* any more than you can bring back high-buttoned shoes and there's no point in your wasting your time for the empty exercise of fighting Cutter. He's won and you might as well accept it. Put it behind you, take that 'kick me' sign off your back, and start being Maxi again."

"For a bat you sound like a wimp," Maxi answered angrily.

"I am a brilliant businessman, which means I face reality every day. I'd like a little respect from you since I'm probably the most eligible bachelor in New York, but hard to get because I don't give a shit about what a girl looks like and I still haven't found anyone whose soul I want to hang out with for the rest of my life."

"A vain, tactless, mean old wimp who isn't even thoughtful enough to offer me a drink when I need it most," Maxi said mournfully.

"It's more like time for Saturday breakfast, babe, or hadn't you noticed?"

"The trouble with you, Tobias, is you're too literal-minded, as your mother would *never* say to you," Maxi said angrily.

"Breakfast calls for a drink, don't you agree?"

"Now that you mention it, why not?"

India West glared at herself malevolently in the mirror on the dressing table of her Beverly Hills bedroom. She made minuscule adjustments in her mind, and her eyes, which were that special brilliant blue of rare Persian turquoises, seemed to deepen or lighten to her order. Supremely delicate muscles moved under her skin and enough happened there to fill the pages of *Les Cahiers du Cinéma*. She fell deeply in love, she endured a quiet depression, was tormented by a secret terror, grew joyful, changed from wanton to nun and was illuminated by a gentle anticipation of rapture. All systems, she noted lugubriously, were still functioning at will, in spite of her catastrophic hangover.

As she gazed, deeply unimpressed by her image, unmoved at that composition of extraordinary features whose perfection bored no one but India herself, she decided that there was something fundamentally and deeply *dumb* about being called the most beautiful movie actress in the world. What kind of a job was that for an adult? Did anybody have any idea what a racket it was? She reminded herself of nothing so much as a Greta Garbo film, with that divine face hardly registering a change of expression and the conditioned response of an audience reading vast emotions into it. Had Garbo ever felt the same way as she did about herself? India suspected that she had, and had quit before anyone else caught on.

"You're no Meryl Streep, you silly bitch," she said out loud to her glorious reflection, "but you *can* do that thing they call acting." She tied back her shivery waves of amber blond hair and looked in disgust at the Bloody Mary on the table. India West almost never drank but last night had been a horrible exception for which there was only one remedy which would make her liver consider the possibility of going back to work. She swallowed the drink, a goddess resigned to her minute of mortality, shuddered and tottered back to bed.

All her strength had gone into opening the tomato juice and finding the Tabasco, for on Sunday she was alone. There were no maids, no secretaries, no cook in the huge house, all phones were quiet as the great ones of The Industry slept or thought vaguely about brunch as they watched people condemned to live in other places play football on television. Still, India reflected, if it weren't Sunday she'd have to go to her regular workout with her gym teacher, the arbiter of her life, Mike Abrums. If that man even suspected that she had a hangover, and God knows, you could keep nothing from him, he would make her very sorry indeed. He might even *take away her appointments.*

In spite of a well-founded rumor that he possessed-somewhere—a heart of gold, Mike Abrums ruled his pupils with the relentless discipline that he had perfected during his years in the Marines, teaching men how to kill other men with their bare hands. Now he maintained meticulously selected and worshipfully obedient Hollywood bodies in a state of perfection and had a waiting list of hundreds of supplicants. Mike had forbidden her to eat red meat, sugar, salt, fats and liquor, in any amount or form whatever. Last night, in an outburst of rebellion, India had copiously ingested every single item on his list of taboo foods.

"If I weren't so beautiful I could eat a hamburger every day," she said pathetically, addressing the ceiling. "If I weren't a major star I wouldn't have to be perfect. If I weren't rich I couldn't afford to go to that magnificent dictator six times a week, if I weren't famous nobody would give a damn. I have a very bad case of the sort of problems that people always sneer at and say they would like to have, but just because everyone would like my problems doesn't mean *I* have to like them. They are not a transferable asset. A banal thought, I admit, but in my condition I can't rise above it."

India's voice, even though she was only speaking to the ceiling, was winelike, with its infinite shades and range, from darkly potent Burgundy to icy, brilliant champagne; from warm, mellow Bordeaux to the unearthly sweetness of Sauternes. After six years of Hollywood stardom, India no longer found it strange to be talking out loud to herself. One of the less recognized problems of being a star was that there were very few people in the world to whom she could speak frankly. The urge to bask in the glory of being her confidant was all but irresistible and if she confided in any but a trusted few she was likely to read about it in the columns the next day.

"If only my ceiling were more interesting," she observed. A hangover severely limited her options. She couldn't stand the noise of music, she didn't have the strength to focus on print, and worst of all there was nobody she wanted to talk to on the phone. At that thought she began to feel tears forming. She eased herself painfully out of bed, clasped a robe around her, and headed slowly for her pool. Anything was better than lying around feeling sorry for herself.

India threaded her way along the path of her back garden. It had been intended to look tropical and after spending two hundred thousand dollars, her landscape decorator had managed to achieve an unreal Rousseau-like landscape of monumentally exotic plants that seemed, in India's present mood, to be menacing and grotesque. Uneasily she wondered about tigers, sleeping gypsies, and snakes. Suddenly the network of underground sprinklers everywhere sprang to life with an ominous series of thuds. They were only supposed to work during the night. As she stood there, buffeted by a dozen different nozzles, three enormous German shepherds, barking wildly, sprang out of the giant ferns, almost knocking her over.

"Down! Down, you revolting creeps!" she screamed, trying to sound authoritative. They slavered at her ambiguously.

"Bonnie-Lou! Sally-Ann! Debbie-Jane! Down, I say!" They were all males but it helped a little to pretend they were girls. The huge beasts terrified her but a consultation with the Beverly Hills Police had convinced her business manager and her agent that she had to have them. Apparently the fences and the electrically controlled gates and the television camera at the end of the driveway, plus all the complicated electric eyes and beams that were installed throughout the house, weren't worth even one German shepherd, for real protection.

Muscles aquiver, India continued dripping her way toward the pool, hair drenched, robe soaking, slobbering wet dogs stepping on her feet and licking her hands in what she hoped was affection. Oh God. Had they been fed? She felt increasingly unsure of the future of this particular Sunday.

She finally fought her way out of the rain forest and stopped with a cry of disbelief and outrage. The water of the pool had turned overnight into a vile shade of murky green. Killer dogs, killer sprinklers and now killer algae. It was too much. She fled back to the house and pulled the bedcovers over her head, cursing the pool man who had skipped a visit. "Human beings were not meant to live in Beverly Hills,"

India groaned into her now damp sheets. "The whole place is a desert, made to bloom only by water stolen from decent, hardworking farmers by the evil founding fathers of Los Angeles. An abomination in the eyes of the Lord. Repent ye sinners."

She poked her head out of the covers and considered the possibility of another Bloody Mary. No. Absolutely not. One was clearly medicinal but two? She would count her blessings instead as her mother had taught her to. First, as ever, health. The only blessing that really mattered. Hangovers didn't count as being sick since they were temporary. Second, her sheets, the smoothest possible pure cotton, from Pratasi, the borders embroidered with tiny scallops, at six hundred dollars the pair. She had a closet full of them, they were her pride and joy—could you be addicted to sheets? Still it was a harmless pleasure surely since you couldn't eat or drink them. Or were the sheets a case of transference?

During the last year she had worked herself out of her transference to her shrink, Doctor Florence Florsheim, psychoanalyst to the stars, and now she seemed to have transferred her affections to her linen closet. Could this be called progress? She'd have to check it out with Doctor Florsheim but she doubted it. What were her next blessings? Beautiful, rich, famous and talented. Even John Simon agreed about her talent, an opinion she allowed to convince her whenever she began to feel self-doubt. But she'd covered all that already and found them less than comforting. Still that made six blessings. Lovers? She didn't have one currently and the last one she'd had was, without the slightest qualification, an error in taste on a scale so great that she blushed at the memory. The *absence* of lovers was perhaps a blessing in disguise. Count it as half a blessing, making a total of six and a half, not too bad for someone with a life-threatening hangover. Youth? She was only just twenty-seven. Yes, youth, if you didn't remember that *thirty* was only three years away. Three years were ages and ages. More than a thousand days. A *thousand days were nothing!* She must not think about it. Christ, but it wasn't easy to be the most beautiful movie actress in the world, it was stress on a major scale, even Doctor Florsheim had to admit that.

India thought of a remark made by Nijinsky when an admirer of the great dancer asked him if it wasn't difficult to hang in the air as he literally seemed to do. He'd answered that it wasn't difficult, "It's just climbing up there and staying up for a little." As good a description of a movie career as she'd heard, India reflected, and poor Nijinsky had died insane. Still, what else was she fit for? She'd wanted her career, worked hard for it, and now she just had to stay up there, defying gravity. Self-pity began to overwhelm India West once more. The phone rang just as she was about to get out of bed and comfort herself with pillowcases.

"Miss West. This is Jane Smith of 'Sixty Minutes.' We've decided to investigate the India West Syndrome and I'll be out next week with a crew to follow you around for a month or so. My particular interest is in the problem of stardom, starting, of course, with the pimple on your ass . . ."

"MAXI! You angel, you blessing . . . how could you go away for so long . . . where are you calling from? . . . Are you really coming here? I'm all by myself and so very lonely."

"No, I'm in New York and I'm not going anywhere, probably for the rest of my life. I have such a hangover that I don't think I'll live. I called you up to say goodbye forever."

"You too? I'm curing mine with a Bloody Mary. Go make one—I'll hold on."

"What a sickening idea . . . I'd throw up."

"Look, chemically tomato juice is half salt and half potassium. It replaces your electrolytes quicker than a transfusion and you can't smell the vodka if you use enough Tabasco. The best internist in Beverly Hills told me to do it, honest."

"All right . . . but don't go away. I'll hurry."

As she waited by the phone India felt reborn. With Maxi back on the same continent, even a sinister Beverly Hills Sunday seemed filled with promise. Maxi couldn't enter a room without creating a fiesta.

Over the clinking of ice cubes Maxi returned to the phone. "I know why I got drunk but why did you?"

"It was the party last night. I went by myself and there wasn't anybody there I wanted to talk to, Then a definitely fascinating guy walked in and I perked up until he got close enough so that I could read his T-shirt."

"India, I've warned you never to read T-shirts. They're pure aggression. What did it say?" Maxi asked, breathless with curiosity.

"Life is Shit and Then You Die."

"You've got to get out of that place! When T-shirts start to drive you to drink . . ."

"And eat," India said on a dire note. "Everything in sight."

"Think of it this way," Maxi advised. "One night's eating isn't going to show on your thighs and if you don't get compulsive and *confess* to Mike Abrums, he can't read your mind and you can reveal all the awful things you did when you see Doctor Florsheim because she never makes judgments."

"Oh, Maxi, you're right! When you're not here there's nobody to put me in perspective except myself and I'm not good at it yet."

"It takes two for perspective."

"Maybe *that* could be the title for my novel," India said excitedly.

"Are you writing a novel?"

"I'm going to start as soon as I get the right title. I have a feeling that it's what I should be doing. I've always wanted to write and half the people in town are being published—so why not me?"

"Instead of being the most beautiful movie star in the world?"

"Exactly. What do you think of '*If Hell Is Other People, Then Heaven Is Smoked Fish*'?"

"*India!*" Maxi sputtered. "Not while I'm drinking."

"Then you like it?"

"It's divine, but a little too esoteric. Anything more mass market?"

"How about a science-fiction novel? I rather like '*Chateau Margaux 2001.*' "

"No, India, no."

"Well then, '*Married Men Don't Have Wet Dreams.*' "

"A hard case to prove."

"How about '*Hamlet Was An Only Child*'?"

"What does it mean?"

"I think it speaks for itself," India said with dignity.

"Look, India, I'm worried about you—seriously. Going to parties alone, getting drunk, thinking up novel titles, next thing you know you'll be counting your sheets again. And you know what that means. It's not healthy for you to be alone in that monster house. What ever happened to that heavenly housekeeper who used to do tarot cards with you?"

"Doctor Florsheim told me I had to stop relying on friendships I paid for, so that means no live-in help."

"Are you sure you're neurotic enough to suffer such deprivation?" Maxi asked anxiously.

"If I wasn't when I started, I am now."

"I think you should tell Doctor Florsheim that you need sick leave and come visit me. I need you desperately."

"I would in a second but I'm in the middle of a picture."

"I was afraid of that," Maxi said in tones of utter despair.

"Is it a man?"

"Ten times worse than the worst man I ever met, or even married. Worse than Laddie Kirkgordon."

"Nothing could be that bad . . . you're not sick, are you?" India asked.

"No, not unless you count stupidity as a terminal disease. And arrogance and misjudgment, lack of information, acting like an idiot and jumping off the deep end into an empty pool."

"But that sounds exactly like you when you fall in love. I knew it was a man," India insisted, her hangover cured by the sound of Maxi's voice, and the familiar delight of hearing about Maxi's improbable problems.

"If you hold on while I make myself another Bloody Mary," Maxi said in resignation, "I'll tell you the whole hideous story."

"Goody!" India cried and settled down for a lovely long listen.

10

Cutter Amberville's return to San Francisco, after such a relatively short stay in New York, caused little surprise. His friends, all born-and-bred San Franciscans, felt gratified vindication of their own values. They had predicted, before he left, that nowhere in the East would he find the sweetness of life that they enjoyed, and his rejection of Manhattan proved how right they had been. Although some people persisted in calling San Francisco the Wall Street of the West, and others termed it the Paris of the United States, as far as they were concerned it was a city so unique that it need be compared to no other place on earth. Sheer civic pride alone would make San Francisco stand apart, for this quiet Spanish settlement had turned into an international boomtown when gold was discovered at Sutter's Mill in 1848. From that time on successive waves of fortune had deposited millions, indeed billions, in the pockets of the lucky men who led the town, men whose freshly made money grew graciously mellow in less than a century.

None of Cutter's friends—the Bohlings, the Chatfield-Taylors, the Thieriots, the de Guignés and the Blyths—ever knew that be had fled New York because of Lily. He was as welcome as a unicorn, that desirable legendary animal whose horn was reputed to possess magical properties—for was not an eligible yet unattached bachelor almost as rare as a unicorn?

His months in Manhattan had only made Cutter more compelling to look at; deepening the contrast between his blondness and his darkly proud, purposeful manner. He seemed older than twenty-four and more dangerous; a mysterious danger made more seductive by his perfect manners and the unexpectedly warm, rarely won smile that totally changed his expression, that humanized this aloof man. He was well born, he was beginning to be rather respected by the older men in the world of banking but, as the women of the Bay City told themselves, he was apparently not marriage-minded. Cutter Amberville remained resolutely, inexplicably hard to get, fascinatingly, infuriatingly, tantalizingly free of heart. None of the women who gossiped about him suspected that his reason for avoiding an involvement with one of the elegant, unmarried girls of San Francisco was a question of clear-eyed policy: what trouble might Lily cause if she heard about any new romance?

Cutter was absolutely armored against even the most delicious girl—if she represented a Possible entanglement. But, in spite of a degree of emotional control that most men of any age could never achieve, he was utterly unable to dominate his avid, brutal need for sex. He had to have women and he had to have them often and now, after Lily, he had to have them in a condition of risk. Not for him the easy, relatively safe conquest of the women who worked at his office or women he could pick up in bars. Quite logically he recognized that there were women within Society, women who moved in his own world, who were just as restless as he was, who lived with unslaked desire to the same degree as he did, women he could possess at will. But to attract him they had to be women who had too much to lose to become a threat to his public life. He never pursued a woman who could make a claim on him, never stalked a woman who could injure him, and if he sensed in a woman any hint of that crazy, reckless, cap-over-the-windmill view of life that had been Lily's, he never went after her.

But there were so many others! For a man with eyes to see, a man who was surrounded by married couples, there were possible conquests everywhere. Secret swift conquests, made without any ritual of courtship, conquests that were a kind of mutual recognition of an uncomplicated lust. Cutter was the cleverest of lovers. He knew how to make danger work for him, how to seize the most unexpected opportunities, how to sniff out the woman who was as wild and hot as he was under all the proper trappings of their world. With a glance he could tell a mere flirt from a woman in heat, and make his move in a way that drew no attention.

Cutter's reputation as the most elusive single man in the city grew with every year that passed. He went out almost every night: at Ernie's, the Gatti brothers both knew that he liked to begin dinner with the local Dungeness crab, served as simply as possible; at Kans, Johnny Kan himself came to the phone when Cutter called for a reservation; at Trader Vic's his table was always in the Captain's Cabin; but normally he was invited to private homes, not restaurants.

Cutter had realized that the quickest way to total social acceptance in San Francisco was through music. He never failed to attend some twenty of the twenty-six scheduled opera performances and he went to the symphony on both the "fashionable" nights and the "listening" nights. After a few years he was asked to join the Bohemian Club, an institution that was founded in 1872 to promote the arts. By the 1900s it had become a center of all-male power; a club to which the most important men in America were. invited for the annual encampments on the Russian River.

Soon Cutter became known to banking leaders like Richard P. Cooley, president of the Wells Fargo Bank; George Christopher, chairman of the board of the Commonwealth National Bank, and Rudolph A. Peterson, president of the Bank of America. He was careful to maintain his New York banking contacts as well. His months in Manhattan had given him that sort of patina that is comparable to a year spent in the best finishing school in Switzerland for a debutante from a middle-sized American city. He hadn't learned anything to which a specific dollar value could be attached, but he had been thoroughly dipped in the currents of the ocean of major American finance.

On his return Cutter had rejoined his old firm, Booker, Smity and Jameston, but soon moved on to another, larger one. By the time he was thirty, he was seasoned enough to become a junior partner in the firm of Standings and Alexander, one of the most influential in the city.

The head of Cutter's new firm, James Standings III, was a fifth-generation San Franciscan. He had been born as royal as any citizen of a republic can be, and he thoroughly approved of Cutter. He invited him to play golf at the Hillsborough Country Club; he invited him to join the Woodside Hunt, to sail from Sausalito Harbor on his forty-eight-meter yacht, and he proposed him for membership in his town club, the Union League on Nob Hill, for James Standings, like Mr. Bennett in *Pride and Prejudice*, was a man with daughters to marry. Not five, as he often thanked the Deity, only two, and although it pained him to admit it, Candice, his firstborn, was far from a beauty.

Along with its view of the bay, its charm, its culture and its restaurants, San Francisco takes justified pride in the beauty of its women. Such girls as Patsy McGinnis, Penny Bunn, Mielle Vietor, Frances Bowes, Mariana Keean and Patricia Walcott, lovely though each was, were not exceptions in the early 1960s, they were the rule. Compared to the average local belle, Candice Standings was, even in the eyes of her adoring father, just . . . average. Not *desperately* plain, mind you, but no, he had to admit, much as he loved her, she was not even pretty. No one had ever even dreamed of calling her Candy. He and his wife, Sally, also a fifth-generation San Franciscan, were just average too, but they both felt that their older child, a sixth-generation San Franciscan, should somehow have been born beautiful, defying all the laws of genetics. After all, their younger daughter, Nanette, showed definite signs of prettiness and she was only fourteen.

Candice had perfect teeth at last, after years of orthodontia, and glossy hair. She had well-developed arm and leg muscles from practicing all the right sports, but an unfortunately boyish body; she'd graduated from Miss Hamlin's and Finch, her pearls were the best Gump's could offer—but she lacked utterly that certain quality possessed even by girls from that lower-class place called Los Angeles, that unfortunately necessary dash of something sexual that appealed to men.

James Standings III was enormously rich and getting steadily richer. Even if Sally Standings didn't send all her dry-cleaning to Paris by air as did Mrs. W. W. Crocker, or possess a Chinese cook of thirty-seven years standing, like Mrs. Cameron, they lived, when they weren't traveling or vacationing, at the Ramble, a thirty-five-room mansion in patrician Hillsborough, eighteen miles south of the city. The Ramble, inherited from Sally Standings's parents, had terraces and formal gardens that were almost as impressive as Mrs. Charles Blyth's Strawberry Hill, but alas, alas, for Candice, Hillsborough was honeycombed with equally vast houses, populated by equally rich fathers of far too many other girls—less plain, so infinitely, incontestably much less plain than Candice, girls who *all* had to be married off in order to produce seventh-generation San Franciscans.

If James Standings III had ever recognized a buyer's market, it was on those many many evenings when he and Sally dined with twenty-five-year-old Candice and waited, just as anxiously as she did, for the telephone to ring. When it did, as it was beginning to more and more frequently, it was always for Nanette.

Cutter was thirty-one. He had never again felt the emotions he had felt for Lily, and he looked back at that time in his life as a form of clear insanity. But he had made a promise to Lily. He had written her the only kind of letter that he felt sure would ensure her silence. Since that time he had written her other letters, carefully uncompromising, not so many that their arrival in New York would cause comment, far, far fewer letters than the ones she wrote him, but cunningly phrased to keep her from any rash action, for Lily was now more determined than ever that soon they must be together. *They had waited seven years!* Zachary had a mistress, she wrote—everyone knew about it, someone who worked on *Style*, a girl named Nina Stern—so there could be no possibility of his succeeding in keeping the children. Lily was wildly impatient. She hated Cutter's ambiguous letters and thought he was being insanely cautious. Cutter could sense her gathering anger in each letter she sent him, asking what he was waiting for in order to claim her.

Cutter had absolutely no intention of marrying Lily and living with her and her children and making his way, step by step, like any ordinary man. He knew his full value and he planned to capitalize on it. He had decided to marry the girl who could do him the most good. He intended, most precisely, to marry Candice Standings, his boss's daughter. He wanted the fat, easy commissions that would fall to him as her husband.

She was fairly plain, true, but not so outstandingly pudding-faced that people could say, without even thinking twice, that he had only married her for her money. She seemed to have a good disposition, she rode and skied, played tennis and bridge, all with equal competence, and would make an excellent wife. Candice would always be utterly *grateful* to him. Their marriage would just be another example of a good-looking man being united to a less attractive woman, an arrangement accepted for centuries. Candice had a nice smile, after all, and he imagined that she wouldn't run to fat, judging from her mother.

His only problem was Lily. What might she not be capable of saying about him if she heard of an engagement to marry Candice Standings, a Society event that couldn't be kept secret? True, his entanglement with Lily was now old news, no matter how unsavory, and gave her no hold over him. *But that boy?* Justin. His son, Even James Standings III would think twice about giving him even a homely daughter if Lily, in rage, were to tell him about Justin. Ever since Cutter had heard of the child's birth he had tried not to think about him. He had never lain eyes on the child that Lily, damn her, had chosen to have out of arrogance and vanity and selfishness. Justin's existence was entirely her responsibility, no matter how she imagined that the boy was a claim on Cutter.

Discreetly, Cutter began to pay court to Candice Standings; so discreetly that he rarely saw her unless her friends or family were around, but he showed her a special warmth that was just enough to be noticed but not taken seriously enough to become gossip. He knew that Candice was in love with him, with a timid, humble love that put her utterly at his mercy. His only chance, he calculated, was to present Lily with a *fait accompli*, to elope with Candice to Vegas some weekend and then let happen whatever would happen. By that time he would be James Standings's son-in-law and heir apparent, and no one could take that away from him. Lily's only solid weapon was that single letter. Even if she were mad enough to use it they were the words of a boy he no longer was. . . . No other real proof existed.

The Standingses skied at Squaw Valley and at Klosters, in Switzerland, but recently they'd bought a lodge in Aspen. They were all expert enough to negotiate the steep, open meadows and thickly wooded trails without difficulty. James and Sally Standings preferred to ski only in the sunny afternoon, but Cutter and Candice were always the first ones up the mountain, ignoring the freezing air and the possibility of frostbite at the high altitudes in order to get the first run down. In her ski clothes and goggles, Candice was as good-looking as anyone else, Cutter thought, and a better skier than most. She could follow wherever he led and he never had to worry about her ability to check her speed on the narrow trails that cut through the thick forests here and there on the mountains.

A love for skiing was perhaps Cutter's deepest emotion—after hatred for his brother. It was the only sport which made him feel utterly free, unbound for a few downhill minutes from whatever people thought about him, from his past, from his future, from himself, particularly from himself, living entirely in the clean, clear present.

One morning, early, as he skied through the icy crust of newly fallen snow, rejoicing in the untouched surface before him, he suddenly realized that he couldn't hear Candice's skis behind him as usual. He stopped and turned. She was nowhere in sight. Cursing, Cutter began to climb back up the trail which was so narrow that he barely had room to sidestep up the mountain. He called her name but there was no answer. No other skiers appeared. After a few minutes he spotted her body off the trail, dangling, motionless, in the branches of two closely growing pine trees, a foot off the ground as if she had been flung from above. She must have caught an edge and pinwheeled, he realized, using all his skill to clamber up through the dense forest. *Caught an edge and pinwheeled.* He shuddered with the knowledge. Anything could be broken in the wild flight of a pinwheel. Finally he reached her. Cutter had seen enough ski accidents in his many years on the slopes to guess, from her unnatural position, that there was a chance that her back was broken. He took off one of her mitts to feel her pulse. She was alive and that was all he could be sure of, for she was unconscious, and he must not try to move her. Cutter left her there, facedown on the bed of icicle-dripping branches, while he dashed on down the trail to alert the ski patrol.

It wasn't his fault, of course. Nobody could blame him. People hurt themselves skiing all the time. Everybody knew Candice was a good skier. A cold morning, a steep narrow trail. No, nobody, not even her parents, could reasonably blame him. However, he could *choose* to take the blame. He could say that he blamed himself, that it was his fault, that he should have known that the snow was too icy, too risky. He could have stopped her, should have stopped her. Yes, he could take the blame. And he could marry her if she lived. He could have everything Candice Standings could bring him and not even Lily could utter a cry of reproach, if he married a crippled girl, crippled by his fault.

It had taken Nina Stern longer than she would have believed possible to seduce Zachary. After the difficult birth of Justin, the Ambervilles' third and last child, Lily had been very ill for months. Maxi, finding herself the least attention-getting member of her family, had proceeded to outdo herself in inventive acts of naughtiness. Not even Mary Poppins could have handled her, Zachary used to groan to himself, as his heart melted at her genuinely contrite tears when she was eventually caught and had to be punished. Thank God television had been invented. Being deprived of her favorite shows was the only punishment that he could inflict on her. He could never have brought himself to spank Maxi or lock her in her room. How had people disciplined their children before television?

Zachary had been too preoccupied to pay much attention to Nina at the Wednesday staff meetings, caught as he was between the problems at home and the problems at the office, for it was a time when all his magazines had to gird themselves to grow or to go out of business. But eventually, as she had always known it would, the classic moment presented itself: the unexpected dinner invitation, made casually when there are only two people left in an office after a hard, long, but satisfying day. Nina had not spent her life practicing for this minute in order to let the occasion pass and the next morning, when Zachary woke up in her bed, he finally knew why other men played around, knew it in pulverizingly precise and staggering new detail and knew that nothing could stop him from being with her.

During the first months of their affair he had been too obsessed with Nina to feel guilty about Lily and the children. But one day he realized that he could never ask Lily for a divorce, he simply couldn't do that to the exquisite, brave, talented girl he had overwhelmed in a single month when she had still been in her teens, the girl who had abandoned her certain and marvelous future as a prima ballerina for him, who knew no other life than the one he had encouraged her to lead, who had given him his children; Lily who was such a marvelous mother to Toby and to little Justin and even kept her patience with Maxi. Lily Amberville had become a queen in New York and he owed her no diminution of that position. One of the results of Lily's illness had been that they almost never made love, not because she was afraid of getting pregnant again, but because Justin's birth seemed to have caused some profound psychic change in her. All the more reason why he could never abandon her.

Painfully, he explained all this to Nina, knowing that she couldn't want to continue with a man who could offer her no future.

"So, I gather that your idea of my idea of a future is that I expect you to get a divorce and marry me?" she had asked, after listening to him struggle to make his position clear.

"Well. Ah. Yes. I see what you mean, I guess. I mean I *don't* see what you mean! Isn't that more or less what a girl like you *would* expect . . . I mean isn't it? Damn it, Nina, don't you want . . . wouldn't you want . . . you're a 'nice' girl . . . your parents . . . any other girl . . . damn it, I guess I took too much for granted. I thought, well I felt, oh *shit.*"

"It's not that I don't love you," she said, trying as hard as she could not to laugh but having little success.

"If you love me," he said, grabbing her, amazed at the enormity of his relief, "why don't you want to marry me?"

"I'm a weird case. I don't like marriage, it's too obvious, everybody does it and then it becomes something you have to do every single day, like brushing your teeth. What I like is what we do: making love and seeing each other at meetings in the office and knowing we're thinking about each other, and sneaking around corners and getting away for weekends and making love some more when everybody thinks we're someplace else, and all that great, corny backstreet stuff. I like to talk to you, but not necessarily every night."

"Are you *sure* you're Jewish?"

"You sound like my mother. You'd better make love to me again, fast, to make me forget that remark," she said threateningly through her tears of laughter at his shock.

Nina Stern liked her freedom as much as she liked her increasing power at *Style*, a power she knew everybody had to admit she had achieved by merit, not by sleeping with the boss. She adored working hard at work she did brilliantly, she enjoyed being able to work nights without worrying about a family, and she was firm about having no one to please but herself. Every day brought her more invitations than three people could accept; she was one of the half-dozen single women in New York who had achieved the same desirability as a guest at a party as a supremely attractive bachelor. Men of all ages had competed for her throughout her twenties, and now in her thirties she was even more mysteriously, definitively desirable than she had been when she was younger, and just as much a flirt. If anything, fidelity to Zachary made her alluring ways more intriguing since they led to nothing and created a challenge few men could resist; surrounding her with the aura of a beloved, successful, deeply happy woman with a distinctly private, private life. When her mother grumbled about Nina's lack of husband and children all Nina bothered to reply was that she had the most interesting life of any woman she knew, a remark that Mrs. Stern regarded as frivolous and totally irrelevant, but which satisfied Nina completely.

Cutter and Candice Standings were married as soon as possible after it was certain that she was out of danger. The degree of her recovery was still in question but within two years of intensive physical therapy she had almost recovered from her accident. Her back would always give her trouble and frequent pain, but it had not been broken. She would never again be able to participate in any active sports but she walked normally.

During these two years Cutter had not only earned the benefit of his in-laws' almost incredulous gratitude, but Candice's love for him had turned into an emotion that was close to worship. It was an emotion so embarrassingly powerful, she was so totally under his dominion, that she had to hide her feelings for fear of being thought ridiculous. As the years passed, her focus on Cutter grew into an obsession that took the tyrannical, feverish form of jealousy, for never, in her hearts of hearts, was she able to convince herself that Cutter really loved her. *Was* it a proof of love that he had married her when she might have been crippled for life? Or was it merely guilt? He had sworn that yes, he did blame himself for her accident, but blame alone, no matter how great, would never have led him to marry her without love, he had sworn it dozens of times, until, one day, she saw that she must appear to have stopped doubting him for his patience was wearing thin.

She mastered herself, with a strength no one knew she had, and to others, even to Cutter, she seemed to be like many another of those rich young married women who were her friends, women who acted as if they took their husbands for granted. But not for one half hour of one single day was Candice free of a lifelong insecurity based on those many years in which men had ignored her. The jealousy that she drove severely underground possessed her spirit all the more ferociously for being unspoken. Cutter became the only meaning in Candice's life and when they participated in the rites of San Francisco social life, into which she was locked by her birth and position, her eyes forever, secretly, sought him out, checking to see if he was talking to a pretty woman. The jealous words she couldn't allow herself to say turned into a wrinkled glass, like a dirty yellow filter spotted with unnamable filth, through which she saw her privileged world as a place where only misery lay.

Candice Amberville started drinking earlier and earlier every day so that, by the time she had to get dressed for a party or the opera, she could feel relaxed enough to face herself in her mirror without comparing herself to every other woman in town, but it didn't help. She spent a fortune on clothes and became one of the best-dressed women in the city, but it didn't help. She went to the hairdresser every other day so that her good hair was always perfect, but it didn't help. She paid her cook twice what anyone else paid and gave the best, most beautifully organized dinner parties of their group, but it didn't help. She was diseased in a way that nothing could cure. When Cutter lay between her legs, even when he was pulsing inside her, she thought of him doing the same thing to another woman, so when she reached her difficult orgasm, even that momentary relief didn't help. Jealousy was killing Candice Amberville and if Cutter had been faithful to her it would not have helped.

She was so befouled with jealousy that she felt as if she had some vile skin affliction that oozed from every pore—to herself Candice was unclean, tainted, crusty with sores and scabs, each one torn over and over until the blood and pus poured out invisible, disgusting.

In a frantic effort to fill her life with something other than her thoughts she bought a pair of golden retrievers. They gave her some surcease, some brief respite, for into their ears she could pour her suspicions, her words of loathing for her peers who had sat next to Cutter at dinner and laughed with him, who asked him to be their partner at mixed doubles or to spend a day crewing for them in one of the many yacht club races. With no sign of her torment she encouraged him to go, to enjoy all the sports in which she couldn't join. She pretended to be anxious to take ski vacations saying that as far as she was concerned, she welcomed the change, enjoyed walking in the snow and having time to read while he was on the slopes.

If she could have had her way Cutter would have played only polo, for there, in the stands, watching him, she could be sure for hours at a time that he belonged to no one else. But whenever he wasn't playing polo her imagination invented scenarios: Cutter, still dripping with the clean sweat of a tennis match, finding an empty room at the club, stripping off his clothes and plunging, already erect, into his only-too-ready partner; Cutter in the cabin of a becalmed yawl, lying back naked on a bunk, his long, thick penis already half swollen, a woman on her knees before him, following his curt, precise directions; Cutter returning early from the mountain and going, unobserved, to the bedroom of any one of the women who skied with him, watching her undress while he explained exactly what she must do to him, exactly what he intended to do to her, while he grew harder with each word.

Candice enlarged her kennels, bought more champion golden retrievers and started to breed them. She now drank more heavily, keeping bottles in the kennels so that she had a place to go, a private place where she could drink unobserved and tell her dogs all the things she could never tell other people because they would think she was crazy. For Candice there could be no acceptance of her situation, no slow slide into resignation, no truce. Her arid, tortured sense of worth lay entirely in *seeming not to know*, in living as if all were well in her marriage, in presenting a perfectly groomed, superbly dressed, confidently smiling persona to the world in which she was convinced that everyone was aware that her husband was faithless.

Actually Candice Amberville was wrong. Cutter's many affairs, though suspected by some, were not common knowledge. He had picked his partners well; they were outlaws like him, all anxious in their own self-interest to leave no signs that could be read by their husbands; women who were part of an underground that exists in every city in the world.

Candice's father, who advanced Cutter's responsibilities every year, would never have believed that the wife of one of the other partners at Standings and Alexander met Cutter twice a week in a hotel room. Candice's mother would have given the lie to anyone who reported to her that her son-in-law had other women, dozens of them. Only one member of the Standings family knew Cutter for what he was: Nanette, who had been fifteen when Cutter and Candice married and who now was twenty-four, pouting, rosy Nanette who had grown up unscrupulous, amoral and game for anything; Nanette who used other women and cocaine with the same sense of defiant curiosity. Why not do it, if it existed? Life was so dull, San Francisco so provincial, and marriage—for she was married—so boring and predictable that it was worth having at least one hard run at anything.

All undergrounds, even the most clandestine, have grapevines, and that of promiscuity is no exception. Eventually Nanette heard enough hints about Cutter's activities to form a new idea of this blond man, so invincibly cool and so darkly intent, this man who had always acted toward her as if she were nothing more than Candice's baby sister.

How had he managed to convince her that he had overlooked her own sexuality, as visible as a brand on her forehead to the kind of man she now knew he was? Did he find her unattractive? she asked herself, deeply piqued. And just how much of what she'd heard about him was true? A man who needed no arousal, a man who always was ready, a man who left every woman satisfied but with a satisfaction that itched for more—a sexual pirate. Could Cutter be all that? Was her horrid sister, so calm and pulled together, so superior and snobbish and disapproving, so busy with those prizewinning dogs and her famous dinner parties—was Candice so smug because she was getting her fill of such a man? Nanette asked herself in petulant irritation.

Cutter resisted Nanette for as long as he could. She was too close to home, he told himself, refusing to admit that that was part of her attraction. He'd wanted her for years, from the time she turned from another little teenager into a voluptuous woman who reeked of carnality, whose animalism was so wanton that whenever he saw her at family gatherings he had become inflamed, against his will and his judgment, wanting nothing more on earth than to take her immediately, to take her without a smile and without a word, take her the way he knew she wanted to be taken, with brutality and violence. How many nights, in the ski lodge at Aspen, had he thrust himself deeply into his wife's untempting, yielding, yearning body while he thought of luscious Nanette, dark, juicy and flamboyant, whose bedroom was only two doors away?

They stalked each other like creatures in a jungle, each the hunter, each the hunted, until the day came when the only question left was *how soon*? Quickly, it had to be quickly. And after they had wallowed in each other, the only question was how soon *again*? Nanette was inexhaustible with a courtesan's skill he had never known in another woman. She was as voracious as a wolverine and twice as vicious. Cunningly she introduced him to the only experience Cutter had never known with a woman before: the thunderous, forbidden rapture of having two women at the same time; wise Nanette who had understood that this was the only way she was sure to keep Cutter for as long as she wanted him; Nanette who didn't mind sharing him with a woman she had already possessed; Nanette who felt a particular, puissant thrill in showing him exactly what it was like when one woman took another while he watched, watched and waited until she allowed him to take her, take the other, take them both. No matter.

But a secret known to three people is only safe if two of them are dead. And this secret was too good to be confined to the grapevine, this secret was too tasty not to be savored and rolled on the tongue by people to whom debauchery was only a word, a fantasy they would never dare to act out. It became a suspicion, it became almost—but not quite-known, and then, as words written in invisible ink become legible with the application of fire, it came, as inevitably it must, to Candice's ear.

Almost from the beginning of her marriage she had endured the scenarios of Cutter with another woman, but the woman was always faceless. For years all her strength and all her emotional energy had gone into nonacknowledgment; her only solace alcohol, her dogs and her pride. Now her pride could sustain her no longer, for now that faceless woman had a face, that of Nanette. Nanette herself had told her, not showing how much she enjoyed the pseudo-confession. Candice's haughty surface had become so perfect that Nanette couldn't resist—didn't try to resist—shocking Candice out of her self-satisfied contentment. Venomously, as if by accident, she left behind a Polaroid shot of herself and Cutter, his face distorted by his orgasm.

She could not endure more, Candice realized. It was not to be lived with. There was no possible hideous future to a life that contained this certain knowledge. She would never stop seeing that picture. It could never become a memory. It would live before her eyes, the purest of agony. Hell had entered the room and eliminated any doubt and without doubt there was no hope.

Candice dressed herself in a beautiful suit, combed her gleaming hair, put on her makeup, went to a hotel on the far side of Union Square, checked into a room on the sixteenth floor, drank half a bottle of Scotch and jumped out of the window into the empty alley behind the hotel.

It would have been considered a case of temporary insanity, of suicidal depression so well hidden that even her mother hadn't suspected its existence. But while she was swallowing the alcohol that she needed to make it easier to open the window, Candice thought of her dogs and scrawled a letter giving instructions for their care, a rambling letter in which her desire to punish her sister won over her desire to maintain to the end that she did not know what sort of husband Cutter had been, a letter in which she accused Nanette.

The detective who found the letter gave it to James Standings III. He had no choice but to believe that Candice was wrong about Nanette, for he had only one child left. All his vengeance turned toward Cutter, now senior vice-president of his firm. In order to avoid a further scandal out of what he could still manage to have treated as a tragedy, all that James Standings III could do was to expel Cutter from the firm and vow that never again would he be hired by any other of the many San Francisco banking houses in which he exerted considerable influence.

James Standings III never realized it but his vengeance was as effective as any other he could have achieved, without a gun, for he took away from Cutter that sure future presidency of Standings and Alexander toward which he had been purposefully moving in so many ways from the day he first met Candice.

Jumbo Booker had never given up the borrowed glory he derived from his position as Cutter's best friend. Enclosed as Jumbo was in the tight pattern of a comfortable marriage, the sinfully exciting life that he could only imagine that Cutter led—for Cutter never boasted—gave him the illusion of participation without the problems that actual participation would have posed. Now, with Cutter so abruptly and inexplicably out of a job, Jumbo exerted himself to find something for his friend, enjoying this welcome sign that his own position, if less glamorous, was still superior.

Jumbo had fund-raising connections with the Nixon administration and he found Cutter an appointment in Belgium within the complicated bureaucracy of the Agency for International Development. Brussels, hospitable if singularly gloomy in its almost perpetual fog, suited Cutter's state of mind and he was soon involved in the complicated diplomatic life of the busy, well-fed capital. Eventually Jumbo got him the opportunity to work for an investment bank in London and there, after a few years, the faithful Jumbo got him an opportunity to return to New York and work in the local office of Booker, Smity and Jameston. It was 1981 and Cutter judged that it was time to go home. Neither the welcome of the NATO wives nor the friendliness of the British quite made up for the advantages he could still hope for as an Amberville on his native soil.

In 1969, twelve years before Cutter came back to Manhattan, Nina Stern had turned thirty-five. Her love affair with Zachary had been conducted so quietly that it had become part of the mosaic of Manhattan life, taken for granted by those in the know and undreamed of by anyone else. Whatever tidal waves of gossip there must certainly have been some ten years earlier had become mere wavelets as Lily and Zachary remained undramatically married. Nina and Zachary were like a minor, little-known institution, some obscure historical society located on a side street which had no fund-raising functions and no inquiring scholars. Only the two of them knew the treasures concealed behind the façade they had built, and as far as Zachary was concerned he asked no greater happiness.

But Nina Stern at thirty-five was not the same free spirit as Nina Stern at twenty-five. She was just as beloved, daily more successful, sure to succeed Zelda Powers as Editor-in-chief of *Style*, but her loathing of everything domestic had not resisted the attack of her hormonal heritage. She had reached the age at which the unmarried career woman faces that classic, unavoidable realization: *now or never*. On the eve of her thirty-fifth birthday Nina had taken stock, asking herself where she would be in ten years, and the answer hadn't pleased her: exactly where she was now, still successful, still with Zachary, but forty-five years old. With fifty fast approaching. Atavistic voices sounded in her mind. *Now or never*. Could she reconcile herself to the *never*? Must she change her mind about what she had believed she wanted just because the sands of time kept running? Nina Stern took a long, honest look at herself. Unclouded by illusion, she realized that, alas, she too was just like other women after all. She wanted the *now*—she couldn't hold on to the *never*. Even if marriage and children would not, in the end, make her happy, she must find out for herself. She was disappointed in this evidence of her ordinary humanity but a little relieved at the same time . . . perhaps, just perhaps, it would turn out to be an interesting experiment.

She broke with Zachary as quickly, as neatly and as sweetly as she knew how, and soon married the most eligible of the many men who had continued to pursue her over the years.

Only her daughter Nina, Mrs. Stern triumphantly told her friends, could have produced twin boys and held on to her job in the first year of marriage. Only Nina, thought Zachary, could have made the break with such decency and such honesty that he was able to go to the wedding and—almost—feel happy for her. Only Nina, thought Nina, could continue to care so deeply for Zachary and yet give her new husband the exclusive—almost exclusive—love he deserved. It was, after all, possible to have the best of both worlds . . . it was all a question of having the right sense of timing.

Lily Amberville saw an opportunity and did not fail to take advantage of it. The wedding invitation would have told her that Zachary was free of his mistress even if she hadn't been able to read the poignant loneliness in his eyes. From the time of Cutter's marriage, six years before, she had lived in a gilded, adorned, extravagantly bedecked emptiness. Now Zachary was as lonely as she and slowly the two of them came together and made their peace with each other, a silent peace—since there had never been any formal rupture to repair—a peace that grew more solid year by year, a peace of dry, resigned, but somehow rewarding contentment. They had each had their great romance. Now they had each other and their children and it was better, so very much better, than being alone.

11

One spring day in 1972 Zachary Amberville and Nina Stern Heller had lunch together, meeting unselfconsciously at one of the restaurants they had often gone to during the years of their love affair, an unfashionable place where it was unlikely that they would be seen by anyone who knew either of them. During the years that they had been together they had discovered that there were dozens of such places in Manhattan, neighborhood places, comfortable and warm, with fairly decent food. Now, there was no longer a reason to avoid attention, nor was there a reason to abandon the restaurants they both liked. If an element of nostalgia, a few moments of remembered pain, of remembered joy, crept into these lunches of the Editor-in-chief of *Style* and the head of Amberville Publications it only added a particularly bittersweet flavor to the feast.

"You have to admit," Nina said, choosing her words carefully, "that Maxi has potential."

"So did Bonnie and Clyde."

"Come on, Zachary, don't be too hard on her. I think she needs to be motivated, focused on something so she can use everything she has. After all, when she's interested in a subject in school she can get straight A's . . ."

"And when she isn't, she just won't bother to study, which adds up to a D-plus average. What kind of college is going to accept her with that record?" Zachary wondered miserably.

Nina considered Maxi and sighed. A most perplexing, puzzling minx, deeply and fundamentally lovable yet always in some kind of trouble, managing, even in this permissive society, to get herself thrown out of a succession of schools and summer camps; not for drugs or stealing or cheating, but for organizing groups of her peers into inspired, effective mischief. "She's always elected president of her class," Nina reminded him cheerfully.

"Usually just before she's bounced. All the future I can see for her is to be voted Miss Congeniality but she's not a type they allow in the Miss America contest."

"If only . . ." Nina ventured and then stopped.

"Yup." They both knew that they didn't want to discuss, yet again, the difficulties that existed between Maxi and Lily which made Zachary almost totally responsible for his daughter.

From the time Lily found out about Toby's inexorable eye disease she seemed to have abandoned her unquenchable healthy daughter for the boy who needed her. Maxi was barely three when this happened and, as the months and years passed, she never stopped yearning with all her heart for her mother's inaccessible affection. On Toby, Lily lavished a possessive, watchful, anxious love that was on alert as long as he was awake.

After Justin's birth, her youngest child too became an object of an adoring, excessive passion. Consumed by her two boys, who, like lovers, changed the colors of her world and demanded infidelity, Lily no longer even tried to make the time to read to her intrusive small girl child or let her play dress-up with her jewels.

Maxi had her father all to herself, Lily thought in self-justification when Maxi tried to claim her attention. If she had to cope with Maxi, it would be just too much for her sanity. The child was indestructible, she assured herself as she gave brief, firm, fruitless instruction to one of the procession of nannies she hired for her daughter, and turned quickly back to Toby's learning problems and Justin's health, for he had been premature and frighteningly frail for long after his birth.

But at no point during her childhood did Maxi stop craving and needing Lily's love. She strove for her mother's consideration in every naughty way she could think of, but only managed to get herself punished by her father, whose heart wasn't in it, as well she knew.

She never tried being a "good girl," for she understood that the better she was, the less chance she had to be noticed. Yet from birth Maxi had been bound by the rules of fair play. Some tangible thing called "fairness" was utterly and indelibly precious to her and as she grew older she tried to convince herself that it was "fair" that Toby and Justin should so preoccupy her mother. She had tried very hard indeed to make herself believe this, but she'd never totally succeeded and, at some early time in her life, she began to stop hoping for Lily's love. She never gave up completely but her hope diminished year by year until it was buried so deep that it almost stopped hurting.

Nina stopped eating her osso buco and turned to Zachary.

"There's one thing you've never tried. Every summer you send Maxi away to some new place . . . tennis camp, theater camp, wilderness survival camp, riding camp . . . and every year she's returned to you by air mail. Why not give her a real challenge—I'll bet she'd rise to it."

"What I love about you, among a billion other things, is your optimism." Zachary smiled at her. A beautiful, warmhearted wonderful woman, damn that husband of hers.

"A job, a summer job," Nina continued excitedly. "It would use up all of that crazy energy of hers on something she could sink her teeth into, something that would give her a sense of accomplishment."

"Who would hire her?" Zachary asked. He couldn't imagine anyone deliberately adding Maxi to any business endeavor.

"You, Zachary, you."

"Oh no! Not me! Not Maxi!"

"You know perfectly well that you always have summer jobs available for kids with pull, kids of major advertisers. It's an understood thing. I've got a half-dozen set for this summer on my staff alone, Miss Better Dresses, Miss Panty Hose, and four others, not any one of them as smart as Maxi."

"Pull is one thing, nepotism is another."

"That's a cop-out. I'll talk to Pavka and between us we'll find a place for her. At least try it . . . you've got nothing to lose."

"Nothing to lose?" Zachary asked, amused by her Girl Scout madness.

"What's the worst that can happen?" Nina demanded.

"She'll fuck up," he said.

"But it's worth a try, isn't it?" Nina insisted, looking at him with a special kind of love that her husband had never seen, would never see, in her eyes.

"Are you asking me or telling me?"

"Telling you."

"Then it's worth a try."

Amberville Publications now included three more successful magazines. *Savoir Vivre*, a magazine devoted to the art of living well through cultivation of ever more sophisticated taste buds; *Sports Week*, which had become rapidly indispensable to every man, woman and child in America who had ever worn out a pair of sneakers, and *Indoors*, a magnificent monthly for well-heeled masochists that made its buyers, no matter how rich, feel that they lived like pigs and attracted large numbers of fans who looked at the photographs in each issue with a magnifying glass so as not to miss a single mortifying detail of other people's homes.

Pavka Mayer, who was on the masthead of each of the publications as Artistic Director, sat in his office and contemplated Nina with relish. Even her latest idea hadn't astonished him. He thought Nina capable of anything.

"It boils down to where Maxi can do the least harm," he said thoughtfully.

"*Style* is out because it's fashion and fashion leads to photographers and photographers lead to sex," Nina brooded.

"We can't hide her on *T.V. Week*—those gangsters there won't put up with her. And they might send her to interview Warren Beatty just as a gag," Pavka added.

"On *Seven Days* she'll meet too many other kids. We don't want to encourage our darling's ringleader tendencies and all the editors at *Sports Week* are jocks or ex-jocks or would-be jocks and I don't think it would be a good idea to expose Maxi to so many older men all at once."

"You can't mean you think she's still a virgin?" Pavka asked, shocked.

"I don't know. I've made it a point never to ask. It's none of my business, Pavka. Nothing is impossible no matter how unlikely," Nina replied.

"So that leaves only *Savoir Vivre* and *Indoors*," Pavka realized. "You decide."

"No, you decide. I don't want to be totally responsible."

"Neither do I," Pavka said stubbornly. He pushed a button and spoke to his secretary. "Miss Williams, would you rather work on *Savoir Vivre* or *Indoors*?"

There was a long pause and finally his secretary blurted, "Have I done something wrong, Mr. Mayer?"

"No, just answer my question. Please, if you would be so kind."

"Does this mean I'm fired?" she quavered.

"Oh, my God. No, it's just an election bet."

"Did you win or lose?"

"Miss Williams, I beg of you. Toss a coin if you don't have an opinion."

"I'd rather work on *Savoir Vivre* because I'd rather see pictures of roast pork than of somebody's dining room."

"Thank you, Miss Williams. Well done."

"Oh, you're so welcome, Mr. Mayer. Any time."

Pavka beamed at Nina. "Can I help it if women adore me?"

Maxi was in heaven. Every summer of her life she had been forced into banishment in the country. Beaches, lakes, trees, fresh air and group sports, all were considered to be absolutely necessary for her well-being. Left to herself, a quick trip to Central Park was more than enough contact with nature.

On those rare occasions when she'd been in New York in the summer, for a few hours she'd been conscious of another Manhattan, one that was a hot tropical island where everything moved to a different beat, a city whose rhythm had somehow altered and, in its transformation, had become languid, mysterious, more exciting than ever. Although the office buildings seemed to have the same number of people dashing in and out, there was something different about the people themselves. They dressed differently and they smiled more. A sense of holiday, of a potential party just about to happen reigned in the business district, and in the residential parts of town there was a lazy emptiness, as well-dressed housewives, well-dressed children and well-dressed nannies vanished as completely as if plague stalked the streets.

Now this alluring, throbbing Manhattan in its summer metamorphosis was going to be hers, except for weekends when she and her father would join the family in Southampton. She would go to work with her father in the morning and then—lovely conspiracy—drift away from his side without a goodbye and take another elevator to the offices of *Savoir Vivre* where she would be known as Maxi Adams. Both Pavka and Nina had insisted on the necessity of concealing her identity from everyone but Carl Koch, the Editor-in-chief of the magazine. If her co-workers knew she was Zachary Amberville's daughter, at best they would think she was a spoiled rich bitch who was slumming her way into the magazine business, and at worst they would suspect her of being a spy, planted by the management to see what they were up to, reporting back to her father. Since *Savoir Vivre* was a magazine that had been published for only a little over two years, Maxi was unknown to everyone who worked there and they had decided to plant her in the art department, where she could be put to work on layouts. "She should be able to do wonders with glue and rubber cement and Scotch tape and a ruler," Nina had assured Pavka.

"Maxi and a pot of glue? It won't last two days," Pavka muttered. "But better that than the test kitchens or, God forbid, the wine department. Glue you can always clean up. Glue you can re-glue."

On that first Monday morning of July Maxi woke early and began to prepare herself for her entrance into the world of major corporative responsibility. She was enchanted with the idea of a job, a grown-up job. She had decided to add two necessary years to Maxi Adams's age and tell everybody that she was nineteen.

She walked around in her biggest closet, looking for her oldest pair of jeans, the most paint-splotched, the ones that spoke the most of real work of all the many jeans she owned. She had worn them while painting scenery at her next-to-last school and it seemed to her that they gave off an artistic aura, for was she not going to be working in an art department? With them she put on a clean, pale blue, but equally well-worn denim shirt which seemed to say that she had never spent an unproductive minute in her life, a shirt that she felt was sensible, down-to-earth and adult, above all adult. She wanted so much to make a good first impression. Maxi bound a thick silver-and-turquoise Arizona Indian belt tightly around her eighteenth-century waist. After all, any art department would expect that even its most humble employee would still have a sense of decoration. Shoes? No. She put on one of her many pairs of treasured high-heeled Western boots, four hundred and fifty dollars by mail order from Tony Lama, boots that she was convinced added three inches to her height.

Satisfied with her body she attacked her face and hair. No female, in 1972, ever considered that she had enough hair. Maxi had let hers grow down long beyond her shoulders and liked to fling it around, often adding to it with one of the many hunks of fake hair she had accumulated in the last few years. But today called for seriousness and dignity. She combed all her hair back from her face so that her streak of white was prominent. Makeup? Maxi had as much experience with makeup as any demonstrator on the first floor of Bloomingdale's. Today she wanted to look *old.* The less makeup she used, the younger she looked, so she set about skillfully applying base, powder, blusher, mascara, eye liner, lipstick and eye shadow with a steady hand born of long hours of solitary practice. She added chunky nuggets of turquoise earrings and studied the finished product. She used an eyebrow pencil to darken the beauty mark above the bow of her upper lip.

No, still not *quite* old enough, Maxi decided, and dove into her closet and produced a pair of large horn-rimmed glasses she always wore when she played poker. They had plain glass for lenses but it helped to have some sort of mask, no matter how transparent, when bluffing. Something was *still* missing, she fretted, looking into a triple mirror. It was all that hair, of course. What good did it do to have white hair in front if the rest of it all hung down in the back? She pulled it all into a neat chignon and fastened it securely. Perfection, she thought. The portrait of the artist as an almost-middle-aged woman.

Zachary greeted her appearance at the breakfast table as impassively as possible. Perhaps, he thought prayfully, she didn't look any different from any other girl of her age . . . he didn't go around staring at them so he didn't know for sure. But wasn't there something almost . . . depraved? . . . about the way her jeans and shirt clung to her body? Didn't Maxi realize that she looked sexier in those damn jeans than if she'd pranced around in black lace panties? Shouldn't a girl with such a tiny waist and such . . . a well-developed . . . pair of tits, for want of a less parental phrase, not wear a limp denim shirt that hugged each blossoming inch of her? And those glasses? Since when did she need glasses? They only made the rest of her more—whatever it was that disturbed him. And what had she done to her face? And her hair? Nothing he could figure out for sure, but there was something different about his daughter this morning. Was he going crazy or did she look almost . . . mature? No, not Maxi. Not mature, it couldn't be. *Ripe.* By God, *ripe*!

"Maxi, you look ripe, damn it."

"Thank you, Daddy," she said demurely.

"Don't you think you should wear a dress . . . maybe?"

"Daddy, nobody wears dresses anymore," she said with gentle reproof.

She was right, Zachary realized. Nina wore pants, his secretary wore pants, all his female editors wore pants. The last woman he had seen in a dress was Lily, and hers were all that new mid-calf length. He sighed, hoping dresses would come back soon, and returned to his eggs.

"This is Maxi Adams, your summer trainee," Carl Koch, Editor-in-chief of *Savoir Vivre,* said to his clever, capable art director, Linda Lafferty. "Do with her what you will." He disappeared hastily, and with considerable relief, leaving Linda, who was close to six feet tall and still managed to be dumpy, to cope with the trainee.

Carl Koch had good instincts and he'd been immediately convinced that Maxi was a problem. He just wasn't sure of what magnitude. Those summer kids always were a pain in the ass to deal with. But Pavka had given him firm, not-to-be-questioned orders and *Savoir Vivre* was stuck with her for the summer. But now she was Linda Lafferty's problem.

Linda inspected Maxi with growing wonder. This young person looked to her like a budding intellectual who had somehow become a hooker in Santa Fe, or perhaps an apprentice Simone de Beauvoir who'd strayed into a stag party.

"Howdy pardner," she said finally.

"Howdy, Miz Lafferty."

"Where do you . . . hail from?"

"The East," Maxi answered, skillfully avoiding this leading question.

"East?" Linda persisted. "Far East or Near East?"

"East Seventies," she admitted.

"Oh. Any art training?"

"Only school and camp."

"Camp?"

"Summer camp," Maxi murmured, suddenly unable to find a substitute that would sound more impressive.

Why me, thought Linda Lafferty. *Why me?*

Nothing she had ever done in her life, Maxi decided after a week of work, could compare to the office for sheer fun. The potential for making merry in the art department of *Savoir Vivre* was beyond anything she had imagined. How come she had never guessed that people went to work in order to stand around and tell each other much better dirty jokes than she'd ever heard at school—really good ones—and horse around like crazy and get friendly with each other and goof off and sneak joints in the john and gossip like wild about sex? They all seemed to be making it with each other. To do that all day and get paid for it too—this was the secret grown-ups never told you when they spoke so seriously of something called "business." Business was play on a major scale.

All her new friends worked on layouts, which reminded her of kindergarten, pasting pictures on heavy paper. She loved helping them, leaning over their shoulders and straightening out edges, handing them Magic Markers and sharpening their pencils and making them laugh if they ever got too annoyed with some photograph that wouldn't fit right on a page. She'd shown them things they'd never thought of—the story on foie gras for instance, with photographs of seventeen different slices of foie gras, each one from a different French restaurant—nobody had been able to tell which part of which slice was the top and which was the bottom by the time she'd finished rearranging them.

Maxi's very favorite part of the day was when the bagel-and-doughnut wagon came around, and everybody stopped pretending to be busy and gathered around like nomads stoking up before a trek across the desert. She even came back from lunch early for the afternoon bagel wagon halt at three o'clock. Nobody really needed her till then anyway. Lunch was such a groovy invention! Three free hours to shop. She was on a diet so she didn't bother to eat. Instead, she systematically combed the stores, boutiques as well as department stores.

Maxi had been picking out her own clothes for years but always before she'd had to wait till September to shop. But now the city was full of early fall merchandise and there wasn't anything Maxi didn't try on. When she finally finished her daily bout of pillage and plunder, all charged to Lily's accounts, she brought stacks of packages back to her brightly lit cubicle and pulled all her purchases out of their boxes and modeled them for her co-workers who had such terrific taste about things like colors and shapes and were teaching her a lot about what to wear. She'd stopped using her glasses and doing dumb things to her hair once she'd been firmly established as nineteen, going on twenty, and part of the gang.

The idea of starting her last year of high school in September was too revolting to think about. Maxi had decided to go to art school instead and everyone had advice for her about which school to pick and they were so great about coming back to her office and sitting around telling her about their days in art school and the hell-raising they'd gotten up to there. She hated the end of the day when she had to refuse all the offers of drinks at the bars that surrounded the office and disappear back home, even though she could usually con her father into taking her out to dinner with him.

Linda Lafferty simmered with midsummer rage. Productivity in her art department—*her* department!—had fallen off precipitously since the advent of Maxi. All her workers, who at best had never been as dependable as she would have liked, had turned into randy goats who spent most of their time thinking up excuses to have yet another long conversation with that . . . that . . . she couldn't think of the right word. Maxi was outside of her previous experience, and none of the words she knew managed to satisfactorily categorize that sexy, funny, absolutely lawless, disruptive and yet somehow, in spite of it all—admit it, Linda, you like to talk to her too, she told herself in disgust. The kid was a daily bacchanal. She must be Miss Seagram's or Miss General Foods or Miss Coca-Cola to be allowed such a range of nuisance value, for Carl Koch simply refused to listen to her complaints about the new trainee.

However, Linda Lafferty had a department to run, a department that had always been the single most overworked department at the magazine. Much of the body of the book was given over to photographs and the rest of the thick magazine was stuffed with ads for luxury products. The readers of *Savoir Vivre* were rich people and the magazine, printed on glossy, thick, fifty-pound paper, was expected to drip visual riches that would make its rich readers feel even richer. All the responsibility for the quality and originality of this monthly cornucopia lay squarely on the art department. The text barely mattered although the food and wine articles were all written by top literary figures who were paid enormous sums of money by magazine standards.

She needed a new assistant art director, Linda Lafferty decided in desperation, someone fast and good who would be tough enough to speed things up. A lot of severe ass-kicking could do wonders to kill Maxi-lust, she thought, but something about being so tall made it almost impossible for her to kick ass effectively. She hadn't decided if it was her desire to be liked or fear of killing someone, but at least she was smart enough to know when she needed help.

When she put her request to Carl Koch she was surprised at how quickly he agreed to let her hire a new top assistant. Although *Savoir Vivre* was clearly a money-machine, Koch, like most editors, didn't like to add any staff if he could help it. In her last job Linda had worked with a young man who was as single-mindedly work-oriented as he was brilliant. She had wanted to hire him for a long time and now Maxi Adams, queen of the rubber cement, Lorelei of paste-up, catnip sorceress of the ruler, was going to give her the opportunity to offer Rocco Cipriani a salary he couldn't resist, for he had always said that only a lot of money could get him away from Condé Nast. Maxi Adams would serve a purpose, would make a contribution in spite of herself.

Linda Lafferty looked at Rocco Cipriani severely. "I'm taking a vacation. I haven't had one minute off since I came to *Savoir Vivre.* I won't be there when you start tomorrow. I don't want people coming to me about you and complaining. You're going to be in absolute charge. They'll all have memos to that effect."

"You want a new broom, mixed with Captain Queeg and a few floggings?"

"Precisely. There isn't one of my bums who's doing a full day's work. I have a major discipline problem on my hands. I'm absolutely counting on you to beat and whack and knock them back into shape while I'm away having that thirty-day nervous breakdown Carl said I was entitled to, and when I get back I want to be ahead of schedule . . . or else." She had decided not to pinpoint Maxi as the source of the trouble. Let him find out for himself. On-the-job training.

"You're cute as hell, Linda, when you get threatening."

"That's why I've hired you, that's why we've spent all weekend going over this disgusting backload of undone work. You're going to save my ass because you're not at all cute."

"And I thought you liked me."

"You're all right for a kid," she said primly, cursing her never-give-up Irish lust that didn't have the good sense to stop raging at the sight of that young and completely untouchable Rocco Cipriani. She looked at him closely, trying to decide how any man so absurdly gorgeous could still command as much respect as he did. He had an indecent chaos of black curls, heavily hooded dark eyes that were both dreamy and glowing in their intensity, as well as the nose of a Medici prince. In his strong features, for all her acuteness, she could find no single fault. She didn't even dare to look at his mouth. A girl had only so much self-control. Everything about Rocco worked together, relentlessly, powerfully, insistently. It was difficult to turn away from him. He was, she decided, like the model for a great Renaissance painter's masterpiece, a vision of a proud Saint Sebastian. All that was lacking were the arrows piercing his body at those interestingly vulnerable places. Rocco Cipriani explained as much about the high period of Italian art as a trip to the Met.

Yet, at barely twenty-three, he was doing so well at Condé Nast that it was only a question of having a little more seniority, a little more seasoning before he would be the art director of his own magazine. She knew full well that he would never stay at Amberville. This was simply one of those sharp, strategic, sideways moves that some of the best and most ambitious art directors made in order to go ahead faster than they would if they stayed at one company during their entire career . . . she'd done it herself. It made you more appreciated than total loyalty ever did, and it was only risky if you were not very, very, *very* good. Rocco had nothing to worry about.

There are as many kinds of art directors in Manhattan as there are publications and agencies and commercial-makers. Rocco was one of a very special kind, one who never wanted to work on anything but magazines. He harbored no itch to work in advertising in spite of the desirable big bucks those poor bastards who called themselves "creative directors" made. They were bound by the demands of clients and he was bound by nothing but the limits of his own imagination. For Rocco the ultimate joy in life was pages and pages of an empty magazine, pure glorious white space, space without end, space renewed each month by advertising department magic, waiting for him to fill it with layouts that had never been dreamed of before, combinations of type that had never been put together since typography was invented, graphics that would make history, photographs hitherto unimagined, cropped in ways no one had ever cropped before, drawings commissioned from artists who had never been thought of except in terms of gallery and museum walls. Each page of editorial space was to him like a blank canvas to a painter: a new chance to impose his vision of what *could* be, and like a painter, he was never totally satisfied.

Rocco was the not-yet-satiated Alexander the Great of the magazine world, still on the rampage, not with armies but with torrents of talent. He worked at least ten hours a day at his desk and then went home to empty his mailbox into which were stuffed magazines from all over the world, each one of which he devoured page by page, cursing horribly when he saw a new idea he hadn't thought of himself, raping the magazines of the pages he wanted to study, which he taped to the walls of his big Soho loft until they went from floor to eye level, and were gradually covered over by other pages so that being in the room was like living inside a collage of the best international graphic design.

There were only two men in the world whom Rocco Cipriani envied: Alexander Liberman, the genius who was Artistic Director of Condé Nast, and Pavka Mayer. One day he felt sure he was destined to replace one or the other of them, but he also knew he still had a lot to learn, so Linda Lafferty's job offer had an additional allure: he'd be working for Pavka for the first time, indirectly it was true, but still there was always the potential opportunity of picking the man's great brain.

Rocco started at *Savoir Vivre* on a Monday in mid-July. By Friday, Linda couldn't stand it anymore and let herself give in to the temptation to telephone him and find out how things were going.

"We've cleared up all that major lot of undone work and Monday I'm attacking the November issue," he said.

"Already? Are you sure?"

"Well, nobody was thrilled about working till midnight every night all week, but they did it."

"What about the Maxi problem?"

" 'Maxi problem?' You mean my trainee?"

"If you want to describe her that way, yes."

"Christ, Linda, she's no problem at all. I can't believe what a help that kid is. Doesn't even take her lunch hour, just bolts a hard-boiled egg out of a paper bag and goes right back to sweeping up and getting rid of eraser crumbs and making sure that everyone has fresh supplies when they come back from lunch. She seems very grown-up for only nineteen. In on time every morning, last one out at night, doesn't fool around in the bagel breaks, brings coffee just before anyone begins to itch for it, keeps my Magic Markers arranged just right, in fact I've never had such an organized desk anywhere. Doesn't smoke, wears those demure little dresses, doesn't indulge in idle chat and doesn't even seem to take time to pee. Maybe she's a Mormon? She's always there when I want her . . . yet she's never a nuisance. A good lady, that one. Not bad-looking too, now that I come to think about it . . . in fact . . . not bad at all . . ."

"Oh SHIT."

"What's that about?"

"Forget it. Just forget it. Carry on, Rocco. I'm going back to the beach and walk into the ocean until I drown."

"If you're planning on working all weekend, Rocco, maybe I can help out?" Maxi suggested casually, holding her breath. She would die for him, she would not just walk on burning coals for him, she would cover herself with them and lie down quietly until it was all over. There wasn't anything in the lexicon of human behavior that she would not do for Rocco Cipriani beginning with leaving home and crossing continents on foot and starving in the wilderness. He had only to ask.

"I don't want to interrupt your weekend plans," he said.

"I don't have any actually. And I could learn a lot while I kept your stuff straight. You know how your layouts disappear under each other when you're working hard. And . . . I could go out for pizza," she added, a suggestion that grew from every bit of wisdom she had absorbed in her life.

"Good thought. I usually forget to eat. And there's that pizza place right next door that takes so long to deliver that the cheese is always cold. O.K., come by on Saturday morning about nine. I'll give you the address."

She took the paper and put it in her handbag to keep forever. She already knew where he lived, she knew his phone number, she knew all about his big family in Hartford, his scholarship to art school, his prizes, his promotions. The advent of Rocco had started a storm of speculation in the art department of *Savoir Vivre* and Maxi had listened carefully, saying nothing but registering every morsel, weeding out the bits that overlapped or didn't seem to go together and ending up with a fair idea of the truth. She knew he had had a lot of girls but no long-lasting one, she knew his enemies and his friends, she knew as much about this stranger she had met for the first time five days before as it is possible to learn and intuit. Maxi's intuition of Rocco was far more than the act of mental contemplation or recognition or consideration. It went deeper than that philosophical definition which claims for intuition a spiritual perception and immediate knowledge that can be ascribed to angelic or spiritual beings. Hers went further and was a good deal shorter. It was Hawthorne's definition: "A miraculous intuition of what ought to be done just at the right time for action."

The first Saturday and Sunday Maxi spent in Rocco's loft were busy ones. Whenever she saw that Rocco was lost in thought before his drawing table she moved about the room, so quietly that he never heard her, finding out where he kept his household supplies. She made his bed with fresh sheets and bundled up all his dirty linen and shirts for a trip to that laundromat which, for the first time in her life, she was sure she would be able to find and figure out. She washed her first sinkful of dirty dishes and put them away; she went through his pantry and made lists of the basics that were missing; but she didn't have time to tackle his drawers or closets. While she bent to these divine tasks she always had one eye on him, and whenever he looked up, needing something, she had it ready for him, with much of the expertise of an operating-room nurse. He gulped down the pizza and sandwiches she brought back for him, sharing them with her of course, but silently, as he thought about the design problems that confronted him. Now that the backlog of old work had been cleared up, Rocco wanted to impose his own style on *Savoir Vivre* before Linda Lafferty came back from her vacation.

He was immediately concerned with the problems created by a magazine devoted to food and wine. He had worked with models and clothes so long that the presentation of objects, whose main relation to the readers was to cause them to salivate, provided him with a challenge which made him oblivious to all else.

"*One* grain, just one grain," he muttered as Maxi sliced another pizza on Sunday night.

"Not hungry?" she asked, worried.

"One single grain of golden caviar, on a full-bleed double spread. The obvious thing to do would be to have Penn photograph it but Penn means Condé Nast and anyway I don't do the obvious. Laser photography? Photomicrography? You can't *draw* caviar—or can you? Maybe, yeah, maybe . . . with gold leaf covering both pages and Andrew Wyeth to draw the caviar . . . maybe . . . is that pepperoni?"

"I asked for everything on it."

"Good." He lapsed back into silence and soon afterwards, seeing that he was about to stop working, Maxi left, so quietly that he didn't notice she was gone.

During the following week anyone coming into the art department of *Savoir Vivre* might have thought himself in the manuscript room of a medieval monastery as the workers bent over their desks with concentrated industry, trying out all the ideas that Rocco flung at them in his search for ever newer, ever more exciting pages.

Zachary was thrilled as Maxi told him about her modest but necessary part in this work and even more delighted when she asked him questions that showed how closely she had been watching the whole process of putting a magazine together. Yet he was slightly concerned by the sheer intensity of her interest . . . if she were so involved, might it not all be over as quickly as it had started? He didn't trust Maxi's enthusiasm. He was relieved that at least she had spent the weekend visiting her school friend India West, in Connecticut, and was going back there again this coming Saturday.

Sunday night Rocco put down his tools, yawned and stretched.

"That's it! That ought to be it," he said victoriously to Maxi who had just finished putting his recently washed and dried and rolled socks in military order in a drawer where he couldn't miss them. The loft was as immaculate as she could make it without actually disturbing any of the magazines or books or portfolios.

"Pizza time?" she asked.

"Not again. Not another one. I couldn't stand it." He grinned at her. Best assistant he'd ever had, he thought. And he could swear that she'd done something, he couldn't figure out what, which made it easier to get dressed in the morning.

"I could cook a steak, make a salad and put a potato in the oven to bake," Maxi offered.

"Where are you going to find all that stuff on Sunday night?"

"In here," Maxi said, opening the refrigerator which she had stocked the day before. Wilderness survival camp had included basic cooking lessons.

"Great. I'm beat. I think I'll grab a nap while the potato bakes. Wake me in time for dinner, O.K.?"

"Sure."

Rocco sank into a deep sleep almost immediately. It was so late in the day that the setting sun just dusted the air of the loft, but midsummer light still filled the room. Maxi crept close to Rocco's bed and carefully sank to her knees beside it. She had to clench her fists to prevent herself from reaching out and touching his hair. What if he woke up as suddenly as he had fallen asleep? She had never before been able to gaze directly at him for more than a few seconds except when he was talking to someone at the office, and even then she had been aware that if he looked up and caught her staring she would blush humiliatingly. During their two Saturdays and Sundays in the loft she had been particularly circumspect, knowing that if she distracted him in any way he'd throw her out.

Maxi was so much in love and so much in awe of Rocco that her normal reaction had been frozen. She realized that she hadn't been herself since she first laid eyes on him but she didn't know *how* to become herself with this man, who certainly had not been affected by her in the same way as any other man or boy she'd ever met. Love had generated in Maxi a condition in which every ordinary act of Rocco's was invested with absolute charm. If he scratched his head she was charmed. If he bit on his knuckles in thought she was charmed. When he hummed to himself she caught a glimpse of paradise. Maxi's eyes traced the perfect lines of his lips with a mixture of reverence and desperate longing. Her heartstrings pulled her toward him but she stayed immobile, wildly yearning, yearning with a violence that she knew she would never feel for any other man as long as she lived. She was filled with all the unutterable confusion and single-minded passion of first love. If she could just lift one of the soft black curls on his forehead and touch, just touch the skin underneath. If she could just rub the back of her hand against his cheek. But she didn't dare. The risk was too great.

As she knelt there, paralyzed with longing, Rocco's words suddenly hit her.

"Well, that ought to do it," he'd said, and stopped working. She knew him well enough to realize that he had finished with the November issue. Of course the December issue would be attacked next week but without the same need to invent a new graphic style that had been pushing him to work seven-day weeks. She had never thought about this moment before. Somehow she had let herself believe that these weekends in the loft would continue on . . . but her summer job would last only another five weeks. Panic struck Maxi. Tomorrow she would go back to work, just another body in the crowded art department, fetching and carrying and bringing coffee, and that right minute she had never been able to clearly imagine would never present itself—that absolutely necessary minute when Rocco would finally *see* her.

With panic Maxi became Maxi again. The enchantment that had rendered her ineffective, inert, was lifted, a spell broken. Her motto, discovered in French class, was the words of Danton: "Boldness, again boldness and ever boldness." For a minute she paced silently about the loft, and then, whispering "Boldness" to herself, she stripped off her T-shirt and her jeans and her underwear in a few silent but resolute motions. She untied her espadrilles and stood naked, as rosy and voluptuous as a Boucher, with her full, well-separated breasts that were so young that in spite of their weight they tilted upward from her narrow rib cage. Below her tiny, firm waist, where her white flesh was marked by the belt she had just dropped on the floor, her hips swelled out deliciously, in an excellent yet immoderate curve.

Nakedness was as natural to Maxi as to Eve. She was so perfectly proportioned that without clothes she seemed taller than when she was dressed. She ran her fingers through her long hair, shaking her head slightly, unable to move for a second. Boldness, she thought, *boldness*! She tiptoed over to the bed and bent over Rocco, reassured to see that he was in the deepest possible sleep. Carefully, as lightly as a flower, she lay down next to him, her delicate yet lavish body finding a place to nestle. She lifted herself up so that she hung over his face. Boldness, she prayed as she began to kiss him awake, so softly, so sweetly, so gently that it was many minutes before he began to stir and mutter complainingly. She undid the buttons of his shirt and kissed his chest and his throat until he floated up to consciousness, and when she saw him open his eyes she finally kissed him on his mouth, kissed him once and then kept on kissing his lips, moving higher so that her breasts rested on his bare chest, lightly holding his shoulders down on the bed until he woke up completely and tried to sit up.

"Maxi? *Maxi?*" he said in amazement.

She rolled over on her back and looked up at him through the tangle of her hair, looked right into his astonished eyes. She laughed her great, deep, free, joyous laugh that he'd never heard before.

"I hope you weren't expecting somebody else," she answered as he bent toward her and eagerly pulled her to him.

12

"As we used to say in the RAF," India West remarked thoughtfully, "you've bought the farm, Maxi."

"And just exactly what does that mean?" Maxi asked anxiously. India West was never, *never* wrong. She was only fifteen, two years younger than Maxi, but from the moment the two of them had met in school, while trying, as usual, to avoid gym class, they had been best friends, joined by an instantaneous appreciation of each other which included a decided preference for heightened versions of the truth. People sometimes took them for liars, as Maxi once explained to India, but they were only rearranging life to make it more interesting for everybody, a public service, as it were.

"Crashed your plane," India said absently, looking at herself in the mirror. "I think I'm getting rather . . . well, beautiful. What do you think?"

"You know you're beautiful. When haven't you been divinely beautiful? Stop trying to change the subject. We were talking about me."

India had just come back from Saratoga where she had spent the summer with her family. Lily Amberville, the boys and the servants were expected back from Southampton at the end of August. Finally Maxi had somebody she could talk to about Rocco. Rocco was besotted, infatuated, fascinated, her captive. They had been together every minute of the summer, at work and after work, since the first night in July. He was in love with her, truly in love, seriously in love. He had told her so, and Rocco, unlike Maxi, never told anything but the truth. Maxi, in her rapture, couldn't understand why India, usually so insouciant, saw a problem in her flawless love.

"Seventeen is not nineteen. An Amberville is not an Adams," India said.

"My birthday's tomorrow, I'll be eighteen, and I'm exactly the same person he's in love with," Maxi protested.

"Not really."

"You mean you think he won't love me when he finds out? India! That's ridiculous."

"No, I mean something else, and you know perfectly well what I mean. Just because we go to a school which is politely called 'an alternative form of education' doesn't mean that either of us is an idiot," India said severely.

"So, O.K. My father is a rich man . . ."

"Ha!"

"One of the richest men in America, all right? And I don't go to Vassar, after all. I'm still in high school. Do two mere years and a father with tons of money make me a leper?"

"You lied to him."

"I lie to *everybody*."

"So do I . . . but you said Rocco always tells the truth. That means he won't trust you anymore. How can a self-respecting, hardworking young man from a nice conservative Italian family with a strong sense of his own values carry on a flaming affair with teenaged Miss Amberville, his boss's daughter? What does that make him? You're supposed to be his 'trainee.' What does that do to his career? Apparently the man cares a lot about his work. How can he ever trust you again? You've taken him in completely, poor sucker, and if it had started a year ago you'd be jailbait. And God knows what the consequences will be when Pa and Ma Amberville find out."

India used her voice as effectively as a master bellringer, ringing changes in tones so that no one of any age could ignore her when she spoke. Even Maxi felt effectively subdued, accustomed as she was to the India phenomenon.

"I wish you wouldn't talk to me like that," Maxi said, taking her streak of white hair and twisting it between her thumb and forefinger and pulling it until it hurt. She was, in spite of her bravado, aware that she'd painted herself into corners before, but this corner didn't have any floor left.

"India, I need you," she said nervously. "I have a terrible practical problem. My family's due back here in a week and my freedom will be gone. I've been telling Rocco that they're still in Europe. If I tell him they're back he'll expect to meet them . . . he's old-fashioned about things like meeting parents."

"Ah, so," said India impassively.

"School doesn't start for three more weeks," Maxi continued. "I can tell him they're still away until then if you'll cover for me. I'll tell them I'm with you when I'm with Rocco, and on the nights when I simply have to show my face for dinner at home, I'll tell Rocco I'm with you. Does that make sense?"

"If he's so old-fashioned, wouldn't he expect you to introduce him to your best friend?"

"I'll say that . . . that you have a phobia. You're afraid to leave the house. Agoraphobia, it's well known."

"Why wouldn't he come to see me? You said he's wonderfully compassionate."

"You're afraid to meet strangers. It's another one of your phobias. He can talk to you on the phone. Reassuringly."

"That takes care of him. What about Pa and Ma? How come we're virtually inseparable?"

"I'll tell them that I'm helping you study so you can skip into my class."

"*You're* helping *me* study?"

"Sure. They know I can when I want to. It would be a good deed. And if they call your house to talk to me you answer, and make something up about why I'm not there." India was a much more inventive and believable liar than even Maxi could ever hope to be.

"Which means I have to spend the next three weeks hanging around my telephone," India grumbled. "And what happens when school really starts? And you really have homework? You won't be able to get out of the house so easily."

"Just give me these three weeks with him . . . by then I'll have figured something out."

"There's always the truth."

"India, please," Maxi pleaded, horrified. "You don't seem to understand. This is the most important thing that's ever happened to me. Nothing like this will ever happen to me again . . . I *have* to make it work out. The *truth* . . . please don't even *think* that word. It's too late for the . . . you know what."

"The highest compact we can make with our fellow man is 'Let there be truth between us two forevermore,' " India intoned.

"Why are you torturing me?"

"It's Emerson, Ralph Waldo. I'm reading him. Can I help it if I have a trick memory?"

"Could you please try to remember things on your own time?"

"He also said, 'Keep cool; it will be all one a hundred years hence.' "

"You're a comfort to me, India, you really are. Why did I pick a precocious brat for a best friend?"

" 'In skating over thin ice our safety is our speed.' "

"Emerson again?"

"Is he boring you?"

"No, he's making me feel nervous." Maxi's jade-green eyes, widened by anxiety, seemed to absorb all the light in the room into their tantalizing depths.

"Listen, Maxi, is it really all that much fun to fool around?" India asked, with sudden timidity.

"Fooling around," said Maxi, "is the *ultimate fun*."

"Damn, I was afraid you'd say that."

It wasn't until early October that the truth caught up with Maxi. She had spent so much of her mental energy on hopping and skipping between the lies she and India were telling an increasingly large number of people that she had overlooked one of the normal concerns of most females who are making love as often as is humanly possible. She was at least a month, perhaps two, gone with child, as India delicately put it, when together they counted the weeks since Maxi's last period. They looked at each other in solemn, awed, horrified silence for some time. For the first time since they'd met, neither one of them was trying to interrupt the other. Suddenly the suggestion of a smile that always shaped Maxi's lower lip turned into a huge grin and her delicate, wicked, witty face radiated uncomplicated delight.

"Fun," she breathed, "what heavenly, groovy, fabulous fun. Incredible fun. Oh, WHAT FUN!" She jumped up, lifted India, who was already an inch taller than she, and whirled her around the room in glee.

"Fun?" India squeaked indignantly. "Put me down, you damn fool! Fun?"

"A baby. A darling little baby. A little boy who looks just like Rocco. A bambino all pink and white and chubby with black curls. Oh, I can't wait! I'll learn to knit, I'll take lessons in natural childbirth, I wish he could be born tomorrow . . . didn't I tell you something would happen and everything would be all right? And to have all this fun too, on top of it . . . I can't believe how lucky I am!"

"Lord have mercy." India collapsed in a chair, disbelief in every bone.

"Is that your only reaction? What's wrong with you?" Maxi demanded. "I thought you knew how to have fun."

"Maybe my idea of fun isn't the same as yours," India said faintly. "And, Miz Scarlett, I don't know nothin' 'bout birthin' babies."

"It's my fault," said Nina. "I was the one who thought she should have a job."

"It's my fault," Zachary insisted. "I was the one who agreed."

"It's my fault," Pavka insisted. "I was the one who put her in that art department. And Linda Lafferty says it's entirely her fault."

"Actually, Pavka," said Nina, "it's your secretary's fault, the one who worships you. She picked *Savoir Vivre*."

"Listen, you two, it isn't anybody's fault except Maxi's. God knows Rocco can't be blamed . . . the poor bastard never had a chance once Maxi made up her mind," Zachary said.

"What does Lily think?" Pavka asked Zachary.

"She's too busy with the wedding arrangements to have time to think. As far as she's concerned, barely eighteen is a good age to get married if you're not doing anything else with your life. She wasn't much older when we got married. But she insists on a big English wedding with all the nonessentials: bridesmaids, flower girls strewing rose petals, pages in velvet pants, the house turned upside down for the reception. The only problem is one of time . . . they should be married as soon as possible. They'd be married by now if it weren't for Lily's plans. But Maxi doesn't care one way or the other . . . she's having too much 'fun' to worry about how premature the baby will be . . . I'm beginning to have visions of her doing a two-step down the aisle carrying the baby instead of a bouquet."

"And Rocco?" Pavka said curiously.

"What about him? Linda Lafferty says that the two of you agree that he's doing a fine job," Zachary said, slightly on the defensive.

"I don't mean his work . . . what about his family?"

"They think anything he does is perfect," Zachary replied. "We finally got everybody together for dinner and it went as well as any first-time meeting of future in-laws, better maybe. Joe Cipriani was in the Air Force in Korea, so we told war stories and Anna, Rocco's mother, and Lily talked silver patterns and china patterns and wedding dresses, and Maxi just sat there looking as if she'd accomplished a miracle and won the Nobel Prize for reproduction, and Rocco didn't have anything to say. He looked as if he'd been hit over the head with a club, or run over by a train, or both."

"Then why on earth," Nina wondered, "are the three of us sitting around here and worrying about something that everyone else thinks is perfectly fine?"

"Because we all know Maxi," Zachary answered grimly.

Angelica Amberville Cipriani entered the great world in April of 1973, just a little more than six months after Maxi and Rocco were married, a perfectly respectable degree of prematurity in any society high or low, since the world began counting on its fingers. Rocco had snapped out of his catatonic state once the wedding actually took place and Maxi had delightedly given up her senior year of high school to prepare Rocco's loft for the arrival of the baby.

Lily and Zachary had both tried to insist that the baby should come home from the hospital to a comfortable apartment where Maxi could have a nanny to help her and someone in the kitchen to cook and someone else to clean. They took it for granted that they would buy and furnish the apartment and subsidize the salaries of the staff, but Rocco had firmly refused to take anything from them other than a traditional wedding present of a silver service. He was making thirty-five thousand dollars a year, and the habit of total financial independence was deeply rooted in him. His own parents had contributed nothing to his upkeep from the day he won his first scholarship to art school, and he had no worries about earning enough to support a wife and child. Maxi was now eighteen, and many other girls in the world in which he had grown up were capable mothers by that age, in competent charge of their modest households.

Maxi approached the future with blissful energy. She went to three different cooking schools so that she could offer Rocco a choice of French, Italian and Chinese food; she took classes in two separate methods of giving birth, just in case she changed her mind in mid-process; she shopped at Saks and Bloomingdale's and even ventured all the way to Macy's, in order to buy a layette complete in every detail. Sensibly, she stored the dozens of barrels of wedding gifts in a warehouse, except for pots and pans, a set of pottery, stainless-steel tableware and inexpensive glass goblets.

Fortunately, Rocco's loft was spacious enough so that with the help of two neighborhood carpenters they were able to divide it into three separate areas: the baby's corner, a kitchen and storage section, and a third space in which they would live, eat, sleep, and in which Rocco would have his work table. Rocco had suggested that the third room be further divided to give him a separate workroom, but, as Maxi pointed out, she intended to continue being helpful to him when he needed her, so that didn't make sense. It would be the perfect harmony of last summer, she thought, with the additional joy of the bambino sleeping snugly away in its own little domain.

Maxi sat on a hard bench in a small neighborhood park with two scrawny trees, rocking the English pram, conspicuous by its size, its brilliant blue finish, its high, elegant wheels and the fringe on the canvas cover that kept the sun out of Angelica's eyes. It was August, and hot and humid as only August in Manhattan can be; the city lay enclosed in a monstrous bowl of airless, evil-smelling gray-yellow stuff that might be air but would kill most Amazonian Indians. Maxi wore shorts and a halter top and flat sandals. Although she'd pinned up her hair on top of her head to keep it off her neck, sweat-wet strands kept escaping. She fanned herself to no avail with a copy of *Rolling Stone*, fighting the urge to foam at the mouth, howl like a dog and demand a recount.

I will think about the fun things, she said to herself rigidly. Rocco is fun when he isn't working on that double sized Christmas issue. Angelica is fun when she isn't screaming, and keeping us awake. Being married is fun when Angelica is sleeping and Rocco isn't working. Cooking is fun when . . . no, cooking wasn't really what you could call fun. Not when you had to clean up afterwards. That makes about one fun hour in every forty-eight hours. At least one hour that might have been fun if it weren't so hot and humid. NOTHING is fun in New York in August, she thought savagely, unless the fucking air conditioning works.

Their two inadequate window units had both blown from old age when the heat wave started three weeks earlier, and getting new ones in the middle of the hottest summer in years was proving impossible. Day after day Maxi waited for their promised arrival and day after day she was forced to realize that once again they weren't going to be delivered.

Each morning Zachary phoned to beg her to go out to Southampton with the baby, every night Rocco assured her that she was crazy to stay in town, that he'd be perfectly all right on his own during the week, and promised to come out every weekend, but Maxi, stubborn as she had never been before in a lifetime dedicated to having things her own way, refused to budge.

The first summer, she told herself, was the time of testing, the exam that she knew everybody expected her to flunk. But she was going to stick it out in the city; she wasn't going to run off to her parents' like a child and abandon her husband when he was working so hard, leaving him bereft of wife and child and tender care.

She didn't intend him to be a weekend husband who missed seeing his baby grow up during these few precious months. To turn tail and run off to the cool breezes and the ocean and servants bringing cold glasses of freshly squeezed fruit juice . . . No! She took out a damp wad of Kleenex and mopped up the rivulets of sweat that crept down her neck.

Why couldn't she stop thinking about white? White linen, white sand, little dabs of white clouds in a blue sky over a blue sea, virgin white Pampers, white tennis shoes, maids in white aprons, big, white wooden houses, white wicker tables set with crisp white lace cloths and white Limoges china. White seemed the last thing Manhattan had to offer this particular August, except for the filthy litter of once-white paper that blew about her feet.

Angelica woke up howling. Maxi picked her up and fanned her frantically. In spite of constant sponging and cool baths the baby had heat rash or prickly heat or some sort of other irritation in half the folds of her plump, four-month-old body. She was a pretty baby, except when her face was screwed up in misery, as it had been for most of the summer. "Poor baby," Maxi crooned, and felt tears come into her own eyes. "Poor, poor little baby. I feel so sorry for you, really I do," she sobbed into Angelica's neck, "oh, poor, unfortunate, brave little baby, what a good little girl you are, and nobody gives you any credit for it, no they don't, they don't, they don't!" Angelica stopped crying and opened her eyes and pulled on a stray piece of Maxi's hair and smiled at her. "*Oh,*" wept Maxi harder than ever, seeing the smile, "you poor little thing!"

She leapt up from the bench and, running, wheeled the pram out of the park. A small cab stopped, seeing her frenzied wave, and Maxi simply abandoned the imported, five-hundred-dollar object on the corner without a second thought, scooped up Angelica and slid into the taxi.

"The Saint Regis Hotel," she told the driver. "Hurry, it's an emergency."

Amberville Publications kept a permanent suite at the St. Regis for visiting customers and everyone at the reception desk knew Maxi on sight. She was escorted to the five-room suite with as much chucking and concern as if she had just been pulled into a lifeboat from engulfing waves. Maxi flopped down on one of the beds, clutching her baby, and for a while nothing mattered except the cool air. As soon as she felt enough energy returning, she filled a tub full of tepid water, took off everything she and Angelica were wearing, unpinned her hair and stepped cautiously into the water with the baby in her arms. She lay back in the big tub and floated Angelica above her breasts, supporting her under her armpits and nuzzling her tiny nose. She made little crooning noises and swished Angelica back and forth; a mermaid and her young.

Soon, restored to full efficiency, Maxi bundled herself and the baby into huge towels and attacked the telephone. First she called Saks for baby shirts and nighties, a crib, another pram, baby bed linen and a rocking chair. Then she called Bonwit's for an assortment of negligees, short silk pajamas and cotton shirts and shorts for herself. Next she telephoned the hotel florist and told him to send up a dozen white vases filled with white flowers. The druggist was instructed to bring up baby oil, baby powder, Pampers and shampoo. Then she phoned F. A. O. Schwarz and ordered a mobile to hang over the crib and duplicates of all her own favorites among Angelica's stuffed animals. She called the hotel desk and dispatched bellboys in every direction to pick up her purchases immediately, and then she called room service and ordered lunch. Yes, they could puree carrots and white meat of chicken, they assured her. Finally, Maxi called Rocco at the office.

"Darling," she said excitedly, "I've just discovered the most marvelous place for us to spend the summer, and it's only a few blocks from your office."

August heat waves are normal in New York but, as any native knows, they can be almost as bad in September. "Autumn in New York" is a song that should clearly specify October, just as "April in Paris" is a song that should mention the necessity to bring umbrellas, warmly lined raincoats and waterproof boots. Maxi, Rocco and Angelica were sheltered by the friendly walls of the St. Regis for another five weeks. Although Rocco couldn't help realizing that the room-service bills alone were more than his weekly salary, he forced himself not to protest. No matter how he felt, he reasoned, he couldn't insist that the baby be subjected to the heat of the loft. Time enough for them to go home when it was cool again.

"I think we should move back tonight," Maxi said to him one morning in late September, as he left for work.

"I thought you were trying to hold out till the first snow," Rocco said, smiling at her flushed, happy face, and nibbling the tip of her impudently pointed nose.

"I'm tired of room service," she murmured, licking his chest as high up as she could reach between two of his shirt buttons, underneath his necktie, a maneuver at which she had become expert while holding the baby.

"I'll try to come home as early as I can and help you pack."

"Don't bother, sweetheart, I have all day and the hotel staff promised to do most of it for me . . . just come back and pick the two of us up."

That evening, when he reached the hotel, he found Maxi and Angelica waiting in the lobby to meet him.

"Everything's done," she said triumphantly. They got into a cab and the doorman gave the driver an address and waved them farewell.

"Why is he going uptown?" Rocco asked.

"I wanted to stop by and see my family first," Maxi said gaily.

"Then why has he passed your parents' house?" Rocco said patiently, realizing that Maxi had planned one of the surprises she loved so much: learning to make tortellini for instance, or framing a group of his sketches with her own inexpert hands, or finding an old dress for Angelica in a thrift shop and producing the baby trailing a cascade of Victorian lace.

"Because they're visiting Toby," she said vaguely.

"And Toby's visiting a friend?"

"Right. You're so smart. Did you know I married you for your acute intelligence and not merely for your impossible brooding beauty?"

"I thought *I* married you because I knocked you up. That's more or less the general opinion," Rocco said, delighted with the mischief in her eyes. He had surrendered to her as he would to a girl in a most improbable, happy dream. Sometimes his young wife was, as tonight, the embodiment of a delightful practical joke.

"Not in front of the baby!" Maxi whispered.

The cab finally came to a stop before a handsome apartment building on Seventy-sixth Street, between Fifth and Madison. They took the elevator up to the fifth floor and walked along a wide corridor until Maxi rang a doorbell. A uniformed maid opened the door with a smile of greeting.

"Nobody here?" Rocco asked, looking around the big, white-walled, well-shaped room, all brown and terra-cotta and burnt umber, furnished in a way he immediately liked although he didn't know exactly why.

"They must be somewhere," Maxi said, wandering away from him toward a hallway. "Anybody home?" she called.

"Don't you think we should wait in the living room?"

"Come on, sweetheart, they must be here somewhere," Maxi answered from the hall, and Rocco followed her as she flitted through charmingly furnished but unpeopled rooms: a baby's room, a huge bedroom with a four-poster bed covered with an antique quilt, and a shining kitchen, where the maid was cooking busily. In the red-walled little dining room, where the round French provincial table was laid for two, he finally grabbed her and tried to make her stop. "Sit down and wait. You can't just go through someone's house like this, not even you. Or is this some kind of a surprise party?" She eluded him, still carrying Angelica.

"Wait, there's one more room. Maybe they're in there, hiding." She opened another door and Rocco found himself standing in a well-lit room bare of all but his work table, his chair and all his working equipment, everything arranged perfectly, not one familiar item missing.

Maxi faced him, absolutely delighted with herself. "Don't think this happened overnight," she said proudly.

"This . . . ?"

"Is *our* house. 'Surprise party!' You aren't as smart as I thought," she teased.

"You know what I said about not taking anything from your parents . . . how could you do this, Maxi?" Rocco asked quietly.

"I fully respect what you said. This has nothing to do with it," she answered, beaming with satisfaction.

"Then where does it come from?"

"Me. From me to you, from me to me, from me to Angelica."

"What do you mean, 'me'?"

"My very own trust fund. The one Daddy set up when I was born. I came into it on my last birthday. There's another one I'll get when I'm twenty-one and another when I'm twenty-five . . . Justin and Toby have them too, of course. It's a way to give your kids something while you're still alive so that the government doesn't get it all when you die," Maxi explained, not too sure of the precise details.

"Your father, *knowing you*, gave you a large sum of money?" Rocco said, disbelief clear in his voice.

"Oh, once it was set up there wasn't anything he could do to change it. Otherwise I guess he might not have trusted me with so much. But, you see, he would have been wrong, wouldn't he? I haven't done anything wildly extravagant, considering."

"Considering what?"

"That I got five million dollars."

"Five million dollars."

"Honestly, Rocco, including the price of buying the apartment, all I've spent isn't even three-quarters of a million."

"Three-quarters of a million."

"Well, it's not a big apartment . . . just enough for the three of us," Maxi explained patiently. Rocco didn't seem to be too bright tonight. "We'll move when we have another baby."

"Are you expecting another baby?" Rocco asked in a tightly neutral tone of voice. "Is that another surprise for tonight?"

"Not yet, for heaven's sake!"

"Let's go."

"Go where?"

"Back to Soho. If I won't take anything from your parents, how could you possibly imagine I'd take this . . . this place . . . from you?" he asked, pale with outraged fury, insulted to the marrow of his bones.

"But it has nothing to do with my parents. It's totally *different*—I bought and furnished this apartment with *my own money*. Surely I have a right to spend my own money, Rocco? After all, it's for *us*, for us to share."

"I can't do it. I'm sorry, Maxi, but there is no way I can do it. It goes against everything I believe in."

"You're just being stubborn and old-fashioned Italian, and typically male," she said, her patient tone wearing thin.

"I'm being me. You should have known me better when we got married. I haven't changed."

"Neither have I," Maxi flashed at him, outraged.

"And that," said Rocco, "is the whole problem. One of us is going to have to change." His hands were balled into fists. He should have known. He'd had warning after warning but ignored them, soft fool that he was, not wanting to believe that she was so deeply spoiled, so thoughtlessly capricious.

"Don't look at me, Rocco Cipriani," Maxi shouted.

"Goodbye, Maxi," he said briefly, afraid that any other words would be irremediably cruel, even more cruel than the end of their marriage. He'd feared this minute from the beginning, but he had tried to overlook his uneasy intuition of Maxi's true character. "I'll send for my stuff."

Openmouthed, Maxi looked at the empty room. She heard the front door close quietly, she waited a few minutes for the doorbell to ring and then she carried Angelica into the lovingly furnished living room and sat down on one of the big, russet velvet sofas. "He'll be back, Angelica," she said to the baby. "He just needs to understand that he can't boss me around like that. Who does he think he is, anyway? *Nobody* talks to me like that, do you hear, nobody!" and she burst into tears of a fearful grief, for she knew already that neither one of them was going to change, neither was capable of change. He couldn't even try, because of his absurd, unnecessary pride, that stubborn bastard, and she would not, would, absolutely, not! She was Maxi Amberville, after all. *So why the hell should she?*

13

Maxi never spent so much as one single night in the apartment she had decorated with such disastrous joy. She arranged for Rocco's work table and supplies to be sent back to him the next day and instructed her real estate agent to sell everything, including the last copper-bottomed saucepan, as quickly as possible, at whatever price was first offered.

The divorce was handled with tactful dispatch and without publicity by the Amberville corps of legal experts. Once Rocco had achieved joint custody of Angelica he agreed that the baby should live with Maxi on a full-time basis. He had returned to work at Condé Nast, and the only alternative arrangement possible for him was to hire a nurse to care for Angelica while he was away at the office, which made no sense since the baby had a perfectly good mother. However, as often as possible, he exercised his right to take Angelica for the weekend, joining the legion of divorced fathers in the park nearby with the doubtful distinction of having the youngest child in his group.

Maxi tried to get through the period of her divorce by concentrating ferociously on each detail of raising her daughter. She became an expert on denial; not thinking, not remembering, not asking herself questions, not wondering "what if" while she conferred with six different but patient Madison Avenue grocers on the quality of their juice oranges and the provenance of their chicken breasts. Nevertheless an appalling, punishing pain located in the very middle of her being vibrated like a tuning fork except when she was actually communing with Angelica, but that healthy baby spent far too much of her first year asleep. Maxi endured the raw torment with silence, for she understood that she had no alternative. Meanwhile she would bathe and feed Angelica and take her downstairs to visit with Lily and Zachary. She had returned home the night Rocco had walked out of the new apartment, seeking the surest refuge she knew.

This period of mourning lasted throughout the fall of 1973 and the winter of 1974. It wasn't until late in the spring of her nineteenth year that finally there came a day on which Maxi realized that she could now dare to take stock. She prepared herself for this process by piling her bed high with pillows and lying back on them after she'd applied the warm, sweet-smelling sleeping body of Angelica on her chest like a mustard plaster. The little girl was over a year old and satisfactorily big enough to provide considerable protection for an adult unfortunate enough to have to examine her own mental condition.

What was her exact position in life? Maxi wondered. How should she define herself? She had a daughter, she was divorced and in a few months she'd be twenty. She was no longer an adolescent, she would never be a debutante, she was not a college girl, nor was she an unwed mother. On the other hand she wasn't a working woman with a career. It seemed that she was left with only one category to fill: that of the interesting, no, make that the *fascinating*, young divorcée. If people still used that word.

What then were the options of this young divorcée who possessed millions from her first installment of her trust fund? In principle the world must be full of endless options for someone with so much money and so much time. Obviously she could stay on living in this great gray house, safe, secure and cared for, yet able to come and go as she chose, since she now had the status of adult rather than that of schoolgirl. Using her parents' home as a base she could venture forth at will to . . . to . . . do what?

In the first place she could—and probably should—go to college in Manhattan, Maxi ruminated, but damn it, first she'd have to finish high school. Years of bouncing around the backwaters and byways of the educational system had taught her that there would always be a high school that could be persuaded to accept her for the senior year she'd missed. Therefore college was a distinct possibility. But did she really feel like taking on the burden of any additional education? Wasn't it now somehow too late and yet too early to return to academia? Scratch college.

Of course there was travel. She could take Angelica and hire a nanny and spend six months or a year in England where her grandparents would introduce her to the world. Maxi's eyes almost closed as she imagined herself conquering London. She'd buy the wildest dresses Zandra Rhodes had ever designed, she'd rent a big flat on Eaton Square, she'd keep a Rolls—no, a Bentley—no, a Daimler, the kind of car the Queen always used that was too wide for American roads, and she'd plunge into all the delights of London society that her mother hadn't bothered about, with the help of the good offices of the nineteenth Baronet and second Viscount Adamsfield. Ah, if only the sixties weren't over. Yet somewhere they must still be lurking, even if the swinging had stopped. Yes . . . London . . . Maxi smiled into the dimness of canopied chintz above her bed until suddenly her eyes popped wide open in surprised pique as reality returned. Rocco, that impossible, doting Italian papa, would never allow her to take Angelica away from him for six months at one time. Never. So travel was not an option except for a week or two at the longest. Scratch travel.

A job? A willingness to do the lowliest task in the art department had landed her where she was now. Perhaps the working world was not for her? Anyway she had a child to take care of. Scratch work.

She seemed to be stuck right here, lying on her bed back at home. And that was out. Out! It *felt* wrong, no matter how much her parents obviously wanted her to stay.

Maxi blew carefully into Angelica's hair and nibbled on one dark curl. Her parents didn't trust her to exist on her own. She could see it in their eyes although they were careful not to say anything to indicate that the present arrangement was anything but temporary. But she could read their anxious minds. They'd like her to stay here until another man, a more appropriate one, appeared to lure her back into a domesticity that Maxi had no intention of attempting again.

The process of elimination had left her with only one option. She must have her *own* place in Manhattan. Out! If she didn't move she'd fall back into the comfortable, familiar, but decidedly outgrown role of the daughter of the house. Maxi felt a licking, brief bite of apprehension. She'd never lived alone. She had gone right from her father's house to her husband's house and then straight back to her father's house.

All the more reason, Maxi thought, her lips tightened defiantly, to get on with it. She'd start house hunting tomorrow. She wanted a town house since she couldn't have London, a dear little brownstone in which she could entertain her friends. What friends? Since that day—oh diabolic day—that she'd walked into the art department of *Savoir Vivre*, two years ago, she'd been so involved in the unfolding drama of her own life that she'd lost touch with everybody she knew of her own age except India who had so selfishly gone to college. Still, she must know *someone.* Hadn't a famous hostess once said that all you had to do to attract guests was to open a can of sardines and spread the word? She would buy a can opener, Maxi resolved, and a case of sardines. If life had taught her anything it was that one thing led to another. If there had been any other lessons along the way, she'd missed them.

Once Maxi had resolved to leave her parents' protection she'd quickly found the perfect small town house and discovered a team of decorators, Ludwig and Bizet, to help her turn it into a setting that had nothing to do with chronology. It was not the home of an impulsive girl but of a serene heiress with a leaning toward eclectic interiors that cunningly defrosted Louis XV with Venetian touches of high fantasy, the combination mellowed with English chintz.

After Maxi's first timid venture into introspection she brooded long and often about her future. She had discarded the category of young divorcée almost as quickly as she had thought of it. There were so many other divorced women in Manhattan, forming a vast, unchartered club she'd rather not join. With far more art and discipline than she had employed in preparing herself for her first day at work, she carefully went about creating a new Maxime Emma Amberville Cipriani, one who would be immediately recognizable as a *widow*. Widowhood—early, cruel, accidental and mysterious widowhood—was a condition so much more desirable than any other open to her. It was a state that combined a certain mournfully elegant status with a distinction and an aura of—poetry?—yes, poetry, if you did it right, she thought, her lips quivering with a suppressed grin.

Maxi worked her way toward widowhood by the elegiac tempering of her smile; by the suddenly tremulous silences into which she fell unexpectedly; by a finely tuned, brave dignity in which she wrapped herself. She dimmed the field of energy in which she usually moved and turned it inward, so that it was obvious—but never immediately or painfully obvious—that she was suffering from an unspoken sorrow with which she would trouble no one. Now she dressed in black at all times: quiet, serious, expensive, indecently becoming black. The only jewelry she wore had been her parents' wedding present, a glorious double strand of Burmese pearls, graduated from twelve to nineteen millimeters, each perfectly round globe radiating a matchless luster, and of course, the widow's necessary ornament, a modest, plain wedding band she longed to throw in the garbage. As soon as Maxi found herself alone at home she changed immediately into old jeans and worn T-shirts but she never left the house unless she was raven-clad from head to toe, even if she were going to the country in black pants and a black silk blouse. Maxi used her makeup skills to achieve a delicious pallor, she threw away her collection of blushers and lipsticks and concentrated on demurely darkening the area around her eyes with smoky grays and taupes. If only India were around to appreciate her efforts, she thought longingly, as she staged her effects.

Just as Maxi forbade herself her belly laugh she made a rule never to talk about herself. Instead she grew adept at drawing people out on their all-time favorite subject: themselves. She learned to subtly sidestep all questions about her private life and automatically refused two out of every three of her many invitations—for the sardines had worked marvelously well—in order to stay home with Angelica.

Although she was deeply, constantly tempted, she never went so far as to tell anyone that Rocco Cipriani was dead—stone-cold dead—but she never referred to a former husband, or a previous marriage.

Since the length of time people bother to remember details of each other's private lives in Manhattan is determined by how much fuel is flung on the fire, Maxi achieved established widowhood within a year, by her twenty-first birthday.

It was not a widowhood without distractions. She took with utmost discretion, a baker's dozen of lovers, in not too rapid succession; each one impeccable, eligible, eager to marry her and free of any problems presented by an alliance with a man who might not understand that her money was her own to spend as she liked. Yet not one of them had seemed somehow *necessary* enough to keep longer than a few months. Maxi became convinced that she'd never fall in love again and the thought, although melancholy, was balanced by the freedom it gave her. She had become, she flattered herself, an updated Henry James heroine, a woman with a past that was only dimly known; whose present was tantalizingly private yet illuminated by the blaze of her independence, her family, her fortune, and—why not be blunt—her face; a woman whose future held infinite promise.

One fragrant August in 1978, Maxi drifted toward the entrance to the Casino in Monte Carlo. She idled along alone in the darkness, relaxed in the knowledge that the principality had one policeman for every five visitors and every woman could safely wear all her jewelry in public on the darkest street of the little city. In her bones she felt there was a lucky seat at the chemin de fer table just waiting for her but she wasn't in a hurry to get into the action.

This was Maxi's first evening in Monte Carlo and literally the first time in her life that she was utterly free to come and go as she pleased, alone and on her own, unquestioned, unaccounted for and accountable to no one. Her parents were in Southampton. Rocco had finally been able to arrange matters at the magazine so that he had August off and he had taken Angelica to visit his parents in the country outside of Hartford.

Maxi had refused a number of proposals to be a houseguest or to join traveling friends, and quietly reserved a suite for herself at the Hotel de Paris in Monte Carlo, a corner suite, majestically proportioned, with a great semicircular balcony off the sitting room from which she had watched the sunset. Far below her she could see the crowded port of Monte Carlo; beyond it on a jutting, rocky promontory, rose the palace and beyond the palace was the remarkable sky, meeting the remarkable sea on which dozens of pleasure craft were coming into the harbor. There was no hint from the view from Maxi's suite that every week one more of the charming Edwardian villas that, for so long, were the enchantment of the city, was demolished, each to be replaced by yet another, Miami modern high-rise apartment building; no hint that every last square inch of Grimaldi territory was being exploited with an unsentimental thoroughness that was far more Swiss than Mediterranean.

August, no matter how hot, is *the* season for Monte Carlo, the month of balls and fireworks, of ballet and of a gathering together of a particular—and often peculiar—assortment of royalty-groupie rich from all over who never miss that once-a-year visit to Monaco. August is the one thirty-one-day bonus period during which those tax exiles from ninety-nine countries whose lawyers and accountants command them to become residents of Monaco, can rent their expensive dwellings and make enough to pay for their upkeep during the other eleven months; the one month during which the harbor yacht moorings are at a premium, the one month in which the myth of Monte Carlo is annually reborn.

Maxi felt intoxicatingly reborn herself. In anticipation of her trip she had assembled a new wardrobe that filled seven suitcases, a wardrobe from which all black was banished; she had armed herself with an enormous letter of credit to a local bank and just that afternoon she had changed so many dollars into francs that her evening bag bulged.

A certain Beekman Place high-stakes poker game, which took place nightly in New York, had occasionally enlivened her sumptuous early widowhood, but Maxi had always had a yen to visit a real casino that would in no way resemble Las Vegas. Gambling, she thought, was a little like shopping . . . you couldn't really do it right as part of a couple. Call it what you will—a question of skill, a matter of luck, or even just picking numbers—all gambling boiled down to choice, and choice was not a collaborative or a cooperative pursuit, arrived at with someone looking over your shoulder and making suggestions. It would be good for her, Maxi thought virtuously, to have a fling. Widowhood was so constricting. She *deserved* a fling, and obviously everyone in the crowd that pressed toward the entrance to the Casino felt equally festive.

The first large rooms of the ornate building were disappointing; filled with casually clad tourists playing slot machines, the high, painted ceilings seeming to look down in grief on such ignoble goings-on. But once past the stern men who guarded the entrance to the private rooms, Maxi discovered that the legend of the Casino of Monte Carlo still existed, as uncompromisingly authentic, as firmly locked into history as if it were a four-masted sailing ship that had somehow sailed out of the past. An Edwardian glamour, voluptuous and unashamed, showered down in gilded splendor; a sweeping waltztime drowned out the mad jazz tempo of the first rooms, a pink glow replaced the popping lights of the slot machines. Low-voiced, purposeful, well-dressed people moved here and there in the air that was charged with an almost unbearable excitement, the thrill that can only be imprinted on a space devoted to gaming, wagering, playing, betting, in short, gambling. No one was immune to its spell, least of all Maxi Amberville.

Curbing her quick New Yorker's pace, Maxi moved into the Casino with felicitous poise, with the self-assurance that can never be feigned, of a beautiful woman who is perfectly at ease *without* an escort. She wore a long, strapless, chiffon dress that was one shade lighter than the green of her eyes and diaphanous to the point of cruelty. Her black hair, which she wore pulled back severely from her face in New York, had been allowed to fall freely over her shoulders. She had transformed her double strand of pearls into one long rope that hung down over her bare white back, she'd thrust a spray of tiny white orchids between her breasts. Nothing about her suggested widowhood . . . nor maidenhood. She looked as fastidiously haughty as she felt; a fine feline female out on the town.

It was too early in the evening for baccarat or chemin de fer she decided. She'd try roulette just to warm up and orient herself. She'd never played it but it looked like a silly, easy kids' game in which no skill was involved.

Maxi went to the cashier and bought chips for ten thousand dollars, receiving a hundred big black chips in exchange, each worth five hundred francs. She couldn't do much damage with that little lot, Maxi thought, as she slid into a chair at the nearest roulette table. She decided to play her age and asked the croupier to put ten chips on twenty-three black. The wheel spun, finally stopped and Maxi was a thousand dollars poorer. Perhaps her next birthday? The twenty-four black yielded nothing. Nevertheless, she thought, if it had come up, she would have made thirty-five thousand dollars since all the numbers paid off at thirty-five to one. Where was the beginner's luck to which she was entitled? On the other hand, roulette was not normally considered an investment, she reminded herself as she pondered her next choice. The man next to her spoke to the croupier.

"Ten on zero," he said in an accent that Maxi couldn't identify. She glanced at him curiously. He was slumped on one elbow as if only that bone was holding him up and he wore the most miserably threadbare dinner jacket that she had ever seen. His dark hair needed cutting, his hollow cheeks needed shaving, and his eyes needed opening, for his lids were so low and his black lashes so long that it seemed impossible that he could see. He looked like a scarecrow, a bored yet oddly elegant scarecrow who had been left out in the fields until the birds had picked him almost to pieces. She drew slightly away. Obviously this was the sort of riffraff to whom a foolhardy fling at roulette was the final episode in a sordid history of debauchery. Surely there was something decadent about his finely cut profile? Yet he had the most beautiful hands she'd ever seen, with immaculate nails. A professional card-sharp? Probably not, for what self-respecting professional could dream of looking so down at the heels, so pathetically scruffy?

Maxi absently lost seventy more chips as she continued to take inventory of the man who had only given her the briefest of glances. Somewhere in his thirties, she decided, and probably Irish, for who but the Irish combined such white skin and such black hair? If his eyes were blue that would be final proof, but they were still hooded. He lost his ten five-hundred-franc chips and lazily put the equivalent of another thousand dollars on the zero again. His expression didn't change and he seemed to take no interest in the rollicking dance of the ball as the wheel turned, first quickly, then gradually slowing to a stop. Maxi lost again as she noted, fascinated, that the man wore ancient tennis shoes and baggy white socks, and that his dinner jacket was worn over a white T-shirt over which he'd looped the necessary tie as casually as if it were a piece of string. It probably *was* a piece of string, and frayed string at that.

Maxi realized that she had only ten chips left. She beckoned to the attendant who hovered by the table and gave him the money to buy another fifty chips. Her neighbor looked up at the sound of her voice.

"Ten for me, please," he said casually, without offering money. Obviously he was hoping for credit from the Casino, Maxi realized.

"Sorry, sir," the attendant said, refusing his request.

"No more?"

"I'm afraid not, sir."

"Not my night." He offered the comment in infinite expressionlessness.

"No, sir," the attendant agreed, going to get Maxi her chips.

So he was Irish, she thought. There was no disguising the classic deep blue of his eyes during the brief exchange. An Irish wharf rat, probably off the crew of one of the yachts in the harbor, who'd come to the Casino in a borrowed dinner jacket and lost his last franc or dime or farthing or whatever he'd had when he came in. Still there wasn't an Irish lilt to his voice but some other accent—English but not British, whatever that meant she thought confusedly.

He reached into his socks and pulled out five black chips from each one with the kind of supremely indifferent look that Maxi knew must mean that he had been saving this stash for just this moment. She felt sorry for the feckless creature, she realized. There was something gallant and touching in the way he refused to show his absolute desperation. He was obviously at the end of the line. Who knew what fate awaited him after he'd lost his last chips? He'd probably borrowed the money he had been playing with. Or even stolen it. Yet he'd put all ten big chips on the zero again, not even holding back a single one to give himself a chance to play one more time. She held her breath as the wheel slowed, as the little ball finally dropped to rest. On the zero. Maxi clapped both hands loudly in delight. Thirty-five thousand dollars—that should keep him from shooting himself. She smiled at him in congratulation and saw, to her disbelief, that his eyelids were not even raised. Should she nudge him? Hadn't he seen?

There was a rustle of interest as the croupier took the next bets but the man next to Maxi never moved. Finally, the croupier said, "Still on zero, sir?"

"Yep."

He was going to let the money ride, Maxi realized in horror. The odds that the zero would come up twice in a row were beyond reckoning. Was he mad, drunk, doped, or didn't he understand the game?

Maxi forgot to bet as she fought not to say something and when the croupier barked "*Rien ne va plus*" she realized that it was too late to give advice. She sighed and waited for the inevitable as the wheel spun, as the ball hopped and skipped, as the wheel slowed and the ball fell. On the zero. A gasp rose from the crowd that stood around the table. The scarecrow had won thirty-five times one hundred and seventy-five thousand francs. Even Maxi's rusty multiplication table told her that it was over a million American dollars. Considerably over. This should make him open his eyes, this should make him look a little less hopeless, she thought, turning toward him and meeting his glance for a second. Was that a smile on his lips? Was that a raising of his lids? Was there a flush of color in his cheeks? No. Absolutely not. He was still slumped on one elbow, he hadn't reached for his chips, he didn't look any less removed or detached than when the attendant had refused him credit. Clearly a mental case.

"Take those chips *off* the board," she commanded him in a low voice.

"Why?" he asked mildly.

"Because otherwise you'll lose the lot, you damn fool. Don't argue. It's the chance of a lifetime," Maxi hissed at him furiously.

"And play it safe?" he asked, almost sounding faintly amused.

Action at the table had been stopped as the croupier waited for a casino official to permit him to accept the bet. The official arrived, looked at the scarecrow with an indefinable expression and reluctantly nodded at the croupier to go ahead. As a big, buzzing crowd immediately gathered around the table, Maxi, in her agitation, again forgot to bet. The man was clearly insane. Criminally insane. The law of averages hadn't been suspended for his sake and there was no possibility that the ball would come back to zero a third time. The Casino knew that as well as she did or they would never have allowed the game to continue. How many men had really been given a chance to break the bank at Monte Carlo? The croupier busied himself with the other players and only when they had all placed their bets did he look again at the scarecrow.

"Will you stay on the zero, sir?"

"Why not?" he asked with a hint of a yawn.

Maxi watched in outrage as the croupier began to set the wheel in motion. There wasn't a sound from the crowd. The croupier's lips opened to say the words "*Rien ne va plus*," and in that split second Maxi catapulted herself wildly onto the pile of chips on the zero. She scooped them all off the table, scattering them around the man at her side before the bet could be finalized and the chips lost forever.

A roar of scandalized disbelief rose from the crowd. Her breach of casino etiquette was so unthinkable that their attention was switched from the wheel to Maxi. Indignantly she glared at the watchers. Barbarians, she fumed to herself, just waiting to see someone thrown to the lions. Well this isn't going to be your day, you bastards, even if I do look silly. She stared down the jabbering mob in righteous certainty until she realized that the scarecrow was still watching the wheel, not touching a single one of the chips that she had saved for him. Cold sweat covered her in a flash. She had just remembered something else about the law of averages. Each spin of the wheel was a fresh start, as if it had never spun before. Oh no, she prayed, no, *please.* In the sudden utter silence of the Casino only the wheel could be heard. Maxi closed her eyes. A wild incredulous sound came from the bystanders. Zero. Again. Maxi sat frozen, waiting to die. She deserved it. Murder was too good for her. A hand reached out and closed on her upper arm. He was going to break it. Yes, bone by bone, every bone in her body. He had every right. She wouldn't defend herself.

"Nobody will ever call you a cheap date," the scarecrow commented mildly as he rose from his seat, lifting her with him, leaving the chips Maxi had swept off the table to be gathered up by an attendant.

Maxi opened her eyes and burst into tears. She was going to live. He was even more insane than she had realized but not *criminally* insane.

"I don't like to see a woman cry," he remarked kindly.

Maxi stopped immediately. She didn't dare not to. He gave her a surprisingly clean handkerchief and helped her blow her nose and dry her eyes.

"It's only money," he said, smiling for the first time.

"*Only money*! Over forty million dollars?"

He shrugged. "I'd inevitably have lost it back to the house another day. You don't imagine that they'd have let me bet if they didn't know that for sure, did you? You're not working for the house by any chance? No, I didn't think so. But they do owe you a free drink. Come on, sit down here and I'll order. Champagne?"

"Something much stronger," Maxi begged.

"Good girl. Tequila then, Buffalo Grass tequila." He motioned to a waiter. "My usual, Jean-Jacques, and one for the lady. A double."

"Bad luck, Monsieur Brady," the waiter said sympathetically.

The scarecrow looked closely at Maxi. "Not necessarily, Jean-Jacques, not necessarily." He turned to Maxi. "Drink up and I'll take you home."

"Oh, no, you don't have to do that," she protested.

"Might as well. After all, I *own* you now. Forty million dollars worth anyway."

"Oh."

"You *do* agree?" he asked politely.

"Yes. Of course. It's only . . . fair." And Maxi thought, there could be worse fates. Far far worse. But she'd absolutely have to do something about his clothes.

Dennis Brady was the first remittance man that Australia had sent back to the old country. A century earlier his ancestor, Black Dan Brady, emigrated to Australia from Dublin and struck it rich when he discovered an enormous silver deposit at Wasted Valley in the New South Wales Outback. In the decades that followed, the Wasted Valley Proprietary Company found vast amounts of iron ore, coal and manganese. By 1972, in addition to the mine operations, its assets included huge steel mills and oil ventures which accounted for three percent of Australia's gross domestic product, and a cash flow of close to a billion dollars a year. Its chief liability was its rebellious chief stockholder and orphaned only heir to the Brady fortune, Bad Dennis Brady, who was bored, bored, *bored* with Melbourne; bored, bored, *bored* with being the richest man in Australia; bored, bored, *bored* with discussions about drilling for oil off the coast of China, finding copper in Chile, or mining gold in South Africa. Dennis Brady had not the slightest interest in extracting another ounce or gram or droplet of anything whatsoever out of this planet. On the other hand he dearly loved a wager. But gambling is not permitted in Australia and the closest casino in Tasmania had lost so much money to him that they had barred him from play forever.

They couldn't call him a black sheep, he told the board of directors meeting of Wasted Valley that he had convened, because a black sheep doesn't pay his debts, nor could they call him a wastrel because he often ended up winning, and, over the long haul, was almost even, although he knew perfectly well that the odds would always be with the house, but no one could call him an asset to the company either. And there was no need to take a vote on that, gentlemen, thank you very much indeed. He'd tried, God knows he'd tried, for twenty-nine miserable years, to be a credit to the Brady dynasty but it just wasn't going to work out. Too bloody *boring* by half. Wouldn't it be better for everyone if he cleared out, went back to wherever it was that Bradys had come from in the first place and left them to get on with the family business? All those in favor say aye—no never mind the formalities—he'd just remembered that he owned more than enough stock to cast the deciding vote. Could he buy anyone a farewell drink?

"What happened next?" Maxi asked, fascinated with his story.

"They said it was too early in the day for a drink but they rather thought I had the right idea and they all shook hands. Good chaps. They're undoubtedly still drilling and smelting and forging away and looking for new companies to buy. They're as industrious as a bunch of giant Santa's helpers . . . motivated, businesslike, patriotic, good to their mothers—useful but all so terribly tedious."

"Did you go back to Ireland?"

"Good Lord, no. Never cared for racing or breeding the beasts—I'm allergic to horses and I can't endure rain. Came straight here and bought this lovely yacht and I've been here ever since. It's not quite the biggest one in the port but it's nothing to be ashamed of and it's the happiest ship in the harbor."

"But what do you *do*, Dennis?"

"Do? Well . . . I just . . . live, you know? A little here, another bit there. Water ski, drink a little, drink a lot, listen to music, sail, fly my helicopter—sometimes we even take the ship out for a day or two. It's a full life. Occasionally I'm so busy I don't even get to the Casino before midnight. I've put myself on a strict credit limit there . . . it might get boring otherwise."

"Are you never bored anymore?"

"Let's say that I'm not bored *now*. I've never owned a forty-million-dollar girl before. I wonder what I should do with you first?"

"Maybe if you thought of me as just a girl . . ." Maxi murmured, trying to make out his face in the darkness of the deck. Most of the other yachts in the port had put out all but their running lights while they talked, and Bad Dennis Brady had almost disappeared in the moonless night. She missed being able to watch his half-tragic, half-fey face, she realized, rather more than she'd expected.

"But if you were 'just' a girl I'd never have told you all this," he protested.

"What do you talk about with girls you don't own?"

"Not much," he said wistfully.

"You're shy," Maxi diagnosed.

"No, basically just Australian. Australian men prefer action to talk when it comes to women. At least that's the general notion."

"But according to you, no one was ever a less typical Australian."

"Well I can't be can I? Poor eye-to-hand coordination, you know. I never was any good at games, particularly soccer. My guardians, when my parents died, sent me to England for quite a while so I don't even sound right. A half-assed Australian and an all-around total misfit, I'm afraid." He sighed pathetically in the darkness and reached out and took Maxi's hand in both of his. The minute she felt his touch she knew that there was at least one sport in which Dennis Brady had won high marks. Feckless, whimsical, admittedly fit only for loafing, but not, oh no decidedly not harmless. Every warning bell in her system went off.

"Ah, poor Bad Dennis, that's a sad story and no mistake," she crooned. "But as much as it pains me to have to remind you—the meter's running."

"The meter? Oh, of course . . . I'd almost forgotten. How much?"

"One million dollars."

"Per week?" he asked hopefully.

"No, Dennis," she said patiently.

"Per day?" He tried to sound incredulous.

"Per hour . . . and you've just spent two of them talking."

"Good Lord! I think that's a bit high. On the other hand, it is slower than roulette. Or should be, if done properly. Well, if you're sure?"

"I am," Maxi answered crisply.

"In that case, perhaps you might . . . care to go below?" he said, springing to his feet.

"I'm yours to command," Maxi answered.

"I like this game," Dennis Brady announced happily. "Even if you can't bet on it."

"Would you consider marrying someone like me, Maxi?" Dennis Brady asked humbly. Startled, Maxi turned toward him as he lay, long, lean and unexpectedly strong, beside her on the bed of the main cabin of the yacht. Without his deplorable garments he was a superlatively well made man and all the energy he had been too bored to turn toward mineral rights had apparently been saved just for her, to judge by the last day and a half.

"Someone '*like*' you? . . . there isn't anyone like you, Dennis, or the world would be a different place—no aggression, no ambition, just sex and casinos . . . maybe paradise is like that." She ached exquisitely in every major and most minor muscles and her mind was so blissfully unhinged that it was almost impossible to speak, much less think.

"Well, actually, to come right down to it, I meant me in particular, yes, just me, Maxi."

"Would I? Marry you?"

"That's the general idea, yes."

"What time is it, Dennis?" Maxi mumbled, remembering.

"It's ten in the morning."

"How long have we been on board?" she asked, yawning hugely.

"Exactly thirty-four hours. Oh, Maxi darling, come on and answer me," he pleaded.

Maxi made an effort to consider. This seemed important. "Let's see. Thirty-four hours plus the two hours you spent talking makes thirty-six so that leaves you four more hours . . . so . . . if you can manage to arrange it before the time's up, what choice do I have?"

"I did hope you'd see it that way," Dennis Brady said joyfully, wrapping a towel around his middle and grabbing the phone at the side of the bed. "Captain, how long will it take you to get out into international waters? What? No, I don't give a damn about the harbor master. *How* many of the crew went ashore? Well, make do, man, make do. By the way, you are a real captain aren't you? I know, I know, of course I've seen your Master's Certificate—have you ever performed a wedding? Just a burial at sea? Well if you can do one you can do the other. Break out your Bible Captain, and let's get under way."

"I don't have anything to wear," Maxi said automatically, choking with laughter. Mrs. Bad Dennis Brady. What would people think? What did it matter? What a dear he was. What *fun* they would have! She simply wasn't responsible. Everyone understood that a debt of honor had to be paid or you lost your good reputation.

14

"Poor dear sweetie, old Bad Dennis," Maxi said thoughtfully as she and India sat over a frivolous dinner at Spago, their favorite Hollywood restaurant. "He still sends me the saddest postcards and it's over a year since I left him."

India paused in the middle of lifting a forkful of goat cheese pizza to her lips. "Why do you sound even faintly regretful? I clearly remember your telling me that you couldn't take life in Monte Carlo another minute. I even remember your quoting Emerson. 'To live without duties is obscene'—wasn't that it?"

"It was. It still would be. I deeply regret another divorce but I'll never forget waking up and realizing that the darling lad hadn't had a dull moment during the few months we'd been married and I was going out of my mind. Oh, India, it was so boring, boring, *boring* to live with a man who didn't do anything in particular but hang about being an utterly lackadaisical, perfectly joyous good-for-nothing and didn't even feel the smallest twinge of guilt about it. I suppose I kept comparing him to my father, which wasn't fair, of course, because Dennis had warned me what he was like. You know how much my father accomplishes every day and how charged up and enthusiastic he is about his work, and how he communicates that energy, and how much I admire him? I guess he's ruined me for a man who isn't at least trying to *do* something, no matter what. What's more, shuttling poor little Angelica and Nanny Grey back and forth from Monte Carlo to Manhattan every month was just about impossible but that bastard, Rocco, simply wouldn't, under any circumstances, let her spend more than half the time with me. He took a much bigger apartment with plenty of room for Angelica and Nanny and since he has joint custody what could I do? Still, Angelica might have been on the verge of getting too much attention with a crew of twenty all doting on her."

"Did the lovemaking get boring too?"

"No," sighed Maxi. "I wish it had. But you can't base your entire future on sexual attraction."

"*You* can't?" India asked suspiciously.

"Not beyond a certain limit and I didn't want to reach that day so I left before it happened."

"Are you sure you're not still a little bit in love with him?" India said dubiously.

"Actually I don't think I ever was 'in love' with him . . . I just plain loved him . . . he was so needy and lost and . . . lusty. I loved the Australian in him. If only he hadn't been so totally determined to be *shiftless*." Maxi sighed deeply. "I did care for him, but not enough, India, not nearly enough." She looked severely at her mesquite broiled salmon and wished it were pizza too.

Maxi had flown to Los Angeles to visit India who had a free weekend between pictures. India had slipped into movie stardom with the irritating ease with which she'd gone through school with straight A's and Maxi felt jealous of the demanding film industry that imprisoned her friend so far from New York, or sent her on location to impossible places; jealous of the fun she was certain that India was having in spite of her complaints that making movies was irksome drudgery, comparable at best to being a privileged inmate in a minimum-security prison.

"Well, forget Dennis Brady," India advised, tackling a huge plateful of pasta with wild Japanese mushrooms and duck sausage.

"I did, a long time ago. You were the one who brought him up."

"I simply asked if there were any new men in your life and you said not even one who was worth comparing with Bad Dennis."

"India, how come you've started going to a shrink yet you're still giving me advice?" Maxi asked sharply.

"What does my being neurotic have to do with my ability to help someone else?" India asked, offended. People never understood about psychoanalysis, not even Maxi.

"I don't understand why you've started to think of yourself as neurotic," Maxi replied. "You're no different than you used to be as far as I can tell—precocious, flaky, much too beautiful and kind of weird. But now you're famous."

"I'm a ten-foot-pole neurotic, the kind who won't let a man get emotionally close to her until she meets a guy who's a seven-foot-pole neurotic with a three-foot feather duster attached to his head," India said broodingly. "And fame only makes it worse."

"What's this Doctor Florence Florsheim going to do about you?"

"Do? She's not supposed to *do* anything—I'm the one who has to change. The best thing about her is that she validates."

"You mean that she's supportive, that she believes in you?" Maxi asked excitedly.

"No, Maxi, she validates my parking ticket for the lot next to her office," India explained patiently. "*You're* supportive, *you* believe in me, because you're my friend and you don't know any better. She's my shrink, not my buddy. She listens and doesn't make judgments and every two weeks or so she might ask a question. Also she doesn't give a hoot in hell what I look like, which is the most marvelous relief. There's no point in not telling her the truth because she can't read my mind and if I lie it costs me time and money, since eventually I *have* to tell the truth or I'm not playing fair and won't get helped. I can tell her anything I want to and know she'll never be shocked because there's nothing she hasn't heard already. If I should say anything important she'll certainly remember it."

"Are you absolutely sure about that?"

"No. It's an article of faith. You have to have faith in your shrink, Maxi, and if you start to doubt her you have to tell her all about it which takes another year. The main thing, I guess, is that she's my *ally*. I pay her for it admittedly but still I've got to have a staunch day-to-day ally, especially in this town."

"Did she say she was on your side? How do you know she's your ally?"

"I *feel* it . . . and stop asking for guarantees because she doesn't pass them out. Now, could we stop trying to explain the inexplicable and talk about what you plan to do next with the life you've utterly wasted except for producing Angelica?" India asked kindly.

"I'm going to London next week. I've wanted to spend time there for years and Angelica's going to be with Rocco all of July this year."

"Where are you staying?"

"With my grandparents, of course. They'd be terribly offended if I didn't. They're in their late sixties now and more alarmingly vigorous than ever. They've planned all sorts of things for me involving jolly entertainment and meeting people including cousins in the second, third and fourth degree, none of whom I know."

"That sounds . . . interesting," India said.

"You mean it sounds perfectly awful."

"That too, that too," India agreed cheerfully.

"There's no point in trying to do anything about it," Viscountess Adamsfield said to her husband in a gloomy tone that was at odds with her feeble attempt at philosophy.

"But of all men to choose, of all possible Scots, and god knows, I like the Scots almost more than any other people on earth, your granddaughter had to pick a *Kirkgordon*! Laddie Kirkgordon no less, and after knowing him less than two months—his family lost almost everything at Flodden Field well over four hundred years ago and they've been going downhill ever since," her husband growled.

"She's your granddaughter too and he is, after all, Oswald Charles Walter Angus, Earl of Kirkgordon, ruined or not."

"Oswald! No wonder he's called Laddie," Evelyn Gilbert Basil Adamsfield fumed. He'd been lucky to extract a miserable "Bertie" out of his name after two dozen fistfights at school.

"Oswald was king of Northumbria from 635 to 642. Apparently the name is a family tradition," Lady Adamsfield said sadly. "Oswald was king for only seven years, unfortunately, but he must have been a very holy man, sending out all those missionaries to convert the heathen, you know."

"No I did not. And I don't care. Why didn't Oswald mind his own business? I suppose Maxi's been educating you? Is that girl bucking for sainthood this time around?"

"She's in love, Bertie. She told you herself. I think you're being perfectly vile about it."

"I'm not going to pretend that I like it, Maxime, and that's that. I had a splendid husband picked out for her, as well you know."

"Maxi said he was a twit."

"No marquis is a twit, and most particularly not one who's practically a duke. His father won't last out the year. He's a bit dim, perhaps, but not a twit. What's more, *his* family has always been loyal to the crown and those wild, daft Kirkgordons are still loyal to the House of Stuart. As far as they're concerned a descendent of Mary Queen of Scots should be on the throne. No wonder they're down and out; idealistic, unrealistic, notoriously eccentric, the whole crazy, stubborn pack of them. And her Laddie the worst of the lot."

"I rather think that's what Maxi sees in him. She said he had a strong sense of destiny, something to live and fight for, a deep meaning to everything he did, a passionate striving, a . . ."

"Spare me, Maxime, my darling. I was at the wedding too and what Maxi sees in him is obvious."

"You have to admit that he is rather gorgeous," Lady Adamsfield said dreamily. "In fact, I haven't seen a better-looking creature in a long, long time . . . that noble head, those *blue, blue* eyes, that wonderfully fresh, ruddy coloring, that sandy hair, almost golden, when you come to think about it, that great height, those *shoulders* . . ."

"That crumbling castle, those barren acres . . ."

"Those historic, twelve-feet-thick walls, that breath-taking view . . ."

"He doesn't have a shilling and she could have been a duchess . . ."

"She's quite rich enough in her own right, pet, she *is* a countess and he absolutely adores her . . ."

"Maxime," said Viscount Adamsfield, "you're a hopeless romantic. I used to think you were a sensible woman."

"Well, I just hope she's settled down for good this time."

"Maxi? Settled with a *Kirkgordon*? I very much doubt it, my dear. Settled down indeed!"

"What's *that*, for heaven's sake?" Milton Bizet demanded, recoiling.

"What does it look like?" his partner, Leon Ludwig, said smugly.

"A telephone-book-sized telegram. It must be from Maxi. Hand it over."

"If you knew, Milton, why did you ask me what it was?"

"To indicate my alarm, curiosity and feverish delight. I've actually been wondering why we hadn't heard from her except for the announcement of her wedding to that utterly glorious-looking Kirkgordon person. Our Maxi and her indecently macho earl must have bought a marvelous house in London by now, I said to myself, and she certainly isn't going to be unfaithful to us and let some English decorators get their beastly little hands on it. Where is it? In Mayfair, of course, but where in Mayfair? Now give me that telegram."

"It's a castle," Ludwig announced, handing over the pages.

"Trust Maxi. We taught her to think big."

"In Scotland," Ludwig said ominously.

"Oh, no."

"Oh, yes. Somewhere between Kelso and Ettrick Forest, so she says, as if we'd know where *that* was, no heating at all except for a few fireplaces that are big enough to roast a whole sheep in, no minstrel galleries, no follies, no marvelous paneling, no family heirlooms, no tapestries, no pictures, almost no bathrooms, tiny little windows so that it could be defended from the invading Royalist troops, whatever that means, Lord knows how long ago. And the whole damn thing has been falling to pieces for at least a thousand years and even when it was in its glory it wasn't vaguely comfortable . . . not a stately home, Milton, oh no, a bloody fortress. She calls it 'Castle Dread.' Maxi wants us to get over there as soon as possible, preferably tomorrow, so we can start to make it *cozy*. Apparently she's found a horrendous problem with dry rot and you know what *that* can lead to. She says the decor consists of a hundred stags' heads and hoards of horrid stuffed fish hanging on the walls and that there isn't even any decent family silver except for some sort of sacred chalice or other. *Poor* Maxi." Ludwig subsided with a tiny sigh.

"Why 'poor Maxi' when money's no object?" Milton Bizet inquired. "I remember when we had to fly to Monaco to redecorate Blissful Dennis's yacht . . . he didn't care what we spent. I did love that job. In fact I rather loved Dennis, didn't you? He looked just like Peter O'Toole in *Lawrence of Arabia*."

"Only not as well dressed," Leon Ludwig pointed out, with a small, nostalgic smile.

"And will you ever forget the job we did on Maxi's second town house, after we talked her into getting rid of that first little brownstone?" Bizet continued. "She really went the distance on that place. I suppose that she'll keep the new apartment she's bought in Trump Tower for a *pied à terre* when she gets tired of deer stalking or whatever it is she intends to do in Scotland, don't you?"

"All I'm sure of is that money isn't the problem. It never is with Maxi. It's *us*

... we're going to have to spend months and months in Scotland. What does Scotland mean to you, Milton? Besides deer stalking?"

"Cashmere sweaters, plaids, whiskey, ah . . . shetland sweaters, tartans, Drambuie, ah . . . haggis, bagpipes, trout . . . *kilts*! Leon, is this a quiz show?"

"Rain, cold, fog, wind, discomfort, lonely moors, the hound of the Baskervilles—if Castle Dread doesn't have central heating and decent bathrooms, who in the neighborhood will?"

"Leon, you have no vision. You panic too easily. There's got to be a hotel somewhere and if not we'll just camp out at Claridge's and pop up to Scotland when it's absolutely necessary. But I do wish Claridge's had better lighting in the bathrooms. I can never see well enough to get a decent shave, but where else can we stay?"

"Nowhere," Leon Ludwig sighed. "If we did, people might think we were slumming, and slumming in London isn't chic anymore, alas."

"I'll tell my secretary to make reservations immediately. Maxi sounds desperate. She says she has to have the central heating in by next week and for some reason she can't seem to make the local contractor understand. This is a crisis, Leon. She needs us."

"Milton, when didn't Maxi need us? We're indispensable to her."

"Well, I just hope she's settled down for good this time."

"Who, Maxi?! Really, Milton, you've taken leave of your senses. *Settled down*, indeed!"

Angelica ate her hamburger, looking, Rocco thought, more thoughtful than a seven-year-old should look.

"Is there something wrong, sweetheart?" he asked.

"Oh, no, Daddy, I was just wondering if I liked Laddie as much as I liked Dennis, that's all."

"Oh."

"Dennis was so funny but Laddie can play a twelve-string guitar and sing old songs; Dennis taught me to swim but Laddie is going to get me a Shetland pony and teach me how to ride; Dennis had a great big wonderful boat but Laddie has an enormous castle; Dennis showed me how to play Go Fish and he always let me beat him but Laddie gave me a little red fishing rod and when the trout season comes he's going to show me how to . . ."

"It sounds as if they're both simply perfect, two absolutely wonderful guys," Rocco interrupted. "Would you like another hamburger, Angelica?"

"Oh, yes, please, Daddy. That's one thing they can't make right in Monte Carlo or Scotland. I *miss* hamburgers."

"Really."

"Yes, and I miss tuna fish sandwiches and turkey with cranberry sauce," Angelica said sadly.

"Are those the only things that you miss, Angelica?"

"Well, I suppose I still miss Dennis, a little bit. I don't know Laddie quite well enough yet to stop missing Dennis, even though Laddie's so very very tall and so very very handsome."

"I see."

"That's O.K., Daddy," Angelica assured him earnestly. "Maybe people always miss people they like, even when they meet other new people they like."

"Maybe."

"Please pass the ketchup, Daddy. Remember when Mommy was married to Dennis? Remember how every month Nanny and I used to take the helicopter from Monte Carlo to Nice and then the little jet from Nice to Paris and then the Concorde from Paris to New York to be with you? But I was just a little kid then and I didn't have to learn things. Now I'm in second grade and I can't change schools every month."

"I know, sweetheart."

"So once I start school in Scotland, I won't get to visit you until we have a vacation that's long enough for me to come back to New York," Angelica explained with a look of concern.

"I understand, baby. Your mother and I discussed it for a long time and I had to agree with her that I couldn't interrupt your schooling."

"But I'm worried about you, Daddy."

"Why, Angelica?"

"Because you're going to miss me."

"A lot, God damn it! *One hell of a lot.* But you'll have your mother and Laddie what's-his-name and a pony and a castle and probably dozens of pretty little plaid kilts to wear to school, so you'll be too busy to miss me, darling."

"I miss you all the time I'm not with you, Daddy," she said reproachfully.

"More than Dennis?"

"Don't be silly! It's not at all the same thing. I liked Dennis. I *love* you."

"I was just making a little joke."

"Well, I don't think it was funny. Not at all! Take it back, right away," Angelica said severely.

"I take it back," Rocco mumbled.

"O.K. Could I have a chocolate fudge sundae, please?"

"Of course. You can have anything you want."

"Well, I just hope that Mommy is going to stay settled down with Laddie this time. I don't want to have to miss him too."

"Settled down? Your mother? *Ha!*"

"What does that 'ha' mean, Daddy?"

"I was coughing, Angelica. Just coughing."

"Zachary, just listen to this letter from my mother," Lily said in a tone of alarm, putting down her piece of buttered toast.

"What's bothering her?" Zachary ate his egg patiently.

"It's Maxi."

"I know it's Maxi. Obviously your mother's too sensible to get upset about anything minor. What's Maxi done now? I assume people have gotten over being shocked about the indoor swimming pool she installed in the dungeon and the bathroom she insisted on for every bedroom, even though the castle is a historic monument."

"It's nothing that petty. Mother says that Maxi's becoming the talk of London and that's not easy to do when you live in the Border Country. Apparently she's giving house parties that last for weeks."

"Why the hell not?" Zachary stopped eating in quick defense of his daughter. "It took her at least a year to get the old barrack modernized and decorated and it certainly cost her millions. Naturally, she'll want to amortize that, and what better way than surrounding herself with friends?"

"I suppose you're right, Zachary, but it seems that her house parties are simply notorious. They say that Maxi is growing a huge crop of marijuana in the greenhouse and she fills the Kirkgordon Chalice that the Archbishop of Glasgow presented to the family in the fifteenth century with a never-ending supply of home-rolled, Good Lord, Mother writes 'joints'—I didn't think she knew that word—and that Maxi is running a high-stakes poker game every day *including* Sunday in the late earl's trophy room . . . for heaven's sake, dear, put down your butter knife . . . and that she lights great blazing fires on top of the castle tower to celebrate Saint Patrick's Day and Columbus Day and Kosciusko Day and I Am an American Day and every single other American holiday and the local fire department can't get her to stop. She still persists in driving her Ferrari on the wrong side of the road and, Zachary, worst of all, when she was invited to visit her neighbors, the Duke and Duchess of Buccleuch at Bowhill House, she said that she wasn't absolutely convinced that their Leonardo is authentic! That's quite unpardonable, Zachary, and, of course, untrue and she must have known it." Lily flung the letter down in exasperation.

"She's unhappy, Lily. The marriage isn't working out. That's what all this means and I'm not surprised. I always thought that brute of a Kirkgordon was much too beautiful. I don't trust men who look like that, and now he's made her miserable. I admit that Maxi's a little spoiled at times but she's never been self-destructive," Zachary said, taking off his glasses absently and shaking his head in concern. "The only part of that letter that seriously worries me is her driving on the wrong side of the road. I'm going to phone her and find out what's going on. I'd just hoped, I really had, that maybe Maxi had finally settled down this time."

"I know you're a doting father but there should be *some* limits to your wishful thinking. 'Settled down'? Your daughter? Maxi? Really, Zachary!"

"What was it exactly that went wrong this time, Maxi?" India questioned breathlessly. "Tell me everything, take it from the top."

"If you'd ever been able to visit, you wouldn't have to ask. But you were too busy even to pop over for a weekend," Maxi said accusingly. "So, here I am, back on the coast, just to see you."

"That's a bum rap. I didn't have the time for jet lag in both directions and you know it perfectly well. It's not as if you've been living in San Francisco. Come on, stop stalling."

"Basically, it was the dreich."

"Of course it was," India said soothingly. "What's he like this dreich person?"

"It's a Scots word, India, and it means very, very wet, very, very dark, very, very dim and very, very cold. The weather, India, the weather was *fucking* dreich." Maxi reached over and took some pizza off of India's plate. She was thin enough now to risk anything, and the pizza at Spago was irresistible.

"So you got divorced for the third time because of the weather? Interesting. This is the first time I've heard that one. Of course, if you see enough Bergman movies you can begin to understand that gloomy weather does create a definite morbidity and melancholy, but in less than two years? Maxi, leave my plate alone. Wouldn't you like to order your *own* pizza? What about all those tons of central heating you put in?"

"India, what about being generous enough to share your pizza? I gave you half my angel hair pasta, didn't I? What if I told you that my taste in men is probably the worst in the whole world, that I shouldn't be allowed out by myself without a keeper?"

"I'd be forced to disagree. Rocco was, as I well remember, one of the all-time greats, Bad Dennis Brady was, in his own way, supremely delicious, and according to your letters Laddie Kirkgordon was sheer heaven. I quote: 'He has all the best points of King Arthur, Tarzan and Warren Beatty.' Didn't his being an earl even account for something?"

"You try waking up in the middle of the night and telling yourself that you're a countess and see how much difference that makes," Maxi snapped.

"And just why were you waking up in the middle of the night and talking to yourself?"

"All right, India, all right. I give up. I see you've been taking Doctor Florence Florsheim lessons, getting right down to the roots of things, isn't that it?"

"More or less," India answered in a deliberate monotone.

"Laddie is a certifiable lunatic," Maxi said, and fell silent.

"That's it? That's all there is to it? Most men are lunatics, Maxi. Stark, raving lunatics. But you don't divorce them because of it, you learn to live with them. That's probably why I've never married. I know too much up front, in advance. Laddie just wasn't *your kind* of lunatic."

"Damn right, he wasn't. I think he was an overreaction to poor Dennis, but in the beginning I really fell for it: that glorious tradition handed down from generation to generation; the purpose in life; the meaningfulness of being Scots, Scottish, Scotch, you can call it what you will; ancestor worship, the House of Stuart, patriotism, I fell for the lot. But once we got out of bed long enough for me to listen clearly to him, and that took a year, I found out I was much more of an American than I'd ever realized. Laddie began to sound quite obsessed, and finally I realized he was decidedly mad, bonkers, living in another century. He refused to have anything to do with the real world, with one single exception: winning the Selkirk Silver Arrow—I think it's the only thing he cares about."

"Huh?"

"It's an archery trophy, the oldest there is, and every seven years there's a competition of the Queen's Bodyguard of Archers to win the Arrow. Laddie spent at least six hours every day practicing with his bow and don't say it was just a hobby, it was *life* to him, even though the Queen he was doing it for was not Elizabeth the Second. If he'd had better weather he'd have spent more time at it than that, but what with the dreich and all . . ."

"Why didn't you bail out earlier? Between the wet and the target practice I don't understand why you stuck around for so long."

"I was simply just too *embarrassed* to admit I'd made another mistake. I never knew one of my three husbands for more than a month or two before I married him—I only knew poor, sweet, Bad Dennis for thirty-odd—very odd—*hours*, India. What does that tell you about me? Don't bother to answer. Don't say one single word, that wasn't a question."

"What did Angelica think?"

"Oh, she was having too good a time to notice that the laird was a wee bit peculiar. She loved the indoor swimming pool, she loved the local school and she really became quite good with a bow and arrow. Laddie gave her lessons, I'll say that for him. Fortunately I got her off in time, before she started thinking that Bonnie Prince Charlie was going to come riding out of the mists on a white horse and carry her away. I believe Angelica could thrive underwater. I'm the one who isn't adaptable."

"You're just impulsive," India said lovingly.

"Do you think *I* should go to Doctor Florence Florsheim?" Maxi asked with a look of despair. "You can't say that I'm leading life in the fast lane—it feels like oncoming traffic."

"That happens to be the one kind of advice I can't give you. People in analysis are not supposed to go around telling their friends that they should go into analysis too. Anyway, Doctor Florsheim wouldn't take you because you've heard too much about her and she knows too much about you, to say nothing of our being best friends. It would be strictly unkosher."

"Do you talk to her about me?" Maxi asked, with a delighted expression. "I didn't know that! What do you say?"

"When I'm trying to avoid talking about something I don't want to talk about, I do have a tendency to discuss you, yes. But since you're not one of my problems it's just another waste of my time and by now I know that whenever I even *mention* you it's because I'm avoiding something really awful."

"Oh."

"Don't try to understand."

"I won't, India, I truly promise not to."

"What do you intend to do now, Maxi?"

"First of all I'm going to make you a solemn and binding commitment, India. I'm going to vow, with you as my witness, that I will never, ever marry another man. *Never ever another man*, India, do you hear?"

"I hear but I don't believe you. Just because you don't intend to get married again doesn't mean that you won't. You're too young to make such a vow. I warn you not to do it."

"You let me decide that! India, if I get married to another man I'll . . . I'll take out an ad, a full-page ad, saying that I'm not responsible for my actions, that I have no sense when it comes to men, that I'm doing it against my better judgment, that I'm acting in haste and will repent in leisure, that I'm sure in advance that it's going to turn out to be a mistake and that you, India West, are my witness, the only one in the world who knows that I have made a vow to myself, an absolute vow, never, ever to marry *another* man."

"Where will the ad run?" India asked through her fit of giggles.

"In the *New York Times*, in . . . in *Women's Wear Daily*, in the *New York Post*, in the *London Times*, in *Le Figaro*—that should cover just about everybody I know, don't you think?"

"*Weekly Variety* too," India suggested. "You've met a few people in the business."

"Done. I'm absolutely dead serious about this, India."

"I know you are. Oh, Maxi, I did hope that this time you'd settled down for good."

"India, *me*? You should know better than that!"

15

In spite of the discouragement in which she had briefly wallowed over the weekend and on the phone with India, Maxi approached the offices of *Buttons and Bows* on Monday with a tickle of irrepressible excitement. After her long therapeutic talk with her best friend she had convinced herself that the former editor, Bob Fink, was simply too superannuated to understand that something could be made of her magazine, no matter how low it had fallen. He didn't believe in it anymore, if indeed he ever had, he had no competitiveness left, he lacked vision, he had made too much money in real estate to be hungry for improvement, except when it was time for his daily free lunch, Maxi assured herself as she opened the door to the suite of offices, a door that she resolved to have painted as soon as possible.

She stood inside and surveyed the unprepossessing chamber. On the walls of the reception area were framed covers of *Trimming Trades* when it had still been the thriving, prosperous magazine on which Zachary Amberville built his empire. The old-fashioned covers from the forties and fifties just reinforced her conviction that bringing the magazine back to life was a question of using her imagination. The skimpy, recent issue of *Buttons and Bows* that she had put into her handbag and taken home had a cover that was basically similar to those on the walls. Surely something as important as a cover could have been, should have been, totally changed in the course of forty years?

"Miss Amberville, welcome to hard times."

Maxi spun around. It was the receptionist who had announced her arrival last week.

"You're still here? Bob Fink said everyone couldn't wait to leave."

"My salary is paid through the end of the week, and I'm not old enough to retire."

"What's your name?"

"Julie Jacobson."

"Call me Maxi," she said, sitting down in front of the battered desk. "About your clothes, Julie, shall we put our cards on the table?"

"I guess that would be best," Julie answered carefully.

They were wearing identical outfits: miniskirts in a screaming red, with crisp white blouses and exaggeratedly long, black men's ties around their necks. They both had on black tights and high-heeled black pumps. A wool Chesterfield that matched the skirt was hanging behind the receptionist's desk. Maxi was wearing its double. The ensemble was Stephen Sprouse's newest, freshest, and brightest, exactly what a fashion addict with superb legs would choose to wear on this particular day of this particular month of this particular year. Since they were roughly the same height, the two young women looked absolutely alike from the chin down.

"I think we should stop meeting like this," Maxi said, "or else try to make a point of it." Bob Fink had said that his receptionist was overpaid but this suit and blouse had cost over a thousand dollars, not counting the shoes. Just how overpaid was she?

Julie was Maxi's height, but she had little breasts and narrow hips that meant she would always look taller than Maxi in the same clothes. Her short hair was tinted an otherworldly color between Bordeaux and orange that stopped precisely short of punk. It was brushed back uncompromisingly from her forehead to reveal a face that belonged to an impertinent doe: huge challenging eyes, darkly rimmed in charcoal liner and shadow; a slender nose with nostrils so sensitive that they looked as if they could twitch at any minute; delicate lips painted a bright crimson; a chin that was just small enough to give the impression that she shared some forest animal's timidity and yet firm enough to let the world know that Julie Jacobson didn't let anyone order her around.

"But let's discuss wardrobe later," Maxi continued. "I'm going to look around my office. Then maybe you could show me the rest of the establishment?"

Julie sprang up and stood with her back protectively barring the door that led to Uncle Bob Fink's former office.

"I don't think you really want to go in there," she said.

"I don't?"

"It might not be the best way to start the day."

"Don't tell me he didn't get rid of all his stuff," Maxi sputtered. "He promised, damn it."

"No, it's all been carted away."

"Then what's the problem?" Maxi said blithely as she entered. She stopped in her tracks in shock.

The room was completely empty, except for one old black leather chair with a rump-sprung seat. The entire carpet was covered, many inches deep, with layer upon layer of half-disintegrated bits of paper, a mess ten times worse than Broadway after a ticker-tape parade. Cobwebs, she thought in a daze, real honest-to-God cobwebs hung in the corners of the room. Did New York have *spiders*? The walls, now that Uncle Bob's nine towering desks no longer concealed them, were mottled and filthy. There had been leaks over the years and paint had fallen from the walls in long zigzag strips that lay in pieces over the other debris. The windows were so dirty that scarcely any sun lit up the scene, but whatever light came through the grime was desolate.

"At least in *Great Expectations* Mrs. Havisham had *furniture* to hold up her cobwebs," Maxi said when she could find her voice.

"The last desk, the one he was working at, collapsed when they tried to move it," Julie explained.

"There isn't a broom, there isn't a vacuum cleaner, there isn't any instrument known to man that could clean up this . . . I don't even know what to call it," Maxi said faintly.

"There's always motivation." Julie sounded as if she'd meditated on the problem.

"Motivation?" Maxi was horrified. "You don't mean *me*!"

"In *our* clothes? I was thinking of Hank, from the building. He's been known to become highly motivated by the palm of his hand. Do you have fifty bucks?"

"In cash . . . I don't think so. Will he take a credit card?"

"I'll lend it to you. You can pay me back tomorrow."

"Bless you, Julie! Let's get out of here. It's morbid."

"You're the boss."

"Right? Right! Now where can the boss sit down and discuss the future of *Buttons and Bows* with her staff?"

"Maxi, you don't have a staff."

"What about you?"

"No way. I don't mind lending you money, but that's as far as it goes. I'm purely temporary, not staff, God forbid, in this place."

"Couldn't you just pretend? Till the end of the week. You could put it on your résumé, when you go for your next job."

"I am planning on leaving *Buttons and Bows* off my résumé entirely. But if it makes you feel any better, you can call me a consultant and let me buy you a cup of coffee to cheer us both up. Don't look for a coffee maker, it's broken."

"The nearest coffee shop?"

"You're on."

"Julie," Maxi said earnestly, leaning over the table, "have you ever stopped to think of the possibilities? Every rock group in the world is trimming-crazy, tons of gold braid, uniforms, everything they wear is trimmed to high heaven. Medals are back all over the place. Shoulder pads have never been more important. Claude Montana. Just think of Claude Montana's shoulder pads! The T-shirt craze. What is punk but the inspired use of trimming? And just look at the evening dresses this year . . . if they don't glitter, forget them. Sonia Rykiel's things—all trim. Why, we could do a whole issue on . . . on Joan Collins's puffed sleeves!"

"Hmmm."

"What does that mean?"

"I've only been here two weeks because the assistant editor's job I was supposed to have at *Mademoiselle* fell through at the last minute, but I do know who still subscribes to *Buttons and Bows*. Basically, it's your Mr. Lucas who is worried about selling five thousand yards of passementerie and your Mr. Spielberg whose main business in life is fringe. I don't think they would be intensely fascinated by Joan Collins's sleeves. They would hardly notice if Joan Collins herself appeared stark naked on the cover of the magazine. *Buttons and Bows*, if it's about anything, is about a few of the nuts and bolts of the fashion business. For fashion, Spielberg and Lucas stick to *WWD*. That's not subject to change by you."

"Then we have to widen our base of circulation, appeal to somebody other than Lucas and Spielberg."

"Not *we*, Maxi, *you*," Julie insisted. "*You*."

"Anyway, that's tomorrow's problem," Maxi said, pushing it away into the air. "Tell me about you. All the vital statistics you care to have known."

"I'm twenty-two. I graduated from Smith last year. My mother always insisted that I have secretarial skills to fall back on. For three generations the women of my family have had secretarial skills and I'm the first one who's ever had to fall back on them. I do not enjoy it. In two weeks I'm starting at *Redbook* as assistant to the assistant to the fashion editor."

"Are you a New Yorker?" Maxi asked curiously. Julie was as businesslike a creature as she'd ever met and crisply self-confident.

"Cleveland, Shaker Heights. My father's a neurosurgeon and my mother teaches English literature at the university. Her speciality is Virginia Woolf and the Bloomsbury Group. My sister's working for a double Ph.D. in French and philosophy so that she can teach Pascal, Montaigne and Voltaire, heaven only knows to whom, and my brother's a city planner and chief aide to the mayor of Cleveland. I'm my parents' only failure."

"What is your crime?" Maxi gaped. It must be the color of her hair. Everything else about her was so impressive.

"I'm nuts about fashion. No one in the Jacobson family thinks fashion is a proper way to spend the only life you have. It's frivolous, poorly paid, and doesn't add to universal knowledge."

"It's the fourth or fifth biggest industry in the country."

"They don't think much of industry either."

"They sound a bit . . . Bostonian."

"There's another branch of the family that's lived in Boston forever. They make the Cleveland Jacobsons look like television game show producers."

"I didn't even graduate from high school," Maxi confessed.

"Is that why you've been sent to *Buttons and Bows*—to teach you what happens to people who fail to complete their education?"

"It was my own idea. And I'm not giving it up," Maxi said grimly.

"I don't understand why, with all the other Amberville publications, you should care what happens to pathetic old *Buttons and Bows*. In your place I'd be at *Style* like a shot."

"Let's talk about clothes," Maxi suggested. She liked Julie but she wasn't about to bare her heart and her loss to satisfy her curiosity. The reasons were too emotional, too bound up with her love for her father to explain.

"Clothes Milan? Clothes Bendel's? Clothes American designers?" Julie's eyes lit up with anticipation.

"You're buying the coffee so you get to pick," Maxi said generously.

For several hours that afternoon Maxi sat in what had once been the art department, where two bare L-shaped layout tables and several tottering chairs had been abandoned on a dirty, peeling linoleum floor. In the reception room, from time to time, she could hear Julie answering the phone and coping with the reluctantly motivated maintenance man.

Maxi had supplied herself with a yellow legal pad and a box of ballpoint pens and she decided that the first thing she had to do was to plot the future of a new, revitalized, expanded, explosive *Buttons and Bows*. She had the intention of making lists and sketches and more lists and more sketches. She walked around the room, looked out of the window, sat down, looked at her yellow legal pad, got up and walked around the room some more. Inspiration proved elusive. Maybe it was the fault of the decor, maybe it was the terrible ham-and-cheese sandwiches she and Julie had shared in a coffee shop that had been sold out of her favorite, tuna salad, maybe it was the antics of the full moon or the diabolical influence of Saturn or maybe it just wasn't her day. Maybe it was Lucas and Spielberg. She wished that Julie had never told her about them. None of the ideas that came into her head seemed good when viewed from the Lucas-Spielberg angle, and they were, after all, the faithful core that was left of the readers of *Buttons and Bows*. The magazine, if it were to rise from the ashes, had to appeal to many thousands of Lucases and Spielbergs, wherever they were to be found. Hundreds of thousands. Millions!

"Jesus Christ Almighty!" Maxi said out loud.

"You spoke?" Julie asked, standing in the doorway.

"There *aren't* millions of Lucases and Spielbergs!"

"One of each, I believe. On your subscription list in any case."

"Julie, I'm going for a walk. I think better on my feet."

"It's nice outside," Julie said, eyeing the virgin yellow pad meaningfully. "Oxygen stimulates the brain."

"And it's nice outside. See you tomorrow."

Elie was waiting with the limo downstairs.

"The center of the universe, Elie," she ordered. He made his rapid, illegal way to the corner of Fifty-seventh and Fifth, stopped and opened the door for her. "When will you need me tonight, Miss Amberville?"

"I'm not sure, Elie, but call in around six."

She walked briskly down Fifth Avenue, breathing deeply, relishing the nimble temper of the September city, that perpetual urban high-wire act. She loved the incomparable tension of this island metropolis that felt as if it were perched on the top of an active volcano. "I'll take Manhattan, the Bronx and Staten Island too," Maxi sang, although she had known for years that the song her father had taught her had been skewed to suit his determination since the first three words of the lyric really were "We'll have Manhattan."

Never had Fifth Avenue seemed broader or brighter to her than after the dismal hours she'd spent in her new office, never had the passing throng, pushing and shoving and overtaking each other in the aggressive, *con brio* New York version of a stroll, seemed more fascinating and varied than after the fruitless afternoon she'd spent with her yellow pad. Everyone had a destination, a goal, a reason for being here, in this place, on this street, at this hour.

What, Maxi wondered, what did they all want? *Wanting* was the very essence of the New Yorker. She knew what she wanted. She wanted to make a smashing success of *Buttons and Bows* and quite suddenly she admitted to herself that she knew it could not be done. Not with *Buttons and Bows*. No way, nohow. There was no *major* demand in this city, where there was a market for everything, for a magazine that was devoted to articles, no matter how well executed, on the mystery of the hand-embroidered glitz on Julio's three-thousand-dollar dresses or the ruffles on Prince's clothes or the definitive word on Linda Evans's paillettes. Probably there was a market for a magazine for contact lens wearers, or a magazine for left-handed people, perhaps even a magazine for people who collected string, but they would always be *small* magazines. Maxi wasn't about to pour her energy into a small magazine.

Scratch trimming, she thought. She needed to find a new idea—a—a *concept*. That was all she needed, a concept, Maxi thought, as she almost danced down Fifth Avenue, in her red miniskirt, a smile on the perfect bow of her mouth. Just a new concept, merely a new, fresh concept that hadn't already been done. That was all. As she sped by, every man who saw her ached to follow.

When Elie called in tonight she'd tell him that tomorrow morning she wanted him to make the rounds of all the newsstands in the city and bring her a copy of every single magazine on sale. She might as well know what was out there already before she invented her new magazine.

"Ma," said Angelica in a voice of supplication, "when are you going to stop torturing yourself? I can't take this much longer."

"Tough shit, kid."

"Ma, that's not a nice way to talk to your little girl."

"I don't have time to be nice. If you want a nice person go find somebody else, I'm working."

"Ma, why are you doing this to me?"

"Because. And stop whining . . . other girls have working mothers and they don't complain."

"Working mothers!" Angelica sputtered. "You're like some kind of loony, a robot, a crazed robot."

"Go play Trivial Pursuit."

"You've been shut up with these magazines for three days now, you haven't had more than a bite to eat, you read till you drop, you grind your teeth when you're asleep . . ."

"How do you know?"

"Because you fell asleep on top of that pile of magazines last night and I heard you grinding away."

"Just a little stress, just normal stress, Angelica."

"But you've always avoided stress, you hate stress, Ma. Stop it!"

"To be stressed is human, kid, don't you know that? Maybe you're too young, but according to what I read, every female in this country is operating under unendurable stress and it's getting worse even as we sit here and waste time talking. Now go away and let me get back to my work."

"Ma, I'm going to call Toby and get you committed to an institution."

"It takes three doctors to commit somebody and all the doctors in the country are busily writing articles on stress for magazines, so you won't find any who have the time, but you're free to try."

Angelica folded her lanky frame in sections and sat down protectively next to Maxi. Three days before, when Elie had arrived at the apartment with the first shift of magazines, her mother had been like a kid opening Christmas presents. She had installed herself in her new library, with its solar-gray mirrored walls, its book-crowded shelves and its big armchairs covered in off-white glove leather. She had opened each new magazine with anticipation, pounced on it and leafed through it page by page, leaving out nothing from cover to cover. When she had wrung a magazine dry Maxi carefully added it to one or another of the piles of different types of magazines that were beginning to collect around her. Elie kept returning from his expeditions with his arms piled high. From expectation, Maxi's mood grew more subdued. By lunch she began to look slightly dismayed and by the end of that first day she was annoyed. By the evening of the following day she had progressed to outrage, and her outrage had mounted ever since. Still the magazines kept coming, the piles now tumbling down the sides of all but the window wall of the room.

Many of them had been sent away, carried off by the weary Elie: the only-for-men magazines; the sports magazines; the computer magazines; the car-owner magazines; the audio-freak magazines; the motorcycle-nut magazines; the weekly news magazines; the movie magazines; the soap-opera fan magazines; the magazines for male homosexuals; the aerospace magazines; the business magazines of all kinds and sorts.

Maxi had, by now, cleared a place for herself on the red and white hand-loomed carpet and sat cross-legged, hemmed in by dozens and dozens of publications.

"I haven't found one for lesbians yet," she said in a tired but thoughtful tone of voice.

"Ma! Is that what you're planning?"

"It may be the only major virgin market left."

"Would lesbians go out to a newsstand and buy a special magazine?" Angelica wondered. She heard the front door open. It must be Elie with more dreaded magazines, because the footsteps were those of a man.

"In a country with fifty-nine million single people and a magazine like *Bride's* that claims to reach just over three million, it stands to reason that there's got to be a big lesbian audience out there somewhere," Maxi answered, trying for a tone of sweet reasonableness.

A man entered the carpeted library where they sat so engrossed in print that they didn't hear him. He stood leaning on the doorjamb, casually poised. The mocking cock of his head, the tough jut of his chin, the skeptical glint in his eyes, the clearly bellicose way in which his short, pointy, ash-blond hair stood up from his head, all indicated someone who viewed the world with a certain disdain. He wore battered leather so worn that it seemed a collection of bits and pieces, three Nikons were slung around his neck, and his smile was both knowing and deeply loving. It was evident that he found both Maxi and Angelica very funny, objects of his benevolence, and it was just as evident that only a very few people in the world fell into that category.

"Could I interest you ladies in a subscription to *Boy's Life*?" he said quietly.

"Justin!" Maxi whooped and launched herself across the room into his arms, scattering magazines in every direction. "Justin, you beast, where the fuck have you been for a year, you rotten bastard, you shithead! Justin, darling!"

"Give me a chance at him," Angelica cried, and grabbed him tightly, trying to climb up him like a monkey as she used to when she was a little girl, almost toppling him over in the process. Eventually he extricated himself from the two excited, babbling creatures, separated them and put an arm around each of them. "Let's look at you," Justin said, and they immediately fell silent and subjected themselves to his scrutiny. "Still the ultimate best in the kingdom," he said after a few seconds. He inspected his sister and his niece keenly, his dark gray eyes missing nothing, but whatever his real thoughts were he kept them, as always, to himself.

Soon after Zachary Amberville died so suddenly, so horribly, Justin had taken off without a word to any member of his family. He had a record of disappearing for months at a time since he was fifteen, and the Ambervilles had become accustomed to his comings and goings. He never wrote or telephoned while he was away but, from time to time, photographs would crop up in a variety of publications with the photo credit "Justin": photographs from tiny islands so distant that no travel agent knew them, from mountaintops so unexplored that they had no names, from jungles that were only empty space on most maps; photographs of surfers in Australia, of Brazilian transvestites in the Bois de Boulogne, of the inside of the Royal Enclosure at Ascot; photographs that had nothing to connect them to each other except the unexpected viewpoint of the brain beyond the lens of the camera that captured images that couldn't be skipped over, even in an era when it seemed that the most extraordinary photographs must all have been taken.

His last "trip," as the family called Justin's mysterious wanderings, had been longer than any other he had made, and his photographs had been infrequent, but still no one worried, for by now it was accepted as a fact that Justin was invulnerable.

In his early teens, he had seemed utterly ill at ease in his own skin, jumpy, awkward, and seeking every opportunity to avoid attention. Then, when he was twelve, he had started to study the martial arts and self-defense, embracing a schedule of relentless training that had reminded Lily of the single-mindedness of the ballet. Slowly Justin's bearing, even when he stood still, began to convey an unstated menace. Everything that had earlier seemed vague and alienated in him had been collected into the strength and speed with which he knew he could move.

Today he was a presence to reckon with, all dexterity, all sinewy grace; a man of twenty-four, of medium height, whose lean body nevertheless had more density than that of other young men.

Justin looked both lionhearted and unpredictable although he disdained any outward trappings of toughness. His familiar leathers were not studded body armor, just relaxed, well-worn, shabby garments in which he could travel anywhere. When he could be coaxed into a game of croquet in Southampton he exuded the same potential for dauntlessness, wearing white linen trousers and a pastel crew sweater; the quality was built into his hard muscles, into his lack of relaxation, as if he were ready to do battle at any minute.

Maxi had never seen Justin touch another person except with tenderness, yet she often realized that she knew remarkably little about her younger brother although they loved each other unreservedly. He was the most highly defended man she had ever met and whatever went on behind his high rounded forehead, whatever unspoken need made him drift away from home so often was a bafflement to her. Even Toby, with the acuity of his senses, with his way of reading unspoken thoughts, had no clues to the perplexing conundrum of Justin's motivations. It seemed to both of them that he stalked some invisible goal that eluded them, a goal he never had explained, never had described yet a goal that inexorably lured him on and on.

"What," Justin demanded, grinning, "are the two of you doing? I want an explanation. Toby said I'd find you here but he didn't say in what condition. He said you'd tell me all about it."

"Ma's looking for a new magazine concept," Angelica answered with a shrug of her shoulders, "and I'm trying to make sure she doesn't starve to death in the process. The new cook quit yesterday."

"Maxi, why?" Justin said, astonished. "Who needs another magazine?"

"I'm not sure yet, that's the problem. But the rockbottom reason has to do with Cutter, and a matter of not letting him make an ass out of me."

"In that case, you can count on my full cooperation," Justin said with as much overt ferocity in his voice as he ever displayed.

While Maxi and Toby could have explained in detail what they distrusted and disliked in their uncle, only Justin had always hated Cutter and yet could not have said why. It was an instinctive loathing that went too deep for words, a question of absolute mutual antipathy. Justin had been curious, as they all were, about his father's brother who never seemed to leave San Francisco. When Justin was almost eleven, Cutter and Candice Amberville finally came through New York, stopping for a few days on their way to Europe. The first time Justin met Cutter his curiosity had been transformed into a visceral disgust, a disgust he didn't try to understand. It existed as solidly as a boulder, it was not something to question or ponder, it just *was*, as powerful as his love for Zachary, as obvious as his caring for Toby and Maxi.

"I accept your offer," Maxi said delightedly. For the last three days Angelica had been her only sounding board. Julie was busy at the office winding up the business of putting *Buttons and Bows* into the limbo where all dead magazines still float, items of rare, plaintive nostalgia and trivia quizzes. Maxi had not called on any of the professionals at Amberville Publications who would have been glad to lend her a hand. Pride had prevented her, pride and an irresistible need to do this thing by *herself*, to see it through to the absolute end and then, if she ran dry after giving it her unreserved best, to admit defeat if necessary. But she didn't want to lean on the obviously available expertise of Pavka or Nina or Linda Lafferty, or any of many others who were among the editorial board members. She was twenty-nine and she'd never accomplished much alone in her life except bringing up Angelica. However, Justin's help was different. He was family.

"Where do we start?" Justin asked, shedding several layers of soft leather and making a place for himself on the floor with Maxi and Angelica.

"Don't you want to know why I'm looking for a concept?" Maxi demanded.

"Not necessarily, as long as it has to do with screwing Cutter. How far have you come? Do you have a glimmer of a glimmer?"

"I know what I can't do. I have eliminated all the glossy magazines: the *Vogues* and *Architectural Digests* and *House & Gardens*. Not only are they too expensive to publish, but Amberville already has *Style* and *Indoors* and I don't want to compete with the company. Also they make me so *angry*!"

"Since when? I thought you loved them."

"I used to, I was addicted to my monthly fix of slippery paper, but the more I looked at them, the more I read them, the more furious I got. Justin, do you realize that the glossy books just make you feel like a piece of *junk*? Almost nobody can look like that; wear those damn clothes; use that crazy new makeup; have houses like that or gardens like that . . . you can aspire, you can spend the rest of your life trying to be someone photographed in that one perfect minute, which is the only thing they *ever* show, but you'll never make it for real. They're not selling dreams, they're selling putdowns. They're selling heartache, dissatisfaction with what you have, above all they're selling *envy*."

"Hey, Maxi, take it easy. They're selling clothes and furniture and cosmetics . . . the editorial pages are just the vehicle for the ads. They make the wheels of American business turn. You know that as well as I do."

"That doesn't make me like them," Maxi said obdurately.

"But you *are* their reader, you of all people. You know perfectly well that you can buy just about anything that you see in those magazines. Look at this apartment . . . four million dollars, or was it five? Look in your overstuffed closets, look in your jewel box, and then take a good look in the mirror. Just what don't *you* have? Except for a fourth husband?"

"I'm thinking about my readers," Maxi said impatiently.

"Oh, so you have readers do you? I knew there was something different about this place but I thought it was the view."

"I intend to have them, Justin, and I'm not going to give them another overdose of how rich people live."

"Bravo! What other kinds of magazines have you decided not to publish?" Justin asked, his curiosity piqued by her vehemence.

"All those damn service books: *Good House, Family Circle, Woman's Day, Redbook, McCall's*, and anything else that digs, digs and digs some more at every woman's guilt. Just look at this *Ladies' Home Journal* ad . . . they surveyed 86,000 women and eighty-seven percent of them said that 'women can do anything.' "

"Well, can't they? You've always acted as if you thought *you* could."

"Look what *else* it says—'We're here as she presses herself for physical excellence. Offering her sensible diet, exercise and beauty plans . . . and we're there as she presses to be better in other ways too. At home. On the job. In her community . . . pressing just as hard for excellence as the seventeen and a half million women who read us every month.' It's a big, lousy, fucking conspiracy, a *tyranny*, Justin, no poor bitch is allowed to be anything but bloody excellent at all times, in all situations. Press on, press on, and if you drop dead from sheer *pressing* for excellence, at least you won't have let your subscription lapse!"

"Angelica, go get your mother a Miltown."

"It's all right, Justin, I just gave her one. It doesn't help. Can it kill you to foam at the mouth?"

"I doubt it, sweetheart, your mother's just suffering from stress."

"Justin," Angelica shrieked in alarm, "please don't use that word."

"Oh, balls," Maxi muttered, throwing down a copy of *Family Circle.* "It's only September, and they've got '101 Christmas Gifts to Make' and 'All-Time Favorite Cookie Recipes' on the cover and Doctor Art Ulene's book on *How to Stop Family Problems Before They Start.* . . . What if you don't bake, what if you buy your presents and don't want to know more about your family problems at Christmastime than you do already? How *guilty* will this cover make you feel? And it's the world's largest-selling women's magazine according to the masthead. And look at this magazine, just look. It's called *Lady's Circle* and it's really a joyful book: a piece on stomach-stapling that didn't work, an article about a teenager with a rare, fatal liver disease, another stress article that contains a test on how you rate as a heart-attack victim; and then, for fun, how to crochet a holiday tablecloth. Is crochet a stress antidote? Or a stress add-on?"

"Maxi, why are you even bothering with service books?" Justin asked. "That's not exactly your line of country. I've never seen you making anything more complicated than a vodka gimlet and I remember your being furious that limes had seeds."

"I have to know what people are buying, what *women* are reading, or I won't know what to give them that they don't *already* have," Maxi explained, looking as if she had suddenly turned into a toadstool. "It's obvious."

"But you can't be planning to compete with a *Good House.* . . . Where are your test kitchens, Maxi, where's your money-back guarantee, where's your well-earned readers' confidence? Where's your reputation for excellence and your position as a trusted friend, not a magazine?"

"Justin, how come you know so much?" Maxi inquired suspiciously.

"I had lunch with someone from Hearst once," he said evasively.

"I like to bake cookies," Angelica announced. "Could I have that copy of *Woman's Day*, Ma?"

"With my blessings," Maxi said, smiling for the first time that morning. She turned to Justin and raised astonished eyebrows. Baking cookies?

"What's in that pile?" he asked, pointing to the heap of magazines closest to her.

"I call them the 'so what else is wrong with you?' books. Their premise is simply that things are going so badly that you're desperate for help. Here we have *Woman* and *Complete Woman*, with typical cover lines: 'Why Do You Let Him Walk All Over You?'; 'Beat Those Menstrual Blahs'; 'Conquering Your Shyness'; 'If Sex Leaves You Wondering "What's Wrong with Me?" '; 'So You Are Not Interested in Sex . . . '; 'Banish Boredom, Overcome Hurts, Fight Insecurity, Beat Loneliness'; 'How to Save Yourself from Yourself.' I could go on . . ."

"Don't! Please don't. Or I'll scream," Justin said, unable to repress a guffaw.

"Ma's overreacting," Angelica whispered to him.

"The hell I am," Maxi snapped. "I'm just seeing what's being sold on the newsstands and having *normal* reactions."

"Like grinding your teeth in your sleep?" Angelica asked.

"Precisely! How about this piece on 'The Number-One Stress Stopper' by Michael Korda. Guess what it is."

"Relaxation?" asked Justin.

"Deep breathing and chocolate cake?" Angelica hazarded.

"No, no, my children . . . 'Do More . . . or How to Be a Confirmed, Happy, Unapologetic Overachiever.' That *SUCKS*!" Maxi flopped on the floor and groaned aloud. " 'Do More,' the man says. *More*."

"Let me rub your back, Maxi, it's probably killing you," Justin said, rolling up his sleeves and flexing his strong fingers.

"How about a brownie, Ma? They say chocolate makes you happy, releases some kind of hormone or something," Angelica suggested anxiously.

"No, don't try to make me feel better." Maxi jumped up from the carpet and picked up the magazines around her and pitched them violently at the magazines that were piled against the walls. "Enough guilt! Enough of your guilt trips about everything from your extra pounds to how you've changed your lover into a tyrant; enough guilt trips about how pathetically little you know about how to handle money, about how you can't accessorize your clothes, keep a neat closet, don't take enough calcium, haven't been promoted at work, can't manage a job and a family too, and need your marriage saved; enough about your nutrition mistakes and how to handle failure; enough about how boring your sex life is and it's probably your fault; enough guilt about your whole life being depressing and why men are unwilling to commit; enough about why you fuck up job interviews. . . . *No more guilt trips!*"

"We agree, don't we, Justin?" Angelica said hurriedly as Maxi whirled around faster and faster but Maxi didn't hear her and kept on talking louder and louder, her bare feet thudding on the thick carpet like enraged hooves.

"All they do is undermine your self-confidence while trying to tell you how to be, seem, and feel *more* self-confident; they make you feel that it's impossible for your body to ever be attractive *enough*, that you can and should be doing better, better, *better*, in the kitchen, the bedroom, the boardroom—what, you mean you haven't been promoted yet? How come you're not an executive and if so what horrible things does your office furniture reveal about your character and when will you learn how to manipulate your boss and make office politics pay? And if you don't work, how come you aren't at home making a new kind of stuffing for the turkey, how come you're such a poor pathetic creature that without this magazine you'd never make it through the night? Oh, thank them—thank the good editors for making you feel better about that heel you married, the dozen men who've left you, the seventeen different things you do wrong in bed, the only man—naturally a shit—whom you can't forget; all of which are your fault, bad girl. *BAD GIRL*! Guilt, guilt, guilt! WOULD ANY MAN BUY A MAGAZINE THAT TOLD HIM EVERY MONTH WHAT A SCHMUCK HE WAS? No, my children, he would not. *If I read one more article about bulimia I'll throw up*. God damn it to hell, isn't there a single magazine a woman can buy that loves her just the way she is? What did I just say?"

"You'd throw up if . . ." Angelica cried hysterically.

"No, after."

"Doesn't any magazine like women?" Justin ventured.

Maxi jumped up and down. "THAT'S IT! That is fucking it! The reader-friendly magazine, the magazine that loves you and doesn't try to change you, the magazine that wants to amuse you, that exists for your pleasure and *only* your pleasure. FUN. The magazine that doesn't give a shit if you eat too much or can't find a guy, or should have known better or need help. Fun, I say! There's already more help out on the newsstands than anybody could possibly use. FUN! Did you hear me? FUN!" She opened her arms wide and jumped up and down, flinging the last of the magazines away, kicking as high as any Texas cheerleader, strutting her stuff.

"We heard you, Ma. Everybody in Trump Tower heard you."

"What is this fun book going to be called?" Justin said with a flashing look of pleasure at the sight of his adored sister back to normal form again.

"It's already got a name, Justin. I picked *Buttons and Bows* when I had my chance. But times have changed," Maxi said gleefully, "and so has the name. I'm shortening it to *B and B*."

"*B and B*? What kind of name is that?" Angelica asked.

"Do I know? Does it matter? Bread and Butter, Bosoms and Bottoms, Benedictine and Brandy, Balls and Bums, whatever suits your fancy. It's called *B and B* and that means F-U-N!"

16

"Zap-proof. Fucking zap-proof!" Rocco said, angrily throwing down the issue of *Adweek* he'd been reading. He looked out of the window of his office on the forty-third floor of Dag Hammarskjold Plaza and noted with annoyance the red neon sign of the Pepsi bottling plant on the other side of the East River. Coca-Cola was his client and Pepsi was the loathed enemy, until the almost certain day when Pepsi would become the client and Coke the enemy. "Anyway," he added, "this story is totally sick. Imagine having to go for zap-proof by shooting eight and a half hours of film and editing it down to a thirty-second television spot. No matter how good it might turn out to be, I say it's a sign of something fundamentally wrong."

"We have nothing to do with that spot, Rocco," Rap Kelly said soothingly. "It's for somebody's deodorant soap. You should stop reading the trades."

"Don't turn into a philosopher, Rocco," added Man Ray Lefkowitz, the third partner of the firm of Cipriani, Lefkowitz and Kelly, the hottest advertising agency in New York. "When you give the public remote-control units for their TV sets, it stands to reason that they're going to zap the commercials."

"If it *had* been us, I'd have killed whoever directed that soap commercial with my bare hands," Rocco said somberly. "Hitchcock he wasn't."

Manny and Rap exchanged glances. Was Rocco going into another of his occasional phases which they privately called yearning-for-print-freakouts? When the two of them had lured him away from Condé Nast three years ago it had been the hardest selling job either of them had ever gone through, including the battle to get the Chevrolet account. Rocco hadn't wanted to admit that magazines were dodo birds as far as getting graphics to the attention of the masses was concerned. He had wanted to stay buried in print forever, Rocco had, until together they'd wrestled him out of his fixation.

Manny Lefkowitz, that brilliant copywriter, still remembered his winning argument. "Rocco," he'd said, "it takes more time and energy and decision to turn the page of an ad, particularly when you've *paid* for a magazine, than it does to zap a commercial, since it is your right, as an American, to see a commercial coming at you for *free* every time you turn on the television. Who's the bigger challenge to an art director? The willing consumer, the veritable captive audience of a magazine who's intent on amortizing his investment, or the absolutely fed-up-with-commercials audience watching television who only wants the show to come back on? Don't bother to answer—it's obvious. So if you're the best art director in the world, as Rap and I think you are, then television advertising is the only medium worthy of you. It's your next step, Rocco, you can't help but admit that."

"I admit it . . . but I just don't know . . . where's the *white space*, Man Ray, where's the layout?"

"On that blank screen, Rocco, and you know it. It means you'll be grabbing people quicker and grabbing more of them . . . millions and millions more. And you have to sell them something, not just entertain them. The major difference, Rocco, is that magazine layouts are essentially the print equivalent of jerking off—all you're doing is making pretty pages for the advertisers to plant their ads *around*... it's pure self-indulgence. With commercials you live or die in that split second before forty percent of the viewing audience decides to zap you. So you have to be better than in print. Not just good, *great*."

"Jerking off?" Rocco said, offended.

"With all due apologies to the magazine business, it's a century behind its time. A page doesn't *move* or speak to you and nothing is ever going to make it do so. Get off the pot, Rocco, don't be like that guy who said nobody would ever go to talkies."

"Yeah, Rocco, don't be totally dumb," Rap Kelly chimed in. He was the cat-burglar, business-getter of the threesome, who specialized in being indecently smarter than he sounded, and won many an account that too-slick talk had lost.

Rocco had looked at the two of them, Manny, the monster-talented chief copywriter and vice-president at BBD&O, and Rap, who was the king of the hill at Young and Rubicam, and realized that the adventure of starting a new advertising agency with these two advertising geniuses was irresistible. The top creative agency job that they were proposing to him had never before been offered to a Madison Avenue art director. Traditionally that job always went to someone who came up through the copy department.

He had been thirty-three then and, except for his brief experience at Amberville Publications, he'd always worked for Condé Nast. But his idol, Alexander Liberman, was going as strong as ever, showing no signs of age, and Rocco suddenly felt that perhaps the time had come to move away from the printed page, at least for a time; perhaps Manny and Rap were right about the challenge. To say nothing about the money. No one in magazines had a chance of making the money that he knew he could make in an ad agency and it was time to think realistically about money.

From the time Rocco and Maxi had been divorced, only a little more than nine years before, he had chosen not to think about money, knowing that it was un-American and unnatural and in some basic way ridiculous not to think about money, as if he'd taken some sort of vow. It was more difficult to work in New York and not think about money than it was not to think about sex or food, but for someone whose life had been as screwed up by money—Maxi's money—as his had been, it was a revolting topic.

And he'd been right about the money he'd make. CL&K, as their new agency was known, was a gold mine from the day it opened its door. They pulled down out of trees clients that supposedly belonged to the venerable giants of Madison Avenue as if they'd been ripe bananas; fickle advertising directors of Fortune 500 companies beat at their doors before they'd finished raiding the other agencies in town for much of their prime talent, for Cipriani, Lefkowitz and Kelly had something extra going for them that no other agency in town had: all three were bachelors without attachments. And much of the prime Madison Avenue talent was female. Man Ray Lefkowitz was a jolly redheaded giant with violently blue eyes which he insisted were a sign that he was of some special tribe directly descended from the Queen of Sheba; and Kelly was a redheaded Irishman with violently blue eyes who had been an all-American quarterback for UCLA and could sing tear-bringing whorehouse tenor when he wanted to, and all three of them had never lost a hair off their scalps or been rude to a lady or failed to observe Valentine's Day. Last year their bill for Valentine's Day flowers from Robert Homma had been over eighty thousand dollars. They had sent his antique Japanese storage jars filled with tall, graceful branches of flowering quince, and it had come back to them as Kelly reverently said, "a million fold."

"Let's go get drunk," Rocco said suddenly, when the Pepsi sign blinked on. "Didn't we just get the Cutty Sark account?"

"Last week . . ." Rap Kelly answered. "It wasn't easy prying them loose from that old boat. I thought you hated Scotch, Rocco."

"Not if they're a client. I'm going to develop a taste. Come, kids, it's that time of day." He put on his tie and jacket and led the way, while behind him, Lefkowitz and Kelly exchanged worried glances. Rocco rarely drank.

"Just a touch of delicious New York vulgarity—just short of actually rough, a hint, merely a hint, of tough chic," said Leon Ludwig, one of Maxi's interior decorators.

"I don't agree. We're talking middle-America; all Mumsy and English country-cottage, tons of glazed floral chintz, and slightly tatty settees," replied Milton Bizet, the other half of Ludwig and Bizet, the decorating team Maxi had used for her last two town houses and the renovation of the Earl of Kirkgordon's castle in the Border Country.

They had not, nevertheless, been able to really impose themselves on the Trump Tower apartment. Their efforts rejected the geometry of the building, since Maxi insisted on keeping favorite pieces bought in her wandering, the spoils of a careless, rich nomad with the instincts of a bazaar keeper. They'd opened up the walls of the adjoining apartment she acquired and done what they could, but the job had left them feeling that their client had not been satisfactorily tamed or subdued.

"Boys," Maxi interrupted, "hold it right there. We're talking office furniture, we're talking state-of-the-art steno chairs. We are not trying to make a design statement."

The three of them were approaching the area in which the office of *Buttons and Bows* was located and when Elie stopped the limousine in front of the building off Seventh Avenue, Ludwig and Bizet stood on the sidewalk in disbelief.

"Here?" asked Leon Ludwig, recoiling.

"Here. The lease has three years to run, all the space on the rest of the floor is available, the rent is much lower than in any of the new buildings, and the neighborhood has associations for me," Maxi said firmly.

"It isn't even Art Deco," Milton Bizet breathed in amazement. He'd never seen this part of New York before, not even on his way to the theater.

"It isn't art anything," Maxi snapped, "unless it's Depression Repugnant. It's a mess and it's utterly inefficient . . . that's what I want you two to fix up. I need it last week. I can't use staff effectively until I have a decent place for them to work."

"Maybe one of those companies that specialize in offices . . . those Itkins or whatever their name is—would suit your purposes better than . . ." Leon Ludwig ventured, unwilling to confide his elegant person to the interior of the building.

"Boys, I have no relationship with the Itkins and I assume you want to continue yours with me?"

"Naturally, Maxi, my delicious, but . . ."

"Then get your bodies upstairs and stop whimpering," she said with her most alarming smile. "It's going to be fun for you, making it all work on a budget," she added thoughtfully.

"And just how much is the budget?" asked Milton arching his eyebrows. It wasn't like Maxi to talk of budget except as something disposable that they would throw guiltlessly to the winds as they went along digging up blissful things without which she couldn't live. He'd known there'd be trouble, ever since Trump Tower had come into her life.

"*Half* of the rock bottom minimum you can come up with," she answered.

"Funny girl," Leon purred.

"I have this sinking feeling that she's not joking," Milton said in unfeigned horror, observing the strangely serious expression on the face of their favorite, if marginally difficult, client.

"I'm not. This magazine is going to take a pot of money to produce and I don't want to see it wasted on the walls of the office. On the other hand, cows give more milk in happy surroundings, as do people, so it's essential that the whole office be cheerful, gay, *fun* to work in. I want windows that open, no fluorescent lighting except where it's absolutely necessary, a smashing reception room—do it with mirrors, *cheap* mirrors, Leon, no bevels . . ."

"Maxi, haven't you ever heard that you have to spend money to make money?" Leon said in a last-ditch stand against the all too foreseeable agonies of a strict budget.

"Too often. The money will go into salaries. How else can I get the best people away from their present jobs to work on a new magazine? Well, here we are." Maxi opened the door of the office. The reception room was empty and she vanished immediately in search of Julie. She didn't like to watch grown men cry.

"Welcome back," Julie said in relief. "I've got your keys right here, all the old business is wound up, all debts paid, my desk is cleared out, the phone's still working, and the only thing still hanging around is a blank yellow legal pad and the pencils you left here last week."

"What about my sweater?" inquired Maxi looking at her strangely.

"What sweater? You didn't leave one here."

"I know." Eyes like slits, Maxi studied Julie's new Perry Ellis sweater and skirt costume, the one that would set the standard of adventure for American ready-to-wear that year, two extraordinary ways to use cashmere; one a dazzling tunic, a tapestry of reds, blues, and yellows, inspired by the Cubist work of Sonia Delaunay; the other a longish wrapped black skirt that worked absolutely with Julie's flat black shoes and magenta tights. The sweater, for Maxi too had bought one on Saturday, was eight hundred dollars, and it was too eye-poppingly, too specifically and memorably fall-of-1984 to be worn for more than one season. You couldn't even wear it more than once every two weeks in an office. The skirt, at three hundred bucks, could become a classic, but the sweater was a bravura gesture, the sign either of someone so rich that she could afford it without thinking of price, or someone so clothes-mad that she would buy it, wear it a few glorious times, and then keep it forever for her private pleasure.

Julie Jacobson couldn't be all that rich, Maxi calculated, or she wouldn't have had to take a job as a secretary while she waited for her minor assistant's appointment at *Redbook*. She had undertaken the dreary labor of funeral director of *Buttons and Bows* with tact, dispatch, energy, and remarkable good spirits, setting up her command post in what had been the old art department. As Maxi had fled from witnessing the vapors of Leon and Milton, she had noticed that the offices were now as spotless as they could be, granted their state of decrepitude. Julie was two girls and a half.

"I have a proposal to make to you," Maxi said, sitting down next to Julie.

"No," Julie answered shuddering. "Really, truly, no."

Maxi ignored her. "How much are you going to be paid at *Redbook*?"

"A hundred and seventy-five a week, but that's not the point."

"The point is that you'll be in the fashion department, as assistant to the assistant to the fashion editor."

"Exactly," Julie answered, her eyes gleaming with a vision of herself at some time in a far hazy future, sitting in the front row at the New York fashion collections, pencil poised to make notes of whatever she judged worthy.

"Have you ever played Monopoly?" Maxi asked. Julie nodded, still in her dream. "Remember when you got to pass 'Go' and whiz ahead on the board and collect two hundred dollars from the bank? Didn't it feel good?"

Julie snapped back to reality. "Maxi, what are you trying to con me into? I don't work for you anymore, thank God. As of last Friday I'm not even on the payroll here. What's more there isn't a payroll anymore."

"But there is a payroll, a new payroll, and I'm going to be meeting it every week."

"How many people are you employing?" Julie asked suspiciously.

"So far, none. Eventually dozens and dozens. Hundreds."

"Doing what?"

"Putting out a new magazine."

"But that's *exactly* what you were planning to do last week! Oh really, Maxi!"

"This has nothing to do with last week. You were absolutely right about my idea for *Buttons and Bows*. It was youthful folly. Since then I've aged a thousand years in wisdom and experience."

"Is that a fact?"

"Trust me."

"I never trust people who say 'trust me.' "

"That was a test," said Maxi smugly. "And you've passed. Therefore I'm officially offering you the job of fashion editor of *B and B* combined with the job of my chief personal assistant in charge of all other details until I find someone who can take them off your hands and leave you totally free to plan the fashion pages."

" 'All other details'? Why do I smell snake oil? What is *B and B*? Another remake of *Buttons and Bows*? How many fashion pages would there be? And how much authority would I really have? And what about salary? And what if the magazine doesn't make it and I blow the job at *Redbook*?"

"Three hundred a week, to start with, *you go wholesale for your clothes*, absolute authority within the basic philosophy of *B and B*, which is simply that women are great the way they are—you can't argue about that, can you?—and, oh, there you are! This is Justin, your photographic consultant, Justin, this is Julie Jacobson, the new fashion editor of *B and B*. You two will be working closely together."

Julie spun around and gaped at Justin who had soundlessly materialized in the doorway and stood leaning against the wall with such compact and tightly coiled power that it looked as if he were holding the building up with his shoulder. He advanced toward Julie, who was hypnotized by the battery of Nikons that he wore as familiarly as if they were a scarf tossed around his neck, took her hand and shook it.

"Justin, *the Justin*, is working for this magazine too?" Julie gasped.

"*The Justin*. I said trust me. That didn't necessarily mean that you couldn't," Maxi laughed. "And here—'hi guys'—as Mary Tyler Moore used to say—here are Milton Bizet and Leon Ludwig who are designing our offices—come in, boys, and greet Julie Jacobson, my fashion editor. She'll be going over your bills, so be nice to her. Julie, you don't have to be nice to them at all. In fact, I would advise the utmost caution. Leon, what color office do you see for Julie, assuming that she doesn't change her hair?"

"A forest atmosphere, lots of batik, tapa on the walls, obviously a kilim on the floor, fishtail palms . . ."

"Leon, I meant the color of the *paint.* We do not have fabric walls at *B and B*, we do not have fabric anywhere. Fabric is too expensive and gets dirty. The fabric-free office is about to make interior design history, isn't it, Justin? Zen and the art of office maintenance. It might get you a story in *Architectural Digest* and then again it might get you the cover of *Plastics Weekly* . . . it all depends on your imagination and talent. If you show enough of it, I may make the two of you my decorating editors, but first you have to prove yourselves."

"An all-white office," Milton offered, deeply offended, "with a large box of Ajax and a gross of sponges."

"Can I just bring one white rose in a white bud vase for my desk?" Julie begged, blushing with excitement. *Wholesale! Justin!*

"I'll supply the rose," Justin announced.

"I'll *lend* you an onyx vase," Leon announced. "White vase indeed."

"Hmm," sniffed Maxi, "I rather thought *I'd* like an all-white office to go with the streak in my hair. We can't have two."

"Julie gets it," Leon decreed, feeling much better. "She's the only one we have to be nice to now."

"Pavka, I'm so glad you asked me to lunch. I haven't seen you in, oh, much too long." Maxi had rushed into his arms in an effervescent swirl of plaid pleats and a sweep of her fine limbs that proved forever that the knee is, under some circumstances, far, far from an unlovely joint.

"I've missed you, but I knew you were busy," Pavka said, careful not to sound reproachful. He was perfectly aware that she had been avoiding him. There were rumors all over Amberville Publications about Maxi's plan, but no one had a single solid detail to contribute.

"We've been painting the office," Maxi said demurely.

"Well . . . that's a beginning."

"I think so." Maxi studied the menu at the Four Seasons Grill Room which had developed into a virtual club of the top executives and agents in publishing, people so important that their perks included the limousines which jammed Fifty-second Street off Park Avenue as if a gangster's funeral were going on inside. As well it may have been, in certain subtle senses of the phrase.

"And when the offices are painted," Pavka continued patiently, after they had ordered, "you will hang curtains, bring in furniture, put down rugs?"

"We'll most likely get around to doing something like that, or at least drifting in that general direction," Maxi admitted gravely, giving the question her most serious consideration.

"And, if I understand correctly, eventually you will publish a magazine?" Pavka pounced, but she didn't flinch.

"Ah, that. I imagine so, eventually. Of course, eventually is never tomorrow, but I suppose that sooner or later we'll putter along and see if we can manage to squeeze out a little . . . a nice little . . . magazine."

"Which doesn't, by any chance, have a name yet?"

"Not a name really. No, I don't think you could say it had a name." Maxi's Imperial Jade eyes had suddenly turned as uncompromisingly and flatly green as a color sample. She was determined not to reveal any details to Pavka. She felt like a mother bird who was being disturbed in her nest while she was hatching her first egg.

"But, my darling, surely you intend it to have a name?"

"In time. In time." She looked sinfully, blissfully lazy. Time was to be ignored, she seemed to say without words . . .

"But Maxi, you do understand the importance of a name?"

"*Good Housekeeping, Reader's Digest, National Geographic, Playboy*—of course I do."

"I assume you're looking for a name that tells the reader what the magazine is about, hmm?"

"More or less in that general area, yes. Pavka, did you know that Russell Baker says there are only six subjects: sex, God, marriage, children, politics and baseball?"

"So may I conclude that your magazine is about sex?" he pressed.

"I'd never ignore it, not completely. Marriage is good too. So is divorce."

"Maxi! Why won't you tell me anything? You're teasing me, you sound like somebody in a bad off-Broadway play. Don't you know that you have to have an *informative* title so that you can get people to even *glance* through the first issue, which is only one of your problems, and at that, only the *first* of the *dozens* of problems involved in launching a new magazine. You have to get them to open it, Maxi, much less actually buy it."

"Pavka, angel Pavka, I have the most enormous favor to ask of you." Maxi tossed him a look of cosmic prettiness. His heart melted. She really didn't have to bother, she had always had his devotion.

"Anything you want. You know I'll help, whatever it is—do you want to discuss your plans in detail? Or can I help you with the dummy? Nothing is too much trouble for my Maxi."

"All I want you to do is *not* to tell me about my dozens of problems," Maxi answered in her sweetest voice. "I know how much marvelous advice you could give me, but Pavka, you *know too much*, you've seen too many magazines fail. Would you tell a baby who's about to take her first step about the dangers in downhill skiing? About hang-gliding? Ice dancing?"

"Have it your way, my darling, but there is one thing you can't stop me from insisting on saying—you need to hire someone experienced to handle traffic control, someone usually called an executive editor, or managing editor, someone who won't impose his opinion about what goes into the magazine, but who will steer ideas through the many tedious stages from conception to completion, and then get the copy and photos and ads to the printer on time. He should be a pessimist who never believes anything will go right unless he does it himself. A beast of burden, if you will, but a beast you can trust with your life. Otherwise your magazine will be a boat without a rudder."

"I'm the rudder."

"No, Maxi, you're the boat—and the ocean and certainly the wind that fills the sails, but your temperament isn't that of a rudder."

"Hmm." Maxi didn't know whether to be irritated or placated but she rather fancied herself as a boat—a trim forty-eight-meter, three-masted racing yacht. "I suppose you have someone in mind?"

"There's a man I can put my hands on. He was managing editor of *Wavelength* before Cutter's massacre, and he took a vacation when he was fired so he's still available . . . a man named Allenby Montgomery. Allenby *Winston* Montgomery."

"Do I have to call him 'General'?"

"*Évidemment*—by now he doesn't answer to any other name. But there's no need to salute if you don't want to."

"He sounds like an easygoing guy," Maxi gloomed, resignation in her voice. She knew Pavka was right. She needed someone utterly steady around, so she could do all the unsteady parts herself.

"I hope you've thought about an art director," Pavka continued cautiously. If Maxi had been at all clear about what she planned to do, she'd never have been able to keep from unfolding it to him, even if she didn't want his advice. She'd have been too pleased with herself. Did she even have a concept? If she did, and he doubted it, whatever it was, it existed on some half-baked drawing board in the back of her little delicious, maddening head, somewhere under that cockatoo hairdo which went every which way including up and made her look as if she were actively in bed with a few very close, energetic friends.

"An art director?" Maxi murmured vaguely. "Of course I've thought about one . . . but that's as far as I've got. We're still waiting for the paint to dry—I don't need an art director yet."

"I asked a great editor once what was the worst single thing his enemies in the publishing business could do to destroy him and he answered, 'Steal my art director,' " Pavka said, almost to himself.

"What editor?"

"Your father. I was the art director."

"*Évidemment.* And *touché.* But I *am* considering it, Pavka, I just haven't made any decisions. Trust me."

"How could I not? So tell me, how are you coming with the dummy?"

"Brilliantly, just . . . brilliantly. I feel just like the cowboy who jumped into the cactus bush. When they asked him why he'd done it, he answered, 'It seemed like a good idea at the time.' "

Laughing, Pavka was able to hide this confirmation of his conviction that Maxi was lying to him. Her summer job at *Savoir Vivre* had indeed led to major events, marriage and motherhood among them; but he doubted that she'd been allowed anywhere near a dummy, much less become capable of making one. He sighed but he was far from surprised.

"Remember, my darling, I'm here if you need any kind of help," he said, keeping up the pretense since she wanted it that way. "And I'll tell the General to call you as soon as he gets back."

"Thank you, Pavka. You're too good to me." The two of them finished lunch laughing at the atmosphere of the Four Seasons, that hotbed of sexual possibilities. They observed editors seducing writers, writers seducing editors, publishers seducing editors and editors seducing publishers, but never saw a writer seducing another writer, for that would be like two professional football linebackers falling in love. In the dignity of the marble room half the people present had been married two and a half times to the other half and were working on the third alliance. Their only permanent relationships were with the headwaiters.

After lunch Maxi found Elie right in front of the revolving door, stolidly resisting the efforts of the doorman to make him move the limousine farther up the street. As she was driven back to her office, she felt relieved that she hadn't been provoked into telling Pavka anything, tempting as it had been. When all was said and done, he was just a little old-fashioned, a bit of a pessimist. He might not have understood that now that she had found her concept the rest of it was *all out there*, all waiting for her. It merely needed a spot of pinning down. Nothing more. Just a little more . . . thought . . . a touch of . . . oh, work . . . yes, face it, work.

That night, refusing three invitations for dinner, Maxi stayed home. She wished that the men she knew hadn't all hooted when she told them that she couldn't join them because she had to work. She frowned as she settled herself in the center of her enormous bed, propping herself firmly on the least floppy of her many pillows, pulling up the white mink throw that lay at the end of the bed so that her knees made a little fur desk.

All the materials she thought would be necessary for the fabrication of a dummy lay neatly beside her. She'd bought ten packages of the thickest paper she could find in a rainbow of vivid colors, five types of Scotch tape, two boxes of special number-three Dutch pencils, a miniature portable pencil sharpener from Sanyo, a vast assortment of ballpoint pens in every color that existed on the market, a complete calligraphy set, and close at hand were the latest issues of all the women's magazines published in the United States. She looked at the magazines scornfully. She had never seen a complete dummy, only scattered pages of layouts, but obviously it must be a magazine-shaped object. She intended to use the other magazines to clip out ads to put into her dummy so the finished product wouldn't just be text and pictures. In fact, she decided, hefting the long, expensive, Swiss-made scissors, why not clip a good assortment of the best-looking ads now, to have easily at hand? Then she could get the magazines out of the way and into the wastepaper basket where they belonged.

Soon she had a thick sheaf of ads, most of them in color. After deliberation, Maxi added a few in black and white; Bill Blass, Blackglama, Lancôme and Germaine Monteil, just for contrast. She shoved the magazines off the bed with a sign of good riddance and, feeling efficient, clipped the ads together in two groups with the paper clips she had not forgotten to buy.

Now.

Now for the dummy.

Perhaps she should just check up first on Angelica, make sure she was doing her homework. No, Angelica's school didn't begin until next week. She'd be in the library waiting impatiently for "Hill Street Blues" to begin. Perhaps she should call India and tell her what she was doing. No, they'd just talk for hours and the evening would disappear. Resolutely she took one of the steel-tipped quill pens from the calligraphy set and experimented drawing an ampersand on a sheet of stiff red paper. The ampersand was tricky to draw but she did a fairly neat job on her fifth attempt. Eventually she inked boldly, *B&B*. At the bottom of the page she made a small circle and carefully inked in the letter C in the middle of the circle. Now she had the copyright on her title; that was all it took. Extraordinary. Perhaps it had something to do with the Library of Congress? Once published it would belong to her. Once published. She never believed the person who had told her you can't copyright titles. She'd like to see the person who could take *B&B* away from her.

Well. So far so good. Now for the text and pictures. Text first, it stood to reason, or how would she know what pictures she needed? Or if they should be photographs or illustrations? Yes, text. No, not text! She wasn't going to write the magazine herself, after all. That was what writers were for. All she needed were headlines.

Titles of articles. How lucky she was that she knew what she didn't want, that she'd spent so much time eliminating the sort of thing that made women envious or depressed or guilty. She'd already done most of the work, actually, when you came to think about it. Perhaps she'd join Angelica in the library and see what they were doing up on the Hill this week. Maybe Mick had bought a new suit. Maybe Furillo would fall in love with a blond. Maybe Renko would take up bodybuilding. Maybe Joyce would get a different hairstyle. Maxi sighed deeply. She should have waited till tomorrow to start this dummy. Any day was good for a dummy but only Thursdays brought the Hill. She could just stay to watch the opening shots.

No. She would, *she had to* stay right here. The program was probably a repeat anyway. She reached for the still-empty yellow legal pad that had been malevolently half-hiding under a pillow, picked up a pencil and slowly wrote "Why Short, Fat Men Are Better in Bed, by Nancy Kissinger." Nancy should be glad to get a chance to tell the world, Maxi thought, and breathed deeply for the first time since she'd arranged herself on the bed. She licked the pencil and reflected deeply. She tugged three times at her white streak and slowly wrote "I Was Wrong About Penis Envy: An Unpublished Manuscript, by Sigmund Freud." A little long, that title, Maxi decided, but it did jump off the page at you. Her stomach rumbled. She had never realized how hungry it made you to think. Resisting the urge to go into the kitchen she scribbled "Why You Must Have Lots of Chocolate in Your Daily Diet." Who was head of the space program? She would get him to do it. Or Jane Fonda. Which one was the greatest authority figure? Jane, of course.

She slipped off the bed and started to walk in circles in front of the window, not even noticing the lights of Manhattan spread below as if she were an alien in a spaceship about to land in Central Park. Suddenly she jumped back on the bed and wrote quickly "The Ultimate Love-Hate Relationship: You and Your Hairdresser, by Boy George." She skipped a few lines, groaned a few times and then grabbed the pencil again. "Real Men Never Fantasize About Thin Women, by . . . by . . . Clint Eastwood . . . no, Mel Gibson . . . no, Mikhail Baryshnikov."

"Monthly column," Maxi said out loud. "Monthly column." She messed about with her hair, scratched her ears, tugged at her toes and finally wrote "Let's Talk Sex, by Tom Selleck." She smiled. The same amount of effort that went into thinking up a one-shot article could make a monthly column. It was an economy of effort, she realized, and decided to give it another try to see if it worked. She closed her eyes for a few minutes, poking around in her brain as if it were Santa's big white bag. After a little while she rubbed her eyes vigorously, opened them and carefully inscribed the words "The First Twenty-five Things I Adore About Women Over Thirty, by Warren Beatty." For another issue it could be women over forty, or fifty or twenty-five, with different writers like Richard Gere or Bill Murray or Sam Shepard or Prince or any particularly attractive man. Even if a reader weren't over the age that was under consideration, she could look forward to it or figure that she was prematurely adorable. "The Best Divorce I've Ever Had, by Liz Taylor." No column in that one, unless you added a Gabor another month and, no, it didn't have staying power. Most people didn't get divorced that often. Some people never got divorced even once, like the Queen of England for instance. Maxi wrote quickly "Queen: The Worst job in the World, by Anthony Haden-Guest." She paused, wondering if her readers would know who Haden-Guest was, and decided that they probably wouldn't. She crossed out his name and wrote in its place, "by Prince Philip." She sneezed vigorously. This was a dusty business. "Where Do They Put the Kleenex Box? or What Five Famous Women's Bathrooms Really Look Like

When They've Finished Dressing, a photo essay by Helmut Newton." With amazement she saw that she'd come to the bottom of the page. "Sex in a Moving Vehicle," she scratched on the next page. By John De Lorean. No. By Paul Newman.

"Ma!" The door to her bedroom opened suddenly.

"What is it, Angelica? Can't you see I'm working?"

"Come quick. Lucy's pregnant. Nobody knows who the father is, or what this will do to her career. Hurry or you'll miss it!"

"I can't stop now. Let me know when you find out. And shut the door after you."

"What happened to your compassion?" Angelica looked stunned. Was this the same mother whose only dream had been to be abandoned on a desert island with all the guys on the Hill?

"They're just actors," Maxi replied and wrote "Twenty Good Reasons Not to Have Children" at the top of another page.

Alone again, Maxi stretched cautiously. All her equipment was still surrounding her. She hadn't made a dent in the dummy yet but she had a strange yet familiar feeling in her stomach. This was . . . making these lists was . . . almost exactly, in fact *exactly* exactly like . . . having . . . *FUN*!

She popped off her bed in excitement at the realization and went to her bathroom mirror to take a good look at herself. She needed something familiar to calm her down from discovering that this thing that she had been avoiding even thinking about, this thing she hadn't told Pavka she was utterly terrified of, this actual writing down of ideas that related to her concept of a magazine that liked its readers, in their natural, imperfect state, was possible after all. She looked pale and messy and all her makeup was gone. The mascara had smeared where she'd rubbed her eyes and if she didn't know how pretty she was she'd have been worried.

"The Ten Top Models—What They *Really* Look Like,' " she said out loud. Justin could get those photos. Steal them . . . because no model would let him take a picture like that on purpose. But if he snapped them quickly before the makeup people and hair people went to work, the girls would never notice when they automatically signed the usual release forms. That would make a good start for the beauty pages for the first issue and make millions of women happy. Beauty pages, she mused. Yes, there would be all those departments filling out *B&B*, Beauty and Decorating and Fashion and even Health. Health sounded so institutional . . . why not call it "Living Well: Eating, Drinking and Having Sex" and begin with "The Ten Best Hangover Remedies"? A true public service, that was what it would be. Decorating? She'd make Milton and Leon do a piece on "Think Twice Before You Redecorate," with pages of horrible examples to illustrate the theme, and as for fashion, something soothing. Fashion always tended to make everyone so anxious. "The Ten Indispensable Things Every Woman ALREADY Owns, by Yves Saint-Laurent." With pictures showing how to use them. Maxi tapped her teeth with her pencil as she thought about the pictures.

"Ma, Lucy had a miscarriage," Angelica said sadly, popping her head in through the door. "She must have met a really wrong guy . . . she still won't say who he was."

"Wonderful Mr. Wrong Guy, the Essential Not-to-Be-Missed Fun Experience in Every Woman's Life," said Maxi.

"I don't get it," Angelica said.

"You will, after Don Johnson explains it to you," Maxi assured her.

17

Paper cuts. Nothing helps paper cuts. There is no unguent or pill known to medicine that relieves the tiny but maddeningly painful presence of dozens of paper cuts on every fingertip. Backache. Nothing helps backache except a change of position, exercise and massage, so, if your work requires you to handle many pieces of paper while maintaining a certain back-straining position, you learned to endure backache and paper cuts. Eyestrain. When things got blurry you went to the bathroom and held a cold, wet wash-cloth over your eyelids, put in a few eye drops and returned to the task because the only thing that would remove eyestrain was to stop work, and that wasn't possible. Not until the dummy was gone, because without the dummy *B&B* wouldn't be real.

"I suppose," Maxi said wearily to Angelica who was hovering over her anxiously, "this has built my character." She pushed the dummy aside, got up from her desk and flopped down flat on the carpet of her bedroom.

"You were perfect the way you were," Angelica retorted. She was so accustomed to feeling slightly superior to her screwball of a mother that this new serious incarnation, which of course couldn't possibly last longer than any other of Maxi's fads, was a little frightening. It had all started when she'd canceled that trip to Venice . . . nothing had been the same since. It couldn't possibly last more than another week, she thought. True, Maxi had stuck it out in the Border Country of Scotland for almost two years as Countess of Kirkgordon but this was different; that had been a marriage and this was just a magazine. Angelica shivered, remembering the biting winds of the moors, the drafts at Castle Dread, and then smiled thinking kindly of her loony second stepfather. Had Ma understood he was nuts? Nicely nuts?

"When will it be finished, Ma?"

"What do you mean 'when'? Can't you tell it's finished now?" Maxi asked indignantly. "Why do you suppose I've stopped worrying? Could you please rub my back? Please, *please* rub my back. Walk on it in your bare feet, do something about my back, Angelica, if you love me."

"You're lying on your back. Turn over."

"I can't. I don't have the strength."

"Ma, come on, just roll over."

"I will, in a minute. Angelica, isn't it gorgeous? Don't you think my dummy is fabulous?"

Angelica took a look at the object she had grown to loathe. It didn't look any different from the way it had in her mother's first four attempts at making a dummy. It was hugely fat and bulgy and sloppy and exceptionally uninviting to the eye. Just looking at it, she felt that it would fall apart if she touched it. Obscurely it reminded Angelica of school. She was sure she'd made something very much like it in third grade, only smaller and a great deal more attractive.

"It's awesome, Ma, really awesome. I like the red cover. That's a very nice, bright red, definitely eyecatching."

Maxi rolled over, groaning, and looked squarely at her daughter. "What's wrong with it?" she demanded.

"Nothing's wrong with it, honestly. It's hot, I mean I don't know what a dummy is supposed to look like anyway so I don't have any basis for comparison, but the cover is a great red . . . a humpy red."

Maxi stood up and went over to the desk on which the dummy sat.

"It looks like shit," she said quietly. "A bundle of red shit. And it's the best I can fucking do."

"Ma!"

"I'm sorry, Angelica, but I'm not employing any words you don't know . . . and use, from time to time."

"It's not your language, Ma, it's what you said. You've worked so hard. It's *got* to be good. You couldn't be wrong about it—you're just tired. You're not a fair judge."

"You don't have to be a judge of shit. When you see it you know it. I need help. Specifically I need an art director. Who's the best art director in the world, Angelica?"

"Why ask silly questions that you know the answer to as well as I do?"

"Who can always get your father on the phone, at any time of day or night?"

"Me, but you wouldn't want *me* to ask *him* to help *you*! You've always said you wouldn't ask him for a crust of bread if you were dying of hunger or a sip of water if you were dying of thirst."

"I don't want bread or water. I want the best art director in the world."

"Would you settle for second best . . . please?"

"Angelica, that's unworthy of you."

"Well then, call him and ask him yourself. The two of you always talk on the phone. What's the big deal?"

"We only talk about you, Angelica, and who is going to pick you up, and where and when. We never talk about anything else, not even the weather."

"That's too dumb for words."

"But that's the way it is."

"Well. I don't approve. And I'm late for my guitar lesson. Adults!" Angelica said in disgust and disappeared so quickly that when Maxi went running after her, all she saw were the doors of the elevator closing swiftly and soundlessly on the brown and beige carpet of the corridor.

Maxi marched back to her room, not bothering even to glance into any of the many rooms of her new apartment, each one so expensively appointed by Bizet and Ludwig, each one filled with the collection of furniture and paintings and sculpture she had tracked down all over the world, hundreds of quickly purchased objects that had seemed necessary to her until the minute she owned them. She hadn't used any room of the apartment except her bedroom since she'd started work on the dummy a week ago. She'd had her meals standing up in the kitchen, eating whatever the new cook had seen fit to leave for her in the fridge and returning to work immediately with a quick wave to Angelica if her daughter happened to be home.

Her lips tight—talk about the ingratitude of children!—she dialed the number of Cipriani, Lefkowitz and Kelly. Rocco's secretary told her that Mr. Cipriani was in a meeting with some gentlemen from General Foods and couldn't possibly be disturbed. And after that he was due at Avedon's studio. A Calvin Klein commercial.

"But this is an emergency, Miss Haft," Maxi explained. She was put through immediately.

"What's happened to Angelica?" Rocco demanded, in alarm.

"She's fine. Impossible but fine."

"Then . . . why did you call?" he asked coldly.

"Rocco, I need your help."

"Something *has* happened to Angelica! Damn it, Maxi . . ."

"Rocco, your daughter is in perfect mental and physical health. But I have to have your professional assistance on a business matter and I need it fast. When can you come here? I can't bring it to your office. You'll understand when you see it."

"Maxi, whatever it is you 'have to have,' get it from somebody else."

"No."

"I'm in a meeting. Goodbye."

"Rocco—if you don't come to my house and help me I'm going to . . . to . . . put Angelica on the pill."

"She's only eleven, for Christ's sake!"

"Ah, but soon she'll be twelve and she's awfully mature—you know how precocious she is. Girls are ready for motherhood much earlier these days and with your rampaging Latin blood in her, well, anything might happen. Better safe than sorry. Have you read the latest statistics on teenage pregnancies? I remember when I was her age . . ." Maxi's voice trailed off, full of improvised memories.

"Tonight at nine." Rocco hung up without another word.

Humming happily, Maxi called her masseuse and made an appointment. Hilda would be over within a half hour. Then a long bath—she could wash her hair in the shower and take a nice nap. Why, she wondered, did men make life so difficult for themselves? If they would only always be pleasant and agreeable and helpful. But no, their characters were such that they simply forced you to employ alternative means of persuasion. It went against her better nature not to be direct, but in an emergency you had to use whatever methods were available. Angelica didn't even like boys. It would be another, oh, at least six years before they had to think about the pill. Or perhaps she'd want to remain a virgin until she married. Virginity was coming back in. Maxi picked up her yellow pad and wrote absently, "Try Celibacy and See, by Dan Aykroyd and Chevy Chase."

"It's a *what?*" Rocco said incredulously, staring at the red heap.

"You heard me the first time. I want you to fix it and I want it to be the most beautiful fucking dummy ever made on the face of the earth," Maxi said in a businesslike tone.

"I don't do dummies anymore, Maxi. I believe you're aware of that fact," he said, shaking with rage. This rotten bitch needed a good spanking so badly that it made his teeth ache just thinking about it. To think that he had once married a creature so evil, so low, so utterly vile. So selfish, so self-centered, so . . . to say nothing of using outright blackmail. How Angelica managed to be as lovable, as perfect as she was, coming from a mother like this, was a miracle of the supremacy of his own gene pool. No wonder he'd never even been tempted to marry again. This—this disgrace to her gender would turn any man against marriage for life.

"Why the hell *should* I do it?" he asked. "There are dozens of guys I can recommend who can turn that thing into a dummy. There's no mystery to it."

"Because you'll do a better job," Maxi said inexorably.

"Better by a few degrees, maybe, but what difference does it make? What counts is what's *in* the magazine, not just the dummy. People aren't fooled by a pretty page, they look for content."

"The content is O.K. I didn't ask you for help on the content, only on the presentation."

"Just like that, hm? O.K.? All from your little brain? Would it interest you to know that Time, Inc. has a super high-powered magazine-development group working on new ideas? They've got eighteen top people, including Stolley who founded *People* and Fier from *Rolling Stone* plus seventeen free-lancers and fifteen business types all working like crazy with a budget of over three million a year? Fifty people, headed by Marshall Loeb who made a success of *Money*, the best brains Time could buy. They've already got a finished dummy on something called *Women's Week* and another called *Investor's Weekly*, plus a number of others with covers and boards? What do you say to that?"

"It doesn't bother me. I don't believe in committees. Henry Luce probably didn't believe in committees either, when he was alive. My father didn't believe in committees. Do you have all night to sit around talking shop, Rocco, or do you want to get started on my dummy?" Maxi said evenly. Her ruffled, artfully messed hair remained firmly on her head and Rocco couldn't see her scalp prickling in horror. What if one of Time, Inc.'s brain trust had come up with *her* concept?

"I'm leaving here as soon as I've talked to Angelica about the pill and what taking it too young can do to her."

"Don't bother," Maxi said indignantly. "I'd never let her near it, you ass. You never did know when I was joking, that was your problem. One of the many. Anyway tonight is the night Angelica is allowed to watch MTV and she won't like to be disturbed." She went over to the dummy, picked it up and thrust it into Rocco's arms so quickly that he automatically held on to it.

"Shit!"

"I know, that's why I need you. Sit down, and read it."

"I'll give you three minutes, you lying bitch. And only because Angelica knows I'm here and you'd bad-mouth me if I don't look at this mess. What the hell is *B&B*? That stinks for openers. It's a brand name of an after-dinner drink made by monks, not a magazine name," Rocco puffed, struggling with the floppy mass.

He sat down at Maxi's desk, put the thing on the desktop, and began leafing rapidly through the pages. Maxi held her breath, watching him closely for the sign of any reaction. She had not actually laid eyes on Rocco for over four years. When Angelica was seven she had been quite grown-up enough to be picked up and delivered from Maxi's apartment to Rocco's apartment by one or the other of them, or by Elie, without their having to have the slightest contact. Christ, she thought, the mistakes a girl can make because a man is impossibly beautiful. He looks almost exactly as he did when I first saw him and it just simply couldn't matter less . . . it's as if he were invisible. He has as little appeal as a bottle of gin does to someone who's been in A.A. for twenty years. I wonder when he'll start losing his hair and getting fat? It's inevitable, just a question of time. There must be something fundamentally wrong with him anyway, all those girls he sees, the ones Angelica talks about, and he hasn't managed to settle down. Yet he's thirty-six if he's a day. He'll be a sad, lonely old bachelor soon . . . bad for Angelica because old bachelors die young. Why isn't he reacting? He looked right through the Kissinger article with all those blissfully snooty pictures of Nancy, and didn't even blink, the son of a bitch.

He just doesn't want to give me the satisfaction. Well, I don't give a fart about his opinion . . . *B&B* is for women, not sell-out magazine men who've lowered themselves to make commercials. I'm glad he's successful, for Angelica's sake, but obviously the bugger couldn't possibly enjoy his life, not with that pinched, set look he's got on his face.

Rocco flipped through the dummy, came to the end and slapped his hand down on it, closing it firmly, and pushing it away.

"How much is this going to sell for?"

"Rocco! You mean it has a chance? Oh, Rocco! You'd never have asked me that if you didn't think it was good." Maxi jumped up and down, more relieved than she could have believed possible.

"It has a certain . . . quality. I don't mean it has 'quality,' God knows, I mean there's something catchy about it . . . a reflection of your twisted mind. It might sell a few copies."

"I want it to sell for a dollar fifty."

"You're raving. Much too cheap."

"That's what *People* costs, and everyone buys it."

"Maxi, I really don't like to break this news to you but you're talking about one of the biggest-circulation books in the country and it sits at the supermarket checkout counters at point-of-sale where women just automatically put it into their shopping carts."

"That's where *B&B* will be," Maxi said calmly. "It's meant for the same audience, plus the *Cosmo* audience and the *Good House* audience. *Women*, Rocco, women. There are a lot of women in this country who will buy a magazine that likes them *just the way they are*, a magazine that they can have fun with, a magazine that guarantees a good time."

"Where'd you steal that concept?" Rocco demanded.

"Oh, it just came to me. One day. Out of the blue."

"For a buck fifty you have to have enormous circulation—at least four—no, make that five million, to make money. And ads and more ads. You're living in a dream. You haven't even got a distributor, I'll bet."

"I wouldn't take your money," Maxi said with dignity. "I'm quite aware that it's a crapshoot, but then I like to gamble. I'm not interested in special groups; *Bon Appétit* this isn't . . . I'm going for the mass market and if it doesn't work, well, back to the drawing board."

"Big talk, big talk. Whose money are you going to be losing? Lily's?"

"I don't intend to lose. Now let's stop haggling. I want you to make this dollar-fifty magazine look like a million. You can do it with graphics even if the paper isn't up to *Town & Country* standards, even if the binding is perfected instead of saddled. Think of it as a chance to do your tricks with white space again, to do the things you used to do without General Foods and General Motors getting into your act. Freedom, Rocco. I'm offering you complete artistic freedom! You can be honest again. I'm doing you a favor, Rocco, although you don't seem to realize it. In fact, you might show a little gratitude."

"Bitch!"

"But you can't resist this challenge, can you?"

"Easily. I'll send you a first-class free-lancer. I've got forty major clients to service. What kind of megalomania does it take for you to think that I have time to diddle around with the dummy of a new magazine—it's a *huge* job."

"No, I want you."

"You still think you can have everything you want, don't you? It's really extraordinary, it's almost admirable, to be so stuck in the past, like the survival of some prehistoric animal, still breathing even though it's up to its ears in ooze."

"Have it your way," Maxi sighed. "Just send me somebody really good. Oh, and Rocco, before you go, I have some brochures to show you."

"Brochures? What about?"

"Swiss boarding schools. There are about a half-dozen good ones. It's time Angelica went away to school. It's not just for the French and the skiing. She's subject to all sorts of bad influences in the city. I don't have to tell you that they sell pot and LSD and angel dust in the playgrounds. And the kids she knows are too hip. She really should be in Switzerland. You can see her in the summer—when she is not at camp—even go over for Christmas, if you miss her."

"You . . . you . . ." He was wordless with rage. He'd kill the creature.

"Oh, I *am* pleased that you changed your mind," Maxi said, cooing. "When can I expect the finished product?"

"In three shakes of a lamb's tail," he said, between his clenched teeth.

"What exactly does that mean? A week? Two weeks?"

"I'll show you," Rocco screamed and grabbed her, turned her upside down on her bed and smacked her as hard as he could on her bottom. "*One*," he shouted, "and *two*." He hit her again. "And *three*!"

"Coward," Maxi panted, and tried to punch him in the balls. He grunted and hit her again, falling on the bed from her strong blow which had landed on one knee. Maxi grabbed his hair and pulled it as viciously as she could while he tried to gain a purchase on the mattress to give her a shaking that would break her spine. She slithered away just before his hands could close on her shoulders, did a sort of semi-jackknife and grabbed his penis firmly in both hands. He went totally immobile. God knew what she might do, starting with emasculation. Neither of them moved a muscle, waiting in a silence broken only by their breathing, for the next move. The silence grew longer and, to his utter disgust, Rocco felt his penis hardening in Maxi's unrelenting grip. Harder and harder. There was nothing on earth he could do to stop the damn thing from reacting. He tried mightily to pull away but she had him too tightly. After half a minute it became slightly less important to get out of her hands, and as soon as she felt the change in him she used one of her hands to unzip his fly while, with the other, her grip changed from that of a prison warden to that of a woman, opening and closing her fingers around him in a rhythm he'd never been able to resist.

"Bitch," he grunted.

"Shut up," she replied, and began to caress his penis with delicate feathery strokes, while she cuddled his balls with the hand that had unzipped his fly. He attacked his belt buckle and pushed his trousers and tight jockey shorts down below his knees to give her more room to move in, but Maxi concentrated her attention on his penis, never straying away to touch the rest of his body. She didn't intend to give him an instant to think. A penis, as every woman knows, has no brain. It was jerking strongly as it grew bigger, almost twitching away from her while she lapped it with her tongue until she heard his unwilling groan of pleasure. She dragged her tongue slowly up from the base of his penis, pausing every now and then as if wondering whether to go further, putting her entire open mouth around his shaft as far as it would go, sucking hard for just an instant, and then resumed her leisurely progress toward the full, pronounced and tender line at the base of the tip. There she paused and made her tongue into a hot little arrow that circled the swelling head, but she didn't take it into her mouth. He'd have to ask for it, she thought, as she slid out of her underwear without his noticing her rapid movement beneath her skirt.

"Please," she heard him breathe, "*please.*" At his words, she raised herself slightly and lowered her mouth down on the enormous head of his penis, first just holding it and exploring the hot pulsing shape with the whole of the inside of her lips and her now-flattened tongue. He pushed his hips up from the mattress in strong demanding movements and at that well-remembered signal Maxi began to suck with all the power she had, maddened now by the need to possess this flesh, to own it, to draw it into herself. From a distance she heard his breath coming faster and faster. At that she pulled her mouth away but still held his penis. With a quick move she slid upward on the bed, and put one knee on each side of his body. Quickly she lowered herself down onto him, so that he was totally enfolded in her wet, waiting nest. Savagely intent, she rode him, raising and lowering her pelvis, eluding his grasping hands that tried to slow her down, moving faster and faster, giving it to him, giving it to him good, caught up in a relentless rhythm as she felt her own orgasm growing with each thrust she made, with each time she plunged down onto his body and her clitoris came into contact with the base of his penis, rubbing quickly and deeply before she rose up again. Madly they moved in unison, until their backs tensed, arched, held still for a tiny instant and then, bodies remembering, came together in a wildness, a long, drawn-out, shaking, heaving burst of magnificent release.

Maxi collapsed on top of Rocco. His eyes were closed and he had gone completely limp. She mustered up the force to roll off his body. Both of them still had their shoes on, she noticed in part of her mind, as well as all their clothes except for her panties. His lips moved but she couldn't hear what he had said. She pulled herself up closer and his lips moved again.

"Grudge fuck," he croaked.

"Mercy hump," she hissed, and pushed him with the little energy she had left, so that he almost fell off the edge of the bed. Weaving, he managed to get to his feet. With difficulty he pushed his shirt into his trousers and zipped them and stumbled around, disoriented.

"You forgot the dummy," Maxi murmured. He picked it up wordlessly and stumbled toward the door.

"How many ad pages can I count on from CL&K?" she called as he fumbled for the doorknob.

"God help me," he muttered and tried to slam the door after him, with no success.

Maxi lay on the bed and rolled her eyes at the ceiling. Every man has a weak point, she thought, and it was the same one with all of them. If you understood that simple fact, you could beat the odds every time. What's more, she had discovered the cure for paper cuts.

18

"Cut. And . . . print!" The director's valedictory tone marked the final second, the final take of India West's latest picture.

She almost ran to her dressing room, radiant with liberty and the unprecedented fact that her shrink, Dr. Florence Florsheim, was on vacation at the same time as the picture wrapped. This conjunction of events hadn't happened in the years since she'd become a star. She was at liberty to rush to the aid of Maxi whose last phone call had been so disturbing. There must be something seriously wrong. Maxi hadn't called in two weeks and since that Sunday, whenever India tried to telephone her the only person she could reach was Angelica who had developed an interesting talent of lying convincingly. "Ma's working and absolutely can't be disturbed," she'd said each time, and if India didn't have a profound knowledge of her friend's character she would have believed the child. Well, it was probably hereditary, that talent for lying. Angelica was as believable as Maxi herself.

But whatever sinister mystery was going on "back East" as she found herself saying, in the same way the English stuck for life in some Indian garrison town used to say "home" when they meant Britain, India intended to find out about it at first hand. Tomorrow she was flying to New York, her bags were packed, the beastly dogs were in a kennel that charged only a little less than the Beverly Hills Hotel, and by evening she'd know what was up with her oldest and her only best friend.

Maxi couldn't have been serious about that absurd plan she had to publish a magazine about . . . zippers? Her story had been hard to follow, interrupted as it had been by bouts of self-recrimination and violent outbursts against her wretched uncle. Except for Lily, who was so often photographed, it was hard to visualize Maxi's family, India thought. She'd caught glimpses of Toby and Justin a few brief times all those years ago when she and Maxi were both teenagers doing their homework together. After Maxi's first marriage, her contact with the Amberville family had been maintained purely through what her friend told her. If Maxi hadn't visited from time to time during these last six years in California they would scarcely have laid eyes on each other since Maxi's first divorce, when India was in the process of leaving Manhattan for her freshman year at college. She had managed to catch up with Maxi and to spend a few days on board the yacht when her friend had decided to take on heavenly Bad Dennis Brady, in Monte Carlo, but she'd missed the miserable Scottish years entirely. A shame about that; the Countess of Kirkgordon must have been a priceless, not-to-be-forgotten piece of miscasting.

Now Maxi *was* her family, India reflected. Her own parents were dead, but Maxi had remained the one fixed point in her life. Even though ninety-nine percent of their contact was by phone, they could read each other's minds through the receivers. What's more, she was Angelica's godmother, and made up for her lack of physical attendance by sending her marvelous presents. You wouldn't think a nice little girl would lie like that to her own darling, lovable, gift-sending godmother, would you? She'd have to have a long talk with the youngster about Emerson and the importance of the truth. With Maxi for a mother there was no way of knowing what bad habits she might have fallen into, India told herself with a dubious shake of her head. She'd straighten the kid out. Give her the benefit of some of Doctor Florsheim's insights, buy her some decent sheets.

Maxi was having a Rolodex housewarming. Everyone listed in her Rolodex had been invited, and had accepted. Working through one morning with Julie, neither of them off the phone for a minute, out of sheer *joie de vivre* at the thought of her precious dummy being transformed by Rocco, she had put the party together in the way she liked best. "Parties should just pop up out of nowhere, for the same night," she said to Julie. "If you give people time to plan what they're going to wear and get their hair done and wonder who else will be there, you take the bloom off the rose. And if they've made other plans, they can always bring their friends with them. It's like a marvelous surprise package."

It was a zoo, a very choice zoo for only the best species. Gazelles, peacocks, antlered stags, superb panthers, sleek seals, self-satisfied lions and, here and there, a delicate monkey. Manhattan animals all, the decibel level of their voices reaching a pitch that no group in any major city of the world could, or would desire, to produce.

The front door was left wide open because the doorbell could not be heard inside. India, followed by the elevator man carrying her luggage, paused on the threshold, bewildered. She started to turn around and leave. Obviously this was no time for a surprise visit. She'd go to the suite the studio kept at the Palace and call tomorrow. Parties made her more horribly shy than usual.

"Godmother!" Angelica, as reverently as possible, lifted her six inches off the floor and looked at her, stunned. "It's you! You yourself, in person. Totally awesome! Ma tried to call but you weren't home. How did you know about the party?"

"You . . . are . . . Angelica?"

"I know, I've grown. I'll put you down. I didn't hurt you, did I?"

"Of course not. You just—surprised—me. Now, listen here, Angelica, you told me your mother couldn't be disturbed because she was working and I walk in on a madhouse. What's going on?"

"She *was* working, Godmother, until last night. Macabre! Now she's relaxing."

"And why do you have three holes punched in each of your ears, Angelica? And why are you wearing feather-tufted studs in them? Have you joined a religious cult?" India asked as severely as possible in the face of the consternation Angelica's unexpected beauty caused. Had she any idea of what she would become?

"I went for it, Godmother," Angelica explained. "Do you think it was a mistake? I feel like a freakazoid, to tell you the truth. But do you like my to-die-for denims? Hot, huh? I think they were made in a leper colony somewhere. Macabre!"

"I can relate to them," India said carefully, reaching as far back as she could into the seventies for a suitable response. "The holes in your ears will grow back together if you take the studs out and could you please stop calling me Godmother?"

"If you insist," Angelica agreed, a little crestfallen. "I'll take your bags to the guest bedroom . . . India." Angelica lifted them easily and began to lead the way into the apartment.

"No. Stop. I couldn't possibly stay here. It's jammed," India said, ready to flee.

"The bottom line, India, is that I will clear the guest room out for you in five seconds. You're the guest of honor. Could you be totally into that?"

"Do you always talk this way, Angelica?"

"I try. I try," Angelica said, picking up India's luggage and clearing a pathway for her.

That child needs help, India thought, as she quickly changed her clothes in the locked guest room. It was lucky she had come. It might not be too late. Obviously Maxi had neglected her education. India wafted out of the room, wearing a dress of white lace and white chiffon from Judyth van Amringe that floated so lightly that it seemed to be held together only by her brooch, an antique Greek coin set in cabochon sapphires and emeralds, which she'd pinned just above one hipbone. Her beauty was a creature of seasons, lacking only a winter; a changeable, endlessly mesmerizing parade as she flowed from the embodiment of bewitching spring to full summer to ripe autumn, depending on the demands of the director or the script. Today, left to her own decision, she was springtime in all its promise, all its freshness.

Shy as she was, India was realistic. There was no way to find clothes that would make her disappear at parties so she might just as well look like a star. People expected it and essentially it aroused less attention than did the tatty, ratty, why-should-I-bother-to-dress-for-*you*, Diane Keaton look that just made people curious and hostile. Nor, in a year in which clothes glittered, would she give in to it, because anything that sparkled made her feel like an Oscar presenter and she was, after all, an Oscar winner.

India went in search of Maxi, moving with a deliberate drift, a technique she'd perfected for parties, designed to keep her in motion at all times. If stopped, she still suggested constant movement by the way she leaned away from the person who talked to her. She never carried a glass so that if she found herself stuck in conversation she could say, "Oh, I must find a drink, I'll be right back," and disengage herself. Or she could ask the man she was talking to—women never seemed to want to say anything to her—to be an angel and get her a drink and then escape in another direction. If India actually wanted a drink she went to the bar, got it from the bartender, drank it straight down and gave the glass back immediately.

India always looked into the air above people so that they couldn't catch her eye, zigzagged slightly as she drifted, so that she presented a moving target, and wore an expression that instantly conveyed that she was intent on joining someone she knew terribly well on the other side of the room. This combination enabled her to attend the necessary Hollywood parties without actually having to speak to anyone except the agents from Creative Artists who were everywhere and who ignored her act and tended to hug her a lot. As a client, she didn't intimidate them, for how could they be intimidated by any woman, no matter how fabled a beauty, when that beauty was theirs to sell and her income was automatically reduced by their commission?

Actually, India thought, as she drifted, hoping that she was insulated by her mannerisms, she never felt shy with her agents or the men who were physically involved in the making of movies. They knew she was just another girl, once they'd graduated from apprenticeship and reached the stage of second assistant to a second assistant to someone or other. Doctor Florence Florsheim said that there was no difference between being an elusive motion-picture star and a plain, everyday wallflower, India thought, fighting the beginning of panic.

"What was the worst thing that could happen if you did get involved in a conversation?" Dr. Florsheim always wanted to know. India couldn't explain to her own satisfaction. Her mind blanked out at the conversation itself. It *was* the worst thing. Something about the way she looked stopped conversation dead, leaving the burden of human exchange on her incurably reluctant shoulders. The best thing about Dr. Florsheim was that she never looked at India, except when she came in and when she left the office, and she never permitted small talk.

Maintaining her seemingly purposeful course, but picking up speed, India went from room to room, panic mounting as Maxi didn't appear. Soon she'd have to start looking at people instead of above them, and that meant the risk of catching someone's eye.

"I'm *sorry*!" She had bumped directly into a man, causing him to spill the two glasses he was holding all over his suit. "My God, I'm clumsy, I wasn't looking, let me help mop up, oh dear," she babbled, blushing with confusion.

"It's just vodka, don't worry. No harm done," he reassured her, and there was something in the resonance of his voice, something that she caught at his first words that utterly dissolved her panic. He would probably be in control of the situation if *he'd* spilled the drinks on *her*, she thought, amazed at his ability to calm her down. Only a few film directors had ever been able to do that with so few words, and they had been the great ones.

"You seem to be looking for somebody," he remarked. "Can I help?"

"No," India heard herself answering. "I was just wandering around." Maxi could wait, she decided, daring to actually look at the man she'd just drenched. He was almost a head taller than she was, probably in his early thirties, and as he stood there calmly, ignoring his wet jacket, she found herself wondering what he'd look like if he were in love. A passing waiter took away the two glasses he was still holding. She grabbed a handful of cocktail napkins. "Couldn't I just . . . you're dripping on the carpet," she laughed, making a tentative swabbing motion. He took the napkins out of her hand and held them.

"Vodka evaporates and doesn't leave a stain. There's enough body heat in this room to make it disappear in a minute." The words were simple enough but there was a meditative expression on his face, as if, somehow, he were dreaming and as if the dream were one of gallantry. So fascinated that she forgot her habitual fear of anyone unknown, India found herself looking at him as particularly inquisitive and tactless people sometimes looked at her, as if they could learn something just from the way her features connected with each other. There's a courtliness to him, she thought, something to do with being kind and firm and confident, something about his mouth, formed for . . . no, *by* bravery. And an impatience at the same time. There was a kind of impact of . . . was it concentration? He was, somehow, electrokinetic. She hoped he wouldn't go away to whomever he had been bringing the drinks, but he seemed disinclined to move. They stood together in the middle of the restlessly busy room, an island of two tall, isolated people. She peered into his eyes and it seemed to her that he was looking at her urgently, with intensity, yet with no sign of recognition, of the deference or bedazzlement she was resigned to seeing.

"I like your voice," he said.

"Thank you." For the first time in her life she didn't feel that she had to apologize for a compliment. His confidence seemed to be contagious.

"It makes love to the air," he added.

"Well, you know that there's always the chance that perhaps it's just a trick," she answered, using, in a sudden, unexpected rush of her old sense of mischief, the accent she had learned to play Blanche DuBois, slurring her pronouns with a kind of breathless, giddy emphasis on the verbs, ending the sentence with her voice vaguely going up at the end of the phrase.

He smiled as if she were deliciously, childishly silly, and India felt ridiculously proud of herself.

"A plantation voice," he said, "I've always liked a girl with a plantation voice, but it's not precisely suitable to you. You're too timid to be Southern . . . that's their charm . . . they never let their shyness show so they don't arouse it in others."

"And mine shows?" she asked, downcast: She'd always believed that she hadn't been really good as Blanche, even if everybody said she had been.

"Instantly. To me, anyway. But I like that too. To be timid at times is universal to the human race, but in this city people become aggressive just so that their natural, normal, inevitable shyness won't be revealed. The result"—he gestured—"is what you hear. It's tiring to listen to, and hard to combat. Half the time I whisper . . . you can be heard more easily under the noise than above it."

"I had a coach once who told me that."

"A coach?" He bent toward her and peered at her even more closely.

"A . . . vocal coach," she said, bewildered.

"Are you a singer?"

"I've been known to sing," India answered, utterly astonished. It had been so many years since she had met someone who didn't know who she was that she hardly knew how to treat this fact. Her eyes sharpened with sudden suspicion. Oh Lord, let him not be one of those people who pretended not to recognize her. They were worse than gawkers. No, whatever he was he simply wasn't a moviegoer or a magazine reader. In his household she obviously wasn't a household word.

'What else do you do?" he asked, giving her no time to ask about him. He had a habit of command, she realized as she replied.

"I . . . work . . . and, well, you know, live, like everybody else. I feed my dogs and go to exercise class and read a lot and swim and, well, go to a few parties, and that's about it. I guess that doesn't sound like a very full life . . . oh, and I go to my shrink, of course, Doctor Florence Florsheim . . . stop laughing! I don't see what's so funny about that, it's a name like any other, she can't help it though . . . with Florence for a first name perhaps she shouldn't have . . . married Mr. Florsheim." India was reduced to a puddle of giggles. "She must have been madly in love, or maybe it's her maiden name."

"Did you ever ask her?" he wanted to know.

"She rarely answers questions. She's very orthodox about that anyway."

"My shrink answers questions."

"Then he's not a Freudian," she pronounced with a superior air.

"He told me that, like every other shrink, he stood on Freud's shoulders, but he'd thrown away the stuff he didn't believe in . . . if you say you hate your mother he assumes that your old lady was a tough number, until proven otherwise, not that you wanted to make love to her when you were three."

"I like the sound of that. But I'm stuck with Doctor Florsheim . . . she knows too much," India said darkly.

"Other people's shrinks always sound better than your own. It's the first rule of analysis. However, I agree about your life, it doesn't seem exactly full. What about a husband and children?"

"Nonexistent. And you?"

"Never married, no kids."

"Aren't you interested or haven't you had the time?" India inquired cautiously.

There had to be something wrong. There always was.

"It's just never happened yet, but it will. Meanwhile I'm available, shamelessly available, and I'd like to get out of this hellhole and take you to dinner. Shall we go?"

"Oh, *yes*," India replied.

"*India! What* are you doing here?" Maxi asked, so surprised that she squeaked.

"Hello, darling. I'll tell you later. I have to go out to dinner now," India said ruthlessly, trying in one glance to convey love, support, and the absolute necessity of Maxi's letting her escape the party with this man, this heavenly, heavenly man, before another second passed and someone—perhaps the person he'd been getting the drinks for—appeared and tried to get him away from her, because she would not, could not run that risk.

"But Toby, you just can't disappear with India like that," Maxi wailed, outraged. "She is *my* friend, damn it, not yours, and nobody ever even told me she was here."

"Toby?" India whispered in a voice of wonder that held both shock and the beginning of choice.

"India? *That* friend? The one who's the most beautiful girl in the world?" Toby stopped dead, a complex set of emotions appearing on his face, hesitation first among them.

"Oh, shut up!" India said, timid no longer. "You said you *liked* me four times. So don't act like a . . . dumbbell. Anyway, it's too late now, isn't it?"

"My, my," Maxi cooed, "I think the two of you are going to have your first fight. Oh, good! Can I listen?"

19

Cutter Amberville seemed intent on retracing his exact path, as if he were putting his feet into footprints he'd made on a wet and sandy beach, as he walked back and forth on the carpet that lay in front of the window behind his desk. His hands were clasped tightly together behind his back, his knuckles cutting off the circulation to his fingertips so that they were much redder than his fingers. Maxi watched him as he walked, perched on the arm of the chair she had chosen, refusing the low chair he had offered. Instead, taking her time, she had picked out a chair with a reasonably wide arm, and pulled it to precisely the spot she intended to be in, at a distance too far away from his desk for his comfort.

She swung her legs, clad in high shining riding boots and brown velvet jodhpurs laced from boot-top to knee. She caressed the frilled neck of the Victorian lace blouse she wore under a brown velvet, shawl-collared jacket, nipped in at the waist, a Chantal Thomass fantasy that was never meant to come near the saddle of a horse.

"Cutter," she said, breaking his fuming silence, "my driver is double-parked downstairs. Would you disgorge whatever you seemed so anxious to see me about, so that he doesn't get a ticket?"

Cutter turned and finally stopped his pacing, leaning with both hands on the top of his enormous desk.

"I can see that I underestimated you, Maxi," he said.

"Couldn't you have told me that on the phone? I'm a busy woman, and this trip downtown has fouled up my morning. Time is money, Cutter, time is money!"

Weeks had passed since Rocco had finished the miraculous dummy, dozens of expensive people were on Maxi's payroll, the work of completing the first issue and laying out those to follow was going on at top speed, all propelled by Maxi's flood of energy, working seven days out of seven.

Not only was the door to her office always open, the room did not, by her instructions, even have a door, nor did Maxi have a desk. There was a big table in the middle of her office covered with cases of cold soft drinks and urns of coffee, tea and Sanka which were always kept full by the cateress Maxi had hired for that task; a woman who kept platters piled with cookies and brownies and made stacks of thick, delicious sandwiches that were constantly replenished. A number of high, round tables surrounded the feast, with bar stools invitingly placed about them. The tables could easily be pushed together when the group around them grew larger. Her office was as close to the kind of eighteenth-century coffeehouse in which Samuel Johnson would have felt at home as Maxi could devise, and the result was the one she had planned for: everyone on her brilliant, young, constantly growing, highly paid staff wandered in at least once or twice a day, knowing that they were permanently welcome and would be royally fed. They tended to hang around and talk about *B&B*, people from all departments getting to know each other; and from this constant rubbing together of the best talent in the magazine business, from these excited "why the hell not?" conversations, came a steady stream of new ideas for the magazine, not one of which was ever lost, for Maxi noted them all down, unobtrusively perched on one or another of the stools. When she was busy elsewhere, or on the phone, one of her rotating staff of three secretaries replaced her. The only reason that Maxi had agreed to come down to Cutter's office was that she wouldn't let him see her own. He'd contaminate it.

"I never would have believed you had it in you," Cutter continued. "No, not even you."

"But you haven't even seen the first layouts," Maxi answered, annoyed. Could someone have leaked him pages? Did he have a spy planted on her staff?

"I'm not talking about your magazine, Maxi, whatever it may be." Cutter looked her full in the face and she realized that he was flushed, almost crimson, with suppressed rage. He pushed a pile of paper across the desk to her.

"These are what I'm talking about, *these*! Bills for millions of dollars, bills that those damn fool accountants have been paying automatically, because they were signed for by an Amberville, paying without asking me, without questioning them, bills for paper, for rent, for furnishings, for salaries, for photos, for articles, for expenses, for . . ."

"Food," Maxi interrupted. "Start-up money is always more than you expect," Maxi added with composure. "It won't be as expensive once *B&B* is actually out and, naturally, as soon as we start making money the whole picture will change."

"No, don't play that game with me, Maxi. I know, and you know that I know, what we agreed on. *Buttons and Bows!* That was the magazine you wanted and that was the one you got. A trimming magazine with almost no budget at all. This thing, this *B&B*, whatever it is, has absolutely nothing to do with the deal we made."

"Not so," Maxi said coolly. "It's as much *Buttons and Bows* as *Buttons and Bows* was *Trimming Trades Monthly*. It even says so on the masthead. You never said I couldn't update the magazine, Cutter. You didn't utter a word about not changing it into something more viable. You gave me a year and I'm taking my year, and that year has barely begun."

"*I never gave you the right to spend millions*," Cutter said violently, hitting the desk with his fists.

"I hope that desk isn't valuable," Maxi commented with a tiny yawn. "It looks authentic, but then they make such good copies these days."

"*Millions of dollars* . . . I never said . . ."

"Ah, but you didn't say I couldn't, did you, Cutter?" Maxi smiled lazily at him, and readjusted the lace at her neck, preening, and then flicked a spot of dust off one of her boots. Her eyebrows rose in amusement until they were hidden by her bangs. "It's too late now, you see. I've already—and in person—sold six months of advertising, at very special introductory rates, to dozens of major advertisers. They also all advertise in the other Amberville publications, and, naturally, they have every reason to believe that when an Amberville comes to them with a splendid concept for a new magazine and an absolutely smashing dummy, they're spending their money safely. Amberville Publications is *committed* to *B&B*, Cutter, totally committed as far as the advertising and business community is concerned. As long as the magazine is being published we *have* to run those ads, or else give them their money back and look, at the very least, frivolous, unbusinesslike. Especially since you just took it upon yourself to fold three other books. They all know that *B&B* has your special blessing, Cutter. I've made sure they realized that. You can't *touch* my magazine without making everyone suspect that the entire company is about to go under."

"Do you have any idea what the money you spent is going to do to our balance sheet?" he demanded.

"Punch a giant hole in it, I imagine. And, Cutter," Maxi said, rising and moving toward the door, "about those bills, it's only fair to tell you, because your blood pressure looks dangerously high to me, the bills on your desk are only the beginning. I've gone way out on a big, long, lovely limb for the first six months—you have to spend money to make it, and I can't risk disappointing my readers. 'First catch them, then keep them,' as my father used to say." Maxi reached the door and held it open while Cutter sat immobilized by sheer rage behind his desk. "Another thing, I've taken a series of ads in all the major magazines and newspapers that are read by media people, telling them about *B&B* and our plans for the future, an introduction to the newest Amberville Publication as it were. You should be getting those bills very soon. Don't bother to get up—I'll see myself out . . . as usual." She went through the door and half-closed it behind her. Then she turned, cast a glance at him, looked closer, shook her head and made a little tut-tut sound of concern. "Goodness gracious, Cutter, you *do* look upset." She shut the door softly but not until she'd asked, "Was it something I said?"

"Lily, love, come and sit closer to me," Cutter said, patting the space at his side on the couch. Obediently, Lily left her chair and took the offered place, her pliant, slender body curving into his side.

She sighed in a satisfaction almost deeper than love. These moments together, when he came home from his office, these long-awaited moments were, she often reflected, the reward for her years of patience. Even more of a reward than physical passion, although the endurance of that unquenchable, living connection of their two bodies was her great pride. The years that had separated them had left the embers of a fire that needed only a breath of wind, another match, a twist of paper and a bit of wood, to make it flame into hot life. But to be able to sit together at the end of a day and talk quietly, as she had never totally enjoyed doing with Zachary . . . ah, that was the even more delicious joy. It was at moments like this, when the easy comfort of their long-sought, so-long-delayed intimacy, was combined with the new happiness of being married to Cutter, that she knew that she finally had what she had always wanted, had always *deserved*.

"Darling, something happened today at the office that suddenly made me think about you, about the future of our life together," Cutter said.

Alarmed at the gravity of his tone, Lily lifted her head from his shoulder abruptly.

"No, no," he laughed, "nothing to worry about. Something to dream about, something that I would never have initiated on my own, but still, a piece of business I can't not tell you about."

"Business?" Lily asked. "You promised that we wouldn't waste our time together talking business. I've never understood it and when Zachary used to drone on and on, I'd get a headache just from having to sit and listen."

"It is business, and yet, in a way, it isn't. Not boring business. You have to listen, darling."

"All business is boring," Lily said willfully, "but I'm the patient sort, as you should know."

"I had an extraordinary phone call today from a man at the United Broadcasting Company, a perfect stranger to me. He wanted to know if there was any possibility of your meeting with him to discuss . . . to talk about an eventual sale of Amberville Publications."

"What! But he's mad! Who on earth does he think he is? *What utter nerve.* What makes him think the company's for sale? I just can't imagine anyone rude enough to make a call like that out of the blue," Lily said, stung into indignation, as if her jewelry had been stolen while she looked on helplessly.

Cutter laughed indulgently. "That man from UBC's not trying to take advantage of you, my darling. He's just doing his job. It's not some sort of attack. In fact, it's an enormous compliment. All I have to do is to call him tomorrow and say you're not interested, that Amberville Publications isn't for sale. And he'll go away, or maybe he won't. But one way or another you can expect to get more and more calls like that."

"Because Zachary's dead?"

"Even if Zachary were alive, it wouldn't make any difference. He'd be getting the same queries. It's the trend of the times. Lots of companies, particularly major conglomerates, are all out looking for magazines to buy."

"Well, I'm not interested. Why should I be? Anyway, I only own seventy percent of the stock. You know the children have ten percent each."

"They can't sell their stock except to you and you're the majority stockholder. You can do absolutely anything you want, Lily. They can't stop you. When I explained why we had to stop publication of those magazines that were losing money, I thought you understood."

"I did. You convinced me that it was necessary. But selling . . . I never thought of selling. Zachary spent his whole life building the magazines . . . he never sold one. I don't know if he ever would have, under any circumstances, for any amount of money."

"Oh, Lily, you can't stop being loyal, can you? Have you ever thought of the many ways you were sacrificed to those magazines? *You*, Lily? All that business talk that bored you so, all those business trips when you were left alone, all the times you had to cope with the children and their problems by yourself because Zachary was working, the endless weekends he spent shut up in his office, all that business entertaining and being charming to people who didn't interest you? Those magazines were built on *your life*, Lily. Years and years of the only life you'll ever have. And now you're still thinking about what Zachary would do with them if he were still alive. *He is not.* There's no one who's in charge whom you can trust but me. Would you put your shares in the hands of Pavka? He's an old man; brilliant, yes, but old. He'll retire soon, I imagine. And the rest of the editorial board? Could you rely on them to keep the magazines afloat? They're just employees, creative employees, I grant you, but not managers. Zachary was a manager, but he never built a second rank of managers to replace himself."

"I hadn't really thought . . ."

"I know you hadn't, darling. I've been keeping things going so that you wouldn't have anything to worry about. I left Booker, Smity and Jameston and opened my own office just to keep your affairs in order. Still in my heart of hearts I'm not at all convinced that the magazine business is necessarily the one you should be in."

"Is there something going on, something I don't know? Some reason why I should sell?" Lily sat up very straight at the faintly ominous tone of his voice.

"Lily, the magazines are all doing well . . . at the moment . . . but the reality of 1985 publishing economics will include great increases in paper costs and much higher distribution expenses. That doesn't have to mean that we'll make less money next year than we did this year, but it makes it a damn sight more difficult. Right now our profit-and-loss statement, our balance sheet, is still perfectly healthy. I can't begin to imagine how much money you could get tomorrow for Amberville Publications—a great deal. However, in a few years . . . who knows? I don't have a crystal ball, and I hate like hell to see you chained to something that doesn't even interest you, even if Maxi is infatuated by it to the point of . . ."

"Maxi?" Lily questioned. "What's she up to now?"

"Nothing for you to worry about—a little of her usual overenthusiasm. I'll manage Maxi, darling, so that she doesn't get burnt. Of course, if you sold, the children would all be able to realize their inheritances."

"But what about you, Cutter? Are you trying to say that *you* don't want to be in the magazine business? That you wished you hadn't left Booker?"

"If it's what you need, my love, then I'm more than willing to stick it out. I never wanted to join Zachary, you know that. He suggested it a dozen times but I always refused. However, since that phone call from UBC today, coming out of the blue, I've been asking myself if it weren't some kind of sign, some kind of . . . turning point . . . something to which we should pay attention."

"Sign? Sign of what?"

"A new life. A life for us together, without being tied down to worrying every month about page rate increases and the rising cost of pension plans and the million and one other details involved in Amberville Publications. You *could* sell, darling, if you wanted to. And then we'd both be free. There wouldn't be anything in the entire world you couldn't do. You could have your own ballet company . . . no? . . . we could spend the best months of the year in England, we could buy the most wonderful house in the South of France, we could start to become *serious* collectors of everything you love. Oh, Lily, there's got to be more to life than my sitting in an office in New York, able to be with you only after a long day's work is done. But it's not my stock, it's not my company, it's for you to decide if you're even interested in the possibility. That's why I had to talk to you about that phone call. Business, 'boring' business, if you will, but I could hardly keep it a secret."

"No, no, you couldn't," Lily said slowly.

"Think about it, darling, or don't think about it. It's entirely up to you. You've given as much of your blood and your heart to Amberville Publications as anyone possibly could, and perhaps you should keep on that way. I only want to see you happy."

"I will think about it. I promise. It's not something . . . I could decide about right away . . . is it? No, of course not."

"It's important to take all the time you need, Lily. It's a very serious step," Cutter answered, and rose to make himself another gin and tonic.

Amberville Publications, he thought, Amberville Publications, that enormous creation of his hated brother, would soon be just another item on the balance sheet of a giant conglomerate; its identity lost, its key employees scattered, its real estate sold, and, most important, Zachary Amberville himself quickly forgotten, with the disappearance of his name. Within a matter of years it would only evoke a nod of recognition from a few people with long memories. *Thank God he was still young enough to wipe out Amberville Publications*, to fling it to the winds, to rid himself of its hold, to be free of his brother at last, to destroy what was left of him. As for UBC, he'd call its president tomorrow and make a lunch date, find out if they really were in the market. There were dozens of potential suitors out there. That much was absolutely true. He had foreseen this day when he'd shut down publication of all the magazines that were losing money. All except one.

"You know, Justin, it isn't easy being fashion editor of a magazine that exists to tell women that they're just fine the way they are. Fashion is what hasn't been seen *before*, damnation. Fashion pages should make you itch to buy."

Julie spoke rebelliously but her voice was like a slightly electrified love song. Her infatuation with Justin had reached the point where she could list each separate and virtually identical piece of clothes he wore, she could even tell each of his three Nikons apart. She knew when he'd cut his nails. Every detail of the man was under her constant but imperceptible scrutiny and the very fact that her emotions seemed to be unreciprocated made them more profound. If Justin had shown a lively interest there would have had to be a progression, for better or worse, in their relationship. She would have been miserable, or in some stage of happiness. But in the weeks they'd worked together he treated her with a pleasant and maddeningly *un-fraught* mixture of friendliness and working cooperation that Julie Jacobson of Shaker Heights, who had never, since first grade, failed to get her man, no longer regarded as a challenge. It had become a painful longing for some sign that they might have a future.

"Do you wish you were on a conventional magazine?" Justin asked idly. "Do you regret not taking that job at *Redbook*?"

"Never. But this idea . . . I mean after all, imagine a whole fashion feature that tells about why you should never, ever throw away your favorite bathing suit? How am I going to explain that to Cole and Gottex and O. M. O. Kamali and all the other bathing suit manufacturers who've given us ads?"

"Explain Maxi's theory—that when a woman feels good about herself, after she's read an issue of *B&B*, she's got to react to their advertising in a positive way, even if the editorial material doesn't make the reader believe that she has to rush out and spend money just to survive the weekend."

"Do you believe that? Or is it just Maxi?"

"As a matter of fact, I do too. Basic, acquisitive human nature will take care of the shopping instinct and *B&B* will put women in the right mood to pay attention to the advertising."

Justin surveyed his studio, the first he'd ever had, with well-hidden consternation. He'd always shot on location before, traveling light with just a couple of duffel bags and camera cases, but in order to turn out the work Maxi asked of him for *B&B* he'd rented a studio with all the infinite variety of equipment it contained, and hired the necessary assistants to answer the phone, work in the darkroom, and help him with lights and props. Of course it was all paid for by *B&B* but it was the first time in his life that he'd had the impression of being attached to a particular place of work. It made him uneasy and restless, but since he'd taken a proprietary interest in the success of *B&B*, he couldn't just disappear again until he was sure that Maxi had managed to get the magazine off the ground and running smoothly. Or until it turned out to be a failure. And either possibility, he thought, was still very alive. He was used to Maxi's new projects, he'd observed the frenetic pace of her life, the ceaseless search for something that was more fun than the last thing, and he was far from convinced that she had the staying power to do more than launch a magazine. She'd probably be sick of the thing in six months.

No one, he often thought, understood her better than he did, for he was like her. He too had never found whatever it was that could tempt him to settle down and stick around. He too was an impermanent person with few long-lasting attachments. He had loved his father deeply and his death had been a tragedy to Justin. He would always miss Zachary Amberville, yet they had rarely had intimate conversations. Justin had avoided them and Zachary, understanding, hadn't sought them out, hadn't forced them on him. There had been a mutual but unspoken understanding between the two of them that Justin's desire for privacy must be respected.

On the other hand, he thought grimly, his mother seemed to have been after his soul from the day he was born. "Justin, come here and talk to me." Every day when he'd come home from school he'd heard her irresistibly lovely voice, so grave, so poignant, calling to him from her sitting room. There hadn't been any choice but to go in and give her the kiss she reached up for and let her smooth his hair and try, without squirming, to give satisfactory answers to all the questions she persisted in asking him. "How was the math test, Justin? Weren't you cold in just that sweater? Why didn't you take your coat? Who's your best friend this year? And who's your second best? What about that new boy who moved from Chicago? Do you like him? When do you have to turn in your English paper? If you need any help you can always show it to me, you know that, don't you?" Her constantly probing, gentle, devoted, poetic voice, wanting to know everything he did, everything he thought.

He had never told her that he didn't have a best friend, or a second-best friend, or really any friends he cared about at all because that would only have led to more questions, to concern, to trying to do something about it, when he wanted only to be left in peace to try to deal with his fears of growing up, to learn to live with the idea that there was no one he could count on to solve his problems except himself. Yet he had never refused to lend his presence, never had the heart to turn his back on his mother because he sensed keenly how deeply needy she was, how somehow bereaved, like a young widow, in spite of her beauty and her jewels and her never-ending social life. In her devotion to him Lily was, he knew without words, really begging that he take care of her. And he had done his best.

Only when he'd discovered the martial arts and started taking lessons, had he managed to spend the late afternoons free of the burden of the maternal emotion that his mother hadn't shown his sister; a kind of emotion that seemed tinged, even tainted, by a feeling he couldn't quite define but had learned to hate in spite of his love for her. Almost a kind of . . . worship. It was because he was the youngest child, he had decided. Maxi had been in constant trouble with their mother and Toby had been so independent, so special, in spite of his slowly approaching blindness, that perhaps he had been the only one left for her to lavish her feelings on . . . but still he, Justin, had had to bear the particular burden of that special child, the *favorite*.

As soon as he knew clearly that *B&B* was either a failure or a success, he'd be off again, to someplace he'd never been before, resuming the only role in which he'd learned to feel comfortable: that of the inconspicuous observer, a part of every scene, the quiet outsider who nevertheless, because of his camera, was at home everywhere. And nowhere.

"Justin," Julie cried, holding up a flowered bikini that could only have been made in the late 1950s, "do you *believe* this? And it's still in such perfect shape that it probably never even hit the water."

"Maybe most favorite bathing suits don't," he said, shrugging.

"That's what Maxi says. 'If a woman ever finds a suit that really flatters her, that hides what she wants to hide and shows off what she wants to show off, she won't get it wet unless she's forced to, and even if she gets too fat to wear it, she'll keep it somewhere, with the idea that eventually she'll fit into it again,' " Julie quoted. "Maxi is just encouraging magical thinking, if you ask me," Julie added in disapproval.

"Whatever you think, love, we've still got those dozen old suits to shoot. How many models did you book?"

"Three girls and two dozen boys."

"You're mad. Why so many boys?"

"That was Maxi's idea too. Each girl is going to have a big bunch of assorted guys around her, darting flattering looks," Julie said tartly. She hadn't had time to go wholesale for an entire week, thanks to the hunt for ancient bathing suits.

"What are you putting the boys into?"

"I have four dozen identical—objects—from Ralph Lauren Bodywear in a million different colors. Identical but not exactly old-fashioned. I don't know if they're bathing suits or underwear but they don't waste fabric, do they?" Julie held up just enough of a garment to cover a man's pelvis and give him something to put his legs through. "Bellybutton City. It's a disgrace. We're encouraging women not to buy new suits and men are allowed to parade around all but naked."

"Where are we going to put that mob?"

"The girls get the dressing room to themselves—what with the hairdressers and makeup people they need all that space—the boys will just have to use your office, Justin. This studio isn't big enough."

"How often do you book twenty-seven models at the same time?" he asked reasonably.

"This is a first, but I still think you should find someplace with a second dressing room."

"I probably will," said Justin, knowing he wouldn't. He had chosen the studio precisely because it demanded improvisation. This interior space set aside exclusively for his work made him nervous. The smaller it was the better, the less likely to seem to be a commitment or an announcement that he had come to stay. This place was only rented on a month-to-month basis, although Maxi had given him a free hand. His own office contained little more than a desk, a chair, a phone and a couch where he could flop and relax after a session was over.

The girls all arrived at once and Justin looked them over critically. Julie had booked them for the neutrality of their good looks. They were beautiful but not too beautiful. Their hair was new—no Farrah Fawcett flowing manes—but not so short as to be alarming, and the two makeup men had been instructed not to try anything outrageously different with their faces. "No pink eyelids and no blue lipsticks," Julie had ordered. "We're not trying to sell any one of those awful new looks in cosmetics. We're trying for your average American woman if she knew how to put on basic makeup."

The three girls passed his inspection and as the two dozen anonymously handsome male models started to arrive, while the girls were being made ready, he busied himself with his cameras. Like many photographers, he never let his assistant touch the cameras before a shoot, and only permitted him to reload film while he was working. Soon the first girl was ready, and for the next half hour Justin, Julie and the models all worked steadily, yet without managing to achieve the certain rhythm that would make each girl, surrounded by a dozen almost unclad men, look perfectly at ease.

"Wet them down, Julie," Justin finally said.

"Why?"

"They're still too stiff. Bathing suits indoors look posed and that's no good. There are some buckets in the darkroom. Boys, some of you go and fill the buckets with water and we'll try it that way."

"Are we going to get *wet*?" one of the girls asked in disbelief. "Nobody at the agency said anything about water. I'm going to call my booker."

"Relax, I'm just wetting down the boys," Justin said curtly. He wished he were back on some unknown street in some unknown city, free to take a picture or not, instead of here with twenty-seven of the most expensive-per-hour bodies in the United States, each refusing to flow naturally, the way real people did in real surroundings. The Ganges, that's where he could shoot them. In fact it would be a pleasure to push them all in and hold them under for a while. Meanwhile he'd have to make do.

The water did the trick. It loosened them up as nothing else could have, turned them all into kids again, dumping buckets of water on each other and on themselves in a competition to get wetter than anyone else, creating the illusion of a swimming pool or beach that no amount of props could have achieved.

Jon, a male model with shaggy dark red hair and a grin full of animal vitality, was the ringleader. It was he who threw the first bucket of water on one of the female models. "Don't you dare!" she shrieked, and received another bucket of water over her head. After that it became a free-for-all, the two dozen boys and three girls awash, forgetting the camera totally, the hairdressers standing by shaking their heads but not discontented, since they could still be paid their usual seven hundred and fifty dollars an hour. Julie, at a nod from Justin, pulled out each dripping girl when he'd finished a shot and took her to change her suit, not an easy job on a wet body. She should have booked a dozen girls or at least brought towels, she thought, but who had anticipated a water fight?

Finally the sitting was over, all the wet suits were collected, the girls had been blotted with paper towels and dried down by the blow dryers and everyone including the assistants had been sent home. Julie looked wearily around the studio, pleased with what she knew would be an exciting set of pictures.

"Don't worry. I'll get it cleaned up tomorrow. Go on home, Julie," Justin said gently.

"I should stay, but . . ."

"Don't be silly, you're beat. Out, love, out."

Finally alone, pushing aside sheets of wet and dirty paper, Justin put his cameras away carefully. He opened the closed door of his office, wondering what kind of shambles the boys had left it in.

"You took your sweet time, Justin. I thought you were lost." Jon, his red hair still slightly damp, sat behind the desk, his bad-boy grin appearing as he saw Justin enter. He looked as much at ease behind the desk as if it belonged to him.

"Couldn't you find your clothes?" Justin asked quietly, his composed tone belying his stance, the posture of a man trained and ready to defend himself.

"They're exactly where I left them when I came in."

"Do you enjoy sitting around in a wet bathing suit?" he said sharply.

"I'm not. I took it off." Jon smiled again and stretched, as lazily as a big jungle cat.

"You can't be comfortable," Justin said, his expression tightly vigilant. "And that happens to be my chair."

"I'd be more comfortable on the couch, as a matter of fact," Jon answered, but made no move to stand up.

"I'm sure you would be," Justin said, as if decoding the statement with his deepest concentration. "But what makes you think that I want you there?"

"Justin," Jon mocked him, half reproachfully, "do you think I don't know what you want? Do you think I don't know how much you want me? On the couch or on the floor or anywhere you can have me? Do you think I don't know what you wish you could do to me, what I need—and intend—to do to you? Do you think I'm stupid?"

"Just what gave you that idea about me?" Justin asked, the menace with which he always moved more in evidence than ever, without his having to take a step in any direction.

"Nothing you said, nothing about the way you look, or walk or talk. Nothing 'gave' me that idea . . . I know it. I have very good instincts."

"Do you? Are you really sure? Or aren't you just trying it on for size? Something you pull with any photographer on the off-chance that you'll be right? And that there'll be something in it for you?"

"I don't want anything, Justin, except the same thing you're aching for. I love it, just as much as you do, only, unlike you, I'm not afraid to ask. I've been hurting for you since I walked in here . . . it wasn't easy not letting it show in that bathing suit. I'm so hard now, Justin, I'm as hard as I've ever been before, and *so are you.* I can see just how much you want me all the way from behind this desk. So come here and stop playing games. Come, give it to me, Justin. Any way that makes you happy. Any way, anything—I can take it all."

Wordlessly, Justin moved toward Jon, wordlessly and willingly.

20

"The trouble with you, Maxime, is that you're too impulsive," Lily said, her opal eyes narrowing as she inspected her daughter with her familiar air of withheld criticism.

"Mother, I know I have a history of recklessness and I'm not proud of it, I promise you, but *B&B* is something absolutely different. It's not fair of you to assume that this is just another toy until you've seen how I mean to make it work. Look, I've brought you the dummy of the first issue so that you can see for yourself." Eagerly, Maxi held the dummy out to Lily.

"No, Maxime, I can't judge anything from looking at that. I've never been a clever judge of magazines, particularly new ones. Even your father had to admit that, try as he would. Put it back in your attaché case, dear, so you don't forget it here when you leave."

"Please, Mother, just take a quick look. It might make you laugh," Maxi pleaded. Somehow she had to *reach* Lily. Since her return from Europe they had barely seen each other. Maxi had been too busy to meet her mother for the occasional lunch and ballet matinee that had, over the years, developed as the easiest and least abrasive way of maintaining their relationship. Today, however, she'd had to make time to accept her mother's unmistakable summons to come for tea, the one resolutely British ritual that Lily had maintained since she'd arrived in Manhattan more than thirty years ago.

"I'd prefer not to, dear. Of course I'll read it when it's properly printed, but until then I'd rather wait. I'm hoping for a pleasant surprise. The reason I asked you to interrupt your work today, Maxime, is that I've been giving some thought to Amberville Publications recently and I was curious to find out just how much money is being spent on this sudden whim of yours . . . this notion that you have turned into a publisher, or an editor, or whatever it is you think you are."

"Do you mean Cutter hasn't told you?" Maxi asked, astonished. It had been several days since her interview with Cutter in his office and she had assumed that he would have told her mother the whole story.

"No. As a matter of fact he was very vague about it. It seemed to me that he was avoiding the subject. That's precisely what made me wonder what was going on, wonder if there weren't something in the air—something between you—that I should know about."

"In the air? You mean am I having a problem with Cutter? Is that what you mean?"

"Precisely," Lily answered, pouring Maxi another cup of tea.

"We're having a bit of a hassle, Mother. He thinks that I'm spending too much money and I *know* that I can't spend a penny less and hope to have a success. If I stop now all the start-up money will be a total loss. It's either do it right or not at all and I haven't been able to make him understand that. Father would have known exactly what I'm doing. It's only fair to say that I haven't been exactly tactful with

Cutter—in fact, not tactful at all—but Mother, he's just *not* a magazine person, he's got a Wall Street balance sheet mentality. That's natural considering that he's always been an investment banker but it makes a reasonable conversation impossible with him. If Father . . ."

"Maxime, your father is dead. Your problem with Cutter stems from your personal resentment of him, an illogical grudging resistance that's made me very unhappy, a problem that doesn't come from any lack of knowledge or interest on his part."

"Mother, it's not that at all . . ."

"Just one minute, Maxime. Let me finish. I've tried to understand your deep . . . antagonism . . . toward Cutter. I know that anyone at all who presumed to come into my life after your father died would have aroused those primitive feelings in you. You always were a daddy's girl and you'll never get over it." An old, familiar bitterness had crept into Lily's voice, into that voice she kept under such delicate control; the voice that told Maxi that her mother was entitled to everything she wanted without having to even ask for it.

"You don't appreciate what Cutter means to me," Lily continued, "or, if by some miracle you do, you don't care. I'm fifty years old, Maxime, and in January I'll be fifty-one. I'm sure you think that I'm too old to be concerned with my emotions. What must fifty seem to you, at twenty-nine, with most of your life ahead of you and a past that wasn't exactly uneventful? At twenty-nine what can you even guess of my feelings?"

"For God's sake, Mother, fifty isn't old! And I'm not stupid enough to think that you don't have a heart and a body. Give me some credit at least. Maybe fifty sounded old to you when you were my age, but times have changed." Maxi put her cup of tea down in such agitation that Lily flinched when the porcelain hit the table.

"Times have changed, but only in principle. Human nature remains the same," Lily continued relentlessly. "And it's human nature to classify your own mother as a bloodless antique. It's inescapable, although, heaven knows, you've tried to avoid it with Angelica and so far you've succeeded. You're so breathtakingly unpredictable that she just participates in your life and you take that for granted—she's the tail to your comet. But one day she'll classify you too, Maxime, mark my words."

"How did Angelica get into this conversation?" Maxi, said, deeply annoyed. "I thought you wanted to talk about the money I'm spending on *B&B*."

"One day, Maxime, you'll know what it feels like to be young forever in the trap of a body that grows older no matter what you do to preserve it," Lily continued as if Maxi hadn't answered her. "I look at the models in the fashion magazines and I think, ah, yes, *now*—but in twenty years those photographs will be *unendurable.* To *have been* beautiful is a life sentence, not a blessing. To have been *anything* wonderful that you've lost . . ."

"Mother, you're getting morbid. You are beautiful, you were beautiful, you will always be beautiful. What does it have to do with this tea party?"

"I should have known it was hopeless." Lily sighed and ran her hands over her smooth, heavy chignon. "I've been trying to explain something about Cutter and me, but your insensitivity, as usual, makes it difficult. Well, Maxime, how much is this whole magazine business costing?"

"I can't give you a final figure, not yet. Because it will cost one amount if it works and a very different amount if it doesn't."

"Then just tell me how much you've spent so far."

"Somewhere close to five million dollars has been committed, over the next six months."

"Is that a normal amount of money to spend before you know the results of your venture?"

"Absolutely. In fact it's on the low side. Take Mort Zuckerman for example. He's poured eight million into *The Atlantic* and doesn't expect to see a profit for more than a year, and then there's Gannett's enormous investment in *USA Today*, even with that terrific Cathie Black publishing it, and the fortune it took to make *Self* work . . ."

"Spare me, Maxime. I can't endure it when you talk numbers like that. You sound like a parrot of your father but at least he knew what he was doing. So you've spent five million dollars since you came back from Europe, five million dollars of Amberville Publications' money."

"Yes, Mother, I have. Five million and I wouldn't try to pretend that I've finished yet. You won't regret it, I promise." If Lily had been studying Maxi's face she would have recognized Zachary's expression of eager resolution.

"You promise." Lily shrugged her shoulders with a movement almost too faint for irony. "Well then, I won't worry about it anymore. Can I give you another cup of tea?"

"No thanks, Mother. I really have to get back to the office."

"I understand, dear. Give Angelica my love. If she's free next week I have ballet tickets on Saturday afternoon."

"I'm sure she'd love it." Maxi kissed Lily goodbye. It was no good. It had never been any good. The trouble with you, Maxime, is that you're insensitive, that you don't appreciate Cutter, that you are a daddy's girl, that you want me to care about your work. The trouble with you, Maxime, is you expect too much from your mother.

As Lily rang for the maid to take away the tea tray she thought how wise she had been to have had this interview with Maxime. Her daughter was running true to form. Five million spent and nothing but a dummy to show for it. Lily might not like to talk business but she knew that if Maxi admitted that she'd not finished spending money yet there was no telling how much could be lost. A dangerous toy in the hands of a thoughtless extravagant child, who'd never had to make a penny in her life. Five million dollars thrown out of the window in a matter of a few months. There was no point in getting upset about it, not when Cutter assured her that the balance sheet was still healthy. It was merely a confirmation, if she had actually needed one, that with Zachary dead, the Amberville family should get out of the magazine business.

It wasn't merely the loss of money, Lily thought, as she walked upstairs to her dressing room, it was the wear and tear on Cutter. It had been typically unselfish of him not to have told her the dismaying details of Maxime's spending spree. He must have been wild with anger, and yet he hadn't wanted to disturb her with the maddening account of her daughter's pretensions. He was consideration itself, almost to a fault. He should have told her. Maxi running berserk as publisher of a magazine, indeed! She scanned her closets critically. How she missed darling Mainbocher. And just who, she asked herself, could tell what Toby and Justin, much as she loved them, would decide to do in the future? Together they owned thirty percent of the Amberville stock. No, thank you, she didn't want her children for partners. She might not know much about business, Lily thought with the shrewd, self-centered practicality she had always managed to hide from everyone including herself, but she knew that much.

"Get away from here," the man behind the pushcart snarled at Angelica.

"How come you're selling leather whips?" she asked him curiously.

"Never mind, kid, just beat it." Sadomasochistic paraphernalia would never move if brats hung around. This tall one with all that long hair would drive away trade. "Here," he said, and gave her a dollar. "Go buy yourself a hot dog."

"Thanks." Angelica walked away to the Sabrett man directly in front of the entrance to the residential section of Trump Tower. She'd have to bring her gang, the Trump Tower Troops, to visit the pushcart tomorrow. A free hot dog each? Why not? As she ate her hot dog she inspected the various pushcarts on Fifth Avenue. Wallets, belts, scarves, jewelry, all made halfway across the world and laid out on the once-immaculate sidewalk in front of the finest retail stores in the world. The Troops had never seen Fifth Avenue in the days of its glory. That roving gang, who varied from eleven to fifteen members, were the only children who lived in the building, and to them the street vendors were a constant source of amusement and interest, part of their world, a natural counterpoint to their multimillion-dollar apartments.

The Troops knew everything about Trump Tower. They knew how to get through the concealed security booth, manned twenty-four hours a day, which led from the dignified, small, luxurious, basically beige lobby of their building into the vast, six-story-high, pink marble atrium of the building's retail arcade where a truly marvelous waterfall ran by magic and there was always someone in a tailcoat playing the grand piano in the entrance. Tired New Yorkers gratefully entered to sit down for a while, listen to the familiar songs and perhaps eat a sandwich while in one of the many wildly expensive boutiques only a few floors above them, four-thousand-dollar nightgowns were being sold to women from many lands. The Troops knew every store, they knew about the floor where the live-in maids' rooms were located, they knew the beautiful blond Mrs. Trump and had persuaded her to let them visit the garden of her triplex which covered the entire top of the Tower and was planted with full-grown trees.

Angelica was the leader of the gang because she was American and had the biggest apartment, an "L" combined with an "H." Most of the others were foreign and their apartments were only considered *pieds-à-terre* by their parents who were forever on the move from one capital city to another. However today Angelica wasn't in the mood to seek out any of her cronies. She was worried about her mother, and she wasn't exactly sure why.

For one thing, she mused, as she bought another hot dog with her own money, Maxi was getting so bizarrely organized. She'd found a cook who actually showed every sign of staying on the job since Maxi now left her detailed lists of everything that was to be done in the course of each day and had provided her with a cleaning woman to do the heavy work. Maxi—who had never planned anything—had started to plan meals a week ahead so that the shopping could be done efficiently. As a result Angelica was certain that they had the only cook in Trump Tower who didn't just telephone Gristede's but actually picked out the produce herself on Lexington Avenue. Where were the last-minute phone calls to the places that delivered? Angelica wondered. She remembered years of odd and ethnic improvised feasts, or former careless, carefree meals, often eaten right out of the cartons in which the food had been delivered. Her kind of eating.

And it wasn't just the fact that she and her mother sat down to dinner together at night. Maxi had actually begun to supervise Angelica's homework. Not to understand it necessarily, for today's math naturally was beyond Ma, like yesterday's math, but to make sure that it got done on time. What's more, she had started to take an interest in Angelica's wardrobe instead of letting her wear whatever she wanted to, charging it at any of the stores in town as she had been in the habit of doing since she was ten. "Appropriate clothes," she'd said just the other day, "aren't necessarily all bad." Now what kind of macabre statement was that for Ma to make?

And then there was the matter of her love life. Ma didn't seem to have any and she didn't seem to care. Could she be in menopause? Angelica considered Maxi's age and decided that twenty-nine was probably too young. But as long as she could remember there had been a man in Ma's life, one right after another, and sometimes, Angelica suspected, two at the same time. Humpy guys as older men went. But *B&B* left her no time for anyone, humpy or not. When she wasn't at the office or with Angelica she spent every evening working with Justin or Julie or one or another of the people from the office, or, astonishingly, often alone, actually alone, in her own bedroom bent over a yellow legal pad, occasionally letting out great hoots of laughter, at her own wit, Angelica supposed, since the television wasn't on. Was this what people meant by obsession? And wasn't obsession supposed to be bad for you?

Yet she couldn't see any signs that Maxi was beginning to fall apart, Angelica ruminated. It was just the opposite; she was getting it all together, going for it, totally going for it, and that was the worst part of all, because a Ma who was going for it wasn't as much fun as a cute, crazy Ma who had to be *supervised.* A grown-up Ma with a whole bunch of grown-up ideas about how to do things wasn't what Angelica had bargained for. Ma was changing, that was for sure, and Angelica didn't like it. No. Not one little bit. Because, if Ma was the grown-up in this family, what did that make her?

No Cipriani in memory had ever bitten through his own bottom lip, Rocco suddenly realized and made himself ease up on the painful grip of his upper jaw.

"Obviously I've avoided the classic mistake," Maxi said, attacking her codfish gumbo in its incendiary sauce as if it were as bland as mashed potatoes.

"Which classic mistake?" Rocco asked, wondering why he had let her talk him into having dinner. He supposed it was curiosity. After all the work he'd put into the dummy, after he'd found her Brick Greenfield, a stunningly good young art director, to carry on where he'd blazed the trail, he felt a reluctant interest in the future of *B&B*, but Maxi's insouciance was turning his temper as hot as the Creole cuisine of Chez Leonie whose smiling Haitian proprietor had taken them under her wing and ordered for them.

Rocco had already heard, from entirely too many people, how Maxi had visited most of the major advertisers in person, using his—*his*—dummy as her calling card, and talked them into taking space in her magazine, using every bit of guile she possessed, every ounce of wile and winsomeness, all of her Amberville credentials. Even he had to admit that the basic concept of *B&B* could sound logical when presented by Maxi at her most devious, if you had no previous experience with her. If she were a stranger, for example, and you could be conned into thinking that a reader-friendly magazine was what you needed to round out the kind of totally balanced media buy that a top agency like Cipriani, Lefkowitz and Kelly would provide with the help of a highly trained team of people whose whole life was media buying. If you happened to be some damn foolish horse's ass of a national advertiser and some ditsy girl who called herself a publisher and acted as her own ad manager as well came along, bypassed your rightful ad agency, and sweet-talked you into making commitments you'd never have made in your right mind.

"Rocco, why are you doing that with your teeth? You're drawing blood, or is it only this red sauce?" Maxi offered him her napkin in concern.

"Put that away, I've got my own napkin, damn it! I think I bit right through a giant hot pepper. Hell!"

"I warned you to be careful." Maxi looked around Chez Leonie, a First Avenue restaurant only big enough to hold six tables but full of an atmosphere she loved: old records of old Caribbean melodies being played on an old phonograph somewhere in the back; candelabras everywhere, dripping wax as if it were a Cocteau movie; the softest, almost yellow walls on which Leonie's family photographs were hung here and there. It made Maxi feel as if she'd gone on an Island holiday. Obviously Rocco had become so Madison Avenue that he didn't understand the poetry of this place. And that from a man who used to live on hot peppers. Sad.

"Which classic mistake?" Rocco asked again, his dignity restored.

"Of not understanding that I have two customers for each copy: the reader and the advertiser. You can't get the ads without the readers and you can't get readers without ads, because they're suspicious of a thin magazine. That's why I practically *gave* away the advertising space for the first six months. Well, I didn't give it entirely, but it is much, *much* cheaper than it should be. Absurdly cheap. The first issue is going to be nice and heavy and reassuring, like a great plump chicken. My reader will be able to just heft it and know that at a dollar fifty she's getting a bargain. Rocco, leave some room for the main course."

"Isn't this it?"

"Wait," said Maxi with a particularly provoking smile, her beauty spot riding above the perfect bow of her upper lip in a way that made Rocco feel the impulse to give her a good slap and see what would happen.

"There's only one problem you don't seem to think you have all figured out," he said, "and that's how to get your magazine distributed. You can have the world's most beautiful book, with every other page a four-color ad, and you still have to scare up those millions of readers you've been assuming you'll get. And if people can't find *B&B* how can they buy it?"

"Rocco, did you ever hear of a man named Joe Shore?"

"Nope."

Maxi sighed. "He was a wonderful old man but he's been dead for, oh, fifteen years I guess. I used to go to the track with him right up to the end. He let me have as many hot dogs as I could eat. He died the way he would have wanted to, in his box at Belmont Park, with a winner. Of course he'd only bet two dollars, but still he'd won."

"Maxi, what are you talking about?"

"Uncle Joe, Uncle Barney's father. Well, naturally I've never lost touch with Uncle Barney. He was awfully upset when I divorced Laddie Kirkgordon . . . he loved my being a countess. He and his wife came to visit us at Castle Dread and they had a wonderful time."

"Uncle Barney? J. Bernard Shore? The head of Crescent?" Rocco waved away the enormous platter of braised pork ribs, chicken, yellow rice and roast duck. "*Crescent*?" His voice cracked.

"Well of course, Crescent. You have to have a national distributor, Rocco," Maxi explained with sweet patience.

"I'm fully aware of that, Maxi," Rocco said carefully. She *was* trying to kill him. Creole food and aggravation, red hot peppers and deliberate malice. He wondered if he had an ulcer yet or was he just getting one now? Crescent was the most important national distributor in the United States. Naturally Amberville Publications was an important account for them, but as for *B&B*, they'd just laugh. Or should, if they had any sense.

"Anyway, I went to see Uncle Barney and told him my problem. He knows that I've always been able to pick a winner, ever since I was three, and so I signed a contract with him. Of course they get their usual ten percent of the cover price, he couldn't do anything to lower that, but he did put me onto the Front Line Rack. *Rocco*! Leonie! Come quick, I think he's choking. My God, Leonie, were there fishbones in that gumbo? Rocco, put your arms above your head, no, Leonie, don't hit him on the back, Rocco, do you want the Hug of Life? The Heimlich maneuver? Oh, make up your mind! Run your fingers across your throat if you can't breathe . . . oh, you're O.K. . . . Christ . . . you frightened me. I'll never bring you here again, so help me. Leonie, could I have some of your Haitian cognac, please? I feel faint."

"The Front Line Rack?" Rocco whispered, gasping between each word. "Are you sure that's what he said?"

"Absolutely. He said he'd make the space if he had to build bigger racks himself."

"How much?"

"Well, that's another problem. I have to pay the retailer directly for that. About five dollars every three weeks. Per store, I mean. Surely you don't think that the supermarkets put magazines at the checkout counter out of charity, Rocco? Is that how *People* and the *National Inquirer* and *Cosmo* get up front where you can't miss them? After all, business is business," Maxi said briskly, recovering from the shock of Rocco's choking fit by eating his portion of chili-flavored ribs as well as her own.

"You're going to lose a fucking fortune!" he roared.

"Rocco, will you keep your voice down—or at least moderate your language? Maybe I will lose a fortune but my eyes are open and I'm betting on me. And so is Uncle Barney . . . he's acting as my banker for the Front Line Racks for a year. I picked an Exacta for him once. The only time it ever happened in his whole life . . . and I was only three, couldn't even read. Oh, Rocco, for heaven's sake, have some of my cognac . . . I'm worried about you. Have you thought of having a checkup? I know a good internist who specializes in nervous advertising men, as if there were any other kind."

It was a solemn group that descended from the plane at the airport in Lynchburg, Virginia, on the day that the first issue of *B&B* was to go to press, printed at the gigantic Meredith/Burda plant located outside of Lynchburg. On arrival, they separated into two groups because one rental car wasn't big enough to hold all seven of them. Justin, who had come along to lend Maxi moral support, drove the first car, with Maxi beside him and Julie and Brick Greenfield in the back. The second car was driven by Allenby Winston Montgomery, the managing editor suggested by

Pavka. His long, gloomy face was set in its normal expression of someone who, with resignation, dignity and patience, is mounting the steps of the guillotine, but his personality had changed a little on the day that Maxi decided that "Monty" suited him better as a nickname than "General." He had actually smiled at her once, and although he hadn't smiled since, he seemed, to those who observed him, quite likely to smile again before the year was out. He was accompanied by Angelica, who had refused to let Maxi get on the plane without her, school or no school, and by Harper O'Malley from Editorial Control, whose job it would be, every month, to stay at the printing plant during the entire printing process, inspecting copies as they came off the presses and making sure that they were being printed correctly, and, if not, making immediate changes.

Maxi clutched the precious bundle of First Color Proofs on which she, Brick Greenfield and Monty had made their final corrections, after the two preliminary sets of "Blues" and Second Color Proofs had already undergone the process of correction and been returned to Meredith/Burda. Maxi's eyes didn't register the Virginia countryside as she tried to remember when she had last felt the same set of emotions that she was now enduring, and which she would have scorned to call fear if she honestly could.

Yes, she had it now. It had happened before, about three days before Angelica's birth. She and Rocco had gone to a movie and suddenly, during the film, she had been overcome by the knowledge that the baby inside her, the baby she had blithely carried for almost nine months, had no exit from her body except one. This unspeakably absolute fact, which somehow she had managed to ignore until that moment, had struck her with such force that she had only one thought: how to get out of it. There must be, there simply had to be some way to *avoid* having the baby. But as she looked at her enormous lap, even Maxi had had to bow to a certain incontrovertible logic. There was no way around the fear. She had to go through with it. The pile of proofs that lay on her lap now had to go to press just as Angelica had had to come into the world. She relaxed slightly and patted the proofs lovingly. Whatever their future, she had given them the best she could give.

Except to Harper O'Malley and Brick Greenfield, who had been to the plant when they had worked for other magazines, the sheer size of Meredith/Burda was enough to inspire awe if not downright terror. Inside the plant the gigantic automated presses snaked around the vast room, five stories high, where a few of the top printers waited to greet them. The noise, drowning, deafening, almost unimaginable, made conversation impossible, but they all shook hands and mimed greetings as Maxi handed over the proofs. It was like being trapped inside of Chaplin's *Modern Times*, she thought, with *Star Wars* improvements. Computers blinked here and there, constantly checking the yellows, reds and blues of the inks, and the little group from *B&B* waited, huddled together, tense and unsmiling, for the first copy to come off the press. In spite of automation and computers, there was still the need, there would always be the need, of a human eye to scan each page and make sure that the page looked as it had been intended to look. When the first copy appeared they all crowded around and flipped through it.

Except for Angelica and Justin, they each thought that they knew exactly what to expect, for they had gone over every word and picture many hundreds of times, but it was a totally different experience to see the magazine bound and trimmed, between covers, than it had been to see it in segments and double spreads; almost as different, Maxi thought, as the mound she'd seen in her lap at the movies and the baby she'd seen in the delivery room. Almost but not quite.

After she, Monty, O'Malley and Greenfield had each given their final approval, the first run of *B&B* started to come off the press, bound by huge machines into big bales tied in plastic strips and conveyed on belts to an outside loading dock where a great fleet of trucks was standing ready. Within four days of distribution there would be copies of the new magazine on every major newsstand and in every major supermarket and drugstore chain in the United States.

Maxi, followed by the others, walked out to the loading dock to watch the first trucks leave. Monty shattered the sudden silence as, with a note in his voice that almost broke, he said, "Well, there they go." Suddenly he smiled as if watching a flock of baby birds taking their first flight. Maxi sighed deeply and Angelica, who was standing next to her, turned and lifted her a few inches off the dock, gave her a crushing hug and a kiss on each cheek.

"Hey, Ma," she said, "what's going on? You're crying!"

21

Maxi prowled around the Eastern newsstand in the Pan Am Building. It is one of the largest and best stocked in Manhattan since many hundreds of thousands of people pass it every morning and evening, looking for something to read. It is located at one of the key intersections of New York, a building that must be crossed or entered to get to a hundred different places, including the subway and Grand Central Station. Every publisher, from Newhouse to Annenberg, from Forbes to Hearst, has its representatives checking out the sales situation at the Eastern newsstand a dozen times a day whenever the new issue of its magazine goes on sale. Experts with searching eyes circle the newsstand, people who can calculate the number of copies left in a stack and, returning in an hour, recount and know immediately whether the cover photo or blurbs have pulled a big audience or bombed out, or performed as usual.

It had been four full days since *B&B* hit the loading dock in Virginia and Maxi had forced herself to wait till this evening before going to the Eastern newsstand. She had refused to let anybody from the office go with her. This was not a communal effort as putting together the first issue had been. This was a solitary affair. Playing roulette was something you did in a group but when you went to cash in your winning chips or else rose nonchalantly from your chair after you'd lost everything, it was better to do it without company or fanfare.

Slowly circling, she moved in closer and closer, at first confused by the sheer abundance of magazines and the hurly-burly of customers around the newsstand, but little by little the scene came into close focus. Uncle Barney had told Meredith/Burda how many copies to send to each of the local wholesalers in different parts of the United States. Normally the wholesalers decided how many to send to each retailer, on the basis of past experience. In the case of *B&B*, since the magazine was brand-new, Uncle Barney himself had indicated the numbers he thought should be distributed. A newsstand doesn't have the same few choice checkout positions as a supermarket, but it will inevitably group the fastest-selling magazines together so that customers don't have to hunt for them. To give *B&B* a fighting chance it was supposed to be stacked—for this month only, since even Uncle Barney, with all his power, could do no more—next to *Cosmo*. *Cosmo* sold ninety-two percent of its copies as individual newsstand or supermarket purchases and just being next to it would give *B&B* a special opportunity to be noticed by women.

Maxi located the stacks of *Cosmo*, which had come out a few days earlier, and realized that they were half-depleted compared to the still-high stacks of most of the other women's magazines. She inched closer, peering anxiously right and left, but nowhere could she spot the screaming red cover of *B&B* that Rocco had chosen because it was precisely the color of a stop sign, the one color everyone had to pause and notice except the color-blind. And she damn well wasn't color-blind, Maxi thought. Could the magazine not have been delivered yet? That seemed impossible. Four days was the period in which every single city and bus stop in the country was supposed to have its copies. The Eastern newsstand had unquestionably had them as soon as, or sooner than, anyone else.

Was it possible, she asked herself, that the newsstand boss had left the bundles of *B&B* unopened, so busy with his sure-to-sell merchandise that he hadn't bothered to unstrip the new bales? Monty, in his infinite wisdom, had told her a dozen horror stories like that: when it happened, for whatever reason, you were dead. Dead. Stone-cold dead in the water. No matter how carefully you had planned every detail in the entire publishing business it all depended, in the end, on that special unknown person who opened the bale of magazines or box of books or bundle of newspapers and put them out for sale. If that person had the flu and had been replaced by someone less experienced, you were dead. Or if he were tired or had had a fight with his wife and didn't hustle as he usually did . . . dead. *Damn the human factor*, Maxi thought as she grew more agitated. These things should be done by computer and robots.

Unable to control herself, she stood directly in front of the pile of *Cosmo.* She gaped, gasped and blinked. A tall stack of *The New York Review of Books* was nestled right next to *Cosmo*, where *B&B* should have been. She should have known! Double-cross! The beastly New York newsdealer, some kind of weirdo intellectual, with utterly phony, pseudo-liberal pretensions, who probably had a son who wrote poetry or even intended to be a harpsichord critic—the bastard had usurped her place! Gaining brownie-points with *NYRB* for his rotten kid. She'd see about that! Maxi pushed her way into the sacrosanct center of the newsstand, swarming with busy newsboys falling over each other as they tried to make change for impatient customers.

"Where's the boss?" she demanded at large. "Show me the boss, and fast!"

"You're not allowed in here, miss. And I'm the boss. Would you move outside?" A large man made a shooing gesture, and almost turned away. New York must be full of beautiful, loony girls, with messed-up hair and furious green eyes.

"The hell I will." Maxi pulled him around. "Where'd you put *B&B*, God damn it? Why aren't they out there next to *Cosmo*? And don't try and tell me you didn't get them because I'm sure you . . ."

"Did. Yeah, we did, and whatever they are they're all sold. I called the rep for the retailer and he's bringing me another couple hundred. So don't blame me, lady, I'm saving its place with that fink sissy newspaper and that really hurts."

"They're gone?" Maxi whispered. "*People bought them?*"

"Don't look at me like that, lady. I don't know any more about them than you. They just melted away. Never saw anything like it in my life. Hey, lady, stop it! I don't even know you . . . stop kissing me, lady . . . well, all right, just stop crying all over my shirt . . . mascara, lipstick . . . sure, I agree, it's wonderful that I'm not a robot." Too bad she was crazy, with legs like that: they were gams, real old-fashioned gams like you used to see on Marilyn and Rita and Cyd Charisse. Too bad he was too old for her . . . anyway she was holding up traffic.

Pavka Mayer and Barney Shore barely knew each other. Although Crescent had been the national distributor for Amberville Publications for almost thirty-seven years the sophisticated, profoundly elegant Artistic Director had had little contact with the rough-and-tumble tycoon whose chief reading material remained the *Racing Form.* Yet, three days after Maxi went to the newsstand in the Pan Am Building, Pavka Mayer found himself being taken to lunch by Barney Shore at *Le Veau d'Or*, the kind of small French restaurant in which they both felt at home, a restaurant that had surely been in business longer than either of them, a restaurant as urbane as Pavka, as down-to-earth as Barney, an un-fancy and excellent restaurant not known to non–New Yorkers.

"I had to celebrate with somebody who'd feel the same way I do," Barney said.

"I'm glad you called me," Pavka agreed gravely.

"It's been a week now and it's sold out in every major city in the country. Nobody's seen anything like it since that first issue of *Life.* My computers are going crazy. It didn't do anything to make peace in the war between Fort Worth and Dallas when the Dallas ladies drove all the way to Fort Worth and the Fort Worth ladies drove to Dallas, all assuming that the other place would have copies. Couldn't even bribe the clerks at the checkout counters . . . they couldn't sell what they'd sold out. Same story in Chicago, L.A., San Diego, Boston, Milwaukee . . . same story everywhere. I miscalculated, should have printed five times as many . . . or ten. We persuaded Meredith/Burda to go back to press—they kicked and screamed and we paid double time—so you'd better keep your copy as a first edition, a collector's item." Barney Shore's grin grew broader.

"You don't happen to have any extras at your place, do you?" asked Pavka.

"Sorry, but my wife graciously passed them out to her friends, without asking me, every last one . . . my daughters are ready to strangle her," Barney replied, chuckling in delight. God, he loved to follow a hunch, and Maxi had always brought him luck.

"I was afraid you'd say that. My wife's friends never do their own shopping and when they finally resigned themselves to enter a supermarket it was too late. The gals at the office who were too blasé to be interested, who spend their lives knee-deep in magazines, are taking turns going to the newsstand in the building to be there in time when the next batch is coming in. Wouldn't you think that Meredith/Burda might have been thoughtful enough to save a special bale for us?" Pavka's delighted eyes and triumphant expression belied his grumble.

"My secretary had the idea of stealing one out of the folder at her hairdresser's but the owner of the shop had already taken it home for himself and won't bring it back. Says his clients are all confirmed kleptomaniacs and they won't enjoy it as much as he does anyway. Well, Pavka, here are our drinks."

The two men raised their glasses and touched the rims briefly. Their eyes met and their smiles faded.

"To Zachary Amberville," Pavka said.

"To Zachary Amberville," echoed Barney Shore.

Rocco buzzed his secretary. "Where are Lefkowitz and Kelly?" he asked.

"In Mr. Lefkowitz's office. Shall I ring them?"

"Never mind, Miss Haft, I'll go in."

He found his redheaded, blue-eyed partners just returned from lunch and not even out of their coats. Kelly, who slept with a copy of *Gentleman's Quarterly* on his night table, was wearing a tailored dark gray Chesterfield overcoat with velvet lapels and a homburg, its brim curled to the side and dipped at the front and back. Lefkowitz, who had been deeply marked in his early twenties by the Belmondo movie *Stavisky*, wore a Borsalino, which, as he frequently reminded Kelly, was made by Borsalino Giuseppe e Fratello of Alessandria, Italy, and not one of your average wide-brimmed felt makers. He turned down its brim on one side only so that one would confuse him with F. Scott Fitzgerald, and he too still wore his reversible tweed raincoat from Cesarani.

"You guys cold?" Rocco asked, "or auditioning for a remake of *The Sting*?"

"Rocco, look at this thing!" Lefkowitz said excitedly.

"We almost trampled a couple of broads but we got one," Kelly said triumphantly. "Rocco, take a look. What do you think . . . wasn't it worth being half clawed to death?"

They made room for Rocco to look as they turned the pages of *B&B*, with the fine-tuned perception only possible to men whose whole lives were defined by the necessity to sell people things they had not yet realized they needed.

"Nice," Rocco commented.

"Nice?" Rap Kelly snorted. "Thank God we made those page buys at the right price. 'Nice' is all Rocco finds to say. Do I detect a little jealousy, pal?"

"Come off it, Rap. Why the hell should you think a dumb thing like that?" Lefkowitz asked.

"Man Ray, let's face it, the look of this book is very, very special. I haven't seen anything that comes within light-years of it. Christ, just look at that use of white space, at that typography, those graphics, the layout . . . maybe you guys think that all I know how to do is get new business, but I'm not blind."

"I said it was nice," Rocco repeated heatedly, looking at the pages he'd laid out for Maxi, pages he could never now claim as his own, at the risk of looking an absolute fool.

"He said it was nice, Rap, what more do you want?" Lefkowitz said hurriedly. "Listen, Rap, back when Rocco was doing magazines, he was at least as good as the guy who laid out this book, easily as good, anybody will tell you."

"Yeah," said Kelly, "if there's anybody who still remembers."

Justin, dressing rapidly, hours late for Maxi's office party, to celebrate the success of the first issue, didn't hear the first knock on the door of his modest, walk-up apartment. The second knock was louder, more impatient.

"Open up, police."

What the hell, Justin thought, and hurried to open the door. Two men, casually dressed, stood there.

"You Justin Amberville?"

"Yes. Why?"

They showed him their badges. "New York City Police. We have a warrant to search your apartment."

"Search? What for? What's going on?" Justin said in surprise, moving swiftly to block them from coming into his apartment. Expertly they shouldered him aside and when he fought back violently with all his sinewy strength it took both detectives to pin him to the wall. "Harry," one of them said to the other, "you look the place over. Justin here thinks he's pretty tough and he has objections, so let's make sure we really give the place a going-over he won't forget. Here's the warrant, Justin baby. Cool it." The scorn in his voice when he said Justin's name was blatant, provocative, but at the sight of the paper Justin realized that there was no point in struggling with the man and, in any case, he had nothing to hide.

He watched, momentarily silenced by sheer disbelief, in the muteness of a dreamer, as the first policeman rapidly searched his living room, slitting open all the couch and chair pillows, sweeping all the books off the shelves, taking apart the speakers of his stereo. Still immobile against the wall he listened to the noisy, exhaustive wrecking of his bedroom. Harry came out. "Not there, Danny, unless it's under the floor. I'll try the other room."

"That's my darkroom. There's thousands of dollars of valuable stuff . . . for Christ's sake, be careful."

"Sure thing, Justin. That's what we're here for, to be careful," Harry sneered. He flung open the darkroom door, turned on the light and started his search, violently flinging down everything that didn't interest him. One by one Justin watched his Nikons hit the floor, their lenses shattered. As the third camera was tossed out he broke Danny's strong hold in a single swift, fluid movement and went after Harry, easily tossing the heavy man on his back. Harry grunted in pain, unable to move for a moment. "Bastard!" Justin spat and turned quickly to face Danny. His kick shattered Danny's elbow. The fight that followed was short, ugly and brutish. Without their illegal saps the detectives would both have found themselves doubled up, on the floor, unable to breathe, but instead it was Justin who was finally beaten into semiconsciousness, and handcuffed.

"Harry, you missed that little closet," Danny gasped, nursing his elbow. "This slick fucker has to have the stuff somewhere." The second detective, panting from the damage Justin had inflicted, jerked down a pile of boxes from the closet shelf and riffled through the photographs that had been carefully filed in them. He unbuckled Justin's empty camera cases and threw them away in disgust. Finally he unzipped the duffel bag that Justin had put away after his last trip.

"Pay dirt," he grunted, lifted the bag and put it down on the floor so that the other detective could see its contents. "How much does it look like to you, Danny? Whataya say, Justin, huh, whataya say, creep?" He kicked Justin hard in the ribs. "Looks like about three kilos of blow to me, the whole fucking side pocket's jammed full of the stuff. Millions of bucks worth, on the street. He must have thought he found the perfect hiding place. Too obvious to bother about, huh, Justin? Come on, Danny, I'll take him in, read him the Miranda. You just get downstairs. I'll come back for the bag. You gotta be hurting bad." Viciously he pulled Justin upright by his handcuffed wrists.

"Come on, Mr. Amberville, we've got a date downtown."

After Justin had been booked for possession of cocaine, with suspicion of intent to sell, fingerprinted and photographed, he was allowed one phone call. Bewildered, dazed, hurting badly, instinctively reaching out to the one person he dared to call, he dialed Maxi's number.

When the phone rang she had just finished putting a woozy Angelica to bed. Maxi sat at her desk, weary in every bone, yet so euphoric, so utterly content that she didn't want to go to bed herself and end the celebration that had lasted until long after dinner.

"Justin! Why didn't you come to the party? We all waited . . . What? *What*! No, it's impossible . . . I don't understand . . . of course, I'll be right down. Jesus, Justin, shall I bring a doctor too? A lawyer then? No? you're sure? All right. I promise I won't say anything to anybody. I'll be there as fast as possible . . . yes, my checkbook. Just hang on, I'm on my way."

It was after eleven when Maxi reached the Midtown North precinct house, yet only a quarter of an hour after she left her apartment; a quarter of an hour of nightmare, nightmare conjecture, nightmare streets glimpsed from the taxi window, a quarter of an hour in which the precise conditions of a nightmare were duplicated;

something hideous, not quite known, yet long dreaded had happened. It was more than the fact of Justin's arrest; it was the feeling that somehow she had expected it for reasons she had avoided looking at. There was a revolting whiff of the familiar, something of the half-understood, the half-suspected, the unseen that had been hidden, just out of sight, deliberately, even scrupulously unacknowledged, something more frightening than anything she had ever thought about in the light of day. Her thoughts weren't clear and she shivered uncontrollably in spite of her fur coat. Her checkbook. It was in her handbag, the one solid reference point in the universe.

In the crowded, confusing station Maxi finally located the sergeant who was in charge.

"No, ma'am, no way you can get him out on bail. Bail hasn't been set yet. He's not here, ma'am. After booking he was taken down to One Police Plaza to await arraignment before a judge. The man should have called his lawyer, not his sister. What's the charge? Possession, it says here, and suspected dealing. How much drugs? Enough, a lot more than enough. That's all I can tell you. No, of course you can't see him. Not till arraignment. And bring a lawyer with you. What's that? He doesn't want one? Well, you listen to me, lady, he needs one. Bad."

After another half hour of fruitless quest in the police station for someone who might be able to tell her more, Maxi was stopped by a young stranger.

"Miss Amberville? I understand that your brother was arrested tonight . . ." the man said sympathetically.

"Who are you?" Maxi demanded.

"Perhaps I can help. I saw him brought in. He definitely needed medical attention and I thought you should know."

"Who are you?"

"Apparently a large amount of cocaine was found in his apartment. He claimed that it wasn't his, that it must belong to somebody else. Do you have any idea who could have put it there? Could it have been someone he trusted, some acquaintance, some friend, somebody—"

"Go away," Maxi screamed. She raced down the stationhouse stairs, waving frantically for a taxi. A friend? An acquaintance? Someone who hid cocaine in that apartment where even she had never been invited, where Justin guarded his privacy as though it were a fragile, infinitely precious object. *Oh, Justin, what kind of people do you call friends*? Who knows you better than I do? Poor, sweet, lost Justin . . . I've tried so hard not to guess. Wasn't that what you wanted, more than anything else in the world, that none of us should guess?

There was no help for it, Maxi thought, as she picked up the phone by her bed to telephone Lily. The only lawyers Maxi herself could contact immediately specialized in divorce. Justin obviously needed the highest-powered law firm that Amberville Publications could summon and, in any case, Lily would have to be told as gently as possible before she read about Justin's arrest in the newspaper tomorrow.

"Hello, Mother."

"Do you have any idea of the time, Maxime?" Lily's voice said drowsily.

"Yes, it's after midnight. I'm terribly sorry to wake you but . . . something's happened, something . . . no, *nobody's* been hurt, Mother, it's something else, Justin's been arrested."

"Let me take this on another phone," Lily whispered. In a few seconds she had picked up another extension. "I didn't want to wake Cutter. Where is Justin now?"

"He's in jail. They've taken him down to One Police Plaza."

"What did they arrest him for, Maxime? Was it . . . was it soliciting?" Lily asked in a low, terrified tone.

"My God, Mother!"

"I've been afraid of that for so long. Was it that, Maxime? Tell me," Lily implored.

"No, Mother, not that. It's some kind of terrible mistake. They say that they found cocaine in his apartment. They suspect him of dealing. It's all utterly impossible. The only thing that I was able to find out was that he said someone hid the drugs in his place."

"If that's what he said, that's what happened." Lily's voice was relieved, calmer. "Justin is not a liar. And of course he's not a drug dealer. I'll call Charlie Salomon right now. He'll know exactly what to do, how to fight this. We'll get him out of jail in the morning, first thing."

"Mother, more than anything Justin didn't want anybody to hear—to guess. But there was a reporter there and he got a photo of me . . . he knew the essentials, about the drugs."

"We have to be prepared for that." Lily's grave, silver voice had never sounded this note of lament, not even for herself.

"Oh, Mother, I feel so horribly sorry for him, poor, loving, harmless Justin. Why did this have to happen to him?" Maxi asked, and as she asked she knew how childish the question was.

"Maxime, something—like this—has been waiting to happen to Justin for a long time. It's not his fault, dear, but it was bound to come. Try not to worry. Charlie Salomon's the best lawyer in town and thank God, Cutter is here for all of us. Goodnight, Maxime, and . . . thank you, darling. Thank you for going to help."

Before she went to wake Cutter, Lily telephoned Charlie Salomon, chief counsel to Amberville Publications, at home, finding him still watching television. Precisely, displaying almost no emotion she told him what had happened, as far as she was aware of the facts, and made an appointment to meet him at One Police Plaza in the morning.

Then, wrapping her robe around her she walked slowly from her sitting room to the bedroom she shared with her husband. He had had a particularly tiring day and she knew that he had to get up early for a breakfast appointment, but she couldn't put off waking him any longer. The reassurance she had given Maxi, the short conversation she had had with the lawyer had left her with an intense need to be held in Cutter's arms and told that everything was going to be all right, that he would carry on for her now, that she was no longer alone.

She looked at his sleeping face, as distinguished in unconsciousness as it was in wakefulness, for the relaxation of his lean facial muscles left the clean, fine, aristocratic line of his bones and his skull unchanged. Only the dark, brooding sternness, that perpetual bull-killer's watchfulness had disappeared from his expression. She sighed with unconscious pleasure. Even in this moment of long-dreaded trouble there was joy for her in looking at him.

Gently she ran her fingertips over his forehead. He turned to one side to avoid her touch but she continued and eventually he woke, dazed, from the depth of sleep. "What? Lily? What's happening?" he muttered, not fully awake.

"Wake up, my darling, I need you."

"Lily, are you sick?" He sat up in bed, alarmed.

"I'm fine. It's one of the children, one of them is in trouble . . ."

"Maxi. What's she done now?"

"No, it's Justin, our child, Cutter. Oh, Cutter, hold me tight, hug me hard, I've been so afraid, so afraid for so long, and now it's happened." Lily flung herself into Cutter's arms and tried to burrow into a safe place. He held her and kissed the top of her head and comforted her for a minute, but then he pushed her away far enough so that he could see her face.

"Tell me, Lily. What about Justin? What's happened, for God's sake?"

"He's been arrested. The police searched his apartment and found drugs—cocaine. They've taken him to jail. He called Maxi but it was too late to do anything tonight. I've already talked to Charlie Salomon and he'll get him out first thing tomorrow."

"Wait a minute. How much cocaine did they find?"

"Maxi didn't know, they wouldn't tell her, just that it was 'enough'—enough to book him as a suspected dealer."

"Christ!" Cutter jumped out of bed and tied his bathrobe around his waist. "Christ almighty, as if that kid didn't have enough money! How the hell could he have been so stupid? I could strangle him with my bare hands . . . suspected of dealing cocaine? An Amberville dealing cocaine! Do you have any idea of the disgrace that is? It's as low as—"

"Wait! *He's not guilty*, Cutter*!* Justin couldn't possibly be guilty of that. He's not evil, he's not a criminal, how can you even think it?" Lily was panting with outrage. "Somebody left it, concealed it, in his apartment. He didn't know it was there. Maxi learned that much."

"Oh, Lily. Couldn't that dumb kid have thought up a lie that sounded a little more convincing?"

"You assume it's a *lie*?" Lily's voice rose.

"Justin is somebody with something to hide. I knew it from the minute I first saw him. He's never been honest with me or with you or anybody else in the family. He vanishes for months without saying where he's going, he has an apartment we've never even seen; it all adds up, Lily. I know you don't want to admit it, but it adds up. And now we get the whole rotten mess dumped in our laps. Justin's a lousy rich dilettante drifter whose dividends and trust funds aren't enough, so he sells coke on the side and gets caught, the little prick."

Lily looked at Cutter, striding up and down the bedroom, ruthlessly throwing his words like stones at her feet.

"Cutter, listen to me." She forced herself to speak as calmly as possible. "You don't know Justin, but even so, surely you must understand that he would never ever do anything to hurt anyone but himself. Unfortunately, he does know the kind of people who would hide drugs in his place. When I realized that the two of you didn't get along with each other, when you and Justin never grew close, when you made no effort to get to know him better—*your own son*, Cutter—I thought the reason was because you knew, because you sensed, well—because somehow you instinctively realized that he was homosexual. And I thought that perhaps you blamed yourself in some crazy way, thought that—"

"Homosexual?" There was a moment of dead silence. The word seemed to bounce back and forth from one wall to another of the bedroom that was filled with Cutter's stunned disbelief and Lily's incredulous realization that he had *not* known, not seen, never even bothered perhaps, to be sensitive to his son, to wonder at

Justin's evasive mode of life and ask himself why.

"He can't be a homosexual, Lily. It's not possible," Cutter finally said in harsh denial.

"You believed he was a cocaine dealer. Immediately, with no questions asked. Why can't you believe he's a homosexual?"

"My son a faggot! No, never. If it had been Toby . . . but not *mine.* God damn it, Lily, I never wanted you to have him, but you, no, you wanted what you wanted. *He should never have been born.*"

"Never been born?" Lily looked straight at Cutter as she echoed his words and he saw a face he had not dreamed could exist, contorted, ready to strike out at him, the face of a woman stripped down to the bones of an emotion he'd never seen before.

Swiftly he walked toward her and forced her, struggling, into his grip. "Lily, Lily, beloved, I'm sorry, Jesus I didn't mean it, not a word, not a single word. I just went crazy for a minute—I have a thing about . . . homosexuals . . . a phobia, I guess. It's some kind of primitive reaction, I just couldn't take it when you said that Justin . . . Lily, it sounds nuts but it's my problem and I'm ashamed of it. I don't blame you for being upset. You know how people can say things when they've had a shock, things they don't mean. Lily, I'm glad we have a son—truly, deeply glad. So glad, my Lily." He felt her relax in his hold and begin to weep. "O.K. now, darling? I love you so much. Please say you forgive me. Look, I'm going to get us both a drink and we'll talk about it, about what we can do to help the poor guy, about what I can do for my son."

As he made his way down the stairs to the bar Cutter swore at himself for being the worst kind of a fool, a man who let his tongue slip when dealing with a woman. No amount of anger was an excuse. Since the minute he'd first made love to Lily he'd schooled her to be controlled, to be dominated, so that now he could turn her in any direction that suited his purpose. To carry out his intention to break up Amberville Publications meant that he must continue to have Lily's complete confidence, her entire trust. He'd managed to make her stop publication of three magazines but there were seven more still left whose identities must be wiped out as fully as possible. He'd almost blown it. That wouldn't happen again, he vowed, as he carried the glasses back to the bedroom. Not even if it meant saving Justin's ass, that sick, sullen little faggot. He'd always hated him and now he knew why.

22

At breakfast time there is always a traffic jam at Park and Sixty-first Street, for in front of the Regency Hotel the police allow limousines to triple-park while less privileged taxis are forced into a single file to pass this expensive but basically unremarkable hotel. Its dining room has, for reasons unclear, become the most popular place for powerful men to do business with each other over coffee and dry toast. The Plaza is too far downtown, the Carlyle too far uptown, the Waldorf too far east, the new Plaza Athenée too new, so it has fallen to the Regency to garner the Tisches, the Rohatyns, the Newhouses and the Sulzbergers of the city, who often accomplish more real trading in the course of a one-hour breakfast than they may do in the rest of their day. No two men ever meet for breakfast at the Regency just to eat, unless they are a pair of rare, unaware tourists who can't bother to wait for room service.

Cutter Amberville had, by virtue of consistent and precisely right overtipping—never so much that he seemed insecure, yet never so little that it failed to impress—nailed down the second banquette on the right facing the Sixty-first Street windows. He had picked this table three years ago when he first came back from England, because it allowed him to sit with his back to the wall. He could not understand the men who allowed themselves to be seated at the center tables, exposed to all eyes. Obviously they knew that they would be observed, since the Regency breakfast was a declaration of courtship, potential or protracted, but why, he wondered, go out of your way to attract attention? Cutter made sure to arrive several minutes before his guest, Leonard Wilder of the United Broadcasting Company, thereby establishing subliminal proprietary rights from the beginning of the conversation. He concentrated on the man he was going to meet, sparing no thought for Lily, who had already left to get Justin out of jail.

Leonard Wilder was a man famous for his impatience. He wore two watches and constantly checked them; he normally made two breakfast dates in a morning, one at eight and one at nine, and he never bothered to eat. He had been important for too long to bother with the courtesy rituals, the minuetlike to-ing and fro-ing of corporate affairs, and his favorite phrase was known to be "Cut the baloney, what's the bottom line?"

Cutter rose as Wilder was brought over to the table by the headwaiter.

"I'm delighted to meet you, Mr. Wilder," Cutter said as they shook hands, "and I'm particularly pleased that you could find time for breakfast on such short notice. My wife and I watched your 'Ragtime Special' last night, and we both agreed that it was excellent entertainment."

"Wasn't bad, did well." Wilder replied in his rapid-fire, impatient way.

"Well then, shall we order?" Cutter studied the menu critically, giving it his complete attention. "Henry, I'll start with the fresh strawberries and Mr. Wilder will have—no, nothing to begin with? After that, the English porridge with fresh cream. Let's see—ah, yes, I'll have the buckwheat cakes with Canadian bacon. Be sure the bacon is lean and cooked to a crisp, and remind the chef that my buckwheat cakes must be freshly made." He turned to Wilder. "I'd have the same if I were you. No? They make a batch all at once every morning and then put them on a steam table to keep them warm . . . they're no good that way so the chef always makes a fresh batch for me." Wilder grunted. "And hot coffee, really hot. You can bring that right now. What will you have, Mr. Wilder? Only coffee? I guess it's the transplanted ex-Westerner in me, but I find that with a decent breakfast I can do twice as much work before lunch than if I only gulp a cup of coffee. You're sure? All right, Henry, just coffee for Mr. Wilder."

Leonard Wilder glanced at Cutter's trim waistline. Cutter intercepted his look. "Breakfast like a rich man, dine like a pauper. I've always followed that advice. Still, diet isn't enough, you have to keep in shape too. My wife and I are both ardent weekend athletes and we have a gym in the house so that we can work out every day. What do you do for exercise?"

"Walk to work."

"Ah, there's nothing like walking," Cutter agreed, "but I don't find it exercises the whole body unless you run and in this city you can't do that, unless you're willing to be killed by a taxi driver."

He sat back and sipped his coffee. "Waiter, this isn't really hot. Could you bring another pot, please, and fresh cups? And take away Mr. Wilder's coffee too. It's only lukewarm."

Leonard Wilder ground his teeth and checked his watches. Cutter relaxed and waited for the fresh coffee.

"I knew your brother," Leonard Wilder said abruptly. "Wonderful man."

Cutter sighed. "We all miss him. It's been a great loss."

"One-man show. Best in town. Things a mess now?"

Cutter chuckled. "Well, Mr. Wilder, that can happen in a privately owned corporation. We both know too many cases where the founder of a business died and the business fell apart at the seams. But fortunately Amberville Publications is in a different situation. Henry, these strawberries aren't ripe. Take them back, please, and bring me a compote of mixed fruit." He turned back to Wilder. "That's the trouble with out-of-season strawberries, you can never be sure. Usually there are good ones from Algeria or Israel this time of year, but those really weren't worth eating."

"Amberville's all right, then?"

"As a matter of fact, our profits will be up considerably this year. My brother loved to tinker with the magazines. He had lost interest in the bottom line years ago. His passion was starting new magazines and giving them all the time they needed to prove themselves. You know how costly that can be. And risky. When my wife—as majority shareholder—asked me to mind the store, I decided to cut losses to a minimum. I'm afraid I had to make an unpopular decision—nobody likes to lose his job—but it turned out for the best. Henry, you can clear the fruit away. Sure you won't join me for porridge, Mr. Wilder? It's particularly good here. No? Henry, bring another pitcher of cream. This one is only half full." Cutter attacked his porridge with relish, adding a judicious amount of butter and sugar to the steaming bowl.

"Profits up, you say?"

"Definitely. Every one of our magazines is showing increases in ad revenue and, as you know, that's where the money is."

" 'Up' can mean anything with a privately owned company," Wilder said, repressing the desire to peek at his watches.

"I don't feel it's indiscreet to tell you, Mr. Wilder. I'm talking about fourteen or fifteen percent, possibly more."

"Hmm. Nice going."

"Yes, it's been a most satisfactory experience. On the other hand, Lily, my wife, is British and she misses England. She's been really stuck in New York, except for whirlwind trips to Europe when Zachary went on business, for more than thirty years. She's still a young woman and she'd like to spend more time abroad. Hunting, theater, all of that . . . Lily says there has to be more to life than the magazine business. You're married, aren't you, Mr. Wilder?"

"Call me Leonard. Yes, married twenty-five years. You said up fourteen or fifteen percent, Cutter?"

"Right. Ah, thank you, Henry. Those look good."

Leonard Wilder wriggled on the banquette. He was already late for his nine-o'clock breakfast and Cutter Amberville had just started on his buckwheat pancakes.

"Could we talk round figures?" Wilder asked.

"Round figures?" Cutter poured some maple syrup on the pancakes. "I don't see why not. You're known never to repeat things. Something near one hundred and seventy million in pretax profits."

"Near? Which way? Up or down?"

"I don't like to overstate, Leonard, but I expect a higher figure. There's still some deadwood to be trimmed here and there."

"Business for sale, Cutter? That's why you called me?"

"Yes, as a matter of fact, there is that possibility. As I said, my wife is longing for a change and she deserves whatever she wants. I've urged her not to rush into any decision, told her to take her time, but spring's in the air and she's always been impulsive."

"So the business *is* for sale."

"It wouldn't be fair to make any promises . . . but it might be. It might very well be. At the right price."

"Naturally."

"Now take Bill Ziff for instance, and his company," Cutter said, between bites. "Interesting deal he just made. If you'll forgive me for mentioning the competition, Leonard, CBS just bought twelve magazines from him for three hundred and sixty-two million dollars, books like *Popular Photography* and *Yachting.* Then he sold Murdoch twelve trade publications, *Aerospace Daily* for one, and *Hotel and Resort Guide* for another, for an additional three hundred and fifty million. Twenty-four magazines in all. Now, admittedly we've only got six books to sell, but each is the leader in its field, each a classic. Major magazines, Leonard. We can leave *B&B* out of the discussion—it's an experiment, at the moment, unproven. But the others have revenues well above Ziff's, far, far above. So you have to understand that we're discussing a very large sum of money, certainly near a billion. Henry, more hot coffee, please."

"UBC is cash-rich, Cutter. That's not a problem. You talked to anyone else?" Wilder demanded, his other breakfast date utterly forgotten.

"No. Not yet. Lily only brought up the matter a few weeks ago and I didn't see any reason to hurry. I like to give new ideas time to mature, to ripen. All in good time and no regrets."

"Cutter, I don't believe in kidding around. I'm interested. Been looking for a major magazine group for years. Always liked Amberville. Got a three-man executive committee. They can commit whole board. Only ask one thing; don't speak to anyone else before we have a chance to get together on this."

"That sounds fair enough, particularly since I'm in no hurry. In fact, our next statement isn't due for almost three months and I'm so sure that it's going to show an interesting jump that I'd prefer to wait until then. If Lily is still of the same mind, then your accountants can go to work, and judge the values for themselves."

" . . . Three months . . . you're sure you want to wait? We could get started a lot sooner."

"I'm sure, Leonard. But during that time, why don't we get together for dinner with our wives? I feel I owe you something decent to eat. You missed a wonderful breakfast."

"Does anybody else know about this?" Toby asked India suspiciously, running his fingers down her belly.

"Could you be more specific?" she asked lazily, drifting up from the glowing globe of great joy in which she floated, feeling the complicated, compelling sense of bliss she experienced at the sound of his voice.

"This tiny scar, right here, below your bellybutton and to the right."

"Appendix, when I was eight. Even Barbara Walters doesn't know about it. On the other hand, she never asked."

"That's the one hundred and seventeenth thing I know about you that nobody else knows. Your ears are distinctly different sizes; your nose is out of line to the right, only by a hair but still nobody could call it straight; you have thinner eyelashes on your left eye than on the right, and correspondingly, less hair under your left arm than under your right, shave your armpits though you will; there's a tiny mole under your pussy hair on the left outer labia—"

"Toby!"

"I suppose it's not your fault if you're not perfect. You were billed as being perfect but, good Lord, the things I've found would fill a book, and I've barely begun to look. And as for taste, let me tell you, young lady, you don't taste the same way two days in a row. A man likes a little consistency in his woman."

"Am I your woman?" India wondered, knowing she shouldn't ask, but unable to resist.

"My woman of the moment. The only woman of the only moment. But you know how I feel . . . I've never—"

"Spare me . . . never committed yourself. Coward! Revolting, timid coward. I wish I had a penny for every fink man in the country who goes around counting pussy hair and not committing himself. Have you no shame?"

"I didn't count your pussy hair, I counted your underarm hairs."

"It comes to the same thing and you know it. How did women get into this? Why are you allowed to make me love you and then refuse to love me back?"

"I do love you back," Toby said in a low voice. "You know I do. I loved you as soon as you threw those drinks over me to attract my attention five months ago. But commitment is something else."

"Where I come from, when you love somebody and she loves you and there's no reason why you can't agree to hope to keep on loving each other for good, logically that will lead to a commitment for some kind of permanent arrangement . . . called marriage," India said with the same dogged persistence which had kept her flying back and forth from Los Angeles to New York almost every weekend since she'd met Toby. She had moved half her wardrobe, little by little, to his closets and now even his bed, on which they were lying, was covered with her very own hand-ironed Porthault sheets.

"Is not marriage an open question, when it is alleged, from the beginning of the world, that such as are in the institution wish to get out, and such as are out wish to get in?"

India sat up fuming. "You dare to quote Emerson to *me*—I invented quoting Emerson, you skunk."

" 'By necessity, by proclivity, and by delight, we all quote,' " Toby declaimed in perfect Emersonian dignity.

"It's Maxi, I know it's got to be Maxi. She told you how I used to torment her with Emerson, didn't she?"

"She may have mentioned it, in passing, as an example of girlish affection."

"Then the two of you have been talking about me?"

"Naturally. It wouldn't be in Maxi's character to maintain a discreet silence, when her brother is in love with her best friend."

"What does she think?"

"She thinks that I'll have to make up my own mind."

"Some best friend," India said bitterly. The phone rang and startled her.

"Don't answer it," she said.

"It might be from one of my managers," Toby sighed. "The restaurant business never sleeps." He picked up the bedside phone, listened for a moment and then hung up angrily and abruptly.

"Not him?" India asked anxiously.

"I'm afraid so, darling. It was your 'biggest fan' again. And my unlisted number was changed only last month."

"Oh, Toby, I'm sorry. That crazy guy. He writes me three times a week, and tries to call long distance. My secretary just tells him I'm not available. Forget him, it's the price of fame."

Toby unplugged the phone and turned back to India.

"Now listen, my love, you really have the most extraordinary and admirable facility to avoid facing facts," he said, resuming the interrupted conversation. "Let's cut to the chase. I'm blind, we can't pretend that I'm not."

"You're not really blind," India said stubbornly. "You can see something, you told me that your field of vision was less than five degrees, but that's still *something*."

"Less than five degrees out of a normal field of one hundred and forty in each eye, and that's only when I put together a tiny bit here and a tiny bit there, where there are still a few cones functioning in my retina. It's all fragmented, a nothing, not even black, just a kind of flickering, a now-and-then reality that has no color, no borders or stability. And it will probably get worse, certainly no better. And there's no cure, no hope at all."

"But your blindness skills, everything you learned at Saint Paul's! You can do so much, Toby, you learned so much while you could still see . . . all those *years* of seeing, more than twenty-five good years. You told me yourself that you have an enormous number of visual clues, thousands of memories that help to piece things together, to make a pattern recognizable, it isn't as if you'd been born blind. Anyway, what difference does the exact percentage matter, when you can function? When you can work? What does it have to do with the two of us? So what if you've never seen me? When I get old and wrinkled and lose my looks you won't care about it. You don't love me just because I'm beautiful. Don't you realize how much that means? Besides Maxi you're the only person I know who doesn't base some of his feelings about me on my particular face, you're the only person I can trust to *like* me for no other reason than that I'm me. Doesn't that make a difference to you? Don't I make sense?"

"Perfect sense, up to a certain point. I don't think it's fair to you to involve you in my problems."

"Fair? What's fair is to take the happiness you know exists for you, now, this very minute, without doing any harm to anyone else, the happiness that exists if you just stretch out your hand," India said, her voice trembling.

"You have an incredible ability to oversimplify, India, sweet, imperfect India. I can't allow you to choose a man with my particular handicap, for it is a handicap, say what you will, even if you're convinced, at this particular time, that it's what you want. You have no idea of what the future holds, you can't know how long I'll be able to make you happy."

"I *know* you're the man I want," India said, her voice golden with the intensity of her sureness, "and I know I'm not going to change my mind."

"What, may I ask, does Doctor Florence Florsheim have to say about us?" Toby asked.

"Don't change the subject."

"She must have said something, analyst or not."

"She said that it wasn't recommended to make major life changes during the analytic process. Not that I couldn't, just that it wasn't recommended."

"That's all?"

"Word for word."

"Well, I think she's right."

"Oh *rats*!" India howled, pounding her fists against his bare chest. "I knew you'd say that. You make fun of her all the time and suddenly when it suits you, you decide to agree with her."

"Just because she's your shrink doesn't mean she's necessarily wrong. Hey, what's this I've found? Oh, oh, India, poor baby, I think you've got a crow's foot in its earliest stages. It probably won't be noticeable on the screen for a few years, maybe even five if you never smile from now on. Let me kiss it and make it well."

"You're a first-class sadist, Toby. You know something? For the first time I'm absolutely convinced that you and Maxi are brother and sister."

The morning of Cutter's breakfast meeting with Leonard Wilder, Charlie Salomon had called and told Lily to meet him at the courthouse. He had used his considerable influence to arrange for Justin's hearing to take place immediately following the judge's arrival.

"I'll go with you, darling," Cutter said, "just let me cancel my breakfast date."

"No, I don't really think it's a good idea," Lily answered. "Not that I don't want you there, but I believe it would be easier on Justin if we treated this as . . . routinely . . . as possible. Anyway, I promised Maxi to let her know as soon as he could get out of that awful place. I'll call her and tell her to come with me."

"Maxi, for moral support?"

"Well, you know how close she is to him."

"All right, Lily, if you're sure, but—"

"I'm positive. I'll call you as soon as I'm back home."

Lily picked up Maxi on the way downtown to the courthouse. There they met

Charlie Salomon and two young lawyers from his office whom he had brought along. When Justin was brought in, handcuffed, Lily grasped Maxi's hand tightly, and lowered her eyes so that if Justin happened to glance at her he wouldn't see her watching him until the handcuffs were removed. How stubbornly defiant he looked, Maxi thought. His stance was as dangerous as it had always been, his head tilted at his characteristically aggressive angle but he limped slightly and no amount of toughness could disguise the dark bruises around his eyes, forehead and chin where the detectives had hit him with their saps. His spiky blond hair was matted in several places. Maxi flicked a glance at her brother and caught his eye. On impulse she winked broadly and smiled as if she were remembering a private joke between them, but Justin looked away, without acknowledging her.

"The defendant is a very rich man, Your Honor," they all heard the assistant district attorney say. "Two detectives found almost three kilos of cocaine in his possession and he forcibly resisted arrest. If found guilty of conspiracy to distribute cocaine he will certainly face years in prison. Under these circumstances there is every reason to expect him to leave the country rather than stand trial. The state asks for one million dollars bail."

Bring your checkbook, Maxi thought. Oh, Justin, how naive we both were last night. The reporter who had accosted her the day before was scribbling away in the row behind them.

"That's an unreasonable amount, Your Honor," Charlie Salomon said. "My client has no record of any previous offense."

After a few more minutes of argument the judge made his decision.

"Bail is set at two hundred and fifty thousand dollars."

Justin was handcuffed again and taken to a holding cell in the courthouse until the money could be produced. Lily telephoned her bank manager and made arrangements for a cashier's check, to be delivered by a messenger on a motorcycle. After an hour and a quarter of waiting the check finally arrived and was handed over. The necessary paperwork for release took another half hour.

"Charlie, thank you so much for your help," Lily said. "I think you and your colleagues should go now. Maxime and I will go back uptown with Justin."

"I think I should stay here with you till he comes out. I have to talk to him anyway, Lily."

"Tomorrow, Charlie," Lily commanded and the lawyers left.

"That reporter from last night is here again today, Mother, and he's got a photographer with him today," Maxi warned.

"Justin is not guilty, Maxime. If they want to take pictures, there's nothing we can do about it."

"Shall we both smile for the camera, Mother?"

"Why not, Maxime? There's nothing to be ashamed of."

"All I need is a good hot shower and something to eat," Justin insisted when Lily suggested that she call her doctor and ask him to examine Justin in case there was serious damage to his skull from the saps the detectives had used. Nothing could sway him so the three Ambervilles went back to the great gray stone house and eventually found themselves sitting, at Lily's insistence, over the lunch table making conversation as if nothing more serious than an unremarkable head cold were at issue. Even Maxi felt gripped by the compelling force of Lily's superbly maintained composure, yet without looking at her mother or her brother she felt the hurt that suffused their souls. As a rack of lamb followed the cream of asparagus soup the tension in the room grew greater with every evasive word they each uttered, with the mounting total of essential words that hadn't been spoken. The servants came and went.

"Mother, could we skip the dessert and have coffee, just the three of us, in your sitting room?" Maxi asked.

"Certainly, dear," Lily answered as if this were the most normal request in the world.

They went upstairs, Justin moving with the tightly controlled restraint of a man who is keeping all his capacities for action in reserve. He looked as psychically remote from his sister and his mother as if he were a bullfighter being dressed in his suit of lights just before the *corrida*. It was almost, Maxi thought, as if he weren't there at all.

"Sugar?" Lily asked.

"Please," he answered and took two lumps with the close attention a heart surgeon might give to opening a chest.

"Tomorrow," Lily said, with no change of tone, "I'll have Charlie Salomon look into the question of defense lawyers, the best ones available. The fact that you're innocent is hardly a sufficient defense."

"Thank you, Mother," Justin said with a lopsided shadow of his go-to-the-devil smile.

"Of course, you realize," Lily said nervously, fiddling with the handle of the coffeepot, her words tumbling out in a way that wasn't natural to her, "that whatever life-style you choose will never make any difference to us, that we love you anyway—very much—no matter what."

"Life-style? You mean even if I were a vegetarian or took up computer fraud? How about murder-for-hire?" Justin challenged her.

"What the hell are the two of you talking about?" Maxi burst out. "This isn't a time for twenty questions, Justin. We know that there's only one reason that cocaine was found in your place."

"Maxime," Lily said warningly.

"Mother, we can't keep waltzing around." Maxi got up and took away Justin's demitasse and put it down on a side table. She knelt on the floor by his side and wrapped her arms around him and gave him a deliberately loud smacking kiss on the cheek. "Look, kiddo, there's got to be a guy who has a key to your place or who's been staying with you, somebody who put that stuff there without telling you, some guy you're *involved* with. Can't we just get this out in the open, Justin, so Mother and I can stop trying to act as if we didn't know that you're gay?"

Justin leapt up savagely and stalked to the window without a word, turning his back on them. Maxi ran after him and grabbed him around the waist. "*Gay*, Justin, or whatever word you prefer. *We know*, we've known for a long time, Mother and I, and we don't give a fuck! Come back and sit down. It's not the end of the world. Gay is one thing, stupid is another, and in either case going to jail is not recommended. So turn around so we can discuss this sensibly."

"You don't know anything. You can't possibly know anything," Justin said, his voice corrosive, his back still turned, gripping the windowsill. He stood as if he felt contempt for them rather than any stronger, more personal emotion.

"But I do, darling," Lily said, more evenly now. "I've known for years. I saw no reason to talk about it with anyone, ever. It was your private life, until now."

"I had no idea that Mother realized anything until last night when I had to call her," Maxi said, without slackening her grasp. "Nobody but people who love you very much and know you as well as we do, and God knows, you've made sure there are damn few of us, would even begin to wonder. But this is a tough conversation to have with your shoulder blades. Please?" She planted a row of delicate kisses on the back of his neck, holding on to him as hard as she could, all the while.

"Justin, who do you think put the drugs in your closet? That's really the point, isn't it?" Lily spoke as if she were asking him if she should dismiss a light-fingered butler.

He turned, finally. Only two patches of red on his sharp cheekbones and the long, thin muscle that worked in his throat displayed any emotion. "I haven't the slightest idea." His tone was almost ironic, formal.

"But there is somebody, *some man*, who can get into your place when you're not there?" Maxi persisted.

His face twisted in a spasm of shame so mixed with pain that it brought tears to Lily's eyes.

"Yes." The one word so quietly spoken hung in the air like a long sigh. Briskly, Maxi broke the silence that threatened to overtake them all.

"Do you think he did it?"

"No. No, he couldn't have. Absolutely not. He's simply not like that. He's just a guy I met on a shoot. But we've done a lot of . . . entertaining . . . people always dropping in—it could have been anyone. That duffel bag's been sitting there empty since the last time I came back to town." His voice was so empty that they felt fear.

"Do you know where he is now?" Maxi asked. "What's his name?"

"He's out of town," Justin said. "It must have been somebody else. And his name is none of anybody's business. I refuse to start blaming someone I trust just to prove I'm innocent. *Christ, I hate this city!*"

Maxi and Lily sat silently after Justin had rushed out of the room.

"Thank you, Maxime. Without your kind of directness I don't think I could have persuaded him to say anything. But it must have seemed unfair, the two of us cornering him like that," Lily said. "I feel somehow ashamed, not for him, for us."

"Unfair? Yes, but only if we'd wanted to know for any other reason than to keep him out of jail. But in these circumstances, no, absolutely not. And, Mother, he must have some sense of relief now that it's out and he knows we love him just as much as we ever did, that it doesn't make any difference. He's been guarding that secret all alone for much too long a time."

"Oh, but Maxime, you saw his face . . . he looked . . . oh, as if he wanted to vanish, as if he didn't believe in anyone or anything in the world and never would again. He's always been so alone, so apart, he's always kept so much to himself. I've worried about him all of his life but I could never break through to him."

"It's not your fault, Mother. Not mine. Not Justin's. It just is and it has to be dealt with. It's reality and nothing could have changed it."

"I wish I could believe that," Lily said wistfully.

"Mother, do you really imagine that on one particular day when Justin was just a little boy you could have said, 'Now darling, when you grow up, the only people you'll want to touch will be girls,' the way you taught him good table manners?"

Lily smiled slowly, reluctantly and ruefully. "That would have been too good to be true, but what a wonderful idea. You do have a way of getting straight to the point, Maxime."

"Thank you, Mother," Maxi said almost shyly. "I have to rush to the office now, but what's the next step? How can we help Justin?"

"I'm going to call Charlie Salomon at once and tell him what Justin just told us. But, on one hand he didn't tell us much that would help, as far as I can see, and on the other hand wouldn't it be better not to use it? I so desperately hope that we can keep that part of his life out of the newspapers . . . the man with the key to his apartment, the parties. If only we could do that much, at least."

"Every paper in the country is going to have the drug story, Mother. Plus the *Star* and the *Inquirer* and the news magazines. I don't see how we can keep it from being a media circus. It's only a question of time before they sniff out the rest of what Justin told us. There's nothing we can do to protect him. All it will take will be one lead, one person talking to one reporter. I don't think there's much hope."

"I thought . . . if only he could keep that bit of dignity. He cares so terribly much," Lily said soberly.

"I don't think you should be optimistic about protecting Justin's private life. The most important thing is to prove him innocent of drug dealing. He's an Amberville after all, and the media is going to be out in full force, dancing on his head."

Lily sighed as Maxi got up to leave. The two women embraced, a little awkwardly, with more warmth than either of them could remember showing each other in years. Lily, in her familiar gesture, pushed Maxi's hair back from her forehead.

"It's still wrong, isn't it, Mother?" Maxi asked wryly.

"The trouble with you, Maxime, is that you always jump to conclusions. I was just thinking how charmingly you wear your hair. It wouldn't really look like *you* any other way, would it?"

23

As Maxi and Lily were saying goodbye to each other, Cutter was meeting in his Wall Street office with Lewis Oxford, Vice-President for Financial Affairs of Amberville Publications. Cutter could more easily have established himself in a suite of offices in the Amberville Building uptown but he found it useful to force everyone who worked on the magazines to make a time-consuming trek to see him, and it kept him at a useful remove from anyone who wanted to talk about minor matters.

"Oxford, I wish you would stop doing that," Cutter rapped out.

"Sorry, Mr. Amberville. It helps me to reflect," Lewis Oxford answered, regretfully putting away the pencil with which he had been tapping his teeth.

"There's nothing to reflect about. My wife's orders are clear enough."

"Clear, perfectly clear. The only thing I was wondering was if it wouldn't be better to follow her instructions over a period of six months, or even a year. Three months isn't much time and I'm going to have to make a lot of waves."

"I've given you three months, Oxford, and if you can't manage I'll find someone who can. I'm sure you know that it's more merciful to cut off a dog's tail in one clean sweep than bit by bit. Every single one of the Amberville magazines has a thick strip of fat running through it and I want that fat cut out, starting immediately. Our next profit statement must reflect this change. By my estimates at least fourteen percent of our operating costs can be eliminated. Maybe more. Preferably more."

Lewis Oxford shook his head. "I still think it may be a mistake to move so rapidly."

"I'm not interested in anything but results, Oxford. Mrs. Amberville wants the paper quality on each and every magazine to go down one level. No more fifty-pound free sheet for *Style*—it doesn't have to look like *Town & Country* to sell. Everything that's being printed on forty-pound stock will be printed on thirty-four-pound stock from now on, as soon as you've used up the paper already in inventory. *T.V. Week* goes to thirty-four-pound ground-wood stock. Is that understood?"

"Yes, Mr. Amberville."

"As for the bulge on each magazine; the staff salaries, writers' fees and photo fees, I expect to see impressive results. Cut all staff by fifteen percent immediately. Mrs. Amberville wants every article and photo story you have in inventory to be used. *Eat up that inventory*, Oxford. You have hundreds of thousands of dollars worth that's just getting out of date. What's more, no more expensive writer's fees are to be approved. This article by Norman Mailer on 'Miami Vice'—can you give me one good reason why we should be paying for Mailer instead of some unknown freelance we can get at a cut-rate price?"

"It's classy, Mr. Amberville, and it might attract readers we wouldn't ordinarily have."

"We don't need class in a television magazine with seven million readers. It's sheer editorial ego to use class writers."

"Excuse me, sir, but that's not quite fair. The editor of *T.V. Week* feels strongly that Mailer and other name writers will impress Madison Avenue. He's ordered a series of ads in *Adweek* and *Advertising Age*—"

"Cancel them. For the next three months Amberville Publications is not blowing its own horn. We've been around for almost forty years and the advertising community is hardly unaware of us. I want promotion and publicity eliminated."

"Yes, sir."

"These photographers' bills are insane, Oxford. Insane."

"That's what all the top photographers are getting, now, Mr. Amberville."

"Send out a notice to the Editor-in-chief of each magazine that they are to stop using the same photographers they've been relying on for years. One of our editors' problems is that they've been letting the photographers do the imaginative work they should be doing themselves. I want them to use new photographers, the least expensive they can find, particularly women, people who will work for a great deal less and work harder. What's more, I want thirty percent fewer color spreads, replaced by black and white. That can be just as effective as color, used properly. As for models' fees, they're killing us. Whenever possible I want celebrities to be used for models—they don't cost us anything at all."

"Mr. Amberville, I must object. There's a limit to how many celebrities you can use before the magazines will all begin to look like *People.* Mr. Zachary Amberville never—"

"I'm not interested in repeating the past, Oxford. Readers want to see celebrities and we're going to give them what they want. I'm very disappointed in our profit for the last quarter. It has to come *up*, Oxford."

"It will, sir."

"Won't advertisers supply free articles and pictures if their products are plugged?" Cutter asked.

"It's been known to happen, but not at Amberville."

"Well, make it happen, Oxford. As often as you can. And another thing, just look at these travel expense accounts for our ad and sales representatives," Cutter went on. "They're an absolute scandal. Let each rep know that we're watching him and tell them that we expect a reduction of thirty-five percent in the next set of figures."

"Hell, Mr. Amberville, the reps live off their T-and-E's—everybody knows that."

"They're living too high, Oxford. Every rep who doesn't change his ways will be replaced. Be sure and put that in the memo."

"But the reps have to maintain relationships . . ." Lewis Oxford's voice trailed off at the mounting rage he saw in Cutter's face.

"Amberville Publications is not a God damned gravy train, Oxford! I can see that these cuts are long overdue. I blame you for letting things go on in this way. And do *not*, if you value your job, tell me that Mr. Zachary Amberville wanted it that way. My brother was a great editor, Oxford, but I can see he wasn't keeping a tight ship, as Mrs. Amberville and I have suspected. Do you have any more suggestions, Oxford? or have I covered everything?"

"There are small things, tables we take at magazine industry dinners, the lunches we give for major advertisers, things like that."

"Leave those alone. They don't amount to enough to make a difference and I want our presence maintained on that particular level. Don't worry, Oxford, when the profit is up, we'll take out media ads and let everyone know about it. Three months from now."

Cutter waited a few seconds and Lewis Oxford, hoping that the conversation was over, began to pull his papers together in preparation for departure.

"One more thing, Oxford. *B&B*. How much are we losing on it every month?"

"I'd need time to get the exact figures, Mr. Amberville. But I'll send Miss Amberville all your cost-cutting directives."

"No, don't bother. How long will it take for *B&B* to break even, assuming that every issue does as well as the first one?"

"Many months, I'm afraid. As you know, every startup is a major hemorrhage of money, sir. But that's only normal. Once they're back in the black profits should be tremendous."

"Stop publication of *B&B*, Oxford."

"What?"

"Don't you understand English? Cancel it, eliminate it, finish it! No more *B&B*, Oxford. Give the printers instructions not to print any more copies. Let all the creditors know that they'll be paid in full for whatever is currently owed, but beyond that Amberville Publications will not honor a single bill that Miss Amberville runs up. Warn them, Oxford. Not a dime. And fire the whole staff except for Miss Amberville. She's not on salary."

"But the magazine is a success, Mr. Amberville! The biggest success story since *Cosmo* or *Life* or *Seven Days*."

"It was a successful experiment, Oxford. But we can't afford the loss over the next year, or even over the next six months, not if we plan to raise our profit to where it should be. Even you would have to admit that whatever you save everywhere else will be more than offset by *B&B*'s losses."

"Well, yes, in fact I assumed that those losses were why you were taking such drastic measures."

"Never assume, Oxford," Cutter said with a pleasant smile, and rose to show the man to the door. "Never assume anything in a privately owned company."

Angelica stood on Fifth Avenue, between Fifty-sixth and Fifty-seventh streets, leaning disconsolately against a tall, metal city sign. "Don't Even THINK of Parking Here," it said, and added, for emphasis, "Red Zone, Tow Fine, $100 Minimum. No Standing at Any Time." Behind the sign, sitting around the fountain of the Steuben Glass Building, were the usual collection of waifs, drunks and tourists, some of them eating falafel, schnitzel or chicken nuggets from the pushcarts that stood conveniently at hand, others dipping their aching feet in the fountain, and still others studying the contents of the shopping bags they had just filled up and down the avenue. It was an affluent North American version of Calcutta.

The stern no-parking sign was Elie's favorite place to sit in the limo when he waited for Maxi. He had reached a tacit agreement with the cops on the street to start the motor and pull up a symbolic inch or so whenever they came along. But this afternoon he was late in bringing Maxi home and Angelica scanned the passing traffic with impatience.

Finally the long blue limo pulled up and Maxi hopped out.

"Oh, no," she groaned, seeing Angelica and the copy of the *New York Post* that she was holding, open to the story of Justin's arrest. How could she not have realized that there was the chance that Angelica would see the story in the paper before she'd been told about it? The lunch with Justin and Lily, followed by a few hectic hours at the office, making up for the work she hadn't done that morning, had driven the thought of warning her daughter out of her head.

"Ma?" Angelica's voice was blurred with tears.

"Baby, it's all crap. A giant setup. Uncle Justin has absolutely nothing to do with selling cocaine. Don't worry about it for a second. He's totally innocent," Maxi said in a rush.

"I know he's innocent, Ma, for goodness' sake, you don't have to tell me that. But how come you and Granny are smiling in that picture? That's what I want to know. How could you be so heartless? You look like two freaked-out beauty queens—Miss North Carolina and her lovely mother. *Honestly*."

"How do you think we should have looked? Frightened, miserable, horrified?"

"A little cool wouldn't have hurt. I mean, after all, you're not supposed to be thrilled about a bum rap. At least Uncle Justin handled himself properly . . . he looks terrific, tough, grim, indifferent, just like Sting, yeah, exactly like Sting."

"Angelica, I think you should seriously consider a career in public relations. Come on, let's go home."

"Can I have a falafel first?"

"You'll ruin your dinner. But go ahead, if you can pronounce it you can eat it, as far as I'm concerned," Maxi said, too exhausted to argue.

"You're losing your grip," Angelica said in relief, "but I'm not surprised. Today I found out that Cyndi Lauper's thirty years old. She's older than you are, Maxi."

"Please, a little respect," Maxi said, stung into firmness.

"I'll try," Angelica said hastily, feeling better. Cyndi Lauper might be older but Ma was . . . her mother.

Rocco opened the *Post*, his head snapped upright and Angelo, the barber downstairs at the St. Regis, who dispensed his forty-dollar haircuts to a chosen circle, narrowly missed nicking him with his scissors, although his reflexes were finely conditioned to the aberrant reactions of executives under stress.

"Hey, Rocco, trying to lose an ear?"

"I have to get to a phone. Don't bother to finish." Rocco stood up and started to undrape himself.

"Sit! I'm half through. You can't leave here like that."

"The hell I can't." Brushing off hairs, Rocco ran up the staircase. The phone booths in the lobby were all occupied. He rushed out of the hotel and saw that even if he could get a cab it couldn't move in the late-afternoon traffic. Where could he get a phone? All of the booths on the street were permanently out of order, vandalized as soon as they were repaired. The office was too far to run to. Angelo! He ran back to the hotel, descended the stairs three at a time and took unasked possession of Angelo's private phone. The barber, who could get a president of a Fortune 500 company a previously unobtainable reservation at the Hotel du Cap at Antibes during the busiest week of the year, merely raised an eyebrow. Rocco was crazy but his hair was a pleasure to cut. Old Country hair, thick, curly, healthy, the real thing, should last him till he didn't need it anymore.

"Maxi, I just read about Justin. What can I do to help?"

"I don't know. Mother's busy mobilizing legal talent but Justin hasn't the first idea of how the cocaine got there. Apparently he's been doing a lot of entertaining . . . he insists that it could be any one of dozens of people. However, he did say there had been some guy who had a key to his place but all he would tell us was it was someone he met on a shoot and that it couldn't possibly be him."

"Why not?"

"Apparently he's just too perfect a person," Maxi said dryly. "And Justin absolutely refused to tell us this saint's name. What's more the wonderful human being is out of town."

"Can you follow it up?"

"That's exactly what I've been asking myself. The first bathing-suit shoot Justin did for me used twenty-four male models. The next fashion feature was the one called 'Celebrity Closets, or The Positive Effects of Creative Disorder,' and the following month we had Bill Blass showing you thirty different ways to wear your oldest sweaters. Besides the fashion shots, Justin's done a lot of other stuff for us . . . I'm looking over the pictures now."

"Twenty-four male models? All from the same agency?"

"No, Julie booked them from four different agencies, or maybe even five."

"Look, get hold of the bills. They must be there at your office. Then give them to me and let me make a few phone calls. I'll let you know if anything checks out."

"I'll go get the bills now."

"Tomorrow morning is soon enough. I have to talk to people in their offices, people I can't call at home."

"I'll have them delivered first thing. Rocco, look, this is really extraordinarily sweet of you, and I'm deeply, deeply grateful," Maxi said. "I won't ever forget it."

"What the hell," Rocco said, ignoring her emotion. "You know I've always liked Justin. That poor bastard. How's Angelica taking it?" he asked, his voice suddenly anxious.

"In her own way."

"What's that supposed to mean?"

"If anyone survives this, it will be my daughter," Maxi sniffed.

"You don't understand her," Rocco said, "my daughter's an exceptionally sensitive little girl."

"Angelica has finer feelings I couldn't possibly comprehend, I suppose."

"Exactly. She's probably suffering a trauma you wouldn't even recognize, much less cope with."

"Rocco, I have an idea. Why don't I have Elie bring her over to your place? You can take her out to dinner tonight and help her deal with the shock."

"Uh. Well. As a matter of fact I have a date. Of course Angelica could join us, I guess, or maybe that wouldn't be such a great idea. No, probably not, on second thought. Angelica's going to be spending the weekend with me. We'll talk it all out then."

"You do that. Thanks anyway, Rocco. Talk to you." Maxi hung up softly, and looked around for something to throw at the wall, something guaranteed to break into a billion pieces and make one hell of a lot of noise. But nothing too valuable. That miserable pissant wasn't worth it.

"Sue, this is Rocco Cipriani."

"Oh, hi there, Mr. Cipriani. What can I do for you?" she chirped.

"There's a little question I'd like to ask about four of your guys," Rocco said lightly. Sue was the best booker of models at her agency.

"Sure thing. Which of our glorious boys interests you?"

"I'll tell you in a minute. It's a little delicate, Sue, but I'm sure you understand that sometimes I have to ask a, well, a somewhat hard question."

"That's what I'm here for," Sue proclaimed perkily.

Rocco gave her the names of the models from her agency who had been in the bathing-suit shoot and added, as if he were asking their chest measurements, "I'd like to know if one or more of them uses cocaine."

"Is this a complaint, Mr. Cipriani?" Sue asked after a tiny pause.

"No, Sue, nothing like that. Nothing to be alarmed about. But I figured that if anyone else had been having trouble with one or more of the guys, if there had just possibly been some complaints, you'd know about it before anyone else."

"Mr. Cipriani, you know as well as I do that if a model is on dope he won't last long. If we get enough complaints we drop him." Her upbeat voice had disappeared completely, replaced by the firmness that had made her a power in the industry.

"Of course you do. On the other hand, Sue, it's not impossible to get away with a few complaints here and there if you're really hot. A model in real demand can get away with murder, much less a few toots."

"Not here," she insisted. "This isn't Hollywood."

"Your people are special, Sue, we've always known that." Rocco's voice curled sweetly around the compliment. "I also want to find out if any of the guys I'm curious about are living high, spending more money than they could be earning."

"I still don't understand what you're driving at," she said, managing not to sound defensive.

"Why don't we put it this way?" Rocco said soothingly. "My instinct tells me that among the male models in this city, there are a few who are either heavy users or dealers in cocaine or both. One way or another, I really need the information."

"Not a model with this agency, Mr. Cipriani, no way, absolutely not."

"Maybe not. I'm pretty sure you're right. But something is going on. I'd also like to just suggest that the best interests of the entire modeling agency industry would be served if it polices itself. Call it a pre-police action, because, Sue, if, for some reason or another, I don't get those special names, I'm awfully afraid that the police are going to be out in force, crawling under and over every agency in the city," Rocco said. "In fact you can count on it," he added gently.

"I'll do everything I can to help," Sue said, determinedly businesslike. "I'll definitely ask around."

"Right, you do that little thing. By the way, I've been checking out the bookings CL&K did with your agency last year. Four hundred thousand dollars, wasn't it? No, actually quite a bit more than that. What do you know? You people really can pick 'em. Goodbye, Sue, and oh, if by some remote chance, you should happen to learn anything helpful, let me know fast, won't you?"

"Of course, Mr. Cipriani."

"By three-thirty or four this afternoon, let's say, in fact no later than the close of business today. And Sue, I'm really looking for a dealer, not just your dime-a-dozen user. I know that you're far too bright not to have realized that, aren't you? I'm not all that interested in your ordinary users—but I want their names anyway, just in case."

"In case?"

"Just in case. A *dealer and the people he sells to*. That's what I'm after, Sue. And that's what I'd better get. We're all equally concerned, aren't we? I'll be hearing from you, one way or the other, won't I?" The smile in Rocco's voice grew deeper.

"Sure thing. Absolutely. You can count on it. One way or the other. Oh, and thanks for calling, Mr. Cipriani."

"It's always nice to talk to you," Rocco said pleasantly. "A dealer, Sue, and the people he sells to."

Rocco spent the morning making four similar phone calls to the four other agencies who had supplied the, models for the bathing-suit story. All of them did a great deal of business with CL&K. He got the same set of resolutely negative answers but by five in the afternoon he had a longer list of names than he had anticipated and behind the scenes at five agencies a lot of very worried executives were consulting each other. This sort of thing wasn't supposed to be going on except at other agencies, they told each other. They could afford to lose CL&K's business if it came to that, but none of them could afford a scandal in the modeling industry. They had given Rocco every name they could pry or threaten out of their male models and their bookers, as well as the names of every model they had had vague suspicions about themselves. But exactly what had Cipriani meant by a "pre-police action"? they wondered. And why had he been so uncharacteristically pleasant? So terrifyingly *mild*?

Two days later Rocco telephoned Maxi at her office.

"Justin's in the clear, Maxi. I thought you'd like to know. All charges have been dropped."

"Rocco! Are you sure? Are you absolutely sure?"

"I just had a call from Charlie Salomon. He confirmed it."

"What did you do? How did you do it?" She was so excited that she almost dropped the phone.

"Oh, I just asked around."

"Rocco, don't drive me crazy. Oh shit, you're so wonderful—"

"Cut it out, Maxi. It was no big deal. I asked around for names and I got names and figured out who the guy was from your list and I gave the name to Salomon, plus the names of some people who'd been buying from Justin's friend and who were . . . urged . . . strongly urged, by their agencies, to agree to testify against him . . . nothing your average amateur detective couldn't do if he knew where to look."

"You're so incredible, you're the most marvelous—who was he?"

"Some beauty named Jon, a relatively minor-league dealer who was caught doing a little business with some much bigger fish down in Florida. He tried to cop a plea, putting the blame on Justin. He'd left his merchandise at Justin's place, unfortunately for Justin. Jon's not a very nice guy, basically. As Angelica would say, he has a massive attitude problem. Anyway, the cops managed to pick him up. A relatively simple matter once they knew who he was, or so I gather."

"Why do I have the feeling that there's something you're not telling me?"

"You always had a suspicious nature. Too bad Justin didn't. Anyway, that's that. I'm glad it's over. Goodbye, Maxi."

"Rocco, wait! Don't just hang up. Please let me thank you," Maxi pleaded. "You don't have the faintest idea of what this means to me. I'm just . . . I don't know what to say . . ." Her words fell over each other in a cry of thanksgiving. She sounded almost childish in her immense joy and gratitude.

"Oh, come on, cool it. I did it for Angelica and Justin. And your mother, of course. Salomon's calling her right now. Justin will be in the office sometime Monday, business as usual. He said to tell you."

"When did you talk to him?" Maxi asked incredulously.

"A few minutes ago. I figured he should be the first to hear the good news."

"What did he say?"

"Not much. He was relieved, naturally, but more than anything else he didn't want to believe that Jon had been the one to set him up. He had some very serious illusions about that creep. Your brother is one of the last of the great romantics. So, if I were you, I wouldn't act all bubbly and Mary Tyler Moore and thrilled when he shows up for work. Just try to act natural, like it's not the end of the world or something. Make it easy for the poor son of a bitch."

"I'll do my best," Maxi said softly.

"Try not to be too sloppy, O.K.?"

"Right, Rocco. Will do." Maxi looked for something satisfactorily resistant to grind under the four-inch heels of her new Mario Valentine pumps. "Good show. Well done. The family appreciates your efforts on our behalf and there will be a turkey for you in your Christmas basket, my good man."

All right, thought Maxi, all right, probably she had sounded as if he were Superman and she were Lois Lane tied to the railroad tracks, maybe she had let her happiness get out of control, but wasn't it normal to be grateful? How could anybody, even someone as thoroughly crusty and grumpy as Rocco Cipriani, not want to be thanked? How did a man get so contemptible? she asked herself furiously, sitting in a lump in the middle of her bed, her chin resting on her folded hands, her elbows on her knees, unmoving, brooding, a solid mass of resentment. He never lost a chance to try to make her feel feeble-minded, even when he was doing a good deed. He had actually accused her of insensitivity, warning her how to treat Justin, as if he expected her to be gauche and goofy. He'd always had that arrogant streak, that unbending vein of sheer shitheaded vanity that made him think that his way was the only right way. His trouble was that he thought he was the center of the universe. Nothing had ever really happened to him to make him realize that he was just a pinheaded pretty face who was clever with a pencil. Humility. Rocco needed to learn humility. She said the word out loud, savoring it, tasting the sweetness of it. But, unlike him, she was not a small-minded, petty, grudging, miserly person. She was happy to see that the father of her child was good in a crisis. He had done the Amberville family a gigantic service, and he was going to be rewarded for it whether he wanted to be or not. Rewarded royally, rewarded until it made him sick!

Suddenly gleeful, Maxi reached out for her now ever-present yellow pad and started to make notes. First, an Alfa-Romeo Spider convertible. What did it matter that he wouldn't be able to find a parking place for it and that a car like that was an invitation to vandals? She'd take whatever color was immediately available although she'd prefer black because it showed dirt faster. Next; that set of delicately etched antique crystal wineglasses she'd seen at James Robinson. Three thousand dollars and they had to be washed by hand, preferably in a rubber-lined basin, and dried with exquisite care. He'd probably break the lot in six months. What else? Why not a full set of antelope suede luggage from Loewe? The Spanish leather-goods makers had a shop downstairs and she'd been eyeing covetously their soft-sided pale gray bags, trimmed in burgundy, but of course they were too fragile for airplane travel; they'd be ruined in one trip. The smallest carry-on bag alone was almost six hundred dollars—maybe he could manage to keep that one looking decent for a while. Ah-ha, she had it, that glorious Art-Deco sterling silver and coffee set from Puiforcat. So what if it was forty thousand dollars—it had to be kept polished if it were to look like anything, just like any ordinary piece of silver. But you couldn't say it wasn't thoughtful.

A string of polo ponies? No, Maxi decided regretfully. They were only ten thousand each but even Rocco, unsophisticated as he was, would realize that they were inappropriate. Ponies needed a groom and boxes and regular feeding—either she'd have to throw in all the upkeep or not give them to him at all. Anyway he knew that she knew he couldn't ride. It would be delicious to give him a small Learjet 23 but three hundred thousand dollars seemed just a bit too much to spend to indicate her everlasting gratitude. Still, the list lacked something. It was skimpy. Why not a pair of tickets for a long Caribbean cruise? It would be good therapy for a devoted workaholic like Rocco. Perhaps two, no, make it three dozen of those lace-edged bath towels she'd seen at Barney's the last time she'd shopped retail. In beige, of course, or, better yet, plain white. Not an obviously feminine color. He should be able to find a fine hand laundry somewhere, if he looked hard enough. And just to show that she harbored nothing in her heart but sincere generosity, a case of Glenfiddich, his favorite pure malt whiskey. That should confuse him nicely, Maxi thought. What she'd really like to give him would be a folio of drawings by Leonardo da Vinci. That would show him the extent of his tiny talent as nothing else could. But the Queen of England had cornered the best of them and the Morgan Library had most of the rest.

There was a tap on her door and Angelica came in.

"Why aren't you with your father?" Maxi asked in surprise. It was Angelica's weekend to be with Rocco. "Don't tell me he canceled on you?"

"No, Ma, you know he'd never do that. He's got the most awful cold in the head. He just called and said he was sure he was contagious, swarming with germs and that I should ask if he could trade weekends with you."

"Sure you can," Maxi answered. Angelica looked even more doleful than before. "Don't you want to?"

"Well, actually, the Troop had planned something special for today because a lot of kids are home for spring vacations and I kind of hate to miss it. I mean, it's happenin' *this* weekend, not next weekend and anyway I'd like to have some time to myself, you know, to jam a little. Nothing bogus, Ma, just a little time raging with my people."

"You make it sound like rape and pillage," Maxi said, hairs lifting on her nape. "Raging?"

"I am referring," Angelica said with dignity, "to an afternoon at the circus followed by a dim sum rage, or, as you would put it, a nice time with nice young ladies and gentlemen, including refreshments."

"Be my guest," Maxi assured her. She had the greatest faith in the Troop and their activities. Angelica vanished skipping in a resounding whoop of joy, free from her guilt-ridden parents who took up far too much of her private life making up to her for their divorce. Didn't they know that everybody got divorced sooner or later?

Maxi started to get dressed for her shopping trip to buy Rocco's thank-you presents. Maybe he'd still be home sick when they were delivered. A terrible head cold could last a week. Spring vacations? Hadn't Angelica just said something about spring vacations? She looked out of the bathroom window and verified that spring had come to Central Park without notice, as surprisingly overnight as it had in *Mary Poppins*. A head cold and spring vacations. Why hadn't she realized it sooner? The malignant Cipriani hay fever had struck and Rocco, clinging stubbornly to his traditions, had refused to admit it, insisting, as he did every year, that it was unthinkable that he should suffer from such a sissy ailment since no Cipriani in history had ever had it. How could you get hay fever in Venice? Maxi had asked once, many years ago. She felt that the question was still valid.

Standing, rocking with laughter, in her pale lavender satin chemise, one foot about to be thrust into the right leg of a pair of sheer black stockings embroidered here and there with butterflies, Maxi was struck by a most kindly, most charitable, most openhearted impulse. She would just dart over and make Rocco more comfortable in his misery, like a higher form of visiting nurse. Indeed an angel of mercy.

She knew where Angelica kept the key to his place and she knew just the treatment for the Cipriani hay fever. There are some things you never forget. On her way to Rocco's, Maxi speculated about his apartment. He lived barely three blocks away, in a duplex on Central Park South, but she had never deigned to ask Angelica to describe it. She remembered Rocco's old longing for someplace monastic, austere and calm, as if he were a Japanese monk. Perhaps by now he had mastered the minimalist school of decorating, subtracting everything that made a house livable and spending all his money on fanatical detailing that nobody else would ever notice. Or else he'd gone in for hideously uncomfortable Mackintosh chairs and black-and-white tiles from the 1930s that had been ugly to begin with and hadn't improved with age in spite of their highly touted, inexplicable Andrée Putman chic. Maybe he was heavily invested in industrial objects, steel pipe sections and neon tubing, and slept on a mat on the floor. On the other hand that was all démodé. Perhaps by now he'd gone in for the Santa Fe Calvin Klein look—a nightmare out of Georgia O'Keeffe, with three meaningful stones on the mantel whose magic arrangement must never be changed, adobe walls on which the plaster was encouraged to flake and one perfect cactus, dying slowly. Or possibly he just lived like half the design snobs she knew, with all white walls and horribly boring and expensive Mies and Breuer furniture, punctuated by the obligatory Frank Stellas and Roy Lichtensteins. It was too much to hope that he was into the truly atrocious 1950s and laminated plywood. Probably, like most old bachelors, his place was bound to be basically a mess.

Quietly, Maxi used Angelica's key to open the front door. The entrance hall was a good-sized room she observed disapprovingly. How odd of him to have used fine old parquet, rubbed to a golden glow. What a strange place to put a life-sized Maillol torso of Venus, a powerful, darkly gleaming presence that held its own, magnificent against the melting magic, the receding rainbow tides of the two large Helen Frankenthalers on facing walls. No furniture, she noted, with the exception of a superb Regency table against the third wall, all curves and carving and unquestionably authentic to her experienced eye. Well, it's not all that difficult to buy good art if you have the money, she thought, closing the door softly behind her, and she disapproved of the art-gallery school of decorating on theory. Maxi listened for the sound of life in the apartment but heard nothing. Cautiously she made her way into the living room. Well, Rocco had certainly developed a taste for luxury that was quite out of keeping with his mingy highmindedness, a luxury that seemed to be set with a divine incongruity in an old barn in the country instead of on Central Park South. Sunlight poured into the two-story room and turned the walls, covered with wooden siding, into a source of subtle information on the beauty that weather can work on wood. Deep, downy, gray velvet sofas, separated by a Parsons table lacquered in Chinese red, turned their backs on each other in the center of the long room and faced the great twin fireplaces that were on each of the side walls. Old

Indian cashmere paisley in tones of biscuit, red and coral covered the supremely elegant Regency armchairs; here and there on the old brick floor were scattered Chinese silk rugs in muted, rare colors that echoed the sunlight.

Maxi sniffed as scornfully as possible. The most valuable piece in the room was clearly the Egyptian sculpture she'd given Rocco for their first Christmas together, an early Ptolemaic piece, a statue of Isis almost two feet tall, made from red quartzite. You could see every detail of her body, for the Egyptian goddesses wore robes more sheer than any Bob Mackie creation and the Isis had the most delicious breasts and bellybutton, almost as nice as her own, but no head. And the Maillol Venus had no arms. Apparently Rocco didn't like women enough to have one around who didn't lack a part of her anatomy.

She jumped at the sound of a violent sneeze, and a smile of anticipatory relish curved her tightly appraising mouth into a dangerous weapon, the particular smile that even Maxi was not vain enough to know drove men mad.

She crept softly upstairs toward the sound of sneezing and swearing and the blowing of a nose. All ugly and swollen she knew it would be, like a caricature of W. C. Fields at his worst.

The door to Rocco's bedroom was three-quarters closed. Inside she could see that it was dim, almost dark. He must have drawn the draperies and gone to ground under as many covers and quilts as he owned. No man had ever been brought so low by a head cold as Rocco Cipriani. Bad Dennis Brady treated them by switching from tequila to hot grogs and Laddie, Earl of Kirkgordon, simply ignored anything less than pneumonia. It was the weather, he explained. His ancestors had *always* had colds and what was good enough for Bonnie Prince Charlie was good enough for him.

Maxi coughed lightly to warn Rocco. There was no point in sending him into cardiac arrest when she'd come to make him feel better.

"Angelica, I told you not to come near me."

"It's just me," Maxi assured him. "Angelica was so worried about you that she insisted that I come over and make sure that you didn't need a doctor."

"Bugger off," he snarled, sneezing deliberately in her direction. All she could see of him was a gloomy hump of Dickensian churliness.

"Now Rocco," Maxi said soothingly, "you're just making yourself miserable. There's no need to act as if you're at death's door just because you have a little head cold."

"Go ahead, gloat, but get the fuck out of my house."

"Isn't that a little paranoid? Why would I gloat over the suffering of any human being? Particularly the father of my child? I only came to reassure Angelica. However," Maxi said cheerfully, throwing open draperies, "since I am here, I'll do what I can to make you more comfortable."

"I don't want to be comfortable. I want to be alone! In the dark!"

"Typical, typical, everyone knows how men love to suffer. I bet you haven't even taken any vitamin C," Maxi said, eyeing the giant sprays of budding forsythia that stood in a superb Florentine jar on a table near his bed. Renaissance majolica unless she was badly mistaken. There was the source of his cold, although he'd never believe it.

"Vitamin C's a crock. It's never been proven," Rocco wheezed, sliding farther down under the covers and trying to pull a pillow over his head.

"But we don't know for sure, do we? Anyway even you know you need liquids. I'm going to make you a pitcher of fresh orange juice and leave it for you."

"Just leave. I don't have any oranges. Out. Out!"

Maxi disappeared, closing his door, before he could actually rouse himself to throw her out bodily. She had brought a bag of oranges from home, anticipating this deplorable state of gender-specific need. Men, in her experience, never had oranges at hand. Lemons, yes, apples sometimes, but not oranges. She tiptoed down the stairs and found the kitchen. It was, she saw at once, four times as big as her own, and much more cheerful. Of course, it didn't have a view of the World Trade Center, she told herself while she squeezed the oranges, but it did have a highly polished eight-burner cast-iron range, a floor of golden travertine marble, a huge wooden worktable that looked Pennsylvania Dutch and a burnished bronze refrigerator full of champagne. She peeked into the freezer. As she had thought, many bottles of vodka, all frozen to that thick, glacial condition that makes it go down the throat like a kiss blown by a friendly iceberg. Thoughtfully she added three-quarters of one entire bottle to the pitcher of juice and tasted it. You couldn't even tell it was there because of the sweetness of the fruit. She put the pitcher in the refrigerator to get colder and went in search of the linen closet. Nothing made a sick person feel better than clean crisp sheets. Well! So India wasn't the only person she knew who was depraved on the subject of linen. Rocco had everything you could buy at Pratesi, all in solid white with severe geometric borders in dark brown, navy blue and deep purple. Did himself well, didn't he? Pratesi could be even more expensive than Porthault although if you flew to Milan for it the trip paid for itself. She gathered up thousands of dollars worth of pure Egyptian cotton and returned to the kitchen for the juice and a big glass and made her way back upstairs.

Noiselessly she opened his door. As she had thought, he was fast asleep. Maxi burrowed under the covers and found Rocco's big toe. It was the gentlest way to be awakened. She tugged on his toe with a light touch until he stirred, and kept tugging until he emerged from under his pillow.

"Juice time," she trilled as prettily as Julie Andrews.

"I don't fucking believe it," he moaned and sneezed ferociously. She gave him a fresh Kleenex and a full glass of orange juice, holding it with impersonal dignity. He drank deeply and grunted something that could be taken for thanks. She poured another full glass and put it into his hand.

"You're dehydrated. That can be dangerous," Maxi warned him.

"Later. Just put it down. And go."

"I will, but only when you've finished," she promised. He drank it quickly, to show her how anxious he was for her to leave, and then fell back on his pillow and closed his eyes. Maxi waited a few minutes for the vodka to have its calming effects on his nervous system.

"Rocco?"

"Yeah."

"Feel any better?"

"Maybe. A little."

"In that case I suggest that you take a nice long shower, and while you're doing that I'll make your bed."

"Shower? You're crazy. Change of temperature at a time like this could kill me. Kill me."

"Don't take a hot shower, take a room-temperature shower. I guarantee it'll make you feel so much better, honestly."

"Sure?"

"Positive. And fresh, cool, lovely sheets . . . wouldn't they feel good?"

"Couldn't hurt. Since you're here. Then you'll go? You promise?"

"Of course. More orange juice?"

"Maybe—try another glass. Seems to help." He tottered happily toward the bathroom, carrying the glass with him. Maxi bustled about. One thing she could do was make a damn good bed. She heard him in the shower, not singing but not sneezing either. She moved the forsythia to the hallway with the pile of discarded bed linen and pulled the draperies almost shut.

Ten minutes later Rocco emerged to find an empty bedroom, with just enough light in it for him to make out his newly made bed with the quilt pulled high, just the way he liked it. With a sigh of relief he flung himself into the heavenly sheets and stretched out, groaning with pleasure.

"*Aiiiii!*" He bounded off the mattress. His foot had just touched something—alive.

"For goodness' sake, it's only me," Maxi whispered. "I thought you could see. Sorry."

"Whatcha doing in my bed?"

"I must have fallen asleep. It's such a big bed to make, so hard to get around."

"You're naked," he pointed out.

"I am?" she said sleepily.

"Uh-huh."

"Hmm . . . that's odd, so I am." She yawned. "I must have thought I was at home. Do forgive me."

"Don't scare me again. Hate being scared."

"Of course you do," Maxi murmured maternally, pulling his head to her marvelous breasts like sun-warmed fruit of the gods. "Of course you do, poor thing, poor, *poor* Rocco, it's so terrible to have a cold."

"I'm catching," he sighed, starting to suck on one of her nipples.

"No, no, don't worry, I never caught your colds." She was kissing his shoulder and a particularly tender spot at the back of his neck where he was especially fond of being kissed if memory served.

Memory served. Blissfully, sweetly, and soon irresistibly, memory served, lulled by Russia's gift to the world and assisted by Maxi's dexterous lips and limbs, memory was gloriously celebrated.

Hours later, toward twilight, Rocco woke up with a floatingly light head and a profound sense of uneasiness. Something had happened. He wasn't sure what. He wasn't sure when or how but *something* had happened. Instinctively, with inching caution he explored his bed. It was empty. Something was still wrong. He turned on his bedside light and looked around the room. Nobody was there. He got out of bed and listened to the sounds of his apartment. He could tell at once that he was entirely alone. Why did he feel so worried? He returned to his bed and gazed at the ceiling. Memory returned. Oh God. Oh no. *That bitch.* Memory unveiled itself further, disclosing details. Not once, not twice, but three times. He knew it. She was trying to kill him. Three times in a row. What was he supposed to be, fourteen fucking years old? She'd raped him, that's what she'd done, or was it sexual harassment? Could you claim rape three times in one afternoon? Angrily he realized that he was grinning like an imbecile. Rocco whacked his pillow until the feathers flew out of it. How like her, to take advantage of a sick man. A vampire, that's what she was. She knew, that vicious, unpardonable, victimizing, manipulative, unspeakably evil creature, she knew perfectly well that when he had a head cold he always got horny.

"So, schmuck," he said out loud to himself, "how come you're not sneezing?"

24

"Maxi, could you come into my office for a minute?" Monty asked, grabbing her by the arm. "Your office is a madhouse and we have to talk."

It was early in the morning of Monday, April 15, and Maxi had just started working on the final corrections of the proofs of the September issue of *B&B* which was to go to press in a week. The article by Madonna called "The Easy-to-Come-by Joys of Narcissism" needed more pictures and Dan Rather's piece, "Nobody Knows How Shy I Am," had developed into a regular column, with celebrities vying with each other to expose the adolescent terrors they still endured. "Those Necessary Lies: Why You Must Never Feel Guilty" by Billy Graham had brought so many readers' letters that more of them had to be reprinted on the letter page than anyone had expected and the "I Wish I Were" monthly article for September, in which Johnny Carson wished he were Woody Allen and Elizabeth Taylor wished she were Brooke Shields, had somehow gotten screwed up, so the way it read now Woody Allen wished he were Brooke Shields. What was more disturbing, something in the "pace" of the issue that was laid out, pinned page by page on the walls of her office, was slightly off to Maxi's eye.

"Couldn't it be after lunch, Monty?" she pleaded. "This stuff is urgent."

"Now, please." When Monty said something in that emphatically unalarmed tone of voice, Maxi had learned to question him no further. She led the way to his office, tucked away in a far corner of the additional space she'd rented after the first issue had sold out. On the way she passed Julie's all-white office where her fashion editor was huddled over the telephone. Ever since the story linking Jon and Justin had appeared in the newspapers Julie had tried to avoid her, but Maxi had seen her proudly concealed anguish and immediately guessed at its cause. She felt intense sympathy for Julie but to express it would be to show her that she knew why her friend was so deeply wounded, and Maxi judged it was best to let her be for a little while. Eventually time would heal, Maxi thought, as she walked along the busy corridor and responded to greetings. It was an old cliché, cold comfort indeed, but it happened to be true. If she had found out that Rocco was gay when she worked on *Savoir Vivre*, how much time would it have taken her to get over him? Six months? No. More. A year? Probably more. Her reverie was interrupted by Monty who ushered her into his office, closed the door firmly behind him, and stood with his back to it so that nobody could come in.

"Lewis Oxford just called. He must have gone crazy but he sounded sane. He told me that he was putting us on notice that Amberville Publications is shutting down *B&B*. Everybody here is fired as of the end of this business day. He has already called Meredith/Burda to notify them that Amberville will not authorize payment for printing the September issue. They're calling all our suppliers to tell them not to extend us a penny's credit. He's acting on direct orders from Cutter Amberville, who is acting for your mother."

"She would not do that. He's simply wrong." Maxi spoke with the anesthetized coldness of shock.

"When was the last time you talked to her?"

"Just last week, when Justin was freed. We're on the best terms we've been on in years. Look, Monty, this is some trick of Cutter's. He's trying some new tactic that I can't understand until I talk to her. You just sit on this absurdity until I go uptown and see her—she's always home in the mornings. And keep your lip buttoned, or whatever."

"Obviously. But I'm worried about the printer. If we lose our time on the presses, if they've already replaced us for next week, we won't get the issue out in time even when you straighten things out. They sell their time months in advance."

"Call Mike Muller, the Burda business guy at the plant, and tell him that I personally guarantee payment. Me, Maxime Amberville."

"Will do," Monty said, looking as if he would like to ask more questions. Maxi hurried out of his office and rushed downstairs to where Elie was waiting for her.

She burst in on Lily who was conferring with her chef about a dinner party.

"Mother, we have to talk right away."

"Maxime, I've been trying to reach you all weekend. Jean-Philippe, I'll finish this menu later. Where were you, Maxime? I've been so anxious to speak to you."

"Out," Maxi answered mechanically. "Mother, Lewis Oxford just called to say we didn't have any more credit, that *B&B* was out of business."

"Oh dear, oh dear, this is exactly what I didn't want to have happen! That fool Oxford! I warned Cutter that I wanted to have a meeting with you and Toby and Justin all together, first, but obviously Oxford didn't check with me to make sure it had taken place."

"What does that mean, 'first'? Why do you want to talk to the three of us? What does it have to do with *B&B?*"

"Maxime, do stop shouting. Oh, dear, I *so* wanted this to be an orderly event, and now it's spoiled." Lily actually wailed in distress.

"Mother, you are going to drive me out of my mind. What in holy hell are you talking about?"

"I can understand that you're upset, dear, hearing it like that. I wanted to tell you all at the same time." She paused for a few seconds and then continued, resolutely, "I have decided to sell Amberville Publications to the United Broadcasting Corporation, but now it's been announced in the worst possible way." Lily twisted the head off a rose in a silver bowl.

"Mother! I don't give a damn what form this decision comes in! *How can you sell?* I . . . I don't understand anything you're saying. Sell our business? Sell Father's business? Sell Amberville? It's . . . it's—you just can't do it—it's—*unthinkable.*" Maxi sat down opposite her mother, her legs drained of strength, her heart sinking as she read the stubborn expression on Lily's face, only agitated by the way in which she had to present a decision on which Maxi could see she was determined.

"Now, Maxime, do listen to me and stop saying the first thing that comes into your mind. It's not at all unthinkable. It makes great sense. Since your father died the company has been without its founder. It's kept on going by momentum but that momentum can't last forever. UBC is interested in buying the company and Cutter believes that in three months, when the sale will take place, the price will be close to—well, more or less a billion dollars. This is an opportunity that may never come again and it's obvious that I have to act on it. Maxime, you and Toby and Justin will receive a hundred million dollars each. There's no way in which any of you can realize your ten percent unless I sell, but that's not the only reason I'm doing it."

"Mother . . ."

"No, *wait,* Maxime, don't interrupt until you hear me out. I can't run a magazine publishing company, Cutter doesn't want the responsibility and I don't blame him, Toby obviously has his own life, Justin has his, and although you're having fun with your fling at turning out a magazine, you obviously aren't cut out to run a vast enterprise. If the company is ever to be sold, the time is now, not later. I know that *B&B* is having a dear little boom but you have to admit that it's costing the company a fortune. Cutter reluctantly had to tell me how much money *B&B* loses each month and I was horrified. It's too expensive a toy even for you, Maxime, and UBC will be buying Amberville on the basis of what Cutter called a very sick-looking balance sheet if it continues to be published."

"So it *was* on your orders that Oxford called?"

"Yes, of course, but I had intended to explain it all to you before any of you heard from him. Nobody is supposed to know about the sale until it's gone through, except the family. I'm deeply distressed that you had this shock. If only I'd been able to reach you over the weekend . . ."

"I was out," Maxi repeated. "Mother, don't you understand that a new magazine automatically loses money no matter how big a success it is, until it starts getting enough income from the advertisers? I literally almost *gave* away the advertising to get the magazine off the ground, and it costs more to print an issue than I can sell it for on the racks."

"That was clever of you, I suppose, although I'm no judge . . . it sounds to me as if you willfully took a big risk. But that's neither here nor there, Maxime, since the decision to sell is mine to make, and I've made it. I'm being guided by Cutter in how to handle Amberville affairs until the sale is official and he is quite adamant about stopping publication of *B&B* right now. I'm sorry for your disappointment, dear—"

"Disappointment." Maxi's echo was flat. The gap between the way she and her mother felt about *B&B* was so vast that no words could bridge it, no emphasis of tone could make any difference. Her mother would never be convinced by anything she could say that *B&B* was not just a plaything but the only tribute that was in her power to make to Zachary Amberville and the great love she had for him.

"Well, I know you've been having a terribly amusing time and I'm really proud of how well it's selling, but obviously you couldn't have done it without using the company's money, could you?" Lily continued.

"No, as a matter of fact, I couldn't. No way," Maxi admitted.

"Well then, you do see, don't you? It's not like a real magazine, is it, dear? It's subsidized, it's not paying its own way."

"No. that's wrong, Mother. It is a *real* magazine. *Millions* of women pay a dollar fifty for it every month. I have a fantastic staff working their hearts out. *B&B* exists, it's growing like mad, the September issue has two hundred and fifty pages, it's crammed with ads and photographs and articles and we get thousands of letters from our readers, it's as real as any other magazine, it's just *young,*" Maxi said passionately.

Lily laughed indulgently. "Maxime, Maxime, I'm pleased to see you sticking to something for such a long time, and if your father were alive he would have been delighted, but you just have to accept the reality of the sale of Amberville. It's in all of our best interests."

"Mother, look. If, *before* the sale goes through, I can show you that Amberville Publications isn't losing money because of *B&B*, if the company is worth just as much as it would be without *B&B*, would you reconsider your decision to sell?" Maxi asked quietly.

"First of all, you don't know how Justin and Toby will feel. I've told you how Cutter and I feel. No, Maxime, I can't promise to reconsider."

"If I don't ask you to 'promise' to reconsider; if, just before the three months are up, I come to you and just ask you *to think about it again* . . ." Maxi asked imploringly.

"I'm afraid that the answer will still be no, dear, but, of course, you can always come and ask," Lily said gently. She found it hard to refuse Maxime absolutely when she obviously cared so much and was being so reasonable. There was no harm in letting her "ask" again since it was obvious that she couldn't accomplish the impossible and publish without money. And if she didn't insist that her daughter accept her decision right now, it would end this upsetting interview so much more quickly and pleasantly. She'd have time to finish planning the menu for her dinner party before lunch.

"Where to now, Miss A. ?" Elie asked.

"The Amberville Building," Maxi answered. She must talk to Pavka. He was the only person to whom she could go for advice. At the offices of *B&B* everyone would be looking to her for leadership but she needed help herself as she had never needed it before. She prayed that he was in his office and not out enjoying one of the long lunches for which publishing was more guilty than Hollywood. She had to talk to Pavka before she went to speak to her accountants to get the money to keep *B&B* operating.

"Is he in?" she asked Pavka's secretary anxiously, skidding to a halt before her desk.

"He's in your father's office," the secretary answered and Maxi could see that she was puzzled. "He's been in there for a half hour and he asked me not to put through any calls. But of course he'd see you—perhaps if I just knock—" Maxi was gone before she could even get up, headed at a half-run down the corridor to the door of the office which nobody had used or changed since Zachary Amberville's death.

"Pavka?" she questioned softly. His back was turned to her and he was standing at one of the windows, his head bowed, leaning on the sill with both hands in a position she had never seen him in before, a posture of helplessness. He turned and the amused and knowing look she was so used to seeing on his alert, dandy's face was gone. In its place there was a gravity that matched hers and something she recognized as deep grief. And yet he could not possibly know about the proposed sale yet. Lily had said that only the family would be told now.

"You must have received one of these too," Pavka said, holding out a sheet of paper, without even greeting her.

"No, nobody's sent me anything—not on paper anyway. Aren't you going to give me a kiss?"

"A kiss?" he asked absently. "Did I not kiss you?" He gave her a brief peck, very unlike his traditionally close and appreciative embrace and for the first time since she'd gone to see Lily, Maxi felt real terror.

"Read this," he said, handing her the memo from the office of the Vice-President for Financial Affairs. It listed all the changes and cuts that Cutter had outlined to

Oxford. Copies had been sent to the editors and managing editors and art directors of all six Amberville publications. Maxi read it in silence. Nothing was said about the sale of the company.

"I intend to resign," he told her abruptly. "I don't have the power to prevent these measures but I refuse to have my name associated with them; using the cheapest writers and photographers we can find; cutting the number of color pages; throwing everything to celebrity models; getting editorial pages from advertisers for plugs; using inferior paper and eating up everything in inventory, including those many projects that didn't turn out well enough to come up to our standards. This memo is vile, Maxi, *vile!*" He quivered with rage and frustration.

"Pavka, please sit down and talk to me," Maxi implored, *B&B* forgotten in the shamefulness of what she had just read. They both sank into the weathered leather armchairs that faced Zachary Amberville's desk and fell silent. In spite of their anger and concern, as soon as they stopped speaking they became aware that in the office something was still happening. They felt it immediately. Some activity was continued within the room that didn't need a human presence, something alive and powerful and joyous, imprinted in the very walls; a sense memory of Zachary Amberville hung in the air, as robust and enthusiastic as he had been when they'd last seen him. Pavka and Maxi both drew deep breaths and, for the first time, smiled at each other. Still they didn't begin to speak as they looked around the big, always disordered, wood-paneled room, its walls covered with the originals of some of the famous covers and illustrations that he had published over the years and, here and there, signed photographs of Presidents of the United States, of writers, photographers and illustrators. Nowhere was there a photograph of Zachary Amberville himself, but the memory of his excited, amused, vibrant, living voice seemed to echo in the room, his appetite for excellence, his belly laugh, his roar of approval when an associate made a good suggestion, the outpouring of his energy, ardor and fervor that had been concentrated on every issue of each magazine he had ever published—all this lived on without him.

"Pavka," Maxi said, "am I right in thinking that the price paid for a company is based on how much profit it's making at the time of sale?"

"Normally yes. Why do you ask?"

"If," Maxi continued, not answering his question, "you resigned, but the magazines continued to be published, incorporating all the changes that Oxford has ordered, how soon would the economies show up as profit?"

"On the next balance sheet, in three months. But, Maxi, that's beside the point. The magazines would be cheaper to produce but they could never be the *same.* We'd know it right away as we worked on the new issues, and in time our readers would see the difference, no matter how cleverly it was done. They might not be able to tell you exactly what was wrong with *Seven Days* or *Indoors* or the others but they wouldn't look forward to a new issue with the same excitement, they wouldn't read them with the same satisfaction, and eventually, after a year or so, they would either accept them in their diminished, cheapened state—as so much *is* accepted by consumers—or stop buying them altogether. We've never settled for less than our highest possible degree of excellence, but this memo takes the idea of excellence and spits on it."

"My mother intends to sell Amberville Publications based on the earnings shown in the next balance sheet," Maxi said tonelessly.

"Ah." There was a world of sadness and disillusionment in his sigh. "So that explains it. I should have guessed. What a fool I am, not to have thought of that:

It is the only possible explanation for destroying what your father stood for. Still, I'm amazed that she's doing it this way. The magazines could be sold untouched, intact and proud. There would be no dishonor then in selling them if that's what she has decided to do."

"But less money?"

"Oh, yes, less, unquestionably somewhat less, but still enough for any family until the end of time," he said bitterly. "She'll have my resignation within an hour. I predict that many other people will resign too. I came in here to escape their outraged phone calls. They don't realize that even I can't fight this. Soon the editors who knew your father best and longest, the key people, will decide that they don't want to have any part of it, if they haven't made that decision already. Also, they've been around long enough to know that inevitably they'd be on their way out after the sale. The new owners, whoever they are, will change the magazines to suit themselves, put in their own people. In a few years you won't know that this group of magazines was once Amberville Publications although the magazines will probably have the same names. That's all that's being sold now: brand names."

"How can you be so sure that the new owners won't want to keep on the people who made the magazines great?"

"Oh, Maxi, perhaps they will try, after all. Perhaps they will be wise. But good editors must spend money and this memo makes that impossible. When a Company that has been created by one man is sold, the heart goes out of it, the soul if you will, the spirit of the founder, the vision of that one man can't possibly be retained. Look, right here, on this memo, it's started already. I'm appalled by your mother, Maxi, appalled. As long as Amberville Publications lived, so did your father." He shook his head with something far deeper than sadness as he thought of the high hearts and great plans with which he and Zachary Amberville had embarked on their publishing adventure almost forty years ago.

Slowly Maxi rose and walked the few paces to her father's desk and sat down in the chair that nobody but he had ever used. In her mind she turned over everything her mother had said. *B&B*'s future was only a small part of the puzzle. What was happening was the willful dismembering of Zachary Amberville's achievement, an achievement that had continued on past his death, that had lived and prospered for a year and could endure indefinitely with the group of loyal people he had drawn together around him, far into the future. Six enormously prosperous, powerful magazines were to be cheapened, degraded and then sold to no necessary purpose. A lifetime's achievement was being destroyed, her father's lifetime. The dividends that came from Amberville Publications had supported his family in luxury until now, and would do so as long as people could still read.

Cutter. There was only one person whose interests could be served by tearing down the monument that Amberville Publications was to her father's memory. Cutter. Everything Maxi knew or had observed about Cutter, everything she sensed, everything her instincts told her, everything she and Toby and Justin had felt about this younger brother who had married their mother, gathered into a cloud and the cloud began to take a form, to solidify into a shape, the shape of a great hate. *A great envy*. Envy even more potent than hatred. First he had taken his brother's wife. Then Cutter had strangled the last of Zachary Amberville's new creations, those three magazines that hadn't yet hit their stride. And now he was sucking the guts out of the sturdy giants and selling them as quickly as he could. Only envy could answer for his actions, only her father's death had given him the chance to first mutilate and then betray a life's work he could never have matched.

She wasn't going to let him do it.

"Pavka, don't resign," Maxi said. "Please, for me, don't resign. I'm going to fight this sale. I think I can influence my mother not to do it. If you can keep everybody calmed down and working for the next few months, making these infernal changes as slowly and as imaginatively as humanly possible, trimming here and there but not enough to seriously compromise the October and November issues, dragging your heels on absolutely everything, making Oxford pin you to the wall on the tiniest detail, commissioning articles and photographs by the best people you know, *as of yesterday*, if you can do all that, Pavka, I'm going to fight Cutter."

"Cutter?"

"None of this started as my mother's idea, Pavka. Cutter has led her into it, I promise you. It could never have happened without his influence."

Pavka came close to the desk and inspected Maxi gravely, without the familiar overtone of flirtation and mutual charm that had always colored their relationship. She sat there, where he had never seen anyone but Zachary Amberville sit, with an unthinking ease, a sureness, a right of possession. He would not have dared to use that chair, yet she had taken it unconsciously. And she spoke with a firmness, a cleverness, a cold purpose, a gathering together of forces, that he had never dreamed she could call upon. This was not the girl he had watched so long as she flitted after fun, living as if her life were a gigantic sack of brightly colored lollipops, to each of which she'd give one experimental lick before discarding it for another. He had rarely caught sight of Maxi since her return, he realized, and in the months since that shocking board meeting she had changed profoundly. She had not, he thought, aged, no, that wasn't the word. She had grown up. Maxi Amberville had become a woman.

"Why are you going to fight Cutter? If you leave things alone the only thing that can happen to you is that you will become richer," Pavka said, and there was a warning in his tone. Maxi, grown up, was still not a match for Cutter, with Lily under his domination. "I know you detest him, but that is no reason to engage yourself in a corporate battle."

"It's not a personal vendetta, Pavka. I'm doing it for my father," Maxi said simply. "I'm doing it because I loved him more than anyone in the world and this is the one way I can show how much he meant—how much he *means*—to me."

"In that case, I too will do my best. For my dear friend, your father."

Maxi had telephoned her accountants from Pavka's office and made an appointment to see Lester Maypole, of Maypole and Maypole, who had acted as her personal accountant from the days she had first had the spending of her own trust fund. On the drive downtown Maxi thought about money. It was not a topic on which she usually spent much time. It was as familiar as one of her senses, taken for granted as much as touch or smell. Her mother had talked about a hundred million dollars but Maxi did not see why, when she had always had everything she wanted, she should be interested in such a sum, impossible to comprehend. It would only create problems. Right now she was rich in the same way that she had ten fingers and ten toes. A hundred million dollars would be like having two heads.

She had been born rich, she reflected, as the limousine slipped through traffic like a long, blue snake, and she'd grown up rich, and when she'd been poor, or living as if she were poor, during the time she and Rocco were married, she hadn't liked it at all so she had simply arranged to stop being poor. It had been the same as taking off an uncomfortable pair of new shoes endured during a necessary hike; she had just stepped out of poorness and resumed the comfort of the richness that had been there waiting for her all along. Of course the detour into an early marriage and early motherhood had kept her from getting trapped in the rich girl's world; the silliness of debutantes and fortune hunters; or else the obvious solution of a solid match with somebody appropriate, followed by the accumulation of country houses and dogs and horses. Instead, she supposed, she had fallen into the category that the late-night movies would label "madcap heiress."

B&B had taught her what it cost to budget a magazine but it hadn't influenced her habits of private spending. Nameless people in Lester Maypole's office paid all her bills and since she'd had no complaints from them she could only assume that there was more than enough to sustain her style of living: to pay for the upkeep on the apartment; the travel; the servants who cooked and laundered and cleaned and drove; the garage; the caterers who did the parties; the florists who sent in flowers twice a week for every room in the apartment; the clothes she wore for the season in which they were fashionable and then replaced; the buckets of jewelry she hadn't had time to add to since *B&B* started. And then there was Angelica. Rocco paid for half of Angelica's clothes and school because he insisted on it, so Angelica really was one of the least expensive items in her life, somewhere between food and flowers, so much more necessary than one, so much more beautiful than the other. Of course, there were her collections, Maxi reminded herself. The antiques, the precious boxes, the old silver; so many collections that had had to be put into storage when she moved to the Trump Tower from her old town house in the East Sixties.

What, Maxi asked herself, did her accountants do with all of the money she received that she didn't spend? Did they reinvest it in stocks and bonds? Did they risk it in the market or buy the safest possible securities? She had no head for the subject and no need to force herself to take an interest in it. That was what she paid Maypole for. But it stood to reason that she must have pots of money. And anyone with money could always get more, everybody knew that.

Lester Maypole looked at Maxi as if she were a cross between a mermaid and a hippogriff, a mythological creature who had materialized in his office with a list of what would have been perfectly reasonable questions if it weren't for one fact: Maxime Amberville had always lived up to her huge income, from her trusts and her Amberville dividends. Not beyond it, just within it. And she didn't seem to realize this fact which had been writ large on the bottom of every month's statement they had ever sent her.

"But you never *warned me*, Mr. Maypole," Maxi protested, disbelieving, just beginning to be angry.

"Miss Amberville, we're accountants, not keepers. We just receive your monies and pay your bills. There's never been any reason for us to think that you didn't know that you were spending up to the limit so long as you didn't exceed it. You never expressed any interest in investments or we would have told you that you had none. Your art objects and your apartment and your jewelry are all assets, of course, but as for the rest—" He waved his hand expressively.

"I've just pissed it away."

"Oh, don't be too hard on yourself. After all it did cost you almost three million dollars to refurnish Castle Kirkgordon . . ."

"Laddie Kirkgordon had sold practically everything but his bed to pay death duties . . . it seemed the least I could do . . . and there wasn't any central heating, none at all," Maxi explained, remembering those frozen, titled years.

"And then, in Monte Carlo, your pearls were stolen . . . twice. The double strands were worth almost nine hundred thousand dollars and you didn't have insurance. Each time you *replaced* the pearls."

"It wasn't really *in* Monte Carlo. The police there are very effective. It was pirates on the high seas . . . or at least that's what they looked like to me. I couldn't get insurance, Mr. Maypole. Any wife of Bad Dennis Brady's, even a short-term one, was considered to be a bad insurance risk, with good reason, but a girl *has* to have her wedding pearls," Maxi said indignantly. It wasn't as if they had been diamonds after all.

"On top of that, you're in the highest possible tax bracket, you give very large amounts to charity and you've lost several major fortunes in casinos." He coughed, just short of disapprovingly.

"It's such fun to gamble, but nobody sensible expects to *win*," Maxi explained.

"That's more or less my point," Lester Maypole said quietly.

"It's *all* gone?"

"I would hardly put it that way. You are a very rich young woman. You own ten percent of a great company. Why shouldn't you spend your money freely?"

"Pissed it away," Maxi repeated furiously.

"You could have employed someone who specialized in estate management . . ."

"But it's too late now, isn't it?"

"For the past, I'm afraid so, but there's enough in your account to carry you until the next yearly dividends are declared in June, unless you've just bought something I don't know about."

"How much will the dividends amount to?" she pounced, hope suddenly restored.

"That will depend on your mother. The owner of the controlling interest in any company declares dividends as he or she sees fit."

"Would you care to bet on the size of this year's dividends, Mr. Maypole? Never mind. What about my ten percent of Amberville? I'd like to borrow on that up to the maximum."

"That stock can't be sold to anyone but your mother," Lester Maypole said. Surely she must know that much.

"It's still stock," Maxi objected wildly. She felt as if Maypole were torturing her for his own pleasure.

"You can't borrow on it, Miss Amberville. Not a penny."

"You mean it is as if it didn't exist? It doesn't *count?*"

"Miss Amberville, please, don't get so upset. It exists, it counts, it belongs to you. You just can't *borrow* on it, because you can't *sell* it to an outsider."

"You're saying that I don't have any money."

"You could put it that way, for the moment, yes, I suppose you don't actually have any, well, any *cash*."

"Thank you, Mr. Maypole." Maxi was gone like lightning striking too close, leaving Lester Maypole sweating in alarm. She didn't seem to understand the difference between money and cash and he, for once, had lost track of it himself. He looked in his wallet. Twenty-four dollars. He buzzed his secretary. "Linda," he said, his heart beating ridiculously, "get me my investment portfolio, right away. And then take a check to the bank. No, I just want some cash in fives. And make it snappy."

Maxi pushed her way through the crowds listening to a pianist and violinist playing "Alice Blue Gown" in the lobby of the Trump Tower. She didn't notice the eighty-foot-tall waterfall which was running at the highest of its three speeds, or the walls and floor of shrimp-pink and mango-colored Breccia Perniche marble, nor did she spare a glance for thriving ponytail palms and the lovers kissing on the escalators. She took the first elevator to the right and went straight up to the large suite of offices from which the building was run.

"Louise," she asked the warm, blond woman who was vice-president of Trump, "can I hock my apartment?"

Louise Sunshine didn't look surprised. Years of working with restless, unpredictable Donald Trump had made her immune to shock of any kind. "The Residential Board doesn't like liens on apartments, Maxi. What's the matter, gal, want to buy the Pentagon?"

"More or less. Is Donald available?"

"To you, always. Just let me check and make sure he's not on the phone."

Maxi waited impatiently but her heart contracted as she looked out of the window. There, but at a much lower height than her sixty-third floor, was the view that she loved so intensely; the view invented to drive people to extremes of adoration or hate, a view of a city that everyone took personally, as an affront or as a challenge or as something to which it was virtuous to be indifferent. New York was never *just* a city, it was a place that had to belong to you or be chased from your consciousness. And from no other location could the city look so heartbreakingly beautiful, so truly the dream and not the reality.

"Go right on in," Louise Sunshine said, startling her.

Donald Trump, the brilliant, ambitious young real-estate man whom even his enemies had to admit was disarmingly unaffected, rose to greet Maxi.

"Hey you, pretty girl, what's the problem?"

"I need cash, and I need it fast."

"That happens in the best of families," he grinned.

"Can you sell my apartment, Donald? This week?"

"Hold on a minute, Maxi, are you sure you want to do that?" Suddenly he looked totally serious. "I've always got a waiting list for your apartment—next to mine it's the best and biggest in the whole tower, but once it's gone, it's gone forever. And there will never be another great one like it. It's an 'L' and an 'H' thrown together—almost four thousand square feet." His concern was genuine. There was a certain normal amount of turnover in apartments in the building but generally they were those which had been bought specifically for investment. Maxi, who loved her apartment the way he loved his, as a part of herself, as an extension of her capacity for life, would never sell unless she was in serious trouble and had nothing else left to sacrifice.

"Can you promise I'll get my money this week?"

"Maxi, how much money do you need exactly? Maybe there's another way . . ."

"I don't know the exact amount, a minimum of six million dollars—probably more."

"That much? And right away?" He considered a moment and then he said, "No, there's no other way. Look, it will take me a little time to make the best possible deal for you but if you want to turn the apartment over to me I'll write you a check for six million. Then, if I can sell it for more, and I hope that I can, I'll give you the rest when the deal closes."

"Where do I sign?" Maxi asked.

"I just hope it's worth it, whatever it is," he said, shaking his head, and picking out a checkbook from his desk drawer.

"It's worth trying, Donald, even if I don't win. Give me your pen, damn it. And a fucking Kleenex."

25

Once Maxi had found herself, after two hours of intense looking, at the far end of the great second floor of the Louvre, the longest gallery of paintings in the world. She had been overcome by a staggering case of total visual overload. She knew that if she saw another masterpiece she would never want to go into a museum again, yet three hundred and fifty yards separated her from the exit. She had solved the problem by walking back the length of the gallery as quickly as her tired feet would allow, with her head bent so far down that all she could see was the floor. Not even the edge of a frame entered her peripheral vision and she made it to the Winged Victory and down the marble steps to the exit without mishap.

It was in this fashion that she walked through her apartment, her ex-apartment, and headed straight to the telephone next to her bed, which was still her bed, and made arrangements for an expert from Sotheby's to come as soon as possible to take inventory of every valuable she owned, including the objects in storage, and put them up for auction as quickly as possible. Now, she thought as she put the telephone back, she was sitting on her ex-bed, for the carved and gilded eighteenth-century *lit à la Polonaise* hung with its original crownlike pouf of embroidered silk would bring a good price. Was she sitting on her ex-mattress? Probably, she thought, not quite sure if she had ever seen a mattress up at auction with the bed it belonged to. Better not to know.

"Maxi? Where are you?" she heard a voice calling.

"I'm in here, in the bedroom," she answered, suddenly unable to say "*my* bedroom."

Angelica, flushed from her day's adventures, appeared at the door.

"Have you hugged a mother today?" Maxi asked, in a small voice.

"You don't look as if you need a hug," Angelica observed, approaching her cautiously, "you look as if you need intensive care. Maybe a transfusion. You've been working too hard."

"Try a hug," Maxi advised. Angelica enveloped her in her strong, athletic grip, lifted her up, twirled her around a few times and then flopped back on the bed with her mother still pinioned in her arms.

"Did that help?" she asked Maxi anxiously, peering at her closely with her truthful, undefended eyes.

"Very much. Thank you, darling. I have something not nice to tell you."

"You *are* sick!" Angelica said, stricken, sitting up abruptly.

"No, damn it. I'm not sick at all. I'm perfectly fine. But I had to sell the apartment. We can't live here anymore."

"You promise you're not sick?"

"I swear on—what do I have to swear on for you to believe me?"

"My head."

"I swear on your head that I'm a totally healthy mother. Satisfied?"

"Yup. So why did you sell the apartment?" Angelica asked, vastly relieved.

"It's a long, very complicated story, but basically I need the money."

Angelica's face wrinkled up in an attempt to understand words she'd never heard her mother utter in her entire life.

"To buy something with?" she asked finally.

"Yes . . . and no."

"Ma," Angelica said patiently, "I really think it would be helpful if you'd tell me the whole story, long though it may be. I'm old enough to understand."

When Maxi was finished there was a silence while Angelica considered the situation.

"The way I see it," she said finally, "is that you did what you had to do. This is just like real life. In fact—it *is* real life. That's—interesting. It's not exactly fun but it's chewy. Now, the next problem is where do we live? I'd pick Columbus Avenue because that's where it's happenin', but I know you'd never go for it. And anyway we should really live on nothing, right? So why not invite ourselves to Uncle Toby's? It's free, he's got some extra room and the food will be great. He'd probably be glad of the company. And another thing, after school every day I can come down to *B&B* and work at anything that needs doing, delivering packages or mailing letters or helping out in the art department."

"Don't you go *near* the art department!"

"What's in there, snakes? O.K., I won't, but there's no reason I can't pitch in, lend a hand, is there?"

"None." Maxi looked for Donald Trump's damp pocket handkerchief, for he carried nothing as common as a Kleenex, and applied it as inconspicuously as possible to her streaming eyes.

"And the third and final thing, and I don't care if you do disapprove of my choice of language," Angelica pronounced. "In my honest opinion, Ma, Cutter eats shit."

Maxi looked around and wondered what it was that was familiar about her surroundings. She and Angelica had been immediately welcomed at Toby's but they'd had to cram themselves into the two small rooms on the fourth and top floor of his long but narrow brownstone. The first floor was devoted to the swimming pool and kitchen; the second floor was all one big living room. The third floor was Toby's domain. Somehow Maxi had imagined that they would be given the big extra bedroom next to Toby's but that was before she discovered that India and Toby were living together on alternate weekends. The extra bedroom's closets were full of India's clothes and, Lord have mercy, even some of India's sheets. Not for anything in the world would Maxi want to be on the same floor as a couple delicately involved in tentative nest-building. In fact, if she had actually realized that India was spending so much time in New York she wouldn't have called Toby at all, but once she had, he had insisted on her moving in with Angelica.

Did she feel as if she were their chaperone, she wondered? No, nothing that adult. Summer camp! That was it. She felt as if she and Angelica were at summer camp together, uprooted from their familiar surroundings and bunking in a strange place, with only a few stuffed animals of Angelica's, her school books, and some of Maxi's framed photographs to make them feel a sense of familiarity. Her own clothes hung on the cumbersome metal racks she'd had to buy because the closets weren't big enough. Yes, a cross between summer camp and a tiny, overcrowded designer's showroom, she decided.

Thank God she'd bought all her spring and summer clothes before the ax had fallen, Maxi thought, looking at the laden racks. They took up almost all the space in the room. She needed to look expensive and authoritative and totally carefree at the daily lunches she spent wooing potential advertisers, but fortunately for the female editors of many magazines, the public-relations people at most ready-to-wear houses will "do a personal" and bring up the designer's clothes to the editor's office for her to choose from, at wholesale, of course. But tonight she could relax, she thought, putting on Zoran's baggy pull-on ivory cashmere pants and his ivory cashmere and silk boat-necked pullover, cut short and ribbed all over, the two pieces three times too expensive and worn, as they should be, about three sizes too big. Cashmere was as comforting as mother's milk and a good deal easier to come by, Maxi reflected as she laced up her sneakers. She wasn't anxious for the rainy April weather to turn into a warm spring. If she could, she'd wear six layers of cashmere at once until she won her battle with Cutter. Maxi sighed as she realized that the most costly wool couldn't warm away the worry she lived with now. A wave of infinitely sad longing for Uncle Nat and Aunt Minnie swept over her. She could have confided in them as in no one else, but after Uncle Nat had died of a heart attack in his early fifties, Aunt Minnie had gone to live in the Landauer family compound in Palm Beach. Now it wouldn't be fair to disturb her with the convoluted problems of *B&B* but, oh, how she missed the two of them.

Maxi padded downstairs and stopped outside the entrance to the kitchen-dining room in which Toby was busy cooking. She heard him say, "It's a meat loaf, and you can consider yourself lucky to get anything that complex at a chef's own table." Was Toby talking to himself at such a young age? They were supposed to be having dinner alone together since Angelica was with Rocco and India was in Hollywood. Curious, Maxi peeked into the big double-purpose room. A trail of tattered leather oddments, shed here and there in the kitchen, informed her immediately of Justin's presence.

Maxi swooped on him with joy, for she'd been so busy with Monty working on the budgets for future issues of *B&B* that she hadn't seen him for days.

"I wanted to surprise you," Toby said, pleased with the success of his invitation.

"Have you got anyone else up your sleeve?" Maxi asked.

"No, just the three of us. I don't think that we've had dinner together alone like this since we were kids," Toby answered. "After I went away to college and you got married there were always other people, mainly one or another of your husbands. This is a post-nursery evening for cultivated adults who like meat loaf, and have a certain special common interest."

"Such as?" Maxi questioned.

"The future of Amberville Publications," Justin answered. "You don't think you're the only one who's concerned about it, do you?"

"Of course not."

"You never came to us for help, Goldilocks," Toby said seriously. "Don't you think that you should have, before you went and sold your apartment and planned to strip yourself of everything you own?"

"No, I don't," Maxi countered. "It's a fight I volunteered for. What's more, I'm not at all sure that if I win it, you won't be disappointed. Maybe each of you would rather have the cash you'd get if the sale goes through. That's what I really *should* have asked you about."

"Whatever it was you should have asked us about, you didn't. And we're both peeved, to put it mildly. This dinner is a setup, in case you haven't realized it yet," Toby said pleasantly, basting the meat loaf with a fresh-tomato-and-basil sauce.

"I was beginning to have my suspicions. So you wouldn't mind if Mother sold the company? You want me to cave in and fold *B&B* and stop making a fuss and, in general, act like it's all right with me?"

"Toby, have you noticed that Maxi has a tendency to overreact?" Justin asked.

"Actually, since you've brought it up, I'd say that the trouble with Maxi is that she jumps to conclusions," Toby answered.

"Or," Justin added, "you could say that the trouble with Maxi is that she jumps overboard and never looks around to see if there's a life preserver on board."

"No, that's not quite it. The trouble with Maxi is that she confuses herself with General de Gaulle. *L'Etat c'est moi*, you know. Amberville, *c'est elle*, or something like that."

"De Gaulle didn't say that, Louis the Fourteenth said it," Justin corrected. "He too had a tendency toward grandiosity, but that was so long before the Revolution that he could be forgiven, but Maxi, no."

"I don't think you're as funny as you both seem to think you are," she said, annoyed.

"The trouble with Maxi is that she doesn't know when people are trying to lend her money," said Toby.

"Oh, so that's what this is all about. *No way* am I going to come to the two of you for money! You've got your own lives, you've got your separate interests, why should I expect you to lend me money for something that is totally a decision that I made myself? Keeping my magazine afloat until it can swim by itself is a personal problem, and the money *has* to come from me."

"I work for *B&B*—doesn't that give me a say?" Justin asked.

"Look, Justin, I know you hate doing magazine photography and that you're only sticking with it for my sake. That's as much of a contribution as I'd ever expect you to make and I'm very aware of what it costs you to be tied down like this," Maxi said severely. "So don't expect me to hit you up for a loan on top of that."

"What about me? I'm your older brother, Goldilocks. You might have tried me," Toby insisted.

"Come on Bat, you've never had the slightest interest in the magazines," Maxi replied. "You can't convince me that you do. No, Toby, this one is my baby. It just wouldn't be fair to rely on either of you. Surely you two are sensitive enough to understand that, for once in my life, I want to win something *on my own, by myself.* I've had a free ride in life and I haven't made much out of it. This time it's different!"

"Hear, hear," Justin said with a slanting, loving, ironic and surprised glance.

"The real trouble with Maxi," she continued, "is that she's always starving, always hungry, always needing to eat. Such a bore, that girl. She gets mad when she gets hungry, so butt out of my business, you guys! Back off, you bums. When is the overrated, probably overcooked meat loaf going to be ready?"

"Maybe you should have taken their money," Monty said doggedly, for the third time, as he watched Maxi sign checks. "Or, at the very least, you could have asked them how much they had in mind."

Maxi shook her head. She couldn't explain to Monty that Lily was planning to sell the entire company. This meant that she couldn't tell him about the hope she had pinned on the survival of *B&B*, about the possibility that Lily would change her mind. It was a thin possibility, she knew, but the only one she had. If she allowed herself to indulge in self-doubt now, all would be lost without question. Maxi changed the subject to lure Monty away from his lust for her brothers' money.

"Monty, our last month's circulation figures were hovering at four million copies. If we can maintain that number, when those six-month advertising contracts are up, we'll be able to renew them at a huge hike in page rates, isn't that so?"

"Yeah, if all your advertisers are willing to stand still for the size of the increases you plan to ask for, which is by no means certain and you'd better not count on it. After all, you still don't really know precisely who those four million dames are, and what their income level and age level are. *Demographics*, Maxi, demographics. Madison Avenue buys specific audience with specific needs. But assuming that the advertisers do renew, you'll start to begin to see daylight with the seventh issue. Right now every copy we're selling at a dollar fifty is costing us two dollars and five cents to produce, not including the money Barney Shore is putting up for rack space. You're such a raving success that you're losing fifty-five cents a copy four million times a month or, to make it easier to understand, two million, two hundred thousand dollars monthly."

Maxi raised her eyebrows so high that they disappeared under her rumpled bangs. "With three more issues to go, that's over seven million dollars . . . still, it's not as bad as the Defense Department. My auction had better break some records."

"Don't try to increase your circulation," Monty warned her. "Success kills."

"Don't worry. I do understand that much. Is this the only business in the world where the product costs the manufacturer more to make than it costs the person who buys it?"

"Ever heard of movies?" Monty asked sadly. "Or theater? Or ballet or opera or concerts? Or television shows that don't work?"

"So, essentially, we're in show business?" Maxi summed up.

"Damn right we are," Monty brooded.

"If you had money, would you put it into show business?"

"No," Monty mourned. "Show business is two dirty words."

"If you don't cheer up, I'll goose you!" Maxi threatened. He gave her a bleak grimace that tried to pass for a smile.

"We'd better pray that the price of paper or printing or distribution doesn't go up," Maxi said thoughtfully.

"And that Barney Shore doesn't drop dead," Monty added helpfully.

"I hope you can run faster than I can, you bastard," Maxi exclaimed, charging at him, her middle finger already in position. "Here I come!"

"Frankly, Maxi, I think you're bonkers, obsessed, over the hill," India said as she unpacked the nine suitcases she had brought for a week's stay. "If someone wanted to buy my family business, and the payoff meant that I'd have more money than I've ever heard of, I'd jump at the chance. You can't even be sure that your father wouldn't have sold if UBC had made him an offer."

"He was only sixty-one when he died. I'm positive that, he would never have sold and retired. What would he have done with the rest of his life? He lived for his magazines. They were his anchor, and he was my anchor. Don't you understand?"

"And you identify with him? A sort of transference?"

"I guess someone like you would feel the need to put it into that particular, simple-minded jargon. I see you've discussed it with Doctor Florence Florsheim."

"Naturally," India said with dignity. "I try not to talk about you, but it's getting more and more difficult since I met Toby."

"And what did the good woman say?"

"She said maybe you didn't want a hundred million dollars."

"Oh, so she's started to have opinions, has she?"

"About other people, sure. She's human, after all. She just doesn't have opinions about *me*, or at least she doesn't tell me about them bluntly. She lets me arrive at my own conclusions about her opinions."

"India, would it surprise you to know that she's right? I don't want a hundred million dollars."

"Why ever not?"

"Ever since you became a movie star you've been complaining about how being publicly beautiful is a drag. How many women do you know who would understand that problem? And sympathize? You keep moaning about how this special and particular arrangement of your chromosomes has turned you into some kind of freak; how strangers get all sorts of delusional notions about you because of the particular way your cheekbones slant, because of the size of your eyes and their color; how millions of people project impossible dreams on your frail little shoulders based on the shape of your chin, the length of your nose, the color of your hair, and God knows what else. You say that no one can see 'the real you' but an old friend like me, or Toby, who's blind, or your analyst, who doesn't care. You complain that you intimidate people just because of an accident of birth; that they make you shy because you know what they're thinking; that you can't make friends with other women because of envy; that your looks invite the unwelcome attention of all kinds of sick creeps like that guy who keeps phoning and writing you those awful letters. Are you still getting them, by the way?"

"Unfortunately, yes. *Please* don't mention it in front of Toby—my 'fan' called here today, he's getting crazier by the minute. But let's not talk about him. And anyway, what do weird types like that have to do with money?"

"Money invites the same kind of fantasies, only worse. You used to be smarter, India. People would read about the sale in the papers—whenever a private company is sold the details get spread all over the financial pages and leak over into the regular press, and I'd never seem even remotely human again. I'd be one of those immensely rich women whose fortunes get listed in magazines and any chance I still have of leading a normal life would disappear. As it is, it's bad enough. When people meet me for the first time I can actually see the pupils of their eyes change, as if I glowed in the dark, had a halo or an aura. They can never see me without it; it taints every word they say, and makes them shut up and listen when I make the most banal remark. Money is great and it's also a serious barrier to being allowed to join the rest of the human race." Maxi sighed, and twisted her white streak into a corkscrew curl.

"There are times, particularly at the office, when I'm genuinely just one of the gang, and it's heaven. Being an Amberville obviously means being rich, but nobody knows exactly *how* rich, and it's that particular detail, that number, that dollar value, that Americans get off on. And not just Americans. Everybody. It makes them crazy. And as bad as it would be for me, it would be much worse for Angelica, because at least I'm my own person, I more or less know who I am, and who my friends are, but Angelica would be so exposed, so much in the spotlight as she grew up. Now she's still a regular little girl."

"She may be regular but she's not a little girl anymore. Not the last time I looked, which was this morning," India said.

"She's only twelve and a bit," Maxi said defensively.

"Going on thirteen and watch out! Raging hormones. She'll be rich *and* insanely beautiful. She's got Rocco's looks, that kid. You're still terribly pretty, Maxi, even if you are almost thirty," India said, giving her a slow, professional, critical assessment, "but nothing to compare with Angelica. No offense meant."

"No offense taken, creep. After all I only married Rocco because he was so handsome."

"If I remember correctly, there was just a bit more to it than that."

"The worst thing about old friends is that they don't have the grace to disremember. Rocco always was a miserable grouch but as he gets older he gets worse. He's so flawed that it's hard to pick out his worst aspect but I think that probably it's his ingratitude. I cured his head cold and he's never called to thank me."

"Do you know how to cure head colds? That could be valuable; science has been looking for a way for years," India commented dubiously.

"Only certain head colds. What's more I almost gave him a bunch of presents for something he did for Justin. I didn't because that's when my money ran out, but it's just as well. He has a basically odious, nature."

"I always liked Rocco," India announced with determination. "He must still be divine to look at, at least."

"Some people might think so, I suppose, but it won't last much longer, no beauty does, you know," Maxi said. "Not even yours," she added in a compassionate voice.

"Tell me, Maxi, how's your sex life?" India inquired, her turquoise eyes unswervingly observant. "Something seems to be biting your ass. I detect a little oversensitivity, a degree of irritability. Knowing you, it's got to be a new man."

"Ha! Who has time for sex? I've forgotten about it. When you're as busy as I am, sexual appetites just go away somewhere and you don't miss them."

"So that's what it is, lack of libido. On the other hand it's the only thing I can think of to keep you out of trouble. Remember, you've taken a vow never to marry another man."

"Who would I marry? And more to the point, *why* would I marry? Who was it who said, 'I've been a man and I've been a woman and there's got to be something better'? That's the way I feel about marriage."

"I think you're scrambled. Didn't Tallulah Bankhead say, 'I've *had* a man and I've *had* a woman and there's got to be something better'?"

"Never mind," Maxi said. "You know what I mean."

"Actually not. I can't think of anything I want more than marriage," India said wistfully.

"Not having tried it, naturally you're tempted. Anyway, Toby is a hundred times superior to any of my husbands. If you can only manage to talk him into it."

"That would make us sisters-in-law and I don't know if I could live with your currently pessimistic view of the world. Cheer up. If everything falls apart at *B&B* and you end up wildly, ridiculously rich you can give it all away to charity. Or you could start your own cult. You could buy the Getty—no, you wouldn't have enough for that. Well, you could buy a movie studio and get rid of the money that way, faster than you think."

"Why don't you write a novel called *Unsolicited Advice*? Or maybe one called *I Also Do Windows?*" Maxi suggested, tweaking India's famous nose. "I appreciate your thoughts and comments, but, you see, I am in show business already."

Man Ray Lefkowitz and Rap Kelly, Rocco's partners, having lunch together, sat in the Perigord Park eating shad roe and covertly eavesdropping on Maxi who was at the next table working over the most important space buyer on the Seagram account. Her voice, as it drifted over to them, was as potent as a dose of nitroglycerine wafting up a man's spine, yielding, addictive and yet businesslike, maintaining a firm borderline that never crossed over into the overtly seductive.

"We've finally got the demographics, George," Maxi said. "You're one of the first to know." She sounded almost clandestine yet somehow ingenuous. "Naturally it took time to collect them, but our four million readers are, on the average, working women as well as wives and mothers. She's between nineteen and forty-four years old and last year she personally earned over twenty-six thousand dollars, which is roughly twenty-two percent of all the income earned by all the women in America put together. And George, teetotaler she most definitely is not. She buys *B&B* because it makes her feel good—that you know already. But did you know that seventy percent of our readers read *B&B* while they're enjoying a drink? Maybe relaxing from their work, maybe just sitting around waiting for their guys to arrive, maybe making dinner—we don't have the breakdown on that yet, but the figures should be in soon. *B&B* is simply not the sort of magazine you read when you're on a diet and have decided to cut out wine and liquor—our reader is too busy being nice to herself, day in, day out. She's the sort who celebrates . . . and if there's nothing to celebrate, she decides to celebrate anyway."

"Are you sure she's not an alcoholic, Maxi?" George asked. Maxi turned slightly toward him, with the faintest necessary movement, the minimal successful movement of someone who knows that she has the best legs, the best posture that shows off the best breasts, the best shoulder pads and the best haircut of any woman in the room.

"You have a delightful sense of humor for such an attractive man," Maxi said, with enough of a twist of diabolical mockery mixed into her winsome flattery to make him wonder exactly what she had meant . . . all that night long. "So many otherwise sensational men lack humor. They take themselves so seriously."

"I know what you mean," George assured her, pedaling like mad. Where exactly was she coming from? "Interesting demographics. Very interesting. Four million women, all sipping a drink and reading *B&B*."

"Now, George, I never said that. Only seventy percent of my four million readers drink *while* they read *B&B*. The others do other things. *Then* they drink. That's why I have so many liquor clients who want to buy next year's run of the back cover."

At the next table the two men eyed each other with faces that were a study in willful blankness.

"Kelly, she can't get away with that," whispered Lefkowitz. "George won't buy it. Nobody would buy such a blatant lie."

"Wanna bet?" Kelly hissed at him.

"Actually, no. I mean, look at her, for goodness' sakes. Yum."

"After all, what does it cost him? He's not spending his own money," said Kelly, finally laughing.

"Where do you suppose she gets the demographics?"

"*Pravda*?" Kelly ventured.

"They're more accurate. Listen, let's do her a good deed," proposed Lefkowitz. "Rocco's been awfully uncreative lately. We've only pulled down two new accounts since that magazine of Maxi's started. All right, they each bill about twenty-five million a year, but I still think something is bothering him. I wouldn't be surprised if it isn't connected to worrying about the success of *B&B*—you know what it's like to have an ex-wife who goes into business."

"Tell me. No, don't tell me, I know," Kelly amended quickly.

"Let's be nice to her."

"Rocco said that we weren't to give her any favored nations treatment."

"I just said nice," Man Ray Lefkowitz said, "nothing extravagant."

They paid their check and rose to leave, passing Maxi's table as they turned toward the door.

"Miss Amberville, I didn't see you there," Kelly said. "Oh, hi, George, how'd you get so lucky? Trying to get the jump on the rest of the space buyers? Naughty boy—but I don't blame you. I hope you're paying for lunch. Miss Amberville, may I say how pleased we are with our buys in *B&B*? Best deals we ever made."

"Just a minute, Kelly," said Lefkowitz, who saw, not to his surprise, that Kelly had cast him in the role of the bad cop. "Just one tiny minute. I think that *B&B* owes us a favor. We bought in before the first issue was published. That showed confidence and the willingness to take a risk on a new book. I think that as far as the proposed changes in ad rates are concerned, we should get some sort of break. Something, I don't know what, but something, damn it! I'm not suggesting that we can renew at those start-up giveaway prices . . . but I'll be very unhappy if we don't deserve some kind of favored-nations treatment. After all, Miss Amberville is almost a member of the family."

"Hey, guys, take it easy," Maxi said sweetly. "I'll split the difference . . . on one buy. Tell Rocco that there's no way, no way in the world, that I'm about to give away space in my magazine this time around. I suppose he told you to hit on me?"

"Those weren't his exact words," Kelly said sheepishly.

"No, Rocco always speaks of you with respect. He did say that this was the time to buy, if you were selling, but he wasn't taking anything for granted, just because . . . well, because of old times' sake," Lefkowitz finished delicately.

"Where," asked Maxi, "are the snow jobs of yesteryear?"

"Do you fellows intend to join our table or just stand there?" George asked in irritation. "I'm trying to do a little business here. See you two around, huh?"

"I hope that your auction is coming up soon," Monty said, watching Maxi sign checks toward the end of May. "Tomorrow would be good. Today would be better."

"It isn't exactly tomorrow," Maxi said, carefully casual. "I thought all I had to do was make a phone call and it would happen like that—sort of a superior garage sale. But no, Sotheby's tells me that the jewelry can't be sold until their next jewelry sale in the fall—it's past the season now, there aren't enough rich people in town, it's too soon to be pre-Christmas, all sorts of silly reasons. And my collections are just too varied: the pictures have to wait till exactly the right big picture sale; the boxes won't bring as much until they're included in a major box sale. Boring. Almost the only thing that they can sell in June is my furniture. Auction-arranging is some sort of fine art in itself and they refuse to let me rush them into anything. Apparently I didn't have quite enough of everything to warrant their doing a special auction of all my possessions at the same time; unless I'd dropped dead, which, I gather, would have given everything a certain cachet and brought in more money." Maxi shrugged it off: a petty problem.

"June! You're not getting any more money until then?"

"You heard me. And who knows how much it will be after they finish taking out their commission? The apartment turns out to have been my major asset and Donald was only able to sell it for almost the six million he gave me. I returned the difference. It had something to do with the overvalued dollar. Almost half of Trump Tower is owned by foreigners and last month they weren't spending dollars. Ah—go figure the economy. It's a waste of time."

"We're in very deep into . . . waste products, Maxi."

"Eighty-five percent—maybe more—of the advertisers have renewed at the new rates."

"Some of them don't go into effect until July, many of them not till August or September."

"Why don't we borrow from a bank against the page rate increases? Our advertisers are all major companies. They're good for the money. No, Monty, don't tell me we can't. I know it already . . . I've tried."

"If it were up to me, I'd lend you anything but I'm not a bank. I wish I were." Monty sighed as if he were about to be embalmed. "Don't you think it's time to ask the staff to take pay cuts?"

"Even if they worked for nothing, their salaries are a drop in the bucket compared to our other costs. And if word of pay cuts got around on Madison Avenue people might think we were in trouble and start to renege on the advertising commitments they've made. No, nothing gets cut, not the free, lunch, not the quality of the photographs, not the amounts we pay to get celebrity writers. It would be fatal. We'll go down in glory or continue in glory, but no in-between measures."

Maxi finished signing the checks with a brave flourish and smiled so encouragingly at Monty that he decided not to jump out of the window. The May sunlight seemed to scatter like drops of water off her shiny, dark, messy hair when she moved and although she was down to her very last million she refused to let Monty know how desperate she felt until it was necessary. Each issue of *B&B* that was sold proved to her that she'd been right in her idea about the need for a magazine that didn't count on women's everpresent supply of depression, guilt and anxiety for its subject matter. "Admit it, Monty, don't you get just a tiny kick out of being on the cutting edge?" Maxi asked, laughing, her eyes so green that he blinked.

"Of what?" he asked, almost smiling back.

"Bankruptcy."

A week later, in the first days of June, Maxi sat down by herself to leftovers in Toby's kitchen. Everybody was out with springtime projects, but as worn out as she felt, she hated to find herself alone. During the working day Maxi still managed to present a picture of confident leadership but more and more frequently, when she found herself without an audience, even an audience of one, she felt beset with anxiety. For the first time since her struggle with Cutter began she wondered if she weren't being ridiculously quixotic, if she hadn't started a fight that was impossible to finish, a struggle whose dimensions she had never anticipated when she first went to see Cutter to try to use moral suasion on him. Who, after all, had appointed her trustee of her father's heritage? He had left control to her mother. Could that have possibly meant that he wanted her mother's wishes to be followed strictly, even if they did involve the destruction of Amberville Publications? Why was she, Maxi, the only one in the family who knew—or thought she knew—as absolutely as if she could hear Zachary Amberville talking to her, that nothing must be left undone to keep the magazines together? Oh, she had had a special closeness to her father that not even the boys had felt. He had been the one person in the world who had always believed in her, stood up for her, no matter what escapade she had been involved in, but did that mean that she could know *now* what he would have wanted?

The only person with whom she could share a part of her worries was Pavka and she'd seen him that day for lunch. She made a point of meeting him at least once a week so that she could keep track of what was happening on all the other Amberville publications. The picture he reported grew steadily worse. Every shrewd, ingenious and experienced move he had made to keep up the excellence of the magazines during the last few months since Cutter's edict had been accomplished only by the exercise of utmost cunning and patience. Nevertheless half of the things he had tried to do had been detected and countermanded by Lewis Oxford who was in touch with Cutter every day. Only his promise to Maxi not to resign kept Pavka on a job in which he was no longer in control, and Maxi, who knew how close to the end of the line she was, felt guilty for the struggle he was undergoing. Yet neither of them was acting out of selfish or ambitious motives; they were both doing it for Zachary Amberville, or, to be accurate, for his memory.

It couldn't last much longer, she realized. The sale to UBC, if it were made, would take place at the end of June, when the quarter's profits were known. The struggle couldn't go on for more than another month in any case. By the end of June she might not have the money left to go to press. It all depended on the auction of her furniture that was scheduled for the following week. If that went exceptionally well she could just scrape by, and if she were sure she could publish the next issue she could ask Lily to reconsider.

That afternoon Maxi had decided to take her jewelry and her precious boxes out of the unhurried, deliberately careful hands of Sotheby's and sell them herself to anyone who would buy them. To hock them if she couldn't sell them, although how she'd find the time to do it she didn't know. She didn't begin to know how you hocked things or where. If only she'd bought real estate instead of beautiful playthings. If only she'd worn fake pearls. If only she'd invested in the safest possible bonds instead of buying old furniture with uncertain market value. If only she hadn't put central heating into Castle Dread but had frozen to death without protest. If only she'd acted like the squirrel in the fable and had stored away nuts for winter instead of like the feckless grasshopper. If only. If only she hadn't acted like herself, she thought angrily. Too late now, and a pointless exercise. The doorbell rang and interrupted her fruitless replay of her life.

"Justin? Am I glad to see you! I can offer you pâté, five kinds, all original and still nameless, of Toby's own making. I haven't started to eat yet—come on and I'll put another plate on the kitchen table."

Justin followed her, sat down but only accepted a glass of wine. "How's the news from the front?" he asked.

"We're not taking prisoners."

"So I've heard. That's the word that's around."

"What are people saying?" Maxi asked, frowning.

"Oh, it goes all the way from rumors of the sale, which might have come out of UBC, to outraged denial. You name it, people are saying it. Confusion in the ranks, civil disorder, darkness at noon. Listen. I don't want you to think that I'm avoiding the showdown but I've *got* to get out of New York, New York, it's a hell of a town.

And too much for me, Maxi. I can't take all these stones any longer, now that the weather is so beautiful. There are so many other places I want to be. Better places. I'm going to hit the trail, kid, before the monsoon season starts. I like a Gershwin tune, but babe, I *hate* New York in June." He tried to speak lightly but his expression was mordant.

"I know you feel that way and, truly, I understand. At least I know you'll always come back, sooner or later."

"I'm going to miss your birthday."

"So what, darling? You always miss my birthday. But honestly, it doesn't hurt my feelings. Oh, you're worried about my turning thirty, you think I'm going to go into a decline or something. That's it, isn't it? Oh, Justin, what's thirty? What's forty? Betty Friedan is what forty looks like, for God's sake."

"Gloria Steinem," Justin corrected her.

"You see, it doesn't matter. And I've got other things to think about, believe me."

"Well anyway, what the hell, I wanted to give you an advance birthday present to take the pain out of leaving your outrageous, picaresque, lust-filled twenties." Justin casually pulled out a piece of paper and put it down on the table. Maxi didn't reach for it.

"Since when," she asked, "do you give your own sister a check?"

"When she's grown up," Justin answered, "enough to know what to do with it." He took it, and delicately deposited it on her empty plate. She looked down and read the figures. It was enough to keep publishing *B&B* until all the new space she'd sold had been paid for, enough to save the magazine.

"Didn't I tell you I wouldn't borrow from you? Would not, could not and will not," she reminded him somberly, picking up the check and pushing it back across the table. "I have to see this through by myself."

"Don't be too proud, Maxi. We're a proud bunch, you and Toby and I—it must be Mother's influence. I ask you, if Father had been in money trouble with a magazine he believed in, wouldn't he have done anything, short of dishonesty, to save it? Don't get carried away by pride, Maxi. Anyway, this is a present, not a loan. A nonreturnable gift. There's nothing you can do about it except say, 'Thank you, Justin.' "

"But why? I don't understand."

"Because this is the only way I can find to join the fight. We're all in this together, we're a family and we're doing this for the family name. I've got to be part of that! Zachary Amberville was my father too, Maxi. You aren't the only who loved him, you know. If you don't win, at least I won't feel that I didn't do as much as I could have. *Let me help!* It's for all of us. Please, Maxi, take it," he begged, showing more emotion than she had ever seen on his ironic, remote, withdrawn face.

Maxi snatched the check back, as full of expectation and excitement as if she were watching the arrival of a comet.

"Thank you, darling, darling Justin! And while you're in this generous mood, could you possibly let me have ten dollars till payday?"

26

"Cutter, can't you really go up to Canada without me?" Lily asked. "We've seen Leonard and Gerry Wilder for dinner at least three times since the two of you met. Isn't that enough courtship, even for a major business transaction? Why is my presence necessary on this trip?"

"I thought you liked Gerry."

"I do, she's a perfectly agreeable woman, but this weekend trip with them up to look over the timberlands that the company owns—don't you realize that it brings up difficult memories for me?"

There was a change in Cutter's expression, below the surface of his polished and almost absolute charm, something seemed to be happening, a tightening of resolution.

"Darling, you're being just a bit self-indulgent, changing your mind at the last minute, aren't you? The fact that Zachary died in Canada shouldn't make the place impossible to visit—you've never even been there. You still live in the house you shared with him all those years, yet that isn't too painful for you. So why should this make any difference? You know I've planned this trip for weeks. Gerry is counting on your company while Leonard and I inspect the stands of timber."

"Oh, really," Lily complained, "this does drag on so."

"It's the kind of weekend that consolidates a relationship in a way that no number of New York dinners ever can," Cutter explained. "When the time comes, two weeks from now, to sit down and talk business at UBC, my personal relationship with Leonard will make a difference. He won't admit it, he won't even be aware of it, but I know it's true. So much hinges on you. You're the star of our little group. You *own* Amberville, I only speak for you. Be a big girl, my darling. You're so important in the end game. Remember, no deal is consummated until the papers are signed."

Lily sighed. She wanted to get this difficult, overdue sale over with and behind her. She was so weary of being looked at and standing in as the symbol of ownership, so tired of constantly having to watch herself in her mind's eye, that most difficult judge of all, ever alert to the position Cutter put her in at the center of the Amberville Publications stage, always the gracious soloist. She knew that Gerry Wilder, pleasant as she was, was still slightly awed by her, as impressed as a member of a *corps de ballet* would feel about the ballerina. Still, she was accustomed to enduring that central role that once she had coveted beyond all else, and Cutter was evidently intent on her being part of this weekend.

"All right, I'll go. Will I need a heavy coat or just lots of sweaters?"

"Bring everything you think you'll need. We're going in the UBC company jet so baggage is no problem."

"Good. That's something. I'll just go and tell my maid what to pack."

The interior of the UBC jet was so arranged that it didn't look like a flying boardroom. Intimate conversations were possible at both ends of the cabin. Cutter and Leonard Wilder sat together talking while their wives chatted up front.

"This timberland, thousands of acres, was one of the last things that my brother bought before he died," Cutter said. "He felt that the more independent Amberville was from paper manufacturers, the better. Hell, he'd have bought a printing plant next, and then a distribution business. That might be something for UBC to consider."

"One thing at a time," Leonard chuckled. Now that he had every intention of buying Amberville Publications his normally brusque manner had mellowed. "Speaking of things to consider, I've been giving a lot of thought to *B&B*. When we first met we only talked about the established books. I didn't give *B&B* another month's life. Since then your offbeat experimental baby has begun to fascinate me. At first I thought it would bring down your profits; then I saw the circulation figures, and lately I've started to ask myself if the first thing we should do is pour money into it or, on the other hand, shut it down. Any suggestions, Cutter?"

"Leonard, I've been going through all of that questioning myself, multiplied by ten. I've been tinkering with the magazine personally, doing all the fine-tuning and I promise you I've managed to get it over the hump. It was a challenge I took personally. But the jury's still out. As I do on any new project, I've let it go just so far and no further. It keeps our people on their toes and it's good for the company."

"I heard Lily's daughter speak at the dinner for Women in Publishing and I was damned impressed. Does she come with the package?"

"Maxi's a wonder. A chip off the old block. You'd have to cut your own deal with her, Leonard. I couldn't speak for her . . . but I'm not convinced that she's necessarily in it for the long haul. Still, who knows?"

"Won't the start-up losses distort your profit picture?"

"Less than you'll ever guess. I've been personally riding herd on Maxi and I think you're going to be pleasantly surprised. I'm satisfied with the Amberville balance sheet. I think you will be too."

"The figures will tell the story, won't they?" He stretched agreeably. "Ah, it's nice to be getting away. I've never been to the wilds of Canada."

"We have flush toilets for VIPs."

"Somehow I'd imagined you would."

"Leonard and I never had any children," Gerry Wilder told Lily, as she did each time they talked. "I envy you so much. And not just three children, even a granddaughter. You must be so proud."

"I am . . . but recently I began to realize something. I can't take the credit for them when they're being wonderful and so I shouldn't blame myself when they're being . . . difficult. It's taken years to even begin to reach that conclusion. I always thought that they had to be perfect or else it meant that I wasn't perfect. Well, I'm not and they're not. We're all just human."

Gerry Wilder tried to hide her astonishment. She'd never heard Lily talk about herself so intimately before. She seized the opportunity to delve further into the character of the woman whose manner and breeding had always caused most of the other women of New York to think of her as set apart from them.

"Are you closer to one of your children than to the others?"

Lily smiled gently at the question. Only a woman without children could imagine that such a question could be answered simply, or even at all. She said the obvious and satisfactory thing. "They're each different and I'm close to each one in a different way."

"It must be wonderful having a daughter," Gerry said wistfully.

"Actually I'm more optimistic about Maxime than I've ever been before," Lily said, surprised at her own words.

"Optimistic?" Gerry Wilder said, puzzled.

"Oh," Lily laughed at her impulsive remark. "She's had three husbands, you know. That's a bit worrying for a mother. She seems to have finally settled down. Happily unmarried."

"Goodness, *yes*. Leonard took me to the Women in Publishing dinner and I thought she was marvelous. So businesslike. That combination of intelligence and beauty bowled us over. And I do adore that magazine of hers. I even go out to buy it—I can't wait to read it at the hairdresser's. It always makes me feel so—well, pleased with myself. I suppose she shows it to you before it comes out every month?"

"Actually she's quite private about it. I have to go to the newsstand to get it too."

"For heaven's sake," Gerry said, mystified by the world of publishing. After all, Lily Amberville owned the company. You'd think she'd get advance copies of every magazine. It sounded as if she knew as little about her own business as Gerry herself did about next season's pilots. Leonard wouldn't let her look at them because she couldn't conquer her habit of comparing them to "Masterpiece Theatre." But then she didn't own UBC.

Soon the small jet landed on the airstrip that had been carved out of the forest. The passengers left the plane, pulling on the heavy coats they had brought along. It was windy and bright but still very chilly up in this part of Northern Ontario. A tall, obviously young man in spite of his fine red beard stood waiting for them with a new jeep. He approached the group, shyly. "Mr. Amberville?" he asked, looking questioningly at the two men.

"I'm Mr. Amberville," Cutter answered. "You must be Bob Davies. You look like your dad."

"Yes sir. Nice to meet you, sir."

"This is Mrs. Amberville and our guests, Mr. and Mrs. Wilder. Bob's just learning the ropes, Leonard. His father used to be in charge of the camp here but he retired last year, went down to Florida. Just out of college, aren't you, Bob? How's your dad?"

"Fine, sir. Thank you. Why don't you all get into the jeep while I stow those bags? I don't like to keep you waiting in this wind. It's about a half-hour ride to the guest house."

Leonard Wilder entered the enclosed jeep reluctantly. He wanted to drink in the sight of the dark green, towering trees that, like the sea, had the power to awe a city man. Network television had never given him such a heady sense of being in touch with the real world, with growing things. This particular, surprising asset of Amberville Publications, he decided, was going to become his private fiefdom. The next time he flew up here it would be as host, not as a guest. He'd let Gerry redecorate the guest house, whatever shape it was in, so that she'd stop complaining about his never sharing the pilots with her. She refused to realize how lucky she was that he didn't.

On the same Saturday that Cutter and Lily were up north, Toby and India, in New York, were getting dressed for the first night of a Broadway play that had been written by Sam Shepard, India's costar in her last film. They had invited Angelica and Maxi to go with them but Maxi had promised to spend the evening with Julie who was kicking up an alarming fuss, digging in her heels about her growing conviction that a magazine that thought women were fine just the way they were didn't need a fashion editor at all, but rather a resident bag lady. When they found themselves with an extra ticket, they had told Angelica that she could bring a friend so long as the girl was properly dressed for an important theatrical event that was sure to draw a crowd of the usual curious civilians as well as a covey of photographers.

Impatiently India changed her dress at the last minute. She had fallen into the trap of this particular spring and bought a number of the chintz-printed gowns that looked heavenly on the hanger and turned their wearers into walking English country sofas. "Cabbage roses on the body don't work like cabbage roses on cushions," India said out loud to herself, ransacking her closets, and coming up with Nile-green satin Saint-Laurent evening pajamas, sashed at the waist in the palest pink, and a brighter pink satin raincoat that went with it, that must never be worn if it looked at all like rain.

"Angelica's friend is here, I heard the doorbell," Toby said.

"How do I look?" India asked.

"Come closer. Yeah—like the sky in the moment between sunset and sunrise in Norway, on Midsummer's Night."

"How did you know?"

"From the sound of the fabric, from the color I see out of a tiny tunnel, from the sound of your walk, from the way you smell, from the tone of your voice. By the way, when we go downstairs, try not to say the very first thing that comes into your mind about Angelica's friend."

"Toby, don't be mysterious. You've just picked up her voice, haven't you?"

"Right. This bat has super-sensitive hearing. Just keep your head." He touched her lips. "Lipstick. I'm going to kiss you anyway, but I won't smudge—I also specialize in super-sensitive, ultrasonic, laser-beam kissing."

"Go on, smudge," she invited. "Otherwise how will I know you've touched me?"

"You'll know . . . you know, don't you? Oh yes, you know. Come on now, we'll be late." Together they walked down to the living room where Angelica was waiting.

"Oh, what lovely cabbage roses, Angelica," India said automatically. It was true even when spoken out of stunned surprise. On Angelica the slipcovers were like a garden just coming into bloom.

"Thank you, Godmother," Angelica said with the utmost formality. "May I present Henry Eagleson, a friend from school. My godmother, India West, and my Uncle Toby."

"How do you do," the young man said.

"Basketball," India said wildly. "You must play basketball."

"He's the tallest boy in the eighth grade, Godmother," Angelica said, a note of triumph creeping into her tremulous voice.

"Center?" asked Toby.

"Yes sir. But if I stop growing I'll have to give it up."

"How old are you?" India finally ventured to ask.

"Fourteen, ma'am."

"Why should you stop growing at fourteen?" Toby wondered.

"I'm over six feet three already, sir. I have to stop sometime, at least I hope so."

"Not necessarily," Angelica said, grasping this neutral topic with both hands. "He could keep growing until he's twenty-one or -two, couldn't he? What do you think, Uncle Toby?"

"Why don't we wait and see? And why don't you call us India and Toby, Henry?"

"Swell. If you call me Dunk. Chip knows everybody calls me Dunk but tonight she's being proper or something. What's with you, Chip?"

"Nothing, nothing," India rushed into the breach. "Chip's been brought up by a very old-fashioned mother, you know, Dunk, of the old school. *Vieille* New York."

"Punctilious, hum? My mother gets that way too. Tonight I thought she'd have a complete breakdown before I left the house. She made me change my tie three times and my socks twice. Listen, Mom, I said, just because this is my first date doesn't mean that *you* have to get nervous. I don't understand parents at times. In most cases I do, but not always."

"My mother was the same way when I had my first date," Angelica said. "Wasn't she, Godmother?" She looked imploringly at India.

"Oh, indeed she was, Goddaughter. I thought she'd turn green. Or was it blue? But that was *ever so long ago*, wasn't it, Uncle Toby?"

"Years, must have been years. So far in the past that I can't even seem to remember it. Shall we go? It's getting late."

Toby had borrowed Maxi's limousine for the evening. It had survived her great purge of possessions because it was the only practical way to get around New York. Cabs were never available at lunchtime in the neighborhood of *B&B* and Maxi had to race uptown for lunch and then race back to work. And her blue limo was part of her essential image of unquestioned success.

Elie ushered Angelica and her first date into the big car with not the slightest change of expression. They might have been an aged duke and duchess on their way to church, for all his solemnity. What Miss A. would say about it, he thought, he couldn't say. He supposed that Angelica had to start carrying on sometime, but with a giant? Maybe he was younger than he looked. At least they had chaperones, although Miss West and Mr. A. were too much in love to notice anyone but themselves, in his opinion. What *a terrible* family. He sighed in pure pleasure.

There was a large crowd gathered in front of the theater. "I wouldn't do this for anyone but Sam," India said. "I'm going to withdraw into being oblivious until we're inside the theater. Just don't let go of my arm, Toby, because I'll be walking straight ahead as if there weren't anyone watching me, O.K.?"

"Right. Chip can take your bows. Elie, see if you can let us off right in front of the theater, please."

"Yes, Mr. A.," Elie answered. You could see he wasn't used to a good driver, asking a damn fool thing like that. Where did he think he'd be left off, halfway down the block?

Angelica and Dunk got out of the limousine first, two tall, magnificent, unknown young people who were scanned by the crowd and then ignored as if they didn't exist. Then Toby stepped out and waited for India.

As they crossed to the entrance to the theater, so many flashbulbs went off, combined with the lights of the local television minicam crews, that India was blinded. Voices shouted out greetings to her but she didn't hear them in her condition of willed nonresponse.

"India, India, I've got something for you," one voice called, almost lost in the commotion caused by her appearance. She walked on but Toby instantly dropped her arm, whirled toward the voice and threw himself into the crowd like a linebacker, bringing a man crashing down to the street. They fought frantically for an instant, and before people started to scream there was the sound of a pop and a grunt. As if in slow motion Toby continued to struggle with the man on the pavement while the crowd stood milling, hysteria mounting, but directionless and ineffectual. Using all his great strength to hold the man down, Toby forced his fingers open until the gun he held dropped out of his hand. It was only then that India turned and screamed. It had happened so quickly that, like all such attempts, it seemed as if it were over before it had started. Only the bright arterial blood pouring out of Toby's arm was real. And the loaded gun that Dunk picked up carefully and held until a policeman took it away from him.

"How did you know, how did you know?" India wept, holding Toby's hand tightly as the ambulance careened through the streets.

"Recognized his voice—the nut who kept phoning you at the house, knew it right away. Didn't figure you'd want whatever he had for you." Toby was still in shock and seemed not to notice the ambulance attendant who was trying to stop the flow of blood.

"He was going to kill me. I knew he was crazy but I never thought he'd try to shoot me."

"Nobody is ever going to hurt you while I'm around."

"How did you know *where* he was? Oh, Toby, how did you know?"

"Training, orientation training. Comes in handy lots of times . . ."

"Lady, would you stop talking? I'm trying to fix this man up till we can get him to the hospital. Ask questions later. Oh, Oh! India West! Say, do you think I could have an autograph when we get there? It's for my wife . . . otherwise I wouldn't bother you at a time like this but she's a fan, see, a real big fan."

Lily would have been content to spend the morning in the neighborhood of the guest house but Gerry was clearly anxious to see more of the surrounding forest.

"Shall we ride?" Lily proposed.

"Horses terrify me. Don't you think we could ask that nice young man to take us for a tour in his jeep?" Gerry asked.

"Why not? Cutter left him here in case we wanted him for anything."

Soon they were in the jeep with Bob Davies who had overcome his first attack of shyness with the city visitors. Lily soon realized that this particular woodsman was far from silent. He was impossible to shut up without downright rudeness as he regaled them with tales of the towns that existed on the outskirts of the wild lumbering country, where the local workers got pig-drunk every Saturday night and fistfights were the normal end of the evening.

"Goodness," said Gerry, fascinated by this rough aspect of her new domain, "have you ever been involved in a fight, Bob?"

"No, Mrs. Wilder. My father wouldn't let me go near one of those bars when I was in high school. After that I was away at forestry school, and then I came straight here to work. That was when he retired, so suddenly. Out of the blue a relative died, someone he hadn't even known about, and he had enough money to buy a little place in Florida. That was always my mother's dream—she didn't like the cold. They just packed up and left. He's got a little boat rental business down there now and they're as happy as newlyweds. Mr. Amberville let me take over here without even interviewing me. I really appreciated that, believe me. This is the first time I've had the pleasure of seeing any of the Amberville family. The old owners were always around; bringing friends up with them for the hunting season and the fishing season, using the horses, having big cookouts, just having a great old time. Do you think you'll be back often, now that you've seen the spread, Mrs. Amberville?"

"I have no idea," Lily said distantly.

"It sounds wonderful," Gerry remarked thoughtfully. Lily knew that Gerry was thinking that as soon as the deal went through she and Leonard would immediately begin to entertain their friends up here. She felt a sharp pang of annoyance, as if Gerry's obviously proprietary interest were an attack on her own territory. Yet, when UBC bought Amberville none of this would still belong to her. So why not just accept it? What on earth did it matter?

The jeep drove slowly along the trail, in the shadow of the thickly planted great trees. It was a sunny day and light struck down into every space that the trees would grant its entrance.

"Oh look, Lily, there's a sort of clearing up ahead. Why don't we get out of the jeep and take a little walk in that direction? It seems a shame not to get some exercise," Gerry proposed.

"Bob, could you stop here for a minute? We're going to take a stroll," Lily agreed.

"Will do, Mrs. Amberville." He braked carefully to a halt and slid out of his seat to help them down. "I'd better come with you ladies. There's a ravine on the edge of that clearing."

"That won't be necessary, Bob," Lily said coldly. She wanted to have a little time this morning ungarnished by his life's story. Reluctantly he let them go on without him and the two women walked energetically along the trail for hundreds of feet, breathing deeply of the pine-scented air. When they reached the grassy clearing they found that it was almost hot in the sun trap and they took off their coats and sat on the grass for a few minutes, enjoying the silence and the peace of the moment.

"Let's go look for the ravine," Gerry suggested, her eyes sparkling with interest. She'd never owned a ravine and she wanted to see it for herself. It was a feature of the place, like the horses and the lake that was reputed to be full of fish anxious to be caught. The air itself was part of the deal, the grass, the trails, the guest house. She couldn't be less concerned with the timber except as a background for her future pleasure parties.

"I'd rather not, if you don't mind," Lily answered. She had had enough of Gerry Wilder for the morning. "I'm feeling a bit tired. But you go on. I'll wait for you."

"You're sure?"

"Absolutely."

Gerry wandered off and Lily forgot her, almost falling asleep. Suddenly she heard a sharp cry. "Oh, my God!" She opened her eyes and saw Gerry on the grass at a distance, backing rapidly away. "Lily! There's the most godawful drop there. You can't imagine. 'Ravine' my eye! It looks like an opening into hell . . . all jagged boulders and a terrible steep drop . . . and you can't even tell it's there until you're almost right on top of it. Those places should be marked, for heaven's sake. They should have railings around them."

"Well, you'll put them there, won't you?" Lily muttered to herself. "Come on back, Gerry. Let's get into that jeep. It must be almost lunchtime."

"Bob," said Gerry, as soon as they were on their way back to the guest house, "I think it's terribly dangerous not to mark that ravine. Why isn't there a fence there?"

"There are so many of them, Mrs. Wilder. There must have been an earthquake here once. There are dozens just like that, but not a one that's nearly as close to the guest house. Everyone who works in these woods knows about them. It's only strangers who are surprised. That's why I warned you. In fact . . . well, it's not a story I should tell you ladies . . . it happened just before the old owners finally sold the place. My dad told me about it, but in confidence . . ."

"Oh, come on, Bob," Gerry said eagerly. She wanted to know everything about this new future toy of hers and if there was a local mystery, so much the better.

"Well . . . I don't know . . ." He was obviously dying to regale them with the story.

"Oh, Bob, what difference can it make? Tell!" Gerry insisted.

"See, my dad, he used to fly a little one-engine plane, like the new pilot who's taking your husbands around. He was up in it one day, on his way to an emergency in a camp all the way on the other edge of the forest—a lumberjack had been injured real bad and had to be picked up and rushed to the hospital. Anyway, he spotted two guys, visitors from the city like you ladies. He never told me who they were but they were on horses. They got off the horses in the clearing back there and they must have had some sort of argument. Not so different from the boys here on Saturday night, because they got into a fistfight. One of them must have thrown a hell of a punch because the other ended up at the bottom of that ravine."

"What did your dad do?" Gerry asked breathlessly.

"He couldn't stop, see, not enough room to land, and he was real worried about that lumberjack I told you about. Anyway he knew that the accident was real close to the guest house and he figured the other guy would ride back as fast as possible and get help. But when he finally got back here, a day later, they still hadn't located that poor fellow in the ravine. There was all sorts of confusion, search parties going out in every direction but the right one. Nobody seemed to be in charge or know what was going on. Dad was fit to be tied. He led them to the ravine right away but it was, well . . . it was too late. The visitor from the city was dead. Nobody ever did know if it was from the fall or from being out all night in the cold. See, it was below zero that night when it happened. Anyway . . ."

"Stop the car!" Gerry screamed. Lily had fainted and slumped sideways, halfway out of the vehicle, and it was taking all of her strength to keep Lily from falling out onto the trail.

Lily sat in the semidarkness in the main bedroom of the guest house. She'd asked Gerry Wilder to draw the curtains and insisted, in a way that permitted nothing but obedience, that she be left alone. She hadn't attempted to explain her brief descent into unconsciousness to the other woman. "Let me rest. I don't want lunch. Please do not come back upstairs to see how I am," she had ordered in a tone so absolute that Gerry Wilder had not dared to ask a single question.

Throughout the afternoon Lily sat by the window in a straight-backed chair while her memory and her vision turned in upon herself. In the passage of a few hours she grew old and bent and drained of pride and beauty. She was desperately cold, as if the flow of blood in her veins had stopped, yet she lacked the will to rouse herself to put on another sweater. At moments she muttered a few words out loud and then fell silent. From time to time she doubled over, her hands cramped painfully over her mouth to silence her spasms of howling grief, her attacks of brutish anger. She had to summon all her strength to quiet those hands. They wanted to rend her, to tear her flesh, to pluck out her hair, to damage her forever.

Eventually, as the afternoon grew to a close, she mastered her emotions and concentrated on the door to the bedroom. Soon, as she knew he must, Cutter opened it quietly, obviously expecting that she would be resting on one of the twin beds. Lily made no sound.

"Lily?" he asked, not seeing her in the gathering darkness. He walked a few steps into the room and then turned to snap on a standing lamp. "Where are . . . Lily, what are you doing there like that?" He approached her and stopped dead at the sight of the ugly woman whose face was contorted in a grimace of some unnameable emotion, an old woman wearing Lily's clothes, a woman with Lily's hair, who glared at him with savage, slashing eyes.

"Good God, Lily, what's happened?" he asked in horror. "Gerry told me about the ravine. What the *hell* kind of stunt was that, Lily, to go and look at it, of all stupid things to do. How could you *do* that to yourself? Just look at you . . ."

"No." Her voice was dry and broken by the tears she had shed, hoarse and ancient. "Don't bother to look at me. It doesn't matter what I look like. Look in the mirror, look at yourself."

"What kind of riddle is that supposed to be?" Cutter asked, disgust and ferocity mixed. "Damn! I should never have brought you to Canada. If I'd known that you were so morbid—"

"You shouldn't have. But you didn't anticipate everything, for once in your life. You didn't know that I'd find out." Lily's voice had faded to a whisper.

"Find out'? There's nothing here for you to find out. What are you talking about?"

"How . . . how did Zachary die?" she hissed.

"Lily," Cutter said in a reasonable way, "Lily, you have *always* known how Zachary died. Darling, everyone knows. You've had a shock, that's all, from being so near the place where it happened. Come on, let me help you up and get you into a warm bath. You're going to make yourself ill if . . ."

"*Murderer,*" she screamed.

"Lily! Stop that at once! You're hysterical!" In a bound he reached the chair and pulled her to her feet, trapping her flailing arms behind her back with one powerful hand.

"*Murderer!*"

"Shut up! The Wilders are in the next room, they'll hear you . . ."

"*MURDERER!*"

Cutter clapped his other hand over her mouth and she bit deeply into the pad of his thumb. Roughly he pushed her away so that she fell onto one of the beds. "That's enough! That's more than enough out of you. You're out of control, don't you understand that, Lily? It's this place, that's all, it's making you hysterical."

Lily shook her head violently and rose, standing to confront him. "You were there, at the ravine, yes, you were there. *It was you!* You knocked him in and you left him to die." She looked at Cutter in bitter wonder and there was steady accusation in her voice now as she only stated the facts that she had spent the hours facing.

"That's the most . . . the most purely, utterly *insane* thing you've ever said in your life, you've gone mad, completely mad—"

"You can bluster all you like, it's all the same to me." Lily kept looking at him as if she were trying to assemble his separate parts into one human being, looking in bewilderment as if she were trying to persuade herself that he was Cutter Amberville, the man she had loved, trying and failing utterly. Yet she continued to speak firmly, without faltering, and her voice seemed to come from far away, from inside a death's head, primitive, hollow and devoid of life. "Bob Davies told me. He didn't know what he was saying. Now I understand why his father was able to retire at forty-seven. I know who gave him the money to go to Florida. Only one man saw what happened but he was as talkative as his son. We heard it all, Gerry and I. Two men in the clearing, two men who got off their horses, two men who got into a fistfight, one man who was hit—or was he pushed?—into the ravine and one man who came back and *did not* send a rescue party for his brother. In subzero weather. The closest ravine to the house. You must have been terrified when Davies came back the next day and told you he'd seen what happened. But you didn't get him out of the way quickly enough. He told his son and he'd tell any court in the world. I'll make sure of that."

"Lily, you can't believe that story! That kid is full of wild stories, lies—"

"Shall I call his father down in Florida? It's only one little long-distance call. He'll admit everything when I tell him he's an accessory to a murder." Lily reached for the telephone. "I have his number. I asked Bob for it when Gerry wasn't listening. I said I wanted to tell him what a nice, helpful son he had."

"Wait! Put that phone down. I can explain—"

"No, I don't think you can." Lily's voice made Cutter go cold with fear but she put the phone back in its cradle. He drew a deep breath.

"Lily, something did happen that day. I hoped you'd never have to know. I *was* with Zachary when he fell into the ravine. We did have a fight, *but it was an accident*, Lily, an accident!"

"But why didn't you send back a rescue party?" Lily asked relentlessly.

"I still don't understand it. I was in total shock, Lily. I don't remember what happened for hours afterwards. I was out of my head with grief. I looked over the edge and I could tell he was dead just by the way he lay there. Even if he'd been rescued right away it wouldn't have made any difference. I found my way back here somehow and I just blanked out. I couldn't function. My brother was dead . . . my brother . . . I just couldn't believe it. That's why I had to get rid of Davies—sure I bribed him. I knew nobody would believe what had happened. Oh, but Lily, *you* have to believe me! You know I would never have harmed Zachary on purpose. Why should I have done such a thing? *Why?* It doesn't make any sense. Admit that it doesn't make sense. It would have been insane." Cutter stopped, his eyes searching her face pleadingly.

"What did you fight about?" Lily asked.

"You. I don't know what had given him the idea or why he suddenly picked that particular time to bring it up but, Lily, he had suspicions about us. He got violent. Raging mad. He accused me of having been your lover when we were young. He said he was beginning to think that Justin was my son and not his. I can't imagine what might have made him sniff out our secrets so many years after they'd happened but I couldn't take the risk of reacting in any way but as if he were insulting *you*. I swung that first punch for you, Lily. It was so out of character that it was the only way I could think of showing Zachary how wrong he was. I did it to protect you. I did it for your sake, my darling. If I hadn't, who knows what might have happened? How he might have taken it out on you and Justin? I admit I did it, but it was for you, only for you, Lily."

"You can't *stop* lying, can you?" she said, wearily, no surprise left, only contempt.

"Lying?—Lily, what else would have made me fight my own brother?"

"*I told him about us thirteen years ago.* He knew about you and me and Justin all those last years. We made our peace with each other, Zachary and I, but before we did I wanted to start fresh or not at all. So I told him everything. *Everything.* He forgave me completely. He had always loved Justin as his son and he kept right on loving him until the day you killed him. He was hurt, but he hadn't exactly been a saint himself. So we made it up and went on to create a good life together. You're the last person in the world to whom he would have admitted that he knew." As empty and dead as Lily's voice was, her tone was irrefutable. Truth rang through every word. Cutter turned his back to her.

"Whatever your reason for killing my husband, it doesn't matter. Envy and hatred were at the root of it. That's why you made me love you. To take something of his away. I was almost as bad as you, then. But I'm not a murderer. Or a liar. Not anymore."

"Lily . . ."

"Not another word. Never, *never* another lying word. I'm leaving now, back to New York. You can tell the Wilders whatever lie you choose. I'll send the plane back for them as soon as it lands. Zachary Amberville was murdered by his brother. I know the truth. Nobody else will. I won't try to punish you. It would serve no purpose. You're not worth it. Unless . . ."

"Unless?" Cutter said, still unable to believe that she really meant what she was saying.

"Unless you ever try to come into contact with any member of the Amberville family again. If you do, I'll bring you to trial. I swear it, by all that's dear to me."

"Wait, stop—" he cried, but she had already gone.

27

Every other time that Maxi had crossed the lobby of the Amberville Building in the last year it had been at a run. Today she lagged, finding more than enough unwelcome time to inspect the giant ferns that flourished under their special health-giving lights, many minutes to sneer at the lusty condition of the bromeliads, to count with disdain the ranks of huge palms and reflect on the greening of corporate America. What was wrong with the city fathers of her Manhattan who permitted more and more builders to reduce the amount of sunlight that could reach the streets so long as they guaranteed that each new, ever-taller building was to have a mere token indoor green space? Greener lobbies, darker streets, she thought to herself, aware that her mood was generated by the dread with which she approached the summons she had received to talk to Lily, a meeting for which she was early, due to Elie's overly skillful driving. Still, even if she had been precisely on time—even if, unthinkably, she had been late—the outcome of this interview had already been decided, she thought as she took the elevator to the executive floor.

"Mrs. Amberville is waiting for you in Mr. Amberville's office," the receptionist said to her as soon as she appeared. The full treatment, Maxi realized, backed up by the authority of Zachary Amberville. Good news didn't come hedged by such a display of legitimate command, of absolute jurisdiction.

She went in. Here, at least, the prodigal sun could enter and rollick, here the two rivers that clasped Manhattan like the arms of a giant lover could both be perceived, one running darker than the other, but both running to the ocean. She looked around, momentarily dazzled, and could not distinguish her mother's presence until her eyes adjusted to the light. Lily was sitting on the lower step of a library ladder and she held a bound volume of copies of *Seven Days* from the 1960s, open to pages of photographs from the Kennedy-Nixon campaign, taken by the many Amberville photographers who followed every step of the national drama. She put the heavy book down when Maxi approached her and looked up almost unchanged in her still moonlit beauty and intensely studied elegance. Yet there was something battered, something blighted in the flesh around her eyes that Maxi had never seen before, as if a flower had been sucked of its freshness overnight, grown limp, tired, faded.

"Who ran for Vice-President with Nixon?" Lily asked.

"Damn," Maxi said. She couldn't remember, except that it certainly wasn't Spiro Agnew. Or was it?

"I didn't know either, Maxime."

"That's reassuring . . . How was your weekend?" she added, since small talk seemed to be the first thing on the agenda.

" . . . Illuminating. And yours?"

"Horrible. Poor Toby. I think I'm still in shock," Maxi answered.

"I went to see him at his house yesterday but you weren't back with Angelica yet. Thank God he's going to be as good as new as soon as he heals. Tell me, just who is Dunk and what is a Dunk?"

"Angelica's first boyfriend. He's fourteen, very polite, and eats like an army, Napoleon's army. But he has excellent table manners."

"Toby and India spoke highly of him."

"Angelica's not *their* daughter. He'd just better treat her properly," Maxi said in a warlike tone, her fists clenched.

"Or?"

"I'll get Rocco to deal with him. Imagine Angelica sneaking off on her first date when she knew perfectly well I wasn't going to be home. She'd never have dared try that with her father. I'm still fuming."

"The trouble with you, Maxime, is you forget what it's like to be young," Lily said, brushing her objections aside.

"Mother! I'm not even thirty yet! Not for a few weeks. And I didn't start dating until I was . . . sixteen."

"Ah, but when you did . . ."

"I remember, that's what I'm worried about."

"Angelica's a very different kind of person than you were. She's sensible and well balanced. If I were you, I wouldn't worry about her."

"Thank you," Maxi said with dignity, refusing to rise to the bait. She had no intention of trying to defend her teenaged self. If Lily still thought of her that way, there was nothing she could do about it.

"Of course," Lily continued, "she'll change, in all sorts of ways as time goes on—we all do, we all have to, don't we? But Angelica's character is pretty well formed. I can imagine her almost as she'll be in ten years' time, unlike you, Maxime. I could never be sure just what was going to happen to you. You were a rather difficult child, you know, but I had no idea that you'd be a late bloomer."

"A late bloomer? Just what is that supposed to mean?"

"Now don't be defensive, Maxime. I simply mean that you hadn't reached your full potential . . . no, you hadn't started to reach your potential . . . until very recently." Lily's voice was as neutral as clear water, and as difficult to read meaning into as a night without stars.

"I suppose that you're leading up to the letdown with these kind words?" Maxi said, barely listening to Lily, burning over the description of herself as a "difficult child" and the implied comparison to Angelica who had managed to escape being judged in any way by her doting grandmother. Not that Angelica wasn't ideal. More or less.

"If you would just sit down, Maxime, we could discuss this more comfortably," Lily remarked, settling in one of the chairs in front of the desk.

Maxi, who had been standing throughout the conversation, went to the desk and automatically sat down in her father's chair, where she had sat when she asked Pavka not to resign. Lily allowed a little silence to fall.

"Do you feel comfortable there?" she finally asked Maxi.

"Oh. I'm sorry!" Maxi stood up abruptly, confused. "I wasn't thinking."

"I know. I'm quite aware of that." Lily smiled at her, an involuntary smile. "That chair's been empty for so long. You almost fit it."

"Mother?" What was this cat-and-mouse game, Maxi asked herself, thrown off balance.

"I told you that you forget what it's like to be young, really young, Maxime. Well, so do I. But sometimes I'm smart enough to remember. Your father was younger than you are now by the time he had founded his first magazines. You're the age he was when I met him. You've already founded one magazine and made a roaring success out of it, if we ignore your untraditional financial methods. Why shouldn't you be able to take over the others . . . with the help of all the people who've been running them since your father died? That is, if you want to."

"*Take over the others?* But—but I never asked for, never dreamed of—that," Maxi stammered, turning pale.

"But surely you realize that if I don't sell Amberville someone in the family has to take over? And you're the only possible person, aren't you? That's finally, at long last, obvious even to me. Late bloomer that I am."

"*You're not going to sell?*"

"You didn't think I'd brought you here to tell you that I was? Good God, Maxime, I wouldn't have done anything so unfeeling. I would have told you, but not here, not in your father's office. Sometimes I think you don't understand me at all." Lily sighed with bafflement. "But let's not talk about that . . . it's a problem we may never settle, and it has no bearing on your answer. Do you want to take over? As publisher of all the magazines?"

"But what . . . I don't understand . . . what will Cutter say?" Maxi's normally nimble, skeptical tone had dissolved into the utter disarray of surprise.

"He will never have anything to say about how your father's magazines are to be run, *ever*. He is . . . gone. I have sent him away. I intend to divorce him. His future is no concern of mine. None of us will ever see him again and I trust that we will never discuss him, never mention his name." The liquid surface of Lily's voice, as she spoke these abrupt, curt phrases of absolute banishment, was flawed, for the first time in Maxi's memory, by whirlpools of raw emotion of complex, unpolished pain.

Another silence fell. Neither woman looked at each other, but in the dust motes that danced in the sun-striped air, questions were asked, answers were refused, questions were withdrawn and put away for all time.

Of all the rare and desirable luxuries that Zachary Amberville's money had bestowed on her in her lifetime, Lily thought, this power to cast Cutter out of her life was finally the most valuable, the most necessary. The same power enabled her to impose silence on her children, to keep from ever having to explain to them. But one thing money could not buy, the only cessation that no coin could purchase, was freedom from her own knowledge of the kind of man he was. How could she have chosen such a man? Where did her faults begin? For how much of the tangled story had she been responsible? Why had she maintained that wild, irrational connection, unwilling to change her stubborn fantasies about him, no matter how often he had disappointed her? Just how evil had he been? Had he ever really loved her? Worse—*how could it still matter to her*? She was certain of one thing. Somehow she was as much to blame as he except in one vital way: Cutter had not left Zachary to die *because of her*, and in that fact she would have to find her strength, no matter how hard were the questions that tormented her. "Well, Maxime," she asked again, "do you want the job?"

Maxi's head was as light as if she had rapidly scaled a mountain peak and breathed deeply of the light, bright exhilaration of the air of the summit. She saw nothing except the vastness of the shining temptation, the immensity of the horizon, the infinite vistas that opened before her. She stayed there a moment, dazzled, and then she forced herself to return to practical things, coming back to the reality of the office, trying to visualize herself here every day, dealing with all the decisions, demands, problems and responsibilities that would fall to the lot of whoever was the head of Amberville Publications. She understood suddenly that she couldn't possibly know what it would be like in advance. When she had so blithely demanded that Cutter give her a poor old rag called *Trimming, Trades Monthly*, had she had any idea of what it would be like to actually publish *B&B* month after month? Publisher? *Head of the company*?

"Oh, yes, Mother! *I want it!*" she exclaimed, out of a whole heart. She wanted it and she knew that her father would have wanted it for her.

"Good. I'm glad, Maxime. Very glad. I wouldn't have offered the job to you if I didn't think you could do it," Lily said calmly, yet with a deep note of tenderness. "The sale was always possible, it is still possible. But I'd like to keep Amberville Publications in the family. I was once told that I'd sacrificed my life to the company, that I'd been deprived of my freedom by all the different ways in which I helped your father while he was running the magazines. I believed that interpretation of my life. I thought that my birthright, whatever that means, had been taken away from me." She paused for a moment, as if pondering the meaning of "birthright."

"Father believed in you," Maxi said, "or he wouldn't have left you control of his business. He would never have done that unless he'd thought you were worthy of the responsibility."

"I don't know about being worthy, Maxime, but I've done a lot of thinking in the last day, enough for years, and I know now that the magazines have enriched my life. Being part of them has become part of my life, a part that is much too meaningful to permit me to sell them to strangers, to see them pass out of Amberville control. I'm proud of the magazines, Maxime, *damn proud* and I want them to be better than they've ever been before—"

"Mother!" Maxi interrupted, "do you have any idea—"

"Indeed I do, more than an idea. I spent the morning with Pavka. I know what's been going on behind my back. That's over, once and for all. All those disgraceful orders have been revoked. But no others have been given. I was waiting to see what you'd decide. Now the only person who will give orders in the future will be you. You'll have Pavka's guidance, but I imagine you'll have to earn the support of the old editorial board. Some of them may very well resent you. I won't interfere—but you can always use me . . . for window dressing. I'm very, very good at it."

"Don't say that!" Maxi protested. "You gave up a great career as a prima ballerina! Oh, Mother . . . you could have had *that*."

"Not necessarily," Lily murmured, with a small, mysterious, inward smile. "Not necessarily. I'll never know, never *have* to know. Surely that was the *point*?" She shook her head and came back from the past. "However, as window dressing I was the very best and I intend to continue to be. Every window needs dressing, otherwise it's just a bare and naked piece of glass. Never underestimate the power of window dressing." Lily sounded matter-of-fact now, but there was a newly perceptive expression on the perfect oval of her face and a mourning, rueful look in her gray-green-blue eyes, a look that contained all the shrewdness that she had always hidden, the shrewdness that she now shared with this daughter whom she admitted to her confidence for the first time in their lives.

"Angelica once told me that Father said that she was the only one in the family with a head for publishing," Maxi confided.

"He was wrong about that . . . even Zachary Amberville could be wrong. Even I can be wrong on occasion," Lily said with a gossamer smile, in which relief vied with the beginning of self-mockery.

"The trouble with you, Mother, is that you always like to have the final word on any question," Maxi said.

"Like you."

"Like me. Just like me. Come on, Mother, give me a kiss."

"Toby," Maxi asked, "would your feelings be hurt if Angelica and I moved out of your attic? Now that I've got job security and a regular paycheck I can afford to pay rent. Nothing fancy, but just a little bigger. More closet space of course, a bigger room for Angelica, somewhere to put a few bits and pieces."

"A few? You never had 'a few' of anything," Toby retorted.

"Well, I will have," Maxi insisted. "You know that I never did get around to auctioning anything? Even the furniture hasn't been sold yet. I've decided to keep only the very few things I like best. Now that I've gotten used to living without all those objects I'm going to try the pared-down look for a while . . . just a couple of marvelous pieces, each one set off by its relationship to the space around it. Of course I'll need a really top lighting designer . . ."

"Spare me, please spare me your decorating plans," Toby begged. "Don't you have Ludwig and Bizet to discuss this with? I thought they did all your places for you."

"They used to but I feel as if I'm ready for a change."

"Does it make the slightest sense to undertake a job that's going to consume your life and try to redecorate a new apartment at the same time?"

"Put like that, no," Maxi answered. Toby was lying in his favorite Eames chair, his feet up, his arm in an embroidered sling that India had somehow fashioned out of one of her sacred pillowcases, ruthlessly wielding a pair of scissors while Maxi vainly offered any scarf from a drawer full. "Still, we do have to move, now that the emergency is over. Angelica is miserable about it. She loves being here and the Troop really enjoys your pool."

"It would have been nice if they'd brought their own towels, but somehow they never remembered to," Toby said thoughtfully.

Maxi ignored him. "I don't really want to move either. It's so cozy up there and the leftovers are even better than the meals, and, oh Lord, you're right about the job. I won't even have time to do a proper job of apartment hunting. I won't have time to do anything until I get the job under control. I'd better start going in early and staying late and working weekends and . . ."

"Don't be dumb. You're having an attack," Toby cut in. "A stupidity attack. It comes over people when they're faced with enormous changes in their lives, especially people like you who are all-or-nothing people, no compromises, no halfway measures, no doing things a little bit at a time. Now it's your compulsive career. It used to be the compulsive search for fun, so that means that if you work it has to be compulsive work without any time off."

"My compulsive career, as you charmingly call it, also happens to be the most marvelous fun in the world," Maxi sputtered, outraged. "Instant analysis—disgusting."

"May I remind you," Toby said, "that you're only almost thirty—"

"Why does everybody pick this time to remind me of my age all of a sudden?"

"Thirty," Toby continued, "in the prime of life, with, I should imagine, from my memories of your scandalous past, a normal need for male companionship."

"Men," Maxi snorted.

"You sound just like Dad," Angelica piped up from her place on the floor at Maxi's feet. "That's what he says, 'women' in that same contemptuous tone of voice. He isn't even dating anymore. Remember the girl I used to tell him smelled like vanilla? Well, she's been gone for months and actually she wasn't bad if you don't mind funny smells. And that exceptionally pretty one I told him I just instinctively *knew* was a wrong broad, he hasn't called her in ages, and she wasn't really all that bad, just not my type. And there were a whole bunch of others who were after him because he's so successful—at least that was my opinion—or only interested in his looks. Superficial ladies. I always let Dad know my true feelings about them so he wasn't in danger of being taken in—well, he's not seeing anybody at all now. I wonder if I gave him some sort of complex?"

"Adolescence," India ruminated, "was invented by a psychologist named G. Stanley Hall in a book he wrote in 1905. Eighty years ago, Angelica, before we knew about adolescence, somebody would have put you in the corner or made you write things on the blackboard a hundred times, like 'I will not meddle in my father's love life.' Or maybe put you on bread and water. Even the ducking stool. I don't know which you would have hated more."

"I didn't meddle, I just made observations. If he hadn't paid any attention to me, like a regular father, it wouldn't have affected him. And 'love life' is such an old-fashioned expression. He was just seeing them."

"*Seeing,*" Toby growled bitterly. "Now it's become a word for all sorts of relationships, from the casual to the engaged-to-be-engaged. Just yesterday one of your gossips told me that Julie Jacobson was 'seeing' that young art director at *B&B*—does that mean nightly, semi-nightly, twice a week? I wonder what damn fool invented that miserable *perverted* usage of a word?"

"Well, whoever did, I don't know about Julie and Brick Greenfield but all *Dad* was doing was casual seeing," Angelica answered him as Maxi and India exchanged worried glances. "It wasn't as if he'd saved one of their lives and he was seriously in love, like you are with India. Anyway, I have to get dressed. Dunk is coming to pick me up in half an hour. We're going to a revival of *Wuthering Heights*."

"I'll come help you dress," Maxi said hastily, ignoring Angelica's surprised eyebrows. She knew how to dress, for heaven's sake.

"Well, you did, you know," India said after a pause.

"So you've mentioned. Several times. Does saving your life make me your captive?"

"If you were Chinese and you'd saved my life you'd owe me all sorts of things because I'd become your responsibility or something like that."

"I'm not Chinese."

"No, you're a full-fledged member of the Running Wounded," India said angrily. "I'm going to pack. I'm sick of not being appreciated."

"What the hell is that—the 'Running Wounded'—what's that supposed to mean?"

"You know what the walking wounded are—soldiers who've been wounded but don't have to be carried off the battlefield. You're different—you're wounded but you're running away from it, running around in meaningless circles, running so hard that you don't feel the pain or you can pretend that it doesn't exist. I'd thought you were different. You seem to have come to terms with being blind and you can do more than most men who can see. You'll always be able to do more. Blindness is finite . . . it's not going to get worse. But you've decided to cut yourself off from the rest of life. The harder part maybe. The human part. The part where I come in. *I'm not interested in your reasons anymore*! I'm only interested in what it does to me to be in love with you. Without hope. I'm not willing to put up with it. I refuse to become one of the Running Wounded myself."

"Doctor Florsheim?"

"I haven't seen her for months. My analysis is finished. I'm leaving you, Toby. For good."

"Hey, wait a minute."

"Now what?" India said from the doorway.

"Are you taking your sheets?" He looked meditative, with the beginning of concern.

"Of course."

"Pillowcases? And all the little baby pillows with the scalloped edges?"

"What is the point of this?" India snapped. "Just because I finished my analysis doesn't mean that I have to give up my bed linen. One thing has nothing to do with the other."

"I don't think I'd be comfortable sleeping on no-iron, fifty-percent manmade fiber anymore," Toby grinned, as if he'd solved a weighty problem that had bothered him for years.

"Oh?" India's heart started to beat so loudly that she thought that even a man with sight must be able to hear it.

"So let's make a deal. We'll get married and I'll get custody of your hope chest." Under his casual words was the tensile strength of a stubborn man who had finally changed his mind.

"My hope chest? Do you mean my linen?" India asked, approaching him slowly, carefully, so as not to betray her sudden tumult, the wild fluttering of her hands.

"Aren't they the same thing?"

"I don't believe so. Certainly not. Hope chest indeed!" India said, sounding deeply affronted, in the best acting of her short but glorious career.

"Well, let's get married and sleep on your sheets." He spoke with his habitual tone of command but India could detect a tremble in his voice.

"Is that your idea of a proposal?" She almost achieved a sneer but failed, failed utterly.

"Yep."

"You can't do better than that?"

"I saved your life, didn't I?" he said, too impatient to try for courtliness.

"You can't use that line forever, Toby Amberville," she whispered, the sweet wine of her voice denying her words.

Toby got out of his chair and walked over to her and held her tightly against him with his good arm. He gazed at her intently, his amber-brown eyes happier than she'd ever seen them, abandoned to utter tenderness. "If there were a moor nearby, I'd take you up on it and fill your arms with heather and tell you how much I love you, Cathy . . . but there's only Central Park. I love you, Cathy, and I want to live with you forever and ever and have a dozen children and take my chances with life."

"Heathcliff!"

"Does that mean yes?"

"I'll have to call my agent first, but . . . I think we can work something out."

In San Francisco, two weeks later, Jumbo Booker's secretary buzzed him.

"It's Mr. Amberville," she said, "calling from New York. Shall I put him through?"

Jumbo was not surprised by the call. He'd been expecting it ever since the word had reached him that Cutter was out of Amberville Publications. During the two years that had passed since Cutter had left his job with Booker, Smity and Jameston, of which Jumbo was now president, he had all but lost touch with his high-flying former employee. However, the extraordinary news of Cutter's unannounced, abrupt and unexplained departure from the publishing world had reached him through the corporate grapevine, a grapevine just as effective as the one that had passed on the knowledge of Cutter's sexual exploits during his marriage.

Jumbo was perfectly aware that Cutter had not been able to find another job in all of investment banking. Cutter had had a dozen job interviews but nothing had materialized for him and Jumbo knew why even if Cutter did not. A third grapevine had slowly operated on the highest levels of San Francisco society and many influential people had become gradually aware that Candice Amberville had killed herself. A number of them had guessed why, and from that number arrows of gossip had flown to Manhattan; gossip that would always be contained within a small group; gossip that would never leak beyond a certain circle; gossip so shocking, so vile, that it made anyone who heard it unwilling to ever have anything to do with Cutter Amberville again.

It no longer suited Jumbo Booker's needs for superiority to do favors for his former roommate. He wished that he had never laid eyes on the man, that he had never had any association with him. It was embarrassing, no, worse than embarrassing. It was shameful to be known as his friend.

"Tell him I won't take his call, Miss Johnson," Jumbo said to his secretary.

"When shall I tell him he can reach you?"

"Tell him he can't," Jumbo answered.

"I don't quite understand, Mr. Booker. Do you mean you'll be out all day?"

"No, I mean that I will not speak to him on the phone now or at any time in the future. Not on the phone and not in person. Make it perfectly clear, Miss Johnson."

"Oh," she said blankly, astonished and not sure what to do.

"Don't worry about being rude. Just repeat what I've just said and then hang up the phone. Don't wait for an answer."

"Mr. Booker?"

"And if he ever calls again, under any circumstances, tell him the same thing."

"Yes, Mr. Booker, I'll remember."

"Thank you, Miss Johnson."

Cutter put the phone down slowly. During all the humiliations of the past days he'd prevented himself from calling Jumbo Booker. He'd counted on Jumbo all along. He had felt certain that he would welcome him back to a job, if not his former job, then another, equally good. He'd made money for Booker, Smity and Jameston in his years with them, he'd always had Jumbo in his back pocket, but he'd grown tired of being patronized by someone he'd known too long. After giving the orders and running the show at Amberville Publications he had preferred to deal with strangers than to go to Jumbo with his hat in his hands; Jumbo, that talentless, boring, stuffy man who'd lived through him for so long; Jumbo, who had everything only because he'd been born an heir; Jumbo, who even now lacked the guts to insult him and had made his secretary do it for him.

Cutter lay back on the bed in his hotel room. It was all Zachary's fault, of course, as it always had been. Zachary's fault that he'd gone to San Francisco in the first place; Zachary's fault for marrying Lily; Zachary's fault that he'd had to marry Candice; Zachary's fault for being so unbearably forgiving and smugly understanding, so sickeningly unmoved by the revelations about Lily and Justin. It had been necessary to smash him up, necessary to leave him to die. Yes, to die. Yes, to die finally, because there was no other way to get rid of him, no other way to get even at last. It had been only fair, only just, only what he *deserved.*

Justin. Yesterday, in some gossip column, he had read that Justin had come back to New York to do the pictures for Toby's wedding to that actress. What had the columnist written about him? "An American Lord Snowden shooting the marriage of the year," something like that. Justin. The child Lily adored, Justin who didn't know that his real father wasn't dead, Justin who owed him life.

An hour later Justin answered his doorbell and found Cutter standing there, looking as confident as if he were an eagerly awaited guest at a party. Justin recoiled and Cutter took advantage of his movement to walk into the living room and shut the door behind him.

"Hello, Justin," he said, putting out his hand to be shaken. Justin moved backward another step. "All right, Justin, I understand if you're hostile, believe me I do. I know what's been going on since I had that flare-up with your mother . . . she hasn't wanted to see me, she's probably been saying things about me to all of you children that aren't true, poisoning your minds against me, but it isn't her fault, Justin. She had a bad shock, a serious trauma that was caused by hearing a pack of lies when she went up to Canada."

Justin stood still, not looking at Cutter. "I decided that I should leave her alone long enough for her to realize that nothing she had heard would stand up under the exercise of common sense, or even under any investigation. God knows she was free to make one if she'd chosen. Now listen, Justin, I've come to talk to you because I think you're the most sensible and the most sensitive of all of Lily's children, and I'm worried about her."

Justin retreated farther into his room, speechless.

"O.K., if you don't want to discuss it, I do. I think it's too important to just let matters stay as they are. This separation from your mother is as bad for her as it is for me. She loves me deeply, Justin, and I love her far more than she knows. We have a long, happy future together if only she can be made to see it. I know she said that she doesn't want to lay eyes on me again, but by now, and I know my Lily, she wishes that she hadn't been so hasty. Still she's a proud woman and won't make the first step. That's why I've come to you. You're the one person I think she'd listen to with an open mind."

Justin turned and looked out of the window, his shoulders tense with the effort not to say anything to Cutter, not to dignify his presence in any way.

"Justin, just consider the situation. Isn't your mother going to be a very lonely woman without me? She's never existed without a man to guide her, to be devoted to her happiness, to protect her. As soon as my brother died she turned to me in such need, in such utter loneliness, that it broke my heart. I never failed her, not for an instant." Cutter took a step toward the window and then stopped as he saw the tight control in which Justin's slender, powerful body was clenched, a study in utter rejection.

"Look, Justin, you're never around town for more than a few weeks at a time. Toby is getting married and probably moving to California and Maxi, God knows, is going to be busy with running the company. . . . Who will have time for Lily if I'm not there for her? Justin, I came here to ask you to do something, not for me, but for your mother. I want you to go to her and ask her to talk to me . . . just talk to me."

Justin moved away from the window, picked up a camera, sat down, and began to examine it closely.

"I don't blame you for giving me the silent treatment, Justin. For some reason we've never managed to have a decent, warm relationship, but we should have been friends a long time ago . . . more than friends." Cutter stood over Justin, speaking quietly, as if to gentle down a wild animal.

"I have a *right* to come here and talk to you, Justin. I would never have intruded on your privacy if I didn't have that right. I would never tell you what I'm going to tell you if I didn't think that the time had come for you to know the truth, to know why I feel entitled to ask you to do something for me and for your mother that I wouldn't ask anyone else in the family to do. No, don't shake your head, Justin, don't refuse to listen, don't shut me out."

Cutter's voice took on a pleading tone. Justin sat tensely, only looking at the camera now, using all the fierce concentration of his martial arts training to remain absolutely immobile.

"Justin . . . this is not easy to say. I know how much you love your mother. She's a woman who's impossible not to love. Years ago, when she and I were very young, both of us no more than twenty-four, younger than you are now, we fell in love with each other."

Justin dropped the camera he'd been holding, stood up and turned toward the blank wall, like a prisoner in a cell.

"We fell in love, we loved each other in all the ways a man and woman love each other, and we had a child . . . you, Justin. You're my son."

"I know." Justin spoke quickly, throwing the words away.

"What! Did Lily tell you?"

"I read that letter you wrote to her when you left her to go to California. I figured it out from the date on the letter and my birthday. I was just a kid, sneaking around looking at things in her desk the way kids do and I found it, hidden away. After I read it I put it back. It's probably still there."

"But . . . then, if you *know* . . . if you've *known*! Why did you never . . . how could you have . . . just, just kept it all to yourself?"

Justin turned around and walked toward the door. At last he raised his eyes to Cutter. "*Zachary Amberville was my father.* He was the only father I ever wanted, the only father I've ever *had.* He is still my father and he always will be. Please leave."

"Justin! You know the truth and you don't even deny it! Blood is blood. *I'm* your father, Justin! And I'm *alive* . . . doesn't that mean anything to you, for God's sake?"

"Just get out of here. Go away." Justin opened the door and gestured toward it with a shaking hand. Slowly, reluctantly, Cutter moved toward it and then, when he stood next to Justin, he hesitated. Suddenly, playing his last card, he clasped his arms around his son.

"NO!" With an instinctive movement, swift and powerful, Justin pulled away and, using all his dangerous strength, chopped the edges of his hands down on the arms that tried to hold him. Cutter staggered backward, his broken forearms dangling uselessly, unable to steady himself or regain his footing.

As he fell backward, screaming in pain, down the long, steep staircase, above him a door was closed and bolted.

28

A few days later, when the excitement over Toby and India's wedding, which was planned for the following weekend, was at its peak, Maxi left Toby's house without being noticed. India, Angelica and Lily were too deep in conversation about what they would wear to see her slip out after dinner and Toby had taken refuge in one of his restaurants to avoid the fuss.

Maxi had put on an old pair of jeans and a plain white T-shirt. Her feet were bare, in flat sandals, and she wore no makeup. A sublime sprite, battle-ready. She made a stop on the way to her destination and finally arrived at Rocco's apartment carefully carrying a large, flat package.

"What's in that box?" Rocco said suspiciously, as he answered the doorbell and she foamed into the room. "And how come you dropped in? New Yorkers don't just drop in. They telephone first."

"I simply had to get away from Toby's . . . they're going loony over there talking about heirloom lace and white satin slippers and all that nonsense . . . weddings seem to drive even sensible women crazy. I thought that since you were home—Angelica told me you were in tonight—you wouldn't mind if I came by and discussed some things. Her relationship to Dunk for instance. I mean, Rocco, he's going to be an usher, for goodness' sakes."

"That's hardly a lifetime commitment." Rocco sniffed deeply. "Is that a pizza?"

"Oh, just a little one. I thought you might be hungry. Shall I go put it in the kitchen?"

"What kind of pizza?" Rocco demanded.

"With everything on it. Would I ever bring you any other kind of pizza, Rocco?" Maxi asked. Her enchantress eyes, her straight dark eyebrows, even her bow-shaped upper lip all expressed innocent reproach.

"No, I guess not. You were always very good at pizza. A consummate artist. By the way, congratulations, sincere congratulations. I think you'll be a great publisher. I mean it. You needed the right outlet for your energies and at last you've got it. I'm happy for you, Maxi. You'll do a terrific job. Just don't try to make another dummy by yourself."

"Thank you," Maxi said modestly. "Should we eat this right away while it's still hot?"

"So we're going to share it, are we?" Rocco shrugged. "In that case I'm not in favor of reheating it. The cheese will get all stringy and the crust will get too dry. Anyway I didn't have any dinner. I've been too busy working to stop to eat." Rocco deftly set the kitchen table and cut large slices out of the enormous pizza for both of them. For a while they ate in the reverent, utterly greedy silence that a really good pizza commands, prudently leaving the crusts for later when there would be nothing else left, for no pizza, however disappointing, had ever remained unfinished by Rocco Cipriani and this was a prime pizza, a definitive pizza. With it they drank beer out of the bottle and the pile of paper napkins in the center of the kitchen table steadily diminished.

"Funny thing about pizza," Rocco said, "you can actually feel your stomach saying 'thank you' to the rest of your body. It's not like regular food, it's more like a transfusion. I guess that's what soul food does . . . although it never does it for me."

"Hot dogs at the track, that's what works for me," Maxi said dreamily. "With tons of icky yellow mustard, those lukewarm white buns and that tepid flabby pink sausage . . . nothing can ever replace them."

"Maybe it's a religious difference."

"Childhood, it all has to do with childhood. Or so I believe," Maxi replied.

"How do you feel about soup?" Rocco asked earnestly.

"Soup? I'm not against soup, by any means, but it's still not my number-one thing."

"If you were sick, or cold, or just needed comforting?" Rocco persisted.

"And there wasn't any alcohol around?"

"Right . . . for some mysterious reason you can't get any booze. Then would you go for soup?"

"Only out of a can," Maxi said decidedly. "It would have to come right out of a can, none of the homemade, it's good-for-you stuff. That's too European."

" 'I'm in the mood for soup,' " Rocco sang off-key to the tune of "I'm in the Mood for Love." " 'Only because you're near me, darling, and when you're near me, I'm in the mood for soup.' "

"What's the background?" Maxi asked, sensing the creation of a commercial. Rocco never used to sing in the kitchen.

"Lovers, every kind of lovers, all ages, sizes, shapes, white, black, yellow, brown, red, extraterrestrials, animals, three seconds on each pair, kissing, hugging, caressing, with Julio Iglesias singing the lyric."

"Do you see the product?" Maxi asked.

"Never. It's for the American Soup Canning Association. A full minute. Like it?"

"I think it's brilliant. But not Julio . . . I like him but his English just isn't convincing. What about Kenny Rogers? No, too Western. It's a ballad and Ol' Blue Eyes is too obvious—to say nothing of what he'd charge to do it—I know—Tony Bennett!"

"Perfect! Romantic, warm, familiar—perfect. So you like the concept? You really like it?"

"It would make me go into the kitchen, like a brainwashed zombie, and open a can of any kind of soup and heat it up and drink it before I knew what had happened," Maxi assured him, giving him the last slice of pizza, and all the crusts.

"That's what I've been working on," Rocco said, between bites. "I just wasn't sure if people really liked soup, or if they just thought it was good for them."

"What does that matter to the Soup Canning Association?"

"I have to feel emotional about a commercial before I get it right. And my mother always made her own soup. She'd never let us touch the canned kind, so I couldn't trust my gut on this."

"Your mother did make the most incredibly good soup. She gave me her recipe for chicken soup once but it started with buying a whole chicken and a veal knuckle. I wasn't ready for that. So I went out and bought Campbell's instead," Maxi remembered sadly.

"Well, you were only eighteen, after all. Or were you seventeen? I never was absolutely sure."

"I don't think I was, either. Anyway, I still can't cook."

"My mother can't run a publishing company. To each his own," Rocco said fairly, putting the plates in the sink and finding two more bottles of beer. "But damn it, she made her own wine too—I'm having problems with the Gallo account but I'll get over them. Thank God Mama couldn't make beer, or cars or soap. Let's go in the living room. What about Dunk? I thought he seemed like a good guy when Angelica dragged him over to meet me. You can't really believe that Angelica's in danger of being seduced by him?"

"Probably not. My mother pointed out that she's a different and wiser teenager than I was. I guess I should relax."

"Would you have been seduced by him when you were twelve?" Rocco wondered, standing by the window and looking out at all of Central Park, spread before him from his tall windows.

"Of course not. I was waiting for you." There was great art in her simple statement.

"Wouldn't you even have necked with him? . . . Dunk's pretty attractive."

"I never necked. Not with kids," Maxi answered, gazing at the reflection of the fine, well-lit room that floated in front of the windows, the Isis suspended in midair, timelessly queenly; the majestic croup of Rocco's Han Dynasty horse visible on a table. "You were the first man I ever kissed," she added after a pause. She batted her lashes until they quarreled but avoided looking at him.

"Oh."

"You always knew that."

"No I didn't. I thought you had experience—not real experience since you were a virgin, but something. You were a hot number, as we used to say in the old neighborhood."

"All an act," Maxi confessed, hanging her impertinently frivolous head.

"No, you *were* a hot number," Rocco insisted.

"The experience part—that was an act. The hot part—that was you." She raised her head and subjected him to her unruly matchless green gaze, the lips of her sorceress's mouth slightly parted, suddenly girlish, mysterious, as if every minute of their mutual past had been abolished, as if they were meeting for the first time.

"Oh. Well, thanks."

"Rocco—"

"*No*, Maxi. Absolutely *not*!"

"No? How do you know what I was going to say?" Maxi said, beautifully indignant. "How can you be so negative when you don't even know if I was going to say something that required an answer?"

"I've gotten smarter over the years. When you pop up on my doorstep in virtually the same clothes you used to wear to my loft the summer we met, looking young enough to be jailbait and so fucking pretty that it's criminal—except to someone who knows you as well as I do—and then you bring me a pizza with *everything* on it, and are so interested and sweet and helpful about my soup commercial, do you honestly think that I wouldn't *have* to know that you're setting me up for something? A major con? Come on, Maxi. Admit it."

"Don't you believe that people can change their characters as they grow up?" she asked reasonably, tugging her white streak. "Don't you think that I might just want to have a better relationship with the father of my child, a friendly interchange between two adults, a laying to rest of all the anger and hostility that has come between us? A new start, Rocco, so that aside from Angelica and our mutual love for her, we could coexist in the same city with some kindness and regard? Do I have to be coming over here with anything else in mind?"

"Maxi, shape up. Who blackmailed me—viciously—into making the dummy for *B&B*? Who got me drunk when I had a head cold and raped me three times? Well—the first time anyway."

"That's absurd!"

"Maybe it can't be proved, but I know what I know. You never show up unless you want something. What is it this time? Wait, let me guess. Pavka is going to retire in a few years and you want me to come over and get ready to take over for him. That's it, isn't it? Actually I'd do it too, except it would mean working for you, no matter how much freedom you gave me. So—I won't. No way. What else could it be? Maybe—"

"Rocco! You're absolutely right, I admit it. I am a con artist. It's my nature, it's always been more fun to get places by twisting the odds. I can't seem to stop trying to bend the truth in my favor, and what's more, sometimes I have a bad temper when I don't get what I want."

"That's hard to believe," he grunted.

"But I *have* changed. In this last year I've changed more than in the rest of my whole life put together. I've learned so much, Rocco, I've discovered that if I work very hard and sink my teeth in and don't give up, I can get what I want the honest way, right down the middle—with a lot of help from my friends."

"And you want me to be one of them?" he asked suspiciously.

"No." Maxi faced him, standing squarely but, at last, speaking the unadorned truth, looking him straight in the eye, all determination, all conviction, all fire. "I want you to love me again, Rocco."

"Why?" He didn't move a fraction of an inch toward her. Did she think that all she had to do was ask and he'd fall at her feet?

"You don't have any idea, do you, how I *yearn* for you? Oh, Rocco, it started way back when I first laid eyes on you and now it's a thousand times worse than it ever was when I was seventeen. It's such a yearning, such a *need*—it's unspeakable, impossible to find the right words. It's more than I can stand anymore, Rocco, for you not to love me," Maxi cried out in a voice that concealed no tricks, nothing but her pure emotion. "There's never been another man I've cared about, not deeply, not truly. Oh, if only I'd met you when I was older! I wouldn't have been so impossible, I wouldn't have made all the thoughtless, teenage, rich-girl mistakes I made. I wouldn't have made that one unforgivable mistake—I would have understood you better and realized how proud you were. We could have managed, we'd still be married to each other. Please, Rocco, please at least give me another chance. Just a chance, that's all I'm asking for. Oh, how can you look at me like that, as if you haven't any idea how I'm feeling? I love you so much I can't *endure* it."

Rocco continued to stare at Maxi impassively, brooding darkly down at her with a long, slow look that confirmed everything he already knew about this fantastical creature he had been unable to forget, unable to replace, since the day he had walked out on their marriage. She'd ruined him for other women, deliberately of course. Once you'd been wholly in love with Maxi you were done for, he guessed. He *knew*. She'd always had good stuff. She'd always be trouble, outrageous trouble, sure, but nothing that he couldn't handle. Anyway, who was he kidding, *he adored her*. He worshiped this wonderfully surprising little fiend with her bottomless bag of tricks. He'd *died* each time she'd married those two fruitcakes. There wasn't anyone else for him either. Never had been, never would be.

Rocco was caught up in such a flashflood of disorderly rejoicing that he could barely articulate. "O.K. Fair enough."

"You *will* give me another chance?" Maxi faltered, suddenly unsure. "Where do we start? From scratch, as if we didn't know each other at all?"

"Why do things halfway," Rocco answered munificently, suddenly finding his voice. "Let's go all out—get married again. It's not as if I don't love you like an absolute madman. It's not as if I've ever stopped—I'm not sure I even tried. We've wasted so many years growing up—or maybe it had to be that way? You're going to move in here with me, you and Angelica, and right away. But no fuss, no big wedding, no heirloom lace this time," he added, taking her into the indisputably jubilant grip he'd made himself hold back for so long, so very long.

"No fuss," Maxi promised. "It's not as if I'm marrying *another* man."

"You're marrying me. For good, damn it, for better, forever! The same man you started with," Rocco stated possessively, abandoning himself to her magic without another backward thought.

"Exactly, that's what I'll tell India . . . not another man," Maxi crooned in her most witching song.

"Tell India?" he muttered in surprise. "Aren't you going to tell Angelica first?"

"Angelica? Oh, her. Of course I'll tell her first," Maxi answered vaguely through the celebration of finding herself back home where she belonged.

"If only you still didn't have to go back to Toby's to get your things. You can't move in just with jeans and a T-shirt," Rocco murmured, rocking her tightly in his impatient arms. He picked her up urgently and started to carry her up the stairs. "After all, you have to go to work tomorrow morning. My baby Maxi, my beauty, my little publisher, my wife."

"That's all right," Maxi assured him breathlessly as he besieged her with kisses. "We run an informal shop." Somehow it didn't seem like quite the right moment to tell him that Elie was waiting patiently downstairs in the limousine with all her luggage. Later—yes, much later, would be soon enough. Or, perhaps . . . never?

About the Author

JUDITH KRANTZ has written many #1 *New York Times* bestsellers. Her other novels include *Scruples*, *Till We Meet Again* and *Dazzle*. Her travels and early career as a fashion editor and magazine editor help her with the totally authentic scenes she provides as a background for her scandalously entertaining novels.